"Wow," Holden said to himself, "I really don't want to do this."

The sound echoed in his helmet, competing only with the faint hiss of his radio.

"I tried to talk you out of it," Naomi replied, her voice somehow managing to be intimate even flattened and distorted by his suit's small speakers.

"Sorry, I didn't think you were listening."

"Ah," she said. "Irony."

Holden tore his eyes way from the slowly growing sphere that was his destination and spun around to look for the *Rocinante* behind him. She wasn't visible until Alex fired a maneuvering thruster and a gossamer cone of steam reflected some of the sphere's blue glow. His suit told him that the *Roci* was over thirty thousand kilometers away—more than twice as far as any two people on Earth could ever be from each other—and receding. And here he was, in a suit of vacuum armor, wearing a disposable EVA pack that had about five minutes of thrust in it. He'd burned one minute accelerating toward the sphere. He'd burn another slowing down when he got there. That left enough to fly back to the *Roci* when he was done.

Optimism expressed as conservation of delta V.

ABADDON'S GATE

BOOK THREE OF THE EXPANSE

JAMES S. A. COREY

orbit

www.orbitbooks.net

Copyright © 2013 by James S. A. Corey
Excerpt from *Cibola Burn* copyright © 2014 by James S. A. Corey
Excerpt from *War Dogs* copyright © 2014 by Greg Bear

Orbit
Hachette Book Group
1290 Avenue of the Americas
New York, NY 10104
www.orbitbooks.net

Printed in the United States of America

RRD-C

First U.S. edition: June 2013

10

Orbit is an imprint of Hachette Book Group.
The Orbit name and logo are trademarks of Little, Brown Book Group Limited.

The Hachette Speakers Bureau provides a wide range of authors for speaking events. To find out more, go to www.hachettespeakersbureau.com or call (866) 376-6591.

The publisher is not responsible for websites (or their content) that are not owned by the publisher.

Library of Congress Cataloging-in-Publication Data:
Corey, James S. A.
Abaddon's Gate / James S. A. Corey. — First Edition.
pages cm. — (The Expanse ; Book Three)
ISBN 978-0-316-12907-7 (trade pbk.) — ISBN 978-0-316-23542-6 (ebook)
1. Science fiction.   I. Title.
PS3601.B677A64 2013
813'.6—dc23
                                                    2012041860

*For Walter Jon Williams, who showed us how
to do it, and for Carrie Vaughn, who made
sure we didn't screw it up too badly*

Prologue: Manéo

Manéo Jung-Espinoza—Néo to his friends back on Ceres Station—huddled in the cockpit of the little ship he'd christened the *Y Que*. After almost three months, there were maybe fifty hours left before he made history. The food had run out two days before. The only water that was left to drink was half a liter of recycled piss that had already gone through him more times than he could count. Everything he could turn off, he'd turned off. The reactor was shut down. He still had passive monitors, but no active sensors. The only light in the cockpit came from the backsplash of the display terminals. The blanket he'd wrapped himself in, corners tucked into his restraints so it wouldn't float away, wasn't even powered. His broadcast and tightbeam transmitters were both shut off, and he'd slagged the transponder even before he'd painted the name on her hull. He hadn't flown this far just to have some kind of accidental blip alert the flotillas that he was coming.

Fifty hours—less than that—and the only thing he had to do was not be seen. And not run into anything, but that part was in *las manos de Dios*.

His cousin Evita had been the one who introduced him to the underground society of slingshots. That was three years ago, just before his fifteenth birthday. He'd been hanging at his family hole, his mother gone to work at the water treatment plant, his father at a meeting with the grid maintenance group that he oversaw, and Néo had stayed home, cutting school for the fourth time in a month. When the system announced someone waiting at the door, he'd figured it was school security busting him for being truant. Instead, Evita was there.

She was two years older, and his mother's sister's kid. A real Belter. They had the same long, thin bodies, but she was *from* there. He'd had a thing for Evita since the first time he saw her. He'd had dreams about what she'd look like with her clothes off. What it would feel like to kiss her. Now here she was, and the place to himself. His heart was going three times standard before he opened the door.

"Esá, unokabátya," she said, smiling and shrugging with one hand.

"Hoy," he'd said, trying to act cool and calm. He'd grown up in the massive city in space that was Ceres Station just the way she had, but his father had the low, squat frame that marked him as an Earther. He had as much right to the cosmopolitan slang of the Belt as she had, but it sounded natural on her. When he said it, it was like he was putting on someone else's jacket.

"Some coyos meeting down portside. Silvestari Campos back," she said, her hip cocked, her mouth soft as a pillow, and her lips shining. "Mit?"

"Que no?" he'd said. "Got nothing better."

He'd figured out afterward that she'd brought him because Mila Sana, a horse-faced Martian girl a little younger than him, had a thing, and they all thought it was funny to watch the ugly inner girl padding around after the half-breed, but by then he didn't care. He'd met Silvestari Campos and he'd heard of slingshotting.

Went like this: Some coyo put together a boat. Maybe it was salvage. Maybe it was fabbed. Probably at least some of it was stolen. Didn't need to be much more than a torch drive, a crash couch, and enough air and water to get the job done. Then it was all about plotting the trajectory. Without an Epstein, torch drive burned pellets too fast to get anyone anywhere. At least not without help. The trick was to plot it so that the burn—and the best only ever used one burn—would put the ship through a gravity assist, suck up the velocity of a planet or moon, and head out as deep as the push would take them. Then figure out how to get back without getting dead. Whole thing got tracked by a double-encrypted black net as hard to break as anything that the Loca Greiga or Golden Bough had on offer. Maybe they ran it. It was illegal as hell, and somebody was taking the bets. Dangerous, which was the point. And then when you got back, everyone knew who you were. You could lounge around in the warehouse party and drink whatever you wanted and talk however you wanted and drape your hand on Evita Jung's right tit and she wouldn't even move it off.

And just like that, Néo, who hadn't ever cared about anything very much, developed an ambition.

"The thing people have to remember is that the Ring isn't magical," the Martian woman said. Néo had spent a lot of time in the past months watching the newsfeeds about the Ring, and so far he liked her the best. Pretty face. Nice accent. She wasn't as thick as an Earther, but she didn't belong to the Belt either. Like him. "We don't understand it yet, and we may not for decades. But the last two years have given us some of the most interesting and exciting breakthroughs in materials technology since the wheel. Within the next ten or fifteen years, we're going to start seeing the applications of what we've learned from watching the protomolecule, and it will—"

"Fruit. Of. A poisoned. Tree," the old, leathery-looking coyo beside her said. "We cannot allow ourselves to forget that this was built from mass murder. The criminals and monsters at Protogen and Mao-Kwik released this weapon on a population of innocents. That slaughter began all of this, and profiting from it makes us all complicit."

The feed cut to the moderator, who smiled and shook his head at the leathery one.

"Rabbi Kimble," the moderator said, "we've had contact with an undisputed alien artifact that took over Eros Station, spent a little over a year preparing itself in the vicious pressure cooker of Venus, then launched a massive complex of structures just outside the orbit of Uranus and built a thousand-kilometer-wide ring. You can't be suggesting that we are morally required to ignore those facts."

"Himmler's hypothermia experiments at Dachau—" the leathery coyo began, wagging his finger in the air, but now it was the pretty Martian's turn to interrupt.

"Can we move past the 1940s, please?" she said, smiling in a way that said, *I'm being friendly but shut the fuck up.* "We're not talking about space Nazis here. This is the single most important event in human history. Protogen's role in it was terrible, and they've been punished for it. But now we have to—"

"Not *space* Nazis!" the old coyo yelled. "The Nazis aren't from *space*. They are right here among us. They are the beasts of our worst nature. By profiting from these discoveries, we *legitimize* the path by which we came to them."

The pretty one rolled her eyes and looked at the moderator like she wanted help. The moderator shrugged at her, which only made the old one angrier.

"The Ring is a temptation to sin," the old coyo shouted. There were little flecks of white at the corners of his mouth that the video editor had chosen to leave visible.

"We don't know what it is," the pretty one said. "Given that it was intended to do its work on primordial Earth with single-celled organisms and wound up on Venus with an infinitely more complex substrate, it probably doesn't work at all, but I can say that temptation and sin have nothing to do with it."

"They are victims. Your 'complex substrate'? It is the corrupted bodies of the innocent!"

Néo turned down the feed volume and just watched them gesture at each other for a while.

It had taken him months to plan out the trajectory of the *Y Que*, finding the time when Jupiter, Europa, and Saturn were all in the right positions. The window was so narrow it had been like throwing a dart from a half klick away and pinning a fruit fly's wing with it. Europa had been the trick. A close pass on the Jovian moon, then down so close to the gas giant that there was almost drag. Then out again for the long trip past Saturn, sucking more juice out of its orbital velocity, and then farther out into the black, not accelerating again, but going faster than anyone would imagine a little converted rock hopper could manage. Through millions of klicks of vacuum to hit a bull's-eye smaller than a mosquito's asshole.

Néo imagined the expressions of all the science and military ships parked around the Ring when a little ship, no transponder and flying ballistic, appeared out of nowhere and shot straight through the Ring at a hundred and fifty thousand kilometers per hour. After that, he'd have to move fast. He didn't have enough fuel left to kill all his velocity, but he'd slow down enough that they could get a rescue ship to him.

He'd do some time in slam, that was sure. Maybe two years, if the magistrates were being pissy. It was worth it, though. Just the messages from the black net where all his friends were tracking him with the constant and rising chorus of *holy shit it's going to work* made it worth it. He was going down in history. In a hundred years, people were still going to be talking about the biggest-balled slingshot ever. He'd lost months building the *Y Que*, more than that in transit, then jail time after. It was worth it. He was going to live forever.

Twenty hours.

The biggest danger was the flotilla surrounding the Ring. Earth and Mars had kicked each other's navies into creaky old men months ago, but what was left was mostly around the Ring. Or else down in the inner planets, but Néo didn't care about them. There were maybe twenty or thirty big military ships watching each other while every science vessel in the system peeked and listened and floated gently a couple thousand klicks from the Ring. All the navy muscle there to make sure no one touched. Scared, all of them. Even with all that metal and ceramic crammed into the same little corner of space, even with the relatively tiny thousand klicks across what was the inner face of the Ring, the chances that he'd run into anything were trivial. There was a lot more nothing than something. And if he did hit one of the flotilla ships, he wasn't going to be around to worry about it, so he just gave it up to the Virgin and started setting up the high-speed camera. When it finally happened, it would be so fast, he wouldn't even know whether he'd made the mark until he analyzed the data. And he was making sure there was going to be a record. He turned his transmitters back on.

"Hoy," he said into the camera, "Néo here. Néo solo. Captain and crew of souverän Belt-racer *Y Que*. Mielista me. Got six hours until biggest slipper since God made man. Es pa mi mama, the sweet Sophia Brun, and Jesus our Lord and Savior. Watch close. Blink it and miss, que sa?"

He watched the file. He looked like crap. He probably had time; he could shave the ratty little beard off and at least tie back his hair. He wished now he'd kept up with his daily exercises so he wouldn't look so chicken-shouldered. Too late now. Still, he could mess with the camera angle. He was ballistic. Wasn't like there was any thrust gravity to worry about.

He tried again from two other angles until his vanity was satisfied, then switched to the external cameras. His introduction was a little over ten seconds long. He'd start the broadcast twenty seconds out, then switch to the exterior cameras. More than a thousand frames per second, and it still might miss the Ring between images. He had to hope for the best. Wasn't like he could get another camera now, even if a better one existed.

He drank the rest of his water and wished that he'd packed just a little more food. A tube of protein slush would have gone down really well. It'd be done soon. He'd be in some Earther or Martian brig where there would be a decent toilet and water to drink and prisoner's rations. He was almost looking forward to it.

His sleeping comm array woke up and squawked about a tightbeam. He opened the connection. The encryption meant it was from the black net, and sent long enough ago that it would reach him here. Someone besides him was showing off.

Evita was still beautiful, but more like a woman now than she'd been when he'd started getting money and salvage to build the *Y Que*. Another five years, she'd be plain. He'd still have a thing for her, though.

"Esá, unokabátya," she said. "Eyes of the world. Toda auge. Mine too."

She smiled, and just for a second, he thought maybe she'd lift her shirt. For good luck. The tightbeam dropped.

Two hours.

"I repeat, this is Martian frigate *Lucien* to the unidentified ship approaching the Ring. Respond immediately or we will open fire."

Three minutes. They'd seen him too soon. The Ring was still three minutes away, and they weren't supposed to see him until he had less than one.

Néo cleared his throat.

"No need, que sa? No need. This is the *Y Que*, racer out sa Ceres Station."

"Your transponder isn't on, *Y Que*."

"Busted, yeah? Need some help with that."

"Your radio's working just fine, but I'm not hearing a distress beacon."

"Not distressed," he said, pulling the syllables out for every extra second. He could keep them talking. "Ballistic is all. Can fire up the reactor, but it's going to take a couple minutes. Maybe you can come give a hand, eh?"

"You are in restricted space, *Y Que*," the Martian said, and Néo felt the grin growing on his face.

"No harm," he said. "No harm. Surrender. Just got to get slowed down a little. Firing it up in a few seconds. Hold your piss."

"You have ten seconds to change trajectory away from the Ring or we will open fire."

The fear felt like victory. He was doing it. He was on target for the Ring and it was freaking them out. One minute. He started warming up the reactor. At this point, he wasn't even lying anymore. The full suite of sensors started their boot sequence.

"Don't fire," he said, as he made a private jacking-off motion. "Please, sir, please don't shoot me. I'm slowing down as fast as I can."

"You have five seconds, *Y Que*."

He had thirty seconds. The friend-or-foe screens popped up as soon as the full ship system was on. The *Lucien* was going to pass close by. Maybe seven hundred klicks. No wonder they'd seen him. At that distance, the *Y Que* would light up the threat boards like it was Christmas. Just bad luck, that.

"You can shoot if you want, but I'm stopping as fast as I can," he said.

The status alarm sounded. Two new dots appeared on the display. *Hijo de puta* had actually launched torpedoes.

Fifteen seconds. He was going to make it. He started broadcast and the exterior camera. The Ring was out there somewhere, its thousand-kilometer span still too small and dark to make out with the naked eye. There was only the vast spill of stars.

"Hold fire!" he shouted at the Martian frigate. "Hold fire!"

Three seconds. The torpedoes were gaining fast.

One second.

As one, the stars all blinked out.

Néo tapped the monitor. Nothing. Friend-or-foe didn't show anything. No frigate. No torpedoes. Nothing.

"Now that," he said to no one and nothing, "is weird."

On the monitor, something glimmered blue and he pulled himself closer, as if being a few inches closer to the screen would make it all make sense.

The sensors that triggered the high-g alert took five hundredths of a second to trip. The alert, hardwired, took another three hundredths of a second to react, pushing power to the red LED and the emergency Klaxon. The little console telltale that pegged out with a ninety-nine-g deceleration warning took a glacial half second to excite its light-emitting diodes. But by that time Néo was already a red smear inside the cockpit, the ship's deceleration throwing him forward through the screen and into the far bulkhead in less time than it took a synapse to fire. For five long seconds, the ship creaked and strained, not just stopping, but being stopped.

In the unbroken darkness, the exterior high-speed camera kept up its broadcast, sending out a thousand frames per second of nothing.

And then, of something else.

Chapter One: Holden

When he'd been a boy back on Earth, living under the open blue of sky, one of his mothers had spent three years suffering uncontrolled migraines. Seeing her pale and sweating with pain had been hard, but the halo symptoms that led into it had almost been worse. She'd be cleaning the house or working through contracts for her law practice and then her left hand would start to clench, curling against itself until the veins and tendons seemed to creak with the strain. Next her eyes lost their focus, pupils dilating until her blue eyes had gone black. It was like watching someone having a seizure, and he always thought *this* time, she'd die from it.

He'd been six at the time, and he'd never told any of his parents how much the migraines unnerved him, or how much he dreaded them, even when things seemed good. The fear had become familiar. Almost expected. It should have taken the edge off the terror, and maybe it did, but what replaced it was a sense of being trapped. The assault could come at any time, and it could not be avoided.

It poisoned everything, even if it was only a little bit.

It felt like being haunted.

"The house always wins," Holden shouted.

He and the crew—Alex, Amos, Naomi—sat at a private table in the VIP lounge of Ceres' most expensive hotel. Even there, the bells, whistles, and digitized voices of the slot machines were loud enough to drown out most casual conversation. The few frequencies they weren't dominating were neatly filled in by the high-pitched clatter of the pachinko machines and the low bass rumble of a band playing on one of the casino's three stages. All of it added up to a wall of sound that left Holden's guts vibrating and his ears ringing.

"What?" Amos yelled back at him.

"In the end, the house always wins!"

Amos stared down at an enormous pile of chips in front of him. He and Alex were counting and dividing them in preparation for their next foray out to the gaming tables. At a glance, Holden guessed they'd won something like fifteen thousand Ceres new yen in just the last hour. It made an impressive stack. If they could quit now, they'd be ahead. But, of course, they wouldn't quit now.

"Okay," Amos said. "What?"

Holden smiled and shrugged. "Nothing."

If his crew wanted to lose a few thousand bucks blowing off steam at the blackjack tables, who was he to interfere? The truth was it wouldn't even put a dent in the payout from their most recent contract, and that was only one of three contracts they'd completed in the last four months. It was going to be a very flush year.

Holden had made a lot of mistakes over the last three years. Deciding to quit his job as the OPA's bagman and become an independent contractor wasn't one of them. In the months since he'd put up his shingle as a freelance courier and escort ship, the *Rocinante* had taken seven jobs, and all of them had been profitable. They'd spent money refitting the ship bow to stern. She'd had a tough couple of years, and she'd needed some love.

When that was done and they still had more money in their general account than they knew what to do with, Holden had asked for a crew wish list. Naomi had paid to have a bulkhead in their quarters cut out to join the two rooms. They now had a bed large enough for two people and plenty of room to walk around it. Alex had pointed out the difficulty in buying new military-grade torpedoes for the ship, and had requested a keel-mounted rail gun for the *Roci*. It would give them more punch than the point defense cannons, and its only ammunition requirements were two-pound tungsten slugs. Amos had spent thirty grand during a stopover on Callisto, buying them some after-market engine upgrades. When Holden pointed out that the *Roci* was already capable of accelerating fast enough to kill her crew and asked why they'd need to upgrade her, Amos had replied, "Because this shit is awesome." Holden had just nodded and smiled and paid the bill.

Even after the initial giddy rush of spending, they had enough to pay themselves salaries that were five times what they'd made on the *Canterbury* and keep the ship in water, air, and fuel pellets for the next decade.

Probably, it was temporary. There would be dry times too when no work came their way and they'd have to economize and make do. That just wasn't today.

Amos and Alex had finished counting their chips and were shouting to Naomi about the finer points of blackjack, trying to get her to join them at the tables. Holden waved at the waiter, who darted over to take his order. No ordering from a table screen here in the VIP lounge.

"What do you have in a scotch that came from actual grain?" Holden asked.

"We have several Ganymede distillations," the waiter said. He'd learned the trick of being heard over the racket without straining.

He smiled at Holden. "But for the discriminating gentleman from Earth, we also have a few bottles of sixteen-year Lagavulin we keep aside."

"You mean, like, actual scotch from Scotland?"

"From the island of Islay, to be precise," the waiter replied. "It's twelve hundred a bottle."

"I want that."

"Yes sir, and four glasses." The waiter tipped his head and headed off to the bar.

"We're going to play blackjack now," Naomi said, laughing. Amos was pulling a stack of chips out of his tray and pushing them across the table to her. "Want to come?"

The band in the next room stopped playing, and the background noise dropped to an almost tolerable level for a few seconds before someone started piping Muzak across the casino PA.

"Guys, wait a few minutes," Holden said. "I've bought a bottle of something nice, and I want to have one last toast before we go our separate ways for the night."

Amos looked impatient right up until the bottle arrived, and then spent several seconds cooing over the label. "Yeah, okay, this was worth waiting for."

Holden poured out a shot for each of them, then held his glass up. "To the best ship and crew anyone has ever had the privilege of serving with, and to getting paid."

"To getting paid!" Amos echoed, and then the shots disappeared.

"God damn, Cap," Alex said, then picked up the bottle to look it over. "Can we put some of this on the *Roci*? You can take it out of my salary."

"Seconded," Naomi said, then took the bottle and poured out four more shots.

For a few minutes, the stacks of chips and the lure of the card tables were forgotten. Which was all Holden had wanted. Just to keep these people together for a few moments longer. On every other ship he'd ever served on, hitting port was a chance to get away from the same faces for a few days. Not anymore. Not with this crew. He stifled an urge to say a maudlin, *I love you guys!* by drinking another shot of scotch.

"One last hit for the road," Amos said, picking up the bottle.

"Gonna hit the head," Holden replied, and pushed away from the table. He weaved a bit more than he expected on his walk to the restroom. The scotch had gone to his brain fast.

The restrooms in the VIP lounge were lush. No rows of urinals and sinks here. Instead, half a dozen doors that led to private facilities with their own toilet and sink. Holden pushed his way into one and latched it behind him. The noise level dropped almost to nothing as soon as the door closed. A little like stepping outside the world. It was probably designed that way. He was glad whoever built the casino had allowed for a place of relative calm. He wouldn't have been shocked to see a slot machine over the sink.

He put one hand on the wall to steady himself while he did his business. He was mid-stream when the room brightened for a moment and the chrome handle on the toilet reflected a faint blue light. The fear hit him in the gut.

Again.

"I swear to God," Holden said, pausing to finish and then zip up. "Miller, you better not be there when I turn around."

He turned around.

Miller was there.

"Hey," the dead man started.

"'We need to talk,'" Holden finished for him, then walked to the sink to wash his hands. A tiny blue firefly followed him and landed on the counter. Holden smashed it with his palm, but when he lifted his hand nothing was there.

In the mirror, Miller's reflection shrugged. When he moved, it was with a sickening jerkiness, like a clockwork ticking through its motions. Human and inhuman both.

"Everyone's here at once," the dead man said. "I don't want to talk about what happened to Julie."

Holden pulled a towel out of the basket next to the sink, then leaned against the counter facing Miller and slowly dried his hands. He was trembling, the same as he always did. The sense of threat and evil was crawling up his spine, just the same way it always did. Holden hated it.

Detective Miller smiled, distracted by something Holden couldn't see.

The man had worked security on Ceres, been fired, and gone off hunting on his own, searching for a missing girl. He'd saved Holden's life once. Holden had watched when the asteroid station Miller and thousands of victims of the alien protomolecule had been trapped on crashed into Venus. Including Julie Mao, the girl Miller had searched for and then found too late. For a year, the alien artifact had suffered and worked its incomprehensible design under the clouds of Venus. When it rose, hauling massive structures up from the depths and flying out past the orbit of Neptune like some titanic sea creature translated to the void, Miller rose with it.

And now everything he said was madness.

"Holden," Miller said, not talking to him. Describing him. "Yeah, that makes sense. You're not one of them. Hey, you have to listen to me."

"Then you have to say something. This shit is out of hand. You've been doing your random appearing act for almost a year now, and you've never said even one thing that made sense. Not one."

Miller waved the comment away. The old man was starting to breathe faster, panting like he'd run a race. Beads of sweat glistened on his pale, gray-tinged skin.

"So there was this unlicensed brothel down in sector eighteen. We went in thinking we'd have fifteen, twenty in the box. More, maybe. Got there, and the place was stripped to the stone. I'm supposed to think about that. It means something."

"What do you want from me?" Holden said. "Just tell me what you *want*, all right?"

"I'm not crazy," Miller said. "When I'm crazy, they kill me.

God, did they kill me?" Miller's mouth formed a small O, and he began to suck air in. His lips were darkening, the blood under the skin turning black. He put a hand on Holden's shoulder, and it felt too heavy. Too solid. Like Miller had been remade with iron instead of bones. "It's all gone pear-shaped. We got there, but it's empty. The whole sky's empty."

"I don't know what that means."

Miller leaned close. His breath smelled like acetate fumes. His eyes locked on Holden, eyebrows raised, asking him if he understood.

"You've got to help me," Miller said. The blood vessels in his eyes were almost black. "They know I find things. They know you help me."

"You're dead," Holden said, the words coming out of him without consideration or planning.

"Everyone's dead," Miller said. He took his hand from Holden's shoulder and turned away. Confusion troubled his brow. "Almost. Almost."

Holden's terminal buzzed at him, and he took it out of his pocket. Naomi had sent DID YOU FALL IN? Holden began typing out a reply, then stopped when he realized he'd have no idea what to say.

When Miller spoke, his voice was small, almost childlike with wonder and amazement.

"Fuck. It *happened*," Miller said.

"What happened?" Holden said.

A door banged as someone else went into a neighboring stall, and Miller was gone. The smell of ozone and some rich organic volatiles like a spice shop gone rancid were all the evidence that he had been there. And that might only have been in Holden's imagination.

Holden stood for a moment, waiting for the coppery taste to leave his mouth. Waiting for his heartbeat to slow back down to normal. Doing what he always did in the aftermath. When the worst had passed, he rinsed his face with cold water and dried it with a soft towel. The distant, muffled sound of the gambling decks rose to a frenzy. A jackpot.

He wouldn't tell them. Naomi, Alex, Amos. They deserved to have their pleasure without the thing that had been Miller intruding on it. Holden recognized that the impulse to keep it from them was irrational, but it felt so powerfully like protecting them that he didn't question it much. Whatever Miller had become, Holden was going to stand between it and the *Roci.*

He studied his reflection until it was perfect. The carefree, slightly drunk captain of a successful independent ship on shore leave. Easy. Happy. He went back out to the pandemonium of the casino.

For a moment, it was like stepping back in time. The casinos on Eros. The death box. The lights felt a little too bright, the noises sounded a little too loud. Holden made his way back to the table and poured himself another shot. He could nurse this one for a while. He'd enjoy the flavor and the night. Someone behind him shrieked their laughter. Only laughter.

A few minutes later, Naomi appeared, stepping out of the bustle and chaos like serenity in a female form. The half-drunken, expansive love he'd felt earlier came back as he watched her make her way toward him. They'd shipped together on the *Canterbury* for years before he'd found himself falling in love with her. Looking back, every morning he'd woken up with someone else had been a lost opportunity to breathe Naomi's air. He couldn't imagine what he'd been thinking. He shifted to the side, making room for her.

"They cleaned you out?" he asked.

"Alex," she said. "They cleaned Alex out. I gave him my chips."

"You are a woman of tremendous generosity," he said with a grin.

Naomi's dark eyes softened into a sympathetic expression.

"Miller showed up again?" she asked, leaning close to be heard over the noise.

"It's a little unsettling how easily you see through me."

"You're pretty legible. And this wouldn't be Miller's first bathroom ambush. Did he make any more sense this time?"

"No," Holden said. "He's like talking to an electrical problem. Half the time I'm not sure he even knows I'm there."

"It can't really be Miller, can it?"

"If it's the protomolecule wearing a Miller suit, I think that's actually creepier."

"Fair point," Naomi said. "Did he say anything new, at least?"

"A little bit, maybe. He said something happened."

"What?"

"I don't know. He just said, 'It happened,' and blinked out."

They sat together for a few minutes, a private silence within the riot, her fingers interlaced with his. She leaned over, kissing his right eyebrow, and then pulled him up off the chair.

"Come on," she said.

"Where are we going?"

"I'm going to teach you how to play poker," she said.

"I know how to play poker."

"You think you do," she said.

"Are you calling me a fish?"

She smiled and tugged at him.

Holden shook his head. "If you want to, let's go back to the ship. We can get a few people together and have a private game. It doesn't make sense to do it here. The house always wins."

"We aren't here to win," Naomi said, and the seriousness in her voice made the words carry more than the obvious meaning. "We're here to play."

The news came two days later.

Holden was in the galley, eating takeout from one of the dockside restaurants: garlic sauce over rice, three kinds of legumes, and something so similar to chicken, it might as well have been the real thing. Amos and Naomi were overseeing the loading of nutrients and filters for the air recycling systems. Alex, in the pilot's seat, was asleep. On the other ships Holden had served aboard, having the full crew back on ship before departure required it was almost unheard of, and they'd all spent a couple of nights in dockside hotels before they'd come home. But they were home now.

Holden ran through the local feeds on his hand terminal, sipping news and entertainment from throughout the system. A security flaw in the new Bandao Solice game meant that financial and personal information from six million people had been captured on a pirate server orbiting Titan. Martian military experts were calling for increased spending to address the losses suffered in the battle around Ganymede. On Earth, an African farming coalition was defying the ban on a nitrogen-fixing strain of bacteria. Protesters on both sides of the issue were taking to the streets in Cairo.

Holden was flipping back and forth, letting his mind float on the surface of the information, when a red band appeared on one of the newsfeeds. And then another. And then another. The image above the article chilled his blood. The Ring, they called it. The gigantic alien structure that had left Venus and traveled to a point a little less than 2 AU outside Uranus' orbit, then stopped and assembled itself.

Holden read the news carefully as dread pulled at his gut. When he looked up, Naomi and Amos were in the doorway. Amos had his own hand terminal out. Holden saw the same red bands on that display.

"You seen this, Cap'n?" Amos asked.

"Yeah," Holden said.

"Some mad bastard tried to shoot the Ring."

"Yeah."

Even with the distance between Ceres and the Ring, the vast empty ocean of space, the news that some idiot's cheapjack ship had gone in one side of the alien structure and hadn't come out the other should have only taken about five hours. It had happened two days before. That's how long the various governments watching the Ring had been able to cover it up.

"This is it, isn't it?" Naomi said. "This is what happened."

Chapter Two: Bull

Carlos c de Baca—Bull to his friends—didn't like Captain Ashford. Never had.

The captain was one of those guys who'd sneer without moving his mouth. Before Ashford joined up with the OPA full-time, he'd gotten a degree in math from the Lunar Campus of Boston University, and he never let anyone forget it. It was like because he had a degree from an Earth university, he was better than other Belters. Not that he wouldn't be happy to bad-mouth guys like Bull or Fred who really had grown up down the well. Ashford wasn't one thing or another. The way he latched on to whatever seemed like it made him the big man—education, association with Earth, growing up in the Belt—made it hard not to tease him.

And Ashford was going to be in command of the mission.

"There's a time element too," Fred Johnson said.

Fred looked like crap. Too thin. Everyone looked too thin

these days, but Fred's dark skin had taken on an ashy overtone that left Bull thinking about things like autoimmune disorders or untreated cancer. Probably it was just stress, years, and malnutrition. Same thing that got everyone if nothing else did. Point of fact, Bull was looking a little gray around the temples too, and he didn't like the crap LEDs that were supposed to mimic sunlight. That he was still darker than an eggshell had more to do with a nut-brown Mexican mother than anything ultraviolet.

He'd been out in the dark since he was twenty-two. He was over forty now. And Fred, his superior officer under two different governments, was older than he was.

The construction gantry sloped out ahead of them, the flexible walls shining like snake scales. There was a constant low-level whine, the vibrations of the construction equipment carried along the flesh of the station. The spin gravity here was a little less than the standard one-third g on Tycho Station proper, and Ashford was making a little show of speeding up and then slowing down for the Earthers. Bull slowed his own steps down just a little to make the man wait longer.

"Time element? What's that look like, Colonel?" Ashford asked.

"Not as bad as it could be," Fred said. "The Ring hasn't made any apparent changes since the big one during the incident. No one else has gone through, and nothing's come out. People have backed down from filling their pants to just high alert. Mars is approaching this as a strictly military and scientific issue. They've got half a dozen science vessels on high burn already."

"How much escort?" Bull asked.

"One destroyer, three frigates," Fred said. "Earth is moving slower, but larger. They've got elections coming up next year, and the secretary-general's been catching hell about turning a blind eye to rogue corporate entities."

"Wonder why," Bull said dryly. Even Ashford smiled. Between Protogen and Mao-Kwikowski, the order and stability of the solar system had pretty much been dropped in a blender. Eros

Station was gone, taken over by an alien technology and crashed into Venus. Ganymede was producing less than a quarter of its previous food output, leaving every population center in the outer planets relying on backup agricultural sources. The Earth-Mars alliance was the kind of quaint memory someone's grandpa might talk about after too much beer. The good old days, before it all went to hell.

"He's putting on a show," Fred went on. "Media. Religious leaders. Poets. Artists. They're hauling them all out to the Ring so that every feed he can reach is pointed away from him."

"Typical," Ashford said, then didn't elaborate. Typical for a politician. Typical for an Earther. "What are we looking at out there?"

The gantry sang for a moment, an accident of harmonics setting it ringing and shaking until industrial dampers kicked in and killed the vibration before it reached the point of doing damage.

"All we've confirmed is that some idiot flew through the Ring at high ballistic speeds and didn't come out the other side," Fred said, moving his hands in the physical shrug of a Belter. "Now there's some kind of physical anomaly in the Ring. Could be that the idiot kid's ship got eaten by the Ring and converted into something. The ring sprayed a lot of gamma and X-rays, but not enough to account for the mass of the ship. Could be that he broke it. Could be that it opened a gate, and there's a bunch of little green men in saucers about to roll through and make the solar system into a truck stop."

"What—" Bull began, but Ashford talked over him.

"Any response from Venus?"

"Nothing," Fred said.

Venus was dead. For years after a corrupted Eros Station fell through its clouds, all human eyes had turned to that planet, watching as the alien protomolecule struggled in the violence and heat. Crystal towers kilometers high rose and fell away. Networks of carbon fibers laced the planet and degraded to nothing. The weapon had been meant to hijack simple life on Earth, billions of years before. Instead, it had the complex ecosystem of human bodies and the structures to sustain them in the toxic oven of Venus. Maybe it had taken longer to carry out its plan. Maybe having complex life to work with had made things easier. Everything pointed to it being finished with Venus. And all that really mattered was it had launched a self-assembling ring in the emptiness outside the orbit of Uranus that sat there dead as a stone.

Until now.

"What are we supposed to do about it?" Bull asked. "No offense, but we don't got the best science vessels. And Earth and Mars blew the crap out of each other over Ganymede."

"Be there," Fred said. "If Earth and Mars send their ships, we send ours. If they put out a statement, we put out one of our own. If they lay a claim on the Ring, we counterclaim. What we've done to make the outer planets into a viable political force has reaped real benefits, but if we start letting them lead, it could all evaporate."

"We planning to shoot anybody?" Bull asked.

"Hopefully it won't come to that," Fred said.

The gantry's gentle upward slope brought them to a platform arch. In the star-strewn blackness, a great plain of steel and ceramic curved away above them, lit by a thousand lights. Looking out at it was like seeing a landscape—this was too big to be something humans had made. It was like a canyon or a mountain. The meadow-filled caldera of some dead volcano. The scale alone made it impossible to see her as a ship. But she was. The construction mechs crawling along her side were bigger than the house Bull had lived in as a boy, but they looked like football players on a distant field. The long, thin line of the keel elevator stretched along the body of the drum to shuttle personnel from engineering at one end to ops at the other. The secondary car, stored on the exterior, could hold a dozen people. It looked like a grain of salt. The soft curve was studded with turreted rail guns and the rough, angry extrusions of torpedo tubes.

Once, she'd been the *Nauvoo*. A generation ship headed to the stars carrying a load of devout Mormons with only an engineered ecosystem and an unshakable faith in God's grace to see them through. Now she was the *Behemoth*. The biggest, baddest weapons platform in the solar system. Four *Donnager*-class battleships would fit in her belly and not touch the walls. She could accelerate magnetic rounds to a measurable fraction of *c*. She could hold more nuclear torpedoes than the Outer Planets Alliance actually had. Her communications laser was powerful enough to burn through steel if they gave it enough time. Apart from painting teeth on her and welding on an apartment building–sized shark-fin, nothing could have been more clearly or effectively built to intimidate.

Which was good, because she was a retrofitted piece of crap, and if they ever got in a real fight, they were boned. Bull slid a glance at Ashford. The captain's chin was tilted high and his eyes were bright with pride. Bull sucked his teeth.

The last threads of weight let go as the platform and gantry matched to the stillness of the *Behemoth*. One of the distant construction mechs burst into a sun-white flare as the welding started.

"How long before we take her out?" Ashford asked.

"Three days," Fred said.

"Engineering report said the ship'll be ready in about ten," Bull said. "We planning to work on her while we're flying?"

"That was the intention," Fred said.

"Because we could wait another few days here, do the work in dock, and burn a little harder going out, get the same arrival."

The silence was uncomfortable. Bull had known it would be, but it had to be said.

"The crew's comfort and morale need as much support as the ship," Fred said, diplomacy changing the shapes of the words. Bull had known him long enough to hear it. *The Belters don't want a hard burn.* "Besides which, it's easier to get the in-transit work done in lower g. It's all been min-maxed, Bull. You ship out in three."

"Is that a problem?" Ashford said.

Bull pulled the goofy grin he used when he wanted to tell the truth and not get in trouble for it.

"We're heading out to throw gang signs at Earth and Mars while the Ring does a bunch of scary alien mystery stuff. We've got a crew that's never worked together, a ship that's half salvage, and not enough time to shake it all down. Sure it's a problem, but it's not one we can fix, so we'll do it anyway. Worst can happen is we'll all die."

"Cheerful thought," Ashford said. The disapproval dripped off him. Bull's grin widened and he shrugged.

"Going to happen sooner or later."

Bull's quarters on Tycho Station were luxurious. Four rooms, high ceilings, a private head with an actual water supply. Even as a kid back on Earth, he hadn't lived this well. He'd spent his childhood in a housing complex in the New Mexican Shared Interest Zone, living with his parents, grandmother, two uncles, three aunts, and about a thousand cousins, seemed like. When he turned sixteen and declined to go on basic, he'd headed south to Alamogordo and worked his two-year service stripping down ancient solar electricity stations from the bad old days before fusion. He'd shared a dorm with ten other guys. He could still picture them, the way they'd been back then, all skinny and muscled with their shirts off or tied around their heads. He could still feel the New Mexican sun pressing against his chest like a hand as he basked in the radiation and heat of an uncontrolled fusion reaction, protected only by distance and the wide blue sky.

When his two-year stint was up, he tried tech school, but he'd gotten distracted by hormones and alcohol. Once he'd dropped out, his choices were pretty much just the military or basic. He'd chosen the one that felt less like death. In the Marines, he'd never had a bunk larger than the front room of his Tycho Station quarters. He hadn't even had a place that was really his own until he mustered out. Ceres Station hadn't been a good place for him. The hole he'd taken had been up near the center of spin, low g and high Coriolis. It hadn't been much more than a place to go sleep off last night's drunk, but it had been his. The bare, polished-stone walls, the ship surplus bed with restraining straps for low g. Some previous owner had chiseled the words BESSO O NADIE into the wall. It was Belter cant for *better or nothing*. He hadn't known it was a political slogan at the time. The things he'd gotten since coming to Tycho Station—the frame cycling through a dozen good family pictures from Earth, the tin Santos candleholder that his ex-girlfriend hadn't taken when she left, the civilian clothes—would have filled his old place on Ceres and not left room for him to sleep. He had too much stuff. He needed to pare it down.

But not for this assignment. The XO's suite on the *Behemoth* was bigger.

The system chimed, letting him know someone was at the door. From long habit, Bull checked the video feed before he opened the door. Fred was shifting from one foot to the other. He was in civilian clothes. A white button-down and grandpa pants that tried to forgive the sag of his belly. It was a losing fight. Fred wasn't out of shape any more than Bull was. They were just getting old.

"Hey," Bull said. "Grab a chair anywhere. I'm just getting it all together."

"Heading over now?"

"Want to spend some time on the ship before we take her out," Bull said. "Check for stray Mormons."

Fred looked pained.

"I'm pretty sure we got them all out the first time," he said, playing along. "But it's a big place. You can look around if you want."

Bull opened his dresser, his fingers counting through T-shirts. He had ten. There was a sign of decadence. Who needed ten T-shirts? He pulled out five and dropped them on the chair by his footlocker.

"It's going to be all kinds of hell if they get rights to the *Nauvoo* back," he said. "All the changes we're making to her."

"They won't," Fred said. "Commandeering the ship was perfectly legal. It was an emergency. I could list you ten hours of precedent."

"Yeah, but then we salvaged it ourselves and called it ours," Bull said. "That's like saying I've got to borrow your truck, but since I ran it into a ditch and hauled it back out, it's mine now."

"Law is a many-splendored thing, Bull," Fred said. He sounded tired. Something else was bothering him. Bull opened another drawer, threw half his socks into the recycler, and put the others on his T-shirts.

"Just if the judge doesn't see it that way, could be awkward," Bull said.

"The judges on Earth don't have jurisdiction," Fred said. "And the ones in our court system are loyal to the OPA. They know the big picture. They're not going to take our biggest ship off the board and hand it back over. Worst case, they'll order compensation."

"Can we afford that?"

"Not right now, no," Fred said.

Bull snorted out a little laugh. "Ever wonder what we did wrong that got us here? You're driving one of the biggest desks in the OPA, and I'm XO to Ashford. That ain't a sign we've been living our lives right, man."

"About that," Fred said. "We've had a little change of plan."

Bull opened his closet, his lips pressing thin. Fred hadn't just come to chew the fat. There was a problem. Bull took two suits out of the closet, both still wrapped in sticky preservative film. He hadn't worn either one in years. They probably didn't fit.

"Ashford thought it would be better to have Michio Pa as the XO. We talked about it. I'm reassigning you as chief security officer."

"Third-in-command now," Bull said. "What? Ashford think I was going to frag him and take his chair?"

Fred leaned forward, his fingers laced. The gravity of his

expression said he knew it was a crap situation but was making the best of it.

"It's all about how it looks," Fred said. "This is the OPA's navy. The *Behemoth* is the Belt's answer to Mars' and Earth's heaviest hitters. Having an Earther on the bridge doesn't send the right message."

"All right," Bull said.

"I'm in the same position. You know that. Even after all this time, I have to work twice as hard to command loyalty and respect because of where I'm from. Even the ones who like having me around because they think I make Earth look weak don't want to take orders from me. I've had to earn and re-earn every scrap of respect."

"Okay," Bull said. Security officer was going to mean less time in uniform. With a sigh, he put both suits on the chair.

"I'm not saying that you haven't," Fred said. "No one knows better than I do that you're the best of the best. There are just some constraints we have to live with. To get the job done."

Bull leaned against the wall, his arms crossed. Fred looked up at him from under frost-colored brows.

"Sir, I been flying with you for a long time," Bull said. "If you need to ask me something, you can just do it."

"I need you to make this work," Fred said. "What's going on out there is the most important thing in the system, and we don't know what it is. If we embarrass ourselves or give the inner planets some critical advantage, we stand to lose a lot of ground. Ashford and Pa are good people, but they're Belters. They don't have the same experience working with Earth forces that you and I do."

"You think they're going to start something?"

"No. Ashford will try his hardest to do the right thing, but he'll react like a Belter and be surprised when other people don't."

"Ashford has only *ever* done a right thing because he's afraid of being embarrassed. He's a pretty uniform surrounding vacuum. And you can't rely on that."

"I'm not," Fred agreed. "I'm sending you out there because I trust you to make it work."

"But you're not giving me command."

"But I'm not giving you command."

"How about a raise?"

"Not that either," Fred said.

"Well, heck," Bull said. "All the responsibility and none of the power? How can I turn down an offer like that?"

"No joking. We're screwing you over, and the reasons are all optics and political bullshit. But I need you to take it."

"So I'll take it," Bull said.

For a moment, the only sound was the quiet ticking of the air recycler. Bull turned back to the task of putting his life in a foot-locker again. Somewhere far above him, hidden by tons of steel and ceramic, raw stone and vacuum, *Behemoth* waited.

Chapter Three: Melba

When she walked into the gambling house, Melba felt eyes on her. The room was lit by the displays on the game decks, pink and blue and gold. Most of them were themed around sex or violence, or both. Press a button, spend your money, and watch the girls put foreign and offensive objects inside themselves while you waited to see whether you'd won. Slot machines, poker, real-time lotteries. The men who played them exuded an atmosphere of stupidity, desperation, and an almost tangible hatred of women.

"Darling," an immensely fat man said from behind the counter. "Don't know where you think you come to, but you come in the wrong place. Maybe best you walk back out."

"I have an appointment," she said. "Travin."

The fat man's eyes widened under their thick lids. Someone in the gloom called out a vulgarity meant to unease her. It did, but she didn't let it show.

"Travin in the back, you want him, darling," the fat man said, nodding. At the far end of the room, through the gauntlet of leers and threat, a red metal door.

All of her instincts came from before, when she was Clarissa, and so they were all wrong now. From the time she'd been old enough to walk, she'd been trained in self-defense, but it had all been anti-kidnapping. How to attract the attention of the authorities, how to deescalate situations with her captors. There had been other work, of course. Physical training had been part of it, but the goal had always been to break away. To run. To find help.

Now that there was no one to help her, nothing quite applied. But it was what she had, so it was what she used. Melba—not Clarissa, *Melba*—nodded to the fat man and walked through the close-packed, dim room. The full gravity of Earth pulled on her like an illness. On one of the gambling decks, a cartoon woman was being sexually assaulted by three small gray aliens while a flying saucer floated above them. Someone had won a minor jackpot. Melba looked away. Behind her, an unseen man laughed, and she felt the skin at the back of her neck tighten.

Of all her siblings, she had most enjoyed the physical training. When it ended, she began studying tai chi with the self-defense instructor. Then, when she was fourteen, her father had made a joke about it at a family gathering. How learning to fight might make sense—he could respect that—but dancing while pretending to fight looked stupid and wasted time. She'd never trained again. That was ten years ago.

She opened the red door and walked through it. The office seemed almost bright. A small desk with a built-in display tuned to a cheap accounting system. White frosted glass that let in the sunlight but hid the streets of Baltimore. A formed plastic couch upholstered with the corporate logo of a cheap brand of beer that even people on basic could afford. Two hulking men sat on the couch. One had implanted sunglasses that made him look like an insect. The other wore a T-shirt that strained at his steroidal shoulders. She'd seen them before.

Travin was at the desk, leaning his thigh against it. His hair was cut close to the scalp, a dusting of white at the temples. His beard was hardly longer. He wore what passed for a good suit in his circles. Father wouldn't have worn it as a costume.

"Ah, look, the inimitable Melba."

"You knew I was here," she said. There were no chairs. No place to sit that wasn't already occupied. She stood.

" 'Course I did," Travin said. "Soon as you came off the street."

"Are we doing business?" she asked. Her voice cut the air. Travin grinned. His teeth were uncorrected and gray at the gums. It was an affectation of wealth, a statement that he was so powerful mere cosmesis was beneath him. She felt a hot rush of scorn. He was like an old cargo cultist; imitating the empty displays of power and no idea what they really meant. She was reduced to dealing with him, but at least she had the grace to be embarrassed by it.

"It's all done, miss," Travin said. "Melba Alzbeta Koh. Born on Luna to Alscie, Becca, and Sergio Koh, all deceased. No siblings. No taxation indenture. Licensed electrochemical technician. Your new self awaits, ah?"

"And the contract?"

"The *Cerisier* ships out, civilian support for the grand mission to the Ring. Our Miss Koh, she's on it. Senior class, even. Little staff to oversee, don't have to get your hands dirty."

Travin pulled a white plastic envelope from his pocket. The shadow of a cheap hand terminal showed through the tissue.

"All here, all ready," he said. "You take it and walk through the door a new woman, ah?"

Melba took her own hand terminal out of her pocket. It was smaller than the one in Travin's hand, and better made. She'd miss it. She thumbed in her code, authorized the transfer, and slid it back in her pocket.

"All right," she said. "The money's yours. I'll take delivery."

"Ah, there is still *one* problem," Travin said.

"We have an agreement," Melba said. "I did my part."

"And it speaks well of you," Travin said. "But doing business with you? I enjoy it, I think. Exciting discoveries to be made. Creating this new you, we have to put the DNA in the tables. We have to scrub out doubled records. I think you haven't been entirely honest with me."

She swallowed, trying to loosen the knot in her throat. The insect-eyed man on the couch shifted, his weight making the couch squeak.

"My money spends," she said.

"As it should, as it should," Travin said. "Clarissa Melpomene Mao, daughter to Jules-Pierre Mao of Mao-Kwikowski Mercantile. Very interesting name."

"Mao-Kwikowski was nationalized when my father went to jail," Melba said. "It doesn't exist anymore."

"Corporate death sentence," Travin said as he put the envelope on the desk display. "Very sad. But not for you, ah? Rich men know money. They find ways to put it where little eyes can't find. Get it to their wives, maybe. Their daughters."

She crossed her arms, scowling. On the couch, the bodybuilder stifled a yawn. It might even have been genuine. She let the silence stretch not because she wanted to pressure Travin to speak next, but because she didn't know what to say. He was right, of course. Daddy had taken care of all of them as best he could. He always had. Even the persecution of the United Nations couldn't reach everything. Clarissa had had enough money to live a quiet, retiring life on Luna or Mars and die of old age before the capital ran out. But she wasn't Clarissa anymore, and Melba's situation was different.

"I can give you another ten thousand," she said. "That's all I've got."

Travin smiled his gray smile.

"All that pretty money flown away, ah? And what takes you out into the darkness, eh? I wondered. So I looked. You are very, very good. Even knowing to squint, I didn't see more than shadows. Didn't hear more than echoes. But—" He put the envelope on the desk before him, keeping one finger on it the way her brother Petyr did when he was almost sure of a chess move but hadn't brought himself to commit. It was a gesture of ownership. "I have something no one else does. I know to look at the Ring."

"Ten thousand is all I have. Honestly. I've spent the rest."

"Would you need more, then?" Travin asked. "Investment capital, call it? Our little Melba can have ten thousand, if you want it. Fifty thousand if you need it. But I will want more back. Much more."

She felt her throat tighten. When she tilted her head, the movement felt too fast, too tight. Birdlike. Scared.

"What are you talking about?" she asked, willing her voice to sound solid. Formless threat hung in the air like bad cologne: masculine and cheap. When he spoke again, false friendliness curved all of his vowels.

"Partners. You are doing something big. Something with the Ring and the flotilla, ah? All these people heading out in the dark to face the monsters. And you are going with them. It seems to me that such a risk means you expect a very great return. The sort one expects from a Mao. You tell me what is your plan, I help you how I can help you, and what comes your way from this, we divide."

"No deal." The words were like a reflex. They came from her spine, the decision too obvious to require her brain.

Travin pulled back the envelope, the plastic hissing against the table. The soft tutting sound of tongue against teeth was as sympathetic as it was false.

"You have moved heaven and earth," he said. "You have bribed. You have bought. You have arranged. And when you say that you have held nothing in reserve, I believe you. So now you come to my table and tell me no deal? No deal is no deal."

"I paid you."

"I don't care. We are partners. *Full* partners. Whatever you are getting from this, I am getting too. Or else there are other people, I think, who would be very interested to hear about what the infamous Mao have been so quietly doing."

The two men on the couch were paying attention to her now. Their gazes were on her. She turned to look over her shoulder. The door to the gamblers' den was metal, and it was locked. The window was wide. The security wire in it was the sort that retracted if you wanted the glass to open and let the filthy breeze of the city in to soil the air. The insect-eyed one stood up.

Her implants were triggered by rubbing her tongue against the roof of her mouth. Two circles, counterclockwise. It was a private movement, invisible. Internal. Oddly sensual. It was almost as easy as just thinking. The suite of manufactured glands tucked in her throat and head and abdomen squeezed their little bladders empty, pouring complex chemistry into her blood. She shuddered. It felt like orgasm without the pleasure. She could feel conscience and inhibition sliding away like bad dreams. She was fully awake and alive.

All the sounds in the room—the roar of street traffic, the muffled cacophony of the gambling decks, Travin's nasty voice—went quieter, as if the cocktail flowing into her had stuffed foam in her ears. Her muscles grew tense and tight. The taste of copper filled her mouth. Time slowed.

What to do? What to do?

The thugs by the couch were the first threat. She moved over to them, gravity's oppressive grip forgotten. She kicked the bodybuilder in the kneecap as he rose, the little beer coaster of bone ripping free of its tendons and sliding up his thigh. His face was a cartoon of surprise and alarm. As he began to crumple, she lifted her other knee, driving it up into his descending larynx. She'd been aiming for his face. *Throat just as good*, she thought as the cartilage collapsed against her knee.

The insect-eyed one lunged for her. He moved quickly, his own body modified somehow. Fused muscular neurons, probably. Something to streamline the long, slow gap when the neurotransmitters floated across the synapses. Something to give him an edge when he was fighting some other thug. His hand fastened on her shoulder, wide, hard fingers grabbing at her. She turned in toward him, dropping to pull him down. Palm strike to the inside of the elbow to break his power, then both her hands around his wrist, bending it. None of her attacks were conscious or intentional. The movements came flowing out of a hindbrain that had been freed of restraint and given the time to plan its mayhem. It was no more a martial art than a crocodile taking down a water buffalo was; just speed, strength, and a couple billion years of survival instinct unleashed. Her tai chi instructor would have looked away in embarrassment.

The bodybuilder sloped down to the floor, blood pouring from his mouth. The insect-eyed man pulled away from her, which was the wrong thing to do. She hugged his locked joints close to her body and swung from her hips. He was bigger than she was, had lived in the gravity well all his life. He buffed up with steroids and his own cheap augmentations. She didn't need to be stronger than him, though. Just stronger than the little bones in his wrist and elbow. He broke, dropping to his knee.

Melba—not Clarissa—swung around him, sliding her right arm around his neck, then locking it with the left, protecting her own head from the thrashing that was about to come. She didn't need to be stronger than him, just stronger than the soft arteries that carried blood to his brain.

Travin's gun fired, gouging a hole in the couch. The little puff of foam was like a sponge exploding. No time. She shrieked, pulling the power of the scream into her arms, her shoulders. She felt the insect-eyed man's neck snap. Travin fired again. If he hit her, she'd die. She felt no fear, though. It had been locked away where she couldn't experience it. That would come soon. Very soon. It had to be done quickly.

He should have tried for a third bullet. It was the smart thing. The wise one. He was neither smart nor wise. He did what his body told him to and tried to get away. He was a monkey, and millions of years of evolution told him to flee from the predator. He didn't have time for another mistake. She felt another scream growing in her throat.

Time skipped. Her fingers were wrapped around Travin's neck. She'd been driving his skull into the corner of his desk. There was blood and scalp adhering to it. She pushed again, but he was heavy. There was no force behind her blow. She dropped him, and he fell to the floor moaning.

Moaning.

Alive, she thought. The fear was back now, and the first presentiment of nausea. He was still alive. He couldn't still be alive when the crash came. He'd had a gun. She had to find what had happened to it. With fingers quickly growing numb, she pulled the little pistol from under him.

"Partners," she said, and fired two rounds into his head. Even over the gambling decks, they had to have heard it. She forced herself to the metal door and checked the lock. It was bolted. Unless someone had a key or cut through it, she was all right. She could rest. They wouldn't call the police. She hoped they wouldn't call the police.

She slid to the floor. Sweat poured down her face and she began shaking. It seemed unfair that she'd lose time during the glorious and redemptive violence and have to fight to stay conscious through the physiological crash that followed, but she couldn't afford to sleep. Not here. She hugged her knees to her chest, sobbing not because she felt sorrow or fear, but because it was what her flesh did when she was coming down. Someone was knocking at the door, but the sound was uncertain. Tentative. Just a few minutes, and she'd be...not all right. Not that. But good enough. Just a few minutes.

This was why glandular modification had never taken root in the military culture. A squad of soldiers without hesitation or doubt, so full of adrenaline they could tear their own muscles and not care, might win battles. But the same fighters curled up and mewling for five minutes afterward would lose them again. It was a failed technology, but not an unavailable one. Enough money, enough favors to call in, and enough men of science who had been cured of conscience. It was easy. The easiest part of her plan, really.

Her sobs intensified, shifted. The vomiting started. She knew from experience that it wouldn't last long. Between retching, she watched the bodybuilder's chest heaving for air through his ruined throat, but he was already gone. The smell of blood and puke thickened the air. Melba caught her breath, wiping the back of her hand against her lips. Her sinuses ached, and she didn't know if it was from the retching or the false glands that lay in that tender flesh. It didn't matter.

The knocking at the door was more desperate now. She could make out the voice of the fat man by the door. No more time. She took the plastic envelope and shoved it in her pocket. Melba Alzbeta Koh crawled out the window and dropped to the street. She stank. There was blood on her hands. She was trembling with every step. The dim sunlight hurt, and she used the shadows of her hands to hide from it. In this part of Baltimore, a thousand people could see her and not have seen anything. The blanket of anonymity that the drug dealers and pimps and slavers arranged and enforced also protected her.

She'd be okay. She'd made it. The last tool was in place, and all she had to do was get to her hotel, drink something to put her electrolytes back in balance, and sleep a little. And then, in a few days, report for duty on the *Cerisier* and begin her long journey out to the edge of the solar system. Holding her spine straight, walking down the street, avoiding people's eyes, the dozen blocks to her room seemed longer. But she would do it. She would do whatever had to be done.

She had been Clarissa Melpomene Mao. Her family had controlled the fates of cities, colonies, and planets. And now Father sat in an anonymous prison, barred from speaking with anyone besides his lawyer, living out his days in disgrace. Her mother lived in a private compound on Luna slowly medicating herself to death. The siblings—the ones that were still alive—had scattered to whatever shelter they could find from the hatred of two worlds. Once, her family's name had been written in starlight and blood, and now they'd been made to seem like villains. They'd been destroyed.

She could make it right, though. It hadn't been easy, and it wouldn't be now. Some nights, the sacrifices felt almost unbearable, but she would do it. She could make them all see the injustice in what James Holden had done to her family. She would expose him. Humiliate him.

And then she would destroy him.

Chapter Four: Anna

Annushka Volovodov, Pastor Anna to her congregation on Europa—or Reverend Doctor Volovodov to people she didn't like—was sitting in the high-backed leather chair in her office when the wife beater arrived.

"Nicholas," she said, trying to put as much warmth into her voice as she could manage. "Thank you for taking the time."

"Nick," he said, then sat on one of the metal chairs in front of her desk. The metal chairs were lower than her own, which gave the room a vaguely courtroom-like setting, with her in the position of judge. It was why she never sat behind the desk when meeting with one of her parishioners. There was a comfortable couch along the back wall that was much better for personal conversations and counseling. But every now and then, the air of authority the big chair and heavy desk gave her was useful.

Like now.

"Nick," she said, then pressed her fingertips together and rested her chin on them. "Sophia came to see me this morning."

Nick shrugged, looking away like a schoolboy caught cheating on an exam. He was a tall man, with the narrow, raw-boned look outer planets types got from hard physical labor. Anna knew he worked in surface construction. Here on Europa, that meant long days in a heavy vacuum suit. The people who did that job were as tough as nails. Nick had the attitude of a man who knew how he looked to others, and used his air of physical competence to intimidate.

Anna smiled at him. *It won't work on me.*

"She wouldn't tell me what happened at first," she said. "It took a while to get her to lift her shirt. I didn't need to see the bruises, I knew they'd be there. But I did need pictures."

When she said *pictures*, he leaned forward, his eyes narrowing and shifting from side to side. He probably thought it made him look tough, threatening. Instead it made him look like a rodent.

"She fell—" he started.

"In the kitchen," Anna finished for him. "I know, she told me. And then she cried for a very long time. And then she told me you'd started hitting her again. Do you remember what I said would happen if you hit her again?"

Nick shifted in his chair, his long legs bouncing in front of him with nervous energy. His large, bony hands squeezing each other until the knuckles turned white. He wouldn't look directly at her. "I didn't mean to," he said. "It just happened. I could try the counseling again, I guess."

Anna cleared her throat, and when he looked at her she stared back until his legs stopped bouncing. "No, too late. We gave you the anger counseling. The church paid for you to go right up until you quit. We did that part. That part is done."

His expression went hard.

"Gonna give me one of those Jesus speeches? I am sick right up to here"—Nick held his hand under his chin—"with that shit. Sophia won't shut up about it. 'Pastor Anna says!' You know what? Fuck what Pastor fucking Anna says."

"No," Anna said. "No Jesus speeches. We're done with that too."

"Then what are we doing here?"

"Do you," she said, drawing the words out, "remember what I said would happen if you hit her again?"

He shrugged again, then pushed up out of the chair and walked away, putting his back to her. While pretending to stare at one of the diplomas hanging on the wall he said, "Why should I give a fuck what you say, *Pastor Anna*?"

Anna breathed a quiet sigh of relief. Preparing for this meeting, she'd been unsure if she'd actually be able to do what was needed. She had a strong, visceral dislike of dishonesty, and she was about to destroy someone by lying. Or if not lying, at least deceit. She justified it to herself by believing that the real purpose was to save someone. But she knew that wouldn't be enough. She'd pay for what she was about to do for a long time in sleepless nights and second-guessing. At least his anger would make it easy in the short term.

Anna offered a quick prayer: *Please help me save Sophia from this man who's going to kill her if I don't stop him.*

"I said," Anna continued at Nick's back, "that I would make sure you went to jail for it."

Nick turned around at that, a rodent's low cunning back on his face. "Oh yeah?"

"Yes."

He moved toward her in the low-gravity version of a saunter. It was intended to look threatening, but to Anna, who'd grown up down the well on Earth, it just looked silly. She suppressed a laugh.

"Sophia won't say shit," Nick said, walking up to her desk to stare down at her. "She knows better. She fell down in the kitchen, and she'll say it to the magistrates."

"That's true," Anna said, then opened the drawer of her desk and took the taser out. She held it in her lap where Nick couldn't see it. "She's terrified of you. But I'm not. I don't care about you at all anymore."

"Is that right?" Nick said, leaning forward, trying to frighten her by pushing into her personal space. Anna leaned toward him.

"But Sophia is a member of this congregation, and she is my friend. Her children play with my daughter. I love them. And if I don't do something, you're going to kill her."

"Like what?"

"I'm going to call the police and tell them you threatened me." She reached for her desk terminal with her left hand. It was a gesture meant to provoke. She might as well have said, *Stop me.*

He gave her a feral grin and grabbed her arm, squeezing the bones in her wrist together hard enough to ache. Hard enough to bruise. She pointed the taser at him with her other hand.

"What's that?"

"Thank you," she said, "for making this easier."

She shot him, and he drifted to the ground spasming. She felt a faint echo of the shock through his hand on her arm. It made her hair stand up. She pulled up her desk terminal and called Sophia.

"Sophia, honey, this is Pastor Anna. Please listen to me. The police are going to be coming to your house soon to ask about Nick. You need to show them the bruises. You need to tell them what happened. Nick will already be in jail. You'll be safe. But Nick confronted me when I asked him about what happened to you, and if you want to keep us both safe, you need to be honest with them."

After a few minutes of coaxing, she finally got Sophia to say she would talk to the police when they came. Nick was starting to move his arms and legs feebly.

"Don't move," Anna said to him. "We're almost done here."

She called the New Dolinsk Police Department. The Earth corporation that had once had the contract was gone, but there still seemed to be police in the tunnels, so someone had picked it up. Maybe a Belter company. Or the OPA itself. It didn't matter.

"Hello, my name is Reverend Doctor Annushka Volovodov. I'm the pastor at St. John's United. I'm calling to report an assault on my person. A man named Nicholas Trubachev tried to attack me when I confronted him about beating his wife. No, he didn't hurt me, just a few bruises on my wrist. I had a taser in my desk and used it before he could do anything worse. Yes, I'd be happy to give a statement when you arrive. Thank you."

"Bitch," Nick spat, trying to get off the floor on shaky limbs.

Anna shot him again.

"Tough day?" Nono asked when Anna finally got home. Nono was dandling their daughter on her lap, and little Nami gave a squeal and reached for Anna as soon as she closed the door behind her.

"How's my girl?" Anna said, and dropped onto the couch next to them with a long sigh. Nono handed the baby to her, and Nami immediately set about undoing Anna's bun and trying to pull her hair. Anna squeezed her daughter and took a long sniff off the top of her head. The subtle and powerful scent Nami had given off when they'd first brought her home had faded, but a faint trace of it was still there. Scientists might claim that humans lacked the ability to interact at the pheromonal level, but Anna knew that was baloney. Whatever chemicals Nami had been pumping out as a newborn were the most powerful drug Anna had ever experienced. It made her want to have another child just to smell it again.

"Namono, no hair pulling," Nono said, trying to untwist Anna's long red hair from the baby's fist. "Don't want to talk about it?" she said to Anna.

Nono's full name was Namono too. But she'd been Nono ever since her older twin had been able to speak. When Anna and Nono named their daughter after her, the name had somehow morphed into Nami. Most people probably had no idea the baby was named after one of her mothers.

"Eventually, yes," Anna said. "But I need baby time first."

She kissed Nami on her pug nose. The same broad flat nose as Nono, just below Anna's own bright green eyes. She had Nono's coffee-colored skin, but Anna's sharp chin. Anna could sit and stare at Nami for hours at a time, drinking in the astonishing melding of herself and the woman she loved. The experience was so powerful it bordered on the sacred. Nami stuck a lock of Anna's hair in her mouth, and Anna gently pulled it back out again, then blew a raspberry at her. "No eating the hair!" she said, and Nami laughed as though this was the funniest thing ever spoken.

Nono took Anna's hand and held it tightly. They didn't move for a long time.

Nono was cooking mushrooms and rice. She'd put some reconstituted onion in with it, and the strong scent filled the kitchen. Anna cut up apples at the table for a salad. The apples were small and not very crisp. Not good for munching, but they'd be fine in a Waldorf with enough other flavors and textures to hide their imperfections. And they were lucky to have them at all. The fruit was part of the first harvest to come off of Ganymede since the troubles there. Anna didn't like to think how hungry everyone would be without that moon's remarkable recovery.

"Nami will be asleep for at least another hour," Nono said. "Are you ready to talk about your day?"

"I hurt someone and I lied to the police today," Anna said. She pushed too hard on the knife and it slipped through the soft apple and scored her thumb. It wasn't deep enough to bleed.

"Well...okay, you'll have to explain that," Nono said, stirring a small bowl of broth into her rice and mushroom mix.

"No, I really can't. Some of what I know was told in confidence."

"This lie you told, it was to help someone?"

"I think so. I hope so," Anna said, putting the last bits of apple in the bowl, then adding nuts and raisins. She stirred in the dressing.

Nono stopped and turned to stare at her. "What will you do if you get caught in the lie?"

"Apologize," Anna said.

Nono nodded, then turned back to the pot of rice. "I turned on your desk terminal today to check my mail. You were still logged in. There was a message from the United Nations about the secretary-general's humanitarian committee project. All those people who they're sending out to the Ring."

Anna felt the sharp twist of guilt. Of having been caught out at something.

"Shit," she said. She didn't like profanity, but some occasions demanded it. "I haven't responded yet." It felt like another lie.

"Were we going to talk about it before you decided?"

"Of course, I—"

"Nami is almost two," Nono said. "We've been here two years. At some point, deciding to stay is deciding who Nami is going to be for the rest of her life. She has family in Russia and Uganda who've never seen her. If she stays here much longer, they never will."

Nami was being fed the same drug cocktail all newborns in the outer planets received. It encouraged bone growth and fought off the worst of the effects low-gravity environments had on childhood development. But Nono was right. If they stayed much longer, Nami would begin to develop the long, thin frame that came with life out there. To life in low gravity. Anna would be sentencing her to a life outside her home world forever.

"Europa was always supposed to be temporary," Anna said. "It was a good posting. I speak Russian, the congregation here is small and fragile..."

Nono turned off the stove and came to sit by her, holding her hand on the table. For the first time, the faux wood tabletop looked cheap to Anna. Tacky. She saw with startling clarity a future in which Nami never lived anywhere with real wood. It felt like a punch to the stomach.

"I'm not mad at you for coming here," Nono said. "This was our dream. Coming to places like this. But when you asked for the transfer out here, you were three months pregnant."

"I was so unlikely to be chosen," Anna said, and she could hear the defensiveness in her own voice.

Nono nodded. "But you *were* chosen. And this thing for the UN. Flying out to the Ring as part of the secretary-general's advisory group. And our baby not even two."

"I think two hundred people signed up for the same slot," Anna said.

"They chose you. They want you to go."

"It was so unlikely—" Anna started.

"They always choose you," Nono interrupted. "Because you are very special. Everyone can see it. I can see it. I saw it the first time I met you, giving your speech at the faith conference in Uganda. So nervous you dropped your notes, but I could've heard a pin drop in that auditorium. You couldn't help but shine."

"I stole you from your country," Anna said. It was what she always said when Nono brought up how they met. "The Ugandan church could have used a young minister like you."

"I stole you," Nono said, like she always said, only this time it had a disconcertingly pro forma feel. As though it were an annoying ritual to be rushed through. "But you always say this. 'There were so many others. I was so unlikely to be picked.'"

"It's true."

"It's the excuse you use. You've always been one to ask for forgiveness rather than permission."

"I won't go," Anna said, pushing her hand against her eyes and the tears that threatened there. Her elbow banged into the salad bowl, nearly knocking it off the table. "I haven't said yes to them. I'll tell them it was a mistake."

"Annushka," Nono said, squeezing her hand. "You *will* go. But I am taking Nami back to Moscow with me. She can meet her grandparents. Grow up in real gravity."

Anna felt a white-hot spike of fear shoot through her stomach. "You're leaving me?"

Nono's smile was a mix of exasperation and love.

"No. *You're* leaving *us*. For a little while. And when you come back, we will be waiting for you in Moscow. Your family. I will find us a nice place to live there, and Nami and I will make it a home. A place where we can be happy. But we will not go with you."

"Why?" was all Anna could think to say.

Nono got up and took two plates out of the cupboard, then dished up dinner and put it on the table. As she spooned Waldorf salad onto her plate she said, "I'm very afraid of that thing. The thing from Venus. I'm afraid of what it will mean for everything we care about. Humanity, God, our place in His universe. I'm afraid of what it will do, of course, but much more afraid of what it *means*."

"I am too," Anna said. It was the truth. In fact, it was part of the reason she'd asked to join the expedition when she heard it was being assembled. That same fear Nono was talking about. Anna wanted to look it in the eye. Give God a chance to help her understand it. Only then could she help anyone else with it.

"So go find the answers," Nono said. "Your family will be waiting for you when you get back."

"Thank you," Anna said, a little awed by what Nono was offering her.

"I think," Nono said around a mouthful of mushrooms and rice, "that maybe they will need people like you out there."

"Like me?"

"People who don't ask permission."

Chapter Five: Bull

It's not in the budget," Michio Pa, executive officer of the *Behemoth*, said. If she'd been an Earther, she would have been a small woman, but a lifetime in microgravity had changed her the way it did all of them. Her arms, legs, and spine were all slightly elongated—not thin exactly. Just put together differently. Her head was larger than it would have been, and walking in the mild one-third-g thrust gravity, she stood as tall as Bull but still seemed perversely childlike. It made him feel shorter than he was.

"We might need to adjust that," he said. "When they put in the rail gun, they were treating it like we had standard bulkheads and supports. Thing is, the Mormons were really trying to cut back on mass. They used a lot of ceramics and silicates where the metals usually go. Directional stuff. We fire a round right now, we could shear the skin off."

Pa walked down the long, curving corridor. The ceiling arched above her, white and easily twice as high as required, an aesthetic gesture by designers who hadn't known they were building a warship. Her stride a little wider than his, moving a little more comfortably in the low g and making him trot slightly to keep up. It was one of a thousand small ways Belters reminded earthborn men and women that they didn't belong here. The XO shook her head.

"We came out here with an operational plan," she said. "If we start rewriting it every time we find an adjustment we'd like to make, we might as well not have bothered."

Privately, Bull thought the same thing, but with a different inflection. If he'd been XO, the operational plan would have been called a suggested guideline and only opened when he wanted a good laugh. Pa probably knew that. They reached the transit ramp, a softly sloping curve that led from the command and control levels at the head of the *Behemoth* down to the massive drum of her body. From Pa's domain to his.

"Look," Pa said, her mouth twitching into a conciliatory smile, "I'll make note of it for the refit, but I'm not going to start reallocating until I have an idea of the big picture. I mean, if I start pulling resources out of environmental control to cover this, and next week we find something that needs doing there, I'll just be pushing it back, right?"

Bull looked down the ramp. Soft lights recessed in the walls filled the air with a shadowless glow like a cheesy vision of heaven. Pa put her hand on his shoulder. She probably meant it to be sympathetic, but it felt like condescension.

"Yeah, okay," he said.

"It'll be all right, chief," she said, giving his trapezius a little squeeze. He nodded and walked down the ramp to the transfer platform. Her footsteps vanished behind him, submerging in the hum of air recyclers. Bull fought the urge to spit.

The *Behemoth*, back when she'd been the *Nauvoo*, had been built with a different life in mind. Most ships built for travel between the planets were like massive buildings, one floor above another with the thrust of the Epstein drive at the bottom providing the feeling of weight for whole voyages apart from a few hours in the middle when the ship flipped around to change from acceleration to slowing down. But Epstein or not, no ship could afford the power requirements or the heat generated by accelerating forever. Plus, Einstein had a thing or two to say about trying to move mass at relativistic speeds. The *Nauvoo* had been a generation ship, its journey measured in light-years rather than light-minutes. The percentage of its life span it could afford to spend under thrust was tiny by comparison. The command and control at the top of the ship and the main engines and the associated parts of engineering at the bottom could almost have belonged to a standard craft connected by a pair of kilometers-long shafts, one for a keel elevator to move people and another that gave access to the skin of the drum.

Everything else was built to spin.

For the centuries out to Tau Ceti, the body of the *Nauvoo* was meant to turn. Ten levels of environmental engineering, crew quarters, temples, schools, wastewater treatment, machine shops, and forges, and at the center, the vast interior. It would have been a piece of Earth curved back on itself. Soil and farmland and the illusion of open air with a central core of fusion-driven light and heat as gentle and warm as a summer day.

All the rooms and corridors in the body section—the vast majority of the ship—were built with that long, slow, endless season in mind. The brief periods of acceleration and deceleration at the journey's ends hardly mattered. Except that they were all the ship had now. Those places that should have been floors were all walls, and would be forever. The vast reinforced decks meant to carry a tiny world's worth of soil were the sides of a nearly unusable well. Someone slipping from the connection where the command and control levels met the great chamber could fall for nearly two full kilometers. Water systems built to take advantage of spin gravity and Coriolis stood on their sides, useless. The *Nauvoo* had been a marvel of human optimism and engineering, a statement of faith in the twinned powers of God and rigorous engineering. The *Behemoth* was a salvage job with mass accelerators strapped to her side that would do more damage to herself than to an enemy.

And Bull wasn't even allowed to fix the problems he knew about.

He passed through the transfer station and down toward his office. The rooms and corridors here were all built aslant, waiting for the spin gravity that would never come. Stretches of bare metal and exposed ducting spoke of the rush to finish it, and then to salvage and remake it. Just walking past them left Bull depressed.

Samara Rosenberg, longtime repair honcho on Tycho Station and now chief engineer on the *Behemoth*, was waiting in the anteroom, talking with Bull's new deputy. Serge, his name was, and Bull wasn't sure what he thought of the man. Serge had been part of the OPA before that was a safe thing to be. He had the traditional split circle insignia tattooed on his neck and wore it proudly. But like the rest of the security force, he'd been recruited by Michio Pa, and Bull didn't know exactly how things stood. He didn't trust the man yet, and distrust kept him from thinking all that well of him.

Sam, on the other hand, he liked.

"Hey, Bull," she said as he dropped onto the foam-core couch. "Did you get a chance to talk to the XO?"

"We talked," Bull said.

"What's the plan?" Sam said, folding her arms in a way that meant she already knew.

Bull ran a hand through his hair. When he'd been younger, his hair had been soft. Now it was like he could feel each strand individually against his fingertips. He pulled out his hand terminal and scrolled through. There were five reports waiting, three routine security reports and two occasionals—an injury report and a larceny complaint. Nothing that couldn't wait.

"Hey, Serge," Bull said. "You hold the fort here for an hour?"

"Anything you want, chief," Serge said with a grin. It was probably just paranoia that left Bull hearing contempt in the words.

"All right, then. Come on, Sam. I'll buy you a drink."

In a Coalition ship, back when there'd been an Earth-Mars Coalition, there would have been a commissary. In the OPA, there was a bar and a couple mom-and-pop restaurants along with a bare-bones keep-you-alive supply of prepack meals that anyone could get for the asking. The bar was in a wide space that might have been meant for a gymnasium or a ball court, big enough for a hundred people but Bull hadn't seen it with more than a couple dozen. The lighting had been swapped out for blue-and-white LEDs set behind sand-textured plastic. The tables were flat black and magnetized to hold the bulbs of beer and liquor to them. Nothing was served in glasses.

"Che-che!" the bartender called as Bull and Sam stepped through the door. "Moergen! Alles-mesa, you."

"Meh-ya," Sam replied, as comfortable with the mishmash Belter patois as Bull was with Spanish or English. It was her native tongue.

"What're you having?" Bull asked as he slid into one of the booths. He liked the ones where he could see the door. It was an old habit.

"I'm on duty," she said, sitting across from him.

Bull leaned forward, catching the barkeep's eye, and held up two fingers.

"Lemonades," he said.

"Sa sa!" the barkeep replied, lifting a fist in the equivalent of a nod. Bull sat back and looked at Sam. She was a pretty enough woman. Cute, with pixie-cut hair and a quick smile. There had been about a minute when they'd first met that Bull had seriously considered whether he found her attractive. But if he'd seen the same calculus in her, they'd gotten past it.

"Didn't go so good?" Sam asked.

"No."

Sam lifted her eyebrows and leaned her elbows against the tabletop. He sketched out Pa's objections and rationale, and Sam's expression shifted slowly into a fatalistic amusement.

"Waiting for the refit's all well and good," she said when he was done, "but if we try and test-fire that bad boy, it's going to make an awfully big owie."

"You're sure about that?"

"Not a hundred percent," she said. "High eighties, though."

Bull sighed out a tired obscenity as the barkeep brought the bulbs of lemonade. They were about the size of Bull's balled fists, citrus yellow with Плодоовощ малыша потехи printed on the side in bright red script.

"Maybe I should talk to her," Sam said. "If it came straight from me…"

"It came straight from you, probably it would work," he said, "and they get to tell me no on everything from now on. 'Bull asked for it? Well, if it was important, he'd have sent the Belter.' Right?"

"You really think it's about you not getting born up here?"

"Yeah."

"Well…you're probably right," Sam said. "Sorry about that."

"Comes with the territory," Bull said, pretending that it didn't bother him.

Sam plucked her lemonade off the table and took a long, thoughtful drink. The bulb clicked when the magnet readhered to the tabletop. "I've got nothing against inners. Worked with a lot of you guys, and didn't run into a higher percentage of assholes than when I'm dealing with Belters. But I have to get that rail gun's mounts reinforced. If there's a way to do that without undercutting you, I'm all for it."

"But if it's that or mess up the ship," Bull said, nodding. "Gimme a little time. I'll think of something."

"Start when you want to shoot someone and count back eighteen days," Sam said. "That's my deadline. Even if everyone's sober and working balls-out, my crew can't get it done faster than that."

"I'll think of something," Bull said.

The larceny complaint turned out to be from a repair and maintenance crew who couldn't agree how to store their tools. The injury report was a kid who got caught between a stretch of deck plating and someone driving a salvage mech. The cartilage in the kid's knee had gotten ground into about a dozen different bits of custard; the medic said a good clean bone break would have been better. The injured man would be fine, but he was off active duty for at least a month while all his pieces got glued back together.

The security reports were boilerplate, which either meant that things were going well or that the problems were getting glossed over, but probably they were going well. The trip out to the Ring was a shakedown cruise, and that always meant there'd be a little honeymoon period when the crew were all figuratively standing shoulder to shoulder and taking on the work. Everyone expected there'd be problems, so there was a grace period when morale didn't start heading down.

Chief security officer on an OPA ship was a half-assed kind of position, one part cop, one part efficiency expert, and pretty much all den mother to a crew of a thousand people with their own agendas and petty power struggles and opinions on how he should be doing his job better. A good security chief kept bullshit off the captain's plate as a full-time job.

The worst part, though, was that all Bull's formal duties were focused inward, on the ship. Right now, a flotilla of Earth ships was burning out into the deep night. A matching force of Martian war vessels—the remnants of the navy that had survived two let's-not-call-them-wars—was burning out on a converging path. The *Behemoth* was lumbering along too with a head start that came from being farther from the sun and the hobble of low-g acceleration to keep her slow. And all of it was focused on the Ring.

Reports would be filling Captain Ashford's queue, and as his XO, Pa would be reading them too. Bull had whatever scraps they let him have or else the same mix of pabulum and panic that filled the newsfeeds. Ashford and Pa would be in conference for most of their shifts, working over strategies and options and playing through scenarios for how things might go down when they reached the Ring. Bull was going to worry about all the trivial stuff so that they didn't have to.

And somehow, he was going to make the mission work. Because Fred had asked him to.

"Hey, chief," Serge said. Bull looked up from the terminal feed in his desk. Serge stood in the office doorway. "Shift's up, and I'm out."

"All right," Bull said. "I still got some stuff. I can lock up when I'm done."

"Bien alles," Serge said with a nod. His light, shuffling footsteps hissed through the front room. In the corridor, Gutmansdottir stroked his white beard and Casimir said something that made them both chuckle. Corin lifted her chin to Serge as he stepped out. The door closed behind him. When he was sure he was alone, Bull pulled up the operational plan and started hunting. He didn't have authority to change it, but that didn't mean he couldn't change anything.

Two hours later, when he was done, he turned off the screen and stood. The office was dark and colder than he liked it. The hum of the ventilation system comforted him. If it were ever completely silent, that would be the time to worry. He stretched, the vertebrae between his shoulder blades crunching like gravel.

They would still be in the bar, most likely. Serge and Corin and Casimir. Macondo and Garza, so similar they could have been brothers. Jojo. His people, to the degree that they were his. He should go. Be with them. Make friends.

He should go to his bunk.

"Come on, old man," he said. "Time to get some rest."

He had closed and locked the office door before Sam's voice came to him in his memory. *Even if everyone's sober and working balls-out, my crew can't get it done faster than that.* He hesitated, his wide fingers over the keypad. It was late. He needed food and sleep and an hour or so checking in with the family aggregator his cousin had set up three years before to help everyone keep track of who was living where. He had a container of flash-frozen green chile from Hatch, back on Earth, waiting for him. It was all going to be there in the morning, and more besides. He didn't need to make more work for himself. No one was going to thank him for it.

He went back in, turned his desk back on, and reread the injury report.

Sam had a good laugh. One that came from the gut. It filled the machining bay, echoing off ceiling and walls until it sounded like there was a crowd of her. Two of the techs on the far side turned to look toward her, smiling without knowing what they were smiling about.

"Technical support?" she said. "You've got to be kidding."

"Rail gun's a pretty technical piece of equipment," Bull said. "It needs support."

"So you redefined what I do as technical support."

"Yeah."

"That's never going to fly," she said.

"Then get the job done quick," Bull said.

"Ashford will pull you up for disciplinary action," she said, the amusement fading but not quite gone yet.

"He has that right. But there's this other thing I wanted to talk about. You said something yesterday about how long it would take to do the job if everyone on your crew was sober?"

It was like turning off a light. The smile left Sam's face as if it had never been there. She crossed her arms. Tiny half-moon shapes dented in at the corners of her mouth, making her look older than she was. Bull nodded to her like she'd said something.

"You've got techs coming to work high," he said.

"Sometimes," she said. And then, reluctantly, "Some of it's alcohol, but mostly it's pixie dust to make up for lack of sleep."

"I got a report about a kid got his knee blown out. His blood was clean, but it doesn't look like anyone tested the guy who was driving the mech. Driver isn't even named in the report. Weird, eh?"

"If you say so," she said.

Bull looked down at his feet. The gray-and-black service utility boots. The spotless floor.

"I need a name, Sam."

"You know I can't do that," she said. "These assholes are my crew. If I lose their respect, we're done here."

"I won't bust your guys unless they're dealing."

"You can't ask me to pick sides. And sorry for saying this, but you already don't have a lot of friends around here. You should be careful how you alienate people."

Across the bay, the two technicians lifted a broken mech onto a steel repair hoist. The murmur of their conversation was just the sound of words without the words themselves. If he couldn't hear them, Bull figured they couldn't hear him.

"Yeah. So Sam?"

"Bull."

"I'm gonna need you to pick sides."

He watched her vacillate. It only took a few seconds. Then he looked across the bay. The technicians had the mech open, pulling an electric motor out of its spine. It was smaller than a six-pack of beer and built to put out enough torque to rip steel. Not the sort of thing to play with drunk. Sam followed his gaze and his train of thought.

"For a guy who bends so many rules, you can be pretty fucking uncompromising."

"Strong believer in doing what needs to get done."

It took her another minute, but she gave him a name.

Chapter Six: Holden

Uranus is really far away," Naomi said as they walked along the corridor to the docking bay. It was the third objection to the contract that she'd listed so far, and something in her voice told Holden there were a lot more points on her list. Under other circumstances, he would have thought she was just angry that he'd accepted the job. She *was* angry. But not *just*.

"Yes," he said. "It is."

"And Titania is a shitty little moon with one tiny little science base on it," Naomi continued.

"Yes."

"We could *buy* Titania for what it cost these people to hire us to fly out there," Naomi said.

Holden shrugged. This part of Ceres was a maze of cheap warehouse tunnels and even cheaper office space. The walls were the grungy off-white of spray-on insulation foam. Someone with a pocketknife and a few minutes to kill could reach the bedrock of Ceres without much effort. From the ratty look of the corridor, there were a lot of people with knives and idle time.

A small forklift came down the corridor toward them with an electric whine and a constant high-pitched beep. Holden backed up against the wall and pulled Naomi to him to get her out of its way. The driver gave Holden a tiny nod of thanks as she drove by.

"So why are they hiring us?" she asked. Demanded.

"Because we're awesome?"

"Titania has, what, a couple hundred people living at the science base?" Naomi said. "You know how they usually send supplies out there? They load them into a single-use braking rocket, and fling them at Uranus' orbit with a rail gun."

"Usually," Holden agreed.

"And the company? Outer Fringe Exports? If I was making a cheap, disposable shell corporation, you know what I'd call it?"

"Outer Fringe Exports?"

"Outer Fringe Exports," she said.

Naomi stopped at the entry hatch that opened to the rental docking bay and the *Rocinante*. The sign overhead listed the present user: Outer Fringe Exports. Holden started to reach for the controls to cycle the pressure doors open, but Naomi put a hand on his arm.

"These people are hiring a warship to transport something to Titania," she said, lowering her voice as though afraid someone might be listening. "How can they possibly afford to do that? Our cargo hold is the size of a hatbox."

"We gave them a good rate?" Holden said, trying for funny and failing.

"What would someone be sending to Titania that requires a fast, stealthy, and heavily armed ship? Have you asked what's in those crates we signed up to carry?"

"No," Holden said. "No, I haven't. And I normally would, but I'm trying really hard not to find out."

Naomi frowned at him, her face shifting between angry and concerned. "Why?"

Holden pulled out his hand terminal and called up an orbital map of the solar system. "See this, all the way on this edge? This is the Ring." He scrolled the display to the other edge of the solar system. "And this is Uranus. They are literally the two spots furthest from each other in the universe that have humans near them."

"And?" Naomi said.

Holden took a deep breath. He could feel a surge of the anxiety he always tried to deny leaping up in him, and he pushed it back down.

"And I know I don't talk about it much, but something really unpleasant and really big with a really high body count knows my name, and it's connected to the Ring."

"Miller," Naomi said.

"The Ring opened, and he *knew when it happened*. It was the closest thing to making sense he's done since..."

Since he rose from the dead. The words didn't fit in his throat, and Naomi didn't make him say them. Her nod was enough. She understood. In an act of legendary cowardice, he was running away to the other side of the solar system to avoid Miller and the Ring and everything that had to do with them. If they had to transport black market human organs or drugs or sexbots or whatever was in those crates, he'd do it. Because he was scared.

Her eyes were unreadable. After all this time, she could still keep her thoughts out of her expression when she wanted to.

"Okay," Naomi said, and pushed the entry door open for him.

At the outer edge of Ceres where the spin gravity was greatest, Holden almost felt like he could have been on Luna or Mars. Loading gantries fed into the skin of the station like thick veins, waiting for the mechs to load in the cargo. Poorly patched scars marked the walls where accidents had marred them. The air smelled of coolant and the kind of cheap air filters that reminded Holden of urinal cakes. Amos lounged on a small electric power lift, his eyes closed.

"We get the job?"

"We did," Naomi said.

Amos cracked an eye open as they came near. A single frown line drew itself on his broad forehead.

"We happy about that?" he asked.

"We're fine with it," Naomi said. "Let's get the lift warmed up. Cargo's due in ten minutes and we probably want to get it off station as quickly as we can without raising suspicion."

There was a beauty in the efficiency that came from a crew that had flown together as long as they had. A fluidity and intimacy and grace that grew from long experience. Eight minutes after Holden and Naomi had come in, the *Roci* was ready to take on cargo. Ten minutes later, nothing happened. Then twenty. Then an hour. Holden paced the gantry nearest the entry hatch with an uncomfortable tingling crawling up the back of his neck.

"You *sure* we got this job?" Amos asked.

"These guys seemed really sketchy to me," Naomi said over the comm from her station in ops. "I'd think we've been scammed, except we haven't given anyone our account numbers."

"We're on the clock here, boss," Alex said from the cockpit. "These loading docks charge by the minute."

Holden bit back his irritation and said, "I'll call again."

He pulled out his terminal and connected to the export company's office. Their messaging system responded, as it had the last three times he'd requested a connection. He waited for the beep that would let him leave another message. Before he could, his display lit up with an incoming connection request from the same office. He switched to it.

"Holden here."

"This is a courtesy call, Captain Holden," the voice on the other end said. The video feed was the Outer Fringe Exports logo on a gray background. "We're withdrawing the contract, and you might want to consider leaving that dock very, very soon."

"You can't back out now," Holden said, trying to keep his voice calm and professional against the rising panic he felt. "We've signed the deal. We've got your deposit. It's non-refundable."

"Keep it," his caller said. "But we consider your failure to inform us of your current situation as a prior breach."

Situation? Holden thought. They couldn't know about Miller. He didn't think they could. "I don't—"

"The party that's tracking you left our offices about five minutes ago, so you should probably get off Ceres in a hurry. Goodbye, Mr. Holden—"

"Wait!" Holden said. "Who was there? What's going on?"

The call ended.

Amos was rubbing his pale, stubble-covered scalp with both hands. He sighed and said, "We got a problem, right?"

"Yep."

"Be right back," Amos replied, and climbed off the forklift.

"Alex? How long till we can clear this dock?" Holden asked. He loped across the bay to the entry hatch. There didn't seem to be any way to lock it from his side. Why would there be? The bays were temporary rental space for loading and unloading cargo. No need for security.

"She's warmed up," Alex replied, not asking the obvious question. Holden was grateful for that. "Gimme ten to run the decouplin' sequence, that should do it."

"Start now," Holden said, hurrying back toward the airlock. "Leave the 'lock open till the last minute. Amos and I will be out here making sure no one interferes."

"Roger that, Cap," Alex replied, and dropped the connection.

"Interferes?" Naomi said. "What's going on...Okay, why is Amos going out there with a shotgun?"

"Those sketchy, scary gangster types we just signed on with?"

"Yes?"

"They just dropped *us*. And whatever scared them into doing it is coming here right now. I don't think guns are an overreaction."

Amos ran down the ramp, holding his auto-shotgun in his right hand and an assault rifle in his left. He tossed the rifle to Holden, then took up a cover position behind the forklift and aimed at the bay's entry hatch. Like Alex, he didn't ask why.

"Want me to come out?" Naomi asked.

"No, but prepare to defend the ship if they get past me and Amos," Holden replied, then moved over to the forklift's recharging station. It was the only other cover in the otherwise empty bay.

In a conversational tone, Amos said, "Any idea what we're expecting here?"

"Nope," Holden said. He clicked the rifle to autofire and felt a faint nausea rising in his throat.

"All right, then," Amos said cheerfully.

"Eight minutes," Naomi said from his hand terminal. Not a long time, but if they were trying to hold the bay under hostile fire, it would seem like an eternity.

The entry warning light at the cargo bay entrance flashed yellow three times, and the hatch slid open.

"Don't shoot unless I do," Holden said quietly. Amos grunted back at him.

A tall blond woman walked into the bay. She had an Earther's build, a video star's face, and couldn't have been more than twenty. When she saw the two guns pointed at her, she raised her hands and wiggled her fingers. "Not armed," she said. Her cheeks dimpled into a grin. Holden tried to imagine why a supermodel would be looking for him.

"Hi," Amos said. He was grinning back at her.

"Who are you?" Holden said, keeping his gun trained on her.

"My name's Adri. Are you James Holden?"

"I can be," Amos said, "if you want." She smiled. Amos smiled back, but his weapon was still in a carefully neutral position.

"What've we got down there?" Naomi asked, her voice tense in his ear. "Do we have a threat?"

"I don't know yet," Holden said.

"You are, though, right? You're James Holden," Adri said, walking toward him. The assault rifle in his hands didn't seem to bother her at all. Up close, she smelled like strawberries and vanilla. "*Captain* James Holden, of the *Rocinante*?"

"Yes," he said.

She held out a slim, throwaway hand terminal. He took it automatically. The terminal displayed a picture of him, along with his name and his UN citizen and UN naval ID numbers.

"You've been served," she said. "Sorry. It was nice meeting you, though."

She turned back to the door and walked away.

"What the fuck?" Amos said to no one, dropping the muzzle of his gun to the floor and rubbing his scalp again.

"Jim?" Naomi said.

"Give me a minute."

He paged through the summons, jumping past seven pages of legalese to get to the point: The Martians wanted their ship back. Official proceedings had been started against him in both Earth and Martian courts challenging the salvage claim to the *Rocinante*. Only they were calling it the *Tachi*. The ship was under an order of impound pending adjudication, effective immediately.

His short conversation with Outer Fringe Exports suddenly made a lot more sense.

"Cap?" Alex said through the connection. "I'm getting a red light on the docking clamp release. I'm puttin' a query in. Once I get that cleared, we can pop the cork."

"What's going on out there?" Naomi asked. "Are we still leaving?"

Holden took a long, deep breath, sighed, and said something obscene.

The longest layover the *Rocinante* had taken since Holden and the others had gone independent had been five and a half weeks. The twelve days that the *Roci* spent in lockup seemed longer. Naomi and Alex were on the ship most of the time, putting inquiries through to lawyers and legal aid societies around the system. With every letter and conversation, the consensus grew. Mars had been smart to begin legal proceedings in Earth courts as well as their own. Even if Holden and the *Roci* slipped the leash at Ceres, all major ports would be denied them. They'd have to skulk from one gray-market Belter port to the next. Even if there was enough work, they might not be able to find supplies to keep them flying.

If they took the case before a magistrate, they might or might not lose the ship, but it would be expensive to find out. Accounts that Holden had thought of as comfortably full suddenly looked an order of magnitude too small. Staying on Ceres Station made him antsy; being on the *Roci* left him sad.

There had been any number of times in his travels on the *Roci* that he'd imagined—even expected—it all to come to a tragic end. But those scenarios had involved firefights or alien monstrosities or desperate dives into some planetary atmosphere. He'd imagined with a sick thrill of dread what it would be like if Alex died, or Amos. Or Naomi. He'd wondered whether the three of them would go on without him. He hadn't considered that the end might find all of them perfectly fine. That the *Rocinante* might be the one to go.

Hope, when it came, was a documentary streamcast team from UN Public Broadcasting. Monica Stuart, the team lead, was an auburn-haired freckled woman with a professionally sculpted beauty that made her seem vaguely familiar when he saw her on the screen of the pilot's deck. She hadn't come in person.

"How many people are we talking about?" Holden asked.

"Four," she said. "Two camera jockeys, my sound guy, and me."

Holden ran a hand across eight days' worth of patchy beard. The sense of inevitability sat in his gut like a stone.

"To the Ring," he said.

"To the Ring," she agreed. "We need to make it a hard burn to get there before the Martians, the Earth flotilla, and the *Behemoth*. And we'd like some measure of safety once we're out there, which the *Rocinante* would be able to give us."

Naomi cleared her throat, and the documentarian shifted her attention to her.

"You're sure you can get the hold taken off the *Roci*?" Naomi asked.

"I am protected by the Freedom of Journalism Act. I have the right to the reasonable use of hired materials and personnel in the pursuit of a story. Otherwise, anyone could stop any story they didn't like by malicious use of injunctions like the one on the *Roci*. I have a backdated contract that says I hired you a month ago, before I arrived at Ceres. I have a team of lawyers ten benches deep who can drown anyone that objects in enough paperwork to last a lifetime."

"So we've been working for you all along," Holden said.

"Only if you want to get that docking lock rescinded. But it's more than just a ride I'm looking for. That's what makes it reasonable that I can't just hire a different ship."

"I knew there was a but," Holden said.

"I want to interview the crew too. While there are a half dozen ships I could get for the trip out, yours is the one that comes with the survivors of Eros."

Naomi looked across at him. Her eyes were carefully neutral. Was it better to be here, trapped on Ceres while the *Roci* was pulled away from him by centimeters, or flying straight into the abyss with his crew? And the Ring.

"I have to think about it," he said. "I'll be in touch."

"I respect that," Monica said. "But please don't take long. If we're not going with you, we've still got to go with someone."

He dropped the connection. In the silence, the deck seemed larger than it was.

"This isn't coincidence," Holden said. "We just *happen* to get locked down by Mars, and the only thing that can get us out of the docking clamps just *happens* to be heading for the Ring? No way. We're being manipulated. Someone's planning this. It's him."

"Jim—"

"It's him. It's Miller."

"It's not Miller. He can barely string together a coherent sentence," Naomi said. "How is he going to engineer something like this?"

Holden leaned forward and the seat under him shifted. His head felt like it was stuffed with wool.

"If we leave, they can still take her away from us," he said. "Once this story is done, we won't be in any better position than we are right now."

"Except that we wouldn't be locked on Ceres," Naomi said. "And it's a long way out there. A long way back. A lot could change."

"That wasn't as comforting as you meant it to be."

Naomi's smile was thin but not bitter.

"Fair point," she said.

The *Rocinante* hummed around them, the systems running through their automatic maintenance checks, the air cycling gently through the ducts. The ship breathing and dreaming. Their home, at rest. Holden reached out a hand, lacing his fingers with Naomi's.

"We still have some money. We can take out a loan," she said. "We could buy a different ship. Not a good one, but…It wouldn't have to be the end of it all."

"It would be, though."

"Probably."

"No choice, then," Holden said. "Let's go to Nineveh."

Monica and her team arrived in the early hours of the morning, loading a few small crates of equipment that they carried themselves. In person, Monica was thinner than she seemed on screen. Her camera crew were a sturdy Earth woman named Okju and a brown-skinned Martian man who went by Clip. The cameras they carried looked like shoulder-mounted weapons, alloy casings that could telescope out to almost two meters or retract to fit around the tightest corner in the ship.

The soundman was blind. He had a dusting of short white hair and opaque black glasses. His teeth were yellowed like old ivory, and his smile was gentle and humane. According to the paperwork, his name was Elio Casti, but for some reason the documentary team all called him Cohen.

They assembled in the galley, Holden's four people and Monica's. He could see each group quietly considering the other. They'd be living in one another's laps for months. Strangers trapped in a metal-and-ceramic box in the vast ocean of the vacuum. Holden cleared his throat.

"Welcome aboard," he said.

Chapter Seven: Melba

If the Earth-Mars alliance hadn't collapsed, if there hadn't been a war—or two wars depending on how the line between battles was marked—civilian ships like the *Cerisier* would have had no place in the great convoy. The ships lost at Ganymede and in the Belt, the skirmishes to control those asteroids best placed to push down a gravity well. Hundreds of ships had been lost, from massive engines of war like the *Donnager,* the *Agatha King,* and the *Hyperion* to countless small three- and four-person support ships.

Nor, Melba knew, were those the only scars. Phobos with its listening station had become a thin, nearly invisible ring around Mars. Eros was gone. Phoebe had been subjected to a sustained nuclear hell and pushed into Saturn. The farms at Ganymede had collapsed. Venus had been used and abandoned by the alien protomolecule. Protogen and the Mao-Kwikowski empire, once one of the great shipping and transport companies in the system, had been gutted, stolen, and sold.

The *Cerisier* began her life as an exploration vessel. Now she was a flying toolshed. The bays of scientific equipment were machine shops now. What had once been sealed labs were stacked from deck to deck with the mundane necessities of environmental control networks—scrubbers, ducting, sealants, and alarm arrays. She lumbered through the uncaring vacuum on the fusion plume of her Epstein drive. The crew of a hundred and six souls was made of a small elite of ship command—no more than a dozen, all told—and a vast body of technicians, machinists, and industrial chemists.

Once, Melba thought, this ship had been on the bleeding edge of human exploration. Once it had burned through the skies of Jovian moons, seeing things humanity had never seen before. Now it was the handservant of the government, discovering nothing more exotic than what had been flushed into the water reclamation tanks. The degradation gave Melba a sense of kinship with the ship's narrow halls and gray plastic ladders. Once, Clarissa Melpomene Mao had been the light of her school. Popular and beautiful, and suffused with the power and influence of her father's name. Now her father was a numbered prisoner in a nameless prison, allowed only a few minutes of external connection every day, and those to his lawyer, not his wife or children.

And she was Melba Koh, sleeping on a gel couch that smelled of someone else's body in a cabin smaller than a closet. She commanded a team of four electrochemical technicians: Stanni, Ren, Bob, and Soledad. Stanni and Bob were decades older than her. Soledad, three years younger, had been on two sixteen-month tours. Ren, her official second, was a Belter and, like all Belters, passionate about environmental control systems the way normal people were with sex or religion. She didn't ask how he'd ended up on an Earth ship, and he didn't volunteer the information.

She had known the months going out to the Ring would be hard, but she'd misunderstood what the worst parts would be.

"She's a fucking bitch, right?" Stanni said. It was a private channel between him and Ren. If she'd been who she pretended to be, she wouldn't have been able to hear it. "She doesn't know dick."

Ren grunted, neither defending her nor joining the attack.

"If you hadn't caught that brownout buffer wrong way on the *Macedon* last week, it would have been another cascade failure, si no? Would have had to throw off the whole schedule to go back and fix it."

"Might've," Ren said.

She was a level above them. The destroyer *Seung Un* muttered around her. The crew was on a maintenance run. Scheduled, routine, predictable. They'd left the *Cerisier* ten hours earlier in one of the dozen transports that clung to the maintenance ship's skin. They would be here for another fifteen hours, changing out the high-yield scrubbers and checking the air supply continuity. The greatest danger, she'd learned, was condensation degrading the seals.

It was the kind of detail she should have known.

She pulled herself through the access shaft. Her tool kit hung heavy on her front in the full-g thrust gravity. She imagined it was what being pregnant would feel like. Unless something strange had happened, Soledad and Bob were sleeping in the boat. Ren and Stanni were a level down, and going lower with every hour. They were expecting her to make the final inspection of their work. And, it seemed, they were expecting her to do it poorly.

It was true, of course. She didn't know why a real electrochemical technician seeing her inexperience should embarrass her as deeply as it did. She'd read a few manuals, run through a few tutorials. All that mattered was that they think she was an authentic semicompetent overseer. It didn't matter whether they respected her. They weren't her friends.

She should have switched to the private frequencies for Soledad and Bob to be certain neither had woken unexpectedly and might come looking for her. This part of the plan was important. She couldn't let any of them find her. But somehow, she couldn't bring herself to shift away from Ren and Stanni.

"She don't do anything is all. Keeps to her cabin, don't help on the project. She just come out the end, look up, look down, sign off, and go back to her cabin."

"True."

The junction was hard to miss. The bulkhead was reinforced and clearly marked with bright orange safety warnings in five languages. She paused before it, her hands on her hips, and waited to feel some sense of accomplishment. And she did, only it wasn't as pure as she'd hoped. She looked up and down the passageway, though the chances of being interrupted here were minimal.

The explosive was strapped against her belly, the heat of her skin keeping it malleable and bright green. As it cooled to ambient, the putty would harden and fade to gray. It surprised her again with its density. Pressing it along the seams of the junction, she felt like she was forming lead with her bare hands. The effort left her knuckles aching before she was halfway done. She'd budgeted half an hour, but it took her almost twice that. The detonator was a black dot four millimeters across with ten black ceramic contacts that pressed into the already stiffening putty. It looked like a tick.

When she was done, she wiped her hands down with cleaning towelettes twice, making sure none of the explosive was caught under her fingernails or on her clothes. She'd expected to skip her inspection of just the one level, but Ren and Stanni had made good time, and she took the lift down two levels instead. They were still talking, but not about her now. Stanni was considering getting a crush on Soledad. In laconic Belt-inflected half phrases, Ren was advising against it. Smart man, her second.

The lift paused and three soldiers got on it, all men. Melba pressed herself back to make room for them, and the nearest nodded his polite gratitude. His uniform identified him as Marcos. She nodded back, then stared hard at her feet, willing them not to look at her. Her uniform felt like a costume. Even though she knew better, it felt like they would see through her disguise if they looked too close. Like her past was written on her skin.

My name is Melba Koh, she thought. *I've never been anyone else.*

The lift stopped at her level and the three soldiers made way for her. She wondered, when the time came, whether Marcos would die.

She had never been to her father's prison, and even if he'd been allowed visitors, the visit would have been in a prescribed room, monitored, transcribed. Any real human emotion would have been pressed out of it by the weight of official attention. She would never have been permitted to see the hallways he walked down or the cell where he slept, but after his incarceration by the United Nations, she'd researched prison design. Her room was three centimeters narrower, a centimeter and a half longer. The crash couch she slept in was gimbaled to allow for changes in acceleration, while his would be welded to the floor. She could squeeze out whenever she wanted and go to the gang showers or the mess. Her door locked from the inside, and there were no cameras or microphones in her room.

In every way that mattered, she had more freedom than her father. That she likely spent as much time in isolation was a matter of choice for her, and that made all the difference. Tomorrow would be a fresh rotation out. Another ship, another round of maintenance that she could pretend to oversee. Tonight she could lie in her couch dressed in the simple cotton underclothes that she'd bought as the kind of thing Melba would wear. Her hand terminal had fifteen tutorials in local memory and dozens more on the ship's shared storage. They covered everything from microorganic nutrient reclamation to coolant system specifications to management policies. She should have been reading them through. Or if not that, at least she shouldn't have been reviewing her own secret files.

On the screen, Jim Holden looked like a zealot. The composite was built from dozens of hours of broadcast footage of the man taken over the previous years, with weight given to the most recent images and stills. The software she'd used to make a perfect visual simulacrum of the man cost more than her Melba persona had. The fake Holden had to be good enough to fool both people and computers, at least for a little while. On the screen, his brown eyes squinted with an idiot's earnestness. His jaw had the first presentiment of jowls, only half hidden by the microgravity. The smarmy half smile told her everything she needed to know about the man who had destroyed her family.

"This is Captain James Holden," he said. "What you've just seen is a demonstration of the danger you are in. My associates have placed similar devices on every ship presently in proximity to the Ring. You will all stand down as I am assuming sole and absolute control over the Ring in the name of the Outer Planets Alliance. Any ship that approaches the Ring without my *personal* permission will be destroyed without—"

She paused it, freezing her small, artificial Holden in mid-gesture. Her fingertip traced the outline of his shoulder, across his cheek, and then stabbed at his eyes. She wished now that she'd picked a more inflammatory script. On Earth, making her preparations, it had seemed enough to have him take unilateral control of the Ring. Now each time she watched it, it seemed tamer.

Killing Holden would have been easier. Assassinations were cheap by comparison, but she knew enough about image control and social dynamics to see where it would have led. Martyrdom, canonization, love. A host of conspiracy theories that implicated anyone from the OPA to her father. That was precisely not the point. Holden had to be humiliated in a way that passed backward in time. Someone coming to his legacy had to be able to look back at all the things Holden had done, all the pronouncements he'd given, all the high-handed, self-righteous decisions made on behalf of others while never leaving his control and see that of course it had all led to this. His name put in with the great traitors, con men, and self-aggrandizing egomaniacs of history. When she was done, everything Holden had touched would be tainted by association, including the destruction of her family. Her father.

Somewhere deep in the structure of the *Cerisier*, one of the navigators started a minor correction burn and gravity shifted a half a degree. The couch moved under her, and she tried not to notice it. She preferred the times when she could pretend that she was in a gravity well to the little reminders that she was the puppet of acceleration and inertia.

Her hand terminal chimed once, announcing the arrival of a message. To anyone who didn't look carefully, it would seem like just another advertisement. An investment opportunity she would be a fool to ignore with a video presentation attached that would seem like corrupted data to anyone who didn't have the decryption key. She sat up, swinging her legs over the edge of the couch, and leaned close to the hand terminal.

The man who appeared on her screen wore black glasses dark enough to be opaque. His hair was cropped close to his skull, but she could see from the way it moved that he was under heavy burn. The soundman cleared his throat.

"The package is delivered and ready for testing. I'd appreciate the balance transfer as soon as you've confirmed. I've got some bills coming due, and I'm a little under the wire." Something in the background hissed, and a distant voice started laughing. A woman. The file ended.

She replayed it four more times. Her heart was racing and her fingers felt like little electric currents were running through them. She'd need to confirm, of course. But this was the last, most dangerous step. The *Rocinante* had been cutting-edge military hardware when it had fallen into Holden's hands. There could also have been any number of changes made to the security systems in the years since. She set up a simple remote connection looped through a disposable commercial account on Ceres Station. It might take days for the *Rocinante*'s acknowledgment to come back to her saying that the back door was installed and functioning, that the ship was hers. But if it did...

It was the last piece. Everything in place. A sense of almost religious well-being washed over her. The thin room with its scratched walls and too-bright LEDs had never seemed so benign. She levered herself up out of the couch. She wanted to celebrate, though of course there was no one she could tell. Talk to might be enough.

The halls of the *Cerisier* were so narrow that it was impossible to walk abreast or to pass someone coming the opposite way without turning sideways. The mess would fit twenty people sitting with their hips touching. The nearest thing to an open area was the fitness center off the medical bay. The treadmills and exercise machines required enough room that no one would be caught in the joints and belts. Safety regulations made it the widest, freest air in the ship, and so a good place to be around people.

Of her team, only Ren was present. In the usual microgravity, he would probably have been neck deep in a tank of resistance gel. With the full-g burn, he was on a regular treadmill. His pale skin was bright with sweat, his carrot-orange hair pulled back in a frizzed ponytail. It was strange watching him. His large head was made larger by his hair, and the thinness of his body made him seem more like something from a children's program than an actual man.

He nodded to her as she came in.

"Ren," she said, walking to the front of his machine. She felt the gazes of other crewmen on her, but on the *Cerisier* she didn't feel as exposed. Or maybe it was the good news that carried her. "Do you have a minute?"

"Chief," he said instead of yes, but he thumbed down the treadmill to a cool-down walk. "Que sa?"

"I heard some of the things Stanni was saying about me," she said. Ren's expression closed down. "I just wanted..."

She frowned, looked down, and then gave in to the impulse welling up in her.

"He's right," she said. "I'm in over my head with this job. I got it because of some political favors. I'm not qualified to do what I'm doing."

He blinked rapidly. He shot a glance around her, checking to see if anyone had overheard them. She didn't particularly care, but she thought it was sweet that he did.

"Not so bad, you," he said. "I mean, little off here, little off there. But I've been under worse."

"I need help," she said. "To do all the work the way it should be done, I need help. I need someone I can trust. Someone I can count on."

Ren nodded, but his forehead roughened. He blew out his breath and stepped off the treadmill.

"I want to get the work done right," she said. "Not miss anything. And I want the team to respect me."

"Okay, sure."

"I know you should have had this job."

Ren blew out another breath, his cheeks ballooning. It was more expressive than she'd ever seen him before. He leaned against the wall. When he met her gaze, it was like he was seeing her for the first time.

"Appreciate you saying it, chief, but we're both of us outsiders here," he said. "Stick together, bien?"

"Good," she said, leaning against the wall next to him. "So. The brownout buffers? What did I get wrong?"

Ren sighed.

"The buffers are smart, but the design's stupid," he said. "They talk to each other, so they're also a separate network, yah? Thing is, you put one in the wrong way? Works okay. But next time it resets, the signal down the line looks wrong. Triggers a diagnostic run in the next one down, and then the next one down. Whole network starts blinking like Christmas. Too many errors on the network and it fails closed, takes down the whole grid. And then you got us going through checking each one by hand. With flashlights and the supervisor chewing our nuts."

"That's...that can't be right," she said. "Seriously? It could have shut down the *grid*?"

"I know, right?" Ren said, smiling. "And all it would take

is change the design so it don't fit in if you got it wrong. But they never do. A lot of what we do is like that, boss. We try to catch the little ones before they get big. Some things, you get them wrong, it's nothing. Some things, and it's a big mess."

The words felt like a church bell being struck. They resonated. She was that fault, that error. She didn't know what she was doing, not really, and she'd get away with it. She'd pass. Until she didn't, and then everything would fall apart. Her throat felt tighter. She almost wished she hadn't said anything.

She was a brownout buffer pointed the wrong way. A flaw that was easy to overlook, with the potential to wreck everything.

"For the others…don't take them harsh. Blowing off steam, mostly. Not you so much as it's anything. Fear-biting."

"Fear?"

"Sure," he said. "Everyone on this boat's scared dry. Try not to show it, do the work, but we all getting nightmares. Natural, right?"

"What are they afraid of?" she asked.

Behind her the door cycled open and shut. A man said something in a language she didn't know. Ren tilted his head, and she had the sick, sinking feeling that she'd done something wrong. She hadn't acted normal, and she didn't know what her misstep was.

"Ring," he said at last. "It's what killed Eros. Could have killed Mars. All that weird stuff it did on Venus, no one knows what it was. Deaded that slingshot kid who went through. Half everyone thinks we should be pitching nukes at it, other half thinks we'd only piss it off. We're going out as deep as anyone ever has just so we can look in the devil's eye, and Stanni and Solé and Bob? They're all scared as shit of what we see in it. Me too."

"Ah," she said. "All right. I understand that."

Ren tried on a smile.

"You? It don't scare you?"

"It's not something I think about."

Chapter Eight: Anna

Nami and Nono left for Earth a week before Anna's shuttle. Those last days living alone in those rooms, knowing that she would never be back—that they would never be back—was like a gentle presentiment of death: profoundly melancholy and, shamefully, a little exhilarating.

The shuttle from Europa was one of the last to join the flotilla, and it meant eighteen hours of hard burn. By the time she set foot on the deck of the UNN *Thomas Prince*, all she wanted was a bunk and twelve hours' sleep. The young yeoman who'd been sent to greet and escort her had other plans, though, and the effort it would have taken to be rude about it was more than she could muster.

"The *Prince* is a *Xerxes*-class battleship, or what we sometimes refer to as a third-generation dreadnought," he said, gesturing to the white ceramic-over-gel of the hangar's interior walls. The shuttle she'd arrived on nestled in its bay looking small under the cathedral-huge arch. "We call it a third-generation battleship because it is the third redesign since the buildup during the first Earth-Mars conflict."

Not that it had been much of a conflict, Anna thought. The Martians had made noises about independence, the UN had built a lot of ships, Mars had built a few. And then Solomon Epstein had gone from being a Martian yachting hobbyist to the inventor of the first fusion drive that solved the heat buildup and rapid fuel consumption problems of constant thrust. Suddenly Mars had a few ships that went really, really fast. They'd said, *Hey, we're about to go colonize the rest of the solar system. Want to stay mad at us, or want to come with?* The UN had made the sensible choice, and most people would agree: Giving up Mars in exchange for half of the solar system had probably been a pretty good deal.

It didn't mean that both sides hadn't kept on designing new ways to kill each other. Just in case.

"...just over half a kilometer long, and two hundred meters wide at its broadest point," the yeoman was saying.

"Impressive," Anna replied, trying to bring her wandering attention back.

The yeoman pulled her luggage on a small rolling cart to a bank of elevator lifts.

"These elevators run the length of the ship," he said as he punched a button on the control panel. "We call them the keel elevators—"

"Because they run along the belly of the ship?" Anna said.

"Yes! That's what the bottom of seagoing vessels was called, and space-based navies have kept the nomenclature."

Anna nodded. His enthusiasm was exhausting and charming at the same time. He wanted to impress her, so she resolved to be impressed. It was a small enough thing to give someone.

"Of course, the belly of the ship is largely an arbitrary distinction," he continued as the elevator climbed. "Because we use thrust gravity, the deck is always in the direction thrust is coming from, the aft of the ship. Up is always away from the engines. There's not really much to distinguish the other four directions from each other. Some smaller ships can land on planetary surfaces, and in those ships the belly of the ship contains landing gear and thrusters for liftoff."

"I imagine the *Prince* is too large for that," Anna said.

"By quite a lot, actually! But our shuttles and corvettes are capable of surface landings, though it doesn't happen very often."

The elevator doors opened with another ding, and the yeoman pushed her luggage out into the hall. "After we drop off your baggage at your stateroom, we can continue the tour."

"Yeoman?" Anna said. "Is that the right way to address you?"

"Certainly. Or Mister Ichigawa. Or even Jin, since you're a civilian."

"Jin," Anna continued. "Would it be all right if I just stayed in my room for a while? I'm very tired."

He stopped pulling her baggage and blinked twice. "But the captain said all of the VIP guests should get a complete tour. Including the bridge, which is usually off-limits to non-duty personnel."

Anna put a hand on the boy's arm. "I understand that's quite a privilege, but I'd rather see it when I can keep my eyes open. You understand, don't you?" She gave his arm a squeeze and smiled her best smile at him.

"Certainly," he said, smiling back. "Come this way, ma'am."

Looking around her, Anna wasn't sure if she actually wanted to see the rest of the ship. Every corridor looked the same: Slick gray material with something spongy underneath covered most walls. Anna supposed it was some sort of protective surface, to keep sailors from injury if they banged into it during maneuvers. And anything that wasn't gray fabric was gray metal. The things that would be impressive to most people about the ship would be its various mechanisms for killing other ships. Those were the parts of the ship she was least interested in.

"Is that okay?" Ichigawa said after a moment. Anna had no idea what he was talking about. "Calling you ma'am, I mean. Some of the VIPs have titles. Pastor, or Reverend, or Minister. I don't want to offend."

"Well, if I didn't like you I'd ask you to call me Reverend Doctor, but I do like you very much, so please don't," she said.

"Thank you," Jin said, and the back of his neck blushed.

"And if you were a member of my congregation, I'd have you call me Pastor Anna. Buddhist?"

"Only when I'm at my grandmother's house," Jin said with a wink. "The rest of the time I'm a navy man."

"Is that a religion now?" Anna asked with a laugh.

"The navy thinks so."

"Okay." She laughed again. "So why don't you just call me Anna?"

"Yes, ma'am," Jin said. He stopped at a gray door marked OQ 297-11 and handed her a small metal card. "This is your room. Just having the card on you unlocks the door. It will stay locked when you're inside unless you press the yellow button on the wall panel."

"Sounds very safe," Anna said, taking the key from Jin and shaking his hand.

"This is the battleship *Thomas Prince*, ma'am. It's the safest place in the solar system."

Her stateroom was three meters wide by four meters long. Luxurious by navy standards, normal for a poor Europan, coffinlike to an Earther. Anna felt a brief moment of vertigo as the two different Annas she'd been reacted to the space in three different ways. She'd felt the same sense of disconnection when she'd first boarded the *Prince* and felt the full gravity pressing her down. The Earther she'd been most of her life felt euphoric as, for the first time in years, her weight felt *right*. The Europan in her just felt tired, drained by the excessive pull on her bones.

She wondered how long it would take Nono to get her Earth legs back. How long it would take before Nami could walk there. They were both spending the entire trip back pumped full of muscle and bone growth stimulators, but drugs can only take a person so far. There would still be the agonizing weeks or months as their bodies adapted to the new gravity. Anna could almost see little Nami struggling to get up onto her hands and knees like she did on Europa. Could almost hear her cries of frustration while she built up the strength to move on her own again. She was such a determined little thing. It would infuriate her to lose the hard-won physical skills she'd developed over the last two years.

Thinking about it made Anna's chest ache, just behind her breastbone.

She tapped the shiny black surface of the console in her room, and the room's terminal came on. She spent a moment learning the user interface. It was limited to browsing the ship's library and to sending and receiving text or audio/video messages.

She tapped the button to record a message and said, "Hi Nono, hi Nami!" She waved at the camera. "I'm on the ship, and we're on our way. I—" She stopped and looked around the room, at the sterile gray walls and spartan bed. She grabbed a pillow off of it and turned back to the camera. "I miss you both already." She hugged the pillow to her chest, tight. "This is you. This is both of you."

She turned the recording off before she got teary. She was washing her face when the console buzzed a new-message alert. Even though it didn't seem possible Nami could have gotten the message and replied already, her heart gave a little leap. She rushed over and opened the message. It was a simple text message reminding her of the VIP "meet and greet" in the officers' mess at 1900 hours. The clock said it was currently 1300.

Anna tapped the button to RSVP to the event and then climbed under the covers of her bed with her clothes on and cried herself to sleep.

"Reverend Doctor Volovodov," a booming male voice said as soon as she walked into the officers' mess.

The room was laid out for a party, with tables covered in food ringing the room, and a hundred or more people talking in loose clumps in the center. In one corner, an ad hoc bar with four bartenders was doing brisk business. A tall, dark-skinned man with perfectly coiffed white hair and an immaculate gray suit walked out of the crowd like Venus rising from the waves. Anna wondered how he managed the effect. He reached out and took her hand with his. "I'm so happy to have you with us. I've heard so much about the powerful work you're doing on Europa, and I don't see how the Methodist World Council could have chosen anyone else for this important trip."

Anna shook his hand, then carefully extricated herself from his grasp. Doctor Hector Cortez, Father Hank on his live streamcasts that went out to over a hundred million people each week, and close personal friend and spiritual advisor to the secretary-general himself. She couldn't imagine how he knew anything about her. Her tiny congregation of less than a hundred people on Europa wouldn't even be a rounding error to his solar system–wide audience. She found herself caught between feeling flattered, uncomfortable, and vaguely suspicious.

"Doctor Cortez," Anna said. "So nice to meet you. I've seen your show before, of course."

"Of course," he said, smiling vaguely and already looking around the room for someone else to talk to. She had the sense that he'd come to greet her less out of the pleasure of her arrival than as a chance to extricate himself from whatever conversation he'd been having before, and she didn't know whether to be relieved or insulted. She settled on amused.

Like a smaller object dragged into some larger gravity well, an elderly man in formal Roman Catholic garb pulled away from the central crowd and drifted in Doctor Cortez's direction.

She started to introduce herself when Doctor Cortez cut in with that booming voice and said, "Father Michel. Say hello to my friend Reverend Doctor Annushka Volovodov, a worker for God's glory with the Europa congregation of Methodists."

"Reverend Volovodov," the Catholic man said. "I'm Father Michel, with the Archdiocese of Rome."

"Oh, very nice to meet—" Anna started.

"Don't let him fool you with that humble old country priest act," Cortez boomed over the top of her. "He's a bishop on the short list for cardinal."

"Congratulations," Anna said.

"Oh, it's nothing. All exaggeration and smoke." The old man beamed. "Nothing will happen until it fits with God's plan."

"You wouldn't be here if that were true," Cortez said.

The bishop chuckled.

A woman in an expensive blue dress followed one of the uniformed waiters with his tray of champagne. She and Father Michel reached for a glass at the same moment. Anna smiled a no at the offered champagne, and the waiter vanished into the crowd at the center of the room.

"Please," the woman said to Anna. "Don't leave me to drink alone with a Catholic. My liver can't take it."

"Thank you, but—"

"What about you, Hank? I've heard you can put down a few drinks." She punctuated this with a swig from her glass. Cortez's smile could have meant anything.

"I'm Anna," Anna said, reaching out to shake the woman's hand. "I love your dress."

"Thank you. I am Mrs. Robert Fagan," the woman replied with mock formality. "Tilly if you aren't asking for money."

"Nice to meet you, Tilly," Anna said. "I'm sorry, but I don't drink."

"God, save me from temperance," Tilly said. "You haven't seen a party till you get a group of Anglicans and Catholics trying to beat each other to the bottom of a bottle."

"Now, that's not nice, Mrs. Fagan," Father Michel said. "I've never met an Anglican that could keep up with me."

"Hank, why is Esteban letting you out of his sight?" It took Anna a moment to realize that Tilly was talking about the secretary-general of the United Nations.

Cortez shook his head and feigned a wounded look without losing his ever-present toothy grin. "Mrs. Fagan, I'm humbled by the secretary-general's faith and trust in me, as we speed off toward the single most important event in human history since the death of our Lord."

Tilly snorted. "You mean his faith and trust in the hundred million voters you can throw his way in June."

"Ma'am," Cortez said, turning to look at Tilly's face for the first time. His grin never changed, but something chilled the air between them. "Maybe you've had a bit too much champagne."

"Oh, not nearly enough."

Father Michel charged in to the rescue, taking Tilly's hand and saying, "I think our dear secretary-general is probably even more grateful for your husband's many campaign contributions. Though that does make this the most expensive cruise in history, for you."

Tilly snorted and looked away from Cortez. "Robert can fucking afford it."

The obscenity created an awkward silence for a few moments, and Father Michel gave Anna an apologetic smile. She smiled back, so far out of her depth that she'd abandoned trying to keep up.

"What's he getting with them, I wonder?" Tilly said, pointing attention at anyone other than herself. "These artists and writers and actors. How many votes does a performance artist bring to the table? Do they even vote?"

"It's symbolic," Father Michel said, his face taking on a well-practiced expression of thoughtfulness. "We are all of humanity coming together to explore the great question of our time. The secular and the divine come to stand together before that overwhelming mystery: What is the Ring?"

"Nice," Tilly said. "Rehearsal pays off."

"Thank you," the bishop said.

"What is the Ring?" Anna said with a frown. "It's a wormhole gate. There's no question, right? We've been talking about these on a theoretical basis for centuries. They look just like this. Something goes through it and the place on the other side isn't here. We get the transmission signals bleeding back out and attenuating. It's a wormhole."

"That's certainly a possibility," Father Michel said. Tilly smiled at the sourness in his voice. "How do you see our mission here, Anna?"

"It isn't what it *is* that's at issue," she said, glad to be back in a conversation she understood. "It's what it *means*. This changes everything, and even if it's something wonderful, it'll be displacing. People will need to understand how to fit this in with their understanding of the universe. Of what this means about God, what this new thing tells us about Him. By being here, we can offer comfort that we couldn't otherwise."

"I agree," Cortez said. "Our work is to help people come to grips with the great mysteries, and this one's a doozy."

"No," Anna started, "explaining isn't what I—"

"Play your cards right, and it might get Esteban another four years," Tilly said over the top of her. "Then we can call it a miracle."

Cortez grinned a white grin at someone across the room. A man in a small group of men and women in loose orange robes raised his hand, waving at them.

"Can you *believe* those people?" Tilly asked.

"I believe those are delegates from the Church of Humanity Ascendant," Anna said.

Tilly shook her head. "Humanity Ascendant. I mean, really. Let's just make up our own religion and pretend we're the gods."

"Careful," Cortez said. "They're not the only ones."

Seeing Anna's discomfort, Father Michel attempted to rescue her. "Doctor Volovodov, I know the elder of that group. Wonderful woman. I'd love to introduce you. If you all would excuse us."

"Excuse me," Anna started, then stopped when the room suddenly went silent. Father Michel and Cortez were both looking toward something at the center of the gathering near the bar, and Anna moved around Tilly to get a better view. It was hard to see at first, because everyone in the room was moving away toward the walls. But eventually, a young man dressed in a hideous bright red suit was revealed. He'd poured something all over himself; his hair and the shoulders of his jacket were dripping a clear fluid onto the floor. A strong alcohol scent filled the room.

"This is for the people's Ashtun Collective!" the young man yelled out in a voice that trembled with fear and excitement. "Free Etienne Barbara! And free the Afghan people!"

"Oh dear God," Father Michel said. "He's going to—"

Anna never saw what started the fire, but suddenly the young man was engulfed in flames. Tilly screamed. Anna's shocked brain only registered annoyance at the sound. Really, when had someone screaming ever solved a problem? She recognized her fixation on this irritation as her own way of avoiding the horror in front of her, but only in a distant and dreamy sort of way. She was about to tell Tilly to just shut up when the fire-suppression system activated and five streams of foam shot out of hidden turrets in the walls and ceiling. The fiery man was covered in white bubbles and extinguished in seconds. The smell of burnt hair competed with the alcohol stench for dominance.

Before anyone else could react, naval personnel were streaming into the room. Stern-faced young men and women with holstered sidearms calmly told everyone to remain still while emergency crews worked. Medical technicians came in and scraped foam off the would-be suicide. He seemed more surprised than hurt. They handcuffed him and loaded him onto a stretcher. He was out of the room in less than a minute. Once he was gone, the people with guns seemed to relax a little.

"They certainly put him out fast," Anna said to the armed young woman closest to her. "That's good."

The young woman, looking hardly older than a schoolgirl,

laughed. "This is a battleship, ma'am. Our fire-suppression systems are robust."

Cortez had darted across the room and was speaking to the ranking naval officer in a booming voice. He sounded upset. Father Michel seemed to be quietly praying, and Anna felt a strong urge to join him.

"Well," Tilly said, waving at the room with her empty champagne glass. Her face was pale apart from two bright red dots on her cheeks "Maybe this trip won't be boring after all."

Chapter Nine: Bull

It would have gone faster if Bull had asked for more help, but until he knew who was doing what, he didn't want to trust too many people. Or anyone.

A thousand people in the crew more or less made things a little muddier than they would have been in some ways. With a crew that big, the security chief could look for things like crew members from unlikely departments meeting up at odd times. Deviations from the pattern that every ship had. Since this was the shakedown voyage, the *Behemoth* didn't have any patterns yet. It was still in a state of chaos, crew and ship getting to know one another. Making decisions, forming habits and customs and culture. Nothing was normal yet, and so nothing was strange.

On the other hand, it was only a thousand people.

Every ship had a black economy. Someone on the *Behemoth* would be trading sex for favors. Someone would run a card game or set up a pachinko parlor or start a little protection racket. People would be bribed to do things or not do things. It was what happened when you put people together. Bull's job wasn't to stamp it all out. His job was to keep it at a level that kept the ship moving and safe. And to set boundaries.

Alexi Myerson-Freud was a nutritionist. He'd worked mid-level jobs on Tycho, mostly in the yeast vats, tuning the bioengineering to produce the right mix of chemicals, minerals, and salts for keeping humans alive. He'd been married twice, had a kid he hadn't seen in five years, was part of a network war-gaming group that simulated ancient battles, pitting themselves against the great generals of history. He was eight years younger than Bull. He had mouse-ass brown hair, an awkward smile, and a side business selling a combination stimulant and euphoric the Belters called pixie dust. Bull had worked it all until he was certain.

And even once he knew, he'd waited a few days. Not long. Just enough that he could follow Alexi around on the security system. He needed to make sure there wasn't a bigger fish above him, a partner who was keeping a lower profile, or a connection to Bull's own team—or else, God forbid, Ashford's. There wasn't.

Truth was, he didn't want to do it. He knew what had to happen, and it was always easier to put it off for another fifteen minutes, or until after lunch, or until tomorrow. Only every time he did, it meant someone else was going on shift stoned, maybe making a stupid mistake, breaking the ship, getting injured, or getting killed.

The moment came in the middle of second shift. Bull turned down his console, stood up, took a couple of guns from the armory, and made a connection on his hand terminal.

"Serge?"

"Boss."

"I'm gonna need you and one other. We're going to go bust a drug dealer."

The silence on the line sounded like surprise. Bull waited. This would tell him something too.

"You got it," Serge said. "Be right there."

Serge came into the office ten minutes later with another security grunt, a broad-shouldered, grim-faced woman named Corin. She was a good choice. Bull made a mental note in Serge's favor, and handed them both guns. Corin checked the magazine, holstered it, and waited. Serge flipped his from hand to hand, judging the weight and feel, then shrugged.

"What's the plan?" he asked.

"Come with me," Bull said. "Someone tries to keep me from doing my job, warn them once, then shoot them."

"Straightforward," Serge said, and there was a sense of approval in the word.

The food processing complex was deep inside the ship, close to the massive, empty inner surface. In the long voyage to the stars, it would have been next to the farmlands of the small internal world of the *Nauvoo*. In the *Behemoth*, it wasn't anywhere in particular. What had been logical became dumb, and all it took was changing the context. Bull drove them, the little electric cart's foam wheels buzzing against the ramps. In the halls and corridors, people stopped, watched. Some stared. It said something that three armed security agents traveling together stood out. Bull wasn't sure it was something good.

Near the vats, the air smelled different. There were more volatiles and unfiltered particulates. The processing complex itself was a network of tubs and vats and distilling columns. Half of the place was shut down, the extra capacity mothballed and waiting for a larger population to feed. Or else waiting to be torn out.

They found Alexi knee deep in one of the water treatment baths, orange rubber waders clinging to his legs and his hands full of thick green kelp. Bull pointed to him, and then to the catwalk on which he, Serge, and Corin stood. There might have been a flicker of unease in Alexi's expression. It was hard to say.

"I can't get out right now," the dealer said, holding up a broad wet leaf. "I'm in the middle of something."

Bull nodded and turned to Serge.

"You two stay here. Don't let him go anywhere. I'll be right back."

"Sa sa, boss," Serge said.

The locker room was down a ladder and through a hall. The bank of pea-green private storage bins had been pulled out of the wall, turned ninety degrees, and put back in to match the direction of thrust. Blobs and filaments of caulk still showed at the edges where it failed to sit quite flush. Two other water processing techs were sitting on the bench in different levels of undress, talking and flirting. They went silent when Bull walked in. He smiled at them, nodded, and walked past to a locker on the far end. When he reached it, he turned back.

"This belong to anyone?" he asked.

The two techs looked at each other.

"No, sir," the woman said, pulling her jumpsuit a little more closed. "Most of these are just empty."

"Okay, then," Bull said. He thumbed in his override code and pulled the door open. The duffel bag inside was green and gray, the kind of thing he'd have put his clothes in when he went to work out. He ran a finger along the seal. About a hundred vials of yellow-white powder, a little more grainy than powdered milk. He closed the bag, put it on his shoulder.

"Is there a problem?" the male tech asked. His voice was tentative, but not scared. Curious, more. Excited. Well, God loved rubberneckers, and so did Bull.

"Myerson-Freud just stopped selling pixie dust on the side," Bull said. "Should go tell all your friends, eh?"

The techs looked at each other, eyebrows raised, as Bull headed out. Back at the kelp tank, he dropped the bag, then pointed to Alexi and to the catwalk beside him, the same motions he'd used before. This time Alexi's face went grim. Bull waited while the tech slogged through the deep water and pulled himself up.

"What's the problem?" Alexi said. "What's in the bag?"

Bull shook his head slowly, and only once. The chagrin on Alexi's face was like a confession. Not that Bull had needed one.

"Hey, ese," Bull said. "Just want you to know, I'm sorry about this."

He punched Alexi in the nose. Cartilage and bone gave way under his knuckle and a bright red fountain of blood spilled slowly past the tech's startled mouth.

"Put him on the back of the cart," Bull said. "Where folks can see him."

Serge and Corin exchanged a look that was a lot like the pair in the locker room.

"We heading to the brig, boss?" Serge asked, and his tone of voice meant he already knew the answer.

"We have a brig?" Bull asked as he scooped up the duffel bag.

"Pretty don't."

"Then we're not going there."

Bull had planned the route to pass through all the most populated public areas between the innermost areas of the ship and its skin. Word was already going around, and there were spectators all along the way. Alexi was making a high keening sound when he wasn't shouting or begging or demanding to see the captain. Bull had the sudden, visceral memory of seeing a pig carried to the slaughter when he'd been younger. He didn't know when it had happened; the memory was just there, floating unconnected from the rest of his life.

It took almost half an hour to reach the airlock. A crowd had gathered, a small sea of faces, most of them on wide heads and thin bodies. The Belters watching the Earther kill one of their own. Bull ignored them. He keyed in his passcode, opened the inner door of the lock, walked back to the cart, and hefted Alexi with one arm. In the low gravity it should have been easy, but Bull felt himself getting winded before he got back to the lock. It didn't help that Alexi was thrashing. Bull pushed him in, closed the inner door, put in the override code, and opened the exterior door without evacuating the air first. The pop rang through the metal deck like a distant bell. The monitor showed that the lock was empty. Bull closed the exterior door. While the lock refilled, he walked back to the cart. He stood on the back of the cart where Alexi had been, the duffel bag over his head in both hands. Blood stained his sleeve and his left knee.

"This is pixie dust, right?" he said to the crowd. He didn't use his terminal to amplify his voice. He didn't need to. "I'm gonna leave this in the airlock for sixteen hours, then I'm spacing it. Any other dust comes in to join it before then, well, it just happened. No big deal. Any of this goes away, and that's a problem. So everybody go tell everybody. And the next pendejo signs on shift high comes and talks to me."

He walked back to the airlock slowly, letting everyone see him. He opened the inner door, slung the bag through, and turned away, leaving the door open behind him. Climbing back behind the wheel of the cart, he could feel the tension in the crowd, and it didn't bother him at all. Other things did. What he'd just done was the easy part. What came next was harder, because he had less control over it.

"You want to set a guard on that, boss?" Serge asked.

"Think we need to?" Bull asked. He didn't expect an answer, and he didn't get one. The cart lurched forward, the spectators parting before it like a herd of antelope before a lion. Bull aimed them back toward the ramps that would take him to the security offices.

"Hardcore," Corin said. She made it sound like a good thing.

Religious art decorated the captain's office. Angels in blue and gold held the parabolas of the archways that rose overhead to meet at the image of a calm and bearded God. A beneficent Christ looked down from the wall behind Ashford's desk, Caucasian features calm and serene. He didn't look anything like the bloody, bent, crucified man Bull was familiar with. Arrayed at the Savior's side were images of plenty: wheat, corn, goats, cows, and stars. Captain Ashford paced back and forth by Jesus' knees, his face dark with blood and fury. Michio Pa was seated in the other guest chair, carefully not looking at Ashford or at Bull. Whatever the situation was with the Martian science ships and their military escort, with the massive Earth flotilla, it was forgotten for the moment.

Bull didn't let the anxiety show in his face.

"This is unacceptable, Mister Baca."

"Why do you think that, sir?"

Ashford stopped, put his wide hands on the desk, and leaned forward. Bull looked into his bloodshot eyes and wondered whether the captain was getting enough sleep.

"You killed a member of my crew," Ashford said. "You did it with clear premeditation. You did it in front of a hundred witnesses."

"Shit, you want witnesses, there's surveillance footage," Bull said. It wasn't the right thing to do.

"You are relieved of duty, Mister Baca. And confined to quarters until we return to Tycho Station, where you will stand trial for murder."

"He was selling drugs to the crew."

"Then he should have been *arrested*!"

Bull took a deep breath, exhaling slowly through his nose.

"You think we're more running a warship or a space station, sir?" he asked. Ashford's brow furrowed, and he shook his head. To Bull's right, Pa shifted in her seat. When neither of them spoke, Bull went on. "Reason I ask is if I'm a cop, then yeah, I should have taken him to the brig, if we had a brig. He should have gotten a lawyer. We could have done that whole thing. Me? I don't think this is a station. I think it's a battleship. I'm here to maintain military discipline in a potential combat zone. Not Earth navy discipline. Not Martian navy discipline. OPA discipline. The Belter way."

Ashford stood up.

"We aren't anarchists," he said, his voice dripping with scorn.

"OPA tradition, maybe I'm wrong, is that someone does something that intentionally endangers the ship, they get to hitchhike back to wherever there's air," Bull said.

"You hauled him out of a water vat. How was he endangering the ship? Was he going to throw kelp at it?" Pa said, her voice brittle.

"People been coming on shift high," Bull said, lacing his fingers together on one knee. "Don't trust me. Ask around. And, c'mon. Of course they are, right? We've got three times as much work needs to get done as we can do. Pixie dust, and they don't feel tired. Don't take breaks. Don't slow down. Get more done. Thing about bad judgment? You got to have good judgment to notice you've got it. We already got people hurt. Matter of time before someone died. Or worse."

"You're saying this man was responsible for all those other people performing badly at their work, so you killed him?" Ashford said, but the wind was out of his sails. He was going to fold like wet cardboard. Bull recognized that Ashford's weakness was going to work to his advantage this time, but he still hated it.

"I'm saying he was putting the ship at risk for his own financial gain, just like he was stealing air filters. And sure he did. There was a demand, he filled it. If I lock him up, that makes it so that the risk is higher. Prices are higher. Get caught, you maybe go to jail when we get back to Tycho."

"And you made it so that the risk is death."

"No," Bull said. "I mean, yeah, but I don't shoot him. I do what you do to people who risk the ship. Belters know what getting spaced means, right? It frames the issue."

"This was a mistake."

"I've got a list of fifty people he sold to," Bull said. "Some of them are skilled technicians. A couple are mid-level overseers. We could lock 'em all up, but then we've got less people to do the work. And anyway, they won't be doing it anymore. Supply's gone. But if you want I could talk to them. Let 'em know I'm keeping an eye open."

Pa's chuckle was mirthless.

"That would be difficult if you're in the brig on charges," she said.

"We don't have a brig," Bull said. "Plan was the church elders were just gonna talk everything out." He kept his tone carefully free of sarcasm.

Ashford waffled. It was like watching a cat trying to decide whether to jump from one tree limb to another. His expression was calculating, internal, uncertain. Bull waited.

"This never happens again," Ashford said. "You decide someone needs to go out the airlock, you come to me. I'll be the one that pushes the button."

"All right."

"All right, what?" Ashford bit the words. Bull lowered his head, looking at the deck. He'd gotten what he came for. He could let Ashford feel like he'd gotten a little win too.

"I mean, yes, sir, Captain. Solid copy. I understand and will comply."

"You're damn right you will," Ashford said. "Now get the hell back to work."

"Yes, sir."

When the door closed behind him, Bull leaned against the wall and took a few deep breaths. He was intensely aware of the sound of the ship—low hum of the air recyclers, the distant murmur of voices, the chimes and beeps of a thousand different system alerts. The air smelled of plastic and ozone. He'd taken his calculated risk, and he'd pulled it off.

Walking back down, level by level, he felt the attention on him. In the lift, a man tried not to stare at him. In the hall outside the security office, a woman smiled at him and nodded, nervous as a mouse that smells cat. Bull smiled back.

In the security office, Serge and another man from the team—a Europan named Casimir—lifted their fists, greeting him in the physical idiom of the Belt. Bull returned the gesture and ambled over.

"What we got?" Bull asked.

"A couple dozen people came to pay respects," Serge said. "I figure about half a kilo more dust just appeared out of nowhere."

"Okay, then."

"I've got a file of everyone who went in. You want me to flag them in the system?"

"Nope," Bull said. "I told them it was no big deal. It's no big deal. You can kill the file."

"You got it, boss."

"I'll be in my office," Bull said. "Let me know if something comes up. And somebody start a pot of coffee."

He sat down on the desk, his feet resting on the seat of his chair, and leaned forward. He was suddenly exhausted. It had been a long, bad day, and losing the dread he'd been carrying for the weeks leading up to it was like being released from prison. It took a minute or two to notice he had a message waiting from Michio Pa. The XO hadn't requested a connection. She didn't want to talk to him, then. She just wanted to say something.

In the recording, her face was lit from below with the back-splash of her hand terminal screen. Her smile was thin and tight and sort of faded away somewhere around her cheekbones.

"I saw what you did there. That was very nice. Very clever. Wrapping yourself in the OPA flag, making the old man wonder if the crew wouldn't take your side. More-Belter-than-thou. It was *graceful*."

Bull scratched his chin. The stubble that had grown in since morning made his fingernails sound like a rasp. It was probably too much to ask that he not make any enemies with this, but he was sorry it was Pa.

"You can't sugarcoat it with me. We both know that killing someone doesn't make you admirable. I'm not about to forget this. I just hope you have enough soul left that what you've done still bothers you."

The recording ended, and Bull smiled at the blank screen wearily.

"Every time," he told the hand terminal. "And next time too."

Chapter Ten: Holden

The *Rocinante* was not a small ship. Her normal crew complement was over a dozen navy personnel and officers, and on many missions she'd also carry six marines. Running the *Roci* with four people meant each of them did several jobs, and that didn't leave a lot of downtime. It also meant that it was pretty easy at first to avoid the four strangers living on the ship. With the documentary crew restricted from entering ops, the airlock deck, the machine shop, or engineering, they were stuck on the two crew decks with access only to their quarters, the head, the galley, and sick bay.

Monica was a lovely person. Calm, friendly, charismatic. If even a part of her charm translated to the other side of the camera, it was easy to see how she'd succeeded. The others—Okju, Clip, Cohen—made clear overtures of friendship, cracking jokes with the *Rocinante*'s crew, making dinners. Reaching out, but it wasn't clear to Holden whether it was the usual honeymoon period that came when any crew first came together for a long voyage or something more calculated. Maybe a little of both.

What he did see was his own crew drawing back. After two days of the documentary team being on board, Naomi simply retreated to the ops deck where she couldn't be found. Amos had made a halfhearted pass at Monica, and a slightly more serious attempt with Okju. When both failed, he began spending most of his time in the machine shop. Of them all, only Alex took time to socialize with their passengers, and him not all that often. He'd taken to sometimes sleeping in the pilot's couch.

They'd agreed to being interviewed, and Holden knew they couldn't avoid it forever. They hadn't been out for a full week yet, and even on a fairly high burn it would be months to their destination. Besides, it was in their contract. The discomfort of it was almost enough to distract him from the fact that every day brought them closer to the Ring and whatever it was that Miller wanted him out there for. Almost.

"It's Saturday," Naomi said. She was lounging in a crash couch near the comm station. She hadn't cut her hair for a while, and it was getting long enough to become an annoyance to her. For the last ten minutes, she'd been trying to braid it. The thick black curls resisted her efforts, seeming to move with a will of their own. Based on past experience, Holden knew this was the precursor to cutting half of it off in exasperation. Naomi liked the idea of growing her hair very long, but not the reality. Holden sat at the combat ops panel watching her struggle with it and letting his mind drift.

"Did you hear me?" she said.

"It's Saturday."

"Are we inviting our guests to dinner?"

It had become custom on the ship that no matter what else was going on, the crew tried to have dinner as a group once a week. By unspoken agreement it was usually Saturday. Which day of the week it happened to be didn't really matter much on a ship, but by holding their dinner on Saturday, Holden thought they were doing some small bit to celebrate the passing of a week, the beginning of another. A gentle reminder that there was still a solar system outside of the four of them.

But he hadn't considered inviting the documentary crew to join them. It felt like an invasion. The Saturday dinner was for *crew*.

"We can't keep them out of it." He sighed. "Can we?"

"Not unless we want to eat up here. You did give them the run of the galley."

"Dammit," he said. "Should have confined them to quarters."

"For four months?"

"We could have shoved ration bars and catheter bags under the door to them."

She smiled and said, "It's Amos' turn to cook."

"Right, I'll call and let him know it's dinner for eight."

Amos made pasta and mushrooms, heavy on the garlic, heavy on the Parmesan. It was his favorite, and he always splurged to buy real cloves of garlic and actual Parmesan cheese to grate. Another small luxury they wouldn't be able to afford if they wound up in a courtroom battle with Mars.

While Amos finished sautéing the mushrooms and garlic, Alex set the table and took drink orders. Holden sat next to Naomi on one side of the table, while the documentary crew sat together on the other. The banter was polite and friendly, and if there was an uncomfortable undercurrent to it all, he still wasn't quite sure why.

Holden had asked them not to bring cameras or recording equipment to the dinner table, and Monica had agreed. Clip, the Martian, was talking about sports history with Alex. Okju and Cohen, sitting across from Naomi, were telling stories about the last assignment they'd been on, covering a new scientific station that was in stationary orbit around Mercury. It should have been almost pleasant, and it just wasn't.

Holden said, "We don't usually eat this well while flying, but we try to do something nice for our weekly dinner together."

Okju smiled and said, "Smells lovely." She was wearing half a dozen rings, a blouse with buttons on it, a silver pendant, and an ivory-colored comb holding back her frizzy brown hair. The soundman gazed serenely at nothing, his black glasses hiding the top of his face, his expression calm and open. Monica watched him look over her crew, saying nothing, a faint smile on her lips.

"Chow," Amos said, then began putting bowls of food on the table. While the meal was handed around in a slow circuit, Okju bowed her head and mumbled something. It took Holden a moment to realize she was praying. He hadn't seen anyone do it for years, not since he'd left home. One of his fathers, Caesar, had sometimes prayed before meals. Holden waited for her to finish before he started eating.

"This is very nice," Monica said. "Thank you."

"You're welcome," said Holden.

"We're a week out of Ceres," she said, "and I think we're all settled in. Was wondering if we could start scheduling some preliminary interviews? It's mostly so we can test out the equipment."

"You can interview me," Amos said, not quite hiding his leer.

Monica smiled at him and speared a mushroom with her fork, then stared at him while she popped it into her mouth and chewed slowly.

"Okay," she said. "We can start with background work. Baltimore?"

The silence was suddenly brittle. Amos started to stand, but a gentle hand on his arm from Naomi stopped him. He opened his mouth, closed it, then looked down at his plate while the pale skin on his scalp and neck turned bright red. Monica looked down at her plate, her expression at the friction point between embarrassed and annoyed.

"That's not a good idea," Holden said.

"Captain, I'm sensitive to privacy issues for you and your crew, but we have an agreement. And with all respect, you've been treating me and mine like we're unwelcome."

Around the table, the food was starting to cool off. It had hardly been touched. "I get it. You held up your end of the deal," Holden said. "You got me out of Ceres, and you put money in our pockets. We haven't been holding up our end. I get it. I'll set aside an hour tomorrow for starters, does that work?"

"Sure," she said. "Let's eat."

"Baltimore, huh?" Clip said to Amos. "Football fan?"

Amos said nothing, and Clip didn't press it.

After the uncomfortable dinner, Holden wanted nothing more than to climb into bed. But while he was in the head brushing his teeth, Alex pretended to casually wander in and said, "Come on up to ops, Cap. Got something to talk about."

When Holden followed him up, he found Amos and Naomi already waiting. Naomi was leaning back with her hands behind her head, but Amos sat on the edge of a crash couch, both feet on the floor and his hands clenched into a doubled fist in front of him. His expression was still dark with anger.

"So, Jim," Alex said, walking over to another crash couch and dropping into it, "this ain't a good start."

"She's looking stuff up about us," Amos said to no one in particular, his gaze still on the floor. "Stuff she shouldn't know."

Holden knew what Amos meant. Monica's reference to Baltimore was an allusion to Amos' childhood as the product of a particularly nasty brand of unlicensed prostitution. But Holden couldn't admit he knew it. He himself only knew because of an overheard conversation. He had no interest in humiliating Amos further.

"She's a journalist, they do background research," he said.

"She's more than that," Naomi said. "She's a nice person. She's charming and she's friendly, and every one of us on this ship wants to like her."

"That's a problem?" Holden said.

"That's a big fucking problem," Amos said.

"I was on the *Canterbury* for a reason, Jim," Alex said. His Mariner Valley drawl had stopped sounding silly, and just seemed sad instead. "I don't need someone diggin' up my skeletons to air them out."

The *Canterbury*, the ice hauler they'd all worked on together before the Eros incident, was a bottom-of-the-barrel job for those who flew for a living. It attracted people who'd failed down to the level of their incompetence, or those who couldn't pass the background checks a better job might require. Or, in his own case, those who had a dishonorable military discharge staining their record. After having served with his small crew for years, Holden knew it wasn't incompetence that had put any of them on that ship.

"I know," he started.

"Same here, Cap'n," Amos said. "I got a lot of past in my past."

"So do I," Naomi said.

Holden started to reply, then stopped when the import of her words hit him. Naomi was hiding something that had driven her to take a glorified mechanic's job on the *Canterbury*. Well, of course she was. Holden hadn't wanted to think about it, but it was obvious. She was about the most talented engineer he'd ever met. He knew she had degrees from two universities, and had completed her three-year flight officer training in two. She'd started her career on an obvious command track. Something had happened, but she'd never talked about what it had been. He frowned a question at her, but she stopped him with a tiny shake of her head.

The fragility of their little family struck him full force. The paths that had pulled them all together had been so diverse, as improbable and unlikely as those kinds of things ever were. And the universe could just as easily take them apart. It left him feeling small and vulnerable and a little defensive.

"Everyone remembers why we did this, right?" Holden asked. "The lockdown? Mars coming after the *Rocinante*?"

"We didn't have a choice," Naomi replied. "We know. We all agreed to take this job."

Amos nodded in agreement. Alex said, "No one's sayin' we shouldn't have taken the job. What we're sayin' is that you're the frontman for this band."

"Yes," Naomi said. "You need to be so interesting that this documentary crew forgets all about the rest of us. That's your job for the rest of this flight. That's the only way this works."

"No," Amos said, still not looking up. "There *is* another way, but I've never tossed a blind man out an airlock. Don't know how I'd feel about that. Might not be fun."

"Okay," Holden said, patting the air with his hands in a calming motion. "I get it. I'll keep the cameras out of your faces as much as I can, but this is a long trip. Be patient. When we get to the Ring, maybe they'll be tired of us and we can pawn them off on some other ship."

They were silent for a moment, then Alex shook his head.

"Well," he said, "I think we just found the only thing that'll make me look forward to getting *there*."

Holden woke with a start, rubbing furiously at an itch on his nose. He had a half-remembered feeling of something trying to climb inside it. No bugs on the ship, so it had to have been a dream. The itch was real, though.

As he scratched, he said, "Sorry, bad dream or something," and patted the bed next to him. It was empty. Naomi must have gone to the bathroom. He inhaled and exhaled loudly through his nose several times, trying to get rid of the itchy sensation inside. On the third exhale, a blue firefly popped out and flew away. Holden became aware of a faint scent of acetate in the air.

"We need to talk," said a familiar voice in the darkness.

Holden's throat went tight. His heart began to pound. He pulled a pillow over his face and suppressed an urge to scream as much from frustration and rage as the old familiar fear that tightened his chest.

"So. There was this rookie," Miller started. "Good kid, you'd have hated him."

"I can't take this shit," Holden said, yanking the pillow away from his face and throwing it in the direction of Miller's voice. He slapped the panel by the bed and the room's lights came on. Miller was standing by the door, the pillow behind him, wearing the same rumpled gray suit and porkpie hat, fidgeting like he had a rash.

"He never really learned to clear a room, you know?" Miller continued. His lips were black. "Corners and doorways. I tried to tell him. It's always corners and doorways."

Holden reached for the comm panel to call Naomi, then stopped. He wanted her to be there, to make the ghost vanish the way it always had before. And he was also afraid that this time, it wouldn't.

"Listen, you've gotta clear the room," Miller said, his face twisted with confusion and intensity, like a drugged man trying to remember something important. "If you don't clear the room, the room *eats* you."

"What do you want from me?" Holden said. "Why are you making me go out there?"

A thick exasperation twisted Miller's expression.

"What the hell are you hearing me *say*? You see a room full of bones, only thing you know is something got *killed*. You're the predator right up until you're prey." He stopped, staring at Holden. Waiting for an answer. When Holden didn't respond, Miller moved a step closer to the bed. Something on his face made Holden think of the times he'd watched the cop shoot people. He opened a cabinet by the bed and took out his sidearm.

"Don't get any closer," Holden said, not pointing the gun at Miller yet. "But be honest, if I shot you, would you even die?"

Miller laughed. His expression became almost human. "Depends."

The door opened and Miller blinked out. Naomi came in wearing a robe and carrying a bulb of water.

"You awake?"

Holden nodded, then opened the cabinet and put the gun away. His expression must have told Naomi everything.

"Are you all right?"

"Yeah. He vanished when you opened the door."

"You look terrified," Naomi said, putting her water down and sliding under the covers next to him.

"He's scarier now. Before, I thought...I don't know what I thought. But ever since he knew about the gate, I keep trying to figure out what he really means. It was easier when I could think it was some kind of static. That it didn't...that it didn't mean anything."

Naomi curled up against his side, putting her arms around him. He felt his muscles relaxing.

"We can't let Monica and her crew ever know about this," he said. Naomi's smile was half sorrow. "What?"

"James Holden not telling everyone everything," she said.

"This is different."

"I know."

"What did he say?" Naomi asked. "Did it make sense?"

"No. But it was all about death. Everything he says is about death."

Over the course of the following weeks, the ship fell into a routine that, while not comfortable, was at least collegial. Holden spent time with the documentary crew, being filmed, showing them the ship, answering questions. What was his childhood like? Loving and complex and bittersweet. Had he really saved Earth by talking the half-aware girl who'd been the protomolecule's seed crystal into rerouting to Venus? No, mostly that had just worked out well. Did he have any regrets?

He smiled and took it and pretended he wasn't holding anything back. That the only thing leading him out to the Ring was his contract with them. That he hadn't been chosen by the protomolecule for something else that he hadn't yet begun to understand.

Sometimes, Monica turned to the others, but Alex and Naomi kept their answers friendly, polite, and shallow. Amos laced his responses with cheerful and explicit profanity until it was almost impossible to edit into something for a civilized audience.

Cohen turned out to be more than a sound engineer. The dark glasses he wore were a sonar feedback system that allowed him to create a three-dimensional model of any space he occupied. When Amos asked why he didn't have prosthetics instead, Cohen had told them that the accident that claimed his eyes also burned the optic nerves away. The attempted nerve regrowth therapy had failed and almost killed him with an out-of-control brain tumor. But the interface that allowed his brain to translate sonar data into a working 3D landscape also made him an extraordinary visual effects modeler. While Monica spun a narrative of Holden's life following the destruction of his ship the *Canterbury*, Cohen created beautiful visual renderings of the scenes. At one point, he showed the crew a short clip of Holden speaking, describing the escape from Eros after the initial protomolecule infection, all while he appeared to be moving down perfectly rendered Erosian corridors filled with bodies.

Part of Holden had almost come to enjoy the interviews, but he could only watch the Eros graphics for a few seconds before he asked Cohen to turn it off. He'd been sure that seeing it would somehow invoke Miller, but it hadn't. Holden didn't like the memories that came with their story. The documentary crew made accommodations, not forcing him further than he was willing to go. Their being nice about it somehow only made him feel worse.

A week out from the Ring, they caught up to the *Behemoth*. Monica was sitting on the ops deck with the crew when the massive OPA ship finally got close enough for the *Roci*'s telescopes to get a good view of her. Holden had allowed the restrictions on where the documentary crew were permitted to just sort of fade away.

They were doing a slow pan of the *Behemoth*'s hull when Alex whistled and pointed at a protrusion on the side. "Damn, boss, the Mormons are better armed than I remember. That's a rail gun turret right there. And I'd bet a week's desserts those things are torpedo tubes."

"I liked her better when she was a generation ship," Holden replied. He called up combat ops and told the *Rocinante* to classify the new hull as the *Behemoth*-class dreadnought and add all the hardpoints and weapons to her threat profile.

"That's the kind of stealing only governments can get away with," Amos said. "I guess the OPA is a real thing now."

"Yeah," Alex replied with a laugh.

"Mars is making a similar claim against us," Holden said.

"And if *we'd* been the ones to blow up their battleship before we flew off in this boat, they'd have an argument to make," Amos said. "Last I checked, that was the bad guys, though."

Naomi didn't chime in. She was working at something on the comm panel. Holden could tell it was a complex problem because she was quietly humming to herself.

"You've been on the *Nauvoo* before, right?" Monica asked.

"No," Holden said. The *Rocinante* began rapidly throwing data onto his screen. The ship's calculations of the *Behemoth*'s actual combat strength. "They were still working on it the first time I was on Tycho Station. By the time I started working for Fred Johnson, they'd already shot the *Nauvoo* at Eros, and she was on her way out of the solar system. I did get to walk through the ship they sent to catch her, once."

The *Rocinante* was displaying puzzling projections at him. The ship seemed to think that the *Behemoth* didn't have the structural strength to support the number and size of weapon hardpoints she currently sported. In fact, she seemed to think that if the OPA battleship ever actually fired two of its six capital-ship-class rail guns at the same time, there was a 34 percent chance the hull would rip apart. Just to have something to do, Holden told the *Roci* to create a tactical package for fighting the *Behemoth* and send it to Alex and Naomi. Probably, they'd never need it.

"You didn't like working for the OPA?" Monica asked. She had the little smile she got when she asked a question she already knew the answer to. Holden suspected the documentarian was also a terrible poker player, but so far he hadn't been able to get her into a game.

"It was a mixed bag," he said, forcing himself to smile. To be the James Holden that Monica wanted and expected. To sacrifice himself to her attention so she'd leave the others be.

"Jim?" Naomi said, finally looking up from her panel. "You know that memory leak in comms that I've been hunting for a month? It's getting worse. It's driving me nuts."

"How bad?" Alex asked.

"Fluctuating between .0021 and .033 percent," she said. "I'm having to flush and reboot every couple of days now."

Amos laughed. "Do we care about that? Because I'll raise you a power leak in the head that's almost a whole percent."

Naomi turned to look at him with a frown. "You didn't tell me?"

"I'll bet you a month's pay it's a worn lead to the lights. I'll yank the fucker out when I get a chance."

"Do those things happen a lot?" Monica asked.

"Hell no," Alex replied before Holden could. "The *Roci* is solid."

"Yeah," Amos chimed in. "She's so well put together, we gotta obsess over bullshit like crusty memory bubbles and shitty light bulbs just to have something to do." The smile he aimed at Monica was indistinguishable from the real thing.

"So you didn't really answer my question about the OPA," Monica said, swiveling her chair to face Holden. She pointed at the threat map the *Roci* had created of the *Behemoth*, the weapon hardpoints like angry red blisters dotting her skin. "Everything okay between you?"

"Yeah, everyone's still friends," Holden said. "Nothing to worry about."

A proximity light flashed as the *Behemoth* bounced a ranging laser off the *Roci*'s hull. She returned the favor. Not targeting lasers. Just two ships making sure they weren't in any danger of getting too close.

Nothing to worry about.

Yeah, right.

Chapter Eleven: Melba

Stanni stood just behind Melba's left shoulder, looking at the display. His palm rubbed against the slick fabric of his work trousers like he was trying to sooth a cramped quadriceps. Melba had learned to read it as a sign the man was nervous. The narrow architecture of the *Cerisier* put him so close to her, she could feel the subtle warmth of his body against the back of her neck. In any other context, being this close to a man would have meant they were sharing an intimate moment. Here, it meant nothing. She didn't even find it annoying.

"Mira," Stanni said, flapping his hand. "La. Right there."

The monitor was old, a constant green pixel burning in the lower left corner where some steady glitch had been irreparable and not worth replacing. The definition was still better than a hand terminal. To the untrained eye, the power demand profile for the UNN *Thomas Prince* could have been the readout of an

EEG or a seismological reading or the visual representation of a bhangra recording. But over the course of weeks—months now—Melba's eye wasn't untrained.

"I see it," she said, putting her finger on the spike. "And we can't tell where it came from?"

"Fucks me," Stanni said, rubbing his thigh. "I'm seeing it, but I don't know what I'm looking at."

Melba ran her tongue against the back of her teeth, concentrating, trying to remember what the tutorials had shown about tracking power spikes. In an odd way, her inexperience had shifted into an asset for the team. Stanni and Ren, Bob and Soledad all had more hands-on experience than she did, but she'd only just learned the basics. Sometimes she would know some simple thing that all of them had known once, and only she hadn't forgotten. Her analysis was slower, but it didn't skip steps, because she didn't know which steps could be skipped.

"Did it start at the deceleration flip?" she asked.

Stanni grunted like a man struck by a sudden pain.

"They hit null g and one of the regulators reset," he said. "Least it's nothing serious. Embarrassing to blow up all they preachers y sa. We'll need to get back over there and check them, though."

Melba nodded and made a mental note to read through what that process required. All she'd known was the truism repeated in three of her tutorials that when a ship cut thrust halfway through a journey, flipped, and began accelerating in the opposite direction it was a time for especial care.

"I'll put it on the rotation," she said, and pulled up her team's schedule. There was a slot in ten days when there would be enough time to revisit the big ship. She blocked out the time, marked it, and posted it to the full group. All of it felt easy and natural, like the sort of thing she had been doing her whole life. Which in a sense, she had.

The flotilla was coming to the last leg of its journey. They had passed the orbit of Uranus weeks ago, and the sun was a bright star in an overwhelming abyss of night sky. All the plumes of fire were pointed toward the Ring now, bleeding off their velocity with every passing minute. Even though it was the standard pattern for Epstein drive ships, Melba couldn't quite shake the feeling that they were all trying to flee from their destination and being pulled in against their will.

Unless they were discussing work, the only conversation— in the mess hall, on the exercise machines, on the shuttles to and from the ships they maintained—was about the Ring. The Martian science ships and their escort were already there, peering through the void. There had been no official reports given, so instead rumors sprang up like weeds. Every beam of light that passed through the Ring and hit something bounced back, just like in normal space. But a few troubling constants varied as you got close to it. The microwave background from inside the Ring was older than the big bang. People said if you listened carefully to the static from the other side of the Ring, you could hear the voices of the dead of Eros, or of the damned. Melba heard the dread in other people's voices, saw Soledad crossing herself when she thought no one was looking, felt the oppressive weight of the object. She understood their growing fear not because she felt it herself but because her own private crisis point was coming.

The OPA's monstrous battleship was on course to arrive soon, almost at the same time as the Earth flotilla. It wasn't a matter of days yet, but it would be soon. The *Rocinante* had already passed the slower *Behemoth*. She and Holden were rising up out of the sun's domain, and soon their paths would converge. Then there would be the attack, and the public humiliation of James Holden, and with it, his death. And after that...

It was strange to think of an afterward. The more she imagined it, the more she could see herself relaxing back into Melba's life. There was no reason not to. Clarissa Mao had nothing, commanded nothing, was nothing. Melba Koh had work, at least. A history. It was a pretty thought, made prettier by being impossible.

She would go home, become Clarissa again, and do whatever else she could to restore her family's name. Honor required it. If she'd stayed, it would have meant being like Julie.

Growing up, Clarissa had admired and resented her older sister. Julie the pretty one. The smart one. The champion yacht racer. Julie who could make Father laugh. Julie who could do no wrong. Petyr was younger than Clarissa and so would always be less. The twins Michael and Anthea had always been a world unto themselves, sharing jokes and comments that only they understood, and so seemed at times more like long-term guests of the family than part of it. Julie was the oldest, the one Clarissa longed to be. The one to beat. Clarissa hadn't been the only one to see Julie that way. Their mother felt it too. It was the thing that made Clarissa and her mother most alike.

And then something happened. Julie had walked away from them all, cut her hair, dropped out of school, and disappeared up into the darkness. She remembered her father hearing the news over dinner. They'd been having kaju murgh kari in the informal dining room that overlooked the park. She'd just come back from her riding lesson and still smelled a little of horse. Petyr had been talking about mathematics again, boring everyone, when her mother looked up from her plate with a smile and announced that Julie had written a letter to say she'd quit the family. Clarissa's mouth had dropped open. It was like saying that the sun had decided to become a politician or that four had decided to be eight. It wasn't quite incomprehensible, but it lived on the edge.

Her father had laughed. He'd said it was a phase. Julie'd gone to live like the common people and sow a few wild oats, and once she'd had her fill, she'd come home. But she'd seen in his eyes that he didn't believe it. His perfect girl was gone. She'd rejected not only him, but the family. Their name. Forever after, cashews and curry had tasted like victory.

And so Melba would have to be folded up when she was done here. Put back in a box and buried or burned. Clarissa could go live with one of her siblings. Petyr had his own ship now. She could work on it as an electrochemical engineer, she thought with a smile. Or, in the worst case, stay with Mother. If she told them what she'd done, how she'd saved the family name, then Clarissa could start to rebuild the company. Remake their empire in her own name. Possibly even free her father from imprisonment and exile.

The thought left her feeling both hopeful and tired.

A loud clang and the distant sound of laughter brought her back to herself. She reviewed the maintenance schedule for the next ten-day cycle—maintenance on the electrical systems of three of the minor warships and a physical inventory of the electrical cards—marked the ship's time, and shut down her terminal. The mess hall was half full when she got there, members of half a dozen other teams eating together and talking and watching the newsfeeds about the Ring, about themselves going to meet it. Soledad was sitting by herself, gaze fixed on her hand terminal while she ate a green-brown paste that looked like feces but smelled like the finest-cooked beef in the world. Melba told herself to think of it as pâté, and then it wasn't so bad.

Melba got herself a plate and a bulb of lemon water and slid in across from Soledad. The other woman's eyes flicked up with a small but genuine smile.

"Hoy, boss," she said. "How's it go?"

"Everything's copacetic." Melba smiled. She smiled more than Clarissa did. That was an interesting thought. "What did I miss?"

"Report from Mars. Data, this time. The ship that went through? Not on the drift."

"Really?" Melba said. After they'd picked up the faint transmission from the little cobbled-together ship that had started all this, the assumption had been that it had been crippled by something that lived on the other side of the Ring. That it was floating free. "It's under power?"

"Maybe," Soledad said. "Data shows it's moving, and a lot slower than it went in. And the probes they sent in? One of *them* got grabbed too. Normal burn, and then boom, stopped.

The signal's all fucked up, but it looks like the same course that the ship's on. Like they're being...taken to the same place. Or something."

"Weird," Melba said. "But I guess weird is kind of what we expect. After Eros."

"My dad was on Eros," Soledad said, and Melba felt a strange tightening in her throat. "He worked one of the casinos. Security to make sure no one hacked the games, right? Been there fifteen years. Said he was going to retire there, get a little hole up where he didn't weigh so much and just live off his retirement."

"I'm sorry."

Soledad shrugged.

"Everyone dies," she said gruffly, then wiped the back of her hand against her eyes and turned back to the screen.

"My sister was there," Melba said. It was truth, and more than truth. "My sister was one of the first ones it took."

"Shit," Soledad said, looking up at her now, terminal forgotten.

"Yeah."

The two were quiet for a long moment. At another table, a Belter man no more than twenty barked his knees against the edge of the table and started cursing squat little Earth designers, to the amusement of his friends.

"You think they're still there?" Soledad said softly, nodding at her terminal. "There were those voices. The transmissions that came off Eros. You know. After. It was people, right?"

"They're dead," Melba said. "Everyone on Eros died."

"Changed, anyway," Soledad said. "Some guy said it took the patterns off them, right? Their bodies. Their brains. I think about maybe they never really died. Just got *remade*, you know? What if their brains never stopped working and just got..."

She shrugged, looking for a word, but Melba knew what she meant. Change, even profound change, wasn't the same as death. She was proof enough of that.

"Does it matter?"

"What if their souls never got loose?" Soledad said, with real pain in her voice. "What if it caught them all, right? Your sister. My dad. What if they aren't dead, and Ring's got all their souls still?"

There are no souls, Melba thought with a touch of pity. *We are bags of meat with a little electricity running through them. No ghosts, no spirits, no souls. The only thing that survives is the story people tell about you. The only thing that matters is your name.* It was the kind of thing Clarissa would think. The kind of thing her father would have said. She didn't say it aloud.

"Maybe that's why Earth's bringing all those priests," Soledad said and took a scoop of her food. "To put them all to rest."

"Someone should," Melba agreed, and then she turned to her meal.

Her hand terminal chimed: Ren requesting a private conversation. Melba frowned and accepted the connection.

"What's up?" she said.

His voice, when it came, was strained.

"I got something I was wondering if you could look at. An anomaly."

"On my way," Melba said. She dropped the connection and downed her remaining meat paste in two huge swallows, then dropped the plate into the recycler on her way out. Ren was at a workstation in one of the storage bays. It was one of the new spaces he could work in that had a ceiling high enough that he wouldn't have to hunch. Around him, blue plastic crates stood fixed to the floor or one another with powerful electromagnets. Her footsteps were the only sound.

"What've you got?" she asked.

He stood back and nodded at the monitor.

"Air filter data from the *Seung Un*," he said.

Her blood went cold.

"Why?" she said too sharply, too quickly.

"It's catching a lot of outliers. Raised a flag. I'm looking at the profile, and it's all high-energy ganga. Nitroethenes y sa."

She hadn't thought of this. She'd known that the ships did passive gas monitoring, but it had never occurred to her that stray molecules of her explosive would get caught in the filters, or that anyone would check. Ren took her silence as confusion.

"Built a profile," he said. "Ninety percent fit with a moldable explosive."

"So they've got explosives on board," Melba said. "It's a warship. Explosives is what they do, right?" Despair and embarrassment warred in her chest. She'd screwed up. She just wanted Ren to be quiet, to not say the things he was saying. That he was *going* to say.

"This is more like what they'd use for mining and excavation," he said. "You inspected that deck. You remember seeing anything funny? Might have been hard to see. This stuff's putty until it hits air."

"You think it's a bomb?" she said.

Ren shrugged.

"Inners hauling full load of gekke. A guy tried to light himself on fire. Hunger strike lady. The one coyo did that thing with the camera."

"That wasn't political," she said. "He's a performance artist."

"All I mean, we put together a lot of different kinds of people think a lot of different kinds of things. Doesn't bring out the best in people. I was a kid, I watched me eltern end a marriage over whether the madhi was going to be a Belter. And everybody know everybody back down the well's watching. That kind of attention changes people, and it don't make them better. Maybe someone's planning to make a statement, si no?"

"Did you alert their security?" she asked.

"Check with you first. But something like this, shikata ga nai. We got to."

I have to kill him, she thought like someone whispering in her ear. She saw how to do it. Get him to look at his screen, hunch over it just a little. Enough to bare the back of his neck. Then she would press her tongue against the roof of her mouth, the rough of the tastebuds tickling her palate a little, and the strength would come. She'd break him here and then...take him back to her quarters. She could clear out her locker, fit him in. And there was packing sealant that would keep the smell of the body from getting out. She'd file a report, say he was missing. She could act as confused as anyone. By the time she gave up the room and they found him, Melba would already be gone. Even if they worked out that she'd also planted the bomb, they'd just assume she was one of Holden's agents.

Ren was looking at her, his brown eyes mild, his carrot-orange hair back in a wiry ponytail that left the skin of his neck exposed. She thought of him explaining about the brownout buffers. The gentleness in his expression. The kindness.

I'm sorry, she thought. *This isn't my fault. I have to.*

"Let's check the data again," she said, angling her body toward the monitor. "Show me where the anomalies are."

He nodded, turning with her. Like everything on the *Cerisier*, the controls were built for someone a little shorter than Ren. He had to bend a little to reach them. A thickness rose up at the back of her neck, filled her throat. Dread felt like drowning. Ren's ponytail shifted, pulled to the side. There was a mole, brown and ovoid, just where his spine met his skull, like a target.

"So I'm looking on this report here," he said, tapping the screen.

Melba pressed her tongue against the roof of her mouth. What about Soledad? She'd been there when Ren called her. She knew Melba had gone to see him. She might have to kill her too. Where would she put that body? There would have to be an accident. Something plausible. She couldn't let them stop her. She was so close.

"It's not going up, though," he said. "Steady levels."

She circled her tongue counterclockwise once, then paused. She felt light-headed. Short of breath. One of the artificial glands leaking out, maybe, in preparation for the flood. Ren was speaking, but she couldn't hear him. The sounds of her own breath and the blood in her ears was too loud.

I have to kill him. Her fingers were jittering. Her heart raced.

He turned to her, blew a breath out his nostrils. He wasn't a person. He was just a sack of meat with a little electricity. She could do this. For her father. For her family. It needed to be done.

When Ren spoke, his voice seemed to come from a distance.

"Was denkt tu? You want to make the call, you want me to?"

Her mind moved too quickly and too slowly. He was asking if they should alert the *Seung Un* about the bomb. That was what he meant.

"Ren?" she said. Her voice sounded small, querulous. It was the voice of someone much younger than she was. Someone who was very frightened, or very sad. Concern bloomed in his expression, drew his brows together.

"Hey? You all right, boss?"

She touched the screen with the tip of her finger.

"Look again," she said softly. "Look close."

He turned, bending toward the data as if there were something there to discover. She looked at his bent neck like she might have looked at a statue in a museum: an object. Nothing more. She circled her tongue against the roof of her mouth twice, and calm descended on her.

His neck popped when it broke, the cartilaginous disks ripping free, the bundle of nerves and connective tissue that his life had run through coming apart. She kept striking the base of his skull until she felt the bone give way beneath her palm, and then it was time to move the body. Quickly. Before anyone walked in on them. Before the crash came.

Fortunately, there was only a little blood.

Chapter Twelve: Anna

Two hours into an interfaith prayer meeting, and for the very first time in her life, Anna was tired of prayer. She'd always found a deep comfort in praying. A profound sense of connection to something infinitely larger than herself. Her atheist friends called it awe in the face of an infinite cosmos. She called it God. That they might be talking about the same thing didn't bother her at all. It was possible she was hurling her prayers at a cold and unfeeling universe that didn't hear them, but that wasn't how it felt. Science had given mankind many gifts, and she valued it. But the one important thing it had taken away was the value of subjective, personal experience. That had been replaced with the idea that only measurable and testable concepts had value. But humans didn't work that way, and Anna suspected the universe didn't either. *In God's image*, after all, being a tenet of her faith.

At first, the meeting had been pleasant. Father Michel had a lovely deep voice that had mellowed with age like fine wine. His lengthy and heartfelt prayer for God's guidance to be upon those who would study the Ring had sent shivers down her spine. He was followed by an elder of the Church of Humanity Ascendent who led the group through several meditations and breathing exercises that left Anna feeling energized and refreshed. She made a note in her hand terminal to download a copy of their book on meditation and give it a read. Not all of the faiths and traditions represented on board took a turn, of course. The imam would not pray in front of non-Muslims, though he did give a short speech in Arabic that someone translated for her through her earbud. When he ended with *Allah hu akbar*, several people in the audience repeated it back. Anna was one of them. Why not? It seemed polite, and it was a sentiment she agreed with.

But after two hours, even the most heartfelt and poetic of the prayers had begun to wear on her. She began counting the little plastic domes that hid fire-suppression turrets. She'd gotten good at spotting them since the attempted suicide at the first party. She found her mind wandering off to think about the message she'd send to Nono later. The chair she sat in had a very faint vibration that she could almost hear if she remained very still. It must have been the ship's massive drive, and as Anna listened for it, it began to develop a rhythmic pulse. The pulse turned into music, and she began humming under her breath. She stopped when an Episcopalian in the seat next to her pointedly cleared his throat.

Hank Cortez was, of course, scheduled to go last. In the weeks and months Anna had been on the *Prince*, it had become apparent that while no one was officially in charge of the interfaith portion of the Ring expedition, Doctor Hank was treated as a sort of "first among equals." Anna suspected this was because of his close ties to the secretary-general, who'd made the whole mission possible. He also seemed to be on a first-name basis with many of the important artists, politicians, and economic consultants in the civilian contingent of the group.

It didn't really bother her. No matter how egalitarian a group might start out, someone always wound up taking a leadership role. Better Doctor Hank than herself.

When the Neo-Wiccan priestess currently at the podium finally finished her rites, Doctor Hank was nowhere to be seen. Anna felt a little surge of hope that the prayer service would end early.

But no. Doctor Hank made his entrance into the auditorium trailed by a camera crew and bulled his way up to the podium like an actor taking the stage. He flashed his gleaming smile across the audience, making sure to end with the section the camera people had set up in.

"Brothers and sisters," he said, "let us bow our heads and offer thanks to the Almighty and seek His counsel and guidance as we draw ever closer to the end of this historic journey."

He managed to rattle on that way for another twenty minutes.

Anna started humming again.

After, Anna met Tilly for lunch at the officers' mess that had been set aside for civilian use. Anna wasn't exactly sure how she'd wound up being Tilly's best and only friend on the trip, but the woman had latched on to her after their first meeting and burrowed in like a tick. No, that wasn't really fair. Even though the only thing she and Tilly had in common was their carbon base, it wasn't like Anna had a lot of friends on the ship either. And while Tilly could appear flighty and exasperating, Anna had gradually seen through the mask to the deeply lonely woman underneath. Her husband's obscene contributions to the secretary-general's reelection campaign had bought her way onto the flight as a civilian consultant. She had no purpose on the mission other than to be seen, an extended reminder of her husband's enormous wealth and power. That she had nothing else to offer the group only made the real point clearer. She knew it, and everyone else knew it too. Most of the other civilians on the flight treated her with barely concealed contempt.

While they waited for their food to arrive, Tilly popped a

lozenge in her mouth and chewed it. The faint smell of nicotine and mint filled the air. No smoking on military ships, of course.

"How'd your thing go?" Tilly asked, playing with her silver-inlaid lozenge box and looking around the room. She was wearing a pants and blouse combination that probably cost more than Anna's house on Europa had. It was the kind of thing she wore when she wanted to appear casual.

"The prayer meeting?" Anna said. "Good. And then not as good. Long. Very, very long."

Tilly looked at her, the honesty getting her attention. "God, don't I know it. No one can blather on like a holy man with a trapped audience. Well, maybe a politician."

Their food arrived, a navy boy acting as waiter for the VIP civilians. Anna wondered what he thought of that. The UN military was all volunteer. He'd probably had a vision of what his military life would be like, and she doubted this was it. He carefully placed their food in front of them with the ease of long practice, gave them both a smile, and vanished back into the kitchen.

Galley. They called it a galley on ships.

Tilly picked halfheartedly at a farm-grown tomato and real mozzarella salad that Anna could have afforded on Europa by selling a kidney, and said, "Have you heard from Namono?"

Anna nodded while she finished chewing a piece of fried tofu. "I got another video last night. Nami gets bigger in every one. She's getting used to the gravity, but the drugs make her cranky. We're thinking about taking her off of them early, even if it means more physical therapy."

"Awww," Tilly said. It had a pro forma feel to it. Anna waited for her to change the subject.

"Robert hasn't checked in for a week now," Tilly said. She seemed resigned rather than sad.

"You don't think he—"

"Cheating?" Tilly said with a laugh. "I wish. That would at least be interesting. When he locks himself away in his office at 2 a.m., you know what I catch him looking at? Business reports, stock values, spreadsheets. Robert is the least sexual creature I've ever met. At least until they invent a way to fuck money."

Tilly's casual obscenity had very quickly stopped bothering Anna. There was no anger in it. Like most of the things Tilly did, it struck her as another way to be noticed. To get people to pay attention to her. "How's the campaign coming?" Anna said.

"Esteban? Who knows? Robert's job is to be rich and have rich friends. I'm sure that part is coming along just fine."

They ate in silence for a while, then without planning to, Anna said, "I don't think I should have come."

Tilly nodded gravely, as though Anna had just quoted gospel at her. "None of us should have."

"We pray, and we get photographed, and we have meetings about interfaith cooperation," Anna continued. "You know what we never talk about?"

"The Ring?"

"No. I mean yes. I mean we talk about the Ring all the time. What is it, what's it for, why did the protomolecule make it."

Tilly pushed her salad away and chewed another lozenge. "Then what?"

"What I thought we came here to do. To talk about what it *means*. Nearly a hundred spiritual leaders and theologians on this ship. And none of us is talking about what the Ring means."

"For God?"

"Well, at least *about* God. Theological anthropology is a lot simpler when humans are the only ones with souls."

Tilly waved at the waiter and ordered a cocktail Anna had never heard of. The waiter seemed to know, though, and darted off to get it. "This seems like the kind of thing I'll need a drink for," she said. "Go on."

"But how does the protomolecule fit into that? Is it alive? It murders us, but it also builds amazing structures that are astonishingly advanced. Is it a tool used by someone more like us, only smarter? And if so, are they creatures with a sense of the divine? Do they have faith? What does that look like?"

"If they're even from the same God," Tilly said, using a short straw to mix her drink, then taking a sip.

"Well, for some of us there's only one," Anna replied, then asked the waiter for tea. When he'd left again, she said, "It calls into question the entire concept of Grace. Well, not entirely, but it complicates it at the very least. The things that made the protomolecule are intelligent. Does that mean they have souls? They invade our solar system, kill us indiscriminately, steal our resources. All things we would consider sins if we were doing them. Does that mean they're fallen? Did Christ die for them too? Or are they intelligent but soulless, and everything the protomolecule's done is just like a virus doing what it's programmed for?"

A group of workers in civilian jumpsuits came into the dining area and sat down. They ordered food from the waiter and talked noisily among themselves. Anna let them distract her while her mind chewed over the worries she hadn't let herself articulate before today.

"And, really, it's all pretty theoretical, even to me," she continued. "Maybe none of that should matter to *our* faith at all, except that I have this feeling it will. That to most people, it will matter."

Tilly was sipping her drink, which Anna knew from experience meant she was taking the conversation seriously. "Have you mentioned this to anyone?" Tilly said, prompting her to continue.

"Cortez acts like he's in charge," Anna replied. Her tea arrived and she blew on it for a while to cool it. "I guess I should talk to him."

"Cortez is a politician," Tilly said with a condescending smirk. "Don't let his folksy Father Hank bullshit snow you. He's here because as long as Esteban is in office, Cortez is a powerful man. This dog and pony show? This is all about votes."

"I hate that," Anna said. "I believe you. You understand this all better than I do. But I hate that you're right. What a waste."

"What would you ask Cortez for?"

"I'd like to organize some groups. Have the conversation."

"Do you need his permission?" Tilly asked.

Anna thought of her last conversation with Nono and laughed. When she spoke, her voice sounded thoughtful even to her.

"No," she said. "I guess I don't."

That night Anna was awakened from a dream about taking Nami to Earth and watching her bones break as the gravity crushed her, to a blaring alarm. It lasted only a few seconds, then stopped. A voice from her comm panel said, "All hands to action stations."

Anna assumed this didn't mean her, as she had no idea what an action station was. There were no more alarms, and the voice from the comm panel didn't return with more dire pronouncements, but being startled out of her nightmare left her feeling wide awake and jumpy. She climbed out of her bunk, sent a short video message to Nono and Nami, and then put on some clothes.

There was very little traffic in the corridor and lifts. The military people she did see looked tense, though to her relief, not particularly frightened. Just aware. Vigilant.

Having nowhere else to go, she wandered into the officers' mess and ordered a glass of milk. When it arrived, she was stunned to discover it was actual milk that had at some point come out of a cow. How much was the UN spending on this civilian "dog and pony show"?

The only other people in the mess hall were a few military people with officers' uniforms, and a small knot of the civilian contractors drinking coffee and slumping in their seats like workers in the middle of an all-nighter. A dozen metal tables were bolted to the floor with magnetic chairs at their sides. Wall displays scrolled information for the ship's officers, all of it gibberish to her. A row of cutouts opened into the galley, letting through plates of food and the sounds of industrial dishwashers and the smell of floor cleaner. It was like sitting too near the kitchen in a very, very clean restaurant.

Anna drank her milk slowly, savoring the rich texture and ridiculous luxury of it. A bell chimed on someone's hand terminal, and two of the civilian workers got up and left. One stayed, a beautiful but sad-faced woman who looked down at a terminal on the table with a vacant, thousand-yard stare.

"Excuse me, ma'am," said a voice behind her, almost making Anna jump out of her chair. A young man in a naval officer's uniform moved into her field of view and gestured awkwardly at the chair next to her. "Mind if I sit?"

Anna recovered enough to smile at him, and he took it as assent, stiffly folding himself into the seat. He was very tall for an Earther, with short blond hair and the thick shoulders and narrow waist all of the young officers seemed to have regardless of gender.

Anna reached across the table to shake his hand and said, "Anna Volovodov."

"Chris Williams," the young officer replied, giving her hand a short but firm shake. "And yes, ma'am, I know who you are."

"You do?"

"Yes, ma'am. My people in Minnesota are Methodists, going back as far as we can trace them. When I saw you listed on the civilian roster, I made sure to remember the name."

Anna nodded and sipped her milk. If the boy had singled her out because she was a minister of his faith, then he wanted to talk to her as a member of the congregation. She mentally shifted gears to become Pastor Anna and said, "What can I do for you, Chris?"

"Love your accent, ma'am," Chris replied. He needed time to build up to whatever it was that he'd approached her about, so Anna gave it to him.

"I grew up in Moscow," she replied. "Though after two years on Europa I can almost do Belter now, sa sa?"

Chris laughed, some of the tension draining out of his face. "That's not bad, ma'am. But you get those guys going at full speed, I can't understand a word the skinnies say."

Anna chose to ignore the slur. "Please, no more 'ma'am.' Makes me feel a hundred years old. Anna, please, or Pastor Anna if you have to."

"All right," Chris said. "Pastor Anna."

They sat together in companionable silence for a few moments while Anna watched Chris work up to whatever he needed to say.

"You heard the alarm, right?" he finally said. "Bet it woke you up."

"It's why I'm here," Anna replied.

"Yeah. Action stations. It's because of the dusters— I mean, Martians, you know."

"Martians?" Anna found herself wanting another glass of the delicious milk, but thought it might distract Chris, so she didn't wave at the waiter.

"We're in weapons range of their fleet now," he said. "So we go on alert. We can't share sky with the dusters anymore without going on alert. Not since, you know, Ganymede."

Anna nodded and waited for him to continue.

"And that Ring, you know, it's already killed somebody. I mean, just a dumb as sand skinny slingshotter, but still. Somebody."

Anna took his hand. He flinched a bit, but relaxed when she smiled at him. "That scares you?"

"Sure. Of course. But that ain't it."

Anna waited, keeping her face carefully neutral. The pretty civilian girl across the room got up suddenly, as though leaving. Her lips moved, talking to herself, then she sat back down, put her arms on the table, and leaned her head on them. Someone else scared, waiting out the long watches of the night, all alone in a room full of people.

"I mean," Chris said, breaking into her reverie, "that ain't all of it anyway."

"What else?" Anna said.

"The Ring didn't put us on alert," he said. "It's the Martians. Even with that thing out there, we're still thinking about shooting each other. That's pretty fucked up. Sorry. Messed up."

"It seems like we should be able to see past our human differences when we're confronted with something like this, doesn't it?"

Chris nodded and squeezed her hand tighter, but said nothing.

"Chris, would you like to pray with me?"

He nodded and lowered his head, closing his eyes. When she'd finished, he said, "I know I'm not the only Methodist on the ship. Do you, you know, hold services?"

I do now.

"Sunday, at 10 a.m., in conference room 41," she said, making a mental note to ask someone if she could use conference room 41 on Sunday mornings.

"I'll see if I can get the time off," Chris said with a smile. "Thank you, ma'am. Pastor Anna."

"It was nice talking to you, Chris." *You just gave me a reason to be here.*

When Chris left, Anna found herself very tired, ready to return to her bed, but the pretty girl across the room hadn't moved. Her head was still buried in her arms. Anna walked over to her and gently touched her on the shoulder. The girl's head jerked up, her eyes wild, almost panicked.

"Hi," Anna said. "I'm Anna. What's your name?"

The girl stared up, as if the question were a difficult one. Anna sat down across from her.

"I saw you sitting here," Anna said. "It looked like you could use some company. It's okay to be afraid. I understand."

The girl jerked to her feet like a malfunctioning machine. Her eyes were flat, and her head tilted a degree. Anna felt suddenly afraid. It was like she'd gone to pet a dog and found herself with her hand on a lion. Something in the back of her head told her, *This is a bad one. This one will hurt you.*

"I'm sorry," Anna said, standing up with her hands half raised. "I didn't mean to disturb you."

"You don't know me," the girl replied. "You don't know anything." Her hands were clenched into fists at her sides, the tendons in her neck quivering like plucked guitar strings.

"You're right," Anna said, still backing up and patting the air with her hands. "I apologize."

Other people in the room were staring at them now, and Anna felt a surge of relief that she wasn't alone with the girl. The girl stared at her, trembling, for a few more seconds, then darted out of the room.

"What the fuck was that all about?" someone behind Anna said in a quiet voice.

Maybe the girl had woken up from a nightmare too, Anna thought. Or maybe she hadn't.

Chapter Thirteen: Bull

Arriving at the Ring was a political fiction, but that didn't keep it from being real. There was no physical boundary to say that this was within the realm of the object. There was no port to dock at. The *Behemoth*'s sensory arrays had been sucking in data from the Ring since before they'd left Tycho. The Martian science ships and Earth military forces that had been there before the doomed Belter kid had become its first casualty were still there, where they had been, but resupplied now. The new Martian ships had joined them, matched orbit, and were hanging quietly in the sky. The Earth flotilla, like the *Behemoth*, was in the last part of the burn, pulling up to whatever range they'd chosen to stop at. To say, *We have come across the vast abyss to float at this distance and now we are here. We've arrived.*

As far as anyone could tell, the Ring didn't give a damn.

The structure itself was eerie. The surface was a series of twisting ridges that spiraled around its body. At first they appeared uneven, almost messy. The mathematicians, architects, and physicists assured them all that there was a deep regularity there: the height of the ridges in a complex harmony with the width and the spacing between the peaks and valleys. The reports were breathless, finding one layer of complexity after another, the intimations of intention and design all laid bare without any hint of what it all might mean.

"The official Martian reports have been very conservative," the science officer said. His name was Chan Bao-Zhi, and on Earth, he'd have been Chinese. Here, he was a Belter from Pallas Station. "They've given a lot of summary and maybe a tenth of the data they've collected. Fortunately, we've been able to observe most of their experiments and make our own analysis."

"Which Earth will have been doing too," Ashford said.

"Without doubt, sir," Chan said.

Like any ritual, the staff meeting carried more significance than information. The heads of all the major branches of the *Behemoth*'s structural tree were present: Sam for engineering, Bull for security, Chan for the research teams, Bennie Cortland-Mapu for health services, Anamarie Ruiz for infrastructure, and so on, filling the two dozen seats around the great conference table. Ashford sat in the place of honor, another beneficent Christ painted on the wall behind him. Pa sat at his right hand, and Bull—by tradition—at his left.

"What have we got?" Ashford said. "Short form."

"It's fucking weird, sir," Chan said, and everyone chuckled. "Our best analysis is that the Ring is an artificially sustained Einstein-Rosen bridge. You go through the Ring, you don't come out the other side here."

"So it's a gate," Ashford said.

"Yes, sir. It appears that the protomolecule or Phoebe bug or whatever you want to call it was launched at the solar system several billion years ago, aiming for Earth with the intention of hijacking primitive life to build a gateway. We're positing that whoever created the protomolecule did it as a first step toward making travel to the solar system more convenient and practical later."

Bull took a deep breath and let it out slowly. It was what everyone had been thinking, but hearing it spoken in this official setting made it seem more real. The Ring was a way for something to get here. Not just a gateway. A beachhead.

"When the *Y Que* went through it, the mass and velocity of the ship triggered some mechanism in the Ring," Chan said. "The Martians have a good dataset from the moment it happened, and there was a massive outpouring of energy within the Ring structure and a whole cascade of microlevel conformation changes. The entire object went up to about five thousand degrees Kelvin, and it has been cooling regularly ever since. So it took a lot of effort to get that thing running, but it looks like not much to maintain."

"What do we know about what's on the other side?" Pa asked. Her expression was neutral, her voice pleasant and unemotional. She could have been asking him to justify a line item in his budget.

"It's hard to know much," Chan said. "We're peeking through a keyhole, and the Ring itself seems to be generating interference and radiation that makes getting consistent readings difficult. We know the *Y Que* wasn't destroyed. We're still getting the video feed that the kid was spewing when he went through, it's just not showing us much."

"Stars?" Ashford said. "Something we can start to navigate from?"

"No, sir," Chan said. "The far side of the Ring doesn't have any stars, and the background microwave radiation is significantly different from what we'd expect."

"Meaning what?" Ashford said.

"Meaning, 'Huh, that's weird,'" Chan said. "Sir."

Ashford's smile was cool as he motioned the science officer to continue. Chan coughed before he went on.

"We have a couple of other anomalies that we aren't quite sure what to make of. It looks like there's a maximum speed on the other side."

"Can you unpack that, please?" Pa said.

"The *Y Que* went through the Ring going very fast," Chan said. "About seven-tenths of a second after it reached the other side, it started a massive deceleration. Bled off almost all its speed in about five seconds. It looks like the nearly instant deceleration was what killed the pilot. Since then, it seems as if the ship is being moved out away from the Ring and deeper into whatever's on the other side."

"We know that when the protomolecule's active, it's been able to...alter what we'd expect from inertia," Sam said. "Is that how it stopped the ship?"

"That's entirely possible," Chan said. "Mars has been pitching probes through the Ring, and it looks like we start seeing the effect right around six hundred meters per second. Under that, mass behaves just the way we expect it to. Over that, it stops dead and then moves off in approximately the same direction that the *Y Que* is going."

Sam whistled under her breath.

"That's *really* slow," she said. "The main drives would be almost useless."

"It's slower than a rifle shot," Chan said. "The good news is it only affects mass above the quantum level. The electromagnetic spectrum seems to behave normally, including visible light."

"Thank God for small favors," Sam said.

"What else are the probes telling us?"

"There's something out there," Chan said, and for the first time a sense of dread leaked into his voice. "The probes are seeing objects. Large ones. But there's not much light except what we're shining through the Ring or mounting on the probes. And, as I said, the Ring has always given inconsistent returns. If whatever's in there is made of the same stuff, who knows?"

"Ships?" Ashford said.

"Maybe."

"How many?"

"Over a hundred, under a hundred thousand. Probably."

Bull leaned forward, his elbows on the table. Ashford and Pa were looking around the table at the graying faces. They'd known before, because they weren't going to wait for a staff meeting to get their information. Now they were judging the reactions. So he'd give them a reaction. Control the fall.

"Be weirder if there wasn't anything there. If it was an attack fleet, they'd have attacked by now."

"Yeah," Ruiz said, latching on to the words.

Ashford opened the floor for questions. How many probes had Mars fired through? How long would it take something going at six hundred meters per second to reach one of the structures? Had they tried sending small probes in? Had there been any contact from the protomolecule itself, the stolen voices of humans, the way there had been with Eros? Chan did his best to be reassuring without actually having anything more that he could say. Bull assumed there was a deeper report that Ashford and Pa were getting, and he wondered what was in it. Being kept out chafed.

"All right. This is all interesting, but it's not our focus," Ashford said, bringing the Q-and-A session to a halt. "We're not here to send probes through the Ring. We're not here to start a fight. We're just making sure that whatever the inner planets do, we're at the table. If something comes out of the Ring, we'll worry about it then."

"Yes, sir," Bull said, throwing his own weight behind Ashford's. It wasn't like there was another strategy. Better that the crew see them all unified. People were watching how this all came down, and not just the crew.

"Mister Pa?" Ashford said. The XO nodded and glanced at Bull. Instinct dropped a weight in his gut.

"There have been some irregularities in the ship's accounting structure," Pa said. "Chief Engineer Rosenberg?"

Sam nodded, surprise on her face. "XO?" she said.

"I'm afraid I'm going to have to restrict you to quarters and

revoke your access privileges until this is all clarified. Chief Wata-
nabe will relieve you. Mister Baca, you'll see to it."

The room was just as silent, but the meaning behind it was different now. Sam's eyes were wide with disbelief and rising fury.

"Excuse me?" she said. Pa met her gaze coolly, and Bull understood all of it in an instant.

"Records show you've been drawing resources from work and
materials budgets that weren't appropriate," Pa said, "and until
the matter is resolved—"

"If this is about the tech support thing, that's on me," Bull said.
"I authorized that. It's got nothing to do with Sam."

"I'm conducting a full audit, Mister Baca. If I find you've been
drawing resources inappropriately, I'll take the actions I deem
appropriate. As your executive officer, I am informing you that
Samara Rosenberg is to be confined to quarters and her access to
ship's systems blocked. Do you have any questions about that?"

She'd waited until they'd made the trip, until they'd gotten
where they were going, and now it was time to establish that she
was in control. To get back at him for the drug dealer he'd spaced
and punish Sam for being his ally. Would have been stupid to do
until their shakedown run was over. But now it was.

Bull laced his fingers together. The refusal was on the back
of his tongue, waiting. It would have been insubordination, and
it would have been easy as breathing out. There were years—
decades even—when he'd have done it, and taken the consequences as a badge of honor. It had been his call, and standing by
while Sam was punished for it was more than dishonorable, it was
disloyal. Pa knew that. Anyone who'd read his service records
would know it. If it had just been his mission, his career on the
line, he'd have done it, but Fred Johnson had asked him to make
this work. So there was only one play to make.

"No questions," he said, rising from his chair. "Sam. You
should come with me now."

The others were silent as he led her out of the conference room.
They all looked stunned and confused, except Ashford and Pa. Pa

wore a poker face, and Ashford had a little shadow of smugness in the corners of his mouth. Sam's breath shook. Outrage and adrenaline left her skin pale. He helped her into the side seat of his security cart, then got behind the controls. They lurched into motion, four small engines whirring and whining. They were almost at the elevators when Sam laughed. A short, mirthless sound as much like a cry of pain as anything.

"Holy shit," Sam said.

Bull couldn't think of anything to say that would pull the punch, so he only nodded and took the cart into the wide elevator car. Sam wept, but there was nothing that looked like sorrow in her expression. He guessed that she'd never suffered that kind of disciplinary humiliation before. Or if she had, it hadn't been often enough to build up a callus. The dishonor of letting her take the hit was like he'd swallowed something before he'd chewed it enough, and now it wouldn't go down.

Back at the security office, Serge was at the main desk. The man's eyebrows rose as Bull came in the room.

"Hoy, bossman," the duty officer said. A hardcore OPA bruiser named Jojo. "Que pasa?"

"Nothing good. What did I miss?"

"Complaint from a carnicería down by engineering about a missing goat. Got a note from one of the Earth ships lost one of their crew, wondering if we'd come up with an extra. A couple coyos got shit-faced and we locked 'em in quarters, told 'em we'd sic the Bull on 'em."

"How'd they take that?"

"We had them mop up after."

Bull chuckled before he sighed.

"So. I've got Samara Rosenberg in the cart outside," he said. "XO wants her confined to quarters for unauthorized use of resources."

"I want a pony in a wetsuit." Jojo grinned.

"XO gave an order," Bull said. "I want you to take her to her quarters. I'll get her access pulled. We'll need to set a guard while we're at it. She's pissed."

Jojo scratched at his neck. "We're doing it?"

"Yeah."

Jojo's face closed. Bull nodded toward the door. Jojo left, and Bull took his place at the desk, identifying himself to the system and starting the process of locking Sam out of her own ship. While the security system ran its check against each of the *Behemoth*'s subsystems, he leaned on his elbows and watched.

The first time Fred Johnson saved Bull's life, he'd done it with a rifle and a mobile medical unit. The second time, he'd done it with a credit chip. Bull had mustered out at thirty and took his pension to Ceres. For three years, he'd just lived. Ate cheap, drank too much, slept in his own bed not knowing if he was sick from the alcohol or the spin. Not caring much. He got into a few fights, had a few disagreements with the local law. He didn't see that he had a problem until it was unmistakable, and by then it was a hell of a problem.

Depression ran in his family. Self-medicating did too. His grandfather had died of the pair. His mother had been in therapy a couple times. His brother had graduated to heroin and lived five years in a treatment center in Roswell. None of it had seemed to have anything to do with Bull. He was a marine. He'd turned away from a life on basic to live in the stars, or if not the stars, at least the rocks that floated free in the night sky. He'd killed men. Bottle couldn't beat him. But it almost had.

The day Fred Johnson had appeared at his door, it had been stranger than a dream. His former commanding officer looked different. Older, stronger. Truth was, their birthdays weren't all that far apart, but Johnson had always been the Old Man. Bull had followed the news about the fallout from Anderson Station, and Fred's changing sides. Some of the other marines he knew on Ceres had been angry about it. He'd just figured the Old Man knew what he was doing. He wouldn't have done it without a reason.

Bull, Fred had said. Just that, at first. He could still remember Fred's dark eyes meeting his. The shame had made Bull try to stand straighter, to suck in his gut a little. In that moment, he saw how far he'd fallen. Two seconds of seeing himself through Fred Johnson's eyes was all it took for that.

Sir, Bull had replied, then stood back and let Johnson into the hole. The place stank of yeast and old tofu. And flop sweat. Fred ignored it all. *I need you back on duty, soldier.*

Okay, Bull had said. And the secret he carried with him, the one he'd take to his grave, was this: He hadn't meant it. In that moment, all he'd wanted was for Fred Johnson to go away and let Bull forget him again. Lying to his old commanding officer, to the man who'd kept him from bleeding out under fire, came as naturally as breathing. It didn't have anything to do with Earth or the Belt or Anderson Station. It wasn't some greater loyalty. He just wasn't done destroying himself. And even now, sitting alone at the security desk betraying Sam, he thought that Fred had known. Or guessed.

Fred had pressed a credit chip into his palm. It was one of the cheap, vaguely opalescent ones that the OPA had used to keep its funds untraceable, back in the bad old days. *Get yourself a new uniform.* Bull had saluted, already thinking about the booze he could buy.

The chit carried six months' wages at his old pay grade. If it had been less, Bull wouldn't have gone. Instead, he shaved for the first time in days, got a new suit, packed a valise, and threw out anything that didn't fit in it. He hadn't had a drink since, even on the nights he'd wanted one more than oxygen.

The security system chimed that the lockout was finished. Bull noted it and leaned back in the chair, reading the be-on-alert notice from the *Cerisier* and letting his mind wander. When Gathoni arrived to take the next shift, he walked two corridors down to a little mom-and-pop bodega, bought a blister-pack with four bulbs of beer, and headed over to Sam's quarters. The guard on duty nodded to him. Legally, Bull didn't have to knock. As head of security, he could have walked into Sam's rooms at any time, with or without being welcome. He knocked.

Sam was wearing a simple sweater and black workpants with magnetic strips down the sides. Bull held up the beer. For a long moment, Sam glared at him. She stepped back and to the side. He followed her in.

Her rooms were clean, neat, and cluttered. The air smelled like industrial lubricant and old laundry. She leaned against the arm of a foam couch.

"Peace offering?" she said bitterly.

"Pretty much," Bull said. "Pa's pissed off at me, and she's taking it out on you. She figured either I do it and I lose my best ally or I don't and I'm the one confined to quarters, right? No way to lose for her."

"This is bullshit."

"It is," Bull said. "And I'm sorry as hell about the whole damn thing."

Sam's breath rattled with anger. Bull accepted it. He had it coming. She walked across to him, grabbing the four-pack out of his hand, twisting it to shatter the plastic, and plucking one of the bulbs free.

"You want one?" she asked.

"Just water for me," he said.

"What chafes me," Sam said, "is the way Ashford just sits there like he's so happy about the whole thing. He knows the score. He's as much a part of it as Pa. Or you. Don't think you can buy me off with a few cheap brews. You're just as much at fault as they are."

"I am."

"I got into engineering because I didn't want all the petty social birdshit. And now look at me."

"Yeah," Bull said.

Sam dropped to the couch with a sigh and said something obscene and colorful. Bull sat down across from her.

"Okay, stop that," she said.

"What?"

"That looking repentant thing. I feel like I'm supposed to genu-flect or something. It's creepy." She took a long pull at the bulb, the soft plastic collapsing under the suction, then expanding out a little as the beer outgassed. "Look, you and Pa are both doing what you think you ought to, and I'm getting screwed. I get it. Doesn't mean I have to be happy about it. Thing is, you're right. She wants you to lose allies. So no matter how much I want to tell you to go put your dick in a vise? I'm not going to, just because it would mean Pa won."

"Thank you for that, Sam."

"Go put your dick in a vise, Bull."

Bull's hand terminal chimed.

"Mister Baca?" Gathoni's voice said. "You should come back to the office, maybe."

Sam's expression sobered and she put down the bulb. Bull's belly tightened.

"What's going on?" he asked. When Gathoni answered, her voice was controlled and calm as a medic calling for more pressure.

"Earth destroyer *Seung-Un*? It just blew up."

Chapter Fourteen: Melba

When she'd thought about it, planning the final, closing stages of her vengeance, she'd pictured herself as the conductor of a private symphony, moving her baton to the orchestrated chaos. It didn't happen that way at all. The morning she went to the *Thomas Prince*, she didn't know that the day had finally come.

"Active hands to stations," a man's voice announced over the general channel.

"Wish to fuck they'd stop doing that," Melba said. "Always makes me feel like I should be doing something."

"Savvy, boss. When they start paying me navy wages, I'll start jumping for their drills," Soledad said, her voice pressed thin by the hand terminal's speaker. "I've got nothing on this couple. Unless Stanni's got it, we got to move down a level, try again."

"Copy that," Melba said. "Stanni, what are you seeing?"

The channel went silent. Melba looked around the service

corridor at a half kilometer of nothing: conduit and pipes and the access grating that could shift to accommodate any direction of thrust. The only sounds were the creaking, hissing, and muttering of the *Thomas Prince*. The seconds stretched.

"*Stanni?*" Soledad said, dread in her voice, and the channel crackled.

"Perdón," Stanni said. "Looking at some weird wiring, but it's not the goose we're hunting. Lost in my head, me. I'm fine. I'm here."

Soledad said something obscene under her breath.

"Sorry," Stanni said again.

"It's okay," Melba said. "Did you check the brownout buffers?"

"Did."

"Then let's just keep moving. Next level."

The thing that surprised her, the one she hadn't seen coming, was how everyone on the *Cerisier* was ready to put Ren's disappearance at the foot of the Ring. It was rare for people to go missing on a ship. The *Cerisier*, like any other long-haul vessel, was a closed system. There was nowhere to go. She'd assumed there would be the usual, human suspicions. Ren had crossed someone, stolen something, slept with the wrong person, and he'd been disposed of. Thrown out an airlock, maybe. Fed into the recycling and reduced to his basic nutrients, then passed into the water or food supply. It wasn't that there were no ways to hide or dispose of a body, it was that there were so few ways for it to go unnoticed. Traveling between the planets had never eliminated murder. So many highly evolved primates in the same box for months on end, a certain death rate had to be expected.

This time, though, it was different. It made sense to people that someone would go missing, vanish, as they approached the Ring. It felt right. The voyage itself was ill-omened, and strange things were supposed to happen when people drew too near the uncanny, the dangerous, the haunted. The others were all on edge, and that gave her cover too. If she started weeping, they'd think they understood why. They'd think it was fear.

Melba packed her diagnostic array back in its sleeve, stood, and headed down to the lift. The internal service lifts were tiny, with hardly enough room for one person and the gear. Traveling between decks here was like stepping into a coffin. As she shifted down to the next level, she imagined the power failing. Being trapped there. Her mind flickered, and for a moment, she saw her own storage locker. The one in her quarters. The one filled with sealant foam and Ren. She shuddered and forced her mind elsewhere.

The *Thomas Prince* was one of the larger ships in the Earth flotilla, the home of the civilian horde that the UN had put together. Artists, poets, philosophers, priests. Even without changing the physical structures of the ship, it gave her the feeling of being less a military vessel and more a poorly appointed, uncomfortable cruise liner. Clarissa had been on yachts and luxury ships most of the times she'd traveled outside Earth's gravity well, and she could imagine the thousand complaints the ship's captain would suffer about the halls not being wide enough and the screens on the walls too low a quality. It was the sort of thing she would have been concerned with, in her previous life. Now it was less than nothing.

It shouldn't have bothered her. One more death, more or less. It shouldn't have mattered. But it was Ren.

"In position," Stanni said.

"Give me a second," Melba said, stepping out of the lift. The new corridor was nearly identical to the one above it. These decks were all quarters and storage, with very little of the variation that she'd see when they reached the lowest levels—engineering, machine shops, hangar bays. Tracking down the electrical anomaly, they'd started here because it was easy. The longer it took, the harder it would get. Like everything.

She found the junction, took the diagnostic array out of its sleeve, and plugged it in.

"Solé?"

"In place," Soledad said.

"Okay," Melba said. "Start the trace."

When it had happened, she'd gotten Ren to her quarters and laid him out on the floor. She'd already felt the crash coming on, so she'd lain down on her bunk and let it come. It might only have been her imagination that made that one seem worse than the ones before. For a long horrified moment at the end, she thought that she'd voided herself, but her uniform was clean. She'd gone then, Ren still on her floor, gotten a bulb of coffee, put Ren's hand terminal in a stall of the group head, and found the security officer. He was a thin Martian named Andre Commenhi, and he'd listened to her informal report with half an ear. Ren had called her and asked her to consult with him. When she'd gone to see him at his usual workstation, he wasn't there. She'd been through the ship, but she hadn't found him, and he wasn't answering connection requests. She was starting to get concerned.

While they'd done a sweep of the ship, she'd gotten the tubes of sealant foam, gone back to her quarters, and entombed him. His hair had seemed brighter, the orange like something from a coral reef. His skin was pale as sunlight where the blood had drained away from it. Purple as a bruise where it had pooled. Rigor hadn't set in, so she was able to fold him together, curled like a fetus, and fill the spaces around him with foam. It had taken minutes to harden. The foam was engineered to be airtight and pressure-resistant. If she'd done it right, the corpse smell would never leak out.

"Nadie," Soledad said, sounding resigned. "You guys got anything?"

"Hey!" Stanni said. "Think I do. I've got a ten percent fluctuation on this box."

"Okay," Melba said. "Let's reset it and see if that clears the issue."

"On it," Stanni said. "Grab some lunch while it run?"

"I'll meet you in the galley," Melba said. Her voice seemed almost normal. She sounded like someone else.

The galley was nearly empty. By the ship's clock, it was the middle of the night, and only a few officers lurked at their tables watching the civilians as they passed. The terms of the service contract meant they got to use the officers' mess. She'd heard there was a certain level of distrust among the navy crews for civilians like her and her team. She would have resented it more if she hadn't been the living example of why their suspicions were justified. Soledad and Stanni were already at a table, drinking coffee from bulbs and sharing a plate of sweet rolls.

"I'm gonna miss these when we cut thrust," Stanni said, holding one of the rolls up. "Best cook flying can't bake right without thrust. How long you think we're going to be on the float?"

"As long as it takes," Melba said. "They're planning for two months."

"Two months at null g," Soledad said, but her voice and the grayness of her face were clear. Two months at the Ring.

"Yeah," Stanni said. "Any word on Bob?"

The fifth of the team—fourth now—was still back on the *Cerisier*. It turned out he and Ren had both been having a relationship with a man on the medical team, and security were rounding up the usual suspects. Most times someone went missing, it was domestic. Melba felt her throat going thick again.

"Nothing yet," she said. "They'll clear him. He wouldn't have done anything."

"Yeah," Soledad said. "Bob wouldn't hurt anyone. He's a good man. Everyone knew about everything, and he loved Ren."

"Could stop the passato," Stanni said. "We don't know he's dead."

"With esse coisa out there, dead's the best thing he could be," Soledad said. "I've been having bad dreams since we flipped. I don't think we're making it back from this run. Not any of us."

"Talking like that won't help," Stanni said.

A woman walked into the galley. Middle-aged, thick red hair pulled into a severe-looking bun that competed with her smile. Melba looked at her to try not to be at the table, then looked away.

"Whatever happened to Ren," she said, "we've got our job to do. And we'll do it."

"Damn right," Stanni said, and then again with a catch in his voice. "Damn right."

They sat together quietly for a moment while the older man wept. Solé put a hand on his arm, and Stanni's shuddering breath slowed. He nodded, swallowed. He looked like an icon of grief and courage. He looked noble. It struck Melba for the first time that Stanni was probably her father's age, and she had never seen her father weep for anyone.

"I'm sorry," she said. She hadn't planned to speak the words, but there they were, coughed up on the table. They seemed obscene.

"It's okay," Stanni said. "I'm all right. Here, boss, have a roll."

Melba reached out, fighting herself not to weep again. Not to speak. She didn't know what she'd say, and she was afraid of herself. The alert chimed on her hand terminal. The diagnostic was finished. It only took a second to see that the spike was still there. Stanni said something profane, then shrugged.

"No rest for the wicked, no peace for the good," he said, standing.

"Go ahead," Melba said. "I'll catch up."

"Pas problema," Soledad said. "You hardly got to drink your coffee, sa sa?"

She watched them go, relieved that they wouldn't be there and wanting to call them back, both at the same time. The thickness in her throat had traveled to her chest. The sweet rolls looked delicious and nauseating. She forced herself to take a few deep breaths.

It was almost over. The fleets were there. The *Rocinante* was there. Everything was going according to her plan, or if not quite that, at least near enough to it. Ren shouldn't have mattered. She'd killed men before him. It was almost inevitable that people would die when the bomb went off. Vengeance called forth blood, because it always did. That was its nature, and she had made herself its instrument.

Ren wasn't her fault, he was Holden's. Holden had killed him by making her presence necessary. If he had respected the honor of her family, none of this would have happened. She stood up, squared herself, prepared to get back to the job of fixing the *Thomas Prince*, just the way the real Melba would have.

"I'm sorry, Ren," she said, thinking it would be the last time, and the sorrow that shook her made her sit back down.

Something was wrong. This wasn't how it was supposed to be. Her control was slipping. She wondered if after all she'd done, she simply wasn't strong enough. Or if there was something else. Maybe the artificial glands had begun to leak their toxins into her bloodstream without being summoned. She was getting more emotionally labile. It could be a symptom. She rested her head on her arms and tried to catch her breath.

He'd been kind to her. He'd been nothing but kind. He'd helped her, and she'd killed him for it. She could still feel his skull giving way under her hand; crisp and soft, like standing at the bank of a river and feeling the ground fall away. Her fingers smelled like sealant foam.

Ren touched her shoulder, and her head snapped up.

"Hi," someone said. "I'm Anna. What's your name?"

It was the redhead who'd been talking to the naval officer a moment ago.

"I saw you sitting here," she said, sitting down. "It looked like you could use some company. It's okay to be afraid. I understand."

She knows.

The thought ran through Melba's body like a sheet of lightning. Even without her tongue touching her palate, she felt the glands and bladders hidden in her flesh engorging. Her face and hands felt cold. Before the woman's eyes could widen, Melba's sorrow and guilt turned to a cold rage. She knew, and she would expose everything, and then all of it would have been wasted.

She didn't remember rising to her feet, but she was there now. The woman stood and took a step back.

I have to kill her.

"I'm sorry. I didn't mean to disturb you."

The woman's hands were half raised, as if that were enough to ward off a blow. It would be simple. She didn't look strong. She didn't know how to fight. Kick her in the gut until she bled out. Nothing simpler.

A small voice in the back of Melba's mind said, *She's one of those idiot priests looking for someone to save. She doesn't know anything. You're in public. If you attack her, they'll catch you.*

"You don't know me," Melba said, struggling to keep her voice calm. "You don't know anything."

At one of the tables nearest the door, a young officer stood up and took two steps toward them, ready to interfere. If this woman got her thrown in the brig, they'd look into Melba's identity. They'd find Ren's body. They'd find out who she was. She had to keep it together.

"You're right. I apologize," the woman said.

Hatred surged up in Melba's mind, pure and black where it wasn't red. A swamp of obscenities rose in her throat, ready to pour out on the idiot priest who was putting everything— everything—in jeopardy. Melba swallowed it all and walked quickly away.

The corridors of the *Thomas Prince* were a vague presence in the unquiet of her mind. She'd let the thing with Ren throw her. It stole her focus and led her into risks she didn't need to take. She hadn't been thinking straight, but now she was. She got into the elevator and selected the level where Stanni and Soledad were checking the electrical system, chasing down the failing component. Then she deselected it and picked the hangar.

"Stanni? Solé?" she said into her hand terminal. "Hold it together for me here. I've got a thing I need to do."

She waited for the inevitable questioning, the prying and suspicion.

"Okay," Soledad said. And that was all.

At the hangar, Melba authorized the flight of her shuttle, waited ten minutes for clearance, and launched out the side of the *Thomas Prince* and into the black. The shuttle monitors were cheap and small, the vastness of space compressed into fifty centimeters by fifty centimeters. She had the computer figure the fastest burn for the *Cerisier*. It was less than an hour. She leaned into the thrust like she was riding a roller coaster and let the torch engines burn. The *Cerisier* appeared in the dusting of stars as a small gray dot that hurtled toward her. The ship, like all the others in the flotilla, was in the last of the deceleration burn to put them at the Ring. Somewhere out past all the glowing drive plumes, it waited. Melba pushed the thought from her mind. It made her think of Stanni and Soledad and their quiet fears. She couldn't think of them now.

Impatience to arrive made it hard to start the flip and the deceleration burn. She wanted to get there, to be there already. She wanted to speed into the *Cerisier* like a witch on a broom, screaming in at speeds that wouldn't have been possible in atmosphere. She waited too long, and did the last half of the jump at almost two g. When she docked, she had a headache and her jaw felt like someone had punched her.

No one asked why she was back early and alone. She listed personal reasons in the log. Walking through the cramped corridors, squeezing past the other crewmen, felt oppressive, familiar, and comforting. It took coming back to recognize how much the wider spaces of the *Thomas Prince* had bothered her. It felt too much like freedom, and she was all about necessity.

Her cell was a mess. All of her things—clothes, terminal jack, tampons, communications deck, toothbrush—were scattered on the floor. She'd have to find a way to secure them all before the burn stopped, or they'd be floating out into the corridor. People would wonder why they weren't packed away. She let herself glance at the metal door under her crash couch. A tiny golden curl of sealant foam stuck out from one corner. She'd get some kind of mesh bag and some magnets. That would do. It didn't matter. That was later. Nothing later mattered.

She picked up the comm deck, turned it on. Ping times to the *Rocinante* were under thirty seconds. Melba loaded the sequence she'd been waiting to load for months. Years. It was a short script. It didn't take a second to prompt her to confirm.

The fear was gone. The hatred was too. For a moment, the tiny room was filled with a sense of having just woken from a dream, and her body felt relaxed. Almost light. She'd come so far and worked so hard, and despite all of the mistakes and screwups and last-minute improvisations, she'd done it. Everything in her life had been aiming toward this moment, and now that she was here, it was almost hard to let it all go. She felt like she was graduating from university or getting married. This moment, this action that fulfilled all the things she'd fought for, and then her world would never be the same.

Carefully, savoring each keystroke, she put in the confirmation code—JULES-PIERRE MAO—and thumbed the send button. The comm deck LED glowed amber. At the speed of light, a tiny packet of information was pulsing out, hardly more than a bit of background static. But the software on the *Rocinante* would recognize it. The communications array on Holden's ship would be slaved to the virtual machine already installed and impossible to stop without scraping the whole system clean. The *Rocinante* would send a clearly recognizable trigger code to the *Seung Un*, wait fifty-three seconds, and announce Holden's responsibility and his demands. And then the virtual machine would power up the weapons and targeting systems. And nothing, no power in the universe, could stop it from happening.

The comm deck got the confirmation response, and the amber LED shifted to red.

Chapter Fifteen: Bull

Bull's hand terminal sat on the cart's thin plastic dashboard, jiggling with every bump in the corridor floor. The siren blatted its standard two-tone, scattering people from his path and calling them out behind him. If they didn't know yet, they all would in minutes. The death of the *Seung Un* wasn't the sort of thing you could overlook.

On the small, jittering screen, the destroyer exploded again. At first it was only a flicker of orange light amidships, something that could have been electrical discharge or a gauss gun finishing its maintenance regimen. Half a second later, sparkles of yellow radiated out from the site. Two seconds after, the major detonation. Between one frame and the next, the destroyer's side bloomed open. Then nothing for ten full seconds before the fusion reactor core emerged slowly from the back, brighter than the sun. Bull watched the intense white gases begin to diffuse out and fade into a massive golden aurora, a drop of gold losing cohesion in the oceanic black.

He looked up to make the turn onto the ramp that would take him back to the office. A young man ambled slowly out of his path, and Bull leaned on the cart's horn.

"There's a siren," Bull yelled as he passed the young man, and got an insolent nod in reply.

"Okay," Serge said from the terminal. "We're getting the first security analysis. Best guess, something blew out in one of the power conduits, fused the safety systems so they couldn't shut it down. Would have taken about that long to turn the whole starboard main circuit to molten slag."

"What blew?" Bull demanded.

"Probably a maneuvering thruster. About the right place for one. Get it hot enough, water skips steam and just goes straight to plasma. Cuts right through the bulkheads around it."

Bull turned the cart around a tight corner and slowed to let a half dozen pedestrians get out of his way.

"Why'd they dump core?"

"Don't know, but probably they thought they'd lose containment. They got six ships diverting now to keep from plowing into that mierda."

"If they'd lost containment it'd be worse. They'd be diverting to avoid bodies and shrapnel. Are there survivors?"

"Yeah. They're putting out the distress request. Medical and evacuation. Sounds pretty fucked up, que no?"

"What about trace data. Can we tell who shot 'em?"

"No one shot 'em. Either it was a straight accident, or . . ."

"Or?"

"Or it wasn't."

Bull bit his lip. An accident would be bad enough. People on all sides of the system's power structure were on edge, and a reminder that Earth's fleet was aging and poorly maintained wouldn't make anything easier. Sabotage would be worse. The closest thing to good news was that everyone had seen it and there wouldn't be any accusations of enemy action. If there'd been a gauss round or a lucky missile that had slipped through the *Seung Un*'s defenses undetected, the scientific mission could turn into a shooting war faster than Bull wanted to think about.

"Are we offering assistance?" Bull asked.

"Give us a breath, boss," Serge said. "Ashford ain't hearing any of this faster than us."

Bull leaned forward, his hands wrapping the steering controls until his knuckles went white. Serge was right. What happened outside the ship was Ashford's problem. And Pa's. He was security chief, and he needed to think about what needed doing inside the *Behemoth*. People would be scared, and it was his job to make sure that fear didn't turn into hysteria. Watching a ship blow out—even an enemy ship—reminded everyone how tenuous life was with only a thin skin of steel and ceramic to keep the vacuum at bay. It reminded him. The cart hit a larger bump than usual, and his hand terminal slipped onto its side.

"Okay," Bull said. "Look, we're going to need to get relief supplies ready in case the captain decides to offer assistance. How many survivors can we take on?"

Serge's laughter rasped.

"All of them. We're the pinche *Behemoth*. We got enough room for a city, us."

"Okay," Bull said, smiling a little despite himself. "It was a stupid question."

"The only thing we got to worry about is—"

The line went dead.

"Serge? Not funny," Bull said. And then, "Talk to me, mister."

"We got something. Broadcast coming from a private corvette called the *Rocinante*."

"Why do I know that name?" Bull asked.

"Yeah," Serge said. "I'm putting it to you."

The handset screen blacked out, jumped, and then a familiar face appeared. Bull let the cart slow as James Holden, the man whose announcement about the death of the ice hauler *Canterbury* started the first war between Earth and Mars, once again made things worse.

"...ship that approaches the Ring without my *personal* permission will be destroyed without warning. Do not test my resolve."

"Oh no," Bull said. "Oh shit no."

"It has always been a personal mission of mine to assure that information and resources remain free to all people. The efforts of individuals and corporate entities may have helped us to colonize the planets of our solar system and make life possible where it was inconceivable before, but the danger of someone unscrupulous taking control of the Ring is too great. I have proven myself worthy of the trust of the people of the Belt. It is a moral imperative that this shining artifact be protected, and I will spill as much blood as I have to in order to do so."

Bull scooped up the hand terminal and tried to connect to Ashford. The red trefoil of command block blinked on the screen and shunted him to a menu that let him record a message for later. He tried Pa and got the same thing. Holden's message was looping now, the replayed words just as idiotic and toxic the second time through. Bull said something obscene through clenched teeth. He pulled on the cart, turning the wheels as far as they would go, and stamped on the accelerator. The central lifts were only a minute or two away. He could get there. Just please God let Ashford not do anything stupid before he got to the bridge.

"That true, boss?" Serge said. "Did Holden just claim us all the Ring?"

"I want everyone on security mobilized right now," Bull said. "Enemy action protocols. Corridors clear and bulkheads closed. Anyone on a weapons or damage control team, wake 'em up and get 'em dressed. You're in charge of that."

"You got it, boss," Serge said. "Someone asks, where are you?"

"Trying to keep from needing them."

"Bien."

The familiar corridors seemed longer than usual, the awkwardness of floors built to be walls and walls intended as ceilings

more surreal. If he'd been on a real battleship, there would have
been a simple, direct path. If the Behemoth's great belly had been
spinning, it would have been better than this. He willed the cart
faster, pushing the engine past what it could do. The alert Klaxon
sounded: Serge calling everyone to brace for battle.

A crowd had formed at the lift: men and women trying to get
back to their stations. Bull pushed through them, the shortest
person there. An Earther, like Holden. At the lift, he activated the
security override, called the first car, and stepped in. A tall, dark-
skinned man tried to follow him. Bull put a hand on the man's
chest, stopping him.

"Take the next one," Bull said. "I'm not going where you want
to be."

As the lift rose toward the bridge like it was ascending to
heaven, Bull used his hand terminal to grasp for any information.
He didn't have access to the secure channels—only the captain
and the XO had those—but there was more than enough public
chatter. He ran through the open feeds, grasping for a sense of the
situation, watching for a few seconds here, a few seconds there.

The Martian science team and their escort were raging at
Holden on every feed, calling him a terrorist and a criminal. The
Earth flotilla's reaction was quieter. Most of the public conversation was coordinating the rescue efforts on the *Seung Un*. The
high-energy gas from the core dump was confusing some of the
relief crew's comms, and someone fairly smart had started using
the public feeds to coordinate them. It had the grim efficiency of a
military operation, and it gave Bull hope for the Earth navy crew
still alive on the *Seung Un* as much as it scared him about what
was going to come after.

Holden's message was repeating, spilling out over the public
feeds. At first it just came from the *Rocinante*, but soon it was
being relayed on other feeds along with commentary. Once the
signal got back to the Belt and the inner planets, it was going to be
the only thing anyone talked about. Bull could already imagine
the negotiations between Earth and Mars, could practically hear

them reaching the conclusion that the OPA had gotten too confident and needed to be taken down a notch.

Someone on the *Behemoth* put out a copy of Holden's message with the split circle emblem over it and a commentary track saying that it was about time that the Belt take its place and demand the respect it deserved. Bull told Serge to find the feed and shut it down.

After what felt like hours and probably wasn't more than four minutes, the lift reached the bridge, the doors opening silently before him, and let Bull out.

The bridge wasn't designed for battle. Instead of a real war machine's system of multiple stations and controlled lines of command, the *Behemoth*'s bridge was built like the largest tugboat ever made, only with angels blowing golden trumpets adorning the walls. The stations—single stations with a rotating backup scheme—were manned by Belters looking at each other and chatting. The security station was through a separate door and stood unmanned. The bridge crew were acting like children or civilians, their expressions were bright and excited. People who didn't recognize danger when they saw it and assumed that whatever the crisis was, it would all work out in the end.

Ashford and Pa were at the command station. Ashford was speaking into a camera, talking with someone on one of the other ships. Pa, scowling, strode toward Bull. Her eyes were narrow and her lips bloodless.

"What the hell are you doing here, Mister Baca?"

"I've got to talk to the captain," Bull said.

"Captain Ashford's busy right now," Pa said. "You might have noticed we have a situation on our hands. I would have expected you to be at your duty station."

"Yes, XO, but—"

"Your station isn't on the bridge. You should leave now."

Bull clenched his jaw. He wanted to shout at her, but this wasn't the time for it. He was here to make it work, and that wasn't going to help.

"We've got to shoot him, ma'am," Bull said. "We've got to fire on the *Rocinante*, and we've got to do it now."

All heads had turned toward them. Ashford ended his transmission and stepped toward them. Uncertainty made him look haughty. The captain's eyes flickered toward the crew members at their stations and back again. Bull could see how aware Ashford was that he was being watched. It deformed all his decisions, but there wasn't time for privacy.

"I have this under control, Mister Baca," Ashford said.

"All respect, Captain," Bull said, "but we've got to shoot down Holden, and we have to do it before anyone else does."

"We're not going to do a damn thing until we know what's going on, mister," Ashford said, his voice taking a dangerous buzz. "I've sent back a request for clarification to Ceres to see whether the higher-ups authorized Holden's action, and I am monitoring the activity of the Earther fleet."

The slip was telling. Not UN. Earther. Bull felt the blood in his neck. Ashford's casual racism and incompetence was about to get them all killed. He gritted his teeth, lowered his head, and raised his voice.

"Sir, there's a calculation happening right now with Earth and Mars both—"

"This is a potentially volatile situation, Mister Baca—"

"—where they have to decide whether to take direct response or let Holden win—"

"—and I am not going to be the one to throw gas on the fire. Escalating to violence at this point—"

"—and once they start shooting at *him*, they're going to start shooting at *us*."

Pa's voice cut through the air like a single flute in a bass symphony.

"He's right, sir."

Bull and Ashford turned toward her. Ashford's surprise was a mirror of his own. The man at the sensor station muttered something to the woman next to him, the hiss of his voice carrying in the sudden silence.

"Mister Baca's right," Pa said. "Holden's identified himself as a representative of the OPA. He's taken violent action against the Earth forces. The opposing commanders will have to look on us as his backup."

"Holden isn't a representative of the OPA," Ashford said. The bluster made him sound unsure.

"You called Ceres," Bull said. "If you're not sure, they're not either."

Ashford's face flushed red.

"Holden hasn't had any official status with the OPA since Fred Johnson fired him over his handling of Ganymede. If there's a question, I can clarify with the other commanders that Holden doesn't speak for us, but no one's taking any action. The best thing is to wait and let things cool down."

Pa looked down, then up again. It didn't matter that she'd humiliated Bull and Sam in front of the command staff. All that counted was doing this next part right. Bull wanted to reach out, touch her arm, lend her the courage to stand up to Ashford.

It turned out she didn't need it.

"Sir, if we don't take the initiative, someone else will, and then it's going to be too late for clarifications. Denials are fine if they're believed, but Holden and his crew were known to be working with us previously and they're claiming to represent us now. We're four hours' lag to Ceres. We can't wait for answers. We have to make the division between us and Holden unequivocal. Mister Baca's right. We need to engage the *Rocinante*."

Ashford's face was gray.

"I'm not going to start a shooting war," he said.

"You listening to the same feeds as me, Captain?" Bull asked. "Everyone already thinks we did."

"The *Rocinante*'s one ship. We can take her out," Pa said. "If we fight Earth or Mars, we'll lose."

The truth lay on the floor between them. Ashford put a hand to his chin. His eyes were flickering back and forth like he was reading something that wasn't there. Every second he didn't respond, his cowardice showed through, and Bull could see that the man knew it. Resented it. Ashford was responsible, and didn't want the responsibility. He was more afraid of looking bad than of losing.

"Mister Chen," Ashford said. "Get a tightbeam to the *Rocinante*. Tell Captain Holden that it's an urgent matter."

"Yes, sir," the communications officer said, and then a moment later, "The *Rocinante* isn't accepting the connection, sir."

"Captain?" the man at the sensor array said. "The *Rocinante*'s changing course."

"Where's she going?" Ashford demanded, his gaze still locked on Bull.

"Um. Toward us? Sir?"

Ashford closed his eyes.

"Mister Corley," he growled. "Power up the port missile array. Mister Chen, I want tightbeam connections to the Earth and Mars command ships, and I want them now."

Bull let himself sag back. The sense of urgency giving way to relief and a kind of melancholy. *One more time, Colonel Johnson. We dodged the bullet one more time.*

"Weapons board is green, sir," the weapons officer said, her voice crisp and excited as a kid at an arcade.

"Lock target," Ashford said. "Do I have those tightbeams yet?"

"We're acknowledged and pending, sir," Chen said. "They know we want to talk."

"That'll do," Ashford said, and began pacing the bridge like an old-time captain on a wooden quarterdeck. His hands were clasped behind his back.

"We have lock," the weapons officer said. Then, "The *Rocinante*'s weapons systems are powering up."

Ashford sank into his couch. His expression was sour. He'd been hoping, Bull realized, that it might be true. That the OPA might be making a play to control the Ring.

The man was an idiot.

"Should we fire, sir?" the weapons officer asked, the strain in her voice like a dog on a leash. She wanted to. Badly. Bull didn't think better of her for it. He glanced at Pa, but she was making a point of not looking at him.

"Yes," Ashford said. "Go ahead. Fire."

"One away, sir," the weapons officer said.

"I'm getting an error code," the operations officer said. "We're getting feedback from the launcher."

Bull's mouth tasted like a penny. If Holden had put a bomb on the *Behemoth* too, their problems might only be starting.

"Is the missile out?" Pa snapped. "Tell me we don't have an armed torpedo stuck in the tube."

"Yes, sir," the weapons officer said. "The missile is away. We have confirmation."

"The *Rocinante* is taking evasive maneuvers."

"Is she returning fire?" Ashford said.

"No, sir. Not yet, sir."

"I'm getting errors in the electrical grid, sir. I think something's shorted out. We might—"

The bridge went dark.

"—lose power. Sir."

The monitors were black. The lights were off. The only sound was the hum of the air recyclers, running, Bull imagined, off the battery backups. Ashford's voice came out of the darkness.

"Mister Pa, did we ever test-fire the missile systems?"

"I believe it's on the schedule for next week, sir," the XO said. Bull tuned his hand terminal screen to its brightest, lifting it like a torch. He glanced up at the emergency lighting set into the walls all around the room, sitting there as dark as everything else. Another system that hadn't been tested yet.

A few seconds later, half of the bridge crew pulled flashlights out of recessed emergency lockers. The light level came up as beams played across the room. No one spoke. No one needed to. If the *Rocinante* fired back, they were a dead target, but the chances were that they wouldn't lose the whole ship. If they'd waited until they were in pitched battle against Earth or Mars or both, the *Behemoth* would have died. Instead, they'd just shown the whole system how unprepared they were. It was the first time Bull was really glad to be just the security officer.

"XO?" Bull said.

"Yes."

"Permission to release the chief engineer from house arrest?"

Pa's face was monochrome gray in the dim light, and solemn as the grave. Still, he thought he saw a glint of bleak amusement in her eyes.

"Permission granted," she said.

Chapter Sixteen: Holden

Well," Amos said. "That's just fucking peculiar."

The message began to repeat.

"This is Captain James Holden. What you've just seen is a demonstration of the danger you are in..."

The ops deck was in a stunned silence, then Naomi began working the ship ops panel with a quiet fury. In Holden's peripheral vision, Monica motioned to her crew and Okju lifted a camera. The tacit decision to let the "no civilians on the ops deck" rule slide suddenly seemed like it might have been a mistake.

"It's a fake," Holden said. "I never recorded that. That's not me."

"Sort of sounds like you, though," Amos said.

"Jim," Naomi said, panic beginning to distort her voice. "That broadcast is coming from us. It's coming from the *Roci* right now."

Holden shook his head, denying the assertion outright. The

only thing more ridiculous than the message itself was the idea that it was coming from *his* ship.

"That broadcast is coming from us," Naomi said, slamming her hand against her screen. "And I can't stop it!"

Everything seemed to recede from Holden, the noises in the room coming from far away. He recognized it as a panic reaction, but he gave in to it, accepted the short moment of peace it brought. Monica was shouting questions at him he could barely hear. Naomi was furiously pounding on her workstation, flipping through menu screens faster than he could follow. Over the ship's comm, Alex was shouting demands for orders. From across the room, Amos was staring at him with a look of almost comical puzzlement. The two camera operators, equipment still clutched in one hand, were trying to belt themselves into crash couches with the other. Cohen floated in the middle of the room, lips pursed in a faint frown.

"This was the setup," Holden said. "This is what it was for."

Everything: the Martian lawsuit, the loss of his Titania job, the camera crew going to the Ring, all leading to this. The only thing he couldn't imagine was why.

"What do you mean?" Monica asked, pushing close to get into the shot with him. "What setup?"

Amos put a hand on her shoulder and shook his head once.

"Naomi," Holden said, "is the only system you've lost control of comms?"

"I don't know. I think so."

"Then kill it. If you can't, help Amos isolate the entire comm system from the power grid. Cut it out of the damn ship if you have to."

She nodded again and then turned to Amos.

"Alex," Holden said. Monica started to say something to him, but he held up one finger to silence her, and she closed her mouth with a snap. "Get us burning toward the *Behemoth*. We're not really claiming the Ring for the OPA, but as long as everyone thinks we are, they're the team least likely to shoot us."

"What can you tell me about what's going on?" Monica said. "Are we in danger here? Is this dangerous?" Her usual smirk was gone. Open fear had replaced it.

"Strap in," Holden said. "All of you. Do it now."

Okju and Clip were already belted into crash couches, and Monica and Cohen quickly followed suit. The entire documentary crew had the good sense to stay quiet.

"Cap," Alex said. His voice had taken on the almost sleepy tone he got when in a high-stress situation. "The *Behemoth* just lit us up with their targeting laser."

Holden belted himself into the combat ops station and warmed it up. The *Roci* began counting ships within their threat radius. It turned out to be all of them. The ship asked him if any should be marked as hostiles.

"Your guess is as good as mine, honey."

"Huh?" Naomi asked.

"Um," Alex said. "Are you guys warming up the weapons?"

"No," Holden said.

"Oh, I'm really sorry to hear that," Alex said. "Weapons systems are coming online."

"Are we shooting at anyone?"

"Not yet?"

Holden told the *Roci* to mark anything that hit them with a targeting system as hostile and was relieved when the system actually responded. The *Behemoth* shifted to red on the display. Then, after a moment's thought, he told the ship to lump all the Martians and Earth ships into two groups. If they wound up fighting with one ship in a group, they'd be fighting them all.

There were too many. The *Roci* was caught between Fred Johnson's two-kilometer-long OPA overcompensation and most of the remaining Martian navy. And beyond the Martians, the Ring.

"Okay," he said, desperately trying to think of what to do now. They were as far from a hiding spot as it was possible to be in the solar system. It was a two-month trip just to the nearest rock bigger than their ship. He doubted he could outrun three fleets and all their torpedoes for two months. Or two minutes, really, if it came to that. "How's that radio coming?"

"Down," Amos said. "Easy enough to just pull the plug."

"Do we have any way to tell everyone that the broadcast wasn't us? I will happily signal full and complete surrender at this point," Holden said.

"Not without turning it back on," Amos replied.

"Everyone out there is probably trying to contact us," Holden said. "The longer we don't answer, the worse this will look. What about the weapons?"

"Warmed up, not shooting," Amos said. "And not responding to us."

"Can we pull power on those too?"

"We can," Amos said, looking pained. "But damn, I sure don't want to."

"Fast mover!" Naomi yelled.

"Holy shit," Alex said. "The OPA just fired a torpedo at us."

On Holden's panel, a yellow dot separated from the *Behemoth* and shifted to orange as it took off at high g.

"Go evasive!" Holden said. "Naomi, can you blind it?"

"No. No laser," she replied, her voice surprisingly calm now. "And no radio. Countermeasures aren't responding."

"Fuck me," Amos said. "Why did someone drag us all the way out here just to kill us? Coulda done that at Ceres, saved us the trip."

"Alex, here's your course." Holden sent the pilot a vector that would take them right through the heart of the Martian fleet. As far as he knew, the Martians only wanted to arrest him. That sounded okay. "Has the *Behemoth* fired again?"

"No," Naomi replied. "They've gone dark. No active sensors, no drives."

"Kinda big and kinda close to be trying for sneaky," Alex said without any real humor. "Here comes the juice."

While the couches pumped them full of drugs to keep the high g from killing them, apropos of nothing Cohen said, "Fucking *bitch*."

Before Holden could ask what he meant, Alex opened up the *Roci*'s throttle and the ship took off like a racehorse feeling the spurs. The sudden acceleration slammed Holden into his couch hard enough to daze him for a second. The ship buzzed him back to his senses when a missile proximity alarm warned him the *Behemoth*'s torpedo was getting closer. Helpless to do anything about it, Holden watched the orange dot that meant all their deaths creeping ever closer to the fleeing *Rocinante*. He looked up at Naomi, and she was looking back, as helpless as he was, all her best tricks taken away when the comm array was powered down.

The gravity dropped suddenly. "Got an idea," Alex said over the comm, then the ship jerked through several sharp maneuvers, and the gravity went away again. The *Rocinante* had added a new alarm to her song. A collision warning was sounding. Holden realized he'd never actually heard a collision alarm outside of drills. When do spaceships run *into* each other?

He turned on the exterior cameras to a field of uniform black. For a second, he thought they were broken, but then Alex took control of them, panning out along the vast expanse of a Martian cruiser's skin. The target lock buzzer cut out, the missile losing them.

"Put this Martian heavy between us and the missile," Alex said, almost whispering it, as though the missile might hear if he spoke too loud.

"How close are we to them?" Holden asked, his voice matching Alex's.

" 'Bout ten meters," Alex said, pride in his voice. "More or less."

"This is really going to piss them off if the missile keeps coming," Amos said. Then, almost meditatively, "I don't even know what a point defense cannon does at a range like this."

As if in answer, the cruiser hit them with a targeting laser. Then all of the other Martian ships did as well, adding a few dozen more alarms to the cacophony.

"Shit," Alex said, and the gravity came back like a boulder rolled onto Holden's chest. None of the Martian ships fired, but the original missile shot back into view on the scope. The Martians were guiding it in, now that the *Behemoth* seemed to be out of action. Holden marveled that he'd lived *just* long enough to finally see real Martian-OPA cooperation. It wasn't as gratifying as he'd hoped.

Martian ships whipped past on both sides as the *Rocinante* accelerated through the main cluster of their fleet. Holden could imagine the targeting arrays and point defense cannons swiveling to track them as they went by. Once past them, there was nothing but the Ring and infinite star-speckled black all around it.

The plan came to mind with the sick, sinking feeling of something horrible he'd always known and tried to forget. The missile was coming, and even if they avoided it, there would be others. He couldn't dodge forever. He couldn't surrender. For all he knew, his weapons might start firing at any second. For a moment, the ops deck seemed to go still, time slowing the way it did when something catastrophic was happening. He was intensely aware of Naomi, pressed back in her couch. Monica and Okju, their eyes wide with fear and thrust. Clip, his hand pressed awkwardly into the gel by his side. Cohen's slack jaw and pale face.

"Huh," Holden gurgled to himself, the g forces crushing his throat when he vocalized. He signaled Alex to cut thrust, and the gravity dropped away again.

"The Ring," Holden said. "Aim for the Ring. Go."

The gravity came back with a slap, and Holden rotated his chair to his workstation and brought up the navigational console. Watching the rapidly approaching orange dot out of the corner of his eye, he built a navigational package for Alex that would take them at high speed to the Ring, then spin them for a massive and almost suicidally dangerous deceleration burn just before they went in. He could slide them in under the velocity cap that had stopped the *Y Que* and all the fast-moving probes since. With any luck, the missile would be caught by whatever was on the other side, and the *Roci*, going slower, wouldn't. The ship warned him that such high-g forces had a 3 percent chance to kill one of the crew members even during a short burn.

The missile would kill them all.

Holden sent the nav package to Alex, half expecting him to refuse. Hoping. Instead, the *Roci* accelerated for an endless twenty-seven minutes, followed by a nauseating zero-g spin that lasted less than four seconds, and a deceleration burn that lasted four and a half minutes and knocked every single person on the ship unconscious.

"Wake up," Miller said in the darkness.

The ship was in free fall. Holden began coughing furiously as his lungs attempted to find their normal shape again after the punishing deceleration burn. Miller floated beside him. No one else seemed to be awake yet. Naomi wasn't moving at all. Holden watched her until he could see the gentle rise and fall of her rib cage. She was alive.

"Doors and corners," Miller said. His voice was soft and rough. "I tell you check your doors and corners, and you blow into the middle of the room with your dick hanging out. Lucky sonofabitch. Give you this, though, you're consistent."

Something about the way he spoke seemed saner than usual. More controlled. As if guessing his thoughts, the detective turned to look at him. Smiled.

"Are you here?" Holden asked. His mind was still fuzzy, his brain abused by thrust and oxygen loss. "Are you real?"

"You're not thinking straight. Take your time. Catch up. There's no hurry."

Holden pulled up the exterior cameras and blew out one long exhale that almost ended in a sob. The OPA missile was floating outside the ship, just over a hundred meters from the nose of the *Roci*. The torpedo's drive was still firing, its tail a furious white torch stretching nearly a kilometer behind it. But the missile hung in space, motionless.

Holden didn't know if the missile had been that close when they went through. He suspected not. More likely, they'd just wound up that close once they'd both stopped moving. Even so, the sight of the massive weapon, engine burning as it still fought to reach him, made a shiver go down his spine and his balls creep up into his belly. Ten meters closer and they'd have been in proximity. It would have detonated.

As he watched, the missile was slowly pulled away, dragged off to who knew where by whatever power set the speed limit on this side of the Ring.

"We made it," he said. "We're through."

"Yeah," Miller said.

"This is what you wanted, isn't it? This is why you did it."

"You're giving me too much credit."

Amos and Naomi both groaned as they started to wake. The documentary crew was motionless. They might even be dead. Holden couldn't tell without unstrapping, and his body wouldn't allow that yet. Miller leaned close to the screen, squinting at it like he was searching for something. Holden pulled up the sensor data. A host of information flooded in. Numerous objects, clustered within a million kilometers, close as seeds in a pod. And past them, nothing. Not even starlight.

"What are they?" Holden asked. "What's out there?"

Miller glanced down at the display. His face was expressionless.

"*Nothing*," the dead man said. And then, "It scares the shit out of me."

Chapter Seventeen: Bull

The hell are we?" Serge said, floating gently by the security desk. "Security or fucking babysitters?"

"We're whatever gets the job done," Bull said, but he couldn't put much force behind the words.

It was thirty hours since the *Behemoth* had gone dark, and he had slept for six of them. Serge, Casimir, Jojo, and Corin had been trading off duty at the desk, coordinating the recovery. The rest of the security staff had been in ad hoc teams, putting down two little panic riots, coordinating the physical resources to free a dozen people trapped in storage bays where the air recycler hadn't booted back up, arresting a couple of mech jockeys who'd taken the chaos as opportunity to settle a personal score.

The lights were on all across the ship now. The damage control systems, woken from their coma, were working double time to catch up. The crews were exhausted and frightened and on edge, and James fucking Holden had escaped through the Ring into whatever was on the other side. The security office smelled like old sweat and the bean curd masala that Casimir had brought in yesterday. For the first day, there had been an unconscious effort to keep a consistent physical orientation—feet toward the floor, head toward the ceiling. Now they all floated in whatever direction they happened to fall into. It seemed almost natural to the Belters. Bull still suffered the occasional bout of vertigo.

"Amen alles amen," Serge said with a laugh. "Lube for the machine, us."

"Least fun I've ever had with lube," Corin said. Bull noted that when Corin got tired, she got raunchy. In his experience, everyone dealt with pushing too hard differently. Some got angry and irritable, some got sad. At a guess, it was all loss of inhibition. Wear down the façade with too much work or fear or both, and whoever was waiting underneath came out.

"All right," Bull said. "You two go take a rest. I'll watch the shop until the others get back. You two have done more than—"

The security desk chimed. The connection request was from Sam. Bull lifted a finger to Serge and Corin, and pulled himself over to the desk.

"Sam?" he said.

"Bull," she replied, and the single syllable, short and sharp, carried a weight of annoyance and anger that verged on rage. "I need you to come down here."

"You can call whoever you want," a man's voice said in the background. "I don't care, you hear? I don't care anymore. You do whatever you want."

Bull checked the connection location. She was down near the machine shops. It wasn't too far.

"I need to bring a sidearm?" Bull asked.

"I won't stop you, sweetie," Sam said.

"On my way," he said, and dropped the connection.

"Gehst du," Corin said to Serge. "You've been up longer. I'll keep the place from burning."

"You going to be all right?" Serge asked, and it took Bull a second to realize the man was talking to him.

"Unstoppable," Bull said, trying to mean it.

Being exhausted in zero gravity wasn't the same as it was under thrust or down a gravity well. Growing up, Bull had been dead tired pretty often, and the sense of weight, of his muscles falling off the bone like overcooked chicken, was what desperate fatigue meant. He'd been off of Earth for more years now than he'd been on it, and it still confused him on an almost cellular level to be worn to the point of collapse and not feel it in his joints. Intellectually, he knew it left him feeling that he could do more than he actually could. There were other signs: the grit against his eyes, the headache that bloomed slowly out from the center of his skull, the mild nausea. None of them had the same power, and none of them convinced.

The corridors weren't empty, but they weren't crowded. Even at full alert, with every team working double shifts and busting ass, the *Behemoth* was mostly empty. He moved through the ship, launching himself handhold to handhold, sailing down each long straightaway like he was in a dream. He was tempted to speed up, slapping at the handholds and ladders as they passed and adding just a touch of kinetic energy to his float the way he and his men had back in his days as a marine. More than one concussion had come out of the game, and he didn't have time for it now. He wasn't young anymore either.

He found Sam and her crew in a massive service bay. Four men in welding rigs floated near the wall, fixing lengths of conduit to the bulkhead with showers of sparks and lights brighter than staring at the sun. Sam floated nearby, her body at a forty-five-degree angle from the work. A young Belter floated near her, his body at an angle that pointed his feet toward her. Bull understood it was an insult.

"Bull," Sam said. The young man's face was a pale mask of rage. "This is Gareth. He's decided laying conduit's icky."

"I'm an *engineer*," Gareth said, spitting out the word so violently it gave him a degree of spin. "Did eight years on Tycho Station! I'm not going to get used like a fucking *technician*."

The other welders didn't turn from their work, but Bull could see them all listening. He looked at Sam, and her face was closed. Bull couldn't tell if calling him in for help had been hard for her or if it was part of how she expected him to make things right to her after the thing with Pa. That it had been the shortest detention on record didn't pull the sting of being caught up in his political struggles. Either way, she'd escalated the problem to him, and so it was his now.

Bull took a deep breath.

"So what are we working on here?" he asked, less because he cared than that it would give him a few extra seconds to think and his brain wasn't at its best.

"I've got a major line faulting out," Sam said. "I can take three days and diagnose the whole thing or I can take twenty hours and put up a workaround."

"And the conduit's for the workaround?"

"Is."

Bull lifted his fist in the Belter's equivalent of a nod and then turned his attention to the boy. Gareth was young and he was tired and he was an OPA Belter, which meant he'd never been through any kind of real military indoctrination. Bull had to figure Sam had yelled at him enough before she'd called for backup.

"All right, then," Bull said.

"Está-hey bullshit is," the man said, his educated grammar fracturing.

"I understand," Bull said. "You can go. Just help me get your rig on first."

Gareth blinked. Bull thought he saw the ghost of a smile in the corners of Sam's bloodshot eyes, but that could have meant anything. Pleasure at the weariness in Bull's voice or at Gareth's confusion, or maybe she'd understood what Bull was doing and she thought he was really clever.

"I talk to the guys on the other ships some," Bull said. "Earth or Mars. Someone'll be sending a ship back. I'll see if I can't get you a ride as far as Ceres anyway."

Gareth's mouth opened and closed like a goldfish. Sam pushed off, hooking the welder's rig with one hand, pulling it close to speed up the turn and then extending her arm to slow it. Bull took it from her and started pulling on the straps.

"You know how to do this?" Sam asked.

"Good enough to hang conduit," Bull said.

"Security can lose you?"

"Shift's done," Bull said. "I was just heading for my bunk, but this needs doing, I can do it."

"All right, then," Sam said. "Take the length at the end, and I'll have someone join it up with Marca's. I'll come check your work in a minute."

"Sounds good," Bull said. He was spinning just a few degrees each second and he let the momentum carry him around to face the boy. The rage was still there, but it was sinking under a layer of embarrassment. All his arguments and bluster about not doing something because it was beneath him, and now the head of security was using his off-shift to do the same work. Bull could feel the attention of the other welders on them. Bull lit his torch, just testing it out, and the air between them went white for a second. "Okay, then. I got this. You can go if you want."

The boy shifted, getting ready to launch himself back across the bay and out into the ship. Bull tried to remember the last time he'd actually welded something with no gravity. He was pretty sure he could do it, but he'd have to start slow. Then Gareth's shoulders cupped forward, and he knew he wouldn't have to. Bull started taking off the straps, and Gareth moved forward to help him.

"You're tired," Bull said, his voice low enough not to carry to the others. "You been working too hard, and it got to you a little. Happens to everyone."

"Bien."

He put the torch in the boy's hand and squeezed it there.

"This is a privilege," Bull said. "Being out here, doing this bullshit, working our asses off for no one to give a shit? It's a privilege. Next time you undermine Chief Engineer Rosenberg's authority, I will ship your ass home with a note that says you couldn't handle it."

The boy muttered something Bull couldn't make out. The flare from the other torches made the boy's face dance white and brown and white again. Bull put a hand on his arm.

"Yes, sir," Gareth said. Bull let go, and the boy pushed off to the wall, situating himself over the length of pipe that was waiting there for him. Sam appeared at Bull's elbow, sliding down from the blind spot above and behind him.

"That worked," she said.

"Yeah."

"Didn't hurt that you're an Earther."

"Didn't. How's it all coming?"

"Apart," Sam said. "But we'll stick it back together with bubblegum if we have to."

"Least no one was shooting at us."

Sam's laugh had some warmth in it.

"They wouldn't have had to do it twice."

The alert tone came from all their hand terminals at once, simultaneous with the ship address system. Bull felt his lips press thin.

"Well, that timing's a little ominous," Sam said before Captain Ashford's voice rang out through the ship. The openness of the spaces and the different speakers made the words echo like the voice of God.

"This is your captain speaking. I have just received confirmation from the OPA central authority that the actions undertaken by the criminal James Holden were unauthorized by any part of the Outer Planets Alliance. His actions put not only this ship but the reputation and good standing of the alliance in threat. I have informed the central authority that we took swift and decisive action against Holden, and that he escaped from us only by retreating through the Ring."

"Thanks for that, by the way," Sam said.

"De nada."

"I have requested and received," Ashford continued, "the authority to continue action to address this insult as I deem fit. The evidence of our own sensors and of the Martian and Earth feeds to which we have access all show that the *Rocinante* has passed through the Ring in good condition and appears to have sustained no damage despite the physical anomalies on the other side.

"In light of that, I have made the decision to follow Holden through the Ring and take him and his crew into custody. I will be sending out specific instructions to all department heads outlining what preparations we will need to complete before we begin our burn, but I expect to be in pursuit within the next six hours. It is imperative for the pride, dignity, and honor of the OPA that this insult not go unanswered and that the hands that bring Holden to justice be ours.

"I want you all to know that I am honored to serve with such a valiant crew, and that together we will make history. Take these next hours, all of you, to rest and prepare. God bless each and every one of you, and the Outer Planets Alliance."

With a resounding click from a hundred speakers, Ashford dropped the connection. The flashing white light of the welding torches was gone, and the bay was darker. Laughter warred against despair in Bull's gut.

"Is he drunk, do you think?" Sam said.

"Worse. Embarrassed. He's trying to save face," Bull said.

"The *Behemoth* filled its diddies in front of God and everyone, so now we're going to be the biggest badass in the system to make up for it?"

"Pretty much."

"Gonna talk him out of it?"

"Gonna try."

Sam scratched her cheek.

"Could be hard to back down after that little once-more-into-the-breach thing."

"He won't," Bull said. "But I've got to try."

The inner planets came out to the black with an understanding that they were soldiers sent to a foreign land. Bull remembered the feeling from when he'd first shipped out: the sense that his home was behind him. For the inners, the expansion out into the solar system had always had the military at its core.

The Belters didn't have that. They were the natives here. The forces that had brought their ancestors out to the Belt had roots in trade, commerce, and the overwhelming promise of freedom. The OPA had begun its life more like a labor union than a nation. The difference was subtle but powerful, and it showed in strange ways.

If they had been in any of the Earth or Mars ships that floated now in the darkness near the Ring, Bull would have come from his thorough and profound dressing down by the captain to seek out XO Pa in a galley or mess hall. But this was the *Behemoth*, so he found her in a bar.

It was a small place with bulbs of alcohol, chocolate, coffee, and tea all set with temperature controls in the nipple, so the uniformly tepid drinks could come out anywhere from almost boiling to just this side of ice. The décor was cheap nightclub, with colored lights and cheap graphic films to hide the walls. Half a dozen people floated on handholds or tethers, and Pa was one of them.

His first thought as he pulled himself toward her was that she needed a haircut. With the false gravity of acceleration gone, her hair floated around her, too short to tie back but still long enough to interfere with her vision and creep into her mouth. His second thought was that she looked as tired as he was.

"Mister Baca," Pa said.

"XO. You mind if I join you?"

"I was expecting you. You've been to see the captain?"

Bull wished he could sit down, not for any actual reason so much as the small physical punctuation it would have given their conversation.

"I have. He wasn't happy to see me. Showed me the proposal you'd built up on how to remove me from my position."

"It was a contingency plan," she said.

"Yeah. So this idea where we take the *Behemoth* through the Ring? We can't do that. We start any kind of serious burn, we're going to have two navies on our butts. And we don't know what's on the other side except that it's way more powerful than we are."

"Do you want an alien civilization taking its ideas of humanity from Jim Holden?"

Ashford had said the same thing, word for word. It had been his most cogent argument, and now Bull knew where he'd borrowed it from. He'd had the long trip down in the lift to let his sleep-deprived brain come up with its counterargument.

"That's not even going to come into play if they shoot our nuts off before we get there," he said. "You really think Earth and Mars are going to go for the whole 'we're just playing sheriff' line? There's going to be a bunch of them who still think whatever Holden was up to, we were in on it. But even if they don't, the part where they stand to the side and let us take the lead isn't going to happen. You can bet your ass the head of the Mars force is asking his XO if they want an alien civilization taking its ideas of humanity from Ashford."

"That was nice," Pa said. "The reversal thing? That was good."

"The inner planets may not be making threats yet," Bull said, "but—"

"They are. Mars has threatened to open fire on us if we get within a hundred thousand kilometers of the Ring."

Bull put his hand to his mouth. He could feel his mind struggling to make sense of the words. The Martian navy had already laid down an ultimatum. Ashford hadn't even mentioned it.

"So what the hell are we doing?"

"We're preparing for burn in four and three-quarter hours, Mister Baca," Pa said. "Because that's what we've been ordered to do."

The bitterness wasn't only in her voice. It was in her eyes and the angle of her mouth. Sympathy and outrage battled in Bull's mind, and underneath them a rising panic. He was too tired to be having this conversation. Too tired to be doing what had to get done. It had stripped away all the protections that would have made him hesitate to speak. If he could have gotten just one good cycle's rest, maybe he could have found another way, but this was the hand he'd been dealt, so it was the hand he'd play.

"You don't agree with him," Bull said. "If it was your call, you wouldn't do it."

Pa took a long pull at her bulb, the flexible foil buckling under the suction. Bull was pretty sure she wasn't drinking for the taste, and the urge to get some whiskey for himself came on him like an unexpected blow.

"It doesn't matter what I would or wouldn't do," Pa said. "It's not my command, so it's not my decision."

"Unless something happens to the captain," Bull said. "Then it would be."

Pa went still. The sound of the music, the shifting patterns of lights, all of it seemed to recede. They were in their own small universe together. Pa thumbed on the bulb's magnet and stuck it to the wall beside her.

"There are still hours before the burn starts. And then travel time. The situation may change, but I won't take part in mutiny," she said.

"Maybe you wouldn't have to. Doesn't have to have anything to do with you. But unless you're going to specifically order me not to—"

"I am specifically ordering you, Mister Baca. I am ordering you not to take any action against the captain. I am ordering you to respect the chain of command. And if that means I have to commit to following through on Ashford's orders, then I'll make that commitment. Do you understand me?"

"Yeah," Bull said slowly. "Either we're all going to die, or we're going through the Ring."

Chapter Eighteen: Anna

Eleven people showed up for Anna's first worship service. The contrast with her congregation on Europa was unsettling at first. On Europa, she'd have had twenty or so families straggling in over the half hour before the service began, and a few drifting in late. They'd have been all ages, from grandparents rolling in on personal mobility devices to screaming children and infants. Some would come in their Sunday best formal wear, others in ratty casual clothes. The buzz of conversation prior to the service would be in mixed Russian, English, and outer planets polyglot. By the end of the worship meeting, a few might be snoring in their pews.

Her UNN congregation showed up in a single group at exactly 9:55 a.m. Instead of walking in and taking seats, they floated in as a loose clump and then just hovered in a disconcerting cloud in front of her podium. They wore spotless dress uniforms so crisply pressed they looked sharp enough to cut skin. They didn't speak, they just stared at her expectantly. And they were all so young. The oldest couldn't have been more than twenty-five.

The unusual circumstances rendered her standard worship service inappropriate—no need for a children's message or church announcements—so Anna launched directly into a prayer, followed by a scripture reading and a short sermon. She'd considered doing a sermon on duty and sacrifice; it seemed appropriate in the martial setting. But she had instead decided to speak mostly on God's love. Given the fear Chris had expressed a few days prior, it felt like the better choice.

When she'd finished, she closed with another prayer, then served communion. The gentle ritual seemed to ease the tension she felt in the room. Each of her eleven young soldiers came up to her makeshift table, took a bulb of grape juice and a wafer, and returned to their prior position floating nearby. She read the familiar words in Matthew and Luke, then spoke the blessing. They ate the bread and drank from the bulb. And, as had always happened since the very first church service she could remember, Anna felt something vast and quiet settle on her. She also felt the shiver that tried to crawl up her spine competing with a threatening belly laugh. She had a sudden vision of Jesus, who'd asked His disciples to keep doing this in remembrance of Him, watching her little congregation as they floated in microgravity and drank reconstituted grape beverage out of suction bulbs. It seemed to stretch the boundaries of what He'd meant by *this*.

A final prayer and the service was over. Not one of her congregation pushed toward the door to leave. Eleven young faces stared at her, waiting. The oppressive aura of fear she'd managed to push away during the communion crept back into the room.

Anna pulled herself around the podium and joined their loose cloud. "Should I expect anyone next week? You guys are making me nervous."

Chris spoke first. "No, it was real nice." He seemed to want to say more, but stopped and looked down at his hands instead.

"Back on Europa, people would have brought snacks and coffee for after the service," Anna said. "We could do that next time, if you want."

A few halfhearted nods. A muscular young woman in a marine uniform pulled her hand terminal halfway out of her pocket to check the time. Anna felt herself losing them. They needed something else from her, but they weren't going to ask for it. And it definitely wasn't coffee and snacks.

"I had a whole sermon on David," she said, keeping her tone casual. Conversational. "On the burden we place on our soldiers. The sacrifices we ask you to make for the rest of us."

Chris looked up from his hands. The young marine put her hand terminal away. With her podium behind her, the meeting room was just a featureless gray box. The little knot of soldiers floated in front of her, and suddenly the perspective shifted and she was above them, falling toward them. She blinked rapidly to break up the scene and swallowed to get the lemony taste of nausea out of her throat.

"David?" a young man with brown hair and dark skin said. He had an accent that she thought might be Australian.

"King of Israel," another young man said.

"That's just the nice version," the marine countered. "He's the guy who killed one of his own men so he could sleep with his wife."

"He fought for his country and his faith," Anna cut in, using the teacher's voice she used in Bible classes for teenagers. The one that made sure everyone knew she was the voice of authority. "That's the part I care about right now. Before he was a king, he was a soldier. Often unappreciated by those he served. He put his body over and over again between danger and those he'd sworn to protect, even when his leaders were unworthy of him."

A few more nods. No one looking at hand terminals. She felt herself getting them all back.

"And we've been asking that of our soldiers since the beginning of time," she continued. "Everyone here gave up something to be here. Often we're unworthy of you and you do it anyway."

"So why didn't you?" Chris asked. "You know, do the David sermon?"

"Because I'm scared," Anna said, taking Chris' hand with her left, and the hand of the Australian boy with her right. Without anyone saying anything, the loose cloud became a circle of held hands. "I'm so afraid. And I don't want to talk about soldiers and sacrifice. I want to talk about God watching me. Caring about what happens to me. And I thought maybe other people would too."

More nods. Chris said, "When the skinnies blew that ship, I thought we were all dead."

"No shit," the marine said. She gave Anna an embarrassed look. "Sorry, ma'am."

"It's okay."

"They say they didn't," another woman said. "They shot at Holden."

"Yeah, and then their whole ship mysteriously turned off. If the dusters hadn't pinged Holden, he'd have flown off scot free."

"They're gonna follow him," the young marine said.

"Dusters say they'll smoke them if they go in."

"Fuck the dusters," the Australian said. "We'll grease every one of them if they start anything."

"Okay," Anna cut in, keeping her voice gentle. "Dusters are Martians. They prefer Martians. And calling people from the outer planets skinnies is also rude. Epithets like that are an attempt to dehumanize a group so that you won't feel as bad about killing them."

The marine snorted and looked away.

"And," Anna continued, "fighting out here is the last thing we should be doing. Am I right?"

"Yeah," Chris said. "If we fight out here, we'll all die. No support, no reinforcements, nothing to hide behind. Three armed fleets and nothing bigger than a stray hydrogen atom for cover. This is what we call the kill box."

The silence stretched for a moment, then the Australian sighed and said, "Yeah."

"And something may come out of the Ring."

Saying the thing out loud and then acknowledging it drained the tension out of the air. With everyone floating in microgravity, no one could slump. But shoulders and foreheads relaxed. There were a few sad smiles. Even her angry young marine ran a hand through her blond crew cut and nodded without looking at anyone.

"Let's do this again next week," Anna said while she still had them. "We can celebrate communion, then maybe just chat for a while. And in the meantime, my door is always open. Please call me if you need to talk."

The group began to break up, heading for the door. Anna kept hold of Chris' hand. "Could you wait a moment? I need to ask you about something."

"Chris," the marine said with a mocking singsong voice. "Gonna get a little preacher action."

"That's not funny," Anna said, using the full weight of her teacher voice. The marine had the grace to blush.

"Sorry, ma'am."

"You may leave," Anna said, and her marine did. "Chris, do you remember the young woman who was in the officers' mess that first time we met?"

He shrugged. "There were lots of people coming and going."

"This one had long dark hair. She looked very sad. She was wearing civilian clothes."

"Oh," Chris said with a grin. "The cute one. Yeah, I remember her."

"Do you know her?"

"No. Just a civvy contractor fixing the plumbing, I'd guess. We have a couple ships full of them in the fleet. Why?"

That was a good question. She honestly wasn't sure why the angry young woman weighed on her mind so much over the last few days. But something about her stuck in Anna's memory like a burr in her clothing. She'd feel irritated and antsy and suddenly the girl's face would pop into her mind. The anger, the sense of threat she'd radiated. The proximity of that encounter to the sudden hostilities and damaged ships and people shooting at each other. There was nothing that tied them all together, but Anna couldn't shake the feeling that they were connected.

"I'm worried about her?" Anna finally said. At least it wasn't a lie.

Chris was tinkering with his hand terminal. After a few seconds, he said, "Melba Koh. Electrochemical engineer. She'll probably be on and off the ship here and all the way home. Maybe you'll run into her."

"Great," Anna said, wondering if she actually wanted that to happen.

"You know what sucks?" Tilly asked. Before Anna could say anything, Tilly said, "*This* sucks."

She didn't have to elaborate. They were floating together near a table in the civilian commissary. A small plastic box was attached to the table with magnetic feet. Inside it was a variety of tubes filled with protein and carbohydrate pastes in an array of colors and flavors. Next to the box sat two bulbs. Anna's held tea. Tilly's coffee. The officers' mess, with its polite waiters, custom-cooked meals, and open bar, was a distant memory. Tilly hadn't had an alcoholic drink in several days. Neither of them had eaten anything that required chewing in as long.

"The oat and raisin isn't bad. I think it might actually have real honey in it," Anna said, holding up one of the white plastic squeeze packs. Tilly was no stranger to space travel. Her husband owned estates on every major rock in the solar system. But Anna suspected she'd never eaten food out of a plastic tube in her entire life before this. Any pilot who had the poor planning to put Tilly's ship at null g during one of her meals was probably fired at the next port.

Tilly picked up a packet of the oat mush, wrinkled her lip at it, and flicked it away with her fingers. It sat spinning next to her head like a miniature helicopter.

"Annie," Tilly said. "If I wanted to suck vile fluids out of a flaccid and indifferent tube, I'd have stayed on Earth with my husband."

At some point Anna had become Annie to Tilly, and her objection to this nickname hadn't fazed Tilly at all. "You have to eat, eventually. Who knows how long we'll be out here."

"Not much longer, if I have anything to say about it," said a booming voice from behind Anna.

If she'd been touching the floor, she would have jumped. But floating in the air, all she managed was an undignified jerk and squeak.

"Sorry to startle you," Cortez continued, sliding into her field of view. "But I had hoped we might speak."

He was scuffing across the floor wearing the magnetic booties the navy had handed out. Anna had tried them, but drifting free while your feet remained pinned to the floor had given her an uncomfortable underwater sensation that made her even sicker than just floating around did. She never used them.

Cortez nodded to Tilly, his too-white smile beaming at her in his nut-brown face. Without asking if he could join them, he used the menu screen on the table to order himself a soda water. Tilly smiled back. It was the fake *I don't really see you* smile she used on people who carried her luggage or waited on her table. Their mutual contempt established, Tilly sipped her coffee and ignored his presence. Cortez placed one large hand on Anna's shoulder and said, "Doctor Volovodov, I am putting together a coalition of the important civilian counselors on this ship to make a request of the captain, and I'd like your support."

Anna admired the absolute sincerity Cortez managed to pack into a sentence that was almost entirely composed of flattery. Cortez was here because he was the spiritual advisor to the UN secretary-general. Anna was here because the United Methodist

Council could spare her, and her home happened to be on the way. If she was on any list of important counselors, then the bar was set pretty low.

"I'm happy to talk about it, Doctor Cortez," Anna said, then reached for her tea bulb. It gave her an excuse to extricate her arm from his grip. "How can I help?"

"First, I have to commend you on your initiative in arranging worship services for the women and men on the ship. I'm ashamed I didn't think of it first, but I'm happy to follow your lead. We're already arranging for similar meetings with leaders of the various faiths on board."

Anna felt a blush come up, even though she suspected that everything Cortez said was manipulative. He was so good, he could get the response he wanted even when you knew exactly what he was up to. Anna couldn't help but admire it a little.

"I'm sure the sailors appreciate it."

"But there is other work we can be doing," Cortez said. "Greater work. And that's what I came to ask you about."

Tilly turned back to the table and gave Cortez a sharp look. "What are you up to, Hank?"

Cortez ignored her. "Anna, may I call you Anna?"

"Here it comes, Annie," Tilly said.

"Annie?"

"No," Anna cut in. "Anna is fine. Please call me Anna."

Cortez nodded his big white-and-brown head at her, blinding her with his smile. "Thank you, Anna. What I want to ask you to do is sign a petition I'm circulating, and add your voice to ours."

"Ours?"

"You know that the *Behemoth* has begun to burn toward the Ring?"

"I'd heard."

"We're asking the captain to accompany it."

Anna blinked twice, then opened her mouth to speak and found nothing to say. She closed it with a snap when she realized both Cortez and Tilly were staring at her. Go *into* the Ring? Holden had made it inside, and it looked like he was still alive. But actually entering the Ring had never been part of the mission plan, at least not for the civilian contingent.

No one had any idea what the structures were that waited beyond the Ring, or what changes passing through the wormhole might make on humans. Or even if the Ring would stay open. It might have a preset mass limit, or a limited power supply, or anything. It might just slam shut after enough ships had gone through. It might slam shut with half a ship going through. Anna pictured the *Prince* cut in half, the two pieces drifting in space a billion light-years apart, humans spilling into vacuum from both sides.

"We're also asking the Martians to come with us," Cortez continued. "Now hear me out. If we join together in this—"

"Yes," Anna said before she knew she was going to say it. She didn't know why Cortez was pushing for it, and she didn't care. Maybe it was to get votes in the Earth elections. Maybe it was a way for Cortez to exert control over the military commanders. Maybe he felt it was his calling. They hadn't come here as explorers, not really. They'd come here to be seen by the people back at home who were watching. It was why they'd had so many protests and dramas on the way out. Once, this had been about the spectacle, but now things had changed, and this was the answer to the fear she'd seen at church.

The immediate danger wasn't the Ring. At least not right now. It was humans taking their anxiety out on the nearest enemy they could actually see: each other. If the OPA went ahead with its plan to follow Holden into the Ring, and the UN and Martian forces joined together to follow, no one would have any reason to shoot anyone else. They'd be what they'd started out as again. They'd be a joint task force exploring the most important discovery in human history. If they stayed, they were three angry fleets trying to keep one another from getting an advantage. The whole thing spilled into Anna's mind feeling very much like relief.

"Yes," she said again. "I'll sign it. The things we need to know, the things we need to learn and take back with us to all those frightened people back home. That's where we'll learn them. Not here. On the other side. Thank you for asking me, Doctor Cortez."

"Hank, Anna. Please call me Hank."

"Oh," Tilly said, her coffee bulb floating forgotten in the air in front of her. "We are *so* fucked."

"Hi Nono," Anna said to the video camera in her room's communication panel. "Hi Nami! Mom loves you. She loves you so much." She hugged her pillow to her chest, squeezing it tight. "This is you. This is both of you."

She put the pillow down, taking a moment to compose herself.

"Nono, I'm calling to apologize again."

Chapter Nineteen: Melba

The injustice of it shrieked in the back of her skull; it wouldn't let her sleep. It had come so close to working. So much of it *had* worked. But then Holden dove into the Ring, and something had saved him, and Melba felt a huge invisible fist drive itself into her gut. And it was still there.

She'd watched the whole thing unfold in her quarters, sitting cross-legged on her crash couch, her hand terminal seeking information from any feed. The network had been so swamped with other people doing the same thing, her own signal wouldn't stand out. No one would wonder why she was watching when everyone else was doing the same. When the OPA had opened fire, she'd heard the Earth forces bracing for a wave of sabotage explosions that never came. The anger at Holden, the condemnations and recriminations had been like pouring cool water on a burn. Her team had been called up on an emergency run to the *Seung Un*, repairing the damage she'd done, but she'd checked in whenever there was a free moment. When Mars had turned its targeting lasers on the *Rocinante*, guiding the missile to him, she'd laughed out loud. Holden had stopped her outgoing message, but at the expense of killing his whole communications array. There was no way he could send out a retraction in time.

When he'd passed through the Ring, she'd been in three conversations simultaneously and watching an electrical meter for dangerous fluctuations. She didn't find out until they were being rotated back to the *Cerisier* that Holden hadn't died. That he wasn't going to. The missile had been stopped and the enemy had been spared.

Back on her ship, she'd gone straight to her bunk, curled up on the crash couch, and tried not to panic. Her brain felt like it had come untied; her thoughts ran in random directions. If the Martians had just launched a few missiles of their own instead of waiting for the OPA's to do the job, Holden would be dead. If the *Rocinante* had been a few thousand kilometers closer to the *Behemoth* when it fired, Holden would be dead. The gimbaling under her couch hushed back and forth in the last of the deceleration burn, and she realized she was shaking her body, banging her back against the gel. If the thing that made the protomolecule—the nameless, evil thing that was hunched in the abyssal black on the other side of the Ring—hadn't changed the laws of physics, Holden would be dead.

Holden was alive.

She'd always known that the destruction of James Holden was a fragile thing. Discrepancies would be there if anyone looked closely. She couldn't match her announcement to the exact burn that the *Rocinante* would be on when she sprang her trap. There would be artifacts in the video that a sufficiently close analysis would detect. By the time that happened, though, it would have been too late. The story of James Holden would have been set. New evidence could be dismissed as crackpots and conspiracy theorists. But it required that Holden and his crew be *dead*. It was something she'd always heard her father say. If the other man's dead, the judge only has one story to follow. When he put his communication array back together, the investigation would begin. She'd be caught. They'd find out it was her.

And—the thought had the copper taste of fear—they'd find Ren. They'd know she killed him. Her father would know. Word would reach him in his cell that she had beaten Ren to death, and that would be worse than anything. Not that she'd done it, Melba thought. That she'd been caught doing it.

The sound came from her door, three hard thumps, and she screamed despite herself. Her heart was racing, the blood tapping at the inside of her throat, banging at her ribs.

"Miss Koh?" Soledad's voice came. "You in there? Can I...I need to talk if you've..."

Hearing fear in someone else's voice felt like vertigo. Melba got to her feet. Either the pilot was repositioning the ship or she was just unsteady. She couldn't tell which. She looked in her mirror, and the woman looking out could almost have been a normal person woken from a deep sleep.

"Just a minute," she said, running her fingers through her hair, pressing the dark locks against her scalp. Her face felt clammy. Nothing to be done. She opened the door.

Soledad stood in the thin, cramped corridor. The muscles in her jaw worked like she was chewing something. Her wide eyes skittered over Melba, away and back, away and back.

"I'm sorry, Miss Koh, but I can't...I can't do it. I can't go there. They can fire me, but I can't go." Melba reached out and put her hand on the woman's arm. The touch seemed to startle them both.

"All right," she said. "It'll be all right. Where can't you go?"

The ship shifted. That one wasn't her imagination, because Solé moved too.

"The *Prince*," she said. "I don't want...I don't want to volunteer."

"Volunteer for what?" Melba asked. She felt like she was coaxing the girl back from some sort of mental break. There was enough self-awareness left in her to appreciate the irony.

"Didn't you get the message? It's from the contracts supervisor."

Melba looked back over her shoulder. Her hand terminal was on the crash couch, a green-and-red band on the screen showing that there was a priority message waiting. She raised a finger, keeping Soledad out of the room and away from the locker, and grabbed the terminal. The message had come through ten hours before, marked URGENT AND MUST REPLY. Melba wondered how long she'd been lying in her couch, lost in her panic fugue. She thumbed the message accept. A stream of tight legal script poured onto the screen, brash as a shout.

Danis General Contracting, owners and operators of half the civilian support craft in the fleet, including the *Cerisier*, was invoking the exceptional actions clause of the standard contract. Each functional team would choose a designated volunteer for temporary duty on the UNN *Thomas Prince*. The remuneration would remain at the standard level until completion of the contract, when any hazard bonuses or exemptions would be assessed.

Melba had to read the words three times to understand them.

"I can't go in there," Soledad was saying, somewhere away to her left. The voice had taken on an irritating whine. "My father. I told you about him. You understand. Your sister was there too. You have to tell Bob or Stanni to do it. I can't."

They were going after Holden. They were going through the Ring after Holden. Her panic didn't fall away so much as click into focus.

"None of you are going," Melba said. "This one's mine."

The official transfer was the easiest thing she'd done since she came aboard. She sent a message to the contracts officer with her ID number and a short message saying that she'd accept transfer to the *Prince*. Two minutes later, she had her orders. Three hours to finish her affairs on the *Cerisier*, then into the transport and gone. It was intended, she knew, as a time to meet with her team, make the transition easy. She had other fish to fry.

Filling a locker with industrial sealant was one thing. The foam was made to apply quickly and remain malleable for a few seconds before the yellow mush dimmed to gold and set. The excess could be cut away with a sharp knife for the next hour. After that, nothing would move it except the right kind of solvent, and even that was an ugly, arduous process.

But leaving the body where it could be found wasn't an option. Someone would be assigned to her bunk, and they'd want to use the locker. Besides which, leaving Ren behind seemed somehow wrong. And so with two and a half hours before she left the ship, Melba took a pair of shoulder-length latex gloves, three cans of solvent, a roll of absorbent towels, and a vacuum-rated large personal tool case into her room and locked the door behind her.

The locker door didn't want to open at first, fixed in place by a drop of sealant she hadn't noticed, but a few sprays of solvent degraded it until she could pull it open with her fingers. The sealant was a single rough-textured face of gold, like a cliff made small. She opened the tool case, took a deep breath, and faced the grave.

"I'm sorry about this," she said. "I'm really, really sorry."

At first the solvent spray didn't seem to do anything beyond a sharp smell, but then the sealant began ticking, like a thousand insects walking over stone. Gouges and crevasses formed in the sealant wall, then a small runnel of slime. She rolled up a few of the towels, setting them on the floor to catch the flow.

Ren's knee was the first part to appear, the round cap of the bone and death-blackened skin emerging from the melting foam like a fossil. The fabric of his uniform was soaked with fluid rot. The smell hit her, but it wasn't as bad as she'd expected. She'd imagined herself retching and weeping, but it was gentler than that. When she took his legs to draw him out, they fell away from his pelvis, so she cut the trousers, wrapped the legs in towels, and put them in the toolbox. Her mind was quiet and still, like an archaeologist pulling the dead of centuries before out into the light. Here was his spine. This was the vile slush where the hydrochloric acid in his gut, no longer held in check by the mechanisms of life, had digested his stomach, his liver, his intestines. She drew out his head last, the bright red hair darkened and flecked with matter like an overused kitchen mop.

She lifted the bones into the toolbox, packed them with the gore- and corruption-soaked towels, then closed his new coffin, triggered the seal, and set the lock combination. She had forty minutes left.

She spent another ten minutes cleaning out the locker where Ren had spent his death, then stripped off the gloves and threw them in the recycler. She bathed, trying to scrub off the stink, and noticed distantly that she was sobbing. She ignored the fact, and by the time she'd changed into her new uniform, the crying seemed to have stopped. She picked up the last of her things, threw them in a pack, put her still-wet hair in a ponytail, and hauled Ren to the loading bay where the other supplies would be taken across to the *Prince*. It didn't allow her time to say her goodbyes to Soledad or Stanni or Bob. She was sorry for that, but it was a burden she could bear.

There were about thirty of them, all told. Men and women she'd seen around the ship, heard their names once or twice, nodded to in the galley or on the exercise machines. Once they reached the *Prince*, they were all brought into a small white conference room with benches that bolted to the floor like pews. They were already under thrust, already moving for the Ring and whatever was on the other side. While the overly enthusiastic yeoman prattled on about the *Thomas Prince*, she glanced at the faces around her. An old man with a scruffy white beard and ice-blue eyes. A stocky blond woman who was probably younger than she was with poorly applied eyeliner and a grim look about the jowls. They'd all come here of their own free will. Or free will as bounded by the terms of their work contracts. They were all going through the Ring, into the mouth of whatever was on the other side. She wondered what would motivate them to do it, what kinds of secrets they'd hidden in *their* tool chests.

"You will need to keep your identification cards with you at all times," the yeoman was saying, holding up a white plastic card on a lanyard. "Not only are these the keys to get into your quarters, they'll also get you food in the civilian commissary. And they'll let you know if you're where you're supposed to be."

The blond woman turned toward Melba and glared. Melba looked away, blushing. She hadn't intended to stare. Never be rude unintentionally, her father had always said.

The yeoman's white card turned a deep, bloody red.

"If you see this," he said, "it means you're in a restricted area and need to leave immediately. Don't worry too much. She's a big ship, and we all get a little turned around sometimes. I got buzzed four times the first week I was here. No one's going to get bent out of shape over an honest mistake, but security will be following up on them, so be prepared."

Melba looked at her own white card. It had her name, a picture of her unsmiling face. The yeoman was talking about how much they were appreciated, and how their service was an honor to the ship and to themselves. All in this together, one big team. The first stirring of hatred for the man shifted in her gut, and she tried to distract herself.

She didn't know what she'd do once they were all on the other side, but she had to find Holden. She had to destroy him. The soundman too. Anything that led back to her had to be destroyed or discredited. She wondered if there was a way to get a fake card, or one that belonged to someone with a lot more clearance than Melba Koh would have. Maybe one that could check out a shuttle. She'd need to look into it. She was improvising now, and getting the best tools she could manage would be critical.

Around her, people began standing up. From the bored looks and the quiet, she figured they were beginning the walking tour. She'd been through the *Thomas Prince* before. She was already familiar with the high ceilings and wide corridors where three people could walk abreast. She might not know where everything was, but she could fake it. She fell in line with the others.

"In case of emergency, all you'll have to do is get back to your quarters and strap in," the yeoman said, walking backward so that he could keep lecturing them while they all moved, bumping against each other like cattle. Someone behind her made a soft mooing sound, and someone else chuckled. The joke had gone out to the darkness of space even where cows hadn't.

"Now, through here is the civilian commissary," the yeoman said as they passed through a pair of sliding steel doors. "Those of you who were working here before might be used to getting your food and coffee from the officers' mess, but now that we're on a military operation, this is going to be the place to go."

The civilian commissary was a low gray box of a room with tables and chairs bolted to the floor, and a dozen people of all ages and dress sat scattered around. A thin man with improbably pale hair leaned against a crash-padded wall, drinking something from a bulb. Two older men in black robes and clerical collars sat huddled together like the unpopular kids at a cafeteria. Melba was already beginning to turn inward again, ignoring them all, when something caught her. A familiar voice.

Twenty feet away, Tilly Fagan leaned in toward an older man who looked like he was struggling between annoyance and flirtation. Her hair was up and her laughter caustic in a way that recalled long, uncomfortable dinner parties with both of their families. Melba felt a sudden atavistic shame at being so underdressed. For a sickening moment, her false self slipped away and she was Clarissa again.

Forcing herself to move slowly, calmly, she drifted to the back of the crowd, making herself as small and difficult to notice as she could. Tilly glanced over at the nattering yeoman and his herd of technicians with undisguised annoyance, but didn't notice Melba. Not this time. The yeoman led them all back out of the commissary, down the long hallway to their new quarters. Melba took her ponytail down and brushed her hair in close around her face. She'd known, of course, that the *Prince* had the delegation from Earth, but she'd discounted them. Now she wondered how many other people here knew Clarissa Mao. She had the horrible image of turning a corner and seeing Micha Krauss or Steven Comer. She could see their eyes going wide with surprise, and she wondered whether she could bring herself to kill them too. If she couldn't, the brig and the newsfeeds and a prison cell like her father's would follow.

The yeoman was talking about their quarters, assigning them out one by one to all the volunteer technicians. They were tiny, but the need for each person to have a crash couch in case of emergency meant they wouldn't be hot-bunking. She could stay in there, bribe one of the others to bring her food. Except, holed up like a rat, tracking and killing Holden became exponentially more difficult. There had to be a way...

The yeoman called her name, and she realized it wasn't the first time.

"Here," she said. "Sorry."

She scuttled into her room, the door recognizing her white card and unlocking for her, then closing once she was inside. She stood for a long moment, scratching her arm. The room was bright and clean and as unlike the *Cerisier* as Nepal was from Colombia.

"You came to improvise," she said, and her voice sounded like it came from someone else. "Well, here you are. Start improvising."

Chapter Twenty: Holden

Instead of putting him at ease, the weeks and months of interviews had given Holden a new persona. A version of himself that stood in front of a camera and answered questions. That explained things and told stories in ways entertaining enough to keep the focus on himself. It wasn't the sort of thing that he'd have expected to have any practical application.

One more surprise among many.

"This," Holden said, gesturing to the large video monitor behind him on the operations deck, "is what we are calling the slow zone."

"That's a terrible name," Naomi said. She was at the ship operations panel, just out of view of the documentary crew's cameras. "Slow zone? Really?"

"You have a better name?" Monica asked. She whispered something to Clip and he shifted a few degrees to his left, camera moving with him in a slow pan. The burst blood vessel in his eye was starting to fade. The high-g burn through the Ring had been hard on all of them.

"I still like Alex's name," Naomi replied.

"Dandelion sky?" Monica said with a snort. "First of all, only people from Earth and Mars have even the slightest idea what a dandelion is. And second of all, no, it sounds stupid."

Holden knew he was still on camera, so he just smiled and let the two of them hash it out. The truth was, he'd been partial to Alex's name. Where they sat, looking out, it did sort of look like being at the center of a dandelion, the sky filled with fragile-looking structures in an enormous sphere around them.

"Can we finish this?" Monica asked, shooting the comment at Naomi without looking at her.

"Sorry I interrupted," Naomi replied, not looking sorry at all. She winked at Holden and he grinned back.

"And, three...two..." Monica pointed at him.

"The slow zone, based on the sensor data we're able to get, is approximately one million kilometers across." Holden pointed at the 3D representation on the screen behind him. "There are no visible stars, so the location of the zone is impossible to determine. The boundary is made up of one thousand three hundred and seventy-three individual rings evenly spaced into a sphere. So far, the only one we've been able to find that's 'open' is the one we came through. The fleets we traveled out with are still visible on the other side, though the Ring seems to distort visual and sensor data, making readings through it unreliable."

Holden tapped on the monitor, and the center of the image enlarged rapidly.

"We're calling this Ring Station, for lack of a better term. It appears to be a solid sphere of a metallic substance, measuring about five kilometers in diameter. Around it is a slow-moving ring of other objects, including all of the probes we've fired into the slow zone, and the Belter ship *Y Que*. The torpedo that chased us through the Ring is headed toward the station in a trajectory that seems to indicate it will become part of the garbage ring too."

Another tap and the central sphere took up the entire screen. "We're calling it a station pretty much only because it sits at the center of the slow zone, and we're making the entirely unfounded assumption that some sort of control station for the gates would be located there. The station has no visible breaks in its surface. Nothing that looks like an airlock, or an antenna, or a sensor array, or anything. Just that big silvery blue glowing ball."

Holden turned off the monitor and both of the camera operators swiveled to put him at the center of their shots.

"But the most intriguing factor of the slow zone, and the one that gives it its name, is the absolute speed limit of six hundred meters per second. Any object above the quantum level traveling faster than that is locked down by what seems to be an inertial dampening field, and then dragged off to join the garbage circling the central station. At a guess, this is some sort of defensive system that protects the Ring Station and the gates themselves. Light and radar still work normally, but radiation made up of larger particles like alpha and beta radiation does not exist inside the slow zone. At least outside the ship, that is. Whatever controls the speeds here only seems concerned by the exterior of the objects, not the interior. We've done radiation and object speed tests inside the ship, and so far everything works as normal. But the last probe we fired was immediately grabbed by the field and is now making its way down to the garbage ring. The lack of alpha and beta radiation leads me to believe that there's a thin cloud of loose electrons and helium nuclei orbiting that station as part of the garbage ring."

"Can you tell us what your plan is now?" Monica said from off camera. Cohen pointed his mic at her, then back at Holden.

"Our plan now is to remain motionless, avoid attracting the Ring Station's attention, and keep studying the slow zone using what instruments we have. We can't leave until we repair the comm array and let everyone outside know that we aren't psychotic murderers bent on claiming the Ring for ourselves."

"Great!" Monica said, giving him the thumbs-up. Clip and

Okju moved around the room getting shots to cut in later. They shot the instrument panels, the monitor behind Holden, even Naomi lounging in her ops station crash couch. She smiled sweetly and flipped them off.

"How's everyone doing after the burn?" Holden asked, Clip's blood-pinked eye still drawing his attention.

Cohen touched his side and grimaced. "Got a rib that I think just slid back into place this morning. I've never been on a ship doing maneuvers that violent before. It gave me a little more respect for the navy."

Holden pushed off the bulkhead and drifted over to Naomi. In a low voice he said, "Speaking of the navy, how's that comm array coming along? I'd really love to start protesting my innocence before someone figures out a way to lob a slow-moving torpedo in here after us."

She blew out an exasperated breath at him and started tugging on her hair like she did when she was lost in a complex problem. "That little Trojan horse that keeps grabbing control? Every time I wipe and reboot, it finds its way back in. I've got comms totally isolated from the other systems, and it's still getting in."

"And the weapons?"

"They keep on powering up, but they never fire."

"So there has to be some connection."

"Yes," Naomi said, and waited. Holden felt a self-conscious discomfort.

"That doesn't tell you anything you didn't know."

"No."

Holden pulled himself down into the crash couch next to hers and buckled in. He was trying to play it cool, but the truth was the longer they went without presenting a defense or at least a denial to the fleets outside, the more risk there was that someone would find a way to destroy the *Roci*, slow zone or not. The fact that Naomi couldn't figure it out only added to the worry. If whoever was doing this was clever enough to outsmart Naomi with an engineering problem, they were in a lot of trouble.

"What's the next plan?" he asked, trying to keep the impatience out of his voice. Naomi heard it anyway.

"We're taking a break from it," she said. "I've got Alex doing ladar sweeps of all the other rings that make up the boundary of the slow zone. Just to see if one is different in some way. And I've got Amos fixing that light bulb in the head. There's nothing else to do, and I wanted him out of my hair while I come up with another way to attack this comm problem."

"What can I do to help?" Holden asked. He'd already gone through every other system on the ship three times looking for malicious and hidden programs. He hadn't found any, and he couldn't think of anything else that might be useful.

"You're doing it," Naomi said, subtly moving her head toward Monica without actually looking at her.

"I feel like I've got the shit job here."

"Oh, please," Naomi said with a grin. "You love the attention."

The deck hatch slid open with a bang, and Amos came up the crew ladder. "Mother*fucker*!" he yelled as the hatch closed behind him.

"What?" Holden started, but Amos kept yelling.

"When I peeled that twitchy power circuit open in the head, I found this little bastard hiding in the LED housing, sucking off our juice."

Amos threw something, and Holden barely managed to catch it before it hit him in the face. It looked like a small transmitter with power leads coming off one end. He held it up to Naomi, and her face darkened.

"That's it," she said, reaching out to take it from Holden.

"You're fucking right that's it," Amos bellowed. "Someone hid that in the head, and it's been loading the software hijacker onto our system every time we boot up."

"Someone with access to the ship's head," Naomi said, looking at Holden, but he'd already gone past that and was unbuckling his restraints.

"Are you armed?" Holden asked Amos. The big mechanic

pulled a large-caliber pistol out of his pocket and held it against his thigh. In the microgravity it would shove Amos around if he fired it, but surrounded by bulkheads that wouldn't be too much of a problem.

"Hey," Monica said, her face shifting from confusion to fear.

"One of you hijacked my comm array," Holden said. "One of you is working for whoever is doing this to us. Whoever it is should really just tell me now."

"You forgot to threaten us," Cohen said. He sounded almost ill.

"No. I didn't."

Naomi had unbuckled her harness as well, and was floating next to him now. She tapped a wall panel and said, "Alex, get down here."

"Look," Monica said, patting the air with her hands. "You're making a mistake blaming us for this." Clip and Okju moved behind her, pulling Cohen to them. The documentary crew formed a small circle facing outward, unconsciously creating a defensive perimeter. More Pleistocene-age behavior that humans still carried with them. Alex drifted down from the cockpit; his usually jolly face had a hard expression on it. He was carrying a heavy wrench.

"Tell me who did it," Holden repeated. "I swear by everything holy that I will space the whole damn lot of you to protect this ship if I have to."

"It wasn't *us*," Monica said, the fear on her face draining the bland video star prettiness away, making her look older, gaunt.

"Fuck this," Amos said, pointing the gun at them. "Let me drag one of 'em down to the airlock and space them right now. Even if only one of them did it, I got me a twenty-five percent chance to get the right one. Got a thirty-three percent chance with the second one I toss. Fifty-fifty by the third, and those are odds I'll take any day."

Holden didn't acknowledge the threat, but he didn't argue with it either. Let them sweat.

"Shit," Cohen said. "I don't suppose it will matter that I got set up just as bad as you guys, will it?"

Monica's eyes went wide. Okju and Clip turned to stare at the blind man.

"You?" Holden said. It didn't make any sense not to, not really, but he honestly hadn't suspected the blind guy. It made him feel betrayed and guilty of his prejudices at the same time.

"I got paid to stick that rig on the ship," Cohen said, moving out of the defensive circle and floating a half meter closer to Holden. Pulling himself out of the group, so that if anything happened, they wouldn't get hurt. Holden respected him for that. "I had no idea what it would do. I figured someone was spying on your comms, is all. When that broadcast went out and the missiles started flying, I was just as surprised as you guys. And my ass was just as much on the line."

"Motherfucker," Amos said again, this time without the heat. Holden knew him well enough to know that angry Amos was not nearly as dangerous as cold Amos. "I was thinking I'd have a tough time spacing a blind guy, but turns out I'm gonna be just fine with it."

"Not yet," Holden said, waving Amos off. "Who paid you to do this. Lie to me and I let Amos have his way."

Cohen held up both hands in surrender. "Hey, you got me, boss. I know my ass is hanging by a thread right now. I got no reason not to come clean."

"Then do."

"I only met her once," Cohen continued. "Young woman. Nice voice. Had lots of money. Asked me to plant this thing. I said, 'Sure, get me on that ship and I plant whatever you want.' Next thing I know Monica's got a gig doing this doc about you and the Ring. Damned if I know how she swung that."

"Son of a bitch," Monica said, clearly as surprised by this revelation as anyone else. That actually made Holden feel a little better.

"Who was this young woman with all the money?" Holden asked. Amos hadn't moved, but he wasn't pointing the gun at anyone anymore. Cohen's tone didn't have a hint of deception in it. He sounded like a man who knew that his life hung on every word.

"Never got a name, but I can sculpt her pretty easy."

"Do that," Holden said, then watched as Cohen plugged his modeling software into the big monitor. Over the next several minutes, the image of a woman slowly formed. It was all one color, of course, and the hair was a sculpted lump, not individual strands. But when Cohen had finished, Holden had no doubt about who it was. She was changed, but not so much that he couldn't recognize the dead girl.

Julie Mao.

The ship was quiet. Monica and her two camera operators had been confined to the crew decks again, and last time Holden had checked they were together in the galley, not talking. Cohen's betrayal had taken them by surprise as well, and they were still working through it. Cohen himself was in the airlock. It was the closest thing they had to a brig. Holden had to assume the man was quietly panicking.

Alex was back in the cockpit. After Amos had thrown Cohen into the airlock he'd disappeared back down to his machine shop to brood. Holden had let him go. Of them all, Amos took betrayal the hardest. Holden knew that Cohen's life was hanging on whether Amos could get past it or not. If he decided to take action, Holden wouldn't be able to stop him, and didn't even know if he'd want to try.

So he and Naomi sat alone together on the ops deck as she made the last few adjustments to get the comm array back up and running. With Cohen's device disabled, they'd been able to reboot it without being hijacked.

Naomi was waiting for him to speak. He could feel the tension in her shoulders from across the room. But he had no idea what to say. For a year, Miller had been a confused phantasm that appeared randomly and spouted nonsense. Now everything

Miller had said over the last year took on the weight of dark portents. Prophetic riddles whose meaning must be teased out or risk catastrophe. And Miller wasn't the only ghost haunting Holden.

Julie Mao had joined the game.

Somehow, while Miller had followed Holden around the solar system, the protomolecule had been using Julie, working on its own secret plans. Julie had arranged for the Martian lawsuit that stripped him of safe ports and employment. She'd arranged to have a documentary crew placed on his ship to send him to the Ring. And now it appeared she'd engineered an elaborate betrayal that forced him to actually go through the Ring to stay alive. The ghost Julie didn't resemble his Miller at all. It was working with very specific purpose. It had access to money and powerful connections. The only thing it had in common with Miller was that it seemed to be focused on him. And if this was all true, then everything it had done had been with a single purpose in mind.

To bring him here. To *force* him to go through the Ring.

A shiver crawled its way up his spine, sending all the hairs on his arms and neck standing straight up. He turned on the closest workstation and brought up the external telescopes. Nothing at all in this starless void except a lot of inactive rings and the massive blue ball at its center. As he watched, the missile that had chased them through the gate drifted into view and joined the slowly circling ring of flotsam that orbited the station.

Everything comes to me, eventually, the station seemed to be saying.

"I have to go there," he said out loud even as the thought popped into his head.

"Where?" Naomi asked, turning away from her work on the comm. The relief he could see on her face now that he'd finally said something wouldn't last long. He felt a pang of guilt for that.

"The station. Or whatever it is. I have to go there."

"No you don't," she said.

"Everything that's happened over the last year has been to bring me here, now." Holden rubbed his face with both hands, itching his eyes and hiding from Naomi's scrutiny at the same time. "And that thing is the only place in here. There's nothing else. No other open gates, no planets, no other ships. Nothing."

"Jim," Naomi said, a warning in her voice. "This thing where you always have to be the guy who goes..."

"I'll never know why the protomolecule is talking to me until I get there, face-to-face."

"Eros, Ganymede, the *Agatha King*," Naomi continued. "You always think you have to go."

Holden stopped rubbing his face and looked at her. She stared back, beautiful and angry and sad. He felt his throat threaten to close up, so he said, "Am I wrong? Tell me I'm wrong and we'll think of something else. Tell me how all of what's happened means something else and I'm just not seeing it."

"No," she said again, meaning something else this time.

"Okay." He sighed. "Okay then."

"It's getting old being the one who stays behind."

"You're not staying behind," Holden said. "You're keeping the crew alive while I do something really stupid. It's why we're an awesome team. You're the captain now."

"That's a shit job and you know it."

Chapter Twenty-One: Bull

In the last hours before they shot the Ring, a kind of calm descended on the *Behemoth*. In the halls and galleries, people talked, but their voices were controlled, quiet, brittle. The independent feeds, always a problem, were pretty subdued. The complaints coming to the security desk fell to nothing. Bull kept an eye on the places people could get liquored up and stupid, but there were no flare-ups. The traffic going through the comm laser back toward Tycho Station and all points sunward spiked to six times its usual bandwidth. A lot of people on the ship wanted to say something to someone—a kid, a sister, a dad, a lover—before they passed through the signal-warping circumference and into whatever was on the other side.

Bull had thought about doing it too. He'd logged into the family group feed for the first time in months, and let the minutiae of the extended Baca family wash over him. One cousin was engaged, another one was divorcing, and they were trading notes and worldviews. His aunt on Earth was having trouble with her hip, but since she was on basic, she was on a waiting list to get a doctor to look at it. His brother had dropped a note to say that he'd gotten a job on Luna, but he didn't say what it was or anything about it. Bull listened to the voices of the family he never saw except on a screen, the lives that didn't intersect his own. The love he felt for them surprised him, and kept him from putting his own report in among them. It would only scare them, and they wouldn't understand it. He could already hear his cousins telling him to jump ship, get on something that wasn't going through. By the time the message got there, he'd already have gone anyway.

Instead, he recorded a private video for Fred Johnson, and all he said in it was, "After this, you owe *me* one."

With an hour to go before they passed through, Bull put the whole ship on battle-ready status. Everyone in their couches, one per. No sharing. All tools and personal items secured, all carts in their stations and locked down, the bulkheads closed between major sections so that if something happened, they'd only lose air one deck at a time. He got a few complaints, but they were mostly just grousing.

They made the transit slowly, the thrust gravity hardly more than a tendency for things to drift toward the floor. Bull couldn't say whether that was a technical decision on Sam's part meant to keep them from moving too quickly in the uncanny reduced speed beyond the ring, or Ashford giving the Earth and Mars ships the time to catch up so that they'd all be passing through at more or less the same time. Only if it was that, it wouldn't have been Ashford. That kind of diplomatic thinking was Pa.

Probably it was just that the main drive couldn't go slow enough, and this was as fast as the maneuvering thrusters could move them.

Bull wasn't that worried about the Earth forces. They'd been the ones to broker the deal, and they had civilians on board. Mars, on the other hand, might call itself a science mission, but its escort was explicitly military, and until Earth stepped in they'd been willing to poke holes in the *Behemoth* until the air ran out.

Too many people with too many agendas, and everyone was worried that the other guy would shoot them in the back. Of all the ways to go and meet the God-like alien whatever-they-were that built the protomolecule, this was the stupidest, the most dangerous, and—for Bull's money—the most human.

The transit actually took a measurable amount of time, the great bulk of the *Behemoth* sulking through the Ring in a few seconds. An eerie fluting groan passed through the ship, and Bull, in his crash couch at the security office waiting for the next disaster, felt the gooseflesh on his arms and neck. He flipped through the security monitors like a dad walking through the house to see if the windows were all locked, all the kids safely in their beds. Memories of the Eros feed tugged at the back of his mind: black whorls of filament covering the corridors; the bodies of the innocent and the guilty alike warping, falling apart, and becoming something else without actually dying in between; the blue firefly glow that no one had yet explained. With every new monitor, he expected to see the *Behemoth* in that same light, and every time he didn't, his dread moved on to the one still to come.

He moved to the external sensor feed. The luminous blue object in the center of a sphere of anomalies that the computers interpreted as being approximately the same size as the Ring. Gates to God knew where.

"I don't know what the hell we're doing here," he said under his breath.

"A-chatté-men, brother," Serge said, pale-faced, from his desk.

A connect request popped on Bull's hand terminal, the alert-red of senior staff. With dread growing at the back of his throat, Bull accepted it. Sam appeared on the screen.

"Hey," she said. "This whole act-like-we're-in-a-battle thing where we aren't supposed to get out of our crash couches? I'd really appreciate it if you could ease up enough to let us make sure the ship isn't falling apart."

"You getting alerts?"

"No," Sam admitted. "But we just sailed the *Behemoth* into a region of space with different, y'know, laws of *physics* and stuff? Makes me want to take a peek."

"We got eight ships coming in right behind us," Bull said. "Hold tight until we see how that shakes down."

Sam smiled in a way that expressed her annoyance with him perfectly.

"You can get the teensiest bit paternalistic sometimes, Bull. You know that?"

A new alert popped up by Sam's face. A high-priority message was coming into the comm array. From the *Rocinante*.

"Sam, I got something here. I'll get back to you."

"I'll be sitting here in my couch doing nothing," she said.

He flipped over to the incoming message. It was a broadcast. A Belter woman, with black hair pulled back from her face in a style that gave Bull the impression she'd been welding something before she'd begun the broadcast and would be again as soon as she was finished, looked into the camera.

"...Nagata, executive officer of the *Rocinante*. I want to make it very clear that the previous broadcast claiming our ownership of the Ring was a fake. Our communications array was hijacked, and we were locked out of it. The saboteur on board has confessed, and I am including a datafile at the end of this transmission with all the evidence we have about the real perpetrator of these crimes. I am also including a short documentary presentation on what we've discovered in the time we've been here that Monica Stuart and her team produced. I want to reiterate here, Captain Holden had no mandate from anyone to claim the Ring, he had no intention of doing so, and none of us had any participation in or knowledge of the bomb on the *Seung Un* or on any other ship. We were here solely as transport and support for a documentary team, and pose no intentional threat whatsoever to any other vessel."

Serge grunted, unconvinced. "You think they fragged him?"

"Keep Jim Holden from grabbing the camera? Fragged him or

tied him up," Bull said. It was a joke, but there was something in it. Why *wasn't* the *Rocinante*'s captain the one making the announcement?

"We will not surrender our ship," the Belter said, "but we will invite inspectors aboard to verify what we've reported, with the following conditions. First, the inspectors will have to comply with basic safety—"

Five more communication alerts popped up, all from different ships. All broadcast. If they were flying into the teeth of a vast and malefic alien intelligence, by God, they we're going to go down squabbling.

"—unacceptable. We demand the immediate surrender of the *Tachi* and all accompanying—"

"—what confirmation you can provide that—"

"—James Holden at once for interrogation. If your claims are verified, we will—"

"—Message repeats. Please confirm and clarify EVA activity, *Rocinante*. Who've you got out there, and where are they going?"

Bull pulled up the sensor array and began a careful sweep of the area around Holden's ship. It took him half a minute to find it. A single EVA suit, burning away from the ship and heading for the blue-glowing structure in the center of the sphere. He said something obscene. Five minutes later, the XO of the *Rocinante* spoke again to confirm Bull's worst suspicions.

"This is Naomi Nagata," she said, "executive officer and acting captain of the *Rocinante*. Captain Holden is not presently available to take questions, meet with any representatives, or surrender himself into anybody's custody. He is..." She looked down. Bull couldn't tell if it was fear or embarrassment or a little of both. The Belter took a deep breath and continued, "He is conducting an EVA approach of the base at the middle of the slow zone. We have reason to believe he was...called there."

Bull's laughter pulled Serge's attention. Serge lifted his hand, the physical Belter idiom for asking a question. Bull shook his head.

"Just trying to think of a way we could be doing this worse," he said.

Ashford insisted that they meet in person, so even though Bull had ordered that all crew members not performing essential functions remain in their couches, he himself floated to the lift and headed to the bridge.

The crew was a muted cacophony. Every station was juggling telemetry and signal switching and sensor data, even though basically nothing was going on. It was just that the excitement demanded that everything be busy and serious and fraught. The excitement or else the fear. The monitors were set to a tactical display, Earth in blue, Mars in red, the *Behemoth* in orange, and the artifact at the center of the sphere in a deep forest green. The debris ring was marked in white. And two dots of gold: one for the *Rocinante*, well ahead of the other ships, and another for her captain. The scale was so small, Bull could see the shapes of the larger ships, boxy and awkward in the way that structures built for vacuum could be. The universe, shrunk down to a knot smaller than the sun and still unthinkably vast.

And in that bubble of darkness, mystery, and dread, two matched dots—one blue, the other red—moving steadily toward the little gold Holden. Marine skiffs, hardly more than a wide couch strapped on the end of a fusion drive. Bull had ridden on boats like them so long ago it seemed like a different lifetime, but if he closed his eyes, he could still feel the rattle of the thrusters transferred through the shell of his armor. Some things he would never forget.

"How long," Ashford said, "until you can put together a matching force?"

Bull rubbed his palm against his chin, shrugged.

"How long'd it take to get back to Tycho?"

Ashford's face went red.

"I'm not interested in your sense of humor, Mister Baca. Earth and Mars have both launched interception teams against the outlaw

James Holden. If we don't have a force of our own out there, we look weak. We're here to make sure the OPA remains the equal of the inner planets, and we're going to do that, whatever it takes. Am I clear?"

"You're clear, sir."

"So how long would it take?"

Bull looked at Pa. Her face was carefully blank. She knew the answer as well as he did, but she wasn't going to say it. Leaving the shit job for the Earther. Well, all right.

"It can't be done," Bull said. "Each one of those skiffs is carrying half a dozen marines in full battle dress. Powered armor. Maybe Goliath class for the Martians, Reaver class for the Earthers. Either way, I don't have anything in that league. And the soldiers inside those suits have trained for exactly this kind of combat every day for years. I've got a bunch of plumbers with rifles I could put on a shuttle."

The bridge went quiet. Ashford crossed his arms.

"Plumbers. With rifles. Is that how you see us, Mister Baca?"

"I don't question the bravery or commitment of anyone on this crew," Bull said. "I believe that any team we sent over there would be willing to lay down their lives for the cause. Of course, that would only take about fifteen seconds, and I won't send our people into that."

The implication floated in the air as gently as they did. *You're the captain. You can make the order, but you'll own the consequences. And they'll know the Earther told you what would happen.* Pa's eyes were narrow and looked away.

"Thank you, Mister Baca," Ashford said. "You're dismissed."

Bull saluted, turned, and launched himself for the lift. Behind him, the bridge crew started talking again, but not as loud. Probably they'd all get reamed once Bull was gone just because they'd been in the room when Ashford got embarrassed. The chances were slim that they'd be sending anyone to the thing. Nucleus, base, whatever it was. Bull couldn't think of a way to do any better than that, so that would count for a win.

On the way back to his station, he looked over the datafile the *Rocinante* had sent out. The saboteur seemed legitimate enough. Bull had seen enough faked confessions to recognize the signs, and this didn't have them. After that, though, the whole damn thing turned into a fairy tale. A mysterious woman who manipulated governments and civilians, who was willing to kill dozens of people and risk thousands in order to…do what? Put James Holden through the Ring, where he was going now?

The image the prisoner had built looked like it had been carved from ice. No one had added color. Bull put on an even olive flesh tone and brown hair, and the face didn't look familiar. Juliette Mao, they said. She hadn't been the first person infected with the protomolecule, but everyone before her had gotten thrown in an autoclave one way or the other. She'd been the seed crystal that Eros had used to make itself, to make the Ring. So who was to say she couldn't be wandering around hiring traitors and placing bombs?

The problem with living with miracles was that they made everything seem plausible. An alien weapon had been lurking in orbit around Saturn for billions of years. It had eaten thousands of people, hijacking the mechanisms of their bodies for its own ends. It had built a wormhole gate into a kind of haunted sphere. So why not the rest? If all that was possible, everything was.

Bull didn't buy it.

Back at the security desk, he checked the status. The skiff of Earth marines had gone too fast, trying to race ahead of the Martian force. The slow zone had caught them, and the skiff was drifting off toward the ring of debris. Chances were that all the men in it were dead. The Martian skiff was still on track, but Holden would reach the structure before they got to him. It was too bad, in a way. The Martians had been the trigger-happy ones all along. Chances of someone getting to question Holden were looking pretty long.

Bull sucked his teeth, half-formed ideas shifting in the back of his mind. Holden wasn't getting interrogated, but that didn't mean no one would. He checked his security codes. Ashford hadn't blocked him from using the comm laser. Protocol would have been to discuss this with Ashford or at least Pa, but they had their hands full right now anyway. And if it worked, it would be hard for them to object. They'd have a bargaining chip.

The *Rocinante's* XO appeared on the screen.

"What can I do for you, *Behemoth*?"

"Carlos Baca here. I'm security chief. Wanted to talk about maybe taking a problem off your hands."

She hoisted her eyebrows, her head shaking like she was trying to stay awake. She had a smart face.

"I've got a lot of problems right now," she said. "Which one were you thinking about?"

"You got a bunch of civvies on your ship. One of 'em under arrest. Mars is still saying you're flying their ship. Earth is wondering whether you blew the shit out of one of theirs. I can take custody of your prisoner and give the rest of them a safer place than you can."

"Last I checked, the OPA was the only one that's actually shot at us so far," she said. She had a good smile. Too young for him, but ten years ago he'd have been asking her if he could make her dinner around now. "Doesn't put you at the top of my list."

"That was me," Bull said. "I won't do it this time." It got him a chuckle, but it was the bleak kind. The one that came from someone wading through hell. "Look, you got a lot going on, and you've got a bunch of people on there who aren't your crew. You got to keep them safe, and it's a distraction. You send 'em over here, and everyone'll see you aren't trying to control access to them. Makes this whole thing about how it wasn't you that blew the shit out of the *Seung Un* that much easier for people to believe."

"I think we're past goodwill gestures," she said.

"I think goodwill gestures are the only chance you have to avoid a field promotion," Bull said. "They're sending killers after your captain. Good ones. No one's thinking straight here. You and me, we can start cooling things down. Acting like grown-ups. And if we do, maybe they do too. No one else needs to get killed."

"Thin hope," she said.

"It's all the hope I got. You got nothing to hide, then show them that. Show everyone."

It took her twenty seconds.

"All right," she said. "You can have them."

Chapter Twenty-Two: Holden

Wow," Holden said to himself, "I really don't want to do this." The sound echoed in his helmet, competing only with the faint hiss of his radio.

"I tried to talk you out of it," Naomi replied, her voice somehow managing to be intimate even flattened and distorted by his suit's small speakers.

"Sorry, I didn't think you were listening."

"Ah," she said. "Irony."

Holden tore his eyes way from the slowly growing sphere that was his destination and spun around to look for the *Rocinante* behind him. She wasn't visible until Alex fired a maneuvering thruster and a gossamer cone of steam reflected some of the sphere's blue glow. His suit told him that the *Roci* was over thirty thousand kilometers away—more than twice as far as any two people on Earth could ever be from each other—and receding.

And here he was, in a suit of vacuum armor, wearing a disposable EVA pack that had about five minutes of thrust in it. He'd burned one minute accelerating toward the sphere. He'd burn another slowing down when he got there. That left enough to fly back to the *Roci* when he was done.

Optimism expressed as conservation of delta V.

Ships from the three fleets had begun coming through the gate even before he'd started his trip. The *Roci* was now protected from them only by the absolute speed limit of the slow zone. She was drifting off at just under that limit to put as much space between her and the fleets as possible. They had a sphere a million kilometers in diameter to play with, even without going beyond the area marked by the gates. The gates had close to fifty thousand kilometers of empty space between them, but the idea of flying out of the slow zone and into that starless void beyond made Holden's skin crawl. He and Naomi had agreed it would be a maneuver of last resort.

As long as no one could fire a ballistic weapon, the *Roci* should be plenty safe with five hundred quadrillion square kilometers to move around in.

Holden spun back around, using two quarter-second blasts from his EVA pack, and took a range reading to the sphere. He was still hours away. The minute-long burst he'd fired from the pack to start his journey had accelerated him to a slow crawl, astronomically speaking, and the *Roci* had come to a relative stop before releasing him. He'd never have had enough juice in the EVA pack to stop himself if the ship had flung him out at the slow zone's maximum speed.

Ahead in the middle of all that starless black, the blue sphere waited.

It had waited for two billion years for someone to come through his particular gate, if the researchers were right about how long ago Phoebe had been captured by Saturn. But lately the strangeness surrounding the protomolecule and the Ring left Holden with the disquieting feeling that maybe all of the assumptions they'd made about its origins and purpose were wrong.

Protogen had named the protomolecule and decided it was a tool that could redefine what it meant to be human. Jules-Pierre Mao had treated it like a weapon. It killed humans, therefore it was a weapon. But radiation killed humans, and a medical X-ray machine wasn't intended as a weapon. Holden was starting to feel like they were all monkeys playing with a microwave. Push a button, a light comes on inside, so it's a light. Push a different button and stick your hand inside, it burns you, so it's a weapon. Learn to open and close the door, it's a place to hide things. Never grasping what it actually did, and maybe not even having the framework necessary to figure it out. No monkey ever reheated a frozen burrito.

So here the monkeys were, poking the shiny box and making guesses about what it did. Holden could tell himself that in his case the box was asking to be poked, but even that was making a lot of assumptions. Miller looked human, had *been* human once, so it was easy to think of him as having human motivations. Miller wanted to communicate. He wanted Holden to know or do something. But it was just as likely—more likely, maybe—that Holden was anthropomorphizing something far stranger.

He imagined himself landing on the station, and Miller saying, *James Holden, you and only you in the universe have the correct chemical composition to make a perfect wormhole fuel!* then stuffing him into a machine to be processed.

"Everything okay?" Naomi asked in response to his chuckle.

"Still just thinking about how incredibly stupid this is. Why didn't I let you talk me out of it?"

"It looks like you did, but it took a couple of hours for it to process. Want us to come get you?"

"No. If I bail out now, I'll never have the balls to try it again," Holden said. "How's it look out there?"

"The fleets came through with about two dozen ships, mostly heavies. Alex has figured out the math on doing short torpedo burns to get one up to the speed limit but not over. Which means everyone on those other ships are doing the same thing. So far no one has fired at us."

"Maybe your protestations of my innocence worked?"

"Maybe," she said. "There were a couple of small ships detaching from the fleet on an intercept course with you. The *Roci* is calling them landing skiffs."

"Shit, they're sending the Marines after me?"

"They've burned up to the speed limit, but the *Roci* says you make stationfall before they catch you. But *just* before."

"Damn," Holden said. "I really hope there's a door."

"They lost the UN ship. The other is Martian. So maybe they brought Bobbie. She can make sure the others are nice to you."

"No," Holden said with a sigh. "No, these will be the ones that are still mad at me."

Knowing the marines were following made the back of his neck itch. Being in a space suit just added that to his already lengthy list of insoluble problems.

"On the good news level, Monica's team is getting evacuated to the *Behemoth*."

"You never did like her."

"Not much, no."

"Why not?"

"Her job is digging up old things," Naomi said, the lightness of her tone almost covering her anxieties. "And digging up old things leads to messes like this one."

When Holden was nine, Rufus the family Labrador died. He'd already been an adult dog when Holden was born, so Holden had only ever known Rufus as a big black slobbering bundle of love. He'd taken some of his first steps clutching the dog's fur in one stubby fist. He'd run around their Montana farm not much bigger than a toddler with Rufus as his only babysitter. Holden had loved the dog with the simple intensity only children and dogs share.

But when he was nine, Rufus was fifteen, and old for such a big dog. He slowed down. He stopped running with Holden, barely managing a trot to catch up, then gradually only a slow walk. He stopped eating. And one night he flopped onto his side next to a heater vent and started panting. Mother Elise had told him that Rufus probably wouldn't last the night, and even if he did they'd have to call the vet in the morning. Holden had tearfully sworn to stay by the dog's side. For the first couple of hours, he held Rufus' head on his lap and cried, as Rufus struggled to breathe and occasionally gave one halfhearted thump of his tail.

By the third, against his will and every good thought he'd had about himself, Holden was bored.

It was a lesson he'd never forgotten. That humans only have so much emotional energy. No matter how intense the situation, or how powerful the feelings, it was impossible to maintain a heightened emotional state forever. Eventually you'd just get tired and want it to end.

For the first hours drifting toward the glowing blue station, Holden had felt awe at the immensity of empty starless space around him. He'd felt fear of what the protomolecule might want from him, fear of the marines following him, fear that he'd made the wrong choice and that he'd arrive at the station to find nothing at all. Most of all fear that he'd never see Naomi or his crew again.

But after four hours of being alone in his space suit, even the fear burned out. He just wanted it all to be over with.

With the infinite and unbroken black all around him, and the only visible spot of light coming from the blue sphere directly ahead, it was easy to feel like he was in some vast tunnel, slowly moving toward the exit. The human mind didn't do well with infinite spaces. It wanted walls, horizons, limits. It would create them if it had to.

His suit beeped at him to let him know it was time to replenish his O2 supply. He pulled a spare bottle out of the webbing clipped to his EVA pack and attached it to the suit's nipple. The gauge on his HUD climbed back up to four hours and stopped. The next time he had to refill, he'd be on the station or in Marine custody.

One way or the other, he wouldn't be alone anymore, and that was a relief. He wondered what his mothers would have thought about all this, whether they would have approved of the choices he'd made, how he could arrange to have a dog for their children since Naomi wouldn't be able to live at the bottom of the gravity well. His attention wandered, and then his mind.

He awoke to a harsh buzzing sound, and for a few seconds slapped his hand at empty space trying to turn his alarm off. When he finally opened sleep-gummed eyes, he saw his HUD flashing a proximity warning. He'd somehow managed to fall asleep until the station was only a few kilometers away.

At that distance, it loomed like a gently curving wall of metallic blue, glowing with its own inner light. No radiation alarms were flashing, so whatever made it glow wasn't anything his suit thought was dangerous to him. The flight program Alex had written for him was spooling out on the HUD, counting down to the moment when he'd need to do his minute-long deceleration burn. Waving his hand around when he first woke up had put him into a gentle rotation, and the flight program was prompting him to allow it to make course corrections. Since he trusted Alex completely on matters of navigation, Holden authorized the suit to handle the descent automatically.

A few quick bursts of compressed gas later, he was facing out into the black, the sphere at his back. Then came a minute-long burn from the pack to slow him to a gentle half meter per second for landing. He kicked on his boot magnets, not knowing if they'd actually help or not—the sphere looked like metal, but that didn't mean much—and turned around.

The wall of glowing blue was less than five meters away. Holden bent his knees, bracing for the impact of hitting the surface, and hoping to absorb enough energy that he didn't just bounce off. The half meters ticked away, each second taking too long and passing too quickly. With only a meter before impact, he realized he'd been holding his breath and let out a long exhale.

"Here we go," he said to no one.

"Hey, boss?" Alex said in a burst of radio static.

Before Holden could reply, the surface of the sphere irised open and swallowed him up.

After Holden passed through the portal into the interior of the sphere he landed on the gently curving floor of a room shaped like an inverted dome. The walls were the metallic blue of the sphere's exterior. The surfaces were textured almost like moss, and tiny lights seemed to flicker in and out of existence like fireflies. His suit reported a thin atmosphere made mostly of benzene compounds and neon. The ceiling irised closed again, its flat unbroken surface showing no sign that there had ever been an opening.

Miller stood a few meters from where Holden landed, his rumpled gray suit and porkpie hat made both mundane and exotic by the alien setting. The lack of breathable air didn't seem to bother him at all.

Holden straightened his knees, and was surprised to feel something like gravity's resistance. He'd felt the weight of spin and of thrust, and the natural deep pull of a gravity well. The EVA pack was heavy on his back, but the quality of it was different. He almost felt like something was pushing down on him from above instead of the ground coming up to meet him.

"Hey, boss?" Alex repeated, a note of worry in his voice. Miller held up a hand in a don't-mind-me gesture. Wordless permission for Holden to answer.

"Receiving, Alex. Go ahead."

"The sphere just swallowed you," Alex said. "You okay in there?"

"Yep, five by five. But you called before I went in. What's up?"

"Just wanted to warn you that company's comin' pretty close on. You can expect them in about five minutes at best guess."

"Thanks for the report. I'm hoping Miller won't let them in."

"Miller?" Alex and Naomi said at the same time. She must have been monitoring the exchange.

"I'll call when I know more," Holden said with a grunt as he finished getting the EVA pack off. It fell to the floor with a thud.

That was odd.

Holden turned on the suit's external speakers and said, "Miller?" He heard the sound of his own voice echoing off of the walls and around the room. The atmosphere shouldn't have been thick enough for that.

"Hey," Miller replied, his voice unmuffled by the space suit, as if they were standing together on the deck of the *Roci*. He nodded slowly, his sad basset hound face twisting into something resembling a smile. "There are others coming. They yours?"

"Not mine, no," Holden replied. "That would be the skiff full of Martian recon marines that are coming to arrest me. Or maybe just shoot me. It's complicated."

"You've been making friends without me," Miller said, his tone sardonic and amused.

"How are you doing?" Holden asked. "You seem more coherent than usual."

Miller gave a short Belter shrug. "How do you mean?"

"Usually when we talk, it's like only half the signal's getting through."

The old detective's eyebrows rose in surprise.

"You've seen me before?"

"On and off for the last year or so."

"Well, that's pretty disturbing," Miller said. "If they're planning to shoot you, we'd better get going."

Miller seemed to flicker out of existence, reappearing at the edge of the mosslike walls. Holden followed, his body fighting with the nauseating sense of being weightless and heavy at the same time. When he drew close, he could see the spirals within the moss on the walls. He'd seen something like this before where the protomolecule had been, but this was lush by comparison. Complex and rich and deep. A vast ripple seemed to pass over the wall like a stone thrown in a pond, and despite having his own isolated air supply, Holden smelled something like orange peels and rain.

"Hey," Miller said.

"Sorry," Holden said. "What?"

"We better get going?" the dead man said. He gestured toward what looked like a fold of the strange moss, but when Holden came close, he saw a fissure behind it. The hole looked soft as flesh at the edges, and it glistened with something. It wept.

"Where are we going?"

"Deeper," Miller said. "Since we're here, there's something we should probably do. I have to tell you, though, you got a lot of balls."

"For what?" Holden said, and his hand slid against the wall. A layer of slime stuck to the fingers of his suit.

"Coming here."

"You told me to," Holden said. "You brought me. Julie brought me."

"I don't want to talk about what happened to Julie," the dead man said.

Holden followed him into the narrow tunnel. Its walls were slick and organic. It was like crawling through a deep cave or down the throat of a vast animal.

"You're definitely making more sense than usual."

"There are tools here," Miller said. "They're not...they're not right, but they're here at least."

"Does this mean you might still say something enigmatic and vanish in a puff of blue fireflies?"

"Probably."

Miller didn't expand on this, so Holden followed him for several dozen meters through the tunnel until it turned again and Miller led him into a much larger room.

"Uh, wow," he managed to say.

Because the floor of the first room and the tunnel that led out of it had both had a consistent "down," Holden had thought he was moving laterally just under the skin of the station. That couldn't have been right, because the room the tunnel opened into had a much higher ceiling than was possible if that were true. The

space stretched out from the tunnel into a cathedral-vast opening, hundreds of meters across. The walls slanted inward into a
domed ceiling that was twenty meters off the floor in the center.
Scattered across the room in seemingly random places were two-
meter-thick columns of something that looked like blue glass with
black, branching veins shooting through it. The columns pulsed
with light, and each pulse was accompanied by a subsonic throb
that Holden could feel in his bones and teeth. It felt like enormous
power, carefully restrained. A giant, whispering.

"Holy shit," he finally said when his breath came back. "We're
in a lot of trouble, aren't we?"

"Yeah," Miller said. "You should not have come."

Miller walked off across the room, and Holden hurried to catch
up. "Wait, what?" he said. "I thought you wanted me here!"

Miller walked around something that from a distance had
looked like a blue statue of an insect, but up close was a massive
confusion of metallic limbs and protrusions, like a construction
mech folded up on itself. Holden tried to guess at its purpose and
failed.

"Why would you think that?" Miller said as he walked. "You
don't know what's *in* here. Doors and corners. Never walk into a
crime scene until you know there's not someone there waiting to
put you down. You've got to clear the room first. But maybe we
got lucky. For now. Wouldn't recommend doing it again, though."

"I don't understand."

They came to a place in the floor that was covered in what
looked like cilia or plant stalks, gently rippling in a nonexistent
wind. Miller walked around it. Holden was careful to do the same.
As they passed, a swarm of blue fireflies burst out of the ground
cover and flew up to a vent in the ceiling where they vanished.

"So there was this unlicensed brothel down in sector 18. We
went thinking we'd be hauling fifteen, twenty people in. More,
maybe. Got there, and the place was stripped to the stone," Miller
said. "It wasn't that they'd gotten wind of us, though. The Loca
Greiga had heard about the place, sent their guys to clean it up.

Took about a week to find the bodies. According to forensics, they'd all been shot twice in the head pretty much while we were getting one last cup of coffee. If we'd been a little bit faster, we'd have walked in on it. Nothing says fucked like opening the door on a bunch of kids who thought they'd make a quick buck off the sex trade and having an organized kill squad there for the meet and greet instead."

"What has that got to do with anything?"

"This place is the same," Miller said. "There was supposed to be something. A lot of something. There was supposed to be... shit, I don't have the right words. An empire. A civilization. A home. More than a home, a *master*. Instead, there's a bunch of locked doors and the lights on a timer. I don't want you charging into the middle of that. You'll get your ass killed."

"What the hell do you mean?" Holden said. "You, or the proto-molecule, or Julie Mao, or whatever, *you* set this whole thing up. The job, the attack, all of it."

That stopped Miller. He turned around with a frown on his face. "Julie's dead, kid. *Miller's* dead. I'm just the machine for finding lost things."

"I don't understand," Holden said. "If you didn't do this, then who did?"

"See now, *that's* a good question, on several levels. Depending on what you mean by 'this.'" Miller's head lifted like a dog catching an unfamiliar scent on the wind. "Your friends are here. We should go." He moved off at a faster walk toward the far wall of the room.

"The marines," Holden said. "Could you stop them?"

"No," Miller said. "I don't protect anything. I can tell the station they're a threat. There'd be consequences, though."

Holden felt a punch of dread in his gut.

"That sounds bad."

"It wouldn't be good. Come on. If we're going to do this, we need to stay ahead of them."

The halls and passages widened and narrowed, meeting and

falling away from each other like blood vessels of some massive organism. Holden's suit lights seemed almost lost in the vast darkness, and the blue firefly flickers came in waves and vanished again. Along the way they passed more of the metallic blue insect-like constructs.

"What are these?" Holden asked, pointing to an especially large and dangerous-looking model as they passed it.

"Whatever they need to be," Miller replied without turning around.

"Oh, great, so we're back to inscrutable, are we?"

Miller spun around, a worried look on his face, and blinked out of existence. Holden turned.

Far across the huge room, a form was coming out of the tunnel. Holden had seen similar armor before. A Martian marine's powered armor was made of equal parts efficiency and threat.

There was no escaping it. Anyone in those suits could run him down without trying. Holden switched his suit to an open frequency.

"Hey! I'm right here. Let's talk about this," he said, then started to walk toward the group. As one, all eight marines raised their right arms and opened fire. Holden braced himself for death even while part of his mind knew that he shouldn't have time to brace for death. At the distance they were, the rounds from their high-velocity guns would be hitting in a fraction of a second. He'd be dead long before the sound of the shots reached him.

He heard the rapid and deafening buzzsaw sound of the guns firing, but nothing hit him.

A diffuse cloud of gray formed in front of the marines. When the firing finally stopped, the cloud drifted away toward the walls of the room. Bullets. They'd stopped centimeters from the gun barrels, and were now being drawn away just like the objects outside the station.

The marines broke into a fast run across the room, and Holden tried to scramble away. They were beautiful in their way, the lethal power of the suits harnessed by years of training to make their movements seem like a dance. Even without their weapons, they could tear him limb from limb. One punch from that armor would break all the bones he had and change his viscera to a thin slurry. His only chance was to outrun them, and he couldn't outrun them.

He almost didn't see the movement when it came. His focus was locked on the Martians, on the danger he knew. He didn't consciously notice that one of the insectlike things had started moving until the marines turned to it.

The alien thing's movements were fast and jagged, like a clockwork mechanism that only had full speed and full stop. It clicked toward the marines, jerking with each step, and it loomed larger than the tallest of them by almost half a meter.

They panicked in the way that people trained to expect violence panic. Two started firing, with the same results as before. Another marine's suit shifted something in its arm, and a larger barrel appeared. Holden scooted away from the confrontation. He was sure there was shouting going on in those armored suits, but it wasn't a frequency he had access to. The large barrel went white with muzzle flash, and a slow-arcing slug of metal the size of Holden's fist took to the strange air.

A grenade.

The ticking monster ignored it, stepping closer to the marines, and the grenade detonated at its insectile feet where it landed. The alien thing jerked back, its appendages flailing and dust falling from its severed limbs like a smoke of fungal spores. The complex carpet of moss glowed with orange embers where the blast had burned it.

And all around the marines, a dozen other alien statues came to life. They moved faster this time. Before the marines could begin to react, the one who'd launched the grenade was lifted gently up and ripped apart. Blood sprayed up into the air, hanging, Holden thought numbly, too long before it drifted back to the ground. The surviving marines began to fall back, their guns pointing to the alien creatures that were swarming the dead man. While

Holden watched, the marines retreated into the far tunnel, falling back. Regrouping.

The alien things fell on their own injured fellow, ripping and clawing, slaughtering it as if it were the enemy as much as the marines had been. And then, when it was gone, five of the monsters gathered together in the burned spot where the explosion had been. They shuddered, went still, shuddered again, and then from all five of them, a thin stream of opaque yellow goo spattered out onto the scar. Holden felt fascination and revulsion as the moss grabbed on to the stuff, regrowing like it had never been damaged. Like the attack hadn't even existed.

"Consequences," Miller said at his side. He sounded tired.

"Did they...did they just turn that poor bastard into spackle?"

"They did," Miller said. "He had it coming, though. That guy got happy with his grenade launcher? Just killed a lot of people."

"What? How?"

"He taught the station that something moving as fast as a good baseball pitch might still be a threat."

"Is it going to take revenge?"

"No," Miller said. "It's just going to protect itself. Reevaluate what counts as dangerous. Take control of all the ships that might be a problem."

"What does that even mean?"

"Means a really bad day for a whole lot of people. When it slows you down, it ain't gentle."

Holden felt a cold hand close on his heart.

"The *Roci*..."

A look of sorrow, even sympathy, passed over the detective's face.

"Maybe. I don't know," Miller said with a rueful shrug. "One way or the other, a whole lot of people just died."

Chapter Twenty-Three: Melba

Julie saved her. There was no other way to look at it.

True to style, Holden's proxy had given everything away. Cohen, discovered, told everything he knew, and put the image he'd stolen along with it. Melba had it on her hand terminal: a portrait of the young woman as ice sculpture. She hadn't known the soundman had taken the data when she'd met with him, but she should have guessed he would. The mistake was obvious in retrospect.

It ought to have ended the chase. The people in power should have seen it, shrugged, and thrown her out an airlock. Except that it came with its own misinterpretation. *Here*, Holden said, *is Julie Mao*, and that's what everyone saw. The differences that were obvious to her became invisible to others. They expected to see the protomolecule infiltrating and threatening and raising the dead, and so they saw it.

She did what she could to keep anyone from noticing the similarities. She'd met Cohen on Earth with a full g pulling down. With the *Thomas Prince* already close to the Ring's velocity limit, there was no acceleration thrust. Her cheeks looked fuller, her face round. She'd had her hair down then, so now she pulled it back in a braid. The image had no color, so she wore a little makeup to alter the shape of her eyes and lips. Doing something radical would only call attention, so she went small. She might not even have needed to do that.

Her schedule in the *Thomas Prince* was full. They were going to work her—work all of them—like dogs. She didn't care. The service gantries and accessways would be safe. No one who knew Clarissa Mao would be there. She would stay away from the public parts of the ship as much as she could, and more often than not she could get one of the other techs to grab a tube of something from the commissary and bring it to her.

In the off-shifts, she would build her arsenal.

Holden was beyond her reach for the time being. It was almost funny. She'd gone to so much effort to make him seem like an unrepentant megalomaniac, and then left to his own devices, he named himself de facto ambassador of the whole human race. Julie had fooled him too. With any luck at all, he'd die in a firefight or get killed by the protomolecule. Her work had narrowed to destroying the evidence of Holden's innocence. It wouldn't be hard.

The *Rocinante* had begun its life as an escort corvette on the battleship *Donnager*. It was well designed and well constructed, but also now years past its last upgrade. The weaknesses in its defense were simple: The cargo doors nearest the reactor had been damaged and repaired, and would almost certainly be weaker than the original. The forward airlock had been built with a software glitch vulnerable to hacking; real Martian naval ships would have been updated as a matter of course, but Holden might have been sloppy.

Her first hope was the airlock. A short-range access transmitter built for troubleshooting malfunctioning airlocks had found its way in among her things. If that failed, getting through the cargo door was harder. She hoped for something explosive, but the *Thomas Prince* took its munitions very seriously. The equipment manifests did include a half-suit exoskeleton mech. It would fit over her chest and arms—it wasn't designed for legs—and with a cutting torch to make the initial breach, it could probably bend the plating enough to let her through. It was also small and lightweight enough to carry, and her access card was a high enough grade for the system to let her take one away.

Once she was on, it would be simple. Kill everyone, overload the reactor, and blow the ship to atoms. With any luck at all, it would reignite suspicions about the bomb on the *Seung Un*. If she got out, fine. If she didn't, she didn't.

The only tricks now were getting there, and waiting like everyone else to hear what happened on the station.

She was dreaming when catastrophe came.

In it, she was walking through a field outside a schoolhouse. She knew that it was on fire, that she had to find a way in. She heard fire engine sirens, but their dark shapes never appeared in the sky. There were people trapped inside and she was supposed to get to them. To free them or to keep them from escaping or both.

She was on the roof, going down through a hole. Smoke billowed out around her, but she could still breathe because she'd been immunized against flames. She stretched down, fingertips brushing against low-g handholds. She realized someone was holding her wrist, supporting her as she strained in toward the darkness and fire. Ren. She couldn't look at him. Sorrow and guilt welled up in her like a flood and she collapsed into a blue-lit bar with crash couches where all the tables should have been. Couples ate dinner and talked and screwed in the dim around her. The man across from her was both Holden and her father. She tried to speak, to say that she didn't want to do this. The man took her by the shoulders, pressing her into the soft gel. She was afraid for a moment that he'd crawl on top of her, but he brought his fists down on her chest with a killing impact and she woke up to the sound of Klaxons and droplets of blood floating in the air.

The pain in her body was so profound and inexplicable that it didn't feel like pain; it was only the sense that something was wrong. She coughed, launching a spray of blood across the room. She thought that somehow she'd triggered her false glands in her sleep, that what was wrong was only her, but the ship alarms argued that it was something worse. She reached for her hand terminal, but it wasn't in its holder. She found it floating half a meter from the door, rotating in the air. A star-shaped fracture in the resin case showed where it had hit something hard enough to break. The network access displayed a bright red bar. No status. System down.

Melba pulled herself to the door and cycled it open.

The dead woman floating in the corridor had her arms out before her, her hair splayed around her like someone drowned. The left side of her face was oddly shaped, softer and rounder and bluer than it should have been. Her eyes were half open, the whites the bright red of burst vessels. Melba pushed past the corpse. Farther down the corridor, a sphere of blood the size of a soccer ball floated slowly toward the air intake with no sign where it had come from.

In the wider corridors toward the middle of the ship, things were worse. Bodies floated at every door, in every passageway. Everything not bolted down floated now by the walls, thrown toward the bow. The soft gray walls were covered with dents where hand terminals and tools and heads had struck them. The air smelled like blood and something else, deeper and more intimate.

Outside the commissary, three soldiers were using sealant foam to stick the dead to the walls, keeping them out of the way. In gravity, they would have been stacking bodies like cordwood.

"You all right?" one of them said. It took Melba a second to realize that the woman was speaking to her.

"I'm okay," Melba said. "What happened?"

"Who the fuck knows? You're one of the maintenance techs, yes?" the woman said sharply.

"I am," Melba said. "Melba Koh. Electrochemical."

"Well, you can get your ass to environmental, Koh," the woman said. "I'm guessing they need you there."

Melba nodded, the motion sending her spinning a little until the woman put out a hand to steady her.

She'd never been in a battle or at the scene of a natural disaster. The nearest had been a hurricane that hit São Paulo when she was eight, and her father had hidden the family in the corporate shelters until the flooding was gone. She'd seen more of that damage on the newsfeeds than in person. The *Thomas Prince* was a scene from hell. She passed knots of people working frantically, but the dead and dying were everywhere. Droplets of blood and chips of shattered plastic formed clouds where the eddies of the recyclers pushed them together. In zero g, blood pooled in the wounds and wouldn't clear. Inflammation was worse. Lungs filled with fluid more easily. However many had died already, more would. Soon. If she hadn't been in her crash couch, she'd have been thrown into a wall at six hundred meters per second, just like all the others. No, that couldn't be right. No one would have survived that.

She hadn't spent much of her time on environmental decks. Most of her work before with Stanni and Soledad had been with power routing. The air and water systems had technicians of their own, specialists at a higher pay grade than hers. The architecture of the rooms kept everything close without being as cramped as the *Cerisier*. She floated in with a sense of relief, as if reaching her goal accomplished something in itself. As if it gave her some measure of control.

The air smelled of ozone and burned hair. A young man, face covered with blue-black bruises, was stuck to the bulkhead with a rope and two electromagnets. He waved something similar to a broom with a massive mesh of fabric on the end like a gigantic fly swatter. Clearing blood from the air. His damaged face was impassive, shocked. A thickening layer of tears encased his eyes, blinding him.

"You! Who the hell are you?"

Melba turned. The new man wore a navy uniform. His right leg was in an inflatable pressure cast. The foot sticking out the end was a bluish purple, and his breath was labored in a way that made her think of pneumonia, of internal bleeding.

"Melba Koh. Civilian electrochemical tech off the *Cerisier*."

"Who do you answer to?"

"Mikelson's my group supervisor," she said, struggling to remember the man's name. She had only met him once, and he hadn't left much of an impression on her.

"My name's Nikos," the broken-legged man said. "You work for me now. Come on."

He pushed off more gracefully than should have been possible. She followed him a little too fast and had to grab a handhold to keep from running into his back. He led her through a long passageway into engineering. A huge array of thin metal and ceramic sheets stood at one wall, warnings in eight languages printed along its side. Scorch marks drew circles on the outermost plate, and the air stank of burnt plastic and something else. A hole two feet across had been punched through the center. A human body was still in it, held in place by shards of metal.

"You know what that is, Koh?"

"Air processing," she said.

"That's the primary atmosphere processing unit," he said as if she hadn't spoken. "And it's a big damn problem. Secondary processor's still on fire just at the moment, and the tertiary backups will get us through for about seven hours. Everyone on my team is busted or dead, so you're about to rebuild this one. Understand?"

I can't do that, she thought. *I'm not really an electrochemical technician. I don't know how to do this.*

"I'll...get my tools."

"Don't let me stop you," he said. "If I find someone can help out, I'll send 'em your way."

"That would be good," she said. "What about you? Are you all right? Can you help?"

"At a guess? Crushed pelvis, maybe something worse going on in my gut. Keep passing out a little," he said with a grin. "But I'm high as a kite on the emergency speed, and there's work. So hop to."

She pushed off. Her throat was tight, and she could feel her mind starting to shut down. Overstimulation. Shock. She made her way through the carnage and wreckage to the storage bay where the toolboxes from the *Cerisier* were. Her card unlocked them. One had shattered, the remains of a testing deck floating in the air, green ceramic shards and bits of gold wire. Ren was there, his coffin toolbox shifted in place despite the electromagnetic clamps. For a moment, the dream of the fire washed over her. She wondered if she might still be sleeping, the wave of death just part of the same blackness in her own brain. She put her hand on Ren's box, half expecting to feel him knocking back. A sudden vertigo washed through her, and the sense that she and the ship were falling, that it would land on her. Crush her. All the blood and all the terror, every dead person held in place to keep the corpses from floating, they all began here. Every sin she'd committed, backward and forward in time, had its center in the bones beneath her hand.

"Stop," she said. "Just stop."

She took her tool chest, the real one, and sped back to engineering and the shattered air processing controller. Nikos had found two other people, a man in civilian dress and an older woman in naval uniform.

"You're Koh?" the woman said. "Good, grab his legs."

Melba set her toolbox against the deck and activated the magnets, then pushed over to the hole in the atmosphere processor. The machine had been loosened from its housing, giving the body a little more room to move. Melba put her hands on the dead man's thighs, wadding the cloth of his trousers in her fists. She braced herself against the metal siding of the unit.

"Ready?" the man asked.

"Ready."

The woman counted down from three, and Melba pulled. For a long moment, she thought the corpse wouldn't come out, but then something tore, the vibrations of it transferring through to her hands. The body slid free.

"Score one for the good guys," Nikos said from across the bay. His face was developing an ashy gray tone. Like he was dying. She wished he would go to the medical bays, but they were probably swamped. He could die here doing his work, or there waiting for an open bay. "Clear him away. Got him out, we don't need him drifting back."

Melba nodded, took a firm grip, and pushed off on a trajectory that would land them on the far bulkhead. The back of the corpse's head had been crushed almost flat, but death had come so swiftly, there was very little blood. At the wall, she secured him with a spray of foam and held him for a moment while it set. The dead man's face was close to hers. She could see the whiskers he'd missed when he'd shaved. The brown of his empty eyes. She felt a sudden urge to kiss him and then pushed the impulse away, disgusted.

From his uniform, he'd been an officer. Lieutenant, maybe. The white identity card on the lanyard around his neck had a picture of him looking solemn. She took it in her fingers. Not lieutenant. Lieutenant commander. Lieutenant Commander Stepan Arsenau, who would never have come through the Ring if it weren't for her. Who wouldn't have died here. She tried to feel guilt, but there wasn't room for him inside of her. She had too much blood already.

She was reaching out to tuck his card back in place when the small voice in the back of her mind said, *I bet he could get an EVA pack with this.* Melba blinked. Her mind seemed to click back into focus, and she looked around her, the last wisps of dream or delirium leaving her mind. She had access to the equipment she needed. The ship was in chaos. This was it. This was the opportunity she'd been waiting for. She plucked the card off its lanyard and slipped it in her pocket, then looked around nervously.

No one had noticed.

She licked her lips.

"I'm going to need something to crack this," the young man was saying. "The bolt head's sheared round. I can't get it out."

The older woman swore and turned to her.

"Got anything that'll do the trick?"

"Not here," Melba said. "I have an idea where I could get something to drill it out, though."

"Move fast. We don't want this place gettin' stuffy."

"Okay. You guys do what you can. I'll be right back," Melba lied.

Chapter Twenty-Four: Anna

Eschatology had always been Anna's least favorite study of theology. When asked about Armageddon, she'd tell her parishioners that God Himself had been pretty circumspect on the topic, so it didn't do much good to worry about it. Have faith that God will do what's best, and avoiding His vengeance against the wicked should be the least compelling reason for worship.

But the truth was that she'd always had a deeply held disagreement with most futurist and millennialist interpretations. Not the theology itself, necessarily, since their guess at what the end times prophecies really meant was as good as anyone else's. Her disagreement was primarily with the level of glee over the destruction of the wicked that sometimes crept into the teachings. This was especially true in some millennialist sects that filled their literature with paintings of Armageddon. Pictures of terrified people running away from some formless fiery doom that burned their world down behind them, while smug worshipers—of the correct religion, of course—watched from safety as God got with the smiting. Anna couldn't understand how anyone could see such a depiction as anything but tragic.

She wished she could show them the *Thomas Prince*.

She'd been reading when it happened. Her hand terminal had been propped on her chest with a pillow behind it, her hands behind her head. A three-tone alarm had sounded a high-g alert, but it was late to the party. She was already being mashed into her crash couch so hard that she could feel the plastic of the base right through twenty centimeters of impact gel. It seemed to last forever, but it was probably just a few seconds. Her hand terminal had skidded down her chest, suddenly heavier than Nami the last time she'd picked her daughter up. It left a black-and-blue trail of bruises up her breastbone and slammed into her chin hard enough to split the skin. The pillow mashed into her abdomen like a ten-kilo sandbag, filling her mouth with the taste of stomach acid.

But worst of all was the pain in her shoulders. Both arms had snapped back flat against the bed, temporarily dislocating them. When the endless seconds of deceleration were over, both joints popped back into place with a pain even worse than when they'd come out. The gel of the couch, stressed beyond its design specifications, hadn't gripped her the way it was meant to. Instead, it rebounded back into its prior shape and launched her in slow motion toward the ceiling of her cabin. Trying to put her hands in front of her sent bolts of agony through her shoulders, so she drifted up and hit the ceiling with her face. Her chin left a smear of blood on the fabric-covered foam.

Anna was a gentle person. She'd never in her life been in a fight. She'd never been in a major accident. The worst pain she'd ever felt before was childbirth, and the endorphins that had followed had mostly erased it from her memory. To suddenly be so hurt in so many different places at once left her dazed and with a sort of directionless anger. It wasn't fair that a person could be hurt so much. She wanted to yell at the crash couch that had betrayed her by letting this happen, and she wanted to punch the ceiling for hitting her in the face, even though she'd never thrown a punch in her life and could barely move her arms.

When she could finally move without feeling light-headed she went looking for help and found that the corridor outside her room was worse.

Just a few meters from her door, a young man had been crushed. He looked as though a malevolent giant had stomped on him and then ground him under its heel. The boy was not only smashed, but torn and twisted in ways that barely left him recognizable as a human. His blood splashed the floor and walls and drifted around his corpse in red balls like grisly Christmas ornaments.

Anna yelled for help. Someone yelled back in a voice filled with liquid and pain. Someone from farther down the corridor. Anna carefully pushed off the doorjamb of her room and drifted toward the voice. Two rooms down, another man was half in and half out of his crash couch. He must have been in the process of getting out of bed when the deceleration happened, and everything from his pelvis down was twisted and broken. His upper torso still lay on the bed, arms waving feebly at her, his face a mask of pain.

"Help me," he said, and then coughed up a glob of blood and mucus that drifted away in a red-and-green ball.

Anna drifted up high enough to push the comm panel on the wall without using her shoulder. It was dead. All the lights were the ones she'd been told came on in emergency power failures. Nothing else seemed to be working.

"Help me," the man said again. His voice was weaker and filled with even more of a liquid rasp. Anna recognized him as Alonzo Guzman, a famous poet from the UN's South American region. A favorite of the secretary-general, someone had told her.

"I will," Anna said, not even trying to stop the tears that suddenly blinded her. She wiped her eyes on her shoulder and said, "Let me find someone. I've hurt my arms, but I'll find someone."

The man began weeping softly. Anna pushed back into the corridor with her toes, drifting past the carnage to find someone who wasn't hurt.

This was the part the millennialists never put in their paintings. They loved scenes of righteous Godly vengeance on sinful mankind. They loved to show God's chosen people safe from harm, watching with happy faces as they were proved right to the world. But they never showed the aftermath. They never showed weeping humans, crushed and dying in pools of their own fluids. Young men smashed into piles of red flesh. A young woman cut in half because she was passing through a hatchway when catastrophe hit.

This was Armageddon. This is what it looked like. Blood and torn flesh and cries for help.

Anna reached an intersection of corridors and ran out of strength. Her body hurt too badly to continue. And in all four directions, the corridor floors and walls were covered with the aftermath of violent death. It was too much. Anna drifted in the empty space for a few minutes, and then she gently floated to the wall and stuck to it. Movement. The ship was moving now. Very slow, but enough to push her to the wall. She pushed away from it and floated again. Not still accelerating, then.

She recognized that her interest in the relative movements of the ship was just her mind trying to find a distraction from the scene around her, and started crying again. The idea that she might never come home from this trip crashed in on her. For the first time since coming to the Ring, she saw a future in which she never held Nami again. Never smelled her hair. Never kissed Nono, or climbed into a warm bed beside her and held her close. The pain of those things being ripped away from her was worse than anything physical she'd suffered. She didn't wipe away the tears that came, and they blinded her. That was fine. There was nothing here she wanted to see.

When something grabbed her from behind and spun her around, she tensed, waiting for some new horror to reveal itself.

It was Tilly.

"Oh, thank God," the woman said, hugging Anna tight enough to send new waves of pain through her shoulders. "I went to your room and there was blood on the walls and you weren't there and someone was dead right outside your door..."

Unable to hug back, Anna just put her cheek against Tilly's for a moment. Tilly pushed her out to arm's length, but didn't let go. "Are you okay?" She was looking at the gash on Anna's chin.

"My face is fine. Just a little cut. But my arms are hurt. I can barely move them. We need to get help. Alonzo Guzman's in his room, and he's hurt. Really hurt. Do you know what happened?"

"I haven't met anyone yet who knows," Tilly said, rotating Anna first one way, then the other, looking her over critically. "Move your hands. Okay. Bend your elbows." She felt Anna's shoulders. "They're not dislocated."

"I think they were for a second," Anna said after the gasp of pain Tilly's touch brought. "And everything else hurts. But we have to hurry."

Tilly nodded and pulled a red-and-white backpack off one shoulder. When she opened it, it was filled with dozens of plastic packages with tiny black text on them. Tilly pulled a few out, read them, put them back. After several tries, she stripped the packaging off of three small injection ampules.

"What is that?" Anna said, but Tilly just jabbed her with all three in answer.

Anna felt a rush of euphoria wash over her. Her shoulders stopped hurting. *Everything* stopped hurting. Even her fear about never seeing her family again seemed a distant and minor problem.

"I was sleeping when it happened," Tilly said, tossing the empty ampules into the first aid pack. "But I woke up feeling like a forklift had run over me. I think my ribs were popped out of place. I could barely breathe. So I dug up this pack from the emergency closet in my room."

"I didn't think to look there," Anna said, surprised she hadn't. She had a vague memory of being disoriented by pain, but now she felt *great*. Better than ever before. And sharp. Hyper-aware. Stupid not to think of the emergency supplies. This being, after all, an emergency. She wanted to slap herself on the forehead for being so stupid. Tilly was holding her arms again. Why was she doing that? They had work to do. They had to find the medics and send them after the poet.

"Hey, kiddo," Tilly said, "takes a second for that first rush to ease down a bit. I spent a full minute trying to resuscitate a pile of red paste before I realized how wired I was."

"What is this?" Anna asked, moving her head from side to side, which made the edges of Tilly's face blurry.

Tilly shrugged. "Military-grade amphetamines and painkillers, I'm guessing. I gave you an anti-inflammatory too. Because what the hell."

"Are you a doctor?" Anna asked, marveling at how *smart* Tilly was.

"No, but I can read the directions on the package."

"Okay." Anna nodded, her face serious. "Okay."

"Let's go find someone who knows what's going on," Tilly said, pulling Anna down the corridor with her.

"And after, I need to find my people," Anna said, letting herself be pulled.

"I may have given you too much. Nono and Nami are at home, in Moscow."

"No, my *people*. My congregation. Chris and that other guy and the marine. She's angry, but I think I can talk to her. I need to find them."

"Yeah," Tilly said. "May have overdosed you a bit. But we'll find them. Let's find help first."

Anna thought of the poet and felt her tears threatening to return. If she was sad, maybe the initial rush of the drugs was wearing off a little. She found herself regretting that for a moment.

Tilly stopped at a printed deck map on the wall. It was right next to a black and unresponsive network panel. Of course military ships would have both, Anna thought. They were built with the expectation that things would stop working when the ship got shot. That thought made Anna sad too. Some distant part of her consciousness recognized the drug-fueled emotional roller coaster she was on, but was powerless to do anything about. She started weeping again.

"Security station." Tilly tapped on a spot on the map, then yanked Anna down the corridor after her. They made two turns and wound up at a small room filled with people, guns, and computers that seemed to still be working. A middle-aged man with salt-and-pepper hair and a grim expression on his face pointedly ignored them. The other four people in the room were younger, but equally uninterested in their arrival.

"Get 35C open first," the older man said to the two young men floating to his left. He pointed at something on a map. "There were a dozen civvies in there."

"EMT?" one of the young men asked.

"Don't have them to spare, and that galley doesn't have crash couches. Everyone in there is pasta sauce, but the El Tee says look anyway."

"Roger that," the young man replied, and he and his partner pushed out of the room past Anna and Tilly, barely glancing at them as they went.

"You two do a corridor sweep," the older man said to the other two young sailors in the room. "Tags if you can find them, pictures and swabs if you can't. Everything sent to OPCOM on red two one, got me?"

"Aye-aye," one of them said, and they floated out of the room.

"The man in 295 needs help," Anna said to the security officer. "He's hurt badly. He's a poet."

He tapped something onto his desk terminal and said, "Okay, he's in the queue. EMTs will get there as soon as they can. We're setting up a temporary emergency area in the officers' mess. I suggest you two ladies get there double time."

"What happened?" Tilly asked, and gripped a handhold on the wall like she meant to stay a while. Anna grabbed on to the nearest thing she could find, which turned out to be a rack of weapons.

The security officer looked Tilly up and down once, and seemed to come to the conclusion that giving her what she wanted was the easiest solution. "Hell if I know. We decelerated to a dead stop in just a shade under five seconds. The damage and injuries are all high-g trauma. Whatever grabbed us only grabbed the skin of the ship and didn't give a shit about the stuff inside."

"So the slow zone changed?" Tilly was asking. Anna looked over the guns in the rack, her emotions more under control, but her mind was still racing. The rack was full of pistols of various kinds. Big blocky ones with large barrels and fat magazines. Smaller ones that looked like the kind you saw on cop shows. And in a special rack all their own, tasers like the one she'd had on Europa. Well, not really like it. These were military models. Gray and sleek and efficient-looking, with a much bigger power pack than hers. In spite of their non-lethal purpose, they managed to appear dangerous. Her old taser at home had looked like a small hair dryer.

"Don't touch those," the security officer said. Anna hadn't even realized she was reaching for one until he said it.

"That could mean a damn lot of casualties," Tilly said. Anna had the feeling she was reentering the conversation after having missed a lot of it.

"Hundreds on the *Prince*," the security officer said. "And we weren't going anywhere near the old speed limit. Some of the ships were. We get no broadcasts from those now."

Anna looked at the various terminals working in the office around her. Damage reports and security feeds and orders. Anna couldn't understand much of them. They used a lot of acronyms and numbers for things. Military jargon. One small monitor was displaying pictures of people. Anna recognized James Holden in one, then another version of him with a patchy beard. Wanted posters? But she didn't recognize any of the other people until the sculpture of the girl that Naomi, Holden's second-in-command, had blamed for the attack.

"Maybe it was the space girl," Anna said before she'd realized she was going to. She still felt stoned, and suppressed an urge to giggle.

The security officer and Tilly were both staring at her.

Anna pointed at the screen. "Julie Mao, the girl from Eros. The one the *Rocinante* blamed. Maybe she did this."

Both the security officer and Tilly turned to look at the screen. A few seconds later the image of Julie the space girl disappeared and was replaced by someone Anna didn't recognize.

"Someone's going to get James Holden in an interrogation room for a few hours, and then we'll have a much better idea of where to put the blame."

Tilly just laughed.

"Is that who they blamed?" she said when she'd finished. "That isn't Julie Mao. And there's no way Claire's out here."

"Claire?" Anna and the officer said at the same time.

"That's Claire. Clarissa Mao. Julie's little sister. She's living on Luna with her mother, last I heard. But that's definitely not Julie."

"Are you sure?" Anna said. "Because the executive officer from the *Rocinante* said—"

"I dandled both those girls on my knee back in the day. The Maos used to be regular guests at our house in Baja. Brought the kids out during the summers to swim and eat fish tacos. And that one is Claire, not Julie."

"Oh," said Anna as her drug-enhanced mind ran out the entire plot. The angry girl she'd seen in the galley, the explosion of the UN ship, the ridiculous message from Holden's ship, followed by the protestations of innocence. "It was her. She blew up the ship."

"Which ship?" the officer asked.

"The UN ship that blew up. The one that made the Belter ship shoot at Holden. And then we all went through the Ring and she's *here*! She's on this ship right now! I saw her in the galley and I *knew* there was something wrong with her. She scared me but I should have said something but I didn't because why would I?"

Tilly and the security man were both staring at her. She could feel her mind running away with her, and her mouth seemed to be working all on its own. They were looking at her like she'd gone insane.

"She's here," Anna said, clamping her mouth shut with an effort.

"Claire?" Tilly asked with a frown.

"I saw her in the galley. She threatened me. She was on this ship."

The security man scowled and tapped something on his terminal, swore, then tapped something else. "I'll be a sonofabitch. Shipwide face recognition says we've got a match in hangar B right now."

"You have to go arrest her," Anna shouted.

"Hangar B is a designated emergency area," the officer said. "She's probably there with the other survivors and broken in five different places. If it's even her. Shitty reproduction like that makes for a lot of false positives."

"You have software that could have found her at any time?" Tilly asked in disbelief. "You didn't *check*?"

"Ma'am, we don't ask 'how high' when James fucking Holden says jump," the officer growled back.

"There's an airlock in there," Anna said, stabbing her hand at the display. "She could leave. She could go anywhere."

"Like *where*?" the officer replied.

As if on cue, a green airlock cycling alarm appeared on the display.

"We have to go get her," Anna said, pulling on Tilly's arm.

"You have to go to the officers' mess," the security man said. "I'll send people to pick her up for questioning as soon as we stop bleeding. Don't worry about it. We've got plenty enough to sort out now. That one'll wait."

"But—"

A young man floated into the room. The left half of his face was covered in blood.

"Need the EMTs to six-alpha, sir. We've got ten civvies."

"I'll see who I can pry free," the officer said. "Do we know anything about the condition of the injured?"

"Bones sticking out, but they're not dead."

Anna pulled Tilly into the corridor.

"We can't wait. She's dangerous. She's already killed people when she blew up the other ship."

"You're stoned," Tilly said, pulling her arm free and drifting across the corridor to bump into the wall. "You're not acting rationally. What are you going to do even if Claire Mao *is* on this ship and has become some sort of terrorist? She blew up a ship. Gonna hit her with your Bible?"

Anna pulled the taser halfway out of her pocket. Tilly sucked in a whistling breath through her teeth. "You *stole* that? Are you insane?" she asked in a loud whisper.

"I'm going to go find her," Anna replied, the drugs singing in her blood having focused down to a fine point. She felt like if she could stop this Claire person, she could save herself from losing her family forever. She recognized this idea as utterly irrational, and gave in to its power anyway. "I have to talk to her."

"You're going to get killed," Tilly said. She looked like she might start crying. "You told security. You did your part. Let it go. You're a minister, not a cop."

"I'll need an EVA pack. Do you know where they keep those? Are they near the airlocks?"

"You're insane," Tilly said. "I can't be part of this."

"It's okay," Anna said. "I'll be back."

Chapter Twenty-Five: Holden

Naomi," Holden said again. "Come in. Please. Please respond."

The silent radio felt like a threat. Miller had paused, his face bleak and apologetic. Holden wondered how many other people had looked at that exact expression on Miller's face. It seemed designed to go with words like *There's been an accident* and *The DNA matches your son's*. Holden could feel his hands trembling. It didn't matter.

"*Rocinante*. Naomi, come *in*."

"Doesn't mean anything," Miller said. "She could be just fine, but the comm array went down. Or maybe she's busy fixing something."

"Or maybe she's dying by centimeters," Holden said. "I've got to go. I have to get back to her."

Miller shook his head.

"It's a longer trip back out than it was getting here. You can't go as fast anymore. By the time you get back, she'll have figured out whatever needed figuring."

Or she'll be dead, Miller didn't say. Holden wondered what it meant that the protomolecule could put Miller on its hand like a puppet and the detective could still be thoughtful enough to leave out the possibility that everyone on the *Roci* was gone.

"I have to try."

Miller sighed. For a moment, his pupils flickered blue, like there were tiny bathypelagic fish swimming in the deep trenches of his eyeballs.

"You want to help her? You want to help all of them? Come with me. Now. You run back home, we won't get to find out what happened. And you may not get the chance to come back here. Plus, you can bet your friends are regrouping back there, and they can still gently rip your arms off if they catch you."

Holden felt like there were two versions of himself pulling at his mind. Naomi might be hurt. Might be dead. Alex and Amos too. He had to be there for them. But there was also a small, quiet part of himself that knew Miller was right. It was too late.

"You can tell the station that there are people on those ships," he said. "You can ask it to help them."

"I can tell a rock that it ought to be secretary-general. Doesn't mean it's gonna listen. All this?" Miller waved his hands at the dark walls. "It's dumb. Utilitarian. No creativity or complex analysis."

"Really?" Holden said, his curiosity peeking through the panic and anger and fear. "Why not?"

"Some things, it's better if they're predictable. No one wants the station coming up with its own bad ideas. We should hurry."

"Where are we going?" Holden said, pausing for a few deep breaths. He'd been at low g for too long without taking the time for exercise. His cardio had suffered. The dangers of growing rich and lazy.

"I'm going to need you to do something for me," Miller replied. "I need access to the...shit, I don't know. Call 'em records."

Holden finished his panting, then straightened and nodded for Miller to resume their walk. As they moved down the gently sloping corridor he said, "Aren't you already plugged in?"

"I'm aware. The station is in lockdown, and they didn't exactly give me the root password. I need you to open it up for me."

"Not sure what I can do that you can't," Holden said. "Other than be a charming dinner guest."

Miller stopped at another seeming dead end, touched the wall, and a portal irised open. He gestured Holden through, then followed and closed the door behind them. They were in another large chamber, vaguely octagonal and easily fifty meters long on each face. More of the insectile mechs littered the space, but the glass pillars were not in evidence. Instead, at the center of the chamber stood a massive construct of glowing blue metal. It was octagonal, a smaller version of the dimensions of the room, but only a few meters wide on each face. It didn't glow any brighter than the rest of the room, but Holden could feel something coming off of it, an almost physical pressure that made walking toward it difficult. His suit said that the atmosphere had changed, that it was rich with complex organic chemicals and nitrogen.

"Sometimes, having a body at all means you've got a certain level of status. If you aren't pretty damn trusted, you don't get to walk around in the fallen world."

"The fallen world?"

Miller shuddered and leaned his hand out against the wall. It was a profoundly human gesture of distress. The glowing moss of the wall didn't respond at all. Miller's lips were beginning to turn black.

"Fallen world. The substrate. *Matter.*"

"Are you all right?" Holden asked.

Miller nodded, but he looked like he was about to vomit. "There's time's I start knowing things that are too big for my head. It's better in here, but there're going to be some questions that don't fit in me. Just thinking with all this crap connected to the back of my head is a full contact sport, and if I get too much,

I'm pretty sure they'll...ah...call it reboot me. I mean, sure, consciousness is an illusion and blah blah blah, but I'd rather not go there if we can help it. I don't know how much the next one would remember."

Holden stopped walking, then turned and gave Miller a hard shove. Both of them staggered backward. "You seem pretty real to me."

Miller held up his finger. "Seem. Good verb. You ever wondered why I leave as soon as anyone else shows up?"

"I'm special?"

"Yeah, I wouldn't go that far."

"Fine," Holden said. "I'll bite. Why doesn't anyone else see you?"

"I'm not sure we've got time for this, but..." Miller took off his hat and scratched his head. "So your brain has a hundred billion brain cells and about five hundred trillion synapses."

"Will this be on the test?"

"Don't be an asshole," Miller said conversationally, and put his hat back on. "And that shit is custom grown. No two brains are exactly alike. Guess how much processing power it takes to really model even one human brain? More than every human computer ever built put together, and that's before we even start getting to the crap that goes on inside the cells."

"Okay."

"Now picture those synapses as buttons on a keyboard. Five hundred trillion buttons. And say that a brain looking at something and thinking, 'That's a flower' punches a couple billion of those keys in just the right pattern. Except it ain't near that easy. It isn't just a flower, it's a pile of associations. Smells, the way a stem feels in your fingers, the flower you gave your mom once, the flower you gave your girl. A flower you stepped on by accident and it made you sad. And being sad brings on a whole pile of other associations."

"I get it," Holden said, holding up his hands in surrender. "It's complicated."

"Now picture you need to push exactly the right buttons to make someone think of a person, hear them speaking, remember the clothes they wore and the way they smelled and how they would sometimes take off their hat to scratch their head."

"Wait," Holden said. "Are there bits of protomolecule in my brain?"

"Not exactly. You may have noticed I'm non-local."

"What the hell does that even mean?"

"Well," Miller said. "Now you're asking me to explain microwaves to a monkey."

"That's a metaphor I've never actually spoken aloud. If you're aiming for not creeping me the hell out, you need more practice."

"So, yeah. The most complex simulation in the history of your solar system is running right now so that we can pretend I'm here in the same room with you. The correct response is being flattered. Also, doing what the fuck I need you to do."

"That would be?"

"Touching that big thing in the middle of the room."

Holden looked at the construct again, felt the almost subliminal pressure coming off of it. "Why?"

"Because," said Miller, lecturing to a stupid child. "The place is in lockdown. It's not accepting remote connections without a level of authorization I don't have."

"And I do?"

"You're not making a remote connection. You're actually here. In the substrate. In some quarters, that's kind of a big deal."

"But I just walked in here."

"You had some help. I calmed some of the security down to get you this far."

"So you let the marines in too?"

"Unlocked is unlocked. C'mon."

The closer Holden got to the octagon, the harder it was to approach. It wasn't just fear, though the dread swam at the back of his throat and all down his spine. It was physically difficult, like pushing against a magnetic field.

The shape was chipped at the edges, marked with hair-thin lines in patterns that might have been ideograms or patterns of fungal growth or both. He reached out his hand, and his teeth itched.

"What will happen?" he asked.

"How much do you know about quantum mechanics?"

"How much do you?" Holden replied.

"A lot, turns out," Miller said with a lopsided grin. "Do now, anyway."

"I'm not going to burst into flames or something, right?"

Miller gave a small Belter shrug with his hands. "Don't think so. I'm not up on all the defense systems. But I don't *think* so."

"So," Holden said. "*Maybe?*"

"Yeah."

"Okay." Holden sighed and started to reach for the surface. He paused. "You didn't really answer the question, you know."

"You're stalling," Miller said. And then, "Which question was that?"

"I get why no one else sees you. But the real question is 'why me' at all? I mean, okay, you're screwing with my brain and that's hard work, and if there's other people for me to interact with it's too hard and all like that. But why *me*? Why not Naomi or the UN secretary-general or something?"

Miller nodded, understanding the question. He frowned, sighed.

"Miller kind of liked you. Thought you were a decent guy."

"That's it?"

"You need more?"

Holden placed his palm flat against the closest surface. He didn't burst into flames. Through the gloves of his EVA suit, he felt a short electric tingle and then nothing, because he was floating in space. He tried to scream and failed.

Sorry, a voice said in his head. It sounded like Miller. *Didn't mean to drag you in here. Just try and relax, all right?*

Holden tried to nod, but failed at that too. He didn't have a head.

His sense of his own body had changed, shifted, expanded past anything he'd imagined before. The simple extent of it was numbing. He felt the stars within him, the vast expanses of space contained by him. With a thought, he could pull his attention to a sun surrounded by unfamiliar planets like he was attending to his finger or the back of his neck. The lights all tasted different, smelled different. He wanted to close his eyes against the flood of sensation, but he couldn't. He didn't have anything so simple as eyes. He had become immeasurably large, and rich, and strange. Thousands of voices, millions, billions, lifted in chorus and he was their song. And at his center, a place where all the threads of his being came together. He recognized the station not by how it looked, but by the deep throb of its heartbeat. The power of a million suns contained, channeled. Here was the nexus that sat between the worlds, the miracle of knowledge and power that gave him heaven. His Babel.

And a star went out.

It wasn't especially unique. It wasn't beautiful. A few voices out of quadrillions went silent, and if the great chorus of his being was lessened by them, it wasn't perceptible. Still, a ripple passed through him. The colors of his consciousness swirled and darkened. Concern, curiosity, alarm. Even delight. Something new had happened for the first time in millennia.

Another star flickered and failed. Another few voices went silent. Now, slowly and instantly both, everything changed. He felt the great debate raging in him as a fever, an illness. He had been beyond anything like a threat for so long that all the reflexes of survival had weakened, atrophied. Holden felt a fear that he knew belonged to him—the man trapped within the machine—because his larger self couldn't remember to feel it. The vast parliament swirled, thoughts and opinions, analysis and poetry blending together and breaking apart. It was beautiful as sunlight on oil, and terrifying.

Three suns failed, and now Holden felt himself growing smaller. It was still very little, almost nothing. A white spot on the back of his hand, a sore that wouldn't heal. The plague was still only a symptom, but it was one his vast self couldn't ignore.

From the station at his core, he reached out into the places he had been, the darkened systems that were lost to him, and he reached out through the gates with fire. The fallen stars, mere matter now, empty and dead, bloated. Filled their systems in a rage of radiation and heat, sheared the electrons from every atom, and detonated. Their final deaths echoed, and Holden felt a sense of mourning and of peace. The cancer had struck, and been burned away. The loss of the minds that had been would never be redeemed. Mortality had returned from exile, but it had been cleansed with fire.

A hundred stars failed.

What had been a song became a shriek. Holden felt his body shifting against itself, furious as a swarm of bees trapped and dying. In despair, the hundred suns were burned away, the station hurling destruction through the gates as fast as the darkness appeared, but the growing shadow could not be stopped. All through his flesh, stars were going out, voices were falling into silence. Death rode the vacuum, faster than light and implacable.

He felt the decision like a seed crystal giving form to the chaos around it, solid, hard, resolute. Desperation, mourning, and a million farewells, one to the other. The word *quarantine* came to him, and with the logic of dreams, it carried an unsupportable weight of horror. But within it, like the last voice in Pandora's box, the promise of reunion. One day, when the solution was found, everything that had been lost would be regained. The gates reopened. The vast mind restored.

The moment of dissolution came, sudden and expected, and Holden blew apart.

He was in darkness. Empty and tiny and lost, waiting for the promise to be fulfilled, waiting for the silent chorus to whisper again that Armageddon had been stopped, that all was not lost. And the silence reigned.

Huh, Miller thought at him. *That was weird.*

Like being pulled backward through an infinitely long tunnel of light, Holden was returned to his body. For one vertiginous moment he felt too small, like the tiny wrapping of skin and meat would explode trying to contain him.

Then he just felt tired, and sat down on the floor with a thump.

"Okay," Miller said, rubbing his cheek with an open palm. "I guess that's a start. Sort of explains everything, sort of nothing. Pain in the ass."

Holden flopped onto his back. He felt like someone had run him through a shredder and then badly welded him back together. Trying to remember what it felt like to be the size of a galaxy gave him a splitting headache, so he stopped.

"Tell me everything it explains," he said when he could remember how to speak. Being forced to move moist flaps of meat in order to form the words felt sensual and obscene.

"They quarantined the systems. Shut down the network to stop whatever was capping the locals."

"So, behind each of those gates is a solar system full of whatever made the protomolecule?"

Miller laughed. Something in the sound of it sent a shiver down Holden's spine. "That seems pretty fucking unlikely."

"Why?"

"This station has been waiting for the all-clear signal to open the network back up for about two billion years. If they'd found a solve, they wouldn't still be waiting. Whatever it was, I think it got them all."

"All of them but you," Holden said.

"Nah, kid. I'm one of them like the *Rocinante* is one of you. The *Roci*'s smart for a machine. It knows a lot about you. It could probably gin up a rough simulation of you if someone told it to. Those things? The ones you felt like? Compared to them, I'm a fancy kind of hand terminal."

"And the nothing it explains," Holden said. "You mean what killed them."

"Well, if we're gonna be fair, it's not really nothing," Miller said, crossing his arms. "We know it ate a galaxy spanning hive consciousness like it was popcorn, so that's something. And we know it survived a sterilization that was a couple hundred solar systems wide."

Holden had a powerfully vivid memory of watching the station hurl fire through the ring gates, of the stars on the other side blowing up like balloons, of the gates themselves abandoned to the fire and disappearing. Even just the echo of it nearly blinded him with remembered pain. "Seriously, did they blow up those *stars* to stop it?"

Holden's image of Miller patted the column at the center of the room, though he knew now that Miller wasn't really touching it. Something was pressing the right buttons on his synaptic keyboard to make him think Miller was.

"Yup. Autoclaved the whole joint. Fed a bunch of extra energy in and popped 'em like balloons."

"They can't still do that, though, right? I mean, if the things that ran this are all gone, no one to pull that trigger. It won't do that to us."

Miller's grim smile chilled Holden's blood. "I keep telling you. This station is in war mode, kid. It's playing for keeps."

"Is there a way we can make it feel better about things?"

"Sure. Now I'm in here, I can take off the lockdown," Miller said, "but you're going to have to—"

Miller vanished.

"To what?" Holden shouted. "I'm going to have to *what*?"

From behind came an electronically amplified voice. "James Holden, by authority of the Martian Congressional Republic, you are placed under arrest. Get down on your knees and place your hands on your head. Any attempt to resist will be met with lethal response."

Holden did as he was told, but turned his head to look behind. Seven marines in recon armor had come into the room. They weren't bothering to point their guns at him, but Holden knew they could catch him and tear him to pieces just using the strength of their suits.

"Guys, seriously, you couldn't have given me five more minutes?"

Chapter Twenty-Six: Bull

Voices. Light. A sense of wrongness deep in places he couldn't identify. Bull tried to grit his teeth and found his jaw already clenched hard enough to ache. Someone cried out, but he didn't know where from.

The light caught his attention. Simple white LED with a sanded backsplash to diffuse it. An emergency light. The kind that came on when power was down. It hurt to look at, but he did, using it to focus. If he could make that make sense, everything else would come. A chiming alarm kept tugging at his attention, coming from outside. In the corridor. Bull's mind tried to slide that way, going into the corridor, out into the wide, formless chaos, and he pulled it back to the light. It was like trying to wake up except he was already awake.

Slowly, he recognized the alarm as something he'd hear in the medical bay. He was in the medical bay, strapped onto a bed. The tugging sensation at his arm was a forced IV. With a moment of nauseating vertigo, his perception of the world shifted—he wasn't standing, he was lying down. Meaningless distinctions without gravity, but human brains couldn't seem to help trying to assert direction on the directionless. His neck ached. His head ached. Something else felt wrong.

There were other people in the bay. Men and women on every bed, most with their eyes closed. A new alarm sounded, the woman in the bay across from him losing blood pressure. Crashing. Dying. He shouted, and a man in a nurse's uniform came floating past. He adjusted something on her bed's control board, then pushed off and away. Bull tried to grab him as he went by, but he couldn't.

He'd been in his office. Serge had already gone for the night. A few minor incidents were piled up from the day, the constant friction of a large, poorly disciplined crew. Like everyone else, he'd been waiting to see whether Holden and the Martians came back out of the station. Or if something else would. The fear had made sleep unlikely. He started watching the presentation that the *Rocinante* had sent, James Holden looking surprisingly young and charming saying, *This is what we're calling the slow zone.* He remembered noticing that everyone had accepted Holden's name for the place, and wondered whether it was just that the man had gotten there first or if there was something about charisma that translated across the void.

And then he'd been here. Someone had attacked, then. A torpedo had gotten past their defenses or else sabotage. Maybe the whole damn ship was just coming apart.

There was a comm interface on the bed. He pulled it over, logged in, and used his security override to open its range to the full ship and not just the nurses' station. He requested a connection to Sam, and a few heartbeats later she appeared on the screen. Her hair was floating around her head. Null g always made him think of drowned people. The sclera of her left eye was the bright red of fresh blood.

"Bull," she said with a grin that looked like relief. "Jesus Christ with a side of chips, but I never thought I'd be glad to hear from you."

"Need a status report."

"Yeah," she said. "I better come by for this one. You in your office?"

"Medical bay," Bull said.

"Be there in a jiff," she said.

"Sam. What happened?"

"You remember that asshole who shot the Ring and got turned into a thin paste when his ship hit the slow zone? Same thing."

"We went too fast?" Bull said.

"We didn't. Something changed the rules on us. I've got a couple techs doing some quick-and-dirty tests to figure out what the new top speed is, but we're captured and floating into that big ring of ships. Along with *everybody* else."

"The whole flotilla?"

"Everybody and their sisters," Sam said. A sense of grim despair undercut the lightness of her words. "No one's under their own power now except the shuttles that were inside the bays when it happened, and no one's willing to send them going too fast either. The *Behemoth* was probably going the slowest when it happened. Other ships, it's worse."

How bad floated in his mind, but something about the words refused to be asked. His mind skated over them, flickering. The deep sense of wrongness welled up in him.

"First convenience," he said.

"On my way," Sam said, and the connection dropped. He wanted to sag back into a pillow, wanted to feel the comforting hand of gravity pressing him down. He wanted the New Mexican sun streaming in through a glass window and the open air and blue sky. None of it was there. None of it ever would be.

Rest when you're dead, he thought, and thumbed the comm terminal on again. Ashford and Pa weren't accepting connections, but they both took messages. He was in the process of connecting to the security office when a doctor came by and started talking with him. Mihn Sterling, her name was. Bennie Cortland-Mapu's second. He listened to her with half his attention. A third of the crew had been in their rest cycle, safely in their crash couches. The other two-thirds—him included—had slammed into walls or decks, the hand terminals they'd been looking at accelerating into projectiles. Something about network regrowth and zero gravity and spinal fluid. Bull wondered where Pa was. If she was dead and Ashford alive, it would be a problem.

Disaster recovery could only go two ways. Either everyone pulled together and people lived, or they kept on with their tribal differences and fear, and more people died.

He had to find a way to coordinate with Earth and Mars. Everyone was going to be stressed for medical supplies. If he was going to make this work, he had to bring people together. He needed to see if Monica Stuart and her team—or anyway the part of her team that wasn't going to be charged with sabotage and executed—were still alive. If he could start putting out his own broadcasts, something along the lines of what she'd done with Holden...

The doctor was getting agitated about something. He didn't notice when Sam came into the room; she was just floating there. Her left leg was in an improvised splint of nylon tape and packing foam. Bull put his palm out to the doctor, motioning for silence, and turned his attention to Sam.

"You've got the report?" he asked.

"I do," Sam said. "And you can have it as soon as you start listening to what she's saying."

"What?"

Sam pointed to Doctor Sterling.

"You have to listen to her, Bull. You have to hear what she's saying. It's important."

"I don't have time or patience—"

"Bull!" Sam snapped. "Can you feel anything—I mean *anything*—lower than your tits?"

The sense of wrongness flooded over him, and with it a visceral, profound fear. Vertigo passed through him again, and he closed his eyes. All the words the doctor had been saying—*crushed spinal cord, diffuse blood pooling, paraplegic*—finally reached his brain. To his shame, tears welled up in his eyes, blurring the women's faces.

"If the fibers grow back wrong," the doctor said, "the damage will be permanent. Our bodies weren't designed to heal in zero g. We're built to let things drain. You have a bolus of blood and spinal fluid putting pressure on the wound. We have to drain that, and we have to get the bone shards out of the way. We could start the regrowth now, but there are about a dozen people who need the nootropics just to stay alive."

"I understand," Bull said around the lump in his throat, hoping she'd stop talking, but her inertia kept her going on.

"If we can stabilize the damage and get the pressure off and get you under at least one-third g, we have a good chance of getting you back to some level of function."

"All right," Bull said. The background of medical alerts and voices and the hum of the emergency air recyclers stood in for real silence. "What's your recommendation?"

"Medical coma," the doctor said without hesitating. "We can slow down your system. Stabilize you until we can evacuate."

Bull closed his eyes, squeezing the tears between the lids. All he had to say was yes, and it was all someone else's problem. It would all go away, and he'd wake up somewhere under thrust with his body coming back together. Or he wouldn't wake up at all. The moment lasted. He remembered walking among the defunct solar collectors. Climbing them. Bracing a ceramic beam with his knees while one of the other men on his team cut it. Running. He remembered a woman he'd been seeing on Tycho Station, and the way his body had felt against her. He could get it back. Or some part of it. It wasn't gone.

"Thank you for your recommendation," he said. "Sam, I'll have that damage report now."

"Bull, no," Sam said. "You know what happens when one of my networks grows back wrong? I burn it out and start over. This is biology. We can't just yank out your wiring and reboot you. And you can't macho your way through it."

"Is that what I'm doing?" Bull said, and he almost sounded like himself.

"I'm serious," Sam said. "I don't care what you promised Fred Johnson or how tough you think you are. You're going to be a big boy and take your nasty medicine and get *better*. You got it?"

She was on the edge of crying now. Blood was darkening her face. Some of her team were surely dead. People she'd known for years. Maybe her whole life. People she'd worked with every day. With a clarity that felt almost spiritual, he saw the depth of her grief and felt it resonate within him. Everyone was going to be there now. Everyone who'd lived on every ship would have seen people they cared about broken or dead. And when people were grieving, they did things they wouldn't do sober.

"Look where we are, Sam," Bull said gently. "Look what we're doing here. Some things don't go back to normal." Sam wiped her eyes with a sleeve cuff, and Bull turned to the doctor. "I understand and respect your medical advice, but I can't take it right now. Once the ship and crew are out of danger, we'll revisit this, but until then staying on duty is more important. Can you keep me cognitively functioning?"

"For a while, I can," the doctor said. "But you'll pay for it later."

"Thank you," Bull said, his voice soft and warm as flannel. "Now, Chief Engineer Rosenberg, give me the damage report."

It wasn't good.

The best thing Bull could say after reading Sam's report and consulting with the doctors and his own remaining security forces was that the *Behemoth* had weathered the storm better than some of the other ships. Being designed and constructed as a generation ship meant that the joints and environmental systems had been built with an eye for long-term wear. She'd been cruising at under 10 percent the slow zone's previous maximum speed when the change came.

The massive deceleration had happened to all the ships at the same time, slowing them from their previous velocity to the barely perceptible drifting toward the station's captive ring in just under five seconds. If it had been instantaneous, no one would have lived through it. Even with the braking spread out, it had approached the edge of the survivable for many of them. People asleep or at workstations with crash couches had stood a chance. Anyone in an open corridor or getting up for a bulb of coffee at the wrong moment was simply dead. The count stood at two hundred dead and twice that many wounded. Three of the Martian ships that had been significantly faster than the *Behemoth* weren't responding, and the rest reported heavy casualties. The big Earth ships were marginally better.

To make matters worse, the radio and laser signals going back out of the Ring to what was left of the flotilla were bent enough that communication was just about impossible. Not that it would have mattered. The slow zone—shit, now he was thinking of it that way too—was doing everything it could to remind them how vast the distances were within it. At the velocities they had available to them now, getting to the Ring would take as long as it had to reach it from the Belt. Months at least, and that in shuttles. All the ships were captured.

However many of them were left, they were on their own.

The station's grip was pulling them into rough orbit around the glowing blue structure, and no amount of burn was able to affect their paths one way or the other. They couldn't speed up and they couldn't stop. No one was under thrust, and it was making the medical crisis worse as zero g complicated the injuries. The *Behemoth*'s power grid, already weakened and patched after the torpedo launch debacle, had suffered a cascading shipwide failure. Sam's team was trekking through the ship, resetting the tripped safeties, adding new patches to the mess. One of the Earth ships had come close to losing core containment and gone through an automatic shutdown that left it running off batteries, another was battling an environmental systems breakdown with the air recyclers. The Martian navy ships might be fine or they might be in ruins, but the Martian commander wasn't sharing.

If it had been a battle, it would have been a humbling defeat. It hadn't even been an attack.

"Then what would you call it?" Pa asked from the screen of his hand terminal. She and Ashford had both survived. Ashford was riding roughshod over the recovery efforts, trying—Bull thought—to micromanage the crisis out of existence. That left Pa at the helm to coordinate with all the other ships. She was better suited for it anyway. There was a chance, at least, that she would listen.

"If I were doing it, I'd call it progressive restraint," Bull said. "That asshole who shot the Ring came through doing something fierce and he got locked down. There's rules about how fast you can go. Then Holden and those marines go to the station, something happens. Whatever's running the station gets its jock in a twist, and things lock down harder. I don't know the mechanism of how they do it, but the logic's basic training stuff. It's allowing us as much freedom as it can, but the more we screw it up, the tighter the choke."

"Okay," Pa said, running a hand through her hair. She looked tired. "I can see that. So as long as it doesn't feel threatened, maybe things don't get worse."

"But if someone gets pissed," Bull said. "I don't know. Some Martian pendejo just lost all his friends or something? He decides to arm a nuke, walk it to the station, and set it off, maybe things get a lot worse."

"All right."

"We've got to get everyone acting together," Bull said. "Earth, Mars, us. Everyone. Because if this was me, I'd escalate from a restraint, to a coercive restraint, to shooting someone. We don't want to get this thing to follow the same—"

"I said *all right*, Mister Baca!" Pa shouted. "That means I understood your point. You can stop making it. Because the one thing I *don't* need right now is another self-righteous male telling me how high the stakes are and that I'd better not fuck things up. I *got* it. *Thank* you."

Bull blinked, opened his mouth, and closed it again. On his screen, Pa pinched the bridge of her nose. He heard echoes of Ashford in her frustration.

"Sorry, XO," he said. "You're right. I was out of line."

"Don't worry about it, Mister Baca," she said, each syllable pulling a weight behind it. "If you have any concrete, specific recommendations, my door is always open."

"I appreciate that," Bull said. "So the captain...?"

"Captain Ashford's doing his best to keep the ship in condition and responsive. He feels that letting the crew see him will improve morale."

And how's that going, Bull didn't ask. Didn't have to. Pa could see him restraining himself.

"Believe it or not, we are all on the same team," she said.

"I'll keep it in mind."

Her expression clouded and she leaned in toward her screen, a gesture of intimacy totally artificial in the floating world of zero g and video connections and still impossible to entirely escape.

"I heard about your condition. I'm sorry."

"It's all right," he said.

"If I ordered you to accept the medical coma?"

He laughed. Even that felt wrong. Truncated.

"I'll go when I'm ready," he said, only realizing after the fact that the phrase could mean two different things. "We get out of the woods, the docs can take over."

"All right, then," she said and her terminal chimed. She cursed quietly. "I have to go. I'll touch base with you later."

"You got it," Bull said and let the connection drop.

The wise thing would have been to sleep. He'd been awake for fourteen hours, checking in with the security staff who were still alive, remaking a duty roster, doing all the things he could do from the medical bay that would make the ship work. Fourteen hours wasn't all that long a shift in the middle of a crisis, except that he'd been crippled.

Crippled.

With a sick feeling, he walked his fingertips down his throat, to his chest, and to the invisible line where the skin stopped feeling like his own and turned into something else. Meat. His mind skittered off the thought. He'd been hurt before and gotten back from it. He'd damn near died four or five different times. Something always happened that got him back on his feet. He always got lucky. This time would be the same. Somehow, somehow he'd get back. Have another story to tell and no one to tell it to.

He knew he was lying to himself, but what else could he do? Apart from stand aside. And maybe he should. Let Pa take care of it. Give Ashford his shot. No one would give him any shit if he took the medical coma. Not even Fred. Hell, Fred would probably have told him to do it. Ordered him.

Bull closed his eyes. He'd sleep or he wouldn't. Or he'd drift into some half-lucid place that wasn't either. One of the doctors was weeping in the corridor, a slow, autonomic sound, more like being sick than expressing sorrow. Someone coughed wetly. Pneumonia was the worst danger now. Null g messed with the sensors that triggered the kinds of coughing that actually cleared lungs until it was too late. After that, strokes and embolisms as the blood that gravity should have helped to drain pooled and clotted instead. On all the other ships, it was the same. Survivable injuries made deadly just by floating. If they could just get under thrust. Get some gravity...

We're all on the same team, Pa said in his half drowse, and Bull was suddenly completely awake. He scooped up his hand terminal, but Ashford and Pa were both refusing connections. It was the middle of their night. He considered putting through an emergency override, but didn't. Not yet. First, he tried Sam.

"Bull?" she said. Her skin looked grayish, and there were lines at the corners of her mouth that hadn't been there before. Her one blood-red eye seemed like an omen.

"Hey, Sam. Look, we need to get all the other crews from all the other ships onto the *Behemoth*. Bring everyone together so no one does anything stupid."

"You want a pony too?"

"Sure," Bull said. "Thing is, we got to give them a reason to come here. Something they need and they can't get anyplace else."

"Sounds great," Sam said, shaking her head. "Maybe I'm not at my cognitive best here, sweetie, but are you asking me for something?"

"They've all got casualties. They all need gravity. I'm asking you how long it would take you to spin up the drum."

Chapter Twenty-Seven: Melba

The darkness was beautiful and surreal. The ships of the flotilla, drawn together by the uncanny power of the station, hugged closer to each other than they ever would have under human control. The only lights came from the occasional exterior maintenance array and the eerie glow of the station. It was like walking through a graveyard in the moonlight. The ring of ships and debris glittered in a rising arc before her and behind, as if any direction she chose would lead up from where she was now.

The EVA suit had limited propellant, and she wanted to conserve it for her retreat. She scuttled through the vacuum, magnetic boots clicking against the hull of the *Prince* until she reached its edge and launched herself into the gap between vessels, aiming toward a Martian supply ship. The half mech and emergency airlock folded on her back massed almost fifty kilos, but with their courses matched, they were as weightless as she was. It was an illusion, she knew, but in the timeless reach between the *Thomas Prince* and hated *Rocinante*, all her burdens seemed light.

The EVA suit had a simple heads-up display that outlined the *Rocinante* with a thin green line. It wasn't the nearest ship. The trip out to it would take hours, but she didn't mind. It was as trapped as all the others. It couldn't go anyplace.

She hummed to herself as she imagined her arrival. Rehearsed it. She let herself daydream that he would be there: Jim Holden returned from the station. She imagined him raging at her as she destroyed his ship. She imagined him weeping and begging her forgiveness, and seeing the despair in his eyes when she refused. They were beautiful dreams, and folded safely inside them, she could forget the blood and horror behind her. Not just the catastrophe on the *Prince*, but all of it—Ren, her father, Julie, everything. The dim blue light of the not-moon felt like home, and the impending violence like a promise about to be kept.

If there was another part of her, a sliver of Clarissa that hadn't quite been crushed yet that felt differently, it was small enough to ignore.

Of course it was just as likely they'd all be dead when she got there. The catastrophe would have hit them as hard as the *Thomas Prince* or any of the other ships. Holden's crew might be nothing but cooling meat already, only waiting for her to come and light their funeral pyre. There was, she thought, a beauty in that too. She ran across the skins of the ships, leaped from one to the next like a nerve impulse crossing a synapse. Like a bad idea being thought by a massive, moonlit brain.

The air in the suit smelled like old plastic and her own sweat. The impact of the magnetic boots pulling her to the ships and then releasing her again translated up her leg, tug and release, tug and release. And before her, as slowly as the hour hand of an analog clock, the ghost-green *Rocinante* grew larger and nearer.

She knew the ship's specs by heart. She'd studied them for weeks. Martian corvette, originally assigned to the doomed *Donnager*. The entry points were the crew airlock just aft of the ops deck, the aft cargo bay doors, and a maintenance port that ran along beneath the reactor. If the reactor was live, the maintenance access wouldn't work. The fore airlock had almost certainly had its security profile changed once the ship fell into Holden's control. Only a stupid man wouldn't change it, and Melba refused to believe a stupid man could bring down her father. The service records she'd gleaned suggested that the cargo bay had been breached once already. Repairs were always weaker than the original structure. The choice was easy.

The attitude of the ship put the cargo bay on the far side of the ship, the body of the *Rocinante* hiding its flaw from the light. Melba stepped into shadow, shivering as if it could actually be colder in the darkness. She fastened the mech to the ship's skin and assembled it for use under the glare of the EVA suit's work lamps. The mech was the yellow of fresh lemons and police tape. The cautions printed in three alphabets were like little Rosetta stones. She felt an inexplicable fondness for the machine as she strapped it across her back, fitting her hands into the waldoes. The mech hadn't been designed for violence, but it was suited for it. That made her and it the same.

She lit the cutting torch and the EVA suit's mask went dark. Melba clung to the ship and began her slow invasion. Sparks and tiny asteroids of melted steel flew off into the darkness around her. The repair work where the bay doors had been bent out and refitted was almost invisible. If she hadn't known to look, she wouldn't have seen the weaknesses. She wondered if they knew she was coming. She imagined them hunched over their security displays, eyes wide with fear at what was digging its way under the *Rocinante*'s skin. She found herself singing softly, snatches of popular songs and old holiday tunes, whatever came to mind. Bits of lyrics and melody matched to the hum of the torch's vibration.

She breached the *Rocinante*, a patch of glowing steel no wider than her finger popping out. No air vented through the gap into the vacuum. They didn't keep the cargo bay pressurized. That meant the atmosphere wasn't dropping inside, and the ship alarms weren't blaring. One problem solved even without her help. It felt like fate. She killed the torch and unfolded the emergency airlock, sealing it against the hatch. She unzipped the outer layer, closed it, unzipped the inner one, and stepped into the small additional room she'd created. She didn't know how much damage she'd have to do to get into the inner areas of the ship. She didn't want an accidental loss of atmosphere to rob her of her vengeance. Holden needed to know who'd done this to him, not gasp out his last breaths thinking his ship had merely broken.

Gently, she slipped the mech's hand into the hole, braced, and peeled back the cargo door, long strips of steel blooming like an iris blossom. When it was wide enough, she took the sides of the hole in her mechanical hands and pulled herself into the cargo bay. Supply crates lined the walls and floors, held in place by electromagnets. One had shattered, a victim of the catastrophe. A cloud of textured protein packets floated in the air. The LED on the panel beside the interior airlock door was green; the bay hadn't been locked down. Why would it? She punched the button to enter the airlock and begin the cycle. Once the green pressure light came on, she slipped her hands out of the mech and lifted off the helmet. No Klaxons were ringing. No voices shouted or threatened. She'd made it on without alarming anyone. Her grin ached.

Back in the mech, she opened the airlock into the interior of the ship and paused. Still no alarms. Melba pulled herself gently, silently into enemy territory.

The *Rocinante* was built floor by floor from the reactor up to the engineering deck, to the machine shop, then the galley and crew cabins and medical bays, storage deck containing the crew airlock, then on up to the command deck and pilot's station farthest forward. Under thrust, it would be like a narrow building. Without thrust, the ship was directionless.

She had choices to make now. The cargo bay was close enough to give her access to engineering and the reactor. She could sneak in there and start the reactor on its overload. Or she could go up, try taking the crew by surprise, and set the ship to self-destruct from the command deck.

She took a deep breath. The *Rocinante* had four regular crew including Holden, and she didn't know whether the documentary crew were still on board. At least two of the regular crew had military training and experience. She might be able to take them in a fight if she got the drop on them or came across them one at a time.

The risk was too high. The reactor was nearest, it was easiest, and she could get out through the cargo bay. She pulled herself along the corridors she knew only from simulations, toward the reactor and the death of the ship.

When she opened the hatch to engineering, a woman floated above an opened control panel, a soldering iron in one hand and a spool of wire in the other. She had the elongated frame and slightly oversized head of someone who'd grown up under low g. Brown skin and dark hair pulled back in a utilitarian knot. Naomi Nagata. Holden's lover.

Melba felt a sudden urge to tear off the mech suit, swirl her tongue across the roof of her mouth, feel the chemical rush. To grab the narrow Belter's neck in her bare hands and feel the bones snap. It would be a yearlong dream of revenge made tactile and perfect. But two other crew members were on the ship, and she didn't know where they were. The terror she'd felt in that sleazy Baltimore casino came rushing back. Crawling helplessly on the floor in the post-drug collapse while people banged at the door to get in. She couldn't risk a crash until she knew where everyone was.

Naomi looked up at the sound of the door, pleasure in the woman's dark eyes as if the interruption were a happy surprise, and then shock, and then a cold fury.

For a moment, neither one moved.

With a yell, the woman launched herself at Melba, spinning the spool of wire in front of her. Melba tried to dodge, but the bulk of the mech and its slow response made it impossible. The wire hit her left cheek with a sound like a brick falling to earth, and for a moment her head rang. She brought up the mech's arm in a rough block, taking the Belter solidly in the ribs and sending them both spinning. Melba grabbed at a handhold, missed it, and then tried for another. The mech's hand latched on, crushing the metal flat and almost pulling it from the wall, but the Belter was ahead of her, skimming through the air at Melba, teeth bared like a shark. Melba tried to get the mech's free arm up to bat her away, but the Belter was already too close. She grabbed the front of Melba's jumpsuit, balling it in a fist, and used the leverage to swing a hard knee into her ribs, punctuating each blow with a word.

"You. Don't. Get. To hurt. My. *Ship*."

Melba felt a rib give way. She reached her tongue for the roof of her mouth, but again she didn't make the small private circles that would flush her blood with fire. She had to be awake and functional when the fight was over. She gritted her teeth and curled the mech's free arm in, bending it against itself, and then snapped her hand closed. The Belter screamed. The mech's claw had her by the shoulder. Melba squeezed again and heard the muffled, wet sound of bone breaking.

She threw the Belter across the room as hard as the motors let her. Where the woman bounced off the far wall, a smear of blood marked it. Melba waited, watching the Belter rotate in the air, directionless and loose as a rag doll sinking to the bottom of a swimming pool. A growing sphere of blood adhered to the woman's shoulder and neck.

"I do what I want," Melba said, and the voice sounded like someone else's.

Carefully, she pulled herself to the control panel. The panel was off, fixed to the deck with a length of adhesive tape. The guts within were a mess of wires and plates. The *Rocinante* had taken some damage in the catastrophe, but not so much that Melba couldn't do what was needed. She shrugged out of the mech, cracked her knuckles, traced the major control nodes, and plugged them back into the panel. The local memory check took only a few seconds, and she overrode the full system check. It was nothing she could have done before she left Earth, but Melba Koh had spent months learning about the guts of military ships. This was just the sort of thing Soledad, Stanni, and Bob would have checked on if they'd been working maintenance. It was something Ren would have taught her.

Her fingers curled, stumbling over the keyboard for a moment, but she got it back.

The control specs of the reactor came up. Releasing the magnetic bottle that kept the core from melting through the ship was deliberately designed to be difficult. Changing the limits on the reaction itself until it would eventually outstrip the bottle's ability to contain it was also hard, but less so. And it would give her a little time to tell Holden what she'd done, then get out of the ship and back toward the *Thomas Prince*. In the chaos of the day, no one might even know that someone had survived the death of the *Rocinante*.

A flicker in her peripheral vision was the only warning she had, but it was enough. Melba twisted out of the way, the Belter's massive wrench hissing through the air where her temple had been. Melba pushed back with her legs, struggling frantically to worm back into the mech. She tensed against the coming attack, but no blows came. She shrugged into the metal and jammed her hands into the waldoes, grabbing the wall and spinning back to the fight just as the Belter looked up from the control panel. Blood was crawling up the woman's neck, held to her by surface tension, and her smile was triumphant. The control panel flashed red and a screen of code crawled over it too fast to read. The lights in the room went off, and the emergency LEDs flickered on. Melba felt her throat go tight.

The Belter had dumped core. The reaction Melba had come to overload was dissipating in a cloud of gas behind the ship. The Belter's smile was feral and triumphant.

"Doesn't change anything," Melba said. It hurt to talk. "You have torpedoes. I'll overload one of those."

"Not in my lifetime," the Belter said, and attacked again.

Her swing was lopsided, though. Clumsy. The wrench clanged against the mech's joint, but it didn't do any damage. The Belter launched herself out of reach just as Melba swung an arm at her. The Belter wasn't using her injured arm at all, and she left spinning droplets of blood whenever she changed direction.

Melba wondered why the woman didn't call for help. On little ships like this, opening a communications channel was often as simple as saying it out loud. Either the computer was down, the rest of the crew dead or incapacitated, or it simply hadn't occurred to her. It didn't matter. It didn't change what Melba had to do. She shifted to her right, sliding through the air, moving handhold to handhold, never giving the other woman the chance to catch her unmoored and spin her into the open air at the center of the room. The Belter perched on the wall, her dark eyes darting one way, then other, searching for advantage. There was no fear in them, no sentimentality. Melba had no doubt that if the opportunity came, Naomi would kill her.

She reached the hatch, setting the mech's claw to grip a handhold, and then slipping one arm free to reach for the door's controls. It was a provocation, and it worked. The Belter jumped, not straight at Melba, but to the deck above her, then turned, kicked, off, and drove down, her heels aiming for Melba's head.

Melba drove her arm back into the mech and snapped the free arm up, catching the Belter in mid-flight. Her handhold broke free of the wall, and the pair of them floated together into the open air of the room. The Belter's injured arm was caught in the mech's clamp, and she kicked savagely with her heels. One blow connected, and Melba's vision narrowed for a moment. She pulled the Belter through the air, worrying at her like a terrier with a rat, and then managed to swing the free arm up and catch the woman by the neck.

The Belter's hand flew up to the clamp, panic in her expression. Her eyes went wide and bright. It would take a twitch of

Melba's fingers to crush the woman's throat, and they both knew it. A sense of triumph and overwhelming joy washed through her. Holden might not be here, but she had his lover. She would take someone he loved from him just the way he'd taken her own father from her. This wasn't even fighting anymore. This was justice.

The Belter's face was flushing red, her breath constricted and rough. Melba grinned, enjoying the moment.

"This is his fault," she said. "All of this is what he had coming."

The Belter scratched at the mech's claw. The blood that came away might have been from the old wound, or the mech's grip might already have broken the skin. Melba closed her fingers a fraction, the pressure feather light. The mech's servos buzzed as it closed a millimeter more. The Belter tried to say something, pushing the word out past her failing windpipe, and Melba knew she couldn't let her speak. She couldn't let her beg or weep and cry mercy. If she did, Melba suddenly wasn't sure she could go through with it, and it had to be done. *Sympathy is for the weak,* her father's voice whispered in her ear.

"You're Naomi Nagata," Melba said. "My name is Clarissa Melpomene Mao. You and your people attacked my family. Everything that's happened here? Everything that's going to happen. It's *your fault.*"

The light was fading from the Belter's eyes. Her breath came in ragged gasps. All it would take was a squeeze. All she had to do was make a fist and snap the woman's neck.

With the last of her strength, the Belter woman lifted her free hand in a gesture of obscenity and defiance.

Melba's body buzzed like she'd stepped into the blast from a firehose. Her head bent back, her spine arching against itself. Her hands flexed open, her toes curled back until it seemed like they had to break. She heard herself scream. The mech spread its arms to the side and froze, leaving her crucified in the metal form. The buzzing stopped, but she couldn't move. No matter how much she willed it, her muscles would not respond.

Naomi came to rest against the opposite wall, a knot of panting and blood.

"Who are you?" the Belter croaked.

I am vengeance, Melba thought. *I am your death made flesh.* But the voice that answered came from behind her.

"Anna. My name's Anna. Are you all right?"

Chapter Twenty-Eight: Anna

The woman—Naomi Nagata—replied by coughing up a red glob of blood.

"I'm an idiot, of course you're not all right," Anna said, then floated over to her, pausing to push the still-twitching Melba to the other side of the compartment. Girl and mech drifted across the room, bounced off a bulkhead, and came to a stop several meters away.

"Emergency locker," Naomi croaked, and pointed at a red panel on one wall. Anna opened it to find flashlights, tools, and a red-and-white bag not too different from the one Tilly had been carrying on the *Prince*. She grabbed it. While Anna extracted a package of gauze and a can of coagulant spray for the nasty wound on Naomi's shoulder, the Belter pulled out several hypo ampules and began injecting herself with them one at a time, her movements efficient and businesslike. Anna felt like something was tearing in her shoulders every time she wrapped the gauze around Naomi's upper torso, and she almost asked for another shot for herself.

Years before, Anna had taken a seminar on ministering to people with drug addictions. The instructor, a mental health nurse named Andrew Smoot, had made the point over and over that the drugs didn't only give pleasure and pain. They changed cognition, stripped away the inhibitions, and more often than not, someone's worst habits or tendencies—what he called their "pathological move"—got exaggerated. An introvert would often withdraw, an aggressive person would grow violent. Someone impulsive would become even more so.

Anna had understood the idea intellectually. Almost three hours into her spacewalk, the amphetamines Tilly had given her began to fade and a clarity she hadn't known she lacked began to return to her. She felt she had a deeper, more personal insight into what her own pathological move might be.

Anna had spent only a few years living among Belters and outer planets inhabitants. But that was long enough to know that their philosophy boiled down to "what you don't know kills you." No one growing up on Earth ever really understood that, no matter how much time they later spent in space. No Belter would have thrown on a space suit and EVA pack and rushed out the airlock without first knowing exactly what the environment on the other side was like. It wouldn't even occur to them to do so.

Worse, she'd run out that airlock without stopping to send a message to Nono. *You don't ask for permission, you ask for forgiveness* echoed in her head. If she died doing this, Nono would have it carved as her epitaph. She'd never get that last chance to say she was sorry.

The brightly colored display, which always seemed to float at the edge of her vision no matter which way her face was pointed, had said that she had 83 percent of her air supply remaining. Not knowing how long a full tank would last robbed that information of some much-needed context.

As she'd tried to slow her breathing back down and keep from panicking, the gauge ticked to 82 percent. How long had it been at 83 percent before it did? She couldn't remember. A vague feeling of nausea made her think about how bad throwing up in her space suit would be, which only made the feeling worse.

The girl, Melba, or Claire now, was far ahead and gaining, moving with the easy grace of long practice. Someone for whom walking in a space suit with magnetic boots was normal. Anna tried to hurry and only managed to kick her boot with her other foot and turn the magnet up high enough to lock it to the hull of the ship. The momentum of her step tugged against the powerful magnetic clamp. After several lost seconds figuring out how to fix that problem, she'd found the controls and slid the grip back down to a normal human range. After that, she gave up on haste and aimed for a safe, consistent pace. Slow and steady, but she wasn't winning the race. She lost sight of the girl, but she'd told herself it didn't matter. She guessed well enough where Clarissa Mao was going. Or Melba Koh. Whoever this woman was.

She had seen images of the *Rocinante* on newsfeeds before. It was probably as famous as a ship could be. James Holden's central role in the Eros and Ganymede incidents along with a peppering of dogfights and antipiracy actions had kept his little corvette mentioned in the media on and off for years. As long as there weren't two Martian corvettes parked next to each other, Anna felt confident she'd be able to spot it.

Fifteen long minutes later, she did.

The *Rocinante* was shaped like a stubby black wedge of metal; a fat chisel laid on its side. The flat surface of the hull was occasionally broken up by a domed projection. Anna didn't know enough about ships to know what they were. It was a warship, so sensors or guns, maybe, but definitely not doors. The tail of the ship had been facing her, and the only obvious opening in it was at the center of the massive drive cone. She walked to the edge of the ship she was on and then from side to side trying to get a better look at the rest of the *Rocinante* before jumping over to it. The irony of looking before she leapt at this late stage of the game made her laugh, and she felt some of the tension and nausea fading.

Just to the right of the drive cone was a bubble of plastic attached to the ship, pale as a blister. A moment later she was through the wound in the ship's cargo doors and inside. It had occurred to her, as she looked at the maze of crates locked against the hull with magnets much like the ones on her own feet, that she hadn't thought her plan through past this. Did this room connect to the rest of the ship? The doors behind her didn't have an airlock, which probably meant that this space was usually kept in vacuum. She had no idea where anyone would be in relation to that room, and more worrisome, she had no idea if the girl she was chasing was still in there, hiding behind one of the boxes.

Anna carefully pulled herself from crate to crate to the other end of the long, narrow compartment. Bits of plastic and freeze-dried food drifted around her like a cloud of oddly shaped insects. The broken crates might have been relics of a fight or debris created by the speed change; she had no way to know. She reached into the small bag tethered to her EVA pack and pulled out the taser. She'd never fired one in microgravity or in vacuum. She hoped neither thing affected it. Another gamble no Belter would ever take.

To her great relief, she found an airlock at the other end of the room, and it opened at a touch of the panel. Cycling it took several minutes, while Anna pulled the heavy EVA pack off her back and played with the taser to make sure she knew how to turn the safety off. The military design was intuitive, but less clearly labeled than the civilian models she was accustomed to. The panel flashed green and the inner doors opened.

No one was in sight. Just a deck that looked like a machine shop with tool lockers and workbenches and a ladder set into one wall. Bookending the ladder were two hatches, one going toward the front of the ship, the other toward the back. Anna was thinking that she was most likely to run into crewmembers by going toward the front of the ship when there was a loud bang from the back and the lights went out.

Yellow LEDs set into the walls came on a moment later, and a genderless voice said, "Core dump, emergency power only," and repeated it several times. Her helmet muffled the sound, but there was clearly still air in the ship. She pulled the helmet off and hung it from her harness.

Anna was fairly certain you only ejected the core in emergencies related to the engine room, so she moved to that hatch instead. With the constant rumble of the ship gone and her helmet removed she could hear faint noises coming through the hatch. It took her several long moments to figure out how to access it, and when she finally did the hatch snapped open so suddenly it made her almost yelp with surprise.

Inside, Melba was murdering someone.

A Belter woman with long dark hair and a greasy coverall was having her throat crushed by the mechanical arms Melba wore. The woman—Anna could see now that it was James Holden's second-in-command, Naomi Nagata—looked like Melba had beaten her badly. Her arm and shoulder were covered in blood, and her face was a mass of scrapes and contusions.

Anna drifted down into the vaulted chamber. The reactor room's walls curving inward like a church, the cathedrals of the fusion age. She felt an almost overwhelming need to hurry, but she knew she'd only get one shot with the taser, and she didn't trust herself to fire on the move.

Naomi's face was turning a dark, bruised purple. Her breath the occasional wet rasp. Somehow, the Belter managed to raise one hand and flip Melba off. Anna's feet hit the decking, and her boots stuck. She was less than three meters behind Melba when her finger pressed the firing stud, aiming for the area of her back not covered by the skeletal frame of the mech, hoping the taser would work through a vacuum suit.

She missed, but the results were impressive anyway.

Instead of hitting the fabric of Melba's suit, the taser's two microdarts hit the mech dead center. The trailing wires immediately turned bright red and began to fall apart like burning string. The taser got so hot Anna could feel it through her glove, so she let go just before it melted into a glob of gooey gray plastic. The mech arced and popped and the arms snapped straight out. The room smelled like burning electrical cables. All of Melba's hair was standing straight up, and even after the taser had died her fingers and legs continued to twitch and jerk. A small screen on the mech's arm had a flashing red error code.

"Who are you?" Naomi Nagata asked, drifting in a way that told Anna she'd be slumping to the floor at the first hint of gravity.

"Anna. My name's Anna," she had said. "Are you all right?"

After the third injection, Naomi took a long, shuddering breath and said, "Who's Anna?"

"Anna is me," she said, then chuckled at herself. "You mean who am I? I'm a passenger on the *Thomas Prince*."

"UN? You don't look like navy."

"No, a passenger. I'm a member of the advisory group the secretary-general sent."

"The dog and pony show," Naomi said, then hissed with pain as Anna tightened the bandage and activated the charge that would keep it from unwinding.

"Everyone keeps calling it that," Anna said as she felt the bandage. She wished she'd paid more attention in the church first aid class. Clear the airway, stop the bleeding, immobilize the injury was about the limit of what she knew.

"That's because it is," Naomi said, then reached up with her good hand to grab a rung of the nearby ladder. "It's all political bullsh—"

She was cut off by a mechanical-sounding voice saying, "Reboot complete."

Anna turned around. Melba was staring at them both, her hair still standing straight out from her head, but her hands no longer twitching uncontrollably. She moved her arms experimentally, and the half mech whined, hesitated, and then moved with her.

"Fuck me," Naomi said. She sounded annoyed but unsurprised.

Anna reached for her taser before she remembered it had melted. Melba bared her teeth.

"This way," Naomi said as the hatch slid open above them. Anna darted through it, with Naomi close behind using her one good arm to pull herself along. Melba surged after them, reaching out with one foot to push off the reactor housing.

Naomi pulled her leg through just in time to avoid being grabbed by the mech's claw, then tapped the locking mechanism with her toe and the hatch slammed shut on the mech's wrist. The hatch whined as it tried to close, crushing the claw in a spray of sparks and broken parts. Anna waited for the scream of pain that didn't come, then realized that the gloves Melba used to control the machine were in the mech's forearms, several centimeters behind the point of damage. They hadn't hurt her, and she'd sacrificed the use of one of the mech's claws in order to keep the hatch open. The other claw appeared in the gap, gripping at the metal, bending it.

"Go," Naomi said, her voice tight with pain, her good hand pointing at the next hatch up the ladder. After they were both through, Anna took a moment to look around at the new deck they were on. It looked like crew areas. Small compartments with flimsy-looking doors. Not a good place to hole up. Naomi flew through the empty air and the dim shadows cast by the emergency lights, and Anna followed as best she could, the feeling of nightmare crawling up her throat.

After they'd passed through the hatch into the next level, Naomi stopped to tap on the small control screen for several seconds. The emergency lights shifted to red, and the panel on the hatch read SECURITY LOCKDOWN.

"She's not trapped down there," Anna said. "She can get out through the cargo bay. There's a hole in the doors."

"That's twice now someone has done that," Naomi replied, pulling herself up the ladder. "Anyway, she's wearing a salvage mech rig, and she's in the machine shop. Half the stuff in there is made to cut through ships. She's not trapped. We are."

This took Anna by surprise. They'd gotten away. They'd locked a door behind them. That was supposed to end it. The monster isn't allowed to open doors. It was fuzzy, juvenile thinking, and Anna became less sure that all the drugs had actually passed through her system. "So what do we do?"

"Medical bay," Naomi said, pointing down a short corridor. "That way."

That made sense. The frail-looking Belter woman was getting a gray tone to her dark skin that made Anna think of massive blood loss, and the bandage on her shoulder had already soaked through and was throwing off tiny crimson spheres. She took Naomi by the hand and pulled her down the corridor to the medical bay door. It was closed, and the panel next to it flashed the security lockdown message like the deck hatches had. Naomi started pressing it, and Anna waited for the door to slide open. Instead, another, heavier-looking door slid into place over the first, and the panel Naomi was working on went dark.

"Pressure doors," Naomi said. "Harder to get through."

"But we're on this side of them."

"Yeah."

"Is there another way in?" Anna asked.

"No. Let's go."

"Wait," Anna said. "We need to get you in there. You're very badly hurt."

Naomi turned to look at her, frowned as if she'd only really seen Anna for the first time. It was a speculative frown. Anna felt she was being sized up.

"I have two injured men in there. My crew. They're helpless," Naomi finally said. "Now they're as safe as I can make them. So you and I are going to go up to the next deck, get a gun, and make sure she follows us. When she shows up, we're going to kill her."

"I don't—" Anna started.

"Kill. Her. Can you do that?"

"Kill? No. I can't," Anna said. It was the truth.

Naomi stared at her for a second longer, then just shrugged with her good hand. "Okay, then, come with me."

They moved through the next hatch to the deck above. Most of the space was taken up by an airlock and storage lockers. Some of the lockers were large enough to hold vacuum suits and EVA packs. Others were smaller. Naomi opened one of the smaller lockers and pulled out a thick black handgun.

"I've never shot anyone either," she said, pulling the slide back and loading a round. To Anna's eye the bullet looked like a tiny rocket. "But those two in the med bay are my family, and this is my home."

"I understand," Anna said.

"Good, because I can't have you—" Naomi started, then her eyes rolled up in her head and her body went limp. The gun drifted away from her relaxed hand.

"No no no," Anna repeated in a sudden wash of panic. She floated over to Naomi and held her wrist. There was still a pulse, but it was faint. She dug through the first aid pack, looking for something to help. One ampule said it was for keeping people from going into shock, so Anna jabbed Naomi with it. She didn't wake up.

The air in the room began to smell different. Hot, and with the melted plastic odor her damaged taser had given off when it died. A spot of red appeared on the deck hatch, then shifted to yellow, then to white. The girl in the mech, coming for them.

The hatch above them, the one that led forward on the ship, was closed and flashing the lockdown message. Naomi hadn't told her what the override code was. The airlock was on their level, but it was locked down too.

The deck hatch began to open in lurching increments. Anna could hear Melba panting and cursing as she forced it. And Naomi's lockdown code hadn't kept the insane woman out, it had only locked them in.

Anna pulled Naomi's limp body over to one of the large vacuum suit storage lockers and put her inside, climbing in after her.
There was no lock on the door. Between the unconscious woman
and the suit, there was hardly enough room for her to close it. She
set both of her feet at the corner where the door of the locker met
the deck and set the magnets up to full. She felt the suit lock onto
the metal, clamping her legs into place and pulling her up close
against the locker door.

On the far side, metal shrieked. Something wet brushed against
the back of Anna's neck. Naomi's hand, limp and bloody. Anna
tried not to move, tried not to breathe loudly. The prayer she
offered up was hardly more than a confusion of fear and hope.

A locker door slammed open off to her left. Then another one,
closer. And then another. Anna wondered where Naomi's gun
had gotten to. It was in the locker somewhere, but there was no
light, and she'd have to unlock the magnets on her boots to look
for it. She hoped they hadn't left it outside with the crazy woman.
Another locker opened.

The door centimeters from Anna's face shifted, but didn't open.
The vents and the cracks in the locker door flared the white of a
cutting torch, then went dark. A mechanical voice said, "Backup
power depleted." The curse from the other side was pure frustration. It was followed by a series of grunts and thumps: Melba taking the mech rig off. Anna felt a surge of hope.

"Open it," Melba said. Her voice was low, rough, and bestial.

"No."

"Open it."

"You...I can hear that you're feeling upset," Anna said, horrified by the words even as she spoke them. "I think we should talk
about this if you—"

Melba's scream was unlike anything Anna had heard before,
deep and vicious and wild. If the id had a throat, it would have
sounded like that. If the devil spoke.

Something struck the metal door and Anna flinched back.
Then another blow. And another. The metal began to bow in, and

droplets of blood clung to the vent slits. *Her fists*, Anna thought. *She's doing this with her hands.*

The screaming was wild now, obscene where it wasn't word-less, and inhuman as a hurricane. The thick metal of the door bent in, the hinges starting to shudder and bend with each new assault. Anna closed her eyes.

The top hinge gave way, shattering.

And then, without warning, silence fell. Anna waited, sure she was being lulled into a trap. No sound came except a small animal gurgle. She could smell the stomach-turning acid stench of fresh vomit. After what felt like hours, she turned off the magnets and pushed the warped and abused door open.

Melba floated curled against the wall, her hands pressed to her belly and her body shuddering.

Chapter Twenty-Nine: Bull

The truth was, distance was always measured in time. It wasn't the sort of thing Bull usually thought about, but his enforced physical stillness was doing strange things with his awareness. Even in the middle of the constant press of events, the calls and coordination, the scolding from his doctor, he felt some part of his mind coming loose. And strange ideas kept floating in, like the way that distance got measured in time.

Centuries before, a trip across the Atlantic Ocean could take months. There was a town near New Mexico named Wheeless where the story was some ancient travelers of the dust and caliche had a wagon break down and decided that it was easier to put down roots than go on. Technologies had come, each building on the ones before, and months became weeks and then hours. And outside the gravity well, where machines were freed from the tyranny of air resistance and gravity, the effect was even more profound. When the orbits were right, the journey from Luna to Mars could take as little as twelve days. The trek from Saturn to Ceres, a few months. And because they were out there with their primate brains, evolved on the plains of prehistoric Africa, everyone had a sense of how far it was. Saturn to Ceres was a few months. Luna to Mars was a few days. Distance was time, and so they didn't get overwhelmed by it.

The slow zone had changed that. Looking at a readout, the ships from Earth and Mars were clustered together like a handful of dried peas thrown in the same bowl. They were drifting now, coming together and spreading apart, taking their places in the captured ring around the eerie station. Compared to the volume of ring-bordered sphere, they seemed huddled close. But the distance between them and the Ring was time, and time meant death.

From the farthest of the ships to the *Behemoth* was two days' travel in a shuttle, assuming that the maximum speed didn't ratchet down again. The closest, he could have jumped to. The human universe had contracted, and was contracting more. With every connection, every stark, frightened voice he heard in the long, frantic hours, Bull grew more convinced that his plan could work. The vastness and strangeness and unreasonable danger of the universe had traumatized everyone it hadn't killed. There was a hunger to go home, to huddle together, back in the village. The instinct was the opposite of war, and as long as he could see it cultivated, as long as the response to the tragedies of the lockdown were to get one another's backs and see that everyone who needed care got it, the grief and fear might not turn to more violence.

The feed went to green, then blue, and then Monica Stuart was smiling professionally into the camera. She looked tired, sober, but human. A face people knew. One they could recognize and feel comfortable with.

"Ladies and gentlemen," she said. "Welcome to the first broadcast of Radio Free Slow Zone, coming to you from our temporary offices here on board the OPA battleship *Behemoth*. I am a citizen of Earth and a civilian, but it's my hope that this program can be of some use to all of us in this time of crisis. In addition to bringing whatever unclassified news and information we can, we will also be conducting interviews with the command crews of the ships, civilian leaders on the *Thomas Prince*, and live musical performances.

"It's an honor to welcome our first guest, the Reverend Father Hector Cortez."

A graphic window opened, and the priest appeared. To Bull's eyes, the man looked pretty ragged. The too-bright teeth seemed false and the blazing white hair had a greasy look to it.

"Father Cortez," Monica Stuart said. "You have been helping with the relief effort on the *Thomas Prince*?"

For a moment, the man seemed not to have heard her. A smile jerked into place.

"I have," the old man said. "I have, and it has been…Monica, I'm humbled. I am…humbled."

Bull turned off the feed. It was something. It was better than nothing.

The Martian frigate *Cavalier*, now under the command of a second lieutenant named Scupski, was shutting down its reactors and transferring all its remaining crew and supplies to the *Behemoth*. The *Thomas Prince* had agreed to move its wounded, its medical team, and all the remaining civilians—poets, priests, and politicians. Including the dead-eyed Hector Cortez. It was a beginning, but it wasn't all he could do. If they were to keep coming, if the *Behemoth* was to become the symbol of calm and stability and certainty that he needed it to be, there had to be more. The broadcast channel could give a voice and a face to the growing consolidation. He'd need to talk to Monica Stuart about it some more. Maybe there could be some sort of organized mourning of the dead. A council with representatives from all sides that could make an evacuation plan and start getting people back through the Ring and home.

Except that when the lockdown came, they'd lost all their long-distance ships to it. And the Ring itself had retreated, because they had to move so slowly, and because distance was measured in time.

His hand terminal chirped, and he came back to wakefulness with a start. Outside his room a woman shouted and a man's tense voice replied. Bull recognized the sound of the crash team rushing to try and revive some poor bastard from collapsing into death. He felt for the team of medics. He was doing the same kind of work, just on a different scale. He shifted his arms, scooped up the terminal, and accepted the connection. Serge appeared on the screen.

"Bist?" he asked.

"I'm doing great," Bull said dryly. "What's up?"

"Mars. They got him. Hauling the cabron back alive."

Instinctively, uselessly, Bull tried to sit up. He couldn't sit and up was a polite abstraction.

"Holden?" he said.

"Who else, right? He's on a skiff puttering slow for the MCRN *Hammurabi*. Should be there in a few hours."

"No," Bull said. "They've got to bring him here."

Serge raised his hand in a Belter's nod, but his expression was skeptical.

"Asi dulcie si, but I don't see them doing it."

Somewhere far away down below Bull's chest, the compression sleeves hissed and chuffed and expanded, massaging the blood and lymph around his body now that movement wouldn't keep his fluids from pooling. He couldn't feel it. If they'd caught fire, he wouldn't feel it. Something deep and atavistic shifted in fear and disgust as his hindbrain rediscovered his injuries for the thousandth time. Bull ground the heel of his palm against the bridge of his nose.

"Okay," he said. "I'll see what I can do. What does Sam say about the project?"

"She got the rail guns off and they're working on cutting back the extra torpedo tubes, but the captain found out and he's throwing grand mal."

"Well, that had to happen sometime," Bull said. "Guess I'll take care of that too. Anything else?"

"Unless tu láve mis yannis, I think you got plenty. Take a breath, we'll take a turn, sa sa? You don't have to do it all yourself."

"I've got to do something," Bull said as the compression sleeves relaxed with a sigh. "I'll be in touch."

Tense, low voices drifted in with the burned-moth stink of cauterized flesh. Bull let his gaze focus on the blue-white ceiling above the bed he was strapped to.

Holden was back. They hadn't killed him. If there was one thing that had the potential to destroy the fragile cooperation he was building, it would be the fight over who got to hold James Holden's nuts to a Bunsen burner.

Bull scratched his shoulder more for the sensation than because it itched and considered the consequences. Protocol was that they'd question him, hold him in detention, and start negotiating extradition with whoever on the Earth side was investigating the *Seung Un*. Bull's guess was they'd beat him bloody and drop him outside. The man was in custody, but he was responsible for too many deaths to assume he'd be safe there.

It was time to try hailing the *Rocinante* again. Maybe this time they'd answer. Since the catastrophe, they'd been silent. Their communications array might have been damaged, they might be staying silent as some sort of political tactic, or they might all be dying or dead. He requested a connection again and waited with no particular hope of being answered.

Later, when they were outside the Ring, people could wrestle for jurisdiction as much as they wanted. Right now, Bull needed them to work together. Maybe if he—

Against all expectation, the connection to the *Rocinante* opened. A woman Bull didn't recognize appeared. Pale skin, unrestrained red hair haloing her face. The smudge on her cheek might have been grease or blood.

"Yes," the woman said. "Hello? Who is this? Can you help us?"

"My name's Carlos Baca," Bull said, swallowing shock and confusion before they could get to his voice. "I'm chief security officer on the *Behemoth*. And yes, I can help you."

"Oh, thank God," the woman said.

"So how about you tell me who you are and what the situation is over there."

"My name is Anna Volovodov, and I have a woman who tried to kill the crew of the *Rocinante* in...um...custody? I used all the sedatives in the emergency pack because I can't get into the actual medical bay. I taped her to a chair. Also, I think she may have blown up the *Seung Un*."

Bull folded his hands together.

"Why don't you tell me about that?" he said.

Captain Jakande was an older woman, silver-haired with a take-no-shit military attitude that Bull respected, even though he didn't like it.

"I still don't have orders to release the prisoner," Captain Jakande said. "I don't see that it's likely that I'll get them. So for the foreseeable future, no."

"I have a shuttle already going to collect his crew and the woman he accused of being the real saboteur," Bull said. "And last time I looked, I have two dozen of your people slated to come over once we have the drum spun up."

Jakande nodded once, confirming everything he'd said without being moved by any of it. Bull knotted his fingers together and squeezed until the knuckles were white, but he did it out of range of the communication deck's cameras.

"It's going to be better for all of us if we can get everyone together," Bull said. "Pool resources and plan the evacuation. If you don't have shuttles, I can arrange transportation for you and your crew. There's plenty of space here."

"I agree that it would be better to be under a single command," Jakande said. "If you are offering to turn over the *Behemoth*, I'm willing to accept control and responsibility."

"Not where I was taking that, no," Bull said.

"I didn't think so."

"Mister Baca," Ashford barked from the doorway. Bull held out a hand in a just-a-minute gesture.

"This is something we're going to have to revisit," he said. "I've got a lot of respect for you and your position, and I'm sure we can find a way to get this done right."

Her expression made it clear she didn't see anything wrong.

"I'll be in touch," Bull said, and dropped the connection. So much for the pleasant part of his day. Ashford pulled himself through the door, coming to rest against the wall nearest the foot of Bull's bed. He looked angry, but it was a different kind of angry. Bull was used to seeing Ashford cautious, even tentative. This man wasn't either. Everything about him spoke of barely restrained rage. *Grief makes people crazy*, Bull thought. Grief and guilt and embarrassment all together maybe did worse.

Maybe it broke people.

Pa floated in behind him, her eyes cast down. Her face had the odd waxy look that came from exhaustion. The doctor followed her, and then Serge and Macondo looking anyplace but at him. The crowd filled the little room past its capacity.

"Mister Baca," Ashford said, biting at each syllable. "I understand you gave the order to disarm the ship. Is that true?"

"Disarm the ship?" Bull said, and looked at Doctor Sterling. Her gaze was straight on and unreadable. "I had Sam take the rail guns off so we could spin up the drum."

"And you did this without my permission."

"Permission for what?"

Blood darkened Ashford's face, and rage roughened his voice.

"The rail guns are a central component of this ship's defensive capabilities."

"Not if they don't work," Bull said. "I had her take apart the thrust-gravity water reclamation system too. Rebuild it at ninety degrees so it'll use the spin. You want me to run through all the stuff I'm having her repurpose because it doesn't work anymore, or are we just caring about the guns?"

"I also understand that you have authorized non-OPA personnel to have access to the communications channels of the ship? Earthers. Martians. All the people we came out here to keep in line."

"Is that why we came out here?" Bull said. It wasn't a denial, and that seemed to be close enough to a confession for Ashford. Besides which, it wasn't like Bull had been hiding it.

"And enemy military personnel? You're bringing them aboard my ship as well?"

Pa had agreed to everything Ashford was listing off. But she stood behind the captain, not speaking up, expression unreadable. Bull wasn't sure what was going on between the captain and his XO, but if they were working out some internal power struggle, Bull knew which side he'd want to end up on. So he bit the bullet and didn't mention Pa's involvement. "Yes, I'm bringing in everyone I can get. Humanitarian outreach and consolidation of control. It's textbook. A second-year would know to do it." Pa winced at that.

"Mister Baca, you have exceeded your authority. You have ignored the chain of command. All orders given by you, all permissions granted by you, are hereby revoked. I am relieving you of duty and instructing that you be placed in a medical coma until such time as you can be evacuated."

"Like fuck you are," Bull said. He hadn't intended to, but the words came out like a reflex. They seemed to float in the air between them, and Bull discovered that he'd meant them.

"This isn't open for debate," Ashford said coldly.

"Damn right it's not," Bull said. "The reason you're in charge of this mission and not me is that Fred Johnson didn't think the crew would be comfortable with an Earther running a Belter ship. You got the job because you kissed all the right political asses. You know what? Good for you. Hope your career takes off like a fucking rocket. Pa's here for the same reason. She's got the right-sized head, though at least hers doesn't seem to be empty."

"That's a racist insult," Ashford said, trying to interrupt, "and I won't have—"

"I'm here because they needed someone who could get the

job done and they knew we were screwed. And you know what? We're still screwed. But I'm going to get us out of here, and I'm going to keep Fred from being embarrassed by what we did here, and you are going to stay out of my way while I do it, you pinche motherfucker."

"That's enough, Mister Baca. I will—"

"You know it's true," Bull said, shifting to face Pa. Her expression was closed, empty. "If he's in charge of this, he's going to get it wrong. You've seen it. You know—"

"You will stop addressing the XO, Mister Baca."

"—what kind of decisions he makes. He'll send them back to their ships, even if it means people die because—"

"You are *relieved*. You will be—"

"—he wasn't the one that invited them. It's going to—"

"—quiet. I do not give you permission—"

"—make all of this more dangerous, and if someone—"

"—to speak to my staff. You will be—"

"—else pisses that thing off, we could all—"

"—*quiet!*" Ashford shouted, and he pushed forward, his mouth in a square gape of rage. He hit the medical bed too hard, pressing into Bull, grabbing him by the shoulder and shaking him hard enough to snap his teeth shut. "I told you to *shut up!*"

The restraints opened under Ashford's attack, the Velcro ripping. Pain lanced through Bull's neck like someone was pushing a screwdriver into his back. He tried to push the captain away, but there was nothing to grab hold of. His knuckles cracked against something hard: the table, the wall, something else. He couldn't say what. People around him were shouting. His balance felt profoundly wrong, the dead weight of his body flowing limp and useless in the empty air, but tugged at by the tubes and the catheters.

When the world made sense again, he was at a forty-degree angle above the table, his head pointing down. Pa and Macondo were gripping Ashford's arms, the captain's hands bent into claws. Serge was bunched against the wall, ready to launch but not sure what direction he should go.

Doctor Sterling appeared at his side, gathering his legs and drawing him quickly and professionally back toward the bed.

"Could we please not assault the patient with the crushed spinal cord," she said as she did, "because this makes me very uncomfortable."

Another vicious flare of pain, hot and sharp and evil, ran through Bull's neck and upper back as she strapped him down. One of the tubes was floating free, blood and a bit of flesh adhering to its end. He didn't know what part of his body it had come out of. Pa was looking at him, and he kept his voice calm.

"We've already screwed up twice. We came through the Ring, and we let soldiers go on the station. We won't get a third. We can get everyone together, and we can get them out of here."

"That's dangerous talk, mister," Ashford spat.

"I can't be captain," Bull said. "Even if I wasn't stuck in this bed, I'm an Earther. There has to be a Belter in charge. Fred was right about that."

Ashford pulled his arms free of Pa and Macondo, plucked his sleeves back into trim, and steadied himself against the wall.

"Doctor, place Mister Baca in a medical coma. That is a direct order."

"Serge," Bull said. "I need you to take Captain Ashford into custody, and I need you to do it now."

No one moved. Serge scratched his neck, the sounds of fingernails against stubble louder than anything in the room. Pa's gaze locked in the middle distance, her face sour and angry. Ashford's eyes narrowed, cutting over toward her. When she spoke, her voice was dead and joyless.

"Serge. You heard what the chief said."

Ashford gathered himself to launch for Pa, but Serge already had a restraining hand on the captain's shoulder.

"This is mutiny," Ashford said. "There'll be a reckoning for this."

"You need to come with us now," Serge said. Macondo took Ashford's other arm and put it in an escort hold, and the three of them left together. Pa stayed against the wall, held steady by a strap, while the doctor, tutting and muttering under her breath, replaced the catheters and checked the monitors and tubes attached to his skin. For the most part, he didn't feel it.

When she was done, the doctor left the room. The door slid closed behind her. For almost a minute, neither of them spoke.

"Guess your opinion on mutiny changed," Bull said.

"Apparently," Pa said, and sighed. "He's not thinking straight. And he's drinking too much."

"He made the decision that brought us all here. He can sign his name to all the corpses on all those ships."

"I don't think he sees it that way," Pa said. And then, "But I think he's putting a *lot* of effort into not seeing it that way. And he's slipping. I don't think...I don't think he's well."

"It'd be easier if he had an accident," Bull said.

Pa managed a smile. "I haven't changed *that* much, Mister Baca."

"Didn't figure. But I had to say it," he said.

"Let's focus on getting everyone safe, and then getting everyone home," she said. "It was a nice career while it lasted. I'm sorry it's ending this way."

"Maybe it is," Bull said. "But did you come out here to win medals or to do the right thing?"

Pa's smile was thin.

"I'd hoped for both," she said.

"Nothing wrong with a little optimism, long as it doesn't set policy," he said. "I'm going to keep on getting everyone on the *Behemoth*."

"No weapons but ours," she said. "We keep taking all comers, but not if it means having an armed force on the ship."

"Already done," Bull said.

Pa closed her eyes. It was easy to forget how much younger than him she was. This wasn't her first tour, but it could have been her second. Bull tried to imagine what he'd have felt like, still half a kid, throwing his commanding officer into the brig. Scared as hell, probably.

"You did the right thing," he said.

"You'd have to say that. I backed your play."

Bull nodded. "I did the right thing. Thank you for supporting me, Captain. Please know that I'll be returning that favor as long as you sit in the big chair."

"We aren't friends," she said

"Don't have to be, so long as we get the job done."

Chapter Thirty: Holden

The marines weren't gentle, but they were professional. Holden had seen Martian powered armor used by a recon marine before. As they moved back through the caverns and tunnels of the station, Holden in thick foam restraints slung across one soldier's back like a piece of equipment, he was aware of how much danger he was in. The men and women in the suits had just watched one of their own be killed and eaten by an alien, they were deep within territory as threatening and unfamiliar as anything he could imagine, and the odds were better than even that they were all blaming him for it. That he wasn't dead already spoke to discipline, training, and a professionalism he would have respected even if his life hadn't depended on it.

Whatever frequencies they were speaking on he didn't have access to, so the furtive journey from the display chamber or whatever it had been back to the surface all happened in eerie silence as far as he was concerned. He kept hoping to catch a glimpse of Miller. Instead, they passed by the insectile machines, now as still as statues, and over the complex turf. He thought he could see something like a pattern in the waves and ripples that passed along the walls and floor, complicated and beautiful as raindrops falling on the surface of a lake, or music. It didn't comfort him.

He tried to get through to the *Rocinante*, to Naomi, but the marine he was strapped to had either disabled his suit radio when they were restraining him or something had jammed the signal. One way or another, he couldn't get anything. Not from the *Roci*, not from the marines, not from anywhere. There was only the gentle loping and an almost unbearable dread.

His suit gave him a low air warning.

He didn't have any sense of where they were or how far they'd gone. The surface of the station might be through the next tunnel or they might not have reached the halfway point. Or, for that matter, the station could be changing around them, and the way they'd come in might not exist. The suit said he had another twenty minutes.

"Hey!" he shouted. He tried to swing his legs against the armor of the person carrying him. "Hey! I'm going to need air!"

The marine didn't respond. No matter how hard Holden tried to thrash, his strength and leverage were a rounding error compared to the abilities of the powered armor. All he could do was hope that he wasn't about to die from an oversight. Worrying about that was actually better than wondering about Naomi and Alex and Amos.

The air gauge was down to three minutes and Holden had shouted himself hoarse when the marine carrying him crouched slightly, hopped up, and the station fell away beneath them. The luminescent surface irised closed behind them, automatic and unthinking. The skiff hung in the vacuum not more than five hundred meters away, its exterior lights making it the brightest thing in the eerie starless sky. They found their way into the mass airlock quickly. Holden's suit was blaring its emergency, the carbon dioxide levels crept up toward the critical level, and he had to fight to catch his breath.

The marine flipped him into a wall-mounted holding bar and strapped him in.

"I'm out of air!" Holden screamed. "Please!"

The marine reached out and cracked the seal on Holden's suit. The rush of air smelled like old plastic and poorly recycled urine. Holden sucked it in like it was roses. The marine popped off his own helmet. His real head looked perversely small in the bulk of the combat armor.

"Sergeant Verbinski!" a woman's voice snapped.

"Yes, sir," the marine who'd been carrying him said.

"There something wrong with the prisoner?"

"He ran out of air a few minutes back."

The woman grunted. Nothing more was said about it.

The acceleration burn, when it came, was almost subliminal. A tiny sensation of weight settling Holden into his suit, gone as soon as it came. The marines murmured among themselves and ignored him. It was all the confirmation he needed. What Miller had said was true. The slow zone's top speed had changed again. And from the expressions on their faces, he guessed that the casualties had been terrible.

"I need to check in with my ship," he said. "Can someone contact the *Rocinante*, please?" No one answered him. He pressed his luck. "My crew may be hurt. If we could just—"

"Someone shut the prisoner up," the woman who'd spoken before said. He still couldn't see her. The nearest marine, a thick-jawed man with skin so black it seemed blue turned toward him. Holden braced himself for a threat or violence.

"There's nothing you could do," the man said. "Please be quiet now."

His cell in the brig of the *Hammurabi* was a little over a meter and a half wide and three meters deep. The crash couch was a dirty blue and the walls and floor a uniform white that gleamed in the harsh light of the overhead LED. The jumpsuit he'd been issued felt like thick paper and crackled when he moved. When the guards came for him, they didn't bother putting the restraints back on his arms and legs.

The captain floated near a desk, her close-cropped silver hair making her look like an ancient Roman emperor. Holden was strapped into a crash couch that was canted slightly forward, so that he had to look up at her, even without the convenience of an up.

"I am Captain Jakande," she said. "You are a military prisoner. Do you understand what that means?"

"I was in the navy," Holden said. "I understand."

"Good. That'll cut about half an hour of legal bullshit."

"I'll happily tell you everything I know," Holden said. "No need for the rough stuff."

The captain smiled like winter.

"If you were anyone else, I'd think that was a figure of speech," she said. "What is your relationship to the structure at the center of the slow zone? What were you doing there?"

He had spent so many months trying not to talk about Miller, trying not to tell anyone anything. Except Naomi, and even then he'd felt guilty putting the burden of the mystery on her. On one hand, the chance to unburden himself pulled at him like gravity. On the other...

He took a deep breath.

"This is going to sound a little strange," he said.

"All right."

"Shortly after the protomolecule construct lifted off from Venus and headed out to start assembling the Ring? I was... contacted by Detective Josephus Miller. The one who rode Eros down onto Venus. Or at least something that looked and talked like him. He's shown up every few weeks since then, and I came to the conclusion that the protomolecule was using him. Well, him and Julie Mao, who was the first one to be infected, to drive me out through the Ring. I thought that they…it wanted me to come here."

The captain's expression didn't change. Holden felt a strange lump in his throat. He didn't want to be having this conversation here. He wanted to be talking with Naomi in their bedroom on the *Rocinante*. Or at a bar on Ceres. It didn't matter where. Only who.

Was she dead? Had the station killed her?

"Go on," the captain said.

"Apparently I was mistaken," Holden said.

He began with the journey out, with the protomolecule's vision of Miller waiting for him at the station. The attack by her marine, and the consequences as Miller explained them. The visions of the vast empire and the darkness that flowed over it, the death of suns. He relaxed as he went along, the words coming easier, faster. He sounded insane even to himself. Visions no one else could see. Vast secrets revealed only to him.

Except it had all been a mistake.

He'd thought he was important. That he was special and chosen, and that what had happened to him and his crew had been dictated by a vast and mysterious power. He'd misunderstood everything. *Doors and corners*, Miller had said, and because he hadn't puzzled out what the dead man meant by it, they'd all come through the Ring. And to the station. His relief and his growing self-disgust mingled with every phrase. He'd been a fool dancing at the edge of the cliff, because he'd been sure that he couldn't fall. Not him.

"And then I was here, talking to you," he said dryly. "I don't know what happens next."

"All right," she said. Her expression gave away nothing.

"You'll want a full medical workup to see if there's anything organically wrong with my brain," Holden said.

"Probably," the captain said. "My medical staff has its hands full at the moment. You will be kept in administrative detention for the time being."

"I understand," Holden said. "But I need to get in contact with my crew. You can monitor the connection. I don't care. I just need to know they're okay."

The angle of the captain's mouth asked why he thought they were.

"I'll try to get a report to you," she said. "Everyone's scrambling right now, and the situation could get worse quickly."

"Is it bad, then?"

"It is."

Time in his cell passed slowly. A guard brought tubes of rations: protein, oil, water, and vegetable paste. Sometimes it had a nearly homeopathic dose of curry. It was food meant to keep you alive. Everything after that was your own problem. Holden ate it because he had to stay alive. He had to find his crew, his ship. He had to get out of there.

He had seen a massive alien empire fall. He'd seen suns blown apart. He'd watched a man overwhelmed and slaughtered by nightmare mechanisms on a space station that human hands hadn't built. All he could think about was Naomi and Amos and Alex. How they were going to keep their ship. How they were going to get home. And home meant anyplace but here. Not for the first time, he wished they were all transporting sketchy boxes of unknown cargo to Titania. He floated in the coffin-sized cell and tried not to go crazy from the toxic combination of inaction and mind-bending fear.

Even if the whole crew was well, he was in custody of Mars now. He hadn't harmed the *Seung Un*, and everyone would know that. He hadn't made the false broadcast. All the things they were accusing him of could fall away, and there would still be the fact that Mars would take away his ship. He tried to focus on that despair, because as bad as it would be, if he kept the ship and lost his crew, that would feel worse.

"You've got lousy taste in friends," Miller said.

"Where the hell have you been?" Holden snapped.

The dead man shrugged. In the cramped quarters, Holden could smell the man's breath. A firefly flicker of blue sped around Miller's head like a low-slung halo and vanished.

"Time's hard," he said, as if the comment carried its own context. "Anyway, we were talking about something."

"The station. The lockdown."

"Right," Miller said, nodding. He plucked off his ridiculous hat and scratched his temple. "That. So the thing is, as long as there's a shitload of high energy floating around, the station's not going to get comfortable. You guys have, what? Twenty big ships?"

"About that, I guess."

"They've all got fusion reactions. They've all got massive internal power grids. Not a big deal by themselves, but the station's been spooked a couple times. It's jumpy. You're going to have to give it a little massage. Show that you're not a threat. Do that, and I'm pretty sure I can get you moving again. That or it'll break you all down to your component atoms."

"It'll what?"

Miller's smile was apologetic.

"Sorry," he said. "Joke. Just get the reactors off-line and the internal grids off. It'll get you below threshold, and I can take it from there. I mean, if that's what you decide you want to do."

"What do you mean, *if*?"

Holden shifted. The ceiling brushed against his shoulders. He couldn't stretch in here. There wasn't room for two people.

There wasn't room for two people.

For a fraction of a second, his brain tried to fit two images—Miller floating beside him and the too-small cell—together and failed. The flesh on his back felt like there were insects crawling all over it. The two things couldn't both be true, and his brain shuddered and recoiled from the fact that they were. Miller coughed.

"Don't do that," he said. "This is hard enough the way it is.

What I mean by *if* is that lockdown's lockdown. I don't get to pick what part of the trap gets unsprung. If I take off the dampening and you all start burning for home or shooting at each other or whatever, that means I also open the gates. All of them."

"Including the ones with the burned-up stars?"

"No," Miller said. "Those gates are gone. Only real star systems on the other side of the ones that are left."

"Is that a problem?"

"Depends on what comes through," Miller said. "That's a lot of doors to kick down all at once." The only sound was the hiss of the air recyclers. Miller nodded as if Holden had said something. "The other option is figure out a way to sneak back home with your tails between your legs and try and pretend this all never happened."

"You think we should do that?"

"I think there was an empire once that touched thousands of stars. The Eros bug? That's one of their tools. It's a wrench. And something was big enough to put a bullet in *them*. Whatever it is could be waiting behind one of those gates, waiting for someone to do something stupid. So maybe you'd rather set up shop here. Make little doomed babies. Live and die in the darkness. But at least whatever's out there stays out there."

Holden put his hand on the crash couch to steady himself. His heart was beating a mile a minute, and his hands were clammy and pale. He felt like he might throw up, and wondered whether he could get the vacuum commode working in time. In his memory, stars died.

"You think that's what we should do?" he asked. "Be quiet and get the hell out of here?"

"No, I want to open 'em. I've learned everything I can get from here, especially in lockdown. I want to figure out what happened, and that means going and taking a look at the scene."

"You're the machine that finds things."

"Yes," Miller said. "Consider the source, right? You might

want to talk about it with someone who's not dead. You people have more to lose than I do."

Holden thought for a moment, then smiled. Then laughed.

"I'm not sure it matters. I'm not in much of a position to set policy," he said.

"That's true," Miller said. "Nothing personal, but you've got lousy taste in friends."

Chapter Thirty-One: Melba

She was in her prison cell when they spun up the drum. In its previous life, the cell had been some sort of veterinary ward for large animals. Horses, maybe. Or cows. A dozen stalls, six to a side, with brushed steel walls and bars. Real bars, just like all the old videos, except with a little swinging door at the top where they could shovel in hay. Everything else was antiseptic white. Everything was locked. Her clothes were gone, replaced by a simple pale pink jumpsuit. Her hand terminal was gone. She didn't miss it. She floated in the center of the space, the walls just out of reach of her fingers and toes. It had taken a dozen attempts, reaching the wall and pushing back more and more gently, to find just the right thrust for the air resistance to stop her out where nothing could touch or be touched. Where she could float and be trapped by floating.

The man in the other cell bounced off his walls. He laughed

and he shouted, but mostly he sulked. She ignored him. He was easy to ignore. The air surrounding her had a slight breeze, the way everything did in a ship. She'd heard a story once on the way out about a ship whose circulation failed in the middle of a night shift. The whole crew had died from the zone of exhausted gas that bubbled around them, drowning in their own recycled air. She didn't think the story was true, because they would have woken up. They would have gasped and thrashed around and gotten up out of their couches, and so they would have lived. People who wanted to live did that. People who wanted to die, on the other hand, just floated.

The Klaxons sounded through the whole ship, the blatting tone resonating through the decks, taking on a voice like a vast trumpet. First, a warning. Then another. Then another. Then, silently, the bars retreated from her, falling away, and the back wall touched her shoulder like it wanted her attention but hesitated to ask. Inch by inch, her skin came to rest against the wall. For almost half a minute, the wall touched her, its energy and her inertia pressing them together like praying hands. The drum's acceleration was invisible to her. She only felt the spin sweeping her forward, and then because forward, down. Her body slid inch by inch, moving down the wall toward the deck. Her body began to take on weight; the joints in her knees and spine shifting, bearing load. She remembered reading somewhere that a woman coming back from a long time at null g could have grown almost two inches just from the disks in her spine never having the fluid pushed out of them. Between that and the muscle atrophy, coming back to weight—spin, thrust, or gravity—was the occasion for the most injury. Spinal disks were supposed to be pushed on, supposed to have the fluids go into them and back out. Without that, they turned into water balloons, and sometimes, they popped.

Her knee brushed the floor, then pressed into it. It had to have been an hour or more since the Klaxons. Up and down existed again, and she let down take her. She folded against herself, empty as damp paper. There was a drain in the floor, white ceramic unstained by any animal's blood or piss. The lights overhead flickered and grew steady again. The other prisoner was shouting for something. Food, maybe. Water. A guard to escort him to the head.

It was natural to think of it as the head now. Not the restroom. Not the water closet. She didn't call for anyone to help her, she just felt her body grow heavier, being pulled down. And because down, out. It wasn't real gravity, so it wasn't real weight. It was her mass trying to fly off into the dark and being restrained. Someone came for the other prisoner. She watched the thick plastic boots flicker across her line of sight. Then voices. Words like *loyal* and *mutiny*. Phrases like *When the time's right* and *Restore order*. They washed over her and she let them go. Her head hurt a little where her temple pushed against the floor. She wanted to sleep, but she was afraid to dream.

More footsteps, the same boots going the other way, passing her. More voices. The boots coming back. The deep metallic clank of the shackle being taken off the stall's door. Her body didn't move, but her attention focused. The guard was different. A woman with broad shoulders and a gun in her hand. She looked at Melba, shrugged, and put a hand terminal into her field of vision.

The man on the screen didn't look like a cop. His skin was pale brown, like cookie dough. There was something strange about the shape of his face—broad chin, dark eyes, wrinkles in his forehead and the corners of his mouth—that she couldn't place until he spoke and she saw him in motion. Then it was clear he was lying down and looking up at the camera.

"My name's Carlos Baca," the lying-down man said. "I'm in charge of security on the *Behemoth*. So this prison you're in? It's mine."

All right, Melba thought.

"You, now. I'm thinking you got a story to tell. The UN records of your DNA says you're Melba Koh. A bunch of people I've got no reason to disbelieve say you're Clarissa Mao. The XO of the *Rocinante* says you tried to kill her, and this Russian priest lady's backing her story. And then there's this sound engineer who says you hired him to place interruption electronics on the *Rocinante*." He went quiet for a moment. "Any of that ringing a bell?"

The case on the hand terminal was green ceramic. Or maybe enameled metal. Not plastic. A hairline scratch in the screen made an extra mark across the man's cheek, like a pirate's dueling scar in a kid's book.

"All right, how about this," he said. "Doctor says you've got a modified endocrine bundle. The kind of things terrorists use when they need to do something showy and hard to detect. And, you know, they don't give a shit if it turns their nervous system into soup in a few years. Not the kind of thing a maintenance tech could afford. Or have much reason to get."

It felt strange, the weight of her head pressing against the floor and looking down from the camera into the man's face both at the same time. Partly, she supposed that was from being weightless for so long. Her brain was still getting used to the spin gravity after relying on visual clues, and now here was this anomalous visual cue. She knew intellectually what it was, but the special analysis part of her brain still gnawed at it.

The man on the screen—he'd said his name, but she didn't remember it—pressed his lips together, then coughed once. It was a wet sound, like he was fighting off pneumonia.

"I don't think you understand how much trouble you're in," he said. "There's people accusing you of blowing up an Earth military vessel, and the case they're building is pretty goddamn good. You can take it from me, the UN has no sense of humor about that kind of thing. They will kill you. You understand that? They'll put you in front of a military tribunal, listen to a couple lawyers for maybe fifteen, twenty minutes. Then they'll blow your brains out. I can help you avoid that, but you have to talk to me.

"You know what I think? I don't think you're a professional. I think you're an amateur. You made a bunch of amateur mistakes, and things got away from you. You tell me if I'm right, and we'll go from there. But you keep playing this catatonia shit, and you're going to get killed. Do you understand what I'm saying?"

He had a good voice. It had what her singing coach would have called a thorough range. Deep as gravel, but with reedy overtones. It was the kind of voice she'd expect in a man who'd been well bruised by the world. Her singing voice had always been a little reedy too, like her father's. Petyr, poor thing, had never been able to hold a melody. The others—Michael, Anthea, Julie, Mother—had all had very pure voices. Like flutes. The problem with a flute was that it couldn't help being pure. Even sorrow sounded posed and over-lovely when the flute was expressing it. Reeds had that deeper buzz, that dirtiness, and it gave the sound authenticity. She and her father were reeds.

"Corin?" the man on the screen said. "Does she understand what I'm saying?"

The woman with the gun picked up the hand terminal, looked down at Melba, and then into the screen.

"I don't think so, chief."

"The doctor said there wasn't any brain damage."

"Did," the woman agreed. "That don't make her right, though."

The sigh carried.

"Okay," the man's voice said. "We're going to have to go from a different angle. I got an idea, but you should come back in first."

"Sa sa," the woman said. She stepped out of the cell. The bars closed again. They were narrow enough to keep a horse's hoof from passing through. She could imagine a horse trying to kick, getting its leg stuck, panicking. That would be bad. Better to avoid the problem. Wiser. Easier to stay out than to get out. Someone had said that to her once, but she didn't know who.

"Hey. Hey," the other prisoner said. He wasn't shouting, just talking loud enough that his voice carried. "Was that true? You have glandular implants? Can you break the door? I'm the captain of this ship. If you can get me out of here, I can help you."

Julie had been the best singer, except that she wouldn't do it. Didn't like performing. Father had been the performer. He'd always been the one to lead when there were songs to be sung. He was always the one to direct the poses when the family pictures were taken. He was a man who knew what he wanted and how to get it. Only he was in prison now. Not even a name, only a number. She wondered whether his cell was like hers. It would be nice if it was. Only his would be under a full g, of course. The spin gravity wasn't even up to a half g. Maybe a third, maybe even less. Like Mars or Ceres. Funny that of all the places humans lived, the Earth was always the highest gravity. It was like if you could escape from home, you could escape from anything.

"Are you there? Are you awake? I saw them bring you in. Help me, and I'll help you. Amnesty. I can get you amnesty. And protection. They can't extradite from Ceres."

That wasn't true, and she knew it. Annoyance almost moved her to speak. Moved her to *move*. But not quite. The floor was a single sheet of polymer plating, formed to slant down to the drain. With her head against the floor like this, the drain was hardly more than a black line in a field of white. A crow on a frozen lake.

"I have been taken prisoner in an illegal mutiny," the man said. "We can help each other."

She wasn't entirely sure that she could be helped. Or if she could, what she would be helped to do. She remembered wanting something once. Holden. That was right. She'd wanted him dead and worse than dead. Her fantasies of it were so strong, they were like memories. But no, she *had* done it. Everyone had hated him. They'd tried to kill him. But something else had gone wrong, and they'd thought that Julie did it.

She'd been so close. If she could have killed the *Rocinante*, they would never have found her. If she'd died on it, they'd never have been sure, and Holden would have gone down in history as the smug, self-righteous bastard that he was. But her father would have known. All that way away, he'd have heard what happened, and he would have guessed that she'd done it. His daughter. The one he could finally be proud of.

It occurred to her that the other prisoner had gone quiet. That was fine. He was annoying. Her knees ached. Her temple hurt where it pressed against the floor. They called bedsores pressure sores. She wondered how long it took for skin to macerate just from not moving. Probably a pretty long time, and she was basically healthy. She wondered how long it had been since she'd moved. It had been a long time. She found she was oddly proud of that.

The footsteps came again. More of them, this time. The plastic boots made a satisfying *clump-clump*, but there were other ones now. High, clicking footsteps, like a dog's claws on tile. She felt a tiny flicker of curiosity, like a candle in a cathedral. The boots came, and with them, little blue pumps. An older woman's ankles. The bars clanked and swung open. The pumps hesitated at the threshold, and then came in. Once they were in motion, the steps were confident. Sure.

The woman in the pumps sat, her back against the wall. Tilly Fagan looked down at her. Her hair was dyed, and her lipstick the same improbable red that made her lips look fuller than they were.

"Claire, honey?" The words were soft and uncomfortable. "It's me."

Tension crawled up her back and into her cheeks. Tension, and resentment at the tension. Aunt Tilly didn't have any right to be here. She shouldn't have been.

Tilly put a hand out, reaching down and stroking her head like it was a cat. The first human touch she could remember since she'd come to. The first gentle one she could remember at all. When Tilly spoke, her voice was low and soft and full of regret.

"They found your friend."

I don't have a friend, she thought, and then something deep under her sternum shifted and went hollow. Ren. They'd found Ren. She pulled her arm out from under her body, pressed the back of her hand against her mouth. The tears were warm and unwelcome and thick as a flood. They'd found Ren. They'd opened her tool chest and found his bones and now Soledad would know. And Bob and Stanni. They'd know what she'd done. The first sob was like a cough, and then the one after it and the one after, and Tilly's arms were around her. And God help her, she was screaming and crying into Tilly Fagan's thighs while the woman stroked her hair and made little hushing sounds.

"I'm *sorry*," she shrieked. The words ripped at her throat. They had hooks on them. "I'm *sorry*. I'm *sorry*."

"I know, honey. I know."

She had her arms around Tilly's waist now, burying her face against her side, holding on to her like Tilly's body could keep her from sinking down. From drowning. The guard said something, and she felt Tilly shaking her head no, the motion translated through their bodies.

"I did it," she said. "I killed him. I thought I had to. I told him to look at the readout so that he'd bend, so that he'd bend his neck, and he *did*. And I—and I—and I— Oh, God, I'm going to puke."

"Trashy people puke," Tilly said. "Ladies are *unwell.*"

It made her laugh. Despite everything, Clarissa laughed, and then she put her head down again and cried. Her chest hurt so badly she was sure something really was breaking. Aortic aneurysm, pulmonary embolism, something. Sorrow couldn't really feel like a heart breaking, could it? That was just a phrase.

It went on forever. And then past that, and then it slowed. Her body was as limp as a rag. Tilly's blouse was soaked with tears and snot and saliva, but she was still sitting just as she'd been. Her hand still ran through Clarissa's hair. Her fingernails traced the curve of her ear.

"You put the bomb on the *Seung Un*," Tilly said, "and framed Jim Holden for it."

It wasn't a question or an accusation. She didn't want Clarissa to confess, just to confirm. Clarissa nodded against Tilly's lap. When she spoke, her voice clicked and her throat felt thick and raw.

"He hurt Daddy. Had to do something."

Tilly sighed.

"Your father is a first-class shit," she said, and because it was her saying it, it didn't hurt to hear.

"I've got to tell the chief," the guard said, apology in her voice. "I mean about what happened. He wants me to report in."

"I'm not stopping you," Tilly said.

"You need to come with me," the guard said. "I can't leave you there with her. It's not safe."

A flash of panic lit her mind. She couldn't be alone. Not now. They couldn't leave her locked up and alone.

"Don't be ridiculous," Tilly said. "You go do whatever it is you need to do. I'll be here with Claire."

"Ah. That girl killed a lot of people, ma'am."

The silence was just a beat, and without shifting her head, Clarissa knew what look was on Tilly's face. The guard cleared her throat.

"I'll have to lock the door, ma'am."

"Do what you need to, Officer," Tilly said.

The bars shifted and crashed. The lock clacked home. The footsteps retreated. Clarissa wept for Ren. Maybe the others would come later. The dead soldiers on the *Seung Un*. Holden's lover whom she'd beaten and brutalized. All the men and women who'd died because they'd followed Holden through the Ring. She might have tears for them, but now it was only Ren, and she didn't think she would stop in her lifetime.

"I deserve to die," she said. "I've become a very bad person."

Tilly didn't disagree, but she didn't stop cradling her either.

"There's someone I'd like you to talk to," she said.

Chapter Thirty-Two: Anna

The security force had come first, three soldiers in a shuttle with guns and restraints for Melba. Or Clarissa. Whoever she was. Then, much later, a medical evacuation had come, taking the *Rocinante*'s crew.

Anna's own ride arrived almost a day later, not an afterthought, but not a priority. The way things had all come about, she thought not being a priority was probably a sign things were going well for her.

When she arrived on the *Behemoth*, she had expected to see someone from that ship's security team. Or, if they were well enough, maybe Naomi and the other two crewmen from the *Rocinante*.

Hector Cortez stood in the shuttle bay. He smiled when he saw her and raised his hand in a little wave of greeting. The motion reminded her of her grandfather in his failing days: careful and a little awkward. She thought Cortez had aged a decade in a few days, then realized he must have been injured in the catastrophe.

"Anna," he said. "I am so glad to see you."

The *Behemoth*'s massive drum section was spinning now, creating a vertigo-inducing false gravity. Anna's feet told her that she was standing on solid ground. Her inner ear argued that she was falling over sideways, and kept trying to get her to tilt her body the other direction. It wasn't enough to make her steps unsteady, but it did make everything feel a little surreal. Having Hector Cortez, celebrity and minister to the powerful, kiss her cheek didn't make things any less dreamlike.

"It's good to see you too," she said. "I didn't know you were on the *Behemoth*."

"We've all come," he said. "They've left the smallest of crews on the *Thomas Prince*, and we've all come here. All of us that are left. We've lost so many. I attended services yesterday for the fallen. Father Michel. Rabbi Black. Paolo Sedon."

Anna felt a little twinge of dread.

"Alonzo Guzman?"

Cortez shook his head.

"Neither alive nor dead," he said. "They have him in a medical coma, but he's not expected to survive."

Anna remembered the man's pleading eyes. If she'd only found help for him sooner...

"I'm sorry to have missed that service," she said.

"I know," Cortez said. "It's why I wanted to meet you. May I walk with you?"

"Of course," Anna said. "But I don't know where I'm going."

"Then I will give you the basic orientation," the old man said, turning a degree and sweeping his hand toward the shuttle bay. "Come with me, and I will bring you to the glory of the lift system."

Anna chuckled and let him lead the way. He walked carefully too. Not mincing, but not striding. He seemed like a different person than the one who'd called the three factions of humanity together to pass through the Ring and into the unknown. It was more than just how he held his body too.

"I thought it was important that those of us who were part of the petition speak at the service," he said. "I wanted our regret to have a voice."

"Our regret?"

He nodded.

"Yours. Mine. All of us who advised that we come to this darkness. It was hubris, and the innocent have suffered because of it. Died for listening to our bad advice. God has humbled me."

His voice still had the richness of a lifetime's practice, but there was a new note in it. A high, childlike whine underneath the grandeur. Sympathy for his distress and an uncharitable annoyance sprang up in her.

"I don't know that I see it that way," she said. "We didn't come here to glorify ourselves. We did it to keep people from fighting. To remind ourselves and each other that we're all together in this. I can't think that's an evil impulse. And I can't see what happened to us as punishment. Time and chance—"

"Befall all men," Hector said. "Yes."

Behind them, a shuttle's attitude rocket roared for a moment, then cut off. A pair of Belters in gray jumpsuits sauntered toward it, toolboxes in their hands. Cortez was scowling.

"But even given what grew from that seed? You still don't think we were punished? The decision was not made out of arrogance?"

"History is made up of people recovering from the last disaster," Anna said. "What happened was terrible. *Is* terrible. But I still can't see God's punishment in it."

"I do," Cortez said. "I believe we have fallen into a realm of evil. And more, Doctor Volovodov, I fear we have been tainted by it."

"I don't see—"

"The devil is here," Cortez said. He shook his head at Anna's protesting frown. "Not some cartoon demon. I'm not a fool. But the devil has always lived in men when they reach too far, when they fail to ask if they *should* do something just because they *can* do it. We have— *I* have fallen into his trap. And worse, we have blazed the trail to him. History will not remember us kindly for what we have done."

Anna knew quite a few members of the Latter-day Saints church. They agreed with the Methodists on a few minor things like not drinking alcohol, which gave them a sense of solidarity at interfaith conventions. They disagreed on some important things, like the nature of God and His plan for the universe, which didn't seem to matter as much as Anna would have thought. They tended to be happy, family-oriented, and unassuming.

Standing in the belly of the *Behemoth*, Anna would never have guessed they would build something like the massive generation ship. It was so big, so extravagant. It was like a rebellious shout at the emptiness of space. *The universe is too big for our ship to move through it in a reasonable time? Fine, we'll stuff all the bits of the universe we need inside of our ship and then go at our own pace.* The inner walls of the rotating drum curved up in the distance, Coriolis effect masquerading as mass, metal ribbing and plates pretending to be substrate, just waiting for soil and plants and farm animals. Through the center of the drum, half a kilometer over Anna's head, a narrow thread of bright yellow light shone down on them all. The sun, stretched into a line in the sky. The entire idea of it was arrogant and defiant and grandiose.

Anna loved it.

As she walked across a wide empty plain of steel that should have been covered in topsoil and crops, she thought that this audaciousness was exactly what humanity had lost somewhere in the last couple of centuries. When ancient maritime explorers had climbed into their creaking wooden ships and tried to find ways to cross the great oceans of Earth, had their voyage been any less dangerous than the one the Mormons had been planning to attempt? The end point any less mysterious? But in both cases, they'd been driven to find out what was on the other side of the long trip. Driven by a need to see shores no one else had ever seen before. Show a human a closed door, and no matter how many open doors she finds, she'll be haunted by what might be behind it.

A few people liked to paint this drive as a weakness. A failing of the species. Humanity as the virus. The creature that never stops filling up its available living space. Hector seemed to be moving over to that view, based on their last conversation. But Anna rejected that idea. If humanity were capable of being satisfied, then they'd all still be living in trees and eating bugs out of one another's fur. Anna had walked on a moon of Jupiter. She'd looked up through a dome-covered sky at the great red spot, close enough to see the swirls and eddies of a storm larger than her home world. She'd tasted water thawed from ice as old as the solar system itself. And it was that human dissatisfaction, that human audacity, that had put her there.

Looking at the tiny world spinning around her, she knew one day it would give them the stars as well.

The refugee camp was a network of tents and prefabricated temporary structures set on the inner face of the drum, the long thin line of sun-bright light pressing down onto them all like a spring afternoon on Earth. It took her almost half an hour to find Chris Williams' tent. The liaison from the *Thomas Prince* let her know that the young naval officer had survived the catastrophe, but had suffered terrible injuries in the process. Anna wanted to find him, and maybe through him the rest of the little congregation she'd formed during the trip out.

A few questions of helpful refugees later, and she found his tent. There was no way to knock or buzz, so she just scratched at the tent flap and said, "Chris? You in there?"

"That you, Pastor? Come on in."

The liaison hadn't been specific in her descriptions of Chris' injuries, so Anna braced herself for the worst when she entered. The young lieutenant was lying in a military-style cot, propped up by a number of pillows. He had a small terminal on his lap that he set aside as she came in. His left arm and left leg both ended at the middle joint.

"Oh, Chris, I'm—"

"If your next word is 'sorry,' " he said, "I'm going to hop over there and kick your ass."

Anna started laughing even as the tears filled her eyes. "I am sorry, but now I'm sorry for being sorry." She sat by the edge of his cot and took his right hand. "How are you, Chris?"

"With a few obvious exceptions"—he waved his shortened left arm around—"I came through the disaster better than most. I didn't even have a bad bruise."

"I don't know how the navy health plan works," Anna started, but Chris waved her off.

"Full regrowth therapy. We ever get out of here and back to civilization, and a few painful and itchy months later I'll have bright pink replacements."

"Well, that's good," Anna said. She'd been about to offer to pay for his treatment, not knowing how she'd actually do that. She felt a moment of relief and shame. "Have you heard from anyone else who was in our group? I haven't had time to find them yet."

"Yeah," Chris said with a chuckle, "I heard. You've been doing commando raids while I've been laid up. If I'd known they trained you guys to take down souped-up terrorists, I'd have paid more attention in church as a kid."

"I ran away from her until she had a seizure, and then I taped her to a chair. Not very heroic."

"I'm getting a medal for falling into a pressure hatch, sacrificing an arm and a leg to keep seven sailors from being trapped in a compromised part of the ship. I was unconscious at the time, but that doesn't seem to matter. Heroism is a label most people get for doing shit they'd never do if they were really thinking about it."

Anna laughed at that. "I've been thinking a lot about that exact thing recently." Chris relaxed back into his pile of pillows and nodded for her to continue.

"Labels, I mean. People are calling the aliens evil, because they hurt us. And without context, how do we know?"

"Yeah," Chris said. "I lose a couple limbs getting drunk and falling into a harvesting combine, I'm an idiot. I lose the same limbs because I happened to be standing next to the right door when the ship was damaged, I'm a hero."

"Maybe it's as simple as that. I don't know. I feel like something really important is about to happen, and we're all making up our minds ahead of time what it will be."

Chris absentmindedly scratched at the stump of his left leg, then grimaced. "Like?"

"We came through the Ring to stop James Holden from talking to the aliens first. But this is the same man that helped send Eros to Venus instead of letting it destroy the Earth. Why did we assume he'd do a bad job of being the first human the aliens met? And now something has slapped us down, taken all our guns away, but not killed us. That should mean something. Certainly anything this powerful could kill us as easily as it declawed us. But it didn't. Instead of trying to figure out what it means, we're hurting so we call it evil. I feel like we're children who've been punished and we think it's because our parents are mean."

"They stopped our ships to...what? Pacify us?" Chris asked.

"Who knows?" Anna said, shrugging. "But I know we're not asking those questions. Humans do bad things when they're afraid, and we're all very afraid right now."

"Tara died," Chris said.

Anna racked her brain trying to remember who Tara was. Chris saw her confusion and added, "Short blond hair? She was a marine?"

"Oh no," Anna replied, feeling the tears well up again. Her angry marine had died. A whole future in which she'd worked with Tara to find out the source of her anger vanished. Conversations she'd already had in her head, lines of questioning, the anticipation of satisfaction she'd get from having the marine open up to her. Gone, as if someone had flicked a switch. It was hard not to sympathize with Cortez's view a little. After all, the aliens had killed one of her congregation now.

But maybe not on purpose, and intent mattered. The universe made no sense to her otherwise.

She managed to finish off her visit without, she hoped, seeming too distracted. Afterward, she went to find her own assigned tent and try to rest. She had no reason to think that sleep would come. After she found her place, Tilly Fagan appeared. Anna lifted her arm in greeting, but before she could get a word out, Tilly threw both arms around her and was squeezing until she could hear her ribs pop. Tilly was surprisingly strong for such a thin woman.

"I was furious with myself for letting you leave," Tilly said, squeezing even tighter and leaning her weight against Anna. She was heavy. They both were in the spinning drum. It took some getting used to.

When Tilly finally let up the pressure a bit, Anna said, "I think I was...altered."

"That was my fault, too," Tilly said, followed by more squeezing. Anna realized the only thing to do was ride it out, and patted Tilly on the lower back until her friend got it out of her system.

After a few moments, Tilly released Anna and stepped back, her eyes shiny but a smile on her face. "I'm glad you didn't die. Everyone else from the *Prince* is a pod." Anna decided not to ask what a pod was. "The *Behemoth* has become the place to be," Tilly continued. "If we never figure out how to escape this trap, it's the place it will take us the longest to die. That makes it the high-rent district of the slow zone."

"Well, that's...important."

Tilly laughed. She pulled a cigarette out and lit it as they walked. At Anna's shocked look she said, "They let you do it here. Lots of the Belters do. They obsess over air filters and then suck poisonous particulates into their lungs recreationally. It's a fabulous culture."

Anna smiled and waved the smoke away from her face.

"So," Tilly said, pretending not to notice. "I demanded they let me go on the first shuttle over. Did you manage to retrieve Holden?"

"I didn't find him," Anna said. "Just his crew. But I think I might have saved their lives."

At first, she thought Tilly's expression had cooled, but that wasn't quite right. It wasn't coldness. It was pain. Anna put her hand on Tilly's arm.

"I have someone I need you to talk to," Tilly said. "And you probably aren't going to like it, but you're going to do it for me. I'll never ask you for anything again, and you're buying a lifetime of expensive markers to trade in with this."

"Whatever I can do."

"You're going to help Claire."

Anna felt like the air had gone out of the room. For a moment, she heard the throat-scarring screams again and felt the blows transferred through the buckling locker door. She heard Chris tell her that Tara had died. She saw Cortez, and heard the buzzsaw despair in his voice. She took a breath.

"Yes," she said. "Of course I am."

Chapter Thirty-Three: Bull

You need to get up," Doctor Sterling said. Spin changed the shape of her face, pulling down her cheeks and hair. She looked older and more familiar.

"I thought I wasn't supposed to move around," Bull said, and coughed.

"That was when I was worried about your spinal cord. Now I'm worried about your lungs. You're having enough trouble clearing secretions, I'm about ready to call it mild pneumonia."

"I'll be fine."

"Spin gravity's not going to do you much good if you're flat on your back," she said, tapping his shoulder for emphasis. "You have to sit up more."

Bull gritted his teeth.

"I can't sit up," he said. "I don't have abdominal muscles. I can't do *anything*."

"You have an adjustable bed," the doctor said, unfazed. "Adjust it. Stay upright as much as you can."

"Isn't that going to screw up my spine even worse?"

"We can brace you," she said. "Anyway, you can live without functioning legs. You can't live without functioning lungs."

The medical wards had changed. Spinning up the drum had meant stripping away as many of the alterations that had changed the generation ship into a weapon of war as they could. The medical stations and emergency showers had all been turned ninety degrees in the refit, prepared to use under thrust or not at all. What had been designed back in what seemed like ancient times to be floors had become walls, and now they were floors again. The whole thing was a hesitation. A stutter-step in industrial steel and ceramic. It was like something that had been broken and grew back wrong.

"I'll do what I can," Bull said, his teeth clenched against another cough. "If I've got to sit up, can I at least get something that travels a little? I'm getting pretty tired of being in the same room all the time."

"I don't recommend it."

"You gonna stop me?"

"I am not."

They paused. Frustration and animosity hung in the air between them. Neither one had slept enough. Both were pushing themselves too hard trying to keep people alive. And they weren't going to make each other happy.

"I'll do what I can, doc," Bull said. "How's it going out there?"

"People are dying. It's slowing down, though. At this point, almost all of the emergent cases are stabilized or dead. Right now it's pretty much the same for everyone. Wound care and support. Keep an eye out for people who had some sort of internal injury we didn't see at the time and try to catch them before they crash. Rest, fluid, light exercise, and prayer."

"All right," he said as his hand terminal chimed. Another connection request. From the *Hammurabi*, the Martian frigate where Captain Jim Holden was being held.

"And how's it going on your end?" Doctor Sterling said. Her lips were pressed thin. She knew the answer. Bull used the controls on his bed, shifting himself up to something approaching a seated position. He could feel a difference in his breath, but if anything it made it harder to keep from coughing.

"Let you know in a minute," he said and accepted the connection. Captain Jakande appeared on the screen.

"Captain," Bull said, making the title a greeting.

"Mister Baca," she said in return. "I got your last message."

"I don't suppose you're calling to arrange the transfer of the prisoner and your remaining crew?"

She didn't smile.

"I wanted to thank you for the staging area you've provided for our medical staff. We will not, however, be transferring any further personnel to your vessel or remanding the prisoner to your custody."

"You don't have a sufficient complement left on your ship to run it. Not even as a skeleton crew. Between the injured and the medics and the injured medics, I've got two-thirds of your people here right now."

"And I thank you for that."

"My point is you have a third or less of your crew left standing. You're pulling double, maybe triple shifts. Earth is still making noise about transferring Holden to them until he's answered charges for the *Seung Un*." He hadn't mentioned Clarissa Mao's confession. That was a card he could play another time. He lifted his hand. "All of us have watched someone we cared about die because of something we don't understand. All of us are grieving and scared. If we don't all come together, someone's going to do something we'll all regret."

"The Martian military code requires—"

"I've got an open investigation here. I'll share all the information we've gathered. Some of it's pretty damn interesting."

Something moved in his chest, and he was coughing so hard he couldn't speak or listen. Phlegm filled his mouth, and he leaned over, supporting himself with his arms, to spit it out. Maybe there was something to this sitting-up thing.

"The Martian military code prohibits the surrender of prisoners except in cases of trades authorized by the government. We can't talk to the MCR, so nothing's getting authorized."

"You could surrender to me."

She laughed that time. The façade of military propriety cracked.

"I wish. I'd be able get a full shift's sleep. But that tin can you're in couldn't take us, even if we *could* fight."

"Which we can't, so we're pretty much down to angry letters at twenty paces. I appreciate the call," he said. "I'll let the captain know it's no-go. But hey, lemme ask you. What are you guys gonna do when Earth sends a couple dozen marines with cutting torches and kitchen knives?"

"Fight with cutting torches and knives," she said. "This is the *Hammurabi* signing off."

Bull watched the dull standby screen for half a minute before he put it down. He'd have to tell Pa, but he wasn't looking forward to that. She had enough on her plate coordinating all the things he couldn't because he was trapped in the medical ward.

No matter what Holden's criminal status with Earth and Mars was, no matter how many people took the blame for the things he was accused of, it didn't matter. It was a pretext. He was the only person not covered by military treaty who could be debriefed about whatever was on the alien station. Earth wanted him. The OPA wanted him. Mars had him, and wouldn't give him up just for the joy of having something other people wanted.

And sooner or later some Martian with too much stress and not enough sleep who thought Holden was responsible for drawing them all through the Ring was going to take revenge for a lover or friend who'd died. Bull scratched at his neck, the stubble rough against his fingertips. His body, empty, splayed out before him in the one-third g.

"Bull?"

He looked up. The nurse seemed, if anything, more tired than the doctor had been.

"You've got a couple visitors, if you're up for it," he said.

"Depends. Who you got?"

"Priest," he said. It took a moment to realize it wasn't a name but a job description.

"The Russian from the *Rocinante*?"

The nurse shook his head. "The politician. Cortez."

"What does he want?"

"As far as I can tell? Save your soul. He's talking about protecting humanity from the devil. I think he wants you to help with that."

"Tell him to talk to Serge at the security office. Who else wants a piece of me?"

The nurse's expression changed. For a moment, Bull couldn't say what was strange about it, then he realized it was the first time in his memory he'd seen the nurse smile.

"Someone's got a little prezzie for you," the nurse said, then leaned back out into the corridor. "Okay. Come on in."

Bull coughed again, bringing up more phlegm. Sam appeared in the doorway, grinning. Behind her, two techs were carrying a blue plastic crate so big he could have put Sam inside it.

"Rosenberg? You been wasting time when you should be fixing my ship?"

"You've still got one more mutiny before it's your ship," Sam said. "And yeah, when the crew heard about what happened with you and Ashford, some of us wanted to put together a little present."

Bull shifted, then caught himself. He was so used to having the muscles in his trunk to hold himself up that every time he began to fall, it was a little surprising. It was one of the things he missed about null g. Sam didn't notice, or pretended not to. She shifted to the side and took hold of the crate's release bar like a stage magician about to reveal an illusion. Doctor Sterling appeared in the doorway, a sly smile haunting her lips. Bull had the uncomfortable feeling of walking in on his own surprise party.

"You're making me nervous," he said.

"You're getting smarter," she said. "Ready?"

"Yeah, I don't think so."

The crate slid open. The mech inside looked complicated, blocky, and thick. Bull laughed for lack of anything he could think to say.

"It's a standard lifting mech," Sam said, "but we carved a bunch of the reinforcing out of its tummy and put in a TLS orthosis the medics gave me. We swapped out the leg actuation with a simple joystick control. It won't take you dancing, and you're still going to need help going potty, but you're not stuck in bed. It's not as comfortable as a top-end wheelchair, but it will get you anywhere in the ship you want to go, whether it was built for accessibility or not."

Bull thought he was about to cough again until he felt the tears welling up in his eyes.

"Aw shit, Sam."

"None of that, you big baby. Let's just get you in and adjust the support plates."

Sam took one shoulder, the nurse the other. The sensation of being carried was strange. Bull didn't know the last time anyone had picked him up. The brace in the guts of the mech was like a girdle, and Sam had put straps along the mech's struts to keep his legs from flapping around. It was an inversion of the usual; instead of using his legs to move the mech, he was using the mech to move his legs. For the first time since the catastrophe, Bull walked down the short hall and into the general ward. Sam kept pace, her gaze on the mechanism like a mother duck taking her ducklings for their first swim. His sense of wrongness didn't leave, but it lessened.

The worst of the injured from all three sides were here, men and women, Belter and Earther and Martian. A bald man with skin an unhealthy yellow struggled to breathe; a woman so young-looking Bull could hardly believe she wasn't a child lay almost naked in a bed, her skin mostly burned away and a distant look in her eyes;

a thick-bodied man with an Old Testament prophet's beard and body hair like a chimp moaned and shifted through his sedation. In the disposable plastic medical gowns, there was nothing to show who belonged to what side. They were people, and they were on his ship, so they were his people.

At the end of the corridor, Corin stood in front of a doorway, a pistol on her hip. Her salute was on the edge between serious and mocking.

"Macht *sly*, chief," she said. "Suits."

"Thank you," Bull said.

"Here to see the prisoners?"

"Sure," Bull said. He hadn't meant to go anywhere in particular, but since he could, he could. The lockdown ward was smaller, but other than one of his security staff at the door, there weren't any signs that the patients here were different. *Prisoners* was a strong word. None of them were legally bound. They ranged from high-value civilians from Earth to the highest-ranking Martian wounded. Anyone whom Bull thought might be particularly useful, now or later. All of the dozen beds were full.

"How's it feeling?" Sam asked.

"Seems like it lists to the right a little," Bull said.

"Yeah, I was thinking maybe—"

The new voice came from the farthest bed, weak and confused but unmistakable:

"Sam?"

Sam's attention snapped to the back, and she took a couple tentative steps toward the woman who had spoken.

"Naomi? Oh holy crap, sweetie. What happened to you?"

"Got in a fight," the XO of the *Rocinante* said through bruised and broken lips. "Whipped her ass."

"You know Nagata?" Bull asked.

"From the bad old days," Sam said, taking her hand. "We were roommates for about six days while she and Jim Holden were having a fight."

"Where," Naomi said. "Where's my *crew*?"

"They're here," Bull said, maneuvering his mech closer to her. "All but Holden."

"They're all right?"

"I've felt better," a balding, slightly pudgy man with skin the color of toast said. He had the drawl of Mariner Valley on Mars or West Texas on Earth. It was hard to tell the difference.

"Alex," Naomi said. "Where's Amos?"

"Next bed over," Alex said. "He's been sleepin' a lot. What happened, anyway? We get arrested?"

"There was an accident," Bull said. "A lot of people got hurt."

"But we ain't arrested," Alex said.

"No."

"Well that's all right, then."

On her bed, Naomi Nagata had visibly relaxed. Knowing her crew were alive and with her carried a lot of weight. Bull filed the information away in case it was useful later.

"The woman who attacked you is under arrest," Bull said.

"She's the one. The bomb," Naomi said.

"We're looking into that," he said, trying to keep his tone reassuring. Another coughing fit spoiled the effect.

Naomi frowned, remembering something. Bull wished he could take her other hand. Build some rapport. The mech was a fine way to walk around, but there were other ways it was limiting.

"Jim?" she said.

"Captain Holden has been taken into custody by the Martian navy," Bull said. "I'm trying to negotiate his release into our custody, but it's not going very well so far."

Naomi smiled as if he'd given her good news and nodded. Her eyes closed.

"What 'bout Miller?"

"Who?" Bull asked, but she was already asleep. Sam shifted to Alex's bed and Bull stepped over to look down on the *Rocinante*'s sleeping mechanic. Amos Burton. They were a pretty sad bunch, and far too small a crew to run a ship like theirs safely. Maybe Jakande could get some pointers from them.

Until he got Holden, they were going to be at a disadvantage. The man was a professional symbol, and creating calm when there was no reason for it was all about symbols. Captain Jakande wouldn't bend, because if she did, she'd be court-martialed when they got back. If they got back. Bull didn't like it, but he understood it. If they'd been anywhere but the slow zone, they'd all have been rattling sabers and baring teeth. Instead, all they could do was talk...

Bull's mouth went dry. Sam was still looking at Naomi Nagata's bed, her face angry and despairing.

"Sam," Bull said. "Got a minute?"

She looked up and nodded. Bull flicked the little joystick, and the mech trod awkwardly around. He steered it back out through the door and back to his own private room. By the time they got there, Sam's expression had shifted to curious. Bull closed the door, coughing. He felt a little light-headed and his heart was racing. Fear, excitement, or being vertical for the first time since they'd passed through the Ring, he didn't know.

"What's up, boss?"

"The comm laser," Bull said. "Say I wanted to make it into a weapon. What's the most power we could put through it?"

Sam's frown was more than an engineer making mental calculations. The spin gravity made her seem older. Or maybe bathing in death and fear just did that to people.

"I can make it about as hot as the middle of a star for a fraction of a second," Sam said. "It'd burn that side of the ship down to a bad smell, though."

"What's the most we could do and get, say, three shots out of it? And not melt our ship?"

"It can already carve through a ship's hull if you've got time to spare. I can probably pare that time down a bit."

"Get that going, will you?"

Sam shook her head.

"What?" Bull asked.

"That big glowy ball out there can turn off inertia when it feels threatened. I don't feel comfortable making light into a weapon. Seriously, what if it decides to stop all the photons or something?"

"If we have it, we won't need to use it."

Sam shook her head again.

"I can't do that for you, Bull."

"What about the captain? Would you do it for a Belter?"

Sam's cheeks flushed. It might have been embarrassment or anger.

"Cheap shot."

"Sorry, but would you take a direct order from Captain Pa?"

"From her, yes. But not because she's a Belter. Because she's the captain and I trust her judgment."

"More than mine."

Sam held up her hands in a Belter shrug.

"Last time I just did whatever you told me to, I wound up under house arrest."

Bull had to give her the point. He fumbled to extricate his arm from the mech, scooped up his hand terminal, and put in a priority connection request to Pa. She took it almost immediately. She looked older too, worn, solid, certain. Crisis suited her.

"Mister Baca," she said. "Where do we stand?"

"Captain Jakande isn't going to bring her people over, even though they all know it would be better. And she won't give up Holden."

"All right," Pa said. "Well, we tried."

"But she might surrender to you," Bull said. "And seems to me it's going to be a lot easier being sheriff if we can get the only gun in the slow zone."

Pa tilted her head.

"Go on," she said.

Chapter Thirty-Four: Clarissa

The guards came, brought thinly rationed food-grade protein and measured bottles of water, led the prisoners to the head with pistols drawn, and then took them back. For the most part, Clarissa lay on the floor or stretched, hummed old songs to herself or drew on the skin of her arms—white fingernail scratches. The boredom would have been crushing if she'd felt it, but she seemed to have unconnected from time.

The only times she cried were when she thought of killing Ren and when she remembered her father. The only things she anticipated at all were another visit from Tilly or her mysterious friend, and death.

The woman came first, and when she did, Clarissa recognized her. With her red hair pulled down by spin, her face looked softer, but the eyes were unforgettable. The woman from the galley on the *Thomas Prince*. And then, later, from the *Rocinante*. Anna. She'd told Naomi that her name was Anna.

Just one more person Clarissa had tried to kill once.

"I have permission to speak with her," Anna said. The guard—a broad-faced man with a scarred arm that he wore like a decoration—crossed his arms.

"She's here, si no? Talk away."

"Absolutely not," Anna said. "This is a private conversation. I can't have it in front of the others."

"You can't have it anywhere else," the guard said. "You know how many people this coya killed? She's got implants. Dangerous."

"She knows," Clarissa said, and Anna flashed a smile at her like they'd shared a joke. A feeling of unease cooled Clarissa's gut. There was something threatening about a woman who could take being attacked and treat it like it was a shared intimacy. Clarissa wondered whether she wanted to talk with her after all.

"It's the risk I came here to take," Anna said. "You can find us a place. An…an interview room. You have those, don't you?"

The guard's stance settled deeper into his knees and hips, immovable.

"Can stay here until the sun burns out," he said. "That door's staying closed."

"It's all right," Clarissa said.

"No it isn't," Anna said. "I'm her priest, and the things we need to talk about are private. Please open the door and take us some-place we can talk."

"Jojo," the captain at the far end of the hall said. Ashford. That was his name. "It's all right. You can put them in the meat freezer. It's not in use and it locks from the outside."

"Then I get a dead preacher, ano sa?"

"I believe that you won't," Anna said.

"Then you believe in vacuum fairies," the guard said, but he unlocked the cell door. The bars swung open. Clarissa hesitated. Behind guard and priest, the disgraced Captain Ashford watched her, peering through his bars to get a look. He needed to shave and he looked like he'd been crying. For a moment, Clarissa gripped the cold steel bars of her door. The urge to pull them closed, to retreat, was almost overwhelming.

"It's all right," Anna said.

Clarissa let go of the door and stepped out. The guard drew his sidearm and pressed it against the back of her neck. Anna looked pained. Ashford's expression didn't shift a millimeter.

"Is that necessary?" Anna asked.

"Implants," the guard said and prodded Clarissa to move forward. She walked.

The freezer was warm and larger than the galley back on the *Cerisier*. Strips of metal ran along floor and ceiling and both walls with notches every few centimeters to allow the Mormon colonists who never were to lock walls and partitions into place. It made sense that the veterinary stalls that had been pressed into service as her prison would be near the slaughterhouse. Harsh white light spilled from LEDs set into the walls, unsoftened and directional, casting hard shadows.

"I'm back in fifteen minutes," the guard said as he pushed Clarissa through the doorway. "Anything looks funny, I'll shoot you."

"Thank you for giving us privacy," Anna said, stepping through after her. The door closed. The latch sounded like the gates of hell, closing. The lights flickered, and the first thought that flashed across Clarissa's mind, rich with disapproval, was, *Shouldn't tie the locking magnet to the same circuit as the control board.* It was like a relic from another life.

Anna gathered herself, smiled, and put out her hand.

"We've met before," she said, "but we haven't really been introduced. My name's Anna."

A lifetime's etiquette accepted the offered hand on Clarissa's behalf. The woman's fingers were very warm.

"My priest?" Clarissa said.

"Sorry about that," Anna said. "I didn't mean to presume. I was getting angry, and I tried to pull rank."

"I know people who do worse. When they're angry."

Clarissa released the woman's hand.

"I'm a friend of Tilly's. She helped me after the ship crashed. I was hurt and not thinking very straight, and she helped me," she said.

"She's good that way."

"She knew your sister too. Your father. The whole family," Anna said, then pressed her lips together impatiently. "I wish they'd given us chairs. I feel like we're standing around at a bus terminal."

Anna took a deep breath, sighing out her nose, then sat there in the middle of the room with her legs crossed. She patted the metal decking at her side. Clarissa hesitated, then lowered herself to sit. She had the overwhelming memory of being five years old, sitting on a rug in kindergarten.

"That's better," Anna said. "So, Tilly's told me a lot about you. She's worried."

Clarissa tilted her head. From just the form, it seemed like the place where she would reply. She felt the urge to speak, and she couldn't imagine what she would say. After a moment, Anna went on, trying again without seeming to.

"I'm worried about you too."

"Why?"

Anna's eyes clouded. For a moment, she seemed to be having some internal conversation. But only for a moment. She leaned forward, her hands clasped.

"I didn't help you before. I saw you just before the *Seung Un* blew up," she said. "Just before you set off the bomb."

"It was too late by then," Clarissa said. Ren had already been dead. "You couldn't have stopped it."

"You're right," Anna said. "That's not the only reason I'm here. I also...I lost someone. When all the ships stopped, I lost someone."

"Someone you cared about," Clarissa said. "Someone you loved."

"Someone I hardly knew, but it was a real loss. And also I was scared of you. I *am* scared of you. But Tilly told me a lot about you, and it's helped me to get past some of my fear."

"Not all of it?"

"No. Not all of it."

Something deep in the structure of the ship thumped, the whole structure around them ringing for a moment like a gigantic bell tolling far, far away.

"I could kill you," Clarissa said. "Before they got the door open."

"I know. I saw."

Clarissa put her hand out, her palm against the notched runner. The finish was smooth and the metal cool.

"You want a confession, then?" she said.

"If you want to offer one."

"I did it," Clarissa said. "I sabotaged the *Rocinante* and the *Seung Un.* I killed Ren. I killed some people back on Earth. I lied about who I was. All of it. I'm guilty."

"All right."

"Are we done, then?"

Anna scratched her nose and sighed. "I came out to the Ring even though it upset my wife. Even though it meant not seeing my baby for months. I told myself that I wanted to come see it. To help people make sense of it and, whatever it was, to not be afraid. You came out here to...save your father. To redeem him."

"Is that what Tilly says?"

"She's not as polite about it."

Clarissa coughed out a laugh. Everything she could say felt trite. Worse, it felt naive and stupid. *Jim Holden destroyed my family* and *I wanted my father to be proud of me* and *I was wrong.*

"I did what I did," Clarissa said. "You can tell them that. The security people. You can tell them I confessed to it all."

"If you'd like. I'll tell them."

"I would. I want that."

"Why did you try to kill Naomi?"

"I wanted to kill all of them," Clarissa said, and each word was hard to speak, as though they were too large to fit through her throat. "They were part of him, and I wanted him not to be. Just not to exist at all anymore. I wanted everyone to know he is a bad man."

"Do you still want that?"

"I don't care," Clarissa said. "You can tell them."

"And Naomi? I'm going to see her. Is there anything you'd want me to tell her in particular?"

Clarissa remembered the woman's face, bruised and bleeding. She flexed her hand, feeling the mech's glove against her fingers. It would have taken nothing to snap the woman's neck, a feather's weight of pressure. She wondered why she hadn't. The difference between savoring the moment and hesitating warred at the back of her mind, and her memory supported both. Or neither.

"Tell her I hope she gets well soon."

"Do you hope that?"

"Or am I just being polite, you mean?" Clarissa said. "Tell her whatever you want. I don't care."

"All right," Anna said. "Can I ask a question?"

"Can I stop you?"

"Yes."

The silence was no more than three long breaths together.

"You can ask me a question."

"Do you want to be redeemed?"

"I don't believe in God."

"Do you want to be redeemed by something other than God, then? If there was forgiveness for you, could you accept it?"

The sense of outrage began in Clarissa's stomach and bloomed out through her chest. It curled her lips and furrowed her brow. For the first time since she'd lost consciousness trying to beat her way through the locker on the *Rocinante*, she remembered what anger felt like. How large it was.

"Why should I be forgiven for anything? I did it. That's all."

"But if—"

"What kind of justice would that be? 'Oh, you killed Ren, but you're sorry now so it's okay'? *Fuck* that. And if that's how your God works, then fuck Him too."

The freezer door clanked. Clarissa looked up at it, resenting the accident of timing and then realizing they'd heard her yelling. They were coming to save the preacher. She balled her hands into fists and looked down at them. They were going to take her back to her cell. She felt in her gut and her throat how little she wanted that.

"It's all right," Anna said as the guard stepped into the freezer, his sidearm trained on Clarissa. "We're okay."

"Yeah, no," the guard said. His gaze was sharp and focused. Frightened. "Time's passed. Meeting's over."

Anna looked at Clarissa with something like frustration in her expression. Not with her, but with the situation. With not getting everything to be just the way she wanted it. Clarissa had some sympathy for that.

"I'd like to talk with you again," Anna said. "If it's all right."

"You know where I live," Clarissa said with a shrug. "I don't go out much."

Chapter Thirty-Five: Anna

Bull wasn't in his office when she arrived. A muscular young woman with a large gun on her hip shrugged when Anna asked if she could wait for him, then ignored her and continued working. A wall screen was set to the Radio Free Slow Zone feed, where a young Earther man was leaning in toward Monica Stuart and speaking earnestly. His skin was a bright pink that didn't seem to be his natural color. Anna thought he looked peeled.

"I haven't changed my commitment to autonomy for the Brazilian shared interest zones," he said. "If anything I feel like I've broadened it."

"Broadened it how?" Monica asked. She seemed genuinely interested. It was a gift. The peeled man tapped at the air with his fingertips. Anna felt sure she'd seen him on the *Thomas Prince*, but she couldn't for the life of her remember his name. She had the vague sense he was a painter. Some kind of artist, certainly.

"We've all changed," he said. "By coming here. By going through the trials that we're all going through, we've all *been* changed. When we go back, none of us will be the people we were before. The tragedy and the loss and the sense of *wonder* changes what it means to be human. Do you know what I mean?"

Oddly, Anna thought she did.

Being a minister meant being in the middle of people's lives. Anna had counseled dating congregation members, presided over their weddings, baptized their babies, and in one heartbreaking case presided over the infant's funeral a year later. Members of the congregation included her in most of the important events of their lives. She was used to it, and mostly enjoyed the deep connection to people it brought. Charting the course of a life was making a map of the ways each event changed the person, leaving someone different on the other side. Passing through the Ring and the tragedies it had brought wouldn't leave any of them the same.

The exodus from the rest of the fleet to the *Behemoth* was in full swing. The tent cities spread across the curved inner surface of the habitation drum like wildflowers on a field of flat, ceramic steel–colored earth. Anna saw tall gangly Belters helping offload wounded Earthers from emergency carts, plugging in IVs and other medical equipment, fluffing pillows and mopping brows. Inners and outers offloaded crates in mixed groups without comment. Anna couldn't help but be warmed by that, even in the face of their recent disaster. Maybe it took real tragedy to get them all working together, but it did. They did. There was hope in that.

Now if they could just figure out how to do it without the blood and screaming.

"Your work has been criticized," Monica Stuart said, "as advocating violence."

The peeled man nodded.

"I used to reject that," he said. "I've come to the conclusion that it may be valid, though. I think when we come home, there will be some readjustment."

"Because of the Ring?"

"And the slow zone. And what's happened here."

"Do you think you would encourage other political artists to come out here?"

"Absolutely."

Chris, her young officer, had asked about organizing mixed-group church services on the *Behemoth*. She'd assumed he meant mixed religions at first, but it turned out he meant a church group with Earthers and Martians and Belters. Mixed, as if God categorized people based on the gravity they'd grown up in. It had occurred to Anna then that there really wasn't any such thing as a "mixed" church group. No matter what they looked like, or what they chose to call Him, when a group of people called out to God together, they were one. Even if there was no God, or one God, or many gods, it didn't matter. *Faith, hope, and love*, Paul had written, *but the greatest of these is love*. Faith and hope were very important to Anna. But she could see Paul's point in a way she hadn't before. Love didn't need anything else. It didn't need a common belief, or a common identity. Anna thought of her child and felt a rush of longing and loneliness. She could almost feel Nami in her arms, almost smell the intoxicating new-baby scent on her head. Nono the Ugandan and Anna the Russian had blended themselves together and made Nami. Not a mix, nothing so crude as that. More than just the sum of her parts and origins. A new thing, individual and unique.

No mixed group, then. Just a group. A new thing, perfect and unique. She couldn't imagine God would see it any other way. Anna was pretty sure she had her first sermon too. She was about halfway through typing up an outline for her "no mixed groups in God's eyes" sermon on her handset when Bull came through the door, his mechanical legs whining and thumping with each step. Anna thought it gave Bull even more gravitas than he'd had before. He moved with a deliberateness caused by mechanical necessity, but easily mistaken for formality and stateliness. The electric whine of the machine and the heavy thump of his tread were a sort of herald calling out his arrival.

Anna imagined the annoyance Bull would feel if she told him this, and giggled a little to herself.

Bull was in the middle of speaking to a subordinate and didn't even notice her. "I don't care how they feel about it, Serge. The agreement was no armed military personnel on the ship. Even if there weren't a shitload of guns built in, those suits would still be weapons. Confiscate their gear or throw them off the damn ship."

"Si, jefe," the other man with him replied. "Take it how, sa sa? Can opener?"

"Charm the bastards. If we can't make them do anything now, while we're all friends, what do we do when they decide we aren't friends? Four marines in recon armor decide they own this ship, they fucking own it. So we take the armor away before they do. I don't even want that stuff in the drum. Lock it in the bridge armory."

Serge looked deeply unhappy at this task. "Some help, maybe?"

"Take as many as you want, but if you don't need them it's only gonna piss the marines off, and if you do, they won't actually help."

Serge paused, mouth open, then closed it with a snap and left. Bull noticed Anna for the first time and said, "What can I do for you, Preacher?"

"Anna, please. I came to talk about Clarissa Mao," she said.

"If you're not her lawyer or her union representative—"

"I'm her priest. What happens to her now?"

Bull sighed again. "She confessed to blowing up a ship. Nothing much good comes after that."

"People say you spaced a man for selling drugs. They say you're hard. Cold."

"Do they?" Bull said. Anna couldn't tell if the surprise in his voice was genuine or mocking.

"Please don't kill her," she said, leaning closer and looking him in the eye. "Don't you let anyone else kill her either."

"Why not?" The way he said it wasn't a challenge or a threat. It was as if he just didn't know that answer, and sort of wondered. Anna swallowed her dread.

"I can't help her if she's dead."

"No offense, but that's not really my concern."

"I thought you were the law and order here."

"I'm aiming for order, mostly."

"She deserves a trial, and if everyone knows what you know about her, she won't get one. They'll riot. They'll kill her. At least help me get her a trial."

The large man sighed. "So are you looking for a trial, or just a way to stall for time?"

"Stall for time," Anna said.

Bull nodded, weighing something in his mind, then gestured for her to precede him into his office. After she sat down next to his battered desk, he clumped around the small space making a pot of coffee. It seemed an extravagance considering the newly implemented water rationing, but then Anna remembered Bull was now the second most powerful person in the slow zone. The privileges of rank.

She didn't want coffee, but accepted the offered cup to allow Bull a moment of generosity. Generosity now might lead to more later, when she was asking for something she really wanted.

"When Holden starts telling people who actually sabotaged the *Seung Un*—and he's Jim Holden, so he will—the UN people are going to ask for Clarissa. And if they give me enough that I can get everyone here, together, and safe until we can get out of this trap, I'm going to give her to them. Not off the ship, but in here."

"What will they do?" Anna took a companionable sip of her coffee. It burned her tongue and tasted like acid.

"Probably, they'll put together a tribunal of flag officers, have a short trial, and throw her in a recycler. I'd say space her, normally, but that seems wasteful considering our predicament. Supplies sent from home will take as long to fly through the slow zone to us as they'll take to get to the Ring."

His voice was flat, emotionless. He was discussing logistics, not a young woman's life. Anna suppressed a shudder and said, "Mister Baca, do you believe in God?"

To his credit, he tried not to roll his eyes. He almost succeeded.

"I believe in whatever gets you through the night."

"Don't be flip," Anna said, and was gratified when Bull straightened a little in his walker. In her experience, most strong-willed men had equally strong-willed mothers, and she knew how to hit some of the same buttons.

"Look," Bull said, trying to reclaim the initiative. Anna spoke over the top of him.

"Forget God for a moment," she said. "Do you believe in the concept of forgiveness? In the possibility of redemption? In the value of every human life, no matter how tainted or corrupted?"

"Fuck no," Bull said. "I think it is entirely possible to go so far into the red you can't ever balance the books."

"Sounds like the voice of experience. How far have you been?"

"Far enough to know there's a too damn far."

"And you're comfortable being the judge of where that line is?"

Bull pulled on the frame of his walker, shifting his weight in the straps that held him. He looked wistfully at the office chair he could no longer use. Anna felt bad for him, broken at the worst possible time. Trying to keep his tiny world in order, and burning through the last reserves of his strength with reckless abandon. The bruised eyes and yellow skin suddenly seemed like a flashing battery indicator, warning that the power was almost gone. Anna felt a pang of guilt for adding to his burden.

"I don't want to kill that girl," he said, taking another sip of the terrible coffee. "In fact, I don't give a shit about her one way or the other, as long as she's locked up and isn't a danger to my ship. The one you should talk to is Holden. He's the one who's gonna get the torches-and-pitchforks crowd wound up."

"But the Martians..."

"Surrendered twenty hours ago."

Anna blinked.

"They've been wanting to for days," Bull said. "We just had to find a way to let 'em save face."

"Save face?"

"They got a story they can tell where they don't look weak. That's all they needed. But if we didn't find something, they'd have stuck to their posts until they all died. Nothing ever killed more people than being afraid to look like a sissy."

"Holden's coming here, then?"

"Already be on a shuttle escorted by four recon marines, which is another fucking headache for me. But how about this? I won't talk about the girl until I have reason to. What Holden does, though, he just does."

"Fine, then I'll talk to him when he arrives," Anna said.

"Good luck with that," Bull said.

Chapter Thirty-Six: Holden

When the Martians came for him—two men and two women, all in uniform and all armed—Holden's isolation-drunk mind had spun out in a dozen directions at once. The captain had found room for him in the medical clinic and she wanted to grill him again about what happened on the station and they were going to throw him out an airlock and they'd had news that Naomi was dead and they'd had news that she wasn't. It felt like every neuron he had from his brain down to his toes was on the edge of firing. It was all he could do not to launch himself off the cell's wall and into the narrow corridor.

"The prisoner will please identify himself," one of the men said.

"James Holden. I mean, it's not like you have very many prisoners here, right? Because I've been trying to find someone to talk with for it feels like about a decade since I got here, and I'm pretty sure there isn't so much as a dust mite in this place besides me."

He bit his lips to stop talking. He'd been alone and scared for too long. He hadn't understood how much it was affecting him. Even if he hadn't been mentally ill when he came to the *Hammurabi*, he was going to be real soon now if nothing changed.

"Record shows prisoner identified himself as James Holden," the man said. "Come along."

The corridor outside the cells was so narrow that two guards ahead and two behind was effectively a wall. The low Martian gravity made their bodies more akin to Belters than to him, and all four of them hunched slightly, bending in over him. Holden had never felt so relieved to be in a tiny, cramped hallway in his life. But even the relief was pushed aside by his anxiety. The guards didn't actually push him so much as start to move with an authority that suggested that he really should match them. The hatch was only five meters away, but after being in his cell, it seemed like a huge distance.

"Was there any word from the *Roci*?"

No one spoke.

"What's...ah...what's going on?"

"You're being evacuated," the man said.

"Evacuated?"

"Part of the surrender agreement."

"Surrender agreement? You're surrendering? Why are you surrendering?"

"We lost the politics," one of the women behind him said.

If the skiff they loaded him onto wasn't the same one that had taken him back from the station, it was close enough that he couldn't tell the difference. There were only four soldiers this time, all of them in full combat armor. The rest of the spaces were taken up by men and women in standard naval uniform. Holden thought at first they were the wounded, but when he looked closer, none of them seemed to have anything worse than minor injuries. It was the exhaustion in their faces and bodies that made them seem broken. The acceleration burn wasn't even announced. The thrust barely shifted the crash couches. All around him, the Martians slept or brooded. Holden scratched at the hard, flexible plastic restraints on his wrists and ankles, and no one told him to stop. Maybe that was a good sign.

He tried to do the math in his head. If the new top speed was about as fast as a launched grenade, then every hour, they'd travel... As tired as he was, he couldn't make the numbers add up to anything. If he'd had his hand terminal, it would have been a few seconds' work. Still, he couldn't see asking to have it. And it didn't matter.

He slept and woke and slept again. The proximity Klaxon woke him from a dream about making bread with someone who was his father Caesar and also Fred Johnson and trying to find the salt. It took him a moment to remember where he was.

The skiff was small enough that when the other ship's crew banged against the airlock, Holden could hear it. From his seat, he couldn't see the airlock open. The first thing he knew was a slightly different scent in the air. Something rich and oddly humid. And then four new people stepped into his view. They were Belters. A broad-faced woman, a thick man with a startling white beard, and two shaven-headed men so similar they might have been twins. The twins had the split circle of the OPA tattooed on their arms. All four wore sidearms.

The *Behemoth*, Holden thought. They'd surrendered to the *Behemoth*. That was weird.

One of the marines, still in battle armor, floated over to them. The Belters didn't show any sign of fear. Holden gave them credit for that.

"I am Sergeant Alexander Verbinski," the Martian said. "I have been ordered to hand over this skiff and her crew and company in accordance with the agreement of surrender."

The woman and white-bearded man looked at each other. Holden thought he could see the question—*You gonna tell them they can't take their suits in?*—pass between them. The woman shrugged.

"Bien alles," she said. "Welcome aboard. Bring them through in sixpacks and we'll get you sorted, sa sa?"

"Yes, ma'am," Verbinski said.

"Corin," one of the twins said. The woman turned to see him gesture toward Holden with his chin. "Pa con esá parlan, si?"

The woman's nod was curt.

"We'll take Holden out now," she said.

"Your show," the marine said. Holden thought from his tone he'd have been as happy to shoot him. That might have been paranoia, though.

The Belters escorted him through the airlock and a long Mylar tube to the engineering deck of the *Behemoth*. A dozen people were waiting with hand terminals at the ready, prepared for the slow, slogging administrative work of dealing with a defeated enemy. Holden got to skip the line, and he wasn't sure it was an honor.

The woman floating near the massive doors at the transition point where the engineering section met the drum looked too young for her captain's insignia. Her hair, pulled back in a severe bun, reminded him of a teacher he'd had once when he'd still been on Earth.

"Captain Pa," the security woman—Corin, one of the twins had called her—said. "You wanted to talk with this one."

"Captain Holden," Captain Pa said with a nod. "Welcome aboard the *Behemoth*. I'm giving you liberty of the ship, but I want you to understand that there are some conditions."

Holden blinked. He'd expected another brig at least. Freedom of the ship was pretty much the same as freedom period. It wasn't like there were a lot of places he could go.

"Ah. All right," he said.

"You are to make yourself available for debriefing whenever you are called upon. No exceptions. You are not to discuss what happened or didn't happen on the station with anyone besides myself or the security chief."

"I know how to shut it off," Holden said.

The younger captain's expression shifted.

"You what?"

"I know how to get the protomolecule to take us all off of lockdown," he said, and went on to explain all of what he'd told Captain Jakande again—seeing Miller, the plan to lull the station into a lower alert level so that the dead man could shut it down—fighting to sound calm, rational, and sane as he did it. He didn't go so far as the massive civilization-destroying invasion that had wiped out the protomolecule's creators. It all sounded bad enough without that.

Pa listened carefully, her face a mask. She wasn't someone he'd want to play poker against. He had the powerful, painful memory of Naomi telling him that she'd teach him how to play poker, and his throat closed.

The security man with the white beard floated up, two angry-looking Martians matching vector behind him.

"Captain?" the Belter said, barely restrained rage in his voice.

"Just a minute, Mister Gutmansdottir," she said, then turned back to Holden. She had to be overwhelmed, but it was only a tightness in her jaw, if it was even that much. "I'll...take that under advisement, but for the immediate future—"

"My crew?"

"They're in the civilian medical bay," Pa said, and the white-bearded man cleared his throat in a way that meant he hadn't needed to. "There are directions posted. If you'll excuse me."

"Captain, there's a load of contraband among the new prisoners," Gutmansdottir said, hitting the last word hard. "Thought you'd want to address that before it got to Bull."

Pa took a deep breath and pushed off after her security man. A few seconds later, Holden realized he hadn't been dismissed so much as forgotten. Fallen down the list of things that the young captain had to do *right now*, and so fuck him. He moved out past the transition point and to the platforms where the axis of the little world spun. There was a long ramp for carts, and he shuffled down it, the spin slowly shifting from pure Coriolis to the sensation of weight. He could feel in his knees how long he'd been on the float and hoped that the medical bays weren't too far away.

If they'd been on the far side of the system, though, he'd have grabbed an EVA suit, as much spare air as he could haul, and started out, though. The idea that he was breathing the same air as Naomi and Alex and Amos was like a drug.

Only Captain Pa hadn't actually said that. All she'd said was that his crew was there. The "remaining" might have been implied. He tried to jog, but got winded after only a couple of minutes and had to pause to catch his breath.

The great body of the drum stretched out before him, a world wrapped into a tube. The long strip of the false sun glowed white above him, now that there was a clear "above," and reached out across two kilometers to a swirling ramp at the other end, the mirror of the one he was on. Thin clouds drifted in tori around the unbearable brightness. The air clung to him, the heat pressing at his skin, but he could imagine the bare metal of the drum's surface covered in green, the air sweet with the scent of apple blossoms, the cycle of evaporation and condensation cooling it all. Or if not, at least making it into a long, permanent summer afternoon.

It was a dream. Someone else's and doomed now to failure, but worthy. Beautiful, even in ruins.

"Captain Holden? Can I speak with you?"

It was a small woman with bright red hair pulled into tight braids, and wearing a plain brown suit. She was the sort of very comfortable middle-aged that always made him think of his mothers.

"My name is Annushka Volovodov," she said with a smile. "But you can call me Anna if you like."

"You can call me Jim," he said, holding out a hand. He almost had his wind back. Anna shook his hand without a hint of fear. His "most dangerous man in the solar system" reputation must not have reached her yet. "Eastern European?"

"Russian," she replied with a nod. "Born in Kimry. But a Muscovite for most of my adult life. North American?"

"Montana. Farming collective."

"I hear Montana is nice."

"Population density is good. Still more cows than people."

Anna nodded and plucked at her suit. Holden got the sense that she actually had something she wanted to say but was having a hard time getting to the point. "Kimry was like that. It's a tourist place you know, the lakes—" Anna started.

"Anna," Holden cut her off gently. "Do you need to say something to me?"

"I do," she said. "I need to ask you not to tell anyone about Clarissa, and what she did."

Holden nodded.

"Okay," he said. "Who's Clarissa and what did she do?"

The woman tilted her head.

"They didn't tell you?"

"I don't think they liked me much," Holden said. "Is there something I should know?"

"Well, this is awkward. Just after the catastrophe, a girl calling herself Melba attacked your ship," Anna said. "It's a long story, but I followed her and tried to help. Your first officer? Naomi? She was hurt in the attack. Badly."

Holden felt the universe contract. Naomi was hurt while he'd been dicking around with Miller on the station. His hands were shaking.

"Where is she?" he asked, not sure if he meant Naomi or the woman who'd hurt her.

"Naomi's here. They brought her over to the *Behemoth*," Anna said. "She's in the medical bay right now receiving treatment. They assure me she'll recover. The rest of your crew is here too. They were hurt earlier. When the speed limit changed."

"They're alive?"

"Yes," Anna said. "They are."

The mix of relief and sorrow and anger and guilt made the ship seem to spin a little beneath him. Anna put a hand on his arm to steady him.

"Who is this Melba and why did she attack my crew?"

"It's not her real name. My friend knows her, knows her family. Apparently she has something of an obsession with you. Her name is Clarissa Mao."

Mao.

The mysterious and powerful Julie. The Julie rebuilt by the protomolecule like his ghostly Miller. The Julie who had hired Cohen the soundman to hack their ship, the Julie he'd sculpted for them later who'd never looked *quite* right. The Julie who'd been manipulating every detail of his life for the last year just to get them through the gate and down to the station.

It wasn't Julie at all.

"She's not well," Anna was saying, "but I believe that she can be reached. If there's time. But if they kill her—"

"Where's Naomi? Do you know where she is?"

"I do," Anna said. And then, "I'm sorry. I may have been a little wrapped up in my own issue. Can I take you there?"

"Please," Holden said.

Fifteen minutes later, Holden stepped into a small room in the medical ward that his little family had to themselves. Naomi lay on a gurney, one arm in an inflatable cast. Her face was mottled with half-healed bruises. Tears stung his eyes, and for a moment he couldn't speak. A killing rage burned in him. This wasn't a disaster. It wasn't an accident. Someone had done this to her.

When she saw him, her smile was gentle and amused.

"Hey," she said. In a moment, he was at her side, holding her good hand, his throat too thick for speech. There were tears in Naomi's eyes too, but no anger. He was amazed how grateful he was for that.

"Anna," Naomi said. She looked genuinely pleased to see her, which was a good start. "Jim, you met Anna? She saved me from the psycho with the demolition mech."

"Saved us too, I guess," Amos said. "So thanks for that, Red. I guess I owe you one."

It took Holden a moment to realize that "Red" meant Anna. She seemed surprised by it too.

"I'm happy I was able to help. I'm afraid I was very stoned

on pain medication at the time. It could have easily gone the other way."

"Just take the marker," Alex said. "Soon as you figure out what Amos is good for, you can trade it in."

"Asshole," Amos said, and threw a pillow at him

"Thank you," Holden said. "If you saved them, I owe you everything."

"I'm happy I was able to help," she repeated. To Naomi she said, "You look better than the last time I saw you."

"Getting better," Naomi replied, then tested her injured arm with a grimace. "We'll see how mobile it is once the bones knit up."

Anna nodded and smiled at her, and then the smile faded.

"Jim? I'm sorry, but I still need to speak to you," she said to him. "Maybe privately?"

"No. I never thought I'd see these people again. I'm staying right here. If you want to talk to me, go ahead and do it."

The woman's eyes shifted between the crewmen. Her expression could have been hope or polite resignation.

"I need something," she finally said.

"Anything," Amos answered instantly, sitting up in bed a bit. Holden knew Anna wouldn't understand how literally Amos meant that. Hopefully a preacher didn't need anyone murdered.

"If we got it," Alex added, "it's yours." Amos nodded agreement.

Anna directed her answer at Holden. "I've talked to the head of security and he's agreed to keep quiet about Clarissa's confession. All that she's done. I need you to keep quiet too."

Holden frowned, but didn't reply. Naomi said, "Why?"

"Well," Anna said. "It's James Holden. He has a reputation for announcing things—"

"Not why ask us?" Naomi said. "Why don't you want people to know?"

Anna nodded. "If it gets out, given our current situation, they'll probably execute her."

"Good," Holden said.

"She does kind of have it coming," Amos added.

Anna held her hands tight in front of her and nodded. She didn't mean that she agreed, only that she heard them. That she understood.

"I need you to forgive her," she said. "If nothing else, as a favor to me. You said I could have anything. That's what I want."

In the pause, Amos let out a long breath. Alex's eyebrows were climbing up his forehead.

"Why?" Naomi said again, her voice calm.

Anna pressed her lips thin. "She's not evil. I believe that Clarissa did what she did out of a love. A sick love, but love. And if she's dead, there won't be any hope for her. And I have to hope."

Holden saw the words wash over Naomi, a sudden pain in her eyes that he didn't understand. She pulled back her lips, baring her teeth. Her whisper was obscene and so quiet that no one but him could hear it. He squeezed her hand, feeling the bones of her fingers against his own.

"Okay," Naomi said. "We'll keep quiet."

The rage flared in his breast. Speaking was suddenly easy.

"I won't," Holden said. "We're talking about an insane member of the Mao clan, the people who've *twice* tried to kill everyone in the solar system, who followed us all the way to the Ring, tried to kill us. To kill you. She blew up a spaceship full of innocent people just to try and make me look bad. Who knows how many other people she's killed? If the UN wants to space her, I'll push the damn button myself."

There was a long moment of silence. Holden watched Anna's face fall as he crushed her hopes. Alex started chuckling, and everyone turned to look at him.

"Yeah," Alex said in his drawling voice. "I mean, Naomi only got beat half to death. She can cut this Clarissa slack, it's no big deal. But the captain's *girlfriend* got hurt. He's the *real* victim here."

The room got quiet again as everyone stopped breathing. Blood flushed into Holden's face, rushing like a river in his ears. It was hatred and pain and outrage. His mind seemed to flicker, and the urge to strike out at Alex for the insult was almost too much to resist.

And then he understood Alex's words, saw Naomi's eyes on his, and it all drained away. *Why*, he wanted to ask, but it didn't matter. It was Naomi, and she'd made her decision. It wasn't his revenge to take.

He was spent. Exhausted. He wanted to curl up on the floor there with his people around him and sleep for days. He tried out a smile.

"Wow," he finally said. "Sometimes I am just a gigantic asshole."

"No," Amos said. "I'm right there with you. I'd kill this Clarissa myself for the shit she's pulled. But Red asked us to let it go, and Naomi's playing along, so I guess we gotta too."

"Don't get me wrong," Holden said to Anna, his voice cold. "I will never forgive this woman for what she's done. Never. But I won't turn her over to the UN, as a favor to you, and because if Naomi can let it go, I guess I have to."

"Thank you," Anna said.

"Things change, Red," Amos said, "you let us know. Because I'll still be happy to kill the shit out of her."

Chapter Thirty-Seven: Clarissa

She didn't know at first what the change was. It presented in little things. The decking she'd been able to sleep on like she was dead suddenly wasn't comfortable. She found herself wondering more what her father did in his cell, five billion kilometers away and, for all she knew, in another universe. She tapped her hands against the bars just to hear the subtle differences in tone that the different bars made when struck. And she hated.

Hatred was nothing new. She'd lived with it for long enough that the memories of the times before all carried the same colors of rage and righteousness. Only before, she'd hated Jim Holden, and now she hated Clarissa Mao. Hating herself had a kind of purity that she found appealing. Cathartic. Jim Holden had shifted out from under her thirst for vengeance, refusing to be consumed by it. She could live in the flames and know she deserved to burn. It was like playing a game on easy.

She tapped the bars. There wasn't enough variation between them to play a melody. If there had been she would have, just for something to distract her. She wondered whether her extra glands would be enough to bend the bars or lift the door off its hinges. Not that it would matter. At best, leaving her cell would have meant being gunned down by an OPA guard. At worst, it would have meant freedom.

The captain had stopped talking to her, at least. She watched the stream of visitors coming to him. She had a pretty clear idea which of the guards answered to him. And there were a couple of Martians in military uniforms who came, and a few UN officers too. They came and met with Captain Ashford, speaking in the low voices of people who took themselves and each other very seriously. She recognized the sound from eavesdropping on her father. She remembered that she had been impressed by it once. Now it made her want to laugh.

She paced her tiny world. She did push-ups and lunges and all the pointless exercises that the light gravity allowed. And she waited for punishment or for the end of the world. When she slept, Ren was there, so she tried not to sleep much.

And slowly, with a sense of growing horror, she understood that the change was her coming back to herself. Falling awake. After her failure on the *Rocinante*, there had been a kind of peace. A disconnection from everything. But even before that, she'd been in a sort of a dream. She couldn't tell if it had started with the day she'd killed Ren or when she'd taken the identification to become Melba Koh. Or earlier, even. When she'd heard her father had been arrested. Whenever she'd lost herself, she was coming back now, and it was like her whole consciousness was suffering pins and needles. It was worse than pain, and it drove her in circles.

The more she thought about it, the clearer the mind games that the red-haired priest had played on her were. The priest and, in her way, Tilly Fagan too. Maybe Anna had come thinking that the promise of forgiveness would need to be dangled in front of her in order to get the confession. If so, the woman was double stupid: first because she'd thought Clarissa wouldn't admit to what she'd done, and second because she'd thought forgiveness was something Clarissa wanted. Or would accept.

I'd like to speak with you again, she'd said, and at the time it had seemed so sincere. So real. Only she hadn't come back. A small rational part of Clarissa's mind knew that it hadn't really been that long. Being in the cell changed the experience of time and made her feel isolated. That was the point of cells. Still, Anna hadn't come back. And neither had Holden. Or Naomi, whom Clarissa hadn't quite killed. They were done with her, and why shouldn't they be? Clarissa didn't have anything else to offer them. Except maybe a warning that the power on the ship was about to change hands again, as if that would even matter. Who got to sit in the doomed ship's captain's chair seemed like a terribly petty thing to worry about. It was like arguing about who was the prettiest girl in the prison camp.

Still, it was the only show playing, so she watched.

The voices from the other cell had taken on a new tone. An urgency. Even before the well-dressed man came down toward her, she knew that their little drama was about to play out. He stood at her door, looking in. His white hair, brilliant and perfectly coiffed, just made him look old. There was a darkness in his professionally avuncular eyes. When he put his hands around the bars, it looked like he was the one imprisoned.

"I'm guessing that you don't remember me," he said. His voice was sad and sweet both.

"Father Cortez," she said. "I remember who you are. You used to play golf with my father."

He chuckled ruefully, stepping his feet back from the bars in a way that brought his forehead closer to them.

"I did, but that was a long time ago. You wouldn't have been more than...what? Seven?"

"I've seen you in the newsfeeds since."

"Ah," he said. His eyes focused on nothing. "That feels like it was a long time ago too. I was just now talking with the captain. He said he's been trying to convince you to join us, only he hasn't had much success."

Two guards came in, walking down the rows of stalls. She recognized them both as Ashford's allies. Cortez didn't take notice of them at all.

"No, he hasn't," she said. And then, "He lies a lot."

Cortez's eyebrows rose.

"Lies?"

"He said he could get me amnesty. When we get back home, he could take me to Ceres and put me under OPA protection. Only he can't do that."

Cortez took a long breath and let it out again. "No. No, he can't. May I be honest with you?"

"I don't see that I'm in a position to stop you," Clarissa said.

"I think that you and I have a great deal in common. You have blood on your hands. The blood of innocents."

She tried to sneer, tried to retreat into a dismissive pose, but it only left her feeling exposed and adolescent. Cortez went on as if he hadn't noticed. Maybe he hadn't.

"I was...instrumental in bringing us through the gate. The combined force, representing all three divisions of humanity, joined gloriously together." Bitterness darkened the words, but then he smiled and she thought maybe there was something as wounded in him as there was in her. "Vainglory is an occupational hazard for men in my profession. It's one I've battled with limited success, I'm afraid."

"I was the one who drove Holden through the Ring," Clarissa said, unsure whether she was confessing a crime or offering Cortez an out.

"Yes. And I led all the others in after him. And so when they died, it was because I had blinded them to the dangers they faced. I led my flock to the slaughterhouse. I thought I was putting my faith in providence, but..."

Tears filled his eyes, and his expression went empty.

"Father?" she said.

"When I was a child," Cortez said, "my cousin found a dead man. The body was in an arroyo out behind our land. She dared me to go and look at it. I was desperately afraid, but I went and I held my head high and I pretended that I wasn't in order not to be. When the medics arrived, we found out the man had died from one of the old hemorrhagic fevers. They put me on prophylactic antivirals for the rest of the summer. So perhaps I've always done this. I thought I was putting my faith in providence, but perhaps I was only covering my own fears. And my own fears led a great many people to die."

"It's not your fault."

"But it is my problem. And perhaps my failings were in the service of a greater good. You were right, my dear. There will be no amnesty for you or for me either. But not for the reason you imagine."

Clarissa stood. Cortez's gaze was on her like a weight. The intimacy of the old man's confession and the fear and grief carried with such dignity made her respect him even though she'd never particularly liked him.

"The dangers that the aliens pose are too great. To think that we could harness them or treat them as equals was hubris, and the deaths we have seen already will be like a raindrop in the ocean. We've delivered ourselves into the hands of the devil. Not everyone understands that, but I think perhaps you do."

To her surprise, she felt dread welling up in her throat. At the far end of the hall, metal clanked. Ashford's stall door swung open. One of the guards said something, but Cortez's full attention was on her and it felt like pouring cool water on a burn.

"I think I do," she said softly.

"Captain Ashford's freedom is my doing because he and I have come to a meeting of the minds that I could not manage with the present captain. When they began to bring the crews of the various ships together here, they did it in part by creating a weapon."

"Weapons don't work here."

"Light does, and they have made a weapon out of it. The communications laser has been made strong enough to cut through hulls. And it can be made stronger. Enough so, we believe, that it will destroy the Ring and close the gate."

"We'll be on the wrong side of it," Clarissa said.

"Yes. But if we wait, others will come. They'll be tempted. 'If we can manipulate the gates,' they'll say, 'what glories would come to us.' I can already hear them."

"You were saying that. You *were* one of them."

"I was, and I've learned a terrible lesson. And you were driven here by hatred. Have you?"

Ashford laughed. One of the guards said, "Welcome back, Captain." Clarissa tapped her fingertips against the bars, and they chimed.

"We were wrong," Cortez said. "But now we have a chance to make it right. We can protect all of humanity from making the mistakes we've made. We can protect them. But there will be a sacrifice."

"Us. All of us."

"Yes. We will die here in the darkness, cut off from all of those we have preserved. And among those who are with us here, we will be reviled. We may be punished. Even put to death." He shifted his hand to touch hers. The contact, skin to skin, was electric. "I'm not lying to you, Clarissa. The things I am asking of you will have no reward in this life."

"What are you asking?" she said. "What do you want me to do about any of this?"

"People will try to stop us. They may try to kill the captain. I understand that the modifications made to your body have the potential to elevate your natural abilities to something exceptional. Come with us. See to it that the captain isn't hurt, and that he isn't stopped. It may be you need do nothing but stand witness. Or you may be the difference between success and failure."

"Either way, I'm dead."

"Yes. But one will only be a death. The other will have meaning."

Captain Ashford and his guards began walking toward them. The click of their heels against the deck was like the soft sounds of a mechanical clock. The moment drew toward its end, and resentment burned a little. She didn't want Ashford to come. She wanted to stay here, talking with the reverend about sacrifice and death. About the burden of having done something so wrong the scales couldn't be balanced while she lived.

Even though his mouth was set, Cortez's pale blue eyes smiled at her. He didn't look like her father at all. His face was too doughy, his jaw was too wide. He was all sincerity where her father always had a sense of laughing at the world from behind a mask. But at that moment, she saw Jules-Pierre Mao in him.

"The people we killed," she said. "If we do this, all of them will have died for a reason too."

"For the noblest of reasons," Cortez agreed.

"We have to get going," Ashford said, and Cortez stepped back from the doorway, folding his hands together. Ashford turned to her. His too-large head and thin Belter's frame made him seem like something from a bad dream. "Last chance," he said.

"I'll go," Clarissa said.

Ashford's eyebrows rose and he glanced from her to Cortez and back. A slow smile stretched his lips.

"You're sure?" he asked, but the pleasure in his voice made it clear he wasn't really looking for her thoughts or justifications.

"I'll make sure no one stops you," she said.

Ashford looked at Cortez for a moment, and his expression showed that he was impressed. He saluted her, and—awkwardly—she saluted back.

She felt a moment's disorientation stepping out of her cell that didn't come from a change in gravity or Coriolis. It was the first free step she'd taken since the *Rocinante*. Ashford walked ahead of her, his two guards talking about action groups and locking down the *Behemoth*. Engineering and command weren't in the rotating drum, and so they would take control of the transfer points at the far north and south of the drum and the exterior elevator that passed between them. How to maintain calm in the drum until they could lock it all down, who was tracking the enemy, who was already a loyalist and who would need persuasion. Clarissa didn't pay much attention. She was more aware of Cortez walking at her side and the sense of having left some kind of burden behind in the cell. She was going to die, and it was going to make all the things she'd done wrong before make sense. Every child born on Earth or Mars or the stations of the Belt would be safe from the protomolecule because of what they were about to do. And Soledad and Bob and Stanni, her father and her mother and her siblings, they would all know she was dead. Everyone who'd known and loved Ren would be able to sleep a little better knowing that his killer had come to justice. Even she'd sleep better, if she got any sleep.

"And she has combat implants," Ashford was saying as he pointed his fist back toward her. One of the guards looked back toward her. The one with off-colored eyes and the scar on his chin. Jojo.

"You sure she's one of us, Captain?"

"The enemy of my enemy, Jojo," Ashford said.

"I will vouch for her," Cortez said.

You shouldn't, Clarissa thought, but didn't say.

"Claro," Jojo said with a Belter gesture equivalent to a shrug. "She's on command deck with tu alles tu."

"That'll be fine," Ashford said.

The hall opened into a larger corridor. White LEDs left the walls looking pale and antiseptic. A dozen people armed with slug throwers, men and women both, sat in electric carts or stood beside them. Clarissa wanted the air itself to smell different, but it didn't. It was all just plastic and heat. Captain Ashford and three armed men jostled in the cart just ahead.

"It will take some time before the ship is fully secured," Cortez said. "We'll have to gather what allies we can. Suppress the resistance. Once we assemble everything we need and get off the drum, they won't be able to stop us." He sounded like he was trying to talk himself into believing something. "Don't be afraid. This has all happened for a reason. If we have faith, there is nothing to fear."

"I'm not afraid," Clarissa said. Cortez looked over at her, a smile in his eyes. When he met her gaze the smile faltered a little. He looked away.

Chapter Thirty-Eight: Bull

Bull tried not to cough. The doctor listened to his breath, moved the stethoscope a few inches, listened some more. He couldn't tell if the little silver disk was cold. He couldn't feel it. He coughed up a hard knob of mucus and accepted a bit of tissue from the doctor to spit it into. She tapped a few notes into her hand terminal. The light from its screen showed how tired she looked.

"Well, you're clearing a little," the doctor said. "Your white count is still through the roof, though."

"And the spine?"

"Your spine is a mess, and it's getting worse. By which I mean it's getting harder to make it better."

"That's a sacrifice."

"When's it going to be enough?" she asked.

"Depends on what you mean by 'it,' " Bull said.

"You wanted to get everyone together. They're together."

"Still got crews on half the ships."

"Skeleton crews," the doctor said. "I know how many people you have on this ship. I treat them. You wanted to bring everyone together. They're together. Is that enough?"

"Be nice to make sure everyone doesn't just start shooting at each other," Bull said.

The doctor lifted her hands, exasperated. "So as soon as humans aren't humans anymore, then you'll let me do my job."

Bull laughed, which was a mistake. His cough was deeper now, rattling in the caverns of his chest, but it wasn't violent. Before he could really work up a good gut-wrencher, he'd need abdominal muscles that fired. The doctor handed him another tissue. He used it.

"We get everything under control," he said, "you can knock me out, all right?"

"Is that going to happen?" she asked. It was the thing everyone wanted to know, whether they came right out and said it or not. The truth was, he didn't like the plan. Part of that was because it came from Jim Holden, part was that it came from the protomolecule, and part was that he badly wanted it to be true. The fallback was that he'd start evacuating who he could with the shuttles he had, except that shuttles weren't built for long-haul work. It wasn't viable.

They had to start making food. Generating soil to fill the interior of the drum. Growing crops under the false strip of sun that ran along the *Behemoth*'s axis. And getting the goddamned heat under control. He had to see to it that they made it, whatever that meant. Medical comas could last a pretty long time when ships slower than a decent fastball made a voyage across emptiness wider than Earth's oceans.

All of the reasons they'd come out—Earth, Mars, the OPA; all of them—seemed almost impossibly distant. Worrying about the OPA's place in the political calculus of the system was like trying to remember whether he'd paid back a guy who bought him a beer when he was twenty. After a certain point, the past becomes irrelevant. Nothing that happened outside the slow zone mattered. All that counted now was keeping things civilized until they found out if Holden's mad plan was more than a pipe dream.

And in order to do that, he had to keep breathing.

"Might pull it off. Captain Pa's got a plan she's looking at might get us burning again. Maybe," he said. "While we're waiting, though, you think you could hook me up?"

She scowled, but she got an inhaler from the pack beside the bed and tossed it to him. His arms still worked. He shook the thing twice, then put the formed ceramics to his lips and breathed. The steroids smelled like the ocean, and they burned a little. He tried not to cough.

"That's not going to fix anything," she said. "All we're doing is masking the symptoms."

"It's just got to get me through," Bull said, trying out a smile. The truth was he felt like crap. He didn't hurt, he just felt tired. And sick. And desperate.

With the inhaler stowed, he angled the walker back out toward the corridor. The medical bays were still full. The growing heat gave everything the sick, close feeling of a tropical summer. The smell of bodies and illness, blood and corruption and fake floral antiseptics made the rooms feel smaller than they were. Practice had made him more graceful with the mechanism. He used the two joysticks to shift out of the way of the nurses and therapists, making himself as unobtrusive as the rig allowed as he made his way back toward the security office.

His hand terminal chimed. He drove to a turn in the corridor, snugging himself into the corner to stay out of the way, then dropped the joysticks and took up the terminal. Corin requesting a connection. He thumbed to accept.

"Corin," he said. "What you got?"

"Boss?" she said. The tension in her voice brought his head up a degree. "You running a drill?"

"What's going on?"

"Jojo and Gutmansdottir just came by and said they were taking over the security office. When I told them they could have it when my shift was up, they drew down on me."

Bull felt a black dread descending upon him. He gripped the terminal and kept his voice low.

"They *what*?"

He pulled up his security interface, but the red border refused him. He was locked out of the command systems. They'd been moving fast.

"Was hoping it was some kind of test. Way they were talking, I got the feeling they were looking to find you there. I'm heading over to Serge's. He's trying to figure out what the hell's going on," she said. "If it was the wrong call—"

"It wasn't. You walked away, you did the right thing. Where were they supposed to be?"

"Sir?"

"They were on shift. Where were they supposed to be?"

For a moment, Corin's wide face was a mask of confusion. He watched her understand, a calm and deadly focus coming into her eyes. She didn't need to say it. Jojo and Gutmansdottir had been guarding the prisoners. Meaning Ashford.

Pa should have let him kill the bastard.

"Okay. Find Serge and anyone you trust. We've got to get this shit contained."

"Bien."

They'd be going for the armory. If they had security, the guns and gear were already theirs. Bull let a thin trickle of conversational obscenities fall from his lips while he tried to think. If he knew how many of his people had turned back to Ashford, he'd know what he had to work with.

"We can't let him get to Monica and the broadcast center," Bull said. "It gets out that we've got fighting in the drum, we'll get a dozen half-assed rescue missions trying to get their people out."

"You want us to concentrate there?" Corin asked.

"Don't concentrate anywhere," Bull said. "Not until we know what we're looking at. Just get as many people and guns as you can and stay in touch."

He had to get a plan. He had to have one now, only his brain wasn't working the way it should. He was sick. Hell, he was dying. It seemed deeply unfair that he should have to improvise at the same time.

"Get to Serge," he said. "We'll worry about it from there. I've got some people I've got to talk to."

"Bien, boss," Corin repeated, and dropped the connection.

A nurse pushed a rolling table around the corner, and Bull had to put his terminal away in order to step out of the man's path. He wished like hell he could walk and hold his terminal at the same damn time. He requested a priority connection to Pa. For a long moment, he was sure she wouldn't pick up, that Ashford had gotten to her already. The screen flickered, and she was there. He couldn't see what room she was in, but there were voices speaking in the background.

"Mister Baca," Pa said.

"Ashford's loose," he said. "I don't know how many people he's got or what he's doing, but a couple of my people just drew weapons and took over the security station."

Pa blinked. To her credit, she didn't show even a moment's fear, only the mental shifting of gears.

"Thank you, Mister Baca," Pa said. He could tell from the movement of her image on the screen that she was already walking away from wherever she'd been. Getting someplace unpredictable. That was what he needed to be doing too.

"I'll try to get in touch when I have a better idea what I'm looking at," he said.

"I appreciate that," she said. "I have a few people nearby that I trust. I'm going there now."

"I figure he's going to try to take over the broadcast station."

"Then we'll try to reinforce them," Pa said.

"Maybe it's just a few assholes," Bull said. "Ashford may be trying to keep his head low too."

"Or he may be getting ready to throw us both into a soil recycler," Pa said. "Which way do you want to bet?"

Bull smiled. He almost meant it.

"Take care of yourself, Captain."

"You too, Mister Baca."

"And hey," he said. "I'm sorry I got you into this."

Now it was Pa's turn to smile. She looked tired. She looked old.

"You didn't make any decisions for me," she said. "If I'm paying for my sins, at least give me that they're mine."

Her gaze jumped up from the terminal's camera toward something off the screen. Her lips pressed thin and the connection dropped. Bull had to fight not to request another connection, just so he could know what happened. But there wasn't time. He had to hurry. He tried connections to Ruiz in infrastructure and Chen without getting replies. He wondered how many supporters Ashford had gotten from the upper ranks of the staff. He cursed himself for having let Ashford pass under his radar. But he'd been so busy...

He tried Sam, and almost as soon as he put in the request, she was there.

"We got a problem," he said. "Ashford's trying to take back the ship. He's got security already."

"And engineering," Sam said.

Bull licked his lips.

"Where are you, Sam?"

"Right now? Funny you should ask. Engineering. Ashford left about five minutes ago. Had a little wish list of things he'd like me to do and about two dozen fellas with guns and scowls. That man's lost his shit, Bull. Seriously. He used to be a prick, but...He wants me to take out the Ring. Your comm laser trick? He wants it overclocked."

"You got to be kidding me."

"Not."

"He's looking to nuke the way *home*?"

"Calls it saving humanity from the alien threat," Sam said sweetly. Her eyes were hard.

"All right," Bull said, even though nothing about this was all right.

"And he's not at all happy with you. Are you someplace safe?"

Bull looked up and down the corridor. There wasn't cover. And even if there was, he was one man in a modified lifting mech and no spinal cord past the middle of his back.

"No," he said. "I don't think I am."

"Might want to get moving."

"I've got no place safe to go," Bull said.

Someone on the other end of the connection shouted and Sam looked up at them.

"I'm trying to scramble up all the technicians I can," she shouted back. "Things have been a tiny bit disorganized. Had a little trouble with the rules of physics changing on us. Maybe you noticed."

The first voice shouted again. Bull couldn't hear the words, but he knew the timbre of the voice. Garza. The guy who'd always gotten bulbs of coffee for whoever was stuck in the security office. Garza was one of theirs. Bull wished he'd gotten to know the man better. Especially after the catastrophe, he should have been checking in with his staff more. He should have seen this all coming.

This was his fault. All of this was his fault.

Sam looked back down at the screen. At him.

"Okay, sweetie," she said. "You should get scarce. Head for the second level, section M. There's a bunch of empty storage there. The door codes are all on default. Straight zeros."

"Why are they on default?"

"Because there's nothing in them, bossypants, and changing the locks on all the empties never made the top of my to-do list. Is this really the time?"

"Sorry," Bull said.

"Don't worry," she said. "Both of us under a little stress right now. Just get your head down before someone knocks it off. And Pa—"

"Pa knows. She's heading for safety too."

"All right, then. I'll try to get you some help."

"No," Bull said. "You don't know who you can trust."

"Yes, I do," Sam said. "Let's don't argue in front of the children."

A voice brought him back to the corridor, the medical center. Not the groans of the wounded, not the professional calm of the nurses. Someone was excited and aggressive. Angry. Someone answered in a lower voice, and the first one came back with *Do I look like I care?* It was trouble, and despite everything, his first impulse was to turn toward it. His job was to get in the middle of things, to make sure that no one got hurt, and if anyone did, it was him. Him first, then the bad guys.

"I got to go," he said, and dropped the connection. It only took a second to stow his hand terminal and get his palms back on the mech's controls. Long enough for him to fight back his instincts. He shifted the mech to head down the corridor, away from the voices. They were Ashford's people. Ashford and whoever was backing him. If he got caught now, he wouldn't be any use to anybody. Chances were they'd just kill him. Might not even get as far as the airlock first. The mech's legs moved slowly. Even full-out, it didn't go more than a modest walk. The voices behind him shifted. Something crashed. He heard his doctor shouting now and waited for the report of gunfire. If they started shooting, he'd have to go back. The mech inched toward the farther door, toward the exit and what passed for safety. Bull pressed the joystick forward so hard his fingers ached, as if the force would make the machine understand the danger.

The voices got louder, coming close. Bull shifted the mech so that it was walking along the wall. If someone came around the corner behind him, it would give him an extra fraction of a second before he was seen. The thick metal legs slid forward, shifted weight, shifted again.

The doorway was six feet away. Four. Three. He let go of the controls and reached out for the door a little too soon and had to inch the mech forward before he tried again. He was sweating, and he hoped it was only fear. If something in his guts had given way, he wouldn't have known. Probably it was just fear.

The door opened, and he slammed the little joystick forward again. The mech took him through, and he closed the door behind him. He didn't have time to wait or think. He angled the mech down another hall toward the internal lifts and the long trip to second level, section M.

The great interior halls and passageways of the *Behemoth* had never seemed less like home. As he descended, the spin gravity grew almost imperceptibly stronger. His numb flesh sat a little heavier in its harness. He was going to have to get someone to change out his piss bag soon unless he could figure out some way to get his arms inside the mech's frame, but his elbows only bent one direction, so that seemed unlikely. And if his spine didn't grow back, if they didn't get the *Behemoth* and everyone else back out of the trap the protomolecule had caught them in, he'd live like this until he died.

Don't think about it, he told himself. *Too far ahead. Don't think about it. Just do your job.*

He didn't take one of the main internal lifts. Chances were too good that Ashford's men would be watching for that. Instead, he found one of the long, spiraling maintenance passages and set the mech to walking on its own. If it drifted too near one wall or the other, he could correct it, but it gave him a few seconds. He pulled out the hand terminal. He was shaking and his skin looked gray under the brown.

Serge answered almost immediately.

"Ganne nacht, boss," the tattooed Belter said. "Was wondering when you were going to check in."

"Ashford," Bull said.

"On top of it," Serge said. "Looks like he's got about a third of our boys and a bunch of crazy-ass coyos from other ships.

Right now they got the transition points off the drum north to command and south to engineering, the security office and the armory, y some little wolf packs going through the drum stirring up trouble."

"How well armed?"

"Nicht so bien sa moi," Serge said, grinning. "They savvy they got us locked out of the communications too, but I got back door open."

"You what?"

"Always ready for merde mal, me. Bust me down later," Serge said. "I'm putting together squads, clean up the drum. We'll get this all smashed flat by bedtime."

"You have to be careful with these guys, Serge."

"Will, boss. Know what we're doing. Know the ship better than anyone. You get safe, let us take care."

Bull swallowed. Giving over control ached.

"Okay."

"We been trying to get the captain, us," Serge said.

"I warned her. She may be refusing connections until she knows more who she can trust," Bull said. He didn't add, *Or they may have found her.*

"Check," Serge said, and Bull heard in the man's voice that he'd had the same thought. "When we track Ashford?"

"We don't have permission to kill him," Bull said.

"A finger slips, think we can get forgiveness?"

"Probably."

Serge grinned. "Got to go, boss. Just when es se cerrado, and they make you XO, keep me in mind for your chair, no?"

"Screw that," Bull said. "When this shit's done, you can be XO."

"Hold you to, boss," Serge said, and the connection went dead.

Chapter Thirty-Nine: Anna

The first sermon Anna had delivered in front of a congregation, fresh out of seminary and filled with zeal, was seventeen pages of single-spaced notes. It had been a lengthy dissection of the first chapter of Malachi, focusing on the prophet's exhortation not to deliver substandard sacrifices to God, and how that related to modern worship. It had been detailed, backed by all of the evidence and argument Anna's studious nature and seven years of graduate school could bring to bear. By the end of it, Anna was pretty sure not one member of the audience was still awake.

She'd learned some important lessons from that. There was a place for detailed Bible scholarship. There was even a place for it in front of the congregation. But it wasn't what people came to church *for*. Learning a bit more about God was part of feeling closer and more connected to Him, and the closeness was what mattered. So Anna's sermons now tended to be just a page or two of notes, and a lot more speaking from the heart. She'd delivered her message on "mixed" churches in God's eyes without looking at the notes once, and it seemed to go over very well. After she concluded with a short prayer and began the sacrament, Belters and Martians and Earthers got into line together in companionable silence. A few shook hands or clapped each other on the back. Anna felt like it might be the most important message she'd ever delivered.

"Well, it wasn't the worst thing I've ever heard," Tilly said once the service was over. She had the twitchy look she got when she wanted a cigarette, but Anna had asked her not to smoke in the meeting tent and she'd agreed. "Though, admittedly, my tolerance for lovey togetherness is low."

"That's very flattering," Anna whispered, then paused to shake hands with a Belter woman who tearfully thanked her for organizing the meeting. Tilly gave the woman her most insincere smile but managed not to roll her eyes.

"I need a drink," Tilly said once the woman had left. "Come with. I'll buy you a lemonade."

"They closed the bar. Rationing."

Tilly laughed. "I have a supplier. The guy running the rationing sold me a bottle of their best Ganymede hooch for the low price of a thousand dollars. He tossed in the lemonade for free."

"A thousand—"

"One of two things will happen," Tilly said, taking out a cigarette and putting it in her mouth but leaving it unlit. "We'll get out of here, back into the solar system where I'm rich and a thousand bucks doesn't matter, or we won't get out and nothing will matter."

Anna nodded because she didn't know what else to say. As much as she'd come to enjoy and rely on Tilly's friendship, she was occasionally reminded how utterly different their worlds were. If she and Nono had an extra thousand UN dollars lying around, it would have immediately gone into Nami's college fund. Tilly had never in her life had to sacrifice a luxury to get a necessity. If there was any actual mixing in the congregation, it was that. The one thing the Belters and inner planet naval people had in common was that none of them would be drinking thousand-dollar alcohol that night, but Tilly would.

God might not care about financial standing, but He was the only one.

"I admit, lemonade sounds nice," Anna said, fanning her face with her hand terminal. The *Behemoth*'s big habitat drum was built to house a lot more people than it currently held, but they'd stripped a lot of the environmental systems out of it when they converted it to a warship. It was starting to seem like they were reaching the atmosphere processing limits. Or maybe just the air conditioning. The temperature was generally higher now than a girl raised in Russia and most recently living on one of Jupiter's icy moons enjoyed.

After one more tour of the tent to say goodbye to the last lingering remnants of her congregation, Anna followed Tilly out. It wasn't much cooler outside the tent, but the spin of the drum and the air recycling system did combine to create a gentle breeze. Tilly looked over her flushed red face and sweat-plastered hair with a critical eye and said, "Don't worry, everyone who's coming over is here. I heard Cortez talking to some OPA bigwig a couple days ago. This is as hot as it's going to be. And as soon as they find a way to cool us down that doesn't involve venting our atmosphere into space, they'll do it."

Anna couldn't help but laugh. When Tilly raised an eyebrow, Anna explained, "We flew across the entire solar system, almost to the orbit of Neptune, a world so cold and distant from the sun we didn't even know it was there until Bouvard noticed that something was bumping Uranus around."

Tilly's eyebrow crept higher. "Okay."

"And when we get here, who knows how far from the sun and with billions of kilometers of empty space in every direction? We somehow manage to be hot and crowded."

"Thank God the Belters thought to bring this rattletrap with them," Tilly said, ducking to enter her tent. She flopped down into a folding chair and started rummaging in a plastic cooler next to it. "Can you imagine trying to stuff everyone onto the *Prince*? We'd be twelve to a bunk there. Lovely culture, these Belters."

Anna pulled her cassock off and laid it over the edge of Tilly's cot. Underneath she was wearing a white blouse and a knee-length skirt that was much less stifling. Tilly pulled a plastic bulb of lemonade out of the cooler and handed it to her, then poured herself a glass of something as clear as water that smelled like hospital cleanser. When Anna took the bulb she was surprised to find it cold. Small drops of condensation were already forming on its surface. She put the cool bottle against the back of her neck and felt a delightful chill run down her spine.

"How did you manage ice?"

"Dry ice," Tilly said around a lit cigarette, then paused to down her first shot. "Apparently it's easy for the people in atmosphere processing to make. Lots of carbon dioxide just lying around."

If Tilly was spending a thousand dollars a bottle for the antiseptic she was drinking, Anna didn't want to know what a steady supply of ice was costing her. They drank in companionable silence for a while, the cool lemonade doing wonders for Anna's heat exhaustion. Tilly brought up the idea of finding something to eat, and they wandered out of her tent in search of a supply kiosk.

There were people walking through the crowded tent city carrying guns.

"This looks bad," Tilly said. It did. These weren't bored security officers with holstered sidearms. These were grim-faced Belter men and women with assault rifles and shotguns carried in white-knuckled grips. The group moving between the tents was at least a dozen strong, and they were looking for something. Or someone.

Anna tugged at Tilly's sleeve. "Maybe we should try to get people to go back to the church tent to wait this out."

"Annie, if the bullets start flying in here, even God can't make that tent a safe place to hide. I want to know what's going on."

Anna reluctantly followed her in a path that paralleled the

armed group, which moved with purpose, occasionally stopping to look in tents or quietly question people. Anna began to feel very frightened without being sure why.

"Oh," Tilly said. "Here we go."

Bull's second-in-command—Serge was his name, Anna thought—rounded one of the larger tents trailing half a dozen security people behind him. They were all armed as well, though only with handguns. Even to Anna's untrained eye, the difference between six people with pistols and twelve people with rifles was dramatic. Serge had a faint smile on his face as though he hadn't noticed. Anna saw the muscular young woman from the security office standing behind him, though her face was a worried scowl. Oddly enough, seeing someone else look worried made Anna feel better.

"No guns in the drum, sa sa?" Serge said to the armed Belter group, though the volume of his voice made it clear he was speaking to the onlookers as well. "Drop 'em."

"You have guns," a Belter woman said with a sneer. She held a rifle at the ready.

"We're the cops," Serge said, placing one hand on the butt of his gun and grinning back at her.

"Not anymore," she replied and in one quick movement shifted her rifle and shot him in the head. A tiny hole appeared in his forehead, and a cloud of pink mist sprayed into the air behind him. He sank slowly to the floor, an expression of vague puzzlement on his face.

Anna felt her gorge rise, and had to double over and pant to keep from vomiting. "Jesus Christ," Tilly said in a strangled whisper. The speed with which the situation had gone from unsettling to terrifying took Anna's breath away. *I've just seen a man have his brains blown out.* Even after the horrors of the slow zone catastrophe, it was the worst thing she'd ever seen. The security man hadn't thought the woman would shoot him, hadn't suspected the true nature of the threat, and the price he'd paid for it was everything.

At that thought, Anna threw up all over her shoes and then sank to her knees, gagging. Tilly dropped down next to her, not even noticing that the knees of her pants were in a pool of vomit. Tilly hugged her for a second then whispered, "We need to go." Anna nodded back because she couldn't open her mouth without fear of losing control again. A few dozen meters away, the Belters were disarming the security team and tying their arms behind their backs with plastic strips.

At least they weren't shooting anyone else.

Tilly pulled her to her feet, and they hurried back to her tent, all thought of food forgotten. "Something very bad is happening on this ship," Tilly said. Anna had to suppress a manic giggle. Given their current circumstances, things would have to be very bad indeed for Tilly to think the situation had gotten worse. Sure, they were all trapped in orbit around an alien space station that periodically changed the rules of physics and had killed a bunch of them, but now they'd decided to start shooting each other too.

Yes, *very bad.*

Hector Cortez came to Tilly's tent about an hour after the shooting. Anna and Tilly had spent the time staying as close to the floor of the tent as possible, arranging Tilly's few bits of furniture into barricades around them. It had the feeling of performing ritual magic. Nothing in the room would actually stop a bullet, but they arranged it anyway. A blanket fort to keep the monsters at bay.

Mercifully, there hadn't been any further sounds of gunfire.

The few times they peeked out of the tent, they saw smaller groups of no more than two or three armed Belters patrolling the civilian spaces. Anna avoided meeting their eyes, and they ignored her.

When Cortez arrived, he cleared his throat loudly outside the tent, then asked if he could enter. They were both afraid to answer, but he came in anyway. Several people waited for him outside, though Anna couldn't see who.

He glanced once around the inside of the gloomy space, looking over their flimsy barricade, then pulled a chair away from it and sat down without commenting on it.

"The shooting is over. It's safe to sit," he said, gesturing at the other chairs. He looked better than he had in a while. His suit had been cleaned and somehow he'd found a way to wash his thick white hair. But that wasn't all of it. Some of his self-assurance had returned. He seemed confident and in charge again. Anna climbed up off the floor and took a chair. After a moment, Tilly did the same.

"I'm sorry you were frightened," Cortez said with a smile that didn't seem sorry at all.

"What's going on, Hank?" Tilly asked, her eyes narrowing. She took out a cigarette and began playing with it without lighting it. "What are you up to?"

"I'm not *up to* anything, Matilda," Cortez said. "What's happening is that the rightful authority on this ship has been restored, and Captain Ashford is once more in command."

"Okay, *Hector*," Tilly replied, "but how are you involved? Seems like internal OPA politics to me. What's your play?"

Cortez ignored her and said to Anna, "Doctor Volovodov, may we speak privately?"

"Tilly can hear anything—" Anna started, but Tilly waved her off.

"I think I'll go outside for a smoke."

When she'd left the tent, Cortez pulled his chair close enough that his knees were almost touching Anna's. He leaned forward, taking her hands in his own. Anna had never had the sense that Hector was interested in her sexually, and still didn't, but somehow the closeness felt uncomfortably intimate. Invasive.

"Anna," he said, giving her hands a squeeze. "Things are about to change dramatically on this ship, and in our calling here. I've been fortunate in that Captain Ashford trusts me and has sought my counsel, so I've had some input on the direction these changes take."

The forced intimacy, combined with the bitter taste still in her mouth from having seen a man murdered, brought up an anger she hadn't expected. She pulled her hands away from him with more violence than she intended, then couldn't help but feel a twinge of satisfaction at the hurt and surprise on his face.

"How nice for you," she said, carefully keeping her tone neutral.

"Doctor Volovodov...*Anna*, I would like your support." Anna couldn't stop the snort of disbelief in time, but he pressed on. "You have a way with people. I'm fine in front of a camera, but I'm not as good one-on-one, and that's where you shine. That's your gift. And we are about to face terrible personal challenges. Things people will have a hard time understanding. I would like your voice there with me to reassure them."

"What are you talking about?" Anna said, barely squeezing the words past a growing lump in her throat. She had the sense of a terrible secret about to be revealed. Cortez shone with the invincible certainty of the true believer.

"We are going to close the gate," he said. "We have a weapon in our possession that we believe will work."

"No," Anna said more in disbelief than in denying his claims.

"Yes. Even now engineers work to refit this vessel's communications laser to make it powerful enough to destroy the Ring."

"I don't mean that," Anna started, but Cortez just continued speaking.

"We are lost, but we can protect those we've left behind. We can end the greatest threat the human race has ever known. All it requires is that we sacrifice any hope of return. A small price to pay for—"

"No," Anna said again, more forcefully. "No, you don't get to decide that for all of these people." *For me*, she thought. *You don't get to take my wife and daughter away like that. Just because you're afraid.*

"In times of great danger and sacrifice such as this, some will step forward to make the difficult decisions. Ashford has done that, and I support him. Now it is our role to make sure the people understand and cooperate. They need to know that their sacrifice will protect the billions of people we've left behind."

"We don't know that," Anna said.

"This station has already claimed hundreds of lives, maybe thousands."

"Because we keep making decisions without knowing what the consequences are. We chased Holden's ship through the Ring, we sent soldiers to the station to hunt him, we keep acting without information and then being angry when it hurts us."

"It didn't hurt us. It killed us. A lot of us."

"We're like children," Anna said, pushing herself to her feet and lecturing down at him. "Who burn their hands on a hot stove and then think the solution is to blow up all the stoves."

"Eros," Cortez started.

"*We* did that! And Ganymede, and Phoebe, all the rest! We did it. We keep acting without thinking and you think the solution is to do it one more time. You have allied yourself with stupid, violent men, and you are trying to convince yourself that being stupid and violent will work. That makes you stupid too. I will never help you. I'll fight you now."

Cortez stood up and called to the people waiting outside. A Belter with protective chest armor and a rifle came into the tent.

"Will you shoot me too?" Anna said, putting as much contempt into the words as she could.

Cortez turned his back on her and left with the gunman.

Anna sank down into her chair, her legs suddenly too shaky to support her. She doubled over, rocking back and forth and taking long shuddering breaths to calm herself. Somehow, she didn't black out.

"Did he hurt you?" Tilly said from behind her. Her friend put a gentle hand on the back of her neck as she rocked.

"No," Anna said. It wasn't technically a lie.

"Oh, Annie. They have Claire. They wouldn't let me talk to her. I don't know if she's a hostage or—"

Before she knew she was going to do it, Anna had jumped to her feet and run out of the tent. They'd be going to the elevator that ran up the side of the drum and connected with the passages to the command decks and engineering. They'd be going to the bridge. Men like Cortez and Ashford, men who wanted to be in charge, they'd be on the bridge. She ran toward the elevator as fast as her legs would carry her. She hadn't actually run in years. Living in a small station tunneled into the ice of Europa, it just hadn't come up. She was out of breath in moments, but pushed on, ignoring the nausea and the stitch in her ribs.

She reached the elevator just as Cortez and his small band of gun-toting thugs climbed inside. Clarissa was standing at the back of the group, looking small and frail surrounded by soldiers in armor. As the doors slid closed, she smiled at Anna and raised one hand in a wave.

Then she was gone.

Chapter Forty: Holden

Hey, Cap?" Amos said from his bed. "That was the third armed patrol that's gone past this room in about three hours. Some shit is going down."

"I know," Holden said quietly. It was obvious that the situation on the *Behemoth* had changed. People with guns were moving through the corridors with hard expressions. Some of them had pulled a doctor aside, had a short but loud argument with her, then taken a patient away in restraints. It felt like a coup in progress, but according to Naomi the security chief Bull had already mutinied and taken the ship from the original Belter captain. And nothing had happened that would explain why he'd suddenly need to put a lot more boots on the ground or begin making arrests.

It felt like a civil war was brewing, or being squashed.

"Should we do something?" Amos asked.

Yes, Holden thought. *We should do something. We should get back to the* Rocinante *and hide until Miller gets done doing whatever he was doing and releases the ships in the slow zone.* Then they should burn like hell out of this place and never look back. Unfortunately, his crew was still laid up and he didn't exactly have a ride waiting to take him to his ship.

"No," he said instead. "Not until we understand what's happening. I just got *out* of jail. Not in a hurry to go back."

Alex sat up in bed, and then moaned at the effort. The top of his head was swathed in bloodstained bandages, and the left side of his face had a mushy, pulpy look to it. The speed limit change had thrown him face first into one of the cockpit's viewscreens. If he hadn't been at least partially belted into his chair, he'd probably be dead.

"Maybe we should find a quieter place than this to hole up," he said. "They don't seem opposed to arresting patients so far."

Holden nodded with his fist. He was starting to pick up Naomi's Belter-style gestures, but whenever he caught himself using one he felt awkward, like a kid pretending to be an adult. "My time on this ship has been limited to the docking bay and this room. I don't have any idea where a quieter place would be."

"Well," Naomi said. "That puts you one up on us. None of us were conscious when they brought us here."

Holden hopped off the edge of her bed and moved to the door, closing it as quietly as possible. He looked around for something to jam it shut with, but quickly decided it was hopeless. The habitation spaces in the *Behemoth*'s drum were built for low weight, not durability. The walls and door of the hospital room were paper-thin layers of epoxy and woven carbon fiber. A good kick would probably bring the entire structure down. Barricading the door would only signal patrols that something was wrong, and then delay them half a second while they broke it.

"Maybe that preacher can help us," Alex said.

"Yeah." Amos nodded. "Red seems like good people."

"No hitting on the preacher," Holden said, pointing at Amos with an accusing finger.

"I just—"

"But it doesn't matter, because if she has even half a brain—and I suspect she has a lot more than that—she'll be busily hiding herself. And she's not from here. We need an insider."

"Sam," Naomi said, just as Holden was thinking the same name. "She's chief engineer on this boat. No one will know it like she does."

"Does she owe you any favors?" Holden asked.

Naomi gave him a sour look and pulled his hand terminal off his belt. "No. I owe her about a thousand," she said as she opened a connection request to Sam. "But she's a friend. Favors don't matter."

She laid the terminal on the bed with the speaker on. The triple beep of an unanswered voice request sounding once a second. Alex and Amos were staring at it intensely, eyes wide. As though it were a bomb that might go off at any moment. In a way, Holden thought, it was. They were about as helpless right now as he could ever remember them being. Holden found himself wishing that Miller would appear and fix everything with alien magic.

"Yo," a voice said from the terminal. "Knuckles."

At some point over the last year, Sam had given Naomi the nickname Knuckles. Holden had never been able to figure out why, and Naomi had never offered to explain.

"Sammy," Naomi replied, the relief in her voice obvious. "We really, really need your help."

"Funny," Sam said. "I was just thinking of coming by to ask for *your* help. Coincidence? Or something more?"

"We were calling you to find a hiding spot," Amos yelled out. "If you were calling us for the same thing, you're fucked."

"No, that's a good idea. I've got a spot you can hole up for a while, and I'll come meet you there. Knuckles, you'll have the layout in just a second. Just follow the map. I'll be there as soon as I can. You kids take care of yourselves."

"You do the same, Sammy," Naomi said, then killed the connection. She worked the terminal for a few seconds. "Okay, I see it. Looks like unused storage just a couple hundred meters aft and spinward."

"You get to navigate," Holden said to her, then added, "Can everyone walk?"

Amos and Alex both nodded, but Naomi said, "Alex's skull is being held together with glue right now. If he gets dizzy and falls, he's not getting up again."

"Now XO," Alex objected. "I can—"

"Naomi can't walk," Amos said. "So you put her on a rolling bed with Alex and push them. I'll take point. Gimme that map."

Holden didn't argue. He picked Naomi up from her bed, trying to jostle her as little as possible, then set her next to Alex on his. "Why am I pushing instead of walking point?"

"He broke his left arm," Naomi said, scooting as close to Alex as possible and then securing the lap restraint across them both. When Amos began to protest she added, "And all the ribs on his left side."

"Right," Holden said, grabbing the push bars at the head of the bed and kicking off the wheel locks. "Lead the way."

Amos led them through the makeshift hospital corridors, smiling at everyone he passed, moving with an easy stride that made him look like a man with a destination but no hurry to get there. Even the armed patrol they passed barely gave him a glance. When they looked curiously at Holden, pushing two injured people on the same bed, he said, "Two to a bed now. That's how crowded we're getting." They just nodded him past, their expressions both sullen and bored.

Holden hadn't had much chance to look around the rest of the hospital. After leaving the docks he'd hurried straight to his crew's room and hadn't left since. But now, as he moved through the halls and intersections toward the exit, he had a chance to look over the full extent of the damage the catastrophic speed limit change had caused.

Every bed in every room was filled with injured people, and sometimes the benches and chairs in the waiting areas. Most of the injuries were contusions or broken bones, but some were more severe. He saw more than one amputation, and quite a few people hanging in traction with serious spinal injuries. But more than the physical damage, there was the stunned look of shock on every face. The sort of expression Holden associated with the recent victims or witnesses of violent crime. The *Rocinante* had tracked and disabled a pirate slaver ship a few months back, and the beaten and starving prisoners pulled from her hold had looked like this. Not just hurt, but robbed of hope.

Someone with a doctor's uniform watched Holden push the bed past, his eyes following their progress, but exhaustion robbing him of curiosity. From a small room to his right, Holden heard the electric popping sound of a cauterizing gun, and the smell of cooking meat filled the air.

"This is horrifying," he whispered to Naomi. She nodded but said nothing.

"None of us shoulda come here," Alex said.

Doors and corners, Miller had warned him. The places where you got killed if you weren't paying attention. Where the ambushes happened. *Could have been a little more explicit*, Holden thought, and then imagined Miller shrugging apologetically and bursting into a cloud of blue gnats.

Amos, half a dozen meters ahead, came to a four-way junction in the corridor and turned right. Before Holden could cross half the distance to the turn, a pair of OPA goons walked into the intersection from the left.

They paused, looking over Naomi and Alex snuggled up in the rolling bed. One of them smirked and half turned to his companion. Holden could almost hear the joke he was about to make about two people to a bed. In preparation, he smiled and readied a laugh. But before the jokester could speak, his companion said, "That's James Holden."

Everything after that happened quickly.

The pair of OPA thugs scrambled to get at the shotguns slung over their shoulders. Holden shoved the rolling gurney into their thighs, knocking them back, and gave the corridor a frantic glance looking for a weapon. One of the thugs managed to fumble his shotgun down off his shoulder and rack it, but Naomi scooted forward on the bed and drove her heel into his groin. His partner stepped back, finished getting his hands on his shotgun, and pointed it at her. Holden started to run forward, knowing he was too slow, knowing he'd watch Naomi blown apart long before he could reach the gunman.

Then both gunmen turned toward each other and slammed their faces together. They slumped to the floor, guns falling from nerveless fingers. Amos stood behind them, grimacing and massaging his left shoulder.

"Sorry, Cap," he said. "Got a little too far ahead there."

Holden leaned against the corridor wall, legs barely able to support him even in the light gravity. "No apologies. Nice save." He nodded toward the shoulder that Amos continued to rub with a pained look. "Thought that was broken."

Amos snorted. "It didn't fall off. Plenty left in here for a couple of idiots like this." He bent down and stripped the two fallen men of their weapons and ammunition. A nurse walked up behind Holden, a plastic case in her hands and a question on her face.

"Nothing to see here," Holden said. "We'll be gone in a minute."

She pointed at a nearby door. "Supply closet. No one will notice them in there for a while." Then she turned and went back the way she came.

"You have a fan," Naomi said from the bed.

"Not everyone in the OPA hates us," Holden replied, moving around the gurney to help Amos drag the unconscious men into the closet. "We did good work for them for over a year. People know that."

Amos handed Holden a compact black pistol and a pair of extra magazines. Holden tucked the gun into the waistband of his pants and pulled his shirt down over it. Amos did the same with a second gun, then put the two shotguns onto the gurney next to Naomi and covered them with the sheet.

"We don't want to get in a gunfight," Holden warned Amos as they began moving again.

"Yeah," Amos said. "But if we're in one anyway, it'll be nice to have guns."

The hospital exit was a short distance down the right-hand hallway, and suddenly they were outside. Or as outside as you could get in the *Behemoth*'s massive habitation drum. From outside, the hospital structure looked cheap and hastily assembled. A football-field-sized shanty made of epoxied carbon and fiberglass. A few hundred meters away, the edge of a city of tents spread out like acne on the drum's smooth skin.

"That way," Naomi said, pointing toward a more permanent-looking steel structure. Holden pushed the gurney, and Amos walked a few meters ahead, smiling and nodding at anyone who looked at them. Something in Amos' face making them scurry away and not look back.

As they approached the squat metal structure, a door opened in the side and Sam's pixie face appeared, waving a hand at them impatiently. A few minutes and some twisty corridors later, they were in a small, empty metal-walled room. Amos immediately dropped to the floor, laying his left arm and back flat against it.

"Ow," he said.

"You hurt?" Sam asked, locking the door behind them with a small metal keycard, and then tossing the card to Naomi.

"Everyone's hurt," Holden said. "So what the hell is going on?"

Sam blew her lips out and ran one greasy hand through her red hair. The streaks of black already in it told Holden she'd been doing a lot of that. "Ashford retook the ship. He's got some sort of coalition of bigwigs from the UN Navy, the Martians, and some of the important civilians."

"Okay," Holden said, realizing that his lack of context made most of that sentence pretty meaningless, but not wanting to waste time with explanations. "So the people roaming the halls with guns are Ashford's?"

"Yep. He's taking out anyone who helped Bull or Pa with the original mutiny, or, y'know, anyone he thinks is a threat."

"From the way they tried to shoot us, we're on that list," Naomi said.

"Definitely." Sam nodded. "I haven't been able to track down Pa, but Bull called me, so I know he's okay."

"Sam," Holden said, patting the air in a calming gesture. "Keep in mind I have no idea who these people are or why they are important, and we don't have time for a who's who. Just tell us the important bits."

Sam started to object, then shrugged and briefly explained the plan to use the comm laser. "If I do what he's asking me to do, we'll be able to get a pulse out of it that'll be hotter than a star for about three-quarters of a second. It will melt that entire side of the ship in the process."

"Does he know that?" Naomi asked, incredulity in her voice.

"He doesn't care. Whether it works on the Ring or not, we have to stop him. There are thousands of people on this ship right now, and they'll all die if he gets his way."

Holden sank down onto the edge of the gurney with a long exhale. "Oh, we're the least of the problem," he said. "This is suddenly much, much bigger than that."

Sam cocked her head at him, frowning a question.

"I've seen what this station does to threats," Holden said. "Miller showed me, when I was there. All this slow zone stuff is non-lethal deterrent as far as it's concerned. If that big blue ball out there decides us monkeys are an actual threat, it will autoclave our solar system."

"Who's Miller?" Sam asked.

"Dead guy," Amos said.

"And he was on the station?"

"Apparently," Amos said with a lopsided shrug.

"Jim?" Naomi said, putting her hand on his arm. This was the first she'd heard him speak of his experiences on the station, and he felt a pang of guilt for not telling her before.

"Something was attacking them, the protomolecule masters or whatever they were. Their defense was causing the star in any... *infected* solar system to go supernova. That station has the power to blow up stars, Naomi.

"If Ashford does this, it will kill every human there is. Everyone."

There was a long silence. Amos had stopped rubbing his arm and grunting. Naomi stared up at him from the bed, eyes wide, the fear on her face mirroring his own.

"Well," Sam finally said. "Good thing I'm not gonna let him, then, isn't it?"

"Say again?" Amos said from the floor.

"I didn't know about this other thing with ghosts and aliens," Sam said in a tone of voice that made it clear she wasn't totally buying Holden's story. "But I've been sabotaging the laser upgrades. Delaying the process while I build in short points. Weaknesses that will blow every time he tries to fire it. It should be easy enough to explain away because of course the system was never designed for this, and the ship is a flying hunk of cobbled-together junk at this point anyway."

"How long can you get us?"

"Day. Maybe a day and a half."

"I think I love you," Alex said, the words coming out in a pain- and medication-induced mumble.

"We all do, Sam," Holden said to cover for him. "That's brilliant, but there aren't very many of us, and it's a big, complicated ship. The question is how we get control of it."

"Bull," she replied. "That's why I called you. Bull's kind of messed up right now and he needs help and I don't know anyone else on this ship I trust." This last part she directed at Naomi.

"We'll do whatever we can," Naomi replied, holding up her hand. Sam crossed the room and took it. "Anything you need, Sammy. Tell us where Bull is, and I'll send my boys to go collect him."

Amos pushed himself up off the floor with a grunt and moved

to the gurney. "Yeah, whatever you need, Sam. We owe you about a million at this point, and this Ashford guy sounds like an asshole."

Sam gave a relieved smile and squeezed Naomi's fingers. "I really appreciate it. But be careful. Ashford loyalists are everywhere, and they've already killed some people. If you run into any more of them, there'll be trouble."

Amos pulled one of the shotguns out from under the sheet and laid it casually across his shoulder.

"Man can hope."

Chapter Forty-One: Bull

The storage cells were too large to be a prison. They were warehouses for the supplies to start again after a hundred ecological collapses. Seed vaults and soil and enough compressed hydrogen and oxygen to recreate the shallow ocean of a generation ship. Bull drove his mech across the vast open space, as wide and tall and airy as a cathedral, but without a single image of God. It was a temple dedicated to utility and engineering, the beauty of function and the grandeur of the experiment that would have launched humanity at the distant stars.

Everything was falling to shit around him. All the information he could put together, hunched close to his hand terminal like he was trying to crawl into it, showed that Ashford had taken over engineering and the reactor at the far south of the drum and command at the north. His squads were moving through the drum with impunity. Pa was missing and might be dead. She still had a lot of people loyal to her, including Bull, to his surprise, but if they found her body in a recycler someplace that would fade quickly. He'd done everything he could. He hadn't had the power, so he'd tried for finesse, and when that didn't work, he'd grabbed the power. He'd taken the massacre of thousands by the proto-molecule's station and gone at least halfway to building a city out of it. A little civilization in the mouth of the void. If he'd been a little more ruthless, maybe he could have made it work. Clanking softly through the massive space, that was the thing that haunted him. Not his sins, not even the people he'd killed, but the thought that if he'd killed just one or two more it might have been enough.

And even with that darkness in his heart, he couldn't keep from feeling moved by the scale of the steel and ceramic. The industrial beauty of design. He wished they'd gone to the stars instead of flying it into the mouth of hell. He wished he'd been able to make it all work out.

He tried to connect with Serge, but got nothing. He tried Corin. He wanted to reach out to Sam again, but he couldn't risk Ashford finding out they were in contact. He checked the broadcast feed or Radio Free Slow Zone, but Monica Stuart and her crew hadn't made any announcements. He let himself hope that Ashford's plan would collapse in on itself the way that all of his own plans had. Not much chance of that, though. Ashford just wanted to blow shit up. That was always easier than making something.

He thought about recording a last message to Fred Johnson, but he didn't know if he wanted to apologize, commiserate, or make the man feel guilty for putting a petulant little boy like Ashford in charge, so instead he waited and hoped for something unexpected. And maybe good for a change.

He heard the footsteps coming from the aftmost access corridor. More than one person. Two. Maybe three. If it was Ashford's men coming for him, he wasn't going to have to worry much about what to say to Fred. He took the pistol out of his holster and checked the magazine. The soft metallic sounds echoed. The footsteps faltered.

"Bull?" a familiar voice called out. "Are you in there?"

"Who's asking?" Bull said, then coughed. He spat on the deck.

"Jim Holden," the voice said. "You aren't planning to shoot me, are you? Because Sam sort of gave us the impression that we were on the same side."

Holden stepped into the storage area. This was who she'd meant when she said she knew who she could trust. And she had a point. Holden was outside every command. His reputation was built on being a man without subtexts. The man behind him with the shotgun was Amos Burton. For a moment, Bull was surprised to see the wounded Earther on his feet, then remembered his own condition and smiled. He lowered his gun, but he didn't put it away.

"And why would she think that?" he asked.

"Same enemies," Holden said. "We have to stop Ashford. If he does what he's planning, we're all trapped in here until we die. And I'm pretty sure the Ring kills everybody on the other side. Earth, Mars. The Belt. Everyone."

Bull felt something deep in his chest settle. He didn't know if it was only the weight of his worst fears coming true or if something unpleasant was happening in his lungs. He put the pistol in his holster, took the joysticks, and angled himself toward the two men. The mech's movements seemed louder now that there were other people to hear them.

"Okay," Bull said. "How about you start at the beginning and tell me what the hell you're going on about."

Bull had been around charisma before. The sense that some people had of moving through their lives in a cloud of likability or power. Fred Johnson had that, and there were glimmers of it in Holden too. In fact, there was something about Holden's open-faced honesty that reminded Bull of the young Fred Johnson's candor. He said things in a simple, matter-of-fact way—the station wouldn't come off lockdown until they turned off all the reactors and enough of the electronics on the ships; the makers of the protomolecule had been devoured by some mysterious force even badder-ass than they were; the station would destroy the solar system if it decided humans and their weapons constituted a real threat—that made them all seem plausible. Maybe it was the depth of his own belief. Maybe it was just a talent some people were born with. Bull felt a growing respect for Jim Holden, the same way he'd respect a rattlesnake. The man was dangerous just by being what he was.

When Holden ran out of steam, repeating himself that they had to stop Ashford, that Sam was buying them time, that the skeleton crews on the other ships had to shut down their reactors and power down their backup systems, Bull scratched his chin.

"What if Ashford's right?" he said.

"I don't understand," Holden said.

"All this stuff you got from the alien? What if it's bullshitting you?"

Holden's jaw went hard, but a moment later he nodded.

"He might be," he said. "I don't have any way of making sure. But Sam says Ashford's going to sacrifice the *Behemoth* when he shoots at the Ring, and if Miller wasn't lying, he's sacrificing everything else along with it. Is that a chance you're willing to take?"

"Taking it either way," Bull said. "Maybe we stop him, and we save the system. Maybe we leave the Ring open for an invasion by things that are going eat our brains on toast. Flip a coin, ese. And we got no time to test it out. No way to make sure. Either way, it's a risk."

"It is," Holden said. "So. What are you going to do?"

Bull's sigh started him coughing again. The mucus that came up into his mouth tasted like steroid spray. He spat. That was what it came down to. It wasn't really a question.

"Figure we got to retake engineering," Bull said. "Probably going to be a bitch of a fight, but we got to do it. With the drum spinning, the only path between engineering and command is the external lift or in through the command transition point, and then all the way through the drum to the engineering transition point with a shitload of people and spin gravity to slow them down. Any reinforcements he's got up top won't make it before the fight's done one way or the other."

"Sammy's already in engineering," Amos said. "Might be she could soften up the terrain for us before we go in."

"That'd be good," Bull said.

"And once we take it?" Holden said.

"Pump an assload of nitrogen into command, and pull 'em all out after they've gone to sleep, I figure," Bull said. "If Captain Pa's still alive, they're her problem."

"What if she ain't?" Amos said.

"Then they're mine," Bull said. Amos' smile meant the man had unpacked Bull's words just the way he'd meant them.

"And the reactor?" Holden said. "Are you going to shut it down?"

"That's the backup plan," Bull said with a grin. "We shut it down. We get everyone else to shut down."

"Can I ask why?"

"Might be that we can get this thing off of lockdown and it won't kill off the sun, even if Ashford does get a shot off," Bull said.

"Fair enough," Holden said. "I've got my crew. We're a little banged up."

"Pure of heart, though," Amos said.

"I don't know how many people I still got," Bull said. "If I can get through to a couple of them, I can find out."

"So where do we set up shop?"

Bull paused. If they were going to try an assault on engineering, a distraction would help. Something that would pull Ashford's attention away from what actually mattered to something else. If there was a way to slap him down. Hurt his pride. Ashford hadn't been the kind of man who thought things through well before the catastrophe, but he had been cautious. If there was a way to make him angry, to overcome that caution. But doing that and getting the word to the other ships that they needed to shut down would be more time than he had, unless…

"Yeah," he said sourly. "I know where we're going. May be a little dangerous getting there. Ashford's people are all through the drum."

"Not as many as there were when we started," Amos said. Bull didn't ask what he meant.

"Lead on," Holden said. "We'll follow you."

Bull tapped his fingers on the joysticks. Embarrassment and shame clawed their way up his guts. A shadow of confusion crossed Holden's face. Bull felt a stab of disgust with himself. He was about to put a bunch of civilians in danger in order to draw Ashford's attention, he was going to do it of his own free will, and he was ashamed of the things that he didn't actually have any control over. He didn't know what that said about him, but he figured it couldn't be good.

Radio Free Slow Zone was in what had once been the colonial administrative offices. The narrow office spaces had been designed into the walls and bulkheads of the original ship, back when it had been the *Nauvoo*, and the amount of work it would have taken to strip the cubicles back until the space could be used for something else had never been worth the effort. Bull had given it to Monica Stuart and her crew because it was a cheap favor. Something he didn't need—the old offices—for something he did: a familiar face and reassuring voice to help make the *Behemoth* into the gathering place for the full and fractured fleet.

The broadcast studio was a sheet of formed green plastic that someone had pried off the floor and set on edge. The lights were jerry-rigged and stuck to whatever surfaces came to hand. Bull recognized most of the faces, though he didn't know many of them. Monica Stuart, of course. Her production team was down to an Earther woman named Okju and a dark-skinned Martian called Clip. Holden had called his crew there, but they hadn't arrived yet.

Bull considered the space from a tactical point of view. It wouldn't be hard to block off accessways. The little half walls provided a lot of cover, and they were solid enough to stop most slug throwers. An hour or two with some structural steel and a couple welders and the place could be almost defensible. He hoped it wouldn't need to be. Except that he hoped it would.

"We went black as soon as the fighting started," Monica said. "Thought it would be better not to go off half-cocked."

"Good plan," Bull said, and his hand terminal chimed. He held up a finger and fumbled to accept the connection. Corin's face flickered to life. She looked pale. Shell-shocked. He knew the expression.

"How bad?"

"I've got about thirty people, sir," Corin said. "Armed and armored. We control the commissary and most of the civilians. Once Ashford got control of the transition points, he mostly fell back."

"Pa?"

"Alive," Corin said. "Pretty beat up, but alive."

"We'll call that a win."

"We lost Serge," Corin said, her voice flat and calm. That was it, then. Bull felt *I'm sorry* coming by reflex and pushed it back. Later. He could offer sympathy later. Right now, he only had room for strong.

"All right," he said. "Bring whoever you can spare to the colonial administrative offices. And weapons. All the weapons we've got, bring them here."

"New headquarters?"

"Security station in exile," Bull said, and Corin almost smiled. There was no joy in it, but maybe a little amusement. Good enough for now. She saluted, and he returned the gesture as best he could before dropping the connection.

"So this is a coup," Monica said.

"Counter-countercoup, technically," Bull said. "Here's what I need you to do. I want you reporting on what's going on here. Broadcast. The *Behemoth*, the other ships in the fleet. Hell, tell the station if you think it'll listen. Captain Ashford was relieved for mental health reasons. The trauma was too much for him. He and a few people who are still personally loyal to him have holed up in command, and the security team of the *Behemoth* is going to extract him."

"And is any of that true?"

"Maybe half," Bull said.

Behind Monica's back, the wide-set Earther woman named Okju looked up and then away.

"I'm not a propagandist," Monica said.

"Ashford's going to get us all killed," Bull said. "Maybe everyone back home too, if he does what he's thinking. The catastrophe? Everything we've been through here? These were the kid gloves. He's trying to start a real fight."

It was strange how saying the words himself made them seem real in a way that hearing from Holden hadn't. He still wasn't sure whether he believed it was true, even. But right now, it needed to be, and so it was. Monica's eyes went a little rounder and bright red splotches appeared on her cheeks.

"When this is over," she said, "I want the full story. Exclusive. Everything that's really going on. Why it came down the way it did. In-depth interviews with all the players."

"Can't speak for anyone but myself right now," Bull said. "But that's a fair deal by me. Also, I need you to talk the other ships in the fleet into shutting down their reactors and power grids, pulling the batteries out of every device they can find that's got them."

"Because?"

"We're trying to get the lockdown on the ships taken off," he said. "Let us go home. And if we can't stop Ashford, getting off lockdown is the only chance we've got to keep the station from retaliating against the folks on the other side of the Ring."

And because if the insults and provocations, the false threats and misdirections all failed, that would be enough. If Ashford could see the other plan coming together, if he could see *his* heroic gesture, *his* grand sacrifice being taken away, he would come. He'd do whatever he could to shut down the studio, and every gun that came here was one less that would be at engineering or command.

Monica looked nonplussed.

"And how am I going to convince them to do that, exactly?"

"I have an idea about that," Bull said. "I know this priest lady who's got people from damn near every ship out here coming to her services. I'm thinking we recruit her."

Even, he didn't say, *if it puts her in the firing line.*

Chapter Forty-Two: Clarissa

The end came. All the running around stopped, and a kind of calm descended on Ashford. On Cortez. All of them. The order went out to secure the transition points. No one was passing into or out of the drum. Not now. Not ever again.

It felt almost like relief.

"I've been thinking about your father," Cortez said as the lift rose toward the transition point, spin gravity ebbing away and the growing Coriolis making everything feel a little bit off. Like a dream or the beginning of an unexpected illness. "He was a very clever man. Brilliant, some would say, and very private in his way."

He tried to turn the protomolecule into a weapon and sell it to the highest bidder, Clarissa thought. The thought should have stung, but it didn't. It was just a fact. Iron atoms formed in stars; a Daimo-Koch power relay had one fewer input than the standard models; her father had tried to militarize the protomolecule. He hadn't known what it was. No one had. That didn't keep them from playing with it. Seeing what they could do. She had the sudden visual memory of a video she'd seen of a drunken soldier handing his assault rifle to a chimp. What had happened next was either hilarious or tragic, depending on her mood. Her father hadn't been that different from the chimp. Just on a bigger scale.

"I'm sorry I didn't have the chance to know him better," Cortez said.

Ashford and seven of his men were on the lift with them. The captain stood at the front, hands clasped behind his back. Most of his men were Belters too. Long frames, large heads. Ren had had that look too. Like they were all part of the same family. Ashford's soldiers had sidearms and bulletproof vests. She didn't. And yet she kept catching them glancing over at her. They still thought of her as Melba. She was the terrorist and murderer with the combat modifications. That she looked like a normal young woman only added to the sense that she was eerie. This was why Ashford had wanted her so badly. She was an adornment. A trophy to show how strong he was and paper over his failure to hold his own ship before.

She wished that one of them would smile at her. The more they acted like she was Melba, the more she felt that version of herself coming back, seeping up into her cognition like ink soaking through paper.

"There was one time your brother Petyr came to the United Nations buildings when I was visiting there."

"That would have been Michael," she said. "Petyr hates the UN."

"Does he?" Cortez said with a gentle laugh. "My mistake."

The lift reached the axis of the drum, slowing gently so that they could all steady themselves with the handrails and not be launched up into the ceiling. Behind them, a series of vast conduits and transformers powered the long, linear sun of the drum. Before she'd come out to the Ring, she'd never seriously thought about balancing power loads and environmental control systems.

That kind of thing had been for other people. Lesser people. Now, with all she'd learned, the scale of the *Behemoth*'s design was awing. She wished the others could have seen it. Soledad and Bob and Stanni. And Ren.

The doors slid open, and the Belters launched themselves into the transition with the grace of men and women who'd spent their childhoods in low or null g. She and Cortez didn't embarrass themselves, but they would never have the autonomic grace of a Belter on the float.

The command decks were beautiful. The soft indirect lighting took everyone's shadows away. Melba launched herself after Ashford and the Belters, swimming through the air like a dolphin in the sea.

The command center itself was beautifully designed. A long, lozenge-shaped room with control boards set into ceramic desks. On one end of the lozenge, a door opened into the captain's office, on the other, to the security station. The gimbaled crash couches looked less like functional necessities than the natural, beautiful outgrowth of the ship. Like an orchid. The walls were painted with angels and pastoral scenes. The effect was only slightly spoiled by the half dozen access panels that stood open, repairs from the sudden stop still uncompleted. Even the guts of the command center were beautiful in their way. Clarissa found herself wanting to go over and just look in to see if she could make sense of the design.

Three men floated at the control boards, all of them Belters. "Welcome back, Captain," one of them said.

Ashford sailed through the empty air to the captain's station. Three of the soldiers drifted out to take positions in the corridor, the others arraying themselves around the room, all with sightlines on the doors leading in. Anyone who tried to take the command center would have to walk through a hailstorm of bullets. Clarissa pulled herself over to the door of the security station, as much to get out of the way as anything, and Cortez followed her, his expression focused, serious, and a little agitated.

Ashford keyed in a series of commands, and his control panel shifted, growing brighter. His eyes tracked over the readouts and screens. Lit from below, he looked less like the man set to save all of humanity at the sacrifice of himself and his crew and more like a lower university science teacher trying to get his simulations to work they way they were meant to.

"Jojo?" he said, and the voice of the prison guard came from the control deck like the man was standing beside them.

"Here, Captain. We've got the engineering transition point locked down. Anyone wants to get in here, we'll give 'em eight kinds of hell."

"Good man," Ashford said. "Do we have Chief Engineer Rosenberg?"

"Yes, sir. She's making the modifications to the comm array now."

"Still?"

"Still, sir."

"Thank you," he said, then tapped the display, his fingertips popping against the screen. "Sam. How long before the modifications are done?"

"Two hours," she said.

"Why so long?"

"I'm going to have to override every safety device in the control path," she said. "This thing we're doing? There's a lot of built-in design that was meant to keep it from happening."

Ashford scowled.

"Two hours," he said, and stabbed the connection closed.

The waiting began. Two hours later, the same woman explained that the targeting system had been shaken out of round by the catastrophe. It just meant a delay getting lock for most purposes, but since this was a one-shot application, she was realigning it. Three more hours. Then she was getting a short loop error that he had to track down. Two more hours.

Clarissa saw Ashford's mood darken with every excuse, every hour that stretched past. She found the toilets tucked at the back of the security station and started wondering about getting a few tubes of food. If the only working commissary was in the drum, that might actually be a problem. Cortez had strapped himself into a crash couch and slept. The guards slowly became more and more restless. Clarissa spent an hour going from access panel to access panel, looking at the control boards and power relays that fed the bridge. It was surprising how many of them were the same as the ones she'd worked with on the Earth ships coming out. Cut an Earther or a Belter, they both bled the same blood. Crack an access panel on the *Behemoth* and the *Prince*, and both ships had the same crappy brownout buffers.

She wondered how the *Behemoth* felt about being the *Behemoth* and not the *Nauvoo*. She wondered how she felt about being Clarissa Mao and not Melba Koh. Would the ship feel the nobility of its sacrifice? Lost forever in the abyss, but with everyone else redeemed by her sacrifice. The symmetry seemed meaningful, but it might only have been the grinding combination of fear and uncertainty that made it seem that way.

Seven hours after they'd taken the bridge, Ashford stabbed at the control console again, waited a few seconds, and punched the console hard enough that the blow pushed him back into his couch. The sound of the violence startled Cortez awake and stopped the muttered conversation between the guards. Ashford ignored them all and tapped at the screen again. His fingertips sounded like hailstones striking rock.

The light from the screen flickered.

"Sir?"

"Where's Sam Rosenberg?" Ashford snapped.

"Last I saw her, she was checking the backup power supply for the reactor bottle, sir. Should I find her?"

"Who's acting as her second?"

"Anamarie Ruiz."

"Get Sam and Anamarie up to command, please. If you have to take them under guard, that's fine."

"Yes, sir."

Ashford closed the connection and pushed away from the console, his crash couch shushing on its bearings.

"Is there a problem, Captain?" Cortez asked. His voice was thick and a little bleary.

"Nothing I can't handle," Ashford replied.

It was almost another hour before Clarissa heard the doors from the external elevator shaft open. New voices came down the hall. The gabble of conversation tried to hide some deeper strain. Ashford tugged at his uniform.

Two women floated in the room. The first was a pretty woman with a heart-shaped face and grease-streaked red hair pulled back in a bun. It made her think of Anna. The second was thin, even for a Belter, with skin the color of dry soil and brown eyes so dark they were black. Three men with pistols followed them in.

"Chief Rosenberg," Ashford said.

"Sir," the red-haired woman said. She didn't sound like Anna.

"We are on our fourth last-minute delay now. The more time we waste, the more likely it is that the rogue elements in the drum will cause trouble."

"I'm doing my best, Captain. This isn't the kind of thing we get to take a second shot at, though. We need to be thorough."

"Two hours ago, you said we'd be ready to fire in two hours. Are we ready to fire now?"

"No, sir," she said. "I looked up the specs, and the reactor's safeties won't allow an output the size we need. I'm fabricating some new breakers that won't screw us up. And then we have to replace some cabling as well."

"How long will that take?" Ashford asked. His voice was dry. Clarissa thought she heard danger in it, but the engineer didn't react to it.

"Six hours, six and a half hours," she said. "The fab printers only go so fast."

Ashford nodded and turned to the second woman. Ruiz.

"Do you agree with that assessment?"

"All respect to Chief Rosenberg, I don't," Ruiz said. "I don't see why we can't use conductive foam instead."

"How long would that take?"

"Two hours," Ruiz said.

Ashford drew a pistol. Almost before the chief engineer's eyes could widen, the gun fired. In the tight quarters, the sound itself was an assault. Sam's head snapped back and her feet kicked forward. A bright red globe shivered in the air, smaller droplets flying out from it. Violent moons around a dead planet.

"Mister Ruiz," Ashford said. "Please be ready to fire in two hours."

For a moment, the woman was silent. She shook her head like she was trying to come back from a dream.

"Sir," she said.

Ashford smiled. He was enjoying the effect he'd just had.

"You can go," he said. "Tick-tock. Tick-tock."

Ruiz and the three guards pulled themselves back out. Ashford put his pistol away.

"Would someone please clean this mess away," he said.

"My God," Cortez said, his voice somewhere between a prayer and blasphemy. "Oh my God. What have you done?"

Ashford craned his neck. Two of the guards moved forward. One of them had a utility vacuum. When he thumbed it on, the little motor whined. When he put it in the blood, the tone of it dropped half a tone from E to D-sharp.

"I shot a saboteur," Ashford said, "and cleared the way to saving humanity from the alien threat."

"You killed her," Cortez said. "She had no trial. No defense."

"Father Cortez," Ashford said, "these are extreme circumstances."

"But—"

Ashford turned, bending his just-too-large Belter head forward.

"With all respect, this is my command. These are my people. And if you think I am prepared to accept another mutiny, you are very much mistaken." There was a buzz in the captain's voice like a drunk man on the edge of a fight. Clarissa put a hand on Cortez's shoulder and shook her head.

The older man frowned, ran a hand across his white hair, and put on a professionally compassionate expression.

"I understand the need for discipline, Captain," Cortez said. "And even some violence, if it is called for, but—"

"Don't make me put you back in the drum," Ashford said. Cortez closed his mouth, his head bowed as if being humbled was old territory for him. Even though she knew that wasn't true, Clarissa felt a warm sympathy for him. He'd seen dead people. He'd seen people die. Seeing someone killed was different. And killing someone was different than that, so in some ways, she was ahead of him.

"Come on," she said. Cortez blinked at her. There were tears in his eyes, floating more or less evenly across his sclera, unable to fall. "The head's this way. I'll get you there."

"Thank you," he said.

Two of the guards were wrapping the dead engineer with tape. The bullet had struck just above her right eye, and a hemisphere of blood adhered to it, shuddering but not growing larger. The woman wasn't bleeding anymore. *She was the enemy*, Clarissa thought, but the idea had a tentative quality about it. Like she was trying on a vest to see how it fit. *She was the enemy and so she deserved to die even though she had red hair like Anna.* It wasn't as comforting as she'd hoped.

In the head, Cortez washed his face and hands with the towelettes and then fed them into the recycler. Clarissa mentally followed them down to the churn and through the guts of the ship. She knew how it would work on the *Cerisier* or the *Prince*. Here, she could only speculate.

You're trying to distract yourself, a small part of herself said. The thought came in words, just like that. Not from outside, not from someone else. A part of her talking to the rest. *You're trying to distract yourself.*

From what? she wondered.

"Thank you," Cortez said. His smile looked more familiar now. More like the man she saw on screens. "I knew that there would be some resistance to doing the right thing here. But I wasn't ready for it. Spiritually, I wasn't ready for it. Surprised me."

"It'll do that," Clarissa said.

Cortez nodded. He was about her father's age. She tried to imagine Jules-Pierre Mao floating in the little space, weeping over a dead engineer. She couldn't. She couldn't imagine him here at all, couldn't picture what he looked like exactly. All of her impressions were of his power, his wit, his overwhelming importance. The physical details were beside the point. Cortez looked at himself in the mirror, set his own expression.

He's about to die, she thought. *He's about to condemn himself and everyone on this ship to dying beyond help, here in the darkness, because he thinks it is the right and noble thing to do.* Was that what Ashford was doing too? She wished now that she'd talked to him more when they'd been prisoners together. Gotten to understand him and who he was. Why he was willing to die for this. And more than that, why he was willing to kill. Maybe it was altruism and nobility. Maybe it was fear. Or grief. As long as he did what needed doing, it didn't matter why, but she found she was curious. She knew why she was here, at least. To redeem herself. To die for a reason, and make amends.

You're trying to distract yourself.

"—don't you think?" Cortez said. His smile was gentle and rueful, and she didn't have any idea what he'd been saying.

"I guess," she said and pushed back from the doorframe to give him room. Cortez pulled himself by handholds, trying to keep his body oriented with head toward the ceiling and feet toward the floor, even though crawling along the walls was probably safer and more efficient. It was something people who lived with weight did by instinct. Clarissa only noticed it because she wasn't doing it. The room was just the room, no up or down, anything a floor or a wall or a ceiling. She expected a wave of vertigo that didn't come.

"You know it doesn't matter," she said.

Cortez smiled at her, tilting his head in a question.

"If we're all sacrifices, it doesn't matter when we go," Clarissa said. "She went a little before us. We'll go a little later. It doesn't even matter if we all go willingly to the altar, right? All that matters is that we break the Ring so everyone on the other side is safe."

"Yes, that's right," Cortez said. "Thank you for reminding me."

An alert sounded in the next room, and Clarissa turned toward it. Ashford had undone his straps and was floating above his control panel, his face stony with rage.

"What's going on, Jojo?"

"I think we've got a problem, sir..."

Chapter Forty-Three: Holden

Everything about the former colonial administrative offices made Holden sad. The drab, institutional green walls, the cluster of cubicles in the central workspace, the lack of windows or architectural flourishes. The Mormons had been planning to run the human race's first extrasolar colony from a place that would have been equally at home as an accounting office. It felt anticlimactic. *Hello, welcome to your centuries-long voyage to build a human settlement around another star! Here's your cubicle.*

The space had been repurposed in a way that at least gave it a lived-in feel. A cobbled-together radio occupied one entire closet, just off the main broadcasting set. The size saying more about the slapdash construction than about the broadcasting power. The current fleet was in a small enough space to pick up a decent handheld set. A touch screen on one wall acted as a whiteboard for the office, lists of potential interviews and news stories listed along with contact names and potential public interest. Holden was oddly flattered to see his name next to the note *Hot, find a way to get this.*

Now the room buzzed with activity. Bull's people were trickling in a few at a time. Most of them brought duffel bags full of weapons or ammunition. A few brought tools in formed plastic cases with wheels on the bottom. They were preparing to armor the former office space into a mini-fortress. Holden leaned against an unused desk and tried to stay out of everyone's way.

"Hey," Monica said, appearing at his side out of nowhere. She nodded her head at the board. "When I heard you were back from the station, I was hoping I could get an interview from you. Guess I missed my chance, though."

"Why?"

"Next to this end-of-the-world shit, you've slipped a couple notches in the broadcast schedule."

Holden nodded, then shrugged. "I've been famous before. It's not so great."

Monica sat on the desk next to him and handed him a drinking bulb. When Holden tasted it, it turned out to be excellent coffee. He closed his eyes for a moment, sighing with pleasure. "Okay, now I'm just a little in love with you."

"Don't tease a girl," she replied. "Will this work? This plan of Bull's?"

"Am I on the record?"

Someone started welding a sheet of metal to the wall, forcing them both to throw up their hands to block the light. The air smelled like sulfur and hot steel.

"Always," Monica said. "Will it?"

"Maybe. There's a reason military ships are scuttled the second someone takes engineering. If you don't own that ground, you don't own the ship."

Monica smiled as if that all made sense to her. Holden wondered how much actually did. She wasn't a wartime reporter. She was a documentary producer who'd wound up in the wrong place at the right time. He finished off the last of his coffee with a pang of regret and waited to see if she had anything else to ask. If he was nice, maybe she'd find him a refill.

"And this Sam person can do that?" she said.

"Sam's been keeping the *Roci* in the air for almost three years now. She was one of Tycho's best and brightest. Yeah, if she's got your engine room and she doesn't like you, you're screwed."

"Want more coffee?"

"Good God, yes," Holden said, holding out his bulb like a street beggar.

Before Monica could take it, Bull came clumping over to them in his mechanical walker. He started to speak and then began a wet, phlegmy cough that lasted several seconds. Holden thought he looked like a man who was dying by centimeters.

"Sorry," Bull said, spitting into a wadded-up rag. "That's disgusting."

"If you die," Monica said, "I won't get my exclusive."

Bull nodded and began another coughing fit.

"If you die," Holden said, "can I have all your stuff?"

Bull gave a grand, sweeping gesture at the office around them. "Someday, my boy, this will all be yours."

"What's the word?" Holden asked, raising the bulb to his lips and being disappointed at its emptiness all over again.

"Corin found the preacher, huddled up with half her congregation in their church tent."

"Great," Holden said. "Things are starting to come together."

"Better than you think. Half the people in that room were UN and Martian military. They're coming with her. She says they'll back her story when she asks the other ships to shut down. It also won't hurt to have a few dozen more able bodies to man the defenses when Ashford comes after us."

As Bull spoke, Holden saw Amos enter the offices pushing the bed Alex and Naomi were on. A knot he hadn't even realized he had relaxed in his shoulders. Bull was still talking about utilizing the new troops for their defensive plans, but Holden wasn't listening. He watched Amos move the gurney to a safe corner at the back of the room and then wander over to stand next to them.

"Nothing new outside," Amos said when Bull stopped talking. "Same small patrols of Ashford goons walking the drum, but they don't act like they know anything's up."

"They'll know as soon as we do our first broadcast," Monica said.

"How's that shoulder?" Holden asked.

"Sore."

"I've been thinking I want you to take command of the defense here once the shit hits the intake."

"Yeah, okay," Amos said. He knew Holden was asking him to protect Naomi and Alex. "I guess that means you're going down to—"

He was interrupted by a loud buzzing coming from Bull's pocket. Bull pulled a beat-up hand terminal out and stared at it like it might explode.

"Is that an alarm?" Holden asked.

"Emergency alert on my private security channel," Bull said, still not answering it. "Only the senior staff can use that channel."

"Ashford, trying to track you down?" Holden asked, but Bull ignored him and answered the call.

"Bull here. Ruiz, I—" Bull started, then stopped and just listened. He grunted a few times, though Holden couldn't tell if they were assents or negations. When he finished the call, he dropped the hand terminal on the desk behind him without looking at it. His brown skin, recently gray with sickness, had turned almost white. He reached up with both hands to wipe away what Holden realized with shock were tears. Holden would not have guessed the man was capable of weeping.

"Ashford," Bull started, then began a long coughing fit that looked suspiciously like sobbing. When he'd finally stopped, his eyes and mouth were covered with mucus. He pulled a rag out of his pocket and wiped most of it off, then said, "Ashford killed Sam."

"What?" Holden asked. His brain refused to believe this could be true. He'd heard the words clearly, but those words could not be, so he must have heard them wrong. "What?"

Bull took a long breath, gave his face one last wipe with the rag, then said, "He brought her up to the bridge to ask about the laser mods, and then he shot her. He made Anamarie Ruiz the chief engineer."

"How do you know?" Monica asked.

"Because that was Ruiz on the line just now. She wants us to get her the hell out of there," Bull said. Almost all traces of his grief were gone from his face. He took another long, shuddering breath. "She knows Ashford has completely gone around the bend, but what can she do?"

Holden shook his head, still refusing to believe it. Brilliant little Sam, who fixed his ship, who was Naomi's best friend, whom Alex and Amos shared a good-natured crush on. *That* Sam couldn't be dead.

Amos was staring at him. The big man's hands were curled into fists, his knuckles a bloodless white.

"We have to hold this ground," Holden said, hoping to head off Amos' next words. "I need you to hold it or this whole thing falls apart."

"Then you kill him," Amos said, his words terrifyingly flat and emotionless. "None of this trial bullshit. No righteous man among the savages bullshit. You fucking kill him, or so help me God…"

Holden felt a sudden nausea almost drive him to his knees. He took a few deep breaths to push it back. This was what they had to offer to Sam's memory. After all she'd done for them. All she'd meant to them. They had violence, arguments about the best way to get revenge. Sam, who as far as he knew had never hurt another person in her life. Would she want this? He could picture her there, telling Amos and Bull to put their testosterone away and act like adults. The thought almost made him vomit.

Monica put a hand on his back. "Are you okay?"

"I have to tell Naomi," was all he could say, then he pushed her hand away and walked across a floor that moved under his feet like the rolling deck of an oceangoing ship.

Naomi reacted only with sorrow, not with anger. She cried, but didn't demand revenge. She repeated Sam's name through her tears, but didn't say Ashford's once. It seemed like the right reaction. It seemed like love.

He was holding Naomi while she gently wept when Bull clumped up behind him. He felt a flash of anger, but swallowed it.

"What?"

"Look," Bull said, rubbing his buzz cut with both hands. "I know this is a shitty time, but we have to talk about where we go from here."

Holden shrugged.

"Sam's gone, and she was pretty central to our plans..."

"I understand," Naomi said. "I'll go."

"What?" Holden said, feeling like they were having a conversation in some kind of code he didn't understand. "Go where?"

"With Sam gone, Naomi is the best engineer we've got," Bull said.

"What about this Ruiz person? I thought she was the chief engineer now."

"She was in charge of infrastructure," Bull said. "And I've seen Nagata's background. She's got the training and the experience. And we trust her. If someone's going to take Sam's place—"

"No," Holden said without thinking about it. Naomi was hurt. She couldn't fight her way into the engine room now. And Sam had been killed.

"I'll go," Naomi repeated. "My arm is for shit, but I can walk. If someone can help me once we get there, I can take out the bridge and shut down the reactor."

"No," Holden said again.

"Yeah, me too," Alex added. He was sitting on the edge of the gurney facing away from them. He'd been shaking like he was crying, but hadn't made a sound. His voice sounded dry, like fallen leaves rustling in the wind. Brittle and empty. "I guess I have to go too."

"Alex, you don't—" Naomi started, but he kept talking over the top of her.

"Nobody pulled the *Roci*'s batteries off-line when we left, so if we're shutting everything down, she'll need someone to do it."

Bull nodded. Holden wanted to smack him for agreeing with any of this.

"And that'll be me," Alex said. "I can tag along as far as engineering, grab an EVA pack there, and use the aft airlock to get out."

Amos moved over behind Bull, his face still flat, emotionless, but his hands in fists. "Alex is going?"

"New plan," Bull said loud enough for everyone to hear. People stopped whatever they were doing and moved over to listen. More must have arrived, because there were almost fifty in the office now. At the back of the room stood a small knot of people in military uniforms. Anna the redheaded preacher was with them. She was holding hands with an aggressively thin woman who alternated smoking and tapping her front teeth with her pinky fingernail. Bull spotted them at the same time Holden did, and waved them forward.

"Anna, come on up here," he said. "Most everyone is here now, so this is how it's going to go down."

The room got quiet. Anna made her way up to Bull and waited. Her skinny friend came with her, staring at the crowd around the preacher with the suspicious eyes of a bodyguard.

"In"—Bull stopped to look at a nearby wall panel with a clock on it—"thirty minutes, I will take a team made up of security personnel and the crew of the *Rocinante* to the southern drum access point. We will retake that access point and gain entrance into the engineering level. Once we control engineering, Monica and her team will begin a broadcast explaining to the rest of the fleet about the need to kill the power. Preacher, that's where you and your people come in."

Anna turned and smiled at her group, a motley collection of people in the uniforms of a variety of services and planetary allegiances. Most of them injured in one way or another. Some quite badly.

"The target for the shutdown is 1900 hours local, about two and a half hours from now. We need them to keep it down for two hours. That's our window. We need the *Behemoth* down during that two hours."

"We'll make it happen," Naomi said.

"But when our broadcast starts, Ashford will probably try to take this location. Amos and the remainder of my team, along with any volunteers from among the rest of you, will hold this position as long as possible. The more bad guys you can tie up here, the fewer we'll have trying to take engineering back from us. But I need you to hold. If we can't keep Anna and her people on the air long enough to get everyone on board with our shutdown plan, this thing ends before it starts."

"We'll hold," Amos said. No one disagreed.

"Once we control engineering, we'll send a team forward to put restraints on the hopefully unconscious people on the bridge and we'll own the ship. The lights go out, the aliens let us go, and we get the fuck out of this miserable stretch of space once and for all. How's that sound?"

Bull raised his voice with the final question, looking for a cheer from the group, and the group obliged. People began to drift back toward their various tasks. Holden squeezed Naomi's uninjured shoulder and moved over to Anna. She looked lost. Along the way he grabbed Amos by the arm.

"Anna," Holden said. "Do you remember Amos?"

She smiled and nodded. "Hello, Amos."

"How you doing, Red?"

"Amos will be here to protect you and the others," Holden continued. "If you need anything, you let him know. I feel safe in saying nothing will get in here to stop you from doing your job as long as he's alive."

"That's the truth," Amos said. "Ma'am."

"Hey, guys," someone called out from the doorway. "Look what followed me home. Can I keep them?"

Holden patted Anna on the arm and gave Amos a meaning-ful look. *Protect this one with your life.* Amos nodded back. He looked vaguely offended.

He left them together and caught up with Bull heading for the door. The security officer Corin, Bull's new second-in-command, was leaning next to the door with a shit-eating grin.

"Come on in, boys," she said, and four Martians with military haircuts came into the room. They stood on the balls of their feet, slowly looking over every inch of the room. Holden had known someone who always entered a room that way. Bobbie. He found himself wishing she were here. The man in the lead was power-fully familiar.

"Sergeant Verbinski," Bull said to one of them. "This is a surprise."

Holden hadn't recognized the man without his armor. He looked big.

"Sir," Verbinski said. "I heard you're about to start a fight to get us all out of here."

"Yeah," Bull said. "I am."

"Sounds like a noble cause," Verbinski replied. "Need four grunts with nothing else to do?"

"Yeah," Bull said with a growing smile. "I really do."

Chapter Forty-Four: Anna

They'd failed.

Anna watched the busy men and women in the radio offices as they strapped on body armor, loaded weapons, hung grenades from their belts, and she felt only sadness and despair.

A history professor at university had once told her, *Violence is what people do when they run out of good ideas. It's attractive because it's simple, it's direct, it's almost always available as an option. When you can't think of a good rebuttal for your opponent's argument, you can always punch them in the face.*

They'd run out of ideas. And now they were reaching for the simple, direct, always available option of shooting everyone they disagreed with. She hated it.

Monica caught her eye from across the room and held up a small thermos of coffee in invitation. Anna waved her off with a smile.

"Are you insane?" Tilly asked. She was sitting on the floor next to her in a back corner of the offices, trying to stay out of everyone's way. "That woman has the only decent coffee on this entire ship." She waved at Monica, pointing at herself.

"I should have spent more time talking to Cortez," Anna said. "The OPA captain might be intractable, but I could have reached Cortez with enough time."

"Life is finite, dear, and Cortez is an asshole. We'll all be better off if someone puts a bullet in him before this is over." Tilly accepted a pour of Monica's coffee with a grateful smile. Monica set the thermos down and sat on the floor next to them.

"Hey, we—" she started, but Anna didn't notice.

"You don't mean that," Anna said to Tilly, annoyance creeping into her voice. "Cortez isn't a bad person. He's frightened and unsure, and has made some bad choices, but at worst he's misguided, not evil."

"He doesn't deserve your sympathy," Tilly said, then tossed back the last of her coffee like she was angry with it.

"Who are we—" Monica started again.

"He does. He does deserve it," Anna said. Watching the young men and women prepare for war, preparing to kill and be killed right in front of her, made her more angry with Tilly than she probably would have been otherwise. But she found herself very angry now. "That's exactly the point. They *all* deserve our sympathy. If Bull's right about Ashford, and he's gone crazy with fear and humiliation and the trauma of seeing his crew killed, then he deserves our sympathy. That's a terrible place to be. Cortez deserves our understanding, because he's doing exactly the same thing we are. Trying to find the right thing to do in an impossible situation."

"Oh," Monica said. "Cortez. He's the—"

"That's a load of crap, Annie. That's exactly how you know who the good guys and the bad guys are: by what they do when the chips are down."

"This isn't about good guys and bad guys," Anna said. "Yes, we've picked sides now, because some of the actions they are about to take will have serious consequences for us, and we're going to try to stop them. But what you're doing is demonizing them, making them the enemy. The problem with that is that once we've stopped them and they can't hurt us anymore, they're still demons. Still the enemy."

"Believe me," Tilly said, "when I get out of here, it will be my mission in life to burn Cortez to the ground for this."

"Why?"

"What do you mean, why?"

"He won't be on a ship trying to destroy the Ring anymore. He won't be supporting Ashford anymore. All of the circumstances that made him your enemy will be gone. What's the value in clinging to the hate?"

Tilly turned away and fumbled around in her pocket for her cigarettes. She smoked one aggressively, pointedly not looking at Anna.

"What's the answer, then?" Monica asked after a few tense moments of silence.

"I don't know," Anna said, pulling her legs close and resting her chin on her knees. She tucked her back as far into the corner of the room as it would go, her body looking for a safe place with a small child's insistence. But the hard green walls offered no comfort.

"So it's all just academic, then," Monica said. Tilly snorted in agreement, still not looking at Anna.

Anna pointed at the people getting ready in the room around them. "How many will be dead by the end of today?"

"There's no way to know," Monica said.

"We owe it to them to look for other answers. We've failed this time. We've run out of ideas, and now we're reaching for the gun. But maybe next time, if we've thought about what led us here, maybe next time we find a different answer. Certainty doesn't have a place in violence."

For a while, they were silent. Tilly angrily chain-smoked. Monica typed furiously on her terminal. Anna watched the others get ready for war, and tried to match faces with names. Even if they won out today, there was a very good chance she'd be presiding over more than one funeral tomorrow.

Bull clunked over to them, his walking machine whining to a stop. He had deteriorated during the few hours they'd spent in the office. He was coughing less, but he'd begun using his inhaler a lot more often. Even the machine seemed ill now, its sounds harsher, its movements jerkier. As though the walker and Bull had merged into one being, and it was dying along with him.

"Everything okay?" he asked.

"Fine," Anna said. She considered telling him he needed rest, then abandoned the idea. She didn't need to lose another argument just then.

"So we're getting pretty close to zero hour here," Bull said, then stifled a wet-sounding cough. "You have everything you need?"

No, Anna thought. *I need an answer that doesn't include what you're about to do.*

"Yes," she said instead. "Monica has been making notes for the broadcast. I've compiled a list of all the ships we have representatives from. We're missing a few, but I'm hoping planetary allegiance will be enough to get their cooperation. Chris Williams, a junior officer from the *Prince*, has been a big help on that."

"You?" Bull asked, jabbing a thick hand toward Monica.

"My team is ready to go," she said. "I'm a bit worried about getting the full broadcast out before Ashford's people stop us."

Bull laughed. It was a wet, unpleasant sound. "Hold on." He called out to Jim Holden, who was busy reassembling a stripped-down rifle of some sort and chatting with one of the Martian marines. Holden put the partly assembled rifle on a table and walked over.

"What's up?"

"These people need reassurance that they'll be protected long enough to finish their broadcast," Bull said.

Holden blinked twice, once at Bull, once at the three women sitting cross-legged on the floor. Anna had to suppress a giggle. Holden was so comically earnest, she just wanted to give him a hug and pat him on the head.

"Amos will make sure you're not interrupted," he finally said.

"Right," Bull said. "Tell them why that's reassuring."

"Oh. Well, when Amos is angry he's the meanest, scariest person I've ever met, and he'd walk across a sea of corpses he personally created to help a friend. And one of his good friends just got murdered by the people who are going to be trying to take this office."

"I heard about that," Anna said. "I'm sorry."

"Yes," Holden said. "And the last people in the galaxy I'd want to be are the ones that are going to try and break in here to stop you. Amos doesn't process grief well. It usually turns into anger or violence for him. I have a feeling he's about to process the shit out of it on some Ashford loyalists."

"Killing people won't make him feel better," Anna said, regretting the words the second they left her mouth. These people were going to be risking their lives to protect her. They didn't need her moralizing at them.

"Actually," Holden said with a half smile, "I think it might for him, but Amos is a special case. You'd be right about most anyone else."

Anna looked across the room at Amos. He was sitting quietly by the front door to the broadcast office, some sort of very large rifle laid across his knees. He was a large man, tall and thick across the shoulders and chest. But with his round shaved head and broad face, he didn't look like a killer to Anna. He looked like a friendly repairman. The kind who showed up to fix broken plumbing or swap out the air recycling filters. According to Holden, he would kill without remorse to protect her.

She imagined trying to explain their current situation to Nono. *I've fallen in with killers, you see, but it's okay because they are the right killers. The good guy killers. They don't shoot innocent chief engineers. They shoot the people who do.*

Monica was asking Holden something. When he started to answer, Anna got up and left with an apology to everyone and no one. She dodged through the crowded office, smiling and patting people on the arm as she passed, distributing gentle reassurance to everyone around her. It was all she had to offer them.

She pulled an unused chair over next to Amos and sat down. "Red," he said, giving her a tiny nod.

"I'm sorry." She put her hand on his arm. He stared down at it as though he couldn't figure out what it was.

"Okay," he said, not asking the obvious question. Not pretending not to understand. Anna found herself liking him immediately.

"Thank you for doing this."

Amos shifted in his chair to face her. "You don't need to—"

"In a few hours, we might all be dead," she said. "I want you to know that I know what you're doing, and I know why, and I don't care about any of that. Thank you for helping us."

"God damn, Red," Amos said, putting his hand on hers. "You must be hell on wheels as a preacher. You're making me feel the best and worst I've felt in a while at the same time."

"That's all I wanted to say," Anna said, then patted his hand once and stood up.

Before she could leave, Amos grabbed her hand in an almost painfully tight grip. "No one's gonna hurt you today."

There was no boast in it. It was a simple statement of fact. She gave him a smile and pulled her hand away. Good-hearted unrepentant killers were not something she'd had to fit into her worldview before this, and she wasn't sure how it would work. But now she'd have to try.

"All right, people, listen up," Bull yelled out over the noise. The room fell silent. "It's zero hour. Let's get the action teams divided up and ready to go."

A shadow fell across Anna. Amos was standing behind her, clutching his large gun. "Defense," he called out. "To me."

A group of maybe two dozen extricated themselves from the general crowd and moved over to Amos. Anna found herself surrounded by heavily armed and armored Belters with a few inner planet types mixed in. She was not a tall woman, and it felt like being at the bottom of a well. "Excuse me," she said, but no one heard her. A strong hand gripped her arm, pulled her through the knot of people, and deposited her outside of it. Amos gave her a smile and said, "Might want to find a quiet corner, Red."

Anna thought about trying to cross the room back to Tilly and Monica, but there were too many people in the way. Amos had a sort of personal field that kept anyone from standing too close to him, so Anna just stayed inside it to keep from getting trampled on. Amos didn't appear to mind.

"Assault team," Holden called out, "to me."

Soon he had a group of two dozen around him, including Naomi and Alex from the *Rocinante*, the four Martian marines, a bunch of Bull's security people, and Bull himself. The only people in the group without obvious physical injuries were the four marines. Alex and Naomi looked especially bad. Naomi's shoulder was bound tight in a harness that immobilized it and her arm, and she winced every time she took a step. Alex's face was swollen so badly that his left eye was almost completely closed. Blood spotted the bandages around his head.

These are the people who helped stop Protogen, who fought the monsters around Ganymede, she told herself. *They're tough, they'll make it.* It sounded thin even in her own head.

"Well," Bull said. The crowd seemed to be waiting for last words from him. "I guess this is it. Good hunting, everyone."

A few people clapped or called out to him. Most didn't. Across the room Monica was talking to her camera people. Anna knew she should join them, but found herself not wanting to. All these people would be risking their lives to buy her time. *Her.* So it was all on her whether the whole plan succeeded or failed. If she couldn't convince an entire flotilla of ships from three separate governments that turning off their power for a couple hours was the right thing to do, then it would all be for nothing. She found herself wanting to delay that moment as long as possible. To keep it from being her responsibility as long as she could.

"Better go, Red," Amos whispered to her.

"What if they're all too scared to shut down their ships?" she replied. "We're in the haunted house, and I'm about to tell everyone that the way to escape is to turn out all the lights. I would find that unconvincing in their shoes."

Amos nodded thoughtfully. Anna waited for the words of encouragement.

"Yeah," he finally said. "That'll be a bitch. My job's a lot easier. Good luck."

Somehow, the honesty in not even trying to sugarcoat it cracked the last of Anna's fear, and she found herself laughing. Before she could reconsider, she grabbed Amos around the middle and gave him a squeeze.

"Again," she said, letting him go after a few seconds, "thank you. I was being a big scaredy-cat. You're a good person, Amos."

"Nah, I'm not. I just hang with good company. Get going, Red. I gotta get my game face on."

The assault team was heading for the door, and Anna moved to the wall to let them by. Holden stopped next to Amos and said, "Be here when I get back, big man."

Amos shook his hand and slapped him on the back once. Holden's face was filled with worry. Anna had a sudden vision of her future, sending Nami off to school one day, being terrified that she wouldn't be there to look after her and having to let her go anyway.

"Keep Naomi and Alex safe," Amos said, pushing Holden toward the door. From Anna's position, she could see the worry lines on Holden's face only deepen at that. He was going to have to let them go too. Even if they all survived the assault on engineering, Alex would be leaving the ship to fly to the *Rocinante*, and Naomi would be left behind to keep the power shut down while Holden continued on toward the bridge. Anna knew the little crew had been together for several years now. She wondered if they'd ever had to split up and fight like this before.

Holden's face seemed to be saying they hadn't.

Anna was watching them file out the door, again trying to memorize faces and names, trying not to think about why. Monica grabbed her and started pulling her toward the makeshift film studio.

"Time to start working," she said. She deposited Anna just outside the camera view and stepped in front of the unadorned green wall they used as a backdrop.

"Welcome," she said, her face and voice shifting into cheery video host mode. "I'm Monica Stuart in the offices of Radio Free Slow Zone. I've got some exciting guests today, including Doctor Anna Volovodov, and a number of UN and Martian military officers. But even more exciting, today we're bringing you the most important broadcast we've ever done.

"Today, we'll tell you how to go home."

Chapter Forty-Five: Bull

Bull felt the time moving past like it was something physical, like he was falling through it and couldn't catch himself. Anamarie Ruiz had an hour left before she had to decide whether to do what Ashford wanted or get killed. If she didn't have to choose, she wouldn't choose wrong, and every minute that he wasn't in the engineering deck took them closer to where they couldn't get back.

They'd left the colonial administration offices in a small convoy. Six electric carts with twenty-five people, including Jim Holden and three-quarters of his crew, the four Martian marines, an even dozen of the *Behemoth*'s crew who'd stayed loyal to Pa, and five Earth soldiers whom Corin had found in the drum and brought along. They had some riot armor that hadn't been taken out of the armory before Ashford's forces occupied it. They had an ugly collection of slug-throwing pistols and shotguns loaded with ballistic gel rounds; a mix of weapons designed to subdue without permanent injury and those meant to assure the enemy's death. The four Martian marines had the four best guns they'd been able to scrounge up, but there were too few of both. The whole thing stank of improvisation.

He couldn't sit down, so he'd taken the canopy off the electric cart and wedged his mech in the back. He sailed through the hot, close air of the drum like a figurehead on the prow of some doomed pirate ship. Corin was at the wheel, hunched over it like she could make it go faster by the raw act of will. The Martian sergeant Verbinski who'd brought Jim Holden to the *Behemoth* in restraints sat at her side looking focused and bemused at the same time.

They passed through the main corridors heading south. The tires made a loud ripping sound against the decking. High above, the long, thin strip of blinding white illuminated the curve of the drum. The southern transfer point loomed ahead of them like a ceramic steel cliff face.

People parted before them, making a path. Bull watched them as he passed. Anger and fear and curiosity. These were his people. They hadn't all been to start with, but he'd brought them here to the *Behemoth*. He'd made the ship important and the OPA's role in the exploration beyond the Ring central. Earthers and Martians and Belters. The ones who'd lived. As the faces turned toward him, watching the convoy pass like flowers back on Earth tracking the arc of the sun, he wondered what Fred Johnson would have thought of all this. It was a clusterfuck from start to finish, no question about that. He hoped that when it came time to settle up accounts, he'd done more good than harm.

"We're a pretty compromised force," Verbinski said, craning his neck back and up to look at Bull. "How many people you think we're going up against?"

"Not sure," Bull said. "Probably a little more than we got, but they're divided between engineering and command."

"They as banged up as we are?"

Bull glanced over his shoulder. The truth was at least half of the people he was about to take into battle were already injured. There were people with pressure casts holding their arms together, with sutures keeping their skin closed. In normal circumstances, half his force would still be in the infirmary. Hell, he didn't have any damn business going into a fire zone either, except that he wasn't going to stay back and send people into a meat grinder he wouldn't step into himself.

"Just about," Bull said.

"You know, if I still had that recon armor you took off of us, I could just go get this done. Not even me and my squad. Just me."

"Yeah. I know that."

"Kind of makes you wish you'd trusted me a little bit, doesn't it?"

"Kind of does," Bull said.

There were two ways to reach the transfer point. The elevator was big enough to fit half the force into a box small enough that when the doors opened at the top, a single grenade would incapacitate nearly all of them. The alternative was a wide, sloping ramp that rose from the floor of the drum and spun up in a tight spiral to the axis. Its curve was going into the drum's spin, so the faster they drove up it, the more the cart tires would push down into the floor. That wouldn't matter down here, but when they reached the top where the fighting would essentially be in free fall, every bit of stability and control they could glean would matter.

The first shots came down from the axis, spraying bits of the ceramic roadway up in front of the lead cart. Bull tried to bend his head back far enough to see whether the attack was coming from the transfer point itself or a barricade closer in.

"Juarez!" Verbinski shouted. "Cover us."

"Yes, sir," a voice called from one of the back carts. Bull swiveled the mech enough to look over his shoulder. On the third cart back, one of the Martian marines was lying on his back, a long scoped rifle pointing up. He looked like he was napping until the rifle fired once. Bull tried to look up again, but the mech prevented him. He took out his hand terminal and used its camera like a mirror. High above them, a body was floating in the null-g zone, a pink cloud of blood forming around its waist.

"One less," Verbinski said.

The firing continued as they took the ramp at speed. The semi-adhesive ripping of the tires against the deck changed its tone as less and less weight pressed against them. Bull felt his body growing lighter in its brace. The edge of the ramp was a cliff now, looking down almost a third of a kilometer to the floor of the drum below. Ashford's men were above them, but not so far now that Bull couldn't see the metal barricades they'd welded to the walls and deck. He was painfully aware of being the highest target. His neck itched.

Two heads popped up from behind the barricades. The muzzle flashes were like sparks. The Martian's rifle barked behind him, and one of the attackers slumped down, the other retreating.

"Okay," Bull said. "This is as close as we get without cover."

Corin spun the cart nose in to the wall and slipped out, taking cover with Verbinski behind it while the next cart came ahead mirroring her. They were in microgravity here. Maybe a tenth of a g. Maybe less. Bull had to turn the magnets on in his mech's feet to keep from floating away. By the time he'd gotten off the cart, the fighting was already far ahead of him. He drove the mech forward, marching up past the improvised barricades of the carts. The closest of them was less than ten meters from the first of Ashford's barricades, and Jim Holden, Corin, and one of the Earthers were already pressed against the enemy's cover, ducking to the side, firing, and falling back. The smell of spent gunpowder soured the air.

"Where's Naomi?" Bull shouted. He didn't have a clear idea whether any of the technical staff in there besides Ruiz were still loyal to Pa, and if they got their only real engineer killed before they made it into engineering, he was going to be pissed. Something detonated behind the barrier and two bodies pinwheeled out into the empty air. The light was behind them, and he couldn't tell if they were his people or Ashford's. At the last of the carts, he stopped. The battle was well ahead of him now, almost at the transfer point itself. That was good. It meant they were winning.

A thin man was still at the cart's wheel. At a guess, he was in his early twenties, brown skin and close-cropped hair. The hole in his chest had already stopped bleeding and his eyes were empty. Bull felt a moment's regret and pushed it away. He'd known. They'd all known. Not just coming to this fight, but when they'd put their boots on the *Behemoth* and headed out past the farthest human habitation, they'd known they might not make it back. Maybe they'd even known that the thing that killed them might not be the Ring, but the people who'd gone out alongside them. People like Ashford. People like him.

"Sorry, ese," Bull said, and drove the joysticks forward.

Ashford's forces were pulling back. There was no question about it now. Verbinski and his team were laying down a withering and professional spray of gunfire. The sniper, Juarez, didn't fire often, but when he did it was always a kill shot. The combination of constant automatic weapons fire and the occasional but lethal bark of Juarez's rifle kept moving the enemy back in toward the transfer point like they were boxing in the queen on a chessboard. Even the most powerful of Ashford's guns couldn't find a safe angle on them, and Verbinski kept the pressure on, pushing back and back and back until Ashford's people broke, running.

The transfer point itself was a short hallway with emergency decompression doors at each end. As Bull watched, the vast red-painted circular hatches groaned and began rolling into place. They wouldn't be enough to stop Bull and his people, but they'd slow things down. Maybe too much.

"Charge!" Bull shouted, then fell into a fit of coughing that was hard to stop. When he could, he croaked, "Come on, you bastards! Get in there before they lock us out!"

They launched through the air, guns blazing. The noise was deafening, and Bull could only imagine what it would sound like from farther away. Distant thunder in a land that had never known rain. He pushed his mech forward, magnetic boots clamping and releasing, as the doors rolled their way nearer to closed. He was the last one into the corridor. At the far end, the air was a cloud of smoke and blood. The farther door was almost closed, but at the side, Naomi Nagata was elbow deep in an access panel, Holden at her back with assault rifle in hand. As Bull approached, the woman pulled something free. A stream of black droplets geysered out into the empty space of the corridor, and the sharp smell of hydraulic fluid cut through the air. The door stopped closing.

In the chaos it was hard to say, but at a guess, Bull thought he still had between fifteen and twenty people standing. It wasn't great, but it could have been worse. Once they got into engineering, things would open up again. There would be cover. The few meters beyond the second door, though, would be a kill zone. It was the space all his people had to go through to get anyplace else. If Ashford's people had any tactical sense at all, they'd be there, waiting for the first sign of movement.

It was a standoff, and he was going to have to be the one to break it. Verbinski skimmed by, as comfortable weightless as a fish in water. He turned, tapped his feet against the wall, and came to something close to a dead stop.

"Going to be a bear making it through there," the Martian said.

"I was just thinking that," Bull said.

Verbinski looked at the half-closed door like a carpenter sizing up a board.

"Be nice if we had some explosives," he said. "Something to clear the area a little. Give us some breathing room."

"You trying to tell me something, Sergeant?"

Verbinski shrugged and took a thin black cassette out of his pocket. Bull hoisted his eyebrows.

"Concussion?" he said.

"Two thousand kilojoules. We call them spine crackers."

"You smuggled arms onto my ship, Sergeant?"

"Just felt a little naked without 'em."

"I'll overlook it this time," Bull said and raised his hands, rallying the troops to him. They took cover behind the half-closed door. Verbinski crawled out onto the surface and peeked over the side, out and back fast as a lizard's tongue. Half a dozen bullets split the air where his head had been. The Martian floated in the air, his legs in lotus position, as he armed the little black grenade. Bull waited, Holden and Corin at his side.

"Just to check," Holden said. "We're throwing grenades into the place that controls the reactor?"

"We are," Bull said.

"So the worst-case scenario?"

"Worst-case scenario is we lose and Ashford kills the solar system," Bull said. "Losing containment on the reactor and we all die is actually second worst."

"Never a sign things have gone well," Holden said.

Verbinski held up a fist, and everyone in the group put their hands over their ears. Verbinski did something sharp with his fingers and flicked the black cassette through the gap between the door and its frame. The detonation came almost at once. Bull felt like he'd been dropped into the bottom of a swimming pool. His vision pulsed in time with his heart, but he pushed the joysticks forward. His ears rang and he felt his consciousness starting to slip a little. As he maneuvered his mech through the space into engineering, it occurred to him that he was going to be lucky if he didn't pass out during the fight. He had a broken spine and his lungs were half full of crap. No one would have thought less of him if he'd stayed behind. Except he didn't care what people thought about him. It was Ashford who cared about that.

The fight on the other side was short. The grenade had been much worse for the defenders. Half of the soldiers had dropped their weapons before all of Bull's people made it in. Only Garza had held out, holding the long corridor between main engineering and the communications array board until Corin had stepped into the space and shot him in the bridge of the nose, doing with a pistol what would have been a difficult shot with a scoped rifle. They took half a dozen of Ashford's men alive, the prisoners zip-tied to handholds in the bulkheads. None of them had been Bull's.

They found Ruiz under a machining table, curled with her arms around her knees. When she came out, her skin had a gray cast to it, and her hands were trembling. Naomi moved around her, shifting from a display panel to the readouts on the different bits of equipment, checking what was being reported in one place against what it said elsewhere. Holden hovered behind her like the tail of a kite.

"Anamarie," Bull said. "You all right?"

Ruiz nodded.

"Thank you," she said, and then before she could say anything else, Naomi sloped in, stopping herself against the desk.

"Was this where Sam was working?" she asked.

Ruiz looked at her for a moment, uncomprehending. When she nodded, it seemed almost tentative.

"What are you seeing?" Bull said. "Can you shut it down?"

"If you just want to drop the core, I can probably do that," Naomi said. "But I don't know if I can get her started again, and there are some folks on the ship who might want to keep breathing. Controlled shutdown would be better."

Bull smiled.

"We need to shut everything down," Holden said. "The reactor. The power grid. Everything."

"I know, honey," Naomi said, and Holden looked chagrined.

"Sorry."

In one of the far corners of the deck, someone yelped. Corin came gliding across the open space, serenely holding in a choke an Earther Bull didn't recognize. It occurred to him that she might be having too much fun with this part. Might not be healthy.

"I don't know what Sam put in place to sabotage the comm laser," Naomi said. "I have to do an audit before I can undo any of it. And without—" Naomi stopped. Her jaw slid forward. She cleared her throat, swallowed. "Without Sam, it's going to be harder. This was her ship."

"Can you just take the laser off-line?" Bull asked.

"Sure," Naomi said. "As long as no one's shooting at me while I'm doing it."

"And how about turning up the nitrogen in the command enough that everyone up there takes a little nap?"

"I can help with that," Ruiz said. Her voice sounded a little stronger.

"All right," Bull said. "Here's what we're doing. Nagata's in charge of engineering. Anything she says, you do." Ruiz nodded, too numb to protest. "Your first priority is get the laser off-line so none of those pendejos in control can fire it. Your second priority is to tweak the environmental controls on the command deck. Your third priority is to shut down the ship so we can bring it back up, see if Mister Holden's ghost is going to keep its promises."

"Sir," Naomi said.

"Corin!" Bull shouted. The coughing stopped him for a moment. It still wasn't violent, and it didn't bring anything up. He didn't know if that was a good sign or a bad one. Corin launched herself to the control board. "You and Holden head up the external elevator shaft with a handful of zip ties. When everyone up there's asleep, you two make sure they don't get confused and hurt themselves."

Corin's smile was cold. Might be that Ashford wasn't a problem he'd have to solve. Bull tried to bring himself to care one way or the other, but his body felt like he'd been awake for a week.

"Why am I doing that?" Holden asked.

"To keep you out of her way," Bull said. "We'll keep your XO safe. We need her."

He could see Holden's objections gathering like a storm, but Naomi stopped them. "It's okay." And that seemed to be that.

"Alex is going to the *Roci* to shut down whatever we left on," Holden said, shrugging. "I'll help him with the EVA suit before I go."

"Okay," Bull said gravely. He was willing to pretend they'd struck some kind of compromise, if that helped. He heard the sound of men laughing and recognized the timbre of Sergeant Verbinski's voice. "Excuse me."

The mech clanked across the deck, magnetic locks clinging and releasing. The others all floated freely in the air, but with three-quarters of his body dead and numb, Bull knew he wouldn't be able to maneuver. It was like he was the only one still constrained by gravity.

Verbinski and his squad were in an alcove near the supply shop. One of the marines had been shot in the elbow. His forearm was a complication of bone and meat, but he was laughing and talking while the others dressed the wound. Bull wondered how much they'd doped him. He caught Verbinski's gaze and nodded him closer.

"You and your people," Bull said when they were out of earshot. "You did good work back there."

"Thank you," Verbinski said. The pride showed right through the humble. "We do what we can. If we'd had our suits, now—"

"Thing is," Bull said. "Those grenades? How many of them you still have on you?"

"Half a dozen," Verbinski said.

"Yeah." Bull sighed. "Nothing personal, but I'm going to need to confiscate those."

Verbinski looked shocked for a moment. Then he laughed.

"Always the hardass," he said.

Chapter Forty-Six: Clarissa

What's going on, Jojo?"

"I think we've got a problem, sir. Take a look."

Monica Stuart appeared on the monitors, her professionally calm face like a being from a different reality.

"Today," she said, her hands folded in her lap and a twinkle in her eye, "we'll tell you how to go home."

"What. The. *Fuck!*" Ashford shouted, dashing his hand across the display. "What is this?"

"They're making a new broadcast, sir," the security man said. Clarissa watched Ashford turn and stare at him, watched the man shrivel under the weight of his gaze.

"Exclusive to Radio Free Slow Zone," Monica said, "we have reason to believe that if we in the united human fleet can reduce our energy output low enough to no longer appear threatening—"

"Shut her down," Ashford said. "Call everyone that's still in the drum and shut that feed off. Get me Ruiz. I want power cut to that whole section if we have to."

"Is this something we need to concern ourselves with?" Cortez asked. His voice had an overtone of whining. "What they do or say can't matter now, can it?"

"This is my ship!" Ashford shouted. "I'm in control."

"Once we've destroyed the Ring, though—"

Clarissa put a hand on Cortez's shoulder and shook her head once.

"He's the father," she said. "The ship is his house."

"Thank you," Ashford said to her, but with his eyes still on Cortez. "I'm glad that someone here understands how this works."

"Suppression team is dispatched," Jojo said. "You want me to pull from the guard units too?"

"Whatever it takes," Ashford said. "I want you to get it done."

On the screen, the view shifted, and Anna's face filled the screen. Her hair was pulled back, and someone had given her makeup in a way that made her look like everyone else in broadcast. Clarissa felt a strange tug in her chest, resentment and alarm. *Get out of there*, she thought at the screen. *God's not going to stop bullets for you.*

"The idea," Anna said, "is that the station has identified us as an ongoing threat. Its actions toward us have been based in a kind of fear. Or, that's wrong. A caution. We are as unknown and unpredictable to it as it is to us. And so we have reason to believe that if we appear to be less threatening, it may relax its constraints."

The camera cut back to Monica Stuart, nodding and looking sober. All the physical cues that would indicate Anna was a serious woman with important opinions.

"And what is your plan, exactly?" Monica asked.

Anna's laughter bubbled. "I wouldn't call the plan mine. What we're thinking is that if we power down the reactors in all the ships and reduce energy being used, the station can be induced to...well, to see us less as a threat and more as a curiosity. I mean, see this all from its perspective. A gate opened, and whatever it had been expecting to come through, instead there came a ship running ballistic at tremendous speed. Then a flotilla of new ships behind that, and armed soldiers who went aboard the station itself with weapons firing. If something came to us that way, we'd call it an invasion."

"And so by giving some indication that we aren't escalating the attack…?"

"We give whatever we're dealing with here the opportunity to not escalate against us," Anna said. "We've been thinking of the protomolecule and all the things that came from it as—"

The screen went dark. Ashford scowled at his control boards, calling up and dismissing information with hard, percussive taps. Cortez floated beside Clarissa, frowning. Humiliated. He had engineered Ashford's escape and reconquest of the *Behemoth*, and she could see in the older man's eyes that it wasn't what he'd expected it to be. She wondered if her own father had that same expression in his cell back on Earth, or wherever it was they'd put him.

"Ruiz," Ashford snapped. "Report. What's our status?"

"I still have half an hour, sir," the woman said through the connection.

"I didn't ask how much time you had left," the captain said. "I asked for a report."

"The conductant is in place and curing," the woman said. "It looks like it'll be done on time. I've found a place in the breaker system that Sam…that Sam put in a power cutout."

"You've replaced that?"

"I did, but I don't know if there are others. She could have sabotaged the whole circuit."

"Well," Ashford said. "You have half an hour to check it."

"That's what I'm doing. Sir."

Ashford tapped the control panel again. Clarissa found herself wishing he'd put the newsfeed back on. She wanted to know what Anna was saying, even if it was only as a way to pass the time.

The air on the bridge wasn't as hot and close as it had been in the drum, but the coolness wasn't comforting. If anything, it seemed to underscore the time they'd been waiting. Her belly was beginning to complain with hunger, and she had to imagine that the others were feeling the same. They were holding the bridge of the largest spacecraft humanity had ever built, trapped in the starless dark by an alien power they barely began to comprehend, but they were still constrained by the petty needs of flesh, and their collective blood sugar was getting pretty low. She wondered what it said about her that she'd watched a women shot to death not two hours before and all she could think about now was lunch. She wondered what Anna would have thought.

"Have we shut those bitches up yet?" Ashford snapped.

"The suppression teams are arriving at the colonial administrative offices, sir," Jojo said. And then, a moment later, "They're encountering some resistance."

Ashford smiled.

"Do we have targeting?" he asked.

"Sir?" one of the other guards said.

"Are the comm laser's targeting systems online?"

"Um. Yes. They're responsive."

"Well, while they mop up downstairs, let's line up our shot, shall we?"

"Yes, sir."

Clarissa kept hold of a handle on the wall absently, watching the captain and his men coordinating. It was hard for her to remember how small the Ring was, and how vast the distances they'd traveled to be here. She had to admire the precision and care that they would need to destroy it. The beauty of it was almost surgical. Behind her, the security station popped and clicked. Among the alerts, she heard the murmur of a familiar voice, lifted in fear. She looked around. No one was paying any attention to her, so she pushed herself gently back.

The security station monitor was still on the newsfeed. Monica Stuart looked ashen under her makeup, her jaw set and her lips thin. Anna, beside her, was squeezing the tip of one thumb over and over anxiously. Another man was propped between them in a medical gurney.

"—anything we can to cooperate," the earnest man was saying into the camera.

"Thank you, Lieutenant Williams," Monica Stuart said. "I hate to add a complicating note to all this, but I've just been informed that armed men have arrive outside the studio and we are apparently under attack at the moment." She laughed nervously, which Clarissa thought was probably newsfeed anchor code for, *Oh my God, I'm going to die on the air.* Anna's voice came in a moment before the cameras cut to her.

"This is an extreme situation," Anna said, "but I think something like this is probably going on in every ship that's listening to us right now. We're at the point where we, as a community, have to make a choice. And we're scared and grieving and traumatized. None of us is sure what the right thing to do would be. And—"

In the background, the unmistakable popping of slug throwers interrupted Anna for a moment. Her face paled, but she only cleared her throat and went on.

"And violence is a response to that fear. I hope very much that we can come together, though, and—"

"She'll go down talking," Cortez said. Clarissa hadn't heard him come in behind her, hadn't sensed him approaching. "I have a tremendous respect for that woman."

"But you think she's wrong."

"I think her optimism is misplaced," Cortez said.

"—if we do escalate our attacks on the station and the Ring," Anna said, "we have to expect that the cycle will go on, getting bigger and more dangerous until one side or the other is destroyed, and I wish—"

"What do you think she'd say about your pessimism?" Clarissa asked.

Cortez looked up at her, his eyes wide with surprise and amusement. "My pessimism?"

Clarissa fought the sudden, powerful urge to apologize. "What else would you call it?"

"We've looked the devil in the eyes out here," Cortez said. "I would call it realism."

You didn't look into the devil's eyes, she thought. *You saw a bunch of people die. You have no idea what real evil is.* Her memory seemed to stutter, and for a moment, she was back on the *Cerisier,* Ren's skull giving way under her palm. *There's a difference between tragedy and evil, and I am that difference.*

"Captain! They're taking fire at engineering!"

Cortez turned back toward the bridge and launched himself awkwardly through the air. Clarissa took a last look at Anna on the screen, leaning forward and pressing the air with her hands as if she could push calm and sanity through the camera and into the eyes of anyone watching. Then she followed Cortez.

"How many down?" Ashford demanded.

"No information, sir," Jojo said. "I have a video feed."

The monitor blinked to life. The engineering deck flickered, pixelated, and came back. A dozen of Ashford's men were training guns at a pressure door that was stuck almost a third of the way closed. Ashford strained against his belts, trying to get closer to the image. Something—a tiny object or a video feed artifact—floated across the screen, and everything went white. When the image came back, Ashford said something obscene.

Armed people poured through the opening like sand falling through an hourglass. Clarissa recognized Jim Holden by the way he moved, the intimacy of long obsession making him as obvious as her own family would have been. And so the tall figure beside him had to be Naomi, whom Melba had almost killed. And then, near the end, the only one walking in the null-g environment, Carlos Baca. Bull. The head of security, and Ashford's nemesis. He walked slowly across the deck, his real legs strapped together and his mechanical ones lumbering step by painful step. One of Ashford's people tried to fire and was shot, his body twisting in the air in a way that reminded her of seeing a caterpillar cut in half. She realized that the sound she was hearing was Ashford cursing under his breath. He didn't seem to stop for breath.

"Lock down the perimeter," Ashford yelled. "Ruiz! Ruiz! We have to fire. We have to fire now!"

"I can't," the woman's voice said. "We don't have a connection."

"I don't care if it's stable, I have to fire now."

"It's not unstable, sir," the woman said. "It's not *there*."

Ashford slammed his fist against the control panel and grimaced. She didn't know if he'd broken his knuckles, but she wouldn't have been surprised. For the next fifteen minutes, they watched the battle play out, the invading force sweeping through the engineering deck. Clarissa tried to keep tabs on where Holden and Naomi were, the way she might watch a dramatic show for one or two favorite minor actors.

"Redirect the suppression teams," Ashford said.

"Yes…ah…"

Ashford turned toward Jojo. The guard's face was pale. "I'm having trouble getting responses from the controls. I think…I think they're locking us out."

Ashford's rage crested and then sank into a kind of deathly calm. He floated in his couch, his hands pressed together, the tips of both index fingers against his lower lip.

"Environmental controls aren't responding," Jojo said, his voice taking on the timbre of near panic. "They're changing the atmosphere, sir."

"Environmental suits," Ashford said. "We'll need environmental suits."

Clarissa sighed and launched herself across the cabin to the open access panels.

"What are you doing?" Ashford shouted at her. She didn't answer.

The internal structure of the *Behemoth* wasn't that different from any other bridge, though it did have more redundancy than she'd expected. If it had been left in its original form, it would have been robust, but the requirements of a battleship were more rigorous than the elegant generation ship had been, and some of the duplicate systems had been repurposed to accommodate the PDCs, gauss guns, and torpedoes. She turned a monitor on, watching the nitrogen levels rise in the bridge. Without the buildup of carbon dioxide, they wouldn't even feel short of breath. Just a little light-headed, and then out. She wondered whether Holden would let them die that way. Probably Holden wouldn't have. Bull, she wouldn't bet on.

It didn't matter. Ren had trained her well. She disabled remote access to their environmental systems with the deactivation of a single circuit.

"Sir! I have atmo control back!" Jojo shouted.

"Well, get us some goddamn air, then!" Ashford shouted.

Clarissa looked at her work with a sense of calm pride. It wasn't pretty, and she wouldn't have wanted to leave it that way for long, but she'd done what needed doing and it hadn't shut down the system. That was pretty good, given the circumstances.

"How much have you got?" Ashford snapped.

"I've got mechanical, atmosphere…everything local to command, sir."

Like a thank-you would kill you, Clarissa thought as she floated back toward the door to the security station.

"Can we do it to them?" Ashford asked. "Can we shut off their air?"

"No," Jojo said. "We're just local. But at least we don't need those suits."

Ashford's scowl changed its character without ever becoming a smile.

"Suits," he said. "Jojo. Do we have access to the powered armor Pa took from those Martian marines?"

Jojo blinked, then nodded sharply. "Yes, sir."

"I want you to find four people who'll fit in them. Then I want you to go down to engineering and get me control of my ship."

Jojo saluted, grinning. "Yes, sir."

"And Jojo? *Anyone* gets in your way, you kill them. Understand?"

"Five by five."

The guard unstrapped and launched himself toward the hallway. She heard voices in the hall, people preparing for battle. *We have to expect the cycle will go on, getting bigger and more dangerous until one side or the other is destroyed.* Who said that? It seemed like something she'd just heard. Under local control the ventilation system had a slightly different rhythm, the exhalations from recyclers coming a few seconds closer together and lasting half as long. She wondered why that would be. It was the sort of thing Ren would have known. It was the sort of thing she only noticed now.

Ren. She tried to imagine him now. Tried to see herself the way he would see her. She was going to die. She was going to die and make everyone else safe by doing it. It wouldn't bring him back to life, but it would make his dying mean something. And it would avenge him. In her mind's eye, she still couldn't see him smiling about it.

Half an hour later, the four people Jojo had selected came into the room awkwardly. The power of the suits made moving without crashing into things difficult. The cowling shone black and red, catching the light and diffusing it. She thought of massive beetles.

"We've got no ammunition, sir," one of them said. Jojo. His voice was made artificially flat and crisp by the suit's speakers.

"Then beat them to death," Ashford said. "Your main objective is the reactor. If all you can get is enough for us to fire the laser, we still win. After that, I want Bull and his allies killed. Anyone who's there that isn't actively fighting alongside you, count as an enemy. If they aren't for us, they're against us."

"Yes, sir."

"Sir!" one of the men at the controls said.

"What?"

"I think we have someone in the external elevator shaft, sir."

"Assault force?"

"No, but they may be trapping it."

Clarissa turned away.

In the security station, the newsfeed was still spooling. Women's voices punctuated by occasional gunfire. Ashford's men hadn't taken the station yet. She wondered whether he'd let his men gun down Monica Stuart and Anna on a live feed where everyone could see it. Then she wondered how he'd prevent it from happening even if he wanted to. It wasn't like there would be any consequences. If they won and blew the Ring, they'd all die here one way or another. A few premature deaths along the way should be neither here nor there. When what came next didn't matter, anybody could do anything. Nothing had consequences.

Except that everyone always dies. You're distracting yourself from something.

Cortez floated in the security booth itself. His face lit from below by the monitor. He looked over as she approached, his smile gentle and calm.

"Ashford's sending men down to retake engineering," she said.

"Good. That's very good."

"—on the *Corvusier*," a brown-skinned woman was saying. "You know me. You can trust me. All we're asking is that you shut down the reactor for a few hours and pull the batteries from the emergency backups. Power down the systems, so we can get out of here."

"They value their own lives so much," Cortez said. "They don't think about the price their survival brings with it. The price for everybody."

"They don't," Clarissa agreed, but something sat poorly with the words. Something itched. "Do you believe in redemption?"

"Of course I do," Cortez said. "Everything in my life has taught me that there is nothing that fully removes us from the possibility of God's grace, though sometimes the sacrifices we must make are painfully high."

"—if we can just come together," Anna said on the screen, leaning in toward the camera. A lock of red hair had come out of place and fell over her left eye. "Together, we can solve this."

"What about you?" Cortez asked. He put his hand against her back. "Do you believe in redemption?"

"No," she said. "Just sacrifice."

"Mao," Ashford barked from the other room. "Get out here."

Clarissa floated to the doorway. The captain looked grayer than he had before. There was swelling around his eyes that would have been dark circles if they'd had any gravity.

"Captain?"

"You understand how all this crap is wired up."

"A little," she said.

"I've got something I need you to do."

Chapter Forty-Seven: Holden

The elevator shaft that ran outside the entire two-kilometer length of the *Behemoth*'s drum section stretched out ahead of him. With Naomi consolidating control over the ship, most of the ancillary systems were down or unsafe to use. The primary elevator was locked at the shaft's midway point. There was a secondary elevator in storage near the top of the shaft, but it could only be activated if the first elevator was removed from the tracks and locked down. So instead of a comfortable four-minute ride, the trip to the bridge was a two-kilometer-long zero-g float through hard vacuum with a big steel-and-ceramic box blocking the midpoint.

It could be worse. From the security camera streams Naomi had been able to dig into, it didn't look like Ashford expected anyone to come at the bridge that way. He'd fortified his position at the command-level transition point once word had gone out about the attack on engineering. But so far they hadn't reinforced the elevator shaft at all. They'd been expecting to hold both ends, and apparently it hadn't occurred to them yet that they didn't.

Bull had warned him that Ashford might be losing his mind under the stress of the situation, but he wasn't a stupid man. He'd had a notably mistake-free career as an OPA captain up to that point, which was why he'd seemed the safe choice to Fred Johnson. Holden couldn't count on him to make mistakes that would make things easy. But if Naomi won out in engineering it wouldn't matter. By the time they reached the bridge everyone there would be blissfully asleep.

Holden had the broadcast from Radio Free Slow Zone playing at low volume in his helmet. Anna and Monica were still explaining to the flotilla about the need to shut down all the power in a back-and-forth sort of interview format while occasional volleys of gunfire popped in the background. Somehow it made the crazy things Anna was saying seem sane. Holden gave Monica points for knowing it would work that way. And, so far, the sounds of fighting seemed light. Amos was probably bored.

They'd made a plan, and so far everything was more or less going the way they'd hoped. The thought left Holden increasingly terrified.

Without warning the wall-mounted LEDs in the shaft went out. Holden turned on his suit lights but didn't slow his climb. He threw a strange double shadow on the bulkhead when Corin's suit lights came on.

"I'm not sure if that means we're winning or losing," he said, just to have something to say.

Corin grunted at him noncommittally. "I see the lift."

Holden tilted his torso back to shine the suit lights farther up the shaft. The bottom of the elevator was visible a hundred meters ahead as a wall of metal and composite.

"There's supposed to be a maintenance hatch we can open."

Corin held up a fist in assent, and while still drifting up the elevator shaft began rummaging around in the duffel she'd brought from engineering. She pulled out a handheld plasma torch.

Holden rotated his body to hit the bottom of the elevator feet first, then kicked on his boot magnets. He walked over to the hatch and tried to open it, but as they suspected it was locked from the inside. Without waiting to be asked Corin started cutting it open with her torch.

"Bull, you there?" Holden asked, switching to the agreed-upon channel.

"Trouble?"

"Just cutting the elevator right now, wanted to check in."

"Well," Bull said, drawing the word out. "We're hitting either home runs or strikes here. We own the essential systems, we've got the laser down, and we're working on killing the reactor."

"What are we missing?" Holden asked. Corin's torch sputtered and went out, and she began a quiet profanity-laced conversation with herself as she replaced the power pack with another from her duffel.

"Naomi can't get into the bridge systems. They've got her totally locked out, which means no knockout gas for the entry."

Which meant, by last count, him and Corin fighting their way past at least fifteen of Ashford's people, and possibly more. Through a narrow doorway, down a long corridor with no cover. It would make the entry into engineering look like a walk in the park.

"We can't do that with two people," Holden said. "There's no chance."

Corin, who'd been listening in on her radio, looked up. She hit the elevator hatch with one gauntleted fist and the cut piece fell inside, edges glowing dull red. She made no move to enter, waiting for the outcome of his conversation with Bull. Her expression was blank; it could have meant anything.

"We're sending some help, so sit tight at the command deck entry hatch and wait for—" He stopped, and Holden could hear someone speaking to him, though the words were too low to make out. It sounded like Naomi.

"What's up?" Holden asked, but Bull didn't answer. An increasingly animated conversation happened on Bull's end for several minutes. Bull's replies were fragments that without context meant nothing to Holden. He waited impatiently.

"Okay, new problem," Bull finally said.

"Bigger than the 'we can't get into the bridge without dying' problem?"

"Yeah," Bull said. Holden felt his stomach drop. "Naomi caught something on a security cam they missed in the corridor outside the bridge. Four people in power armor just left the command deck. It's the armor we took from the Martians. No way to track them, but I can guess where they're headed."

There was only one place Ashford would be sending that much firepower. Engineering.

"Get out," Holden said, more panic in his voice than he'd hoped to hear. "Get out now."

Bull chuckled. It was not a reassuring sound. "Oh, my friend, this will be a problem for you before it is for us."

Holden waited. Corin shrugged with her hands and climbed inside the elevator to open the upper hatch. No need to cut it. The locks were on the inside.

"There are only three ways to get to us," Bull continued. "They can go down through the drum, but that's messy. The maintenance corridor on the other side of the drum can't be accessed when the drum is rotating. That leaves one good way to head south on this beast."

"Right through us," Holden said.

"Yup. So guess what? Your mission just changed."

"Delaying action," Corin said.

"Give the lady a prize. We still might be able to win this thing if we can buy Naomi a little more time. You get to buy it for her."

"Bull," Holden said. "There are two of us with light assault rifles and sidearms here. Those people have force recon armor. I've watched someone work in that gear up close. We won't be a delay. We'll be a cloud of pink mist they fly through at full speed."

"Not quite that fast. I'm not an idiot, I pulled all the ammo from the suits, and as an added precaution I went ahead and yanked the firing contacts in the guns."

"That's good news, actually, but can't they just tear us limb from limb?"

"Yeah," Bull said. "So don't let them grab you if you can avoid it. Buy us as much time as you can. Bull out."

Holden looked at Corin, who was looking back at him, the same blank expression on her broad face. His heart was beating triple time. Everything took on a sense of almost painful reality. It was like he'd just woken up.

He was about to die.

"Last stand time," he said, trying to keep his voice steady.

"This is as good a place as any." She pointed at the boxy and solid-looking elevator. "Use the upper hatch for cover, they'll have to come at us without any cover of their own, and without guns they'll have to close and engage at point blank. We can dump a lot of fire into them as they approach."

"Corin," Holden said. "Have you ever seen one of those suits at work?"

"Nope. Does it change what we need to do here?"

He hesitated.

"No," he said. "I guess it really doesn't." He pulled the assault rifle off his back and left it floating next to him. He checked his ammo. Still the same six magazines it had been when he stuffed them in the bandolier.

Nothing to do but wait.

Corin found a spot by the hatch where she could hook one foot under a handhold set into what would be the wall under thrust. She settled in, staring up the elevator shaft through her sights. Holden tried doing the same, but got antsy and had to start moving around.

"Naomi?" he said, switching to their private channel and hoping she was still on the radio.

"I'm here," she said after a few seconds.

Holden started to reply, then stopped. Everything that came

into his head to say seemed trite. He'd been about to say that he'd loved her since the moment he met her, but that was ludicrous. He'd barely even noticed Naomi when they first met. She'd been a tall, skinny engineer. When he got to know her better, she'd become a tall, skinny, and brilliant engineer, but that was it. He felt like they'd eventually became friends, but the truth was he could barely remember the person he'd been back on the *Canterbury* now.

Everyone had lost something in the wake of the protomolecule. The species as a whole had lost its sense of its own importance. Its primacy in the universal plan.

Holden had lost his certainty.

When he thought back to the man he'd been before the death of the *Cant*, he remembered a man filled with righteous certainty. Right was right, wrong was wrong, you drew the lines thus and so. His time with Miller had stripped him of some of that. His time working for Fred Johnson had, if not removed, then filed down what remained. A sort of creeping nihilism had taken its place. A sense that the protomolecule had broken the human race in ways that could never be repaired. Humanity had gotten a two-billion-year reprieve on a death sentence it hadn't known it had, but time was up. All that was left was the kicking and screaming.

Oddly enough, it was Miller who had given him his sense of purpose back. Or whatever the Miller construct was. He couldn't really remember that version of himself who'd known exactly where all the lines were drawn. He wasn't sure of much of anything anymore. But whatever had climbed up off of Venus and built the Ring, it had built Miller too.

And it had wanted to talk. To him.

A small thing, maybe. The new Miller didn't make much sense. It had an agenda that it wasn't explaining. The protomolecule didn't seem particularly sorry for all the chaos and death it had caused.

But it wanted to talk. And it wanted to talk to him. Holden realized he'd found a lifeline there. Maybe there was a way out of all of the chaos. Maybe he could help find it. He recognized that latching on to the idea that the protomolecule, or at least their agent Miller, had picked him as their contact fed all of his worst inclinations to arrogance and self-importance. But it was better than despair.

And now, only starting to see that murky path out of the hole the protomolecule had dug and humanity had hurled itself into with self-destructive gusto, now he was about to be killed because of yet another petty human with more power than sense. It didn't seem fair. He wanted to live to see how humanity bounced back. He wanted to be part of it. For the first time in a long time he felt like he might be able to turn into the kind of man who could make a difference.

And he wanted to explain this to Naomi. To tell her that he was turning into a better person. The kind of person who would have seen her as more than just a good engineer all those years ago. As if he could, by being a different person now, retroactively fix the shallow, vain man he'd been then. Maybe even make himself worthy of her.

"I like you," he said instead.

"Jim," she replied after a moment. Her voice was thick.

"I've enjoyed your company ever since we met. Even when you were just an engineer and shipmate, you were a very likable one."

There was only a faint static hiss on the radio. Holden pictured Naomi retreating into herself, letting her hair fall across her eyes to hide them in that way she did when she was in an uncomfortable emotional situation. Of course, that was silly. With no gravity her hair wouldn't do that. But the image made him smile.

"Thank you," he said, letting her off the hook. "Thank you for everything."

"I love you, Jim," she finally said. Holden felt his body relax. He saw his coming death, and wasn't afraid of it anymore. He'd miss all the good stuff to follow, but he'd help make it happen. And a very good person loved him. It was more than most people got in a lifetime.

A low screech started, which cycled up into a howl. For a second, Holden thought Naomi was screaming into her headset. He almost started comforting her before he realized he could feel the vibration in his feet. The sound wasn't coming across the radio. It was transmitting through his boots on the elevator wall. The entire ship was vibrating.

Holden placed his helmet against the wall to get a better sound, and the scream of the ship was almost deafening. It stopped after an endless minute with an ear-shattering bang. Silence followed.

"What the fuck?" Corin said under her breath.

"Naomi? Bull? Anyone still on the line?" Holden yelled, thinking that whatever had happened had torn the ship apart.

"Yeah," Bull said. "We're here."

"What—" Holden started.

"Mission change," Bull continued. "That sound was them slamming the brakes on the habitat drum. Catastrophic inertia change 2.0. There are a lot of people in that drum getting thrown around right now."

"Why would they do that? Just to stop the broadcast?"

"Nope," Bull said with a tired sigh. He sounded like a man who'd just been informed he was going to have to pull a double shift. "It means they think we fortified the elevator shaft and they're coming the other way."

"We're on our way back," Holden said, gesturing at Corin to follow him.

"Negative," Bull said. "If they get the laser back online here while Ashford's still sitting at that control panel, we lose."

"So what? We're supposed to get up there, break into the bridge, and shoot everyone while their guys are down there breaking into engineering and shooting all of you?"

Bull's sigh sounded tired.

"Yeah."

Chapter Forty-Eight: Bull

They came out of the maintenance shaft like an explosion. Four black-and-red monsters in roughly human shape. Bull and the people he'd managed to gather opened fire as soon as they saw them. A dozen guns against a maelstrom.

"Don't let them get to the reactor controls," Bull shouted.

"Roger that," one of the Earthers said. "Any idea how we stop them, sir?"

He didn't have one. He unloaded his pistol's clip with one hand, driving the mech backward across the deck with the other. One of the Martian marines cut across overhead, rifle blazing. Small white marks appeared on the breastplate of the nearest attacker, like a child's thumbprints on a window. The man in powered armor reached the nearest workstation, ripped the crash couch out of the decking with one hand, and threw it like a massive baseball.

The couch sang through the air and shattered against the bulk-head where it hit. If there had been anyone in its path, it would have been worse than a bullet.

Bull kept backing up. When his clip ran out, he gave his full attention to driving the mech. The last of the attackers out of the shaft tried to leap across the room, but the armor's amplification made it more like a launch. The red-and-black blur careened off the far wall with a sound like a car wreck.

"And that," Sergeant Verbinski said across the radio, "is why we spend six months training before they put us in those things." He sounded amused. Good thing somebody was.

Fighting in null g complicated the tactics of a firefight, but the basic rule stayed the same. Hold territory, stay behind cover, have someone there to keep the other side busy when you had to move. The problem, Bull saw almost at once, was that they didn't have anything that would damage their opponents. The best they could do was make loud noises and trust the people in the battle armor to give in to their reflexive caution. It wouldn't win the war. Hell, it would barely postpone losing the battle.

"Naomi," Bull said. "How're you doing back there?"

"I can dump the core, power this whole bastard down. Just give me three more minutes," she said. He could hear the focus and drive in her voice. The determination. It didn't count for shit.

"That's not going to happen," he said.

"Just…just hold on."

"They're coming back that way now," Bull said. "And there's not a goddamn thing we can do to stop them."

The four attackers bounced through engineering like grass-hoppers, massive bodies crashing into walls and consoles, shear-ing off bits of the bulkhead where they scraped against it. At this point, their best hope was that the enemy force would beat itself to death against the walls. Bull pulled back toward the entryway to the drum, then took a position behind a crate and started fir-ing at the enemy, trying to draw them toward him. If he could get the enemy out into the habitation drum, he might be able to close down the transition point and make the bastards dig back through. It might even give Naomi the minutes she needed.

The people in power armor didn't seem to notice he was there. One caught a desk, the steel bending in the suit's glove, and started pulling hand over hand toward the reactor controls.

"Can anybody stop that guy?" Bull asked. No one on the frequency answered. He sighed. "Naomi. You got to leave now."

"Core's out. I can drop the grid too. Just a few more minutes."

"You don't have them. Come out now, and I'll try to get you back in when things cool down."

"But—"

"You're no good to anyone dead," he said. The channel went quiet, and for a long moment he thought the Belter had been caught, been killed. Then she came sailing out of the hallway, leading with her chin, her good arm and hair streaming behind her like stabilizing fins. The nearest of the people in power suits grabbed at her, but she was already gone, and they were too timid to try jumping after her.

Bull saw another of the enemy struggling with something. A gun. The massive glove was too thick to fit through the weapon's trigger guard. As Bull watched, the enemy snapped the guard off and settled the gun in its fist, like a child's toy carried by a large man. Bull fired at it a few more times without much hope of doing damage.

Four Earthers shouted with one voice and launched themselves at the one with the gun. The attacker didn't fire. Just swept one big metal arm through the air, scattering Bull's people like they were sparrows.

His people were going to get killed—were *getting* killed—and there was nothing he could do to stop it.

"Okay kids," he said. "Let's pack up and go home. It's getting too hot in here."

"Bull!" Verbinski shouted. "Watch your six!"

Bull tried to swivel in the mech, but something hit him hard in the back. The magnetic feet creaked and lost their grip, and he was floating. The world all around began to shimmer gold and blue as his consciousness slipped away. He was aware distantly of a hand on his shoulder, slowing his fall, and he saw Naomi's face. Something had scraped her cheek, and she had a long bubble of blood clinging to her skin. He tried to turn and failed. That was right. No spine. He should have remembered that.

"What?" he said.

"They cut us off from the drum," Naomi said and turned him so that his mech's feet could touch deck. The air was a debris field. Twists of metal and shattered ceramic, sprays of blood slowly coalescing and growing larger like planets forming out of dust. Electricity arced from the ruins of a control panel, and the shattered glass floated in the tiny play of lightning. Two of the people in power armor stood rooted by the passage to the transition point. One held a rifle by the barrel as a club, the other had pistols with the trigger guard snapped off in either hand. A third was flailing in the air just above the maintenance shaft that they'd arrived through, struggling to get purchase on something. The fourth was shuffling across the deck toward them, its movements deliberate and controlled to keep from kicking off into the air.

"Elevator shaft airlock," Bull said. "Fall back."

"Everyone," Naomi said into her hand terminal. "We're falling back to the elevator shaft on my go. Go!"

Naomi pulled him around, then attached herself to his back in rescue hold and jumped. The enemy's guns opened fire. Bull caught a glimpse of a woman just as a bullet passed through her leg. Saw the grimace on her face and the blood fountaining out of her. *I'm sorry*, he thought.

The wall of the elevator shaft airlock loomed up, and Naomi pushed off from him, landing on the bulkhead with the grace of a woman born to zero g. Two more bodies came through the space, Martian marines, both of them. He recognized the man called Juarez and the woman named Cass. Naomi slapped the controls and the airlock doors began to collapse. Just as the opening seemed too narrow for a human form, two more came through. Sergeant Verbinski and a man from Bull's side of the security force schism.

Bull's head was swimming. He felt like he'd just run twenty miles in the hot New Mexican sun. He clapped his hands together less to command the attention of the people in the lock and more to bring himself back to awareness.

"That shaft's in vacuum," he said. "If that's the way we're going, we need to get suited up. Lockers are over there. Let's see what we've got to work with." A massive blow rang against the airlock door. Then another. "Might want to hurry," he said.

"You aren't going to fit," Verbinski said. "Not with that contraption."

"Yeah," Bull said. "Okay."

"Come on, big boy," the sergeant said. "Let's get you out of that."

No, Bull wanted to say. *I'm all right.* But Juarez and the other marine were already shucking him out of his brace, then out of the mech that Sam had made for him. He was a cripple again. That wasn't true. He'd been crippled ever since the catastrophe. Now he just had one fewer tool.

He'd worked with less.

The banging on the airlock door was getting louder, more intense. Along with the impact, there was something that sounded like tearing. He imagined the powered armor picking up handfuls of steel between massive fingers and pulling back, ripping at the skin of the ship. He clambered over to his mech, his body flowing out behind him, useless as a kite. He popped open the storage and took what was left of his pistol's ammunition and his hand terminal. For a moment, he didn't recognize the flat black package that he took out next. And then he did.

"If we're not staying, we'd best leave," Verbinski said.

"Let's go," Bull said, pushing the grenades into the pouch on the EVA suit's thigh.

Naomi cycled the door to the shaft. The sounds of the attack grew fainter and farther away as the air leaked out, and then the shaft was open below them. A full kilometer's fall to the trapped elevator, and then another past that to...what? Ashford? Certain death? Bull didn't know anymore what he was running from. Or to.

One by one, they pushed off, pulling themselves through the vacuum. Verbinski and the security man, Naomi and the marine, then Bull and Juarez. Without discussing it, they'd all paired off with someone who wasn't theirs. In Bull's sagging mind, that seemed important.

"Juarez?" Verbinski said on the radio, and Bull was surprised to hear his voice.

"Sir."

"If you get a good shot, you think you could crack the visors on those suits?"

"Your suit, maybe," Juarez said. "I keep mine in pretty good condition."

"Do your best," Verbinski said.

Bull felt it when the enemy force breached the airlock. He couldn't even say what it was exactly. Some little press of a shock wave, a whisper-thin breath of atmosphere. He looked down past his dead feet, and there was light at the bottom of the shaft where there shouldn't have been. There were probably about a thousand safety measures slamming down in engineering right now. He hoped so. Far below, he saw a muzzle flash, but they were so far ahead, the bullet almost certainly hit the sides of the shaft and spent itself before it could reach them.

Juarez turned, his rifle steadied between his feet. The man's face went calm and soft and the rifle flashed silently.

"Got one, Verb," he said. And then, "Sergeant?"

Verbinski didn't answer. He was still floating, skimming along the steel tracks that would guide the elevator, but his eyes were closed. His face was slack, and foam flecked his lips and nostrils. Bull hadn't even known the man was injured.

"Sergeant!" Juarez yelled.

"He's gone," Cass said.

The rest of the trip to the elevator was a thing carved from nightmares. Bull's body kept drifting wildly behind him, and his lungs felt full and wet. He'd stopped coughing, though. He didn't know if that was a good thing. Just as they reached the elevator, a lucky shot from their pursuers took the security man in the back, blowing out his air supply. Bull watched the man die, but he didn't hear it. The hatchway Corin had burned through the elevator's base seemed too small to fit through, but he got one arm in and Naomi pulled him the rest of the way.

In the body of the elevator car, Juarez took a position firing down the hole at the pursuers. Bull didn't know how much ammunition the marine had, but it had to be getting close to the end of his supply. Bull would have slouched against the wall if there had been any gravity. Instead he shifted his suit radio to the channel for Naomi.

"Give me a gun," she said before he could speak. "Give me something."

"You keep going," he said. "Get to the top of the shaft."

"But—"

"Maybe you can get the hatch open for them. Get into command."

"You can't access the controls from inside the shaft."

"In this piece-of-shit boat, you never know," Bull said. "Someone might have put a self-destruct button there. Wouldn't surprise me."

"That's your plan B?"

"I think we're pretty much on plan Z at this point," Bull said. "Anyway, you're the engineer. There's fuck-all you can do here. And I heard you with Holden before. You might as well get to see him again. Not like it costs us anything."

He watched her face as she decided. Fear, despair, regret, calm, in that order. Impressive woman. He wished he'd had a chance to know her better. And if she was able to ship with Jim Holden and love him, maybe he wasn't as bad as Bull thought either.

"Thank you," she said, then turned and launched herself along the elevator shaft toward command and her lover. *That was sweet*, Bull thought. Juarez's rifle flashed again and Bull shifted his radio frequencies to include the two marines.

"You two should go too. Head up top. See if you can storm the command."

"You sure?" Cass said, her voice calm and professional. "We've got cover here. There won't be a better place farther up."

"Yeah, pretty sure," Bull said.

"What about you?" Juarez asked.

"I'm staying here," Bull said.

"Okay, bro," Juarez said, then he and Cass were gone too. Bull thought about looking down through the shaft to see how close the enemy had come, but he didn't. Too much energy, and if he got shot in the eye at this point . . . well, that would just be sad. The little box of the elevator was a monochrome non-color, lit only by the backsplash from his own suit light. He took as deep a breath as he could. It was pretty shallow. He drew the grenades out from his pocket, one in either hand, and carefully dialed them down to the shortest fuse.

So he was going to die here. Not what he would have picked, but what the hell. It probably beat going back and having his spine grown back wrong. He'd seen guys who lived their whole lives in a drug haze fighting the pain of a bad regrowth. He hadn't really let himself think about that before. Now it was safe to.

He tried to decide whether he regretted dying, but the truth was he was too fucking tired to care. And he couldn't breathe for crap. He was sorry he hadn't killed Ashford, but that wasn't new. He was sorry he couldn't avenge Sam or find out if Pa was alive. Or whether Ashford would actually be able to destroy the Ring. If he was sad about anything, it was that everything that was in motion now would keep on being in motion without him, and he'd never know how it went. Never know if anything he'd done had made a difference.

His hand terminal blinked. A connection request from Monica Stuart. He wondered for a moment what she wanted with him, and then remembered that Ashford had stopped the drum. Things had to be for shit in there. He routed the request to his suit. No pictures, but the voice connection would be enough.

"Bull," the woman said. "We're being attacked up here. I think Anna's dead. What the hell's going on down there? How much longer?"

"Well, we lost engineering," he said. He felt a pang about Anna, but it was just one of many at that point. "Pretty much everyone in the attack party's dead now. Maybe five folks holed up in the elevator shaft, but the bad guys got the top and the bottom of that, so we're kind of screwed there. Managed to dump the core, but the grid's still up. It'll be enough to fire the laser. Ashford's guys are probably in engineering putting that back online, and I don't see we've got any damn way to stop him."

"Oh my God," Monica breathed.

"Yeah, it kind of sucks."

"What...what are you going to do about it?"

A beam of light shone through the hatch in the floor. Tiny bits of dust and particulate metal glimmered in it like it was swirling in water. He watched it with a half smile on his face. It meant the bad guys were almost there, but it was pretty to look at. He remembered that Monica was on the line. She'd asked him something.

"Yeah," Bull said. "So that thing where we power down the ship and save everyone? We're probably not going to do that."

"You can't give up," she said. "Please. There has to be a way."

Doesn't have to be, he thought, but didn't say. Anna thought there was a way. Where did that get her? *But if there is, I hope one of you folks finds it.*

"How bad is it in there?" he asked.

"It's...it's terrible. It's like the catastrophe happened all over again."

"Yeah, I can see that," Bull said.

"We can't go on," Monica said. "Oh God, what are we going to do?"

The light got stronger. Brighter. He couldn't see the dust motes anymore from the shine of the light.

"Monica?" Bull said. "Look, I'm sorry, but I kind of got to go now, okay? You folks just do your best. Hold it together in there, all right? And hey, if it all works out?"

"Yes?"

"Tell Fred Johnson he fucking owes me one."

He dropped the connection, unplugged his hand terminal. He took a grenade in each hand, his thumbs on the release bars. A head poked up through the hatch, then back down fast. When no one shot at it, the head came back more slowly. Bull smiled and nodded at it, welcoming. The opaque cowling went clear, and he saw Casimir staring at him. Bull grinned. Well, that was a pleasure, at least. A little treat on the way out.

"Hey," Bull said, even though the man couldn't hear him. "Hold this for me."

He tossed the two grenades, and watched the man's expression as he understood what they were.

Chapter Forty-Nine: Anna

Anna returned to consciousness floating in a tangled knot with Okju the camera operator, two office chairs, and a potted ficus plant. Someone was setting off firecrackers in long strings. Someone else was shouting. Anna's vision was blurry, and she blinked and shook her head to clear it. Which turned out to be a mistake, as shaking her head sent a spike of pain up her spine that nearly knocked her unconscious again.

"What?" she tried to say, but it came out as a slushy "bluh" sound.

"Christ, Red, I thought you were cooked there," a familiar voice replied. Rough but friendly. Amos. "I hated to think I broke my promise."

Anna opened her eyes again, careful not to move her head. She was floating in the center of what had been the studio space. Okju floated next to her, her foot tucked into Anna's armpit. Anna extricated her legs from the two office chairs they were twisted up in, and pushed the ficus away from her face.

More firecrackers went off in long, staccato bursts. It took Anna's muddled brain a few seconds to realize the sound was gunfire. Across the room, Amos was leaning against the wall next to the front door, taking a magazine out of his gun and replacing it with the smooth motion of long practice. On the other side of the door one of the UN soldiers they'd picked up was firing at someone outside. Answering gunfire blew chunks of molded fiberglass out of the back wall just a few meters from where Anna floated.

"If you aren't dead," Amos said, then paused to lean around the corner and fire off a short burst. "Then you'll probably want to get out of the middle of the room."

"Okju," Anna said, tugging on the woman's arm. "Wake up. We need to move."

Okju's arm flopped bonelessly when she pulled it, and the woman started slowly rotating in the air. Anna saw that her head was tilted at an acute angle to her shoulders, and her face was slack and her eyes stared at nothing. Anna recoiled involuntarily, the lizard living at the base of her spine telling her to get away from the dead person as quickly as possible. She yelped and pushed against Okju's body with her feet, sending it and herself floating away in opposite directions. When she hit the wall she grabbed on to an LED sconce and held on with all her strength. The pain in her neck and head was a constant percussive throb.

The sounds of gunfire didn't stop. Amos and his small, mixed band of defenders were firing out through every opening in the office space, several of which had been cut as gun ports.

They were under attack. Ashford had sent his people to stop them. Anna's memories of the last few moments came back in a rush. The terrible screeching sound, being hurled sideways at the wall.

Ashford must have shut down the drum to stop them so that his gunmen could finish them off. But if Okju had been killed as a result of the sudden stoppage, then that same effect would have been repeated dozens, maybe hundreds of times throughout the makeshift community on the *Behemoth*. Ashford was willing to kill them all to get his own way. Anna felt a growing rage, and was glad that no one had thought to give her a gun.

"Are we still broadcasting?" she yelled at Amos over the gunfire.

"Dunno, Red. Monica's in the radio room."

Anna pulled herself across the wall to the closet where they'd placed their broadcasting gear. The door was ajar, and she could see Monica floating inside, checking the equipment. The space wasn't large enough for both of them, so Anna just pushed the door open a little farther and said, "Are we still broadcasting? Can we get back on the air?"

Monica gave a humorless laugh but didn't turn around. "I thought you were dead."

"No, but Okju is. I think she broke her neck. I'll take the camera if you need me to. Where's Clip?"

"Clip was helping Amos, and he was shot in the hip. He's bleeding out in a side office. Tilly is helping him."

Anna pushed her way into the small room and put a hand on Monica's shoulder. "We have to get back on the air. We have to keep up the broadcast or this is all for nothing. Tell me what to do."

Monica laughed again, then turned around and swatted Anna's hand off of her arm. "What do you think is happening here? Ashford has men outside trying to break in and kill us. Bull and his people have lost the engine room, and Juarez says Bull's been killed. Who knows how many people he—"

Anna planted her feet against the doorjamb, grabbed Monica by the shoulders, and slammed the reporter up against the wall. "Does the broadcasting equipment still work?" She was amazed at how steady her voice sounded.

"It got banged around some, but—"

"Does. It. Work."

"Yes," Monica said. It came out as a frightened squeak.

"Get me on the channel the assault team was using, and give me a headset," Anna said, then let go of Monica's shoulders. Monica did as she asked, moving quickly and only occasionally giving her a frightened look. *I've become frightening*, Anna thought. Tasting the idea, and finding it less unpleasant than she'd expect. These were frightening times.

"Fuck!" Amos yelled from the other room. When Anna looked out, she saw one of the young Martian officers floating in the middle of the room spraying small globes of red blood into the air around him. Her friend Chris launched across the room by pushing off with his one good leg and grabbed the injured man with his one arm, then pulled him into cover.

"We're running out of time," Anna said to Monica. "Work faster."

Monica's reply was to hand her a headset with a microphone.

"Hello? This is Anna Volovodov at Radio Free Slow Zone. Is anyone left on this channel?"

Someone replied, but they were impossible to hear over the nearby gunfire. Anna turned the volume up to the maximum and said, "Repeat that, please."

"We're here," James Holden said at deafening levels.

"How many are left, and what's the situation?"

"Well," Holden said, then paused and grunted as though exerting himself for several seconds. He sounded out of breath when he continued. "We're holed up in the port elevator shaft just outside the command deck airlock. There are three of us at this position. Bull and the remaining marines are fighting the counterassault team at a position further down the shaft. I have no idea how that's going. We've run out of room to retreat, so unless someone decides to open the hatch and let us onto the bridge, we're sort of out of options."

The last part of his sentence was almost drowned out by a massive wave of incoming gunfire in her office. Amos and his group were hunkered down, leaning against the reinforced armor they'd attached to the walls. The reports of the shots and the sound of bullets hitting metal was deafening. When the fire lessened, a pair of men in *Behemoth* security armor rushed the room, spraying automatic weapons fire as they came. Two of Amos' team were hit, and more globes of red flew into the air. Amos grabbed the second man through the door and yanked him up off his magnetic hold to the floor, then threw him at his partner. They tumbled off across the room together and then Amos fired a long burst from his weapon into both as they spun. The air was filled with so many floating red orbs of various sizes that it became difficult to see. The rest of Amos' team opened fire, and whatever attack Ashford's people had launched was apparently driven back, as no more soldiers charged through the door.

"Is there anything we can do?" Anna yelled at Holden.

"Sounds to me like you're in some shit there yourself, Preacher," Holden replied. His voice was weary. Sad. "Unless you've got the bridge access controls nearby, I'd say you should concentrate on your own problems."

More fire came through the offices, but it was sporadic. Amos had driven off their big attack, and now they were taking petulant potshots. Monica was staring at her, waiting for her to issue another order. Somehow, she'd become the person in charge.

"Set me to broadcast on the Radio Free Slow Zone feed," Anna said. In the end, talking was all she had to offer. Monica nodded at her and pointed a small camera at her face.

"This is Anna Volovodov broadcasting from the offices of Radio Free Slow Zone to anyone on the *Behemoth* that's still listening. We've failed to hold engineering, so our plan to shut down the reactor and get everyone back home is failing as well. We have people trapped in the external elevator shaft, and they can't get onto the bridge.

"So, please, if anyone listening to this can help, we need you. Everyone on this flotilla needs you. The people dying right outside your door need you. Most of all, the people we left behind on Earth and Mars and the Belt need you. If the captain does what he's planning, if he fires the laser at the Ring, everyone back home will die too. Please, if you can hear me, help us."

She stopped, and Monica put down the camera.

"Think that will work?" Monica asked.

Anna was about to say no when the wall comm panel buzzed at her. A voice said, "How do you know that?" A young voice, female, sad. Clarissa. "What you said about destroying Earth if we attack the Ring, how do you know that?"

"Clarissa," Anna said. "Where are you?"

"I'm here, on the bridge. I'm in the security station. I was watching your broadcast."

"Can you open the door and let our people in?"

"Yes."

"Will you do that?"

"How," Clarissa repeated, her tone not changing at all, "do you know what you said?"

A man generally regarded as the instigator of two solar system– wide wars got all this information from a protomolecule-created ghost that no one else can see. It wasn't a particularly compelling argument.

"James Holden got it while he was on the station."

"So *he* told you that this would happen," Clarissa said, her tone doubtful.

"Yes."

"So how do you *know*?"

"I don't, Claire," Anna said, appropriating Tilly's pet name to try and create a connection. "I don't know. But Holden believes it's true, and the consequences if he's right are too extreme to risk. So I'm taking it on faith."

There was a long moment of silence. Then a male voice said, "Clarissa, who are you talking to in here?"

It took Anna a moment to recognize it as Hector Cortez. She'd known he was on the bridge with Ashford, but somehow the reminder that he'd sided with the men who killed Bull was too much. She had to restrain herself from cursing at him.

"Anna wants me to open the elevator airlock and let the other side into the bridge. She wants me to help stop Ashford from destroying the Ring. She says it will kill everyone on Earth if we do."

"Don't listen to her," Cortez said. "She's just afraid."

"Afraid?" Anna yelled. "Do you hear those sounds, Hector? That's gunfire. Bullets are flying by even as we speak. You're locked away safe and snug on the command deck planning to destroy something you don't understand, while I am risking gunshot wounds to stop you. Who's afraid here?"

"You're afraid to make the necessary sacrifices to protect the people we've left behind. You're only thinking of yourself," he yelled back. Anna heard the sound of a door closing in the background. Someone had shut the door to the security station to keep the argument from being overheard. If it was Clarissa, that was a good sign.

"Clarissa," Anna said, keeping her voice as calm as she could with the ongoing sounds of a gunfight behind her. "Claire, the people waiting outside the airlock door are going to be killed if you don't open it. They are trapped there. People are coming to kill them."

"Don't change the subject," Cortez started.

"It's Holden and Naomi out there," Anna continued, ignoring him. "And Bull is there too. Ashford will have them all killed."

"They wouldn't be in danger if they hadn't attacked Ashford's rightful command," Cortez said.

"That's three people who all made the choice to give you a second chance," Anna said. "Bull chose to protect you from the UN fleet's vengeance when he had no reason to. When I asked her to, Naomi forgave you for almost killing her. Holden agreed not to hurt you, in spite of the many provocations you gave him."

"Those people are *criminals*—" Cortez tried to say over the top of her, but she kept her voice level and continued.

"These people, the people who forgive, who try to help others. The people who give their lives to save strangers, they're on the other side of that door, dying. I don't have to take that on faith. That's fact. That's happening right now."

Anna paused, waiting for any sign Clarissa was listening. There was none. Even Cortez had stopped speaking. The comm station hissed faintly, the only sign it was still on.

"Those are the people I'm asking you to help," Anna said. "The person I'm asking you to betray is a man who kills innocent people for expedience's sake. Forget Earth, and the Ring, and everything else you'd have to take on faith. Ask yourself this: Do you want to let Ashford kill Holden and Naomi? No faith. Just that simple question, Claire. Can you let them die? What choice did they make when the same question was asked of them about you?"

Anna knew she was rambling. Knew she was repeating herself. But she had to force herself to stop speaking anyway. She wasn't used to trying to save a person's soul without being able to see them, to measure the effect her words were having by their reaction. She kept trying to fill that empty space with more talking.

"I don't like the idea of those people being killed any more than you do," Cortez said. He sounded sad, but committed to his position. "But there is the necessity for sacrifice. To sacrifice is literally to be made sacred."

"Seriously?" Anna gave a humorless laugh. "We're going to do dueling etymology?"

"What we are facing here is more than humanity is ready for," Cortez said.

"You don't get to decide that, Hank," Anna said, stabbing at the radio as if it were the man. "Think about the people you're killing. Look at who you're working with, and tell me that in clear conscience you know you're doing the right thing."

"Argument by association?" Cortez said. "Really? God's tools have always been flawed. We are a fallen people, but that we have the strength of will to do what we must, even in the face of mortal punishment, is what makes us moral beings. And you of all people—"

The feed went silent for a moment.

"Cortez?" Anna said. But when Cortez's voice came, he wasn't speaking to her.

"Clarissa, what are you doing?"

Clarissa sounded calm, almost half asleep. "I opened the doors."

Chapter Fifty: Holden

Naomi had taken an access panel off the wall next to the command deck airlock. She'd crawled halfway inside, and only her belly and legs were visible. Holden had planted his mag boots next to the airlock's outer door and was awaiting instructions from her. Occasionally she'd ask him to try opening the door again, but every attempt so far had failed. Corin floated next to him, watching down the elevator shaft through her gunsights. They'd seen a quick flash of light down there a few minutes back that had set the bulkheads to vibrating. Something violent and explosive had happened.

Holden, having now moved on to his second last stand of the day, had come to view the whole thing with a weary sense of humor. As far as places to die went, the small platform between the elevator shaft and the airlock was about as good as any other. It was a niche in the wall of the shaft about ten feet on a side. The floor, ceiling, and bulkheads were all the same ceramic steel of the ship's outer hull. The back wall was the airlock door. The front was empty space where the elevator would normally sit. At the very least, when Ashford's people came swarming up the shaft at them, the floor of the niche would offer some cover.

Naomi scooted sideways a bit and kicked one leg. Holden could hear her over the radio as she grunted with the effort of grabbing something just out of reach.

"Gotcha," she said in triumph. "Okay, try it now!"

Holden hit the button to open the outer airlock doors. Nothing happened.

"Are you trying it?" Naomi asked.

He hit the button two more times. "Yeah. Nothing."

"Dammit. I could've sworn..."

Corin shifted enough to give him a sardonic look, but said nothing.

The truth was, Holden was out of emotional gas. He'd gone through his existential moment of truth back when he thought he was making a last stand at the elevator to buy Naomi time. Then he'd been given a reprieve when the attackers chose another path, but Naomi had been put in the firing line, which was actually worse. And then she'd shown up a few minutes ago saying Bull had sent her on ahead to get the door open while he acted as rearguard.

Every plan they'd made had failed spectacularly, with more casualties piling up at every step. And now they were at yet another last stand, with a locked door behind them and Ashford's goons ahead of them and nowhere to go. It should have been terrifying, but at this point Holden just felt sleepy.

"Try it now," Naomi said. Holden jabbed the button a few times without looking at it.

"Nope."

"Maybe..." she said and moved around, kicking her legs again.

"Two incoming," Corin said, her voice harsh and buzzing over the radio. He'd never heard her voice when it wasn't on a suit radio. He wondered whether it would have that same quality naturally. He walked over to the edge of the platform and looked down, magnetic boots having tricked his brain into thinking there was an up and down again.

Looking through his gunsight's magnification, he saw two of the Martian marines hurtling up the shaft as fast as their cheap environment suits would let them. He didn't recognize them yet. Bull wasn't with them.

"Try it now," Naomi said.

"Busy," Holden replied, scanning the space behind the marines for pursuers. He didn't see any.

Naomi climbed out of her access panel and floated over next to him to see what was going on. The marines shot up the shaft toward them at high speed, flipped at the last minute, and hit the ceiling feet first to come to a rapid stop. They pushed off and landed next to Holden, sticking to the floor with magnetic boots.

Holden could see through their faceplates now, and recognized the sniper, Juarez, and a dark-skinned woman whose name he'd never gotten.

"We've lost the hold point," Juarez said. He clutched his long rifle in one hand and a fresh magazine in the other. He loaded the gun and said, "Last mag," to his partner.

She checked her harness and said, "Three."

"Report," Holden said, slipping into military command mode without even meaning to. He'd been a lieutenant in the navy. Juarez was enlisted. The training they'd received about who gave orders and who followed them in combat died hard.

"I took out one hostile with a headshot, I believe a second was neutralized with our remaining explosives. No intel on the other two. They may have been injured or killed by the explosion, but we can't count on that."

"Bull?" Corin asked.

"He was holding the explosives. That second kill was his."

"Bull," Corin said again, choking up. Holden was surprised to see her eyes filling with tears. "We have to go get him."

"Negative," Juarez said. "The elevator has become a barrier. He's inside it. Anything we do to remove his body actively degrades our defensive position."

"Fuck you," Corin said, taking an aggressive step toward Juarez, her hands closing into fists. "We don't *leave* him—"

Before she could take another step, Holden grabbed her by her weapon harness and yanked her off the floor, then spun around to slam her against the closest bulkhead. He heard the air go out of her in a whoosh over the radio.

"Mourn later," he said, not letting her go. "When we're done. Then we mourn for all of them."

She grabbed his wrists in her hands, and for one heartstopping moment Holden thought she might fight him. He seriously questioned his ability to win a zero-g grappling match with the stocky security officer. But she just pulled his hands off her harness, then pushed herself back down to the floor.

"Understood, sir," she said.

"Back on watch," Holden said, keeping his voice as gentle as possible.

She walked back to the edge of the platform. Juarez watched without comment. After a respectful moment he said, "Plan, sir?"

"Naomi is trying to get the door open, but without any success. Blowing the elevator may have bought you two a couple more minutes, but maybe that's all it bought you."

"We'll try to make the most of them," the other marine said with a half smile. Juarez chuckled and slapped her on the back.

"So this is our final defensive position, then. Good cover and field of fire. If I get lucky maybe I can crack another mask. Cass, why don't you take that right corner, Corin can keep the left, and I'll set up here in the center. Holden can rove and back up whichever side is taking the most heat."

He paused, nodding at Holden. "If you agree, sir."

"I agree," Holden said. "In fact, I'm giving you full tactical command of this position. I'm going to be trying to help Naomi with the door. Yell if you get in trouble."

Juarez kicked off his mags, then jumped up to plant his feet on the ceiling. He straightened out, his long rifle pointed over his head, straight down the shaft. From Holden's perspective he looked like a particularly well-armed bat hanging from the roof.

"Movement," he said almost immediately.

"Shit," the marine named Cass said. "They got through the barrier fast."

"Looks like they're not quite through, but the wall is bulging like they're beating their way through it."

"I have an idea," Naomi said and walked over to the edge of the platform, then out onto the wall and over to the opposite side of the elevator shaft.

"Where are you going?" Holden asked.

"Panel," was her only answer before she popped an access hatch off the elevator shaft bulkhead and climbed inside. It was large enough that she completely disappeared. Holden didn't think there would be anything in there that could help them get the airlock door open, but he didn't care. Naomi was hidden while she stayed in there. Ashford's people might not bother to look for her. They probably didn't have good intel on who had engaged in the assault on engineering.

"Here they come," Juarez said, looking down the shaft through his telescopic sight. "Two left." His muzzle flashed once. "Shit, no hit." It flashed twice more. Cass started firing with her assault rifle on single fire, carefully aiming each shot. The bad guys were just under a kilometer away. Holden didn't think he'd be able to hit a stationary transport shuttle at that range, much less a rapidly moving man-sized target. But after having spent some time with Bobbie Draper, Holden knew that if Cass was taking the shots, it was because she thought she had a chance to score hits. He wasn't about to argue with her.

"Eight hundred meters," Juarez said, his voice no different than if he'd been giving a stranger the time. "Seven-fifty." He fired again.

Cass fired off the last of her magazine, then replaced it in one smooth motion. She had one extra left. Holden took three magazines off his own bandolier and left them floating next to her left elbow. She nodded her thanks without pausing in her firing. Juarez fired twice more, then said, "Out." He continued sighting down the scope, calling out ranges for Cass. When he hit five hundred meters, Corin started firing as well.

It was all very brave, Holden thought. None of them were the kind of people who gave up, no matter the odds. But it was also sort of pointless. Juarez had the only gun that was even remotely a threat to troops in state-of-the-art recon armor, and he'd fired it dry and only scored one kill. So they'd throw a lot of bullets at the approaching enemy because that's what people like them did, even when there was no chance. But in the end, Ashford would win. If he wasn't so emotionally drained, Holden would have been pissed.

The LEDs in the elevator shaft came back on, bathing them all with white light. The two soldiers wearing their stolen power armor were flying up the corridor toward them. Before he'd had time to wonder why the power was back on, there was a thud that Holden could feel through his feet. A large section of the elevator bulkhead slid open. The backup elevator slowly moved out into the shaft on hydraulic arms, then locked into place on the wall-mounted tracks. Lights flashed on the elevator's control panel as its systems cycled through warm-up. Then a light on the panel flashed red three times and the elevator launched down the tracks at high speed.

"Huh," Juarez said.

The impact when the hurtling backup elevator slammed into the stationary main elevator shook the bulkheads hard enough to make Holden's helmet ring like a bell.

"Well," Cass said.

Corin leaned out over the edge of the platform, looking down, and yelled, "Fuck you!" through the vacuum.

A few seconds later, Naomi's head popped back out of the open access panel. She looked up at them and waved. "Did that work?"

Holden found that he wasn't too drained to feel relief. "I think so."

"The armor is pretty tough," Juarez said. "It might be okay. But at that speed, whatever's inside it is probably a liquid now."

Naomi walked across the elevator bulkhead and then stepped over and down onto their platform. "I'm not good with guns," she said in an almost apologetic voice.

"No," Juarez said, waving his hands in a gesture of surrender. "You just keep doing your thing. Warn me if I'm in the way."

"Doesn't solve our door problem," Naomi added, still with a tone of apology.

Because he couldn't kiss her in an environment suit, Holden put an arm around her shoulder and hugged her to his side. "I'm happy with you solving the 'about to be ripped to pieces' problem."

Corin, who'd turned to look at the airlock when Naomi mentioned it, said, "Open sesame," and the outer airlock door slid open.

"Holy shit," Holden said. "Did you just magic that door open?"

"The green cycle light was blinking," Corin replied.

"Did you do that?" Holden said, turning to Naomi.

"Nope."

"Then we should be careful." Holden handed his rifle and his remaining magazines to Juarez, then drew his sidearm. "Juarez, when the inner door opens, you have the point."

Cass nodded, and Naomi punched the cycle button. The outer door closed, and for two tense minutes the air pressure equalized. Everyone other than Naomi was pointing a gun at the inner door when it finally opened.

There was nothing on the other side but a short corridor that ended at another elevator, and a second hallway going left at the midway point.

"That's the one that leads to the bridge," Corin said. "Five meters long, a meter and a half or so wide. There's a hatch, but it only closes and locks in the event of emergency decomp. Or if someone in the security station hits the override."

"Then that's our first target," Holden said. "Cass, when we go in you break right and control the security station. Juarez, you go left and try to draw any return fire away from Cass. Corin and I will go right up the gut and try to get our hands on Ashford. If we put a gun to him, I think this ends immediately. Naomi, you stay here but be ready to come running when we call. Taking control of the ship will be your bit."

"Pretty shitty plan, El Tee," Juarez said with a grin.

"You have a better one?"

"Nope, so let's get it done." Juarez pulled the rifle to his shoulder and moved off down the corridor at a quick magnetic boot shuffle. Cass followed close behind, her hand on his back. Holden took third, with Corin bringing up the rear. Naomi waited by the elevator doors, clutching her tool case nervously.

When they reached the junction, Juarez signaled the stop, then leaned around the corner. He pulled back and said, "Looks clear to the bridge entry point. When we go, go fast. Stop for nothing. Maximum aggression wins the day here."

After a round of assents from everyone, he counted down from three, yelled, "Go go go," darted around the corner, and was immediately shot.

It was so unexpected, Cass actually took a step back into Holden. Juarez screamed in pain and launched himself back into their hallway. Bullets slammed into the bulkheads and deck around him. After the long silence of vacuum in the elevator shaft, the sound of gunfire and bullet impacts was disorienting. Deafening.

Cass and Holden grabbed Juarez by his arms and pulled him around the corner out of the gunfire. With Cass covering the intersection, Holden checked Juarez over for injuries. He had gunshot wounds in his hip, upper arm, and foot. None looked instantly lethal, but together they'd bleed him out in short order. Holden pulled him back down the corridor to the airlock. He pointed at the emergency locker until Naomi followed his gesture and nodded.

"Do what you can," he said, and moved back down the hallway to Cass.

When he put his hand on her back to let her know he was there, she said, "Based on volume of fire, I'd guess ten to twelve shooters. Mostly light assault rifles and sidearms. One shotgun. That corridor is a kill box. No way through that."

"Fuck!" Holden yelled in frustration. The universe kept waiting until he was thoroughly beaten, then tossing him a nibble of hope only to yank it away again.

"New plan?" Corin asked.

"Shoot back, I guess," he said, then leaned partway around the corner and fired off three quick shots. He ducked back in time to avoid a fusillade that tore up the bulkhead behind him. When the shooting slowed, Cass launched herself across the opening to the other side. A risky move, but she made it without taking a hit, and started leaning out to lay down fire with her assault rifle. When they drove her back with return fire, Corin leaned around Holden and fired off a few shots.

Before she could pull back out of the line of fire, a round went through the arm of her environment suit, blowing white padding and black sealing gel into the air.

"Not hit, not hit," she yelled, and Cass leaned out to fire again to keep the defenders off balance.

Holden looked back down the corridor, and Naomi was stripping Juarez out of his suit, spraying bandages on his open wounds as she went.

Another wave of fire drove Cass and Corin into cover. When it let up for a second, Holden leaned out and fired a few more shots.

It was what people like them did, even when there was no chance.

Chapter Fifty-One: Clarissa

What the hell did you do?" Ashford shouted. His face was thick and purple. The rage pulled his lips back like a dog baring his teeth. Clarissa knew she should feel fear. Should feel something. Instead, she shrugged the way she had when she was fourteen, and said it again.

"I opened the doors."

A man appeared in the hallway for a fraction of a second, and Ashford's men opened fire, driving him back.

"I've got five in the corridor," one of Ashford's people said. He was looking at the security camera feed. "Three women, two men. One of them's Corin. I think Jim Holden's one of them."

Ashford shook his head in disgust.

"Why the fuck did you let them in here?" he said. His tone dripped acid.

"I didn't kill them," Clarissa said. "So you don't get to."

"She was in distress," Cortez said, moving himself between her and Ashford. Shielding her with his body. "She misunderstood something I said. It wasn't an act of malice, Captain. The girl only—"

"Someone shoot her," Ashford said.

"No!" Cortez cried out. He sounded like someone was about to shoot him.

The guard nearest them turned. The barrel of his gun seemed suddenly enormous, but when the sound of gunfire came, it wasn't from him. A shape—maybe a woman, maybe a man—flickered at the edge of the corridor to the bridge, and the staccato sound of gunfire filled the room. Clarissa, forgotten, pushed herself back through the doorway into the security office. Cortez followed her, his hands up around his ears to block the noise or a bullet or both. He put his hand on her shoulder as if to comfort her, but it only pushed her a little lower to the floor, him a little nearer the ceiling.

"Oh," Cortez murmured, "I wish you hadn't done that. I wish you hadn't done that."

Anna was still speaking on the security station monitor. Radio Free Slow Zone, soldiering on. There was a fresh crackle of gunfire from the bridge. Ashford shouted, "Take them out! Take them all out!" But as far as she could tell, the guards hadn't rushed the corridor. They didn't need to. Sooner or later, Holden and Naomi and whoever they had with them would run out of bullets, and then they'd die. Or Ashford and all his men would, and then Holden would kill them. Either way, she didn't see how it looked good for her. And that was fine. That was what she'd come here for.

Except.

"You heard what she said? What Anna said?"

"Anna Volovodov is seriously mistaken about what is happening here," Cortez said. "It was a mistake letting her into the project in the first place. I knew I should have asked for Muhammed al Mubi instead."

"Did you hear what she *said*?"

"What are you talking about, child?"

"She said if we attack the Ring, it'll take action against the people on the other side. Against everyone."

"She can't know that," Cortez said. "It's just the sort of thing the enemy would say to trick us."

"It wasn't her," Clarissa said. "Holden told her."

"The same James Holden who started a war by 'telling' people things?"

Clarissa nodded. He'd started at least one war. He'd destroyed Protogen, and by doing so set up the dominoes that would eventually topple Mao-Kwik and her father. He'd done all of that.

But.

"He didn't lie. All those other things he did. He never lied once."

Cortez opened his mouth to reply, his face already in a sneer. Before he could, the gunfire boomed again. She could feel Cortez flinch from it. The air was filling with the smell of spent gunpowder, and the air recyclers were moving into high-particulate mode. She could hear the difference in the fans. Probably no one else on the bridge would have any idea what that meant. It would just be a slightly higher whirring to them. If it was anything.

Cortez ran his fingers through his hair.

"Stay out the way," he said. "When it's over, when he's done this, I can speak with Ashford. Explain that you didn't mean to undermine him. It was a mistake. He'll forgive you."

Clarissa bowed her head. Her mind was a mass of confusion, and the hunger and gunfire weren't doing anything to help. Jim Holden was out there in the corridor. The man she'd come so far to disgrace and destroy, and now she didn't want him dead. Her father was back on Earth and she was about to save him and everyone else or possibly destroy them all. She'd killed Ren, and there was nothing she could ever do that would make that right. Not even die for him.

She had been so certain. She'd given so much of herself. She'd given everything, and in the end all she'd felt was empty. And soiled. The money and the time and all of the people she could have been if she hadn't been worshiping at the altar of her family name had already been sacrificed. Now she had offered her life, except that after speaking to Anna, she wasn't sure that wouldn't be an empty sacrifice too.

Her confusion and despair were like a buzzing in her ears and the voice that rose out of it was peculiarly her own: contempt and rage and the one certainty she could hold to.

"Who is *Ashford* to forgive me for anything?" she said.

Cortez blinked at her, as if seeing her for the first time.

"For that matter," she said, "who the hell are *you*?"

She turned and kicked gently for the doorframe, leaving Cortez behind. Ashford and his men were all armed, all waiting for the next round of gunfire. Ashford, stretched out behind his control panel, pistol before him, slammed his palm against the controls.

"Ruiz!" he shouted. His voice was hoarse. How many hours had they been waiting for this apocalypse to come? She could hear the strain in him. "Are we ready to fire? Tell me we're ready to fire!"

The woman's voice came, shrill with fear.

"Ready, sir. The grid is back online. The diagnostics are all green. It should work. Please don't kill me. *Please.*"

This was it, then. And with an almost physical click, she knew how to fix it, if there was time.

She put her tongue to the roof of her mouth and pressed, swirling in two gentle counterclockwise circles. The extra glands in her body leapt into life as if they'd been waiting for her, and the world went white for a moment. She thought that she might have cried out in the first rush, but when she was back to herself—to better than herself—no one had reacted to her. They were all pointing their guns at the corridor. All drawn to the threat of James Holden the way she had been herself. All except Ashford. He was letting go of his weapon, leaving the pistol to hang in the air while he keyed in the firing instructions. That was how long she had. It wasn't enough. Even high as a kite on battle drugs, she couldn't do what needed to be done before Ashford fired the laser.

So he became step one.

She pulled both feet up to the doorframe and pushed out into the open air of the bridge. The air seemed viscous and thick, like water without the buoyancy. A woman ducked out of cover, firing toward Ashford, and Ashford's people returned fire, muzzles blooming flame that faded away to smoke and then bloomed again. She couldn't see the bullets, but the paths they made through the air persisted for a fraction of a second. Tunnels of nothing in nothing. She tucked her knees into her chest. She had almost reached Ashford. His finger was moving down, ready to touch the control screen, ready, perhaps, to fire the comm laser. She kicked out as hard as she could.

The sensation of her muscles straining, ligaments and tendons pushed past their maximum working specifications, was a bright pain, but not entirely without joy. Her timing was only a little off. She didn't hit Ashford in the center of his body, but his shoulder and head. She felt the impact through her whole body, felt her jaw clicking shut from the blow. He slid back through the air away from the control panel, his eyes growing wider. Two of the guards began to swing toward her, but she bent her body against the base of the crash couch and then unfolded, moving away. The guns flashed, one then another, then two together, like watching lightning in a thunderstorm. Bullets flew, and she spun through the air, pulling her arms tight against her to make her spin faster. Rifling herself.

One of the women in the corridor leaned in, spraying gunfire through the room. A bullet caught one of the guards, and Clarissa watched as she moved toward the farthest wall. It was like seeing frames from an old movie. The woman in the corridor, the muzzle of her weapon alive with fire, then Clarissa turned. The guard, unmoved, but blood already splashing out from his neck, the little wave radiating through his skin out from the impact like the ripple of a stone dropped in a pond, then she turned. The guard falling back, blood blooming out of him like a rose blossom. The same would happen to her, she knew. The drugs flowing through her blood, lighting her brain like a seizure, couldn't change the abilities of her flesh. She couldn't dodge a bullet if one found her. So instead she hoped that none would and did what needed to be done.

The access panel was open, the guts of the ship exposed. She grabbed the edge of the panel gently, slowing herself. Blood welled up from her palm where the metal cut into her. She didn't feel it as pain. Just a kind of warmth. A message from her body that she could ignore. The brownout buffer sat behind an array control board. She slid her hand down to it, her fingers caressing the pale formed ceramic. The fault indicator glowed green. She took a breath, gripped the buffer, pushed it down, turned and then pulled. The unit came loose in her hand.

A gun went off. A scar appeared on the wall before her, bits of metal spinning out from it. They were shooting at her. Or near her. It didn't matter. She flipped the unit end for end and reseated it. The buffer's indicator blinked red for a moment, then green. Just the way Ren had showed her. *Terrible design*, she thought with a grin and held down the buffer's reset. Two more guns fired, the sound pushing against her eardrums like a blow. Time stuttered. She didn't know how long she'd been holding the reset, if she'd slipped it off and back on. She thought it should have gone by now, but time was so unreliable. The world stuttered again. She was crashing.

The buffer's readout went red. Clarissa smiled and relaxed. She saw the cascading failure as if she were the ship itself. One bad readout causing the next causing the next, the levels of failure rapid and incremental. The nervous system of the *Behemoth* sensing a danger it couldn't define. Doing what it could to be safe, or at least to be sure it didn't get worse.

Failing closed.

She turned. Ashford stood on his couch, holding the restraint straps in one hand and pressing his feet into the gel. His mouth was a square gape of rage. Two of his people had shifted to face her as well, their guns trained on her, their faces almost blank.

Behind them all, far across the bridge, Cortez was framed by the security office doorway. His face was a mask of distress and surprise. He wasn't, she thought, a man who dealt well with the unexpected. Must be hard for him. She hadn't noticed before how much he looked like her own father. Something about the shape of their jaws, maybe. Or in their eyes.

The lights flickered. She felt her body starting to shudder. It was over. For her, for all of them. The first twitch of the collapse pulled at her back like a cramp. A rising nausea came to her. She didn't care.

I did it, Ren, she thought. *You showed me how, and I did it. I think I just saved everyone.* We *did*.

Ashford caught his pistol out of the air and swung toward her. She heard his screaming like it was meat ripping. Behind him, Cortez was shouting, launching himself through the space. There was a contact taser in the old man's hand, and the grief on the old man's face was gratifying. It was good to know that on some level, he cared what happened to her. The lights flared once and went out as Ashford brought the barrel to bear on her. The emergency lighting didn't kick in.

Everything was darkness, and then, for a moment, light.

And then darkness.

Chapter Fifty-Two: Holden

Holden ejected his spent magazine and reached for a new one. His fingers hit only an empty space where he expected it to be. He hadn't been managing his ammo well. He'd wanted to keep at least one magazine in reserve. Corin was firing around him with her rifle. She had spare pistol ammo on her belt. Without asking, he started pulling magazines off her belt and putting them in his. She fired off a few more shots and waited for him to finish. It was that sort of fight.

Cass was leaning around the corner firing. Answering bullets hit everyplace on her side of the corridor except where she was. Holden was about to shout at her to get back into cover when the lights went out.

It wasn't just the lights. So many things about his physical situation changed all at once that his hindbrain couldn't keep up. It told him to be nauseated just in case he'd been poisoned. It was working with fifty-million-year-old response algorithms.

Holden collapsed to his knees with the nausea, the sudden appearance of gravity being one of the many changes. His knees banged against the floor because he was no longer wearing a heavy environment suit. Which also meant he could smell the air. It had a vaguely swampy, sulfurous odor. His inner ear didn't report any Coriolis, so they weren't spinning. There were no engine sounds, so the *Behemoth* wasn't under thrust.

Holden fumbled at the ground around him. It felt like dirt. Damp soil, small rocks. Something that felt like ground-cover plants.

"Oh, hey, sorry," a voice said. Miller's. The light level came up with no visible source. Holden was kneeling naked on a wide plain of something that looked like a mix of moss and grass. It was as dark as a moonlit night, but no moons or stars shone overhead. In the distance, something like a forest was visible. Beyond that, mountains. Miller stood a few meters away, looking up at the sky, still wearing his old gray suit and goofy hat. His hands were in his pockets, his jacket rumpling around them.

"Where?" Holden started.

"This planet was in the catalog. Most Earth-like one I could find. Thought it'd be calming."

"Am I here?"

Miller laughed. Something in the timbre of his voice had changed since the last time Holden had spoken to him. He sounded serene, whole. Vast. "Kid, *I'm* not even here. But we needed a place to talk, and this seemed nicer than a white void. I've got processing power to spare now."

Holden stood up, embarrassed to be naked even in a simulation, but without any way of changing it. But if this *was* a simulation, then that brought up other issues.

"Am I still in a gunfight?"

Miller turned, not quite facing him. "Hmmm?"

"I was in a gunfight before you grabbed me. If this is just a sim running in my brain, then does that mean I'm still in that gunfight? Am I floating in the air with my eyes rolled back or something?"

Miller looked chagrined.

"Maybe."

"Maybe?"

"Maybe. Look. Don't worry about it. This won't take long."

Holden walked over to stand next to him, to look him in the eyes. Miller gave him his sad basset hound smile. His eyes glowed a bright electric blue.

"We did it, though? We got under the power threshold?"

"Did. And I talked the station into thinking you were essentially dirt and rocks."

"Does that mean we saved the Earth?"

"Well," Miller replied with a small Belter shrug of the hands. "We *also* saved the Earth. Never was the big plan, but it's a nice bonus."

"Good that you care."

"Oh," Miller said with that same vaguely frightening laugh. "I really don't. I mean, I remember being human. The simulation is good. But I remember caring without really caring, if you know what I mean."

"Okay."

"Oh, hey, look at this," Miller said, pointing at the black sky. Instantly the sky was filled with glowing blue Rings. The thousand-plus gates of the slow zone, orbiting around them like Alex's dandelion seeds, seen from the center of the flower. "Shazam!" Miller said. As one, the gates shifted in color and became mirrors reflecting thousands of other solar systems. Holden could actually see the alien stars, and the worlds whirring in orbit around them. He assumed that meant Miller was taking a little artistic license with his simulation.

There was a croaking sound at his feet, and Holden looked down to see something that looked like a long-limbed frog, with grayish skin and no visible eyes. Its mouth was full of sharp-looking little teeth, and Holden became very aware of his bare toes just a few dozen centimeters from it. Without looking down, Miller kicked the frog thing away with his shoe. It blurred away across the field on its too-long limbs.

"The gates are all open out there?"

Miller gave him a quizzical look.

"You know," Holden continued. "In reality?"

"What's reality?" Miller said, looking back up at the swirling gates and the night sky.

"The place where I live?"

"Yeah, fine. The gates are all open."

"And are there invading fleets of monsters pouring through to kill us all?"

"Not yet," Miller said. "Which is kind of interesting in its own way."

"I was joking."

"I wasn't," Miller said. "It was a calculated risk. But it looks clear for now."

"We can go through those gates, though. We can go there."

"Can," Miller said. "And knowing you, you will."

For a moment, Holden forgot about Ashford, the *Behemoth*, the deaths and the violence and the thousand other things that had distracted him from where they really were. What they were really doing.

What it all meant.

He would live to see humanity's spread to the stars. He and Naomi, their children, their children's children. Thousands of worlds, no procreation restrictions. A new golden age for the species. And the *Nauvoo* had made it happen, in a way. Fred could tell the Mormons. Maybe they'd stop suing him now.

"Wow," he said.

"Yeah, well let's not get too happy," Miller said. "I keep warning you. Doors and corners, kid. That's where they get you. Humans are too fucking stupid to listen. Well, you'll learn your lessons soon enough, and it's not my job to nursemaid the species through the next steps."

Holden scuffed at the ground cover with his toe. When it was scraped, a clear fluid that smelled like honey seeped out. This world was in the station's catalog, Miller had said. *I could live here someday.* The thought was astounding.

The sky shifted, and now all the ships that had been trapped around the station were visible. They drifted slowly away from each other. "You let them go?"

"I didn't. Station's off lockdown," Miller said. "And I've killed the security system permanently. No need for it. Just an accident waiting to happen when one of you monkeys sticks a finger where it doesn't belong. Is this Ashford cocksucker really thinking he can hurt the gates?"

"And there are worlds like this on the other side of all those gates?"

"Some of them, maybe. Who knows?" Miller turned to face Holden again, his blue eyes eerie and full of secrets. "Someone fought a war here, kid. One that spanned this galaxy and maybe more. My team lost, and they're all gone now. A couple billion years gone. Who knows what's waiting on the other side of those doors?"

"We'll find out, I guess," Holden replied, putting on a bold front but frightened in spite of himself.

"Doors and corners," Miller said again. Something in his voice told Holden it was the last warning.

They looked up at the sky, watching the ships slowly drift away from them. Holden waited to see the first missiles fly, but it didn't happen. Everyone was playing nice. Maybe what had happened on the *Behemoth* had changed people. Maybe they'd take that change back to where they came from, infect others with it. It was a lot to hope for, but Holden was an unapologetic optimist. Give people the information they need. Trust them to do the right thing. He didn't know any other way to play it.

Or maybe the ships moving was just Miller playing with his simulation, and humanity hadn't learned a thing.

"So," Holden said after a few minutes of quiet sky watching. "Thanks for the visit. I guess I'd better be getting back to my gunfight."

"Not done with you," Miller said. The tone was light, but the words were ominous.

"Okay."

"I wasn't built to fix shit humanity broke," Miller said. "I didn't come here to open gates for you and get the lockdown to let you go. That's incidental. The thing that made me just builds roads. And now it's using me to find out what happened to the galaxy-spanning civilization that wanted the road."

"Why does that matter now, if they're all gone?"

"It doesn't," Miller said with a weary shrug. "Not a bit. If you set the nav computer on the *Roci* to take you somewhere, and then fall over dead a second later, can the *Roci* decide it doesn't matter anymore and just not go?"

"No," Holden said, understanding and finding a sadness for this Miller construct he wouldn't have guessed was possible.

"We were supposed to connect with the network. We're just trying to do that, doesn't matter that the network's gone. What came up off of Venus is dumb, kid. Just knows how to do one thing. It doesn't know how to investigate. But I do. And it had me. So I'm going to investigate even though none of the answers will mean fuck-all to the universe at large."

"I understand," Holden said. "Good luck, Miller, I—"

"I said I'm not done with you."

Holden took a step back, suddenly very frightened about where this might be going. "What does that mean?"

"It means, kid, that I'll need a ride."

Holden was floating in free fall in an environment suit in absolute darkness. People were yelling. There was the sound of a gunshot, then silence, then an electric pop and a groan.

"Stop!" someone yelled. Holden couldn't place the voice. "Everyone stop shooting!"

Because someone was saying it with authority in their voice, people did. Holden fumbled with the controls on his wrist, and his suit's light came on. The rest of his team quickly followed his example. Corin and Cass were still unhurt. Holden wondered how long in actual time his jaunt into the simulation had taken.

"My name is Hector Cortez," the stop-firing voice said. "What's happening out there? Does anyone know?"

"It's over," Holden yelled back, then let his body relax into a dead man's float in the corridor. He was so tired that it was a struggle to not just go to sleep right where he was. "It's all over. You can turn everything back on."

Lights started coming on in the bridge as people took out hand terminals or emergency flashlights.

"Call Ruiz," Cortez said. "Have her send a team up here to fix whatever Clarissa did. We need to get the ship's power back. People will be panicking in the habitation drum right now. And get a medical team up here."

Holden wondered where Ashford was and why this Cortez guy was in charge. But he was saying all the right things, so Holden let it go. He pushed his way into the bridge, ready to help where he could, but keeping his hand near his pistol. Cass and Naomi traded places with Juarez, so Naomi could help with the repairs.

Clarissa, formerly Melba, was floating near an open access panel, blood seeping out of a gunshot wound. Cortez was pressing an emergency bandage to it. Ashford floated across the room, his mouth slack and his muscles twitching. Holden wondered if the captain was dead and then didn't care.

"Naomi. Call down to the radio offices. See if they've got working comms. Find out about Anna and Monica and Amos. Try to raise the *Roci* next. I really really want to get the hell out of here."

She nodded and started trying to make connections.

"Will she live?" Holden asked the white-haired man tending to her.

"I think so," he replied. "She did this," he added, waving a hand around to indicate the lack of lights and power.

"Huh," Holden said. "I guess I'm glad we didn't space her."

Chapter Fifty-Three: Clarissa

She woke up in stages, aware of the discomfort before she knew what hurt. Aware that something was wrong before she could even begin to put together some kind of story, some frame that gave the loose, rattling toolbox of sensations any kind of meaning. Even when the most abstract parts of herself returned—her name, where she was—Clarissa was mostly aware that she was compromised. That something was wrong with her.

The room was dirty, the air a few degrees too hot. She lay in the thin, sweat-stinking bed, an IV drip hanging above her. The significance of that took a long time to come to her. The bag hung there. She wasn't floating. There was gravity. She didn't know if it was spin or thrust, or even the calm pull of mass against mass that being on a planet brought. She didn't have the context to know. Only that it was nice to have weight again. It meant that something had gone right. Something was working.

When she closed her eyes, she dreamed that she had killed Ren, that she'd hidden him inside her own body and so she had to keep anyone from taking an imaging scan for fear they'd find him in her. It was a pleasure to wake up and remember that everyone already knew.

Sometimes Tilly came, sat by her bed. She looked like she'd been crying. Clarissa wanted to ask what was wrong, but she didn't have the strength. Sometimes Anna was there. The doctor who checked on her was a beautiful old woman with eyes that had seen everything. Cortez never came. Sleeping and waking lost their edges. Healing and being ill too. It was difficult if not impossible to draw a line between them.

She woke once to voices, to the hated voice, to Holden. He was standing at the foot of her bed, his arms crossed on his chest. Naomi was next to him, and then the others. The pale one who looked like a truck driver, the brown one who looked like a schoolteacher. Amos and Alex. The crew of the *Rocinante*. The people she hadn't managed to kill. She was glad to see them.

"There is absolutely no way," Holden said.

"Look at her," Anna said. Clarissa craned her neck to see the woman standing behind her. The priest looked older. Worn out. Or maybe distilled. Cooked down to something like her essence. She was beautiful too. Beautiful and terrible and uncompromising in her compassion. It was in her face. It made her hard to look at. "She'll be killed."

Alex, the schoolteacher, raised his hand.

"You mean she'll be tried in a court of law, with a lawyer, for killin' a bunch of folks that we all pretty much know she killed."

I did, Clarissa thought. *It's true*. Above her, Anna pressed her hands together.

"I mean that's what I want to happen," Anna said. "A trial. Lawyers. Justice. But I need someone to get her safely from here to the courts on Luna. With the evacuation starting, you have the only independent ship in the slow zone. You are the only crew that I trust to get her out safely."

Naomi looked over at Holden. Clarissa couldn't read the woman's expression.

"I'm not taking her on my ship," Holden said. "She tried to kill us. She almost *did* kill Naomi."

"She also saved you both," Anna said. "And everybody else."

"I'm not sure being a decent human that one time means I owe her something," Holden said.

"I'm not saying it does," Anna said. "But if we don't treat her with the same sense of justice that we'd ask for ourselves—"

"Look, Red," Amos said. "Everybody in this room except maybe you and the captain has a flexible sense of morality. None of us got clean hands. That's not the point."

"This is a tactical thing," Alex agreed.

"It is?" Holden said.

"It is," Naomi said. "Pretend that she's not a danger in and of herself. Taking her on board, even just to transport her to a safe place, puts us at risk from three different legal systems, and our situation is already...'tenuous' is a nice word."

Clarissa reached up, took Anna's shirt between her fingers, tugging like a child at her mother.

"It's okay," she croaked. "I understand. It's all right."

"How much?" Anna asked. And then, off their blank looks, "If it's just risk versus return, how much would it take to be worth it to you?"

"More than you have," Holden said, but there was an apology in his tone. He didn't want to disappoint Anna and he didn't want to do what she said. No way for him to win.

"What if I bought the *Rocinante*?" Anna said.

"It's not for sale," Holden said.

"Not from you. I know about your legal troubles. What if I bought the *Rocinante* from Mars. Gave you the rights to it, free and clear."

"You're going to buy a warship?" Alex said. "Do churches get to do that?"

"Sure," Holden said, "do that, and I'll smuggle her out."

Anna held up a finger, then pulled her hand terminal out of her pocket. Clarissa could see her hands were trembling. She tapped at the screen, and a few seconds later a familiar voice came from the box.

"Annie," Tilly Fagan said. "Where are you? I'm having cock-tails with half a dozen very important people and they're boring me to tears. The least you can do is come up and let them fawn over you for a while."

"Tilly," Anna said. "You remember that really expensive favor you owe me? I know what it is."

"I'm all ears," Tilly said.

"I need you to buy the *Rocinante* from Mars and give it to Captain Holden." Tilly was silent. Clarissa could practically see the woman's eyebrows rising. "It's the only way to take care of Clarissa."

Tilly's exhalation could have been a sigh or laughter.

"Sure, what the hell. I'll tell Robert to do it. He will. It'll be less than I'd get in a divorce. Anything else, dear? Shall I change the Earth's orbit for you while I'm at it?"

"No," Anna said. "That's plenty."

"You're damn right it is. Get up here soon. Really, everyone's swooning over you, and it'll be much more amusing for me to watch them try to squeeze up next to you in person."

"I will," Anna said. She put her hand terminal back in her pocket and took Clarissa's hand in her own. Her fingers were warm. "Well?"

Holden's face had gone pale. He looked from Clarissa to Anna and back and blew out a long breath.

"Um," he said. "Wow. Okay. We may not be going home right away, though. Is that cool?"

Clarissa held out her hand, astounded by its weight. It took them all a moment to understand what she was doing. Then Holden—the man she'd moved heaven and earth to humiliate and murder—took her hand.

"Pleased to meet you," she croaked.

They installed a medical restraint cuff to her ankle set to sedate her on a signal from any of the crew, or if it detected any of the products of her artificial glands, or if she left the crew decks of the ship. It was three kilos of formed yellow plastic that clung to her leg like a barnacle. The transfer came during the memorial service. Captain Michio Pa, her face still bandaged from the fighting, spoke in glowing terms about Carlos Baca and Samantha Rosenberg and a dozen other names and commended their ashes to the void. Then each of the commanders of the other ships in the flotilla took their turns, standing before the cameras on the decks of their own ships, speaking a few words, moving on. No one mentioned Ashford, locked away and sedated. No one mentioned her.

It was the last ceremony before the exodus. Before the return. Clarissa watched it on her hand terminal when she wasn't looking at the screen that showed the shuttle's exterior view. The alien station was inert now. It didn't glow, didn't react, didn't read to the sensors as anything more than a huge slug of mixed metals and carbonate structures floating in a starless void.

"They're not all going back, you know," Alex said. "The Martian team is plannin' to stay here, run surveys on all the gates. See what's on the other side."

"I didn't know that," Clarissa said.

"Yeah. This right now," the pilot said, gesturing toward the screen where a UN captain was speaking earnestly into the camera, her eyes hard as marbles and her jaw set against the sorrow of listing the names of the dead. "This is the still point. Before, this was all fear. After this, it'll all be greed. But this…" He sighed. "Well, it's a nice moment, anyway."

"It is," Clarissa said.

"So, just to check, are you still plannin' to kill the captain? Because, you know, if you are it seems like you at least owe us a warning."

"I'm not," she said.

"And if you were?"

"I'd still say I wasn't. But I'm not."

"Fair enough."

"Okay, Alex," Holden said from the back. "Are we there yet?"

"Just about to knock," Alex said. He tapped on the control panel, and on the screen the *Rocinante*'s exterior lights came on. The ship glowed gold and silver in the blackness, like seeing a whole city from above. "Okay, folks. We're home."

Clarissa's bunk was larger than her quarters in the *Cerisier*, smaller than the one from the *Prince*. She wasn't sharing it with anyone, though. It was hers as much as anything was.

All she had for clothing was a jumpsuit with the name *Tachi* imprinted in the weave. All her toiletries were the standard ship issue. Nothing was hers. Nothing was her. She kept to her room, going out to the galley and the head when she needed to. It wasn't fear, exactly, so much as the sense of wanting to stay out of the way. It wasn't her ship, it was theirs. She wasn't one of them, and she didn't deserve to be. She was a paid passenger, and not a fare they'd even wanted. The awareness of that weighed on her.

Over time, the bunk began to feel more like her cell on the *Behemoth* than anything else. That was enough to drive her out a little. Only a little, though. She'd seen the galley before in simulations, when she'd been planning how to destroy it, where to place her override. It looked different in person. Not smaller or larger, exactly, but different. The crew moved through the space going from one place to another, passing through in the way she couldn't. They ate their meals and had their meetings, ignoring her like she was a ghost. Like she'd already lost her place in the world.

"Well," Holden said, his voice grim, "we have a major problem. We're out of coffee."

"We still got beer," Amos said.

"Yes," Holden said. "But beer is not coffee. I've put in a request with the *Behemoth*, but I haven't heard back, and I can't see going into the vast and unknown void without coffee."

Alex looked over at Clarissa and grinned.

"The captain doesn't like the fake coffee the *Roci* makes," he said. "Gives him gas."

Clarissa didn't answer. She wasn't sure she was supposed to.

"It does not," Holden said. "That was one time."

"More than once, Cap'n," Amos said. "And no offense, but it does smell like a squirrel crawled up your ass and died there."

"Okay," Holden said, "you've got no room to complain. As I recall, I was the one who cleaned your bunk after that experiment with vodka goulash."

"He's got a point," Alex said. "That was damn nasty."

"I just about shat out my intestinal lining, that's true," Amos said, his expression philosophical, "but I'd still put that against the captain's coffee farts."

Alex made a fake gagging noise, and Amos buzzed his lips against his palm, making a rude sound. Naomi looked from one to the other like she didn't know whether to laugh or smack them.

"I don't get gas," Holden said. "I just like the taste of real coffee better."

Naomi put her hand on Clarissa's forearm and leaned close. Her smile was gentle and unexpected.

"Have I mentioned how nice it is to have another woman on the ship?" she asked.

It was a joke. Clarissa understood that. But it was a joke that included her, and her tears surprised her.

"I appreciate your saying all that about Bull," a man's voice said. Clarissa, moving through the ship, didn't recognize it. An unfamiliar voice in a spaceship caught the attention like a strange sound in her bedroom. She paused. "He was a friend for a lot of years, and...and I'll miss him."

She shifted, angled back toward the other crew cabins. Holden's door was open, and he sat in his crash couch, looking up at his monitor. Instead of the tactical display of the ships, the stations, the Rings, a man's face dominated the screen. She recognized Fred Johnson, traitor to Earth and head of the Outer Planets Alliance. The Butcher of Anderson Station. He looked old, his hair almost all gone to white, and his eyes the yellow color of old ivory.

"I asked a lot from him," the recording went on. "He gave a lot back to me. It...it got me thinking. I have a bad habit, Captain, of asking more than people can give sometimes. Of demanding more than I can fairly expect. I'm wondering if I might have done something like that with you."

"Gee, you think?" Holden said to the screen, though as far as she could see he wasn't recording.

"If I did, I apologize. Just between us. One commander to another. I regret some of the decisions I've made. I figure you can relate to that in your own way.

"I've decided to keep the *Behemoth* in place. We're sending out soil and supplies to start farming on the drum. It does mean the OPA's military fleet just lost its big kahuna. But it looks like we've got a thousand planets opening up for exploration, and having the only gas station on the turnpike is too sweet a position to walk away from. If you and your crew want to help out with the effort, escort some ships from Ganymede out to the Ring, there might be a few contracts in it for you. So that's the official part. Talk about it with the others, and let me know what decisions you come to."

Fred Johnson nodded once to the camera, and the screen fell to the blue emptiness and split circle of the OPA's default. Holden looked over his shoulder. She saw him see her.

"Hey," she said.

"Hey."

They were silent for a moment. She didn't know what to say. She wanted to apologize too, to walk down the path Fred Johnson had just showed her, but she couldn't quite.

She waited to see whether Holden would reach out to her. When he didn't she pulled herself back down toward the crew quarters. Her stomach felt tight and uncomfortable.

They weren't friends. They wouldn't be, because some things couldn't be made right.

She'd have to be okay with that.

Amos smelled of solvent and sweat. Of all the crew, he was the one most like the people she knew. Soladad and Stanni. And Ren. He came into the galley with a welding rig on, the mask pushed up over his forehead. He smiled when he saw her.

"You did a number on the place," Amos said. She knew that if the occasion arose, he would be perfectly willing to kill her. But until that moment, he'd be jovial and casual. That counted for more than she'd expected. "I mean, you had a salvage mech. Those are pretty much built for peeling steel."

"I didn't at the end," she said. "It ran out of power. The locker in the airlock was all me."

"Really?" he said

"Yeah."

"Well," he said, pulling a bulb of the fake coffee from the machine and drifting over to the table. "That was pretty impressive, then."

She imagined him working, the mask down to hide his face, the sparks, the flickering of his great hunched shadow. Hephaestus, the smith of the Gods, laboring in his underworld. It was the kind of association Clarissa Mao would make. Melba Koh would only have thought about the temperature of the arc, the composition of the plates he was fusing together. She could have both of those thoughts, but neither were really hers.

She was on the float now. Later, when the ship was under way and thrust gravity pinned her to the deck, she'd still be on the float. Her world had been constructed around stories about who she was. Jules-Pierre's daughter, Julie Mao's sister, the crew lead on the *Cerisier*, instrument of her father's vengeance. Now she was no one. She was a piece of baggage on her old enemy's ship going from one prison to another, and she didn't even resent it. The last time she'd felt this nameless, she'd probably been in an amniotic sac.

"What was the problem?"

"Hmm?"

"You said I really did a number on something. What's the problem?"

"Deck hatch between the machine shop and here gets stuck. Ever since you crumpled it up. Binds about half open."

"Did you check the retracting arm?"

Amos turned to her, frowning. She shrugged.

"Sometimes these door actuators put on an uneven load when they start to burn out. We probably swapped out four or five of them on the trip out here."

"Yeah?"

"Just a thought," she said. And then a moment later, "When we get back to Luna, they're going to kill me, aren't they?"

"If you're lucky, yeah. UN still has the death penalty on the books, but they don't use it much. I figure you'll be living in a tiny cell for the rest of your life. If it was me, I'd prefer a bullet."

"How long until we get there?"

"About five weeks."

They were silent for a moment.

"I'll miss this place," she said.

Amos shrugged.

"Actuator arm, huh? Worth checking. You want to help me take a look?"

"I can't," she said, gesturing at the clamp on her leg.

"Shit, I can reprogram that. Least enough to get you down to the machine shop. We'll grab you a tool belt, Peaches. Let's crack that thing open."

An hour later, she was running her hand over the frame of the door, looking for the telltale scrape of binding sites. *This was me*, she thought. *I broke it.*

"What'cha think, Peaches?" Amos asked from behind her.

"Feels good to fix something," she said.

Epilogue: Anna

Anna sat in the observation lounge of the *Thomas Prince* and looked out at the stars.

The lounge was a dome-shaped room where every flat surface was a high-definition screen displaying a 360-degree view of the outside. To Anna, sitting in it felt like flying through space on a park bench. It had become her favorite place on the ship, with the stars burning in their bright steady colors, no atmosphere to make them twinkle. They felt so close now. Like she could reach out and touch them.

Her hand terminal beeped at her to remind her that she was in the middle of recording a video message. She deleted the time she'd spent looking at the stars and started the recording again.

"So, that letter from the conference bishop turned out to be a request for a formal meeting. Apparently some people have complained about me. Probably Ashford. Neck deep in his own legal problems with the OPA and still finding time to make trouble for everyone else. But don't worry about it. They'll ask, I'll answer, I've got pretty good reasons for everything I did. I have lots of offers of support from people I worked with on the fleet. I probably won't need them. Speaking of which, I've invited my friend Tilly Fagan to come visit us in Moscow. She's abrasive and cranky and has no social filters at all. You'll love her. She can't wait to meet Nami."

Anna paused to attach a picture she'd taken of Tilly to the message. Tilly was looking at the camera through narrowed eyes, just seconds from telling Anna to "get that fucking thing out of my face." She held a cigarette in one hand; her other was pointing accusingly. It was not the nicest picture of Tilly she had, but it was the most accurate.

"Speaking of Nami, thank you so much for the videos you sent. I can't believe how enormous she's gotten. And crawling around in full gravity like she was born to it. She'll be walking again in no time. Thank you for taking her home. Sometimes I wish I'd just gone with you. Most of the time, actually. But then I think about all the things I did inside the Ring, and I wonder if any of it would have turned out as well if I hadn't helped. It seems arrogant to think that way, but I also believe that God nudges people toward the places they need to be. Maybe I was needed. I still plan on being very contrite when I get back. You, the bishop, Nami, my family, I have a lot of apologizing to do."

As clear as if she'd been in the room, Anna heard Nono say, *You never ask for permission, you just apologize later.* She laughed until her eyes watered. She wiped them and said to the camera, "You're still here, Nono. Still in my head. But I'd trade anything to have you hold me. The *Prince* will take another month to get back. It's an eternity. I love you."

She picked up the pillow she'd brought with her and held it tight to her chest. "This is you and Nami. This is both of you. I love you both so much."

She killed the recording and sent it off, winging ahead of the

Prince to Nono at the speed of light. Still too slow. She wiped away the tears that had accumulated at the corners of her eyes.

Outside, a flare of white light lit the sky, a line of fire a few centimeters long. Another ship in the flotilla, returning home. One of the *Prince's* escort ships, to be so close. Finally going back, but without many of the sailors she'd brought to the Ring. Families would be waiting for her to bring their loved ones home, only to receive flags, posthumous medals, letters of sympathy. It wouldn't be enough to fill the holes those lost people left in their lives. It was never enough.

But the ships from Earth, Mars, and the various stations of the outer planets *were* going home. And they were bringing news of the greatest opportunity humanity had ever been offered. In the midst of all the sadness and tragedy, hope.

Would Nami spend her life at one of those points of light she could see right now? It was possible. Her baby had been born into a world where her parents couldn't afford to give her a sibling, where she'd have to work two years just to prove to the government she was worth receiving an education. Where resources were rapidly diminishing, and the battle to keep the waste from piling up used more and more of what was left.

But she'd grow up in a world without limits. Where a short trip took you to one of the stars, and the bounty of worlds circling them. Where what job you did or what education you pursued or how many children you had was your choice, not a government mandate.

It was dizzying to think of.

Someone walked into the lounge behind her, their footsteps clicking. "Tilly, I just sent—" Anna started, but stopped when she turned around and saw Hector Cortez.

"Doctor Volovodov," he said, his tone a mild apology.

"Doctor Cortez," she replied. The renewed formality between them seemed silly to Anna, but Hector insisted on it. "Please, sit." She patted the bench next to her.

"I hope I'm not disturbing you," he said, sitting and staring out at the stars. Not looking at her. He didn't look her in the eye anymore.

"Not at all. Just recording a message home and enjoying the view."

They sat silently for a few moments, watching the stars.

"Esteban lost," Cortez said, as if they'd been talking about that all along.

"I don't— Oh, the secretary-general. He did?"

"Nancy Gao is the new SG. You can see Chrisjen Avasarala's fingerprints all over that one."

"Who?"

Cortez laughed. It sounded genuine, a nice loud rumble coming up from his belly. "Oh, she would love to hear you say that."

"Who is she?"

"She's the politician no one has ever voted for, that runs the UN like her own personal fiefdom and keeps her name out of the press. The fact that she controls your home government and you've never heard of her means she's very, very good."

"Oh," Anna said. She was not a political creature. She felt that politics was the second most evil thing humanity had ever invented, just after lutefisk.

There was another long silence. Anna wondered where Tilly was, and if she'd show up and rescue her from the awkwardness of the moment.

"You backed the right horse," Cortez finally said. "I picked a bad one. I hope you won't hold that against me. I've grown to respect you a great deal, in spite of our differences. I wouldn't like it if you hated me."

"I don't, Hector," Anna said, taking his hand in both of hers and squeezing it. "Not at all. It was terrible, what we all went through. We all made bad decisions because we were afraid. But you're a good man. I believe that."

Cortez gave her a grateful smile and patted her hand. Anna nodded her head at the star field splashed across the wall.

"So many stars," she said. "Some of them might be ours someday."

"I wonder," Hector replied, his voice low and sad. "I wonder if we should have them. God gave man the Earth. He never promised him the stars. I wonder if He'll follow us out there."

Anna squeezed his hand again, and then let it go. "The God I believe in is bigger than all of this. Nothing we ever learn can be an attack on Him as long as that's true."

Cortez gave a noncommittal grunt.

"I want her to have them," she said, pointing at the spray of light around her. "My little Nami, I want her to have all of that someday."

"Whatever she finds out there," Cortez said, "just remember it's the future *you* chose for her."

His words were full of hope and threat.

Like the stars.

Acknowledgments

Once again, we have more people to thank than space to thank them in. This book and this series wouldn't exist without the hard work of our agent Danny Baror and the support and dedication of Tom Bouman, Susan Barnes, Ellen Wright, Tim Holman, Alex Lencicki, and the whole crew at Orbit. Thanks to the amazing Daniel Dociu for giving us the art that people can't help but pick up off the shelf, and to Kirk Benshoff for creating that wonderful design that ties the whole series together. We'll never be able to adequately express our gratitude to Carrie, Kat, and Jayné for feedback and support, and to Scarlet for allowing us to distract her with *Mythbusters* while we work. Thanks to the *Mythbusters* crew for being so entertaining to scientifically curious six-year-olds. Thanks again to the whole Sake River gang. Much of the cool in the book belongs to them. As always, the errors and infelicities and egregious fudging was all us.

extras

orbit

meet the author

JAMES S. A. COREY is the pen name of fantasy authors Daniel Abraham and Ty Franck. They both live in Albuquerque, New Mexico. Find out more about this series at www.the-expanse.com.

introducing

If you enjoyed
ABADDON'S GATE,
look out for

CIBOLA BURN

Book Four of the Expanse

by James S. A. Corey

Prologue: Bobbie Draper

A thousand worlds, Bobbie thought as the tube doors closed. And not just a thousand worlds. A thousand *systems*. Suns. Gas giants. Asteroid belts. Everything that humanity had spread to, a thousand times over. The screen above the seats across from her showed a newsfeed, but the speakers were broken, the man's voice too fuzzed to make out the words. The graphic that zoomed in and out beside him was enough for her to follow. New data had come in from the probes that had gone through the gates. Here was another image of an unfamiliar sun, circles to mark the orbits of new planets. All of them empty. Whatever had built the protomolecule and fired it toward Earth back in the depths of time wasn't answering calls anymore. The bridge builder had opened the way, and no great gods had come streaming through.

It was astounding, Bobbie thought, how quickly humanity could go from *What unimaginable intelligence fashioned these soul-wrenching wonders?* to *Well, since they're not here, can I have their stuff?*

"'Scuse me," a man's phlegmy voice said. "You wouldn't have a little spare change for a veteran, would you?"

She looked away from the screens. The man was thin, gray-faced. His body had the hallmarks of a childhood in low g: long body, large head. He licked his lips and leaned forward.

"Veteran, are you?" she said. "Where'd you serve?"

"Ganymede," the man said, nodding and looking off with an attempt at nobility. "I was there when it all came down. When I got back here, government dropped me on my ass. I'm just trying to save up enough to book passage to Ceres. I've got family there."

Bobbie felt a bubble of rage in her breast, but she tried to keep her voice and expression calm. "You try veteran's outreach? Maybe they could help you."

"I just need something to eat," he said, his voice turning nasty. Bobbie looked up and down the car. Usually there would be a few people in the cars at this time. The neighborhoods under the Aurorae Sinus were all connected by evacuated tube. Part of the great Martian terraforming project that had begun before Bobbie was born and would go on long after she was dead. Just now, there was no one. She considered what she would look like to the beggar. She was a big woman, tall as well as broad, but she was sitting down, and the sweater she'd chosen was a little baggy. He might have been under the misapprehension that her bulk was fat. It wasn't.

"What company did you serve with?" she asked. He blinked. She knew she was supposed to be a little scared of him, and he was uneasy because she wasn't.

"Company?"

"What company did you serve with?"

He licked his lips again. "I don't want to—"

"Because it's a funny thing," she said. "I could have sworn I knew pretty much everyone who was on Ganymede when the fighting started. You know, you go through something like that, and you remember. Because you see a lot of your friends die. What was your rank? I was gunnery sergeant."

The gray face had gone closed and white. The man's mouth pinched. He pushed his hands deeper into his pockets and mumbled something.

"And now?" Bobbie went on, "I work thirty hours a week with veteran's outreach. And I'm just fucking sure we could give a fine upstanding veteran like you a break."

He turned, and her hand went out to his elbow faster than he could pull away. His face twisted with fear and pain. She drew him close. When she spoke, her voice was careful. Each word clear and sharp.

"Find. Another. Story."

"Yes, ma'am," the beggar said. "I will. I'll do that."

The car shifted, decelerating into the first Breach Candy station. She let him go and stood up. His eyes went a little wider when she did. Her genetic line went back to Samoa, and she sometimes had that effect on people who weren't expecting her. Sometimes she felt a little bad about it. Not now.

Her brother lived in a nice middle-class hole in Breach Candy, not far from the lower university. She'd lived with him for a time after she got back home to Mars, and she was still putting the pieces of her life back together. It was a longer process than she'd expected. And part of the aftermath was that she felt like she owed her brother something. Family dinner nights was part of that.

The halls of Breach Candy were sparse. The advertisements on the walls flickered as she came near, face recognition tracking her and offering up the products and services they thought she might want. Dating services, gym memberships, take-out shwarma, the new Mbeki Soon film, psychological counseling. Bobbie tried not to take it personally. Still, she wished there were more people around, a few more faces to add variety to the mix. To let her tell herself the ads were probably meant for someone walking nearby. Not for her.

But Breach Candy wasn't as full as it used to be. There were fewer people in the tube stations and hallways, fewer people coming to the veteran's outreach program. She heard that enrollment at the upper university was down six percent.

Humanity hadn't managed a single viable colony on the new worlds yet, but the probe data was enough. Humanity had its new frontier, and the cities of Mars were feeling the competition.

As soon as she stepped in the door, the rich scent of her sister-in-law's gumbo thickening the air and making her mouth water, she heard her brother and nephew, voices raised. It knotted her gut, but they were family. She loved them. She owed them. Even if they made the idea of take-out shwarma seem awfully tempting.

"—not what I'm saying," her nephew said. He was in upper university now, but when the family started fighting, she could still hear the six-year-old in his voice.

Her brother boomed in reply. Bobbie recognized the percussive tapping of his fingertips against the tabletop as he made his points. Drumming as a rhetorical device. Their father did the same thing.

"Mars is not optional." Tap. "It is not secondary." Tap. "These gates and whatever's on the other side of them isn't our home. The terraforming effort—"

"I'm not arguing against the terraforming," her nephew said as she walked into the room. Her sister-in-law nodded to her from the kitchen wordlessly. Bobbie nodded back. The dining room looked down into a living space where a muted newsfeed was showing long-distance images of unfamiliar planets with a beautiful black man in wire-rimmed glasses speaking earnestly between them. "All I'm saying is that we're going to have a lot of new data. Data. That's all I'm saying."

The two of them were hunched over the table like there was an invisible chessboard between them. A game of concentration and intellect that wrapped them both up until they couldn't see the world around them. In a lot of ways, that was true. She took her chair without either of them acknowledging she'd arrived.

"Mars," her brother said, "is the most studied planet there is. It doesn't matter how many new datasets you get that aren't about Mars. They aren't about Mars! It's like saying that seeing pictures of a thousand other tables will tell you about the one you're already sitting at."

"Knowledge is good," her nephew said. "You're the one who always told me that. I don't know why you're getting so bent about it now."

"How are things for you, Bobbie?" her sister-in-law said sharply, carrying a bowl to the table. Rice and peppers to use as a bed for the gumbo and a reminder to the others that there was a guest. The two men scowled at the interruption.

"Good," Bobbie said. "The contract with the shipyards came through. It should help us place a lot of vets in new jobs."

"Because they're building exploration ships and transports," her nephew said.

"*David.*"

"Sorry, Mom. But they are," David replied, not backing down. Bobbie scooped the rice into her bowl. "All the ships that are easy to retrofit, they're retrofitting, and then they're making more so that people can go to all the new systems."

Her brother took the rice and the serving spoon, chuckling under his breath to make it clear how little he respected his son's opinion. "The first real survey team is just getting to the first of these places—"

"There are already people living on New Terra, Dad! There were a bunch of refugees from Ganymede—" He broke off, shooting a guilty glance at Bobbie. Ganymede wasn't something they talked about over dinner.

"The survey team hasn't landed yet," her brother said. "It's going to be years before we have anything like real colonies out there."

"It's going to be *generations* before anyone walks on the surface here! We don't have a fucking magnetosphere!"

"Language, David!"

Her sister-in-law returned. The gumbo was black and fragrant with a sheen of oil across the top. The smell of it made Bobbie's mouth water. She put it on the slate trivet and handed the serving spoon to Bobbie.

"And how's your new apartment?" she asked.

"It's nice," Bobbie said. "Inexpensive."

"I wish you weren't living in Innis Shallow," her brother said. "It's a terrible neighborhood."

"No one's going to bother Aunt Bobbie," her nephew said. "She'd rip their heads off."

Bobbie grinned. "Naw, I just look at them mean, and they—"

From the living room, there was a sudden glow of red light. The newsfeed had changed. Bright red banners showed at the top and bottom, and on the screen, a jowly Earth woman looked soberly into the camera. The image behind her was of fire and then a stock image of an old colony ship. The words, black against the white of the flames, read TRAGEDY ON NEW TERRA.

"What happened?" Bobbie said. "What just *happened*?"

Chapter One: Basia

Basia Merton had been a gentle man, once. He hadn't been the sort of man who made bombs out of old metal lubricant drums and mining explosives.

He rolled another one out of the little workshop behind his house and toward one of First Landing's electric carts. The little stretch of buildings spread to the north and south, and then ended, the darkness of the plain stretching to the horizon. The flashlight hanging from his belt bounced as he walked, casting strange moving shadows across the dusty ground. Small alien animals hooted at him from outside the circle of light.

Nights on Ilus—he wouldn't call it New Terra—were very dark. The planet had thirteen tiny, low-albedo moons spaced so consistently in the same orbit that everyone assumed they were alien artifacts. Wherever they'd come from, they were more like captured asteroids than real moons to someone who grew up on the planet-sized satellites of Jupiter. And they did nothing to catch and reflect the light of Ilus' sun once it set. The local nighttime wildlife was mostly small birds and lizards. Or what Ilus' new human inhabitants thought of as birds and lizards. They shared only the most superficial external traits and a primarily carbon base with their terrestrial namesakes.

Basia grunted with effort as he lifted the barrel onto the back of the cart, and a second later an answering grunt came from a few meters away. A mimic lizard, curiosity drawing it right up to the edge of the light, its small eyes glittering. It grunted again, its wide, leathery, bullfrog-shaped head bobbing, and the air sac below its neck inflating and deflating with the sound. It waited for a moment, staring at him, and when he didn't respond, it crawled off into the dark.

Basia pulled elastic straps out of a toolbox and began securing the barrels to the bed of the cart. The explosive wouldn't go off just from falling on the ground. Or that was what Coop said, anyhow. Basia didn't feel like testing it.

"Baz," Lucia said. He flushed with embarrassment like a small boy caught stealing candy. Lucia knew what he was doing. He'd never been able to lie to her. But he'd hoped she would stay inside while he worked. Just her presence made him wonder if he was doing the right thing. If it was right, why did it make him so ashamed to have Lucia see him?

"Baz," she said again. Not insisting. Her voice sad, not angry.

"Lucy," he said, turning around. She stood at the edge of his light, a white robe clutched around her thin frame against the chill night air. Her face was a dark blur.

"Felcia's crying," she said, her tone not making it an accusation. "She's afraid for you. Come talk to your daughter."

Basia turned away and pulled the strap tight over the barrels, hiding his face from her. "I can't. They're coming," he said.

"Who? Who's coming?"

"You know what I mean. They're going to take everything we made here if we don't make a stand. We need time. This is how you get time. Without the landing pad, they've got to use the small shuttles. So we take away the landing pad. Make them rebuild it. No one's going to get hurt."

"If it gets bad," she said, "we can leave."

"No," Basia said, surprised to hear the violence in his voice. He turned and took a few steps, putting her face in the light. She was weeping. "No more leaving. We left Ganymede. Left Katoa and ran away and my family lived on a ship for a year while no one would give us a place to land. We're not running again. Not *ever* running again. *They* took all the children from me they get to take."

"I miss Katoa too," Lucia said. "But these people didn't kill him. It was a war."

"It was a business decision. They made a business decision, and then they made a war, and they took my son away." *And I let them,* he didn't say. *I took you and Felcia and Jacek, and I left Katoa behind because I thought he was dead. And he wasn't.* The words were too painful to speak, but Lucia heard them anyway.

"It wasn't your fault."

Yes, it was floated at the back of his mouth, but he swallowed.

"These people don't have any right to Ilus," he said, struggling to make his voice sound reasonable. "We were here first. We staked claim. We'll get the first load of lithium out, get the money in, then we can hire lawyers back home to make a real case. If the corporations already have roots here when that happens, it won't matter. We just need time."

"If you do this," Lucia said, "they'll send you to jail. Don't do that to us. Don't do that to your family."

"I'm doing this *for* my family," he said softly. It was worse than yelling. He hopped up behind the controls and stomped on the accelerator. The cart lurched off with a whine. He didn't look back, couldn't look back and see Lucy.

"*For* my family," he said again.

He drove away from his house and the ramshackle town that they'd started out calling First Landing back when they'd picked the site off the *Barbapiccola*'s sensor maps. No one had bothered to rename it when it had moved from being an idea to being a place. He drove toward the center of town, two rows of prefab buildings, until he hit the wide stretch of flattened dirt that served as the main road and turned toward the original landing site. The refugees who'd colonized Ilus had come down from their ship in small shuttles, so the only landing pad they'd needed was a flat stretch of ground. But the Royal Charter Energy people, the *corporate* people, who had a UN charter giving the world to them, would be coming down with heavy equipment. Heavy lift shuttles needed an actual landing pad. It had been built in the same open fields that the colony had used as their landing site.

That felt obscene to Basia. Invasive. The first landing site had significance. He'd imagined it someday being a park, with a monument at the center commemorating their arrival on this new world.

Instead, RCE had built a giant and gleaming metal monstrosity right over the top of their site. Worse, they'd hired the colonists to build it, and enough of them had thought it was a good idea that they'd actually done it.

It felt like being erased from history.

Scotty and Coop were waiting for him at the new landing pad when he arrived. Scotty was sitting on the edge of the metal plat-form, legs dangling over the side, smoking a pipe and spitting on the ground below his feet. A small electric lamp that sat beside him colored him with an eerie green light. Coop stood a little way off, looking up at the sky with bared teeth. Coop was an old-school Belter, and the agoraphobia treatments had been harder for him than others. The thin-faced man kept staring up at the void, fight-ing to get used to it like a kid pulling off scabs.

Basia pulled the cart up to the edge of the pad and hopped out to undo the straps holding the barrel bombs down.

"Give me a hand?" he said. Ilus was a large planet, slightly over one gravity. Even after six months of pharma to build his muscles and bones everything still felt too heavy. The thought of lifting the barrels back to the ground made the muscles in his shoulders twitch in anticipated exhaustion.

Scotty slid off the landing pad and dropped a meter and a half to the ground. He pushed his oily black hair out of his eyes and took another long puff on his pipe. Basia caught the pungent, skunky smell of Scotty's bathtub-grown cannabis mixed with freeze-dried tobacco leaves. Coop looked over, his eyes fighting for focus for a moment, and then the thin, cruel smile. The plan had been Coop's from the start.

"Mmm," Coop said. "Pretty."

"Don't get attached," Basia said. "They won't be around long."

Coop made a booming sound and grinned. Together they pulled the four heavy barrels off the cart and stood them in a row next to the pad. By the last one, they were all panting with effort. Basia leaned against the cart for a moment in silence while Scotty smoked off the last of his pipe and Coop set the blasting caps on the barrels. The detonators sat in the back of the cart like sleeping rattlesnakes, the red LEDs dormant for now.

In the darkness, the township sparkled. The houses they'd all built for themselves and one another glittered like stars brought down from the sky. Beyond them, there were the ruins. A long, low alien structure with two massive towers rising up above the landscape like a termite hill writ large. All of it was run through with passageways and chambers that no human had designed. In daylight, the ruins shone with the eerie colors of mother-of-pearl. In the night, they were only a deeper darkness. The mining pits were off past them, invisible as all but the dimmest glow of the work lights on the belly of the clouds. Truth was Basia didn't like the mines. The ruins were strange relics of the empty planet's past, and like anything that was uncanny without posing a threat, they faded from his awareness after the first few months. The mines carried history and expectations. He'd spent half a lifetime in tunnels of ice, and tunnels that ran through alien soil *smelled* wrong.

Coop made a sharp noise and shook his hand, cursing. Nothing blew up, so it couldn't be that bad.

"You think they'll pay us to rebuild it?" Scotty asked.

Basia cursed and spat on the ground.

"We wouldn't have to do this if it wasn't for people wanting to suck on RCE's tit," he said as he rolled the last barrel into place. "They can't land without this. All we had to do was not build it."

Scotty laughed out a cloud of smoke. "They were coming anyway. Might as well take their money. That's what people said."

"People are idiots," Basia said.

Scotty nodded, then smacked a mimic lizard off the passenger seat of the cart with one hand and sat down. He put his feet up on the dash and took another long puff on his pipe. "We gonna have to get gone, if we blow this. That blasting powder makes serious boom."

"Hey, mate," Coop shouted. "We're good. Let's make the place, ah?"

Scotty stood and started walking toward the pad. Basia stopped him, plucked the lit pipe from between his lips, and put it on the hood of the cart.

"Explosives," Basia said. "They explode."

Scotty shrugged, but he also looked chagrined. Coop was already easing the first barrel down onto its side when they reached him. "It's buena work this. Solid."

"Thank you," Basia said.

Coop lay down, back against the ground. Basia lay beside him. Scotty rolled the first bomb gently between them.

Basia climbed under the pad, pulling himself through the tangle of crisscrossed I-beams to each of the four barrels, turning on the remote detonators and syncing them. He heard a growing electric whine and felt a moment of irritation at Scotty for driving off with the cart before he realized the sound was of a cart arriving, not leaving.

"Hey," Peter's familiar voice yelled.

"Que la moog bastard doing here?" Coop muttered, wiping his hand across his forehead.

"You want me to go find out?" Scotty asked.

"Basia," Coop said. "Go see what Peter needs. Scotty hasn't got his back dirty yet."

Basia shifted himself out from under the landing and made room for Scotty and the last of the four bombs. Peter's cart was parked beside his own, and Peter stood between them, shifting from one foot to the other like he needed to piss. Basia's back and arms ached. He wanted this all over and to be back home with Lucia and Felcia and Jacek.

"What?" Basia said.

"They're coming," Pete said, whispering as if there were anyone who could hear them.

"Who's coming?"

"Everyone. The provisional governor. The corporate security team. Science and tech staff. *Everybody.* This is serious. They're landing a whole new government for us."

Basia shrugged. "Old news. They been burning eighteen months. That's why we're out here."

"No," Pete said, prancing nervously and looking up at the stars. "They're coming right now. *Edward Israel* did a braking burn half an hour ago. Got into high orbit."

The copper taste of fear flooded Basia's mouth. He looked up at the darkness. A billion unfamiliar stars, his same Milky Way galaxy, everyone figured, just seen from a different angle. His eyes shifted frantically, and then he caught it. The movement was subtle as the minute hand on an analog clock, but he saw it. The drop ship was dropping. The heavy shuttle was coming for the landing pad.

"I was going to get on the radio, but Coop said they monitor radio spectrum and—" Pete said, but by then Basia was already running back to the landing pad. Scotty and Coop were just pulling themselves out. Coop clapped clouds of dust off his pants and grinned.

"We got a problem," Basia said. "Ship's already dropped. Looks like they're in atmosphere already."

Coop looked up. The brightness from his flashlight threw shadows across his cheeks and into his eyes.

"Huh," he said.

"I thought you were on this, man. I thought you were paying attention to where they were."

Coop shrugged, neither agreeing nor denying.

"We've got to get the bombs back out," Basia said. Scotty started to kneel, but Coop put a restraining hand on his shoulder.

"Why?" he asked.

"They try to land now, they could set it all off," Basia said.

Coop's smile was gentle. "Could," he said. "And what if?"

Basia balled his fists. "They're coming down *now*."

"See that," Coop said. "Doesn't inspire a great sense of obligation. And however you cut it, there ain't time to pull them."

"Can take off the primers and caps," Basia said, hunkering down. He played his flashlight over the pad's superstructure.

"Maybe could, maybe couldn't," Coop said. "Question's should, and it's a limp little question."

"Coop?" Scotty said, his voice thin and uncertain. Coop ignored him.

"Opportunity, looks like to me," Coop said.

"There's people on that thing," Basia said, crawling under the pad. The nearest bomb's electronics were flat against the dirt. He put his aching shoulder against it and pushed.

"Isn't time, mate," Coop called.

"Might be if you got your ass in here," Basia shouted. The blasting cap clung to the barrel's side like a tick. Basia tried to dig his fingers into the sealant goo and pry the cap away.

"Oh shit," Scotty said with something too much like awe in his voice. "Baz, oh *shit*!"

The cap came loose. Basia pushed it in his pocket and started crawling toward the second bomb.

"No time," Coop shouted. "Best we get clear, try and blow it while they can still pull up."

In the distance, he heard one of the carts taking off. Pete, going for distance. And under that, another sound. The bass roar of braking engines. He looked at the three remaining bombs in despair and rolled out from under the pad. The shuttle was massive in the black sky, so close he could make out the individual thrusters.

He wasn't going to make it.

"Run!" he shouted. He and Scotty and Coop sprinted back toward the cart. The roar of the shuttle rose, grew deafening. Basia reached the cart and scooped up the detonator. If he could blow it early, the shuttle could pull out, get away.

"Don't!" Coop shouted. "We're too close!"

Basia slammed his palm on the button.

The ground rose up, hitting him hard, the rough dirt and rocks tearing at his hands and cheek as he came to a stop, but the pain was a distant thing. Some part of him knew he might be hurt very badly, might be in shock, but that seemed distant and easy to ignore too. What struck him most was how quiet everything was.

The world of sound stopped at his skull. He could hear his own breath, his heartbeat. Everything past that had the volume turned down to one.

He rolled onto his back and stared up at the star-speckled night sky. The heavy shuttle streaked overhead, half of it trailing fire, the sound of its engines no longer a bass roar but the scream of a wounded animal that he felt in his belly more than heard. The shuttle had been too close, the blast too large, some unlucky debris thrown into just the right path. No way to know. Some part of Basia knew this was very bad, but it was hard to pay much attention to it.

The shuttle disappeared from view, shrieking a death wail across the valley that came to him as a faint high piping sound, then sudden silence. Scotty was sitting beside him on the ground, staring off in the direction the ship had gone. Basia let himself lie back down.

When the bright spots it had left in his vision faded, the stars returned. Basia watched them twinkle, and wondered which one was Sol. So far away. But with the gates, close too. He'd knocked their shuttle down. They'd have to come now. He'd left them no choice.

A sudden spasm of coughing took him. It felt like his lungs were full of fluid, and he coughed it up for several minutes. With the coughing the pain finally came, wracking him from head to foot.

With the pain came the fear.

If you enjoyed
ABADDON'S GATE,
look out for

WAR DOGS

by Greg Bear

One more tour on the red.

Maybe my last.

They made their presence on Earth known thirteen years ago.

Providing technology and scientific insights far beyond what mankind was capable of. They became indispensable advisors and promised even more gifts that we just couldn't pass up. We called them Gurus.

It took them a while to drop the other shoe. You can see why, looking back.

It was a very big shoe, completely slathered in crap.

They had been hounded by mortal enemies from sun to sun, planet to planet, and were now stretched thin—and they needed our help.

And so our first bill came due. Skyrines like me were volunteered to pay the price. As always.

These enemies were already inside our solar system and were moving to establish a beachhead, but not on Earth.

On Mars.

Down to Earth

I'm trying to go home. As the poet said, if you don't know where you are, you don't know who you are. Home is where you go to get all that sorted out.

Hoofing it outside Skybase Lewis-McChord, I'm pretty sure this is Washington State, I'm pretty sure I'm walking along Pacific Highway, and this is the twenty-first century and not some fidging movie—

But then a whining roar grinds the air and a broad shadow sweeps the road, eclipsing cafés and pawnshops and loan joints—followed seconds later by an eye-stinging haze of rocket fuel. I swivel on aching feet and look up to see a double-egg-and-hawksbill burn down from the sky, leaving a rainbow trail over McChord field . . .

And I have to wonder.

I just flew in on one of those after eight months in the vac, four going out, three back. Seven blissful months in timeout, stuffed in a dark tube and soaked in Cosmoline.

All for three weeks in the shit. Rough, confusing weeks.

I feel dizzy. I look down, blink out the sting, and keep walking. Cosmoline still fidges with my senses.

Here on Earth, we don't say *fuck* anymore, the Gurus don't like it, so we say fidge instead. Part of the price of freedom. Out on the Red, we say fuck as much as we like. The angels edit our words so the Gurus won't have to hear.

SNKRAZ.

Joe has a funny story about *fuck*. I'll tell you later, but right now, I'm not too happy with Joe. We came back in separate ships, he did not show up at the mob center, and my Cougar is still parked outside Skyport Virginia. I could grab a shuttle into town, but Joe told me to lie low. Besides, I badly want time alone—time to stretch my legs, put down one foot after another. There's the joy of blue sky, if I can look up without keeling over, and open air without a helm—and minus the rocket smell—is a newness in the nose and a beauty in the lungs. In a couple of klicks, though, my insteps pinch and my calves knot. Earth tugs harsh after so long away. I want to heave. I straighten and look real serious, clamp my jaws, shake my head—barely manage to keep it down.

Suddenly, I don't feel the need to walk all the way to Seattle. I have my thumb and a decently goofy smile, but after half an hour and no joy, I'm making up my mind whether to try my luck at a minimall Starbucks when a little blue electric job creeps up behind me, quiet as a bad fart. Quiet is not good.

I spin and try to stop shivering as the window rolls down. The driver is in her fifties, reddish hair rooted gray. For a queasy moment, I think she might be MHAT sent from Madigan. Joe warned me, "For Christ's sake, after all that's happened, stay away from the doctors." MHAT is short for *Military Health Advisory Team*. But the driver is not from Madigan. She asks where I'm going. I say downtown Seattle. Climb in, she says. She's a colonel's secretary at Lewis, a pretty ordinary grandma, but she has these strange gray eyes that let me see all the way back to when her scorn shaped men's lives.

I ask if she can take me to Pike Place Market. She's good with that. I climb in. After a while, she tells me she had a son just like me. He became a hero on Titan, she says—but she can't really know that, because we aren't on Titan yet, are we?

I say to her, "Sorry for your loss." I don't say, *Glad it wasn't me.*

"How's the war out there?" she asks.

"Can't tell, ma'am. Just back and still groggy."

They don't let us know all we want to know, barely tell us all we need to know, because we might start speculating and lose focus.

She and I don't talk much after that. Fidging *Titan*. Sounds old and cold. What kind of suits would we wear? Would everything freeze solid? Mars is bad enough. We're almost used to the Red. Stay sharp on the dust and rocks. That's where our shit is at. Leave the rest to the generals and the Gurus.

All part of the deal. A really big deal.

Titan. Jesus.

Grandma in the too-quiet electric drives me north to Spring Street, then west to Pike and First, where she drops me off with a crinkle-eyed smile and a warm, sad finger-squeeze. The instant I turn and see the market, she pips from my thoughts. Nothing has changed since vac training at SBLM, when we tired of the local bars and drove north, looking for trouble but ending up right here. We liked the market. The big neon sign. The big round clock. Tourists and merchants and more tourists, and that ageless bronze pig out in front.

A little girl in a pink frock sits astride the pig, grinning and slapping its polished flank. What we fight for.

I'm in civvies but Cosmoline gives your skin a tinge that lasts for days, until you piss it out, so most everyone can tell I've been in timeout. Civilians are not supposed to ask probing questions, but they still smile like knowing sheep. *Hey, spaceman, welcome back! Tell me true, how's the vac?*

I get it.

A nice Laotian lady and her sons and daughter sell fruit and veggies and flowers. Their booth is a cascade of big and little peppers and hot and sweet peppers and yellow and green and red peppers, Walla Walla sweets and good strong brown and fresh green onions, red and gold and blue and russet potatoes, yams and sweet potatoes, pole beans green and yellow and purple and speckled, beets baby and adult, turnips open boxed in bulk and attached to sprays of crisp green leaf. Around the corner of the booth I see every kind of mushroom but the screwy kind. All that roughage dazzles. I'm accustomed to browns and pinks, dark blue, star-powdered black.

A salient of kale and cabbage stretches before me. I seriously consider kicking off and swimming up the counter, chewing through the thick leaves, inhaling the color, spouting purple and green. Instead, I buy a bunch of celery and move out of the tourist flow. Leaning against a corrugated metal door, I shift from foot to cramping foot, until finally I just hunker against the cool ribbed steel and rabbit down the celery leaves, dirt and all, down to the dense, crisp core. Love it. Good for timeout tummy.

Now that I've had my celery, I'm better. Time to move on. A mile to go before I sleep.

I doubt I'll sleep much.

Skyrines share flophouses, safe houses—refuges—around the major spaceports. My favorite is a really nice apartment in Virginia Beach. I could be heading there now, driving my Cougar across the Chesapeake Bay Bridge, top down, sucking in the warm sea breeze, but thanks to all that's happened—and thanks to Joe—I'm not. Not this time. Maybe never again.

I rise and edge through the crowds, but my knees are still shaky, I might not make it, so I flag a cab. The cabby is white and middle-aged, from Texas. Most of the fellows who used to cab here, Lebanese and Ethiopians and Sikhs, the younger ones at least, are gone to war now. They do well in timeout, better than white Texans. Brown people rule the vac, some say. There's a lot of brown and black and beige out there: east and west Indians, immigrant Kenyans and Nigerians and Somalis, Mexicans, Filipinos and Malaysians, Jamaicans and Puerto Ricans, all varieties of Asian—flung out in space frames, sticks clumped up in fasces—and then they all fly loose, shoot out puff, and drop to the Red. Maybe less dangerous than driving a hack, and certainly pays better.

I'm not the least bit brown. I don't even tan. I'm a white boy from Moscow, Idaho, a blue-collar IT wizard who got tired of working in cubicles, tired of working around shitheads like myself. I enlisted in the Skyrines (that's pronounced SKY-reen), went through all the tests and boot and desert training, survived first orbital, survived first drop on the Red—came home alive and relatively sane—and now I make good money. Flight pay and combat pay—they call it engagement bonus—and Cosmoline comp.

Some say the whole deal of cellular suspension we call timeout shortens your life, along with solar flares and gamma rays. Others say no. The military docs say no but scandal painted a lot of them before my last deployment. Whole bunch at Madigan got augured for neglecting our spacemen. Their docs tend to regard spacemen, especially Skyrines, as slackers and complainers. Another reason to avoid MHAT. We make more than they do and still we complain. They hate us. Give them ground pounders any day.

"How many drops?" the Texan cabby asks.

"Too many," I say. I've been at it for six years.

He looks back at me in the mirror. The cab drives itself; he's in the seat for show. "Ever wonder why?" he asks. "Ever wonder what you're giving up to *them*? They ain't even human." Some think we shouldn't be out there at all; maybe he's one of them.

"Ever wonder?" he asks.

"All the time," I say.

He looks miffed and faces forward.

The cab takes me into Belltown and lets me out on a semicircular drive, in the shadow of the high-rise called Sky Tower One. I pay in cash. The cabby rewards me with a sour look, even though I give him a decent tip. He, too, pips from my mind as soon as I get out. Bastard.

The tower's elevator has a glass wall to show off the view before you arrive. The curved hall on my floor is lined with alcoves, quiet and deserted this time of day. I key in the number code, the door clicks open, and the apartment greets me with a cheery pluck of ascending chords. Extreme retro, traditional Seattle, none of it Guru tech; it's from before I was born.

Lie low. Don't attract attention.

Christ. No way am I used to being a spook.

The place is just as I remember it—nice and cool, walls gray, carpet and furniture gray and cloudy-day blue, stainless steel fixtures with touches of wood and white enamel. The couch and chairs and tables are mid-century modern. Last year's Christmas tree is still up, the water down to scum and the branches naked, but Roomba has sucked up all the needles. Love Roomba. Also pre-Guru, it rolls out of its stair slot and checks me out, nuzzling my toes like a happy gray trilobite.

I finish my tour—checking every room twice, ingrained caution, nobody home—then pull an Eames chair up in front of the broad floor-to-ceiling window and flop back to stare out over the Sound. The big sky still makes me dizzy, so I try to focus lower down, on the green and white ferries coming and going, and then on the nearly continuous lines of tankers and big cargo ships. Good to know Hanjin and Maersk are still packing blue and orange and brown steel containers along with Hogmaw or Haugley or what the hell. Each container is about a seventh the size of your standard space frame. No doubt filled with clever goods made using Guru secrets, juicing our economy like a snuck of meth.

And for that, too—for *them*—we fight.

VISIT THE ORBIT BLOG AT

FEATURING

BREAKING NEWS
FORTHCOMING RELEASES
LINKS TO AUTHOR SITES
EXCLUSIVE INTERVIEWS
EARLY EXTRACTS

AND COMMENTARY FROM OUR EDITORS

WITH REGULAR UPDATES FROM OUR TEAM,
ORBITBOOKS.NET IS YOUR SOURCE
FOR ALL THINGS ORBITAL.

WHILE YOU'RE THERE, JOIN OUR E-MAIL LIST
TO RECEIVE INFORMATION ON SPECIAL OFFERS,
GIVEAWAYS, AND MORE.

The Earth forces weren't attacking.
They were retreating.

It grabbed one UN Marine in its huge hands and tore him in half like paper. Titanium-and-ceramic armor ripped as easily as the flesh inside, spilling broken bits of technology and wet human viscera indiscriminately onto the ice. The remaining five soldiers ran even harder, but the monster chasing them barely slowed as it killed.

"Shoot it shoot it shoot it," Bobbie yelled, and opened fire. Her training and the technology of her combat suit combined to make her an extremely efficient killing machine. As soon as her finger pulled the trigger on her suit's gun, a stream of two-millimeter armor-piercing rounds streaked out at the creature at more than a thousand meters per second. In just under a second she'd fired fifty rounds at it. The creature was a relatively slow-moving human-sized target, running in a straight line. Her targeting computer could do ballistic corrections that would let her hit a softball-sized object moving at supersonic speeds. Every bullet she fired at the monster hit.

It didn't matter.

CALIBAN'S WAR

BOOK TWO OF THE EXPANSE

JAMES S. A. COREY

orbit

www.orbitbooks.net

Orbit
Hachette Book Group
1290 Avenue of the Americas, New York, NY 10104
www.HachetteBookGroup.com

First Edition: June 2012

Orbit is an imprint of Hachette Book Group, Inc. The Orbit name and logo are
trademarks of Little, Brown Book Group Limited.

The Hachette Speakers Bureau provides a wide range of authors for speaking
events. To find out more, go to www.hachettespeakersbureau.com or call (866)
376-6591.

The publisher is not responsible for websites (or their content) that are not
owned by the publisher.

The characters and events in this book are fictitious. Any similarity to real
persons, living or dead, is coincidental and not intended by the author.

Library of Congress Cataloging-in-Publication Data
Corey, James S. A.
  Caliban's war / by James S. A. Corey. — 1st ed.
    p. cm.
  ISBN 978-0-316-12906-0
  I. Title.
  PS3601.B677C35 2012
  813'.6—dc22

                                            2011031646

11

RRD-IN

Printed in the United States of America

To Bester and Clarke, who got us here

CALIBAN'S WAR

Prologue: Mei

Mei?" Miss Carrie said. "Please put your painting work away now. Your mother is here."

It took her a few seconds to understand what the teacher was saying, not because Mei didn't know the words—she was four now, and not a toddler anymore—but because they didn't fit with the world as she knew it. Her mother couldn't come get her. Mommy had left Ganymede and gone to live on Ceres Station, because, as her daddy put it, she needed some mommy-alone-time. Then, her heart starting to race, Mei thought, *She came back*.

"Mommy?"

From where Mei sat at her scaled-down easel, Miss Carrie's knee blocked her view of the coatroom door. Mei's hands were sticky with finger paints, red and blue and green swirling on her palms. She shifted forward and grabbed for Miss Carrie's leg as much to move it as to help her stand up.

"Mei!" Miss Carrie shouted.

Mei looked at the smear of paint on Miss Carrie's pants and the controlled anger on the woman's broad, dark face.

"I'm sorry, Miss Carrie."

"It's okay," the teacher said in a tight voice that meant it wasn't, really, but Mei wasn't going to be punished. "Please go wash your hands and then come put away your painting work. I'll get this down and you can give it to your mother. It is a doggie?"

"It's a space monster."

"It's a very nice space monster. Now go wash your hands, please, sweetheart."

Mei nodded, turned, and ran for the bathroom, her smock flapping around her like a rag caught in an air duct.

"And don't touch the wall!"

"I'm sorry, Miss Carrie."

"It's okay. Just clean it off after you've washed your hands."

She turned the water on full blast, the colors and swirls rushing off her skin. She went through the motions of drying her hands without caring whether she was dripping water or not. It felt like gravity had shifted, pulling her toward the doorway and the anteroom instead of down toward the ground. The other children watched, excited because she was excited, as Mei scrubbed the finger marks mostly off the wall and slammed the paint pots back into their box and the box onto its shelf. She pulled the smock up over her head rather than wait for Miss Carrie to help her, and stuffed it into the recycling bin.

In the anteroom, Miss Carrie was standing with two other grown-ups, neither of them Mommy. One was a woman Mei didn't know, space monster painting held gently in her hand and a polite smile on her face. The other was Doctor Strickland.

"No, she's been very good about getting to the toilet," Miss Carrie was saying. "There are accidents now and then, of course."

"Of course," the woman said.

"Mei!" Doctor Strickland said, bending down so that he was hardly taller than she was. "How is my favorite girl?"

"Where's—" she began, but before she could say *Mommy*, Doctor Strickland scooped her up into his arms. He was bigger than Daddy, and he smelled like salt. He tipped her backward, tickling her sides, and she laughed hard enough that she couldn't talk anymore.

"Thank you so much," the woman said.

"It's a pleasure to meet you," Miss Carrie said, shaking the woman's hand. "We really love having Mei in the classroom."

Doctor Strickland kept tickling Mei until the door to the Montessori cycled closed behind them. Then Mei caught her breath.

"Where's Mommy?"

"She's waiting for us," Doctor Strickland said. "We're taking you to her right now."

The newer hallways of Ganymede were wide and lush and the air recyclers barely ran. The knife-thin blades of areca palm fronds spilled up and out from dozens of hydroponic planters. The broad yellow-green striated leaves of devil's ivy spilled down the walls. The dark green primitive leaves of Mother-in-Law's Tongue thrust up beneath them both. Full-spectrum LEDs glowed white-gold. Daddy said it was just what sunlight looked like on Earth, and Mei pictured that planet as a huge complicated network of plants and hallways with the sun running in lines above them in a bright blue ceiling-sky, and you could climb over the walls and end up anywhere.

Mei leaned her head on Doctor Strickland's shoulder, looking over his back and naming each plant as they passed. *Sansevieria trifasciata. Epipremnum aureum.* Getting the names right always made Daddy grin. When she did it by herself, it made her body feel calmer.

"More?" the woman asked. She was pretty, but Mei didn't like her voice.

"No," Doctor Strickland said. "Mei here is the last one."

"*Chysalidocarpus lutenscens,*" Mei said.

"All right," the woman said, and then again, more softly: "All right."

The closer to the surface they got, the narrower the corridors became. The older hallways seemed dirtier even though there really wasn't any dirt on them. It was just that they were more used up. The quarters and labs near the surface were where Mei's grandparents had lived when they'd come to Ganymede. Back then, there hadn't been anything deeper. The air up there smelled funny, and the recyclers always had to run, humming and thumping.

The grown-ups didn't talk to each other, but every now and then Doctor Strickland would remember Mei was there and ask her questions: What was her favorite cartoon on the station feed? Who was her best friend in school? What kinds of food did she eat for lunch that day? Mei expected him to start asking the other questions, the ones he always asked next, and she had her answers ready.

Does your throat feel scratchy? No.

Did you wake up sweaty? No.

Was there any blood in your poop this week? No.

Did you get your medicine both times every day? Yes.

But this time, Doctor Strickland didn't ask any of that. The corridors they went down got older and thinner until the woman had to walk behind them so that the men coming the other direction could pass. The woman still had Mei's painting in her hand, rolled up in a tube so the paper wouldn't get wrinkles.

Doctor Strickland stopped at an unmarked door, shifted Mei to his other hip, and took his hand terminal out of his pants pocket. He keyed something into a program Mei had never seen before, and the door cycled open, seals making a rough popping sound like something out of an old movie. The hallway they walked into was full of junk and old metal boxes.

"This isn't the hospital," Mei said.

"This is a special hospital," Doctor Strickland said. "I don't think you've ever been here, have you?"

It didn't look like a hospital to Mei. It looked like one of the abandoned tubes that Daddy talked about sometimes. Leftover spaces from when Ganymede had first been built that no one used anymore except as storage. This one had a kind of airlock at the end, though, and when they passed through it, things looked a little more like a hospital. They were cleaner, anyway, and there was the smell of ozone, like in the decontamination cells.

"Mei! Hi, Mei!"

It was one of the big boys. Sandro. He was almost five. Mei waved at him as Doctor Strickland walked past. Mei felt better knowing the big boys were here too. If they were, then it was probably okay, even if the woman walking with Doctor Strickland wasn't her mommy. Which reminded her...

"Where's Mommy?"

"We're going to go see Mommy in just a few minutes," Doctor Strickland said. "We just have a couple more little things we need to do first."

"No," Mei said. "I don't want that."

He carried her into a room that looked a little like an examination room, only there weren't any cartoon lions on the walls, and the tables weren't shaped like grinning hippos. Doctor Strickland put her onto a steel examination table and rubbed her head. Mei crossed her arms and scowled.

"I want Mommy," Mei said, and made the same impatient grunt that Daddy would.

"Well, you just wait right here, and I'll see what I can do about that," Doctor Strickland said with a smile. "Umea?"

"I think we're good to go. Check with ops, load up, and let's release it."

"I'll go let them know. You stay here."

The woman nodded, and Doctor Strickland walked back out the door. The woman looked down at her, the pretty face not smiling at all. Mei didn't like her.

"I want my painting," Mei said. "That's not for you. That's for Mommy."

The woman looked at the painting in her hand as if she'd forgotten it was there. She unrolled it.

"It's Mommy's space monster," Mei said. This time, the woman smiled. She held out the painting, and Mei snatched it away. She made some wrinkles in the paper when she did, but she didn't care. She crossed her arms again and scowled and grunted.

"You like space monsters, kid?" the woman asked.

"I want my mommy."

The woman stepped close. She smelled like fake flowers and her fingers were skinny. She lifted Mei down to the floor.

"C'mon, kid," she said. "I'll show you something."

The woman walked away and for a moment Mei hesitated. She didn't like the woman, but she liked being alone even less. She followed. The woman walked down a short hallway, punched a keycode into a big metal door, like an old-fashioned airlock, and walked through when the door swung open. Mei followed her. The new room was cold. Mei didn't like it. There wasn't an examination table here, just a big glass box like they kept fish in at the aquarium, only it was dry inside, and the thing sitting there wasn't a fish. The woman motioned Mei closer and, when Mei came near, knocked sharply on the glass.

The thing inside looked up at the sound. It was a man, but he was naked and his skin didn't look like skin. His eyes glowed blue like there was a fire in his head. And something was wrong with his hands.

He reached toward the glass, and Mei started screaming.

Chapter One: Bobbie

Snoopy's out again," Private Hillman said. "I think his CO must be pissed at him."

Gunnery Sergeant Roberta Draper of the Martian Marine Corps upped the magnification on her armor's heads-up display and looked in the direction Hillman was pointing. Twenty-five hundred meters away, a squad of four United Nations Marines were tromping around their outpost, backlit by the giant greenhouse dome they were guarding. A greenhouse dome identical in nearly all respects to the dome her own squad was currently guarding.

One of the four UN Marines had black smudges on the sides of his helmet that looked like beagle ears.

"Yep, that's Snoopy," Bobbie said. "Been on every patrol detail so far today. Wonder what he did."

Guard duty around the greenhouses on Ganymede meant

doing what you could to keep your mind occupied. Including speculating on the lives of the Marines on the other side.

The other side. Eighteen months before, there hadn't been sides. The inner planets had all been one big, happy, slightly dysfunctional family. Then Eros, and now the two superpowers were dividing up the solar system between them, and the one moon neither side was willing to give up was Ganymede, breadbasket of the Jovian system.

As the only moon with any magnetosphere, it was the only place where dome-grown crops stood a chance in Jupiter's harsh radiation belt, and even then the domes and habitats still had to be shielded to protect civilians from the eight rems a day burning off Jupiter and onto the moon's surface.

Bobbie's armor had been designed to let a soldier walk through a nuclear bomb crater minutes after the blast. It also worked well at keeping Jupiter from frying Martian Marines.

Behind the Earth soldiers on patrol, their dome glowed in a shaft of weak sunlight captured by enormous orbital mirrors. Even with the mirrors, most terrestrial plants would have died, starved of sunlight. Only the heavily modified versions the Ganymede scientists cranked out could hope to survive in the trickle of light the mirrors fed them.

"Be sunset soon," Bobbie said, still watching the Earth Marines outside their little guard hut, knowing they were watching her too. In addition to Snoopy, she spotted the one they called Stumpy because he or she couldn't be much over a meter and a quarter tall. She wondered what their nickname for her was. Maybe Big Red. Her armor still had the Martian surface camouflage on it. She hadn't been on Ganymede long enough to get it resurfaced with mottled gray and white.

One by one over the course of five minutes, the orbital mirrors winked out as Ganymede passed behind Jupiter for a few hours. The glow from the greenhouse behind her changed to actinic blue as the artificial lights came on. While the overall light level didn't go down much, the shadows shifted in strange and subtle ways.

Above, the sun—not even a disk from here as much as the brightest star—flashed as it passed behind Jupiter's limb, and for a moment the planet's faint ring system was visible.

"They're going back in," Corporal Travis said. "Snoop's bringing up the rear. Poor guy. Can we bail too?"

Bobbie looked around at the featureless dirty ice of Ganymede. Even in her high-tech armor she could feel the moon's chill.

"Nope."

Her squad grumbled but fell in line as she led them on a slow low-gravity shuffle around the dome. In addition to Hillman and Travis, she had a green private named Gourab on this particular patrol. And even though he'd been in the Marines all of about a minute and a half, he grumbled just as loud as the other two in his Mariner Valley drawl.

She couldn't blame them. It was make-work. Something for the Martian soldiers on Ganymede to do to keep them busy. If Earth decided it needed Ganymede all to itself, four grunts walking around the greenhouse dome wouldn't stop them. With dozens of Earth and Mars warships in a tense standoff in orbit, if hostilities broke out the ground pounders would probably find out only when the surface bombardment began.

To her left, the dome rose to almost half a kilometer: triangular glass panels separated by gleaming copper-colored struts that turned the entire structure into a massive Faraday cage. Bobbie had never been inside one of the greenhouse domes. She'd been sent out from Mars as part of a surge in troops to the outer planets and had been walking patrols on the surface almost since day one. Ganymede to her was a spaceport, a small Marine base, and the even smaller guard outpost she currently called home.

As they shuffled around the dome, Bobbie watched the unremarkable landscape. Ganymede didn't change much without a catastrophic event. The surface was mostly silicate rock and water ice a few degrees warmer than space. The atmosphere was oxygen so thin it could pass as an industrial vacuum. Ganymede didn't erode or weather. It changed when rocks fell on it from space, or when warm water from the liquid core forced itself onto the surface and created short-lived lakes. Neither thing happened all that often. At home on Mars, wind and dust changed the landscape hourly. Here, she was walking through the footsteps of the day before and the day before and the day before. And if she never came back, those footprints would outlive her. Privately, she thought it was sort of creepy.

A rhythmic squeaking started to cut through the normally smooth hiss and thump sounds her powered armor made. She usually kept the suit's HUD minimized. It got so crowded with information that a marine knew everything except what was actually in front of her. Now she pulled it up, using blinks and eye movements to page over to the suit diagnostic screen. A yellow telltale warned her that the suit's left knee actuator was low on hydraulic fluid. Must be a leak somewhere, but a slow one, because the suit couldn't find it.

"Hey, guys, hold up a minute," Bobbie said. "Hilly, you have any extra hydraulic fluid in your pack?"

"Yep," said Hillman, already pulling it out.

"Give my left knee a squirt, would you?"

While Hillman crouched in front of her, working on her suit, Gourab and Travis began an argument that seemed to be about sports. Bobbie tuned it out.

"This suit is ancient," Hillman said. "You really oughta upgrade. This sort of thing is just going to happen more and more often, you know."

"Yeah, I should," Bobbie said. But the truth was that was easier said than done. Bobbie was not the right shape to fit into one of the standard suits, and the Marines made her jump through a series of flaming hoops every time she requisitioned a new custom one. At a bit over two meters tall, she was only slightly above average height for a Martian male, but thanks in part to her Polynesian ancestry, she weighed in at over a hundred kilos at one g. None of it was fat, but her muscles seemed to get bigger every time she even walked through a weight room. As a marine, she trained all the time.

The suit she had now was the first one in twelve years of active duty that actually fit well. And even though it was beginning to show its age, it was just easier to try to keep it running than beg and plead for a new one.

Hillman was starting to put his tools away when Bobbie's radio crackled to life.

"Outpost four to stickman. Come in, stickman."

"Roger four," Bobbie replied. "This is stickman one. Go ahead."

"Stickman one, where are you guys? You're half an hour late and some shit is going down over here."

"Sorry, four, equipment trouble," Bobbie said, wondering what sort of shit might be going down, but not enough to ask about it over an open frequency.

"Return to the outpost immediately. We have shots fired at the UN outpost. We're going into lockdown."

It took Bobbie a moment to parse that. She could see her men staring at her, their faces a mix of puzzlement and fear.

"Uh, the Earth guys are shooting at you?" she finally asked.

"Not yet, but they're shooting. Get your asses back here."

Hillman pushed to his feet. Bobbie flexed her knee once and got greens on her diagnostic. She gave Hilly a nod of thanks, then said, "Double-time it back to the outpost. Go."

Bobbie and her squad were still half a kilometer from the outpost when the general alert went out. Her suit's HUD came up on its own, switching to combat mode. The sensor package went to work looking for hostiles and linked up to one of the satellites for a top-down view. She felt the click as the gun built into the suit's right arm switched to free-fire mode.

A thousand alarms would be sounding if an orbital bombardment had begun, but she couldn't help looking up at the sky anyway. No flashes or missile trails. Nothing but Jupiter's bulk.

Bobbie took off for the outpost in a long, loping run. Her squad followed without a word. A person trained in the use of a strength-augmenting suit running in low gravity could cover a lot of ground quickly. The outpost came into view around the curve of the dome in just a few seconds, and a few seconds after that, the cause of the alarm.

UN Marines were charging the Martian outpost. The yearlong cold war was going hot. Somewhere deep behind the cool mental habits of training and discipline, she was surprised. She hadn't really thought this day would come.

The rest of her platoon were out of the outpost and arranged in a firing line facing the UN position. Someone had driven *Yojimbo* out onto the line, and the four-meter-tall combat mech towered over the other marines, looking like a headless giant in power armor, its massive cannon moving slowly as it tracked the incoming Earth troops. The UN soldiers were covering the 2,500 meters between the two outposts at a dead run.

Why isn't anyone talking? she wondered. The silence coming from her platoon was eerie.

And then, just as her squad got to the firing line, her suit squealed a jamming warning at her. The top-down vanished as she lost contact with the satellite. Her team's life signs and equipment status reports went dead as her link to their suits was cut off. The faint static of the open comm channel disappeared, leaving an even more unsettling silence.

She used hand motions to place her team at the right flank, then moved up the line to find Lieutenant Givens, her CO. She spotted his suit right at the center of the line, standing almost directly under *Yojimbo*. She ran up and placed her helmet against his.

"What the fuck is going on, El Tee?" she shouted.

He gave her an irritated look and yelled, "Your guess is as good as mine. We can't tell them to back off because of the jamming, and visual warnings are being ignored. Before the radio cut out, I got authorization to fire if they come within half a klick of our position."

Bobbie had a couple hundred more questions, but the UN troops would cross the five-hundred-meter mark in just a few more seconds, so she ran back to anchor the right flank with her squad. Along the way, she had her suit count the incoming forces and mark them all as hostiles. The suit reported seven targets. Less than a third of the UN troops at their outpost.

This makes no sense.

She had her suit draw a line on the HUD at the five-hundred-meter mark. She didn't tell her boys that was the free-fire zone. She didn't need to. They'd open fire when she did without needing to know why.

The UN soldiers had crossed the one-kilometer mark, still without firing a shot. They were coming in a scattered formation, with six out front in a ragged line and a seventh bringing up the rear about seventy meters behind. Her suit HUD selected the figure on the far left of the enemy line as her target, picking the one closest to her by default. Something itched at the back of her brain, and she overrode the suit and selected the target at the rear and told it to magnify.

The small figure suddenly enlarged in her targeting reticule. She felt a chill move down her back, and magnified again.

The figure chasing the six UN Marines wasn't wearing an environment suit. Nor was it, properly speaking, human. Its skin was covered in chitinous plates, like large black scales. Its head was a massive horror, easily twice as large as it should have been and covered in strange protruding growths.

But most disturbing of all were its hands. Far too large for its body, and too long for their width, they were a childhood nightmare version of hands. The hands of the troll under the bed or the witch sneaking in through the window. They flexed and grasped at nothing with a constant manic energy.

The Earth forces weren't attacking. They were retreating.

"Shoot the thing chasing them," Bobbie yelled to no one.

Before the UN soldiers could cross the half-kilometer line that would cause the Martians to open fire, the thing caught them.

"Oh, holy shit," Bobbie whispered. "Holy *shit*."

It grabbed one UN Marine in its huge hands and tore him in half like paper. Titanium-and-ceramic armor ripped as easily as the flesh inside, spilling broken bits of technology and wet human viscera indiscriminately onto the ice. The remaining five soldiers ran even harder, but the monster chasing them barely slowed as it killed.

"Shoot it shoot it shoot it," Bobbie yelled, and opened fire. Her training and the technology of her combat suit combined to make her an extremely efficient killing machine. As soon as her finger pulled the trigger on her suit's gun, a stream of two-millimeter armor-piercing rounds streaked out at the creature at more than a thousand meters per second. In just under a second she'd fired fifty rounds at it. The creature was a relatively slow-moving human-sized target, running in a straight line. Her targeting computer could do ballistic corrections that would let her hit a softball-sized object moving at supersonic speeds. Every bullet she fired at the monster hit.

It didn't matter.

The rounds went through it, probably not slowing appreciably before they exited. Each exit wound sprouted a spray of black filaments that fell onto the snow instead of blood. It was like shooting water. The wounds closed almost faster than they were created; the only sign the thing had even been hit was the trail of black fibers in its wake.

And then it caught a second UN Marine. Instead of tearing him to pieces like it had the last one, it spun and hurled the fully armored Earther—probably massing more than five hundred kilos total—toward Bobbie. Her HUD tracked the UN soldier on his upward arc and helpfully informed her that the monster had thrown him not *toward* her but *at* her. In a very flat trajectory. Which meant fast.

She dove to the side as quickly as her bulky suit would let her.

The hapless UN Marine swiped Hillman, who'd been standing next to her, and then both of them were gone, bouncing down the ice at lethal speeds.

By the time she'd turned back to the monster, it had killed two more UN soldiers.

The entire Martian line opened fire on it, including *Yojimbo*'s big cannon. The two remaining Earth soldiers diverged and ran at angles away from the thing, trying to give their Martian counterparts an open firing lane. The creature was hit hundreds, thousands of times. It stitched itself back together while remaining at a full run, never more than slowing when one of *Yojimbo*'s cannon shots detonated nearby.

Bobbie, back on her feet, joined in the barrage of fire but it didn't make any difference. The creature slammed into the Martian line, killing two marines faster than the eye could follow. *Yojimbo* slid to one side, far more nimble than a machine of its size should be. Bobbie thought Sa'id must be driving it. He bragged he could make the big mech dance the tango when he wanted to. That didn't matter either. Even before Sa'id could bring the mech's cannon around for a point-blank shot, the creature ran right up its side, gripped the pilot hatch, and tore the door off its hinges. Sa'id was snatched from his cockpit harness and hurled sixty meters straight up.

The other marines had begun to fall back, firing as they went. Without radio, there was no way to coordinate the retreat. Bobbie found herself running toward the dome with the rest. The small and distant part of her mind that wasn't panicking knew that the dome's glass and metal would offer no protection against something that could tear an armored man in half or rip a nine-ton mech to pieces. That part of her mind recognized the futility in attempting to override her terror.

By the time she found the external door into the dome, there was only one other marine left with her. Gourab. Up close, she could see his face through the armored glass of his helmet. He screamed something at her she couldn't hear. She started to lean forward to touch helmets with him when he shoved her backward onto the ice. He was hammering on the door controls with one metal fist, trying to smash his way in, when the creature caught him and peeled the helmet off his suit with one casual swipe. Gourab stood for a moment, face in vacuum, eyes blinking and mouth open in a soundless scream; then the creature tore off his head as easily as it had his helmet.

It turned and looked at Bobbie, still flat on her back.

Up close, she could see that it had bright blue eyes. A glowing, electric blue. They were beautiful. She raised her gun and held down the trigger for half a second before she realized she'd run out of ammo long before. The creature looked at her gun with what she would have sworn was curiosity, then looked into her eyes and cocked its head to one side.

This is it, she thought. *This is how I go out, and I'm not going to know what did it, or why.* Dying she could handle. Dying without any answers seemed terribly cruel.

The creature took one step toward her, then stopped and shuddered. A new pair of limbs burst out of its midsection and writhed in the air like tentacles. Its head, already grotesque, seemed to swell up. The blue eyes flashed as bright as the lights in the domes.

And then it exploded in a ball of fire that hurled her away across the ice and slammed her into a low ridge hard enough for the impact-absorbing gel in her suit to go rigid, freezing her in place.

She lay on her back, fading toward unconsciousness. The night sky above her began to flash with light. The ships in orbit, shooting each other.

Cease fire, she thought, pressing it out into the blackness. *They were retreating. Cease fire.* Her radio was still out, her suit dead. She couldn't tell anyone that the UN Marines hadn't been attacking.

Or that something else had.

Chapter Two: Holden

The coffeemaker was broken again.

Again.

Jim Holden clicked the red brew button in and out several more times, knowing it wouldn't matter, but helpless to stop himself. The massive and gleaming coffeemaker, designed to brew enough to keep a Martian naval crew happy, refused to make a single cup. Or even a noise. It wasn't just refusing to brew; it was refusing to *try*. Holden closed his eyes against the caffeine headache that threatened in his temples and hit the button on the nearest wall panel to open the shipwide comm.

"Amos," he said.

The comm wasn't working.

Feeling increasingly ridiculous, he pushed the button for the 1MC channel several more times. Nothing. He opened his eyes and saw that all the lights on the panel were out. Then he turned around and saw that the lights on the refrigerator and the ovens were out. It wasn't just the coffeemaker; the entire galley was in open revolt. Holden looked at the ship name, *Rocinante*, newly stenciled onto the galley wall, and said, "Baby, why do you hurt me when I love you so much?"

He pulled out his hand terminal and called Naomi.

After several moments, she finally answered, "Uh, hello?"

"The galley doesn't work, where's Amos?"

A pause. "You called me from the galley? While we are on the same ship? The wall panel just one step too far away?"

"The wall panel in the galley doesn't work either. When I said, 'The galley doesn't work,' it wasn't clever hyperbole. It literally means that not one thing in the galley works. I called you because you carry your terminal and Amos almost never does. And also because he never tells me what he's working on, but he always tells you. So, where is Amos?"

Naomi laughed. It was a lovely sound, and it never failed to put a smile on Holden's face. "He told me he was going to be doing some rewiring."

"Do you have power up there? Are we hurtling out of control and you guys were trying to figure out how to break the news to me?"

Holden could hear tapping from Naomi's end. She hummed to herself as she worked.

"Nope," she said. "Only area without power seems to be the galley. Also, Alex says we're less than an hour from fighting with space pirates. Want to come up to ops and fight pirates?"

"I can't fight pirates without coffee. I'm going to find Amos," Holden said, then hung up and put his terminal back in his pocket.

Holden moved to the ladder that ran down the keel of the ship, and called up the lift. The fleeing pirate ship could only sustain about 1 g for extended flight, so Holden's pilot, Alex Kamal, had them flying at 1.3 g to intercept. Anything over 1 g made the ladder dangerous to use.

A few seconds later, the deck hatch clanged open, and the lift whined to a stop at his feet. He stepped on and tapped the button for the engineering deck. The lift began its slow crawl down the shaft, deck hatches opening at its approach, then slamming shut once he had passed.

Amos Burton was in the machine shop, one deck above engineering. He had a complex-looking device half disassembled on the workbench in front of him and was working on it with a solder gun. He wore a gray jumpsuit several sizes too small for him, which strained to contain his broad shoulders when he moved, the old ship name *Tachi* still embroidered on the back.

Holden stopped the lift and said, "Amos, the galley doesn't work."

Amos waved one thick arm in an impatient gesture without stopping his work. Holden waited. After another couple seconds of soldering, Amos finally put down the tool and turned around.

"Yep, it doesn't work because I got this little fucker yanked out of it," he said, pointing at the device he'd been soldering.

"Can you put it back?"

"Nope, at least not yet. Not done working on it."

Holden sighed. "Is it important that we disable the galley to fix this thing just before confronting a bloodthirsty band of space pirates? Because my head is really starting to ache, and I'd love to get a cup of coffee before, you know, doing battle."

"Yep, it was important," Amos said. "Should I explain why? Or you want to take my word for it?"

Holden nodded. While he didn't miss much about his days in the Earth Navy, he did find that he occasionally got nostalgic for the absolute respect for the chain of command. On the *Rocinante* the title "captain" was much more nebulously defined. Rewiring things was Amos' job, and he would resist the idea that he had to inform Holden anytime he was doing it.

Holden let it drop.

"Okay," he said. "But I wish you'd warned me ahead of time. I'm going to be cranky without my coffee."

Amos grinned at him and pushed his cap back on his mostly bald head.

"Shit, Cap, I can cover you on that," he said, then reached back and grabbed a massive metal thermos off the bench. "I made some emergency supplies before I shut the galley down."

"Amos, I apologize for all the mean things I was thinking about you just now."

Amos waved it off and turned back to his work. "Take it. I already had a cup."

Holden climbed back onto the lift and rode it up to the operations deck, the thermos clutched in both hands like a life preserver.

Naomi was seated at the sensor and communications panel, tracking their progress in pursuit of the fleeing pirates. Holden could see at a glance that they were much closer than the last estimate he'd received. He strapped himself into the combat operations couch. He opened a nearby cabinet and, guessing they might be at low g or in free fall in the near future, pulled out a drinking bulb for his coffee.

As he filled it from the thermos's nipple, he said, "We're closing awful fast. What's up?"

"Pirate ship has slowed down quite a bit from its initial one g acceleration. They dropped to half a g for a couple minutes, then stopped accelerating altogether a minute ago. The computer tracked some fluctuations in drive output just before they slowed, so I think we chased them too hard."

"They broke their ship?"

"They broke their ship."

Holden took a long drink out of the bulb, scalding his tongue in the process and not caring.

"How long to intercept now?"

"Five minutes, tops. Alex was waiting to do the final decel burn until you were up here and belted in."

Holden tapped the comm panel's 1MC button and said, "Amos, buckle up. Five minutes to badguys." Then he switched to the cockpit channel and said, "Alex, what's the word?"

"I do believe they broke their ship," Alex replied in his Martian Mariner Valley drawl.

"That seems to be the consensus," Holden said.

"Makes runnin' away a bit harder."

The Mariner Valley had originally been settled by Chinese, East Indians, and Texans. Alex had the dark complexion and jet-black hair of an East Indian. Coming as he did from Earth, Holden always found it strangely disconcerting when an exaggerated Texas drawl came from someone his brain said should be speaking with Punjabi accents.

"And it makes our day easier," Holden replied, warming up the combat ops panel. "Bring us to relative stop at ten thousand klicks. I'm going to paint them with the targeting laser and turn on the point defense cannons. Open the outer doors to the tubes, too. No reason not to look as threatening as possible."

"Roger that, boss," Alex replied.

Naomi swiveled in her chair and gave Holden a grin. "Fighting space pirates. Very romantic."

Holden couldn't help smiling back. Even wearing a Martian naval officer's jumpsuit that was three sizes too short and five sizes too big around for her long and thin Belter frame, she looked beautiful to him. Her long and curly black hair was pulled into an unruly tail behind her head. Her features were a striking mix of Asian, South American, and African that was unusual even in the melting pot of the Belt. He glanced at his brown-haired Montana farm boy reflection in a darkened panel and felt very generic by comparison.

"You know how much I like anything that gets you to say the word 'romantic,'" he said. "But I'm afraid I lack your enthusiasm. We started out saving the solar system from a horrific alien menace. Now this?"

Holden had only known one cop well, and him briefly. During the massive and unpleasant series of clusterfucks that now went under the shorthand "the Eros incident," Holden had teamed up for a time with a thin, gray, broken man called Miller. By the time they'd met, Miller had already walked away from his official job to obsessively follow a missing persons case.

They'd never precisely been friends, but they'd managed to stop the human race from being wiped out by a corporation's self-induced sociopathy and a recovered alien weapon that everyone in human history had mistaken for a moon of Saturn. By that standard, at least, the partnership had been a success.

Holden had been a naval officer for six years. He'd seen people die, but only from the vantage of a radar screen. On Eros, he'd seen thousands of people die, up close and in horrific ways. He'd killed a couple of them himself. The radiation dose he'd received there meant he had to take constant medications to stop the cancers that kept blooming in his tissues. He'd still gotten off lighter than Miller.

Because of Miller, the alien infection had landed on Venus instead of Earth. But that hadn't killed it. Whatever the alien's hijacked, confused programming was, it was still going on under that planet's thick cloud cover, and no one had so far been able to offer any scientific conclusions more compelling than *Hmm. Weird.*

Saving humanity had cost the old, tired Belter detective his life.

Saving humanity had turned Holden into an employee of the Outer Planets Alliance tracking down pirates. Even on the bad days, he had to think he'd gotten the better end of that deal.

"Thirty seconds to intercept," Alex said.

Holden pulled his mind back to the present and called down to engineering. "You all strapped in down there, Amos?"

"Roger, Cap. Ready to go. Try not to get my girl all shot up."

"No one's shooting anyone today," Holden said after he shut the comm link off. Naomi heard him and raised an eyebrow in question. "Naomi, give me comms. I want to call our friends out there."

A second later, the comm controls appeared on his panel. He aimed a tightbeam at the pirate ship and waited for the link light to go green. When it did, he said, "Undesignated light freighter, this is Captain James Holden of the Outer Planets Alliance missile frigate *Rocinante*. Please respond."

His headset was silent except for the faint static of background radiation.

"Look, guys, let's not play games. I know you know who I am. I also know that five days ago, you attacked the food freighter *Somnambulist*, disabled its engines, and stole six thousand kilos of protein and all of their air. Which is pretty much all I need to know about you."

More staticky silence.

"So here's the deal. I'm tired of following you, and I'm not going to let you stall me while you fix your broken ship and then lead me on another merry chase. If you don't signal your full and complete surrender in the next sixty seconds, I am going to fire a pair of torpedoes with high-yield plasma warheads and melt your ship into glowing slag. Then I'm going to fly back home and sleep really well tonight."

The static was finally broken by a boy who sounded way too young to have already decided on a life of piracy.

"You can't do that. The OPA isn't a real government. You can't legally do shit to me, so back the fuck off," the voice said, sounding like it was on the verge of a pubescent squeak the entire time.

"Seriously? That's the best you've got?" Holden replied. "Look, forget the debate about legality and what constitutes actual governmental authority for a minute. Look at the ladar returns you're getting from my ship. While you are in a cobbled-together light freighter that someone welded a homemade gauss cannon onto, I'm in a state-of-the-art Martian torpedo bomber with enough firepower to slag a small moon."

The voice on the other end didn't reply.

"Guys, even if you don't recognize me as the appropriate legal authority, can we at least agree that I can blow you up anytime I want to?"

The comm remained silent.

Holden sighed and rubbed the bridge of his nose. In spite of the caffeine, his headache was refusing to go away. Leaving the channel open to the pirate ship, he opened another channel to the cockpit.

"Alex, put a short burst from the forward point defense cannons through that freighter. Aim for midships."

"Wait!" yelled the kid on the other ship. "We surrender! Jesus *Christ!*"

Holden stretched out in the zero g, enjoying it after the days of acceleration, and grinned to himself. *No one gets shot today* indeed.

"Naomi, tell our new friends how to give remote control of their ship to you, and let's take them back to Tycho Station for the OPA tribunals to figure out. Alex, once they have their engines back up, plot us a return trip at a nice comfortable half g. I'll be down in sick bay trying to find aspirin."

Holden unbuckled his crash couch harness and pushed off to the deck ladder. Along the way, his hand terminal started beeping. It was Fred Johnson, the nominal leader of the OPA and their personal patron on the Tycho corporation's manufacturing station, which was also now doubling as the de facto OPA headquarters.

"Yo, Fred, caught our naughty pirates. Bringing them back for trial."

Fred's large dark face crinkled into a grin. "That's a switch. Got tired of blowing them up?"

"Nope, just finally found some who believed me when I said I would."

Fred's grin turned into a frown. "Listen, Jim, that's not why I called. I need you back at Tycho on the double. Something's happening on Ganymede…"

Chapter Three: Prax

Praxidike Meng stood in the doorway of the staging barn, looking out at the fields of softly waving leaves so utterly green they were almost black, and panicked. The dome arched above him, darker than it should have been. Power to the grow lights had been cut, and the mirrors…He couldn't think about the mirrors.

The flickers of fighting ships looked like glitches on a cheap screen, colors and movements that shouldn't have been there. The sign that something was very wrong. He licked his lips. There had to be a way. There had to be some way to save them.

"Prax," Doris said. "We have to go. Now."

The cutting edge of low-resource agricultural botany, the *Glycine kenon*, a type of soybean so heavily modified it was an entirely new species, represented the last eight years of his life. They were the reason his parents still hadn't seen their only granddaughter in the flesh. They, and a few other things, had ended his marriage. He could see the eight subtly different strains of engineered chloroplasts in the fields, each one trying to spin out the most protein per photon. His hands were trembling. He was going to vomit.

"We have maybe five more minutes to impact," Doris said. "We have to evacuate."

"I don't see it," Prax said.

"It's coming fast enough, by the time you see it, you won't see it. Everyone else has already gone. We're the last ones. Now get in the lift."

The great orbital mirrors had always been his allies, shining down on his fields like a hundred pale suns. He couldn't believe that they'd betray him. It was an insane thought. The mirror plummeting toward the surface of Ganymede—toward his greenhouse, his soybeans, his life's work—hadn't chosen anything. It was a victim of cause and effect, the same as everything else.

"I'm about to leave," Doris said. "If you're here in four minutes, you'll die."

"Wait," Prax said. He ran out into the dome. At the edge of the nearest field, he fell to his knees and dug into the rich black soil. The smell of it was like a good patchouli. He pushed his fingers in as deep as he could, cupping a root ball. The small, fragile plant came up in his hands.

Doris was in the industrial lift, ready to descend into the caves and tunnels of the station. Prax sprinted for her. With the plant to save, the dome suddenly felt horribly dangerous. He threw himself through the door and Doris pressed the control display. The wide metal room of the lift lurched, shifted, and began its descent. Normally, it would have carried heavy equipment: the tiller, the tractor, the tons of humus taken from the station recycling processors. Now it was only the three of them: Prax sitting cross-legged on the floor, the soybean seedling nodding in his lap, Doris chewing her lower lip and watching her hand terminal. The lift felt too big.

"The mirror could miss," Prax said.

"It could. But it's thirteen hundred tons of glass and metal. The shock wave will be fairly large."

"The dome might hold."

"No," she said, and Prax stopped talking to her.

The cart hummed and clanked, falling deeper under the surface ice, sliding into the network of tunnels that made up the bulk of the station. The air smelled like heating elements and industrial lubricant. Even now, he couldn't believe they'd done it. He couldn't believe the military bastards had actually started shooting each other. No one, anywhere, could really be that short-sighted. Except that it seemed they could.

In the months since the Earth-Mars alliance had shattered, he'd gone from constant and gnawing fear to cautious hope to complacency. Every day that the United Nations and the Martians hadn't started something had been another bit of evidence that they wouldn't. He'd let himself think that everything was more stable than it looked. Even if things got bad and there was a shooting war, it wouldn't be here. Ganymede was where the food came from. With its magnetosphere, it was the safest place for pregnant women to gestate, claiming the lowest incidence of birth defects and stillbirth in the outer planets. It was the center of everything that made human expansion into the solar system possible. Their work was as precious as it was fragile, and the people in charge would never let the war come here.

Doris said something obscene. Prax looked up at her. She ran a hand through her thin white hair, turned, and spat.

"Lost connectivity," she said, holding up the hand terminal. "Whole network's locked down."

"By who?"

"Station security. United Nations. Mars. How would I know?"

"But if they—"

The concussion was like a giant fist coming down on the cart's roof. The emergency brakes kicked in with a bone-shaking clang. The lights went out, darkness swallowing them for two hummingbird-fast heartbeats. Four battery-powered emergency LEDs popped on, then off again as the cart's power came back. The critical failure diagnostics started to run: motors humming, lifts clicking, the tracking interface spooling through checksums like an athlete stretching before a run. Prax stood up and walked to the control panel. The shaft sensors reported minimal atmospheric pressure and falling. He felt a shudder as containment doors closed somewhere above them and the exterior pressure started to rise. The air in the shaft had been blown out into space before the emergency systems could lock down. His dome was compromised.

His dome was gone.

He put his hand to his mouth, not realizing he was smearing soil across his chin until he'd already done it. Part of his mind was skittering over the things that needed to be done to save the project—contact his project manager at RMD-Southern, refile the supplemental grant applications, get the data backups to rebuild the viral insertion samples—while another part had gone still and eerily calm. The sense of being two men—one bent on desperate measures, the other already in the numb of mourning—felt like the last weeks of his marriage.

Doris turned to him, a weary amusement plucking at her wide lips. She put out her hand.

"It was a pleasure working with you, Dr. Meng."

The cart shuddered as the emergency brakes retracted. Another impact came from much farther off. A mirror or a ship falling. Soldiers shelling each other on the surface. Maybe even fighting deeper in the station. There was no way to know. He shook her hand.

"Dr. Bourne," he said. "It has been an honor."

They took a long, silent moment at the graveside of their previous lives. Doris sighed.

"All right," she said. "Let's get the hell out of here."

Mei's day care was deep in the body of the moon, but the tube station was only a few hundred yards from the cart's loading dock, and the express trip down to her was no more than ten minutes. Or would have been if they were running. In three decades of living on Ganymede, Prax had never even noticed that the tube stations had security doors.

The four soldiers standing in front of the closed station wore thick plated armor painted in shifting camouflage lines the same shades of beige and steel as the corridor. They carried intimidatingly large assault rifles and scowled at the crowd of a dozen or more pressing in around them.

"I am on the transportation board," a tall, thin, dark-skinned woman was saying, punctuating each word by tapping her finger on one soldier's chest plate. "If you don't let us past, then you're in trouble. Serious trouble."

"How long is it going to be down?" a man asked. "I need to get home. How long is it going to be down?"

"Ladies and gentlemen," the soldier on the left shouted. She had a powerful voice. It cut through the rumble and murmur of the crowd like a teacher speaking to restless schoolchildren. "This settlement is in security lockdown. Until the military action is resolved, there is no movement between levels except by official personnel."

"Whose side are you on?" someone shouted. "Are you Martians? Whose side are you *on*?"

"In the meantime," the soldier went on, ignoring the question, "we are going to ask you all to be patient. As soon as it's safe to travel, the tube system will be opened. Until that time, we're going to ask you to remain calm for your own safety."

Prax didn't know he was going to speak until he heard his own voice. He sounded whiny.

"My daughter's in the eighth level. Her school's down there."

"Every level is in lockdown, sir," the soldier said. "She'll be just fine. You just have to be patient."

The dark-skinned woman from the transportation board crossed her arms. Prax saw two men abandon the press, walking back down the narrow, dirty hall, talking to each other. In the old tunnels this far up, the air smelled of recyclers—plastic and heat and artificial scents. And now also of fear.

"Ladies and gentlemen," the soldier shouted. "For your own safety, you need to remain calm and stay where you are until the military situation has been resolved."

"What exactly is the military situation?" a woman at Prax's elbow said, her voice making the words a demand.

"It's rapidly evolving," the soldier said. Prax thought there was a dangerous buzz in her voice. She was as scared as anyone. Only she had a gun. So this wasn't going to work. He had to find something else. His one remaining *Glycine kenon* still in his hand, Prax walked away from the tube station.

He'd been eight years old when his father had transferred from the high-population centers of Europa to help build a research lab on Ganymede. The construction had taken ten years, during which Prax had gone through a rocky adolescence. When his parents had packed up to move the family to a new contract on an asteroid in eccentric orbit near Neptune, Prax had stayed behind. He'd gotten a botany internship thinking that he could use it to grow illicit, untaxed marijuana only to discover that every third botany intern had come in with the same plan. The four years he'd spent trying to find a forgotten closet or an abandoned tunnel that wasn't already occupied by an illegal hydroponics experiment left him with a good sense of the tunnel architecture.

He walked through the old, narrow hallways of the first-generation construction. Men and women sat along the walls or in the bars and restaurants, their faces blank or angry or frightened. The display screens were set on old entertainment loops of music or theater or abstract art instead of the usual newsfeeds. No hand terminals chimed with incoming messages.

By the central-air ducts, he found what he'd been looking for. The maintenance transport always had a few old electric scooters lying around. No one used them anymore. Because Prax was a senior researcher, his hand terminal would let him through the rusting chain-link fencing. He found one scooter with a sidecar and half a charge still in the batteries. It had been seven years since he'd been on a scooter. He put the *Glycine kenon* in the sidecar, ran through the diagnostic sequence, and wheeled himself out to the hall.

The first three ramps had soldiers just like the ones he'd seen at the tube station. Prax didn't bother stopping. At the fourth, a supply tunnel that led from the surface warehouses down toward the reactors, there was nobody. He paused, the scooter silent beneath him. There was a bright acid smell in the air that he couldn't quite place. Slowly, other details registered. The scorch marks at the wall panel, a smear of something dark along the floor. He heard a distant popping sound that it took three or four long breaths to recognize as gunfire.

Rapidly evolving apparently meant fighting in the tunnels. The image of Mei's classroom stippled with bullet holes and soaked in children's blood popped into his mind, as vivid as something he was remembering instead of imagining. The panic he'd felt in the dome came down on him again, but a hundred times worse.

"She's fine," he told the plant beside him. "They wouldn't have a firefight in a day care. There're kids there."

The green-black leaves were already starting to wilt. They wouldn't have a war around children. Or food supplies. Or fragile agricultural domes. His hands were trembling again, but not so badly he couldn't steer.

The first explosion came just as he was heading down the ramp from seven to level eight along the side of one of the cathedral-huge unfinished caverns where the raw ice of the moon had been left to weep and refreeze, something between a massive green space and a work of art. There was a flash, then a concussion, and the scooter was fishtailing. The wall loomed up fast, and Prax wrenched his leg out of the way before the impact. Above him, he heard voices shouting. Combat troops would be in armor, talking through their radios. At least, he thought they would. The people screaming up there had to be just people. A second explosion gouged the cavern wall, a section of blue-white ice the size of a tractor calving off the roof and falling slowly and inexorably down to the floor, grinding into it. Prax scrambled to keep the scooter upright. His heart felt like it was trying to break out of his rib cage.

On the upper edge of the curving ramp, he saw figures in armor. He didn't know if they were UN or Mars. One of them turned toward him, lifting a rifle. Prax gunned the scooter, sliding fast down the ramp. The chatter of automatic weapons and the smell of smoke and steam melt followed him.

The school's doors were closed. He didn't know if that was ominous or hopeful. He brought the wobbling scooter to a halt, jumped off. His legs felt weak and unsteady. He meant to knock gently on the steel drop door, but his first try split the skin over his knuckle.

"Open up! My daughter's in there!" He sounded like a madman, but someone inside heard him or saw him on the security monitor. The articulated steel plates of the door shuddered and began to rise. Prax dropped to the ground and scrambled through.

He hadn't met the new teacher, Miss Carrie, more than a few times, when dropping Mei off or picking her up. She couldn't have been more than twenty years old and was Belter-tall and thin. He didn't remember her face being so gray.

The schoolroom was intact, though. The children were in a circle, singing a song about an ant traveling through the solar system, with rhymes for all the major asteroid bodies. There was no blood, no bullet holes, but the smell of burning plastic was seeping through the vents. He had to get Mei someplace safe. He wasn't sure where that would be. He looked at the circle of children, trying to pick out her face, her hair.

"Mei's not here, sir," Miss Carrie said, her voice tight and breathy at the same time. "Her mother got her this morning."

"This morning?" Prax said, but his mind fastened on *her mother*. What was Nicola doing on Ganymede? He'd had a message from her two days earlier about the child support judgment; she *couldn't* have gotten from Ceres to Ganymede in two days...

"Just after snack," the teacher said.

"You mean she was evacuated. Someone came and evacuated Mei."

Another explosion came, shaking the ice. One of the children made a high, frightened sound. The teacher looked from him to the children, then back. When she spoke again, her voice was lower.

"Her mother came just after snack. She took Mei with her. She hasn't been here all day."

Prax pulled up his hand terminal. The connection was still dead, but his wallpaper was a picture from Mei's first birthday, back when things were still good. Lifetimes ago. He held up the picture and pointed at Nicola, laughing and dangling the doughy, delighted bundle that had been Mei.

"Her?" Prax said. "*She* was here?"

The confusion in the teacher's face answered him. There'd been a mistake. Someone—a new nanny or a social worker or something—had come to pick up a kid and gotten the wrong one.

"She was on the computer," the teacher said. "She was in the system. It *showed* her."

The lights flickered. The smell of smoke was getting stronger, and the air recyclers were humming loudly, popping and crackling as they struggled to suck out the volatile particulates. A boy whose name Prax should have known whimpered, and the teacher reflexively tried to turn toward him. Prax took her elbow and wrenched her back.

"No, you made a mistake," he said. "Who did you give Mei to?"

"The system said it was her mother! She had identification. It cleared her."

A stutter of muted gunfire came from the hallway. Someone was screaming outside, and then the kids started to shriek. The teacher pulled her arm away. Something banged against the drop door.

"She was about thirty. Dark hair, dark eyes. She had a doctor with her, she was in the system, and Mei didn't make any kind of fuss about it."

"Did they take her medicine?" he asked. "Did they take her *medicine?*"

"No. I don't know. I don't think so."

Without meaning to, Prax shook the woman. Only once, but hard. If Mei didn't have her medicine, she'd already missed her midday dose. She might make it as long as morning before her immune system started shutting down.

"Show me," Prax said. "Show me the picture. The woman who took her."

"I can't! The system's down!" the teacher shouted. "They're killing people in the hallway!"

The circle of children dissolved, screams riding on the backs of screams. The teacher was crying, her hands pressed to her face. Her skin had an almost blue cast to it. He could feel the raw animal panic leaping through his brain. The calm that fell on him didn't take away from it.

"Is there an evacuation tunnel?" he asked.

"They told us to stay here," the teacher said.

"I'm telling you to evacuate," Prax said, but what he thought was *I have to find Mei.*

Chapter Four: Bobbie

Consciousness returned as an angry buzzing noise and pain. Bobbie blinked once, trying to clear her head, trying to see where she was. Her vision was maddeningly blurry. The buzzing sound resolved into an alarm from her suit. Colored lights flashed in her face as the suit's HUD sent her data she couldn't read. It was in the middle of rebooting and alarms were coming on one by one. She tried to move her arms and found that although weak, she wasn't paralyzed or frozen in place. The impact gel in her suit had returned to a liquid state.

Something moved across the window of faint light that was her helmet's face shield. A head, bobbing in and out of view. Then a click as someone plugged a hardline into her suit's external port. A corpsman, then, downloading her injury data.

A voice, male and young, in her suit's internal speakers said,

"Gotcha, Gunny. We gotcha. Gonna be okay. Gonna be all right. Just hang in there."

He hadn't quite finished saying *there* when she blacked out again.

She woke bouncing down a long white tunnel on a stretcher. She wasn't wearing her suit anymore. Bobbie was afraid that the battlefield med-techs hadn't wasted time taking her out of it the normal way, that they'd just hit the override that blew all the seams and joints apart. It was a fast way to get a wounded soldier out of four hundred kilos of armored exoskeleton, but the suit was destroyed in the process. Bobbie felt a pang of remorse for the loss of her faithful old suit.

A moment later, she remembered that her entire platoon had been ripped to pieces before her eyes, and her sadness about the lost suit seemed trivial and demeaning.

A hard bump on the stretcher sent a jolt of lightning up her spine and hurled her back into darkness.

"Sergeant Draper," a voice said.

Bobbie tried to open her eyes and found it impossible to do. Each eyelid weighed a thousand kilos, and even the attempt left her exhausted. So she tried to answer the voice and was surprised and a little ashamed of the drunken mumble that came out instead.

"She's conscious, but just barely," the voice said. It was a deep, mellow male voice. It seemed filled with warmth and concern. Bobbie hoped that the voice would keep talking until she fell back asleep.

A second voice, female and sharp, replied, "Let her rest. Trying to bring her fully awake right now is dangerous."

The kind voice said, "I don't care if it kills her, Doctor. I need to speak to this soldier, and I need to do it now. So you give her whatever you need to give her to make that happen."

Bobbie smiled to herself, not parsing the words the nice voice said, just the kindly, warm tone. It was good to have someone like that to take care of you. She started to fall back asleep, the coming blackness a welcome friend.

White fire shot up Bobbie's spine, and she sat bolt upright in bed, as awake as she'd ever been. It felt like going on the juice, the chemical cocktail they gave sailors to keep them conscious and alert during high-g maneuvers. Bobbie opened her eyes and then slammed them shut again when the room's bright white light nearly burned them out of her sockets.

"Turn off the lights," she mumbled, the words coming out of her dry throat in a whisper.

The red light seeping in through her closed eyelids dimmed, but when she tried to open them again, it was still too bright. Someone took her hand and held it while a cup was put into it.

"Can you hold that?" the nice voice said.

Bobbie didn't answer; she just brought the cup to her mouth and drank the water in two greedy swallows.

"More," she said, this time in something resembling her old voice.

She heard the sounds of someone scooting a chair and then footsteps away from her on a tile floor. Her brief look at the room had told her she was in a hospital. She could hear the electric hum of medical machines nearby, and the smells of antiseptic and urine competed for dominance. Disheartened, she realized she was the source of the urine smell. A faucet ran for a moment, and then the footsteps came toward her. The cup was put back into her hand. She sipped at it this time, letting the water stay in her mouth awhile before swallowing. It was cool and delicious.

When she was finished, the voice asked, "More?"

She shook her head.

"Maybe later," she said. Then, after a moment: "Am I blind?"

"No. You've been given a combination of focus drugs and

powerful amphetamines. Which means your eyes are fully dilated. Sorry, I didn't think to lower the lights before you woke up."

The voice was still filled with kindness and warmth. Bobbie wanted to see the face behind that voice, so she risked squinting through one eye. The light didn't burn into her like it had before, but it was still uncomfortable. The owner of the nice voice turned out to be a very tall, thin man in a naval intelligence uniform. His face was narrow and tight, the skull beneath it pressing to get out. He gave her a frightening smile that didn't extend past a slight upturn at the corners of his mouth.

"Gunnery Sergeant Roberta W. Draper, 2nd Marine Expeditionary Force," he said, his voice so at odds with his appearance that Bobbie felt like she was watching a movie dubbed from a foreign language.

After several seconds, he still hadn't continued, so Bobbie said, "Yes, sir," then glanced at his bars and added, "Captain."

She could open both eyes now without pain, but a strange tingling sensation was moving up her limbs, making them feel numb and shaky at the same time. She resisted an urge to fidget.

"Sergeant Draper, my name is Captain Thorsson, and I am here to debrief you. We've lost your entire platoon. There's been a two-day pitched battle between the United Nations and Martian Congressional Republic forces on Ganymede. Which, at most recent tally, has resulted in over five billion MCR dollars of infrastructure damage, and the deaths of nearly three thousand military and civilian personnel."

He paused again, staring at her through narrowed eyes that glittered like a snake's. Not sure what response he was looking for, Bobbie just said, "Yes, sir."

"Sergeant Draper, why did your platoon fire on and destroy the UN military outpost at dome fourteen?"

This question was so nonsensical that Bobbie's mind spent several seconds trying to figure out what it really meant.

"Who ordered you to commence firing, and why?"

Of course he couldn't be asking why her people had started the fight. Didn't he know about the monster?

"Don't you know about the monster?"

Captain Thorsson didn't move, but the corners of his mouth dropped into a frown, and his forehead bunched up over his nose.

"Monster," he said, none of the warmth gone from his voice.

"Sir, some kind of monster...mutant...something attacked the UN outpost. The UN troops were running to us to escape it. We didn't fire on them. This...this whatever it was killed them, and then it killed us," she said, nauseated and pausing to swallow at the lemony taste in her mouth. "I mean, everyone but me."

Thorsson frowned for a moment, then reached into one pocket and took out a small digital recorder. He turned it off, then set it on a tray next to Bobbie's bed.

"Sergeant, I'm going to give you a second chance. Up to now, your record has been exemplary. You are a fine marine. One of our best. Would you like to start over?"

He picked up the recorder and placed a finger on the delete button while giving her a knowing look.

"You think I'm lying?" she said. The itchy feeling in her limbs resolved itself into a very real urge to reach out and snap the smug bastard's arm off at the elbow. "We all shot at it. There will be gun camera footage from the entire platoon of this thing killing UN soldiers and then attacking us. Sir."

Thorsson shook his hatchet-shaped head at her, narrowing his eyes until they almost disappeared.

"We have no transmissions from the platoon for the entire fight, and no uploaded data—"

"They were jamming," Bobbie interrupted. "I lost my radio link when I got close to the monster too."

Thorsson continued as though she had not spoken. "And all of the local hardware was lost when an orbital mirror array fell onto the dome. You were outside of the impact area, but the shock wave threw you nearly another quarter of a kilometer. It took us some time to find you."

All of the local hardware was lost. Such a sterile way of putting it. Everyone in Bobbie's platoon blown into shrapnel and vapor when a couple thousand tons of mirror fell out of orbit onto them. A monitor started sounding a low, chiming alert, but no one else paid it any attention, so she didn't either.

"My suit, sir. I shot at it too. My video will still be there."

"Yes," Thorsson said. "We've examined your suit's video log. It's nothing but static."

This is like a bad horror movie, she thought. The heroine who sees the monster, but no one will believe her. She imagined the second act, in which she was court-martialed in disgrace, and only got her redemption in the third act, when the monster showed up again and killed everyone who didn't believe—

"Wait!" she said. "What decompression did you use? My suit is an older model. It uses the version 5.1 video compression. Tell the tech that, and have them try it again."

Thorsson stared at her for a few moments, then pulled out his hand terminal and called someone.

"Have Sergeant Draper's combat suit brought up to her room. Send a tech with video gear with it."

He put the terminal away and then gave Bobbie another of those frightening smiles.

"Sergeant, I admit that I am extremely curious about what you want me to see. If this is still a ruse of some kind, you've only bought yourself a few more moments."

Bobbie didn't reply, but her reaction to Thorsson's attitude had finally shifted from frightened through angry to annoyed. She pushed herself up in the narrow hospital bed and turned sideways, sitting on the edge and tossing the blanket to the side. With her size, her physical presence up close usually either frightened men or turned them on. Either way it made them uncomfortable. She leaned toward Thorsson a bit and was rewarded when he pushed his chair back an equal amount.

She could tell from his disgusted expression that he immediately knew what she'd done, and he looked away from her smile.

The door to the room opened and a pair of Navy techs wheeled in her suit on a rack. It was intact. They hadn't wrecked it taking her out. She felt a lump come up in her throat, and swallowed it back down. She wasn't going to show even a moment's weakness in front of this Thorsson clown.

The clown pointed at the senior of the two techs and said, "You. What's your name?"

The young tech snapped off a salute and said, "Petty Officer Electrician's Mate Singh, sir."

"Mr. Singh, Sergeant Draper here is claiming that her suit has a different video compression than the new suits, and that's why you were unable to read her video data. Is this correct?"

Singh slapped himself on the forehead with his palm.

"Shit. Yeah," he said. "I didn't think— This is the old Mark III Goliath suit. When they started making the Mark IV, they completely rewrote the firmware. Totally different video storage system. Wow, I feel pretty stupid—"

"Yes," interrupted Thorsson. "Do whatever you need to do to display the video stored on that suit. The sooner you do, the less time I will have to dwell on the delays caused by incompetence."

Singh, to his credit, did not reply. He immediately plugged the suit into a monitor and began working. Bobbie examined her suit. It had a lot of scratches and dings but appeared otherwise undamaged. She felt a strong urge to go put it on and then tell Thorsson where he could stick his attitude.

A new set of shakes moved up her arms and legs. Something fluttered in her neck like the heartbeat of a small animal. She reached up and touched it. It was her pulse. She started to say something, but the tech was pumping his fist and high-fiving his assistant.

"Got it, sir," Singh said, then began the playback.

Bobbie tried to watch, but the picture kept getting fuzzy. She reached for Thorsson's arm to get his attention, but missed somehow and just kept tipping forward.

Here we go again, she thought, and there was a brief moment of free fall before the blackness.

"God dammit," the sharp voice said. "I goddamn well told you this would happen. This soldier has suffered internal injuries and a nasty concussion. You can't just pump her full of speed and then interrogate her. It's irresponsible. It's fucking criminal!"

Bobbie opened her eyes. She was back in bed. Thorsson sat in the chair by her side. A stocky blond woman in hospital scrubs stood at the foot of her bed, her face flushed and furious. When she saw Bobbie was awake, she moved to her side and took her hand.

"Sergeant Draper, don't try to move. You took a fall and aggravated some of your injuries. We've got you stabilized, but you need to rest now."

The doctor looked up at Thorsson as she said it, her face placing exclamation marks after every sentence. Bobbie nodded at her, which made her head feel like a bowl of water being carried in shifting gravity. That it didn't hurt probably meant they'd shot her full of every pain medication they had.

"Sergeant Draper's assistance was crucial," Thorsson said, not a hint of apology in his lovely voice. "Because of it, she may have just saved us from an all-out shooting war with Earth. Risking one's own life so others don't have to is pretty much the definition of Roberta's job."

"Don't call me Roberta," Bobbie mumbled.

"Gunny," Thorsson said. "I'm sorry about what happened to your team. But mostly I'm sorry for not believing you. Thank you for responding with professionalism. We avoided a serious mistake because of it."

"Just thought you were an asshole," Bobbie said.

"That's my job, soldier."

Thorsson stood up. "Get some rest. We're shipping you out as soon as you're well enough for the trip."

"Shipping me out? Back to Mars?"

Thorsson didn't answer. He nodded to the doctor, then left. The doctor pushed a button on one of the machines near Bobbie's bed, and something cool shot into her arm. The lights went out.

Gelatin. Why do hospitals always serve gelatin?

Bobbie desultorily poked her spork at the quivering mound of green on her plate. She was finally feeling good enough to really eat, and the soft and see-through foods they kept bringing her were growing more unsatisfying. Even the high-protein, high-carbohydrate slop they cranked out on most Navy ships sounded good right then. Or a thick mushroom steak covered in gravy with a side of couscous...

The door to her room slid open and her doctor, who she now knew was named Trisha Pichon but who insisted that everyone call her Dr. Trish, came in along with Captain Thorsson and a new man she didn't know. Thorsson gave her his creepy smile, but Bobbie had learned that it was just the way the man's face worked. He seemed to lack the muscles necessary for normal smiling. The new man wore a Marine chaplain's uniform of indeterminate religious affiliation.

Dr. Trish spoke first.

"Good news, Bobbie. We're turning you loose tomorrow. How do you feel?"

"Fine. Hungry," Bobbie said, then gave her gelatin another stab.

"We'll see about getting you some real food, then," Dr. Trish said, then smiled and left the room.

Thorsson pointed at the chaplain. "This is Captain Martens. He'll be coming with us on our trip. I'll leave you two to get acquainted."

Thorsson left before Bobbie could respond, and Martens plopped himself down in the chair next to her bed. He stuck out his hand, and she shook it.

"Hello, Sergeant," he said. "I—"

"When I marked my 2790 form as 'none' for religious faith, I was serious about that," Bobbie said, cutting him off.

Martens smiled, apparently not offended by her interruption or her agnosticism.

"I'm not here in a religious capacity, Sergeant. I'm also a trained grief counselor, and since you witnessed the death of every person in your unit, and were almost killed yourself, Captain Thorsson and your doctor agree that you might need me."

Bobbie started to make a dismissive reply, which was cut off by the lump in her chest. She hid her discomfort by taking a long drink of water, then said, "I'm fine. Thanks for coming by."

Martens leaned back in the chair, his smile never wavering.

"If you were really all right after what you've been through, it would be a sign that something was wrong. And you're about to be thrown into a situation with a lot of emotional and intellectual pressure. Once we get to Earth, you won't have the luxury of having an emotional breakdown or post-traumatic stress responses. We have a lot of work to—"

"Earth?" Bobbie pounced on the word. "Waitaminute. Why am I going to *Earth*?"

Chapter Five: Avasarala

Chrisjen Avasarala, assistant to the undersecretary of executive administration, sat near the end of the table. Her sari was orange, the only splash of color in the otherwise military blue-and-gray of the meeting. The seven others with seats at the table were the heads of their respective branches of the United Nations military forces, all of them men. She knew their names, their career paths and psychological profiles, pay rates and political alliances and who they were sleeping with. Against the back wall, personal assistants and staff pages stood in uncomfortable still-ness, like the shy teenagers at a dance. Avasarala snuck a pistachio out of her purse, cracked the shell discreetly, and popped the salted nut into her mouth.

"Any meeting with Martian command is going to have to wait until after the situation on Ganymede is stabilized. Official diplo-matic talks before then are only going to make it seem like we've accepted the new status quo." That was Admiral Nguyen, youngest of the men present. Hawkish. Impressed with himself in the way that successful young men tended to be.

General Adiki-Sandoval nodded his bull-wide head.

"Agreed. It's not just Mars we need to think about here. If we start looking weak to the Outer Planets Alliance, you can count on a spike in terrorist activity."

Mikel Agee, from the diplomatic corps, leaned back on his chair and licked his lips anxiously. His slicked-back hair and pinched face made him look like an anthropomorphic rat.

"Gentlemen, I have to disagree—"

"Of course you do," General Nettleford said dryly. Agee ignored him.

"Meeting with Mars at this point is a necessary first step. If we start throwing around preconditions and obstacles, not only is this process going to take longer, but the chances for renewed hostilities go up. If we can take the pressure off, blow off some steam—"

Admiral Nguyen nodded, his face expressionless. When he spoke, his tone was conversational.

"You guys over at Dip have any metaphors more recent than the steam engine?"

Avasarala chuckled with the others. She didn't think much of Agee either.

"Mars has already escalated," General Nettleford said. "Seems to me our best move at this point is to pull the Seventh back from Ceres Station. Get them burning. Put a ticking clock on the wall, then see if the Martians want to stand back on Ganymede."

"Are you talking about moving them to the Jovian system?" Nguyen asked. "Or are you taking them in toward Mars?"

"Taking something in toward Earth looks a lot like taking it in toward Mars," Nettleford said.

Avasarala cleared her throat.

"Do you have anything new on the initial attacker?" she asked.

"The tech guys are working on it," Nettleford said. "But that makes my point. If Mars is testing out new technologies on Ganymede, we can't afford to let them control the tempo. We have to get a threat of our own on the board."

"It was the protomolecule, though?" Agee asked. "I mean, it was whatever was on Eros when it went down?"

"Working on that," Nettleford said again, biting at the words a little. "There are some gross similarities, but there's some basic differences too. It didn't spread the way it did on Eros. Ganymede isn't changing the way the population of Eros did. From the satellite imagery we've got, it looks like it went to Martian territory and either self-destructed or was disposed of by their side. If it's related to Eros at all, it's been refined."

"So Mars got a sample and weaponized it," Admiral Souther said. He didn't talk much. Avasarala always forgot how high his voice was.

"One possibility," Nettleford said. "One very strong possibility."

"Look," Nguyen said with a self-satisfied little smile, like a child who knew he was going to get his way. "I know we've taken first strike off the table here, but we need to talk about what the limits are on immediate response. If this was a dry run for something bigger, waiting may be as good as walking out an airlock."

"We should take the meeting with Mars," Avasarala said.

The room went quiet. Nguyen's face darkened.

"Is that…" he said, but never finished the sentence. Avasarala watched the men look at each other. She took another pistachio from her purse, ate the meat, and tucked the shells away. Agee tried not to look pleased. She really did need to find out who had pulled strings to have him represent the diplomatic corps. He was a terrible choice.

"Security's going to be a problem," Nettleford said. "We're not letting any of their ships inside our effective defense perimeter."

"Well, we can't have it on their terms. If we're going to do this, we want them here, where we control the ground."

"Park them a safe distance away, and have our transports pick them up?"

"They'll never agree to that."

"So let's find out what they will agree to."

Avasarala quietly stood up and headed for the door. Her personal assistant—a European boy named Soren Cottwald—detached himself from the back wall and followed her. The generals pretended not to notice her exit, or maybe they were so wrapped up in the new set of problems she'd handed them, they really didn't. Either way, she was sure they were as pleased to have her out as she was to leave.

The hallways of the United Nations complex in the Hague were clean and wide, the décor a soft style that made everything look like a museum diorama of Portuguese colonies in the 1940s. She paused at an organics recycling unit and started digging the shells out of her bag.

"What's next?" she asked.

"Debriefing with Mr. Errinwright."

"After that?"

"Meeston Gravis about the Afghanistan problem."

"Cancel it."

"What should I tell him?"

Avasarala dusted her hands over the waste container, then turned, walking briskly toward the central commons and the elevators.

"Fuck him," she said. "Tell him the Afghanis have been resisting external rule since before my ancestors were kicking out the British. As soon as I figure out how to change that, I'll let him know."

"Yes, ma'am."

"I also need an updated summary paper on Venus. The latest. And I don't have time to get another PhD to read it, so if it's not in clear, concise language, fire the sonofabitch and get someone who knows how to write."

"Yes, ma'am."

The elevator that rose from the common lobby and meeting rooms up to the offices glittered like spun diamond set in steel and was big enough to seat dinner for four. It recognized them as they stepped in, and began its careful rise through the levels. Outside the windows of the common areas, the Binnenhof seemed to sink and the huge anthill of buildings that was the Hague spread out under a perfect blue sky. It was springtime, and the snow that had touched the city since December was finally gone. The pigeons swirled up from the streets far below. There were thirty billion people on the planet, but they would never crowd out the pigeons.

"They're all fucking men," she said.

"Excuse me?" Soren said.

"The generals. They're all fucking men."

"I thought Souther was the only—"

"I don't mean that they all fuck men. I mean they're all men, the fuckers. How long has it been since a woman was in charge of the armed forces? Not since I came here. So instead, we wind up with another example of what happens to policy when there's too much testosterone in the room. That reminds me: Get in touch with Annette Rabbir in infrastructure. I don't trust Nguyen. If traffic starts going up between him and anyone in the general assembly, I want to know it."

Soren cleared his throat.

"Excuse me, ma'am. Did you just instruct me to spy on Admiral Nguyen?"

"No, I just asked for a comprehensive audit of all network traffic, and I don't give a fuck about any results besides Nguyen's office."

"Of course. My mistake."

The elevator rose past the windows, past the view of the city, and into the dark shaft of the private-office levels. Avasarala cracked her knuckles.

"Just in case, though," she said, "do it on your own initiative."

"Yes, ma'am. That was my thought too."

To those who knew Avasarala only by reputation, her office was deceptively unassuming. It was on the east side of the building, where the lower-ranked officials usually started out. She had a window looking out over the city, but not a corner. The video screen that took up most of the southern wall was left off when it wasn't in active use, leaving it matte black. The other walls were scuffed bamboo paneling. The carpet was industrially short and patterned to hide stains. The only decorations were a small shrine with a clay sculpture of the Gautama Buddha beside the desk, and a cut crystal vase with the flowers that her husband, Arjun, sent every Thursday. The place smelled like fresh blooms and old pipe smoke, though Avasarala had never smoked there and didn't know anyone who had. She walked to the window. Beneath her, the city spread out in vast concrete and ancient stone.

In the darkening sky, Venus burned.

In the twelve years she had been at this desk, in this room, everything had changed. The alliance between Earth and its upstart brother had been an eternal, unshakable thing once. The Belt had been an annoyance and a haven for tiny cells of renegades and troublemakers as likely to die of a ship malfunction as to be called to justice. Humanity had been alone in the universe.

And then the secret discovery that Phoebe, idiosyncratic moon of Saturn, had been an alien weapon, launched at earth when life here was hardly more than an interesting idea wrapped in a lipid bilayer. How could anything be the same after that?

And yet it was. Yes, Earth and Mars were still unsure whether they were permanent allies or deadly enemies. Yes, the OPA, Hezbollah of the vacuum, was on its way to being a real political force in the outer planets. Yes, the thing that had been meant to reshape the primitive biosphere of Earth had instead ridden a rogue asteroid down into the clouds of Venus and started doing no one knew what.

But the spring still came. The election cycle still rose and fell. The evening star still lit the indigo heavens, outshining even the greatest cities of Earth.

Other days, she found that reassuring.

"Mr. Errinwright," Soren said.

Avasarala turned to the dead screen on her wall as it came to life. Sadavir Errinwright was darker skinned than she was, his face round and soft. It would have been in place anywhere in the Punjab, but his voice affected the cool, analytic amusement of Britain. He wore a dark suit and a smart, narrow tie. Wherever he was, it was bright daylight behind him. The link kept fluttering, trying to balance the bright with the dark, leaving him a shadow in a government office or else a man haloed by light.

"Your meeting went well, I hope?"

"It was fine," she said. "We're moving ahead with the Martian summit. They're working out the security arrangements now."

"That was the consensus?"

"Once I told them it was, yes. The Martians are sending their top men to a meeting with officials of the United Nations to personally deliver their apology and discuss how to normalize relations and return Ganymede to blah blah blah. Yes?"

Errinwright scratched his chin.

"I'm not sure that's how our opposites on Mars see it," he said.

"Then they can protest. We'll send out dueling press releases and threaten to cancel the meeting right up to the last minute. High drama is wonderful. It's better than wonderful; it's distracting. Just don't let the bobble-head talk about Venus or Eros."

His flinch was almost subliminal.

"Please, can we not refer to the secretary-general as 'the bobble-head'?"

"Why not? He knows I do. I say it to his face, and he doesn't mind."

"He thinks you're joking."

"That's because he's a fucking bobble-head. Don't let him talk about Venus."

"And the footage?"

It was a fair question. Whatever had made its attack on Ganymede, it had started in the area held by the United Nations. If the back-channel chatter was to be trusted—and it wasn't—Mars had a lone marine's suit camera. Avasarala had seven minutes of high-definition video from forty different cameras of the thing slaughtering the best people Earth had standing for it. Even if the Martians could be convinced to keep it quiet, this was going to be hard to bury.

"Give me until the meeting," Avasarala said. "Let me see what they say and how they say it. Then I'll know what to do. If it's a Martian weapon, they'll show it by what they bring to the table."

"I see," Errinwright said slowly. Meaning he didn't.

"Sir, with all respect," she said, "for the time being, this needs to be something between Earth and Mars."

"High drama between the two major military forces in the system is what we want? How exactly do you see that?"

"I got an alert from Michael-Jon de Uturbé about increased activity on Venus at the *same time* the shooting started on Ganymede. It wasn't a big spike, but it was there. And Venus getting restless just when something happens that looks a damn lot like the protomolecule showed up on Ganymede? That's a problem."

She let that sink in for a moment before she went on. Errinwright's eyes shifted, like he was reading in the air. It was something he did when he was thinking hard.

"Saber rattling we've done before," she said. "We've survived it. It's a known quantity. I have a binder with nine hundred pages of analysis and contingency plans for conflict with Mars, including fourteen different scenarios about what we do if they develop an unexpected new technology. The binder for what we do if something comes up from Venus? It's three pages long, and it begins *Step One: Find God.*"

Errinwright looked sober. She could hear Soren behind her, a different and more anxious silence than he usually carried. She'd laid her fear out on the table.

"Three options," she said softly. "One: Mars made it. That's just war. We can handle that. Two: Someone else made it. Unpleasant and dangerous, but solvable. Three: It made itself. And we don't have anything."

"You're going to put more pages in your thin binder?" Errin-wright said. He sounded flippant. He wasn't.

"No, sir. I'm going to find out which of the three we're looking at. If it's one of the first two, I'll solve the problem."

"And if the third?"

"Retire," she said. "Let you put some other idiot in charge."

Errinwright had known her long enough to hear the joke in her voice. He smiled and tugged absently at his tie. It was a tell of his. He was as anxious as she was. No one who didn't know him would have seen it.

"That's a tightrope. We can't let the conflict on Ganymede become too heated."

"I'll keep it a sideshow," Avasarala said. "No one starts a war unless I say they can."

"You mean unless the secretary-general issues the executive decision and the general assembly casts an affirming vote."

"And I'll tell him when he can do that," she said. "But you can give him the news. Hearing it from an old grandma like me makes his dick shrink."

"Well, we can't have that, certainly. Let me know what you find. I'll speak with the speech-writing staff and make certain that the text of his announcement doesn't color outside the lines."

"And anyone who leaks the video of the attack answers to me," she said.

"Anyone who leaks it is guilty of treason and will be tried before a legitimate tribunal and sent to the Lunar Penal Colony for life."

"Close enough."

"Don't be a stranger, Chrisjen. We're in difficult times. The fewer surprises, the better."

"Yes, sir," she said. The link died. The screen went dark. She could see herself in it as a smudge of orange topped by the gray of her hair. Soren was a blur of khaki and white.

"You need more work?"

"No, ma'am."

"So get the fuck out."

"Yes, ma'am."

She heard his footsteps retreating behind her.

"Soren!"

"Ma'am?"

"Get me a list of everyone who testified at the Eros incident hearings. And run what they said in testimony past the neuro-psych analysts if it hasn't already been."

"Would you like the transcripts?"

"Yes, that too."

"I'll have them to you as soon as possible."

The door closed behind him, and Avasarala sank into her chair. Her feet hurt, and the presentiment of a headache that had haunted her since morning was stepping forward, clearing its throat. The Buddha smiled serenely, and she chuckled at him, as if sharing a private joke. She wanted to go home, to sit on her porch and listen to Arjun practice his piano.

And instead…

She used her hand terminal rather than the office system to call Arjun. It was a superstitious urge that made her want to keep them separate, even in ways as small as this. He picked up the connection at once. His face was angular, the close-cut beard almost entirely white now. The merriness in his eyes was always there, even when he wept. Just looking at him, she felt something in her breast relax.

"I'm going to be late coming home," she said, immediately regretting the matter-of-fact tone. Arjun nodded.

"I am shocked beyond words," he said. Even the man's sarcasm was gentle. "The mask is heavy today?"

The mask, he called it. As if the person she was when she faced the world was the false one, and the one who spoke to him or played painting games with her granddaughters was authentic. She thought he was wrong, but the fiction was so comforting she had always played along.

"Today, very heavy. What are you doing now, love?"

"Reading Kukurri's thesis draft. It needs work."

"Are you in your office?"

"Yes."

"You should go to the garden," she said.

"Because that's where you want to be? We can go together when you're home."

She sighed.

"I may be very late," she said.

"Wake me, and we can go then."

She touched the screen, and he grinned as if he'd felt the caress. She cut the connection. By long habit, they didn't tell each other goodbye. It was one of a thousand small personal idioms that grew from decades of marriage.

Avasarala turned to her desk system, pulling up the tactical analysis of the battle on Ganymede, the intelligence profiles of the major military figures within Mars, and the master schedule for the meeting, already half filled in by the generals in the time since her conference. She took a pistachio from her purse, cracked its shell, and let the raw information wash over her, her mind dancing through it. In the window behind her, other stars struggled through the light pollution of the Hague, but Venus was still the brightest.

Chapter Six: Holden

Holden was dreaming of long twisting corridors filled with half-human horrors when a loud buzzing woke him to a pitch-black cabin. He struggled for a moment with the unfamiliar straps on the bunk before he unbuckled and floated free in the microgravity. The wall panel buzzed again. Holden pushed off the bed to it and hit the button to bring the cabin lights up. The cabin was tiny. A seventy-year-old crash couch above a personal storage locker crammed up against one bulkhead, a toilet and sink built into a corner, and across from the bunk, a wall panel with the name *Somnambulist* etched above it.

The panel buzzed a third time. This time Holden hit the reply button and said, "Where are we, Naomi?"

"Final braking for high orbit. You're not going to believe this, but they're making us queue up."

"Queue up, as in get in line?"

"Yep," Naomi said. "I think they're boarding all the ships that are landing on Ganymede."

Shit.

"Shit. Which side is it?"

"Does it matter?"

"Well," Holden said. "Earth wants me for stealing a couple thousand of their nuclear missiles and handing them over to the OPA. Mars just wants me for stealing one of their ships. I assume those carry different penalties."

Naomi laughed. "They'd lock you up for eternity either way."

"Call me pedantic, then."

"The group we're in line for look like UN ships, but a Martian frigate is parked right next to them, watching the proceedings."

Holden gave a private prayer of thanks for letting Fred Johnson back on Tycho talk him into taking the recently repaired *Somnambulist* to Ganymede rather than try to land in the *Rocinante*. The freighter was the least suspicious ship in the OPA fleet right now. Far less likely to draw unwanted attention than their stolen Martian warship. They'd left the *Roci* parked a million kilometers away from Jupiter in a spot no one was likely to look. Alex had the ship shut down except for air recycling and passive sensors and was probably huddled in his cabin with a space heater and a lot of blankets, waiting for their call.

"Okay, I'm on my way up. Send a tightbeam to Alex and let him know the situation. If we get arrested, he's to take the *Roci* back to Tycho."

Holden opened the locker under the bunk and pulled out a badly fitting green jumpsuit with *Somnambulist* stenciled on the back and the name Philips on the front pocket. According to the ship's records, provided by the tech wizards back at Tycho, he was crewman first class Walter Philips, engineer and general tool pusher on the food freighter *Somnambulist*. He was also third-in-command out of a crew of three. Given his reputation in the solar system, it was thought best that Holden not have a job on the ship that would require him to speak to anyone in authority.

He washed up in his tiny sink—no actual free-flowing water, but a system of moist towels and soaped pads—scratching unhappily at the scraggly beard he'd been growing as part of his disguise. He'd never tried to grow one before, and was disappointed to discover that his facial hair grew in patches of varying length and curl. Amos had grown a beard as well in an act of solidarity and now had a lush lion's mane, which he was considering keeping because it looked so good.

Holden slid the used towel into its cycling chamber and pushed off toward the compartment hatch and up the crew ladder to the operations deck.

Not that it was much of an ops deck. The *Somnambulist* was nearly a hundred years old and definitely at the end of her life cycle. If they hadn't needed a throwaway ship for this mission, Fred's people would probably have just scrapped the old girl out. Her recent run-in with pirates had left her half dead to begin with. But she'd spent the last twenty years of her life flying the Ganymede-to-Ceres food run, and she'd show up in the registry as a regular visitor to the Jovian moon, a ship that might plausibly arrive with relief supplies. Fred thought that with her regular arrivals at Ganymede, she might just get waved past any customs or blockades without a look.

That, it seemed, had been optimistic.

Naomi was belted into one of the operations stations when Holden arrived. She wore a green jumpsuit similar to his, though the name on her pocket read *Estancia*. She gave him a smile, then waved him over to look at her screen.

"That's the group of ships that are checking everyone out before they land."

"Damn," Holden said, zooming the telescopic image in to get a better look at the hulls and identifying marks. "Definitely UN ships." Something small moved across the image from one of the UN ships to the heavy freighter that was currently at the front of the line. "And that looks like a boarding skiff."

"Well, good thing you haven't groomed in a month," Naomi

said, tugging at a lock of his hair. "With that bush on your head and that awful beard, your own mothers wouldn't recognize you."

"I'm hoping they haven't recruited my mothers," Holden said, trying to match her lightness of tone. "I'll warn Amos that they're coming."

Holden, Naomi, and Amos waited in the short locker-filled hallway just outside the inner airlock door for the boarding party to finish cycling the 'lock. Naomi looked tall and stern in her freshly washed captain's uniform and magnetic boots. Captain Estancia had skippered the *Somnambulist* for ten years before the pirate attack that took her life. Holden thought Naomi made a suitably regal replacement.

Behind her, Amos wore a jumpsuit with a chief engineer's patch and a bored scowl. Even in the microgravity of their current orbit around Ganymede, he seemed to be slouching. Holden did his best to emulate his stance and his half-angry expression.

The airlock finished cycling, and the inner doors slid open. Six marines in combat armor and a junior lieutenant in an environment suit clanked out on mag boots. The lieutenant quickly looked over the crew and checked them against something on his hand terminal. He looked as bored as Amos did. Holden guessed that this poor junior officer had been stuck with the shit duty of boarding ships all day and was probably in as big a hurry to be done as they were to leave.

"Rowena Estancia, captain and majority owner of the Ceres-registered freighter *Weeping Somnambulist*."

He didn't make it a question, but Naomi replied, "Yes, sir."

"I like the name," the lieutenant said without looking up from his terminal.

"Sir?"

"The ship name. It's unusual. I swear, if I board one more ship named after someone's kid or the girl they left behind after that magical weekend on Titan, I'm going to start fining people for general lack of creativity."

Holden felt a tension begin at the base of his spine and creep up toward his scalp. This lieutenant might be bored with his job, but he was smart and perceptive, and he was letting them know it up front.

"Well, this one is named after the tearful three months I spent on Titan after he left me," Naomi said with a grin. "Probably a good thing in the long term. I was going to name her after my goldfish."

The lieutenant's head snapped up in surprise; then he began laughing. "Thanks, Captain. That's the first laugh today. Everyone else is scared shitless of us, and these six slabs of meat"—he gestured at the marines behind him—"have had their senses of humor chemically removed."

Holden shot a look to Amos. *Is he flirting with her? I think he's flirting with her.* Amos' scowl could have meant anything.

The lieutenant tapped something on his terminal and said, "Protein, supplements, water purifiers, and antibiotics. Can I take a quick look?"

"Yes, sir," Naomi said, gesturing toward the hatch. "Right this way."

She left, the UN officer and two of the marines in tow. The other four settled into alert-guard poses next to the airlock. Amos elbowed Holden to get his attention, then said, "How you boys doing today?"

The marines ignored him.

"I was saying to my buddy here, I was saying, 'I bet those fancy tin suits those boys wear bind up something awful in the crotch.'"

Holden closed his eyes and started sending psychic messages to Amos to shut up. It didn't work.

"I mean, all that fancy high-tech gear strapped on everywhere, and the one thing they don't allow for is scratching your balls. Or, God forbid, you get outta alignment and gotta give the works a shift to create some space."

Holden opened his eyes. The marines were all looking at Amos now, but they hadn't moved or spoken. Holden shifted to the back corner of the room and tried to press himself into it. No one even glanced in his direction.

"So," Amos continued, his voice full of companionable good cheer. "I got this theory, and I was hoping you boys could help me out."

The closest marine took a half step forward, but that was all.

"My theory is," Amos said, "that to avoid that whole problem, they just go ahead and cut off all those parts that might get caught up in your suit. And it has the added benefit of reducing your temptation to diddle each other during those long cold nights on the ship."

The marine took another step, and Amos immediately took one of his own to close the distance. With his nose so close to the marine's armored faceplate that his breath fogged the glass, Amos said, "So be straight with me, Joe. The outside of those suits, that's anatomically correct, ain't it?"

There was a long, tense silence that was finally broken when someone cleared his throat at the hatch, and the lieutenant came into the corridor. "There a problem here?"

Amos smiled and stepped back.

"Nope. Just getting to know the fine men and women my tax dollars help pay for."

"Sergeant?" the lieutenant said.

The marine stepped back.

"No, sir. No problem."

The lieutenant turned around and shook Naomi's hand.

"Captain Estancia, it has been a pleasure. Our people will be radioing you with landing clearance shortly. I'm sure the people of Ganymede will be grateful for the supplies you're bringing."

"Happy to help," Naomi said, and gave the young officer a brilliant smile.

When the UN troops had cycled back through the airlock and flown away in their skiff, Naomi let out a long breath and began massaging her cheeks.

"If I had to smile one second longer, my face was going to crack apart."

Holden grabbed Amos by the sleeve.

"What. The. Fuck," he said through gritted teeth, "was *that* all about?"

"What?" Naomi said.

"Amos here did just about everything he could to piss the marines off while you were gone. I'm surprised they didn't shoot him, and then me half a second later."

Amos glanced down at Holden's hand, still gripping his arm, but made no move to pull free.

"Cap, you're a good guy, but you'd be a shitty smuggler."

"What?" Naomi said again.

"The captain here was so nervous even I started to think he was up to something. So I kept the marines' attention until you got back," Amos said. "Oh, and they can't shoot you unless you actually touch them or draw a weapon. You were a UN Navy boy. You should remember the rules."

"So..." Holden started.

"So," Amos interrupted. "If the lieutenant asks them about us, they'll have a story to tell about the asshole engineer who got in their faces, and not the nervous guy with the patchy beard who kept trying to hide in the corner."

"Shit," Holden said.

"You're a good captain, and you can have my back in a fight anytime. But you're a crap criminal. You just don't know how to act like anyone but yourself."

"Wanna be captain again?" Naomi said. "That job sucks."

"Ganymede tower, this is *Somnambulist* repeating our request for a pad assignment," Naomi said. "We've been cleared by the UN patrols, and you've had us holding in low orbit for three hours now."

Naomi flicked off her mic and added, "Asshole."

The voice that replied was different from the one they'd been requesting landing clearance from for the last few hours. This one was older and less annoyed.

"Sorry, *Somnambulist*, we'll get you into the pattern as soon as possible. But we've had launches nonstop for the last ten hours, and we still have a dozen ships to get off of the ground before we start letting people land."

Holden turned on his mic and said, "We talking to the supervisor now?"

"Yep. Senior supervisor Sam Snelling if you're making notes for a complaint. That's Snelling with two *L*s."

"No, no," Holden replied. "Not a complaint. We've been watching the outgoing ships flying by. Are these refugee ships? With the tonnage we've seen lifting off, it looks like half the moon is leaving."

"Nope. We do have a few charters and commercial liners taking people off, but most of the ships leaving right now are food freighters."

"Food freighters?"

"We ship almost a hundred thousand kilos of food a *day*, and the fighting trapped a lot of those shipments on the surface. Now that the blockade is letting people through, they're on their way out to make their deliveries."

"Wait," Holden said. "I'm waiting to land with relief food supplies for people starving on Ganymede, and you're launching a hundred thousand kilos of food *off* the moon?"

"Closer to half a million, what with the backup," Sam said. "But we don't own this food. Most of the food production on Ganymede is owned by corporations that aren't headquartered here. Lot of money tied up in these shipments. Every day it sat on the ground here, people were losing a fortune."

"I..." Holden started, then after a pause said, "*Somnambulist* out."

Holden turned his chair around to face Naomi. Her expression was closed in a way that meant she was as angry as he was.

Amos, lounging near the engineering console and eating an

apple he'd stolen from their relief supplies, said, "This surprises you why, Captain?"

An hour later, they got permission to land.

Seen from low orbit and their descent path, the surface of Ganymede didn't look much different than it ever had. Even at its best, the Jovian moon was a wasteland of gray silicate rock and slightly less gray water ice, the entire thing pocked with craters and flash-frozen lakes. It had looked like a battlefield long before humanity's ancestors crawled up onto dry land for the first time.

But humans, with their great creativity and industriousness in the domain of destruction, had found ways to make their mark. Holden spotted the almost skeletal remains of a destroyer stretched across the landscape at the end of a long black scar. The shock wave of its impact had flattened smaller domes as far as ten kilometers away. Tiny rescue ships flitted about its corpse, looking less for survivors than for bits of information or technology that had survived the crash and couldn't be allowed to fall into enemy hands.

The worst damage visible was the complete loss of one of the enormous greenhouse domes. The agricultural domes were gigantic structures of steel and glass with hectares of carefully cultivated soil and meticulously bred and tended crops beneath them. To see one crushed beneath the twisted metal of what looked like a fallen mirror array was shocking and demoralizing. The domes fed the outer planets with their specially bred crops. The most advanced agricultural science in history happened inside them. And the orbiting mirrors were marvels of engineering that helped make it possible. Slamming one into the other, and leaving both lying in ruins, struck Holden as being as stupidly shortsighted as shitting in your water supply to deny your enemy a drink.

By the time the *Somnambulist* had set her creaking bones to rest on their assigned landing pad, Holden had lost all patience with human stupidity.

So, of course, it came out to meet him.

The customs inspector was waiting for them when they stepped out of the airlock. He was a stick-thin man with a handsome face and an egg-shaped bald head. He was accompanied by two men in nondescript security guard uniforms with Tasers in holsters at their belts.

"Hello, my name is Mr. Vedas. I am the customs inspector for port eleven, pads A14 through A22. Your manifest, please."

Naomi, once again playing captain, stepped forward and said, "The manifest was transmitted to your office prior to landing. I don't—"

Holden saw that Vedas wasn't holding an official cargo-inspection terminal, nor were the guards with him wearing Ganymede Port Authority uniforms. He got the tingling premonition of a bad con job about to be played out. He moved up and waved Naomi off.

"Captain, I'll take care of this."

Customs inspector Vedas looked him up and down and said, "And you are?"

"You can call me Mr. Not-putting-up-with-your-bullshit."

Vedas scowled, and the two security guards shuffled closer. Holden smiled at them, then reached behind his back and under his coat and pulled out a large pistol. He held it at the side of his leg, pointed at the ground, but they stepped back anyway. Vedas blanched.

"I know this shakedown," Holden said. "You ask to look at our manifest; then you tell us which items we have *mistakenly* included on it. And while we are retransmitting to your office with our newly amended manifest, you and your goons take the plum items and sell them on what I'm guessing is a thriving black market for food and medicine."

"I am a legally vested administrator of Ganymede Station," Vedas squeaked. "You think you can bully me with your gun? I'll have port security arrest you and impound your entire ship if you think—"

"No, I'm not going to bully you," Holden said. "But I have had it right up to here with idiots profiting from misery, and I'm going to make myself feel better by having my big friend Amos here beat you senseless for trying to steal food and medicine from refugees."

"Ain't bullying so much as stress relief," Amos said amiably.

Holden nodded at Amos.

"How angry does it make you that this guy wants to steal from refugees, Amos?"

"Pretty fucking angry, Captain."

Holden patted his pistol against his thigh.

"The gun is just to make sure 'port security' there doesn't interfere until Amos has fully worked out his anger issues."

Mr. Vedas, customs inspector for port eleven, pads A14 through A22, turned and ran as though his life depended on it, with his rent-a-cops in hot pursuit.

"You enjoyed that," Naomi said. Her expression was odd and evaluating, her voice in the no-man's-land between accusing and not.

Holden holstered his gun.

"Let's go find out what the hell happened here."

Chapter Seven: Prax

The security center was on the third layer down from the surface. The finished walls and independent power supply seemed like luxury items compared with the raw ice of other places on the station, but really they were important signals. The way some plants advertised their poisons by bright foliage, the security center advertised its impregnability. It wasn't enough that it was impossible to tunnel through the ice and sneak a friend or a lover out of the holding cells. Everyone had to *know* that it was impossible—know just by looking—or else someone would try it.

In all his years on Ganymede, Prax had been there only once before, and then as a witness. As a man there to help the law, not to ask help from it. He'd been back twelve times in the last week, waiting in the long, desperate line, fidgeting and struggling with the almost overpowering sense that he needed to be somewhere else doing something, even if he didn't know what exactly it was.

"I'm sorry, Dr. Meng," the woman at the public information counter said from behind her inch-thick wire-laced window. She looked tired. More than tired, more than exhausted even. Shell-shocked. Dead. "Nothing today either."

"Is there anyone I can talk to? There has to be a way to—"

"I'm sorry," she said, and her eyes looked past him to the next desperate, frightened, unbathed person that she wouldn't be able to help. Prax walked out, teeth grinding in impotent rage. The line was two hours long; men and women and children stood or leaned or sat. Some were weeping. A young woman with red-rimmed eyes smoked a marijuana cigarette, the smell of burning leaves over the stink of close-packed bodies, the smoke curling up past the NO SMOKING sign on the wall. No one protested. All of them had the haunted look of refugees, even the ones who'd been born here.

In the days since the official fighting had stopped, the Martian and Earth militaries had retreated back behind their lines. The breadbasket of the outer planets found itself reduced to a waste-land between them, and the collected intelligence of the station was bent to a single task: getting away.

The ports had started out under lockdown by two military forces in conflict, but they'd soon left the surface for the safety of their ships, and the depth of panic and fear in the station could no longer be contained. The few passenger ships that were permitted out were packed with people trying to get anywhere else. The fares for passage were bankrupting people who'd worked for years in some of the highest-paying material science positions outside Earth. The poorer people were left sneaking out in freight drones or tiny yachts or even space suits strapped onto modified frames and fired off toward Europa in hopes of rescue. Panic drove them from risk to risk until they wound up somewhere else or in the grave. Near the security stations, near the ports, even near the abandoned military cordons set up by Mars and the UN, the corridors were thick with people scrambling for anything they could tell themselves was safety.

Prax wished he was with them.

Instead, his world had fallen into a kind of rhythm. He woke at his rooms, because he always went home at night so that he would be there if Mei came back. He ate whatever he could find. The last two days, there hadn't been anything left in his personal storage, but a few of the ornamental plants in the parkways were edible. He wasn't really hungry anyway.

Then he checked the body drops.

The hospital had maintained a scrolling video feed of the recovered dead to help in identification for the first week. Since then, he'd had to go look at the actual bodies. He was looking for a child, so he didn't have to go through the vast majority of the dead, but the ones he did see haunted him. Twice he'd found a corpse sufficiently mutilated that it might have been Mei, but the first had a stork-bite birthmark at the back of her neck and the other's toenails were the wrong shape. Those dead girls were someone else's tragedies.

Once he'd assured himself that Mei wasn't among the lists of the dead, he went hunting. The first night she'd been gone, he'd taken out his hand terminal and made a list. People to contact who had official power: security, her doctors, the warring armies. People to contact who might have information: the other parents at her school, the other parents in his medical support group, her mother. Favorite places to check: her best friend's home, the common-space parks she liked best, the sweet shop with the lime sherbet she always asked for. Places someone might go to buy a stolen child for sex: a list of bars and brothels off a cached copy of the station directory. The updated directory would be on the system, but it was still locked down. Every day, he crossed as many off the list as he could, and when they were all gone, he started over.

From a list, they'd become a schedule. Security every other day, alternating with whoever would talk to him from the Martian forces or the UN on the other days. The parks in the morning after the body checks. Mei's best friend and her family had made it out, so there was nothing to check there. The sweet shop had been burned out in a riot. Finding her doctors was the hardest. Dr. Astrigan, her pediatrician, had made all the right concerned noises and promised him that she would call him if she heard anything and then, when he checked again three days later, didn't remember having spoken to him. The surgeon who'd helped drain the abscesses along her spine when she'd first been diagnosed hadn't seen her. Dr. Strickland from the support and maintenance group was missing. Nurse Abuakár was dead.

The other families from the group had their own tragedies to work through. Mei wasn't the only child missing. Katoa Merton. Gabby Solyuz. Sandro Ventisiete. He'd seen the fear and desperation that shrieked in the back of his head mirrored in the faces of the other parents. It made those visits harder than looking at bodies. It made the fear hard to forget.

He did it anyway.

Basia Merton—KatoaDaddy, Mei called him—was a thick-necked man who always smelled of peppermint. His wife was pencil thin with a nervous twitch of a smile. Their home was six chambers near the water-management complex five levels down from the surface, decorated in spun silk and bamboo. When Basia opened the door, he didn't smile or say hello; he only turned and walked in, leaving the way open. Prax followed him.

At the table, Basia poured Prax a glass of miraculously unspoiled milk. It was the fifth time Prax had come since Mei had gone missing.

"No sign, then?" Basia said. It wasn't really a question.

"No news," Prax said. "So there's that, at least."

From the back of the house, a young girl's voice rose in outrage, matched by a younger boy's. Basia didn't even turn to look.

"Nothing here either. I'm sorry."

The milk tasted wonderful, smooth and rich and soft. Prax could almost feel the calories and nutrients being sucked in through the membranes in his mouth. It occurred to him that he might technically be starving.

"There's still hope," Prax said.

Basia blew out his breath like the words had been a punch in the gut. His lips were pressed thin and he was staring at the table. The shouting voices in the back resolved into a low boyish wail.

"We're leaving," Basia said. "My cousin works on Luna for Magellan Biotech. They're sending relief ships, and when they put off the medical supplies, there's going to be room for us. It's all arranged."

Prax put down the glass of milk. The chambers around them seemed to go quiet, but he knew that was an illusion. A strange pressure bloomed in his throat, down into his chest. His face felt waxy. He had the sudden physical memory of his wife announcing that she'd filed for divorce. Betrayed. He felt betrayed.

"...after that, another few days," Basia was saying. He'd been talking, but Prax hadn't heard him.

"But what about Katoa?" Prax managed to say around the thickness in his throat. "He's here somewhere."

Basia's gaze flickered up and then away, fast as a bird's wing.

"He's not. He's gone, brother. Boy had a swamp where his immune system should've been. You know that. Without his medicine, he used to start feeling really sick in three, maybe four days. I have to take care of the two kids I still got."

Prax nodded, his body responding without him. He felt like a flywheel had come loose somewhere in the back of his head. The grain of the bamboo table seemed unnaturally sharp. The smell of ice melt. The taste of milk going sour on his tongue.

"You can't know that," he said, trying to keep his voice soft. He didn't do a great job.

"I pretty much can."

"Whoever...whoever took Mei and Katoa, they aren't useful to them dead. They knew. They had to know that they'd need medicine. And so it only makes sense that they'd take them somewhere they could get it."

"No one took them, brother. They got lost. Something happened."

"Mei's teacher said—"

"Mei's teacher was scared crazy. Her whole world was making sure toddlers don't spit in each other's mouths too much, and there's a shooting war outside her room. Who the hell knows what she saw?"

"She said Mei's mother and a *doctor*. She said a doctor—"

"And come on, man. Not useful if they're dead? This station is ass deep in dead people, and I don't see anyone getting *useful*. It's a war. Fuckers started a war." There were tears in his wide, dark eyes now, and sorrow in his voice. But there was no fight. "People die in a war. Kids die. You gotta...ah shit. You got to keep moving."

"You don't know," Prax said. "You don't know that they're dead, and until you know, you're abandoning them."

Basia looked down at the floor. There was a flush rising under the man's skin. He shook his head, the corners of his mouth twitching down.

"You can't go," Prax said. "You have to stay and look for him."

"Don't," Basia said. "And I mean *do not* shout at me in my own home."

"These are our kids, and you don't *get* to walk away from them! What kind of father are you? I mean, *Jesus*..."

Basia was leaning forward now, hunched over the table. Behind him, a girl on the edge of womanhood looked in from the hallway, her eyes wide. Prax felt a deep certainty rising in him.

"You're going to stay," he said.

The silence lasted three heartbeats. Four. Five.

"It's arranged," Basia said.

Prax hit him. He didn't plan it, didn't intend it. His arm rolled through the shoulder, balled fist shooting out of its own accord. His knuckles sank into the flesh of Basia's cheek, snapping his head to the side and rocking him back. The big man boiled across the room at him. The first blow hit just below Prax's collarbone, pushing him back, the next one was to his ribs, and the one after that. Prax felt his chair slide out from under him, and he was falling slowly in the low g but unable to get his feet beneath him. Prax swung wild, kicked out. He felt his foot connect with something, but he couldn't tell if it was the table or Basia.

He hit the floor, and Basia's foot came down on his solar plexus. The world went bright, shimmering, and painful. Somewhere a long way away, a woman was shouting. He couldn't make out the words. And then, slowly, he could.

He's not right. He lost a baby too. He's not right.

Prax rolled over, forced himself up to his knees. There was blood on his chin he was pretty sure came from him. No one else there was bleeding. Basia stood by the table, hands in fists, nostrils flared, breath fast. The daughter stood in front of him, interposed between her enraged father and Prax. All he could really see of her was her ass and her ponytail and her hands, flat out at her father in the universal gesture for *stop*. She was saving his life.

"You'd be better off gone, brother," Basia said.

"Okay," Prax said.

He got to his feet slowly and stumbled to the door, still not quite breathing right. He let himself out.

The secret of closed-system botanical collapse was this: *It's not the thing that breaks you need to watch out for. It's the cascade.* The first time he'd lost a whole crop of *G. kenon*, it had been from a fungus that didn't hurt soybeans at all. The spores had probably come in with a shipment of ladybugs. The fungus took hold in the hydroponic system, merrily taking up nutrients that weren't meant for it and altering the pH. That weakened the bacteria Prax had been using to fix nitrogen to the point that they were vulnerable to a phage that wouldn't have been able to take them out otherwise. The nitrogen balance of the system got out of whack. By the time the bacteria recovered to their initial population, the soybeans were yellow, limp, and past repair.

That was the metaphor he used when he thought about Mei and her immune system. The problem was tiny, really. A mutant allele produced a protein that folded left instead of right. A few base pairs' difference. But that protein catalyzed a critical step in signal transduction to the T cells. She could have all the parts of an immune system standing ready to fight off a pathogen, but without twice-daily doses of an artificial catalyzing agent, the alarm would never sound. Myers-Skelton Premature Immunosenescence they called it, and the preliminary studies still hadn't even been able to tell if it was more common outside the well of Earth because of an unknown low-g effect or just the high radiation levels increasing mutations rates generally. It didn't matter. However she'd gotten there, Mei had developed a massive spinal infection when she was four months old. If they'd been anywhere else in the outer planets, she'd have died of it. But everyone came to Ganymede to gestate, so the child health research all happened there. When Dr. Strickland saw her, he knew what he was looking at, and he held back the cascade.

Prax walked down the corridors toward home. His jaw was swelling. He didn't remember being hit in the jaw, but it was swelling, and it hurt. His ribs had a sharp pain on the left that hurt if he breathed in too deep, so he kept his breath shallow. He stopped at one of the parks, scrounging a few leaves for dinner. He paused at a large stand of *Epipremnum aureum*. The wide spade-shaped leaves looked wrong. They were still green, but thicker, and with a golden undertone. Someone had put distilled water in the hydroponic supply instead of the mineral-rich solution long-stability hydroponics needed. They could get away with it for another week. Maybe two. Then the air-recycling plants would start to die, and by the time that happened, the cascade would be too far gone to stop. And if they couldn't get the right water to the plants, he couldn't imagine they'd be able to set all the mechanical air recyclers going. Someone was going to have to do something about that.

Someone else.

In his rooms, his one small *G. kenon* held its fronds up to the light. Without any particular conscious thought, he put his finger in the soil, testing it. The rich scent of well-balanced soil was like incense. It was doing pretty well, all things considered. He glanced at the time stamp on his hand terminal. Three hours had passed since he'd come home. His jaw had gone past aching into a kind of constantly rediscovered pain.

Without her medicine, the normal flora of her digestive system would start overgrowing. The bacteria that normally lived benignly in her mouth and throat would rise against her. After two weeks, maybe she wouldn't be dead. But even in the best case, she'd be so sick that bringing her back would be problematic.

It was a war. Kids died in wars. It was a cascade. He coughed, and the pain was immense and it was still better than thinking. He needed to go. To get out. Ganymede was dying around him. He wasn't going to do Mei any good. She was gone. His baby girl was gone.

Crying hurt worse than coughing.

He didn't sleep so much as lose consciousness. When he woke, his jaw was swollen badly enough that it clicked when he opened his mouth too wide. His ribs felt a degree better. He sat on the edge of his bed, head in his hands.

He'd go to the port. He'd go to Basia and apologize and ask to go along. Get out of the Jovian system entirely. Go someplace and start over without his past. Without his failed marriage and shattered work. Without Mei.

He switched to a slightly less dirty shirt. Swabbed his armpits with a damp cloth. Combed his hair back. He'd failed. It was pointless. He had to come to terms with the loss and move on. And maybe someday he would.

He checked his hand terminal. That day was checking the Martian body drop, walking the parks, checking with Dr. Astrigan, and then a list of five brothels he hadn't been to, where he could ask after the illicit pleasures of pedophilia, hopefully without being gutted by some right-thinking, civic-minded thug. Thugs had children too. Some probably loved them. With a sigh, he keyed in a new entry: MINERALIZE PARK WATER. He'd need to find someone with physical plant access codes. Maybe security could help with that at least.

And maybe, somewhere along the way, he'd find Mei.

There was still hope.

Chapter Eight: Bobbie

The *Harman Dae-Jung* was a *Donnager*-class dreadnought, half a kilometer in length, and a quarter million tons dry weight. Her interior docking bay was large enough to hold four frigate-class escort ships and a variety of lighter shuttles and repair craft. Currently, it held only two ships: the large and almost opulent shuttle that had ferried the Martian ambassadors and state officials up for the flight to Earth, and the smaller and more functional Navy shuttle Bobbie had ridden up from Ganymede.

Bobbie was using the empty space to jog.

The *Dae-Jung's* captain was being pressured by the diplomats to get them to Earth as quickly as possible, so the ship was running at a near-constant one g acceleration. While this made most of the Martian civilians uncomfortable, it suited Bobbie just fine. The corps trained at high g all the time and did lengthy endurance drills at one g at least once a month. No one ever said it was to prepare for the possibility of having to fight a ground war on Earth. No one had to.

Her recent tour on Ganymede hadn't allowed her to get in any high-g exercise, and the long trip to Earth seemed like an excellent opportunity to get back into shape. The last thing she wanted was to appear weak to the natives.

"Anything you can do I can do better," she sang to herself in a breathless falsetto as she ran. "I can do anything better than you."

She gave her wristwatch a quick glance. Two hours. At her current leisurely pace, that meant twelve miles. Push for twenty? How many people on Earth regularly ran for twenty miles? Martian propaganda would have her believe that half of the people on Earth didn't even have jobs. They just lived off the government dole and spent their meager allowances on drugs and stim parlors. But probably *some* of them could run for twenty miles. She'd bet Snoopy and his gang of Earther marines could have run twenty miles, the way they were running from—

"Anything you can do I can do better," she sang, then concentrated on nothing but the sound of her shoes slapping on the metal deck.

She didn't see the yeoman enter the docking bay, so when he called out to her, she twisted in surprise and tripped over her own feet, catching herself with her left hand just before she would have dashed her brains out on the deck. She felt something pop in her wrist, and her right knee bounced painfully off the floor as she rolled to absorb the impact.

She lay on her back for a few moments, moving her wrist and knee to see if there was any serious damage. Both hurt, but neither had any grating sensation in it. Nothing broken, then. Barely out of the hospital and already looking for ways to bang herself up again. The yeoman ran up to her and dropped into a crouch at her side.

"Jesus, Gunny, you took a hell of a spill!" the Navy boy said. "A *hell* of a spill!"

He touched her right knee where the bruise was already starting to darken the bare skin below her jogging shorts, then seemed to realize what he was doing and yanked his hand back.

"Sergeant Draper, your presence is requested at a meeting in conference room G at fourteen fifty hours," he said, squeaking a little as he rattled off his message. "How come you don't carry your terminal with you? They've had trouble tracking you down."

Bobbie pushed herself back up to her feet, gingerly testing her knee to see if it would hold her weight.

"You just answered your own question, kid."

Bobbie arrived at the conference room five minutes early, her red-and-khaki service uniform sharply pressed and marred only by the white wrist brace the company medic had given her for what turned out to be a minor sprain. A marine in full battle dress and armed with an assault rifle opened the door for her and gave her a smile as she went by. It was a nice smile, full of even white teeth, below almond-shaped eyes so dark they were almost black.

Bobbie smiled back and glanced at the name on his suit. Corporal Matsuke. Never knew who you'd run into in the galley or the weight room. It didn't hurt to make a friend or two.

She was pulled the rest of the way into the room by someone calling her name.

"Sergeant Draper," Captain Thorsson repeated, gesturing impatiently toward a chair at the long conference table.

"Sir," Bobbie said, and snapped off a salute before taking the seat. She was surprised by how few people were in the room. Just Thorsson from the intelligence corps and two civilians she hadn't met.

"Gunny, we're going over some of the details in your report; we'd appreciate your input."

Bobbie waited a moment to be introduced to the two civilians in the room, but when it became clear Thorsson wasn't going to do it, she just said, "Yes, sir. Whatever I can do to help."

The first civilian, a severe-looking redheaded woman in a very expensive suit, said, "We're trying to create a better timeline of the events leading up to the attack. Can you show us on this map where you and your fire team were when you received the radio message to return to the outpost?"

Bobbie showed them, then went step by step through the events of that day. Looking at the map they'd brought, she saw for the first time how far she'd been flung across the ice by the impact of the orbital mirror. It looked like it had been a matter of centimeters between that and being smashed into dust like the rest of her platoon…

"Sergeant," Thorsson said, his tone of voice letting her know he'd said it a couple of times before.

"Sir, sorry, looking at these photos sent me woolgathering. It won't happen again."

Thorsson nodded, but with a strange expression Bobbie couldn't read.

"What we're trying to pinpoint is precisely where the Anomaly was inserted prior to the attack," the other civilian, a chubby man with thinning brown hair, said.

The Anomaly they called it now. You could hear them capitalize the word when they said it. *Anomaly*, like something that just happens. A strange random event. It was because everyone was still afraid to call it what it really was. The Weapon.

"So," the chubby guy said, "based on how long you had radio contact, and information regarding loss of radio signal from other installations around that area, we are able to pinpoint the source of the jamming signal as the Anomaly itself."

"Wait," Bobbie said, shaking her head. "What? The monster *can't* have jammed our radios. It had no tech. It wasn't even wearing a damned *space suit* to breathe! How could it be carrying jamming equipment?"

Thorsson patted her hand paternally, a move that irritated Bobbie more than it calmed her.

"The data doesn't lie, Sergeant. The zone of radio blackout moved. And always at its center was the…thing. The Anomaly,"

Thorsson said, then turned away from her to speak to the chubby guy and the redhead.

Bobbie sat back, feeling the energy move away from her in the room, like she was the one person at the dance without a date. But since Thorsson hadn't dismissed her, she couldn't just leave.

Redhead said, "Based on our radio loss data, that puts insertion here"—she pointed at something on the map—"and the path to the UN outpost is along this ridge."

"What's in that location?" Thorsson said with a frown.

Chubby pulled up a different map and pored over it for a few seconds.

"Looks like some old service tunnels for the dome's hydro plant. This says they haven't been used in decades."

"So," Thorsson said. "The kind of tunnels one might use to transport something dangerous that needs to be kept secret."

"Yes," Redhead said, "maybe they were delivering it to that Marine outpost and it got loose. The marines cut and ran when they saw it was out of control."

Bobbie gave a dismissive laugh before she could stop herself.

"You have something to add, Sergeant Draper?" Thorsson said.

Thorsson was looking at her with his enigmatic smile, but Bobbie had worked with him long enough now to know that what he hated most was bullshit. If you spoke up, he wanted to make sure you actually had something useful to say. The two civilians were looking at her with surprise, as though she were a cockroach that had suddenly stood up on two legs and started speaking.

She shook her head.

"When I was a boot, you know what my drill sergeant said was the second most dangerous thing in the solar system, after a Martian Marine?"

The civvies continued to stare at her, but Thorsson nodded and mouthed the words along with her as she next spoke.

"A UN Marine."

Chubby and Redhead shared a look and Redhead rolled her

eyes for him. But Thorsson said, "So you don't think the UN soldiers were running from something that got out of their control."

"Not a fucking chance, sir."

"Then give us your take on it."

"That UN outpost was staffed by a full platoon of Marines. Same strength as our outpost. When they finally started running, there were six left. Six. They fought almost to the last man. When they ran to us, they weren't trying to disengage. They were coming so we could help them *continue* the fight."

Chubby picked a leather satchel up off the floor and started rummaging in it. Redhead watched, as though what he was doing was far more interesting than anything Bobbie had to say.

"If this were some secret UN thing that those Marines were tasked to deliver or protect, they wouldn't have come. They'd have died doing it rather than abandon their mission. That's what we would have done."

"Thank you," Thorsson said.

"I mean, it wasn't even our fight, and *we* fought to the last marine to stop that thing. You think the UN Marines would do less?"

"Thank you, Sergeant," Thorsson said again, louder. "I tend to agree, but we have to explore all possibilities. Your comments are noted."

Chubby finally found what he was looking for. A small plastic box of mints. He took one out, then held the box out to Redhead to take one. The sickly sweet smell of spearmint filled the air. Around a mouthful of mint, Chubby said, "Yes, thank you, Sergeant. I think we can proceed here without taking up more of your time."

Bobbie stood up, snapped another salute at Thorsson, and left the room. Her heart was going fast. Her jaw ached where she was grinding her teeth.

Civvies didn't get it. No one did.

When Captain Martens came into the cargo bay, Bobbie had just finished disassembling the gun housing on her combat suit's right arm. She removed the three-barrel Gatling gun from its mount and placed it on the floor next to the two dozen other parts she'd already stripped off. Next to them sat a can of gun cleaner and a bottle of lubricant, along with the various rods and brushes she'd use to clean the parts.

Martens waited until she had the gun on the cleaning mat, then sat down on the floor next to her. She attached a wire brush to the end of one of the cleaning rods, dipped it in the cleaner, and began running the brush through the gun, one barrel at a time. Martens watched.

After a few minutes, she replaced the brush with a small cloth and swabbed the remaining cleanser out of the barrels. Then a fresh cloth soaked in gun lubricant to oil them. When she was applying lube to the complex mesh of gears that composed the Gatling mechanism and ammo feed system, Martens finally spoke.

"You know," he said, "Thorsson is naval intelligence right from the start. Straight into officer training, top of his class at the academy, and first posting at fleet command. He's never done anything but *be* an intelligence wonk. The last time he fired a gun was his six weeks as a boot, twenty years ago. He's never led a fire team. Or served in a combat platoon."

"That," Bobbie said, putting down her lubricant then standing up to put the gun back together, "is a fascinating story. I really appreciate you sharing it."

"So," Martens continued, not missing a beat. "How fucked up do you have to be before Thorsson starts asking me if maybe you aren't a little shell-shocked?"

Bobbie dropped the wrench she was holding, but caught it with her other hand before it could hit the deck.

"Is this an official visit? Because if not, you can f—"

"Me now? I'm not a wonk," Martens said. "I'm a marine. Ten years as an enlisted man before I was offered OCS. Got dual degrees in psychology and theology."

The end of Bobbie's nose itched, and she scratched it without thinking. The sudden smell of gun oil let her know that she'd just rubbed lubricant all over her face. Martens glanced at it but didn't stop talking. She tried to drown him out by putting the gun together as noisily as possible.

"I've done combat drills, CQB training, war games," he said, speaking a little louder. "Did you know I was a boot at the same camp where your father was first sergeant? Sergeant Major Draper is a great man. He was like a god to us boots."

Bobbie's head snapped up and her eyes narrowed. Something about this headshrinker acting like he knew her father felt dirty.

"It's true. And if he were here right now, he'd be telling you to listen to me."

"Fuck you," Bobbie said. She imagined her father wincing at the use of obscenity to hide her fear. "You don't know shit."

"I know that when a gunnery sergeant with your level of training and combat readiness almost gets taken out by a yeoman still at the tail end of puberty, something is goddamned wrong."

Bobbie threw the wrench at the ground, knocking over the gun oil, which began to spread across her mat like a bloodstain.

"I fucking fell down! We were at a full g, and I just...I fell down."

"And in the meeting today? Yelling at two civilian intelligence analysts about how Marines would rather die than fail?"

"I didn't yell," Bobbie said, not sure if that was the truth. Her memories of the meeting had become confused once she was out of the room.

"How many times have you fired that gun since you cleaned it yesterday?"

"What?" Bobbie said, feeling nauseated and not sure why.

"For that matter, how many times had you fired it since you cleaned it the day before that? Or the one before that?"

"Stop it," Bobbie said, waving one hand limply at Martens and looking for a place to sit back down.

"Have you fired that gun even once since you've come on board the *Dae-Jung*? Because I can tell you that you've cleaned it every single day you've been on board, and several times you've cleaned it twice in one day."

"No, I—" Bobbie said, finally sitting down with a thump on an ammo canister. She had no memory of having cleaned the gun before that day. "I didn't know that."

"This is post-traumatic stress disorder, Bobbie. It's not a weakness or some kind of moral failure. It's what happens when you live through something terrible. Right now you're not able to process what happened to you and your men on Ganymede, and you're acting irrationally because of it," Martens said, then moved over to crouch in front of her. She was afraid for a moment that he'd try to take her hand, because if he did, she'd hit him.

He didn't.

"You're ashamed," he said, "but there's nothing to be ashamed of. You're trained to be tough, competent, ready for anything. They taught you that if you just do your job and remember your training, you can deal with any threat. Most of all, they taught you that the most important people in the world are the ones standing next to you on the firing line."

Something twitched in her cheek just under her eye, and Bobbie rubbed at the spot hard enough to make stars explode in her vision.

"Then you ran into something that your training couldn't prepare you for, and against which you had no defense. And you lost your teammates and friends."

Bobbie started to reply and realized she'd been holding her breath, so instead of speaking, she exhaled explosively. Martens didn't stop talking.

"We need you, Roberta. We need you back. I haven't been where you are, but I know a lot of people who have, and I know how to help you. If you let me. If you talk to me. I can't take it away. I can't cure you. But I can make it better."

"Don't call me Roberta," Bobbie said so quietly that she could barely hear herself.

She took a few short breaths, trying to clear her head, trying not to hyperventilate. The scents of the cargo bay washed over her. The smell of rubber and metal from her suit. The acrid, competing scents of gun oil and hydraulic fluid, old and aged right into the metal no matter how many times the Navy boys swabbed the decks. The thought of thousands of sailors and marines passing through this same space, working on their equipment and cleaning these same bulkheads, brought her back to herself.

She moved over to her reassembled gun and picked it up off the mat before the spreading pool of gun oil could touch it.

"No, Captain, talking to you is not what's going to get me better."

"Then what, Sergeant?"

"That thing that killed my friends, and started this war? Somebody put that thing on Ganymede," she said, and seated the gun in its housing with a sharp metallic click. She gave the triple barrels a spin with her hand, and they turned with the fast oily hiss of high-quality bearings. "I'm going to find out who. And I'm going to kill them."

Chapter Nine: Avasarala

The report was more than three pages long, but Soren had managed to find someone with the balls to admit it when he didn't know everything. Strange things were happening on Venus, stranger than Avasarala had known or guessed. A network of filaments had nearly encased the planet in a pattern of fifty-kilometer-wide hexagons, and apart from the fact that they seemed to carry superheated water and electrical currents, no one knew what they were. The gravity of the planet had increased by 3 percent. Paired whirlwinds of benzene and complex hydrocarbons were sweeping the impact craters like synchronized swimmers where the remains of Eros Station had smashed into the planetary surface. The best scientific minds of the system were staring at the data with their jaws slack, and the reason no one was panicking yet was that no one could agree on what they should panic about.

On one hand, the Venusian metamorphosis was the most

powerful scientific tool ever. Whatever happened did so in plain sight of everyone. There were no nondisclosure agreements or anti-competition treaties to be concerned with. Anyone with a scanner sensitive enough could look down through the clouds of sulfuric acid and see what was going on today. Analyses were confidential, follow-up studies were proprietary, but the raw data was orbiting the sun for anyone to see.

Only, so far, it was like a bunch of lizards watching the World Cup. Politely put, they weren't sure what they were looking at.

But the data was clear. The attack on Ganymede and the spike in the energy expended on Venus had come at exactly the same time. And no one knew why.

"Well, that's worth shit," she said.

Avasarala closed down her hand terminal and looked out the window. Around them the commissary murmured softly, like the best kind of restaurant, only without the ugly necessity of paying for anything. The tables were real wood and arranged carefully so that everyone had a view and no one could be overheard unless they wanted to be. It was raining that day. Even if the raindrops hadn't been pelting the windows, blurring city and sky, she'd have known by the smell. Her lunch—cold sag aloo and something that was supposed to be tandoori chicken—sat on the table, untouched. Soren was still sitting across from her, his expression polite and alert as a Labrador retriever's.

"There's no data showing a launch," Soren said. "Whatever's on Venus would have to have gotten out to Ganymede, and there's no sign of that at all."

"Whatever's on Venus thinks inertia's optional and gravity isn't a constant. We don't know what a launch would look like. As far as we know, they could walk to Jupiter."

The boy's nod conceded the point.

"Where do we stand on Mars?"

"They've agreed to meet here. They've got ships on the way with the diplomatic delegation, including their witness."

"The marine? Draper?"

"Yes, ma'am. Admiral Nguyen is in charge of the escort."

"He's playing nice?"

"So far."

"All right, where do we go from here?" Avasarala asked.

"Jules-Pierre Mao's waiting in your office, ma'am."

"Run him down for me. Anything you think's important."

Soren blinked. Lightning lit the clouds from within.

"I sent the briefing…"

She felt a stab of annoyance that was half embarrassment. She'd forgotten that the background on the man was in her queue. There were thirty other documents there too, and she'd slept poorly the night before, troubled by dreams in which Arjun had died unexpectedly. She'd had widowhood nightmares since her son had died in a skiing accident, her mind conflating the only two men she'd ever loved.

She'd meant to review the information before breakfast. She'd forgotten. But she wasn't going to admit it to some European brat just because he was smart, competent, and did everything she said.

"I know what's in the briefing. I know *everything*," she said, standing up. "This is a fucking test. I'm asking what *you* think is important about him."

She walked away, moving toward the carved oak doors with a deliberate speed that made Soren scramble a little to keep up.

"He's the corporate controlling interest of Mao-Kwikowski Mercantile," Soren said, his voice low enough to carry to her and then die. "Before the incident, they were one of Protogen's major suppliers. The medical equipment, the radiation rooms, the surveillance and encryption infrastructure. Almost everything Protogen put on Eros or used to construct their shadow station came from a Mao-Kwik warehouse and on a Mao-Kwik freighter."

"And he's still breathing free air because…?" she said, pushing through the doors and into the hallway beyond.

"No evidence that Mao-Kwik knew what the equipment was for," Soren said. "After Protogen was exposed, Mao-Kwik was one of the first to turn over information to the investigation committee. If they—and by 'they,' I mean 'he'—hadn't turned over a terabyte of confidential correspondence, Gutmansdottir and Kolp might never have been implicated."

A silver-haired man with a broad Andean nose walking the other way in the hall looked up from his hand terminal and nodded to her as they drew near.

"Victor," she said. "I'm sorry about Annette."

"The doctors say she'll be fine," the Andean said. "I'll tell her you asked."

"Tell her I said to get the hell out of bed before her husband starts getting dirty ideas," she said, and the Andean laughed as they passed. Then, to Soren: "Was he cutting a deal? Cooperation for clemency?"

"That was one interpretation, but most people assumed it was personal vengeance for what happened to his daughter."

"She was on Eros," Avasarala said.

"She *was* Eros," Soren said as they stepped into the elevator. "She was the initial infection. The scientists think the protomolecule was building itself using her brain and body as a template."

The elevator doors closed, the car already aware of who she was and where she was going. It dropped smoothly as her eyebrows rose.

"So when they started negotiating with that thing—"

"They were talking to what was left of Jules-Pierre Mao's daughter," Soren said. "I mean, they think they were."

Avasarala whistled low.

"Did I pass the test, ma'am?" Soren asked, keeping his face empty and impassive except for a small twinkle in the corners of his eyes that said he knew she'd been bullshitting him. Despite herself, she grinned.

"No one likes a smart-ass," she said. The elevator stopped; the doors slid open.

Jules-Pierre Mao sat at her desk, radiating a sense of calm with the faintest hint of amusement. Avasarala's eyes flickered over him, taking in the details: well-tailored silk suit that straddled the line between beige and gray, receding hairline unmodified by medical therapies, startling blue eyes that he had probably been born with. He wore his age like a statement that fighting the ravages of time and mortality was beneath his notice. Twenty years earlier, he'd just have been devastatingly handsome. Now he was that and dignified too, and her first, animal impulse was that she wanted to like him.

"Mr. Mao," she said, nodding to him. "Sorry to make you wait."

"I've worked with government before," he said. He had a European accent that would have melted butter. "I understand the constraints. What can I do for you, Assistant Undersecretary?"

Avasarala lowered herself into her chair. The Buddha smiled beatifically from his place by the wall. The rain sheeted down the window, shadows giving the near-subliminal impression that Mao was weeping. She steepled her fingers.

"You want some tea?"

"No, thank you," Mao said.

"Soren! Go get me some tea."

"Yes, ma'am," the boy said.

"Soren."

"Ma'am?"

"Don't hurry."

"Of course not, ma'am."

The door closed behind him. Mao's smile looked weary.

"Should I have brought my attorneys?"

"Those rat fuckers? No," she said, "the trials are all done with. I'm not here to reopen any of the legal wrangling. I've got real work to do."

"I can respect that," Mao said.

"I have a problem," Avasarala said. "And I don't know what it is."

"And you think I do?"

"It's possible. I've been through a lot of hearings about one damn thing and another. Most of the time they're exercises in ass covering. If the unvarnished truth ever came out at one, it would be because someone screwed up."

The bright blue eyes narrowed. The smile grew less warm.

"You think my executives and I were less than forthcoming? I put powerful men in prison for you, Assistant Undersecretary. I burned bridges."

Distant thunder mumbled and complained. The rain redoubled its angry tapping at the pane. Avasarala crossed her arms.

"You did. But that doesn't make you an idiot. There are still things you say under oath and things you dance around. This room isn't monitored. This is off the record. I need to know anything you can tell me about the protomolecule that didn't come out in the hearings."

The silence between them stretched. She watched his face, his body, looking for signs, but the man was unreadable. He'd been doing this too long, and he was too good at it. A professional.

"Things get lost," Avasarala said. "There was one time during the finance crisis that we found a whole auditing division that no one remembered. Because that's how you do it. You take part of a problem and you put it somewhere, get some people working on it, and then you get another part of the problem and get other people working on that. And pretty soon you have seven, eight, a hundred different little boxes with work going on, and no one talking to anyone because it would break security protocol."

"And you think...?"

"We killed Protogen, and you helped. I'm asking whether you know of any little boxes lying around somewhere. And I'm very much hoping you say yes."

"Is this from the secretary-general or Errinwright?"

"No. Just me."

"I've already said everything I know," he said.

"I don't believe that."

The mask of his persona slipped. It lasted less than a second, nothing more than a shift in the angle of his spine and a hardness in his jaw, here and gone again. It was anger. That was interesting.

"They killed my daughter," he said softly. "Even if I'd had something to hide, I wouldn't have."

"How did it come to be your girl?" Avasarala asked. "Did they target her? Was somebody using her against you?"

"It was bad luck. She was out in the deep orbits, trying to prove something. She was young and rebellious and stupid. We were trying to get her to come home but…she was in the wrong place at the wrong time."

Something tickled at the back of Avasarala's mind. A hunch. An impulse. She went with it.

"Have you heard from her since it happened?"

"I don't understand."

"Since Eros Station crashed into Venus, have you heard from her?"

It was interesting watching him pretend to be angry now. It was almost like the real thing. She couldn't have said what about it was inauthentic. The intelligence in his eyes, maybe. The sense that he was more present than he had been before. Real rage swept people away. This was rage as a gambit.

"My Julie is dead," he said, his voice shaking theatrically. "She died when that bastard alien thing went down to Venus. She died saving the Earth."

Avasarala countered soft. She lowered her voice, let her face take on a concerned, grandmotherly expression. If he was going to play the injured man, she could play the mother.

"Something lived," she said. "Something survived that impact, and everybody knows that it did. I have reason to think that it didn't stay there. If some part of your daughter made it through that change, she might have reached out to you. Tried to contact you. Or her mother."

"There is nothing I want more than to have my little girl back," Mao said. "But she's gone."

Avasarala nodded.

"All right," she said.

"Is there anything else?"

Again, the false anger. She ran her tongue against the back of her teeth, thinking. There was something here, something beneath the surface. She didn't know what she was looking at with Mao.

"You know about Ganymede?" she said.

"Fighting broke out," he said.

"Maybe more than that," she said. "The thing that killed your daughter is still out there. It was on Ganymede. I'm going to find out how and why."

He rocked back. Was the shock real?

"I'll help if I can," he said, his voice small.

"Start with this. Is there anything you didn't say during the hearings? A business partner you chose not to mention. A backup program or auxiliary staff you outfitted. If it wasn't legal, I don't care. I can get you amnesty for just about anything, but I need to hear it now. Right now."

"Amnesty?" he said as if she'd been joking.

"If you tell me now, yes."

"If I had it, I would give it to you," he said. "I've said every-thing I know."

"All right, then. I'm sorry to have taken your time. And…I'm sorry to open old wounds. I lost a son. Charanpal was fifteen. Ski-ing accident."

"I'm sorry," Mao said.

"If you find out something more, bring it to me," she said.

"I will," he said, rising from his seat. She let him get almost to the doorway before she spoke again.

"Jules?"

Turning to glance over his shoulder, he looked like a still frame from a film.

"If I find out that you knew something and you didn't tell me, I won't take it well," she said. "I'm not someone you want to fuck with."

"If I didn't know that when I came in, I do now," Mao said. It was as good a parting line as any. The door closed behind him. Avasarala sighed, leaning back in her chair. She shifted to look at the Buddha.

"Fat lot of help you were, you smug bastard," she said. The statue, being only a statue, didn't reply. She thumbed down the lights and let the gray of the storm fill the room. Something about Mao didn't sit well with her.

It might only have been the practiced control of a high-level corporate negotiator, but she had the sense of being cut out of the loop. Excluded. That was interesting too. She wondered if he would try to counter her, maybe go over her head. It would be worth telling Errinwright to expect an angry call.

She wondered. It was a stretch to believe there was anything human down on Venus. The protomolecule, as well as anyone understood it, had been designed to hijack primitive life and remake it into something else. But if... *If* the complexity of a human mind had been too much for it to totally control, and the girl had in some sense survived the descent, *if* she'd reached out to her daddy...

Avasarala reached for her hand terminal and opened a connection to Soren.

"Ma'am?"

"When I said don't hurry, I didn't mean you should take the whole fucking day off. My tea?"

"Coming, ma'am. I got sidetracked. I have a report for you that might be interesting."

"Less interesting if the tea's cold," she said, and dropped the channel.

Putting any kind of real surveillance on Mao would probably be impossible. Mao-Kwikowski Mercantile would have its own communications arrays, its own encryption schemes, and several rival companies at least as well funded as the United Nations already bent on ferreting out corporate secrets. But there might be other ways to track communications coming off Venus and going to Mao-Kwik installations. Or messages going down that well.

Soren came in carrying a tray with a cast-iron teapot and an earthenware cup with no handle. He didn't comment on the darkness, but walked carefully to her desk, set down the tray, poured out a smoky, dark cupful of still-steaming tea, and put his hand terminal on the desk beside it.

"You could just send me a fucking copy," Avasarala said.

"More dramatic this way, ma'am," Soren said. "Presentation is everything."

She snorted and pointedly picked up the cup, blowing across the dark surface before she looked at the terminal. The date stamp at the lower right showed it as coming from outside Ganymede seven hours earlier and the identification code of the associated report. The man in the picture had the stocky bones of an Earther, unkempt dark hair, and a peculiar brand of boyish good looks. Avasarala frowned at the image as she sipped her tea.

"What happened to his face?" she asked.

"The reporting officer suggested the beard was intended as a disguise."

She snorted.

"Well, thank God he didn't put on a pair of glasses, we might never have figured it out. What the fuck is James Holden doing on Ganymede?"

"It's a relief ship. Not the *Rocinante.*"

"We have confirmation on that? You know those OPA bastards can fake registration codes."

"The reporting officer did a visual inspection of the interior layout and checked the record when he got back. Also, the crew didn't include Holden's usual pilot, so we assume they've got it parked-and-dark somewhere in tightbeam range," Soren said. He paused. "There is a standing detain-on-sight for Holden."

Avasarala turned the lights back on. The windows became dark mirrors again; the storm was pressed back outside.

"Tell me we didn't enforce it," Avasarala said.

"We didn't enforce it," Soren said. "We have a surveillance detail on him and his team, but the situation on the station isn't conducive to a close watch. Plus which, it doesn't look like Mars knows he's there yet, so we're trying to keep that to ourselves."

"Good that someone out there knows how to run an intelligence operation. Any idea what he's doing?"

"So far, it looks a lot like a relief effort," Soren said with a shrug. "We haven't seen him meeting with anybody of special interest. He's asking questions. Almost got into a fight with some opportunists who've been shaking down relief ships, but the other guys backed down. It's early, though."

Avasarala took another sip of tea. She had to give it to the boy; he could brew a fine pot of tea. Or he knew someone who could, which was just as good. If Holden was there, that meant the OPA was interested in the situation on Ganymede. And that they didn't have someone already on the ground to report to them.

Wanting the intelligence didn't in itself mean much. Even if it had been just a bunch of idiot ground-pounders getting trigger-happy, Ganymede was a critical station for the Jovian system and the Belt. The OPA would want their own eyes on the scene. But to send Holden, the only survivor of Eros Station, seemed more than coincidental.

"They don't know what it is," she said aloud.

"Ma'am?"

"They smuggled in someone with experience in the protomolecule for a reason. They're trying to figure out what the hell's going on. Which means they don't know. Which means..." She sighed. "Which means it wasn't them. Which is a fucking pity, since they've got the only live sample we know about."

"What would you like the surveillance team to do?"

"Surveillance," she snapped. "Watch him, see who he talks to and what he does. Daily reports back if it's boring, real-time updates if it runs hot."

"Yes, ma'am. Do you want him brought in?"

"Pull him and his people in when they try to leave Ganymede. Otherwise stay out of their way and try not to get noticed. Holden's an idiot, but he's not stupid. If he realizes he's being watched, he'll start broadcasting pictures of all our Ganymede sources or something. Do not underestimate his capacity to fuck things up."

"Anything else?"

Another flash of lightning. Another roll of thunder. Another storm among trillions of storms that had assaulted the Earth since back in the beginning, when something had first tried to end all life on the planet. Something that was on Venus right now. And spreading.

"Find a way for me to get a message to Fred Johnson without Nguyen or the Martians finding out," she said. "We may need to do some back-channel negotiation."

Chapter Ten: Prax

Pas kirrup es I'm to this," the boy sitting on the cot said. "Pinche *salad*, sa-sa? Ten thousand, once was."

He couldn't have been more than twenty. Young enough, technically, to be his son, just as Mei could have been the boy's daughter. Colt-thin from adolescent growth and a life in low g, his thinness was improbable to begin with. And he'd been starving besides.

"I can write you a promissory note if you want," Prax said.

The boy grinned and made a rude gesture.

From his professional work, Prax knew that the inner planets thought of Belter slang as a statement about location. He knew from living as a food botanist on Ganymede that it was also about class. He had grown up with tutors in accent-free Chinese and English. He'd spoken with men and women from everywhere in the system. From the way someone said *allopolyploidy*, he could tell if they came from the universities around Beijing or Brazil, if they'd grown up in the shadow of the Rocky Mountains or Olympus Mons or in the corridors of Ceres. He'd grown up in microgravity himself, but Belt patois was as foreign to him as to anyone fresh up the well. If the boy had wanted to speak past him, it would have been effortless. But Prax was a paying customer, and he knew the boy was making an effort to dial it back.

The programming keyboard was twice as large as a standard hand terminal, the plastic worn by use and time. A progress bar was slowly filling along the side, notations in simplified Chinese cycling with each movement.

The hole was a cheap one near the surface of the moon. No more than ten feet wide, four rough rooms inched into the ice from a public corridor hardly wider or better lit. The old plastic walls glittered and wept with condensation. They were in the room farthest from the corridor, the boy on his cot and Prax standing hunched in the doorway.

"No promise for the full record," the boy said. "What is, is, sabé?"

"Anything you can get would be great."

The boy nodded once. Prax didn't know his name. It wasn't the sort of thing to ask. The days it had taken to track down someone willing to break through the security system had been a long dance between his own ignorance of Ganymede Station's gray economy and the increasing desperation and hunger in even the most corrupt quarters. A month before, the boy might have been skimming commercial data to resell or hold hostage for easily laundered private credit. Today he was looking for Mei in exchange for enough leafy greens to make a small meal. Agricultural barter, the oldest economy in humanity's record, had come to Ganymede.

"Authcopy's gone," the boy said. "Sucked into servers, buried ass deep."

"So if you can't break the security servers—"

"Don't have to. Camera got memory, memory got cache. Since the lockdown, it's just filling and filling. No one watching."

"You're kidding," Prax said. "The two biggest armies in the system are staring each other down, and they're not watching the security cameras?"

"Watching each other. No one half-humps for us."

The progress bar filled completely and chimed. The boy pulled open a list of identifying codes and started paging through them, muttering to himself. From the front room, a baby complained weakly. It sounded hungry. Of course it did.

"Your kid?"

The boy shook his head.

"Collateral," he said, and tapped twice on a code. A new window opened. A wide hall. A door half melted and forced open. Scorch marks on the walls and, worse, a puddle of water. There shouldn't be free water. The environmental controls were getting further and further away from their safe levels. The boy looked up at Prax. "C'est la?"

"Yes," Prax said. "That's it."

The boy nodded and hunched back over his console.

"I need it before the attack. Before the mirror came down," Prax said.

"Hokay, boss. Waybacking. Tod á frames con null delta. Only see when something happens, que si?"

"Fine. That's fine."

Prax moved forward, leaning to look over the boy's shoulder. The image jittered without anything on the screen changing except the puddle, slowly getting smaller. They were going backward through time, through the days and weeks. Toward the moment when it had all fallen apart.

Medics appeared in the screen, appearing to walk backward in the inverted world as they brought a dead body to lay beside the door. Then another draped over it. The two corpses lay motionless; then one moved, pawing gently at the wall, then more strongly until, in an eyeblink, he staggered to his feet and was gone.

"There should be a girl. I'm looking for who brought out a four-year-old girl."

"Sa day care, no? Should be a thousand of them."

"I only care about the one."

The second corpse sat up and then stood, clutching her belly. A man stepped into the frame, a gun in his hand, healing her by sucking the bullet from her guts. They argued, grew calm, parted peaceably. Prax knew he was seeing it all in reverse, but his sleep- and calorie-starved brain kept trying to make the images into a narrative. A group of soldiers crawled backward out of the ruined door, like a breech birth, then huddled, backed away in a rush. A flash of light, and the door had made itself whole, thermite charges clinging to it like fruit until a soldier in a Martian uniform rushed forward to collect them safely. Their technological harvest complete, the soldiers all backed rapidly away, leaving a scooter behind them, leaning against the wall.

And then the door slid open, and Prax saw himself back out. He looked younger. He beat on the door, hands popping off the surface in staccato bursts, then leapt awkwardly onto the scooter and vanished backward.

The door went quiet. Motionless. He held his breath. Walking backward, a woman carrying a five-year-old boy on her hip went to the door, vanished within, and then reappeared. Prax had to remind himself that the woman hadn't been dropping her son off, but retrieving him. Two figures backed down the corridor.

No. Three.

"Stop. That's it," Prax said, his heart banging against his ribs. "That's her."

The boy waited until all three figures were caught in the camera's eye, stepping out into the corridor. Mei's face was petulant; even in the low resolution of the security camera, he knew the expression. And the man holding her...

Relief warred with outrage in his chest, and relief won. It was Dr. Strickland. She'd gone with Dr. Strickland, who knew about her condition, about the medicine, about all the things that needed to be done to keep Mei alive. He sank to his knees, his eyes closed and weeping. If he'd taken her, she wasn't dead. His daughter wasn't dead.

Unless, a thin demonic thought whispered in his brain, Strickland was too.

The woman was a stranger. Dark-haired with features that reminded Prax of the Russian botanists he'd worked with. She was holding a roll of paper in her hand. Her smile might have been one of amusement or impatience. He didn't know.

"Can you follow them?" he asked. "See where they went?"

The boy looked at him, lips curled.

"For salad? No. Box of chicken and atche sauce."

"I don't have any chicken."

"Then you got what you got," the boy said with a shrug. His eyes had gone dead as marbles. Prax wanted to hit him, wanted to choke him until he dug the images out of the dying computers. But it was a fair bet the boy had a gun or something worse, and unlike Prax, he likely knew how to use it.

"Please," Prax said.

"Got your favor, you. No epressa mé, si?"

Humiliation rose in the back of his throat, and he swallowed it down.

"Chicken," he said.

"Si."

Prax opened his satchel and put a double handful of leaves, orange peppers, and snow onions on the cot. The boy snatched up a half of it and stuffed it into his mouth, eyes narrowing in animal pleasure.

"I'll do what I can," Prax said.

He couldn't do anything.

The only edible protein still on the station was either coming in a slow trickle from the relief supplies or walking around on two feet. People had started trying Prax's strategy, grazing off the plants in the parks and hydroponics. They hadn't bothered with the homework, though. Inedibles were eaten all the same, degrading the air-scrubbing functions and throwing the balance of the station's ecosystem further off. One thing was leading to another, and chicken couldn't be had, or anything that might substitute for it. And even if there was, he didn't have time to solve that problem.

In his own home, the lights were dim and wouldn't go bright. The soybean plant had stopped growing but didn't fade, which was an interesting datapoint, or would have been.

Sometime during the day, an automated system had clicked into a conservation routine, limiting energy use. In the big picture, it might be a good sign. Or it might be the fever break just before the catastrophe. It didn't change what he had to do.

As a boy, he'd entered the schools young, shipping up with his family to the sunless reaches of space, chasing a dream of work and prosperity. He hadn't taken the change well. Headaches and anxiety attacks and constant, bone-deep fatigue had haunted those first years when he needed to impress his tutors, be tracked as bright and promising. His father hadn't let him rest. *The window is open until the window is closed*, he'd say, and then push Prax to do a little more, to find a way to think when he was too tired or sick or in pain to think. He'd learned to make lists, notes, outlines.

By capturing his fleeting thoughts, he could drag himself to clarity like a mountain climber inching toward a summit. Now, in the artificial twilight, he made lists. The names of all the children he could remember from Mei's therapy group. He knew there were twenty, but he could only remember sixteen. His mind wandered. He put the image of Strickland and the mystery woman on his hand terminal, staring at it. The confusion of hope and anger swirled in him until it faded. He felt like he was falling asleep, but his pulse was racing. He tried to remember if tachycardia was a symptom of starvation.

For a moment, he came to himself, clear and lucid in a way he only then realized he hadn't been in days. He was starting to crash. His own personal cascade was getting ahead of him, and he wouldn't be able to keep up his investigation much longer without rest. Without protein. He was already half zombie.

He had to get help. His gaze drifted to the list of children's names. He had to get help, but first he'd check, just check. He'd go to…go to…

He closed his eyes, frowned. He knew the answer. He knew that he knew. The security station. He'd go there and ask about each of them. He opened his eyes, writing *security station* down under the list, capturing the thought. Then *UN outreach station. Mars outreach.* All the places he'd been before, day after day, only now with new questions. It would be easy. And then, when he knew, there was something else he was supposed to do. It took a minute to figure out what it was, and then he wrote it at the bottom of the page.

Get help.

"They're all gone," Prax said, his breath ghosting white in the cold. "They're all his patients, and they're all gone. Sixteen out of sixteen. Do you know the probability of that? It's not random."

The security man hadn't shaved in days. A long, angry ice burn reddened his cheek and neck, the wound fresh and untreated. His face must have touched an uninsulated piece of Ganymede. He was lucky to still have skin. He wore a thick coat and gloves. There was frost on the desk.

"I appreciate the information, sir, and I'll see it gets out to the relief stations—"

"No, you don't understand, he took them. They're sick, and he took them."

"Maybe he was trying to keep them safe," the security man said. His voice was a gray rag, limp and weary. There was a problem with that. Prax knew there was a problem with that, but he couldn't remember what it was. The security man reached out, gently moving him aside, and nodded to the woman behind him. Prax found himself staring at her like he was drunk.

"I want to report a murder," she said, her voice shaking.

The security man nodded, neither surprise nor disbelief in his eyes. Prax remembered.

"He took them first," he said. "He took them before the attack happened."

"Three men broke into my apartment," the woman said. "They... My brother was with me and he tried to stop them."

"When did this happen, ma'am?"

"Before the attack," Prax said.

"A couple hours ago," the woman said. "Fourth level. Blue sector. Apartment 1453."

"Okay, ma'am. I'm going to take you over to a desk here. I need you to fill out a report."

"My brother's dead. They shot him."

"And I'm very sorry about that, ma'am. I need you to fill out a report so we can catch the men who did this."

Prax watched them walk away. He turned back to the line of the traumatized and desperate waiting their turns to beg for help, for justice, for law. A flash of anger lit him, then flickered. He needed help, but there wasn't any to be had here. He and Mei were a pebble in space. They didn't signify.

The security man was back, talking to a tall pretty woman about something horrible. Prax hadn't noticed the man returning, hadn't heard the beginning of the woman's tale. He was starting to lose time. That wasn't good.

The small sane part of his brain whispered that if he died, no one would look for Mei. She'd be lost. It whispered that he needed food, that he'd needed it for days. That he didn't have very much time left.

"I have to go to the relief center," he said aloud. The woman and the security man didn't seem to hear. "Thanks anyway."

Now that he had started to notice his own condition, Prax was astonished and alarmed. His gait was a shuffle; his arms were weak and ached badly, though he couldn't remember having done anything to earn the pain. He hadn't lifted anything heavy or gone climbing. He hadn't done his daily exercise routine any time that he could remember. He didn't remember the last time he'd eaten. He remembered the shudder of the falling mirror, the death of his dome, like it was something that had happened in a previous lifetime. No wonder he was falling apart.

The corridors by the relief center were packed like a slaughterhouse. Men and women, many of them who looked stronger and healthier than he was, pushed against each other, making even the widest spaces feel narrow. The closer he got to the port, the more light-headed he felt. The air was almost warm here, the barn-hot of bodies. It stank of keytone-acrid breath. Saint's breath, his mother called it. The smell of protein breakdown, of bodies eating their own muscles to survive. He wondered how many people in the crowd knew what that scent was.

People were yelling. Shoving. The crowd around him surged back and forth the way he imagined waves might press against a beach.

"Then open the doors and let us look!" a woman shouted, far ahead of him.

Oh, Prax thought. *This is a food riot.*

He pushed for the edges, trying to get out. Trying to get away. Ahead of him, people were shouting. Behind him, they pushed. Banks of LEDs in the ceiling glowed white and gold. The walls were industrial gray. He put a hand out. He'd gotten to a wall. Somewhere, the dam burst, and the crowd flowed suddenly forward, the collective movement threatening to pull him swirling away into the flow. He kept a hand on the wall. The crowd thinned, and Prax staggered forward. The loading bay doors stood open. Beside them Prax saw a familiar face but couldn't place it. Someone from the lab, maybe? The man was thick-boned and muscular. An Earther. Maybe someone he'd seen in his travels through the failing station. Had he seen the man grubbing for food? But no, he looked too well fed. There was no gauntness to his cheeks. He was like a friend and also a stranger. Someone Prax knew and also didn't. Like the secretary-general or a famous actor.

Prax knew he was staring, but he couldn't stop. He knew that face. He *knew* it. It had to do with the war.

Prax had a sudden flashbulb memory. He was in his apartment, holding Mei in his arms, trying to calm her. She was barely a year old, not walking, the doctors still tinkering to find the right pharmaceutical cocktail to keep her alive. Over her colic wail, the news streams were a constant alarmed chatter. A man's face played over and over.

My name is James Holden and my ship, the Canterbury, *was just destroyed by a warship with stealth technology and what appear to be parts stamped with Martian Navy serial numbers.*

That was him. That was why he recognized the face and felt that he'd never seen it before. Prax felt a tug from somewhere near the center of his chest and found himself stepping forward. He paused. Beyond the loading doors, someone whooped. Prax took out his hand terminal, looked at his list. Sixteen names, sixteen children gone. And at the bottom of the page, in simple block characters: *Get help*.

Prax turned toward the man who'd started wars and saved planets, suddenly shy and uncertain.

"Get help," he said, and walked forward.

Chapter Eleven: Holden

Santichai and Melissa Supitayaporn were a pair of eighty-year-old earthborn missionaries from the Church of Humanity Ascendant, a religion that eschewed supernaturalism in all forms, and whose theology boiled down to *Humans can be better than they are, so let's do that.* They also ran the relief depot headquarters with the ruthless efficiency of natural-born dictators. Minutes after arriving, Holden had been thoroughly dressed down by Santichai, a frail wisp of a man with thinning white hair, about his altercation with customs officials at the port. After several minutes of trying to explain himself, only to be shouted down by the tiny missionary, he finally just gave up and apologized.

"Don't make our situation here any more precarious," Santichai repeated, apparently mollified by the apology but needing to drive this point home. He shook a sticklike brown finger in Holden's face.

"Got it," Holden said, holding up his hands in surrender. The rest of his crew had vanished at Santichai's first angry outburst, leaving Holden to deal with the man alone. He spotted Naomi across the large open warehouse space of the relief depot, talking calmly to Melissa, Santichai's hopefully less volatile wife. Holden couldn't hear any shouting, though with the voices of several dozen people and the grinding gears and engine whine and reverse alerts of three lift trucks, Melissa could have been flinging grenades at Naomi and he probably wouldn't have heard it.

Looking for an opportunity to escape, Holden pointed at Naomi across the room and said, "Excuse me, I—"

Santichai cut him off with a curt wave of one hand that sent his loose orange robes swirling. Holden found himself unable to disobey the tiny man.

"This," Santichai said, pointing in the direction of the crates being brought in from the *Somnambulist*, "is not enough."

"I—"

"The OPA promised us twenty-two thousand kilos of protein and supplements by last week. This is less than twelve thousand kilos," Santichai said, punctuating his statement with a sharp poke at Holden's bicep.

"I'm not in charge of—"

"Why would they promise us things they have no intention of delivering? Promise twelve thousand if that is what you have. Do *not* promise twenty-two thousand and then deliver twelve," he said, accompanied by more poking.

"I agree," Holden said, backing out of poke range with his hands up. "I totally agree. I'll call my contact on Tycho Station immediately to find out where the rest of the promised supplies are. I'm sure they're on the way."

Santichai shrugged in another swirl of orange.

"See that you do," he said, then steamed off toward one of the lift trucks. "You! *You!* Do you see the sign that says 'medicine'? Why are you putting things that are not medicine in that place?"

Holden used this distraction to make good his escape, and

jogged over to Naomi and Melissa. Naomi had a form open on her terminal and was completing some paperwork while Melissa watched.

Holden glanced around the warehouse space while Naomi worked. The *Somnambulist* was just one of almost twenty relief ships that had landed in the last twenty-four hours, and the massive room was quickly filling up with crates of supplies. The chill air smelled of dust and ozone and hot oil from the lift trucks, but under it there was a vaguely unpleasant smell of decay, like rotting vegetation. As he watched, Santichai darted across the warehouse floor, shouting instructions to a pair of workers carrying a heavy crate.

"Your husband is something else, ma'am," Holden said to Melissa.

Melissa was both taller and heavier than her tiny husband, but she had the same shapeless cloud of thinning white hair he had. She also had bright blue eyes that nearly disappeared in her face when she smiled. As she was doing now.

"I've never met anyone else in my life who cared more about other people's welfare, and less about their feelings," she said. "But at least he'll make sure everyone is well fed before he tells them all the many things they did wrong."

"I think that does it," Naomi said, hitting the key to send the filled-out form to Melissa's terminal, a charmingly outdated model she pulled out of a pocket in her robe when it chimed receipt.

"Mrs. Supitayaporn," Holden said.

"Melissa."

"Melissa, how long have you and your husband been on Ganymede?"

"Almost," she said, tapping her finger against her chin and staring off into the distance, "ten years? Can it be that long? It must be, because Dru had just had her baby, and he—"

"I'm wondering because the one thing no one outside of Ganymede seems to know is how this"—Holden gestured around him—"all got started."

"The station?"

"The crisis."

"Well, the UN and Martian soldiers started shooting at each other; then we started seeing system failures—"

"Yes," Holden said, cutting in again. "I understand that. But *why*? Not one shot during the entire year that Earth and Mars have jointly held this moon. We had a war before the whole Eros thing, and they didn't bring it here. Then all at once everyone everywhere is shooting? What kicked that off?"

Melissa looked puzzled, another expression that made her eyes almost disappear in a mass of wrinkles.

"I don't know," she said. "I'd assumed they were shooting each other everywhere in the system. We don't get much news right now."

"No," Holden said. "It's just here, and it was just for a couple of days. And then it stopped, with no explanation."

"That is odd," Melissa said, "but I don't know that it matters. Whatever happened, it doesn't change what we need to do now."

"I suppose not," Holden agreed.

Melissa smiled, embraced him warmly, then went off to check someone else's paperwork.

Naomi hooked her arm through Holden's, and they started toward the warehouse exit into the rest of the station, dodging crates of supplies and aid workers as they went.

"How can they have had a whole battle here," she said, "and no one knows why?"

"They know," Holden said. "*Someone* knows."

The station looked worse on the ground than from space. The vital, oxygen-producing plants that lined the corridor walls were turning an unhealthy shade of yellow. Many corridors didn't have lights, and the automatic pressure doors had been hand cranked and then wedged open; if one area of the station suddenly lost pressure, many adjoining sections would as well. The few people they ran into either avoided their eyes or stared at them with open hostility. Holden found himself wishing he were wearing his gun openly, rather than in a concealed holster at the small of his back.

"Who's our contact?" Naomi asked quietly.

"Hmmmm?"

"I assume Fred has people here," she replied under her breath as she smiled and nodded at a passing group of men. All of them openly carried weapons, though most were of the stabbing and clubbing variety. They stared back at her with speculative looks on their faces. Holden moved his hand under his coat and toward his gun, but the men moved on, only giving them a few backward glances before they turned a corner and disappeared from view.

"He didn't arrange for us to meet someone?" Naomi finished in a normal voice.

"He gave me some names. But communication with this moon has been so spotty he wasn't able to—"

Holden was cut off by a loud bang from another part of the port. The explosion was followed by a roar that gradually resolved into people shouting. The few people in the corridor with them began to run, some toward the noise, but most away from it.

"Should we..." Naomi said, looking at the people running toward the commotion.

"We're here to see what's going on," Holden replied. "So let's go see."

They quickly became lost in the twisting corridors of Ganymede's port, but it didn't matter as long as they kept moving toward the noise and along with the growing wave of people running in the same direction. A tall, stocky man with spiked red hair ran alongside them for a while. He was carrying a length of black metal pipe in each hand. He grinned at Naomi and tried to hand her one. She waved it off.

" 'Bout fookin' time," he yelled in an accent Holden couldn't place. He held his extra club out to Holden when Naomi didn't take it.

"What is?" Holden asked, taking the club.

"Fookin' bastahds flingin' the victuals up, and the prols jus gotta shove, wut? Well, fook that, ya mudder-humpin' spunk guzzlas!"

Spiky Redhead howled and waved his club in the air, then took off at a faster run and disappeared into the crowd. Naomi laughed and howled at his back as he ran. When Holden shot her a look, she just smiled and said, "It's infectious."

A final bend in the corridor brought them to another large warehouse space, looking almost identical to the one ruled over by the Supitayaporns, except that this room was filled with a mob of angry people pushing toward the loading dock. The doors to the dock were closed, and a small group of port security officers were trying to hold the mob back. When Holden arrived, the crowd was still cowed by the security officers' Tasers and shock prods, but from the rising tension and anger in the air, he could tell that wouldn't last long.

Just behind the front line of rent-a-cops, with their nonlethal deterrents, stood a small clump of men in dark suits and sensible shoes. They carried shotguns with the air of men who were just waiting for someone to give them permission.

That would be the corporate security, then.

Looking over the room, Holden felt the scene snap into place. Beyond that closed loading bay door was one of the few remaining corporate freighters loaded down with the last food being stripped from Ganymede.

And this crowd was hungry.

Holden remembered trying to escape a casino on Eros when it went into security lockdown. Remembered angry crowds facing down men with guns. Remembered the screams and the smells of blood and cordite. Before he knew he'd made a decision, he found himself pushing his way to the front of the crowd. Naomi followed, murmuring apologies in his wake. She grabbed his arm and stopped him for a moment.

"Are you about to do something really stupid?" she asked.

"I'm about to keep these people from being shot for the crime of being hungry," he said, wincing at the self-righteous tone even as he said it.

"Don't," Naomi said, letting him go, "pull your gun on anyone."

"They have guns."

"Guns plural. You have gun singular, which is why you will keep yours in your holster, or you'll do this by yourself."

That's the only way you ever do anything. By yourself. It was the kind of thing Detective Miller would have said. For him, it had been true. That was a strong enough argument against doing it that way.

"Okay." Holden nodded, then resumed pushing his way to the front. By the time he reached it, two people had become the focus of the conflict. A gray-haired port security man wearing a white patch with the word *supervisor* printed on it and a tall, thin dark-skinned woman who could pass for Naomi's mother were yelling at each other while their respective groups looked on, shouting agreements and insults.

"Just open the damn door and let us look!" yelled the woman in a tone that let Holden know this was something she was repeating again and again.

"You won't get anything by yelling at me," the gray-haired supervisor yelled back. Beside him, his fellow security guards held their shock sticks in white-knuckled grips and the corporate boys held their shotguns in a loose cradle that Holden found far more threatening.

The woman stopped shouting when Holden pushed his way up to the supervisor, and stared at him instead.

"Who...?" she said.

Holden climbed up onto the loading dock next to the supervisor. The other guards waved their shock prods around a little, but no one jabbed him. The corporate thugs just narrowed their eyes and shifted their stances a bit. Holden knew that their confusion about who he was would only last so long, and when they finally got past it, he was probably going to get uncomfortably intimate with one of those cattle prods, if not just blasted in the face with a shotgun. Before that could happen, he thrust his hand out to the supervisor and said in a loud voice that would carry to the crowd, "Hi there, I'm Walter Philips, an OPA rep out of Tycho Station, and here as personal representative of Colonel Frederick Johnson."

The supervisor shook his hand like a man in a daze. The corporate gorillas shifted again and held their guns more firmly.

"Mr. Philips," the supervisor said. "The OPA has no authority..."

Holden ignored him and turned to the woman he'd been shouting at.

"Ma'am, what's all the fuss?"

"That ship," she said, pointing at the door, "has almost ten thousand kilos of beans and rice on it, enough to feed the whole station for a week!"

The crowd murmured agreement at her back and shuffled forward a step or two.

"Is that true?" Holden asked the supervisor.

"As I said," the man replied, holding up his hands and making pushing motions at the crowd as though he could drive them back through sheer force of will, "we are not allowed to discuss the cargo manifests of privately owned—"

"Then open the doors and let us look!" the woman shouted again. While she yelled and the crowd picked up her chant—*let us look, let us look*—Holden took the security supervisor by the elbow and pulled his head close.

"In about thirty seconds, that mob is going to tear you and your men to pieces trying to get into that ship," he said. "I think you should let them have it before this turns violent."

"Violent!" The man gave a humorless laugh. "It's already violent. The only reason the ship isn't long gone is because one of them set off a bomb and blew up the docking-clamp release mechanism. If they try to take the ship, we'll—"

"They will not take the ship," said a gravelly voice, and a heavy hand came down on Holden's shoulder. When he turned around, one of the corporate goons was standing behind him. "This ship is Mao-Kwikowski Mercantile property."

Holden pushed the man's hand off his shoulder.

"A dozen guys with Tasers and shotguns isn't going to stop them," he said, pointing out at the chanting mob.

"Mr."—the goon looked him up and down once—"*Philips*. I don't give a drippy shit what you or the OPA thinks about anything, and especially not my chances of doing my job. So why don't you fuck off before the shooting starts?"

Well, he'd tried. Holden smiled at the man and began to reach for the holster at the small of his back. He wished that Amos were here, but he hadn't seen him since they had gotten off the ship. Before he reached the pistol, his hand was enveloped by long slender fingers and squeezed tightly.

"How about this," Naomi said, suddenly at Holden's side. "How about we skip past the posturing and I just tell you how this is actually going to work?"

Both Holden and the goon turned to look at Naomi in surprise. She held up one finger in a *wait a minute* gesture and pulled out her hand terminal. She called someone and turned on the external speaker.

"Amos," she said, still holding her finger up.

"Yep," came the reply.

"A ship is trying to leave from port 11, pad B9. It's full of food we could really use here. If it makes it off the ground, do we have an OPA gunship close enough to intercept?"

There was a long pause; then, with a chuckle, Amos said, "You know we do, boss. Who'm I actually saying this to?"

"Call that ship and have them disable the freighter. Then have an OPA team secure it, strip it of everything, and scuttle it."

Amos just said, "You got it."

Naomi closed up the terminal and put it back into her pocket.

"Don't test us, boy," she said to the goon, a hint of steel in her voice. "Not one word of that was empty threat. Either you give these people the cargo, or we'll take the whole damned ship. Your choice."

The goon stared at her for a moment, then motioned to his team and walked away. Port security followed, and Holden and Naomi had to dodge out of the way of the crowd rushing up the dock and to the loading bay doors.

When they were out of danger of being trampled, Holden said, "That was pretty cool."

"Getting shot standing up for justice probably seemed very heroic to you," she said, the steel not quite gone from her voice. "But I want to keep you around, so stop being an idiot."

"Smart play, threatening the ship," Holden said.

"You were acting like that asshole Detective Miller, so I just acted like you used to. What I said was the kind of thing you say when you're not in a hurry to wave your gun around."

"I wasn't acting like Miller," he said, the accusation stinging, because it was true.

"You weren't acting like you."

Holden shrugged, noticing only afterward that it was another imitation of Miller. Naomi looked down at the captain's patches on the shoulder of her *Somnambulist* jumpsuit. "Maybe I should keep these…"

A small, unkempt-looking man with salt-and-pepper hair, Chinese features, and a week's growth of beard walked up to them and nodded nervously. He was literally wringing his hands, a gesture Holden had been pretty sure only little old ladies in ancient cinema made.

He gave them another small nod and said, "You are James Holden? Captain James Holden? From the OPA?"

Holden and Naomi glanced at each other. Holden tugged at his patchy beard. "Is this actually helping at all? Be honest."

"Captain Holden, my name is Prax, Praxidike Meng. I'm a botanist."

Holden shook the man's hand.

"Nice to meet you, Prax. I'm afraid we have to—"

"You have to help me," Prax said. Holden could see that the man had been through a rough couple of months. His clothes hung off him like a starving man's, and his face was covered with yellowing bruises from a fairly recent beating.

"Sure, if you'll see the Supitayaporns at the aid station, tell them I said—"

"No!" Prax shouted. "I don't need that. I need you to *help* me!"

Holden shot a glance at Naomi. She shrugged. *Your call.*

"Okay," Holden said. "What's the problem?"

Chapter Twelve: Avasarala

A small house is a deeper kind of luxury," her husband said. "To live in a space entirely our own, to remember the simple pleasures of baking bread and washing our own dishes. This is what your friends in high places forget. It makes them less human."

He was sitting at the kitchen table, leaning back in a chair of bamboo laminate that had been distressed until it looked like stained walnut. The scars from his cancer surgery were two pale lines in the darkness of his throat, barely visible under the powdering of white stubble. His forehead was broader than when she'd married him, his hair thinner. The Sunday morning sun spilled across the table, glowing.

"That's crap," she said. "Just because you pretend to live like a dirt farmer doesn't make Errinwright or Lus or any of the others less human. There's smaller houses than this with six families living in them, and the people in those are a hundred times closer to animals than anyone I work with."

"You really think that?"

"Of course I do. Otherwise why would I go to work in the morning? If someone doesn't get those half-feral bastards out of the slums, who are you university types going to teach?"

"An excellent point," Arjun said.

"What makes them less human is they don't fucking meditate. A small house isn't a luxury," she said, then paused. "A small house and a lot of money, maybe."

Arjun grinned at her. He had always had the most beautiful smile. She found herself smiling back at him, even though part of her wanted to be cross. Outside, Kiki and Suri shrieked, their small half-naked bodies bolting across the grass. Their nurse trotted along a half second behind them, her hand to her side like she was easing a stitch.

"A big yard is a luxury," Avasarala said.

"It is."

Suri burst in the back door, her hand covered in loose black soil and a wide grin on her face. Her footsteps left crumbling dark marks on the carpet.

"Nani! Nani! Look what I found!"

Avasarala shifted in her chair. In her granddaughter's palm, an earthworm was shifting the pink and brown rings of its body, wet as the soil that dripped from Suri's fingers. Avasarala made her face into a mask of wonder and delight.

"That's wonderful, Suri. Come back outside and show your nani where you found that."

The yard smelled like cut grass and fresh soil. The gardener—a thin man hardly older than her own son would have been—knelt in the back, pulling weeds by hand. Suri pelted out toward him, and Avasarala moved along after her at a stroll. When she came near, the gardener nodded, but there was no space for conversation. Suri was pointing and gesturing and retelling the grand adventure of finding a common worm in the mud as if it were a thing of epics. Kiki appeared at Avasarala's side, quietly taking her hand. She loved her little Suri, but privately—or if not that, then only to Arjun—she thought Kiki was the smarter of her grandchildren. Quiet, but the girl's black eyes were bright, and she could mimic anyone she heard. Kiki didn't miss much.

"Darling wife," Arjun called from the back door. "There's someone to talk with you."

"Where?"

"The house system," Arjun said. "She says your terminal's not answering."

"There's a reason for that," Avasarala said.

"It's Gloria Tannenbaum."

Avasarala reluctantly handed Kiki's hand over to the nurse, kissed Suri's head, and went back toward the house. Arjun held the door open for her. His expression was apologetic.

"These cunts are digging into my grandma time," she said.

"The price of power," Arjun replied with a solemnity that was amused and serious at the same time.

Avasarala opened the connection on the system in her private office. There was a click and a moment's dislocation while the privacy screens came up, and then Gloria Tannenbaum's thin, eyebrowless face appeared on her screen.

"Gloria! I'm sorry. I had my terminal down with the children over."

"Not a problem," the woman said with a clean, brittle smile that was as close as she came to a genuine emotion. "Probably for the best anyway. Always assume those are being monitored more closely than civilian lines."

Avasarala lowered herself into her chair. The leather breathed out gently under her weight.

"I hope things are all right with you and Etsepan?"

"Fine," Gloria said.

"Good, good. Now why the fuck are you calling me?"

"I was talking to a friend of mine whose wife is stationed on the *Mikhaylov*. From what he says, it's being pulled off patrol. Going deep."

Avasarala frowned. The *Mikhaylov* was part of a small convoy monitoring the traffic between the deep stations orbiting at the far edge of the Belt.

"Going deep where?"

"I asked around," Gloria said. "Ganymede."

"Nguyen?"

"Yes."

"Your friend has loose lips," Avasarala said.

"I never tell him anything true," Gloria said. "I thought you should know."

"I owe you," Avasarala said. Gloria nodded once, the movement sharp as a crow's, and dropped the connection. Avasarala sat in silence for a long moment, fingers pressed to her lips, mind following the chains of implication like a brook flowing over stones. Nguyen was sending more ships to Ganymede, and he was doing it quietly.

The *why quietly* part was simple. If he'd done it openly, she would have stopped him. Nguyen was young and he was ambitious, but he wasn't stupid. He was drawing conclusions of his own, and somehow he'd gotten to the idea that sending more forces into the open sore that was Ganymede Station would make things better.

"Oh, Nani!" Kiki called. From the lilt of her voice, Avasarala knew there was mischief afoot. She hefted herself up from the desk and headed for the door.

"In here, Kiki," she said, stepping out into the kitchen.

The water balloon hit her in the shoulder without bursting, bobbled down to the floor, and popped at her feet, turning the stone tiles around her dark. Avasarala looked up, rage-faced. Kiki stood in the doorway leading to the yard, caught between fear and delight.

"Did you just make a mess in my house?" Avasarala asked.

Pale-faced, the girl nodded.

"Do you know what happens to bad children who make a mess in their nani's house?"

"Do they get tickled?"

"They get *tickled*!" Avasarala said, and bolted for her. Of course Kiki got away. She was a child of eight. The only time the girl's joints ached, it was from growing too fast. And of course, eventually she let her nani catch her and tickle her until she screamed. By the time Ashanti and her husband came to gather up their children for the flight back to Novgorod, Avasarala had grass stains on her sari and her hair was standing off her scalp in all directions, like the cartoon image of her lightning-struck self.

She hugged the children twice before they left, sneaking bits of chocolate to them each time, then kissed her daughter, nodded to her son-in-law, and waved to them all from her doorway. The security team followed their car. No one so closely related to her was safe from kidnapping. It was just another fact of life.

Her shower was long, using a lavish volume of water almost too hot for comfort. She'd always liked her baths to approach scalding, ever since she was a girl. If her skin didn't tingle and throb a little when she toweled off, she'd done it wrong.

Arjun was on the bed, reading seriously from his hand terminal. She walked to her closet, threw the wet towel into the hamper, and shrugged into a cotton-weave robe.

"He thinks they did it," she said.

"Who did what?" Arjun asked.

"Nguyen. He's thinking that the Martians are behind the thing. That there's going to be a second attack on Ganymede. He knows the Martians aren't moving their fleet there, and he's still reinforcing. He doesn't care if it fucks the peace talks, because he thinks they're crap anyway. Nothing to lose. Are you listening to me?"

"Yes, I am. Nguyen thinks it was Mars. He's building a fleet to respond. You see?"

"Do you know what I'm talking about?"

"As a rule? No. But Maxwell Asinnian-Koh just posted a paper about post-lyricism that's going to get him no end of hate mail."

Avasarala chuckled.

"You live in your own world, dear one."

"I do," Arjun agreed, running his thumb across the hand terminal's screen. He looked up. "You don't mind, do you?"

"I love you for it. Stay here. Read about post-lyricism."

"What are you going to do?"

"The same thing as always. Try to keep civilization from blowing up while the children are in it."

When she'd been young, her mother had tried to teach her knitting. The skill hadn't taken, but there were other lessons that had. Once, the skein of yarn had gotten knotted badly, and Avasarala's frustrated yanking had only made things progressively worse. Her mother had taken the tight-bound clump from her, but instead of fixing it herself and handing it back, her mother sat cross-legged on the floor beside her and spoke aloud about how to solve the knot. She'd been gentle, deliberate, and patient, looking for places where she could work more slack into the system until, seemingly all at once, the yarn spilled free.

There were ten ships in the list, ranging from an ancient transport past due for the scrap heap to a pair of frigates captained by people whose names she'd heard. It wasn't a huge force, but it was enough to be provocative. Gently, deliberately, patiently, Avasarala started plucking it apart.

The transport was first, because it was easiest. She'd been cultivating the boys in maintenance and safety for years. It took four hours for someone with the schematics and logs to find a bolt that hadn't been replaced on schedule, and less than half an hour after that to issue the mandatory recall. The *Wu Tsao*—better armed of the frigates—was captained by Golla Ishigawa-Marx. His service record was solid, workmanlike reading. He was competent, unimaginative, and loyal. Three conversations had him promoted to the head of the construction oversight committee, where he probably wouldn't do any harm. The full command crew of the *Wu Tsao* was requested to come back to Earth to be present when they pinned a ribbon on him. The second frigate was harder, but she found a way. And by then the convoy was small enough that the medical and support ship was a higher rating than the remaining convoy justified.

The knot unspooled in her fingers. The three ships she couldn't pry loose were old and underpowered. If it came to a fight, they wouldn't be significant. And because of that, the Martians would only take offense if they were looking for an excuse.

She didn't think they would. And if she was wrong, that would be interesting too.

"Won't Admiral Nguyen see through all this?" Errinwright asked. He was in a hotel room somewhere on the other side of the planet. It was night behind him, and his dress shirt was unbuttoned at the top.

"Let him," Avasarala said. "What's he going to do? Go crying to his mama that I took his toys away? If he can't play with the big kids, he shouldn't be a fucking admiral."

Errinwright smiled and cracked his knuckles. He looked tired.

"The ships that will get there?"

"The *Bernadette Koe*, the *Aristophanes*, and the *Feodorovna*, sir."

"Those, yes. What are you going to tell the Martians about them?"

"Nothing if they don't bring it up," Avasarala said. "If they do, I can dismiss them. A minor medical support ship, a transport, and an itty-bitty gunship to keep off pirates. I mean, it's not like we're sending a couple of cruisers. So fuck them."

"You'll say it more gently, I hope?"

"Of course I will, sir. I'm not stupid."

"And Venus?"

She took a long breath, letting the air hiss out between her teeth.

"It's the damn bogeyman," she said. "I'm getting daily reports, but we don't know what we're looking at. The network it built across the planetary surface is finished, and now it's breaking down, but there are structures coming up in a complex radial symmetry. Only it's not along the axis of rotation. It's on the plane of ecliptic. So whatever's down there, it's orienting itself with the whole solar system in mind. And the spectrographic analysis is showing an uptick in lanthanum oxide and gold."

"I don't know what that means."

"Neither does anyone else, but the brains are thinking it may be a set of very high-temperature superconductors. They're trying to replicate the crystal structures in the labs, and they've found some things they don't understand. Turns out, the thing down there's a better physical chemist than we are. No fucking surprise there."

"Any link to Ganymede?"

"Just the one," Avasarala said. "Otherwise nothing. Or at least not directly."

"What do you mean, not directly?"

Avasarala frowned and looked away. The Buddha looked back.

"Did you know that the number of religious suicide cults has doubled since Eros?" she said. "I didn't until I got the report. The bond initiative to rebuild the water reclamation center at Cairo almost failed last year because a millennialist group said we wouldn't need it."

Errinwright sat forward. His eyes were narrow.

"You think there's a connection?"

"I don't think there's a bunch of pod people sneaking up from Venus," she said, "but…I've been thinking about what it's done to us. The whole solar system. Them and us and the Belters. It's not healthy having God sleeping right there where we can all watch him dream. It scares the shit out of us. It scares the shit out of *me*. And so we all look away and go about things as if the universe were the same as when we were young, but we know better. We're all acting like we're sane, but…"

She shook her head.

"Humanity's always lived with the inexplicable," Errinwright said. His voice was hard. She was making him uncomfortable. Well, she was making herself uncomfortable too.

"The inexplicable didn't used to eat planets," she said. "Even if the thing on Ganymede didn't come up off Venus on its own, it's pretty damn clear that it's related. And if *we* did it—"

"If we built that, it's because we found a new technology, and we're using it," Errinwright said. "Flint spear to gunpowder to nuclear warheads, it's what we do, Chrisjen. Let me worry about that. You keep your eye on Venus and don't let the Martian situation get out of control."

"Yes, sir," she said.

"Everything's going to be fine."

And, looking at the dead screen where her superior had been, Avasarala decided that maybe he even thought it was true. Avasarala wasn't sure any longer. Something was bothering her, and she didn't yet know what it was. It only lurked there, just underneath her conscious mind, like a splinter in a fingertip. She opened the captured video from the UN outpost on Ganymede, went through the mandatory security check, and watched the Marines die again.

Kiki and Suri were going to grow up in a world where this had happened, where Venus had always been the colony of something utterly foreign, uncommunicative, and implacable. The fear that carried would be normal to them, something they didn't think about any more than they did their own breath. On her screen, a man no older than Soren emptied an assault rifle clip into the attacker. The enhanced images showed the dozens of impacts cutting through the thing, the trails of filament coming out its back like streamers. The soldier died again. At least it had been quick for him. She paused the image. Her fingertip traced the outline of the attacker.

"Who are you?" she asked the screen. "What do you *want*?"

She was missing something. It happened often enough that she knew the feeling, but that didn't help. It would come when it came. All she could do until it did was keep scratching where it itched. She shut down the files, waiting for the security protocols to make sure she hadn't copied anything, then signed out and turned to the window.

She found that she was thinking about the next time. What information they'd be able to get the next time. What kind of patterns she'd be able to glean from the next time. The next attack, the next slaughter. It was already perfectly clear in her mind that what had happened on Ganymede was going to happen again, sooner or later. Genies didn't get put back into bottles, and from the moment the protomolecule had been set loose on the civilian population of Eros just to see what it would do, civilization had changed. Changed so fast and so powerfully that they were still playing catch-up.

Playing catch-up.

There was something there. Something in the words, like a lyric from a song she almost remembered. She ground her teeth and stood up, pacing the length of her window. She hated this part. Hated it.

Her office door opened. When she turned to look at Soren, he flinched back. Avasarala took her scowl down a couple of notches. It wasn't fair to scare the poor bunny. He was probably just the intern who'd pulled the short straw and gotten stuck with the cranky old woman. And in a way, she liked him.

"Yes?" she said.

"I thought you'd want to know that Admiral Nguyen sent a note of protest to Mr. Errinwright. Interference in his field of command. He didn't copy the secretary-general."

Avasarala smiled. If she couldn't unlock all the mysteries of the universe, she could at least keep the boys in line. And if he wasn't appealing to the bobble-head, then it was just pouting. Nothing was going to come of it.

"Good to know. And the Martians?"

"They're here, ma'am."

She sighed, plucked at her sari, and lifted her chin.

"Let's go stop the war, then," she said.

Chapter Thirteen: Holden

Amos, who'd finally turned up a few hours after the food riot carrying a case of beer and saying he'd done some "recon," was now carrying a small case of canned food. The label claimed it was "chicken food products." Holden hoped that the hacker Prax was leading them to would see the offering as at least being in the spirit of his requested payment.

Prax led the way with the manic speed of someone who had one last thing to do before he died, and could feel the end close on his heels. Holden suspected this wasn't far from the truth. The small botanist certainly looked like he'd been burning himself up.

They'd taken him aboard the *Somnambulist* while they'd gathered the supplies they'd need, and Holden had forced the man to eat a meal and take a shower. Prax had begun stripping while Holden was still showing him how to use the ship's head, as if waiting for privacy would waste precious time. The sight of the man's ravaged body had shocked him. All the while, the botanist spoke only of Mei, of his need to find her. Holden realized that he'd never in his life needed anything as badly as this man needed to see his daughter again.

To his surprise, it made him sad.

Prax had been robbed of everything, had all his fat boiled away; he'd been rendered down to the bare minimum of humanity. All he had left was his need to find his little girl, and Holden envied him for it.

When Holden had been dying and trapped in the hell of Eros Station, he had discovered that he needed to see Naomi one last time. Or barring that, to see that she was safe. It was why he hadn't died there. That and having Miller at his side with a second gun. And that connection, even now that he and Naomi were lovers, was a pale shadow compared to the thing driving Prax. It left Holden feeling like he'd lost something important without realizing it.

While Prax had showered, Holden had gone up the ladder to ops, where Naomi had been working to hack her way into Ganymede's crippled security system, pulled her out of her chair, and held her for a few moments. She stiffened with surprise for a second, then relaxed into his embrace. "Hi," she whispered in his ear. It might be a pale shadow, but it was what he had right now, and it was pretty damn good.

Prax paused at an intersection, his hands tapping at his thighs as if he were hurrying himself along. Naomi was back on the ship, monitoring their progress through locators they all carried and with the remnants of the station's security cameras.

At Holden's back, Amos cleared his throat and said in a voice low enough that Prax wouldn't hear, "If we lose this guy, I don't like our chances of finding our way back too quick."

Holden nodded. Amos was right.

Even at the best of times, Ganymede was a maze of identical gray corridors and occasional parklike caverns. And the station certainly wasn't at her best now. Most of the public information kiosks were dark, malfunctioning, or outright destroyed. The pubnet was unreliable at best. And the local citizens moved like scavengers over the corpse of their once-great moon, alternately terrified and threatening. He and Amos were both openly wearing firearms, and Amos had mastered a sort of constant glower that made people automatically put him onto their "not to be fucked with" list. Not for the first time, Holden wondered what sort of life Amos had been leading prior to his signing up for a tour on the *Canterbury*, the old water hauler they'd served together on.

Prax came to a sudden halt in front of a door that looked like a hundred other doors they'd already passed, set into the wall of a gray corridor that looked like every other gray corridor.

"This is it. He's in here."

Before Holden could respond, Prax was hammering on the door. Holden took a step back and to the side, giving himself a clear view of the doorway past Prax. Amos stepped to the other side, tucking the case of chicken under his left arm and hooking his right thumb into his waistband just in front of the holster. A year of patrolling the Belt, cleaning up the worst jackals that the governmental vacuum had left behind, had instilled some automatic habits in his crew. Holden appreciated them, but he wasn't sure he liked them. Working security certainly hadn't made Miller's life any better.

The door was yanked open by a scrawny and shirtless teenager with a big knife in his other hand.

"The fuck—" he started, then stopped when he saw Holden and Amos flanking Prax. He glanced at their guns and said, "Oh."

"I've brought you chicken," Prax replied, pointing back at the case Amos carried. "I need to see the rest of the camera footage."

"Coulda got that for you," Naomi said in Holden's ear, "given enough time."

"It's the 'enough time' part that's a problem," Holden subvocalized back at her. "But that's definitely plan B."

The skinny teen shrugged and opened the door the rest of the way, gesturing for Prax to enter. Holden followed, with Amos bringing up the rear.

"So," the kid said. "Show it, sabé?"

Amos put down the case on a filthy table and removed a single can from the box. He held it up where the kid could see it.

"Sauce?" the kid said.

"How about a second can instead?" Holden replied, moving over to the kid and smiling up at him agreeably. "So go get the rest of the footage, and we'll get out of your hair. Sound good?"

The kid lifted his chin and pushed Holden an arm's length back.

"Don't push up on me, macho."

"My apologies," Holden said, his smile never wavering. "Now go get the damned video footage you promised my friend here."

"Maybe no," the kid said. He flapped one hand at Holden. "Adinerado, si no? Quizas you got more than chicken to pay. Maybe a lot."

"Let me get this straight," Holden replied. "Are you shaking us down? Because that would be—"

A meaty hand came down on his shoulder, cutting him off.

"I got this one, Cap," Amos said, stepping between Holden and the kid. He held one of the chicken cans in his hand, and he was tossing it lightly and catching it.

"That guy," Amos said, pointing at Prax with his left hand while continuing to toss the chicken with his right, "got his baby girl snatched. He just wants to know where she is. He's willing to pay the agreed-upon price for that information."

The kid shrugged and started to speak, but Amos held up a finger to his lips and shushed him.

"And now, when that price is ready to be paid," Amos said, his tone friendly and conversational, "you want to shake him down because you know he's desperate. He'll give anything to get his girl back. This is a fat payday, right?"

The kid shrugged again. "Que no—"

Amos smashed the can of chicken food product into the kid's face so fast that for a moment Holden couldn't figure out why the hacker was suddenly lying on the ground, blood gushing from his nose. Amos settled one knee onto his chest, pinning him to the floor. The can of chicken went up and then pistoned down into the kid's face again with a sharp crack. He started to howl, but Amos clamped his left hand over the boy's mouth.

"You piece of shit," Amos yelled, all the friendliness gone from his voice, leaving just a ragged animal rage that Holden had never heard there before. "You gonna hold a baby girl hostage for more fucking *chicken*?"

Amos smashed the can into the hacker's ear, which immediately bloomed red. His hand came away from the kid's mouth, and the boy started yelling for help. Amos raised the can of chicken one more time, but Holden grabbed his arm and pulled him up off the gibbering kid.

"Enough," he said, holding on to Amos and hoping the big man didn't decide to clobber him with the can instead. Amos had always been the kind of guy who got into bar fights because he enjoyed them.

This was something different.

"Enough," Holden said again, and then held on until Amos stopped struggling. "He can't help us if you bash his brains out."

The kid scooted backward across the floor and had his shoulders up against the wall. He nodded as Holden spoke, and held his bleeding nose between his finger and thumb.

"That right?" Amos said. "You going to help?"

The kid nodded again and scrambled to his feet, still pressed against the wall.

"I'll go with him," Holden said, patting Amos on the shoulder. "Why don't you stay here and take a breather."

Before Amos could answer, Holden pointed at the terrified hacker.

"Better get to work."

"There," Prax said when the video of Mei's abduction came up again. "That's Mei. That man is her doctor, Dr. Strickland. That woman, I don't know her. But Mei's teacher said that she came up in their records as Mei's mother. With a picture and authorization to pick her up. Security is very good at the school. They'd never let a child go without that."

"Find where they went," Holden said to the hacker. To Prax he said, "Why her doctor?"

"Mei is..." Prax started, then stopped and started over. "Mei has a rare genetic disease that disables her immune system without regular treatments. Dr. Strickland knows this. Sixteen other kids with her disorder are missing too. He could keep them...he could keep Mei alive."

"You getting this, Naomi?"

"Yep, riding the hacker's trail through security. We won't need him again."

"Good," Holden said. "Because I'm pretty sure this bridge is thoroughly burned once we walk out the door."

"We always have more chicken," Naomi said with a chuckle.

"Amos made sure the kid's next request will be for plastic surgery."

"Ouch," she replied. "He okay?"

Holden knew she meant Amos. "Yeah. But...is there something I don't know about him that would make this problematic? Because he's really—"

"Aqui," the hacker said, pointing at his screen.

Holden watched as Dr. Strickland carried Mei down an older-looking corridor, the dark-haired woman in tow. They came to a door that looked like an ancient pressure hatch. Strickland did something at the panel next to it, and the three of them went inside.

"No eyes past this," the hacker said, almost flinching as if in expectation of being punished for the failings of the Ganymede security system.

"Naomi, where does that go?" Holden said, patting the air to let the hacker know he wasn't to blame.

"Looks like an old part of the original dig," she said, her words punctuated by pauses as she worked her console. "Zoned for utility storage. Shouldn't be anything beyond that door but dust and ice."

"Can you get us there?" Holden asked.

Naomi and Prax both said, "Yes," at the same time.

"Then that's where we're going."

He gestured for Prax and the hacker to lead the way back out to the front room, then followed them. Amos was sitting at the table, spinning one of the chicken cans on its edge like a thick coin. In the light gravity of the moon, it seemed like it would keep spinning forever. His expression was distant and unreadable.

"You did the job," Holden said to the hacker, who was staring at Amos, his face twitching from fear to rage and back again. "So you'll get paid. We aren't going to stiff you."

Before the kid could reply, Amos stood up and picked up the case of canned chicken. He turned it over and dumped all the remaining cans on the floor, where a few rolled away to various corners of the small room.

"Keep the change, asshole," he said, then threw the empty box into the tiny kitchen nook.

"And with that," Holden said, "we'll take our leave."

After Amos and Prax had gone out the door, Holden backed out, keeping a watchful eye on the hacker to make sure there were no misguided attempts at revenge. He shouldn't have worried. The minute Amos was out the door, the kid just started picking up the chicken cans and stacking them on the table.

As he backed out and closed the door behind him, Naomi said, "You know what it means, don't you?"

"Which thing?" he replied, then said to Amos, "Back to the ship."

"Prax said all the kids with Mei's particular disorder were missing," Naomi continued. "And her doctor is the one who took her out of school."

"So we can probably assume he, or people working with him, took the others," Holden agreed.

Amos and Prax were walking together up the corridor, the big man still wearing his distant look. Prax put a hand on his arm, and Holden heard him whisper, "Thank you." Amos just shrugged.

"Why would he want those kids?" Naomi asked.

"The better question to me is, how did he know to take them just hours before the shooting started?"

"Yeah," Naomi said, her voice quiet. "Yeah, how did he know that?"

"Because he's the reason why things went pear-shaped," Holden replied, saying out loud what they were both thinking.

"If he's got all of those kids, and he or the people he's with were able to start a shooting war between Mars and Earth to cover up the snatch..."

"Starts to feel like a strategy we've seen before, doesn't it? We need to know what's on the other side of that door."

"One of two things," Naomi said. "Nothing, because after the snatch they got the hell off this moon..."

"Or," Holden continued, "a whole lot of guys with guns."

"Yeah."

The galley of the *Somnambulist* was quiet as Prax and Holden's crew watched the video again. Naomi had pieced together all the security footage of Mei's abduction into a single long loop. They watched as her doctor carried her through various corridors, up a lift, and finally to the door of the abandoned parts of the station. After the third viewing, Holden gestured for Naomi to turn it off.

"What do we know?" he said, his fingers drumming on the table.

"The kid's not scared. She's not fighting to get away," Amos said.

"She's known Dr. Strickland all her life," Prax replied. "He would be almost like family to her."

"Which means they bought him," Naomi said. "Or this plan has been going on for..."

"Four years," Prax said.

"Four years," Naomi repeated. "Which is a hell of a long con to run unless the stakes are huge."

"Is it kidnapping? If they want a ransom payment..."

"Doesn't wash. A couple hours after Mei disappears into that hatch," Holden said, pointing at the image frozen on Naomi's screen, "Earth and Mars are shooting each other. Somebody's going to a lot of trouble to grab sixteen sick kids and hide the fact they did it."

"If Protogen wasn't toast," Amos said, "I'd say this is exactly the kind of shit they'd pull."

"And whoever it is has significant tech resources too," Naomi said. "They were able to hack the school's system even before the Ganymede netsec was collapsing from the battle, and insert that woman's records into Mei's file without any trace of tampering."

"Some of the kids in her school had very rich or powerful parents," Prax said. "Their security would have to be top notch."

Holden drummed out a last rhythm on the tabletop with both hands, then said, "Which all leads us back to the big question. What's waiting for us on the other side of that door?"

"Corporate goons," Amos said.

"Nothing," Naomi said.

"Mei," Prax said quietly. "It might be Mei."

"We need to be prepared for all three possibilities: violence, gathering clues, or rescuing a kid. So let's put together a plan.

Naomi, I want a terminal with a radio link that I can plug into whatever network we find on the other side, and give you a doorway in."

"Yep," Naomi said, already getting up from the table and heading toward the keel ladder.

"Prax, you need to come up with a way for Mei to trust us if we find her, and give us details on any complications her illness might cause during a rescue. How quickly do we need to get her back here for her meds? Things like that."

"Okay," Prax said, pulling out his terminal and making notes.

"Amos?"

"Yeah, Cap?"

"That leaves violence to us. Let's tool up."

The smile began and ended at the corners of Amos' eyes.

"Fuck yeah."

Chapter Fourteen: Prax

Prax didn't understand how near he was to collapse until he ate. Canned chicken with some kind of spicy chutney, soft no-crumb crackers of the type usually used in zero-g environments, a tall glass of beer. He wolfed it down, his body suddenly ravenous and unstoppable.

After he finished vomiting, the woman who seemed to take care of all the small practical matters on the ship—he knew her name was Naomi, but he kept wanting to call her Cassandra, because she looked like an intern by that name he'd worked with three years earlier—switched him to a thin protein broth that his atrophied gut could actually handle. Over the course of hours, his mind started coming back. It felt like waking up over and over without falling asleep in between; sitting in the hold of Holden's ship, he'd find himself noticing the shift in his cognition, how much more clearly he could think and how good it felt to come back to himself. And then a few minutes later, some set of sugar-deprived ganglia would struggle back to function, and it would all happen again.

And with every step back toward real consciousness, he felt the drive growing, pushing him toward the door that Strickland and Mei had gone through.

"Doctor, huh?" the big one—Amos—said.

"I got my degree here. The university's really good. Lots of grant money. Or...now I suppose there used to be."

"I was never much for formal education myself."

The relief ship's mess hall was tiny and scarred by age. The woven carbon filament walls had cracks in the enameling, and the tabletop was pitted from years, maybe decades, of use. The lighting was a thin spectrum shifted toward pink that would have killed any plants living under it in about three days. Amos had a canvas sack filled with formed plastic boxes of different sizes, each of which seemed to have a firearm of some kind inside. He had unrolled a square of red felt and disassembled a huge matte-black pistol on it. The delicate metal parts looked like sculpture. Amos dipped a cotton swab into a bright blue cleaning solution and rubbed it gently on a silver mechanism attached to a black metal tube, polishing metal plates that were already bright as a mirror.

Prax found his hands moving toward the disassembled pieces, willing them to come together. To be already cleaned and polished and remade. Amos pretended not to notice in a way that meant he was very much aware.

"I don't know why they would have taken her," Prax said. "Dr. Strickland has always been great with her. He never...I mean, he'd never hurt her. I don't think he'd hurt her."

"Yeah, probably not," Amos said. He dipped the swab into the cleaning fluid again and started on a metal rod with a spring wrapped around it.

"I really need to get there," Prax said. He didn't say, *Every minute here is a minute that they could be hurting Mei. That she could be dying or getting shipped offworld.* He tried to keep his words from sounding like a whine or a demand, but they seemed to come out as both.

"Getting ready's the shitty part," Amos said, as if agreeing to something. "You want to get right out into it right the fuck now. Get it over with."

"Well, yes," Prax said.

"I get that," Amos said. "It's no fun, but you've got to get through it. Going in without your gear ready, you might as well not go. Plus which the girl's been gone for how long now?"

"Since the fighting. Since the mirror came down."

"Chances of another hour making much difference are pretty small, right?"

"But—"

"Yeah," Amos said with a sigh. "I know. This is the tough part. Not as bad as waiting for us to get back, though. That's gonna suck even worse."

Amos put down the swab and started fitting the long black spring back over the spindle of bright metal. The alcohol fumes of the cleaning solution stung Prax's eyes.

"I'm waiting for *you*," Prax said.

"Yeah, I know," Amos said. "And I'll make sure we're real quick about it. The captain's a real good guy, but he can get kind of distracted sometimes. I'll keep him on point. No trouble."

"No," Prax said, "I don't mean I'm waiting for you when you go to that door. I mean I'm waiting for you *right now*. I'm waiting to go there with you."

Amos slid the spring and spindle into the shell of the gun, twisting it gently with his fingertips. Prax didn't know when he'd risen to his feet.

"How many gunfights have you been in?" Amos asked. His voice was low and wide and gentle. "Because I've been in…shit. This'll be eleven for me. Maybe twelve, if you count the one time when the guy got up again as a different fight. Point is, if you want your little girl safe, you don't want her in a tunnel with a guy firing a gun who doesn't know what he's doing."

As if in punctuation, Amos slid the gun together. The metal clacked.

"I'll be fine," Prax said, but his legs were trembling, just standing up. Amos held up the gun.

"This ready to fire?" Amos asked.

"Sorry?"

"If you pick this gun up right now, point it at a bad guy, pull the trigger, does it go bang? You just watched me put it together. Dangerous or safe?"

Prax opened his mouth, then closed it. An ache just behind his sternum grew a notch worse. Amos started to put the gun down.

"Safe," Prax said.

"You sure about that, Doc?"

"You didn't put any bullets in it. It's safe."

"You're *sure*?"

"Yes."

Amos frowned at the gun.

"Well, yeah, that's right," he said. "But you're still not going."

Voices came from the narrow hallway from the airlock. Jim Holden's voice wasn't what Prax had thought it would be. He'd expected him to be serious, grave. Instead, even during the times like now, when the distress clipped his vowels short and tightened his voice, there was a lightness to him. The woman's voice—*Naomi*, not Cassandra—wasn't deeper, but it was darker.

"Those are the numbers," she said.

"They're wrong," Holden said, ducking into the mess. "They've got to be wrong. It doesn't make sense."

"What's the word, Cap'n?" Amos asked.

"Security's not going to be any use," Holden said. "The locals are stretched too thin trying to keep the place from straight-out catastrophe."

"Which is why maybe we shouldn't be going in with guns drawn," Naomi said.

"Please, can we not have that conversation again right now?"

Her mouth hardened and Amos pointedly looked at the gun,

polishing the parts that already shone. Prax had the sense of walking in on a much longer conversation.

"This guy who grabs a gun first and talks later..." Naomi said. "You didn't used to be him. You *aren't* him."

"Well, I need to be him today," Holden said in a voice that closed the subject. The silence was uncomfortable.

"What's wrong with the numbers?" Prax asked. Holden looked at him, confused. "You said there was something wrong with the numbers."

"They're saying that the death rate's going up. But that's got to be wrong. The fighting was...what? One day? Day and a half? Why would things be getting worse now?"

"No," Prax said. "That's right. It's the cascade. It'll get worse."

"What's the cascade?" Naomi asked. Amos slid the pistol into its box and hauled out a longer case. A shotgun maybe. His gaze was on Prax, waiting.

"It's the basic obstacle of artificial ecosystems. In a normal evolutionary environment, there's enough diversity to cushion the system when something catastrophic happens. That's nature. Catastrophic things happen all the time. But nothing we can build has the depth. One thing goes wrong, and there's only a few compensatory pathways that can step in. They get overstressed. Fall out of balance. When the next one fails, there are even fewer paths, and then they're more stressed. It's a simple complex system. That's the technical name for it. Because it's simple, it's prone to cascades, and because it's complex, you can't predict what's going to fail. Or how. It's computationally impossible."

Holden leaned against the wall, his arms folded. It was still odd, seeing him in person. He looked the same as he had on the screens, and he also didn't.

"Ganymede Station," Holden said, "is the most important food supply and agricultural center outside Earth and Mars. It can't just collapse. They wouldn't let it. People come here to have their babies, for God's sake."

Prax tilted his head. A day before, he wouldn't have been able to explain this. For one thing, he wouldn't have had the blood sugar to fuel thought. For another, he wouldn't have had anyone to say it to. It was good to be able to think again, even if it was only so he could explain how bad things had become.

"Ganymede's dead," Prax said. "The tunnels will probably survive, but the environmental and social structures are already broken. Even if we could somehow get the environmental systems back in place—and really, we can't without a lot of work—how many people are going to stay here now? How many would be going to jail? Something's going to fill the niche, but it won't be what was here before."

"Because of the cascade," Holden said.

"Yes," Prax said. "That's what I was trying to say before. To Amos. It's all going to fall apart. The relief effort's going to make the fall a little more graceful, maybe. But it's too late. It's too late, and since Mei's out there, and we don't know what's going to break, I have to go with you."

"Prax," Cassandra said. *No. Naomi.* Maybe his brain wasn't really up to full power even now.

"Strickland and that woman, even if they think they can keep her safe, they can't. You see? Even if they're not hurting her, even if they're not, everything around them is going to fall apart. What if they run out of air? What if they don't understand what's happening?"

"I know this is hard," Holden said. "But shouting about it won't help."

"I'm not shouting. I'm not shouting. I'm just telling you that they took my little girl away, and I need to go and get her. I need to be there when you open that door. Even if she's not there. Even if she's dead, I need to be the one who finds her."

The sound was crisp and professional and oddly beautiful: a magazine slipping into a pistol. Prax hadn't seen Amos take it back out of its box, but the dark metal was in the man's huge hand. Dwarfed by his fingers. While he watched, Amos chambered a round. Then he took the gun by its barrel, careful to keep it pointing at the wall, and held it out.

"But I thought…" Prax said. "You said I wasn't…"

Amos stretched his arms out another half inch. The gesture was unmistakable. *Take it.* Prax took it. It was heavier than it looked.

"Um. Amos?" Holden said. "Did you just give him a loaded gun?"

"Doc needs to go, Cap'n," Amos said with a shrug. "So I'm thinking he should probably go."

Prax saw the look that passed between Holden and Naomi.

"We might want to talk about that decision-making process, Amos," Naomi said, shaping the words carefully.

"You betcha," Amos said. "Soon as we get back."

Prax had been walking through the station for weeks as a native, a local. A refugee with nowhere to flee. He'd gotten used to how the hallways looked, how people's eyes slid over him in case he'd try to lay his burdens on them. Now that Prax was fed and armed and part of a group, the station had become a different place. People's eyes still slid across them, but the fear was different, and hunger fought against it. Holden and Amos didn't have the gray of malnutrition or the haunted look around their eyes of seeing everything they thought was immutable collapse. Naomi was back at the ship, hacked into the local security network and ready to coordinate the three of them in case they got split up.

For the first time perhaps in his life, Prax felt like an outsider. He looked at his hometown and saw what Holden would see: a huge hallway with paints and dyes worked into the ice up high on the wall; the lower half, where people might accidentally touch it, covered in thick insulation. Ganymede's raw ice would strip the flesh from bone with even the briefest contact. The hallway was too dark now, the floodlights beginning to fail. A wide corridor Prax had walked through every day he was at school was a dim chamber filled with the sounds of dripping water as the climate regulation failed. The plants that weren't dead were dying, and the air was getting the stale taste at the back of his throat that meant the emergency recyclers would be coming on soon. Should be coming on soon. Had better.

Holden was right, though. The thin-faced, desperate people they passed had been food scientists and soil technicians, gas exchange experts and agricultural support staff. If Ganymede Station died, the cascade wouldn't stop here. Once the last load of food lifted off, the Belt, the Jovian system, and the myriad long-term bases in their own orbits around the sun would have to find a different way to get vitamins and micronutrients for their kids. Prax started wondering whether the bases on the far planets would be able to sustain themselves. If they had full hydroponics rigs and yeast farms and nothing went wrong...

It was a distraction. It was grasping anything other than the fear of what would be waiting behind that door. He embraced it.

"Hold up! All y'all."

The voice was low and rough and wet, like the man's vocal cords had been taken out and dragged through mud. He stood in the center of the ice tunnels intersecting before them, military-police body armor two sizes too small straining to keep his bulk in. His accent and build said he was Martian.

Amos and Holden paused, turned, looking everywhere but at the man before them. Prax followed their gazes. Other men lurked, half hidden, around them. The sudden panic tasted like copper.

"I make six," Holden said.

"What about the guy with the gray pants?" Amos asked.

"Okay, maybe seven. He's been with us since we left the ship, though. He might be something else."

"Six is still more than three," Naomi said in their ears. "You want me to send backup?"

"Hot damn. We've got backup?" Amos asked. "Gonna have Supitayaporn come down and talk 'em all to death?"

"We can take them," Prax said, reaching for the pistol in his pocket. "We can't let anyone—"

Amos' wide hand closed over his own, keeping the gun in his pocket and out of sight.

"These aren't the ones you shoot," Amos said. "These are the ones you talk to."

Holden stepped toward the Martian. The ease with which he held himself made the assault rifle on his shoulder seem almost innocuous. Even the expensive body armor he wore didn't seem at odds with his casual smile.

"Hey," Holden said. "There a problem, sir?"

"Might be," the Martian drawled. "Might not. That's your call."

"I'll take *not*," Holden said. "Now, if you'll excuse us, we'll be on—"

"Slow down," the Martian said, sidling forward. His face was vaguely like someone Prax had seen before on the tube and never particularly remarked. "You're not from around here."

"I am," Prax said. "I'm Dr. Praxidike Meng. Chief botanist on the RMD-Southern soy farm project. Who are you?"

"Let the cap'n do this," Amos said.

"But—"

"He's pretty good at it."

"I'm thinking you're part of the relief work," the Martian said. "Long way from the docks. Looks like you lost your way. Maybe you need an escort back to where it's safe."

Holden shifted his weight. The assault rifle just happened to slide forward a few inches, not at all provocatively.

"I don't know," Holden said. "We're pretty well protected. I think we can probably take care of ourselves. What kind of fee are you...um, escorts asking?"

"Well now. I count three of you. Call it a hundred in Martian scrip. Five, local."

"How about you follow us down, and I arrange passage for all of you off this ice ball?"

The Martian's jaw dropped.

"That's not funny," he said, but the mask of power and confidence had slipped. Prax had seen the hunger and desperation behind it.

"I'm going to an old tunnel system," Holden said. "Someone

abducted a bunch of kids right before everything went to hell. They took them there. Doc's kid was one of the ones that got snatched. We're going to get her back and politely ask how they knew all this was coming down. Might be resistance. I could use a few people who know what end of the gun points forward."

"You're fucking with me," the Martian said. From the corner of his eye, Prax saw one of the others step forward. A thin woman in cheap protective weave.

"We're OPA," Amos said, then nodded at Holden. "He's James Holden of the *Rocinante*."

"Holy shit," the Martian said. "You are. You're Holden."

"It's the beard," Holden said.

"My name's Wendell. Used to work for Pinkwater Security before the bastards took off, left us here. Way I figure, that voids the contract. You want to pick up some professional firepower, you ain't gonna find better than us."

"How many you got?"

"Six, counting me."

Holden looked over at Amos. Prax felt Amos shrug as much as saw it. The other man they'd been talking about was unrelated after all.

"All right," Holden said. "We tried to talk to local security, but they didn't give us the time of day. Follow me, back us up, and I give you my word you'll get off Ganymede."

Wendell grinned. He'd had one of his incisors dyed red with a small black-and-white design on it.

"Anything you say, boss," he said. Then, lifting his gun: "Form up! We got us a new contract, people. Let's get it done!"

The whoops came from all around them. Prax found the thin woman beside him, grinning and shaking his hand like she was running for office. Prax blinked and smiled back, and Amos put his hand on Prax's shoulder.

"See? Told you. Now let's get moving."

The hallway was darker than it had seemed in the video. The ice had thin melt channels, like pale veins, but the frost covering them was fresh. The door looked like any other of a hundred they'd passed on the way in. Prax swallowed. His stomach ached. He wanted to scream for Mei, to call her name and hear her call back.

"Okay," Naomi said in his ear. "I've got the lock disabled. Whenever you guys are ready."

"No time like the present," Holden said. "Open it up."

The seal around the door hissed.

The door opened.

Chapter Fifteen: Bobbie

Three hours into the first big meeting between the Martian and UN diplomats and they'd only just got past introducing everyone and on to reading the agenda. A squat Earther in a charcoal-gray suit that probably cost more than Bobbie's recon armor droned on about Section 14, Subsection D, Items 1-11, in which they would discuss the effect of past hostilities on commodity pricing pursuant to existing trade agreements. Bobbie looked around, noticed that everyone else at the long oak table was staring with rapt attention at the agenda reader, and stifled the truly epic yawn that was struggling to get out.

She distracted herself by trying to figure out who people were. They'd all been introduced by name and title at some point, but that didn't mean much. Everyone here was an assistant secretary, or undersecretary, or director of something. There were even a few generals, but Bobbie knew enough about how politics worked to know that the military people in the room would be the least important. The people with real power would be the quiet ones with unassuming titles. There were several of those, including a moonfaced man with a skinny tie who'd been introduced as the secretary of something or other. Sitting next to him was someone's grandmother in a bright sari, a splash of yellow in the middle of all the dark brown and dark blue and charcoal gray. She sat and munched pistachios and wore an enigmatic half smile. Bobbie entertained herself for a few minutes by trying to guess if Moonface or Grandma was the boss.

She considered pouring a glass of water from one of the crystal decanters evenly distributed across the table. She wasn't thirsty, but turning her glass over, pouring water into it, and drinking it would burn a minute, maybe two. She glanced down the table and noticed that no one else was drinking the water. Maybe everyone was waiting for someone else to be first.

"Let's take a short break," charcoal-suit man said. "Ten minutes, then we can move on to Section fifteen of the agenda."

People got up and began dispersing toward restrooms and smoking areas. Grandma carried her handbag to a recycling chute and dumped pistachio shells into it. Moonface pulled out his terminal and called someone.

"Jesus," Bobbie said, rubbing her eyes with her palms until she saw stars.

"Problem, Sergeant?" Thorsson said, leaning back in his chair and grinning. "The gravity wearing on you?"

"No," Bobbie said. Then, "Well, yes, but mostly I'm ready to jab a stylus into my eye, just for a change of pace."

Thorsson nodded and patted her hand, a move he was using more often now. It hadn't gotten any less irritating and paternalistic, but now Bobbie was worried that it might mean Thorsson was working up to hitting on her. That would be an uncomfortable moment.

She pulled her hand away and leaned toward Thorsson until he turned and looked her in the eye.

"Why," she whispered, "is no one talking about the goddamned monster? Isn't that why I'm—why *we're* here?"

"You have to understand how these things work," Thorsson said, turning away from her and fiddling with his terminal. "Politics moves slow because the stakes are very high, and no one wants to be the person that screwed it up."

He put his terminal down and gave her a wink. "Careers are at stake here."

"Careers..."

Thorsson just nodded and tapped on his terminal some more.

Careers?

For a moment, she was on her back, staring up into the star-filled void above Ganymede. Her men were dead or dying. Her suit radio dead, her armor a frozen coffin. She saw the thing's face. Without a suit in the radiation and hard vacuum, the red snowfall of flash-frozen blood around its claws. And no one at this table wanted to talk about it because it might affect their careers?

To hell with that.

When the meeting's attendees had shuffled back into the room and taken their places around the table, Bobbie raised her hand. She felt faintly ridiculous, like a fifth-grade student in a room full of adults, but she had no idea what the actual protocol for asking a question was. The agenda reader shot her one annoyed glance, then ignored her. Thorsson reached under the table and sharply squeezed her leg.

She kept her hand up.

"Excuse me?" she said.

People around the table took turns giving her increasingly unfriendly looks and then pointedly turning away. Thorsson upped the pressure on her leg until she'd had enough of him and grabbed his wrist with her other hand. She squeezed until the bones creaked and he snatched his hand away with a surprised gasp. He turned his chair to look at her, his eyes wide and his mouth a flat, lipless line.

Yellow-sari placed a hand on the agenda reader's arm, and he instantly stopped talking. *Okay, that one is the boss,* Bobbie decided.

"I, for one," Grandma said, smiling a mild apology at the room, "would like to hear what Sergeant Draper has to say."

She remembers my name, Bobbie thought. *That's interesting.*

"Sergeant?" Grandma said.

Bobbie, unsure of what to do, stood up.

"I'm just wondering why no one is talking about the monster."

Grandma's enigmatic smile returned. No one spoke. The silence slid adrenaline into Bobbie's blood. She felt her legs starting to tremble. More than anything in the world, she wanted to sit down, to make them all forget her and look away.

She scowled and locked her knees.

"You know," Bobbie said, her voice rising, but she was unable to stop it. "The monster that killed fifty soldiers on Ganymede? The reason we're all here?"

The room was silent. Thorsson stared at her like she had lost her mind. Maybe she had. Grandma tugged once at her yellow sari and smiled encouragement.

"I mean," Bobbie said, holding up the agenda, "I'm sure trade agreements and water rights and who gets to screw who on the second Thursday after the winter solstice is all *very* important!"

She stopped to suck in a long breath, the gravity and her tirade seeming to have robbed her of air. She could see it in their eyes. She could see that if she just stopped now, she'd be an odd thing that happened and everyone could go back to work and quickly forget her. She could see her career not crashing off a cliff in flames.

She discovered that she didn't care.

"But," she said, throwing the agenda across the table, where a surprised man in a brown suit dodged it as though its touch might infect him with whatever Bobbie had, "*what about the fucking monster?*"

Before she could continue, Thorsson popped up from his seat.

"Excuse me for a moment, ladies and gentlemen. Sergeant

Draper is suffering from some post-combat-related stress and needs attention."

He grabbed her elbow and drove her from the room, a rising wave of murmurs pushing at their backs. Thorsson stopped in the conference room's lobby and waited for the door to shut behind him.

"You," Thorsson said, shoving her toward a chair. Normally the skinny intelligence officer couldn't have pushed her anywhere, but all the strength seemed to have run out of her legs, and she collapsed into the seat.

"You," he repeated. Then, to someone on his terminal, he said, "Get down here, now."

"You," he said a third time, pointing at Bobbie, then paced back and forth in front of her chair.

A few minutes later, Captain Martens came trotting into the conference room lobby. He pulled up short when he saw Bobbie slouched in her chair and Thorsson's angry face.

"What—" he started, but Thorsson cut him off.

"This is *your* fault," he said to Martens, then spun to face Bobbie. "And you, Sergeant, have just proven that it was a monumental mistake to bring you along. Any benefit that might have been gained from having the only eyewitness has now been squandered by your . . . your *idiotic* tirade."

"She—" Martens tried again, but Thorsson poked a finger into his chest and said, "You said you could control her."

Martens gave Thorsson a sad smile.

"No, I never said that. I said I could help her given enough time."

"Doesn't matter," Thorsson said, waving a hand at them. "You're both on the next ship to Mars, where you can explain yourselves to a disciplinary board. Now get out of my sight."

He spun on his heel and slipped back into the conference room, opening the door only wide enough for his narrow body to squeeze through.

Martens sat down in the chair next to Bobbie and let out a long breath.

"So," he said. "What's up?"

"Did I just destroy my career?" she asked.

"Maybe. How do you feel?"

"I feel..." she said, realizing how badly she did want to talk with Martens, and becoming angered by the impulse. "I feel like I need some air."

Before Martens could protest, Bobbie stood up and headed for the elevators.

The UN complex was a city in its own right. Just finding a way out took her the better part of an hour. Along the way, she moved through the chaos and energy of government like a ghost. People hurried past her in the long corridors, talking energetically in clumps or on their hand terminals. Bobbie had never been to Olympia, where the Martian congressional building was located. She'd caught a few minutes of congressional sessions on the government broadcast when an issue she cared about was being discussed, but compared to the activity here at the UN, it was pretty low-key. The people in this building complex governed thirty billion citizens and hundreds of millions of colonists. By comparison, Mars' four billion suddenly seemed like a backwater.

On Mars, it was a generally accepted fact that Earth was a civilization in decay. Lazy, coddled citizens who lived on the government dole. Fat, corrupt politicians who enriched themselves at the expense of the colonies. A degrading infrastructure that spent close to 30 percent of its total output on recycling systems to keep the population from drowning in its own filth. On Mars, there was virtually no unemployment. The entire population was engaged either directly or indirectly in the greatest engineering feat in human history: the terraforming of a planet. It gave everyone a sense of purpose, a shared vision of the future. Nothing like the Earthers, who lived only for their next government payout and their next visit to the drugstore or entertainment malls.

Or at least, that was the story. Suddenly Bobbie wasn't so sure.

Repeated visits to the various information kiosks scattered through the complex eventually got her to an exit door. A bored guard nodded to her as she passed by, and then she was outside.

Outside. Without a suit.

Five seconds later she was clawing at the door, which she now realized was an exit only, trying to get back in. The guard took pity on her and pushed the door open. She ran back inside and collapsed on a nearby settee, gasping and hyperventilating.

"First time?" the guard asked with a smile.

Bobbie found herself unable to speak, but nodded.

"Mars or Luna?"

"Mars," she said once her breathing had slowed.

"Yeah, I knew it. Domes, you know. People who've been in domes just panic a bit. Belters lose their shit. And I mean completely. We wind up shipping them home drugged up to keep them from screaming."

"Yeah," Bobbie said, happy to let the guard ramble while she collected herself. "No kidding."

"They bring you in when it was dark outside?"

"Yeah."

"They do that for offworlders. Helps with the agoraphobia."

"Yeah."

"I'll hold the door open a bit for you. In case you need to come back in again."

The assumption that she'd give it a second try instantly won Bobbie over, and she actually looked at the guard for the first time. Earther short, but with beautiful skin so dark it was almost blue. He had a compact, athletic frame and lovely gray eyes. He was smiling at her without a trace of mockery.

"Thank you," she said. "Bobbie. Bobbie Draper."

"Chuck," he replied. "Look at the ground, then slowly look to the horizon. Whatever you do, don't look straight up."

"I think I got it this time, Chuck, but thanks."

Chuck gave her uniform a quick glance and said, "Semper fi, Gunny."

"Oohrah," Bobbie replied with a grin.

On her second trip outside, she did as Chuck had recommended and looked down at the ground for a few moments. This helped reduce the feeling of massive sensory overload. But only a little. A thousand scents hit her nose, competing for dominance. The rich aroma of plants and soil she would expect in a garden dome. The oil and hot metal from a fabrication lab. The ozone of electric motors. All of them hit her at once, layered on top of each other and mixed with scents too exotic to name. And the sounds were a constant cacophony. People talking, construction machinery, electric cars, a transorbital shuttle lifting off, all at once and all the time. It was no wonder it had caused a panic. Just two senses' worth of data threatened to overwhelm her. Add that impossibly blue sky that stretched on forever…

Bobbie stood outside, eyes closed, breathing until she heard Chuck let the door close behind her. Now she was committed. Turning around and asking Chuck to let her back in would be admitting defeat. He'd clearly done some time in the UNMC, and she wasn't going to look weak in front of the competition. Hell no.

When her ears and nose had gotten more accustomed to the barrage of inputs, she opened her eyes again, looking down at the concrete of the walkway. Slowly, she lifted them till the horizon was in view. Ahead of her lay long sidewalks passing through meticulously tended green space. Beyond it in the distance was a gray wall that must have stood ten meters high, with guard towers regularly spaced on it. The UN complex had a surprising amount of security. She wondered if she'd be able to get out.

She needn't have worried. As she approached the guarded gate to the outside world, the security system queried her terminal, which assured it of her VIP status. A camera above the guard post scanned her face, compared it to the picture on file, and verified her identity while she was still twenty meters from the gate. When she reached the exit, the guard snapped her a sharp salute and asked if she'd need a ride.

"No, just going for a walk," she said.

The guard smiled and wished her a good day. She began walking down the street leading away from the UN complex, then turned around to see two armed security personnel following her at a discreet distance. She shrugged and walked on. Somebody would probably lose their job if a VIP like her got lost or hurt.

Once Bobbie was outside the UN compound, her agoraphobia lessened. Buildings rose around her like walls of steel and glass, moving the dizzying skyline far enough up that she no longer saw it. Small electric cars whizzed down the streets, trailing a high-pitched whine and the scent of ozone.

And people were *everywhere*.

Bobbie had gone to a couple of games at Armstrong Stadium on Mars, to watch the Red Devils play. The stadium had seats for twenty thousand fans. Because the Devils were usually at the bottom of the standings, it generally held less than half that. That relatively modest number was the greatest number of humans Bobbie had ever seen in one place at one time. There were billions of people on Mars, but there weren't a lot of open spaces for them to gather. Standing at an intersection, looking down two streets that seemed to stretch into infinity, Bobbie was sure she saw more than the average attendance of a Red Devils game just walking on the sidewalks. She tried to imagine how many people were in the buildings that rose to vertigo-inducing heights in every direction around her, and couldn't. Millions of people, probably in just the buildings and streets she could see.

And if Martian propaganda was right, most of the people she could see right now didn't have jobs. She tried to imagine that, not having any particular place you had to be on any given day.

What the Earthers had discovered is that when people have nothing else to do, they have babies. For a brief period in the twentieth and twenty-first centuries, the population had looked like it might shrink rather than continue to grow. As more and more women went into higher education, and from there to jobs, the average family size grew smaller.

A few decades of massive employment shrinkage ended that.

Or, again, that was what she'd been taught in school. Only here on Earth, where food grew on its own, where air was just a by-product of random untended plants, where resources lay thick on the ground, could a person actually choose not to do anything at all. There was enough extra created by those who felt the need to work that the surplus could feed the rest. A world no longer of the haves and the have-nots, but of the engaged and the apathetic.

Bobbie found herself standing next to a street-level coffee shop and took a seat.

"Can I get you anything?" a smiling young woman with brightly dyed blue hair asked.

"What's good?"

"We make the best soy-milk tea, if you like that."

"Sure," Bobbie said, not sure what soy-milk tea was, but liking those two things separately enough to take a chance.

The blue-haired girl bustled away and chatted with an equally young man behind the bar while he made the tea. Bobbie looked around her, noticing that everyone she saw working was about the same age.

When the tea arrived, she said, "Hey, do you mind if I ask you something?"

The girl shrugged, her smile an invitation.

"Is everyone who works here the same age?"

"Well," she said. "Pretty close. Gotta collect your pre-university credits, right?"

"I'm not from here," Bobbie said. "Explain that."

Blue seemed actually to see her for the first time, looking over her uniform and its various insignias.

"Oh, wow, Mars, right? I want to go there."

"Yeah, it's great. So tell me about the credits thing."

"They don't have that on Mars?" she asked, puzzled. "Okay, so, if you apply to a university, you have to have at least a year of work credits. To make sure you like working. You know, so they don't waste classroom space on people who will just go on basic afterward."

"Basic?"

"You know, basic support."

"I think I understand," Bobbie said. "Basic support is the money you live on if you don't work?"

"Not money, you know, just basic. Gotta work to have money."

"Thanks," Bobbie said, then sipped her milk tea as Blue trotted to another table. The tea was delicious. She had to admit, it made a sad kind of sense to do some early winnowing before spending the resources to educate people. Bobbie told her terminal to pay the bill, and it flashed a total at her after calculating the exchange rate. She added a nice tip for the blue-haired girl who wanted more from life than basic support.

Bobbie wondered if Mars would become like this after the terraforming. If Martians didn't have to fight every day to make enough resources to survive, would they turn into this? A culture where you could actually *choose* if you wanted to contribute? The work hours and collective intelligence of fifteen billion humans just tossed away as acceptable losses for the system. It made Bobbie sad to think of. All that effort to get to a point where they could live like this. Sending their kids to work at a coffee shop to see if they were up to contributing. Letting them live the rest of their lives on *basic* if they weren't.

But one thing was for sure: All that running and exercising the Martian Marines did at one full gravity was bullshit. There was no way Mars could ever beat Earth on the ground. You could drop every Martian soldier, fully armed, into just one Earth city and the citizens would overwhelm them using rocks and sticks.

Deep in the grip of pathos, she suddenly felt a massive weight lift that she hadn't even realized she'd been carrying. Thorsson and his bullshit didn't matter. The pissing contest with Earth didn't matter. Making Mars into another Earth didn't matter, not if this was where it was headed.

All that mattered was finding out who'd put that thing on Ganymede.

She tossed off the last of her tea and thought, *I'll need a ride.*

Chapter Sixteen: Holden

Beyond the door lay a long hallway that looked, to Holden, exactly the same as every other hallway on Ganymede: ice walls with moisture-resistant and insulated structural plates and inset conduit, rubberized walking surface, full-spectrum LEDs to mimic sunlight slanting down from the blue skies of Earth. They could have been anywhere.

"We're sure this is right, Naomi?"

"That's the one we saw Mei go through in the hacker's footage," she replied.

"Okay," he said, then dropped to one knee and motioned for his ad hoc army to do the same. When everyone was in a rough circle around him, he said, "Our overwatch, Naomi, has intel on the layout of these tunnels, but not much else. We have no idea where the bad guys are, or even if they're still here."

Prax started to object, but Amos quieted him with a heavy hand on his back.

"So we could conceivably leave a lot of intersections at our back. I don't like that."

"Yeah," said Wendell, the Pinkwater leader. "I don't like that much either."

"So we're going to leave a lookout at each intersection until we know where we're going," Holden replied, then said, "Naomi, put all their hand terminals on our channel. Guys, put in your earbuds. Comm discipline is don't speak unless I ask a direct question, or someone is about to die."

"Roger," said Wendell, echoed by the rest of his team.

"Once we know what we're looking at, I'll call all the lookouts up to our position if needed. If not, they're our way out of here if we're in over our heads."

Nods all around.

"Outstanding. Amos is point. Wendell, you cover our asses. Everyone else, string out at one-meter intervals," Holden said, then tapped on Wendell's breastplate. "We do this thing clean, and I'll talk to my OPA people about putting a few credits in your accounts in addition to getting you offworld."

"Righteous," the thin woman with the cheap armor said, and then racked a round in her machine pistol.

"Okay, let's go. Amos, Naomi's map says fifty meters to another pressure door, then some warehouse space."

Amos nodded, then shouldered his weapon, a heavy automatic shotgun with a thick magazine. He had several more magazines and a number of grenades dangling from his Martian armor's harness. The metal clicked a little as he walked. Amos headed off down the hallway at a fast walk. Holden gave a quick glance behind, gratified to see the Pinkwater people keeping up the pace and the spacing. They might look half starved, but they knew what they were doing.

"Cap, there's a tunnel coming off to the right just before the pressure door," Amos said, stopping and dropping to one knee to cover the unexpected corridor.

It didn't appear on the map. That meant that new tunnels had been dug *after* the station specs had last been updated. Modifications like that meant he had even less information than he'd thought. It wasn't a good thing.

"Okay," Holden said, pointing at the thin woman with the machine pistol. "You are?"

"Paula," she said.

"Paula, this is your intersection. Try not to shoot anyone that doesn't shoot at you first, but do *not* let anyone past you for any reason."

"Solid copy on that," Paula said, and took up a position looking down the side corridor with her weapon at the ready.

Amos pulled a grenade off his harness and handed it to her.

"Just in case shit goes down," he said. Paula nodded, settled her back against the wall. Amos, taking point, moved toward the pressure door.

"Naomi," Holden said, looking over the door and locking mechanism. "Pressure door, uh, 223-B6. Pop it."

"Got it," she said. A few seconds later, Holden heard the bolts retract.

"Ten meters to the next mapped intersection," he said, then looked at the Pinkwater people and picked one gruff-looking older man at random. "That's your intersection when we get there."

The man nodded, and Holden gestured at Amos. The mechanic took hold of the hatch with his right hand and began counting down from five with his left. Holden took up a position facing the door, his assault rifle at the ready.

When Amos hit one, Holden took a deep breath, and he burst through the door as Amos yanked it open a split second later.

Nothing.

Just another ten meters of corridor, dimly lit by the few LEDs that hadn't failed in the decades since its last use. Years of microfrost melt had built a texture over the surface of the walls like dripping spiderwebs. It looked delicate, but it was mineralized as hard as stone. It reminded Holden of a graveyard.

Amos began advancing to the intersection and the next hatch, his gun aimed down the hallway. Holden followed him, his rifle tracking right as he kept it aimed at the side passage, the reflex to cover every possible ingress point to their position having become automatic over the last year.

His year as a cop.

Naomi had said this wasn't him. He'd left the Navy without seeing live combat outside pirate hunting from the comfort of a warship's operations deck. He'd worked for years on the *Canterbury*, hauling ice from Saturn to the Belt without ever having to worry about something more violent than drunken ice buckers fighting out their boredom. He'd been the peacemaker, the one who always found the way to keep things cool. When tempers flared, he'd keep it calm or keep it funny or just sit for a shift and listen to someone rave and rant whatever it was out of their system.

This new person he'd become reached for his gun first and talked second. Maybe she was right. How many ships had he slagged in the year since Eros? A dozen? More? He comforted himself with the thought that they were all very bad people. The worst kind of carrion eaters, using the chaos of war and the retreat of the Coalition Navy as an opportunity to pillage. The kind of people who'd strip all the expensive parts off your engine, steal your spare air, and leave you adrift to suffocate. Every one of their ships he'd shot down had probably saved dozens of innocent ships, hundreds of lives. But doing it had taken something from him that he occasionally felt the lack of.

Occasions like when Naomi had said, *This isn't you.*

If they tracked down the secret base where Mei had been taken, there was a good chance they'd have to fight to get her back. Holden found himself hoping it would bother him, if for no other reason than to prove that it still could.

"Cap? You okay?"

Amos was staring at him.

"Yeah," Holden said, "I just need a different job."

"Might not be the best moment for a career change, Cap."

"Fair point," Holden said, and pointed to the older Pinkwater man he'd singled out before. "This is your intersection. Same instructions. Hold it unless I call you."

The older guy shrugged and nodded, then turned to Amos. "Don't I get a grenade too?"

"Nah," Amos said, "Paula's cuter than you." He counted down from five, and Holden went through the door, same as last time.

He'd been ready for another featureless gray corridor, but on the other side there was a wide-open space, with a few tables and dusty equipment scattered haphazardly around the room. A massive 3-D copier emptied of resin and partially disassembled, a few light industrial waldoes, the kind of complex automated supply cabinet that usually lurked under desks in scientific labs or medical bays. The mineralized webwork was on the walls but not the boxes or equipment. A glass-walled cube two meters to a side sat off in one corner. One of the tables had a small bundle of sheets or tarps piled on it. Across the room another hatch stood closed.

Holden pointed to the abandoned equipment and said to Wendell, "See if you can find a network access point. If you can, plug this into it." He handed Naomi's hastily rigged network bridge to him.

Amos sent two of the remaining Pinkwater people up to the next hatch to cover it, then came back to Holden and gestured with his gun toward the glass box.

"Big enough for a couple kids," he said. "Think that's where they kept 'em?"

"Maybe," Holden said, moving over to examine it. "Prax, can you—" Holden stopped when he realized the botanist had gone over to the tables and was standing next to the bundle of rags. With Prax standing next to the bundle, Holden's perspective shifted and suddenly it didn't look like a pile of rags at all. It looked very much like a small body under a sheet.

Prax was staring at it, his hand darting toward it and then pulling back. He was shaking all over.

"This...this is..." he said to no one in particular, his hand moving out and back again.

Holden looked at Amos, then gestured at Prax with his eyes. The big mechanic moved over to him and put a hand on his arm.

"How's about you let us take a look at that, okay?"

Holden let Amos guide Prax a few steps away from the table before he moved over to it. When he lifted the sheet to look under, Prax made a sharp noise like the intake of breath before a scream. Holden shifted his body to block Prax's view.

A small boy lay on the table. He was skinny, with a mop of unruly black hair and dark skin. His clothes were bright: yellow pants and a green shirt with a cartoon crocodile and daisies. It wasn't immediately clear what had killed him.

Holden heard a commotion and turned around to see Prax, red-faced and struggling to get past Amos to the table. The mechanic was restraining him with one arm in a grip that was halfway between a wrestling hold and an embrace.

"It's not her," Holden said. "It's a kid, but it's not her. A boy. Four, maybe five years old."

When Amos heard that, he let the struggling Prax go. The botanist rushed to the table, flipping the sheet over and giving one quick cry.

"That's Katoa," Prax said. "I know him. His father..."

"It's not Mei," Holden repeated, putting a hand on Prax's shoulder. "We need to keep looking."

Prax shrugged his hand off.

"It's not Mei," Holden said again.

"But Strickland was here," Prax said. "He was their doctor. I thought if he was with them, they'd be..."

Holden said nothing. He was thinking the same thing. If one of the kids was dead, they could all be.

"I thought that meant they'd keep them alive," Prax said. "But they let Katoa die. They just let him die and they put him under this sheet. Basia, I'm so sorry..."

Holden grabbed Prax and spun him around. The way he imagined a cop would.

"That," he said, pointing at the small body on the table, "is not Mei. Do you want to find her? Then we need to keep moving."

Prax's eyes were filled with tears and his shoulders shook in silent sobs, but he nodded and walked away from the table. Amos watched him carefully. The mechanic's expression was unreadable. The thought came unbidden: *I hope bringing Prax was a good idea.*

Across the room, Wendell whistled and waved a hand. He pointed at Naomi's network access rig plugged into a port in the wall and gave the thumbs-up.

"Naomi, you in?" Holden said while he pulled the sheet back up to cover the dead boy.

"Yep, I'm in," she said, her tone distracted as she worked with the incoming data. "Traffic in this node is encrypted. Got the *Somnambulist* started on it, but she's not nearly as smart as the *Roci*. This could take a while."

"Keep trying," Holden replied, and signaled to Amos. "But if there's traffic on the network, someone's still here."

"If you wait a minute," Naomi said, "I might be able to give you the security cameras and a more up-to-date floor plan."

"Feed us what you can, when you can, but we're not waiting."

Amos ambled over to Holden and tapped the visor of his helmet. Prax was standing alone by the glass cube, staring into it like there was something to see. Holden expected Amos to say something about the man, but Amos surprised him.

"Been paying attention to the temperature, Cap?"

"Yeah," Holden replied. "Every time I check it says 'cold as hell.'"

"I was just over by the door," Amos continued. "It went up about half a degree."

Holden thought about that for a moment, double-checking it on his own HUD and tapping his fingers on his thigh.

"There's climate in the next room. They're heating it."

"Seems likely," Amos said, shifting the big auto-shotgun into both hands and thumbing off the safety.

Holden motioned the remaining Pinkwater people over to them.

"It looks like we've come to the inhabited portion of this base. Amos and I go in first. You three"—Holden pointed at the three Pinkwater people who weren't Wendell—"follow and cover our flanks. Wendell, you cover our asses and make sure we can get back out in a hurry if things go bad. Prax—"

Holden stopped, looking around for the botanist. He had quietly slipped over to the door into the next room. He'd taken the handgun Amos had given him out of his pocket. As Holden watched, he reached out and opened the door, then walked deliberately through.

"Fuck me," Amos said conversationally.

"Shit," Holden said. Then, "Go, go, go," as he rushed toward the now open door.

Just before he got to the hatch, he heard Prax say, "Nobody move," in a loud but quavering voice.

Holden burst through into the room on the other side, going right while Amos came through just behind him and went left. Prax stood a few feet past the door, the large black handgun looking improbable in his pale, shaking hand. The area itself looked a lot like the one they'd just left, except that this one had a small crowd of people in it. Armed people. Holden tried to take in everything that could be used as cover. A half dozen large gray packing crates with scientific equipment in various states of disassembly in them squatted around the room. Someone's hand terminal was propped up on a bench and blaring dance music. On one of the crates sat several open boxes of pizza with most of the slices missing, several of which were still clutched in people's hands. He tried to count them. Four. Eight. An even dozen, all of them wide about the eye and glancing around, thinking about what to do.

It looked to Holden very much like a room full of people packing up to move, taking a short lunch break. Except that the people in this room all had holsters at their sides, and they had left the corpse of a small child to rot in the next room over.

"Nobody! Move!" Prax repeated, this time with more force.

"You should listen to him," Holden added, moving the barrel of his assault rifle in a slow scan across the room. To drive the point home, Amos sidled up to the nearest worker and casually slammed the butt of his auto-shotgun into the man's ribs, dropping him to the floor like a bag of wet sand. Holden heard the tramping of his Pinkwater people rushing into the room behind him and taking up cover positions.

"Wendell," Holden said, not lowering his rifle. "Please disarm these people for me."

"No," said a stern-faced woman with a slice of pizza in her hand. "No, I don't think so."

"Excuse me?" Holden said.

"No," the woman repeated, taking another bite of her pizza. Around a mouthful of food, she said, "There are only seven of you. There are twelve of us just in this room alone. And there are a lot more behind us that will come running at the first gunshot. So, no, you don't get to disarm us."

She smiled a greasy smile at Holden, then took another bite. Holden could smell the cheese-and-pepperoni smell of good pizza over the top of Ganymede's ever-present odor of ice and the scent of his own sweat. It made his stomach give an ill-timed rumble. Prax pointed his handgun at the woman, though his hand was now shaking so badly that she probably didn't feel particularly threatened.

Amos gave him a sidelong glance as if to ask, *What now, chief?*

In Holden's mind, the room shifted into a tactical problem with an almost physical click. The eleven potential combatants who were still standing were in three clusters. None of them were wearing visible armor. Amos would almost certainly drop the group of four to the far left of the room in a single burst from his auto-shotgun. Holden was pretty sure he could take down the three directly in front of him. That left four for the Pinkwater people to handle. Best not to count on Prax for any of it.

He finished the split-second tally of potential casualties, and almost of its own volition, his thumb clicked the assault rifle to full auto.

This is not you.

Shit.

"We don't have to do this," he said, instead of opening fire. "No one has to die here today. We're looking for a little girl. Help us find her, and everyone walks away from this."

Holden could see the arrogance and bravado in the woman's face for the mask it was. Behind that, there was worry as she weighed the casualties her team would suffer against the risks of talking it out and seeing where that went. Holden gave her a smile and a nod to help her decide. *Talk to me. We're all rational people here.*

Except that not all of them were.

"Where's Mei?" Prax yelled, poking the gun at her as if his gesture would be somehow translated through the air. "Tell me where Mei is!"

"I—" she started to reply, but Prax screamed out, "Where's my little girl!" and cocked his gun.

As if in slow motion, Holden saw eleven hands dart down to the holsters at their belts.

Shit.

Chapter Seventeen: Prax

In the cinema and games that formed the basis of Prax's understanding of how people of violence interacted, the cocking of a gun was less a threat than a kind of punctuation mark. A security agent questioning someone might begin with threats and slaps, but when he cocked his gun, that meant it was time to take him seriously. It wasn't something Prax had considered any more carefully than which urinal to use when he wasn't the only one in the men's room or how to step on and off a transport tube. It was the untaught etiquette of received wisdom. You yelled, you threatened, you cocked your gun, and then people talked.

"Where's my little girl!" he yelled.

He cocked his pistol.

The reaction was almost immediate: a sharp, stuttering report like a high-pressure valve failing, but much louder. He danced back, almost dropping the pistol. Had he fired it by mistake? But no, his finger hadn't touched the trigger. The air smelled sharp, acidic. The woman with the pizza was gone. No, not gone. She was on the ground. Something terrible had happened to her jaw. As he watched, her ruined mouth moved, as though she was trying to speak. Prax could hear only a high-pitched squeal. He wondered if his eardrums had ruptured. The woman with the destroyed jaw took a long, shuddering breath and then didn't take another. With a sense of detachment, he noticed that she'd drawn her pistol. It was still clutched in her hand. He wasn't sure when she'd done that. The handset playing dance music transitioned to a different song that only faintly made it past the ringing in his ears.

"I didn't shoot her," he said. His voice sounded like he was in partial vacuum, the air too thin to support the energy of sound waves. But he could breathe. He wondered again if the gunfire had ruptured his eardrums. He looked around. Everyone was gone. He was alone in the room. Or no, they were behind cover. It occurred to him that he should probably be behind cover too. Only nobody was firing and he wasn't sure where to go.

Holden's voice seemed to come from far away.

"Amos?"

"Yeah, Cap?"

"Would you please take his gun away now?"

"I'm on it."

Amos rose from behind one of the boxes nearest the wall. His Martian armor had a long pale streak across the chest and two white circles just below the ribs. Amos limped toward him.

"Sorry, Doc," he said. "Givin' it to you was my bad call. Maybe next time, right?"

Prax looked at the big man's open hand, then carefully put the gun in it.

"Wendell?" Holden said. Prax still wasn't sure where he was, but he sounded closer. That was probably just Prax's hearing coming back. The acrid smell in the air changed to something more coppery. It made him think of compost heaps gone sour: warm and organic and unsettling.

"One down," Wendell said.

"We'll get a medic," Holden said.

"Nice thought, but no point," Wendell said. "Finish the mission. We got most of them, but two or three made it through the door. They'll raise an alarm."

One of the Pinkwater soldiers stood up. Blood was running down his left arm. Another lay on the floor, half of his head simply gone. Holden appeared. He was massaging his right elbow, and the armor showed a new scar at his left temple.

"What happened?" Prax asked.

"You started a gunfight," Holden said. "Okay, let's move ahead before they can set up defenses."

Prax started noticing other bodies. Men and women who had been eating pizza and listening to music. They'd had pistols, but Holden's people carried automatic shotguns and assault rifles and some had military-looking armor. The difference in outcome hadn't been subtle.

"Amos, take point," Holden said, and the big man moved through the doorway and into the unknown. Prax moved to follow, and the head of the Pinkwater people took his elbow.

"Why don't you stay with me, professor," he said.

"Yes. I'll...all right."

On the other side of the door, the nature of the rooms changed. They were still clearly in the old tunnels of Ganymede. The walls still had their webwork of mineralized frost, the lighting was still old-fashioned LED housings, and the gray walls showed where ice had melted and refrozen during some climate system glitch years or decades before. But walking through that doorway was walking from the land of the dead into something living. The air was warmer, and it smelled of bodies and fresh soil and the subtle, sharp scent of phenol disinfectant. The wide hall they entered could have been the common room in any of a dozen labs where Prax had worked. Three metal office doors were closed along the far wall and a rolling metal freight gateway hung open ahead of them. Amos and Holden went to the three closed doors, Amos kicking each in turn. When the third flew open, Holden shouted something, but the words were lost in the bark of a pistol and Amos' return shotgun fire.

The two remaining Pinkwater soldiers who weren't Wendell scuttled forward, pressing their backs to the wall on either side of the freight gateway. Prax started toward them, but Wendell put a restraining hand on his shoulder. The man on the left side of the door ducked his head into the doorway and then out again. A bullet gouged a streak in the wall where it missed him.

"What can you give me?" Holden asked, and for a moment Prax thought he was talking to them. Holden's eyes were hard, and the scowl seemed etched into his skin. Then Naomi said something to make him smile, and he only looked tired and sad. "All right. We've got a partial floor plan. Through there, we've got an open room. It drops down about two meters, with exits to our ten o'clock and one o'clock. It's built like a pit, so if they're setting up defense here, we've got the high ground."

"Makes it a damned stupid place to set up a defense, then," Wendell said.

Gunfire chattered, three small holes appearing in the metal of the freight gateway. The people on the other side were nervous.

"And yet the evidence suggests..." Holden said.

"You want to talk to 'em, Cap?" Amos said. "Or do we head straight for the obvious thing?"

The question meant something more than Prax understood; he could tell that much. Holden started to say something, hesitated, and then nodded toward the doorway.

"Let's get this done," he said.

Holden and Amos jogged toward the gateway, Prax and Wendell close behind. Someone was shouting orders in the room beyond. Prax made out the words *payload* and *evac*, his heart going tight. *Evac.* They couldn't let anyone leave until they found Mei.

"I counted seven," one of the Pinkwater soldiers said. "Could be more."

"Any kids?" Amos asked.

"Didn't see any."

"We should probably look again," Amos said, and leaned out the door. Prax caught his breath, expecting to see the man's head dissolve in a rain of bullets, but Amos was already pulling back when the first shots started.

"What are we working with?" Holden asked.

"More'n seven," Amos said. "They're using this as a choke point, but the fella's right. Either they don't know what they're doing, or there's something in there they can't pull back from."

"So either panicking amateurs or something critical to defend," Holden said.

A metal canister the size of a fist rolled through the gateway, clanking. Amos picked the grenade up casually and tossed it back through the doorway. The detonation lit the room, the report louder than anything Prax had ever heard before. The ringing in his ears redoubled.

"Could be both," Amos shouted conversationally from very far away.

In the next room, something shattered. People were screaming. Prax imagined technicians like the ones from the previous room shredded by shrapnel from their own grenade. One of the Pinkwater soldiers leaned out, peering into the haze of smoke. An assault rifle blatted, and he pulled back, clutching his belly. Blood poured between his fingers. Wendell pushed past Prax, kneeling by his fallen soldier.

"Sorry, sir," the Pinkwater man said. "Got careless. Leave me here and I'll guard the rear as long as I can."

"Captain Holden," Wendell said. "If we're going to do something, we're better off doing it soon."

The screaming in the other room got louder. Someone was roaring inhumanly. Prax wondered if they'd had livestock in there. The bellowing sounded almost like an injured bull. He had to fight the urge to put his hands over his ears. Something loud happened. Holden nodded.

"Amos. Soften them up, then let's head in."

"Aye, aye, Cap," Amos said, putting down his shotgun. He took two grenades of his own, pulled the pink plastic strip-pins, rolled the live grenades through the gateway, and scooped his gun back up. The doubled detonation was deeper than the first one had been, but not as loud. Even before the echo faded, Amos, Holden, Wendell, and the one remaining soldier ducked through the gateway, weapons blazing.

Prax hesitated. He was unarmed. The enemy was just beyond the threshold. He could stay here and tend to the gut-shot man. But the image that wouldn't leave him was Katoa's still body. The dead boy wasn't more than a hundred meters away. And Mei...

Keeping his head down, Prax scuttled through the doorway. Holden and Wendell were to his right, Amos and the other soldier to his left. All four were crouched, weapons at the ready. Smoke stung Prax's eyes and nostrils, and the air recyclers groaned in protest, fighting to clear the air.

"Well now," Amos said, "that's fucking queer."

The room was built on two levels: an upper catwalk a meter and a half wide, and a lower floor two meters below it. A wide passage led away at ten o'clock on the lower level, and a door on the upper level stood open at one o'clock. The pit below them was chaos. Blood soaked the walls and had sprayed up to stipple the ceiling. Bodies lay on the ground below them. A thin steam rose from the gore.

They had been using equipment for cover. Prax recognized a microcentrifuge smashed almost out of its casing. Inch-thick slivers of ice or glass glittered among the carnage. A nitrogen bath was tipped on its side, the alarm indicator showing it had locked down. A massive blot array—easily two hundred kilos—lay at an improbable angle, a child's toy thrown aside in the ecstasy of play.

"What the hell kind of ordnance are you packing?" Wendell asked, his voice awed. From the wide passage at ten o'clock came shrieks and the sound of gunfire.

"I don't think this was us," Holden said. "Come on. Double-time it."

They dropped down to the killing floor. A glass cube like the one they'd seen before stood in shattered glory. Blood made the floor slick underfoot. A hand still wrapping a pistol lay in the corner. Prax looked away. Mei was here. He couldn't lose focus. Couldn't be sick.

He kept going on.

Holden and Amos led the way toward the sound of fighting. Prax trotted along behind them. When he tried to hold back, let Wendell and his compatriot go first, the Pinkwater men gently pushed him forward. They were guarding the rear, Prax realized. In case someone came up from behind. He should have thought of that.

The passageway opened out, broad but low. Industrial loading mechs, amber indicators showing idle, stood beside pallets of foam-coated supply boxes. Amos and Holden moved down the hall with a practiced efficiency that left Prax winded. But with every turn they reached, every door they opened, he found himself willing them to go faster. She was here, and they had to find her. Before she got hurt. Before something happened. And with every body they found, the sick feeling that something had already happened sank deeper in his gut.

They moved forward quickly. Too quickly. When they reached the end of the line—an airlock four meters high and at least seven across—Prax couldn't imagine that there was anyone behind it. Amos let his automatic shotgun hang at his side as he tapped at the airlock controls. Holden squinted up at the ceiling as if something might be written there. The ground trembled and set the hidden base creaking.

"Was that a launch?" Holden said. "That was a launch!"

"Yeah," Amos said. "Looks like they've got a landing pad out there. Monitors aren't showing anything else on it, though. Whatever that was, it was the last train outta here."

Prax heard someone shouting. It took him only a second to

realize it was him. Like he was watching his body move without him, he dashed to the sealed metal doors, pounding them with his clenched fists. She was there. She was just out there, on the ship lifting away from Ganymede. He could feel her like she had a rope tied to his heart and every moment pulled it out of him a little more.

He blacked out for a second. Or maybe longer. When he came back to himself, he was slung over Amos' wide shoulder, the armor biting into his belly. He pushed up to see the airlock receding slowly behind them.

"Put me down," Prax said.

"Can't do it," Amos replied. "Cap says—"

The stuttering of assault rifle fire came, and Amos dropped Prax to the ground and squatted over him, shotgun at the ready.

"What the fuck, Cap?" Amos said.

Prax glanced up in time to see the Pinkwater soldier cut down, blood spraying out of his back. Wendell was on the ground, returning fire around a sharp corner.

"Missed someone," Holden said. "Or else they called in their friends."

"Don't shoot them," Prax said. "What if it's Mei! What if they have her with them?"

"They don't, Doc," Amos said. "Stay down."

Holden was shouting, words rolling out of him too fast to follow. Prax didn't know if he was talking to Amos or Wendell or Naomi back on the ship or him. It could have been any of them. All of them. Four men came around the corner, weapons in hand. They wore the same coveralls that all the others had worn. One had long black hair and a goatee. Another was a woman with skin the color of buttercream. The two in the middle could have been brothers—the same close-cut brown hair, the same long noses.

From somewhere to Prax's right, the shotgun spoke twice. All four fell back. It was like something out of a prank comedy. Eight legs, swept at once. Four people Prax didn't know, had never met, just fell down. They just fell down. He knew they were never getting back up.

"Wendell?" Holden said. "Report?"

"Caudel's dead," Wendell said. He didn't sound sad about it. He didn't sound like anything. "I think I broke my wrist. Anyone know where they came from?"

"Nope," Holden said. "Let's not assume they were alone, though."

They retraced their steps, back through the long, wide passages. Past bodies of men and women they hadn't killed, but who were dead now anyway. Prax didn't try to keep from weeping. There was no point. If he could keep his legs moving, one foot in front of the other, it was enough.

They reached the bloodied pit after a few minutes or an hour or a week. Prax couldn't tell, and all options seemed equally plausible. The ruptured bodies stank, the spilled blood thickening to a black currant jelly, the opened viscera freeing colonies of bacteria usually held in check by the gut. On the catwalk, a woman stood. What was her name? Paula. That was it.

"Why aren't you at your post?" Wendell snapped when he saw her.

"Guthrie called for backup. Said he was gut-shot and about to pass out. I brought him some adrenaline and speed."

"Good call," Wendell said.

"Uchi and Caudel?"

"Didn't make it," Wendell said.

The woman nodded, but Prax saw something pass over her. Everyone here was losing someone. His tragedy was just one among dozens. Hundreds. Thousands. By the time the cascade had run all the way out, maybe millions. When death grew that large, it stopped meaning anything. He leaned against the nitrogen bath, his head in his hands. He'd been so close. So close...

"We have to find that ship," he said.

"We have to drop back ten and punt," Holden said. "We came here looking for a missing kid. Now we've got a covert scientific station halfway to being packed up and shipped out. And a secret landing pad. And whatever third player was fighting with these people while we were."

"Third player?" Paula asked.

Wendell gestured to the carnage.

"Not us," he said.

"We don't know what we're looking at," Holden said. "And until we do, we need to back off."

"We can't stop," Prax said. "I can't stop. Mei is—"

"Probably dead," Wendell said. "The girl's probably dead. And if she's not, she's alive someplace besides Ganymede."

"I'm sorry," Holden said.

"The dead boy," Prax said. "Katoa. His father took the family off Ganymede as soon as he could. Got them someplace safe. Someplace else."

"Wise move," Holden said.

Prax looked to Amos for support, but the big man was poking through the wreckage, pointedly not taking either side.

"The boy was alive," Prax said. "Basia said he knew the boy was dead and he packed up and he left, and when he got on that transport? His boy was here. In this lab. And he was alive. So don't tell me Mei's probably dead."

They were all silent for a moment.

"Just don't," Prax said.

"Cap?" Amos said.

"Just a minute," Holden said. "Prax, I'm not going to say that I know what you're going through, but I have people I love too. I can't tell you what to do, but let me ask you—*ask* you—to look at what kind of strategy is going to be best for you. And for Mei."

"Cap," Amos said. "Seriously, you should look at this."

Amos stood by the shattered glass cube. His shotgun hung forgotten in his hand. Holden walked up to the man's side, following his gaze to the ruined container. Prax pushed away from the nitrogen bath and joined them. There, clinging to the walls of glass that still stood, was a network of fine black filament. Prax couldn't tell if it was an artificial polymer or a natural substance. Some kind of web. It had a fascinating structure, though. He reached out to touch it and Holden grabbed his wrist, pulling him back so hard it hurt.

When Holden spoke, his words were measured and calm, which only made the panic behind them more terrifying.

"Naomi, prep the ship. We have to get off this moon. We have to do it right now."

Chapter Eighteen: Avasarala

W hat do you think?" the secretary-general asked from the upper left pane of the display. On the upper right, Errinwright leaned forward a centimeter, ready to jump in if she lost her temper.

"You've read the briefing, sir," Avasarala said sweetly.

The secretary-general waved his hand in a lazy circle. He was in his early sixties and wore the decades with the elfin charm of a man untroubled by weighty thoughts. The years Avasarala had spent building herself from the treasurer of the Workers Provident Fund to the district governor of the Maharshta-Karnataka-Goa Communal Interest Zone, he'd spent as a political prisoner at a minimum-security facility in the recently reconstructed Andean cloud forest. The slow, grinding wheels of power had lifted him to celebrity, and his ability to appear to be listening lent him an air of gravity without the inconvenience of an opinion of his own.

Had a man been engineered from birth to be the ideal governmental figurehead, he still wouldn't have achieved the perfection that was Secretary-General Esteban Sorrento-Gillis.

"Political briefs never capture the really important things," the bobble-head said. "Tell me what you think."

I think you haven't read the fucking briefs, Avasarala thought. *Not that I can really complain.* She cleared her throat.

"It's all sparring and no fight, sir," Avasarala said. "The players are top level. Michel Undawe, Carson Santiseverin, Ko Shu. They brought enough military to show that it's not just the elected monkeys. But so far, the only one who's said anything interesting is a marine they brought in to be a flower arrangement. Otherwise, we're all waiting for someone else to say something telling."

"And what about"—the secretary-general paused and lowered his voice—"the *alternative hypothesis*?"

"There's activity on Venus," Avasarala said. "We still don't know what any of it means. There was a massive upwelling of elemental iron in the northern hemisphere that lasted fourteen hours. There has also been a series of volcanic eruptions. Since the planet doesn't have any tectonic motion, we're assuming the protomolecule is doing something in the mantle, but we can't tell what. The brains put together a statistical model that shows the approximate energy output expected for the changes we've seen. It suggests that the overall level of activity is rising about three hundred percent per year over that last eighteen months."

The secretary-general nodded, his expression grave. It was almost as if he'd understood any part of what she'd said. Errinwright coughed.

"Do we have any evidence that ties the activity on Venus to the events on Ganymede?" he asked.

"We do," Avasarala said. "An anomalous energy spike at the same time as the Ganymede attack. But it's only one datapoint. It might have been coincidence."

A woman's voice came from the secretary-general's feed, and he nodded.

"I'm afraid I'm called to duty," he said. "You're doing fine work, Avasarala. Damn fine work."

"I can't tell you what that means coming from you, sir," she said with a smile. "You'd fire me."

Half a beat later, the secretary-general barked out a laugh and wagged his finger at the screen before the green connection-ended message took his place. Errinwright sat back, his palms pressed to his temples. Avasarala picked up her cup of tea and sipped it with her eyebrows lifted and her gaze on the camera, inviting him to say something. The tea wasn't quite down to tepid.

"All right," Errinwright said. "You win."

"We're impeaching him?"

He actually chuckled. Wherever he was, it was dark outside his windows, so he was on the same side of the planet that she was. That they were both in night gave the meeting a sense of closeness and intimacy that had more to do with her own exhaustion than anything else.

"What do you need to resolve the Venus situation?" he asked.

"Resolve?"

"Poor choice of words," he said. "From the beginning of this, you've had your eye on Venus. Keeping things calm with the Martians. Reining in Nguyen."

"Noticed that, did you?"

"These talks are stalled, and I'm not going to waste you on baby-sitting a deadlock. We need clarity, and we need it a month ago. Ask for the resources you need, Chrisjen, and either rule Venus out or get us proof. I'm giving you a blank check."

"Retirement at last," she said, laughing. To her surprise, Errinwright took it seriously.

"If you want, but Venus first. This is the most important question either of us has ever asked. I'm trusting you."

"I'll see to it," she said. Errinwright nodded and dropped the connection.

She leaned forward on her desk, fingertips pressed to her lips. Something had happened. Something had *changed*. Either

Errinwright had read enough about Venus to get his own set of the heebie-jeebies, or someone wanted her off the Martian negotiation. Someone with enough pull to get Errinwright to kick her upstairs. Did Nguyen have patrons that powerful?

Yes, it gave her what she wanted. After all she'd said—and meant when she'd said it—she couldn't refuse the project, but the success had a bitter aftertaste. Perhaps she was reading too much into it. God knew she hadn't been getting enough sleep, and fatigue left her paranoid. She checked the time. Ten o'clock p.m. She wouldn't make it back to Arjun that night. Another morning in the depressing VIP quarters, drinking the weak coffee and pretending to care what the latest ambassador from the Pashwiri Autonomous Zone thought about dance music.

Screw it, she thought, *I need a drink.*

The Dasihari Lounge catered to the full range in the complex organism that was the United Nations. At the bar, young pages and clerks leaned into the light, laughing too loud and pretending to be more important than they were. It was a mating dance only slightly more dignified than presenting like a mandrill, but endearing in its own fashion. Roberta Draper, the Martian Marine who'd shat on the table that morning, was among them, a pint glass dwarfed by her hand and an amused expression on her face. Soren would probably be there, if not that night, another time. Avasarala's son would probably have been among them if things had gone differently.

In the center of the room, there were tables with built-in terminals to pipe in encrypted information from a thousand different sources. Privacy baffles kept even the waitstaff from glimpsing over the shoulders of the middle-range administrators drinking their dinners while they worked. And in the back were dark wooden tables in booths that recognized her before she sat down. If anyone below a certain status walked too close, a discreet young man with perfect hair would sweep up and see them to a different table, elsewhere, with less important people.

Avasarala sipped her gin and tonic while the threads of implication wove and rewove themselves. Nguyen couldn't have enough influence to put Errinwright against her. Could the Martians have asked that she be removed? She tried to remember who she'd been rude to and how, but no good suspect came to mind. And if they had, what was she going to do about it?

Well, if she couldn't be party to the Martian negotiations in an official capacity, she could still have contacts on an informal basis. Avasarala started chuckling even before she knew quite why. She picked up her glass, tapped the table to let it know it was permitted to let someone else sit there, and made her way across the bar. The music was soft arpeggios in a hypermodern tonal scale, which managed to sound soothing despite itself. The air smelled of perfume too expensive to be applied tastelessly. As she neared the bar, she saw conversations pause, glances pass between one young fount of ambition and another. *The old lady*, she imagined them saying. *What's she doing here?*

She sat down next to Draper. The big woman looked over at her. There was a light of recognition in her eyes that boded well. She might not know who Avasarala was, but she'd guessed what she was. Smart, then. Perceptive. And fucking hell, the woman was enormous. Not fat either, just...*big*.

"Buy you a drink, Sergeant?" Avasarala asked.

"I've had a few too many already," she said. And a moment later: "All right."

Avasarala lifted an eyebrow, and the bartender quietly gave the marine another glass of whatever she'd been having before.

"You made quite an impression today," Avasarala said.

"I did," Draper said. She seemed serenely unconcerned about it. "Thorsson's going to ship me out. I'm done here. May just be *done*."

"That's fair. You've accomplished what they wanted from you anyway."

Draper looked down at her. Polynesian blood, Avasarala guessed. Maybe Samoan. Someplace that evolution had made humans like mountain ranges. Her eyes were narrowed, and there was a heat to them. An anger.

"I haven't done shit."

"You were here. That's all they needed from you."

"What's the point?"

"They want to convince me that the monster wasn't theirs. One argument they've made is that their own soldiers—meaning you—didn't know about it. By bringing you, they're showing that they aren't afraid to bring you. That's all they need. You could sit around with your thumb up your ass and argue about the offside rule all day. It would be just as good for them. You're a showpiece."

The marine took it in, then raised an eyebrow.

"I don't think I like that," she said.

"Yes, well," Avasarala said, "Thorsson's a cunt, but if you stop working with politicians just for that, you won't have any friends."

The marine chuckled. Then she laughed. Then, seeing Avasarala's gaze on her own, she sobered.

"That thing that killed your friends?" Avasarala said while the marine was looking her in the eye. "It wasn't one of mine."

Draper's inhalation was sharp. It was like Avasarala had touched a wound. Which made sense, because she had. Draper's jaw worked for a second.

"It wasn't one of ours either."

"Well. At least we've got that settled."

"It won't do any good, though. They won't do anything. They won't talk about anything. They don't care. You know that? They don't care what happened as long as they all protect their careers and make sure the balance of power isn't tilted the wrong way. None of them fucking *care* what that thing was or where it came from."

The bar around them wasn't silent, but it was quieter. The mating dance was now only the second most interesting thing happening at the bar.

"I care," Avasarala said. "As a matter of fact, I've just been given a very great deal of latitude in finding out what that thing was."

It wasn't entirely true. She'd been given a huge budget to implicate or rule out Venus. But it was close, and it was the right frame for what she wanted.

"Really?" Draper said. "So what are you going to do?"

"First thing, I'm going to hire you. I need a liaison with the Martian military. That should be you. Can you handle it?"

No one at the bar was talking to anybody now. The room might have been empty. The only sounds were the soft music and Draper's laughter. An older man wearing clove-and-cinnamon cologne walked by, drawn by the quiet spectacle without knowing what it was.

"I'm a Martian Marine," Draper said. "Martian. You're UN. Earth. We aren't even citizens of the same planet. You can't hire me."

"My name's Chrisjen Avasarala. Ask around."

They were silent for a moment.

"I'm Bobbie," Draper said.

"Nice to meet you, Bobbie. Come work for me."

"Can I think about it?"

"Of course," Avasarala said, and had her terminal send Bobbie her private number. "So long as when you're done thinking, you come work for me."

At the VIP apartments, Avasarala tuned the system to the kind of music Arjun might be listening to just then. If he wasn't already asleep. She fought back the urge to call him. It was late already, and she was just drunk enough to get maudlin. Sobbing into her hand terminal about how much she loved her husband wasn't something she longed to make a habit of. She pulled off her sari and took a long, hot shower. She didn't drink alcohol often. Usually she didn't like how it dulled her mind. That night it seemed to loosen her up, give her brain the little extra jazz it needed to see connections.

Draper kept her connected to Mars, even if not to the day-by-day slog of the negotiations. That was a good start. There would be other connections too. Foster, in data services, could be brought in. She'd need to start routing more work through him. Build a relationship. It wouldn't do to march in and insist on being his new best friend just because he happened to be managing the encryption requests for Nguyen. A few no-strings-attached cupcakes first. Then the hook. Who else could she—

Her hand terminal chimed a priority alert. She turned off the water and grabbed a bathrobe, wrapping herself tightly and double-knotting the stay before she accepted the connection. She was years past flashing someone over a hand terminal, no matter how much she'd drunk. The connection came from someone in priority surveillance. The image that flashed up was a middle-aged man with ill-advised mutton-chop whiskers.

"Ameer! You mad dog. What have you done that they make you work so late?"

"Moved to Atlanta, miss," the analyst said with a toothy grin. He was the only one who ever called her miss. She hadn't spoken to him in three years. "I've just come back from lunch. I had an unscheduled report flagged for you. Contact immediately. I tried your assistant, but he didn't answer."

"He's young. He still sleeps sometimes. It's a weakness. Stand by while I set privacy."

The moment of friendly banter was over. Avasarala leaned forward, tapping her hand terminal twice to add a layer of encryption. The red icon went green.

"Go ahead," she said.

"It's from Ganymede, miss. You have a standing order on James Holden."

"Yes?"

"He's on the move. He made an apparent rendezvous with a local scientist. Praxidike Meng."

"What's Meng?"

In Atlanta, Ameer transitioned smoothly to a different file. "Botanist, miss. Emigrated to Ganymede with his family when he was a child. Schooled there. Specializes in partial-pressure low-light soybean strains. Divorced, one child. No known connections to the OPA or any established political party."

"Go ahead."

"Holden, Meng, and Burton have left their ship. They're armed, and they've made contact with a small group of private-security types. Pinkwater."

"How many?"

"The on-site analyst doesn't say, miss. A small force. Should I query?"

"What lag are we at?"

Ameer's brown-black eyes flickered.

"Forty-one minutes, eight seconds, miss."

"Hold the query. If I have anything else, I can send them together."

"The on-site analyst reports that Holden negotiated with the private security, either a last-minute renegotiation or else the whole meeting was extemporaneous. It appears they reached some agreement. The full group proceeded to an unused corridor complex and forced entry."

"A what?"

"Disused access door, miss."

"What the fuck is that supposed to mean? How big is it? Where is it?"

"Should I query?"

"You should go to Ganymede and kick this sorry excuse for an on-site analyst in the balls. Add a clarification request."

"Yes, miss," Ameer said with the ghost of a smile. Then, suddenly, he frowned. "An update. One moment."

So the OPA had something on Ganymede. Maybe something they'd put there, maybe something they'd found. Either way, this mysterious door made things a degree more interesting. While Ameer read through and digested the new update, Avasarala scratched the back of her hand and reevaluated her position. She'd thought Holden was there as an observer. Forward intelligence.

That might be wrong. If he'd gone to meet with this Praxidike Meng, this utterly under-the-radar botanist, the OPA might already know quite a bit about Bobbie Draper's monster. Add the fact that Holden's boss had the only known sample of the proto-molecule, and a narrative about the Ganymede collapse began to take shape.

There were holes in it, though. If the OPA had been playing with the protomolecule, there had been no sign of it. And Fred Johnson's psychological profile didn't match with terrorist attacks. Johnson was old-school, and the monster attack was decidedly new.

"There's been a firefight, miss. Holden and his people have met armed resistance. They've set a perimeter. The on-site analyst can't approach."

"Resistance? I thought this was supposed to be unused. Who the fuck are they shooting at?"

"Shall I query?"

"God *damn* it!"

Forty light-minutes away, something important was going on, and she was here, in a bedroom that wasn't hers, trying to make sense of it by pressing her ear to the wall. The frustration was a physical sensation. It felt like being crushed.

Forty minutes out. Forty minutes back. Whatever she said, whatever order she gave, it would get there almost an hour and a half behind what was clearly a rapidly changing situation.

"Pull him in," she said. "Holden, Burton. Their Pinkwater friends. And this mysterious botanist. Bring them all in. Now."

Ameer in Atlanta paused.

"If they're in a firefight, miss..."

"Then send in the dogs, break up the fight, and take them in. We're past surveillance. Get it done."

"Yes, miss."

"Contact me as soon as it's done."

"Yes, miss."

She watched Ameer's face as he framed the order, confirmed it, sent it out. She could practically imagine the screen, the strokes of his fingers. She willed him to go faster, to press her intent out past the speed of light and get the damn thing done.

"Order's out. As soon as I hear from the on-site analyst, I'll reach you."

"I'll be here. If I don't take the connection, try again until I wake up."

She dropped the link and sat back. Her brain felt like a swarm of bees. James Holden had changed the game again. The boy had a talent for that, but that in itself made him a known quantity. This other one, this Meng, had come from her blind side. The man might be a mole or a volunteer or a stalking goat sent to lead the OPA into a trap. She considered turning off the light, trying to sleep, then abandoned it as a bad bet.

Instead, she set up a connection with the UN's intelligence research database. It was an hour and a half at earliest before she'd hear anything more. In the meantime, she wanted to know who Praxidike Meng was and why he mattered.

Chapter Nineteen: Holden

Naomi, prep the ship. We have to get off this moon. We have to do it *right now*."

All around Holden, the black filaments spread, a dark spider's web with him at the center. He was on Eros again. He was seeing thousands of bodies turning into something else. He thought he'd made it off, but Eros just kept coming. He and Miller had gotten out, but it got Miller anyway.

Now it was back for him.

"What's the matter, Jim?" Naomi said from the distance of the suit radio. "Jim?"

"Prep the ship!"

"It's the stuff," Amos said. He was talking to Naomi. "Like from Eros."

"Jesus, they…" Holden managed to gasp out before the fear welled up in his mind, robbing him of speech. His heart banged against his ribs like it wanted out, and he had to check the oxygen levels on his HUD. It felt like there wasn't enough air in the room.

Out of the corner of his eye, something appeared to scuttle up the wall like a disembodied hand, leaving a trail of brown slime in its wake. When Holden spun and pointed his assault rifle at it, it resolved into a bloodstain below a discolored patch of ice.

Amos moved toward him, a worried look on his broad face. Holden waved him off, then set the butt of his rifle on the ground and leaned on a nearby crate to catch his breath.

"We should probably move out," Wendell said. He and Paula were helping hold up the man who'd been gut-shot. The injured man was having trouble breathing. A small red bubble of blood had formed in his left nostril, and it inflated and deflated with each ragged gasp the man took.

"Jim?" Naomi said in his ear, her voice soft. "Jim, I saw it through Amos' suitcam, and I know what it means. I'm getting the ship ready. That encrypted local traffic? It's dropped way off. I think everyone's gone."

"Everyone's gone," Holden echoed.

The diminished remains of his Pinkwater team were staring at him, the concern on their faces shifting to fear, his own terror infecting them even though they had no idea what the filament meant. They wanted him to do something, and he knew he had to, but he couldn't quite think what it was. The black web filled his head with flashing images, running too quickly to make sense, like video played at high speed: Julie Mao in her shower, the black threads surrounding her, her body twisted into a nightmare; bodies scattered across the floor of a radiation chamber; the zombie-like infected staggering off the trams in Eros, vomiting brown bile on everyone around them, even a drop of the goo a death sentence; video captures of the horror show Eros had become; a torso stripped to a rib cage and one arm dragging itself through the protomolecule landscape on some unknowable mission.

"Cap," Amos said, then moved over to touch Holden's arm. Holden yanked away, almost falling over in the process.

He swallowed the thick lemony-flavored saliva building up in his throat and said, "Okay. I'm here. Let's go. Naomi. Call Alex. We need the *Roci*."

Naomi didn't answer for a moment, then said, "What about the block—"

"Right fucking now, Naomi!" Holden yelled. "Right fucking now! Call Alex right now!"

She didn't reply, but the gut-shot man took one final ragged breath and then collapsed, nearly dragging the wounded Wendell to the floor with him.

"We have to go," Holden said to Wendell, meaning *We can't help him. If we stay, we all die.* Wendell nodded but went to one knee and began taking the man's light armor off, not understanding. Amos pulled the emergency medkit off his harness and dropped down next to Wendell to begin working on the wounded man while Paula watched, her face pale.

"Have to go," Holden said again, wanting to grab Amos and shake him until he understood. "Amos, stop, we have to go right now. Eros—"

"Cap," Amos interrupted, "all due respect, but this ain't Eros." He took a syringe from the medkit and gave the downed man an injection. "No radiation rooms, no zombies puking goo. Just that broken box, a whole lotta dead guys, and these black threads. We don't know *what* the fuck it is, but it ain't Eros. And we ain't leaving this guy behind."

The small rational part of Holden's mind knew Amos was right. And more than that, the person Holden wanted to believe he still was would never consider leaving even a complete stranger behind, much less a guy who'd taken a wound for him. He forced himself to take three deep, slow breaths. Prax knelt by Amos' side, holding the medkit.

"Naomi," Holden said, meaning to apologize for yelling at her.

"Alex is on his way," she replied, her voice tight but not accusing. "He's a few hours out. Running the blockade won't be easy, but he thinks he's got an angle. Where is he putting down?"

Holden found himself answering before he realized he'd made the decision. "Tell him to land in the *Somnambulist*'s berth. I'm giving her to someone. Meet us outside the airlock when we get there."

He pulled the mag-key for the *Somnambulist* out of a pocket on his harness and tossed it to Wendell. "This will get you on the ship you're taking. Consider it a down payment for services rendered."

Wendell nodded and tucked the key away, then went back to his injured man. The man appeared to be breathing.

"Can he be carried?" Holden asked Amos, proud of how steady his voice sounded again, trying not to think about the fact that he would have left the man to die a minute before.

"No choice, Cap."

"Then somebody pick him up," Holden said. "No, not you, Amos. I need you back on point."

"I got him," Wendell said. "I can't shoot for shit with this hand busted."

"Prax. Help him," Holden said. "We're getting the hell out of here."

They moved as quickly as injured people could back through the base. Back past the men and women they'd killed getting in and, more frighteningly, the ones they hadn't. Back past Katoa's small, still corpse. Prax's gaze drifted toward the body, but Holden grabbed his jacket and shoved him toward the hatch.

"It's still not Mei," he said. "Slow us down and I leave you."

The threat made him feel like an ass the moment it left his lips, but it wasn't idle. Finding the scientist's lost little girl had stopped being the priority the instant they found the black filaments. And as long as he was being honest with himself, leaving the scientist behind would mean not being there when they found his daughter twisted into a monster by the protomolecule, brown goo leaking from orifices she hadn't been born with, the black threads crawling from her mouth and eyes.

The older Pinkwater man who'd been covering their exit

rushed over to help carry the injured man without being asked. Prax handed the wounded man off to him without a word and then slid in place behind Paula as she scanned the hallways ahead with her machine pistol.

Corridors that had seemed boring on the trip in took on a sinister feel on the way back out. The frosted texture that had reminded Holden of spiderwebs when he'd come in now looked like the veins of some living thing. Their pulsing had to be caused by adrenaline making his eyes twitch.

Eight rems burning off Jupiter onto the surface of Ganymede. Even with the magnetosphere, eight rems a day. How quickly would the protomolecule grow here, with Jupiter endlessly supplying the energy? Eros had become something frighteningly powerful once the protomolecule had taken hold. Something that could accelerate at incredible speeds without inertia. Something that could, if the reports were right, change the very atmosphere and chemical composition of Venus. And that was with just over a million human hosts and a thousand trillion tons of rocky mass to work with at the beginning.

Ganymede had ten times as many humans and many orders of magnitude more mass than Eros. What could the ancient alien weapon do with such bounty?

Amos threw open the last hatch to the shadow base, and the crew was back in the higher-traffic tunnels of Ganymede. Holden didn't see anyone acting infected. No mindless zombies staggering through the corridors. No brown vomit coating the walls and floor, filled with the alien virus looking for a host. No Protogen hired thugs shepherding people into the kill zone.

Protogen is gone.

An itch at the back of his mind that Holden hadn't even been aware of pushed its way to the front. Protogen was gone. Holden had helped bring them down. He'd been in the room when the architect of the Eros experiment died. The Martian fleet had nuked Phoebe into a thin gas that was sucked into Saturn's massive gravity. Eros had crashed into the acidic and autoclave-hot atmosphere of Venus, where no human ships could go. Holden himself had taken Protogen's only sample of the protomolecule away from them.

So who had brought the protomolecule to Ganymede?

He'd given the sample to Fred Johnson as leverage to be used in the peace talks. The Outer Planets Alliance had gotten a lot of concessions in the chaos that followed the brief inner planets war. But not everything they'd wanted. The inner planets fleets in orbit around Ganymede were proof of that.

Fred had the only sample of the protomolecule left in the solar system. Because Holden had given it to him.

"It was Fred," he said out loud without realizing it.

"What was Fred?" Naomi asked.

"This. What's happening here. He did this."

"No," Naomi said.

"To drive the inner planets out, to test some kind of super-weapon, something. But he did this."

"No," Naomi said again. "We don't know that."

The air in the corridor grew smoky, the nauseating scent of burning hair and flesh choking off Holden's reply. Amos held up a hand to halt the group, and the Pinkwater people stopped and took up defensive positions. Amos moved up the corridor to the junction and looked off to his left for several moments.

"Something bad happened here," he finally said. "I've got half a dozen dead, more than that celebrating."

"Are they armed?" Holden asked.

"Oh yeah."

The Holden who would have tried to talk his way by them, the Holden who Naomi liked and wanted back, barely put up a struggle when he said, "Get us past them."

Amos leaned out around the corner and fired off a long burst from his auto-shotgun.

"Go," he said when the echoes of the gunshots had faded away.

The Pinkwater people picked up their wounded and hurried up the corridor and beyond the battle; Prax jogged along close behind, head down and thin arms pumping. Holden followed, a glance showing him dead bodies on fire at the center of a wide hallway. Burning them had to be a message. It wasn't quite bad enough yet for them to be eating each other. Was it?

There were a few bodies lying outside the fire, bleeding out on the corrugated metal floors. Holden couldn't tell if they were Amos' handiwork. The old Holden would have asked. The new one didn't.

"Naomi," he said, wanting to hear her voice.

"I'm here."

"We're seeing trouble out here."

"Is it..." He heard the dread in her voice.

"No. Not the protomolecule. But the locals may be bad enough. Seal up the 'locks," Holden told her, the words coming to him without thought. "Warm up the reactor. If something happens to us, leave and rendezvous with Alex. Don't go to Tycho."

"Jim," she said, "I—"

"Don't go to Tycho. Fred did this. Don't go back to him."

"No," she said. Her new mantra.

"If we aren't there in half an hour, go. That's an order, XO."

At least she would get away, Holden told himself. No matter what happened on Ganymede, at least Naomi would make it out alive. A vision of the nightmare Julie, dead in her shower, but with Naomi's face flashed in his mind. He didn't expect the little yelp of grief that escaped him. Amos turned and looked back at him, but Holden waved him on without a word.

Fred had done this.

And if Fred had, then Holden had too.

Holden had spent a year playing enforcer to Fred's politician. He'd hunted ships and killed them for Fred's grand OPA government experiment. He'd changed the man he'd been into the man he was now, because some part of him believed in Fred's dream of the liberated and self-governed outer planets.

And Fred had secretly been planning...this.

Holden thought of all the things he'd put off so that he could help Fred build his new solar system order. He'd never taken Naomi to meet his family back on Earth. Not that Naomi herself could have ever gone to Earth. But he could have flown his family up to Luna to meet her. Father Tom would have resisted. He hated travel. But Holden had no doubt that in the end he would have gotten them all to come meet her once he explained how important she'd become to him.

And meeting Prax, seeing his need to find his daughter, made Holden realize how badly he wanted to know what that was like. To experience that sort of hunger for the presence of another human being. To present another generation to his parents. To show them that all the effort and energy they had put into him had paid off. That he was passing it along. He wanted, almost more than he'd wanted anything before, to see the looks on their faces when he showed them a child. His child. Naomi's child.

Fred had taken that from him, first by wasting his time as the OPA's leg breaker, and now by this betrayal. Holden swore to himself that if he made it off Ganymede, Fred would pay for all of it.

Amos halted the group again, and Holden noticed that they were back at the port. He shook himself out of his reverie. He didn't remember how they'd gotten there.

"Looks clear," Amos said.

"Naomi," Holden said, "what does it look like around the ship?"

"Looks clear here," she said. "But Alex is worried that—"

Her voice was cut off by an electronic squeal.

"Naomi? Naomi!" Holden yelled, but there was no response. To Amos he said, "Go, double-time it to the ship!"

Amos and the Pinkwater people ran toward the docks as quickly as their injured bodies and the unconscious teammate would let them. Holden brought up the rear, shouldering his assault rifle and flicking off the safety as he ran.

They ran through the twisting corridors of the port sector, Amos scattering pedestrians with loud shouts and the unspoken threat of his shotgun. An old woman in a hijab scurried away before them like a leaf driven before a storm. She was dead already. If the protomolecule was loose, everyone Holden passed was dead already. Santichai and Melissa Supitayaporn and all the people they'd come to Ganymede to save. The rioters and killers who'd been normal citizens of the station before their social ecosystem collapsed. If the protomolecule was loose, all of them were as good as dead.

So why hadn't it happened?

Holden pushed the thought aside. Later—if there was a later—he could worry about it. Someone shouted at Amos, and Amos fired his shotgun into the ceiling once. If port security still existed outside of the vultures trying to take a cut of every incoming shipment, they didn't try to stop them.

The outer airlock door of the *Somnambulist* was closed when they reached it.

"Naomi, you there?" Holden asked, fumbling in his pockets for the swipe card. She didn't reply, and it took him a moment to remember he'd given the card to Wendell. "Wendell, open the door for us."

The Pinkwater leader didn't reply.

"Wendell—" Holden started, then stopped when he saw that Wendell was staring, wide-eyed, at something behind him. Holden turned to look and saw five men—Earthers, all of them—in plain gray armor without insignias. All were armed with large bore weapons.

No, Holden thought, and brought his gun up and across them in a full auto sweep. Three of the five men dropped, their armor blooming red. The new Holden rejoiced; the old was quiet. It didn't matter who these men were. Station security or inner planet military or just leftover mercenaries from the now destroyed shadow base, he'd kill them all before he let them stop him from getting his crew off this infected moon.

He never saw who fired the shot that took his leg out from under him. One second he was standing, emptying the magazine of his assault rifle into the gray-armored fire-team, and the next a sledgehammer blow hit the armor on his right thigh, knocking him off his feet. As he fell, he saw the two remaining gray-armored soldiers go down as Amos' auto-shotgun unloaded in a single long roar.

Holden rolled to his side, looking to see if anyone else was hurt, and saw that the five on his side had been only half of the enemy team. The Pinkwater people were raising their hands and dropping their weapons as five more gray-armored soldiers came down the corridor from behind.

Amos never saw them. He dropped the expended magazine from his auto-shotgun and was pulling a new one off his harness when one of the mercenaries aimed a large weapon at the back of his head and pulled the trigger. Amos' helmet flew off and he was slapped forward onto the corrugated-metal decking with a wet crunch. Blood splashed across the floor where he hit it.

Holden tried to get a new magazine into his assault rifle, but his hands wouldn't cooperate and before he could reload his gun, one of the soldiers had crossed the distance and kicked the rifle away from him.

Holden had time to see the still standing members of his Pinkwater team disappear into black bags before one came down over his own head and plunged him into darkness.

Chapter Twenty: Bobbie

The Martian delegation had been given a suite of offices in the UN building for their own use. The furniture was all real wood; the paintings on the walls were originals and not prints. The carpet smelled new. Bobbie thought that either everyone in the UN campus lived like a king, or they were just going out of their way to impress the Martians.

Thorsson had called her a few hours after she'd left her run-in with Avasarala at the bar, and had demanded that she meet with him the next day. Now she waited in the lobby of their temporary office suite, sitting in a bergère-style chair with green velvet cushions and a cherry wood frame that would have cost her two years' salary on Mars. A screen set into the wall across from her played a news channel with the sound muted. It turned the program into a confusing and occasionally macabre slide show of images: two talking heads sitting at a desk in a blue room, a large building on fire, a woman walking down a long white hallway while gesturing animatedly to both sides, a UN battleship parked at an orbital station with severe damage scarring its flank, a red-faced man talking directly into the camera against the backdrop of a flag Bobbie didn't recognize.

It all meant something and nothing at the same time. A few hours before, this would have frustrated Bobbie. She would have felt compelled to go find the remote and turn the sound up, to add context to the information being thrown at her.

Now she just let the images flow around her like canal water past a rock.

A young man she'd seen a few times on the *Dae-Jung* but had never actually met hurried through the lobby, tapping furiously on his terminal. When he was halfway across the room, he said, "He's ready for you."

It took Bobbie a moment to realize the young man had been talking to her. Apparently her stock had fallen far enough that she no longer warranted face-to-face delivery of information. More meaningless data. More water flowing past her. She pushed herself to her feet with a grunt. Her hours-long walk at one g the previous day had taken more out of her than she'd realized.

She was vaguely surprised to find that Thorsson's office was one of the smallest in the suite. That meant that either he didn't care about the unspoken status conferred through office size, or he was actually the least important member of the delegation to still rate a private workspace. She felt no compulsion to figure out which. Thorsson did not react to her arrival, his head bent over his desk terminal. Bobbie didn't care about being ignored, or about the lesson he was trying to teach her with it. The size of the office meant that Thorsson had no chair for guests, and the ache in her legs was sufficiently distracting.

"I may have overreacted earlier," he finally said.

"Oh?" Bobbie replied, thinking about where she might find more of that soy-milk tea.

Thorsson looked up at her. His face was trying its mummified-remains version of a warm smile. "Let me be clear. There's no doubt that you damaged our credibility with your outburst. But, as Martens points out, that is largely my fault for not fully understanding the extent of your trauma."

"Ah," Bobbie said. There was a framed photograph on the wall behind Thorsson of a city with a tall metal structure in the foreground. It looked like an archaic rocket gantry. The caption read PARIS.

"So instead of sending you home, I will be keeping you on staff here. You'll be given an opportunity to repair the damage you've done."

"Why," Bobbie said, looking Thorsson in the eye for the first time since coming in, "am I here?"

Thorsson's hint of a smile disappeared and was replaced by an equally understated frown. "Excuse me?"

"Why am I here?" she repeated, thinking past the disciplinary board. Thinking of how hard it would be to get reassigned to Ganymede if Thorsson didn't send her back to Mars. If he didn't, would she be allowed to resign? Just leave the corps and buy her own ticket? The thought of no longer being a marine made her sad. The first really strong feeling she'd had in a while.

"Why are you—" Thorsson started, but Bobbie cut him off.

"Not to talk about the monster, apparently. Honestly, if I'm just here as a showpiece, I think I'd rather be sent home. I have some things I could be doing..."

"You," Thorsson said, his voice getting tighter, "are here to do exactly what I say for you to do, and exactly when I say it. Is that understood, soldier?"

"Yeah," Bobbie said, feeling the water slide past her. She was a stone. It moved her not at all. "I have to go now."

She turned and walked away, Thorsson not managing to get a last word out before she left. As she moved through the suite toward the exit, she saw Martens pouring powdered creamer into a cup of coffee in the small kitchen area. He spotted her at the same time.

"Bobbie," he said. He'd gotten a lot more familiar with her over the last few days. Normally, she'd have assumed it was a buildup to romantic or sexual overtures. With Martens, she was pretty sure it was just another tool in his "how to fix broken marines" tool kit.

"Captain," she said. She stopped. She felt the front door tugging at her with a sort of psychic gravity, but Martens had never been anything but good to her. And she had a strange premonition that she was never going to see any of these people again. She held out her hand to him, and when he took it, she said, "I'm leaving. You won't have to waste your time with me anymore."

He smiled his sad smile at her. "In spite of the fact that I don't actually feel like I've accomplished anything, I don't feel like I wasted my time. Do we part friends?"

"I—" she started, then had to stop and swallow a lump in her throat. "I hope this didn't wreck your career or anything."

"I'm not worried about it," he said to her back. She was already walking out the door. She didn't turn around.

In the hallway Bobbie pulled out her terminal and called the number Avasarala had given her. It immediately went to voice mail.

"Okay," she said, "I'll take that job."

There was something liberating and terrifying about the first day on a new job. In any new assignment, Bobbie had always had the unsettling feeling that she was in over her head, that she wouldn't know how to do any of the things they would ask her to do, that she would dress wrong or say the wrong thing, or that everyone would hate her. But no matter how strong that feeling was, it was overshadowed by the sense that with a new job came the chance to totally recreate herself in whatever image she chose, that—at least for a little while—her options were infinite.

Even waiting for Avasarala finally to notice her couldn't fully dampen that feeling.

Standing in Avasarala's office reinforced Bobbie's impression that the Martian suite was intended to impress. The deputy secretary was important enough to get Bobbie transferred out of Thorsson's command and into a liaison role for the UN with a single phone call. And yet her office had cheap carpet that smelled unpleasantly of stale tobacco smoke. Her desk was old and scuffed. No cherrywood chairs here. The only things that looked lovingly tended in the room were the fresh flowers and the Buddha shrine.

Avasarala radiated weariness. There were dark circles under her eyes that hadn't been there during their official meetings and hadn't been visible in the dim lights of the bar where she'd made her offer. Sitting behind her giant desk in a bright blue sari, she looked very small, like a child pretending to be a grown-up. Only the gray hair and crow's-feet ruined the illusion. Bobbie suddenly pictured her instead as a cranky doll, complaining as children moved her arms and legs and forced her to go to tea parties with stuffed animals. The thought made her cheeks ache from restraining the grin.

Avasarala tapped at a terminal on her desk and grunted with irritation. *No more tea for you, gramma dolly, you've had enough,* Bobbie thought, then stifled a laugh. "Soren, you've moved my fucking files again. I can't find a goddamned thing anymore."

The stiff young man who'd brought Bobbie into the office and then sort of melted into the background cleared his throat. It made Bobbie jump. He was closer behind her than she'd realized.

"Ma'am, you asked me to move a few of the—"

"Yes, yes," Avasarala interrupted, tapping harder on the terminal's screen, as if that would make the device understand what she wanted. Something about that made Bobbie think of people who started talking louder when trying to communicate with someone who spoke a different language.

"Okay, there they are," Avasarala said with irritation. "Why you'd put them…"

She tapped a few more times and Bobbie's terminal chimed.

"That," she said, "is the report and all of my notes on the Ganymede situation. Read them. Today. I may have an update later, once I've had a little polite questioning done."

Bobbie pulled out her terminal and scrolled quickly through the documents she'd just been sent. It went on and on for hundreds of pages. Her first thought was *Did she really mean read all of this today?* This was quickly followed by *Did she really just hand me everything she knows?* It made her own government's recent treatment of her look even worse.

"It won't take you long," her new boss continued. "There's almost nothing there. Lots of bullshit by overpaid consultants who think they can hide the fact that they don't actually know anything by talking twice as long."

Bobbie nodded, but the feeling of being in over her head had started to outcompete her excitement at a new opportunity.

"Ma'am, is Sergeant Draper cleared to access—" Soren said.

"Yes. I just cleared her. Bobbie? You're cleared," Avasarala said right over the top of him. "Stop busting my balls, Soren. I'm out of tea."

Bobbie made a conscious effort not to turn around and look at Soren. The situation was uncomfortable enough without driving home the fact that he'd just been humiliated in front of a foreigner with exactly seventeen minutes on the job.

"Yes, ma'am," Soren said. "But I was wondering whether you should alert the security service about your decision to clear the sergeant. They do like to be in the loop on that kind of thing."

"Meow meow cry meow meow," Avasarala said. "That's all I heard you say."

"Yes, ma'am," Soren said.

Bobbie finally looked back and forth between them. Soren was being dressed down in front of a new team member who was also technically the enemy. His expression hadn't changed. He looked like he was humoring a demented grandmother. Avasarala made an impatient clicking sound with her teeth.

"Was I not clear? Have I lost the ability to speak?"

"No, ma'am," Soren said.

"Bobbie? Can you understand me?"

"Y-yes, sir."

"Good. Then get out of my office and do your jobs. Bobbie, read. Soren, tea."

Bobbie turned to leave and found Soren staring at her, his face expressionless. Which was, in its way, more disconcerting than a little well-justified anger would have been.

As she walked past him, Avasarala said, "Soren, wait. Take this to Foster in data services." She handed Soren what looked like a memory stick. "Make sure you get it to him before he leaves for the day."

Soren nodded, smiled, and took the small black wafer from her. "Of course."

When he and Bobbie had left Avasarala's office, and Soren had closed the door behind them, Bobbie let out a long whistling exhale and smiled at him.

"Wow, that was awkward. Sorry about—" she started, but stopped when Soren held up his hand, casually dismissing her concern.

"It's nothing," he said. "She's actually having a pretty good day."

While she stood gaping and looking at him, Soren turned away from her and tossed the memory stick onto his desk, where it slid under the wrapper of a half-eaten package of cookies. He sat down and put on a headset, then began scrolling through a list of phone numbers on his desktop terminal. If he noticed her continued presence, he gave no sign.

"You know," Bobbie said finally, "I just have some stuff to read, so if you're busy, I could take that thing to the data services guy. I mean, if you're busy with other stuff."

Soren finally looked at her quizzically.

"Why would I need you to do that?"

"Well," Bobbie said, glancing at the time on her terminal, "it's pretty close to eighteen hundred local, and I don't know what time you guys usually close up shop, so I just thought—"

"Don't worry about it. The thing is, my whole job is making her"—he jerked his head toward the closed door—"calm and happy. With her, everything's top priority. And so nothing is, you know? I'll do it when it needs doing. Until then, the bitch can bark a little if it makes her feel happy."

Bobbie felt a cool rush of surprise. No, not surprise. Shock.

"You just called her a bitch?"

"What would you call her, right?" Soren said with a disarming grin. Or was it mocking? Was this all a joke to him, Avasarala and Bobbie and the monster on Ganymede too? An image popped into her head of snatching the smug little assistant out of his chair and snapping him into a zigzag shape. Her hands flexed involuntarily.

Instead, she said, "Madam Secretary seemed to think it was pretty important."

Soren turned to look at her again. "Don't worry about it, Bobbie. Seriously. I know how to do my job."

She stood for a long moment.

"Solid copy on that," she said.

Bobbie was yanked from a dead sleep by sudden blaring music. She lurched upright in an unfamiliar bed in a nearly pitch-black room. The only light she could see was a faint pulsing pearly glow from her hand terminal, all the way across the room. The music suddenly stopped sounding like an atonal cacophony and became the song she'd selected as the audio alarm for incoming phone calls when she went to bed. Someone was calling. She cursed them in three languages and tried to crawl across the bed toward the terminal.

The edge of the bed came unexpectedly and plunged her face-first toward the floor, her half-asleep body not compensating for Earth's heavier gravity. She managed to avoid breaking her head open at the cost of a pair of jammed fingers on her right hand.

Cursing even louder, she continued her trek across the floor to the still glowing terminal. When she finally reached it, she opened the connection and said, "If someone isn't dead, someone *will* be."

"Bobbie," the person on the other end said. It took Bobbie's fuzzy head a moment to place the voice. *Soren.* She glanced at the time on her terminal and saw that it was 0411. She wondered if he was calling to drunkenly upbraid her or apologize. It certainly wouldn't be the strangest thing that'd happened over the last twenty-four hours.

Bobbie realized he was still talking, and put the speaker back up to her ear. "—is expecting you soonest, so get down here," Soren said.

"Can you repeat that?"

He started speaking slowly, as though to a dim child. "The boss wants you to come to the office, okay?"

Bobbie looked at the time again. "Right now?"

"No," Soren said. "Tomorrow at the normal time. She just wanted me to call at four a.m. to make sure you were coming."

The flash of anger helped wake her up. Bobbie stopped gritting her teeth long enough to say, "Tell her I'll be right there."

She fumbled her way to a wall, and then along it to a panel, which lit up at her touch. A second touch brought up the room's lights. Avasarala had gotten her a small furnished apartment within walking distance of the office. It wasn't much bigger than a cheap rent hole on Ceres. One large room that doubled as living space and bedroom, a smaller room with a shower and toilet, and an even smaller room that pretended to be a kitchen. Bobbie's duffel lay slumped in the corner, a few items pulled out of it, but mostly still packed. She'd stayed up till one in the morning reading and hadn't bothered to do anything after that but brush her teeth and then collapse into the bed that pulled down from the ceiling.

As she stood surveying the room and trying to wake up, Bobbie had a sudden moment of total clarity. It was as though a pair of dark glasses she hadn't even known she was wearing were snatched away, leaving her blinking in the light. Here she was, climbing out of bed after three hours of sleep to meet with one of the most powerful women in the solar system, and all she cared about was that she hadn't gotten her quarters shipshape and that she really wanted to beat one of her coworkers to death with his brass pen set. Oh, and she was a career marine who'd taken a job working with her government's current worst enemy because someone in naval intelligence had been mean to her. And not least of all, she wanted to get back to Ganymede and kill someone without having the foggiest idea who that someone might be.

The abrupt and crystal-clear vision of how far off the tracks her life seemed to have fallen lasted for a few seconds, and then the fog and sleep deprivation returned, leaving her with only the disquieting feeling that she'd forgotten to do something important.

She dressed in the prior day's uniform and rinsed her mouth out, then headed out the door.

Avasarala's modest office was packed with people. Bobbie recognized at least three civilians from her first meeting there on Earth. One of them was the moonfaced man who she'd later learned was Sadavir Errinwright, Avasarala's boss and possibly the second most powerful man on Earth. The pair were in an intense conversation when she came in, and Avasarala didn't see her.

Bobbie spotted a small clump of people in military uniforms and drifted in their direction until she saw that they were generals and admirals, and changed course. She wound up next to Soren, the only other person in the room standing alone. He didn't even give her a glance, but something about the way he held himself seemed to radiate that disquieting charm, powerful and insincere. It struck Bobbie that Soren was the kind of man she might take to bed if she was drunk enough, but she'd never trust him to watch her back in a fight. On second thought, no, she'd never be drunk enough.

"Draper!" Avasarala called out in a loud voice, having finally noticed her arrival.

"Yes, ma'am," Bobbie said, taking a step forward as everyone in the room stopped talking to look at her.

"You're my liaison," Avasarala said, the bags under her eyes so pronounced they looked less like fatigue and more like an undiagnosed medical condition. "So fucking *liaise*. Call your people."

"What happened?"

"The situation around Ganymede has just turned into the shit-storm to end all shit-storms," she said. "We're in a shooting war."

Chapter Twenty-One: Prax

Prax knelt, his arms zip-tied securely behind him. His shoulders ached. It hurt to hold his head up and it hurt to let it sink down. Amos lay facedown on the floor. Prax thought he was dead until he saw the zip-ties holding his arms behind his back. The nonlethal round their kidnappers had fired into the back of the mechanic's head had left an enormous blue-and-black lump there. Most of the others—Holden, some of the Pinkwater mercenaries, even Naomi—were in positions much like his own, but not all.

Four years before, they'd had a moth infestation. A containment study had failed, and inch-long gray-brown miller moths had run riot in his dome. They'd built a heat trap: a few dabs of generated pheromones on a heat-resistant fiber swatch under the big long-wave full-spectrum lighting units. The moths came too close, and the heat killed them. The smell of small bodies burning had fouled the air for days, and the scent was exactly like that of the cauterizing drill their abductors were using on the injured Pinkwater man. A swirl of white smoke rose from the formed-plastic office table on which he was laid out.

"I'm just…" the Pinkwater man said through his sedation haze. "You just go ahead, finish that without me. I'll be over…"

"Another bleeder," one of their abductors said. She was a thick-featured woman with a mole under her left eye and blood-slicked rubber gloves. "Right there."

"Check. Got it," said the man with the drill, pressing the metal tip back down into the patient's open belly wound. The sharp tapping sound of electrical discharge, and another small plume of white smoke rising from the wound.

Amos rolled over suddenly, his nose a bloody ruin, his face covered in gore. "I bight be wrong about dis, Cab'n," he said, the words fighting out past the bulbous mess of his nose, "'ut I don'd dink dese fellas are station security."

The room Prax had found himself in when the hood had been lifted had nothing to do with the usual atmosphere of law enforcement. It looked like an old office. The kind a safety inspector or a shipping clerk might have used in the ancient days before the cascade had started: a long desk with a built-in surface terminal, a few recessed lights shining up on the ceiling, a dead plant—*Sanseviera trifasciata*—with long green-brown leaves turning to dark slime. The gray-armored guards or soldiers or whatever they were had been very methodical and efficient. Prisoners were all along one wall, bound at the ankles and wrists; their hand terminals, weapons, and personal effects were stowed along the opposite wall with two guards set to do nothing but make sure no one touched them. The armor they'd stripped off Holden and Amos was in a pile on the floor next to their guns. Then the pair that Prax thought of as the medical team had started working, caring for the most desperately wounded first. They hadn't had time yet to go on to anybody else.

"Any idea who we're dealing with here?" Wendell asked under his breath.

"Not OPA," Holden said.

"That leaves a pretty large number of suspects," the Pinkwater captain said. "Is there somebody you've pissed off I should know about?"

Holden's eyes took on a pained expression and he made a motion as close to a shrug as he could manage, given the circumstances.

"There's kind of a list," he said.

"Another bleeder here," the woman said.

"Check," the drill man said. Tap, smoke, the smell of burning flesh.

"No offense meant, Captain Holden," Wendell said, "but I'm starting to wish I'd just shot you when I had the chance."

"None taken," Holden replied with a nod.

Four of the soldiers came back into the room. They were all squat Earther types. One—a dark-skinned man with a fringe of gray hair and an air of command—was subvocalizing madly. His gaze passed over the prisoners, seeing them without seeing them. Like they were boxes. When his eyes were on Prax, the man nodded but not to him.

"Are they stable?" the dark-skinned man asked the medical team.

"If I had the choice," the woman said, "I wouldn't move this one."

"If you didn't?"

"He'll probably make it. Keep the high g to a minimum until I can get him to a real medical bay."

"Excuse me," Holden said. "Can someone please tell me what the hell's going on?"

He might as well have been asking the walls.

"We've got ten minutes," the dark-skinned man said.

"Transport ship?"

"Not yet. The secure facility."

"Splendid," the woman said sourly.

"Because if you want to ask us any questions," Holden said,

"we should start by getting everybody off Ganymede. If you want your people to still be people, we have to go. That lab we were in had the protomolecule."

"I want them moved two at a time," the dark-skinned man said.

"Yes, sir," the woman replied.

"Are you listening to me?" Holden shouted. "The protomolecule is loose on this station."

"They're not listening to us, Jim," Naomi said.

"Ferguson. Mott," the dark-skinned man said. "Report."

The room was silent as someone somewhere reported in.

"My daughter's missing," Prax said. "That ship took my daughter."

They weren't listening to him either. He hadn't expected them to. With the exception of Holden and his crew, no one had. The dark-skinned man hunched forward, his expression profoundly focused. Prax felt the hair on the back of his neck rise. A premonition.

"Repeat that," the dark-skinned man said. And then a moment later: "*We're* firing? Who's *we*?"

Someone answered. The medical team and the weapons guards had their eyes on the commander too. Their faces were poker-blank.

"Understood. Alpha team, new orders. Get to the port and secure a transport ship. Use of force is authorized. Repeat that: Use of force is authorized. Sergeant Chernev, I need you to cut the prisoners' leg restraints."

One of the gun guards did a double take.

"All of them, sir?"

"All of them. And we're going to need a gurney for this gentleman."

"What's going on, sir?" the sergeant asked, his voice strained by confusion and fear.

"What's going on is I'm giving you an order," the dark-skinned man said, striding fast out the door. "Now *go*."

Prax felt the knife slash as a rough vibration against his ankles.

He hadn't realized his feet were numb until the burning pins-and-needles sensation brought tears to his eyes. Standing hurt. In the distance, something boomed like an empty freight container dropped from a great height. The sergeant cut Amos' legs free from their bonds and moved on to Naomi. One guard still stood by the supplies. The medical team was sealing the gut-shot man's belly closed with a sweet-smelling gel. The sergeant bent over.

The glance between Holden and Amos was the only warning Prax had. As casually as a man heading for the restroom, Holden started walking toward the door.

"Hey!" the weapons guard said, lifting a rifle the size of his arm. Holden looked up innocently, all eyes upon him, while behind him Amos brought his knee up into the sergeant's head. Prax yelped with surprise and the gun swung toward him. He tried to raise his hands, but they were still tied behind him. Wendell stepped forward, put a foot against the medical woman's hip, and pushed her into the guard's line of fire.

Naomi was kneeling on the sergeant's neck; his face was purple. Holden kicked the drill-wielding man in the back of the knee at the same moment that Amos tackled the man with the rifle. The cauterizing drill sparked against the floor with a sound like a finger tapping against glass. Paula had the sergeant's knife in her hands, backing up against one of her compatriots, sawing at the zip line around his wrists. The rifleman swung his elbow, and Amos' breath went out in a whoosh. Holden dropped onto the male half of the medical team, pinning the man's arms with his knees. Amos did something Prax couldn't see, and the rifleman grunted and folded over.

Paula got through the Pinkwater man's zip-tie just as the medical woman scooped up the rifle. The freed man pulled the pistol from the fallen sergeant's holster and leaned forward, pressing the barrel to the medical woman's temple as she swung the rifle up a quarter second too late.

Everyone froze. The medical woman smiled.

"Checkmate," she said, and lowered the rifle to the floor.

It had all taken no more than ten seconds.

Naomi took the knife, quickly, methodically slicing through the wrist bindings while Holden followed along behind, disabling the communication webs in the gray unmarked armor and zip-tying their hands and feet. A perfect inversion of the previous situation. Prax, rubbing the feeling back into his fingers, had the absurd image of the dark-skinned man coming back in and barking orders to him. Another boom came, another huge, resonating container being dropped and sounding out like a drum.

"I just want you to know how much I appreciate the way you looked after my people," Wendell told the pair who made up the medical team.

The woman suggested something obscene and unpleasant, but she smiled while she did it.

"Wendell," Holden said, rummaging in the box of their belongings and then tossing a card-key to the Pinkwater leader. "The *Somnambulist* is still yours, but you need to get to her now and get the hell out of here."

"Preaching to the choir," Wendell said. "Get that gurney. We're not leaving him behind now, and we've got to get out of here before reinforcements come."

"Yessir," Paula said.

Wendell turned to Holden.

"It was interesting meeting you, Captain. Let's not do this again."

Holden nodded but didn't stop putting his armor back on to shake hands. Amos did the same, then distributed their confiscated weapons and items back to them. Holden checked the magazine on his gun and then left through the same door the dark-skinned man had used, Amos and Naomi on his heels. Prax had to trot to catch up. Another detonation came, this one not so distant. Prax thought he felt the ice shake under him, but it might have been his imagination.

"What's . . . what's going on?"

"The protomolecule's breaking out," Holden said, tossing a hand terminal to Naomi. "The infection's taking hold."

"I don'd dink dat' whas habn'ing, Cab'n," Amos said. With a grimace he grabbed his nose with his right hand and yanked it away from his face. When he let go, it looked mostly straight. He blew a bloody-colored plug of snot out of each nostril, then took a deep breath. "That's better."

"Alex?" Naomi said into her handset. "Alex, tell me this link is still up. Talk to me."

Her voice was shaking.

Another boom, this one louder than anything Prax had ever heard. The shaking wasn't imagined now; it threw Prax to the ground. The air had a strange smell, like overheated iron. The station lights flickered and went dark; the pale blue emergency evacuation LEDs came on. A low-pressure Klaxon was sounding, its tritone blat designed to carry through thin and thinning air. When Holden spoke, he sounded almost contemplative.

"Or they might be bombarding the station."

Ganymede Station was one of the first permanent human toe-holds in the outer planets. It had been built with the long term in mind, not only in its own architecture, but also in how it would fit with the grand human expansion out into the darkness at the edge of the solar system. The possibility of catastrophe was in its DNA and had been from the beginning. It had been the safest station in the Jovian system. Just the name had once brought to mind images of newborn babies and domes filled with food crops. But the months since the mirrors fell had corroded it.

Pressure doors meant to isolate atmosphere loss had been wedged open when local hydraulics had failed. Emergency supplies had been used up and not replaced. Anything of value that could be turned into food or passage on the black market had been stolen and sold. The social infrastructure of Ganymede was already in its slow, inevitable collapse. The worst of the worst-case plans hadn't envisioned this.

Prax stood in the arching common space where Nicola and he

had gone on their first date. They'd eaten together at a little *dulcería*, drinking coffee and flirting. He could still remember the shape of her face and the heart-stopping thrill he'd felt when she took his hand. The ice where the *dulcería* had been was a fractured chaos. A dozen passages intersected here, and people were streaming through them, trying to get to the port or else deep enough into the moon that the ice would shield them, or someplace they could tell themselves was safe.

The only home he'd really known was falling apart around him. Thousands of people were going to die in the next few hours. Prax knew that, and part of him was horrified by it. But Mei had been on that ship, so she wasn't one of them. He still had to rescue her, just not from this. It made it bearable.

"Alex says it's hot out there," Naomi said as the four of them trotted through the ruins. "Really hot. He's not going to be able to make it to the port."

"There's the other landing pad," Prax said. "We could go there."

"That's the plan," Holden said. "Give Alex the coordinates for the science base."

"Yes, sir," Naomi said at the same moment Amos, raising a hand like a kid in a schoolroom, said, "The one with the protomolecule?"

"It's the only secret landing pad I've got," Holden said.

"Yeah, all right."

When Holden turned to Prax, his face was gray with strain and fear.

"Okay, Prax. You're the local. Our armor is vacuum rated, but we'll need environment suits for you and Naomi. We're about to run through hell, and not all of it's going to be pressurized. I don't have time to take a wrong turn or look for something twice. You're point. Can you handle it?"

"Yes," Prax said.

Finding the emergency environment suits was easy. They were common enough to have essentially no resale value and stowed at brightly colored emergency stations. All the supplies in the main halls and corridors were already stripped, but ducking down a narrow side corridor that linked to the less popular complex where Prax used to take Mei to the skating rink was easy. The suits there were safety orange and green, made to be visible to rescuers. Camouflage would have been more appropriate. The masks smelled of volatile plastic, and the joints were just rings sewn into the material. The suit heaters looked ill cared for and likely to catch on fire if used too long. Another blast came, followed by two others, each sounding closer than the one before.

"Nukes," Naomi said.

"Maybe gauss rounds," Holden replied. They might have been talking about the weather.

Prax shrugged.

"Either way, a hit that gets into a corridor means superheated steam," he said, pressing the last seal along his side closed and checking the cheap green LED that promised the oxygen was flowing. The heating system flickered to yellow, then back to green. "You and Amos might make it if your armor's good. I don't think Naomi and I stand a chance."

"Great," Holden said.

"I've lost the *Roci*," Naomi said. "No. I've lost the whole link. I was routing through the *Somnambulist*. She must have taken off."

Or been slagged. The thought was on all their faces. No one said it.

"Over this way," Prax said. "There's a service tunnel we used to use when I was in college. We can get around the Marble Arch complex and head up from there."

"Whatever you say, buddy," Amos said. His nose was bleeding again. The blood looked black in the faint blue light inside his helmet.

It was his last walk. Whatever happened, Prax was never coming back here, because *here* wouldn't exist. The fast lope along the service corridor where Jaimie Loomis and Tanna Ibtrahmin-Sook had taken him to get high was the last time he'd see that place. The broad, low-ceilinged amphitheater under the old water treatment center where he'd had his first internship was cracked, the reservoir compromised. It wouldn't flood the corridors quickly, but in a couple of days, the passageways would be filled in. In a couple of days, it wouldn't matter.

Everything glowed in the emergency LEDs or else fell into shadow. There was slush on the ground as the heating system struggled to compensate for the madness and failed. Twice, the way was blocked, once by a pressure door that was actually still functional, once by an icefall. They met almost no one. The others were all running for the port. Prax was leading them almost directly away from it now.

Another long, curved hall, then up a construction ramp, through an empty tunnel, and...

The blue steel door that blocked their way wasn't locked, but it was in safety mode. The indicator said there was vacuum on the other side. One of the God-like fists pummeling Ganymede had broken through here. Prax stopped, his mind clicking through the three-dimensional architecture of his home station. If the secret base was *there*, and he was *here*, then...

"We can't get there," he said.

The others were silent for a moment.

"That's not a good answer," Holden said. "Find a different one."

Prax took a long breath. If they doubled back, they could go down a level, head to the west, and try getting to the corridor from below, except that a blast strong enough to break through here would almost certainly have compromised the level below too. If they kept going to the old tube station, they might be able to find a service corridor—not that he knew there was one, but maybe—and it might lead in the right direction. Three more detonations came, shaking the ice. With a sound like a baseball bat hitting a home run, the wall beside him cracked.

"Prax, buddy," Amos said, "sooner'd be better."

They had environment suits, so if they opened the door, the vacuum wouldn't kill them. But there would be debris choking it. Any strike hard enough to break through to the surface would...

Would...

"We can't get there...through the station tunnels," he said. "But we can go up. Get to the surface and go that way."

"And how do we do that?" Holden asked.

Finding an access way that wasn't locked down took twenty minutes, but Prax found one. No wider than three men walking abreast, it was an automated service unit for the dome exteriors. The service unit itself had long since been cannibalized for parts, but that didn't matter. The airlock was still working under battery power. Naomi and Prax fed it the instructions, closed the inner door, and cycled the outer open. The escaping pressure was like a wind for a moment, and then nothing. Prax walked out onto the surface of Ganymede.

He'd seen images of the aurora from Earth. He'd never imagined he'd see anything like it in the blackness of his own sky. But there, not just above him but in lines from horizon to horizon, were streaks of green and blue and gold—chaff and debris and the radiating gas of cooling plasma. Incandescent blooms marked torch drives. Several kilometers away, a gauss round slammed into the moon's surface, the seismic shock knocking them from their feet. Prax lay there for a moment, watching the water ejecta geyser up into the darkness and then begin to fall back down as snow. It was beautiful. The rational, scientific part of his mind tried to calculate how much energy transfer there was to the moon when a rail-gun-hurled chunk of tungsten hit it. It would be like a miniature nuke without all the messy radiation. He wondered if the round would stop before it hit Ganymede's nickel-iron core.

"Okay," Holden said over the cheap radio in Prax's emergency suit. The low end of the sound spectrum was lousy, and Holden sounded like a cartoon character. "Which way now?"

"I don't know," Prax said, rising to his knees. He pointed toward the horizon. "Over there somewhere."

"I need more than that," Holden said.

"I've never been on the surface before," Prax said. "In a dome, sure. But just *out*? I mean, I know we're close to it, but I don't know how to get there."

"All right," Holden said. In the high vacuum over his head, something huge and very far away detonated. It was like the old cartoon lightbulb of someone getting an idea. "We can do this. We can solve this. Amos, you head toward that hill over there, see what you can see. Prax and Naomi, start going that direction."

"I don't think we need to do that, sir," Naomi said.

"Why not?"

Naomi raised her hand, pointing back behind Holden and Prax both.

"Because I'm pretty sure that's the *Roci* setting down over there," she said.

Chapter Twenty-Two: Holden

The secret landing pad lay in the hollow of a small crater. When Holden crested the lip and saw the *Rocinante* below him, the sudden and dizzying release of tension told him how frightened he'd been for the last several hours. But the *Roci* was home, and no matter how hard his rational mind argued that they were still in terrible danger, home was safe. As he paused a moment to catch his breath, the scene was lit with bright white light, like someone had taken a picture. Holden looked up in time to see a fading cloud of glowing gas in high orbit.

People were still dying in space just over their heads.

"Wow," Prax said. "It's bigger than I expected."

"Corvette," Amos replied, obvious pride in his voice. "Frigate-class fleet escort ship."

"I don't know what any of that means," Prax said. "It looks like a big chisel with an upside-down coffee cup on the back."

Amos said, "That's the drive—"

"Enough," Holden cut in. "Get to the airlock."

Amos led the way, sliding down the crater's icy wall hunched down on his heels and using his hands for balance. Prax went next, for once not needing any help. Naomi went third, her reflexes and balance honed by a lifetime spent in shifting gravities. She actually managed to look graceful.

Holden went last, fully prepared to slip and go down the hill in a humiliating tumble, then pleasantly surprised when he didn't.

As they bounded across the flat floor of the crater toward the ship, the outer airlock door slid open, revealing Alex in a suit of Martian body armor and carrying an assault rifle. As soon as they were close enough to the ship that they could cut through the orbital radio clutter, Holden said, "Alex! Man, is it good to see you."

"Hey, Cap," Alex replied, even his exaggerated drawl not able to hide the relief in his voice. "Wasn't sure how hot this LZ would be. Anyone chasin' you?"

Amos ran up the ramp and grabbed Alex in a bear hug that yanked him off his feet.

"Man, it's fucking good to be home!" he said.

Prax and Naomi followed, Naomi patting Alex on the shoulder as she went by. "You did good. Thank you."

Holden stopped on the ramp to look up one last time. The sky was still filled with the flashes and light trails of ongoing battle. He had the sudden visceral memory of being a boy back in Montana, watching massive thunderheads flash with hidden lightning.

Alex watched with him, then said, "It was a bit hectic, comin' in."

Holden threw an arm around his shoulder. "Thanks for the ride."

Once the airlock had finished cycling and the crew had removed their environment suits and armor, Holden said, "Alex, this is Prax Meng. Prax, this is the solar system's best pilot, Alex Kamal."

Prax shook Alex's hand. "Thank you for helping me find Mei."

Alex frowned a question at Holden, but a quick shake of the head kept him from asking it. "Nice to meet you, Prax."

"Alex," Holden said, "get us warmed up for liftoff, but don't take off until I'm up in the copilot's chair."

"Roger," Alex said, and headed toward the bow of the ship.

"Everything's sideways," Prax said, looking around at the storage room just past the inner airlock door.

"The *Roci* doesn't spend much time on her belly like this," Naomi said, taking his hand and leading him to the crew ladder, which now appeared to run across the floor. "We're standing on a bulkhead, and that wall to our right is normally the deck."

"Grew up in low grav and don't spend much time on ships, apparently," Amos said. "Man, this next part is really gonna suck for you."

"Naomi," Holden said. "Get to ops and get belted in. Amos, take Prax to the crew deck and then head down to engineering and get the *Roci* ready for a rough ride."

Before they could leave, Holden put a hand on Prax's shoulder.

"This takeoff and flight is going to be fast and bumpy. If you haven't trained for high-g flight, it will probably be very uncomfortable."

"Don't worry about me," Prax said, making what he probably thought was a brave face.

"I know you're tough. You couldn't have survived the last couple weeks otherwise. You don't have anything to prove at this point. Amos will take you to the crew deck. Find a room without a name on the door. That will be your room now. Get in the crash couch and buckle in, then hit the bright green button on the panel to your left. The couch will pump you full of drugs that will sedate you and keep you from blowing a blood vessel if we have to burn hard."

"My room?" Prax said, an odd note in his voice.

"We'll get you some clothes and sundries once we're out of this shit. You can keep them there."

"My room," Prax repeated.

"Yeah," Holden said. "Your room." He could see Prax fighting down a lump in his throat, and he realized what the simple offer of comfort and safety probably meant to someone who'd been through what the small botanist had over the last month.

There were tears in the man's eyes.

"Come on, let's get you settled in," Amos said, leading Prax aft toward the crew deck.

Holden headed the other way, past the ops deck, where Naomi was already strapped down into a chair at one of the workstations, then forward into the cockpit. He climbed into the copilot's seat and belted in.

"Five minutes," he said over the shipwide channel.

"So," Alex said, dragging the word out to two syllables while he flicked switches to finish the preflight check, "we're lookin' for someone named Mei?"

"Prax's daughter."

"We do that now? Seems like the scope of our mission is creepin' a bit."

Holden nodded. Finding lost daughters was not part of their mandate. That had been Miller's job. And he'd never be able to adequately explain the certainty he felt that this lost little girl was at the center of everything that had happened on Ganymede.

"I think this lost little girl is at the center of everything that's happened on Ganymede," he said with a shrug.

"Okay," Alex replied, then hit something on a panel twice and frowned. "Huh, we have a red on the board. Gettin' a 'no seal' on the cargo airlock. Might've caught some flak on the way down, I guess. It was pretty hot up there."

"Well, we're not going to stop and fix it now," Holden said. "We keep the bay in vacuum most of the time anyway. If the inner hatch into the cargo area is showing a good seal, just override the alarm and let's go."

"Roger," Alex said, and tapped the override.

"One minute," Holden said over the shipwide, then turned to Alex. "So I'm curious."

"'Bout?"

"How'd you manage to slip through that shit-storm up above us, and can you do it again on the way out?"

Alex laughed.

"Simple matter of never bein' higher than the second-highest threat on anyone's board. And, of course, not bein' there anymore when they decide to get around to you."

"I'm giving you a raise," Holden said, then began the ten-second countdown. At one, the *Roci* blasted off of Ganymede on four pillars of superheated steam.

"Rotate us for a full burn as soon as you can," Holden said, the rumble of the ship's takeoff giving him an artificial vibrato.

"This close?"

"There's nothing below us that matters," Holden said, thinking of the remnants of black filament they'd seen in the hidden base. "Melt it."

"Okay," Alex said. Then, once the ship had finished orienting straight up, he said, "Givin' her the spurs."

Even with the juice coursing through his blood, Holden blacked out for a moment. When he came to, the *Roci* was veering wildly from side to side. The cockpit was alive with the sounds of warning buzzers.

"Whoa, honey," Alex was saying under his breath. "Whoa, big girl."

"Naomi," Holden said, looking at a confusing mass of red on the threat board and trying to decipher it with his blood-starved brain. "Who's firing at us?"

"Everyone." She sounded as groggy as he felt.

"Yeah," Alex said, his tension draining some of the good-old-boy drawl out of his voice. "She's not kidding."

The swarm of threats on his display began to make sense, and Holden saw they were right. It looked like half of the inner planets ships on their side of Ganymede had lobbed at least one missile at them. He entered the command code to set all the weapons to free fire and sent control of the aft PDCs to Amos. "Amos, cover our asses."

Alex was doing his best to keep any of the incoming missiles from catching them, but ultimately that was a lost cause. Nothing with meat inside it could outrun metal and silicon.

"Where are we—" Holden said, stopping to target a missile that wandered into the front starboard PDC's firing arc. The point defense cannon fired off a long burst at it. The missile was smart enough to turn sharply and evade, but its sudden course change bought them a few more seconds.

"Callisto's on our side of Jupiter," Alex said, referring to the next sizable moon out from Ganymede. "Gonna get in its shadow."

Holden checked the vectors of the ships that had fired at them. If any of them were pursuing, Alex's gambit would only buy them a few minutes. But it didn't appear they were. Of the dozen or so that had attacked them, over half were moderately to severely damaged, and the ones that weren't were still busy shooting at each other.

"Seems like we were everyone's number one threat there for a second," Holden said. "But not so much anymore."

"Yeah, sorry about that, Cap. Not sure why that happened."

"I don't blame you," Holden said.

The *Roci* shuddered, and Amos gave a whoop over the ship-wide comm. "Don't be trying to touch my girl's ass!"

Two of the closer missiles had vanished off the threat board.

"Nice work, Amos," Holden said, checking the updated times to impact and seeing that they'd bought another half minute.

"Shit, Cap, the *Roci* does all the work," Amos said. "I just encourage her to express herself."

"Going to duck and cover around Callisto. I'd appreciate a distraction," Alex said to Holden.

"Okay, Naomi, another ten seconds or so," Holden said. "Then hit them with everything you've got. We'll need them blind for a few seconds."

"Roger," Naomi said. Holden could see her prepping a massive assault package of laser clutter and radio jamming.

The *Rocinante* lurched again, and the moon Callisto suddenly filled Holden's forward screen. Alex hurtled toward it at a suicidal rate, flipping the ship and hard burning at the last second to throw them into a low slingshot orbit.

"Three...two...one...now," he said, the *Roci* diving tail first toward Callisto, whipping past it so low that Holden felt like he could have reached out the airlock and scooped up some snow. At the same time, Naomi's jamming package hammered the sensors of the pursuing missiles, blinding them while their processors worked to cut through the noise.

By the time they'd reacquired the *Rocinante*, she'd been thrown around Callisto by gravity and her own drive in a new vector and at high speed. Two of the missiles gamely tried to come about and pursue, but the rest either limped off in random directions or slammed into the moon. When their two pursuers had gotten back on course, the *Roci* had opened up an enormous lead and could take her time shooting them down.

"We made it," Alex said. Holden found the disbelief in his pilot's voice fairly disconcerting. Had it been that close?

"Never doubted it," Holden said. "Take us to Tycho. Half a g. I'll be in my cabin."

When they were finished, Naomi flopped onto her side in their shared bunk, sweat plastering her curly black hair to her forehead. She was still panting. He was too.

"That was...vigorous," she said.

Holden nodded but didn't have enough air to actually speak yet. When he'd climbed down the ladder from the cockpit, Naomi had been waiting, already out of her restraints. She'd grabbed him and kissed him so hard his lip had split. He hadn't even noticed. They'd barely reached the cabin with their clothes on. What had happened afterward was sort of a blur now to Holden, though his legs were tired and his lip hurt.

Naomi rolled across him and climbed out of the bunk.

"I've got to pee," she said, pulling on a robe and heading out the door. Holden just nodded to her, still not quite capable of speech.

He shifted over to the middle of the bed, stretching out his arms and legs for a moment. The truth was the *Roci*'s cabins were not built for two occupants, least of all the crash couches that doubled as beds. But over the course of the last year, he'd spent more and more time sleeping in Naomi's cabin, until it sort of became *their* cabin and he just didn't sleep anywhere else anymore. They couldn't share the bunk during high-g maneuvers, but so far they'd never been asleep anytime the ship had needed to do high-g maneuvering. A trend that was likely to continue.

Holden was starting to doze off when the hatch opened and Naomi came back in. She tossed a cold, wet washcloth onto his belly.

"Wow, that's bracing," Holden said, sitting up with a start.

"It was hot when I left the head with it."

"That," Holden said while he cleaned up, "sounded very dirty."

Naomi grinned, then sat on the edge of the bunk and poked him in the ribs. "You can still think of sex? I would've thought we got that out of your system."

"A close brush with death does wonderful things for my refractory period."

Naomi climbed into the bunk next to him, still wrapped in her robe.

"You know," she said, "this was my idea. And I'm all in favor of reaffirming life through sex."

"Why do I get the feeling that there is a 'but' missing at the end of that sentence?"

"But—"

"Ah, there it is."

"There's something we need to talk about. And this seems a good time."

Holden rolled over onto his side, facing her, and pushed up onto one elbow. A thick strand of hair was hanging in her face, and he brushed it back with his other hand.

"What did I do?" he said.

"It's not exactly anything you've done," Naomi said. "It's more what we're heading off to do right now."

Holden put his hand on her arm but waited for her to continue. The soft cloth of her robe clung to the wet skin beneath it.

"I'm worried," she said, "that we're flying off to Tycho to do something really rash."

"Naomi, you weren't there, you didn't see—"

"I saw it, Jim, through Amos' suitcam. I know what it is. I know how much it scares you. It scares the hell out of me too."

"No," Holden said, his voice surprising him with its anger. "No you don't. You weren't on Eros when it got out, you never—"

"Hey, I was there. Maybe not for the worst of it. Not like you," Naomi said, her voice still calm. "But I did help carry what was left of you and Miller to the med bay. And I watched you try to die there. We can't just accuse Fred of—"

"Right now—and I mean *right now*—Ganymede could be changing."

"No—"

"*Yes.* Yes it could. We could be leaving a couple million dead people behind right now who don't know it yet. Melissa and Santichai? Remember them? Now think of them stripped down to whatever pieces the protomolecule finds most useful at the moment. Think of them as *parts.* Because if that bug is loose on Ganymede, then that's what they are."

"Jim," Naomi said, a warning in her voice now. "This is what I'm talking about. The intensity of your feelings isn't *evidence.* You are about to accuse a man who's been your friend and patron for the last year of maybe killing an entire moon full of people. That isn't the Fred we know. And you owe him better than that."

Holden pushed up to a sitting position, part of him wanting to physically distance himself from Naomi, the part of him that was angry with her for not sympathizing enough.

"*I* gave Fred the last of it. *I gave it to him*, and he swore right to my face he'd never use it. But that's not what I saw down there.

You call him my friend, but Fred has only ever done what would advance his own cause. Even helping us was just another move in his political game."

"Experiments on kidnapped children?" Naomi said. "A whole moon—one of the most important in the outer planets—put at risk and maybe killed outright? Does that make any sense to you? Does that sound like Fred Johnson?"

"The OPA wants Ganymede even more than either inner planet does," Holden said, finally admitting the thing he'd feared since they'd found the black filament. "And they wouldn't give it to him."

"Stop," Naomi said.

"Maybe he's trying to drive them off, or he sold it to them in exchange for the moon. That would at least explain the heavy inner planets traffic we've been seeing—"

"No. Stop," she said. "I don't want to sit here and listen to you talk yourself into this."

Holden started to speak, but Naomi sat up facing him and gently put her hand over his mouth.

"I didn't like this new Jim Holden you've been turning into. The guy who'd rather reach for his gun than talk? I know being the OPA's bagman has been a shitty job, and I know we've had to do a lot of pretty rotten things in the name of protecting the Belt. But that was still you. I could still see you lurking there under the surface, waiting to come back."

"Naomi," he said, pulling her hand away from his face.

"This guy who can't wait to go all *High Noon* in the streets of Tycho? That's not Jim Holden at all. I don't recognize that man," she said, then frowned. "No. That's not right. I do recognize him. But his name was Miller."

For Holden, the most awful part was how calm she was. She never raised her voice, never sounded angry. Instead, infinitely worse, there was only a resigned sadness.

"If that's who you are now, you need to drop me off somewhere. I can't go with you anymore," she said. "I'm out."

Chapter Twenty-Three: Avasarala

Avasarala stood at her window, looking out at the morning haze. In the distance, a transport lifted off. It rode an exhaust plume that looked like a pillar of bright white cloud, and then it was gone. Her hands ached. She knew that some of the photons striking her eyes right now had come from explosions light-minutes away. Ganymede Station, once the safest place without an atmosphere, then a war zone, and now a wasteland. She could no more pick out the light of its death than pluck a particular molecule of salt from the ocean, but she knew it was there, and the fact was like a stone in her belly.

"I can ask for confirmation," Soren said. "Nguyen should be filing his command report in the next eighteen hours. Once we have that—"

"We'll know what he said," Avasarala snapped. "I can tell you that right now. The Martian forces took a threatening position, and he was forced to respond aggressively. *La la fucking la. Where did he get the ships?*"

"He's an admiral," Soren said. "I thought he came with them."

She turned. The boy looked tired. He'd been up since the small hours of the morning. They all had. His eyes were bloodshot, and his skin pallid and clammy.

"I took apart that command group myself," she said. "I pared it down until you could have drowned it in a bathtub. And he's out there now with enough firepower to take on the Martian fleet?"

"Apparently," Soren said.

She fought the urge to spit. The rumble of the transport engines finally reached her, the sound muffled by distance and the glazing. The light was already gone. To her sleep-deprived mind, it was exactly like playing politics in the Jovian system or the Belt. Something happened—she could see it happen—but she heard it only after the fact. When it was too late.

She'd made a mistake. Nguyen was a war hawk. The kind of adolescent boy who still thought any problem could be solved by shooting it enough. Everything he'd done was as subtle as a lead pipe to the kneecap, until this. Now he'd reassembled his command without her knowing it. And he'd had her pulled from the Martian negotiations.

Which meant that he hadn't done any of it. Nguyen had either a patron or a cabal. She hadn't seen that he was a bit player, so whoever called his tune had surprised her. She was playing against shadows, and she hated it.

"More light," she said.

"Excuse me?"

"Find out how he got those ships," she said. "Do it before you go to sleep. I want a full accounting. Where the replacement ships came from, who ordered them, how they were justified. Everything."

"Would you also like a pony, ma'am?"

"You're fucking right I would," she said, and sagged against her desk. "You do good work. Someday you might get a real job."

"I'm looking forward to it, ma'am."

"Is she still around?"

"At her desk," Soren said. "Should I send her in?"

"You better had."

When Bobbie came into the room, a film of cheap paper in her fist, it struck Avasarala again how poorly the Martian fit in. It wasn't only her accent or the difference in build that spoke of a childhood in the lower Martian gravity. In the halls of politics, the woman's air of physical competence stood out. She looked like she'd been rousted out of bed in the middle of the night, just like all of them; it was only that it looked good on her. Might be useful, might not, but certainly it was worth remembering.

"What have you got?" Avasarala asked.

The marine's frown was all in her forehead.

"I've gotten through to a couple of people in the command. Most of them don't know who the hell I am, though. I probably spent as much time telling them I was working for you as I did talking about Ganymede."

"It's a lesson. Martian bureaucrats are stupid, venal people. What did they say?"

"Long story?"

"Short."

"You shot at us."

Avasarala leaned back in her chair. Her back hurt, her knees hurt, and the knot of sorrow and outrage that was always just under her heart felt brighter than usual.

"Of course we did," she said. "The peace delegation?"

"Already gone," Bobbie said. "They'll be releasing a statement sometime tomorrow about how the UN was negotiating in bad faith. They're still fighting out the exact wording."

"What's the hold?"

Bobbie shook her head. She didn't understand.

"What words are they fighting over, and which side wants which words?" Avasarala demanded.

"I don't know. Does it matter?"

Of course it mattered. The difference between *The UN has been negotiating in bad faith* and *The UN was negotiating in bad faith* could be measured in hundreds of lives. Thousands. Avasarala tried to swallow her impatience. It didn't come naturally.

"All right," she said. "See if there's anything else you can get me."

Bobbie held out the paper. Avasarala took it.

"The hell is this?" she asked.

"My resignation," Bobbie said. "I thought you'd want all the paperwork in place. We're at war now, so I'll be shipping back. Getting my new assignment."

"Who recalled you?"

"No one, yet," Bobbie said. "But—"

"Will you please sit down? I feel like I'm at the bottom of a fucking well, talking to you."

The marine sat. Avasarala took a deep breath.

"Do you want to kill me?" Avasarala asked. Bobbie blinked, and before she could answer, Avasarala lifted her hand, commanding silence. "I am one of the most powerful people in the UN. We're at war. So do you want to kill me?"

"I...guess so?"

"You don't. You want to find out who killed your men and you want the politicians to stop greasing the wheels with Marine blood. And holy shit! What do you know? I want that too."

"But I'm active-duty Martian military," Bobbie said. "If I stay working for you, I'm committing treason." The way she said it wasn't complaint or accusation.

"They haven't recalled you," Avasarala said. "And they're not going to. The wartime diplomatic code of contact is almost exactly the same for you as it is for us, and it's ten thousand pages of nine-point type. If you get orders right now, I can put up enough queries and requests for clarifications that you'll die of old age in that chair. If you just want to kill someone for Mars, you're not going to get a better target than me. If you want to stop this idiotic fucking war and find out who's actually behind it, get back to your desk and find out who wants what wording."

Bobbie was silent for a long moment.

"You mean that as a rhetorical device," she said at last, "but it would make a certain amount of sense to kill you. And I can do it."

A tiny chill hit Avasarala's spine, but she didn't let it reach her face.

"I'll try not to oversell the point in the future. Now get back to work."

"Yes, sir," Bobbie said, then stood and walked out of the room. Avasarala blew out a breath, her cheeks ballooning. She was inviting Martian Marines to slaughter her in her own office. She needed a fucking nap. Her hand terminal chimed. An unscheduled high-status report had just come through, the deep red banner overriding her usual display settings. She tapped it, ready for more bad news from Ganymede.

It was about Venus.

Until seven hours earlier, the *Arboghast* had been a third-generation destroyer, built at the Bush Shipyards thirteen years before and later refitted as a military science vessel. For the last eight months, she'd been orbiting Venus. Most of the active scanning data that Avasarala had relied on had come from her.

The event she was watching had been captured by two lunar telescopic stations with broad-spectrum intelligence feeds that happened to be at the correct angles, and about a dozen shipborne optical observers. The dataset they collected agreed perfectly.

"Play it again," Avasarala said.

Michael-Jon de Uturbé had been a field technician when she'd first met him, thirty years before. Now he was the de facto head of the special sciences committee and married to Avasarala's roommate from university. In that time, his hair had fallen out or grown white, his dark brown skin had taken to draping a bit off of his bones, and he hadn't changed the brand of cheap floral cologne he wore.

He had always been an intensely shy, almost antisocial, man. In order to maintain the connection, she knew not to ask too much of him. His small, cluttered office was less than a quarter of a mile from hers, and she had seen him five times in the last decade, each of them moments when she needed to understand something obscure and complex quickly.

He tapped his hand terminal twice, and the images on the display reset. The *Arboghast* was whole once more, floating in false color detail above the haze of Venusian cloud. The time stamp started moving forward, one second per second.

"Walk me through," she said.

"Um. Well. We start from the spike. It's just like the one we saw that last time Ganymede started going to hell."

"Splendid. That's two datapoints."

"This came before the fighting," he said. "Maybe an hour. A little less."

It had come during Holden's firefight. Before she could bring him in. But how could Venus be responding to Holden's raid on Ganymede? Had Bobbie's monsters been part of that fight?

"Then the radio ping. Right"—he froze the display—"here. Massive sweep in three-second-by-seven-second grid. It was looking, but it knew where to look. All those active scans, I'd assume. Called attention."

"All right."

He started the playback again. The resolution went a few degrees grainier, and he made a pleased sound.

"This was interesting," he said, as if the rest were not. "Radiative pulse of some kind. Interfered with all the telescopy except a strictly visible spectrum kit on Luna. Only lasted a tenth of a second, though. The microwave burst after it was pretty normal active sensor scanning."

You sound disappointed perched at the back of Avasarala's tongue, but the dread and anticipation of what would come next stopped it. The *Arboghast*, with 572 souls aboard her, came apart like a cloud. Hull plates peeled away in neat, orderly rows. Superstructural girders and decks shifted apart. The engineering bays detached, slipping away. In the image before her, the full crew had been exposed to hard vacuum. In the moment she was looking at now, they were all dying and not yet dead. That it was like watching a construction plan animation—crew quarters here, the engineering section here, the plates cupping the drive thus and so—only made it more monstrous.

"Now this is especially interesting," Michael-Jon said, stopping the playback. "Watch what happens when we increase magnification."

Don't show them to me, Avasarala wanted to say. *I don't want to watch them die.*

But the image he moved in on wasn't a human being, but a knot of complicated ducting. He advanced it slowly, frame by frame, and the image grew misty.

"It's ablating?" she asked.

"What? No, no. Here, I'll bring you closer."

The image jumped in again. The cloudiness was an illusion created by a host of small bits of metal: bolts, nuts, Edison clamps, O-rings. She squinted. It wasn't a loose cloud either. Like iron filings under the influence of a magnet, each tiny piece was held in line with the ones before and behind it.

"The *Arboghast* wasn't torn apart," he said. "It was disassembled. It looks as though there were about fifteen separate waves, each one undoing another level of the mechanism. Stripped the whole thing down to the screws."

Avasarala took a deep breath, then another, then another, until the sound lost its ragged edge and the awe and fear grew small enough that she could push it to the back of her mind.

"What does this?" she said at last. She'd meant it as a rhetorical question. Of course there was no answer. No force known to humanity could do what had just been done. That wasn't the meaning he took.

"Graduate students," he said brightly. "My Industrial Design final was just the same. They gave us all machines and we had to take them apart and figure out what they did. Extra credit was to deliver an improved design." And a moment later, his voice melancholy: "Of course we also had to put them back together, yes?"

On the display, the rigidity and order of the floating bits of metal stopped, and the bolts and girders, vast ceramic plates and minute clamps began to drift, set in chaotic motion by the departure of whatever had been holding them. Seventy seconds from first burst to the end. A little over a minute, and not a shot fired in response. Not even something clearly to be shot.

"The crew?"

"Took their suits apart. Didn't bother disassembling the bodies. Might have interpreted them as a logical unit or might already know all it needs to about human anatomy."

"Who's seen this?"

Michael-Jon blinked, then shrugged, then blinked again.

"*This* this, or a version of this? We're the only one with both high-def feeds, but it's Venus. Everyone who was looking saw it. Not like it's in a sealed lab."

She closed her eyes, pressing her fingers against the bridge of her nose as if she were fighting a headache while she struggled to keep the mask in place. Better to seem in pain. Better to seem impatient. The fear shook her like a seizure, like something happening to somebody else. Tears welled up in her eyes, and she bit her lip until they went away. She pulled up the personnel locator on her hand terminal. Nguyen was out of the question even if he'd been in conversational range. Nettleford was with a dozen ships burning toward Ceres Station, and she wasn't entirely certain of him. Souther.

"Can you send this version to Admiral Souther?"

"Oh, no. It's not cleared for release."

Avasarala looked at him, her expression empty.

"Are you clearing it for release?"

"I am clearing it for release to Admiral Souther. Please send it immediately."

Michael-Jon bobbed a quick nod, tapping with the tips of both pinkies. Avasarala took out her own hand terminal and sent a simple message to Souther. WATCH AND CALL ME. When she stood, her legs ached.

"It was good seeing you again," Michael-Jon said, not looking at her. "We should all have dinner sometime."

"Let's," Avasarala said, and left.

The women's restroom was cold. Avasarala stood at the sink, her palms flat against the granite. She wasn't used to fear or awe. Her life had been about control, talking and bullying and teasing whoever needed it until the world turned the direction she wanted it to. The few times the implacable universe had overwhelmed her haunted her: an earthquake in Bengal when she'd been a girl, a storm in Egypt that had trapped her and Arjun in their hotel room for four days as the food supplies failed, the death of her son. Each one had turned her constant pretense of certainty and pride against her, left her curled in her bed at night for weeks afterward, her fingers bent in claws, her dreams nightmares.

This was worse. Before, she could comfort herself with the idea that the universe was empty of intent. That all the terrible things were just the accidental convergences of chance and mindless forces. The death of the *Arboghast* was something else. It was intentional and inhuman. It was like seeing the face of God and finding no compassion there.

Shaking, she pulled up her hand terminal. Arjun answered almost immediately. From the set of his jaw and the softness of his eyes, she knew he had seen some version of the event. And his thought hadn't been for the fate of mankind, but for her. She tried to smile, but it was too much. Tears ran down her cheeks. Arjun sighed gently and looked down.

"I love you very much," Avasarala said. "Knowing you has let me bear the unbearable."

Arjun grinned. He looked good with wrinkles. He was a more handsome man now that he was older. As if the round-faced, comically earnest boy who'd snuck to her window to read poems in the night had only been waiting to become this.

"I love you, I have always loved you, if we are born into new lives, I will love you there."

Avasarala sobbed once, wiped her eyes with the back of her hand, and nodded.

"All right, then," she said.

"Back to work?"

"Back to work. I may be home late."

"I'll be here. You can wake me."

They were silent for a moment; then she released the connection. Admiral Souther hadn't called. Errinwright hadn't called. Avasarala's mind was leaping around like a terrier attacking a troop transport. She rose to her feet, forced herself to put one foot in front of the other. The simple physical act of walking seemed to clear her head. Little electric carts stood ready to whisk her back to her office, but she ignored them, and by the time she reached it, she was almost calm again.

Bobbie sat hunched at her desk, the sheer physical bulk of the woman making the furniture seem like something from grade school. Soren was elsewhere, which was fine. His training wasn't military.

"So you're in an entrenched position with a huge threat coming down onto you, right?" Avasarala said, sitting down on the edge of Soren's desk. "Say you're on a moon and some third party has thrown a comet at you. Massive threat, you understand?"

Bobbie looked at her, confused for a moment, and then, with a shrug, played along.

"All right," the marine said.

"So why do you choose that moment to pick a fight with your neighbors? Are you just frightened and lashing out? Are you thinking that the other bastards are responsible for the rock? Are you just that stupid?"

"We're talking about Venus and the fighting in the Jovian system," Bobbie said.

"It's a pretty fucking thin metaphor, yes," Avasarala said. "So why are you doing it?"

Bobbie leaned back in her chair, plastic creaking under her. The big woman's eyes narrowed. She opened her mouth once, closed it, frowned, and began again.

"I'm consolidating power," Bobbie said. "If I use my resources stopping the comet, then as soon as that threat's gone, I lose. The other guy catches me with my pants down. Bang. If I kick his ass first, then when it's over, I win."

"But if you cooperate—"

"Then you have to trust the other guy," Bobbie said, shaking her head.

"There's a million tons of ice coming that's going to kill you both. Why the hell wouldn't you trust the other guy?"

"Depends. Is he an Earther?" Bobbie said. "We've got two major military forces in the system, plus whatever the Belters can gin up. That's three sides with a lot of history. When whatever's going to happen on Venus actually happens, someone wants to already have all the cards."

"And if both sides—Earth and Mars—are making that same calculation, we're going to spend all our energy getting ready for the war after next."

"Yep," Bobbie said. "And yes, that's how we all lose together."

Chapter Twenty-Four: Prax

Prax sat in his cabin. For sleeping space on a ship, he knew it was large. Spacious, even. Altogether, it was smaller than his bedroom on Ganymede had been. He sat on the gel-filled mattress, the acceleration gravity pressing him down, making his arms and legs feel heavier than they were. He wondered whether the sense of suddenly weighing more—specifically the discontinuous change of space travel—triggered some evolutionary cue for fatigue. The feeling of being pulled to the floor or the bed was so powerfully like the sensation of bone-melting tiredness it was easy to think that sleeping a little more would fix it, would make things better.

"Your daughter is probably dead," he said aloud. Waited to see how his body would react. "Mei is probably dead."

He didn't start sobbing this time, so that was progress.

Ganymede was a day and a half behind him and already too

small to pick out with the naked eye. Jupiter was a dim disk the size of a pinky nail, kicking back the light of a sun that was little more than an extremely bright star. Intellectually, he knew that he was falling sunward, heading in from the Jovian system toward the Belt. In a week, the sun would be close to twice the size it was now, and it would still be insignificant. In a context of such immensity, of distances and speeds so far above any meaningful human experience, it seemed like nothing should matter. He should be agreeing that he hadn't been there when God made the mountains, whether it meant the ones on Earth or on Ganymede or somewhere farther out in the darkness. He was in a tiny metal-and-ceramic box that was exchanging matter for energy to throw a half dozen primates across a vacuum larger than millions of oceans. Compared to that, how could anything matter?

"Your daughter is probably dead," he said again, and this time the words caught in his throat and started to choke him.

It was, he thought, something about the sense of being suddenly safe. On Ganymede, he'd had fear to numb him. Fear and malnutrition and routine and the ability at any moment to move, to do something even if it was utterly useless. Go check the boards again, go wait in line at security, trot along the hallways and see how many new bullet holes pocked them.

On the *Rocinante*, he had to slow down. He had to stop. There was nothing for him to do here but wait out the long sunward fall to Tycho Station. He couldn't distract himself. There was no station—not even a wounded and dying one—to hunt through. There were only the cabin he'd been given, his hand terminal, a few jumpsuits a half size too big for him. A small box of generic toiletries. That was everything he had left. And there was enough food and clean water that his brain could start working again.

Each passing hour felt like waking up a little more. He knew how badly his body and mind had been abused only when he got better. Every time, he felt like this had to be back to normal, and then not long after, he'd find that, no, there had been more.

So he explored himself, probing at the wound at the center of his personal world like pressing the tip of his tongue into a dry socket.

"Your daughter," he said through the tears, "is probably dead. But if she isn't, you have to find her."

That felt better—or, if not better, at least right. He leaned forward, his hands clasped, and rested his chin. Carefully, he imagined Katoa's body, laid out on its table. When his mind rebelled, trying to think about something—anything—else, he brought it back and put Mei in the boy's place. Quiet, empty, dead. The grief welled up from a place just above his stomach, and he watched it like it was something outside himself.

During his time as a graduate student, he had done data collection for a study of *Pinus contorata*. Of all the varieties of pine to rise off Earth, lodgepole pine had been the most robust in low-g environments. His job had been to collect the fallen cones and burn them for the seeds. In the wild, lodgepole pine wouldn't geminate without fire; the resin in the cones encouraged a hotter fire, even when it meant the death of the parental tree. To get better, it had to get worse. To survive, the plant had to embrace the unsurvivable.

He understood that.

"Mei is dead," he said. "You lost her."

He didn't have to wait for the idea to stop hurting. It would never stop hurting. But he couldn't let it grow so strong it overwhelmed him. He had the sense of doing himself permanent spiritual damage, but it was the strategy he had. And from what he could tell, it seemed to be working.

His hand terminal chimed. The two-hour block was up. Prax wiped the tears away with the back of his hand, took a deep breath, blew it back out, and stood. Two hours, twice a day, he'd decided, would be enough time in the fire to keep him hard and strong in this new environment of less freedom and more calories. Enough to keep him functional. He washed his face in the communal bathroom—the crew called it the head—and made his way to the galley.

The pilot—Alex, his name was—stood at the coffee machine, talking to a comm unit on the wall. His skin was darker than Prax's, his thinning hair black, with the first few stray threads of white. His voice had the odd drawl some Martians affected.

"I'm seein' eight percent and falling."

The wall unit said something cheerful and obscene. Amos.

"I'm tellin' you, the seal's cracked," Alex said.

"I been over it twice," Amos said from the comm. The pilot took a mug with the word *Tachi* printed on it from the coffee machine.

"Third time's the charm."

"Arright. Stand by."

The pilot took one long, lip-smacking sip from the mug, then, noticing Prax, nodded. Prax smiled uncomfortably.

"Feelin' better?" Alex asked.

"Yes. I think so," Prax said. "I don't know."

Alex sat at one of the tables. The design of the room was military—all soft edges and curves to minimize damage if someone was caught out of place by an impact or a sudden maneuver. The food inventory control had a biometric interface that had been disabled. Built for high security, but not used that way. The name ROCINANTE was on the wall in letters as broad as his hand, and someone had added a stencil of a spray of yellow narcissus. It looked desperately out of place and very appropriate at the same time. When he thought about it that way, it seemed to fit most things about the ship. Her crew, for instance.

"You settlin' in all right? You need anything?"

"I'm fine," Prax said with a nod. "Thank you."

"They beat us up pretty good gettin' out of there. I've been through some ugly patches of sky, but that was right up there."

Prax nodded and took a food packet from the dispenser. It was textured paste, sweet and rich with wheat and honey and the subterranean tang of baked raisins. Prax sat down before he thought about it, and the pilot seemed to take it as an invitation to continue the conversation.

"How long have you been on Ganymede?"

"Most of my life," Prax said. "My family went out when my mother was pregnant. They'd been working on Earth and Luna, saving up to get to the outer planets. They had a short posting on Callisto first."

"Belters?"

"Not exactly. They heard that the contracts were better out past the Belt. It was the whole 'make a better future for the family' idea. My father's dream, really."

Alex sipped at his coffee.

"And so, Praxidike. They named you after the moon?"

"They did," Prax said. "They were a little embarrassed to find out it was a woman's name. I never minded it, though. My wife—my ex-wife—thought it was endearing. It's probably why she noticed me in the first place, really. It takes something to stand out a little, and you can't swing a dead cat on Ganymede without hitting five botany PhDs. Or, well, you couldn't."

The pause was just long enough that Prax knew what was coming and could steel himself for it.

"I heard your daughter went missing," Alex said. "I'm sorry about that."

"She's probably dead," Prax said, just the way he'd practiced.

"It had to do with that lab y'all found down there, did it?"

"I think so. It must have. They took her just before the first incident. Her and several of the others in her group."

"Her group?"

"She has an immune disorder. Myers-Skelton Premature Immunosenescence. Always has had."

"My sister had a brittle bone disorder. Hard," Alex said. "Is that why they took her?"

"I assume so," Prax said. "Why else would you steal a child like that?"

"Slave labor or sex trade," Alex said softly. "But can't see why you'd pick out kids with a medical condition. It true you saw protomolecule down there?"

"Apparently," Prax said. The food bulb was cooling in his hand. He knew he should eat more—he wanted to, as good as it tasted—but something was turning at the back of his mind. He'd thought this all through before, when he'd been distracted and starving. Now, in this civilized coffin hurtling through the void, all the old familiar thoughts started to touch up against each other. They'd specifically targeted the children from Mei's group. Immunocompromised children. And they'd been working with the protomolecule.

"The captain was on Eros," Alex said.

"It must have been a loss for him when it happened," Prax said to have something to say.

"No, I don't mean he lived there. He was on the station when it happened. We all were, but he was on it the longest. He actually saw it starting. The initial infected. That."

"Really?"

"Changed him, some. I've been flyin' with him since we were just fartin' around on this old ice bucket running from Saturn to the Belt. He didn't used to like me, I suspect. Now we're family. It's been a hell of a trip."

Prax took a long pull from his food bulb. Cool, the paste tasted less of wheat and more of honey and raisin. It wasn't as good. He remembered the look of fear on Holden's face when they'd found the dark filaments, the sound of controlled panic in his voice. It made sense now.

And as if summoned by the thought, Holden appeared in the doorway, a formed aluminum case under his arm with electromagnetic plates along the base. A personal footlocker designed to stay put even under high g. Prax had seen them before, but he'd never needed one. Gravity had been a constant for him until now.

"Cap'n," Alex said with a vestigial salute. "Everything all right?"

"Just moving some things to my bunk," Holden said. The tightness in his voice was unmistakable. Prax had the sudden feeling that he was intruding on something private, but Alex and Holden didn't give any further sign. Holden only moved off down the hall. When he was out of earshot, Alex sighed.

"Trouble?" Prax asked.

"Yeah. Don't worry. It's not about you. This has been brewin' for a while now."

"I'm sorry," Prax said.

"Had to happen. Best to get it over with one way or the other," Alex said, but there was an unmistakable dread in his voice. Prax felt himself liking the man. The wall terminal chirped and then spoke in Amos' voice.

"What've you got now?"

Alex pulled the terminal close, the articulated arm bending and twisting on complicated joints, then tapped on it with the fingers of one hand while keeping hold of the coffee with the other. The terminal flickered, datasets converting to graphs and tables in real time.

"Ten percent," Alex said. "No. Twelve. We're moving up. What'd you find?"

"Cracked seal," Amos said. "And yeah, you're very fucking clever. What else we got?"

Alex tapped on the terminal and Holden reappeared from the hallway, now without his case.

"Port sensor array took a hit. Looks like we burned out a few of the leads," Alex said.

"All right," Amos said. "Let's get those bad boys swapped out."

"Or maybe we can do something that doesn't involve crawling on the outside of a ship under thrust," Holden said.

"I can get it done, Cap," Amos said. Even through the tinny wall speaker, he sounded affronted. Holden shook his head.

"One slip, and the exhaust cooks you down to component atoms. Let's leave that for the techs on Tycho. Alex, what else have we got?"

"Memory leak in the navigation system. Probably a fried network that grew back wrong," the pilot said. "The cargo bay's still in vacuum. The radio array's as dead as a hammer for no apparent reason. Hand terminals aren't talking. And one of the medical pods is throwing error codes, so don't get sick."

Holden went to the coffee machine, talking over his shoulder as he keyed in his preferences. His cup said *Tachi* too. Prax realized with a start that they all did. He wondered who or what a Tachi was.

"Does the cargo bay need EVA?"

"Don't know," Alex said. "Lemme take a look."

Holden took his coffee mug out of the machine with a little sigh and stroked the brushed metal plates like he was petting a cat. On impulse, Prax cleared his throat.

"Excuse me," he said. "Captain Holden? I was wondering, if the radio gets fixed or there's a tightbeam available, if maybe there was a way I could use some time on the communications array?"

"We're kind of trying to be quiet right now," Holden said. "What are you wanting to send?"

"I need to do some research," Prax said. "The data we got on Ganymede from when they took Mei. There are images of the woman who was with them. And if I can find what happened to Dr. Strickland...I've been on a security-locked system since the day she went missing. Even if it was just the public access databases and networks, it would be a place to start."

"And it's that or sit around and stew until we get to Tycho," Holden said. "All right. I'll ask Naomi to get you an access account for the *Roci*'s network. I don't know if there'll be anything in the OPA files, but you might as well check them too."

"Really?"

"Sure," Holden said. "They've got a pretty decent face-recognition database. It's inside their secure perimeter, so you might need to have one of us make the request."

"And that would be all right? I don't want to get you in trouble with the OPA."

Holden's smile was warm and cheerful.

"Really, don't worry about that," he said. "Alex, what've we got?"

"Looks like cargo door's not sealin', which we knew. We may

have taken a hit, blown a hole in her. We've got the video feed back up...hold on..."

Holden shifted to peer over Alex's shoulder. Prax took another swallow of his food and gave in to curiosity. An image of a cargo bay no wider than Prax's palm took up one corner of the display. Most of the cargo was on electromagnetic pallets, stuck to the plates nearest the wide bay door, but some had broken loose, pressed by thrust gravity to the floor. It gave the room an unreal, Escher-like appearance. Alex resized the image, zooming in on the cargo door. In one corner, a thick section of metal was bent inward, bright metal showing where the bend had cracked the external layers. A spray of stars showed through the hole.

"Well, at least it ain't subtle," Alex said.

"What hit it?" Holden said.

"Don't know, Cap," Alex said. "No scorching as far as I can see. But a gauss round wouldn't have bent the metal in like that. Just would have made a hole. And the bay isn't breached, so whatever did it didn't make a hole on the other side."

The pilot increased the magnification again, looking closely at the edges of the wound. It was true there were no scorch marks, but thin black smudges showed against the metal of the door and the deck. Prax frowned. He opened his mouth to speak, then closed it again.

Holden said what Prax had been thinking.

"Alex? Is that a handprint?"

"Looks like one, Cap, but..."

"Pull out. Look at the decking."

They were small. Subtle. Easy to overlook on the small image. But they were there. A handprint, smeared in something dark that Prax had the strong suspicion had once been red. The unmistakable print of five naked toes. A long smear of darkness.

The pilot followed the trail.

"That bay's in hard vacuum, right?" Holden asked.

"Has been for a day and a half, sir," Alex said. The casual air was gone. They were all business now.

"Track right," Holden said.

"Yes, sir."

"Okay, stop. What's that?"

The body was curled into a fetal ball, except where its palms were pressed against the bulkhead. It lay perfectly still, as if they were under high g and it was held against the deck, crushed by its own weight. The flesh was the black of anthracite and the red of blood. Prax couldn't tell if it had been a man or a woman.

"Alex, do we have a stowaway?"

"Pretty sure that ain't on the cargo manifest, sir."

"And did that fellow there bend his way through my ship with his bare hands?"

"Looks like maybe, sir."

"Amos? Naomi?"

"I'm looking at it too." Naomi's voice came from the terminal a moment before Amos' low whistle. Prax thought back to the mysterious sounds of violence in the lab, the bodies of guards they hadn't fought, the shattered glass and its black filament. Here was the experiment that had slipped its leash back at that lab. It had fled to the cold, dead surface of Ganymede and waited there until a chance came to escape. Prax felt the gooseflesh crawling up his arms.

"Okay," Holden said. "But it's dead, right?"

"I don't think so," Naomi said.

Chapter Twenty-Five: Bobbie

Bobbie's hand terminal began playing reveille at four thirty a.m. local time: what she and her mates might have grumbled and called "oh dark thirty" back when she'd been a marine and had mates to grumble with. She'd left her terminal in the living room, lying next to the pull-down cot she used as a bed, the volume set high enough to have left her ears ringing if she'd been in there with it. But Bobbie had already been up for an hour. In her cramped bathroom, the sound was only annoying, bouncing around her tiny apartment like radio in a deep well. The echoes were a sonic reminder that she still didn't have much furniture or any wall hangings.

It didn't matter. She'd never had a guest.

The reveille was a mean-spirited little joke Bobbie was playing on herself. The Martian military had formed hundreds of years after trumpets and drums had been a useful means of transmitting information to troops. Martians lacked the nostalgia the UN military had for such things. The first time Bobbie had heard a morning reveille, she'd been watching a video on military history. She'd been happy to realize that no matter how annoying the Martian equivalent—a series of atonal electronic blats—was, it would never be as annoying as what the Earth boys woke up to.

But now Bobbie wasn't a Martian Marine anymore.

"I am not a traitor," Bobbie said to her reflection in the mirror. Mirror Bobbie looked unconvinced.

After the blaring trumpet call's third repetition, her hand terminal beeped once and fell into a sullen silence. She'd been holding her toothbrush for the last half hour. The toothpaste had started to grow a hard skin. She ran it under warm water to soften it back up and started brushing her teeth.

"I'm not a traitor," she said to herself, the toothbrush making the words unintelligible. "Not."

Not even standing here in the bathroom of her UN-provided apartment, brushing her teeth with UN toothpaste and rinsing the sink with UN-provided water. Not while she clutched her good Martian toothbrush and scrubbed until her gums bled.

"Not," she said again, daring mirror Bobbie to disagree.

She put the toothbrush back into her small toiletry case, carried it into the living room, and placed it in her duffel. Everything she owned stayed in the duffel. She'd need to move fast when her people called her home. And they would. She'd get a priority dispatch on her terminal, the red-and-gray border of the MCRN CINC-COM flashing around it. They'd tell her that she needed to return to her unit immediately. That she was still one of them.

That she wasn't a traitor for staying.

She straightened her uniform, slid her now quiet terminal into her pocket, and checked her hair in the mirror next to the door. It was pulled into a bun so tight it almost gave her a face-lift, not one single hair out of place.

"I'm not a traitor," she said to the mirror. Front hallway mirror Bobbie seemed more open to this idea than bathroom mirror

Bobbie had. "Damn straight," she said, then slammed the door behind her when she left.

She hopped on one of the little electric bikes the UN campus made available everywhere, and was in the office three minutes before five a.m. Soren was already there. No matter what time she came in, Soren always beat her. Either he slept at his desk or he was spying on her to see what time she set her alarm for each morning.

"Bobbie," he said, his smile not even pretending to be genuine.

Bobbie couldn't bring herself to respond, so she just nodded and collapsed into her chair. One glance at the darkened windows in Avasarala's office told her the old lady wasn't in yet. Bobbie pulled up her to-do list on the desktop screen.

"She had me add a lot of people," Soren said, referring to the list of people Bobbie was supposed to call in her role as Martian military liaison. "She really wants to get a hold of an early draft of the Martian statement on Ganymede. That's your top priority for the day. Okay?"

"Why?" Bobbie said. "The actual statement came out yesterday. We both read it."

"Bobbie," Soren said with a sigh that said he was tired of explaining simple things to her, but a grin that said he really wasn't. "This is how the game is played. Mars releases a statement condemning our actions. We go back channel and find an early draft. If it was harsher than the actual statement that was released, then someone in the dip corps argued to tone it down. That means they're trying to avoid escalating. If it was milder in the early draft, then they're deliberately escalating to provoke a response."

"But since they know you'll get those early drafts, then that's meaningless. They'll just make sure you get leaks that give you the impression they want you to have."

"See? Now you're getting it," Soren said. "What your opponent wants *you* to think is useful data in figuring out what *they* think. So get the early draft, okay? Do it before the end of the day."

But no one talks to me anymore because now I'm the UN's pet Martian, and even though I'm not a traitor, it is entirely possible that everyone else thinks I am.

"Okay."

Bobbie pulled up the newly revised list and made the first connection request of the day.

"Bobbie!" Avasarala yelled from her desk. There was any number of electronic means for getting Bobbie's attention, but she almost never saw Avasarala use them. She yanked her earbud free and stood up. Soren's smirk was of the psychic variety; his face didn't change at all.

"Ma'am?" Bobbie said, taking a short step into Avasarala's office. "You bellowed?"

"No one likes a smart-ass," Avasarala said, not looking up from her desk terminal. "Where's my first draft of that report? It's almost lunchtime."

Bobbie stood a little straighter and clasped her arms behind her back.

"Sir, I regret to inform you that I have been unable to find anyone willing to release the early draft of the report to me."

"Are you standing at attention?" Avasarala said, looking up at her for the first time. "Jesus. I'm not about to march you out to the firing squad. Did you try everyone on the list?"

"Yes, I—" Bobbie stopped for a moment and took a deep breath, then took a few more steps into the office. Quietly she said, "No one talks to me."

The old woman lifted a snow-white eyebrow.

"That's interesting."

"It is?" Bobbie said.

Avasarala smiled at her, a warm, genuine smile, then poured tea out of a black iron pot into two small teacups.

"Sit down," she said, waving at a chair next to her desk. When Bobbie remained standing, Avasarala said, "Seriously, sit the fuck down. Five minutes talking to you and I can't tilt my head forward again for an hour."

Bobbie sat, hesitated, and took one of the small teacups. It wasn't much larger than a shot glass, and the tea inside it was very dark and smelled unpleasant. She took a small sip and burned her tongue.

"It's a Lapsang souchong," Avasarala said. "My husband buys it for me. What do you think?"

"I think it smells like hobo feet," Bobbie replied.

"No shit, but Arjun loves it and it's not bad once you get used to drinking it."

Bobbie nodded and took another sip but didn't reply.

"Okay, so," Avasarala said, "you're the Martian who was unhappy and got tempted over to the other side by a powerful old lady with lots of shiny prizes to offer. You're the worst kind of traitor, because ultimately everything that's happened to you since you came to Earth was because you were pouting."

"I—"

"Shut the fuck up now, dear, the grown-up is talking."

Bobbie shut up and drank her awful tea.

"But," Avasarala continued, the same sweet smile on her wrinkled face, "if I were on the other team, you know who I'd send misinformation leaks to?"

"Me," Bobbie said.

"You. Because you're desperate to prove your value to your new boss, and they can send you blatantly false information and not really care if they fuck your shit up in the long run. If I were the Martian counterespionage wonks, I'd have already recruited one of your closest friends back home and be using them to funnel a mountain's worth of false data your direction."

My closest friends are all dead, Bobbie thought.

"But no one—"

"Is talking to you from back home. Which means two things. They are still trying to figure out my game in keeping you here, and they don't have a misinformation campaign in place because they're as confused as we are. You'll be contacted by someone in the next week or so. They'll ask you to leak information from my office, but they'll ask it in such a way that winds up giving you a whole lot of false information. If you're loyal and spy for them, great. If not and you tell me what they asked for, also great. Maybe they'll get lucky and you'll do both."

Bobbie put the teacup back on the desk. Her hands were in fists.

"This," Bobbie said, "is why everyone hates politicians."

"No. They hate us because we have power. Bobbie, this isn't how your mind likes to work, and I respect that. I don't have time to explain things to you," Avasarala said, the smile disappearing like it had never been. "So just assume I know what I'm doing, and that when I ask you to do the impossible, it's because even your failure helps our cause somehow."

"*Our* cause?"

"We're on the same team here. Team Let's-Not-Lose-Together. That is us, isn't it?"

"Yes," Bobbie said, glancing at the Buddha in his shrine. He smiled at her serenely. *Just one of the team*, his round face seemed to say. "Yes it is."

"Then get the fuck back out there and start calling everyone all over again. This time take detailed notes on who refuses to help you and the exact words they use in their refusal. Okay?"

"Solid copy on that, ma'am."

"Good," Avasarala said, smiling gently again. "Get out of my office."

Familiarity might breed contempt, but Bobbie hadn't much liked Soren right from the start. Sitting next to him for several days had ratcheted up her dislike to a whole new level. When he wasn't ignoring her, he was condescending. He talked too loud on his phone, even when she was trying to carry on a conversation of her own. Sometimes he sat on her desk, talking to visitors. He wore too much cologne.

The worst thing was he ate cookies all day.

It was impressive, given his rail-thin build, and Bobbie was not generally the kind of person who cared at all about other people's dietary habits. But his preferred brand of cookie came out of the break room vending machine in a foil packet that crinkled every time he reached into it. At first, this had only been annoying. But after a couple of days of the Crinkle, Crunch, Chomp, and Smack Radio Theater, she'd had enough. She dropped her latest pointless connection and turned to stare at him. He ignored her and tapped on his desk terminal.

"Soren," she said, meaning to ask him to dump the damn cookies out on a plate or a napkin so she didn't have to hear that infuriating crinkle sound anymore. Before she could get more than his name out, he held up a finger to shush her and pointed at his earbud.

"No," he said, "not really a good—"

Bobbie wasn't sure if he was talking to her or someone on the phone, so she got up and moved over to his desk, sitting on the edge of it. He gave her a withering glare, but she just smiled and mouthed, "I'll wait." The edge of his desk creaked a little under her weight.

He turned his back to her.

"I understand," he said. "But this is not a good time to discuss— I see. I can probably— I see, yes. Foster won't— Yes. Yes, I understand. I'll be there."

He turned back around and tapped his desk, killing the connection.

"What?"

"I hate your cookies. The constant crinkle of the package is driving me insane."

"Cookies?" Soren said, a baffled expression on his face. Bobbie thought that it might be the first honest emotion she'd ever seen there.

"Yeah, can you put them on a—" Bobbie started, but before she could finish, Soren grabbed up the package and tossed them into the recycling bin next to his desk.

"Happy?"

"Well—"

"I don't have time for you right now, Sergeant."

"Okay," Bobbie said, and went back to her desk.

Soren kept fidgeting like he had more to say, so Bobbie didn't call the next person on her list. She waited for him to speak. Probably the cookie thing had been a mistake on her part. Really, it wasn't a big deal. If she weren't under so much pressure, it wasn't the sort of thing she'd probably even notice. When Soren finally spoke up, she'd apologize for being so pushy about it and then offer to buy him a new package. Instead of speaking, he stood up.

"Soren, I—" Bobbie started, but Soren ignored her and unlocked a drawer on his desk. He pulled out a small bit of black plastic. Probably because she'd just heard him say the name Foster, Bobbie recognized it as the memory stick Avasarala had given him a few days earlier. Foster was the data services guy, so she assumed he was finally getting around to taking care of that little task, which would at least get him away from the office for a few minutes.

Until he turned and headed for the elevators.

Bobbie had done a little gofer work running things back and forth to data services and knew that their office was on the same floor and in the opposite direction of the elevators.

"Huh."

She was tired. She was half sick with guilt and she wasn't even all that sure what she felt guilty about. She disliked the man anyway. The hunch that popped into her head was almost certainly a result of her own paranoia and addled image of the world.

She got up, following him.

"This is really stupid," she said to herself, smiling and nodding at a page who hurried by. She was over two meters tall on a planet of short people. She wasn't going to blend.

Soren climbed into an elevator. Bobbie stopped outside the doors and waited. Through the aluminum-and-ceramic doors, she heard him ask someone to press one. Going all the way to the street level, then. She hit the down button and took the next elevator to the bottom floor.

Of course, he wasn't in sight when she got there.

A giant Martian woman running around the lobby of the UN building would draw a little attention, so she scrapped that as a plan. A wave of uncertainty, failure, and despair lapped at the shoreline of her mind.

Forget that it was an office building. Forget that there were no armed enemy, no squad behind her. *Forget that, and look at the logic of the situation on the ground. Think tactically. Be smart.*

"I need to be smart," she said. A short woman in a red suit who had just come up and pressed the elevator call button overheard her and said, "What?"

"I need to be smart," Bobbie told her. "Can't go running off half-cocked." *Not even when doing something insane and stupid.*

"I...see," the woman said, then pushed the elevator call button again several times. Next to the elevator control panel was a courtesy terminal. *If you can't find the target, restrict the target's degrees of freedom. Make them come to you. Right.* Bobbie hit the button for the lobby reception desk. An automated system with an extremely realistic and sexually ambiguous voice asked how it could assist her.

"Please page Soren Cottwald to the lobby reception desk," Bobbie said. The computer on the other end of the line thanked her for using the UN automated courtesy system and dropped the connection.

Soren might not have his terminal on, or it could be set to ignore incoming pages. Or he might ignore this one all on his own. She found a couch with a sight line to the desk and shifted a ficus to provide her cover.

Two minutes later, Soren trotted up to the reception desk, his hair more windblown than usual. He must have already been all the way outside when he got the page. He began talking to one of the human receptionists. Bobbie moved across the lobby to a little coffee and snack kiosk and hid as best she could. After typing on her desk for a moment, the receptionist pointed at the terminal next to the elevators. Soren frowned and took a few steps toward it, then looked around nervously and headed toward the building entrance.

Bobbie followed.

Once Bobbie was outside, her height was both an advantage and a disadvantage. Being a head and a half taller than most everyone around her meant that she could afford to stay pretty far behind Soren as he hurried along the sidewalk. She could spot the top of his head from half a city block away. At the same time, if he looked behind him, he couldn't miss her face sticking up a good third of a meter out of the crowd.

But he didn't turn around. In fact, he appeared to be in something of a hurry, pushing his way through the knots of people on the busy sidewalks around the UN campus with obvious impatience. He didn't look around or pause by a good reflective surface or backtrack. He'd been nervous answering the page, and he was being pointedly, angrily not nervous now.

Whistling past the graveyard. Bobbie felt her muscles soften, her joints grow loose and easy, her hunch slip a centimeter closer to certainty.

After three blocks he turned and went into a bar.

Bobbie stopped a half block away and considered. The front of the bar, a place creatively named Pete's, was darkened glass. If you wanted to duck in somewhere and see if people were following you, it was the perfect place to go. Maybe he'd gotten smart.

Maybe he hadn't.

Bobbie walked over to the front door. Getting caught following him had no consequences. Soren already hated her. The most ethically suspect thing she was doing was cutting out early to pop into a neighborhood bar. Who was going to rat on her? Soren? The guy who cut out just as early and went to the same damn bar?

If he was in there and doing nothing more than grabbing an early beer, she'd just walk up to him, apologize for the cookie thing, and buy him his second round.

She pushed the door open and went inside.

It took her eyes a moment to adjust from the early-afternoon sunlight outside to the dimly lit bar. Once the glare had faded, she saw a long bamboo bar top manned by a human bartender, half a dozen booths with about as many patrons, and no Soren. The air smelled of beer and burnt popcorn. The patrons gave her one look and then carefully went back to their drinks and mumbled conversations.

Had Soren ducked out the back to ditch her? She didn't think he'd seen her, but she wasn't exactly trained for tailing people. She was about to ask the bartender if he'd seen a guy run through, and where that guy might have gone, when she noticed a sign at the back of the bar that said POOL TABLES with an arrow pointing left.

She walked to the back of the bar, turned left, and found a smaller, second room with four pool tables and two men. One of them was Soren.

They both looked up as she turned the corner.

"Hi," she said. Soren was smiling at her, but he was always smiling. Smiling, for him, was protective coloration. Camouflage. The other man was large, fit, and wearing an excessively casual outfit that tried too hard to look like it belonged in a seedy pool hall. It clashed with the man's military haircut and ramrod-straight posture. Bobbie had a feeling she'd seen his face before, but in a different setting. She tried to picture him with a uniform on.

"Bobbie," Soren said, giving his companion one quick glance and then looking away. "You play?" He picked up a pool cue that had been lying on one of the tables, and began chalking the tip. Bobbie didn't point out that there were no balls on any of the tables, and that a sign just behind Soren said RENTAL BALLS AVAILABLE ON REQUEST.

His companion said nothing but slid something into his pocket. Between his fingers Bobbie caught a glimpse of black plastic.

She smiled. She knew where she'd seen the second man before.

"No," she said to Soren. "It's not popular where I come from."

"Slate, I guess," he replied. His smile became a bit more genuine and a lot colder. He blew the chalk dust off the pool cue's tip and moved a step to the side, shifting toward her left. "Too heavy for the early colony ships."

"Makes sense," Bobbie said, moving back until the doorway protected her flanks.

"Is this a problem?" Soren's companion said, looking at Bobbie.

Before Soren could reply, Bobbie said, "You tell me. You were at that late-night meeting in Avasarala's office when Ganymede went to shit. Nguyen's staff, right? Lieutenant something or other."

"You're digging a hole, Bobbie," Soren said, the pool cue held lightly in his right hand.

"And," she continued, "I know Soren handed you something his boss had asked him to take to data services a couple days ago. I bet you don't work in data services, do you?"

Nguyen's flunky took a menacing step toward her, and Soren shifted to her left again.

Bobbie burst out laughing.

"Seriously," she said, looking at Soren. "Either stop jerking that pool cue off or take it somewhere private."

Soren looked down at the cue in his hand as though surprised to see it there, then dropped it.

"And you," Bobbie said to the flunky. "You trying to come through this door would literally be the high point of my month." Without moving her feet she shifted her weight forward and flexed her elbows slightly.

The flunky looked her in the eye for one long moment. She grinned back.

"Come on," she said. "I'm gonna get blue balls you keep teasing me like this."

The flunky put up his hands. Something halfway between a fighting stance and a gesture of surrender. Never taking his eyes off Bobbie, he turned his face slightly toward Soren and said, "This is your problem. Handle it." He backed up two slow steps, then turned and walked across the room and into a hallway Bobbie couldn't see from where she was standing. A second later, she heard a door slam.

"Shit," Bobbie said. "I bet I'd have scored more points with the old lady if I'd gotten that memory stick back."

Soren began to shuffle toward the back door. Bobbie crossed the space between them like a cat, grabbing the front of his shirt and pulling him up until their noses were almost touching. Her body felt alive and free for the first time in a long time.

"What are you going to do," he said through a forced smirk, "beat me up?"

"Naw," Bobbie replied, shifting to an exaggerated Mariner Valley drawl. "I'm gonna tell on you, boy."

Chapter Twenty-Six: Holden

Holden watched the monster quiver as it huddled against the cargo bay bulkhead. On the video monitor, it looked small and washed out and grainy. He concentrated on his breathing. *Long slow breath in, fill up the lungs all the way to the bottom. Long slow breath out. Pause. Repeat. Do not lose your shit in front of the crew.*

"Well," Alex said after a minute. "There's your problem."

He was trying to make a joke. *Had* made a joke. Normally, Holden would have laughed at his exaggerated drawl and comic obviousness. Alex could be very funny, in a dry, understated sort of way.

Right now, Holden had to clench his hands to stop from strangling the man.

Amos said, "I'm coming up," at the same moment Naomi said, "I'm coming down."

"Alex," Holden said, pretending a calm he didn't feel. "What's the status of the cargo bay airlock?"

Alex tapped twice on the terminal and said, "Airtight, Cap. Zero loss."

Which was good, because as frightened of the protomolecule as he was, Holden also knew that it wasn't magic. It had mass and it occupied space. If not even a molecule of oxygen could sneak out through the airlock seal, then he was pretty sure none of the virus could get in. But...

"Alex, crank up the O2," Holden said. "As rich as we can get it without blowing the ship up."

The protomolecule was anaerobic. If any of it did somehow get in, he wanted the environment as hostile as possible.

"And get up to the cockpit," he continued. "Seal yourself in. If the goo somehow gets loose on the ship, I need your finger on the reactor overrides."

Alex frowned and scratched his thin hair. "That seems a little extreme—"

Holden grabbed him by the upper arms, hard. Alex's eyes went wide and his hands came up in an automatic gesture of surrender. Beside him, the botanist blinked in confusion and alarm. This was not the best way to instill confidence. In other circumstances, Holden might have cared.

"Alex," Holden said, not able to stop himself from shaking even while clutching the pilot's arms. "Can I count on you to blow this ship into gas if that shit gets in here? Because if I can't, consider yourself relieved of duty and confined to quarters immediately."

Alex surprised him, not by reacting in anger, but by reaching up and putting his hands on Holden's forearms. Alex's face was serious, but his eyes were kind.

"Seal myself into the cockpit and prepare to scuttle the ship. Aye, aye, sir," he said. "What's the stand-down order?"

"Direct order from myself or Naomi," Holden replied with a hidden sigh of relief. He didn't have to say, *If that thing gets in here and kills us, you're better off going up with the ship.* He let go of Alex's arms and the pilot took one step back, his broad dark face wrinkled with concern. The panic that threatened to over-whelm Holden might get out of his control if he allowed anyone to feel sympathy for him, so he said, "Now, Alex. Do it now."

Alex nodded once, looked like he wanted to say something else, then spun on his heel and went to the crew ladder and up toward the cockpit. Naomi descended the same ladder a few moments later, and Amos came up from below a short time after that.

Naomi spoke first. "What's the plan?" They'd been intimate long enough for Holden to recognize the barely concealed fear in her voice.

Holden paused to take two more long breaths. "Amos and I will go see if we can't drive it out the cargo bay doors. Get them open for us."

"Done," she said, and headed up the ladder to ops.

Amos was watching him, a speculative look in his eyes.

"So, Cap, how do we 'drive it' out those doors?"

"Well," Holden replied. "I was thinking we shoot the shit out of it and then take a flamethrower to any pieces that fall off. So we better gear up."

Amos nodded. "Damn. I feel like I just took that shit off."

Holden was not claustrophobic.

No one who chose long-flight space travel as a career was. Even if a person could somehow con their way past the psychological profiles and simulation runs, one trip was usually enough to sepa-rate those who could handle long periods in confined spaces from those who went bugfuck and had to be sedated for the trip home.

As a junior lieutenant Holden had spent days in scout ships so small that you literally could not bend over to scratch your feet. He'd climbed around between the inner and outer hulls of war-ships. He'd once been confined to his crash couch for twenty-one days during a fast-burn trip from Luna to Saturn. He never had nightmares of being crushed or being buried alive.

For the first time in his decade and a half of nearly constant space travel, the ship he was on felt too small. Not just cramped, but terrifyingly constricted. He felt trapped, like an animal in a snare.

Less than twelve meters away from where he stood, someone infected with the protomolecule was sitting in his cargo bay. And there was nowhere he could go to get away from it.

Putting on his body armor didn't help this feeling of confinement.

The first thing that went on was what the grunts called the full-body condom. It was a thick black bodysuit, made of multiple layers of Kevlar, rubber, impact-reactive gel, and the sensor network that kept track of his injury and vitals status. Over that went the slightly looser environment suit, with its own layers of self-sealing gel to instantly repair tears or bullet holes. And finally, the various pieces of strap-on armor plating that could deflect a high-velocity rifle shot or ablate the outer layers to shed the energy of a laser.

To Holden, it felt like wrapping himself in his own death shroud.

But even with all its layers and weight, it still wasn't as frightening as the powered armor that recon Marines wore would have been. What the Navy boys called walking coffins. The idea behind the name being that anything powerful enough to break the armor would liquefy the marine inside, so you didn't bother to open it. You just tossed the whole thing into the grave. This was hyperbole, of course, but the idea of going into that cargo bay wearing something that he wouldn't even be able to move without the power-enhanced strength would have scared the shit out of him. What if the batteries died?

Of course, a nice suit of strength-augmenting armor might be handy when trying to throw monsters off the ship.

"That's on backward," Amos said, pointing at Holden's thigh.

"Shit," Holden said. Amos was right. He'd been so far up his own ass that he'd screwed up the buckles on his thigh armor. "Sorry, I'm having a hard time staying focused here."

"Scared shitless," Amos said with a nod.

"Well, I wouldn't say—"

"Wasn't talking about you," Amos said. "Me. I'm scared shitless of walking into the cargo bay with that thing in there. And I didn't watch Eros turn into goo at close range. So I get it. Right there with you, Jim."

It was the first time in Holden's memory that Amos had called him by his first name. Holden nodded back at him, then went about straightening out his thigh armor.

"Yeah," he said. "I just yelled at Alex for not being scared enough."

Amos had finished with his armor and was pulling his favorite auto-shotgun out of his locker.

"No shit?"

"Yeah. He made a joke and I'm scared out of my skull, so I yelled at him and threatened to relieve him."

"Can you do that?" Amos asked. "He's kind of our only pilot."

"No, Amos. No, I can't kick Alex off the ship any more than I can kick you or Naomi off the ship. We're not even a skeleton crew. We're whatever you have when you don't have a skeleton."

"Worried about Naomi leaving?" Amos said. He kept his voice light, but his words hit like hammer blows. Holden felt the air go out of him, and had to focus on breathing again for a minute.

"No," he said. "I mean, yes, of course I am. But that's not what has me freaked out right now."

Holden picked up his assault rifle and looked at it, then put it back in his locker and took out a heavy recoilless pistol instead. The self-contained rockets that were its ammunition wouldn't impart thrust and send him flying all over the place if he fired it in zero g.

"I watched you die," he said, not looking at Amos.

"Huh?"

"I watched you die. When that kidnap team, whoever the hell *they* were, took us. I saw one of them shoot you in the back of the head, and I saw you drop face-first on the floor. There was blood everywhere."

"Yeah, but I—"

"I know it was a nonlethal round. I know they wanted us alive. I know the blood was your broken nose when your head slammed into the floor. I know all of that *now*. At the time, what I knew was that you'd just been shot in the head and killed."

Amos slid a magazine into his shotgun and racked a round but, other than that, didn't make a sound.

"All of this is really fragile," Holden said, waving around at Amos and the ship. "This little family we have. One fuckup, and something irreplaceable gets lost."

Amos was frowning at him now. "This is still about Naomi, right?"

"No! I mean, yes. But no. When I thought you were dead, it knocked all the wind out of me. And right now, I need to focus on getting that thing off the ship, and all I can think about is losing one of the crew."

Amos nodded, slung the shotgun over his shoulder, and sat down on the bench next to his locker.

"I get it. So what do you want to do?"

"I want," Holden said, sliding a magazine into his pistol, "to get that fucking monster off my ship. But please promise me you won't die doing it. That would help a lot."

"Cap," Amos said with a grin. "Anything that kills me has already killed everyone else. I was born to be the last man standing. You can count on it."

The panic and fear didn't leave Holden. They squatted on his chest now just the way they had before. But at least he didn't feel so alone with them.

"Then let's go get rid of this stowaway."

The wait inside the cargo bay airlock was endless as the inner door sealed, the pumps sucked all the air out of the room, and then the outer door cycled open. Holden fidgeted and rechecked his gun half a dozen times while he waited. Amos stood in a relaxed slump, his huge shotgun cradled loosely in his arms. The upside, if there was an upside to the wait, was that with the cargo bay in vacuum, the airlock could make as much noise as it wanted without alerting the creature to their presence.

The last of the external noise disappeared, and Holden could hear only himself breathing. A yellow light came on near the outer airlock door, warning them of the null atmosphere on the other side.

"Alex," Holden said, plugging a hardline into the airlock terminal. Radio was still dead all over the ship. "We're about to go in. Kill the engines."

"Roger that," Alex replied, and the gravity dropped away. Holden kicked the slide controls on his heels to turn up his magnetic boots.

The cargo bay on the *Rocinante* was cramped. Tall and narrow, it occupied the starboard side of the ship, crammed into the unused space between the outer hull and the engineering bay. On the port side, the same space was filled with the ship's water tank. The *Roci* was a warship. Any cargo it carried would be an afterthought.

The downside to this was that while under thrust, the cargo bay turned into a well with the cargo doors at the bottom. The various crates that occupied the space latched on to mounts on the bulkheads or in some cases were attached with electromagnetic feet. With thrust gravity threatening to send a person tumbling seven meters straight down to the cargo doors, it would be an impossible place to fight effectively.

In microgravity, it became a long hallway with lots of cover.

Holden entered the room first, walking along the bulkhead on magnetic boots, and took cover behind a large metal crate filled with extra rounds for the ship's point defense cannons. Alex followed, taking up a position behind another crate two meters away.

Below them, the monster seemed to be asleep.

It huddled motionless against the bulkhead that separated the cargo bay from engineering.

"Okay, Naomi, go ahead and open it up," Holden said. He jiggled the trailing line of cable to get it unhooked from a corner of the crate and gave it a little slack.

"Doors opening now," she replied, her voice thin and fuzzy in his helmet. The cargo doors at the bottom of the room silently swung open, exposing several square meters of star-filled blackness. The monster either didn't notice the doors opening or didn't care.

"They hibernate sometimes, right?" Amos said, the cable running from his suit to the airlock looking like a high-tech umbilical cord. "Like Julie did when she got the bug. Hibernated in that hotel room on Eros for a couple weeks."

"Maybe," Holden replied. "How do you want to approach this? I'm almost thinking we should just go down there, grab the thing, and toss it out the door. But I have strong reservations about touching it."

"Yeah, wouldn't want to take our suits back inside with us," Amos agreed.

Holden had a sudden memory of coming in after playing outside, and taking all his clothes off in the mudroom before Mother Tamara would let him into the rest of the house. This would be pretty much the same, only a lot colder.

"I find myself wishing we had a really long stick," Holden said, looking around at the various objects stored in the cargo bay, hoping to find one that suited his need.

"Uh, Cap'n?" Amos said. "It's looking at us."

Holden turned back around and saw Amos was right. The creature hadn't moved anything but its head, but it was definitely staring up at them now, its eyes a creepy illuminated-from-within blue.

"Well, okay," Holden said. "It's not hibernating."

"You know, if I can knock it off that bulkhead with a shot or two, and Alex kicks on the engine, it might just tumble right out the back door and into the exhaust plume. That oughta take care of it."

"Let's think about—" Holden said, but before he could finish his thought, the room strobed several times with the muzzle flash of Amos' shotgun. The monster was hit multiple times and knocked into a spinning lump floating toward the door.

"Alex, just—" Amos said.

The monster blurred into action. It flung one arm toward the bulkhead, the limb actually seeming to get longer to reach it, and yanked down hard enough to bend the steel plates. The creature hurtled up to the top of the cargo bay so fast that when it hit the crate Holden was hiding behind, the magnetic feet lost their seal. The cargo bay seemed to spin as the impact threw Holden back. The crate, just behind him, matched his velocity. Holden slammed against the bulkhead a split second before the crate did, and the magnetic pallet snapped onto the new wall, trapping Holden's leg beneath it.

Something in his knee bent badly, and the pain turned the world red for a moment.

Amos began firing his gun into the monster at close range, but it casually backhanded him and threw him into the cargo airlock hard enough to bend the inner door. The outer door slammed shut the second the inner door was compromised. Holden tried to move but his leg was pinned by the crate, and with electromagnets rated to hold a quarter ton of weight under a ten-g burn, he wouldn't be moving it anytime soon. The crate controls that would shut the magnets off showed the orange glow of a full seal ten centimeters beyond his reach.

The monster turned back to look at him. Its blue eyes were far too large for its head, giving the creature a curious, childlike look. It reached out one oversized hand.

Holden fired into it until his gun was empty.

The miniature, self-contained rockets the recoilless gun used as ammunition exploded in tiny puffs of light and smoke as they hit the creature, each one pushing it farther back and tearing large chunks of its torso away. Black filaments sprayed out and across the room like a line drawing representation of blood splatter.

When the last rocket hit, the monster was blown off the bulkhead and thrown down the cargo bay toward the open doors.

The black-and-red body tumbled toward the vast swatch of stars and darkness, and Holden let himself hope. Less than a meter from the doors, it reached out one long arm and caught the edge of a crate. Holden had seen what kind of strength was in those hands, and knew it wouldn't lose its grip.

"Captain," Amos was yelling in his ear. "Holden, are you still with us?"

"Here, Amos. In a little trouble."

As he spoke, the monster pulled itself up onto the crate it had caught and sat motionless. A hideous gargoyle turned suddenly to stone.

"Gonna hit the override and get you," Amos said. "The inner door is fucked, so we'll lose some atmo, but not too much—"

"Okay, but do it soon," Holden said. "I'm pinned. I need you to cut the mags on this crate."

A moment later, the airlock door opened in a puff of atmosphere. Amos started to step out into the bay when the monster jumped off the crate it was sitting on, grabbed the heavy plastic container with one hand and the bulkhead with the other, and threw the container at him. It slammed into the bulkhead hard enough that Holden felt the vibration through his suit. It missed taking Amos' head off by centimeters. The big mechanic fell back with a curse and the airlock doors shot closed again.

"Sorry," Amos said. "Panicked. Let me get this open—"

"No!" Holden yelled. "Stop opening the damn door. I'm trapped behind two goddamn crates now. And one of these times, the door is going to cut my cable. I really don't want to be stuck in here without a radio."

With the airlock closed, the monster moved back over to the bulkhead next to the engine room and curled up into a ball again. The tissue in the gaping wounds caused by Holden's gun pulsed wetly.

"I can see it, Cap," Alex said. "If I stomp on the gas, I think I can knock it right out those doors."

"No," Naomi and Amos said at almost the same time.

"No," Naomi repeated. "Look where Holden is under those crates. If we go high g, it'll break every bone in his body, even if he somehow isn't thrown out the door too."

"Yeah, she's right," Amos said. "That plan'll kill the captain. It's off the table."

Holden listened for a few moments to his crew argue about how to keep him alive, and watched the creature snuggle itself up the bulkhead and seem to go back to sleep.

"Well," Holden said, breaking into their discussion. "A high-g burn would almost certainly break me into tiny pieces right now. But that doesn't necessarily take it off the table."

The new words that came over the channel seemed like a thing from another world. Holden didn't even recognize the botanist's voice at first.

"Well," Prax said. "That's interesting."

Chapter Twenty-Seven: Prax

When Eros died, everyone watched. The station had been designed as a scientific data extraction engine, and every change, death, and metamorphosis had been captured, recorded, and streamed out to the system. What the governments of Mars and Earth had tried to suppress had leaked out in the weeks and months that followed. How people viewed it had more to do with who they were than the actual footage. To some people, it had been news. For others, evidence. For more than Prax liked to think, it had been an entertainment of terrible decadence—a Busby Berkeley snuff flick.

Prax had watched it too, as had everyone on his team. For him, it had been a puzzle. The drive to apply the logic of conventional biology to the effects of the protomolecule had been overwhelming and, for the most part, fruitless. Individual pieces were tantalizing—the spiral curves so similar to nautilus shell, the heat signature of the infected bodies shifting in patterns that almost matched certain hemorrhagic fevers. But nothing had come together.

Certainly someone, somewhere, was getting the grant money to study what had happened, but Prax's work wouldn't wait for him. He'd turned back to his soybeans. Life had gone on. It hadn't been an obsession, just a well-known conundrum that someone else was going to have to solve.

Prax hung weightless at an unused station in ops and watched the security camera feed. The creature reached out for Captain Holden, and Holden shot it and shot it and shot it. Prax watched the filamentous discharge from the creature's back. That was familiar, certainly. It had been one of the hallmarks of the Eros footage.

The monster began to tumble. Morphologically, it wasn't very far off from human. One head, two arms, two legs. No autonomous structures, no hands or rib cages repurposed to some other function.

Naomi, at the controls, gasped. It was odd, hearing it only through the actual air they shared and not through the comm channel. It seemed intimate in a way that left him a little uncomfortable, but there was something more important. His mind had a fuzzy feeling, like his head was full of cotton ticking. He recognized the sensation. He was thinking something that he wasn't yet aware of.

"I'm pinned," Holden said. "I need you to cut the mags on this crate."

The creature was at the far end of the cargo bay. As Amos went in, it braced itself with one hand, throwing a large crate with the other. Even in the poor-quality feed, Prax could see its massive trapezius and deltoids, the muscles enlarged to a freakish degree. And yet not particularly relocated. So the protomolecule was working under constraints. Whatever the creature was, it wasn't doing what the Eros samples had done. The thing in the cargo bay was unquestionably the same technology, but harnessed for some different application. The cotton ticking shifted.

"No! Stop opening the damn door. I'm trapped behind two goddamn crates now."

The creature moved back to the bulkhead, near where it had first been at rest. It huddled there, the wounds in its body pulsing visibly. But it hadn't *settled* there. With the engines off-line, there wasn't even a trace of gravity to pull it back in place. If it was comfortable there, there had to be a reason.

"No!" Naomi said. Her hands were on the support rings by the controls. Her face had an ashy color. "No. Look where Holden is under those crates. If we go high g, it'll break every bone in his body, even if he somehow isn't thrown out the door too."

"Yeah, she's right," Amos said. He sounded tired. Maybe that was how he expressed sorrow. "That plan'll kill the captain. It's off the table."

"Well. A high-g burn would almost certainly break me into tiny pieces right now. But that doesn't necessarily take it off the table."

On the bulkhead, the creature moved. It wasn't much, but it was there. Prax zoomed in on it as best he could. One massive clawed hand—clawed but still with four fingers and a thumb—braced it, and the other tore at the bulkhead. The first layer was fabric and insulation and it came off in rubbery strips. Once it was gone, the creature attacked the armored steel underneath. Tiny curls of metal floated in the vacuum beside it, catching the light like little stars. Now why was it doing that? If it was trying to do structural damage, there was any number of better ways. Or maybe it was trying to tunnel through the bulkhead, trying to reach something, following some signal...

The cotton ticking disappeared, resolving into the image of a pale, new root springing from a seed. He felt himself smile. *Well, that's interesting.*

"What is, Doc?" Amos asked. Prax realized he must have spoken aloud.

"Um," Prax said, trying to gather the words that would explain what he'd seen. "It's trying to move up a radiation gradient. I mean…the version of the protomolecule that was loose on Eros fed off radiation energy, and so I guess it makes sense that this one would too—"

"This one?" Alex asked. "What one?"

"This version. I mean, this one's obviously been engineered to repress most of the changes. It's hardly changed the host body at all. There have to be novel constraints on it, but it still seems to need a source of radiation."

"Why, Doc?" Amos asked. He was trying to be patient. "Why do we think it needs radiation?"

"Oh," Prax said. "Because we shut down the drive, and so the reactor is running at maintenance level, and now it's trying to dig through to the core."

There was a pause, and then Alex said something obscene.

"Okay," Holden said. "There's no choice. Alex, you need to get that thing out of here before it gets through the bulkhead. We don't have time to build a new plan."

"Captain," Alex said. "Jim—"

"I'll be in one second after it's gone," Amos said. "If you aren't there, it's been an honor serving with you, Cap."

Prax waved his hands, as if the gesture could get their attention. The movement sent him looping slowly through the operations deck.

"Wait. No. That *is* the new plan," he said. "It's moving up a radiation gradient. It's like a root heading toward water."

Naomi had turned to look at him as he spun. She seemed to spin, and Prax's brain reset to feeling that she was below him, spiraling away. He closed his eyes.

"You're going to have to walk us through this," Holden said. "Quickly. How can we control it?"

"Change the gradient," Prax said. "How long would it take to put together a container with some unshielded radioisotopes?"

"Depends, Doc," Amos said. "How much do we need?"

"Just more than is leaking through from the reactor right now," Prax said.

"Bait," Naomi said, catching hold of him and pulling him to a handhold. "You want to make something that looks like better food and lure that thing out the door with it."

"I just said that. Didn't I just say that?" Prax asked.

"Not exactly, no," Naomi said.

On the screen, the creature was slowly building a cloud of metal shavings. Prax wasn't sure, because the resolution of the image wasn't actually all that good, but it seemed like its hand might be changing shape as it dug. He wondered how much the constraints placed on the protomolecule's expression took damage and healing into account. Regenerative processes were a great opportunity for constraining systems to fail. Cancer was just cell replication gone mad. If it was starting to change, it might not stop.

"Regardless," Prax said, "I think we should probably hurry."

The plan was simple enough. Amos would reenter the cargo bay and free the captain as soon as the bay doors had shut behind the intruder. Naomi, in ops, would trigger the doors to close the moment the creature had gone after the radioactive bait. Alex would fire the engines as soon as doing so wouldn't kill the captain. And the bait—a half-kilo cylinder with a thin case of lead foil to keep it from attracting the beast too early—would be walked out through the main airlock and tossed into the vacuum by the only remaining crewman.

Prax floated in the airlock, bait trap in the thick glove of the environment suit. Regrets and uncertainty flooded through his mind.

"Maybe it would be better if Amos did this part," Prax said. "I've never actually done any extravehicular anything before."

"Sorry, Doc. I've got a ninety-kilo captain to haul," Amos said.

"Couldn't we automate this? A lab waldo could—"

"Prax," Naomi said, and the gentleness of the syllable carried the weight of a thousand *get-your-ass-out-theres*. Prax checked the seals on his suit one more time. Everything reported good. The suit was much better than the one he'd worn leaving Ganymede. It was twenty-five meters from the personnel airlock near the front of the ship to the cargo bay doors at the extreme aft. He wouldn't even have to go all the way there. He tested the radio tether to make sure it was clipped tightly into the airlock's plug.

That was another interesting question. Was the radio-jamming effect a natural output of the monster? Prax tried to imagine how such a thing could be generated biologically. Would the effect end when the monster left the ship? When it was burned up by the exhaust?

"Prax," Naomi said. "Now is good."

"All right," he said. "I'm going out."

The outer airlock door cycled open. His first impulse was to push out into the darkness the way he would into a large room. His second was to crawl on his hands and knees, keeping as much of his body against the skin of the ship as humanly possible. Prax took the bait in one hand and used the toe rings to lift himself up and out.

The darkness around him was overwhelming. The *Rocinante* was a raft of metal and paint on an ocean. More than an ocean. The stars wrapped around him in all directions, the nearest ones hundreds of lifetimes away, and then more past those and more past those. The sense of being on a tiny little asteroid or moon looking up at a too-wide sky flipped and he was at the top of the universe, looking down into an abyss without end. It was like a visual illusion flipping between a vase and then two faces, then back again at the speed of perception. Prax grinned up, spreading his arms into the nothingness even as the first taste of nausea crawled up the back of his tongue. He'd read accounts of extravehicular euphoria, but the experience was unlike anything he'd imagined. He was the eye of God, drinking in the light of infinite stars, and he was a speck of dust on a speck of dust, clipped by his mag boots to the body of a ship unthinkably more powerful than himself, and unimportant before the face of the abyss. His suit's speakers crackled with background radiation from the birth of the universe, and eerie voices whispered in the static.

"Uh, Doc?" Amos said. "There a problem out there?"

Prax looked around, expecting to see the mechanic beside him. The milk-white universe of stars was all that met him. With so many, it seemed like they should sum to brightness. Instead, the *Rocinante* was dark except for the EVA lights and, toward the rear of the ship, a barely visible white nebula where atmosphere had blown out from the cargo bay.

"No," Prax said. "No problems."

He tried to take a step forward, but his suit didn't budge. He pulled, straining to lift his foot from the plating. His toe moved forward a centimeter and stopped. Panic flared in his chest. Something was wrong with the mag boots. At this rate, he'd never make it to the cargo bay door before the creature dug through and into engineering and the reactor itself.

"Um. I have a problem," he said. "I can't move my feet."

"What are the slide controls set to?" Naomi asked.

"Oh, right," Prax said, moving the boot settings down to match his strength. "I'm fine. Never mind."

He'd never actually walked with mag boots before, and it was a strange sensation. For most of the stride, his leg felt free and almost uncontrolled, and then, as he brought his foot toward the hull, there would be a moment, a critical point, when the force took hold and slammed him to the metal. He made his way floating and being snatched down, step by step. He couldn't see the cargo bay doors, but he knew where they were. From his position looking aft, they were to the left of the drive cone. But on the right side of the ship. *No, starboard side. They call it starboard on ships.*

He knew that just past the dark metal lip that marked the edge of the ship, the creature was digging at the walls, clawing through the flesh of the ship toward its heart. If it figured out what was going on—if it had the cognitive capacity for even basic reasoning—it could come boiling up out of the bay at him.

Vacuum didn't kill it. Prax imagined himself trying to clomp away on his awkward magnetic boots while the creature cut him apart; then he took a long, shuddering breath and lifted the bait.

"Okay," he said. "I'm in position."

"No time like the present," Holden said, his voice strained with pain but attempting to be light.

"Right," Prax said.

He pressed the small timer, hunched close to the hull of the ship, and then, with every muscle in his body, uncurled and flung the little cylinder into nothing. It flew out, catching the light from the cargo bay interior and then vanishing. Prax had the nauseating certainty that he'd forgotten a step, and that the lead foil wouldn't come off the way it was supposed to.

"It's moving," Holden said. "It smelled it. It's going out."

And there it was, long black fingers folding up from the ship, the dark body pulling itself up to the ship's exterior like it had been born to the abyss. Its eyes glowed blue. Prax heard nothing but his own panicked breathing. Like an animal in the ancient grasslands of Earth, he had the primal urge to be still and silent, though through the vacuum, the creature wouldn't have heard him if he'd shrieked.

The creature shifted; the eerie eyes closed, opened again, closed; and then it leapt. The un-twinkling stars were eclipsed by its passage.

"Clear," Prax said, shocked by the firmness of his voice. "It's clear of the ship. Close the cargo doors now."

"Check," Naomi said. "Closing doors."

"I'm coming in, Cap'n," Amos said.

"I'm passing out, Amos," Holden said, but there was enough laughter in the words that Prax was pretty sure he was joking.

In the darkness, a star blinked out and then came back. Then another. Prax mentally traced the path. Another star eclipsed.

"I'm heating her back up," Alex said. "Let me know when you're all secure, right?"

Prax watched, waited. The star stayed solid. Shouldn't it have gone dark like the others? Had he misjudged? Or was the creature looping around? If it could maneuver in raw vacuum, could it have noticed Alex bringing the reactor back online?

Prax turned back toward the main airlock.

The *Rocinante* had seemed like nothing—a toothpick floating on an ocean of stars. Now the distance back to the airlock was immense. Prax moved one foot, then the other, trying to run without ever having both feet off the deck. The mag boots wouldn't let him release them both at the same time, the trailing foot trapped until the lead one signaled it was solid. His back itched, and he fought the urge to look behind. Nothing was there, and if something was, looking wouldn't help. The cable of his radio link turned from a line into a loop that trailed behind him as he moved. He pulled on it to take up the slack.

The tiny green-and-yellow glow of the open airlock called to him like something from a dream. He heard himself whimpering a little, but the sound was lost in a string of profanity from Holden.

"What's going on down there?" Naomi snapped.

"Captain's feeling a little under the weather," Amos said. "Think he maybe wrenched something."

"My knee feels like someone gave birth in it," Holden said. "I'll be fine."

"Are we clear for burn?" Alex asked.

"We are not," Naomi said. "Cargo doors are as closed as they're going to get until we hit the docks, but the forward airlock isn't sealed."

"I'm almost in," Prax said, thinking, *Don't leave me here. Don't leave me in the pit with that thing.*

"Right, then," Alex said. "Let me know when I can get us the hell out of here."

In the depth of the ship, Amos made a small sound. Prax reached the airlock, pulling himself in with a violence that made the joints of his suit creak. He yanked on his umbilical to pull it the rest of the way in after him. He flung himself against the far wall, slapping at the controls until the cycle started and the outer door slid closed. In the dim light of the airlock proper, Prax spun slowly on all three axes. The outer door remained closed. Nothing ripped it open; no glowing blue eyes appeared to crawl in after him. He bumped gently against the wall as the distant sound of an air pump announced the presence of atmosphere.

"I'm in," he said. "I'm in the airlock."

"Is the captain stable?" Naomi asked.

"Was he ever?" Amos replied.

"I'm fine. My knee hurts. Get us out of here."

"Amos?" Naomi said. "I'm seeing you're still in the cargo bay. Is there a problem?"

"Might be," Amos said. "Our guy left something behind."

"Don't touch it!" Holden's voice was harsh as a bark. "We'll get a torch and burn it down to its component atoms."

"Don't think that'd be a good idea," Amos said. "I've seen these before, and they don't take well to cutting torches."

Prax levered himself up to standing, adjusting the slides on his boots to keep him lightly attached to the airlock floor. The inner airlock door chimed that it was safe to remove his suit and reenter the ship. He ignored it and activated one of the wall panels. He switched to a view of the cargo bay. Holden was floating near the cargo airlock. Amos was hanging on to a wall-mounted ladder and examining something small and shiny stuck to the bulkhead.

"What is it, Amos?" Naomi asked.

"Well, I'd have to clean some of this yuck off it," Amos said. "But it looks like a pretty standard incendiary charge. Not a big one, but enough to vaporize about two square meters."

There was a moment of silence. Prax released the seal on his helmet, lifted it off, and took a deep breath of the ship's air. He switched to an outside camera. The monster was drifting behind the ship, suddenly visible again in the faint light coming out of the cargo bay, and slowly receding from view. It was wrapped around his radioactive bait.

"A bomb," Holden said. "You're telling me that thing left a *bomb*?"

"And pretty damn peculiar too. If you ask me," Amos replied.

"Amos, come with me into the cargo airlock," Holden said. "Alex, what's left to do before we burn that monster up? Is Prax back inside?"

"You guys in the 'lock?" Alex said.

"We are now. Do it."

"Don't need to say it twice," Alex said. "Brace for acceleration."

The biochemical cascade that came from euphoria and panic and the reassurance of safety slowed Prax's response time so that when the burn began, he didn't quite have his legs under him. He stumbled against the wall, knocking his head against the inner door of the airlock. He didn't care. He felt wonderful. He'd gotten the monster off the ship. It was burning up in the *Rocinante*'s fiery tail even as he watched.

Then an angry god kicked the side of the ship and sent it spinning across the void. Prax was ripped from his feet, the gentle magnetic tug of his boots not enough to stop it. The outer airlock door rushed at him, and the world went black.

Chapter Twenty-Eight: Avasarala

There was another spike. A third one. Only this time, there didn't seem to be any chance of Bobbie's monsters being involved. So maybe...maybe it was coincidence. Which opened the question. If the thing hadn't come from Venus, then where?

The world, however, had conspired to distract her.

"She's not what we thought she was, ma'am," Soren said. "I fell for the little lost Martian thing too. She's good."

Avasarala leaned back in her chair. The intelligence report on her screen showed the woman she'd called Roberta Draper in civilian clothes. If anything, they made her look bigger. The name listed was Amanda Telelé. Free operative of the Martian Intelligence Service.

"I'm still looking into it," Soren said. "It looks like there really was a Roberta Draper, but she died on Ganymede with the other marines."

Avasarala waved the words away and scrolled through the report. Records of back-channel steganographic messages between the alleged Bobbie and a known Martian operative on Luna beginning the day that Avasarala had recruited her. Avasarala waited for the fear to squeeze her chest, the sense of betrayal. They didn't come. She kept turning to new parts of the report, taking in new information and waiting for her body to react. It kept not happening.

"We looked into this why?" she asked.

"It was a hunch," Soren said. "It was just the way she carried herself when she wasn't around you. She was a little too...slick, I guess. She just didn't seem right. So I took the initiative. I said it was from you."

"So that I wouldn't look like such a fucking idiot for inviting a mole into my office?"

"Seemed like the polite thing to do," Soren said. "If you're looking for ways to reward my good service, I do accept bonuses and promotion."

"I fucking bet you do," Avasarala said.

He waited, leaning a little forward on his toes. Waiting for her to give the order to have Bobbie arrested and submitted for a full intelligence debriefing. As euphemisms went, "full intelligence debriefing" was among the most obscene, but they were at war with Mars, and a high-value intelligence agent planted in the heart of the UN would know things that were invaluable.

So, Avasarala thought, *why am I not reacting to this?*

She reached out to the screen, paused, pulled back her hand, frowning.

"Ma'am?" Soren said.

It was the smallest thing, and the least expected. Soren bit at the inside of his bottom lip. It was a tiny movement, almost invisible. Like a tell at a poker table. And as she saw it, Avasarala knew.

There was no thinking it out, no reasoning, no struggle or second-guessing. It was all simply there, clear in her mind as if she had always known it, complete and perfect. Soren was nervous because the report she was looking at wouldn't hold up to rigorous scrutiny.

It wouldn't hold up because it was a fake.

It was a fake because Soren was working for someone else, someone who wanted to control the information getting to Avasarala's desk. Nguyen had re-created his little fleet without her knowing it because Soren was the one watching the data traffic. Someone had known that she would need controlling. Handling. This was something that had been prepared for since well before Ganymede had gone pear-shaped. The monster on Ganymede had been anticipated.

And so it was Errinwright.

He had let her demand her peace negotiations, let her think she'd undermined Nguyen, let her take Bobbie onto her staff. All of it, so that she wouldn't get suspicious.

This wasn't a shard of Venus that had escaped; it was a military project. A weapon that Earth wanted in order to break its rivals before the alien project on Venus finished whatever it was doing. Someone—probably Mao-Kwikowski—had retained a sample of the protomolecule in some separate and firewalled lab, weaponized it, and opened bidding.

The attack on Ganymede had been on one hand a proof of concept assault, on the other a crippling blow to the outer planets' food supply. The OPA had never been on the list of bidders. And then Nguyen had gone to the Jovian system to collect the goods, James Holden and his pet botanist had walked in on some part of it, and Mars had figured out they were about to lose the trade.

Avasarala wondered how much Errinwright had given Jules-Pierre Mao to outbid Mars. It would have had to be more than just money.

Earth was about to get its first protomolecule weapon, and Errinwright had kept her out of the loop because whatever he was going to do with it, she wasn't going to like it. And she was one of the only people in the solar system who might have been able to stop him.

She wondered whether she still was.

"Thank you, Soren," she said. "I appreciate this. Do we know where she is?"

"She's looking for you," Soren said, and a sly smile tugged at his lips. "She may be under the impression that you're asleep. It is pretty late."

"Sleep? Yes, I remember that vaguely," Avasarala said. "All right. I'm going to need to talk to Errinwright."

"Do you want me to have her arrested?"

"No, I don't."

The disappointment barely showed.

"How *should* we move forward?" Soren asked.

"I'll talk to Errinwright," she said. "Can you get me some tea?"

"Yes, ma'am," he said, and practically bowed his way out of the room.

Avasarala leaned back in her chair. Her mind felt calm. Her body was centered and still, like she'd ended a particularly long and effective meditation. She pulled up the connection request and waited to see how long Errinwright or his assistant would take to respond. As soon as she made the request, it was flagged PRIORITY PENDING. Three minutes later, Errinwright was there. He spoke from his hand terminal, the picture jumping as the car he was in bumped and turned. It was full night wherever he was.

"Chrisjen!" he said. "Is anything wrong?"

"Nothing in particular," Avasarala said, silently cursing the connection. She wanted to see his face. She wanted to watch him lie to her. "Soren's brought me something interesting. Intelligence thinks my Martian liaison's a spy."

"Really?" Errinwright said. "That's unfortunate. Are you arresting her?"

"I don't think so," Avasarala said. "I think I'll put my own flag on her traffic. Better the devil we know. Don't you agree?"

The pause was hardly noticeable.

"That's a good idea. Do that."

"Thank you, sir."

"Since I've got you here, I needed to ask you something. Do you have anything that requires you in the office, or can you work on a ship?"

She smiled. Here was the next move, then.

"What are you thinking about?"

Errinwright's car reached a stretch of smoother pavement and his face came into clearer focus. He was wearing a dark suit with a high-collared shirt and no tie. He looked like a priest.

"Ganymede. We need to show that we're taking the situation out there seriously. The secretary-general wants someone senior to go there physically. Report back on the humanitarian angle. Since you're the one who's taken point on this, he thought you'd be the right face to put on it. And I thought it would give you the chance to follow up on the initial attack too."

"We're in a shooting war," Avasarala said. "I don't think the Navy would want to spare a ship to haul my old bones out there. Besides which, I'm coordinating the investigation into Venus, aren't I? Blank check and all."

Errinwright grinned exactly as if he'd meant it.

"I've got you taken care of. Jules-Pierre Mao is taking a yacht from Luna to Ganymede to oversee his company's humanitarian aid efforts. He's offered a berth. It's better accommodations than you get at the office. Probably better bandwidth too. You can monitor Venus from there."

"Mao-Kwik is part of the government now? I hadn't known," she said.

"We're all on the same side. Mao-Kwik is as interested as anyone in seeing those people cared for."

Avasarala's door opened and Roberta Draper loomed into the office. She looked like crap. Her skin had the ashy look of that of someone who hadn't slept in too long. Her jaw was set. Avasarala nodded toward the chair.

"I take up a lot of bandwidth," she said.

"Won't be a problem. You'll get first priority on all communications channels."

The Martian sat down across the desk, well out of the camera's cone. Bobbie braced her hands on her thighs, elbows to the sides, like a wrestler getting ready to step into the cage. Avasarala made herself not glance at the woman.

"Can I think about it?"

"Chrisjen," Errinwright said, bringing his hand terminal closer in, his wide, round face filling the screen. "I told the secretary-general that this might not fly. Even in the best yacht, traveling out to the Jovian system is a hard journey. If you've got too much to do or if you're at all uncomfortable with the trip, you just say so and I'll find someone else. They just won't be as good as you."

"Who is?" Avasarala said with a toss of her hand. Rage was boiling in her gut. "Fine. You've talked me into it. When do I leave?"

"The yacht's scheduled for departure in four days. I'm sorry for the tight turnaround, but I didn't have confirmation until about an hour ago."

"Serendipity."

"If I were a religious man, I'd say it meant something. I'll have the details sent to Soren."

"Better send it to me directly," Avasarala said. "Soren's going to have a lot on his plate already."

"Whatever you like," he said.

Her boss had secretly started a war. He was working with the same corporations that had let the genie out of the bottle on Phoebe, sacrificed Eros, and threatened everything human. He was a frightened little boy in a good suit picking a fight he thought he could win because he was pissing himself over the real threat. She smiled at him. Good men and women had already died because of him and Nguyen. Children had died on Ganymede. Belters would be scrambling for calories. Some would starve.

Errinwright's round cheeks fell a millimeter. His brows knotted just a bit. He knew that she knew. Because of course he did. Players at their level didn't deceive each other. They won even though their opponents knew exactly what was happening. Just like he was winning against her right now.

"Are you feeling all right?" he asked. "I think this is the first conversation we've had in ten years where you haven't said something vulgar."

Avasarala grinned at the screen, reaching out her fingertips as if she could caress him.

"Cunt," she said carefully.

When the connection dropped, she put her head in her hands for a moment, blowing out her breath and sucking it back in hard, focusing. When she sat up, Bobbie was watching her.

"Evening," Avasarala said.

"I've been trying to find you," Bobbie said. "My connections were blocked."

Avasarala grunted.

"We need to talk about something. Someone. I mean, Soren," Bobbie said. "You remember that data you wanted him to take care of a couple days ago? He handed it off to someone else. I don't know who, but they were military. I'll swear to that."

So that's what spooked him, Avasarala thought. Caught with his hands in the cookie jar. Poor idiot had underestimated her pet Marine.

"All right," she said.

"I understand that you don't have any reason to trust me," Bobbie said, "but... Okay. Why are you laughing?"

Avasarala stood up, stretching until the joints in her shoulders ached pleasantly.

"At this moment, you are literally the only one on my staff who I trust as far as I can piss. You remember when I said that the thing on Ganymede wasn't us? It wasn't then but it is now. We've bought it, and I assume we're planning to use it against you."

Bobbie stood up. Her face, once just ashen, was bloodless.

"I have to tell my superiors," she said, her voice thick and strangled.

"No, you don't. They know. And you can't prove it yet any more than I can. Tell them now and they'll broadcast it, and we'll deny it and blah blah blah. The bigger problem is that you're coming back to Ganymede with me. I'm being sent."

She explained everything. Soren's false intelligence report, what it implied, Errinwright's betrayal, and the mission to Ganymede on the Mao-Kwik yacht.

"You can't do that," Bobbie said.

"It's a pain in the ass," Avasarala agreed. "They'll be monitoring my connections, but they're probably doing the same here. And if they're shipping me to Ganymede, you can be dead sure that nothing is going to happen there. They're putting me in a box until it's too late to change anything. Or that's what they're trying, anyway. I'm not giving away the fucking game yet."

"You can't get on that ship," Bobbie said. "It's a trap."

"Of course it's a trap," Avasarala said, waving a hand. "But it's a trap I have to step into. Refuse a request from the secretary-general? That comes out, and everyone starts thinking I'm about to retire. No one backs a player who's going to be powerless next year. We play for the long term, and that means looking strong for the duration. Errinwright knows that. It's why he played it this way."

Outside, another shuttle was lifting off. Avasarala could already hear the roar of the burn, feel the press of thrust and false gravity pushing her back. It had been thirty years since she'd been out of Earth's gravity well. This wasn't going to be pleasant.

"If you get on that ship, they'll kill you," Bobbie said, making each word its own sentence.

"That's not how this game gets played," Avasarala said. "What they—"

The door opened again. Soren had a tray in his hands. The teapot on it was cast iron, with a single handleless enamel cup. He opened his mouth to speak, then saw Bobbie. It was easy to forget how much larger she was until a man Soren's height visibly cowered before her.

"My tea! That's excellent. Do you want any, Bobbie?"

"No."

"All right. Well, put it down, Soren. I'm not drinking it with you standing there. Good. And pour me a cup."

Avasarala watched him turn his back on the marine. His hands didn't shake; she'd give the boy that much. Avasarala stood silent, waiting for him to bring it to her as if he were a puppy learning to retrieve a toy. When he did, she blew across the surface of the tea, scattering the thin veil of steam. He carefully didn't turn to look at Bobbie.

"Will there be anything else, ma'am?"

Avasarala smiled. How many people had this boy killed just by lying to her? She would never know for certain, and neither would he. The best she could do was *not another*.

"Soren," she said. "They're going to know it was you."

It was too much. He looked over his shoulder. Then he looked back, greenish with anxiety.

"Who do you mean?" he said, trying for charm.

"Them. If you're counting on them to help your career, I just want you to understand that they won't. The kind of men you're working for? Once they know you've slipped, you're nothing to them. They have no tolerance for failure."

"I—"

"Neither do I. Don't leave anything personal at your desk."

She watched it in his eyes. The future he'd planned and worked for, defined himself by, fell away. A life on basic support rose in its place. It wasn't enough. It wasn't nearly enough. But it was all the justice she could manage on short notice.

When the door was closed, Bobbie cleared her throat.

"What's going to happen to him?" she asked.

Avasarala sipped her tea. It was good, fresh green tea, brewed perfectly—rich and sweet and not even slightly bitter.

"Who gives a shit?" she said. "The Mao-Kwik yacht leaves in four days. That's not much time. And neither of us is going to be able to take a dump without the bad guys knowing. I'm going to get you a list of people I need to have drinks or lunch or coffee with before we leave. Your job is to arrange it so I do."

"I'm your social secretary now?" Bobbie said, bristling.

"You and my husband are the only two people alive who I know aren't trying to stop me," Avasarala said. "That's how far down I am right now. This has to happen, and there is no one else I can rely on. So yes. You're my social secretary. You're my body-guard. You're my psychiatrist. All of it. You."

Bobbie lowered her head, breathing out through flared nostrils. Her lips pursed and she shook her massive head once quickly—left, then right, then back to center.

"You're fucked," she said.

Avasarala took another sip of her tea. She should have been ruined. She should have been in tears. She'd been cut off from her own power, tricked. Jules-Pierre Mao had sat there, not a meter from where she was now, and laughed down his sleeve at her. Errinwright and Nguyen and whoever else was in his little cabal. They'd tricked her. She'd sat there, pulling strings and trading favors and thinking that she was doing something real. For months—maybe years—she hadn't noticed that she was being closed out.

They'd made a fool of her. She should have been humiliated. Instead, she felt alive. This was her game, and if she was behind at halftime, it only meant they expected her to lose. There was noth-ing better than being underestimated.

"Do you have a gun?"

Bobbie almost laughed.

"They don't like having Martian soldiers walking around the United Nations with guns. I have to eat lunch with a dull spork. We're at war."

"All right, fine. When we get on the yacht, you're in charge of security. You're going to need a gun. I'll arrange that for you."

"You can? Honestly, though, I'd rather have my suit."

"Your suit? What suit?"

"I had custom-fit powered armor with me when I came here.

The video feed of the monster was copied from it. They said they were turning it over to your guys to confirm the original footage hadn't been faked."

Avasarala looked at Bobbie and sipped her tea. Michael-Jon would know where it was. She'd call him the next morning, arrange to have it brought on board the Mao-Kwik yacht with an innocuous label like WARDROBE stamped on the side.

Probably thinking she needed to be convinced, Bobbie kept talking. "Seriously. Get me a gun, I'm a soldier. Get that suit for me, I'm a superhero."

"If we've still got it, you'll have it."

"All right, then," Bobbie said. She smiled. For the first time since they'd met, Avasarala was afraid of her.

God help whoever makes you put it on.

Chapter Twenty-Nine: Holden

Gravity returned as Alex brought the engine up, and Holden floated down to the deck of the cargo bay airlock at a gentle half g. They didn't need to go fast now that the monster was outside the ship. They just needed to put some distance between the ship and it, and get it into the drive's star-hot exhaust plume, where it would be broken down into its various subatomic particles. Even the protomolecule couldn't survive being reduced to ions.

He hoped, anyway.

When he touched down on the deck, he intended to turn on the wall monitor and check the aft cameras. He wanted to watch the thing be torched, but the moment his weight came down, a white-hot spike of pain took his knee. He yelped and collapsed.

Amos drifted down next to him, then kicked off his boot mags and started to kneel. "You okay, Cap?" he said.

"Fine. I mean, for I-think-I-blew-out-my-knee levels of fine."

"Yeah. Joint injury's a lot less painful in microgravity, ain't it?"

Holden was about to reply when a massive hammer hit the side of the ship. The hull rang like a gong. The *Roci*'s engine cut off almost instantly, and the ship snapped into a flat spin. Amos was lifted away from Holden and thrown across the airlock to slam against the outer door. Holden slid along the deck to land standing upright against the bulkhead next to him, his knee collapsing under him so painfully he nearly blacked out.

He chinned a button in his helmet, and his body armor shot him full of amphetamines and painkillers. Within seconds, his knee still hurt, but the pain was very far away and easy to ignore. The threatening tunnel vision vanished and the airlock became very bright. His heart started to race.

"Alex," he said, knowing the answer before he asked, "what was that?"

"When we torched our passenger there, the bomb in the cargo bay went off," the pilot replied. "We've got serious damage to that bay, to the outer hull, and to engineering. Reactor went into emergency shutdown. The cargo bay turned into a second drive during the blast and put us into a spin. I have no control over the ship."

Amos groaned and began moving his limbs. "That sucks."

"We need to kill this spin," Holden said. "What do you need to get the attitude thrusters back up?"

"Holden," Naomi cut in, "I think Prax may be injured in the airlock. He's not moving in there."

"Is he dying?"

The hesitation lasted for one very long second.

"His suit doesn't think so."

"Then ship first," Holden said. "First aid after. Alex, we've got radios again. And the lights are on. So the jamming is gone, and the batteries must still be working. Why can't you fire the thrusters?"

"Looks like…primary and secondary pumps are out. No water pressure."

"Confirmed," Naomi said a second later. "Primary wasn't in the blast area. If it's toast, engineering must be a mess. Secondary's on the deck above. It shouldn't have been physically damaged, but there was a big power spike just before the reactor went off-line. Might have fried it or blown a breaker."

"Okay, we're on it. Amos," Holden said, pulling himself over to where the mechanic lay on the cargo airlock's outer door. "You with me?"

Amos gave a one-handed Belter nod, then groaned. "Just knocked the wind out of me, is all."

"Gotta get up, big man," Holden said, pushing himself to his feet. In the partial gravity of their spin, his leg felt heavy, hot, and stiff as a board. Without the drugs pouring through him, standing on it would have probably made him scream. Instead, he pulled Amos up, putting even more pressure on it.

I will pay for this later, he thought. But the amphetamines made later seem very far away.

"What?" Amos said, slurring the word. He probably had a concussion, but Holden would get him some medical attention later when the ship was back under their control.

"We need to get to the secondary water pump," Holden said, forcing himself to speak slowly in spite of the drugs. "What's the fastest access point?"

"Machine shop," Amos replied, then closed his eyes and seemed to fall asleep on his feet.

"Naomi," Holden said. "Can you control Amos' suit from there?"

"Yes."

"Shoot him full of speed. I can't drag his ass around with me, and I need him."

"Okay," she said. A couple of seconds later, Amos' eyes popped open.

"Shit," he said. "Was I asleep?" His words were still slurred but now had a sort of manic energy to them.

"We need to get to the bulkhead access point in the machine

shop. Grab whatever you think we'll need to get the pump running. It might have blown a breaker or fried some wiring. I'll meet you there."

"Okay," Amos said, then pulled himself along the toe rings set into the floor to get to the inner airlock door. A moment later it was open and he crawled out of view.

With the ship spinning, gravity was pulling Holden to a point halfway between the deck and the starboard bulkhead. None of the ladders and rings set into the ship for use in low g or under thrust would be oriented in the right direction. Not really a problem with four working limbs, but it would make maneuvering with one useless leg difficult.

And of course, once he moved past wherever the ship's center of spin was, everything would reverse.

For a moment, his perspective shifted. The vicious Coriolis rattled the fine bones inside his ears, and he was riding a spinning hunk of metal lost in permanent free fall. Then he was under it, about to be crushed. He flushed with the sweat that came a moment before nausea as his brain ran through scenarios to explain the sensations of the spin. He chinned the suit controls, pumping a massive dose of emergency antinausea drugs into his bloodstream.

Without giving himself more time to think about it, Holden grabbed the toe rings and pulled himself up to the inner airlock door. He could see Amos filling a plastic bucket with tools and supplies he was yanking out of drawers and lockers.

"Naomi," Holden said. "Going to take a peek in engineering. Do we have any cameras left in there?"

She made a sort of disgusted grunt he interpreted as a negative, then said, "I've got systems shorted out all over the ship. Either they're destroyed, or the power is out on that circuit."

Holden pulled himself over to the deck-mounted pressure hatch that separated the machine shop from engineering. A status light on the hatch blinked an angry red.

"Shit, I was afraid of that."

"What?" Naomi asked.

"You don't have environmental readings either, do you?"

"Not from engineering. That's all down."

"Well," Holden said with a long sigh. "The hatch thinks there's no atmosphere on the other side. That incendiary charge actually blew a hole through the bulkhead, and engineering is in vacuum."

"Uh-oh," Alex said. "Cargo bay's in vacuum too."

"And the cargo bay door is broken," Naomi added. "And the cargo airlock."

"And a partridge in a fucking pear tree," Amos said with a disgusted snort. "Let's get the damn ship to stop spinning and I'll go outside and take a look at it."

"Amos is right," Holden said, giving up on the hatch and pushing himself to his feet. He staggered down a steeply angled bulkhead to the access panel where Amos was now waiting, bucket in hand. "First things first."

While Amos used a torque wrench to unbolt the access panel, Holden said, "Actually, Naomi, pump all the air out of the machine shop too. No atmo below deck four. Override the safeties so we can open the engineering hatch if we need to."

Amos ran out the last bolt and pulled the panel off the bulkhead. Beyond it lay a dark, cramped space filled with a confusing tangle of pipes and cabling.

"Oh," Holden added. "Might want to prep an SOS if we can't get this fixed."

"Yeah, because we got a lot of people out there who we really want coming to help us right now," Amos said.

Amos pulled himself into the narrow passage between the two hulls and then out of sight. Holden followed him in. Two meters beyond the hatch loomed the blocky and complex-looking pump mechanism that kept water pressure to the maneuvering thrusters. Amos stopped next to it and began pulling parts off. Holden waited behind him, the narrow space not allowing him to see what the big mechanic was doing.

"How's it look?" Holden asked after a few minutes of listening to Amos curse under his breath while he worked.

"It looks fine here," Amos said. "Gonna swap this breaker anyway, just to be sure. But I don't think the pump's our problem."

Shit.

Holden backed out of the maintenance hatch and half crawled up the steep slope of bulkhead back to the engineering hatch. The angry red light had been replaced with a morose yellow one now that there was no atmosphere on either side of the hatch.

"Naomi," Holden said. "I've got to get into engineering. I need to see what happened in there. Have you killed the safeties?"

"Yes. But I've got no sensors in there. The room could be flooded with radiation—"

"But you have sensors here in the machine shop, right? If I open the hatch and you get radiation warnings, just let me know. I'll shut it immediately."

"Jim," Naomi said, the stiffness that had been in her voice every time she'd spoken to him for the last day slipping a bit. "How many times can you get yourself massively irradiated before it catches up with you?"

"At least once more?"

"I'll tell the *Roci* to prep a bed in sick bay," she said, not quite laughing.

"Get one of the ones that's not throwing errors."

Without giving himself time to rethink it, Holden slapped the release on the deck hatch. He held his breath while it opened, expecting to see chaos and destruction on the other side, followed by his suit's radiation alarm.

Instead, other than one small hole in the bulkhead closest to the explosion, it looked fine.

Holden pulled himself through the opening and hung by his arms for a few moments, examining the space. The massive fusion reactor that dominated the center of the compartment looked untouched. The bulkhead on the starboard side bowed in precariously, with a charred hole in its center, like a miniature volcano had formed there. Holden shuddered at the thought of how much energy had to have been released to bend the heavily armored and radiation-shielded bulkhead in like that, and how close it had come to punching a hole in their reactor. How many more joules to go from a badly dented wall to full containment breach?

"God, this one was close," he said out loud to no one in particular.

"Swapped out all the parts I can think to," Amos said. "The problem is somewhere else."

Holden let go of the rim of the hatch and dropped a half meter to the bulkhead, which angled below him, then slid to the deck. The only other visible damage was a hunk of bulkhead plating stuck in the wall exactly on the other side of the reactor. Holden couldn't see any way that the shrapnel could have gotten there without passing directly through the reactor, or else bouncing off two bulkheads and around it. There was no sign of the first, so the second, incredibly unlikely though it was, had to be what had happened.

"I mean, really close," he said, touching the jagged metal fragment. It was sunk a good fifteen centimeters into the wall. Plenty far enough to have at least breached the shielding on the reactor. Maybe worse.

"Grabbing your camera," Naomi said. A moment later she whistled. "No kidding. The walls in there are mostly cabling. Can't make a hole like that without breaking something."

Holden tried to pull the shrapnel out of the wall by hand and failed. "Amos, bring some pliers and a lot of patch cabling."

"So no on the distress call, then," Naomi said.

"No. But if someone could point a camera aft and reassure me that for all this trouble we actually killed that damned thing, that would be just swell."

"Watched it go myself, Cap," Alex said. "Nothin' but gas now."

Holden lay on one of the sick bay beds, letting the ship look his leg over. Periodically a manipulator prodded his knee, which was swelled up to the size of a cantaloupe, the skin stretched tight as a drum's head. But the bed was also making sure to keep him perfectly medicated, so the occasional pokes and prods registered only as pressure without any pain.

The panel next to his head warned him to remain still; then two arms grabbed his leg while a third injected a needle-thin flexible tube into his knee and started doing something arthroscopic. He felt a vague tugging sensation.

At the next bed over lay Prax. His head was bandaged where a three-centimeter flap of skin had been glued back down. His eyes were closed. Amos, who had turned out not to have a concussion, just another nasty bump on his head, was belowdecks doing makeshift repairs on everything the monster's bomb had broken, including putting a temporary patch on the hole in their engineering bulkhead. They wouldn't be able to fix the cargo bay door until they docked at Tycho. Alex was flying them there at a gentle quarter g to make it easier to work.

Holden didn't mind the delay. The truth was he was in no hurry to get back to Tycho and confront Fred about what he'd seen. The longer he thought about it, the further he got from his earlier blind panic, and the more he thought Naomi was right. It made no sense for Fred to be behind any of this.

But he wasn't sure. And he had to be sure.

Prax mumbled something and touched his head. He started pulling on the bandages.

"I wouldn't mess with those," Holden said.

Prax nodded and closed his eyes again. Sleeping, or trying to. The auto-doc pulled the tube out of Holden's leg, sprayed it with antiseptic, and began wrapping it with a tight bandage. Holden waited until the medical pod was done doing whatever it was doing to his knee, then turned sideways on the bed and tried to stand up. Even at a quarter g, his leg wouldn't support him. He hopped on one foot over to a supply locker and got himself a crutch.

As he moved past the botanist's bed, Prax grabbed his arm. His grip was surprisingly strong.

"It's dead?"

"Yeah," Holden said, patting his hand. "We got it. Thanks."

Prax didn't reply; he just rolled onto his side and shook. It took Holden a moment to realize Prax was weeping. He left without saying anything else. What else was there to say?

Holden took the ladder-lift up, planning to go to ops and read the detailed damage reports Naomi and the *Roci* were compiling. He stopped when he got to the personnel deck and heard two people speaking. He couldn't hear what they were saying, but he recognized Naomi's voice, and he recognized the tone she used when she was having an intimate conversation.

The voices were coming from the galley. Feeling a little like a Peeping Tom, Holden moved closer to the galley hatch until he could make out the words.

"It's more than that," Naomi was saying. Holden almost walked into the galley, but something in her tone stopped him. He had the terrible feeling she was talking about him. About them. About why she was leaving.

"Why does it have to be more?" the other person said. Amos.

"You almost beat a man to death with a can of chicken on Ganymede," Naomi replied.

"Gonna hold a little girl hostage for some food? Fuck him. If he was here, I'd smash him again right now."

"Do you trust me, Amos?" Naomi said. Her voice was sad. More than that. Frightened.

"More than anyone else," Amos replied.

"I'm scared out of my wits. Jim is rushing off to do something really dumb on Tycho. This guy we're taking with us seems like he's one twitch from a nervous breakdown."

"Well, he's—"

"And you," she continued. "I depend on you. I know you've always got my back, no matter what. Except maybe not now, because the Amos I know doesn't beat a skinny kid half to death, no matter how much chicken he asks for. I feel like everyone's losing themselves. I need to understand, because I'm really, really frightened."

Holden felt the urge to go in, take her hand, hold her. The need in her voice demanded it, but he held himself back. There was a long pause. Holden heard a scraping sound, followed by the sound of metal hitting glass. Someone was stirring sugar into coffee. The sounds were so clear he could almost see it.

"So, Baltimore," Amos said, his voice as relaxed as if he were going to talk about the weather. "Not a nice town. You ever heard of squeezing? Squeeze trade? Hooker squeeze?"

"No. Is it a drug?"

"No," Amos said with a laugh. "No, when you squeeze a hooker, you put her on the street until she gets knocked up, then peddle her to johns who get off on pregnant girls, then send her back to the streets after she pops the kid. With procreation restrictions, banging pregnant girls is quite the kink."

"Squeeze?"

"Yeah, you know, 'squeezing out puppies'? You never heard it called that?"

"Okay," Naomi said, trying to hide her disgust.

"Those kids? They're illegal, but they don't just vanish, not right away," Amos continued. "They got uses too."

Holden felt his chest tighten a little. It wasn't something he'd ever thought about. When, a second later, Naomi spoke, her horror echoed his.

"Jesus."

"Jesus got nothing to do with it," Amos said. "No Jesus in the squeeze trade. But some kids wind up in the pimp gangs. Some wind up on the streets..."

"Some wind up finding a way to ship offworld, and they never go back?" Naomi asked, her voice quiet.

"Maybe," Amos said, his voice as flat and conversational as ever. "Maybe some do. But most of them just...disappear, eventually. Used up. Most of them."

For a time, no one spoke. Holden heard the sounds of coffee being drunk.

"Amos," she said, her voice thick. "I never—"

"So I'd like to find this little girl before someone uses her up, and she disappears. I'd like to do that for her," Amos said. His voice caught for a moment, and he cleared it with a loud cough. "For her dad."

Holden thought they were done, and started to slip away when he heard Amos, his voice calm again, say, "Then I'm going to kill whoever snatched her."

Chapter Thirty: Bobbie

Prior to working for Avasarala at the UN, Bobbie had never even heard of Mao-Kwikowski Mercantile, or if she had, she hadn't noticed. She'd spent her whole life wearing, eating, or sitting on products carted through the solar system by Mao-Kwik freighters without ever realizing it. After she'd gone through the files Avasarala had given her, she'd been astonished at the size and reach of the company. Hundreds of ships, dozens of stations, millions of employees. Jules-Pierre Mao owned significant properties on every habitable planet and moon in the solar system.

His eighteen-year-old daughter had owned her own racing ship. And that was the daughter he *didn't* like.

When Bobbie tried to imagine being so wealthy you could own a spaceship just to compete in races, she failed. That the same girl had run away to be an OPA rebel probably said a lot about the relationship of wealth and contentment, but Bobbie had a hard time being that philosophical.

She'd grown up solidly Martian middle class. Her father had done twenty as a Marine noncom and had gone into private security consulting after he'd left the corps. Bobbie's family had always had a nice home. She and her two older brothers had attended a private primary school, and her brothers had both gone on to university without having to take out student loans. Growing up, she'd never once thought of herself as poor.

She did now.

Owning your own racing ship wasn't even wealth. It was like speciation. It was conspicuous consumption befitting ancient Earth royalty, a pharaoh's pyramid with a reaction drive. Bobbie had thought it was the most ridiculous excess she'd ever heard of.

And then she climbed off the short flight shuttle onto Jules-Pierre Mao's private L5 station.

Jules didn't park his ships in orbit at a public station. He didn't even use a Mao-Kwik corporate station. This was an entire fully functioning space station in orbit around Earth solely for his private spaceships, and the whole thing done up like peacock feathers. It was a level of extravagance that had never even occurred to her.

She also thought it made Mao himself very dangerous. Everything he did was an announcement of his freedom from constraint. He was a man without boundaries. Killing a senior politician of the UN government might be bad business. It might wind up being expensive. But it would never actually be risky to a man with this much wealth and power.

Avasarala didn't see it.

"I hate spin gravity," Avasarala said, sipping at a cup of steaming tea. They'd be on the station for only three hours, while cargo was transferred from the shuttle to Mao's yacht, but they'd been assigned a suite of four full-sized bedrooms, each with its own shower, and a massive lounge area. A huge screen pretended to be a window, the crescent Earth with her continent-veiling clouds hung on the black. They had a private kitchen staffed by three people, whose biggest task so far had been making the assistant undersecretary's tea. Bobbie considered ordering a large meal just to give them something to do.

"I can't believe we're about to climb on a ship owned by this man. Have you ever known anyone this wealthy to go to jail? Or even be prosecuted? This guy could probably walk in here and shoot you in the face on a live newsfeed and get away with it."

Avasarala laughed at her. Bobbie suppressed a surge of anger. It was just fear looking for an outlet.

"That's not the game," Avasarala said. "No one gets shot. They get marginalized. It's worse."

"No, it's not. I've seen people shot. I've seen my friends shot. When you say, 'That's not the game,' you mean for people like you. Not like me."

Avasarala's expression cooled.

"Yes, that's what I mean," the old woman said. "The level we're playing at has different rules. It's like playing go. It's all about exerting influence. Controlling the board without occupying it."

"Poker is a game too," Bobbie said. "But sometimes the stakes get so high that one player decides it's easier to kill the other guy and walk away with the money. It happens all the time."

Avasarala nodded at her, not replying right away, visibly thinking over what Bobbie had said. Bobbie felt her anger replaced with a sudden rush of affection for the grumpy and arrogant old lady.

"Okay," Avasarala said, putting her teacup down and placing her hands in her lap. "I hear what you're saying, Sergeant. I think it's unlikely, but I'm glad you're here to say it."

But you aren't taking it seriously, Bobbie wanted to shout at her. Instead, she asked the servant who hovered nearby for a mushroom and onion sandwich. While she ate it, Avasarala sipped tea, nibbled on a cookie, and made small talk about the war and her grandchildren. Bobbie tried to be sure to make concerned noises during the war parts and *awww, cute* noises when the kids were the topic. But all she could think about was the tactical nightmare defending Avasarala on an enemy-controlled space-craft would be.

Her recon suit was in a large crate marked FORMAL WEAR and being loaded onto the Mao yacht even as they waited. Bobbie wanted to sneak off and put it on. She didn't notice when Avasarala stopped speaking for several minutes.

"Bobbie," Avasarala said, her face not quite a frown. "Are my stories about my beloved grandchildren boring you?"

"Yeah," Bobbie replied. "They really are."

Bobbie had thought that Mao Station was the most ludicrous display of conspicuous wealth she'd ever seen right up until they boarded the yacht.

While the station was extravagant, it at least served a function. It was Jules Mao's personal orbital garage, where he could store and service his fleet of private spacecraft. Underneath the glitz there was a working station, with mechanics and support staff doing actual jobs.

The yacht, the *Guanshiyin*, was the size of a standard cheapjack people-mover that would have transported two hundred customers, but it only had a dozen staterooms. Its cargo area was just large enough to contain the supplies they'd need for a lengthy voyage. It wasn't particularly fast. It was, by any reasonable measurement, a miserable failure as a useful spacecraft.

But its job was not to be useful.

The *Guanshiyin*'s job was to be comfortable. Extravagantly comfortable.

It was like a hotel lobby. The carpet was plush and soft underfoot, and actual crystal chandeliers caught the light. Everyplace that should have had a sharp corner was rounded. Softened. The walls were papered with raw bamboo and natural fiber. The first thing Bobbie thought was how hard it would be to clean, and the second thing was that the difficulty was intentional.

Each suite of rooms took up nearly an entire deck of the ship. Each room had its own private bath, media center, game room, and lounge with a full bar. The lounge had a gigantic screen showing the view outside, which would not have been higher definition had it been an actual glass window. Near the bar was a dumbwaiter next to an intercom, which could deliver food prepared by Cordon Bleu chefs any hour of the day or night.

The carpet was so thick Bobbie was pretty sure mag boots wouldn't work. It wouldn't matter. A ship like this would never break down, never have to stop the engines during flight. The kind of people who flew on the *Guanshiyin* had probably never actually worn an environment suit in their lives.

All the fixtures in her bathroom were gold plated.

Bobbie and Avasarala were sitting in the lounge with the head of her UN security team, a pleasant-looking gray-haired man of Kurdish descent named Cotyar. Bobbie had been worried when she first met him. He looked like a friendly high school teacher, not a soldier. But then she'd watched him go through Avasarala's rooms with practiced efficiency, laying out their security plan and directing his team, and her worries eased.

"Well, impressions?" Avasarala asked, leaning back in a plush armchair with her eyes closed.

"This room is not secure," Cotyar said, his accent exotic to Bobbie's ears. "We should not discuss sensitive matters here. Your private room has been secured for such discussions."

"This is a trap," Bobbie said.

"Aren't we finished with that shit yet?" Avasarala said, then leaned forward to give Bobbie a glare.

"She is right," Cotyar said quietly, clearly unhappy to be discussing such matters in an unsecured room. "I've counted fourteen crew on this ship already, and I would estimate that is less than one-third of the total crew of this vessel. I have a team of six for your protection—"

"Seven," Bobbie interrupted, raising her hand.

"As you say," Cotyar continued with a nod. "Seven. We do not control any of the ship's systems. Assassination would be as simple as sealing the deck we are on and pumping out the air."

Bobbie pointed at Cotyar and said, "See?"

Avasarala waved a hand as if she were shooing flies. "What's communications look like?"

"Robust," Cotyar said. "We've set up a private network and have been given the backup tightbeam and radio array for your personal use. Bandwidth is significant, though light delay will be an increasing factor as we move away from Earth."

"Good," Avasarala said, smiling for the first time since they'd come on the ship. She'd stopped looking tired a while ago and had moved on to whatever tired turns into when it became a lifestyle.

"None of this is secure," Cotyar said. "We can secure our private internal network, but if they are monitoring outbound and inbound traffic through the array we're using, there will be no way to detect that. We have no access to ship operations."

"And," Avasarala said, "that is exactly why I'm here. Bottle me up, send me on a long trip, and read all my fucking mail."

"We're lucky if that's all they do," Bobbie said. Thinking about how tired Avasarala looked had reminded her how tired she was too. She felt herself drift away for a moment.

Avasarala finished saying something, and Cotyar nodded and said yes to her. She turned to Bobbie and said, "Do you agree?"

"Uh," Bobbie said, trying to rewind the conversation in her head and failing. "I'm—"

"You're practically falling out of your fucking chair. When's the last time you got a full night's sleep?"

"Probably about the last time you did," Bobbie said. *The last time all my squaddies were alive, and you weren't trying to keep the solar system from catching on fire.* She waited for the next scathing comment, the next observation that she couldn't do her job if she was that compromised. That weak.

"Fair enough," Avasarala said. Bobbie felt another little surge of affection for her. "Mao's throwing a big dinner tonight to welcome us aboard. I want you and Cotyar to come with. Cotyar will be security, so he'll stand at the back of the room and look menacing."

Bobbie laughed before she could stop herself. Cotyar smiled and winked at her.

"And," Avasarala continued, "you'll be there as my social secretary, so you can chat people up. Try to get a feel for the crew and the mood of the ship. Okay?"

"Roger that."

"I noticed," Avasarala said, her tone shifting to the one she used when she was going to ask for an unpleasant favor, "the executive officer staring at you when we did the airlock meet and greet."

Bobbie nodded. She'd noticed it too. Some men had a large-woman fetish, and Bobbie had gotten the hair-raising sense that he might be a member of that tribe. They tended to have unresolved mommy issues, so she generally steered clear.

"Any chance you could talk him up at dinner?" Avasarala finished.

Bobbie laughed, expecting everyone else to laugh too. Even Cotyar was looking at her as though Avasarala had made a perfectly reasonable request.

"Uh, no," Bobbie said.

"Did you say no?"

"Yeah, no. Hell no. Fuck no. *Nein und abermals nein. Nyet. La. Siei,*" Bobbie said, stopping when she ran out of languages. "And I'm actually a little pissed now."

"I'm not asking you to sleep with him."

"Good, because I don't use sex as a weapon," Bobbie said. "I use weapons as weapons."

"Chrisjen!" Jules Mao said, enveloping Avasarala's hand in his and shaking it.

The lord of the Mao-Kwik empire towered over Avasarala. He had the kind of handsome face that made Bobbie instinctively want to like him, and medically untreated male-pattern hair loss that said he didn't care whether she did. Choosing not to use his wealth to fix a problem as treatable as thinning hair actually made him seem even more in control. He wore a loose sweater and cotton pants that hung on him like a tailored suit. When Avasarala introduced Bobbie to him, he smiled and nodded while barely glancing in her direction.

"Is your staff settled in?" he asked, letting Avasarala know that Bobbie's presence reminded him of underlings. Bobbie gritted her teeth but kept her face blank.

"Yes," Avasarala replied with what Bobbie would have sworn was genuine warmth. "The accommodations are lovely, and your crew has been wonderful."

"Excellent," Jules said, placing Avasarala's hand on his arm and leading her to an enormous table. They were surrounded on all sides by men in white jackets with black bow ties. One of them darted forward and pulled a chair out. Jules placed Avasarala in it. "Chef Marco has promised something special tonight."

"How about straight answers? Are those on the menu?" Bobbie asked as a waiter pulled out a chair for her.

Jules settled into his chair at the head of the table. "Answers?"

"You guys won," Bobbie said, ignoring the steaming soup one of the servers placed in front of her. Mao tapped salt onto his and began eating it as though they were just having casual dinner conversation. "The assistant undersecretary is on the ship. No reason to bullshit us now. What's going on?"

"Humanitarian aid," he replied.

"*Bullshit*," Bobbie said. She glanced at Avasarala, but the old woman was just smiling. "You can't tell me that you have time to spend a couple months doing the transit to Jupiter just to oversee handing out rice and juice boxes. And you couldn't get enough relief supplies onto this ship to feed Ganymede lunch, much less make a long-term difference."

Mao settled back in his chair, and the white jackets bustled around the room, clearing the soup away. Bobbie's was whisked away as well, even though she hadn't eaten any of it.

"Roberta," Mao began.

"Don't call me Roberta."

"*Sergeant*, you should be questioning your superiors at the UN foreign office, not me."

"I'd love to, but apparently asking questions is against the rules in this *game*."

His smile was warm, condescending, and empty. "I made my ship available to provide Madam Undersecretary the most comfortable ride to her new assignment. And while you have not yet met them, there are personnel currently on this vessel whose expertise will be invaluable to the citizens of Ganymede once you arrive."

Bobbie had been around Avasarala long enough to see the game being played right in front of her. Mao was laughing at her. He knew this was all bullshit, and he knew she knew it as well. But as long as he remained calm and gave reasonable answers, no one could call him on it. He was too powerful to be called a liar to his face.

"You're a liar, and—" she started; then something he'd said made her stop. "Wait, 'once *you* arrive'? You aren't coming?"

"I'm afraid not," Mao said, smiling up at the white jacket who placed another plate in front of him. This one had what appeared to be a whole fish, complete with head and staring eyes.

Bobbie gaped at Avasarala, who was frowning at Mao now.

"I was told you were personally leading this relief effort," Avasarala said.

"That was my intention. But I'm afraid other business has removed that option. Once we finish with this excellent dinner, I'll be taking the shuttle back to the station. This ship, and its crew, are at your disposal until your vital work on Ganymede is complete."

Avasarala just stared at Mao. For the first time in Bobbie's experience, the old lady was struck speechless.

A white jacket brought Bobbie a fish while her lush prison flew at a leisurely quarter g toward Jupiter.

Avasarala hadn't said a word on the ride down the lift to their suite. In the lounge, she stopped long enough to grab a bottle of gin off the bar, and waggled a finger at Bobbie. Bobbie followed her into the master bedroom, Cotyar close behind.

Once the door was closed and Cotyar had used his handheld security terminal to scan the room for bugs, Avasarala said, "Bobbie, start thinking of a way to either get control of this ship or get us off of it."

"Forget that," Bobbie said. "Let's go grab that shuttle Mao's leaving on right now. It's within range of his station or he wouldn't be taking it."

To her surprise, Cotyar nodded. "I agree with the sergeant. If we plan to leave, the shuttle will be easier to commandeer and control against a hostile crew."

Avasarala sat down on her bed with a long exhale that turned into a heavy sigh. "I can't leave yet. It doesn't work that way."

"The fucking game!" Bobbie yelled.

"Yes," Avasarala snapped. "*Yes*, the fucking game. I've been ordered by my superiors to make this trip. If I leave now, I'm out. They'll be polite and call it a sudden illness or exhaustion, but the excuse they give me will also be the reason I'm not allowed to keep doing my job. I'll be safe, and I'll be powerless. As long as I pretend I'm doing what they asked me to, I can keep working. I'm still the assistant undersecretary of executive administration. I still have connections. Influence. If I run now, I lose them. If I lose them, these fuckers might as well shoot me."

"But," Bobbie said.

"But," Avasarala repeated. "If I continue to be effective, they'll find a way to cut me off. Unexplained comm failure, something. Something to keep me off the network. When that happens, I will demand that the captain reroute to the closest station for repairs. If I'm right, he won't do it."

"Ah," Bobbie said.

"Oh," Cotyar said a moment later.

"Yes," Avasarala said. "When that happens, I will declare this an illegal seizure of my person, and you will get me this ship."

Chapter Thirty-One: Prax

With every day that passed, the question came closer: What was the next step? It didn't feel all that different from those first, terrible days on Ganymede, making lists as a way of telling himself what to do. Only now he wasn't only looking for Mei. He was looking for Strickland. Or the mysterious woman in the video. Or whoever had built the secret lab. In that sense, he was much better off than he had been before.

On the other hand, he had been searching Ganymede. Now the field had expanded to include everywhere.

The lag time to Earth—or Luna, actually, since Persis-Strokes Security Consultants was based in orbit rather than down the planet's gravity well—was a little over twenty minutes. It made actual conversation essentially impossible, so in practice, the hatchet-faced woman on his screen was making a series of promotional videos more and more specifically targeted to what Prax wanted to hear.

"We have an intelligence-sharing relationship with Pinkwater, which is presently the security company with the largest physical and operational presence in the outer planets," she said. "We also have joint-action contracts with Al Abbiq and Star Helix. With those, we can take immediate action either directly or through our partners, on literally any station or planet in the system."

Prax nodded to himself. That was exactly what he needed. Someone with eyes everywhere, with contacts everywhere. Someone who could help.

"I'm attaching a release," the woman said. "We will need payment for the processing fee, but we won't be charging your accounts for anything more than that until we've agreed on the scope of the investigation you're willing to be liable for. Once we have that in hand, I will send you a detailed proposal with an itemized spreadsheet and we can decide the scope of work that works best for you."

"Thank you," Prax said. He pulled up the document, signed off, and returned it. It would be twenty minutes at the speed of light before it reached Luna. Twenty minutes back. Who knew how long in between?

It was a start. He could feel good about that, at least.

The ship was quiet in a way that felt like anticipation, but Prax didn't know exactly what of. The arrival at Tycho Station, but beyond that, he wasn't sure. Leaving his bunk behind, he went through the empty galley and up the ladder toward the ops center and then the pilot's station. The small room was dim, most of the light coming from the control panels and the sweep of high-definition screens that filled 270 degrees of vision with starlight, the distant sun, and the approaching mass of Tycho Station, the oasis in the vast emptiness.

"Hey there, Doc," Alex said from the pilot's couch. "Come up to see the view?"

"If...I mean, if that's all right."

"Not a problem. I haven't been running with a copilot since we got the *Roci*. Strap in right there. Just if somethin' happens, don't touch anything."

"I won't," Prax promised as he scrambled into the acceleration couch. At first, the station seemed to grow slowly. The two counter-rotating rings were hardly larger than Prax's thumb, the sphere they surrounded little more than a gum ball. Then, as they drew nearer, the fuzzy texture at the edge of the construction sphere began to resolve into massive waldoes and gantries reaching toward a strangely aerodynamic form. The ship under construction was still half undressed, ceramic and steel support beams open to the vacuum like bones. Tiny fireflies flickered inside and out: welders and sealant packs firing off too far away to see apart from the light.

"Is that built for atmosphere?"

"Nope. Kinda looks that way, though. That's the *Chesapeake*. Or it will be, anyway. She's designed for sustained high g. I think they're talkin' about running the poor bastard at something like eight g for a couple of months."

"All the way where?" Prax asked, doing a little napkin-back math in his head. "It would have to be outside the orbit of... anything."

"Yep, she'll be going deep. They're going after that *Nauvoo*."

"The generation ship that was supposed to knock Eros into the sun?"

"That's the one. They cut her engines when the plan went south, but she's been cruisin' on ever since. Wasn't finished, so they can't bring her around on remote. Instead, they're buildin' a retriever. Hope they manage too. The *Nauvoo* was an amazin' piece of work. Of course, even if they get her back, it won't keep the Mormons from suing Tycho into nonexistence if they can figure out how."

"Why would that be hard?"

"OPA doesn't recognize the courts on Earth and Mars, and they run the ones in the Belt. So it's pretty much win in a court that doesn't matter or lose in one that does."

"Oh," Prax said.

On the screens, Tycho Station grew larger and more detailed. Prax couldn't tell what detail of it brought it into perspective, but between one heartbeat and the next, he understood the scope and size of the station before him and let out a little gasp. The construction sphere had to be half a kilometer across, like two complete farm domes stuck bottom to bottom. Slowly, the great industrial sphere grew until it filled the screens, starlight replaced by the glow from equipment guides and a glass-domed observation bubble. Steel-and-ceramic plates and scaffolds took the place of the blackness. There were the massive drives that could push the entire station, like a city in the sky, anywhere in the solar system. There were the complex swivel points, like the gimbals of a crash couch made by giants, that would reconfigure the station as a whole when thrust gravity took rotation's place.

It took his breath away. The elegance and functionality of the structure lay out before him, as beautiful and simple and effective as a leaf or a root cluster. To have something so much like the fruits of evolution, but designed by human minds, was awe-inspiring. It was the pinnacle of what creativity meant, the impossible made real.

"That's good work," Prax said.

"Yup," Alex said. And then on the shipwide channel: "We've arrived. Everyone strap in for docking. I'm going to manual."

Prax half rose in his couch.

"Should I go to my quarters?"

"Where you are's as good as anyplace. Just put the web on in case we bump against somethin'," Alex said. And then, his voice changing to a stronger, more clipped cadence: "Tycho control, this is the *Rocinante*. Are we cleared for docking?"

Prax heard a distant voice speaking to Alex alone.

"Roger that," Alex said. "We're comin' in."

In the dramas and action films that Prax had watched back on Ganymede, piloting a ship had always looked like a fairly athletic thing. Sweating men dragging hard against the control bars.

Watching Alex was nothing like it. He still had the two joysticks, but his motions were small, calm. A tap, and the gravity under Prax changed, his couch shifting under him by a few centimeters. Then another tap and another shift. The heads-up display showed a tunnel through the vacuum outlined in a blue and gold that swept up and to the right, ending against the side of the turning ring.

Prax looked at the mass of data being sent to Alex and said, "Why fly at all? Couldn't the ship just use this data to do the docking itself?"

"Why fly?" Alex repeated with a laugh. "'Cuz it's fun, Doc. Because it's fun."

The long bluish lights of the windows in Tycho's observation dome were so clear Prax could see the people looking out at him. He could almost forget that the screens in the cockpit weren't windows: The urge to look out and wave, to watch someone wave back, was profound.

Holden's voice came over Alex's line, the words unidentifiable and the tone perfectly clear.

"We're looking fine, Cap," Alex said. "Ten more minutes."

The crash couch shifted to the side, the wide plane of the station curving down as Alex matched the rotation. To generate even a third of a g on a ring that wide would demand punishing inertial forces, but under Alex's hand, ship and station drifted together slowly and gently. Before Prax had gotten married, he'd seen a dance performance based on neo-Taoist traditions. For the first hour, it had been utterly boring, and then after that, the small movements of arms and legs and torso, shifting together, bending, and falling away, had been entrancing. The *Rocinante* slid into place beside an extending airlock port with the same beauty Prax had seen in that dance, but made more powerful by the knowledge that instead of skin and muscles, this was tons of high-tensile steel and live fusion reactors.

The *Rocinante* eased into her berth with one last correction, one last shifting of the gimbaled couches. The final matching spin had been no more than any of the small corrections Alex had made on the way in. There was a disconcerting bang as the station's docking hooks latched on to the ship.

"Tycho control," Alex said. "This is the *Rocinante* confirming dock. We have seal on the airlock. We are reading the clamps in place. Can you confirm?"

A moment passed, and a mutter.

"Thank you too, Tycho," Alex said. "It's good to be back."

Gravity in the ship had shifted subtly. Instead of thrust from the drive creating the illusion of weight, it now came from the spin of the ring they were clamped to. Prax felt like he was tilting slightly to the side whenever he stood up straight, and had to fight the urge to overcompensate by leaning the other way.

Holden was in the galley when Prax reached it, the coffee machine pouring black and hot, with just the slightest bend to the stream. Coriolis effect, a dimly remembered high school class reminded Prax. Amos and Naomi came in together. They were all together now, and Prax felt the time was right to thank them all for what they'd done for him. For Mei, who was probably dead. The naked pain on Holden's face stopped him.

Naomi stood in front of him, a duffel bag over her shoulder.

"You're heading out," Holden said.

"I am." Her voice was light, but it had meaning radiating from it like harmonic overtones. Prax blinked.

"All right, then," Holden said.

For a few seconds, no one moved; then Naomi darted in, kissing Holden lightly on the cheek. The captain's arms moved out to embrace her, but she'd already stepped away, marching out through the narrow hallway with the air of a woman on her way someplace. Holden took his coffee. Amos and Alex exchanged glances.

"Ah, Cap'n?" Alex asked. Compared to the voice of the man who'd just put a nuclear warship against a spinning metal wheel in the middle of interplanetary space, this voice was hesitant and concerned. "Are we lookin' for a new XO?"

"We're not looking for anything until I say so," Holden said. Then, his voice quieter: "But, God, I hope not."

"Yessir," Alex said. "Me too."

The four men stood for a long, awkward moment. Amos was the first to speak.

"You know, Cap," he said, "the place I've got booked has room for two. If you want the spare bunk, it's yours."

"No," Holden said. He didn't look at them as he spoke, but reached out his hand and pressed his palm to the wall. "I'm staying on the *Roci*. I'll be right here."

"You sure?" Amos asked, and again it seemed to mean something more than Prax could understand.

"*I'm* not going anywhere," Holden said.

"All right, then."

Prax cleared his throat, and Amos took his elbow.

"What about you?" Amos said. "You got a place to bunk down?"

Prax's prepared speech—*I wanted to tell you all how much I appreciate...*—ran into the question, derailing both thoughts.

"I...ah...I don't, but—"

"Right, then. Get your stuff, and you can come with me."

"Well, yes. Thank you. But first I wanted to tell you all—"

Amos put a solid hand on his shoulder.

"Maybe later," the big man said. "Right now, how about you just come with me?"

Holden leaned against the wall now. His jaw was set hard, like that of a man about to scream or vomit or weep. His eyes were looking at the ship but seeing past it. Sorrow welled up in Prax as if he were looking into a mirror.

"Yeah," he said. "Okay."

Amos' rooms were, if anything, smaller than the bunks on the *Rocinante*: two small privacy areas, a common space less than half the size of the galley, and a bathroom with a fold-out sink and toilet in the shower stall. It would have induced claustrophobia if Amos had actually been there.

Instead, he'd seen Prax settled in, taken a quick shower, and headed out into the wide, luxurious passageways of the station. There were plants everywhere, but for the most part they seemed decorative. The curve of the decks was so slight Prax could almost imagine he was back on some unfamiliar part of Ganymede, that his hole was no more than a tube ride away. That Mei would be there, waiting for him. Prax let the outer door close, pulled out his hand terminal, and connected to the local network.

There was still no reply from Persis-Strokes, but it was probably too early to expect one. In the meantime, the problem was money. If he was going to fund this, he couldn't do it alone.

Which meant Nicola.

Prax set up his terminal, turning the camera on himself. The image on the screen looked thin, wasted. The weeks had dried him out, and his time on the *Rocinante* hadn't completely rebuilt him. He might never be rebuilt. The sunken cheeks on the screen might be who he was now. That was fine. He started recording.

"Hi, Nici," he said. "I wanted you to know I'm safe. I got to Tycho Station, but I still don't have Mei. I'm hiring a security consultant. I'm giving them everything I know. They seem like they'll really be able to help. But it's expensive. It may be very expensive. And she may already be dead."

Prax took a moment to catch his breath.

"She may already be dead," he said again. "But I have to try. I know you aren't in a great financial position right now. I know you've got your new husband to think of. But if you have anything you can spare—not for me. I don't want anything from you. Just Mei. For her. If you can give her anything, this is the last chance."

He paused again, his mind warring between *Thank you* and *It's the least you can fucking do*. In the end, he just shut off the recording and sent it.

The lag between Ceres and Tycho Station was fifteen minutes, given their relative positions. And even then, he didn't know what the local schedule there was. He might be sending his message in the middle of the night or during dinnertime. She might not have anything to say to him.

It didn't matter. He had to try. He could sleep if he knew he'd done everything he could to try.

He recorded and sent messages to his mother, to his old roommate from college who'd taken a position on Neptune Station, to his postdoctorate advisor. Each time, the story got a little easier to tell. The details started coming together, one leading into another. With them, he didn't talk about the protomolecule. At best, it would have scared them. At worst, they'd have thought the loss had broken his mind.

When the last message was gone, he sat quietly. There was one other thing he thought he had to do now that he had full communication access. It wasn't what he wanted.

He started the recording.

"Basia," he said. "This is Praxidike. I wanted you to know that I know Katoa is dead. I saw the body. It didn't...it didn't look like he suffered. And I thought, if I was in your place, that wondering...wondering would be worse. I'm sorry. I'm just..."

He turned off the recording, sent it, and crawled onto the small bed. He'd expected it to be hard and uncomfortable, but the mattress was as cradling as crash couch gel, and he fell asleep easily and woke four hours later like someone had flipped a switch on the back of his head. Amos was still gone, even though it was station midnight. There was still no message from Persis-Strokes, so Prax recorded a polite inquiry—just to be sure the information hadn't gotten lost in transit—then watched it and erased it. He took a long shower, washing his hair twice, shaved, and recorded a new inquiry, looking less like a raving lunatic.

Ten minutes after he sent it, a new-message alert chimed. Intellectually, he knew it couldn't be a response. With lag, his message wouldn't even be at Luna yet. When he pulled it up, it was Nicola. The heart-shaped face looked older than he remembered it. There was the first dusting of gray at her temples. But when she made that soft, sad smile, he was twenty again, sitting across from her in the grand park while bhangra throbbed and lasers traced living art on the domed ice above them. He remembered what it had been like to love her.

"I have your message," she said. "I'm...I'm so sorry, Praxidike. I wish there was more I could do. Things aren't so good here on Ceres. I will talk with Taban. He makes more than I do, and if he understands what's happened, he might want to help too. For my sake.

"Take care of yourself, old man. You look tired."

On the screen, Mei's mother leaned forward and stopped the recording. An icon showed an authorized transfer code for eighty FusionTek Reál. Prax checked the exchange rates, converting the company scrip to UN dollars. It was almost a week's salary. Not enough. Not near enough. But still, it had been a sacrifice for her.

He pulled the message back up, pausing it in the gap between two words. Nicola looked out at him from the terminal, her lips parted barely enough for him to see her pale teeth. Her eyes were sad and playful. He'd thought for so long that it was her soul and not just an accident of physiology that gave her that look of fettered joy. He'd been wrong.

As he sat, lost in history and imagination, a new message appeared. It was from Luna. Persis-Strokes. With a feeling somewhere between anxiety and hope, he went to the attached spreadsheet. At the first set of numbers, his heart sank.

Mei might be out there. She might be alive. Certainly Strickland and his people were there. They could be found. They could be caught. There was justice to be had.

He just couldn't afford it.

Chapter Thirty-Two: Holden

Holden sat in a pull-down chair in the *Rocinante*'s engineering bay reviewing the damage and making notes for Tycho's repair crew. Everyone else was gone. *Some more than others*, he thought.

REPLACE STARBOARD ENGINEERING BULKHEAD.

SIGNIFICANT DAMAGE TO PORT-SIDE POWER CABLE JUNCTION, POSSIBLY REPLACE ENTIRE JUNCTION BOX.

Two lines of text representing hundreds of work hours, hundreds of thousands of dollars in parts. It also represented the aftermath of coming within a hand's breadth of fiery annihilation for the ship and crew. Describing it in two quick sentences felt almost sacrilegious. He made a footnote of the types of civilian parts that Tycho was likely to have available that would work with his Martian warship.

Behind him, a wall monitor streamed a Ceres-based news show.

Holden had turned it on to keep his mind occupied while he tinkered with the ship and made notes.

Which was all bullshit, of course. Sam, the Tycho engineer who usually took the lead on their repair jobs, didn't need his help. She didn't need him making lists of parts for her. She was, in every sense, better qualified to be doing what he was doing right now. But as soon as he turned the job over to her, he wouldn't have any reason to stay on the ship. He would have to confront Fred about the protomolecule on Ganymede.

And maybe lose Naomi in the process.

If his early suspicion was correct and Fred actually had bartered using the protomolecule as currency or, worse, as a weapon, Holden would kill him. He knew that like he knew his own name, and he feared it. That it would be a capital offense and would almost certainly get him burned down on the spot was actually less important than the fact that it would be the final proof that Naomi was right to leave. That he'd turned into the man she feared he was becoming. Just another Detective Miller, dispensing frontier justice from the barrel of his gun. But whenever he pictured the scene, Fred's admission of guilt and heartfelt appeal for mercy, Holden couldn't picture not killing him for what he'd done. He remembered being the sort of man who would make a different choice, but he couldn't actually remember what being that man was *like*.

If he was wrong, and Fred had nothing to do with the tragedy on Ganymede, then she'd have been right all along, and he had just been too stubborn to see it. He might be able to apologize for that with sufficient humility to win her back. Stupidity was usually a lesser crime than vigilantism.

But if Fred *wasn't* the one playing God with the alien supervirus, that was much, much worse for humanity in general. It was an unpleasant thought that the truth that would be worst for humanity was the one that would be best for him. Intellectually, he knew he wouldn't hesitate to sacrifice himself or his happiness to save everyone else. But that didn't stop the tiny voice at the back of his head that said, *Fuck everyone else, I want my girl-friend back.*

Something half remembered pushed up from his subconscious and he wrote MORE COFFEE FILTERS on his list of needed supplies.

The wall panel behind him chimed an alert half a second before his hand terminal buzzed to let him know someone was at the airlock, requesting permission to board. He tapped the screen to switch to the airlock's outer door camera and saw Alex and Sam waiting in the corridor. Sam was still the adorable red-haired pixie in the oversized gray coveralls he remembered. She was carrying a large toolbox and laughing. Alex said something else and she laughed harder, almost dropping her tools. With the intercom off, it was a silent movie.

Holden tapped the intercom button and said, "Come on in, guys." Another tap cycled the outer airlock doors open. Sam waved at the camera and stepped inside.

A few minutes later, the pressure hatch to engineering banged open, and the ladder-lift whined its way down. Sam and Alex stepped off, Sam dropping her tools onto the metal deck with a loud crash.

"What's up?" she said, giving Holden a quick hug. "You getting my girl all shot up again?"

"*Your* girl?" Alex said.

"Not this time," Holden replied, pointing out the damaged bulkheads in the engineering bay to her. "Bomb went off in the cargo bay, burned a hole there and threw some shrapnel into the power junction there."

Sam whistled. "Either that shrapnel took the long way around, or your reactor knows how to duck."

"How long, you think?"

"Bulkhead's simple," she said, punching something into her terminal, then tapping her front teeth with its corner. "We can bring a patch in through the cargo bay in a single piece. Makes the job a lot easier. Power junction takes longer, but not a lot. Say four days if I get my crew on it right now."

"Well," Holden said, wincing like a man who had to keep admitting to new wrongdoings. "We also have a damaged cargo bay door that will either have to be fixed or replaced. And our cargo bay airlock is kind of messed up."

"Couple more days, then," Sam said, then knelt down and began pulling things out of her toolbox. "Mind if I start taking some measurements?"

Holden waved at the wall. "Be my guest."

"Been watching the news a lot?" Sam said, pointing at the talking heads on the wall monitor. "Ganymede is fucked, right?"

"Yeah," Alex said. "Pretty much."

"But it's only Ganymede so far," Holden said. "So that means something I haven't quite figured out yet."

"Naomi's staying with me right now," Sam said as if they'd been talking about that all along. Holden felt his face go still and tried to fight against it, forcing himself to smile.

"Oh. Cool."

"She won't talk about it, but if I find out you did something shitty to her, I'm using this on your dick," she said, holding up a torque wrench. Alex laughed nervously for a second, then trailed off and just looked uncomfortable.

"I consider myself fairly warned," Holden said. "How is she?"

"Quiet," Sam said. "Okay, got what I need. Gonna scoot now and get fabrication to work on cutting this bulkhead patch. See you boys around."

"Bye, Sam," Alex said, watching her ride the ladder-lift until the pressure door closed behind her. "I'm twenty years too old, and I'm pretty sure I've got the wrong plumbin', but I like that gal."

"You and Amos just trade this crush back and forth?" Holden said. "Or should I be worried about you two doing pistols at dawn over her?"

"My love is a pure love," Alex said with a grin. "I wouldn't sully it by actually, you know, doin' anything about it."

"The kind poets write about, then."

"So," Alex said, leaning against a wall and looking at his nails. "Let's talk about the XO situation."

"Let's not."

"Oh, let's do," Alex said, then took a step forward and crossed his arms like a man who was not going to give any ground. "I've been flyin' this boat solo for over a year now. That only works because Naomi is a brilliant ops officer and takes up a whole lotta slack. If we lose her, we don't fly. And that's a fact."

Holden dropped the hand terminal he'd been using into his pocket and slumped back against the reactor shielding.

"I know. I *know*. I never thought she'd actually do this."

"Leave," Alex said.

"Yeah."

"We've never talked about pay," Alex said. "We don't get salaries."

"Pay?" Holden frowned at Alex and banged out a quick drumbeat on the reactor behind him. It echoed like a metal tomb. "Every dime that Fred's given us that hasn't gone to pay for operating the ship is in the account I set up. If you need some of it, twenty-five percent of that money belongs to you."

Alex shook his head and waved his hands. "No, don't get me wrong. I don't need money, and I don't think you're stealin' from us. Just pointing out that we never talked about pay."

"So?"

"So that means we aren't a normal crew. We aren't workin' the ship for money, or because a government drafted us. We're here because we want to be. That's all you've got over us. We believe in the cause, and we want to be part of what you're doing. The minute we lose that, we might as well take a real payin' job."

"But Naomi—" Holden started.

"Was your *girlfriend*," Alex said with a laugh. "Damn, Jim, have you *seen* her? She can get another boyfriend. In fact, you mind if I—"

"I take your point. I hear you. I fucked it up, it's my fault. I know that. All of it. I need to go see Fred and start thinking about how to put it all back together again."

"Unless Fred actually *did* do it."

"Yeah. Unless that."

"I've been wondering when you'd finally drop by," Fred Johnson said as Holden walked through his office door. Fred was looking both better and worse than when Holden had first met him a year earlier. Better because the Outer Planets Alliance, the quasi government that Fred was the titular head of, was no longer a terrorist organization, but a de facto government that could sit at the diplomatic table with the inner planets. And Fred had taken to the role of administrator with a relish he must not have felt for being a freedom fighter. It was visible in the relaxed set of his shoulders, and the half smile that had become his default expression.

And worse because the last year and all the pressures of governance had aged him. His hair was both thinner and whiter, his neck a confusion of loose flesh and old, ropy muscle. His eyes had permanent bags under them now. His coffee-colored skin didn't show many wrinkles, but it had a tinge of gray to it.

But the smile he gave Holden was genuine, and he came around the desk to shake his hand and guide him to a chair.

"I read your report on Ganymede," Fred said. "Talk to me about it. Impressions on the ground."

"Fred," Holden said. "There's something else."

Fred nodded to him as he moved back around his desk and sat down. "Go on."

Holden started to speak, then stopped. Fred was staring at him. His expression hadn't changed, but his eyes were sharper, more focused. Holden felt a sudden and irrational fear that Fred already knew everything he was about to say.

The truth was Holden had always been afraid of Fred. There was a duality to the man that left him on edge. Fred had reached out to the crew of the *Rocinante* at the exact moment they'd needed help the most. He'd become their patron, their safe harbor against the myriad enemies they'd gathered over the last year. And yet Holden couldn't forget that this was still Colonel Frederick Lucius Johnson, the Butcher of Anderson Station. A man who had spent the last decade helping to organize and run the Outer Planets Alliance, an organization that was capable of murder and terrorism to further its goals. Fred had almost certainly ordered some of those murders personally. It was entirely possible that the OPA leader version of Fred had killed more people than even the United Nations Marine colonel version of Fred had.

Would he really balk at using the protomolecule to further his agenda?

Maybe. Maybe that would be going too far. And he'd been a friend, and he deserved the chance to defend himself.

"Fred, I—" Holden started, then stopped.

Fred nodded again, the smile slipping off his face and being replaced by a slight frown. "I'm not going to like this." It was a statement of fact.

Holden grabbed the arms of the office chair and pushed himself to his feet. He shoved more violently than he wanted to and, in the low .3 g of station spin, flew off his feet for a second. Fred chuckled and the frown shifted back into a grin.

And that was it. The grin and the laugh broke the fear and turned it into anger. When Holden settled back to his feet, he leaned forward and slammed both palms onto Fred's desk.

"You," he said, "don't get to laugh. Not until I know for sure it wasn't all your fault. If you can do what I think you might have done and still laugh, I will shoot you right here and now."

Fred's smile didn't change, but something in his eyes did. He wasn't used to being threatened, but it wasn't new territory either.

"What I might have done," Fred said, not turning it into a question, just repeating it back.

"It's the protomolecule, Fred. That's what's happening on Ganymede. A lab with kids as experiments and that black webbing shit and a monster that almost killed my ship. That's my fucking *impression on the ground*. Someone has been playing with the bug, and it might be loose, and the inner planets are shooting each other to shit in orbit around it."

"You think I did this," Fred said. Again, just a flat statement of fact.

"*We threw this shit into Venus,*" Holden yelled. "*I gave* you *the only sample.* And suddenly Ganymede, breadbasket of your future empire, the one place the inner navies won't cede control of, gets a fucking outbreak?"

Fred let the silence answer for a beat.

"Are you asking me if I'm using the protomolecule to drive the inner planets troops off Ganymede, and strengthen my control of the outer planets?"

Fred's quiet tone made Holden realize how loud he'd gotten, and he took a moment to take several deep breaths. When his pulse had slowed a bit, he said, "Yes. Pretty much exactly that."

"You," Fred said with a broad smile that did not extend to his eyes, "do not get to ask me that."

"What?"

"In case you've forgotten, you are an employee of this organization." Fred stood up, stretching to his full height, a dozen centimeters taller than Holden. His smile didn't change, but his body shifted and sort of spread out. Suddenly he looked very large. Holden took a step back before he could stop himself.

"I," Fred continued, "owe you nothing but the terms of our latest contract. Have you completely lost your mind, boy? Charging in here? Shouting at me? *Demanding* answers?"

"No one else could have—" Holden started, but Fred ignored him.

"You gave me the only sample we knew of. But you assume that if you don't know about it, it doesn't exist. I've been putting up with your bullshit for over a year now," Fred said. "This idea you have that the universe owes you answers. This righteous indignation you wield like a club at everyone around you. But I don't *have* to put up with your shit.

"Do you know why that is?"

Holden shook his head, afraid if he spoke, it might come out as a squeak.

"It's because," Fred said, "I'm the *fucking boss*. I run this outfit. You've been pretty useful, and you might be again in the future. But I have enough shit to deal with right now without you starting another one of your crusades at my expense."

"So," Holden said, letting the word drag to two syllables.

"So you're fired. This was your last contract with me. I'll finish fixing the *Roci* and I'll pay you, because I don't break a deal. But I think we've finally built enough ships to start policing our own sky without your help, and even if we haven't, I'm just about done with you."

"Fired," Holden said.

"Now get the hell out of my office before I decide to take the *Roci* too. She's got more Tycho parts on her now than originals. I think I might be able to make a good argument I own that ship."

Holden backed up toward the door, wondering how serious that threat might actually be. Fred watched him go but didn't move. When he reached the door, Fred said, "It wasn't me."

Their gazes met for a long, breathless moment.

"It wasn't me," Fred repeated.

Holden said, "Okay," and backed out the door.

When the door slid shut and blocked Fred from view, Holden let out a long sigh and collapsed against the corridor wall. Fred was right about one thing: He'd been excusing himself with his fear for far too long. *This righteous indignation you wield like a club at everyone around you.* He'd seen humanity almost end due to its own stupidity. It had left him shaken to the core. He'd been running on fear and adrenaline ever since Eros.

But it wasn't an excuse. Not anymore.

He started to pull out his terminal to call Naomi when it hit him like a light turning on. *I'm fired.*

He'd been on an exclusive contract with Fred for over a year. Tycho Station was their home base. Sam had spent almost as much time tuning and patching the *Roci* as Amos had. That was all gone. They'd have to find their own jobs, find their own ports, buy their own repairs. No more patron to hold his hand. For the first time in a very long time, Holden was a real independent captain. He'd need to earn his way by keeping the ship in the air and the crew fed. He paused for a moment, letting that sink in.

It felt great.

Chapter Thirty-Three: Prax

Amos sat forward in his chair. The sheer physical mass of the man made the room seem smaller, and the smell of alcohol and old smoke came off him like heat from a fire. His expression couldn't have been more gentle.

"I don't know what to do," Prax said. "I just don't know what to do. This is all my fault. Nicola was just...she was so lost and so angry. Every day, I woke up and I looked over at her, and all I saw was how trapped she was. And I knew Mei was going to grow up with that. With trying to get her mommy to love her when all Nici wanted to do was be somewhere else. And I thought it would be better. When she started talking about going, I was ready for her to do it, you know? And when Mei...when I had to tell Mei that..."

Prax dropped his head into his hands, rocking slowly back and forth.

"You gonna sick up again, Doc?"

"No. I'm fine. If I'd been a better father to her, she'd still be here."

"We talking about the ex-wife or the kid?"

"I don't care about Nicola. If I'd been there for Mei. If I'd gone to her as soon as we got the warning. If I hadn't waited there in the dome. And for what? Plants? They're dead now anyway. I had one, but I lost it, too. I couldn't even save one. But I could have gotten there. Found her. If I'd—"

"You know she was gone before the shit hit the fan, right?"

Prax shook his head. He wasn't about to let reality forgive him.

"And this. I had a chance. I got out. I got some money. And I was stupid. It was her last chance, and I was stupid about it."

"Yeah, well. You're new at this, Doc."

"She should have had a better dad. She deserved a better dad. Was such a good . . . she was such a good girl."

For the first time, Amos touched him. The wide hand took his shoulder, gripping him from collarbone to scapula and bending Prax's spine until it was straight. Amos' eyes were more than bloodshot, white sclera marbled with red. His breath was hot and astringent, the platonic ideal of a sailor on a shore leave bender. But his voice was sober and steady.

"She's got a fine daddy, Doc. You give a shit, and that's more than a lot of people ever do."

Prax swallowed. He was tired. He was tired of being strong, of being hopeful and determined and preparing for the worst. He didn't want to be himself anymore. He didn't want to be anyone at all. Amos' hand felt like a ship clamp, keeping Prax from spinning away into darkness. All he wanted was to be let go.

"She's gone," Prax said. It felt like a good excuse. An explanation. "They took her away from me, and I don't know who they are, and I can't get her back, and I don't understand."

"It ain't over yet."

Prax nodded, not because he was actually comforted, but

because this was the moment when he knew he should act like he was.

"I'm never going to find her."

"You're wrong."

The door chimed and slid open. Holden stepped in. Prax couldn't see at first what was different about him, but that something had happened...had changed...was unmistakable. The face was the same; the clothes hadn't changed. Prax had the uncanny memory of sitting through a lecture on metamorphosis.

"Hey," Holden said. "Everything all right?"

"Little bumpy," Amos said. Prax saw his own confusion mirrored in Amos' face. They were both aware of the transformation, and neither of them knew what it was. "You get laid or something, Cap?"

"No," Holden said.

"I mean, good on you if you did," Amos said. "It just wasn't how I pictured—"

"I didn't get laid," Holden said hesitantly. The smile that came after was almost radiant. "I got fired."

"Just you got fired, or all of us?"

"All of us."

"Huh," Amos said. He went still for a moment, then shrugged. "All right."

"I need to talk to Naomi, but she's not accepting connections from me. Do you think you could track her down?"

Discomfort pursed Amos' lips like he'd sucked on an old lemon.

"I'm not going to pick a fight," Holden said. "We just didn't leave it in the right place. And it's my fault, so I need to fix it."

"I know she was hanging out down in that one bar Sam told us about last time. The Blauwe Blome. But you make a dick of yourself and I'm not the one that told you."

"Not a problem," Holden said. "Thanks."

The captain turned to leave and then stopped in the doorway. He looked like someone still half in a dream.

"What's bumpy?" he asked. "You said it was bumpy."

"The doc was looking to hire on some Luna private security squad to track the kid down. Didn't work out and he kind of took it bad."

Holden frowned. Prax felt the heat of a blush pushing up his neck.

"I thought *we* were finding the kid," Holden said. He sounded genuinely confused.

"Doc wasn't clear on that."

"Oh," Holden said. He turned to Prax. "We're finding your kid. You don't need to get someone else."

"I can't pay you," Prax said. "All my accounts were on the Ganymede system, and even if they're still there, I can't access them. I just have what people are giving me. I can probably get something like a thousand dollars UN. Is that enough?"

"No," Holden said. "That won't buy a week's air, much less water. We'll have to take care of that."

Holden tilted his head like he was listening to something only he could hear.

"I've already talked to my ex-wife," Prax said. "And my parents. I can't think of anyone else."

"How about everyone?" Holden said.

"I'm James Holden," the captain said from the huge screen of the *Rocinante*'s pilot capsule, "and I'm here to ask for your help. Four months ago, hours before the first attack on Ganymede, a little girl with a life-threatening genetic illness was abducted from her day care. In the chaos that—"

Alex stopped the playback. Prax tried to sit up, but the gimbaled copilot's chair only shifted under him, and he lay back.

"I don't know," Alex said from the pilot's couch. "The green background kinda makes him look pasty, don't you think?"

Prax narrowed his eyes a degree, considered, then nodded.

"It's not really his color," Prax said. "Maybe if it was darker."

"I'll try that," the pilot said, tapping at his screen. "Normally it's Naomi who does this stuff. Communications packages ain't exactly my first love. But we'll get it done. How about this?"

"Better," Prax said.

"I'm James Holden, and I'm here to ask for your help. Four months ago..."

Holden's part of the little presentation was less than a minute, speaking into the camera from Amos' hand terminal. After that, Amos and Prax had spent an hour trying to create the rest. Alex had been the one to suggest using the better equipment on the *Rocinante*. Once they'd done that, putting together the information had been easy. He'd taken the start he'd made for Nicola and his parents as the template. Alex helped him record the rest—an explanation of Mei's condition; the security footage of Strickland and the mysterious woman taking her from the day care; the data from the secret lab, complete with images of the protomolecule filament; pictures of Mei playing in the parks; and a short video from her second birthday party, when she smeared cake frosting on her forehead.

Prax felt odd watching himself speak. He had seen plenty of recordings of himself, but the man on the screen was thinner than he'd expected. Older. His voice was higher than the one he heard in his own ears, and less hesitant. The Praxidike Meng who was about to be broadcast out to the whole of humanity was a different man than he was, but it was close enough. And if it helped to find Mei, it would do. If it brought her back, he'd be anyone.

Alex slid his fingers across his controls, rearranging the presentation, connecting the images of Mei to the timeline to Holden. They had set up an account with a Belt-based credit union that had a suite of options for short-term unincorporated nonprofit concerns so that any contributions could be accepted automatically. Prax watched, wanting badly to offer comment or take control. But there was nothing more to do.

"All right," Alex said. "That's about as pretty as I can make it."

"Okay, then," Prax said. "What do we do with it now?"

Alex looked over. He seemed tired, but there was also an excitement.

"Hit send."

"But the review process..."

"There is no review process, Doc. This isn't a government thing. Hell, it's not even a business. It's just us monkeys flying fast and tryin' to keep our butts out of the engine plume."

"Oh," Prax said. "Really?"

"You hang around the captain long enough, you get used to it. You might want to take a day, though. Think it through."

Prax lifted himself on one elbow.

"Think what through?"

"Sending this out. If it works the way we're thinking, you're about to get a lot of attention. Maybe it'll be what we're hoping for; maybe it'll be something else. All I'm saying is you can't unscramble that egg."

Prax considered for a few seconds. The screens glowed.

"It's Mei," Prax said.

"All right, then," Alex said, and shifted communication control to the copilot's station. "You want to do the honors?"

"Where is it going? I mean, where are we sending it?"

"Simple broadcast," Alex said. "Probably get picked up by some local feeds in the Belt. But it's the captain, so folks will watch it, pass it around on the net. And..."

"And?"

"We didn't put our hitchhiker in, but the filament out of that glass case? We're kind of announcing that the protomolecule's still out there. That's gonna boost the signal."

"And we think that's going to help?"

"First time we did something like this, it started a war," Alex said. " 'Help' might be a strong word for it. Stir things up, though."

Prax shrugged and hit send.

"Torpedoes away," Alex said, chuckling.

Prax slept on the station, serenaded by the hum of the air recyclers. Amos was gone again, leaving only a note that Prax shouldn't wait up. It was probably his imagination that made the spin gravity seem to feel different. With a diameter as wide as Tycho's, the Coriolis effect shouldn't have been uncomfortably noticeable, and certainly not when he lay there, motionless, in the darkness of his room. And still, he couldn't get comfortable. He couldn't forget that he was being turned, inertia pressing him against the thin mattress as his body tried to fly out into the void. Most of the time he'd been on the *Rocinante*, he'd been able to trick his mind into thinking that he had the reassuring mass of a moon under him. It wasn't, he decided, an artifact of how the acceleration was generated so much as what it meant.

As his mind slowly spiraled down, bits of his self breaking apart like a meteor hitting atmosphere, he felt a massive welling-up of gratitude. Part of it was to Holden and part to Amos. The whole crew of the *Rocinante*. Half-dreaming, he was on Ganymede again. He was starving, walking down ice corridors with the certainty that somewhere nearby, one of his soybeans had been infected with the protomolecule and was tracking him, bent on revenge. With the broken logic of dreams, he was also on Tycho, looking for work, but all the people he gave his CV to shook their heads and told him he was missing some sort of degree or credential he didn't recognize or understand. The only thing that made it bearable was a deeper knowledge—certain as bone—that none of it was true. That he was sleeping, and that when he woke, he would be somewhere safe.

What did wake him at last was the rich smell of beef. His eyes were crusted like he'd been crying in his sleep, the tears leaving salt residues where they'd evaporated. The shower was hissing and splashing. Prax pulled on his jumpsuit, wondering again why it had TACHI printed across the back.

Breakfast waited on the table: steak and eggs, flour tortillas, and black coffee. Real food that had cost someone a small fortune. There were two plates, so Prax chose one and started eating. It had probably cost a tenth of the money he had from Nicola, but it tasted wonderful. Amos ducked out of the shower, a towel wrapped around his hips. A massive white scar puckered the right side of his abdomen, pulling his navel off center, and a nearly photographic tattoo of a young woman with wavy hair and almond-shaped eyes covered his heart. Prax thought there was a word under the tattooed face, but he didn't want to stare.

"Hey, Doc," Amos said. "You're looking better."

"I got some rest," Prax said as Amos walked into his own room and closed the door behind him. When Prax spoke again, he raised his voice. "I want to thank you. I was feeling low last night. And whether you and the others can actually help find Mei or not—"

"Why wouldn't we be able to find her?" Amos asked, his voice muffled by the door. "You ain't losing respect for me, are you, Doc?"

"No," Prax said. "No, not at all. I only meant that what you and the captain are offering is...it's a huge..."

Amos came back out grinning. His jumpsuit covered scars and tattoos as if they'd never been.

"I knew what you meant. I was just joshing you. You like that steak? Keep wondering where they put the cows on this thing, don't you?"

"Oh no, this is vat-grown. You can tell from the way the muscle fibers grow. You see how these parts right here are layered? Actually makes it easier to get a good marbled cut than when you carve it out of a steer."

"No shit?" Amos said, sitting across from him. "I didn't know that."

"Microgravity also makes fish more nutritious," Prax said around a mouthful of egg. "Increases the oil production. No one knows why, but there are a couple very interesting studies about it. They think it may not be the low g itself so much as the constant flow you have to have so that the animals don't stop swimming, make a bubble of oxygen-depleted water, and suffocate."

Amos ripped a bit of tortilla and dipped it into the yolk.

"This is what dinner conversation's like in your family, ain't it?"

Prax blinked.

"Mostly, yes. Why? What do you talk about?"

Amos chuckled. He seemed to be in a very good mood. There was a relaxed look about his shoulders, and something in the set of his jaw had changed. Prax remembered the previous night's conversation with the captain.

"You got laid, didn't you?"

"Oh hell yes," Amos said. "But that's not the best part."

"It's not?"

"Oh, it's a fucking good part, but there's nothing better in the world than getting a job the day after your ass gets canned."

A pang of confusion touched Prax. Amos pulled his hand terminal out of his pocket, tapped it twice, and slid it across the table. The screen showed a red security border and the name of the credit union Alex had been working with the night before. When he saw the balance, his eyes went wide.

"Is...is that...?"

"That's enough to keep the *Roci* flying for a month, and we got it in seven hours," Amos said. "You just hired yourself a team, Doc."

"I don't know...really?"

"Not just that. Take a look at the messages you've got coming in. Captain made a pretty big splash back in the day, but your kiddo? All that shit that came down on Ganymede just got itself a face, and it's her."

Prax pulled up his own terminal. The mailbox associated with the presentation had over five hundred video messages and thousands of texts. He began going through them. Men and women he didn't know—some of them in tears—offered up their prayers and anger and support. A Belter with a wild mane of gray-black hair gibbered in patois so thick Prax could barely make it out. As near as he could tell, the man was offering to kill someone for him.

Half an hour later, Prax's eggs had congealed. A woman from Ceres told him that she'd lost her daughter in a divorce, and that she was sending him her month's chewing tobacco money. A group of food engineers on Luna had passed the hat and sent along what would have been a month's salary if Prax had still been a botanist. An old Martian man with skin the color of chocolate and powdered-sugar hair gazed seriously into a camera halfway across the solar system and said he was with Prax.

When the next message began, it looked just like the others before it. The man in the image was older—eighty, maybe ninety—with a fringe of white hair clinging to the back of his skull and a craggy face. There was something about his expression that caught Prax's attention. A hesitance.

"Dr. Meng," the man said. He had a slushy accent that reminded Prax of recordings of his own grandfather. "I'm very sorry to hear of all you and your family have suffered. Are suffering." The man licked his lips. "The security video on your presentation. I believe I know the man in it. But his name isn't Strickland…"

Chapter Thirty-Four: Holden

According to the station directory, the Blauwe Blome was famous for two things: a drink called the Blue Meanie and its large number of Golgo tables. The guidebook warned potential patrons that the station allowed the bar to serve only two Blue Meanies to each customer due to the drink's fairly suicidal mixture of ethanol, caffeine, and methylphenidate. And, Holden guessed, some kind of blue food coloring.

As he walked through the corridors of Tycho's leisure section, the guidebook began explaining the rules of Golgo to him. After a few moments of utter confusion—*goals are said to be "borrowed" when the defense deflects the drive*—he shut it off. There was very little chance he was going to be playing games. And a drink that removed your inhibitions and left you wired and full of energy would be redundant right now.

The truth was Holden had never felt better in his life.

He'd messed a lot of things up over the last year. He'd driven his crew away from him. He'd aligned himself with a side he wasn't sure he agreed with in exchange for safety. He might have ruined the one healthy relationship he'd had in his life. He'd been driven by his fear to become someone else. Someone who handled fear by turning it into violence. Someone who Naomi didn't love, who his crew didn't respect, who he himself didn't like much.

The fear wasn't gone. It was still there, making his scalp crawl every time he thought about Ganymede, and about what might be loose and growing there right now. But for the first time in a long time, he was aware of it and wasn't hiding from it. He had given himself permission to be afraid. It made all the difference.

Holden heard the Blauwe Blome several seconds before he saw it. It began as a barely audible rhythmic thumping, which gradually increased in volume and picked up an electronic wail and a woman's voice singing in mixed Hindi and Russian. By the time he reached the club's front door, the song had changed to two men in an alternating chant that sounded like an argument set to music. The electronic wail was replaced by angry guitars. The bass line changed not at all.

Inside, the club was an all-out assault on the senses. A massive dance floor dominated the center space, and the dozens of bodies writhing on it were bathed in a constantly changing light show that shifted and flashed in time to the music. The music had been loud out in the corridor, but inside, it became deafening. A long chrome bar was set against one wall, and half a dozen bartenders were frantically filling drink orders.

A sign on the back wall read GOLGO and had an arrow pointing down a long hallway. Holden followed it, the music fading with each step so that by the time he reached the back room with the game tables, it was back to being muted bass lines.

Naomi was at one of the tables with her friend Sam the engineer and a cluster of other Belters. Her hair was pulled back with a red elastic band wide enough to be decorative. She'd switched out her jumpsuit for a pair of gray tailored slacks he hadn't known she owned and a yellow blouse that made her caramel-colored skin seem darker. Holden had to stop for a moment. She smiled at someone who wasn't him, and his chest went tight.

As he approached, Sam threw a small metal ball at the table. The group at the other end reacted with sudden violent movements. He couldn't see exactly what was happening from where he stood, but the slumped shoulders and halfhearted curses coming from the second group led Holden to believe that Sam had done something good for her team.

Sam spun around and threw up her hand. The group at her end of the table, which included Naomi, took turns slapping her palm. Sam saw him first and said something he couldn't hear. Naomi turned around and gave him a speculative look that stopped him in his tracks. She didn't smile and she didn't frown. He raised his palms in what he hoped was an *I didn't come to fight* gesture. For a moment, they stood facing each other across the noisy room.

Jesus, he thought, *how did I let it come to this?*

Naomi nodded at him and pointed at a table in one corner of the room. He sat down and ordered himself a drink. Not one of the blue liver-killers the bar was famous for, just a cheap Belt-produced scotch. He'd grown to, if not appreciate, at least tolerate the faint mold aftertaste it always had. Naomi said goodbye to the rest of her team for a few minutes and then walked over. It wasn't a casual stroll, but it wasn't the gait of someone going to a dreaded meeting either.

"Can I order you something?" Holden asked as she sat.

"Sure, I'll take a grapefruit martini," she said. While Holden entered the order on the table, she looked him over with a mysterious half smile that turned his belly to liquid.

"Okay," he said, authorizing his terminal to open a bar tab and pay for the drinks. "One hideous martini on its way."

Naomi laughed. "Hideous?"

"A near-fatal case of scurvy being the only reason I can imagine drinking something with grapefruit juice in it."

She laughed again, untying at least one of the knots in Holden's gut, and they sat together in companionable silence until the drinks arrived. She took a small sip and smacked her lips in appreciation, then said, "Okay. Spill."

Holden took a much longer drink, nearly finishing off the small glass of scotch in a single gulp, trying to convince himself that the spreading warmth in his belly could stand in for courage. *I didn't feel comfortable with where we left things, and I thought that we should talk. Kind of process this together.* He cleared his throat.

"I fucked everything up," he said. "I've treated my friends badly. Worse than badly. You were absolutely right to do what you did. I couldn't hear what you were saying at the time, but you were right to say it."

Naomi took another drink of her martini, then casually reached up and pulled out the elastic band holding her masses of black curls behind her head. Her hair fell down around her face in a tangle, making Holden think of ivy-covered stone walls. He realized that for as long as he'd known her, Naomi had always let her hair down in emotional situations. She hid behind it, not literally, but because it was her best feature. The eye was just naturally drawn to its glossy black curls. A distraction technique. It made her suddenly seem very human, as vulnerable and lost as he was. Holden felt a rush of affection for her that must have showed on his face, because she looked at him and then blushed.

"What is this, Jim?"

"An apology?" he said. "An admission that you were right, and that I was turning into my own screwed-up version of Miller? Those at the very least. Hopefully opening the dialogue to reconciliation, if I'm lucky."

"I'm glad," Naomi said. "I'm glad you're figuring that out. But I've been saying this for months now, and you—"

"Wait," Holden said. He could feel her pulling back from him, not letting herself believe. All he had left to offer her was absolute truth, so he did. "I couldn't hear you. Because I've been terrified, and I've been a coward."

"Fear doesn't make you a coward."

"No," he said. "Of course it doesn't. But refusing to face up to it. To not admit to you how I felt. To not let you and Alex and Amos help me. That was cowardice. And it may have cost me you, the crew's loyalty, everything I really care about. It made me keep a bad job a lot longer than I should have because the job was safe."

A small knot of the Golgo players began drifting toward their table, and Holden was gratified when he saw Naomi wave them off. It meant she wanted to keep talking. That was a start.

"Tell me," she said. "Where are you going from here?"

"I have no idea," Holden replied with a grin. "And that's the best feeling I've had in ages. But no matter what happens next, I need you there."

When she started to protest, Holden quickly put up a hand to stop her and said, "No, I don't mean like that. I'd love to win you back, but I'm perfectly okay with the idea that it might take some time, or never happen at all. I mean the *Roci* needs you back. The crew needs you there."

"I don't want to leave her," Naomi said with a shy smile.

"She's your home," Holden said. "Always will be as long as you want it. And that's true no matter what happens between us."

Naomi began wrapping one thick strand of hair around her finger and drank off the last of her drink. Holden pointed at the table menu, but she shook her hand at him.

"This is because you confronted Fred, right?"

"Yeah, partly," Holden said. "I was standing in his office feeling terrified and realizing I'd been afraid for a long, long time. I've screwed things up with him too. Some of that's probably his fault. He's a true believer, and those are bad people to climb into bed with. But it's mostly still mine."

"Did you quit?"

"He fired me, but I was probably going to quit."

"So," Naomi said. "You've lost us our paying gig and our patron. I guess I feel a little flattered that the part you're trying to patch up is me."

"You," Holden said, "are the only part I really care about fixing."

"You know what happens now, right?"

"You move back onto the ship?"

Naomi just smiled the comment away. "Now we pay for our own repairs. If we fire a torpedo, we have to find someone to sell us a new one. We pay for water, air, docking fees, food, and medical supplies for our very expensive automated sick bay. Have a plan for that?"

"Nope!" Holden said. "But I have to say, for some reason, it feels great."

"And when the euphoria passes?"

"I'll make a plan."

Her smile grew reflective and she tugged on her lock of hair.

"I'm not ready to move back to the ship right now," Naomi said, reaching across the table to take his hand in hers. "But by the time the *Roci* is patched up, I'll need my cabin back."

"I'll move the rest of my stuff out immediately."

"Jim," she said, squeezing his fingers once before letting go. "I love you, and we're not okay yet. But this is a good start."

And yes, Holden thought, it really was.

Holden woke up in his old cabin on the *Rocinante* feeling better than he had in months. He climbed out of his bunk and wandered naked through the empty ship to the head. He took an hour-long shower in water he actually had to pay for now, heated by electricity the dock would be charging him for by the kilowatt-hour. He walked back to his bunk, drying skin made pink by the almost scalding water as he went.

He made and ate a large breakfast and drank five cups of coffee while catching up on the technical reports on the *Roci*'s repairs until he was sure he understood everything about what had been done. Holden had switched to reading a column about the state of Mars-Earth relations by a political humorist when his terminal buzzed at him, and a call came through from Amos.

"Hey, Cap," he said, his big face filling the small screen. "You coming over to the station today? Or should we come meet you on the *Roci*?"

"Let's meet here," Holden replied. "Sam and her team will be working today and I want to keep an eye on things."

"See you in a few, then," Amos said, and killed the connection.

Holden tried to finish the humor column but kept getting distracted and having to read the same passage over again. He finally gave up and cleaned the galley for a while, then set the coffee-maker to brew a fresh pot for Amos and the work crew when they arrived.

The machine was gurgling happily to itself like a content infant when the deck hatch clanged open and Amos and Prax climbed down the crew ladder and into the galley.

"Cap," Amos said, dropping into a chair with a thump. Prax followed him into the room but didn't sit. Holden grabbed mugs and pulled two more cups of coffee, then set them on the table.

"What's the news?" he said.

Amos answered with a shit-eating grin and spun his terminal across the table to Holden. When Holden looked at it, it was displaying the account information for Prax's "save Mei" fund. It had just over half a million UN dollars in it.

Holden whistled and slumped into a chair. "Jesus grinned, Amos. I'd hoped we might...but never this."

"Yeah, it was a little under 300k this morning. It's gone up another 200k just over the last three hours. Seems like everyone following the Ganymede shit on the news has made little Mei the poster child for the tragedy."

"Is this enough?" Prax cut in, anxiety in his voice.

"Oh, hell yes," Holden said with a laugh. "Way more than enough. This will fund our rescue mission just fine."

"Also, we got a clue," Amos said, pausing dramatically to sip his coffee.

"About Mei?"

"Yep," Amos said, adding a little more sugar to his cup. "Prax, send him that message you got."

Holden watched the message three times, grinning wider with each viewing. "The security video on your presentation. I believe I know the man in it," the elderly gentleman on the screen was saying. "But his name isn't Strickland. When I worked with him at Ceres Mining and Tech University, his name was Merrian. Carlos Merrian."

"That," Holden said after his final viewing, "is what my old buddy Detective Miller might have called a *lead*."

"What now, chief?" Amos asked.

"I think I need to make a phone call."

"Okay. The doc and I will get out of your hair and watch his money roll in."

They left together, Holden waiting until the deck hatch slammed behind them to send a connection request to the switchboard at Ceres M&T. The lag was running about fifteen minutes with Tycho's current location, so he settled back and played a simple puzzle game on his terminal that left his mind free to think and plan. If they knew who Strickland had been before he was Strickland, they might be able to trace his career history. And somewhere along the way, he'd stopped being a guy named Carlos who worked at a tech school, and became a guy named Strickland who stole little kids. Knowing *why* would be a good start to learning where he might be now.

Almost forty minutes after sending out the request, he received a reply. He was a little surprised to see the elderly man from the video message. He hadn't expected to connect on his first try.

"Hello," the man said. "I'm Dr. Moynahan. I've been expecting your message. I assume you want to know the details about Dr. Merrian. To make a long story short, he and I worked together at the CMTU biosciences lab. He was working on biological development constraint systems. He was never good at playing the university game. Didn't make many allies while he was here. So when he crossed some ethical gray areas, they were only too happy to run him out of town. I don't know the details on that. I wasn't his department head. Let me know if you need anything else."

Holden watched the message twice, taking notes and cursing the fifteen-minute lag. When he was ready, he sent a reply back.

"Thank you so much for the help, Dr. Moynahan. We really appreciate it. I don't suppose you know what happened after he was kicked out of the university, do you? Did he go to another institution? Take a corporate job? Anything?"

He hit send and sat back to wait again. He tried the puzzle game but got annoyed and turned it off. Instead, he pulled up the Tycho public entertainment feed and watched a children's cartoon that was frantic and loud enough to distract him.

When his terminal buzzed with the incoming message, he almost knocked it off the table in his haste to start the video.

"Actually," Dr. Moynahan said, scratching at the gray stubble on his chin while he spoke, "he never even made it in front of the ethics review. Quit the day before. Made a lot of fuss, walking through the lab and yelling that we weren't going to be able to push him around anymore. That he had a bigwig corporate job with all the funding and resources he wanted. Called us small-minded pencil pushers stagnating in a quagmire of petty ethical constraints. Can't remember the name of the company he was going to work for, though."

Holden hit pause and felt a chill go down his spine. *Stagnating in a quagmire of petty ethical constraints.* He didn't need Moynahan to tell him which company would snatch a man like that up. He'd heard almost those exact words spoken by Antony Dresden, the architect of the Eros project that had killed a million and a half people as part of a grand biology experiment.

Carlos Merrian had gone to work for Protogen and disappeared. He'd come back as Strickland, abductor of small children.

And, Holden thought, the murderer too.

Chapter Thirty-Five: Avasarala

On the screen, the young man laughed as he had laughed twenty-five seconds earlier on Earth. It was the level of lag Avasarala hated the most. Too much for the conversation to feel anything like normal, but not quite enough to make it impossible. Everything she did took too long, every reading of reaction and nuance crippled by the effort to guess what exactly in her words and expression ten seconds before had elicited it.

"Only you," he said, "could take another Earth-Mars war, turn it into a private cruise, and then seem pissed off about it. Anyone in my office would give their left testicle to go with you."

"Next time I'll take up a collection, but—"

"As far as an accurate military inventory," he said twenty-five seconds ago, "there are reports in place, but they're not as good as I'd like. Because it's you, I've got a couple of my interns building search parameters. My impression is that the research budget is about a tenth of the money going to actual research. With your clearances, I have rights to look at it, but these Navy guys are pretty good at obscuring things. I think you'll find..." His expression clouded. "A collection?"

"Forget it. You were saying?"

She waited fifty seconds, resenting each individually.

"I don't know that we'll be able to get a definitive answer," the young man said. "We might get lucky, but if it's something they want to hide, they can probably hide it."

Especially since they'll know you're looking for it, and what I asked you to look for, Avasarala thought. Even if the income stream between Mao-Kwikowski, Nguyen, and Errinwright was in all the budgets right now, by the time Avasarala's allies looked, it would be hidden. All she could do was keep pushing on as many fronts as she could devise and hope that they fucked up. Three more days of information requests and queries, and she could ask for traffic analysis. She couldn't know exactly what information they were hiding, but if she could find out what kinds and categories of data they were keeping away from her, that would tell her something.

Something, but not much.

"Do what you can," she said. "I'll luxuriate out here in the middle of nowhere. Get back to me."

She didn't wait fifty seconds for a round of etiquette and farewell. Life was too short for that shit.

Her private quarters on the *Guanshiyin* were gorgeous. The bed and couch matched the deep carpet in tones of gold and green that should have clashed but didn't. The light was the best approximation of mid-morning sunlight that she'd ever seen, and the air recyclers were scented to give everything just a note of turned earth and fresh-cut grass. Only the low thrust gravity spoiled the illusion of being in a private country club somewhere in the green belt of south Asia. The low gravity and the goddamned lag.

She hated low gravity. Even if the acceleration was perfectly smooth and the yacht never had to shift or move to avoid debris, her guts were used to a full g pulling things down. She hadn't digested anything well since she'd come on board, and she always felt short of breath.

Her system chimed. A new report from Venus. She popped it open. The preliminary analysis of the wreckage from the *Arboghast* was under way. There was some ionizing in the metal that was apparently consistent with someone's theory of how the proto-molecule functioned. It was the first time a prediction had been confirmed, the first tiny toehold toward a genuine understanding of what was happening on Venus. There was an exact timing of the three energy spikes. There was a spectral analysis of the upper atmosphere of Venus that showed more elemental nitrogen than expected. Avasarala felt her eyes glazing over. The truth was she didn't care.

She should. It was important. Possibly more important than anything else that was happening. But just like Errinwright and Nguyen and all the others, she was caught up in this smaller, human struggle of war and influence and the tribal division between Earth and Mars. The outer planets too, if you took them seriously.

Hell, at this point she was more worried about Bobbie and Cotyar than she was about Venus. Cotyar was a good man, and his disapproval left her feeling defensive and pissed off. And Bobbie looked like she was about to crack. And why not? The woman had watched her friends die around her, had been stripped of her context, and was now working for her traditional enemy. The marine was tough, in more ways than one, and having someone on the team with no allegiance or ties to anyone on Earth was a real benefit. Especially after fucking Soren.

She leaned back in her chair, unnerved by how different it felt when she weighed so little. Soren still smarted. Not the betrayal itself; betrayal was an occupational hazard. If she started getting her feelings hurt by that, she really should retire. No, it was that she hadn't seen it. She'd let herself have a blind spot, and Errin-wright had known how to use it. How to disenfranchise her. She hated being outplayed. And more than that, she hated that her failure was going to mean more war, more violence, more children dying.

That was the price for screwing up. More dead children.

So she wouldn't screw up anymore.

She could practically see Arjun, the gentle sorrow in his eyes. *It isn't all your responsibility*, he would say.

"It's everyone's fucking responsibility," she said out loud. "But I'm the one who's taking it seriously."

She smiled. Let Mao's monitors and spies make sense of that. She let herself imagine them searching her room for some other transmission device, trying to find who she'd been speaking to. Or they'd just think the old lady was losing her beans.

Let 'em wonder.

She closed out the Venus report. Another message had arrived while she was in her reverie, flagged as an issue she'd requested follow-up on. When she read the intelligence summary, her eyebrows rose.

"I'm James Holden, and I'm here to ask for your help."

Avasarala watched Bobbie watching the screen. She looked exhausted and restless both. Her eyes weren't bloodshot so much as dry-looking. Like bearings without enough grease. If she'd needed an example to demonstrate the difference between sleepy and tired, it would have been the marine.

"So he got out, then," Bobbie said.

"Him and his pet botanist and the whole damned crew," Avasarala said. "So now we have one story about what they were doing on Ganymede that got your boys and ours so excited they started shooting each other."

Bobbie looked up at her.

"Do you think it's true?"

"What is truth?" Avasarala said. "I think Holden has a long

history of blabbing whatever he knows or thinks he knows all over creation. True or not, he believes it."

"And the part about the protomolecule? I mean, he just told everyone that the protomolecule is loose on Ganymede."

"He did."

"People have got to be reacting to that, right?"

Avasarala flipped to the intelligence summary, then to feeds of the riots on Ganymede. Thin, frightened people, exhausted by tragedy and war and fueled by panic. She could tell that the security forces arrayed against them were trying to be gentle. These weren't thugs enjoying the use of force. These were orderlies trying to keep the frail and dying from hurting themselves and each other, walking the line between necessary violence and ineffectiveness.

"Fifty dead so far," Avasarala said. "That's the estimate, anyway. That place is so ass-fucked right now, they might have been going to die of sickness and malnutrition anyway. But they died of this instead."

"I went to that restaurant," Bobbie said.

Avasarala frowned, trying to make it into a metaphor for something. Bobbie pointed at the screen.

"The one they're dying in front of? I ate there just after I arrived at the deployment. They had good sausage."

"Sorry," Avasarala said, but the marine only shook her head.

"So that cat's out of the bag," she said.

"Maybe," Avasarala said. "Maybe not."

"James Holden just told the whole system that the protomolecule's on Ganymede. In what universe is that *maybe not*?"

Avasarala pulled up a mainstream newsfeed, checked the flags, and pulled the one with the listed experts she wanted. The data buffered for a few seconds while she lifted her finger for patience.

"—totally irresponsible," a grave-cheeked man in a lab coat and kufi cap said. The contempt in his voice could have peeled paint.

The interviewer appeared beside him. She was maybe twenty years old, with hair cut short and straight and a dark suit that said she was a serious journalist.

"So you're saying the protomolecule *isn't* involved?"

"It isn't. The images James Holden and his little group are sending have nothing to do with the protomolecule. That webbing is what happens when you have a binding agent leak. It happens all the time."

"So there isn't any reason to panic."

"Alice," the expert said, turning his condescension to the interviewer. "Within a few days of exposure, Eros was a living horror show. In the time since hostilities opened, Ganymede hasn't shown one sign of a live infection. Not one."

"But he has a scientist with him. The botanist Dr. Praxidike Meng, whose daughter—"

"I don't know this Meng fellow, but playing with a few soybeans makes him as much an expert on the protomolecule as it makes him a brain surgeon. I'm very sorry, of course, about his missing daughter, but no. If the protomolecule were on Ganymede, we'd have known long ago. This panic is over *literally* nothing."

"He can go on like that for hours," Avasarala said, shutting down the screen. "And we have dozens like him. Mars is going to be doing the same thing. Saturating the newsfeeds with the counter-story."

"Impressive," Bobbie said, pushing herself back from the desk.

"It keeps people calm. That's the important thing. Holden thinks he's a hero, power to the people, information wants to be free blah blah blah, but he's a fucking moron."

"He's on his own ship."

Avasarala crossed her arms. "What's your point?"

"He's on his own ship and we're not."

"So we're all fucking morons," Avasarala said. "Fine."

Bobbie stood up and started pacing the room. She turned well before she reached the wall. The woman was used to pacing in smaller quarters.

"What do you want me to do about it?" Bobbie asked.

"Nothing," Avasarala said. "What the hell could you do about it? You're stuck out here with me. I can hardly do anything, and I've got friends in high places. You've got *nothing*. I only wanted to talk to someone I didn't have to wait two minutes to let interrupt me."

She'd taken it too far. Bobbie's expression eased, went calm and closed and distant. She was shutting down. Avasarala lowered herself to the edge of the bed.

"That wasn't fair," Avasarala said.

"If you say so."

"I fucking say so."

The marine tilted her head. "Was that an apology?"

"As close to one as I'm giving right now."

Something shifted in Avasarala's mind. Not about Venus, or James Holden and his *poor lost girl* appeal, or even Errinwright. It had to do with Bobbie and her pacing and her sleeplessness. Then she got it and laughed once mirthlessly. Bobbie crossed her arms, her steady silence a question.

"It isn't funny," Avasarala said.

"Try me."

"You remind me of my daughter."

"Yeah?"

She'd pissed Bobbie off, and now she was going to have to explain herself. The air recyclers hummed to themselves. Something far off in the bowels of the yacht groaned like they were on an ancient sailing ship made from timber and tar.

"My son died when he was fifteen," Avasarala said. "Skiing. Did I tell you this? He was on a slope that he'd run twenty, thirty times before. He knew it, but something happened and he ran into a tree. They guessed he was going something like sixty kilometers an hour when he hit. Some people survive an impact like that, but not him."

For a moment, she was there again, in the house with the medic on the screen giving her the news. She could still smell the incense

Arjun had been burning at the time. She could still hear the raindrops against the window, tapping like fingertips. It was the worst memory she had, and it was perfect and clear. She took a long, deep shuddering breath.

"I almost got divorced three times in the next six months. Arjun was a saint, but saints have their limits. We fought about anything. About nothing. Each of us blamed ourselves for not saving Charanpal, and we resented it when the other one tried to take some responsibility. And so, of course, my daughter suffered the worst.

"There was a night when we were out at something, Arjun and I. We got home late, and we'd been fighting. Ashanti was in the kitchen, washing dishes. Washing clean dishes by hand. Scrubbing them with a cloth and this terrible abrasive cleanser. Her fingers were bleeding, but she didn't seem to notice, you know? I tried to stop her, pull her away, but she started screaming and she wouldn't be quiet again until I let her resume her washing. I was so angry I couldn't see. I hated my daughter. For that moment, I hated her."

"And I remind you of her how exactly?"

Avasarala gestured to the room. Its bed with real linen sheets. The textured paper on the walls, the scented air.

"You can't compromise. You can't see things the way I tell you that they are, and when I try and make you, you go away."

"Is that what you want?" Bobbie said. Her voice was crawling up to a higher energy level. It was anger, but it brought her back to being present. "You want me to agree with whatever you say, and if I don't, you're going to hate me for it?"

"Of course I want you to call me on my bullshit. That's what I pay you for. I'm only going to hate you for the moment," Avasarala said. "I love my daughter very much."

"I'm sure you do, ma'am. I'm not her."

Avasarala sighed.

"I didn't call you in here and show you all of this because I was tired of the lag. I'm worried. Fuck it, I'm *scared*."

"About what?"

"You want a list?"

Bobbie actually smiled. Avasarala felt herself smiling back.

"I'm scared that I've been outplayed already," she said. "I'm afraid that I won't be able to stop the hawks and their cabal from using their pretty new toys. And...and I'm afraid that I might be wrong. What happens, Bobbie? What happens if whatever the hell that is on Venus rises up and finds us as divided and screwed up and ineffective as we are right now?"

"I don't know."

Avasarala's terminal chimed. She glanced at the new message. A note from Admiral Souther. Avasarala had sent him an utterly innocuous note about having lunch when they both got back to Earth, then coded it for high-security clearance with a private encryption schema. It would take her handlers a couple of hours at least to crack it. She tabbed it open. The reply was plain text.

LOVE TO.

THE EAGLE LANDS AT MIDNIGHT. PETTING ZOOS ARE ILLEGAL IN ROME.

Avasarala laughed. It was real pleasure this time. Bobbie loomed up over her shoulder, and Avasarala turned the screen so that the big marine could peer down at it.

"What's that mean?"

Avasarala motioned her down close enough that her lips were almost against Bobbie's ear. At that intimate distance, the big woman smelled of clean sweat and the cucumber-scented emollient that was in all Mao's guest quarters.

"Nothing," Avasarala whispered. "He's just following my lead, but they'll chew their livers out guessing at it."

Bobbie stood up. Her expression of incredulity was eloquent.

"This really is how government works, isn't it?"

"Welcome to the monkey house," Avasarala said.

"I think I might go get drunk."

"And I'll get back to work."

At the doorway, Bobbie paused. She looked small in the wide frame. A doorframe on a spaceship that left Roberta Draper looking small. There was nothing about the yacht that wasn't tastefully obscene.

"What happened with her?"

"Who?"

"Your daughter."

Avasarala closed her terminal.

"Arjun sang to her until she stopped. It took about three hours. He sat on the counter and went through all the songs we'd sung to them when they were little. Eventually, Ashanti let him lead her to her room and tuck her into bed."

"You hated him too, didn't you? For being able to help her when you couldn't."

"You're catching on, Sergeant."

Bobbie licked her lips.

"I want to hurt someone," she said. "I'm afraid if it's not them, it's going to wind up being me."

"We all grieve in our own ways," Avasarala said. "For what it's worth, you'll never kill enough people to keep your platoon from dying. No more than I can save enough people that one of them will be Charanpal."

For a long moment, Bobbie weighed the words. Avasarala could almost hear the woman's mind turning the ideas one way and then another. Soren had been an idiot to underestimate this woman. But Soren had been an idiot in a lot of ways. When at length she spoke, her voice was light and conversational, as if her words weren't profound.

"No harm trying, though."

"It's what we do," Avasarala said.

The marine nodded curtly. For a moment, Avasarala thought she might be going to salute, but instead, she lumbered out toward the complimentary bar in the wide common area. There was a fountain out there with sprays of water drifting down fake bronze sculptures of horses and underdressed women. If that didn't make someone want a stiff drink of something, then nothing would.

Avasarala thumbed on the video feed again.

"This is James Holden—"

She turned it off again.

"At least you lost that fucking beard," she said to no one.

Chapter Thirty-Six: Prax

Prax remembered his first epiphany. Or possibly, he thought, the one he remembered as his first. In the absence of further evidence, he went with it. He'd been in second form, just seventeen, and in the middle of a genetic engineering lab. Sitting there among the steel tables and microcentrifuges, he'd struggled with why exactly his results were so badly off. He'd rechecked his calculations, read through his lab notes. The error was more than sloppy technique could explain, and his technique wasn't even sloppy.

And then he'd noticed that one of the reagents was chiral, and he knew what had happened. He hadn't figured anything wrong but he had assumed that the reagent was taken from a natural source rather than generated de novo. Instead of being uniformly left-handed, it had been a mix of chiralities, half of them inactive. The insight had left him grinning from ear to ear.

It had been a failure, but it was a failure he understood, and that made it a victory. The only thing he regretted was that seeing what should have been clear had taken him so long.

The four days since he had sent the broadcast, he'd hardly slept. Instead, he'd read through the comments and messages pouring in with the donations, responding to a few, asking questions of people all over the system whom he didn't know. The goodwill and generosity pouring out to him was intoxicating. For two days, he hadn't slept, borne up on the euphoria of feeling effective. When he had slept, he'd dreamed of finding Mei.

When the answer came, he only wished he'd found it before.

"The time they had, they could have taken her anywhere, Doc," Amos said. "I mean, not to bust your balls or nothing."

"They could," Prax said. "They could take her anywhere as long as they had a supply of her medications. But she's not the limiting factor. The question is where they were coming from."

Prax had called the meeting without a clear idea of where to have it. The crew of the *Roci* was small, but Amos' rooms were smaller. He'd considered the galley of the ship, but there were still technicians finishing the repairs, and Prax wanted privacy. In the end, he'd checked the incoming stream of contributions from Holden's broadcast and taken enough to rent a room from a station club.

Now they were in a private lounge. Outside the wall-screen window, the great construction waldoes shifted by tiny degrees, attitude rockets flaring and going still in patterns as complex as language. Another thing Prax had never thought about before coming here: The station waldoes had to fire attitude rockets to keep their movements from shifting the station they were attached to. Everything, everywhere, a dance of tiny movements and the ripples they made.

Inside the room, the music that floated between the wide tables and crash-gel chairs was soft and lyrical, the singer's voice deep and soothing.

"From?" Alex said. "I thought they were from Ganymede."

"The lab on Ganymede wasn't equipped to deal with serious research," Prax said. "And they arranged things so that Ganymede would turn into a war zone. That'd be a bad idea if they were doing their primary work in the middle of it. That was a field lab."

"I try not to shit where I eat," Amos said, agreeing.

"You live on a spaceship," Holden said.

"I don't shit in the galley, though."

"Fair point."

"Anyway," Prax said, "we can safely assume they were working from a better-protected base. And that base has to be somewhere in the Jovian system. Somewhere nearby."

"You lost me again," Holden said. "Why does it need to be close?"

"Transport time. Mei can go anywhere if there's a good supply of medications, but she's more robust than the...the things."

Holden raised his hand like a schoolboy asking a question.

"Okay, I could be hearing you wrong, but did you just say that the thing that ripped its way into my ship, threw a five-hundred-kilo storage pallet at me, and almost chewed a path straight to the reactor core is more delicate than a four-year-old girl with no immune system?"

Prax nodded. A stab of horror and grief went through him. She wasn't four anymore. Mei's birthday had been the month before, and he'd missed it. She was five. But grief and horror were old companions by now. He pushed the thought aside.

"I'll be clearer," he said. "Mei's body isn't fighting its situation. That's her disease, if you think about it. There's a whole array of things that happen in normal bodies that don't happen in hers. Now you take one of the things, one of the creatures. Like the one from the ship?"

"That bastard was pretty active," Amos said.

"No," Prax said. "I mean, yes, but no. I mean active on a biochemical level. If Strickland or Merrian or whoever is using the protomolecule to reengineer a human body, they're taking one complex system and overlaying another one. We know it's unstable."

"Okay," Naomi said. She was sitting beside Amos and across the table from Holden. "*How* do we know that?"

Prax frowned. When he'd practiced making the presentation, he hadn't expected so many questions. The things he'd thought were obvious from the start hadn't even occurred to the others. This was why he hadn't gone in for teaching. Looking at their faces now, he saw blank confusion.

"All right," he said. "Let me take it from the top. There was something on Ganymede that started the war. There was also a secret lab staffed with people who at the very least knew about the attack before it happened."

"Check," Alex said.

"Okay," Prax said. "In the lab, we had signs of the protomolecule, a dead boy, and a bunch of people getting ready to leave. And when we got there, we only had to fight halfway in. After that, something else was going ahead of us and killing everyone."

"Hey!" Amos said. "You think that was the same fucker that got into the *Roci*?"

Prax stopped the word *obviously* just before it fell from his lips.

"Probably," he said instead. "And it seems likely that the original attack involved more like that one."

"So two got loose?" Naomi asked, but he could see that she already sensed the problem with that.

"No, because they knew it was going to happen. One got loose when Amos threw that grenade back at them. One was released intentionally. But that doesn't matter. What matters is that they're using the protomolecule to remake human bodies, and they aren't able to control it with perfect fidelity. The programming they're putting in fails."

Prax nodded, as if by doing it he could will them to follow his chain of reasoning. Holden shook his head, paused, and then nodded.

"The bomb," he said.

"The bomb," Prax agreed. "Even when they didn't know that the second thing was going to get loose, they'd outfitted it with a powerful incendiary explosive device."

"Ah!" Alex said. "I get it! You figure they knew it was going to go off the rails eventually, so they wired it to blow if it got out of hand."

In the depths of space, a construction welder streaked across the hull of the half-built ship, the light of its flare casting a sudden, sharp light across the pilot's eager face.

"Yes," Prax said. "But it could be also be an ancillary weapon, or a payload that the thing was supposed to deliver. I think it's a fail-safe. It probably is, but it could be any number of other things."

"Okay, but it left it behind," Alex said.

"Given time, it *ejected* the bomb," Prax said. "You see? It chose to reconfigure itself to remove the payload. It didn't place it to destroy the *Roci*, even though it could have. It didn't deliver it to a preset target. It just decided to pop it loose."

"And it knew to do that—"

"It's smart enough to recognize threat," Prax said. "I don't know the mechanism yet. It could be cognitive or networked or some kind of modified immune response."

"Okay, Prax. So if the protomolecule can eventually get out of whatever constraints they're putting on it and go rogue, where does that get us?" Naomi asked.

Square one, Prax thought, and launched in on the information he'd intended to give them in the first place.

"It means that wherever the main lab is—the place they didn't release one of those things on—it has to be close enough to Ganymede to get it there before it slipped its leash. I don't know how long that is, and I'm betting they don't either. So closer is better."

"A Jovian moon or a secret station," Holden said.

"You can't have a secret station in the Jovian system," Alex said. "There's too much traffic. Someone'd see something. Shit, it's where most of the extrasolar astronomy was going on until we got out to Uranus. Put something close, the observatories are gonna get pissed because it's stinking up their pictures, right?"

Naomi tapped her fingers against the tabletop, the sound like the ticking of condensate falling inside sheet metal vents.

"Well, the obvious choice is Europa," she said.

"It's Io," Prax said, impatience slipping into his voice. "I used some of the money to get a tariff search on the kinds of arylamines and nitroarenes that you use for mutagentic research." He paused. "It's all right that I did that, isn't it? Spent the money?"

"That's what it's there for," Holden said.

"Okay, so mutagens that only start functioning after you activate them are very tightly controlled, since you can use them for bioweapons research, but if you're trying to work with that kind of biological cascade and constraint systems, you'd need them. Most of the supplies went to Ganymede, but there was a steady stream to Europa too. And when I looked at that, I couldn't find a final receiver listed. Because they shipped back out of Europa about two hours after they landed."

"Bound for Io," Holden said.

"It didn't list a location, but the shipping containers for them have to follow Earth and Mars safety specifications. Very expensive. And the shipping containers for the Europa shipment were returned to the manufacturer for credit on a transport bound from Io."

Prax took a breath. It had been like pulling teeth, but he was pretty sure he'd made all the points he needed to for the evidence to be, if not conclusive, at least powerfully suggestive.

"So," Amos said, drawing the word out to almost three syllables. "The bad guys are probably on Io?"

"Yes," Prax said.

"Well shit, Doc. Coulda just said so."

The thrust gravity was a full g but without the subtle Coriolis of Tycho Station. Prax sat in his bunk, bent over his hand terminal. There had been times on the journey to Tycho Station when being half starved and sick at heart were the only things that distracted him. Nothing physical had changed. The walls were still narrow and close. The air recycler still clicked and hummed. Only now, rather than feeling isolated, Prax felt he was in the center of a vast network of people, all bent toward the same end that he was.

MR. MENG, I SAW THE REPORT ON YOU AND MY HEART AND PRAYERS ARE WITH YOU. I'M SORRY I CAN'T SEND MONEY BECAUSE I'M ON BASIC, BUT I HAVE INCLUDED THE REPORT IN MY CHURCH NEWS-LETTER. I HOPE YOU CAN FIND YOUR DAUGHTER SAFE AND HEALTHY.

Prax had composed a form letter for responding to all the general well-wishers, and he'd considered trying to find a filter that could identify those messages and reply automatically with the canned response. He held off because he wasn't sure how well he could define the conditions set, and he didn't want anyone to feel that their sentiments were being taken for granted. And after all, he had no duties on the *Rocinante*.

I'M WRITING YOU BECAUSE I MAY HAVE INFORMA-TION THAT WILL HELP WITH THE QUEST TO RECLAIM YOUR DAUGHTER. SINCE I WAS VERY YOUNG, I HAVE HAD POWERFUL PREMONITIONS IN MY DREAMS, AND THREE DAYS BEFORE I SAW JAMES HOLDEN'S ARTICLE ABOUT YOU AND YOUR DAUGHTER, I SAW HER IN A DREAM. SHE WAS ON LUNA IN A VERY SMALL PLACE WITHOUT LIGHT, AND SHE WAS SCARED. I TRIED TO COMFORT HER, BUT I FEEL SURE NOW THAT YOU ARE MEANT TO FIND HER ON LUNA OR IN A NEARBY ORBIT.

Prax didn't respond to *everything*, of course.

The journey to Io wouldn't take much more time than the one to Tycho had. Probably less, since they were unlikely to have the chaos of a stowaway protomolecule construct blowing out the cargo bay this time. If Prax thought about it too long, it made his palm itch. He knew where she was—or where she had been. Every hour was bringing him closer, and every message flowing into his charitable account gave him a little more power. Someone else who might know where Carlos Merrian was and what he was doing.

There were a few he'd set up conversations with, mostly video conversations sent back and forth. He'd spoken with a security broker based out of Ceres Station, who'd run some of his tariff searches and seemed like a genuinely nice man. He'd exchanged a few video recordings with a grief counselor on Mars before he started to get an uncomfortable feeling that she was hitting on him. An entire school of children—at least a hundred of them—had sent him a recording of them singing a song in mixed Spanish and French in honor of Mei and her return.

Intellectually, he knew that nothing had changed. The chances were still very good that Mei was dead, or at least that he would never see her again. But to have so many people—and in such a steady stream—telling him that it would be all right, that they hoped it would be all right, that they were pulling for him made despair less possible. It was probably something like group reinforcement effect. It was something common to some species of crop plant: An ill or suffering plant could be moved into a community of well members of the species and, through proximity, improve, even if soil and water were supplied separately. Yes, it was chemically mediated, but humans were social animals, and a woman smiling up from the screen, her eyes seeming to look deeply into your own, and saying what you wanted to believe was almost impossible to wholly disbelieve.

It was selfish, and he knew that, but it was also addictive. He'd stopped paying attention to the donations that were coming in once he knew there was enough to fund the ship as far as Io. Holden had given him an expense report and a detailed spreadsheet of costs, but Prax didn't think Holden would cheat him, so he'd barely glanced at anything other than the total at the bottom. Once there was enough money, he'd stopped caring about money.

It was the commentary that took his time and attention.

He heard Alex and Amos in the galley, their voices calm and conversational. It reminded him of living in the group housing at university. The awareness of other voices, other presences, and the comfort that came from those familiar sounds. It wasn't that different from reading the comment threads.

I LOST MY SON FOUR YEARS AGO, AND I STILL CAN'T IMAGINE WHAT YOU ARE GOING THROUGH RIGHT NOW. I WISH THERE WAS MORE I COULD DO.

He had the list down to only a few dozen. It was mid-afternoon in the arbitrary world of ship time, but he was powerfully sleepy. He debated leaving the remaining messages until after a nap, and decided to read through them without requiring himself to respond to each one. Alex laughed. Amos joined him.

Prax opened the fifth message.

YOU ARE A SICK, SICK, SICK MOTHERFUCKER, AND IF I EVER SEE YOU, I SWEAR TO GOD I WILL KILL YOU MYSELF. PEOPLE LIKE YOU SHOULD BE RAPED TO DEATH JUST SO YOU KNOW WHAT IT FEELS LIKE.

Prax tried to catch his breath. The sudden ache in his body was just like the aftermath of being punched in the solar plexus. He deleted the message. Another came in, and then three more. And then a dozen. With a sense of dread, Prax opened one of the new ones.

I HOPE YOU DIE.

"I don't understand," Prax said to the terminal. The vitriol was sudden and constant and utterly inexplicable. At least, it was until he opened one of the messages that had the link to a public news-feed. Prax put in a request, and five minutes later, his screen went blank, the logo of one of the big Earth-based news aggregators glowed briefly in blue, and the title of the feed series—The Raw Feed—appeared.

When the logo faded out, Nicola was looking out at him. Prax reached for the controls, part of his mind insisting that he'd some-how slipped into his private messages, even as the rest of him knew better. Nicola licked her lips, looked away, then back at the camera. She looked tired. Exhausted.

"My name's Nicola Mulko. I used to be married to Praxidike Meng, the man who put out a call for help finding our daughter... my daughter, Mei."

A tear dripped down her cheek, and she didn't wipe it away.

"What you don't know—what no one knows—is that Praxi-dike Meng is a monster of a human being. Ever since I got away from him, I've been trying to get Mei back. I thought his abuse of me was between us. I didn't think he'd hurt her. But information has come back to me from friends who stayed on Ganymede after I left that..."

"Nicola," Prax said. "Don't. Don't do this."

"Praxidike Meng is a violent and dangerous man," Nicola said. "As Mei's mother, I believe that she has been emotionally, physi-cally, and sexually abused by him since I left. And that her alleged disappearance during the troubles on Ganymede are to hide the fact that he's finally killed her."

The tears were flowing freely down Nicola's cheeks now, but her voice and eyes were dead as last week's fish.

"I don't blame anyone but myself," she said. "I should never have left when I couldn't get my little girl away too..."

Chapter Thirty-Seven: Avasarala

I don't blame anyone but myself," the teary-eyed woman said, and Avasarala stopped the feed, sitting back in her chair. Her heart was beating faster than usual and she could feel thoughts swimming just under the ice of her conscious mind. She felt like someone could press an ear to her skull and listen to her brain humming.

Bobbie was sitting on the four-poster. She made the thing look small, which was impressive in itself. She had one leg tucked up under her and a pack of real playing cards laid out in formation on the crisp gold-and-green bedspread. The game of solitaire was forgotten, though. The Martian's gaze was on her, and Avasarala felt a slow grin pulling at her lips.

"Well, I'll be fucked," she said. "They're scared of him."

"Who's scared of who?"

"Errinwright is moving against Holden and this Meng bastard, whoever he is. They actually forced him to take action. *I couldn't get that out of him.*"

"You don't think the botanist was diddling his kid?"

"Might have been, but that"—she tapped on the still, tearful face of the botanist's ex-wife—"is a smear campaign. I'll bet you a week's pay that I've had lunch with the woman coordinating it."

Bobbie's skeptical look only made Avasarala smile more broadly.

"This," Avasarala said, "is the first genuinely good thing that's happened since we got on this floating whorehouse. I've got to get to work. Goddamn, but I wish I was back at the office."

"You want some tea?"

"Gin," she said, engaging the camera on her terminal. "We're celebrating."

In the focus window, she looked smaller than she felt. The rooms had been designed to command attention whatever angle she put herself in, like being trapped in a postcard. Anyone who rode in the yacht would be able to brag without saying a word, but in the weak gravity her hair stood out from her head like she'd just gotten out of bed. More than that, she looked emotionally exhausted and physically diminished.

Put it away, she told herself. *Find the mask.*

She took a deep breath, made a rude gesture into the camera, and then started recording.

"Admiral Souther," she said. "Thank you so much for your last message. Something's come to my attention that I thought you might find interesting. It looks like someone's taken a fresh dislike to James Holden. If I were with the fleet instead of floating around the fucking solar system, I'd take you out for a cup of coffee and talk this over, but since that's not happening, I'm going to open some of my private files for you. I've been following Holden. Take a look at what I've got and tell me if you're seeing the same things I am."

She sent the message. The next thing that would have made sense would be contacting Errinwright. If the situation had been what they were both pretending it was, she'd have kept him involved and engaged. For a long moment, she considered following the form, pretending. Bobbie loomed up on her right, putting the glass of gin on the desk with a soft click. Avasarala picked it up and sipped a small taste of it. Mao's private-label gin was excellent, even without the lime twist.

Nah. Fuck Errinwright. She pulled up her address book and started leafing through entries until she found what she wanted and pressed record.

"Ms. Corlinowski, I've just seen the leaked video accusing Praxidike Meng of screwing his cute little five-year-old daughter. When exactly did UN media relations turn into a fucking divorce court? If it gets out that we were behind that, I would like to know whose resignation I'm going to hand to the newsfeeds, and right now I'm thinking it's yours. Give my love to Richard, and get back to me before I fire your incompetent ass out of spite."

She ended the recording and sent it.

"She was the one that arranged it?" Bobbie asked.

"Might have been," Avasarala said, taking another bite of gin. It was too good. If she wasn't careful, she'd drink a lot of it. "If it wasn't, she'll find who it was and serve them up on a plate. Emma Corlinowski's a coward. It's why I love her."

Over the next hour, she sent a dozen more messages out, performance after performance after performance. She started a liability investigation into Meng's ex-wife and whether the UN could be held responsible for slander. She put the Ganymede relief coordinator on high alert, demanding everything she could get about Mei Meng and the search for her. She put in high-priority requests to have the doctor and the woman from Holden's broadcast identified, and then sent a twenty-minute rambling message to an old colleague in data storage, with a small, tacit request for the same information made in the middle of it all.

Errinwright had changed the game. If she'd had freedom, she'd have been unstoppable. As it was, she had to assume that every move she made would be cataloged and acted against almost as soon as she made it. But Errinwright and his allies were only human, and if she kept a solid flow of demands and requests, screeds and wheedling, they might overlook something. Or someone on a newsfeed might notice the uptick in activity and look into it. Or, if nothing else, her efforts might give Errinwright a bad night's sleep.

It was what she had. It wasn't enough. Long years of practice with the fine dance of politics and power had left her with expectations and reflexes that couldn't find their right form there. The lag was killing her with frustration, and she took it out on whomever she was recording for at the moment. She felt like a world-class musician standing before a full auditorium and handed a kazoo.

She didn't notice when she finished her gin. She only put the glass to her mouth, found it empty, and realized it wasn't the first time she'd done it. Five hours had passed. She'd had only three responses so far out of almost fifty messages she'd sent out. That was more than lag. That was someone else's damage control.

She didn't realize that she was hungry until Cotyar came with a plate, the smell of curried lamb and watermelon wafting in with him. Avasarala's belly woke with a roar, and she turned off her terminal.

"You've just saved my life," she told him, gesturing at the desk.

"It was Sergeant Draper's idea," he said. "After the third time you ignored her asking."

"I don't remember that," she said as he put the dish in front of her. "Don't they have servants on this thing? Why are you bringing the food?"

"They do, ma'am. I'm not letting them in here."

"That seems extreme. Feeling jumpy, are you?"

"As you say."

She ate too quickly. Her back was aching, and her left leg was tingling with the pins and needles she got now from sitting too long in one position. As a young woman, she'd never suffered that. On the other hand, she hadn't had the ability to pepper every major player in the United Nations and be taken seriously. Time took her strength but it gave her power in exchange. It was a fair trade.

She couldn't wait to finish her meal, turning on the terminal while she gulped the last of it down. Four waiting messages. Souther, God bless his shriveled little heart. One from someone at the legal council whose name she didn't recognize, and another from someone she did. One from Michael-Jon, which was probably about Venus. She opened the one from Souther.

The admiral appeared on her screen and she had to stop herself from saying hello. It was only a video recording, not a real conversation. She hated it.

"Chrisjen," the admiral said. "You're going to have to be careful with all this information you're sending me. Arjun's going to get jealous. I wasn't aware of our friend Jimmy's part in instigating this latest brouhaha."

Our friend Jimmy. He wasn't saying the name Holden out loud. That was interesting. He was expecting some kind of filtering to be sniffing out Holden's name. She tried to guess whether he thought the filter would be on his outgoing messages or her incoming. If Errinwright had half a brain—which he did—he'd be watching the traffic both ways for both of them. Was he worried about someone else? How many players were there at the table? She didn't have enough information to work with, but it was interesting, at least.

"I can see where your concerns might lead you," Souther said. "I'm making some inquiries, but you know how these things are. Might find something in a minute, might find something in a year. You don't be a stranger, though. There's more than enough going on out here that I can wish I could take you up on that lunch. We're all looking forward to seeing you again."

There was a barefaced lie, Avasarala thought. Still, nice of him to say it. She scraped her fork along the bottom of the plate, a thin residue of curry clinging to the silver.

The first message was some young man with a Brazilian accent explaining to her that the UN had nothing to do with the video footage released of Nicola Mulko, and therefore could not be held responsible for it. The second was the boy's supervisor, apologizing for him and promising a fully formed brief by the end of the day, which was considerably more like it. The smart people were still afraid of her. That thought was more nourishing than the lamb.

As she reached for the screen, the ship shifted under her, gravity pulling her slightly to the side. She put her hand on the desk; the curry and the remnants of gin churned her gut.

"Were we expecting that?" she shouted.

"Yes, ma'am," Cotyar called from the next room. "Scheduled course correction."

"Never happens at the fucking office," she said, and Michael-Jon appeared on her screen. He looked mildly confused, but that could have been just the angle of his face. She felt a sick dread.

For a moment, the *Arboghast* floated before her again, coming apart. Without intending it, she paused the feed. Something in the back of her mind wanted to turn away. Not to know.

It wasn't hard to understand how Errinwright and Nguyen and their cabal would turn their backs on Venus, on the alien chaos that was becoming order and more than order. She felt it too, the atavistic fear lurking at the back of her mind. How much easier to turn to the old games, the old patterns, the history of warfare and conflict, deception and death. For all its horror, it was familiar. It was known.

As a girl, she'd seen a film about a man who saw the face of God. For the first hour of the film, he had gone through the drab life of someone living on basic on the coast of southern Africa. When he saw God, the film switched to ten minutes of the man wailing and then another hour of slowly building himself back up to do the same idiot life he'd had at the beginning. Avasarala had hated it. Now, though, she almost understood. Turning away was natural. Even if it was moronic and self-destructive and empty, it was natural.

War. Slaughter. Death. All the violence that Errinwright and his men—and she felt certain they were almost all of them men—were embracing, they were drawn to because it was comforting. And they were scared.

Well, so was she.

"Pussies," she said, and restarted the playback.

"Venus can think," Michael-Jon said instead of *hello* or any other social pleasantry. "I've had the signal analysis team running the data we saw from the network of water and electrical currents, and we've found a model. It's only about a sixty percent correlation, but I'm comfortable putting that above chance. It's got different anatomy, of course, but its functional structure is most like a cetacean doing spatial reasoning problems. I mean, there's still the problem of the explanatory gap, and I can't help with that part, but with what we've seen, I'm fairly sure that the patterns we saw were it thinking. They were the actual thoughts, like neurons firing off."

He looked into the camera as if expecting her to answer and then looked mildly disappointed when she didn't.

"I thought you'd want to know," he said, and ended the recording.

Before she could formulate a response, a new message from Souther appeared. She opened it with a sense of gratitude and relief that she was slightly ashamed of.

"Chrisjen," he said. "We have a problem. You should check the force assignments on Ganymede and let me know if we're seeing the same things."

Avasarala frowned. The lag now was over twenty-eight minutes. She put in a standard request, expedited it, and stood up. Her back was a solid knot. She walked to the common area of the suite. Bobbie, Cotyar, and three other men were sitting in a circle, the deck of cards distributed among them. Poker. Avasarala walked toward them, rolling through the hips where movement hurt. Something about lower gravity made her joints ache. She lowered herself to Bobbie's side.

"Next hand, you can deal me in," she said.

The order had come from Nguyen, and at first glance it made no sense at all. Six UN destroyers had been ordered off the Ganymede patrol, sent out at high burn on a course that seemed to lead essentially to nowhere. Initial reports showed that after a decent period of wondering what the fuck, a similar detachment of Martian ships matched course.

Nguyen was up to something, and she didn't have the first clue what it could be. But Souther had sent it and thought she would see something.

It took another hour to find it. Holden's *Rocinante* had departed Tycho Station on a gentle burn for the Jovian system. He might have filed a flight plan with the OPA, but he hadn't informed Earth or Mars of anything, which meant Nguyen was watching him too.

They weren't just scared. They were going to kill him.

Avasarala sat quietly for a long moment before she stood up and went back toward the game. Cotyar and Bobbie were at the end of a high-stakes round, which meant the pile of little bits of chocolate candy they were using for chips was almost five centimeters deep.

"Mr. Cotyar," Avasarala said. "Sergeant Draper. With me, please."

The cards all vanished. The men looked at each other nervously as she walked back into her bedroom. She closed the door behind them carefully. It didn't even click.

"I am about to do something that may pull a trigger," she said. "If I do this, the complexion of our situation may change."

Cotyar and Bobbie exchanged looks.

"I have some things I'd like to get out of storage," Bobbie said.

"I'll brief the men," Cotyar said.

"Ten minutes."

The lag between the *Guanshiyin* and the *Rocinante* was still too long for conversation, but it was less than it took to get a message back to Earth. The sense of being so far from home left her a little light-headed. Cotyar stepped into the room and nodded once. Avasarala opened her terminal and requested a tightbeam connection. She gave the transponder code for the *Rocinante*. Less than a minute later, the connection came back refused. She smiled to herself and opened a channel to ops.

"This is Assistant Undersecretary Avasarala," she said, as if there were anyone else on board who it might be. "What the fuck is wrong with your tightbeam?"

"I apologize, Madam Secretary," a young man with bright blue eyes and close-cut blond hair said. "That communication channel isn't available right now."

"Why the fuck isn't it available?"

"It's not available, ma'am."

"Fine. I didn't want to do this on the radio, but I can broadcast if I have to."

"I'm afraid that won't be possible," the boy said. Avasarala took a long breath and let it out through her teeth.

"Put the captain on," she said.

A moment later, the image jumped. The captain was a thin-faced man with the brown eyes of an Irish setter. The set of his mouth and his bloodless lips told her that he knew what was coming, at least in outline. For a moment, she just looked into the camera. It was a trick she'd learned when she'd just started off. Looking at the screen image let the other person feel they were being seen. Looking into the tiny black pinpoint of the lens itself left them feeling stared down.

"Captain. I have a high-priority message I need to send."

"I am very sorry. We're having technical difficulties with the communication array."

"Do you have a backup system? A shuttle we can power up? Anything?"

"Not at this time."

"You're lying to me," she said. Then, when he didn't answer: "I am making an official request that this yacht engage its emergency beacon and change course to the nearest aid."

"I'm not going to be able to do that, ma'am. If you will just be patient, we'll get you to Ganymede safe and in one piece. I'm sure any repairs we need can be done there."

Avasarala leaned close to the terminal.

"I can come up there and we can have this conversation personally," she said. "Captain. You know the laws as well as I do. Turn on the beacon or give me communications access."

"Ma'am, you are the guest of Jules-Pierre Mao, and I respect that. But Mr. Mao is the owner of this vessel, and I answer to him."

"No, then."

"I'm very sorry."

"You're making a mistake, shithead," Avasarala said, and dropped the connection.

Bobbie came into the room. Her face was bright, and there was a hunger about her, like a running dog straining at the leash. Gravity shifted a degree. A course correction, but not a change.

"How'd it go?" Bobbie asked.

"I am declaring this vessel in violation of laws and standards," Avasarala said. "Cotyar, you're witness to that."

"As you say, ma'am."

"All right, then. Bobbie. Get me control of this fucking ship."

Chapter Thirty-Eight: Bobbie

W hat else do you need from us?" Cotyar asked. Two of his people were moving the big crate marked FORMAL WEAR into Avasarala's room. They were using a large furniture dolly and grunting with effort. Even in the gentle quarter g of the *Guanshiyin*'s thrust, Bobbie's armor weighed over a hundred kilos.

"We're sure this room isn't under surveillance?" Bobbie said. "This is going to work a lot better if they have no idea what's about to happen."

Cotyar shrugged. "It has no functioning eavesdropping devices I've been able to detect."

"Okay, then," Bobbie said, rapping on the fiberglass crate with her knuckle. "Open it up."

Cotyar tapped something on his hand terminal and the crate's locks opened with a sharp click. Bobbie yanked the opened panel off and leaned it against the wall. Inside the crate, suspended in a web of elastic bands, was her suit.

Cotyar whistled. "A Goliath III. I can't believe they let you keep it."

Bobbie removed the helmet and put it on the bed, then began pulling the various other pieces out of the webbing and setting them on the floor. "They gave it to your tech guys to verify some video stored in the suit. When Avasarala tracked it down, it was in a closet, collecting dust. No one seemed to care when she took it."

She pulled out the suit's right arm. She hadn't expected them to get her any of the 2mm ammo the suit's integrated gun used, but was surprised to find that they'd completely removed the gun from the housing. It made sense to remove all the weapons before handing the suit off to a bunch of civilians, but it still annoyed her.

"Shit," she said. "Won't be shooting anyone, I guess."

"If you did," Cotyar said with a smile, "would the bullets even slow down as they went through both of the ship's hulls and let all the air out?"

"Nope," Bobbie said, laying the last piece of the suit on the floor, then pulling out the tools necessary to put it all back together again. "But that might be a point in my favor. The gun on this rig is designed to shoot through other people wearing comparable armor. Anything that will shoot through my suit here will probably also hole the ship. Which means—"

"None of the security personnel on this vessel will have weapons capable of penetrating your armor," Cotyar finished. "As you say. How many of my people will you want with you?"

"None," Bobbie said, attaching the fresh battery pack Avasarala's techs had provided to the back of the armor and getting a lovely green "fully charged" light from the panel. "Once I get started, the obvious counterplay will be to grab the undersecretary and hold her hostage. Preventing that is your job."

Cotyar smiled again. There was no humor in it.

"As you say."

It took Bobbie just under three hours to assemble and field prep her suit. It should have taken only two, but she forgave herself the extra hour by remembering that she was out of practice. The closer the suit got to completion, the tighter the knot in her stomach grew. Some of it was the natural tension that came before combat. And her time in the Marines had taught her to use it. To let the stress force her to recheck everything three times. Once she was in the thick of it, it would be too late.

But deep down, Bobbie knew that the possibility of violence wasn't the only thing twisting up her insides. It was impossible to forget what had happened the last time she'd worn this suit. The red enamel of her Martian camouflage was pitted and scraped from the exploding monster and her high-speed skid across Ganymede's ice. A tiny bit of fluid leakage on the knee reminded her of Private Hillman. Hilly, her friend. Wiping off the helmet's faceplate made her think of the last time she'd spoken to Lieutenant Givens, her CO, just before the monster had ripped him in two.

When the suit was finished and lying on the floor, opened up and waiting for her to climb inside, she felt a shudder run up her spine. For the first time ever, the inside looked small. Sepulchral.

"No," she said to no one but herself.

"No?" Cotyar asked, sitting on the floor next to her, holding the tools he thought she might need next. He'd been so quiet during the assembly procedure she'd sort of forgotten he was there.

"I'm not afraid of putting this back on," she said.

"Ah," Cotyar replied with a nod, then put the tools into the toolbox. "As you say."

Bobbie pushed herself to her feet and yanked the black unitard she wore under the armor out of the crate. Without thinking about it, she stripped down to her panties and pulled the skintight garment on. She was pulling the wire leads out of her armor and connecting them to the various sensors on the bodysuit when she noticed that Cotyar had turned his back to her, and that his usually light brown neck was turning beet red.

"Oh," she said. "Sorry. I've stripped down and put this on in front of my squaddies so many times I don't even think about it anymore."

"No reason to apologize," Cotyar said without turning around. "I was only taken by surprise."

He risked a peek over his left shoulder, and when he saw that she was fully covered by the bodysuit, he turned back to help her wire it up to the armor.

"You are," he said, then paused for a beat. "Lovely."

It was her turn to blush.

"Aren't you married?" Bobbie asked with a grin, happy for the distraction. The simple humanity in discomfort with mating signals made the monster in her head seem very far away.

"Yes," Cotyar replied, attaching the final lead to a sensor at the small of her back. "Very. But I'm not blind."

"Thank you," Bobbie said, and gave him a friendly pat on the shoulder. After a few moments' struggle with the tight spaces, she sat down into the suit's open chest and slid down until her legs and arms were fully inside. "Button me up."

Cotyar sealed up the chest as she'd shown him, then put the helmet on her and locked it in place. Inside the suit, her HUD flashed through the boot routine. A gentle, almost subliminal hum surrounded her. She activated the array of micro-motors and pumps that powered the exo-musculature, and then sat up.

Cotyar was looking at her, his face a question. Bobbie turned on the external speaker and said, "Yeah, it all looks good in here. Green across the board."

She pushed herself to her feet effortlessly and felt the old sensation of barely restrained power running through her limbs. She knew if she pushed off hard with her legs, she'd hit the ceiling with enough force to severely damage it. A sudden motion of her arm could hurl the heavy four-poster bed across the room or shatter Cotyar's spine. It made her move with the deliberate gentleness of long training.

Cotyar reached under his jacket and pulled out a sleek black pistol of the slug-throwing variety. Bobbie knew the security team had loaded them with high-impact plastic rounds, guaranteed not to knock holes in the ship. It was the same kind of round Mao's security team would be using. He started to hold it out to her, but then looked at the thickness of her armored fingers, and at the much smaller opening of the trigger guard, and shrugged apologetically.

"I won't need it," she said. Her voice sounded harsh, metallic, inhuman.

Cotyar smiled again.

"As you say."

Bobbie punched the button to call the keel elevator, then walked back and forth in the lounge, letting her reflexes get used to her armor. There was a nanosecond delay between attempting to move a limb and having the armor react. It made walking around feel vaguely dreamlike, as if the act of wanting to move your limbs and the moving of the limbs themselves were separate events. Hours of training and use had mostly overcome the sensation when Bobbie wore her armor, but it always took a few minutes of moving around to get past the oddness of it.

Avasarala walked into the lounge from the room they were using as the communications center and sat down at the bar. She poured herself a stiff shot of gin, then squeezed a piece of lime into it almost as an afterthought. The old lady had been drinking a lot more lately, but it wasn't Bobbie's place to point it out. Maybe it was helping her sleep.

When the elevator didn't arrive after several minutes, she thumped over to the panel and hit the button a few more times. A small display said OUT OF SERVICE.

"Damn," Bobbie said to herself. "They really are kidnapping us."

She'd left the external speakers on, and the harsh voice coming out of her suit echoed around the room. Avasarala didn't look up from her drink but said, "Remember what I said."

"Huh?" Bobbie said, not paying attention. She climbed awkwardly up the crew ladder to the deck hatch above her head and hit the button. The hatch slid open. That meant that everyone was still pretending that this wasn't a kidnapping. They could explain away the elevator. Explaining why the undersecretary was locked out of the rest of the ship would be harder. Maybe they figured a woman in her seventies would be reluctant to climb around the ship on ladders, so killing the lift was good enough. They might have been right. Avasarala certainly didn't look like she was up to a two-hundred-foot climb, even in the low gravity.

"None of these people were on Ganymede," Avasarala said.

"Okay," Bobbie replied to the seeming non sequitur.

"You won't be able to kill enough of them to bring your platoon back," Avasarala finished, tossing off the last of her gin, then pushing away from the bar and heading off to her room.

Bobbie didn't reply. She pulled herself up to the next deck and let the hatch slide shut behind her.

Her armor had been designed for exactly this sort of mission. The original Goliath-class scout suits had been built for Marine boarding parties in ship-to-ship engagements. That meant they were designed for maximum maneuverability in tight spaces. No matter how good the armor was, it was useless if the soldier wearing it couldn't climb ladders, slip through human-sized hatches, and maneuver gracefully in microgravity.

Bobbie climbed the ladder to the next deck hatch and hit the button. The console responded with a red warning light. A few moments of looking at the menus revealed why: They'd parked the crew elevator just above the hatch and then disabled it, creating a barricade. And that meant they knew something was up.

Bobbie looked around the room she was in, another relaxation lounge, nearly identical to the one she'd just left, until she found the likeliest place for them to have hidden their cameras. She waved. *This won't stop me, guys.*

She climbed back down and went into the luxurious bathroom space. On a ship this nice, it couldn't properly be called the head.

A few moments' probing found the fairly well-hidden bulkhead service hatch. It was locked. Bobbie tore it off the wall.

On the other side were a tangle of piping and a narrow corridor barely large enough to stuff her armor into. She climbed in and pulled herself along the pipes for two decks, then kicked the service hatch into the room and climbed in.

The compartment turned out to be a secondary galley, with a bank of stoves and ovens along one wall, several refrigeration units, and lots of counter space, all in gleaming stainless steel.

Her suit warned her that she was being targeted, and changed the HUD so that the normally invisible infrared beams aimed at her became faint red lines. Half a dozen were painting her chest, all coming from compact black weapons held by Mao-Kwik security personnel at the other end of the room.

Bobbie stood up. To their credit, the security goons didn't back up. Her HUD ran through the weapons database and informed her that the men were armed with 5mm submachine guns with a standard ammo capacity of three hundred rounds and a cyclic rate of ten rounds per second. Unless they were using high-explosive armor-piercing rounds, unlikely with the ship's hull right behind her, the suit rated their danger level as low.

Bobbie made sure her external speakers were still on and said, "Okay, fellas, let's—"

They opened fire.

For one long second, the entire galley was in chaos. High-impact plastic rounds bounced off her armor, deflected off the bulkheads, and skipped around the room. They blew apart containers of dried goods, hurled pots and pans off their magnetic hooks, and flung smaller utensils into the air in a cloud of stainless steel and plastic shards. One round took a particularly unlucky bounce and hit one of the security guards in the center of his nose, punching a hole into his head and dropping him to the floor with an almost comic look of surprise on his face.

Before two seconds could tick by, Bobbie was in motion, launching herself across the steel island in the center of the room and plowing into all five remaining guards with her arms out-stretched, like a football player going in for a tackle. They were hurled against the far bulkhead with a meaty thud, then slumped to the ground motionless. Her suit started to put up life-sign indicators on her HUD for them, but she shut it off without looking. She didn't want to know. One of the men stirred, then started to raise his gun. Bobbie gently shoved him, and he flew across the room to crumple against the far bulkhead. He didn't move again.

She glanced around the room, looking for cameras. She couldn't find one but hoped it was there anyway. If they'd seen this, maybe they wouldn't throw any more of their people at her.

At the keel ladder, she discovered that they'd blocked the elevator by jamming the floor hatch open with a crowbar. Basic ship safety protocols wouldn't allow the elevator to move to another deck unless the deck above was sealed. Bobbie yanked out the crowbar and threw it across the room, then hit the call button. The lift climbed up the ladder shaft to her level and stopped. She jumped on and hit the button that would take her to the bridge, eight decks up. Eight more pressure hatches.

Eight more possible ambushes.

She tightened her hands into fists until the knuckles stretched painfully inside her gauntlets. *Bring it.*

Three decks up the elevator stopped, the panel informing her that all the pressure hatches between her and the bridge had been overridden and forced open. They were willing to risk a hole in the ship emptying out half the ship's air rather than let her up to the bridge. It was sort of gratifying to be scarier than sudden decompression.

She climbed off the lift onto a deck that appeared to be mostly crew quarters, though it must have been evacuated. There wasn't a soul in sight. A quick tour revealed twelve small crew cabins and two bathrooms that could reasonably be called heads. No gold plating on the fixtures for the crew. No open bar. No twenty-four-hour-a-day food service. Looking at the fairly Spartan living conditions of the average crew member on the *Guanshiyin* brought home Avasarala's last words to her. These were just sailors. None of them deserved to die for what had happened on Ganymede.

Bobbie found herself glad she didn't have a gun.

She found another access hatch in the head and tore it open. But to her surprise, the service corridor ended just a few feet above her head. Something in the structure of the ship was cutting her off. Having never seen the *Guanshiyin* from the outside, she had no idea what it might be. But she needed to get another five decks up, and she wasn't about to let this stop her.

A ten-minute search turned up a service hatch through the outer hull. She'd torn off two inner hull hatches on two different decks, so if she got it open, those two decks would lose their air. But the central ladder corridor was sealed at Avasarala's deck, so her people would be fine. And the whole reason she was doing this was the sealed hatch to the upper decks, which seemed to be where most of the crew was.

She thought about the six men down in the galley and felt a pang. Sure, they'd shot first, but if any of them were still alive, she had no desire to asphyxiate them in their sleep.

It turned out not to be a problem. The hatch led into a small airlock chamber, about the size of a closet. A minute later it had cycled through and she climbed out onto the outer hull of the ship.

Triple-hulled. Of course. The lord of the Mao-Kwik empire wasn't going to trust his expensive skin to anything that wasn't the safest humans could build. And the ostentatious design of the ship extended to her outer hull as well. While most military ships were painted a flat black that made them hard to spot visually in space, most civilian ships either were left an unpainted gray or were painted in basic corporate colors.

The *Guanshiyin* had a mural painted on it in vivid colors. Bobbie was too close to see what it was, but under her feet were what appeared to be grass and the hoof of a giant horse. Mao had the hull of his ship painted with a mural that included horses and grass. When almost no one would ever see it.

Bobbie made sure her boot and glove mags were set strong enough to handle the quarter-g thrust the ship was still under, and started climbing up the side. She quickly reached the spot where the dead end between the hulls began, and saw that it was an empty shuttle bay. If only Avasarala had let her do this *before* Mao had run off with the shuttle.

Triple hulls, Bobbie thought. Maximum redundancy.

On a hunch, she crawled across the ship to the other side. Sure enough, there was a second shuttle bay. But the ship in it wasn't a standard short-flight shuttle. It was long and sleek, with an engine housing twice as large as that of a normal ship its size. Written in proud red letters across the bow of the ship was the name *Razorback*.

A racing pinnace.

Bobbie crawled back around to the empty cargo bay and used the airlock there to enter the ship. The military override codes her suit sent to the locked door worked, to her surprise. The airlock led to the deck just below the bridge, the one used for shuttle supply storage and maintenance. The center of the deck was taken up by a large machine shop. Standing in it were the captain of the *Guanshiyin* and his senior staff. There were no security personnel or weapons in sight.

The captain tapped his ear in an ancient *can you hear me?* gesture. Bobbie nodded one fist at him, then turned the external speakers back on and said, "Yes."

"We are not military personnel," the captain said. "We can't defend ourselves from military hardware. But I'm not going to turn this vessel over to you without knowing your intentions. My XO is on the deck above us, prepared to scuttle the ship if we can't come to terms."

Bobbie smiled at him, though she didn't know if he could see it through her helmet. "You've illegally detained a high-level member of the UN government. Acting in my role as a member of her security team, I have come to demand that you deliver her immediately to the port of her choosing, at best possible speed."

She shrugged with her hands in the Belter way. "Or, you can blow yourselves up. Seems like a drastic overreaction to having to give the undersecretary her radio privileges back."

The captain nodded and relaxed visibly. Whatever happened next, it wasn't like he had any choice. And since he didn't have any choice, he didn't have any responsibility. "We were following orders. You'll note that in the log when you take command."

"I'll see that she knows."

The captain nodded again. "Then the ship is yours."

Bobbie opened her radio link to Cotyar. "We win. Put Her Majesty on, will you?"

While she waited for Avasarala, Bobbie said to the captain, "There are six injured security people down below. Get a medical team down there."

"Bobbie?" Avasarala said over the radio.

"The ship is yours, madam."

"Great. Tell the captain we need to make best possible speed to intercept Holden. We're getting to him before Nguyen does."

"Uh, this is a pleasure yacht. It's built to run at low g for comfort. I'd bet it can do a full g if it needs to, but I doubt it does much more than that."

"Admiral Nguyen is about to kill everyone that actually might know what the fuck is going on." Avasarala didn't quite yell. "We don't have time to cruise around like we're trying to pick up fucking rent boys!"

"Huh," Bobbie said. Then, a moment later: "If this is a race, I know where there's a racing ship…"

Chapter Thirty-Nine: Holden

Holden pulled himself a cup of coffee from the galley coffeepot, and the strong smell filled the room. He could feel the eyes of the crew on his back with an almost physical force. He'd called them all there, and once they'd assembled and taken their seats, he'd turned his back on them and started making coffee. *I'm stalling for time, because I forgot how I wanted to say this.* He put some sugar in his coffee even though he always drank it black, just because stirring took a few more seconds.

"So. Who are we?" he said as he stirred.

His question was met with silence, so he turned around and leaned back against the countertop, holding his unwanted cup of coffee and continuing to stir.

"Seriously," he said. "Who are we? It's the question I keep coming back to."

"Uh," Amos said, and shifted in his seat. "My name's Amos, Cap. You feeling okay?"

No one else spoke. Alex was staring at the table in front of him, his dark scalp shining through his thinning hair under the harsh white of the galley lights. Prax was sitting on the counter next to the sink and looking at his hands. He flexed them periodically as though trying to figure out what they were for.

Only Naomi was looking at him. Her hair was pulled up into a thick tail, and her dark, almond-shaped eyes were staring right into his. It was fairly disconcerting.

"I've recently figured out something about myself," Holden continued, not letting Naomi's unblinking stare throw him off. "I've been treating you all like you owe me something. And none of you do. And that means I've been treating you like shit."

"No," Alex started without looking up.

"Yes," Holden said, and stopped until Alex looked up at him. "Yes. You maybe more than anyone else. Because I've been scared to death and cowards always look for an easy target. And you're about the nicest person I know, Alex. So I treated you badly because I could get away with it. And I hope you forgive me for that, because I really hate that I did it."

"Sure, I forgive you, Cap," Alex said with a smile and his heavy drawl.

"I'll try to earn it," Holden answered, bothered by the easy reply. "But Alex said something else to me recently that I've been thinking about a lot. He reminded me that none of you are employees. We're not on the *Canterbury*. We don't work for Pur'n'Kleen anymore. And I don't own this ship any more than any of you do. We took contracts from the OPA in exchange for pocket money and ship expenses, but we never talked about how to handle the excess."

"You opened that account," Alex said.

"Yeah, there's a bank account with all of the extra money in it. Last I checked, there was just under eighty grand in there. I said we'd keep it for ship expenses, but who am I to make that decision for the rest of you? That's not *my* money. It's *our* money. *We* earned it."

"But you're the captain," Amos said, then pointed at the coffeepot.

While Holden fixed him a cup, he said, "Am I? I was the XO on the *Canterbury*. It made sense for me to be the captain after the *Cant* got nuked."

He handed the cup to Amos and sat down at the table with the rest of the crew. "But we haven't been those guys for a long time now. Who we are now is four people who don't actually work for anyone—"

Prax cleared his throat at this, and Holden nodded an apology at him. "Anyone long term, let's say. There is no corporation or government granting me authority over this crew. We're just four people who sort of own a ship that Mars will probably try to take back the first chance they get."

"This is legitimate salvage," Alex said.

"And I hope the Martians find that compelling when you explain it to them," Holden replied. "But it doesn't change my point: Who are we?"

Naomi nodded a fist at him. "I see where you're going. We've left a lot of this kind of stuff just up in the air because we've been running full tilt since the *Canterbury*."

"And this," Holden said, "is the perfect time to figure that stuff out. We've got a contract to help Prax find his little girl, and he's paying us so we can afford to run the ship. Once we find Mei, how do we find the next job? Do we go looking for a *next* job? Do we sell the *Roci* to the OPA and retire on Titan? I think we need to know those things."

No one spoke. Prax pushed himself off the counter and started rummaging through the cabinets. After a minute or two, he pulled out a package that read CHOCOLATE PUDDING on the side and said, "Can I make this?"

Naomi laughed. Alex said, "Knock yourself out, Doc."

Prax pulled a bowl out and began mixing ingredients into it.

Oddly enough, because the botanist was paying attention to something else, it created a sense of intimacy for the crew. The outsider was doing outside things, leaving them to talk among themselves. Holden wondered if Prax knew that and was doing it on purpose.

Amos slurped down the last of his coffee and said, "So, you called this meeting, Cap. You have something in mind?"

"Yeah," Holden said, taking a moment to think. "Yeah, kind of."

Naomi put a hand on his arm and smiled at him. "We're listening."

"I think we get married," he said with a wink at Naomi. "Make it all nice and legal."

"Wait," she said. The look on her face was more horrified than Holden would have hoped.

"No, no, that's sort of a joke," Holden said. "But only sort of. See, I was thinking about my parents. They formed their initial collective partnership because of the farm. They were all friends, they wanted to buy the property in Montana, and so they made a group large enough to afford it. It wasn't sexual. Father Tom and Father Caesar were already sexual partners and monogamous. Mother Tamara was single. Fathers Joseph and Anton and Mothers Elise and Sophie were already a polyamorous civil unit. Father Dimitri joined a month later when he started dating Tamara. They formed a civil union to own the property jointly. They wouldn't have been able to afford it if they were all paying taxes for separate kids, so they had me as a group."

"Earth," Alex said, "is a weird freakin' place."

"Eight parents to a baby ain't exactly common," Amos said.

"But it makes a lot of economic sense with the baby tax," Holden said. "So it's not unheard of, either."

"What about people making babies without paying the tax?" Alex asked.

"It's tougher to get away with than you think," Holden said. "Unless you never go to a doctor or only use black markets."

Amos and Naomi shared a quick look that Holden pretended not to see.

"Okay," Holden continued. "Forget babies for a minute. What I'm talking about is incorporating. If we plan to stick together, let's make it legal. We can draft up incorporation papers with one of the independent outer planets stations, like Ceres or Europa, and become joint owners of this enterprise."

"What," Naomi said, "does our little company do?"

"Exactly," Holden said in triumph.

"Uh," Amos said again.

"No, I mean, that's exactly what I've been asking," Holden continued. "Who are we? What do we want to do? Because when this contract with Prax is over, the bank account will be well padded, we'll own a high-tech warship, and we'll be free to do whatever we damn well want to do."

"Jesus, Cap," Amos said. "I just got half a hard-on."

"I know, right?" Holden replied with a grin.

Prax stopped mixing things in his bowl and stuck it in the refrigerator. He turned and looked at them with the careful movements of someone who feared he'd be asked to leave if anyone noticed him. Holden moved over to him and put an arm around his shoulder. "Our friend Prax here can't be the only guy who needs to hire a ship like this, right?"

"We're faster and meaner than just about anything a civvy can dig up," Alex said with a nod.

"And when we find Mei, it will be as high profile as you could hope for," Holden said. "What better advertising could we get than that?"

"Admit it, Cap," Amos said. "You just kind of like being famous."

"If it gets us jobs, sure."

"We're much more likely to wind up broke, out of air, and drifting through space dead," Naomi said.

"That's always a possibility," Holden admitted. "But, man, aren't you ready to be your own boss for a change? If we find we can't make it on our own, we can always sell the ship for a giant sack of money and go our separate ways. We have an escape plan."

"Yeah," Amos said. "Fuck yeah. Let's do this. How do we start?"

"Well," Holden said. "That's another new thing. I think we have to vote. No one of us owns the ship, so I think we vote on important stuff like this from now on."

Amos said, "All in favor of making ourselves into a company to own the ship, raise your hand."

To Holden's delight, they all raised their hands. Even Prax started to, realized he was doing it, and then put it back down.

"I'll get us an attorney on Ceres and start the paperwork," Holden said. "But that leads to something else. A company can own a ship, but a company can't be the registered captain. We'll need to vote for whoever holds that title."

Amos started laughing. "Gimme a fucking break. Raise your hand if Holden isn't the captain."

No hands went up.

"See?" Amos said.

Holden started to speak but stopped when something uncomfortable happened in his throat and behind his sternum.

"Look," Amos said, his face kind. "You're just that guy."

Naomi nodded and smiled at Holden, which only made the ache in his chest pleasantly worse. "I'm an engineer," she said. "There isn't a program on this ship I haven't tweaked or rewritten, and I could probably take her apart and put her back together by myself at this point. But I can't bluff at cards. And I'm never going to be the one that stares down the joint navies of the inner planets and says, 'Back the hell off.'"

"Roger that," Alex said. "And I just want to fly my baby. That's all and that's it. If I get to do that, I'm happy."

Holden started to speak, but to his surprise and embarrassment, the minute his mouth opened, his eyes teared up. Amos saved him.

"I'm just a grease monkey," he said. "I push tools. And I mostly wait for Naomi to tell me when and where to push 'em. I got no desire to run anything bigger than that machine shop. You're the talker. I've seen you face down Fred Johnson, UN naval captains, OPA cowboys, and drugged-up space pirates. You talk out your ass better than most people do using their mouth and sober."

"Thank you," Holden finally said. "I love you guys. You know that, right?"

"Plus which," Amos continued, "no one on this ship will try harder to jump in front of a bullet for me than you will. I find that appealing in a captain."

"Thanks," Holden said again.

"Sounds settled to me," Alex said, getting up and heading toward the ladder. "Gonna go make sure we're not aimed at a rock or somethin'."

Holden watched him go and was gratified to see him wiping his eyes as soon as he got out of the room. It was okay to be a weepy little kid as long as everyone else was being a weepy little kid.

Prax gave him an awkward pat on the shoulder and said, "Come back to the galley in an hour. Pudding will be ready." Then he wandered out and into his cabin. He was already reading messages on his hand terminal as he closed the door.

"Okay," Amos said. "What now?"

"Amos," Naomi said, getting up and walking over to stand in front of Holden. "Please take ops for me for a while."

"Roger that," Amos said, the grin existing only in his voice. He climbed the ladder up and out of sight, the pressure hatch opening for him, then slamming behind him when he went.

"Hi," Holden said. "Was that right?"

She nodded. "I feel like I got you back. I was worried I'd never see you again."

"If you hadn't yanked me out of that hole I was digging for myself, neither of us would have."

Naomi leaned forward to kiss him, and he wrapped his arms around her and pulled her tight. When they stopped to breathe, he said, "Is this too soon?"

She said, "Shut up," and kissed him again. Without breaking the kiss, she pulled her body away from his and began fumbling with the zipper of his jumpsuit. Those ridiculous Martian military jumpsuits that had come with the ship, TACHI stenciled across the back. Now that they were going to have their own company, they'd need to get something better. Jumpsuits made a lot of sense for shipboard life, with changing gravities and oily mechanical parts. But something actually tailored to fit them all, and in their own colors. ROCINANTE on the back.

Naomi's hand got inside the jumpsuit and under his T-shirt, and he lost all thought of fashion choices.

"My bunk or yours?" he said.

"You have your own bunk?"

Not anymore.

Making love to Naomi had always been different than with anyone else. Some of it was physical. She was the only Belter he'd ever been with, and that meant she was physiologically different in some ways. But that wasn't the most notable part for him. What made Naomi different was that they'd been friends for five years before they'd slept together.

It wasn't a flattering testament to his character, and it made him cringe when he thought about it now, but he'd always been pretty shallow when it came to sex. He'd picked out potential sexual partners within minutes of meeting a new woman, and because he was pretty and charming, he usually got the ones he was interested in. He'd always been quick to allow himself to mistake infatuation for genuine affection. One of his most painful memories was the day Naomi had called him on it. Exposed for him the little game he played in which he convinced himself he genuinely cared for the women he was sleeping with so that he wouldn't feel like a user.

But he had been. The fact that the women were using him in turn didn't make him feel better about it.

Because Naomi was so physically different from the ideal that growing up on Earth had created, he had just not seen her as a potential sexual partner when they'd first met. And that meant he'd grown to know her as a person without any of the sexual baggage he usually carried. When his feelings for her grew beyond friendship, he was surprised.

And somehow, that changed everything about sex. The movements might all be the same, but the desire to communicate affection rather than demonstrate prowess changed what everything meant. After their first time together, he'd lain in bed for hours feeling like he'd been doing it wrong for years and only just realized it.

He was doing that again now.

Naomi slept on her side next to him, her arm thrown across his chest and her thigh across his, her belly against his hip and her breast against his ribs. It had never been like this with anyone before her, and this was what it was supposed to be like. This sense of complete ease and contentment. He could imagine a future in which he hadn't been able to prove he'd changed, and in which she never came back to him. He could see years and decades of sexual partners, always trying to recapture this feeling and never being able to because, of course, it wasn't really about the sex.

Thinking about it made his stomach hurt.

Naomi talked in her sleep. Her mouth whispered something mysterious into his neck, and the sudden tickle woke him up enough to realize he'd been drifting off to sleep. He hugged her head to his chest and kissed the top of it, then rolled over onto his side and let himself fade.

The wall monitor over the bed buzzed.

"Who is it?" he said, suddenly as tired as he could remember ever having been. He'd just closed his eyes a second earlier, and he knew he'd never be able to open them now.

"Me, Cap," Alex said. Holden wanted to shout at him but couldn't find the energy.

"Okay."

"You need to see this," was all Alex said, but something in his voice woke Holden up. He sat up, moving Naomi's arm out of the way. She said something in sleep-talk but didn't wake.

"Okay," he said again, turning on the monitor.

A white-haired older woman with very strange facial features looked out at him. It took his addled mind a second to recognize that she wasn't deformed, just being crushed by a heavy burn. With a voice distorted by g-forces mashing down on her throat, she said, "My name is Chrisjen Avasarala. I'm the UN assistant undersecretary of executive administration. A UN admiral has dispatched six Munroe-class destroyers from the Jupiter system to destroy your ship. Track this transponder code and come meet me or you and everyone on your ship will die. This is not a fucking joke."

Chapter Forty: Prax

Thrust pressed him into the crash couch. It was only four g, but even a single full g called for very nearly the full medical cocktail. He had lived in a place that kept him weak. He'd known that, of course, but mostly in terms of xylem and phloem. He had taken the normal low-g medical supplements to encourage bone growth. He had exercised as much as the guidelines asked. Usually. But always in the back of his mind, he'd thought it was idiocy. He was a botanist. He'd live and die in the familiar tunnels, with their comfortable low gravity—less than a fifth of Earth's. An Earth he would never have reason to go to. There was even less reason he would ever need to suffer through a high-g burn. And yet here he lay in the gel like he was at the bottom of an ocean. His vision was blurred, and he fought for every inhalation. When his knee hyperextended, he tried to scream but couldn't catch his breath.

The others would be better. They'd be used to things like this.

They knew that they'd survive. His hindbrain wasn't at all sure. Needles dug into the flesh of his thigh, injecting him with another cocktail of hormones and paralytics. Cold like the touch of ice spread from the injection points, and a paradoxical sense of ease and dread filled his mind. At this point, it was a balancing act between keeping his blood vessels elastic enough that they wouldn't burst and robust enough that they wouldn't collapse. His mind slid out from under him, leaving something calculating and detached in its place. It was like pure executive function without a sense of self. What had been his mind knew what he had known, remembered the things he remembered, but wasn't him.

In this altered state of consciousness, he found himself taking inventory. Would it be okay to die now? Did he want to live, and if he did, on what terms? He considered the loss of his daughter as if it were a physical object. Loss was the soft pink of crushed seashell, where once it had been the red of old, scabby blood. The red of an umbilical cord waiting to drop free. He remembered Mei, what she had looked like. The delight in her laugh. She wasn't like that anymore. If she was alive. But she was probably dead.

In his gravity-bent mind, he smiled. Of course, his lips couldn't react. He'd been wrong. All along, he'd been wrong. The hours of sitting by himself, telling himself that Mei was dead. He'd thought he was toughening himself. Preparing himself for the worst. That wasn't right at all. He'd said it, he'd tried to believe it, because the thought was comforting.

If she was dead, she wasn't being tortured. If she was dead, she wasn't scared. If she was dead, then the pain would be all his, entirely his, and she would be safe. He noticed without pleasure or pain that it was a pathological mental frame. But he'd had his life and his daughter taken from him, had survived in near starvation while the cascade effect ate what was left of Ganymede, had been shot at, had faced a half-alien killing machine, and was now known throughout the solar system as a wife beater and pedophile. He had no reason to be sane. It wouldn't help him.

And on top of that, his knee *really* hurt.

Somewhere far, far away, in a place with light and air, something buzzed three times, and the mountain rolled off his sternum. Coming back to himself was like rising from the bottom of a pool.

"Okay, y'all," Alex said across the ship's system. "We're callin' this dinner. Take a couple minutes for your livers to crawl up off your spinal cords, and we'll meet up in the galley. We've only got fifty minutes, so enjoy it while you can."

Prax took a deep breath, blowing it out between his teeth, and then sat up. His whole body felt bruised. His hand terminal claimed the thrust was at one-third g, but it felt like more and less than that. He swung his legs over the edge, and his knee made a wet, grinding pop. He tapped at his terminal.

"Um, I'm not sure I can walk," he said. "My knee."

"Hang tight, Doc." Amos' voice came from the speaker. "I'll come take a look at it. I'm pretty much the closest thing we've got to a medic unless you wanna hand it over to the med bay."

"Just don't try to weld him back together," Holden said. "It doesn't work."

The link went silent. While he waited, Prax checked his incoming messages. The list was too long for the screen, but that had been true since the initial message had gone out. The message titles had changed.

BABY RAPERS SHOULD BE TORTURED TO DEATH
DON'T LISTEN TO THE HATERS
I BELIEVE YOU
MY FATHER DID THE SAME THING TO ME
TURN TO JESUS BEFORE IT'S TOO LATE

He didn't open them. He checked the newsfeeds under his own name and Mei's and had seven thousand active feeds with those keywords. Nicola's only had fifty.

There had been a time that he'd loved Nicola, or thought that he had. He'd wanted to have sex with her as badly as he'd wanted anything before in his life. He told himself there had been good times. Nights they'd spent together. Mei had come from Nicola's body. It was hard to believe that something so precious and central to his life had also been part of a woman who, by the evidence, he'd never really known. Even as the father of her child, he hadn't known the woman who could have made that recording.

He opened the hand terminal's recording fields, centered the camera on himself, and licked his lips.

"Nicola…"

Twenty seconds later, he closed the field and erased the recording. He had nothing to say. *Who are you, and who do you think I am?* came closest, and he didn't care about the answer to either one.

He went back to the messages, filtering on the names of the people who'd been helping him investigate. There was nothing new since the last time.

"Hey, Doc," Amos said, lumbering into the small room.

"I'm sorry," Prax said, putting his terminal back into its holder beside the crash couch. "It was just that during that last burn…"

He gestured to his knee. It was swollen, but not as badly as he'd expected. He'd thought it would be twice its normal size, but the anti-inflammatories that had been injected into his veins were doing their job. Amos nodded, put a hand on Prax's sternum, and pushed him back into the gel.

"I got a toe that pops out sometimes," Amos said. "Little tiny joint, but get it at the wrong angle on a fast burn, hurts like a bitch. Try not to tense up, Doc."

Amos bent the knee twice, feeling the joint grind. "This ain't that bad. Here, straighten it out. Okay."

Amos wrapped one hand around Prax's ankle, braced the other on the frame of the couch, and pulled slowly and irresistibly. Prax's knee bloomed with pain, and then a deep, wet pop and a nauseating sensation of tendons shifting against bone.

"There you go," Amos said. "We go back into burn, make sure you got that leg in the right place. Hyperextend that again right now, we'll pop your kneecap off, okay?"

"Right," Prax said, starting to sit up.

"I'm sorry as hell to do this, Doc," Amos said, putting a hand on his chest, pushing him back down. "I mean, you're having a lousy day and all. But you know how it is."

Prax frowned. Every muscle in his face felt bruised.

"What is it?"

"All this bullshit they're saying about you and the kid? That's all just bullshit, right?"

"Of course," Prax said.

"Because you know, sometimes things happen, you didn't even mean them to. Have a hard day, lose your temper, maybe? Or shit, you get drunk. Some of the things I've done when I really tied one on? I don't even know about until later." Amos smiled. "I'm just saying if there's a grain of truth, something that's getting all exaggerated, it'd be better if we knew it now, right?"

"I never did anything that she said."

"It's okay to tell me the truth, Doc. I understand. Sometimes guys do stuff. Doesn't make 'em bad."

Prax pushed Amos' hand aside and brought himself up to sitting. His knee felt much better.

"Actually," he said, "it does. That makes them bad."

Amos' expression relaxed, his smile changed in a way Prax couldn't quite understand.

"All right, Doc. Like I said, I'm sorry as hell. But I did have to ask."

"It's okay," Prax said, standing up. For a moment, the knee seemed like it might give, but it didn't. Prax took a tentative step, then another. It would work. He turned toward the galley, but the conversation wasn't finished. "If I had. If I had done those things, that would have been okay with you?"

"Oh, fuck no. I'd have broken your neck and thrown you out the airlock," Amos said, clapping him on the shoulder.

"Ah," Prax said, a gentle relief loosening in his chest. "Thank you."

"Anytime."

The other three were in the galley when Prax and Amos got

there, but it still felt half full. Less. Naomi and Alex were sitting across the table from each other. Neither of them looked as ruined as Prax felt. Holden turned from the wall with a formed-foam bowl in either hand. The brown slurry in them smelled of heat and earth and cooked leaves. As soon as it caught his nose, Prax was ravenous.

"Lentil soup?" Holden asked as Prax and Amos sat on either side of Alex.

"That would be wonderful," Prax said.

"I'll just take a tube of goo," Amos said. "Lentils give me gas, and I can't see popping an intestine next time we accelerate being fun for anyone."

Holden put a fresh bowl in front of Prax and handed a white tube with a black plastic nipple to Amos, then sat beside Naomi. They didn't touch, but the connection between them was unmistakable. He wondered whether Mei had ever wanted him to reconcile with Nicola. Impossible now.

"Okay, Alex," Holden said. "What've we got?"

"Same thing we had before," Alex said. "Six destroyers burning like hell toward us. A matching force burning after them, and a racing pinnace heading away from us on the other side."

"Wait," Prax said. "Away from us?"

"They're matching our course. Already did the turnaround, and they're getting up to speed to join us."

Prax closed his eyes, picturing the vectors.

"We're almost there, then?" he said.

"Very nearly," Alex said. "Eighteen, twenty hours."

"How's it going to play out? Are the Earth ships going to catch us?"

"They're gonna catch the hell out of us," Alex said, "but not before we get that pinnace. Call it four days after, maybe."

Prax took a spoonful of the soup. It tasted just as good as it smelled. Green, dark leaves were mixed in with the lentils, and he spread one open with his spoon, trying to identify it. Spinach, maybe. The stem margin didn't look quite right, but it had been cooked, after all...

"How sure are we this isn't a trap?" Amos asked.

"We aren't," Holden said. "But I don't see how it would work."

"If they want us in custody instead of dead," Naomi suggested. "We are talking about opening our airlock for someone way high up in the Earth government."

"So she is who she says she is?" Prax asked.

"Looks like it," Holden said.

Alex raised a hand.

"Well, if it's talk to some little gramma from the UN or get my ass shot off by six destroyers, I'm thinkin' we can break out the cookies and tea, right?"

"It would be late in the game to go for another plan," Naomi said. "It makes me damn uncomfortable having Earth saving me from Earth, though."

"Structures are never monolithic," Prax said. "There's more genetic variation within Belters or Martians or Earthers than there is between them. Evolution would predict some divisions within the group structures and alliances with out-members. You see the same thing in ferns."

"Ferns?" Naomi asked.

"Ferns can be very aggressive," Prax said.

A soft chime interrupted them: three rising notes, like bells gently struck.

"Okay, suck it down," Alex said. "That's the fifteen-minute warning."

Amos made a prodigious sucking sound, the white tube withering at his lips. Prax put down his spoon and lifted the soup bowl to his lips, not wanting to leave a drop of it. Holden did the same, then started gathering up the used bowls.

"Anyone needs to hit the head, this is the time," he said. "We'll talk again in..."

"Eight hours," Alex said.

"Eight hours," Holden repeated.

Prax felt his chest go tight. Another round of crushing acceleration. Hours of the couch's needles propping up his failing metabolism. It sounded like hell. He rose from the table, nodded to everyone, and went back to his bunk. His knee was much better. He hoped it would still be when he next got up. The ten-minute chime sounded. He lay down on the couch, trying to align his body perfectly, then waited. Waited.

He rolled over and grabbed his hand terminal. Seven new incoming messages. Two of them supportive, three hateful, one addressed to the wrong person, and one a financial statement from the charity fund. He didn't bother reading them.

He turned on the camera.

"Nicola," he said. "I don't know what they told you. I don't know if you really think all those things that you said. But I know I never touched you in anger, even at the end. And if you really felt afraid of me, I don't know why it was. Mei is the one thing that I love more than anything in life. I'd die before I let anyone hurt her. And now half the solar system thinks I hurt her..."

He stopped the recording and began again.

"Nicola. Honestly, I didn't think we had anything left between us to betray."

He stopped. The five-minute warning chimed as he ran his fingers through his hair. Each individual follicle ached. He wondered if this was why Amos kept his head shaved. There were so many things about being on a ship that didn't occur to you until you were actually there.

"Nicola..."

He erased all the recordings and logged into the charity bank account interface. There was a secure request format that could encrypt and send an authorized transfer as soon as light-speed delivered it to the bank's computers. He filled it all out quickly. The two-minute warning sounded, louder and more insistent. With thirty seconds left, he sent her money back. There was nothing else for them to say.

He put the hand terminal in place and lay back. The computer counted backward from twenty, and the mountain rolled back over him.

"How's the knee?" Amos asked.

"Pretty good," Prax said. "I was surprised. I thought there'd be more damage."

"Didn't hyperextend this time," Amos said. "Did okay with my toe too."

A deep tone rang through the ship, and the deck shifted under Prax. Holden, standing just to Prax's right, moved the rifle to his left hand and touched a control panel.

"Alex?"

"Yeah, it was little rough. Sorry about that, but...Hold on. Yeah, Cap. We've got seal. And they're knocking."

Holden shifted the rifle back to his other hand. Amos also had a weapon at the ready. Naomi stood beside him, nothing in her hands but a terminal linked to ship operations. If something went wrong, being able to control ship functions might be more useful than a gun. They all wore the articulated armor of the Martian military that had come with the ship. The paired ships were accelerating at a third of a g. The Earth destroyers still barreled down toward them.

"So I'm guessing the firearms mean you're thinking trap, Cap'n?" Amos asked.

"Nothing wrong with an honor guard," Holden said.

Prax held up his hand.

"You don't ever get one again," Holden said. "No offense."

"No, I was just...I thought honor guards were usually on the same side as the people they're guarding?"

"We may be stretching the definitions a little here," Naomi said. Her voice had just a trace of tension in it.

"She's just a little old politician," Holden said. "And that pinnace can't hold more than two people. We've got her outnumbered. And if things get ugly, Alex is watching from the pilot's seat. You are watching, right?"

"Oh yeah," Alex said.

"So if there are any surprises, Naomi can pop us loose and Alex can get us out of here."

"That won't help with the destroyers, though," Prax said.

Naomi put a hand on his arm, squeezing him gently.

"I'm not sure you're helping, Prax."

The outer airlock cycled open with a distant hum. The lights clicked from red to green.

"Whoa," Alex said.

"Problem?" Holden snapped.

"No, it's just—"

The inner door opened, and the biggest person Prax had seen in his entire life stepped into the room wearing a suit of some sort of strength-augmenting armor. If it weren't for the transparent face-plate, he would have thought it was a two-meter-tall bipedal robot. Through the faceplate, Prax saw a woman's features: large dark eyes and coffee-with-cream skin. Her gaze raked them with the palpable threat of violence. Beside him, Amos took an unconscious step back.

"You're the captain," the woman said, the suit's speakers making her voice sound artificial and amplified. It didn't sound like a question.

"I am," Holden said. "I've got to say, you looked a little different on-screen."

The joke fell flat and the giant stepped into the room.

"Planning to shoot me with that?" she asked, pointing toward Holden's gun with a massive gauntleted fist.

"Would it work?"

"Probably not," the giant said. She took another small step forward, her armor whining when she moved. Holden and Amos took a matching step back.

"Call it an honor guard, then," Holden said.

"I'm honored. Will you put them away now?"

"Sure."

Two minutes later, the guns were stowed, and the huge woman, who still hadn't given her name, tapped something inside the helmet with her chin and said, "Okay. You're clear."

The airlock cycled again, red to green, with the hum of the opening doors. The woman who came in this time was smaller than any of them. Her gray hair was spiking out in all directions, and the orange sari she wore hung strangely in the low thrust gravity.

"Undersecretary Avasarala," Holden said. "Welcome aboard. If there's anything I can—"

"You're Naomi Nagata," the wizened little woman said.

Holden and Naomi exchanged glances, and Naomi shrugged.

"I am."

"How the fuck do you keep your hair like that? I look like a hedgehog's been humping my skull."

"Um—"

"Looking the part is half of what's going to keep you all alive. We don't have time to screw around. Nagata, you get me looking pretty and girlish. Holden—"

"I'm an engineer, not a damned hairstylist," Naomi said, anger creeping into her voice.

"Ma'am," Holden said, "this is my ship and my crew. Half of us aren't even Earth citizens, and we don't just take your commands."

"All right. Ms. Nagata, if we're going to keep this ship from turning into an expanding ball of hot gas, we need to make a press statement, and I'm not prepared to do that. Would you please assist me?"

"Okay," Naomi said.

"Thank you. And, Captain? You need a fucking shave."

Chapter Forty-One: Avasarala

After the *Guanshiyin*, the *Rocinante* seemed dour, mean, and utilitarian. There was no plush carpeting, only fabric-covered foam to soften corners and angles where soldiers might be thrown when the ship maneuvered violently. Instead of cinnamon and honey, the air had the plastic-and-heat smell of military air recyclers. And there were no expansive desk, no wide solitaire-ready bed, and no private space apart from a captain's lounge the size of a public toilet stall.

Most of the footage they'd taken had been in the cargo bays, angled so that no ammunition or weaponry was in the image. Someone who knew Martian military vessels could tell where they were. To everyone else, it would be an open space with cargo crates in the background. Naomi Nagata had helped put the release together—she was a surprisingly good visual editor—and when it became clear that none of the men could manage a professional-sounding voice-over, she'd done that too.

The crew assembled in the medical bay, where the mechanic Amos Burton had changed the feed to display from her hand terminal. Now he was sitting on one of the patient beds, his legs crossed, smiling amiably. If Avasarala hadn't seen the intelligence files on Holden's crew, she'd never have guessed what the man was capable of.

The others were spread out in a rough semicircle. Bobbie was sitting beside Alex Kamal, the Martians unconsciously grouping together. Praxidike Meng stood at the back of the room. Avasarala couldn't tell if her presence made him uncomfortable or if he was always like that.

"Okay," she said. "Last chance for feedback."

"Wish I had some popcorn," Amos said, and the medical scanner flashed once, showed a broadcast code and then white block letters: FOR IMMEDIATE RELEASE.

Avasarala and Holden appeared on the screen. She was speaking, her hands out before her as if illustrating a point. Holden, looking sober, leaned toward her. Naomi Nagata's voice was calm, strong, and professional.

"In a surprising development, the deputy to Undersecretary of Executive Administration Sadavir Errinwright met with OPA representative James Holden and a representative of the Martian military today to address concerns over the potentially earth-shattering revelations surrounding the devastating attack on Ganymede."

The image cut to Avasarala. She was leaning forward to make her neck longer and hide the loose skin under her chin. Long practice made her look natural, but she could almost hear Arjun laughing. A runner at the bottom of the screen identified her by name and title.

"I expect to be traveling with Captain Holden to the Jovian system," Avasarala said. "The United Nations of Earth feel very strongly that a multilateral investigation into this is the best way to restore balance and peace to the system."

The image shifted to Holden and Avasarala sitting in the galley with the botanist. This time the little scientist was talking and she and Holden pretended to listen. The voice-over came again.

"When asked about the accusations leveled against Praxidike Meng, whose search for his daughter has become the human face of the tragedy on Ganymede, the Earth delegation was unequivocal."

Then back to Avasarala, her expression now sorrowful. Her head shaking in an almost subliminal negation.

"Nicola Mulko is a tragic figure in this, and I personally condemn the irresponsibility of these raw newsfeeds that allow statements from mentally ill people to be presented as if they were verified fact. Her abandonment of her husband and child is beyond dispute, and her struggles with her psychological issues deserve a more dignified and private venue."

From off camera, Nagata asked, "So you blame the media?"

"Absolutely," Avasarala said as the image shifted to a picture of a toddler with smiling black eyes and dark pigtails. "We have absolute faith in Dr. Meng's love and dedication to Mei, and we are pleased to be part of the effort to bring her safely home."

The recording ended.

"All right," Avasarala said. "Any comments?"

"I don't actually work for the OPA anymore," Holden said.

"I'm not authorized to represent the Martian military," Bobbie said. "I'm not even sure I'm still supposed to be working with you."

"Thank you for that. Are there any comments that matter?" Avasarala asked. There was a moment's silence.

"Worked for me," Praxidike Meng said.

There was one way that the *Rocinante* was infinitely more expansive than the *Guanshiyin*, and it was the only one that she cared about. The tightbeam was hers. Lag was worse and every hour took her farther from Earth, but knowing that the messages she sent were getting off the ship without being reported to Nguyen and Errinwright gave her the feeling of breathing free. What happened once they reached Earth, she couldn't control, but that was always true. That was the game.

Admiral Souther looked tired, but on the small screen it was hard to tell much more than that.

"You've kicked the beehive, Chrisjen," he said. "It's looking an awful lot like you just made yourself a human shield for a bunch of folks that don't work for us. And I'm guessing that was the plan.

"I did what you asked, and yes, Nguyen took meetings with Jules-Pierre Mao. First one was just after his testimony on Protogen. And yes, Errinwright knew about them. But that doesn't mean very much. I've met with Mao. He's a snake, but if you stopped dealing with men like him, you wouldn't have much left to do.

"The smear campaign against your scientist friend came out of the executive office, which, I've got to say, makes a damn lot of us over here in the armed forces a bit twitchy. Starts looking like there's divisions inside the leadership, and it gets a little murky whose orders we're supposed to be following. If it gets there, our friend Errinwright still outranks you. Him or the secretary-general comes to me with a direct order, I'm going to have to have a hell of a good reason to think it's illegal. This whole thing smells like skunk, but I don't have that reason yet. You know what I'm saying."

The recording stopped. Avasarala pressed her fingers to her lips. She understood. She didn't like it, but she understood. She levered herself up from her couch. Her joints still ached from the race to the *Rocinante*, and the way the ship would sometimes shift beneath her, course corrections moving gravity a degree or two, left her vaguely nauseated. She'd made it this far.

The corridor that led to the galley was short, but it had a bend just before it entered. The voices carried well enough that Avasarala walked softly. The low Martian drawl was the pilot, and Bobbie's vowels and timbre were unmistakable.

"—that tellin' the captain where to stand and how to look. I thought Amos was going to toss her in the airlock a couple of times."

"He could try," Bobbie said.

"And you work for her?"

"I don't know who the hell I work for anymore. I think I'm still pulling a salary from Mars, but all my dailies are out of her office budget. I've pretty much been playing it all as it comes."

"Sounds rough."

"I'm a marine," Bobbie said, and Avasarala paused. The tone was wrong. It was calm, almost relaxed. Almost at peace. That was interesting.

"Does anyone actually like her?" the pilot asked.

"No," Bobbie said almost before the question was done being asked. "Oh hell no. And she keeps it like that. That shit she pulled with Holden, marching on his ship and ordering him around like she owned it? She's always like that. The secretary-general? She calls him a bobble-head to his face."

"And what's with the potty mouth?"

"Part of her charm," Bobbie said.

The pilot chuckled, and there was a little slurp as he drank something.

"I may have misunderstood politics," he said. And a moment later: "You like her?"

"I do."

"Mind if I ask why?"

"We care about the same things," Bobbie said, and the thoughtful note in her voice made Avasarala feel uncomfortable eavesdropping. She cleared her throat and walked into the galley.

"Where's Holden?" she asked.

"Probably sleeping," the pilot said. "The way we've been keepin' the ship's cycle, it's about two in the morning."

"Ah," Avasarala said. For her, it was mid-afternoon. That was going to be a little awkward. Everything in her life seemed to be about lag right now, waiting for the messages to get through the vast blackness of the vacuum. But at least she could prepare.

"I'm going to want a meeting with everyone on board as soon as they're up," she said. "Bobbie, you'll need your formal wear again."

It took Bobbie only a few seconds to understand.

"You'll show them the monster," she said.

"And then we're going to sit here and talk until we figure out what exactly it is they know on this ship. It has the bad guys worried enough they were willing to send their boys to kill them," she said.

"Yeah, about that," the pilot said. "Those destroyers cut back to a cruising acceleration, but they aren't turning back yet."

"Doesn't matter," Avasarala said. "Everybody knows I'm on this ship. No one's going to shoot at it."

In the local morning and Avasarala's subjective early evening, the crew gathered again. Rather than bring the whole powered suit into the galley, she'd copied the stored video and given it to Naomi. The crew members were bright and well rested apart from the pilot, who had stayed up entirely too late talking to Bobbie, and the botanist, who looked like he might just be permanently exhausted.

"I'm not supposed to show this to anyone," Avasarala said, looking pointedly at Holden. "But on this ship, right now, I think we all need to put our cards on the table. And I'm willing to go first. This is the attack on Ganymede. The thing that started it all off. Naomi?"

Naomi started the playback, and Bobbie turned away and stared at the bulkhead. Avasarala didn't watch it either, her attention on the faces of the others. As the blood and carnage played out behind her, she studied them and learned a little more about the people she was dealing with. The engineer, Amos, watched with the calm reserve of a professional killer. No surprise there. At first Holden, Naomi, and Alex were horrified, and she watched as Alex and Naomi slid into a kind of shock. There were tears in the pilot's eyes. Holden, on the other hand, curled in. His shoulders bent outward from each other, and an expression of banked rage smoldered in his eyes and around the corners of his mouth. That was interesting. Bobbie wept openly with her back to the screen, and her expression was melancholy, like a woman at a funeral. A memorial service. Praxidike—everyone else called him Prax—was the only one who seemed almost happy. When at the segment's end, the monstrosity detonated, he clapped his hands and squealed in pleasure.

"That was it," he said. "You were right, Alex. Did you see how it was starting to grow more limbs? Catastrophic restraint failure. It *was* a fail-safe."

"Okay," Avasarala said. "Why don't you try that again with an antecedent. What was a fail-safe?"

"The other protomolecule form ejected the explosive device from its body before it could detonate. You see, these... things—protomolecule soldiers or whatever—are breaking their programming, and I think Merrian knows about it. He hasn't found a way to stop it, because the constraints fail."

"Who's Marion, and what does she have to do with anything?" Avasarala said.

"You wanted more nouns, Gramma," Amos said.

"Let me take this from the top," Holden said, and recounted the attack by the stowaway beast, the damage to the cargo door, Prax's scheme to lure it out of the ship and reduce it to its component atoms with the drive's exhaust.

Avasarala handed over the data she had about the energy spikes on Venus, and Prax grabbed that data, looking it over while talking about his determination of a secret base on Io where the things were being produced. It left Avasarala's head spinning.

"And they took your kid there," Avasarala said.

"They took all of them," Prax said.

"Why would they do that?"

"Because they don't have immune systems," Prax said. "And so they'd be easier to reshape with the protomolecule. There would be fewer physiological systems fighting against the new cellular constraints, and the soldiers would probably last a lot longer."

"Jesus, Doc," Amos said. "They're going to turn Mei into one of those fucking things?"

"Probably," Prax said, frowning. "I only just figured that out."

"But why do it at all?" Holden said. "It doesn't make sense."

"In order to sell them to a military force as a first-strike weapon," Avasarala said. "To consolidate power before…well, before the fucking apocalypse."

"Point of clarification," Alex said, raising his hand. "We have an apocalypse comin'? Was that a thing we knew about?"

"Venus," Avasarala said.

"Oh. That apocalypse," Alex said, lowering his hand. "Right."

"Soldiers that can travel without ships," Naomi said. "You could fire them off at high g for a little while, then cut engines and let them go ballistic. How would you find them?"

"But it won't *work*," Prax said. "Remember? They escape constraint. And since they can share information, they're going to get harder to hold to any kind of new programming."

The room went silent. Prax looked confused.

"They can *share information*?" Avasarala said.

"Sure," Prax said. "Look at your energy spikes. The first one happened while the thing was fighting Bobbie and the other marines on Ganymede. The second spike came when the other one got loose in the lab. The third spike was when we killed it with the *Rocinante*. Every time one of them has been attacked, Venus reacted. They're networked. I'd assume that any critical information could be shared. Like how to escape constraints."

"If they use them against people," Holden said, "there won't be any way to stop them. They'll ditch the fail-safe bombs and just keep going. The battles won't end."

"Um. No," Prax said. "That's not the problem. It's the cascade again. Once the protomolecule gets a little freedom, it has more tools to erode other constraints, which gets it more tools to erode more constraints and on and on like that. The original program or something like it will eventually swamp the new program. They'll revert."

Bobbie leaned forward, her head canted a few degrees to the

right. Her voice was quiet, but it had a threat of violence that was louder than shouting.

"So if they set those things loose on Mars, they stay soldiers like the first one for a while. And then they start dropping the bombs out like your guy did. And then they turn Mars into Eros?"

"Well, worse than Eros," Prax said. "Any decent-sized Martian city is going to have an order of magnitude more people than Eros did."

The room was quiet. On the monitor, Bobbie's suit camera looked up at star-filled sky while battleships killed each other in orbit.

"I've got to send some messages out," Avasarala said.

"These half-human things you've made? They aren't your servants. You can't control them," Avasarala said. "Jules-Pierre Mao sold you a bill of goods. I know why you kept me out of this, and I think you're a fucking moron for it, but put it aside. It doesn't matter now. Just do not pull that fucking trigger. Do you understand what I'm saying? Don't. You will be personally responsible for the single deadliest screwup in the history of humankind, and I'm on a ship with Jim fucking Holden, so the bar's not low."

The full recording clocked in at almost half an hour. The security footage from the *Rocinante* with its stowaway was attached. A fifteen-minute lecture by Prax had to be scrapped when he reached the part about his daughter being turned into a protomolecule soldier, and this time broke into uncontrollable weeping. Avasarala did her best to recapitulate it, but she wasn't at all certain she had the details right. She'd considered bringing Jon-Michael into it, but decided against it. Better to keep it in the family.

She sent the message. If she knew Errinwright, he wouldn't get back to her immediately. There would be an hour or two of evaluation, weighing what she'd said, and then when she'd been left to stew for a while, he'd reply.

She hoped he'd be sane about it. He had to.

She needed to sleep. She could feel the fatigue gnawing at the edges of her mind, slowing her, but when she lay down, rest felt as far away as home. As Arjun. She thought about recording a message for him, but it would only have left her feeling more powerfully isolated. After an hour, she pulled herself up and walked through the halls. Her body told her it was midnight or later, and the activity on board—music ringing out of the machine shop, a loud conversation between Holden and Alex about the maintenance of the electronics systems, even Praxidike's sitting in the galley by himself, apparently grooming a box of hydroponics cuttings—had a surreal late-night feeling.

She considered sending another message to Souther. The lag time would be much less to him, and she was hungry enough for a response that anything would do. When the answer came, it wasn't a message.

"Captain," Alex said over the ship-wide comm. "You should come up to ops and look at this."

Something in his voice told Avasarala that this wasn't a maintenance question. She found the lift to ops just as Holden went up, and pulled herself up the ladder rather than wait. She wasn't the only one who'd followed the call. Bobbie was in a spare seat, her eyes on the same screen as Holden's. The blinking tactical data scrolled down the screen, and a dozen bright red dots displayed changes. She didn't understand most of what she saw, but the gist was obvious. The destroyers were on the move.

"Okay," Holden said. "What're we seeing?"

"All the Earth destroyers hit high burn. Six g," Alex said.

"Are they going to Io?"

"Oh, hell no."

This was Errinwright's answer. No messages. No negotiations. Not even an acknowledgment that she'd asked him to restrain himself. Warships. The despair only lasted for a moment. Then came the anger.

"Bobbie?"

"Yeah."

"That part where you told me I didn't understand the danger I was in?"

"And you told me that I didn't how the game was played."

"That part."

"I remember. What about it?"

"If you wanted to say 'I told you so,' this looks like the right time."

Chapter Forty-Two: Holden

Holden had spent a month at the Diamond Head Electronic Warfare Lab on Oahu as his first posting after officer candidate school. During that time, he'd learned he had no desire to be a naval intelligence wonk, really disliked poi, and really liked Polynesian women. He'd been far too busy at the time to actively chase one, but he'd thoroughly enjoyed spending his few spare moments down at the beach looking at them. He'd had a thing for curvy women with long black hair ever since.

The Martian Marine was like one of those cute little beach bunnies that someone had used editing software on and blown up to 150 percent normal size. The proportions, the black hair, the dark eyes, everything was the same. Only, giant. It short-circuited his neural wiring. The lizard living at the back of his brain kept jumping back and forth between *Mate with it!* and *Flee from it!* What was worse, she knew it. She seemed to have sized him up and decided he was only worth a tired smirk within moments of their meeting.

"Do you need me to go over it again?" she said, the smirk mocking him. They were sitting together in the galley, where she'd been describing for him the Martian intelligence on the best way to engage the Munroe-class light destroyer.

No! he wanted to yell. *I heard you. I'm not a freak. I have a lovely girlfriend that I'm totally committed to, so stop treating me like some kind of bumbling teenage boy who's trying to look down your dress!*

But then he'd look up at her again, and his hindbrain would start bouncing back and forth between attraction and fear, and his language centers would start misfiring. Again.

"No," he said, staring at the neatly organized list of bullet points she'd forwarded to his hand terminal. "I think this information is very...informative."

He saw the smirk widen out of the corner of his eye and focused more intently on the list.

"Okay," Bobbie said. "I'm going to go catch some rack time. With your permission, of course. Captain."

"Permission granted," Holden said. "Of course. Go. Rack."

She pushed herself to her feet without touching the arms of the chair. She'd grown up in Martian gravity. She had to mass a hundred kilos at one g, easy. She was showing off. He pretended to ignore it, and she left the galley.

"She's something, isn't she?" Avasarala said, coming into the galley and collapsing into the recently vacated chair. Holden looked up at her and saw a different kind of smirk. One that said the old lady saw right through him to the warring lizards at the back of his head. But she wasn't a giant Polynesian woman, so he could vent his frustration on her.

"Yeah, she's a peach," he said. "But we're still going to die."

"What?"

"When those destroyers catch us, which they will, we are going to die. The only reason they aren't raining torpedoes down on us already is because they know our PDC network can take out anything fired at this range."

Avasarala leaned back in her chair with a heavy sigh, and the smirk shifted into a tired but genuine smile. "I don't suppose there's any chance you could find an old woman a cup of tea, could you?"

Holden shook his head. "I'm sorry. No tea drinkers on the crew. Lots of coffee, though, if you'd like a cup."

"I'm actually tired enough to do that. Lots of cream, lots of sugar."

"How about," Holden said, pulling her a cup, "lots of sugar, lots of a powder that's called 'whitener.'"

"Sounds like piss. I'll take it."

Holden sat down and pushed the sweetened and "whitened" cup of coffee across to her. She took it and grimaced through several long swallows.

"Explain," she said after another drink, "everything you just said."

"Those destroyers are going to kill us," Holden repeated. "The sergeant says you refuse to believe that UN ships will fire on you, but I agree with her. That's naive."

"Okay, but what's a 'PDC network'?"

Holden tried not to frown. He'd expected any number of things from the woman, but ignorance hadn't been one.

"Point defense cannons. If those destroyers fire torpedoes at us from this distance, the targeting computer for the PDCs won't have any trouble shooting them down. So they'll wait until they get close enough that they can overwhelm us. I give it three days before they start."

"I see," Avasarala said. "And what's your plan?"

Holden barked out a laugh with no humor in it. "Plan? My plan is to die in a ball of superheated plasma. There is literally no way that a single fast-attack corvette, which is us, can successfully fight six light destroyers. We aren't in the same weight class as even one of them, but against one, a lucky shot maybe. Against six? No chance. We die."

"I've read your file," Avasarala said. "You faced down a UN corvette during the Eros incident."

"Yeah, one corvette. We were a match for her. And I got her to back down by threatening the unarmed science ship she was escorting. This isn't even remotely the same thing."

"So what does the infamous James Holden do at his last stand?"

He was silent for a while.

"He rats," Holden said. "We know what's going on. We have all the pieces now. Mao-Kwik, the protomolecule monsters, where they're taking the kids...everything. We put all the data in a file and broadcast it to the universe. They can still kill us if they want to, but we can make it a pointless act of revenge. Keep it from actually helping them."

"No," Avasarala said.

"Uh, no? You might be forgetting whose ship you're on."

"I'm sorry, did I seem to give a fuck that this is your ship? If I did, really, I was just being polite," Avasarala said, giving him a withering glare. "You aren't going to fuck up the whole solar system just because you're a one-trick pony. We have bigger fish to fry."

Holden counted to ten in his head and said, "Your idea is?"

"Send it to these two UN admirals," she said, then tapped something on her terminal. His buzzed with the received file. "Souther and Leniki. Mostly Souther. I don't like Leniki, and he hasn't been in the loop on this, but he's a decent backup."

"You want my last act before being killed by a UN admiral to be sending all of the vital information I have to a UN admiral."

Avasarala leaned back into her chair and rubbed her temples with her fingertips. Holden waited. "I'm tired," she said after a few moments. "And I miss my husband. It's like an ache in my arms that I can't hold him right now. Do you know what that's like?"

"I know exactly what that ache feels like."

"So I want you to understand that I'm sitting here, right now, coming to terms with the idea that I won't see him again. Or my grandchildren. Or my daughter. My doctors said I probably had a good thirty years left in me. Time to watch my grandkids grow up, maybe even see a great-grandchild or two. But instead, I'm going to be killed by a limp-dick, whiny sonofabitch like Admiral Nguyen."

Holden could feel the massive weight of those six destroyers bearing down on them, murder in their hearts. It felt like having a pistol pushed into his ribs from behind. He wanted to shake the old woman and tell her to hurry up.

She smiled at him.

"My last act in this universe isn't going to be fucking up everything I did right up to now."

Holden made a conscious effort to ignore his frustration. He got up and opened the refrigerator. "Hey, there's leftover pudding. Want some?"

"I've read your psych profile. I know all about your 'everyone should know everything' naive bullshit. But how much of the last war was *your* fault, with your goddamned endless pirate broadcasts? Well?"

"None of it," Holden said. "Desperate psychotic people do desperate psychotic things when they're exposed. I refuse to grant them immunity from exposure out of fear of their reaction. When you do, the desperate psychos wind up in charge."

She laughed. It was a surprisingly warm sound.

"Anyone who understands what's going on is at least desperate and probably psychotic to boot. Dissociative at the least. Let me explain it this way," Avasarala said. "You tell everyone, and yeah, you'll get a reaction. And maybe, weeks, or months, or years from now, it will all get sorted out. But you tell the *right* people, and we can sort it out right now."

Amos and Prax walked into the galley together. Amos had his big thermos in his hand and headed straight toward the coffeepot. Prax followed him and picked up a mug. Avasarala's eyes narrowed and she said, "Maybe even save that little girl."

"Mei?" Prax said immediately, putting the mug down and turning around.

Oh, that was low, Holden thought. *Even for a politician.*

"Yes, Mei," Avasarala replied. "That's what this is about, right, Jim? Not some personal crusade, but trying to save a little girl from very bad people?"

"Explain how—" Holden started, but Avasarala kept talking right over the top of him.

"The UN isn't one person. It isn't even one corporation. It's a thousand little, petty factions fighting against each other. Their side's got the floor, but that's temporary. That's always temporary. I know people who can move against Nguyen and his group. They can cut off his support, strip him of ships, even recall and court-martial him given enough time. But they can't do any of that if we're in a shooting war with Mars. And if you toss everything you know into the wind, Mars won't have time to wait and figure out the subtleties; they'll have no choice but to preemptively strike against Nguyen's fleet, Io, what's left of Ganymede. Everything."

"Io?" Prax said. "But Mei—"

"So you want me to give all the info to your little political cabal back on Earth, when the entire reason for this problem is that there are little political cabals back on Earth."

"Yes," Avasarala said. "And I'm the only hope she's got. You have to trust me."

"I don't. Not even a little bit. I think you're part of the problem. I think you see all of this as political maneuvering and power games. I think you want to *win.* So no, I don't trust you at all."

"Hey, uh, Cap?" Amos said, slowly screwing the top onto his thermos. "Ain't you forgetting something?"

"What, Amos? What am I forgetting?"

"Don't we vote on shit like this now?"

"Don't pout," Naomi said. She was stretched out on a crash couch next to the main operations panel on the ops deck. Holden was seated across the room from her at the comm panel. He'd just sent out Avasarala's data file to her two UN admirals. His fingers itched with the desire to dump it into a general broadcast. But they'd debated the issue for the crew, and she'd won the vote. The whole voting thing had seemed like such a good idea when he'd first brought it up. After losing his first vote, not so much. They'd all be dead in two days, so at least it probably wouldn't happen again.

"If we get killed, and Avasarala's pet admirals don't actually do anything with the data we just sent, this was all for nothing."

"You think they'll bury it?" Naomi said.

"I don't know, and that's the problem. I don't know what they'll do. We met this UN politician two days ago and she's already running the ship."

"So send it to someone else too," Naomi said. "Someone who you can trust to keep it quiet, but can get the word out if the UN guys turn out to be working for the wrong team."

"That's not a bad idea."

"Fred, maybe?"

"No." Holden laughed. "Fred would see it as political capital. He'd use it to bargain with. It needs to be someone that has nothing to gain or lose by using it. I'll have to think about it."

Naomi got up, then came over to straddle his legs and sit on his lap facing him. "And we're all about to die. That's not making any of this any easier."

Not all of us.

"Naomi, gather the crew up, the marine and Avasarala too. The galley, I guess. I have some last business to announce. I'll meet you guys there in ten minutes."

She kissed him lightly on the nose. "Okay. We'll be there."

When she disappeared from sight down the crew ladder, Holden opened up the chief of the watch's locker. Inside were a set of very out-of-date codebooks, a manual of Martian naval law, and a sidearm and two magazines of ballistic gel rounds. He took out the gun, loaded it, and strapped the belt and holster around his waist.

Next he went back to the comm station and put Avasarala's data package into a tightbeam transmission that would bounce from Ceres to Mars to Luna to Earth, using public routers all the way. It would be unlikely to send up any red flags. He hit the video record button and said, "Hi, Mom. Take a look at this. Show it to the family. I have no idea how you'll know when the right time to use it is, but when that time comes, do with it whatever seems best. I trust you guys, and I love you."

Before he could say anything else or think better of the whole thing, he hit the transmit key and turned the panel off.

He called up the ladder-lift, because riding it would take longer than climbing the ladder and he needed time to think out exactly how to play the next ten minutes. When he reached the crew deck, he still didn't have it all figured out, but he squared his shoulders and walked into the galley anyway.

Amos, Alex, and Naomi were sitting on one side of the table, facing him. Prax was in his usual perch on the counter. Bobbie and Avasarala sat sideways on the other side of the table so that they could see him. That put the marine less than two meters away, with nothing between her and him. Depending on how this went, that might be a problem.

He dropped his hand to the butt of the gun at his hip to make sure everyone saw it, then said, "We have about two days before elements of the UN Navy get close enough to overwhelm our defenses with a torpedo salvo and destroy this ship."

Alex nodded, but no one spoke.

"But we have the Mao racing pinnace that brought Avasarala to us attached to the hull. It holds two. We're going to stick two people on it and get them away. Then we're going to turn around and head straight for those UN ships to buy the pinnace time. Who knows, we may even take one with us. Get ourselves a few servants in the afterlife."

"Fucking A," Amos said.

"I can support that," Avasarala said. "Who're the lucky bastards? And how do we stop the UN ships from just killing it after they kill this ship?"

"Prax and Naomi," Holden said immediately, before anyone else could speak. "Prax and Naomi go on the ship."

"Okay," Amos said, nodding.

"Why?" Naomi and Avasarala said at the same moment.

"Prax because he's the face of this whole thing. He's the guy who figured it all out. And because when someone finally rescues his little girl, it'd be nice if her daddy was there," Holden said. Then, tapping the butt of the gun with his fingers: "And Naomi because I fucking said so. Questions?"

"Nope," Alex said. "Works for me."

Holden was watching the marine closely. If someone tried to take the gun from him, it would be her. And she worked for Avasarala. If the old lady decided she wanted to be on the *Razorback* when it left, the marine would be the one who tried to make that happen. But to his surprise, she didn't move except to raise her hand.

"Sergeant?" Holden said.

"Two of those six Martian ships that are tailing the UN boys are new Raptor-class fast cruisers. They can probably catch the *Razorback* if they really want to."

"Would they?" Holden asked. "It was my impression that they were there to keep an eye on the UN ships and nothing else."

"Well, probably not, but..." She drifted off mid-sentence with a distant look in her eyes.

"So that's the plan," Holden said. "Prax, Naomi, get whatever supplies you need packed up and get on the *Razorback*. Everyone else, I'd appreciate it if you waited here while they did that."

"Hold on a minute—" Naomi protested, her voice angry.

Before Holden could respond, Bobbie spoke again.

"Hey, you know? I just had an idea."

Chapter Forty-Three: Bobbie

They were all missing something. It was like someone knocking at the back of her mind, demanding to be let in. Bobbie went over it in her head. Sure, that prick Nguyen showed every sign he was willing to kill the *Rocinante*, ranking UN politician on board or not. Avasarala had made a gamble that her presence would back the UN ships off. It seemed she was about to lose that bet. There were still six UN destroyers bearing down on them.

But there were six more ships tailing *them*.

Including, as she'd just pointed out to Holden, two *Raptor*-class fast-attack cruisers. Top-of-the-line Martian military hardware, and more than a match for any UN destroyer. Along with the two cruisers were four Martian destroyers. They might or might not be better than their UN counterparts, but with the two cruisers in their wing, they had a significant tonnage and firepower advantage. And they were following the UN ships to see that they weren't about to do something to escalate the shooting war.

Like killing the one UN politician who wasn't straining at the leash for a war with Mars.

"Hey, you know?" Bobbie said before she realized she was going to say anything. "I just had an idea..."

The galley fell silent.

Bobbie had a sudden and uncomfortable memory of speaking up in the UN conference room and wrecking her military career in the process. Captain Holden, the cute one who was a little too full of himself, was staring at her, a not particularly flattering gape on his face. He looked like a very angry person who'd lost his train of thought mid-rant. And Avasarala was staring at her too. Though, having learned to read the old lady's expression better, she didn't see anger there. Just curiosity.

"Well," Bobbie said, clearing her throat. "There are six Martian ships following those UN ships. And the Martian ships outclass them. Both navies are at high alert."

No one moved or spoke. Avasarala's curiosity had turned to a frown. "So," Bobbie continued, "they might be willing to back us up."

Avasarala's frown had only gotten deeper. "Why," she said, "would the Martians give a fuck about protecting me from being killed by my own damn Navy?"

"Would it hurt to ask?"

"No," Holden said. "I'm thinking no. Is everyone else here thinking it wouldn't hurt?"

"Who'd make the call?" Avasarala asked. "You? The traitor?"

The words were like a gut punch. But Bobbie realized what the old lady was doing. She was hitting Bobbie with the worst possible Martian response. Gauging her reaction to it.

"Yeah, I'd open the door," Bobbie said. "But you're the one that will have to convince them."

Avasarala stared at her for one very long minute, then said, "Okay."

"Repeat that, *Rocinante*," the Martian commander said. The connection was as clear as if they were standing in the room with the man. It wasn't the sound quality that was throwing him. Avasarala spoke slowly, enunciating carefully, all the same.

"This is Assistant Undersecretary Chrisjen Avasarala of the United Nations of Earth," Avasarala said again. "I am about to be attacked by a rogue element of the UN Navy while on my way to a peacekeeping mission in the Jupiter system. Fucking save me! I will reward you by talking my government out of glassing your planet."

"I'm going to have to send this up the chain," the commander said. They weren't using a video link, but the grin was audible in his voice.

"Call whoever you need to call," Avasarala said. "Just make a decision before these cunts start raining missiles down on me. All right?"

"I'll do my best, ma'am."

The skinny one—her name was Naomi—killed the connection and swiveled to look at Bobbie. "Why would they help us, again?"

"Mars doesn't want a war," Bobbie replied, hoping she wasn't talking completely out her ass. "If they find out that the UN's voice of reason is on a ship that's about to be killed by rogue UN war hawks, it only makes sense for them to step in."

"Kind of sounds like you're talking out your ass there," Naomi said.

"Also," Avasarala said, "I just gave them permission to shoot at the UN Navy without political repercussions."

"Even if they help," Holden said, "there's no way they can completely stop the UN ships from taking some shots at us. We'll need an engagement plan."

"We just got this damn thing put back together," Amos said.

"I still say we stick Prax and Naomi on the *Razorback*," Holden said.

"I'm starting to think that's a bad idea," Avasarala said. She took a sip of coffee and grimaced. The old lady was definitely missing her five cups of tea a day.

"Explain," Holden said.

"Well, if the Martians decide they're on our side, that changes the whole landscape for those UN ships. They can't beat all seven of us, if I understand the math right."

"Okay," Holden said.

"That makes it in their interest not to be called a rogue element in the history books. If Nguyen's cabal fails, everyone on his team gets at minimum a court-martial. The best way to make sure that doesn't happen is to make sure I don't survive this fight, no matter who wins."

"Which means they'll be shooting at the *Roci*," Naomi said. "Not the pinnace."

"Of course not," Avasarala said with a laugh. "Because of course I'll be on the pinnace. You think for a second they'll believe that you're desperately trying to protect an escape craft that I'm *not* on? And I bet the *Razorback* doesn't have those PDCs you were talking about. Does it?"

To Bobbie's surprise, Holden was nodding as Avasarala spoke. She'd sort of pegged him as a know-it-all who fell in love only with his own ideas.

"Yeah," Holden said. "You're absolutely right. They'll fling everything they've got at the *Razorback* as she tries to get away, and she'll have no defense."

"Which means we all live or we all die, right here on this ship," Naomi said with a sigh. "As usual."

"So, again," Holden said. "We need an engagement plan."

"This is a pretty thin crew," Bobbie said now that the conversation had moved back to her area of expertise. "Where's everyone usually sit?"

"Operations officer," Holden said, pointing at Naomi. "She also does electronic warfare and countermeasures. And she's a savant, considering she'd never worked it before we got this ship."

"Mechanic—" Holden started, pointing at Amos.

"Grease monkey," Amos said, cutting him off. "I do my best to keep the ship from falling apart when there's holes in it."

"I usually man the combat ops board," Holden said.

"Who's the gunner?" Bobbie asked.

"Yo," said Alex, pointing at himself.

"You fly *and* do target acquisition?" Bobbie said. "I'm impressed."

Alex's already dark skin grew a shade darker. His *aw shucks* Mariner Valley drawl had started to go from annoying to charming. And the blush was sweet. "Aw, no. The cap'n does acquisition from combat ops, generally. But I have to manage fire control."

"Well, there you go," Bobbie said, turning to Holden. "Give me weps."

"No offense, Sergeant..." Holden said.

"Gunny," Bobbie replied.

"Gunny," Holden agreed with a nod. "But are you qualified to operate fire control on a naval vessel?"

Bobbie decided not to be offended and grinned at him instead. "I saw your armor and the weapons you were carrying in the airlock. You found a MAP in the cargo bay, right?"

"Map?" Avasarala asked.

"Mobile assault package. Marine assault gear. Not as good as my Force Recon armor, but full kit for half a dozen ground pounders."

"Yeah," Holden said. "That's where we got it."

"That's because this is a multi-role fast-attack ship. Torpedo bomber is just one of them. Boarding party insertion is another. And gunnery sergeant is a rank with a very specific meaning."

"Yeah," Alex said. "Equipment specialist."

"I'm required to be proficient in all of the weapons systems my platoon or company might need to operate during a typical deployment. Including the weapons systems on an assault boat like this."

"I see—" Holden started, but Bobbie cut him off with a nod.

"I'm your gunner."

Like most things in Bobbie's life, the weapons officer's chair had been made for someone smaller than her. The five-point harness was digging into her hips and her shoulders. Even at its farthest setting, the fire control console was just a bit too close for her to comfortably rest her arms on the crash couch while using it. All of which would be a problem if they had to do any really high-g maneuvering. Which, of course, they would once the fight started.

She tucked her elbows in as close as she could to keep her arms from wrenching out of their sockets at high g, and fidgeted with the harness. It would have to be good enough.

From his seat behind and above her, Alex said, "This'll be over quick one way or the other. You probably won't have time to get too uncomfortable."

"That's reassuring."

Over the 1MC Holden said, "We're inside the maximum-effective weapon range now. They could fire immediately or twenty hours from now. So stay belted in. Only leave your station in life-threatening emergency and at my direct order. I hope everyone got their catheter on right."

"Mine's too tight," Amos said.

Alex spoke behind her, and it was echoed a split second later over the comm channel. "It's a condom catheter, partner. It goes on the *out*side."

Bobbie couldn't help laughing and held one hand up behind her until Alex slapped it.

Holden said, "We have greens across the board down here in ops. Everyone check in with go/no-go status."

"All green at flight control," Alex said.

"Green at electronic warfare," Naomi said.

"We're go down here," Amos said.

"Weapons are green and hot," Bobbie said last. Even strapped into a chair two sizes too small for her, on a stolen Martian war-ship captained by one of the most wanted men in the inner plan-ets, it felt really goddamned good to be there. Bobbie restrained a whoop of joy and instead pulled Holden's threat display up. He'd already marked the six pursuing UN destroyers. Bobbie tagged the lead ship and let the *Rocinante* try to come up with a target solution on it. The *Roci* calculated the odds of a hit at less than .1 percent. She jumped from target to target, getting a feel for the response times and controls. She tapped a button to pull up target info and looked over the UN destroyer specs.

When reading ship specs bored her, she pulled out to the tactical view. One tiny green dot pursued by six slightly larger red dots, which were in turn pursued by six blue dots. That was wrong. The Earth ships should be blue, and the Martians' red. She told the *Roci* to swap the color scheme. The *Rocinante* was oriented toward the pursuing ships. On the map, it looked like they were flying directly at each other. But in reality, the *Rocinante* was in the middle of a deceleration burn, slowing down to let the UN ships catch up faster. All thirteen of the ships in this particular engagement were hurtling sunward. The *Roci* was just doing it ass first.

Bobbie glanced at the time and saw that her noodling with the controls had burned less than fifteen minutes. "I hate waiting for a fight."

"You and me both, sister," Alex said.

"Got any games on this thing?" Bobbie asked, tapping on her console.

"I spy with my little eye," Alex replied, "something that begins with *D*."

"Destroyer," Bobbie said. "Six tubes, eight PDCs, and a keel-mounted rapid-fire rail gun."

"Good guess. Your turn."

"I fucking hate waiting for a fight."

When the battle began, it began all at once. Bobbie had expected some early probing shots. A few torpedoes fired from extreme range, just to see if the crew of the *Rocinante* had full control of all the weapon systems and everything was in working order.

Instead, the UN ships had closed the distance, the *Roci* slamming on the brakes to meet them.

Bobbie watched the six UN ships creep closer and closer to the red line on her threat display. The red line that represented the point at which a full salvo from all six ships would overwhelm the *Roci*'s point defense network.

Meanwhile, the six Martian ships moved closer to the green line on her display that represented their optimal firing range to engage the UN ships. It was a big game of chicken, and everyone was waiting to see who would flinch first.

Alex was juggling their deceleration thrust to try to make sure the Martians got in range before the Earthers did. When the shooting started, he would put the throttle down and try to move through the active combat zone as quickly as possible. It was why they were going to meet the UN ships in the first place. Running away would just have kept them in range a lot longer.

Then one of the red dots—a Martian fast-attack cruiser— crossed the green line, and alarms started going off all over the ship.

"Fast movers," Naomi said. "The Martian cruiser has fired eight torpedoes!"

Bobbie could see them. Tiny yellow dots shifting to orange as they took off at high g. The UN ships immediately responded. Half of them spun around to face the pursuing Martian ships and opened up with their rail guns and point defense cannons. The space on the tactical display between the two groups was suddenly filled with yellow-orange dots.

"Incoming!" Naomi yelled. "Six torpedoes on a collision course!"

Half a second later, the torpedoes' vector and speed information popped up on Bobbie's PDC control display. Holden had been right. The skinny Belter was good at this. Her reaction times were astonishing. Bobbie flagged all six torpedoes for the PDCs, and the ship began to vibrate as they fired in a rapid staccato.

"Juice coming," Alex said, and Bobbie felt her couch prick her in half a dozen places. Cold pumped into her veins, quickly becoming white-hot. She shook her head to clear the threatening tunnel vision while Alex said, "Three...two..."

He never said *one*. The *Rocinante* smashed into Bobbie from behind, crushing her into her crash couch. She remembered at the last second to keep her elbows lined up, and avoided having her arms broken as every part of her tried to fly backward at ten gravities.

On her threat display, the initial wave of six torpedoes fired at them winked out one by one as the *Roci* tracked and shot them down. More torpedoes were in the air, but now the entire Martian wing had opened up on the Earthers, and the space around the ships had become a confusion of drive tails and detonations. Bobbie told the *Roci* to target anything on an approach vector and shoot at it with the point defenses, leaving it up to Martian engineering and the universe's good graces.

She switched one of the big displays to the forward cameras, turning it into a window on the battle. Ahead of her the sky was filled with bright white flashes of light and expanding clouds of gas as torpedoes detonated. The UN ships had decided that the Martians were the real threat, and all six of them had spun to face the enemy ships head-on. Bobbie tapped a control to throw a threat overlay onto the video image, and suddenly the sky was full of impossibly fast blobs of light as the threat computer put a glowing outline on every torpedo and projectile.

The *Rocinante* was coming up fast on the UN destroyers, and the thrust dropped to two g. "Here we go," Alex said.

Bobbie pulled up the torpedo targeting system and targeted the drive cones of two of the ships. "Two away," she said, releasing her first two fish into the water. Bright drive trails lit the sky as they streaked off. The ready-to-fire indicator went red as the ship reloaded the tubes. Bobbie was already selecting the drive cones of the next two UN ships. The instant the ready indicator went green, she fired them both. She targeted the last two destroyers, then checked on the progress of her first two torpedoes. They were both gone, shot down by the destroyers' aft PDCs. A wave of fast-moving blobs of light hurtled toward them, and Alex threw the ship sideways, dancing out of the line of fire.

It wasn't enough. A yellow atmosphere warning light began rotating in the cockpit, and a ditone Klaxon sounded.

"We're hit," Holden said, his voice calm. "Dumping the atmosphere. Hope everyone has their hat on tight."

As Holden shut down the air system, the sounds of the ship faded until Bobbie could hear only her own breathing and the faint hiss of the 1MC channel on her headset.

"Wow," Amos said over the comm. "Three hits. Small projectiles, probably PDC rounds. Managed to go right through us without hitting anything that mattered."

"It went through my room," the scientist, Prax, said.

"Bet that woke you up," Amos said, his voice a grin.

"I soiled myself," Prax replied without a hint of humor.

"Quiet," Holden said, but there was no malice in it. "Stay off the channel, please."

Bobbie let the rational, thinking part of her mind listen to the back-and-forth. She had no use for that part of her brain right now. The part of her mind that had been trained to acquire targets and fire torpedoes at them worked without her interference. The lizard was driving now.

She didn't know how many torpedoes she'd fired when there was an enormous flash of light and the camera display blacked out for a second. When it came back, one of the UN destroyers was torn in two, the rapidly separating pieces of hull spinning away from each other, trailing a faint gas cloud and small bits of jetsam. Some of those things flying out of the shattered ship would be UN sailors. Bobbie ignored that. The lizard rejoiced.

The destruction of the first UN ship tipped the scales, and within minutes the other five were heavily damaged or destroyed. A UN captain sent out a distress call and immediately signaled surrender.

Bobbie looked at her display. Three UN ships destroyed. Three heavily damaged. The Martians had lost two destroyers, and one of their cruisers was badly damaged. The *Rocinante* had three bullet wounds that had let all her air out, but no other damage.

They'd won.

"Holy shit," Alex said. "Captain, we have *got* to get one of these."

It took Bobbie a minute to realize he was talking about her.

"You have the gratitude of the UN government," Avasarala was saying to the Martian commander. "Or at least the part of the UN government I run. We're going to Io to blow up some more ships and maybe stop the apocalypse. Want to come with?"

Bobbie opened a private channel to Avasarala.

"We're all traitors now."

"Ha!" the old lady said. "Only if we lose."

Chapter Forty-Four: Holden

From the outside, the damage to the *Rocinante* was barely noticeable. The three point defense cannon rounds fired by one of the UN destroyers had hit her just forward of the sick bay and, after a short diagonal trip through the ship, exited through the machine shop, two decks below. Along the way, one of them had passed through three cabins in the crew deck.

Holden had expected the little botanist to be a wreck, especially after his crack about soiling himself. But when Holden had checked on him after the battle, he'd been surprised by the nonchalant shrug the scientist had given.

"It was very startling," was all he'd said.

It would be easy to write it off as shell shock. The kidnapping of his daughter, followed by months of living on Ganymede as the social structure collapsed. Easy to see Prax's calm as the precursor to a complete mental and emotional breakdown. God knew the man had lost control of himself half a dozen times, and most of them inconvenient. But Holden suspected there was a lot more to Prax than that. There was a relentless forward motion to the man. The universe might knock him down over and over again, but unless he was dead, he'd just keep getting up and shuffling ahead toward his goal. Holden thought he had probably been a very good scientist. Thrilled by small victories, undeterred by setbacks. Plodding along until he got to where he needed to be.

Even now, just hours after nearly being cut in two by a high-speed projectile, Prax was belowdecks with Naomi and Avasarala, patching holes inside the ship. He hadn't even been asked. He'd just climbed out of his bunk and pitched in.

Holden stood above one of the bullet entry points on the ship's outer hull. The small projectile had left a perfectly round hole and almost no dimpling. It had passed through five centimeters of high-tensile alloy armor so quickly it hadn't even dented it.

"Found it," Holden said. "No light coming out, so it looks like they've already patched it on the inside."

"Coming," Amos said, then clumped across the hull on magnetic boots, a portable welding torch in his hand. Bobbie followed in her fancy powered armor, carrying big sheets of patch material.

While Bobbie and Amos worked on sealing up the outer hull breach, Holden wandered off to find the next hole. Around him, the three remaining Martian warships drifted along with the *Rocinante* like an honor guard. With their drives off, they were visible only as small black spots that moved across the star field. Even with the *Roci* telling his armor where to look, and with the HUD pointing the ships out, they were almost impossible to see.

Holden tracked the Martian cruiser on his HUD until it passed across the bright splash of the Milky Way's ecliptic. For a moment, the entire ship was a black silhouette framed in the ancient white of a few billion stars. A faint cone of translucent white sprayed out from one side of the ship, and it drifted back into the star-speckled black. Holden felt a desire to have Naomi standing next to him, looking up at the same sights, that bordered on a physical ache.

"I forget how beautiful it is out here," he said to her over their private channel instead.

"You daydreaming and letting someone else do all the work?" she replied.

"Yeah. More of these stars have planets around them than don't. Billions of worlds. Five hundred million planets in the habitable zone was the last estimate. Think our great-grandkids will get to see any of them?"

"*Our* grandkids?"

"When this is over."

"Also," Naomi said, "at least one of those planets has the proto-molecule masters on it. Maybe we should avoid that one."

"Honestly? That's one I'd like to see. Who made this thing? What's it all for? I'd love to be able to ask. And at the very least, they share the human drive to find every habitable corner and move in. We might have more in common than we think."

"They also kill whoever lived there first."

Holden snorted. "We've been doing that since the invention of the spear. They're just scary good at it."

"You found that next hole yet?" Amos said over the main channel, his voice an unwelcome intrusion. Holden pulled his gaze away from the sky and back to the metal beneath his feet. Using the damage map the *Roci* was feeding to his HUD, it took only a moment to find the next entry wound.

"Yeah, yeah, right here," he said, and Amos and Bobbie began moving his direction.

"Cap," Alex said, chiming in from the cockpit. "The captain of that MCRN cruiser is lookin' to talk to you."

"Patch him through to my suit."

"Roger," Alex said, and then the static on the radio shifted in tone. "Captain Holden?"

"I read you. Go ahead."

"This is Captain Richard Tseng of the MCRN *Cydonia*. Sorry we weren't able to speak sooner. I've been dealing with damage control and arranging for rescue and repair ships."

"I understand, Captain," Holden said, trying to spot the *Cydonia* again but failing. "I'm out on my hull patching a few holes myself. I saw you guys drive by a minute ago."

"My XO says you'd asked to speak to me."

"Yes, and thank her on my behalf for all the help so far," Holden said. "Listen, we burned through an awful lot of our stores in that skirmish. We fired fourteen torpedoes and nearly half of our point defense ammunition. Since this used to be a Martian ship, I thought maybe you'd have reloads that would fit our racks."

"Sure," Captain Tseng said without a moment's hesitation. "I'll have the destroyer *Sally Ride* pull alongside for munitions transfer."

"Uh," Holden said, shocked by the instant agreement. He'd been prepared to negotiate. "Thanks."

"I'll pass along my intel officer's breakdown of the fight. You'll find it interesting viewing. But the short version is that first kill, the one that broke open the UN defense screen and ended the fight? That was yours. Guess they shouldn't have turned their backs on you."

"You guys can take credit for it," Holden said with a laugh. "I had a Martian Marine gunnery sergeant doing the shooting."

There was a pause; then Tseng said, "When this is over, I'd like to buy you a drink and talk about how a dishonorably discharged UN naval officer winds up flying a stolen MCRN torpedo bomber crewed by Martian military personnel and a senior UN politician."

"It's a damn good story," Holden replied. "Say, speaking of Martians, I'd like to get one of mine a present. Do you carry a Marine detachment on the *Cydonia*?"

"Yes, why?"

"Got any Force Recon Marines in that group?"

"Yes. Again, why?"

"There's some equipment we'll need that you've probably got in storage."

He told Captain Tseng what he was looking for, and Tseng said, "I'll have the *Ride* give you one when we do the transfer."

The MCRN *Sally Ride* looked like she'd come through the fight without a scratch. When she pulled up next to the *Rocinante*, her dark flank looked as smooth and unmarred as a pool of black water. After Alex and the *Ride*'s pilot had perfectly matched course, a large hatch in her side opened up, dim red emergency lighting spilling out. Two magnetic grapples were fired across, connecting the ships with ten meters of cable.

"This is Lieutenant Graves," a girlish voice said. "Prepared to begin cargo transfer on your order."

Lieutenant Graves sounded like she should still be in high school, but Holden said, "Go ahead. We're ready on this end."

Switching channels to Naomi, he said, "Pop the hatches, new fish coming aboard."

A few meters from where he was standing, a large hatch that was normally flush with the hull opened up into a meter-wide and eight-meter-long gap in the skin of the ship. A complicated-looking system of rails and gears ran down the sides of the opening. At the bottom sat three of the *Rocinante*'s remaining ship-to-ship torpedoes.

"Seven in here," Holden said, pointing at the open torpedo rack. "And seven on the other side."

"Roger," said Graves. The long, narrow white shape of a plasma torpedo appeared in the *Ride*'s open hatch, with sailors wearing EVA packs flanking it. With gentle puffs of compressed nitrogen, they flew the torpedo down along the two guidelines to the *Roci*; then, with the help of Bobbie's suit-augmented strength, they maneuvered it into position at the top of the rack.

"First one in position," Bobbie said.

"Got it," Naomi replied, and a second later the motorized rails came to life and grabbed the torpedo, pulling it down into the magazine.

Holden glanced at the elapsed time on his HUD. Getting all fourteen torpedoes transferred and loaded would take hours.

"Amos," he said. "Where are you?"

"Just finishing that last patch down by the machine shop," the mechanic replied. "You need something?"

"When you're done with that, grab a couple EVA packs. You and I will go get the other supplies. Should be three crates of PDC rounds and some sundries."

"I'm done now. Naomi, pop the cargo door for me, wouldja?"

Holden watched Bobbie and the *Ride*'s sailors work, and they had two more torpedoes loaded by the time Amos arrived with two EVA packs.

"Lieutenant Graves, two crew from the *Rocinante* requesting permission to board and pick up the rest of the supplies."

"Granted, *Rocinante*."

The PDC rounds came in crates of twenty thousand and at full gravity would have weighed more than five hundred kilos. In the microgravity of the coasting ships, two people with EVA packs could move one if they were willing to take their time and recharge their compressed nitrogen after every trip. Without a salvage mech or a small work shuttle available, there wasn't any other choice.

Each crate had to be pushed slowly toward the aft of the *Rocinante* through a twenty-second-long "burn" from Amos' EVA pack. When it got to the aft of the ship next to the cargo bay door, Holden would do an equally long thrust from his pack to bring the crate to a stop. Then the two of them would maneuver it inside and lock it to a bulkhead. The process was long, and at least for Holden, each trip had one heart-racing moment when he was firing the brakes to stop the crate. Every time, he had a brief, panicky vision of his EVA pack failing and him and the crate of ammo drifting off into space while Amos watched. It was ridiculous, of course. Amos could easily grab a fresh EVA pack and come get him, or the ship could drop back, or the *Ride* could send a rescue shuttle, or any other of a huge number of ways he'd be quickly saved.

But humans hadn't been living and working in space nearly long enough for the primitive part of the brain not to say, *I'll fall. I'll fall forever.*

The people from the *Ride* finished bringing over torpedoes about the time Holden and Amos had locked the last crate of PDC ammo into the cargo bay.

"Naomi," Holden called on the open channel. "We all green?"

"Everything looks good from here. All of the new torpedoes are talking to the *Roci* and reporting operational."

"Outstanding. Amos and I are coming in through the cargo bay airlock. Go ahead and seal the bay up. Alex, as soon as Naomi gives the all clear, let the *Cydonia* know we can do a fast burn to Io at the captain's earliest pleasure."

While the crew prepped the ship for the trip to Io, Holden and Amos stripped off their gear and stowed it in the machine shop. Six gray disks, three on each bulkhead across the compartment from each other, showed where the rounds had ripped through this part of the ship.

"What's in that other box the Martians gave you?" Amos asked, pulling off one oversized magnetic boot.

"A present for Bobbie," Holden said. "I'd like to keep it quiet until I give it to her, okay?"

"Sure, no problem, Cap'n. If it turns out to be a dozen long-stemmed roses, I don't want to be there when Naomi finds out. Plus, you know, Alex..."

"No, it's a lot more practical than roses—" Holden started, then rewound the conversation in his head. "Alex? What about Alex?"

Amos shrugged with his hands, like a Belter. "I think he might have a wee bit of a thing for our ample marine."

"You're kidding." Holden couldn't picture it. It wasn't as though Bobbie were unattractive. Far from it. But she was also very big, and quite intimidating. And Alex was such a quiet and mild guy. Sure, they were both Martians, and no matter how cosmopolitan a person got, there was something comforting in reminders of home. Maybe just being the only two Martians on the ship was enough. But Alex was pushing fifty, balding without complaint, and wore his love handles with the quiet resignation of a middle-aged man. Sergeant Draper couldn't be more than thirty and looked like a comic book illustration, complete with muscles *on* her muscles. Unable to stop himself, his mind began trying to figure out how the two of them would fit together. It didn't work.

"Wow," was all he could say. "Is it mutual?"

"No idea," Amos replied with another shrug. "The sergeant ain't easy to read. But I don't think she'd do him any deliberate harm, if that's what you're asking. Not that, you know, we could stop her."

"Scares you too, does she?"

"Look," Amos said with a grin. "When it comes to scrapes, I'm what you might call a talented amateur. But I've gotten a good look at that woman in and out of that fancy mechanical shell she wears. She's a pro. We're not playing the same sport."

Gravity began to return in the *Rocinante*. Alex was bringing up the drive, which meant they were beginning their run to Io. Holden stood up and took a moment to let his joints adjust to the sensation of weight again. He clapped Amos on the back and said, "Well, you've got a full load of torpedoes and bullets, three Martian warships trailing you, one angry old lady in tea withdrawal, and a Martian Marine who could probably kill you with your own teeth. What do you do?"

"You tell me, Captain."

"You find someone else for them to fight."

Chapter Forty-Five: Avasarala

As I see it, sir," Avasarala said, "the die is already cast. We effectively have two courses of policy already in play. The question now is how we move forward. So far I've been able to keep the information from getting out, but once it does, it will be devastating. And since it is all but certain that the artifact is able to communicate, the chances of an effective military usage of these protomolecule-human hybrids is essentially nil. If we use this weapon, we will be creating a second Venus, committing genocide, and removing any moral argument against using weapons like accelerated asteroids against the Earth itself.

"I hope you will excuse the language, sir, but this was a cock-up from the start. The damage done to human security is literally unimaginable. It seems clear at this point that the protomolecule project under way on Venus is aware of events in the Jovian system. It's plausible that the samples out here have the information gained from the destruction of the *Arboghast*. To say that makes our position problematic is to radically understate the case.

"If it had gone through the appropriate channels, we would not be in this position. As it stands, I have done all that is presently within my capabilities, given my situation. The coalition I have built between Mars, elements of the Belt, and the legitimate government of Earth are ready to take action. But the United Nations must distance itself from this plan and move immediately to isolate and defang the faction within the government that has been doing this weasel shit. Again, excuse the language.

"I have sent copies of the data included here to Admirals Souther and Leniki as well as to my team on the Venus problem. They are, of course, at your disposal to answer any questions if I am not available.

"I'm very sorry to put you in the position, sir, but you are going to have to choose sides in this. And quickly. Events out here have developed a momentum of their own. If you're going to be on the right side of history on this, you must move now."

If there's any history to be on the right side of, she thought. She tried to come up with something else that she could say, some other argument that would penetrate the layers of old-growth wood that surrounded the secretary-general's brain. There weren't any, and repeating herself in simple storybook rhyme would probably come off as condescending. She stopped the recording, cut off the last few seconds of her looking into the camera in despair, and sent it off with every high-priority flag there was and diplomatic encryption.

So this was what it came to. All of human civilization, everything it had managed, from the first cave painting to crawling up the gravity well and pressing out into the antechamber of the stars, came down to whether a man whose greatest claim to fame was that he'd been thrown in prison for writing bad poetry had the balls to back down Errinwright. The ship corrected under her, shifting like an elevator suddenly slipping its tracks. She tried to sit up, but the gimbaled couch moved. God, but she hated space travel.

"Is it going to work?"

The botanist stood in her doorway. He was stick-thin, with a slightly larger head than looked right. He wasn't built as awkwardly as a Belter, but he couldn't be mistaken for someone who'd grown to maturity living at a full gravity. Standing in her doorway, trying to find something to do with his hands, he looked awkward and lost and slightly otherworldly.

"I don't know," she said. "If I were there, it would happen the way I want it to happen. I could go squeeze a few testicles until they saw it my way. From here? Maybe. Maybe not."

"You can talk to anyone from here, though, can't you?"

"It isn't the same."

He nodded, his attention shifting inward. Despite the differences in skin color and build, the man suddenly reminded her of Michael-Jon. He had the same sense of being a half step back from everything. Only, Michael-Jon's detachment verged on autism, and Praxidike Meng was a little more visibly interested in the people around him.

"They got to Nicola," he said. "They made her say those things about me. About Mei."

"Of course they did. That's what they do. And if they wanted to, they'd have papers and police reports to back it all up, backdated and put in the databases of everywhere you ever lived."

"I hate it that people think I did that."

Avasarala nodded, then shrugged.

"Reputation never has very much to do with reality," she said. "I could name half a dozen paragons of virtue that are horrible, small-souled, evil people. And some of the best men I know, you'd walk out of the room if you heard their names. No one on the screen is who they are when you breathe their air."

"Holden," Prax said.

"Well. He's the exception," she said.

The botanist looked down and then up again. His expression was almost apologetic.

"Mei's probably dead," he said.

"You don't believe that."

"It's been a long time. Even if they had her medicine, they've probably turned her into one of these...things."

"You still don't believe that," she said. The botanist leaned forward, frowning like she'd given him a problem he couldn't immediately solve. "Tell me it's all right to bomb Io. I can have thirty nuclear warheads fired now. Turn off the engines, let them fly ballistic. They won't all get through, but some will. Say the word now, and I can have Io reduced to slag before we even get there."

"You're right," Prax said. And then, a moment later: "Why aren't you doing that?"

"Do you want the real reason, or my justification?"

"Both?"

"I justify it this way," she said. "I don't know what is in that lab. I can't assume that the monsters are only there, and if I destroy the place, I might be slagging the records that will let me find the missing ones. I don't know everyone involved in this, and I don't have proof against some of the ones I do know. It may be down there. I'll go, I'll find out, and then I will reduce the lab to radioactive glass afterward."

"Those are good reasons."

"They're good justifications. I find them very convincing."

"But the reason is that Mei might still be alive."

"I don't kill children," she said. "Not even when it's the right thing to do. You would be surprised how often it's hurt my political career. People used to think I was weak until I found the trick."

"The trick."

"If you can make them blush, they think you're a hard-ass," she said. "My husband calls it the mask."

"Oh," Prax said. "Thank you."

Waiting was worse than the fear of battle. Her body wanted to move, to get away from her chair and walk through the familiar halls. The back of her mind shouted for action, movement, confrontation. She paced the ship top to bottom and back again. Her mind went through trivia about all the people she met in the halls, the small detritus from the intelligence reports she'd read. The mechanic, Amos Burton. Implicated in several murders, indicted, never tried. Took an elective vasectomy the day he was legally old enough to do so. Naomi Nagata, the engineer. Two master's degrees. Offered full-ride scholarship for a PhD on Ceres Station and turned it down. Alex Kamal, pilot. Seven drunk and disorderlies when he was in his early twenties. Had a son on Mars he still didn't know about. James Holden, the man without secrets. The holy fool who'd dragged the solar system into war and seemed utterly blind to the damage he caused. An idealist. The most dangerous kind of man there was. And a good man too.

She wondered whether any of it mattered.

The only real player near enough to talk to without lag turning the conversation utterly epistolary was Souther, and as he was still putatively on the same side as Nguyen and preparing to face battle with the ships protecting her, the opportunities were few and far between.

"Have you heard anything?" he asked from her terminal.

"No," she said. "I don't know what's taking the fucking bobblehead so long."

"You're asking him to turn his back on the man he's trusted the most."

"And how fucking long does that take? When I did it, it was over in maybe five minutes. 'Soren,' I said. 'You're a douche bag. Get out of my sight.' It isn't harder than that."

"And if he doesn't come through?" Souther asked.

She sighed.

"Then I call you back and try talking you into going rogue."

"Ah," Souther said with a half smile. "And how do you see that going?"

"I don't like my chances, but you never know. I can be damned persuasive."

An alert popped up. A new message. From Arjun.

"I have to go," she said. "Keep an ear to the ground or whatever the hell you do out here where the ground doesn't mean anything."

"Be safe, Chrisjen," Souther said, and vanished into the green background of a dead connection.

Around her, the galley was empty. Still, someone might come in. She lifted the hem of her sari and walked to her little room, sliding her door closed before she gave her terminal permission to open the file.

Arjun was at his desk, his formal clothes on but undone at the neck and sleeves. He looked like a man just returned from a bad party. The sunlight streamed in behind him. Afternoon, then. It had been afternoon when he'd sent it. And it might still be. She touched the screen, her fingertips tracing the line of his shoulder.

"So I understand from your message that you may not come home," he said.

"I'm sorry," she said to the screen.

"As you imagine, I find the thought…distressing," he said, and then a smile split his face, dancing in eyes she now saw were red with tears. "But what can I do about it? I teach poetry to graduate students. I have no power in this world. That has always been you. And so I want to offer you this. Don't think about me. Don't take your mind from what you're doing on my account. And if you don't…"

Arjun took a deep breath.

"If life transcends death, then I will seek for you there. If not, then there too."

He looked down and then up again.

"I love you, Kiki. And I will always love you, from whatever distance."

The message ended. Avasarala closed her eyes. Around her, the ship was as close and confining as a coffin. The small noises of it pressed in against her until she wanted to scream. Until she wanted to sleep. She let herself weep for a moment. There was nothing else to be done. She had taken her best shot, and there was nothing to be done but meditate and worry.

Half an hour later, her terminal chimed again, waking her from troubled dreams. Errinwright. Anxiety knotted her throat. She lifted a finger to begin the playback, and then paused. She didn't want to. She didn't want to go back into that world, wear her heavy mask. She wanted to watch Arjun again. Listen to his voice.

Only, of course, Arjun had known what she would want. It was why he'd said the things he had. She started the message.

Errinwright looked angry. More than that, he looked tired. His pleasant demeanor was gone, and he was a man made entirely of salt water and threat.

"Chrisjen," he said. "I know you won't understand this, but I have been doing everything in my power to keep you and yours safe. You don't understand what you've waded into, and you are fucking things up. I wish you had had the moral courage to come to me with this before you ran off like a horny sixteen-year-old with James Holden. Honestly, if there was a better way to destroy any professional credibility you once had, I can't think what it would have been.

"I put you on the *Guanshiyin* to take you off the board because I knew that things were about to go hot. Well, they are, only you're in the middle of them and you don't understand the situation. Millions of people stand in real danger of dying badly because of your egotism. You're one of them. Arjun's another. And your daughter. All of them are in threat now because of *you*."

In the image, Errinwright clasped his hands together, pressing his knuckles against his lower lip, the platonic ideal of a scolding father.

"If you come back now, I might—might—be able to save you. Not your career. That's gone. Forget it. Everyone down here sees that you're working with the OPA and Mars. Everyone thinks you've betrayed us, and I can't undo that. Your life and your family. That's all I can salvage. But you have to get away from this circus you've started, and you have to do it now.

"Time's short, Chrisjen. Everything important to you hangs in the balance, and I cannot help you if you don't help yourself. Not with this.

"It's last-chance time. Ignore me now, and the next time we talk, someone will have died."

The message ended. She started it again, and then a third time. Her grin felt feral.

She found Bobbie in the ops deck with the pilot, Alex. They stopped talking as she came in, a question in Bobbie's expression. Avasarala held up a finger and switched the video feed to display on the ship monitors. Errinwright came to life. On the big screens, she could see his pores and the individual hairs in his eyebrows. As he spoke, Avasarala saw Alex and Bobbie grow sober, leaning in toward the screen as if they were all at a poker table and coming to the end of a high-stakes hand.

"All right," Bobbie said. "What do we do?"

"We break out the fucking champagne," Avasarala said. "What did he just tell us? There is nothing in that message. Nothing. He is walking around his words like they've got poisoned spikes on them. And what's he got? Threats. No one makes threats."

"Wait," Alex said. "That was a good sign?"

"That was excellent," Avasarala said, and then something else, something small, fell into place in the back of her mind and she started laughing and cursing at the same time.

"What? What is it?"

" 'If life transcends death, then I will seek for you there. If not, then there too,' " she said. "It's a fucking haiku. That man has a one-track mind and one train on it. Poetry. Save me from poetry."

They didn't understand, but they didn't need to. The real message came five hours later. It came on a public newsfeed, and it was delivered by Secretary-General Esteban Sorrento-Gillis. The old man was brilliant at looking somber and energetic at the same time. If he hadn't been the executive of the largest governing body in the history of the human race, he'd have made a killing promoting health drinks.

The whole crew had gathered by now—Amos, Naomi, Holden, Alex. Even Prax. They were sandwiched into the ops deck, their combined breaths just slightly overloading the recyclers and giving the deck a feeling of barn heat. All eyes were on the screen as the secretary-general took the podium.

"I have come here tonight to announce the immediate formation of an investigative committee. Accusations have been made that some individuals within the governing body of the United Nations and its military forces have taken unauthorized and possibly illegal steps in dealing with certain private contractors. If these accusations are true, they must be addressed in the most expedient possible manner. And if unfounded, they must be dispelled and those responsible for spreading these lies called to account.

"I need not remind you all of the years I spent as a political prisoner."

"Oh fuck me," Avasarala said, clapping her hands in glee. "He's using the outsider speech. That man's asshole must be tight enough right now to bend space."

"I have dedicated my terms as secretary-general to rooting out corruption, and as long as I have this gavel, I shall continue to do so. Our world and the solar system we all share must be assured that the United Nations honors the ethical, moral, and spiritual values that hold us all together as a species."

On the feed, Esteban Sorrento-Gillis nodded, turned, and strode away in a clamor of unacknowledged questions, and the commentators flowed into the space, talking over each other in all the political opinions of the spectrum.

"Okay," Holden said. "So did he actually say anything?"

"He said Errinwright is finished," Avasarala said. "If he had any influence left at all, that announcement would never have been made. God*damn*, I wish I was there."

Errinwright was off the board. All that left was Nguyen, Mao, Strickland or whoever he was, their half-controlled protomolecule warriors, and the building threat of Venus. She let a long breath rattle through her throat and the spaces behind her nose.

"Ladies and gentlemen," she said, "I have just solved our smallest problem."

Chapter Forty-Six: Bobbie

One of Bobbie's most vivid memories was of the day she got her orders to report to the 2nd Expeditionary Force Spec War training facility. Force Recon. The top of the heap for a Martian ground pounder. In boot camp, they'd trained with a Force Recon sergeant. He'd been wearing a suit of gleaming red power armor, and they'd watched him demonstrate its use in a variety of tactical situations. At the end, he'd told them that the top four boots from her class would be transferred to the Spec War facility on the slopes of Hecates Tholus and trained to wear the armor and join the baddest fighting unit in the solar system.

She decided that meant her.

Determined to win one of those four coveted slots, she'd thrown herself into her boot camp training with everything she had. It turned out that was quite a lot. Not only did she make it into the top four, she was number one by an embarrassing margin. And then the letter came, ordering her to report to Hecate Base for recon training, and it was all worth it. She called her father and just screamed for two minutes. When he finally got her to calm down and tell him what she was calling about, he screamed back for even longer. *You're one of the best now, baby*, he'd said at the end, and the warmth those words put in her heart had never really faded.

Even now, sitting on the gray metal deck in the dirty machine shop on a stolen Martian warship. Even with all her mates torn into pieces and scattered across the frozen surface of Ganymede. Even with her military status in limbo and her loyalty to her nation justifiably in question. Even with all that, *You're one of the best now, baby* made her smile. She felt an ache to call her father and tell him what had happened. They'd always been close, and when neither of her brothers had followed in his footsteps by choosing a military career, she had. It had just strengthened the connection. She knew he'd understand what it was costing her to turn her back on everything she held sacred to avenge her team.

And she had a powerful premonition she'd never see him again.

Even if they made it through to Jupiter with half the UN fleet hunting them, and even if when they got there, Admiral Nguyen and the dozen or more ships he controlled didn't immediately blow them out of the sky, and even if they managed to stop whatever was happening in orbit around Io with the *Rocinante* intact, Holden was still planning to land and save Prax's daughter.

The monsters would be there.

She knew it as surely as she'd ever known anything in her life. Each night she dreamed of facing it again. The thing flexing its long fingers and staring at her with its too-large glowing blue eyes, ready to finish what it had started all those months earlier on Ganymede. In her dream, she raised a gun that grew out of her hand, and started shooting it as it ran toward her, black spiderwebs spilling from holes that closed like water. She always woke before it reached her, but she knew how the dream would end: with her shattered body left cooling on the ice. She also knew that when Holden led his team down to the laboratories on Io where the monsters were made, she'd go along with him. The scene from her dream would play out in real life. She knew it like she knew her father's love. She welcomed it.

On the floor around her lay the pieces of her armor. With weeks of travel on the way to Io, she had time to completely strip and refit it. The *Rocinante*'s machine shop was well stocked, and the tools were of Martian make. It was the perfect location. The suit had seen a lot of use without much maintenance, but if she was being honest with herself, the distraction was the payoff. A suit of Martian reconnaissance armor was an incredibly complex machine, finely tuned to its wearer. Stripping and reassembling it wasn't a trivial task. It required full concentration. Every moment she spent working on it was another moment when she didn't think about the monster waiting to kill her on Io.

Sadly, that distraction was over now. She'd finished with the maintenance, even finding the micro-fracture in a tiny valve that was causing the slow but persistent leak of fluid in the suit's knee actuator. It was time to just put it all back together. It had the feeling of ritual. A final cleansing before going out to meet death on the battlefield.

I've watched too many Kurosawa movies, she thought, but couldn't quite abandon the idea. The imagery was a lovely way of turning angst and suicidal ideation into honor and noble sacrifice.

She picked up the torso assembly and carefully wiped it off with a damp cloth, removing the last bits of dust and machine oil that clung to the outside. The smell of metal and lubricant filled the air. And while she bolted armor plating back onto the frame, the red enameled surface covered with a thousand dings and scratches, she stopped fighting the urge to ritualize the task and just let it happen. She was very likely assembling her death shroud. Depending on how the final battle went, this ceramic and rubber and alloy might house her corpse for the rest of eternity.

She flipped the torso assembly over and began working on the back. A long gouge in the enamel showed the violence of her passage across Ganymede's ice when the monster had self-destructed right in front of her. She picked up a wrench, then put it back down, tapping on the deck with her knuckle.

Why then?

Why had the monster blown itself up at that moment? She remembered the way it had started to shift, new limbs bursting from its body as it watched her. If Prax was right, that was the moment the constraint systems that Mao's scientists had installed failed. And they'd set the bomb up to detonate if the creature was getting out of their control. But that just pushed the question one level back. Why had their control over the creature's physiology failed at that precise moment? Prax said that regenerative processes were a good place for constraint systems to fail. And her platoon had riddled the creature with gunfire as it had charged their lines. It hadn't seemed to hurt it at the time, but each wound represented a sudden burst of activity inside the creature's cells, or whatever it had in place of cells, as the monster healed. Each was a chance for the new growth to slip the leash.

Maybe that was the answer. *Don't try to kill the monster. Just damage it enough that the program starts to break down and the self-destruct kicks in.* She wouldn't even have to survive, just last long enough to harm the monster beyond its ability to safely repair itself. All she needed was enough time to really hurt it.

She put down the armor plate she was working on and picked up the helmet. The suit's memory still had the gun camera footage of the fight on it. She hadn't watched it again after Avasarala's presentation to the crew of the *Roci*. She hadn't been able to.

She pushed herself to her feet and hit the comm panel on the wall. "Hey, Naomi? You in ops?"

"Yep," Naomi said after a few seconds. "You need something, Sergeant?"

"Do you think you can tell the *Roci* to talk to my helmet? I've got the radio on, but it won't talk to civilian stuff. This is one of our boats, so I figure the *Roci* has the keys and codes."

There was a long pause, so Bobbie put the helmet on a worktable next to the closest wall monitor and waited.

"I'm seeing a radio node that the *Roci* is calling 'MCR MR Goliath III 24397A15.' "

"That's me," Bobbie said. "Can you send control of that node down to the panel in the machine shop?"

"Done," Naomi said after a second.

"Thanks," Bobbie said, and killed the comm. It took her a moment to re-familiarize herself with the Martian military video software, and to convince the system to use out-of-date data-unpacking algorithms. After a few false starts, the raw gun camera footage from her fight on Ganymede was playing on the screen. She set it to endless loop and sat back down on the deck with her suit.

She finished bolting the back armor on and began attaching the torso's power supply and main hydraulic system during the first play-through. She tried not to feel anything about the images on screen, nor to attach any significance to them or think of them as a puzzle to be solved. She just concentrated on her work on the suit with her mind and let her subconscious chew on the data from the screen.

The distraction caused her to redo things occasionally as she worked, but that was fine. She wasn't on a deadline. She finished attaching the power supply and main motors. Green lights lit up on the hand terminal she had plugged into the suit's brain. On the wall screen by her helmet, a UN soldier was hurled across the surface of Ganymede at her. A confusion of images as she dodged away. When the image steadied, both the UN Marine and her friend Tev Hillman were gone.

Bobbie picked up an arm assembly and began reattaching it to the torso. The monster had picked up a soldier in a suit of armor comparable to her own and then thrown him with enough force to kill instantly. There was no defense against that kind of strength except not to get hit. She concentrated on putting the arm back together.

When she looked up at the screen again, the feed had restarted. The monster was running across the ice, chasing the UN soldiers. It killed one of them. The Bobbie on the video began firing, followed by her entire platoon opening up.

The creature was fast. But when the UN soldiers suddenly turned to open a firing lane for the Martians, the creature didn't react quickly. So maybe fast in a straight line, but not a lot of lateral speed. That might be useful. The video caught up again to the UN soldier being thrown into Private Hillman. The creature reacted to gunfire, to injuries, even though they didn't slow it down. She thought back to the video she'd seen of Holden and Amos engaging the creature in the *Rocinante*'s cargo hold. It had largely ignored them until Amos started shooting it, and then it had erupted into violence.

But the first creature had attacked the UN troop station. So at least to some degree, they could be directed. Given orders. Once they no longer had orders, they seemed to lapse into a default state of trying to get increased energy and break the constraints. While in that state, they ignored pretty much everything but food and violence. The next time she ran into one, unless it had specifically been ordered to attack her, she could probably pick her own battleground, draw it to her where she wanted to be. That was useful too.

She finished attaching the arm assembly and tested it. Greens across the board. Even if she wasn't sure whom she was working for, at least she hadn't forgotten how to do her job.

On the screen, the monster ran up the side of the big mech *Yojimbo* and tore the pilot's hatch off. Sa'id, the pilot, was hurled away. Again with the ripping and throwing. It made sense. With a combination like enormous strength and virtual immunity to ballistic damage as your tool set, running straight at your opponent, then ripping them in two was a pretty winning strategy. Throwing heavy objects at lethal speeds went hand in hand with the strength. And kinetic energy was a bitch. Armor might deflect bullets or lasers, and it might help cushion impacts, but no one had ever made armor that could shrug off all the kinetic energy imparted by a large mass moving at high speed. At least not in something a human could wear. If you were strong enough, a garbage Dumpster was better than a gun.

So when the monster attacked, it ran straight at its enemy, hoping to get a grip on them, which pretty much ended the fight. If it couldn't do that, it tried to hurl heavy objects at the opponent. The one in the cargo bay had nearly killed Jim Holden by throwing a massive crate. Unfortunately, her armor had a lot of the same restrictions it had. While it made her very fast when she wanted to be, it was not particularly good at lateral movement. Most things built for speed weren't. Cheetahs and horses didn't do a lot of sideways running. She was strong in her suit, but not nearly as strong as it was. She did have an advantage with firearms in that she could run away from the creature while continuing to attack from range. The creature couldn't throw a massive object at her without stopping and anchoring itself. It might be ungodly strong, but it still only weighed what it weighed, and Newton had a few things to say about a light object throwing a heavy one.

By the time she'd finished assembling her suit, she'd watched the video over a hundred times, and the tactics of the fight were starting to take shape in her head. In hand-to-hand combat training, she'd been able to overpower most of her opponents. But the small and quick fighters, the ones who knew how to stick-and-move, gave her trouble. That was who she'd be in this fight. She'd have to hit and run, never stopping for a moment. And even then she'd need a lot of luck, because she was fighting way out of her weight class, and one shot from the monster was a guaranteed knockout.

Her other advantage was that she didn't really have to *win*. She just had to do enough damage to make the monster kill itself. By the time she'd climbed into her newly refurbished suit and let it close around her for a final test, she was pretty sure she could do that.

Bobbie thought her newfound peace about the battle to come would finally let her sleep, but after three hours of tossing and turning in her rack, she gave up. Something still itched at the back of her head. She was trying to find her *Bushido*, and there were still too many things she couldn't let go of. Something wasn't giving her permission yet.

So she pulled on a large fuzzy bathrobe she'd stolen from the *Guanshiyin*, and rode the ladder-lift up toward the ops deck. It was third watch, so the ship was deserted. Holden and Naomi had a cabin together, and she found herself envying that human contact right now. Something certain to cling to amid all the other uncertainty. Avasarala was in her borrowed cabin, probably sending messages to people back on Earth. Alex would be asleep in his room, and for a brief moment she considered waking him. She liked the gregarious pilot. He was genuine in a way she hadn't seen much of since leaving active duty. But she also knew that waking a man up at three a.m. while in her bathrobe sent signals she didn't intend. Rather than try to explain that she just needed to talk to someone, she passed the crew deck by and kept going.

Amos was sitting at a station in ops with his back to her, taking the late watch. To avoid startling him, she cleared her throat. He didn't move or react, so she walked to the comm station. Looking back at him, she saw that his eyes were closed and his breathing was very deep and regular. Sleeping on a duty watch would get you captain's mast, at the least, on an MCRN ship. It seemed Holden had let discipline lapse a bit since his Navy days.

Bobbie opened up the comms and found the closest relay for tightbeam traffic. First she called her father. "Hi, Pop. Not sure you should try and answer this. The situation here is volatile and evolving rapidly. But you may hear a lot of crazy shit over the next few days. Some of it might be about me. Just know that I love you guys, and I love Mars. Everything I did was to try and protect you and my home. I might have lost my way a little bit, because things got complicated and hard to figure out. But I think I see a clear path now, and I'm going to take it. I love you and Mom. Tell the boys they suck." Before she turned off the recording, she reached out and touched the screen. "Bye, Dad."

She pressed send, but something still felt incomplete. Outside her family, anyone who'd tried to help her in the last three months was sitting on the same ship she was, so it didn't make sense.

Except, of course, that it did. Because not *everyone* was on this ship.

Bobbie punched up another number from memory and said, "Hi, Captain Martens. It's me. I think I know what you were trying to help me see. I wasn't ready for it then, but it stuck with me. So you didn't waste your time. I get it now. I know this wasn't my fault. I know I was just at the wrong place at the wrong time. I'm going back to the start now *because* I understand. Not angry, not hurt, not blaming myself. Just my duty to finish the fight."

Something loosened in her chest the moment she hit the send button. All the threads had been neatly tied up, and now she could go to Io and do what she needed to do without regret. She let out a long sigh and slid down in the crash couch until she was almost prone. She suddenly felt bone tired. Like she could sleep for a week. She wondered if anyone would get mad if she just crashed out in ops instead of going all the way back down the lift.

She didn't remember having fallen asleep, but here she was stretched out in the comm station's crash couch, a small puddle of drool next to her head. To her relief, her robe seemed to have remained mostly in place, so at least she hadn't bare-assed everyone walking through.

"Gunny?" Holden said in a tone of voice that meant he was saying it again. He was standing over her, a concerned look on his face.

"Sorry, sorry," she said, sitting up and pulling her robe more tightly around her middle. "I needed to send out some messages last night. Must have been more tired than I thought."

"Yeah," Holden said. "It's no problem. Sleep wherever you like."

"Okay," Bobbie said, backing toward the crew ladder. "With

that, I think I'll go down and take a shower and try to turn back into a human."

Holden nodded as she went, a strange smile on his face. "Sure. Meet me in the machine shop when you're dressed."

"Roger that," she said, and bolted down the ladder.

After a decadently long shower and a change into her clean red-and-gray utility uniform, she grabbed a cup of coffee from the galley and made her way back down to the machine shop. Holden was already there. He had a crate the size of a guitar case sitting on one of the workbenches, and a larger square crate next to his feet on the deck. When she entered the compartment, he patted the crate on the table. "This is for you. I saw when you came on board that you seemed to be missing yours."

Bobbie hesitated a moment, then walked over to the crate and flipped it open. Inside sat a 2mm electrically fired three-barrel Gatling gun, of the type the Marines designated a Thunderbolt Mark V. It was new and shiny and exactly the type that would fit into her suit.

"This is amazing," Bobbie said after catching her breath. "But it's just an awkward club without ammo."

Holden kicked the crate on the floor. "Five thousand rounds of two-millimeter caseless. Incendiary-tipped."

"Incendiary?"

"You forget, I've seen the monster up close too. Armor piercing doesn't help at all. If anything, it reduces soft-tissue damage. But since the lab stuck an incendiary bomb into all of them, I figure that means they aren't fireproof."

Bobbie lifted the heavy weapon out of the crate and put it on the floor next to her newly reassembled suit.

"Oh, *hell* yes."

Chapter Forty-Seven: Holden

Holden sat at the combat control console on the operations deck and watched Ragnarok gather. Admiral Souther, who Avasarala had assured everyone was one of the good guys, had joined his ships with their small but growing fleet of Martians as they sped toward Io. Waiting for them in orbit around that moon were the dozen ships in Admiral Nguyen's fleet. More Martian and UN ships sped toward that location from Saturn and the Belt. By the time everyone got there, there would be something like thirty-five capital ships in the kill zone, and dozens of smaller interceptors and corvettes, like the *Rocinante*.

Three dozen capital ships. Holden tried to remember if there had ever been a fleet action of this size, and couldn't think of one. Including Admiral Nguyen's and Admiral Souther's flagships, there would be four *Truman*-class UN dreadnoughts in the final tally, and the Martians would have three *Donnager*-class battleships of their own, any one of which could depopulate a planet. The rest would be a mix of cruisers and destroyers. Not quite the heavy hitters the battleships were, but plenty powerful enough to vaporize the *Rocinante*. Which, if he was being honest, was the part Holden was most worried about.

On paper, his team had the most ships. With Souther and the Martians joining forces, they outnumbered the Nguyen contingent two to one. But how many Earth ships would be willing to fire on their own, just because one admiral and a banished politician said so? It was entirely possible that if actual shooting started, a lot of UN ships might have unexplained comm failures and wait to see how it all came out. And that wasn't the worst case. The worst case was that a number of Souther's ships would switch sides once Martians starting killing Earthers. The fight could turn into a whole lot of people pointing guns at each other, with no one knowing whom to trust.

It could turn into a bloodbath.

"We have twice as many ships," Avasarala said from her constant perch at the comm station. Holden almost objected but changed his mind. In the end, it wouldn't matter. Avasarala would believe what she wanted to believe. She needed to think all her efforts had been worthwhile, that they were about to pay off when the fleet arrived and this Nguyen clown surrendered to her obviously superior force. The truth was her version wasn't any more or less a fantasy than his. No one would know for sure until everyone knew for sure.

"How long now?" Avasarala said, then sipped at the bulb of weak coffee she'd started making for herself in place of tea.

Holden considered pointing out the navigation information the *Roci* made available at every console, and then didn't. Avasarala didn't want him to show her how to find it herself. She wanted him to tell her. She wasn't accustomed to pressing her own buttons. In her mind, she outranked him. Holden wondered what the chain of command actually looked like in this situation. How many illegal captains of stolen ships did it take to equal one disgraced UN official? That could tie a courtroom up for a few decades.

He also wasn't being fair to Avasarala. It wasn't about making him take her orders, not really. It was about being in a situation that she was utterly untrained for, where she was the least useful person in the room and trying to assert some control. Trying to reshape the space around her to fit with her mental image of herself.

Or maybe she just needed to hear a voice.

"Eighteen hours now," Holden said. "Most of the other ships that aren't part of our fleet will beat us there. And the ones that don't won't show up until it's over, so we can ignore them."

"Eighteen hours," Avasarala said. There was something like awe in her voice. "Space is too fucking big. It's the same old story."

He'd guessed right. She just wanted to talk, so he let her. "What story?"

"Empire. Every empire grows until its reach exceeds its grasp. We started out fighting over who got the best branches in one tree. Then we climb down and fight over a few kilometers' worth of trees. Then someone starts riding horses, and you get empires of hundreds or thousands of kilometers. Ships open up empire expansion across the oceans. The Epstein drive gave us the outer planets..."

She trailed off and tapped out something on the comm panel. She didn't volunteer who she was sending messages to, and Holden didn't ask. When she was done, she said, "But the story is always the same. No matter how good your technology is, at some point you'll conquer territory that you can't hold on to."

"You're talking about the outer planets?"

"Not specifically," she said, her voice growing soft and thoughtful. "I'm talking about the entire fucking concept of empire. The Brits couldn't hold on to India or North America because why should people listen to a king who's six thousand kilometers away?"

Holden tinkered with the air-circulation nozzle on his panel, aiming it at his face. The cool air smelled faintly of ozone and oil. "Logistics is always a problem."

"No kidding. Taking a dangerous trip six thousand kilometers across the Atlantic so you can fight with colonists gives the enemy one hell of a home-court advantage."

"At least," Holden said, "we Earthers figured that out before we picked a fight with Mars. It's even further. And sometimes the sun is in the way."

"Some people have never forgiven us for not humbling Mars when we had the chance," Avasarala said. "I work for a few of them. Fucking idiots."

"I thought the point of your story was that those people always lose in the end."

"Those people," she said, pushing herself to her feet and slowly heading toward the crew ladder, "are not the real problem. Venus might be housing the advance party of the first empire whose grasp is as long as its reach. And this fucking protomolecule has exposed us for the petty, small-town bosses we are. We're getting ready to trade our solar system away because we thought we could build airports out of bamboo and summon the cargo."

"Get some sleep," Holden said to her while she called up the ladder-lift. "We'll defeat one empire at a time."

"Maybe," she said as she dropped out of sight, and the deck hatch banged shut behind her.

"Why isn't anyone shooting?" Prax said. He'd come up to the operations deck trailing after Naomi like a lost child. Now he was sitting at one of the many unused crash couches. He stared up at the main screen, his face a mix of fear and fascination.

The big tactical display showed a muddled mass of red and green dots representing the three dozen capital ships parked in orbit around Io. The *Roci* had marked all the Earth ships green and the Martian ships red. It created a confusing simplicity out of what was in actuality a far more complex situation. Holden knew that friend-or-foe identification was going to be a problem if any-one started shooting.

For now, the various ships drifted quietly above Io, their enor-mous threat merely implied. They made Holden think of the crocodiles he'd seen at the zoo as a child. Huge, armored, filled with teeth, but drifting on the surface of the water like statues. Not even their eyes blinking. When food had been thrown into the pen, they'd exploded out of the water with frightening speed.

We're just waiting for some blood to hit the water.

"Why isn't anyone shooting?" Prax repeated.

"Hey, Doc," Amos said. He was lounging in one of the crash couches next to Prax. He projected a calm laziness that Holden wished he himself felt. "Remember how on Ganymede we were facing down those guys with guns and no one was shooting right up until you decided to cock your gun?"

Prax blanched. Holden guessed he was remembering the bloody aftermath of that fight. "Yes," Prax said. "I remember."

"This is like that," Amos said. "Only no one's cocked their gun just yet."

Prax nodded. "Okay."

If someone finally did break the whole situation loose, Holden knew that figuring out who was shooting at whom would be their first problem. "Avasarala, any word yet on the political landscape? There's a whole lot of green on that board. How many of those dots belong to us?"

Avasarala shrugged and went on listening to the ship-to-ship cross talk.

"Naomi?" Holden said. "Any ideas?"

"So far Nguyen's fleet is targeting only Martian ships," she replied, marking ships on the main tactical board for everyone to see. "The Martian ships are targeting back. Souther's ships aren't targeting anyone, and Souther hasn't even opened his tubes. I'm guessing he's still hoping for a peaceful resolution."

"Please send the intel officer on Souther's ship my compli-ments," Holden said to Naomi. "And ask him to get us some new

IFF data so this doesn't turn into the solar system's biggest clusterfuck."

"Done," Naomi said, and made the call.

"Get everyone buttoned up in their suits, Amos," Holden continued. "Do a hat check here before you go below. I hope we don't start shooting, but what I hope will happen and what actually happens are almost never the same."

"Roger," Amos said, then climbed out of his couch and began clumping around the deck on magnetic boots, checking the seals on everyone's helmets.

"Test test test," Holden said over the crew radio. One by one everyone on the ship responded with the affirmative. Until someone with a higher pay grade than his decided which way things were going to go, there wasn't much else he could do.

"Wait," Avasarala said, then hit a button on her console, and an outside channel started playing on their suit radios.

"—launch immediately against targets on Mars. We have a battery of missiles carrying a lethal biological weapon ready to fire. You have one hour to leave Io orbit or we will launch immediately against targets on Mars. We have a—"

Avasarala turned the channel off again.

"It seems a third party has joined the circle jerk," Amos said.

"No," Avasarala replied. "It's Nguyen. He's outnumbered, so he's ordered his Mao cronies on the surface to make the threat to back us off. He'll— Oh, shit."

She hit her panel again and a new voice spoke over the radio. This one was a woman's voice with a cultured Martian accent.

"Io, this is Admiral Muhan of the Martian Congressional Republic Navy. You fire anything bigger than a bottle rocket and we will glass the whole fucking moon. Do you read me?"

Amos leaned over to Prax. "Now, you see, all this is them cocking their guns."

Prax nodded. "Got it."

"This," Holden said, listening to the barely restrained fury in the Martian admiral's voice, "is about to get seriously out of hand."

"This is Admiral Nguyen aboard the UNN *Agatha King*," a new voice said. "Admiral Souther is here illegally, at the behest of a civilian UN official with no military authority. I hereby order all ships under Admiral Souther's command to immediately stand down. I further order that the captain of Souther's flagship place the admiral under arrest for treason and—"

"Oh, do shut up," Souther replied over the same channel. "I'm here as part of a legal fact-finding mission regarding improper use of UN funds and material for a secret biological weapon project on Io. A project which Admiral Nguyen is directly responsible for in contravention of UN directives—"

Avasarala cut the link.

"Oh, this ain't good," Alex said.

"Well," Avasarala said, then opened the faceplate on her helmet and let out a long sigh. She opened her purse and pulled a pistachio out of it. She cracked it and thoughtfully ate the meat, then put the shell in the nearby recycling chute. A tiny bit of the skin floated away in the microgravity. "No, actually, it should be fine. This is all posturing. As long as they keep comparing dicks, no one will shoot."

"But we can't just wait here," Prax said, shaking his head. Amos was floating in front of him, checking his helmet. Prax shoved him away and tried to get to his feet. He drifted away from his crash couch but didn't think to turn on his boot mags. "If Mei is down there, we have to go. They're talking about glassing the moon. We have to get there before they do it."

There was a high violin-string whine at the back of Prax's voice. The tension was getting to him. It was getting to all of them, but Prax was the one who was going to show it worst and first. Holden shot a look at Amos, but the big man just looked surprised at having been pushed away by the much smaller scientist.

"They're talking about destroying the base. We have to go

down there!" Prax continued, the panic in his voice starting to shine through.

"We're not doing anything," Holden said. "Not until we have a better idea how this is going to shake out."

"We came all this way so that we can not do anything?" Prax demanded.

"Doc, we don't want to be the ones to move first," Amos said, and put a hand on Prax's shoulder, pulling him back down to the deck. The little botanist violently shrugged it off without turning around, then shoved off his couch toward Avasarala.

"Give me the channel. Let me talk to them," Prax said, reaching for her comm panel. "I can—"

Holden launched himself out of his crash couch, catching the scientist mid-flight and hurling them both across the deck and into the bulkhead. The thick layer of anti-spalling padding absorbed their impact, but Holden felt the air go out of Prax when his hip slammed into the smaller man's belly.

"Gah," Prax said, and curled up into a floating fetal ball.

Holden kicked on his boot mags and pushed himself down to the deck. He grabbed Prax and pushed him across the compartment to Amos. "Take him below, stuff him in his bunk, and sedate the shit out of him. Then get to engineering and get us ready for a fight."

Amos nodded and grabbed the floating Prax. "Okay." A moment later the two of them disappeared down the deck hatch.

Holden looked around the room, seeing the shocked looks from Avasarala and Naomi but ignoring them. Prax's need for his daughter to take precedence over everything else had almost put them all in danger again. And while Holden intellectually understood the man's drive, having to stop him from killing them all every time Mei's name came up was stress he didn't need right then. It left him angry and needing to snap at someone.

"Where the hell is Bobbie?" he said to no one in particular. He hadn't seen her since they had put in to orbit around Io.

"Just saw her in the machine shop," Amos replied over the

radio. "She was fieldstripping my shotgun. I think she's doing all the guns and armor."

"That's—" Holden started, ready to yell about something. "That's actually really helpful. Tell her to button up her suit and turn her radio on. Things might be going south in a hurry here."

He took a few seconds to breathe and calm himself down, then returned to the combat operations station.

"You okay?" Naomi asked over their private channel.

"No," he said, chinning the button to make sure only she heard his reply. "No, I'm actually scared to death."

"I thought we were past that."

"Past being scared?"

"No," she said, the smile audible in her voice. "Past blaming yourself for it. I'm scared too."

"I love you," Holden said, feeling that same electric thrill he always got when he told her, part fear, part boast.

"You should probably keep your eye on your station," she said, her tone teasing. She never told him she loved him when he said it first. She'd said that when people did it too often, it made the word lose all its power. He understood the argument, but he'd kind of hoped she'd break her rule this once. He needed to hear it.

Avasarala was hunched over the comm station like an ancient mystic peering into a murky crystal ball. The space suit hung on her like a scarecrow's oversized coveralls. Holden considered ordering her to button up her helmet, then shrugged. She was old enough to decide for herself the relative risks and rewards of eating during a battle.

Periodically she reached into her purse and pulled out another nut. The air around her was a growing cloud of tiny pieces of pistachio skin. It was annoying to watch her cluttering up his ship, but no warship was built so fragile that a little airborne waste would break anything. Either the tiny pieces of shell would be sucked into the air recycling system and trapped by the filters, or they'd go under thrust and all the garbage would fall to the floor, where they could sweep it up. Holden wondered if Avasarala had ever had to clean anything in her life.

While he watched her, the old lady cocked her head to one side, listening with sudden interest to something only she could hear. Her hand darted forward, bird quick, to tap at the screen. A new voice came over the ship's radios, this one with the faint hiss transmissions picked up when traveling for millions of kilometers through space.

"—eneral Esteban Sorrento-Gillis. Some time ago, I announced the formation of an exploratory committee to look into possible misuse of UN resources for illegal biological weapon research. While that investigation is ongoing, and the committee is not prepared to bring charges at this time, in the interests of public safety and to better facilitate a thorough and comprehensive investigation, certain UN personnel in key positions are to be recalled to Earth for questioning. First, Admiral Augusto Nguyen, of the United Nations Navy. Second—"

Avasarala hit the panel to shut off the feed and stared at the console with her mouth open for several seconds. "Oh, fuck me."

All over the ship, alarms started blaring.

Chapter Forty-Eight: Avasarala

I've got fast movers," Naomi said over the blaring alarms. "The UN flagship is firing."

Avasarala closed her helmet, watching the in-suit display confirm the seal, then tapped at the communications console, her mind moving faster than her hands. Errinwright had cut a deal, and now Nguyen knew it. The admiral had just been hung out to dry, and he was taking it poorly. A flag popped up on the console: incoming high-priority broadcast. She thumbed it, and Souther appeared on her terminal and every other one in the ops deck.

"This is Admiral Souther. I am hereby taking command of—"

"Okay," Naomi said. "I need my real screen back now. Got some work to do."

"Sorry, sorry," Avasarala said, tapping at the console. "Wrong button."

"—this task force. Admiral Nguyen is relieved of duty. Any hostilities will be—"

Avasarala switched the feed to her own screen and in the process switched to a different broadcast. Nguyen was flushed almost purple. He was wearing his uniform like a boast.

"—illegal and unprecedented seizure. Admiral Souther is to be escorted to the brig until—"

Five incoming comm requests lit up, each listing a name and short-form transponder ID. She ignored them all for the broadcast controls. As soon as the live button went active, she looked into the camera.

"This is Assistant Undersecretary Chrisjen Avasarala, representing the civilian government of Earth," she said. "Legal and appropriate command of this force is given to Admiral Souther. Anyone rejecting or ignoring his orders will be subject to legal action. I repeat, Admiral Souther is in legally authorized command of—"

Naomi made a low grunting sound. Avasarala stopped the broadcast and turned.

"Okay," Holden said. "That was bad."

"What?" Avasarala said. "What was bad?"

"One of the Earth ships just took three torpedo hits."

"It that a lot?"

"The PDCs aren't stopping them," Naomi said. "Those UN torpedoes all have transponder codes that mark them as friends, so they're sailing right through. They typically don't expect to be getting shot at by other UN ships."

"Three is a lot," Holden said, strapping into the crash couch. She didn't see him touch any of the controls, but he must have, because when he spoke, it echoed through the ship as well as the speakers in her helmet. "We have just gone live. Everyone has to the count of twenty to get strapped in someplace safe."

"Solid copy on that," Bobbie replied from wherever she was on the ship.

"Just got the doc strapped in and happy," Amos said. "I'm on my way to engineering."

"Are we heading into this?" Alex asked.

"We've got something like thirty-five capital ships out there, all of them much, much bigger than us. How about we just try to keep anyone from shooting us full of holes."

"Yes, sir," Alex said from the pilot's deck. Any vestige of democracy and vote taking was gone. That was a good thing. At least Holden had control when there had to be a single voice in command.

"I have two fast movers coming in," Naomi said. "Someone still thinks we're the bad guys."

"I blame Avasarala," Bobbie said.

Before Avasarala could laugh, gravity ticked up and slewed to the side, the *Rocinante* taking action beneath her. Her couch shifted and creaked. The protective gel squeezed her and let her go.

"Alex?"

"On 'em," Alex said. "I wouldn't mind getting a real gunner, sir."

"Are we going to have enough time to get her up here safely?"

"Nope," Alex said. "I've got three more incoming."

"I can take PDC control from here, sir," Bobbie said. "It's not the real thing, but it's something the rest of you won't have to do."

"Naomi, give the PDCs to the sergeant."

"PDC control transferred. It's all yours, Bobbie."

"Taking control," Bobbie said.

Avasarala's screen was a tangle of incoming messages in a flickering array. She started going through them. The *Kennedy* was announcing that Souther's command was illegal. The *Triton*'s first officer was reporting that the captain had been relieved of duty, and requested orders from Souther. The Martian destroyer *Iani Chaos* was trying to reach Avasarala for clarification of which Earth ships it was permitted to shoot at.

She pulled up the tactical display. Circles in red and green marked the swarm of ships; tiny silver threads showed what might have been streams of PDC fire or the paths of torpedoes.

"Are we red or green?" Avasarala asked. "Who's who on this fucking thing?"

"Mars is red, Earth is green," Naomi said.

"And which Earth ones are on our side?"

"Find out," Holden said as one of the green dots suddenly vanished. "Alex?"

"The *Darius* took the safeties off its PDCs, and now it's spraying down everything in range whether it's friend or foe. And... shit."

Avasarala's chair shifted again, seeming to rise from under her, pressing her back into the gel until it was hard to lift her arms. On the tactical screen, the cloud of ships, enemy and friendly and ambiguous, shifted slightly, and two golden dots grew larger, proximity notations beside them counting quickly down.

"Madam Assistant whatever you are," Holden said, "you could respond to some of those comm requests now."

Avasarala's gut felt like someone was squeezing it from below. The taste of salt and stomach acid haunted the back of her tongue. She was beginning to sweat in a way that had less to do with temperature than nausea. She forced her hands out to the control panel just as the two golden dots vanished.

"Thank you, Bobbie," Alex said. "I'm heading up. Gonna try to get the Martians between us and the fighting."

She started making calls. In the heat of a battle, all she had to offer was this: making calls. Talking. The same things she always did. Something about it was actually reassuring. The *Greenville* was accepting Souther's command. The *Tanaka* wasn't responding. The *Dyson* opened the channel, but the only sound was men shouting at each other. It was bedlam.

A message came in from Souther, and she accepted it. It included a new IFF code, and she manually accepted the update. On the tactical, most of the green dots shifted to white.

"Thank you," Holden said. Avasarala swallowed her *You're welcome*. The antinausea drugs seemed to be working for everyone else. She really, *really* didn't want to throw up inside her helmet. One of the six remaining green dots blinked out of existence and another turned suddenly to white.

"Ooh, right in the back," Alex said. "That was cold."

Souther's ID showed up again on Avasarala's console, and she hit accept just as the *Roci* shifted again.

"—the immediate surrender of the flagship *King* and Admiral Augusto Nguyen," Souther was saying. His shock of white hair was standing up off his head as if the low thrust gravity was letting it expand like a peacock's tail. His smile was sharp as a knife. "Any vessel that still refuses to acknowledge my orders as legal and legitimate will forfeit this amnesty. You have thirty seconds from this mark."

On the tactical display, the threads of silver and gold had, for the most part, vanished. The ships shifted positions, each moving along its own complex vectors. As she watched, all the remaining green dots turned to white. All except one.

"Don't be an asshole, Nguyen," Avasarala said. "It's over."

The ops deck was silent for a long moment, the tension almost unbearable. Naomi's voice was the one to break it.

"I've got more fast movers. Oh, I've got a *lot* of them."

"Where?" Holden snapped.

"From the surface."

Avasarala didn't do anything, but her tactical display resized, pulling back until the cluster of ships, red and white and the single defiant green, were less than a quarter of their original size and the massive curve of the moon's surface impinged on the lower edge of the display. Rising like a solid mass, hundreds of fine yellow lines.

"Get me a count," Holden said. "I need a count here."

"Two hundred nineteen. No. Wait. Two hundred thirty."

"What the hell are they? Are those torpedoes?" Alex asked.

"No," Bobbie said. "They're monsters. They launched the monsters."

Avasarala opened a broadcast channel. Her hair probably looked worse than Souther's but she was well past vanity. That she could speak without fear of vomiting was blessing enough.

"This is Avasarala," she said. "The launch you are all seeing right now is a new protomolecule-based weapon that is being used as an unauthorized first strike against Mars. We need to shoot those fuckers out of the sky and do it now. Everyone."

"We've got a coordination override request coming through from Souther's flagship," Naomi said. "Surrender control?"

"The hell I will," Alex said.

"No, but track requests," Holden said. "I'm not handing control of my ship to a military fire-control computer, but we still need to be part of the solution here."

"The *King*'s starting a hard burn," Alex said. "I think he's trying to hightail it."

On the display, the attack from the surface of Io was beginning to bloom, individual threads coming apart in unexpected angles, some corkscrewing, some reaching out in bent paths like an insect's articulated legs. Any one of them was the death of a planet, and the acceleration data put them at ten, fifteen, twenty g's. Nothing human survived at a sustained twenty g. Nothing human had to.

Golden flickers of light appeared from the ships, drifting down to meet the threads of Io. The slow, stately pace of the display was undercut by the data. Plasma torpedoes burning full out, and yet it took long seconds for them to reach the main stem. Avasarala watched the first of them detonate, saw the column of protomolecule monsters split into a dozen different streams. Evasive action.

"Some of those are coming toward us, Cap," Alex said. "I don't think they're designed to hole a ship's hull, but I'm pretty damn sure they'd do it anyway."

"Let's get in there and do what we can. We can't let any of these...Okay, where'd they go?"

On the tactical display, the attacking monsters were blinking out of existence, the threads vanishing.

"They're cutting thrust," Naomi said. "And the RF transponders are going dark. Must have radar-absorbing hull materials."

"Do we have tracking data? Can we anticipate where they're going to be?"

The tactical display began to flicker. Fireflies. The monsters shifting in and out, thrusting in what looked like semi-random directions, but the bloom of them always expanding.

"This is going to be a bitch," Alex said. "Bobbie?"

"I've got some target locks. Get us in PDC range."

"Hang on, kids," Alex said. "We're going for a ride."

The *Roci* bucked hard, and Avasarala pressed back into her seat. The shuddering rhythm seemed to be her own trembling muscles and then the firing PDCs and then her body again. On the display, the combined forces of Earth and Mars spread out, running after the near-invisible foes. Thrust gravity shifted, spinning her couch one way and then another without warning. She tried closing her eyes, but that was worse.

"Hmm."

"What, Naomi?" Holden said. " 'Hmm' what?"

"The *King* was doing something strange there. Huge activity from the maneuvering thrusters and . . . Oh."

" 'Oh' what? Nouns. I need nouns."

"She's holed," Naomi said. "One of the monsters holed her."

"Told you they could do that," Alex said. "Hate to be on the ship right now. Still. Couldn't have happened to a nicer fella."

"His men aren't responsible for his actions," Bobbie said. "They may not even know Souther's in command. We've got to help them."

"We can't," Holden said. "They'll shoot at us."

"Would you all please shut the fuck up?" Avasarala said. "And stop moving the goddamned ship around. Just pick a direction and calm down for two minutes."

Her comm request went ignored for five minutes. Then ten. When the *King*'s distress beacon kicked in, she still hadn't answered. A broadcast signal came in just after.

"This is Admiral Nguyen of the United Nations battleship *Agatha King*. I am offering to surrender to UN ships with the condition of immediate evacuation. Repeat: I am offering surrender to any United Nations military vessel on the condition of immediate evacuation."

Souther answered on the same frequency.

"This is the *Okimbo*. What's your situation?"

"We have a possible biohazard," Nguyen said. His voice was so tight and high it sounded like someone was strangling him. On the tactical display, several white dots were already moving toward the green.

"Hold tight, *King*," Souther said. "We're on our way."

"Like hell you are," Avasarala said, then cursed quietly as she opened a broadcast channel. "Like hell you are. This is Avasarala. I am declaring a quarantine and containment order on the *Agatha King*. No vessel should dock with her or accept transfer of materiel or personnel. Any ship that does will be placed under a quarantine and containment order as well."

Two of the white dots turned aside. Three others continued on. She opened the channel again.

"Am I the only one here who remembers Eros? What the fuck do you people think is loose on the *King*? Do not approach."

The last of the white dots turned aside. When Nguyen answered her comm request, she'd forgotten she still had it open. He looked like shit. She didn't imagine she looked much better. How many wars had ended this way? she wondered. Two exhausted, nauseated people staring at each other while the world burned around them.

"What more do you want from me?" Nguyen said. "I've surrendered. I lost. My men shouldn't have to die for your spite."

"It's not spite," Avasarala said. "We can't do it. The protomolecule gets loose. Your fancy control programs don't work. It's infectious."

"That's not proven," he said, but the way he said it told her everything.

"It's happening, isn't it?" she said. "Turn on your internal cameras. Let us see."

"I'm not going to do that."

She felt the air go out of her. It had happened.

"I am so sorry," Avasarala said. "Oh. I am so sorry."

Nguyen's eyebrows rose a millimeter. His lips pressed, bloodless and thin. She thought there were tears in his eyes, but it might have been only a transmission artifact.

"You have to turn on the transponders," Avasarala said. And then, when he didn't reply: "We can't weaponize the protomolecule. We don't understand what it is. We can't control it. You just sent a death sentence to Mars. I can't save you, I cannot. But turn those transponders back on and help me save them."

The moment hung in the air. Avasarala could feel Holden's and Naomi's attention on her like warmth radiating from the heating grate. Nguyen shook his head, his lips twitching, lost in conversation with himself.

"Nguyen," she said. "What's happening? On your ship. How bad is it?"

"Get me out of here, and I'll turn the transponders on," he said. "Throw me in the brig for the rest of my life, I don't care. But get me off of this ship."

Avasarala tried to lean forward, but it only made her crash couch shift. She looked for the words that would bring him back, the ones that would tell him that he had been wrong and evil and now he was going to die badly at the hands of his own weapon and somehow make it all right. She looked at this angry, small, shortsighted, frightened little man and tried to find the way to pull him back to simple human decency.

She failed.

"I can't do that," she said.

"Then stop wasting my time," he said, and cut the connection.

She lay back, her palm over her eyes.

"I'm gettin' some mighty strange readings off that battleship," Alex said. "Naomi? You seeing this?"

"Sorry. Give me a second."

"What have you got, Alex?" Holden asked.

"Reactor activity's down. Internal radiation through the ship's spiking huge. It's like they're venting the reactor into the air recycling."

"That don't sound healthy," Amos said.

The ops deck went silent again. Avasarala reached to open a channel to Souther but stopped. She didn't know what she'd say. The voice that came over the ship channel was slushy and drugged. She didn't recognize Prax at first, and then he had to repeat himself twice before she could make out the words.

"Incubation chamber," Prax said. "It's making the ship an incubation chamber. Like on Eros."

"It knows how to do that?" Bobbie said.

"Apparently so," Naomi said.

"We're going to have to slag that thing," Bobbie said. "Do we have enough firepower for that?"

Avasarala opened her eyes again. She tried to feel something besides great, oceanic sorrow. There had to be hope in there somewhere. Even Pandora got that much.

Holden was the one who said what she was thinking.

"Even if we can, it won't save Mars."

"Maybe we got them all?" Alex said. "I mean, there were a shitload of those things, but maybe...maybe we got 'em?"

"Hard to tell when they were running ballistic," Bobbie said. "If we missed just one, and it gets to Mars..."

It was all slipping away from her. She had been so close to stopping it, and now here she was, watching it all slip past. Her gut was a solid knot. But they hadn't failed. Not yet. Somewhere in all this there had to be a way. Something that could still be done.

She forwarded her last conversation with Nguyen to Souther. Maybe he'd have an idea. A secret weapon that could come out of nowhere and force the codes out. Maybe the great brotherhood of military men would draw some vestige of humanity out of Nguyen.

Ten minutes later, a survival pod came loose from the *King*. Souther didn't bother contacting her before they shot it down. The ops deck was like a mourning chamber.

"Okay," Holden said. "First things first. We've got to get down to the base. If Mei's there, we need to get her out."

"I'm on that," Amos said. "And we got to take the doc. He ain't gonna outsource that one."

"That's what I was thinking," Holden said. "So you guys take the *Roci* down to the surface."

"*Us* guys?" Naomi asked.

"I'll take the pinnace over to the battleship," Holden said. "The transponder activation codes are going to be in the CIC."

"You?" Avasarala asked.

"Only two people got off Eros," Holden said with a shrug. "And I'm the one that's left."

Chapter Forty-Nine: Holden

Don't do this," Naomi said. She didn't beg, or cry, or make demands. All the power of her request lay in its quiet simplicity. "Don't do it."

Holden opened the suit locker just outside the main airlock and reached for his Martian-made armor. A sudden and visceral memory of radiation sickness on Eros stopped him. "They've been pumping radiation into the *King* for hours now, right?"

"Don't go over there," Naomi said again.

"Bobbie," Holden said over the comm.

"Here," she replied with a grunt. She was helping Amos prep their gear for the assault on the Mao science station. After his one encounter with the Mao protomolecule hybrid, he could only imagine they were going loaded for bear.

"What are these standard Martian armor suits rated for radiation-wise?"

"Like mine?" Bobbie asked.

"No, not a powered suit. I know they harden you guys for close-proximity blasts. I'm talking about this stuff we pulled out of the MAP crate."

"About as much as a standard vacuum suit. Good enough for short walks outside the ship. Not so much for constant exposure to high radiation levels."

"Shit," Holden said. Then: "Thanks." He killed the comm panel and closed the locker. "I'll need a full-on hazard suit. Which means I'll be better in the radiation, and not bullet resistant at all."

"How many times can you get yourself massively irradiated before it catches up with you?" Naomi said.

"Same as last time. At least one more," Holden replied with a grin. Naomi didn't smile back. He hit the comm again and said, "Amos, bring me up a hazard suit from engineering. Whatever's the hardest thing we've got on board."

"Okay," Amos replied.

Holden opened his equipment locker and took out the assault rifle he kept there. It was large, black, and designed to be intimidating. It would immediately mark anyone who carried it as a threat. He put it back and decided on a pistol instead. The hazmat suit would make him fairly anonymous. It was the sort of thing any member of the damage-control team might wear during an emergency. If he was wearing only a service pistol in a hip holster, it might keep anyone from singling him out as part of the problem.

And with the protomolecule loose on the *King*, and the ship flooded with radiation, there would be a big problem.

Because if Prax and Avasarala were right, and the protomolecule was linked even without a physical connection, then the goo on the *King* knew what the goo on Venus knew. Part of that was how human spaceships were put together, ever since it had disassembled the *Arboghast*. But it also meant it knew a lot about how to turn humans into vomit zombies. It had performed that trick a million times or so on Eros. It had practice.

It was entirely possible that every single human on the *King* was now a vomit zombie. And sadly, that was the best-case scenario. Vomit zombies were walking death to anyone with exposed skin, but to Holden, in his fully sealed and vacuum-rated hazmat suit, they would be at worst a mild annoyance.

The worst-case scenario was that the protomolecule was so good at changing humans now, the ship would be full of lethal hybrids like the one he'd fought in the cargo bay. That would be an impossible situation, so he chose to believe it wasn't true. Besides, the protomolecule hadn't made any soldiers on Eros. Miller hadn't really taken the time to describe what he'd run into there, but he'd spent a lot of time on the station looking for Julie and he'd never reported being attacked by anything. The protomolecule was incredibly aggressive and invasive. It would kill a million humans in hours and turn them into spare parts for whatever it was working on. But it invaded at the cellular level. It acted like a virus, not an army.

Just keep telling yourself that, Holden thought. It made what he was about to do seem possible.

He took a compact semiautomatic pistol and holster out of the locker. Naomi watched while he loaded the weapon's magazine and three spares, but she didn't speak. He had just pushed the last round into the final magazine when Amos floated into the compartment, dragging a large red suit behind him.

"This is our best, Cap," he said. "For when shit has gone truly wrong. Should be plenty for the levels they've got in that ship. Max exposure time is six hours, but the air supply only lasts two, so that's not an issue."

Holden examined the bulky suit. The surface was a thick, flexible rubbery substance. It might deter someone attacking with their fingernails or teeth, but it wouldn't stop a knife or a bullet. The air supply was contained under the suit's radiation-resistant skin, so it made for a big, awkward lump on the wearer's back. The difficulty he had pulling the suit to himself and then stopping it told him its mass was considerable.

"Won't be moving fast in this, will I?"

"No," Amos said with a grimace. "They're not made for a fire-fight. If the bullets start flying, you're fucked."

Naomi nodded but said nothing.

"Amos," Holden said, grabbing the mechanic's arm as he turned to leave. "The gunny's in charge once you hit the surface. She's a pro, and this is her show. But I need you to keep Prax safe, because he's kind of an idiot. The only thing I ask you to do is get that man and his little girl safely off the moon and back to this ship."

Amos looked hurt for a moment. "Of course I will, Captain. Anything that gets to him or that baby will already have killed me. And that ain't easy to do."

Holden pulled Amos to him and gave the big man a quick hug. "I feel sorry for anything that tries. No one could ask for a better crewman, Amos. Just want you to know that."

Amos pushed him away. "You act like you're not coming back."

Holden shot a look at Naomi, but her expression hadn't changed. Amos just laughed for a minute, then clapped Holden on the back hard enough to rattle his teeth. "That's bullshit," Amos said. "You're the toughest guy I know." Without waiting for Holden to reply, he headed out to the crew ladder, and then down to the deck below.

Naomi pushed lightly against the bulkhead and drifted over to Holden. Air resistance brought her to a stop half a meter from him. She was still the most agile person in microgravity he'd ever met, a ballerina of null g. He had to stop himself from hugging her to him. The expression on her face told him it wasn't what she wanted. She just floated in front of him for a moment, not saying anything, then reached out and put one long, slender hand against his cheek. It felt cool and soft.

"Don't go," she said, and something in her voice told him it would be the last time.

He backed up and began shrugging his way into the hazmat suit. "Then who? Can you see Avasarala fighting through a mob of vomit zombies? She wouldn't know the CIC from the galley. Amos has to go get that little girl. You know he does, and you know why. Prax has to be there. Bobbie keeps them both alive."

He got the bulky suit over his shoulders and sealed up the front but left the helmet lying against his back. The boot mags came on when he hit them with his heels, and he pushed down to the deck and stuck there.

"You?" he asked Naomi. "Do I send you? I'd bet on you against a thousand zombies any day of the week. But you don't know the CIC any better than Avasarala does. How does that make sense?"

"We just got right again," she said. "That's not fair."

"But," he said, "tell the Martians that me saving their planet makes us even on this whole 'you stole our warship' issue, okay?" He knew he was making light of the moment and immediately hated himself for it. But Naomi knew him, knew how afraid he was, and she didn't call him on it. He felt a rush of love for her that sent electricity up his spine and made his scalp tingle.

"Fine," she said, her face hardening. "But you're coming back. I'll be here on the radio the whole time. We'll work through this together, every step. No hero bullshit. Brains instead of bullets, and we work the problems together. You give me that. You better give me that."

Holden finally pulled her into his arms and kissed her. "I agree. Please, please help me make it back alive. I'd really like that."

Flying the *Razorback* to the crippled *Agatha King* was like taking a race car to the corner market. The *King* was only a few thousand kilometers from the *Rocinante*. It seemed close enough for an EVA pack and a really strong push. Instead, he flew what was probably the fastest ship in the Jupiter system in teakettle mode at about 5 percent thrust through the debris of the recent battle. He could sense the *Razorback* straining at the leash, responding to his tiny bursts of steam with sullen reproach. The distance to the stricken flagship was short enough, and the path treacherous enough, that programming in a course would take more time than just flying by stick. But even at his languid pace, the *Razorback* seemed to have a hard time keeping its nose pointed at the *King*.

You don't want to go there, the ship seemed to be saying. *That's an awful place.*

"No, no, I really don't," he said, patting the console in front of him. "But just get me there in one piece, okay, honey?"

A massive chunk of what must have once been a destroyer floated past, the ragged edges still glowing with heat. Holden tapped the stick and pushed the *Razorback* sideways to get a bit more distance from the floating wreckage. The nose drifted off course. "Fight all you want, we're still going to the same place."

Some part of Holden was disappointed that the transit was so dangerous. He'd never flown to Io before, and the view of the moon at the edge of his screens was spectacular. A massive volcano of molten silicate on the opposite side of the moon was throwing particles so high into space he could see the trail it left in the sky. The plume cooled into a spray of silicate crystals, which caught Jupiter's glow and glittered like diamonds scattered across the black. Some of them would drift off to become part of Jupiter's faint ring system, blown right out of Io's gravity well. In any other circumstance, it would have been beautiful.

But the hazardous flight kept his attention on his instruments and the screens in front of him. And always, the growing bulk of the *Agatha King*, floating alone at the center of the junk cloud.

When he was within range, Holden signaled the ship's automated docking system, but as he'd suspected, the *King* didn't respond. He piloted up to the nearest external airlock and told the *Razorback* to maintain a constant distance of five meters. The racing ship was not designed to dock with another ship in space. It lacked even a rudimentary docking tube. His trip to the *King* would be a short spacewalk.

Avasarala had gotten a master override code from Souther, and Holden had the *Razorback* transmit it. The airlock immediately cycled open.

Holden topped off the hazmat suit's air supply in the *Razorback*'s airlock. Once he got onto Nguyen's flagship, he couldn't trust the air, even in the suit-recharging stations. Nothing from the *King* could be allowed inside his suit. Nothing.

When his stored-air gauge read 100 percent, he turned on the radio and called Naomi. "I'm going in now."

He kicked off his boot mags, and a sharp push against the inner airlock door sent him across the short gap to the *King*.

"I'm getting a good picture," Naomi said. The video link light on his HUD was on. Naomi could see everything he could see. It was comforting and lonely at the same time, like making a call to a friend who lived very far away.

Holden cycled the airlock. The two minutes while the *King* closed the outer door and then pumped air into the chamber seemed to last forever. There was no way to know what would be on the other side of the inner airlock door when it finally opened. Holden put his hand on the butt of his pistol with a nonchalance he didn't feel.

The inner door slid open.

The sudden screech of his hazmat suit's radiation alarm nearly gave him a heart attack. He chinned the control that killed the audible alarm, though he kept the outside radiation level meter running. It wasn't data that actually did him any good, but the suit was reassuring him that it could handle the current levels, and that was nice.

Holden stepped out of the airlock into a small compartment filled with storage lockers and EVA equipment. It looked empty, but a small noise from one of the lockers alerted him, and he turned just in time to see a man in a UN naval uniform burst out of the locker and swing a heavy wrench at his head. The bulky hazmat suit kept him from moving quickly, and the wrench struck a ringing blow off the side of his helmet.

"Jim!" Naomi yelled over the radio.

"Die, you bastard!" the Navy man yelled at the same time. He took a second swing, but he wasn't wearing mag boots, and without the push off the bulkhead to give him momentum, the swing did little more than start spinning the man around in the air. Holden grabbed the wrench out of his hand and threw it away. He caught the man to stop his spinning with his left hand and drew his pistol with his right.

"If you cracked my suit, I'm going to throw you out that airlock," Holden said. He began flipping through suit status screens while keeping his pistol pointed at the wrench enthusiast.

"It looks okay," Naomi said, relief evident in her voice. "No reds or yellows. That helmet is tougher than it looks."

"What the hell were you doing in that locker?" Holden asked the man.

"I was working here when the...it...came on board," the man said. He was a compact-looking Earther, with pale skin and flaming red hair cut close to the scalp. A patch on his suit said LARSON. "All the doors sealed up during emergency lockdown. I was trapped in here, but I could watch what was happening on the internal security system. I was hoping to grab a suit and get out the airlock, but it was sealed too. Say, how'd you get in here?"

"I have admiralty-level overrides," Holden said to him. Quietly, to Naomi he said, "At current radiation levels, what's survival odds for our friend here?"

"Not bad," Naomi said. "If we get him into sick bay in the next couple of hours."

To Larson he said, "Okay, you're coming with me. We're going to CIC. Get me there fast, and you've got a ride off this tub."

"Yes, sir!" Larson said with a salute.

"He thinks you're an admiral." Naomi laughed.

"Larson, put on an environment suit. Do it fast."

"Sir, yes sir!"

The suits they had in the airlock storage lockers would at least have their own air supplies. That would cut down on damage from the radiation the young sailor was absorbing. And an airtight suit would reduce the risk of protomolecule infection as they made their way through the ship.

Holden waited until Larson had shrugged into a suit, then

transmitted the override code to the hatch and it slid open. "After you, Larson. Command information center, as fast as you can. If we run into anyone, especially if they're throwing up, stay away and let me deal with them."

"Yes, sir," Larson said, his voice fuzzy over the static-filled radio, then pushed off into the corridor. He took Holden at his word and led him on a fast trip through the crippled *Agatha King*. They stopped only when a sealed hatch blocked their way, and then only long enough for Holden's suit to convince it to open.

The areas of the ship they moved through didn't look damaged at all. The bioweapon pod had hit farther aft, and the monster had headed straight to the reactor room. According to Larson, it had killed a number of people on the way, including the ship's entire contingent of Marines when they tried to stop it. But once it had entered engineering, it mostly ignored the rest of the crew. Larson said that shortly after it got into engineering, the shipwide security camera system had gone off-line. With no way to know where the monster was, and no way out of the airlock storage room, Larson had hidden in a locker to wait it out.

"When you came in, all I could see was this big, lumpy red thing," Larson explained. "I thought maybe you were another one of those monsters."

The lack of visible damage was a good thing. It meant all the hatches and other systems they came across still worked. The lack of a monster rampaging through the ship was even better. The thing that had Holden worried was the lack of people. A ship this size had over a thousand crew persons. At least some of them should be in the areas of the ship they were passing through, but so far they hadn't run across a single one.

The occasional puddle of brown goo on the floor was not an encouraging sign.

Larson stopped at a locked hatch to let Holden catch his breath. The heavy hazmat suit was not built for long treks, and it was starting to fill up with the stink of his own sweat. While he took a minute to rest and let the suit's cooling systems try to bring his temperature down, Larson said, "We'll be going past the forward galley to one of the elevator bays. The CIC is on the deck just above. Five, ten minutes tops."

Holden checked his air supply and saw that he had burned nearly half of it. He was rapidly approaching the point of no return. But something in Larson's voice caught his ear. It was the way he said *galley*.

"Is there something I should know about the galley?"

Larson said, "I'm not sure. But after the cameras went out, I kept hoping someone was going to come get me. So I started trying to call people on the comm. When that didn't work, I started having the *King* do location checks on people I knew. After a while, no matter who I asked about, the answer was always 'the forward galley.' "

"So," Holden said. "There might be upwards of a thousand infected Navy people crammed into that galley?"

Larson gave a shrug barely visible in his environment suit. "Maybe the monster killed them and put them there."

"Oh, I think that's exactly what happened," Holden said, taking out his gun and working the slide to chamber a round. "But I seriously doubt they stayed dead."

Before Larson could ask what he meant, Holden had his suit unlock the hatch. "When I open this door, you head to the elevator as fast as you can. I'll be right behind you. Don't stop no matter what. You *have* to get me to that CIC. Are we clear?"

Larson nodded inside his helmet.

"Good. On three."

Holden began counting, one hand on the hatch, the other holding his gun. When he hit three, he shoved the hatch open. Larson put his feet against a bulkhead and pushed off down the corridor on the other side.

Tiny blue flickers floated in the air around them like fireflies. Like the lights Miller had reported when he was on Eros the second time. The time he didn't come back from. The fireflies were here now too.

At the end of the corridor, Holden could see the elevator door. He began clumping after Larson on his magnetic boots. When Larson was halfway down the corridor, he passed an open hatch.

The young sailor started screaming.

Holden ran as fast as the clumsy hazmat suit and his magnetic boots would let him go. Larson kept flying down the corridor, but he was screaming and flailing at the air like a drowning man trying to swim. Holden was almost to the open hatch when something crawled out of it and into his path. At first he thought it was the kind of vomit zombie he'd run into on Eros. It moved slowly, and the front of its Navy uniform was covered in brown vomit. But when it turned to look at Holden, its eyes glowed with a faint inner blue. And there was an intelligence in them the Eros zombies hadn't had.

The protomolecule had learned some lessons on Eros. This was the new, improved version of the vomit zombie.

Holden didn't wait to see what it was going to do. Without slowing his pace, he raised his pistol and shot it in the head. To his relief, the light went out of its eyes, and it spun away from the deck, spraying brown goo in an arc as it rotated. When he passed the open hatch, he risked a glance inside.

It was full of the new vomit zombies. Hundreds of them. All their disconcertingly blue eyes were aimed at him. Holden turned back to the corridor and ran. From behind, he heard a rising wave of sounds as the zombies moaned as one and began climbing along the bulkheads and deck after him.

"Go! Get in the elevator!" he screamed at Larson, cursing at how much the heavy hazmat suit slowed him down.

"God, what was that?" Naomi said. He'd forgotten she was watching. He didn't waste breath answering. Larson had come out of his panic-induced fugue and was busily working the elevator doors open. Holden ran up to him and then turned around to look behind. Dozens of the blue-eyed vomit zombies filled the corridor behind him, crawling on the bulkheads, ceiling, and deck like spiders. The floating blue lights swirled on air currents Holden couldn't feel.

"Go faster," he said to Larson, sighting down his pistol at the lead zombie and putting a bullet in its head. It floated off the wall, spraying goo as it went. The zombie behind it shoved it out of the way, which sent it spinning down the corridor toward them. Holden moved in front of Larson to protect him, and a spray of brown slime hit his chest and visor. If they hadn't both been wearing sealed suits, it would have been a death sentence. He repressed a shudder and shot two more zombies. The rest didn't even slow down.

Behind him, Larson cursed as the partially opened doors snapped shut again, pinning his arm. The sailor worked them back open, pushing them with his back and one leg.

"We're in!" Larson yelled. Holden began backing up toward the elevator shaft, emptying the rest of his magazine as he went. Half a dozen more zombies spun away, spraying goo; then he was in the shaft and Larson shoved the doors shut.

"Up one level," Larson said, panting with fear and exertion. He pushed off the bulkhead and floated up to the next set of doors, then levered them open. Holden followed, replacing the magazine in his gun. Directly across from the elevator was a heavily armored hatch with CIC stenciled in white on the metal. Holden moved toward it, having his suit transmit the override code. Behind him, Larson let the elevator doors slam shut. The howling of the zombies echoed up the elevator shaft.

"We should hurry," Holden said, hitting the button to open the CIC and bulling his way in before the hatch had finished cycling open. Larson floated through after him.

There was a single man still in the CIC: a squat, powerfully built Asian man with an admiral's uniform and a large-caliber pistol in one shaky hand.

"Stay where you are," the man said.

"Admiral Nguyen!" Larson blurted out. "You're alive!"

Nguyen ignored him. "You're here for the bioweapon launch vehicle remote codes. I have them here." He held up a hand terminal. "They're yours in exchange for a ride off of this ship."

"He's taking us," Larson said, pointing at Holden. "He said he'd take me too."

"No fucking way," Holden said to Nguyen. "Not a chance. Either give me those codes because there's a scrap of humanity left in you, or give them to me because you're dead. I don't give a shit either way. You decide."

Nguyen looked back and forth from Larson to Holden, clutching the hand terminal and the pistol so tightly that his knuckles were white. "No! *You* have to—"

Holden shot him in the throat. Somewhere in his brain stem, Detective Miller nodded in approval.

"Start working on an alternate route back to my ship," Holden said to Larson as he walked across the room to grab the hand terminal floating by Nguyen's corpse. It took him a moment to find the *King*'s self-destruct switch hidden behind a locked panel. Souther's override code gave him access to that too.

"Sorry," Holden said quietly to Naomi as he opened it. "I know I sort of agreed not to do that anymore. But I didn't have time to—"

"No," Naomi said, her voice sad. "That bastard deserved to die. And I know you'll feel like shit about it later. That's good enough for me."

The panel opened, and a simple button lay on the other side. It wasn't even red, just a plain industrial white. "This is what blows the ship?"

"No timer," Naomi said.

"Well, this is an anti-boarding fail-safe. If someone opens this panel and presses this button, it's because the ship is lost. They don't want it on a timer someone can just disarm."

"This is an engineering problem," Naomi said. She already knew what he was thinking, and she was trying to get an answer out before he could say it. "We can solve this."

"We can't," Holden said, waiting to feel the sorrow but instead feeling a sort of quiet peace. "There are a couple hundred very angry zombies trying to get up the elevator shaft right now. We won't come up with a solution that doesn't leave me stranded in here anyway."

A hand squeezed his shoulder. He looked up, and Larson said, "I'll press it."

"No, you don't have to—"

Larson held out his arm. The sleeve of his environment suit had a tiny tear where the elevator doors had closed on it. Around the tear was a palm-sized brown stain.

"Just rotten fucking luck, I guess. But I watched the Eros feeds like everyone else," Larson said. "You can't risk taking me. Pretty soon I might be..." He paused and pointed back toward the elevator with his head. "Might be one of those."

Holden took Larson's hand in his. The thick gloves made it impossible to feel anything. "I'm very sorry."

"Hey, you tried," Larson said with a sad smile. "At least now I won't die of thirst in a suit locker."

"Admiral Souther will know about this," Holden said. "I'll make sure everyone knows."

"Seriously," Larson said, floating next to the button that would turn the *Agatha King* into a small star for a few seconds. He pulled off his helmet and took a long breath. "There's another airlock three decks up. If they aren't in the elevator shaft yet, you can make it."

"Larson, I—"

"You should go away now."

Holden had to strip off his suit in the *King*'s airlock. It was covered in the goo, and he couldn't risk taking it onto the *Razorback*. He absorbed a few rads while he stole another UN vac suit from one of the lockers and put it on instead. It looked exactly like the one Larson was wearing. As soon as he was back on the *Razorback*, he sent the remote command codes to Souther's ship. He was nearly back to the *Rocinante* when the *King* vanished in a ball of white fire.

Chapter Fifty: Bobbie

The captain just left," Amos said to Bobbie when he came back into the machine shop. She floated half a meter above the deck inside a small circle of deadly technology. Behind her sat her cleaned and refitted recon suit, a single barrel of the newly installed gun gleaming inside the port on its right arm. To her left floated the recently reassembled auto-shotgun Amos favored. The rest of the circle was formed by pistols, grenades, a combat knife, and a variety of weapon magazines. Bobbie took one last mental inventory and decided she'd done all she could do.

"He thinks maybe he's not coming back from this one," Amos continued, then bent down to grab the auto-shotgun. He looked it over with a critical eye, then gave her an appreciative nod.

"Going into a fight where you know you aren't coming back gives you a sort of clarity," Bobbie said. She reached out and grabbed her armor, pulling herself into it. Not an easy thing to do in microgravity. She had to twist and shimmy to get her legs down into the suit before she could start sealing up the chest. She noticed Amos watching her. He had a dopey grin on his face.

"Seriously. Now?" she said. "We're talking about your captain going off to his death, and all that's going through your head right now is 'Ooh, boobies!'"

Amos continued to grin, not chastened at all. "That bodysuit don't leave a lot to the imagination. That's all."

Bobbie rolled her eyes. "Believe me, if I could wear a bulky sweater inside my fully articulated, power-assisted combat suit, I still wouldn't. Because that would be stupid." She hit the controls to seal the suit, and her armor folded around her like a second skin. She closed the helmet, using the suit's external speakers to talk to Amos, knowing it would make her voice robotic and inhuman.

"Better put your big-boy pants on," she said, the sound echoing around the room. Amos took an unconscious step back. "The captain isn't the only one that might not be coming back."

Bobbie climbed onto the ladder-lift and let it take her all the way up to the ops deck. Avasarala was belted into her couch at the comm station. Naomi was in Holden's usual spot at the tactical panel. Alex would be up in the cockpit already. Bobbie opened her visor to speak using her normal voice.

"We cleared?" she asked Avasarala.

The old lady nodded and held up one hand in a *wait* gesture while she spoke to someone on her headset mic. "The Martians have already dropped a full platoon," she said, pushing the mic away from her face. "But their orders are to set up a perimeter and seal the base while someone further up the food chain decides what to do."

"They're not going to—" Bobbie started, but Avasarala cut her off with a dismissive wave of her hand.

"Fuck no," she said. "*I'm* further up the food chain, and I've already decided we're going to glass this abattoir as soon as you're off the surface. I'm letting them think we're still discussing it so you have time to go get the kids."

Bobbie nodded her fist at Avasarala. Recon Marines were trained to use the Belters' physical idiom when in their combat armor. Avasarala just looked baffled at the gesture and said, "So stop playing with your hand and go get the fucking kids."

Bobbie headed back to the ladder-lift, connecting to the ship's 1MC as she went. "Amos, Prax, meet me in the airlock in five minutes, geared up and ready to go. Alex, put us on the deck in ten."

"Roger that," Alex replied. "Good hunting, soldier." She wondered if they might have become friends, given enough time. It was a pleasant thought.

Amos was waiting for her outside the airlock when she arrived. He wore his Martian-made light armor and carried his oversized gun. Prax rushed into the compartment a few minutes later, still struggling to get into his borrowed gear. He looked like a boy wearing his father's shoes. While Amos helped him get buttoned up, Alex called down to the airlock and said, "Heading down. Hang on to something."

Bobbie turned her boot mags to full, locking herself to the deck while the ship shifted under her. Amos and Prax both sat down on chairs that pulled out from the wall, and belted in.

"Let's go over the plan one more time," she said, calling up the aerial photos they'd shot of the facility. She patched into the *Roci* and threw the pictures onto a wall monitor. "This airlock is our entrance. If it's locked, Amos will blast it with explosives to open the outer door. We need to get inside fast. Your armor isn't going to protect you from the vicious radiation belt Io orbits in for long. Prax, you have the radio link Naomi rigged, so once we're inside, you start looking for a network node to plug it into. We have no information about the layout of the base, so the faster we can get Naomi hacking their system, the faster we can find those kids."

"I like the backup plan better," Amos said.

"Backup plan?" Prax asked.

"The backup plan is I grab the first guy we see, and beat him until he tells us where the kids are."

Prax nodded. "Okay. I like that one too."

Bobbie ignored the macho posturing. Everyone dealt with pre-combat jitters in their own way. Bobbie preferred obsessive list making. But flexing and threats were good too. "Once we have a location, you guys move with all haste to the kids, while I ensure a clear path of egress."

"Sounds good," Amos said.

"Make no mistake," Bobbie said. "Io is one of the worst places in the solar system. Tectonically unstable and radioactive as hell. Easy to see why they hid here, but do not underestimate the peril that just being on this shit moon carries."

"Two minutes," Alex said over the comm.

Bobbie took a deep breath. "And that isn't the worst. These assholes launched a couple hundred human-protomolecule hybrids at Mars. We can hope that they shot their entire wad, but I have a feeling they didn't. We might very well run into one of those monsters once we get inside."

She didn't say, *I've seen it in my dreams.* It seemed counterproductive.

"If we see one, *I deal with it.* Amos, you almost got your captain killed blasting away at the one you found in the cargo bay. You try that shit with me, I'll snap your arm off. Don't test me."

"Okay, chief," Amos replied. "Don't get your panties in a twist. I heard you."

"One minute," Alex said.

"There are Martian Marines controlling the perimeter, but they've been given the okay to let us in. If someone escapes past us, no need to apprehend them. The Marines will pick them up before they get far."

"Thirty seconds."

"Get ready," Bobbie said, then pulled up her HUD's suit status display. Everything was green, including the ammo indicator, which showed two thousand incendiary rounds.

The air sucked out of the airlock in a long, fading hiss, leaving only a thin wisp of atmosphere that would be the same density as Io's own faint haze of sulfur. Before the ship hit the deck, Amos jumped up out of his chair and stood on his toes to put his helmet against hers. He yelled, "Give 'em hell, marine."

The outer airlock door slid open, and Bobbie's suit blatted a radiation alarm at her. It also helpfully informed her that the outside atmosphere was not capable of supporting life. She shoved Amos toward the open lock and then pushed Prax after him. "Go, go, go!"

Amos took off across the ground in a weird, hopping run, his breath panting in her ears over the radio link. Prax stayed close behind him and seemed more comfortable in the low gravity. He had no trouble keeping up. Bobbie climbed out of the *Roci* and then jumped in a long arc that took her about seven meters above the surface at its apex. She visually scanned the area while her suit reached out with radar and EM sensors, trying to pinpoint targets. Neither she nor it found any.

She hit the ground next to the lumbering Amos and hopped again, beating them both to the airlock door. She tapped the button and the outer door cycled open. Of course. Who locks their door on Io? No one is going to hike across a wasteland of molten silicon and sulfur to steal the family silver.

Amos plowed past her into the airlock, stopping for breath only once he was inside. Bobbie followed Prax in a second later, and she was about to tell Amos to cycle the airlock when her radio died.

She spun around, looking out across the surface of the moon for movement. Amos came up behind her and put his helmet against her back armor. When he yelled, it was barely audible. "What is it?"

Instead of yelling back, she stepped outside the airlock and pointed to Amos, then pointed at the inner door. She mimed a person walking with her fingers. Amos nodded at her with one hand, then moved back into the airlock and shut the outer door.

Whatever happened inside, it was up to Amos and Prax now. She wished them well.

She spotted the movement before her suit did. Something shifting against the sulfurous yellow background. Something not quite the same color. She tracked it with her eyes and had the suit hit it with a targeting laser. She wouldn't lose track of it now. It might gobble radio waves, but the fact that she could see it meant that light bounced off it just fine.

It moved again. Not quickly, and staying close to the ground. If she hadn't been looking right at it, she'd have missed the motion entirely. Being sneaky. Which probably meant it didn't know she'd spotted it. Her suit's laser range finder marked it as just over three hundred meters away. According to her theory, once it realized it had been spotted, it would charge her, moving in a straight line to try to grab and rip. If it couldn't reach her quickly, it would try to throw things at her. And all she needed to do was hurt it until its program failed and it self-destructed. Lots of theories.

Time to test them out.

She aimed her gun at it. The suit helped her correct for deflection based on the range, but she was using ultrahigh velocity rounds on a moon with fractional gravity. Bullet drop at three hundred meters would be trivial. Even though there was no way the creature could see it through her helmet's darkened visor, she blew it a kiss. "I'm back, sweetie. Come say hi to momma."

She tapped the trigger on her gun. Fifty rounds streaked down-range, crossing the distance from her gun to the creature in less than a third of a second. All fifty slammed into it, shedding very little of their kinetic energy as they passed through. Just enough to burst the tip of each round open and ignite the self-oxidizing flammable gel they carried. Fifty trails of short-lived but very intense flame burned through the monster.

Some of the black filament bursting from the exit wounds actually caught fire, disappearing with a flash.

The monster launched itself toward Bobbie at a dead run that should have been impossible in low gravity. Each push of its limbs should have launched it high into the air. It stuck to the silicate surface of Io as though it were wearing magnetic boots on a metal deck. Its speed was breathtaking. Its blue eyes blazed like lightning. The long, improbable hands reached out for her, clenching and grasping at nothing as it ran. It was all just like in her dreams. And for a split second, Bobbie just wanted to stand perfectly still and let the scene play out to the conclusion she'd never gotten to see. Another part of her mind expected her to wake up, soaking with sweat, as she had so many times before.

Bobbie watched as it ran toward her, and noted with pleasure the burnt black injuries the incendiary bullets had cut through its body. No sprays of black filament and then the wounds closing like water. Not this time. She'd hurt it, and she wanted to go on hurting it.

She turned away and took off in a bounding run at a ninety-degree angle to its path. Her suit kept the targeting laser locked on to the monster, so she could track its location even without turning around to look. As she'd suspected, it turned to follow her, but it lost ground. "Fast on the straightaways," Bobbie said to it. "But you corner like shit."

When the creature realized she wasn't going to just stand still and let it get close to her, it stopped. Bobbie stumbled to a stop, turning to watch it. It reached down and tore up a big chunk of ancient lava bed, then reached down to grip the ground with its other hand.

"Here it comes," Bobbie said to herself.

She threw herself to the side as the creature's arm whipped forward. The rock missed her by centimeters as she hurtled sideways. She hit the moon's surface and skidded, already returning fire. This time she fired for several seconds, sending hundreds of rounds into and through the creature.

"Anything you can do I can do better," she sang under her breath. "I can do anything better than you." The bullets tore great flaming chunks out of the monster and nearly severed its left arm. The creature spun around and collapsed. Bobbie bounced back to her feet, ready to run again if the monster got back up. It didn't. Instead, it rolled over onto its back and shook. Its head began to swell, and the blue eyes flashed even brighter. Bobbie could see things moving beneath the surface of its chitinous black skin.

"Boom, motherfucker!" she yelled at it, waiting for the bomb to go off.

Instead, it bounced suddenly to its feet, tore a portion of its own abdomen off, and threw it at her. By the time Bobbie realized what had just happened, the bomb was only a few meters from her. It detonated and blew her off her feet. She went skidding across Io's surface, her armor blaring warnings at her. When she finally came to a stop, her HUD was flashing a Christmas display of red and green lights. She tried to move her limbs, but they were as heavy as stone. The suit's motion control processor, the computer that interpreted her body's movements and turned them into commands for the suit's actuators, had failed. The suit was trying to reboot it while simultaneously trying to reroute and run the program in a different location. A flashing amber message on the HUD said PLEASE STAND BY.

Bobbie couldn't turn her head yet, so when the monster leaned down over her, it took her completely by surprise. She stifled a scream. It wouldn't have mattered. The sulfur atmosphere on Io was far too thin for sound waves to travel in. The monster couldn't have heard her. But while the new Bobbie was at peace with the idea of dying in battle, enough of the old Bobbie remained that she was not going to go out screaming like a baby.

It leaned down to look at her; its overlarge and curiously child-like eyes glowed bright blue. The damage her gun had done seemed extensive, but the creature appeared not to notice. It poked at her chest armor with one long finger, then convulsed and vomited a thick spray of brown goo all over her.

"Oh, that's *disgusting*," she yelled at it. If her suit had been opened up to the outside, getting that protomolecule shit on her would have been the least of her problems. But still, how the hell was she going to wash this crap off?

It cocked its head and regarded her curiously. It poked again at her armor, one finger wriggling into gaps, trying to find a way in to her skin. She'd seen one of these things rip a nine-ton combat mech apart. If it wanted into her suit, it was coming in. But it seemed reluctant to damage her for some reason. As she watched, a long, flexible tube burst out of its midsection and began probing at her armor instead of the finger. Brown goo dribbled out of this new appendage in a constant stream.

Her gun status light flickered from red to green. She spun up the barrels to test it and it worked. Of course, her suit was still telling her to "please stand by" when it came to actually moving. Maybe if the monster got bored and wandered in front of her gun, she could get some shots off.

The tube was probing at her armor more insistently now. It pushed its way into gaps, periodically shooting brown liquid into them. It was as repulsive as it was frightening. It was like being threatened by a serial killer that was also fumbling at her clothing with a teenager's horny insistence.

"Oh, to hell with *this*," she said to it. She was about through with letting this thing grope her while she lay helpless on her back. The suit's right arm was heavy, and the actuators that made her strong when it was working also resisted movement when it was not. Pushing her arm up was like doing a one-arm bench press while wearing a lead glove. She pressed up anyway until she felt something pop. It might have been in the suit. It might have been in her arm. She couldn't tell yet, because she was too wired for pain to set in.

But when it popped, her arm came up, and she pushed her fist up against the monster's head.

"Buh-bye," she said. The monster turned to look curiously at her hand. She held down the trigger until the ammo counter read zero and the gun stopped spinning. The creature had ceased to exist from the shoulders up. She dropped her arm back to the ground, exhausted.

REROUTE SUCCESSFUL, her suit told her. REBOOTING, it said. When the subliminal hum came back, she started laughing and found she couldn't stop. She shoved the monster's corpse off her and sat up.

"Good thing. It's a really long walk back to the ship."

Chapter Fifty-One: Prax

Prax ran.

Around him, the station walls formed angles at the center to make an elongated hexagon. The gravity was barely higher than Ganymede standard, and after weeks at a full-g burn, Prax had to pay attention to keep himself from rising to the ceiling with each step. Amos loped beside him, every stride low, long, and fast. The shotgun in the man's hands remained perfectly level.

At a T intersection ahead, a woman appeared. Dark hair and skin. Not the one who'd taken Mei. Her eyes went wide and she darted off.

"They know we're coming," Prax said. He was panting a little.

"That probably wasn't their first clue, Doc," Amos said. His voice was perfectly conversational, but there was an intensity in it. Something like anger.

At the intersection, they paused, Prax leaning over and resting elbows on knees to catch his breath. It was an old, primitive reflex. In less than .2 g, the blood return wasn't significantly increased by putting his head even with his heart. Strictly speaking, he would have been better off standing and keeping his posture from narrowing any of his blood vessels. He forced himself to stand.

"Where should I plug in this radio link for Naomi?" he asked Amos.

Amos shrugged and pointed at the wall. "Maybe we can just follow the signs instead."

There was a legend on the wall with colored arrows pointing in different directions. ENV CONTROL and CAFETERIA and PRIMARY LAB. Amos tapped PRIMARY LAB with the barrel of his shotgun.

"Sounds good to me," Prax said.

"You good to go?"

"I am," Prax said, though he probably wasn't.

The floor seemed to shift under him, followed immediately by a long, ominous rumbling that he could feel in the soles of his feet.

"Naomi? You there?"

"I am. I have to keep track of the captain on the other line. I might pop in and out. Everything all right?"

"Might be stretching the point," Amos said. "We got something sounded like someone shooting at us. They ain't shooting at the base, are they?"

"They aren't," Naomi said from the ship, her voice pressed thin and tinny by the attenuated signal. "It looks like some of the locals are mounting a defense, but so far our Marines aren't returning fire."

"Tell 'em to calm that shit down," Amos said, but he was already moving down the corridor toward the primary lab. Prax jumped after him, misjudged, and cracked his arm against the ceiling.

"Soon as they ask me," Naomi said.

The corridors were a maze, but it was the kind of maze Prax had been running through his whole life. The institutional logic of a research facility was the same everywhere. The floor plans were different; budget concerns could change how richly appointed the details were; the fields being supported determined what equipment was present. But the soul of the place was the same, and it was Prax's home.

Twice more, they caught sight of people scattering through the halls with them. The first was a young Belter woman in a white lab coat. The second was a massively obese dark-skinned man with the squat build of Earth. He was wearing a crisp suit, the signature of the administrative class everywhere. Neither one tried to stop them, so Prax forgot about them almost as soon as he saw them.

The imaging suite was behind a set of negative-pressure seals. When Prax and Amos went through, the gust of air seemed to push them faster, urging them on. The rumble came again, louder this time and lasting almost fifteen seconds. It could be fighting. It could be a volcano forming nearby. No way to know. Prax knew this base would have to have been built with tectonic instability in mind. He wondered what the safeguards were for a moment, then put it out of his mind. Nothing he could do about it anyway.

The lab's imaging suite was at least the equal of the one he'd shared on Ganymede, with everything from the spidery full-resonance displays to the inferential gravity lens. In the corner, a squat orange table showed a holographic image of a colony of rapidly dividing cells. Two doors led out apart from the one they'd come through. Somewhere nearby, people were shouting at each other.

Prax pointed at one of the doors.

"This one," he said. "Look at the hinges. It's built to allow a gurney through."

The passageway on the other side was warmer and the air was more humid. It wasn't quite greenhouse level, but near to it. It opened into a long gallery with five-meter ceilings. Fitted tracks on the ceiling and floor allowed for moving high-mass equipment and containment cages. Bays lined it, each, it seemed, with a research bench not so different from the ones Prax had used as an undergraduate: smart table, wall display, inventory control box, specimen cages. The shouting voices were louder now. He was about to say as much, but Amos shook his head and pointed down the gallery toward one of the farther bays. A man's voice came from that direction, his tone high and tight and angry.

"…not an evacuation if there's no place to evacuate to," he was saying. "I'm not giving up the one bargaining chip I have left."

"You don't have that option," a woman said. "Put the gun down, and let's talk this through. I've been handling you for seven years, and I will keep you in business for seven more, but you do not—"

"Are you delusional? You think there's a tomorrow after this?"

Amos pointed forward with his shotgun, then began a slow, deliberate advance. Prax followed, trying to be silent. It had been months since he'd heard Dr. Strickland's voice, but the shouting man could be him. It was possible.

"Let me make this perfectly clear," the man said. "We have nothing. Nothing. The only hope of negotiation is if we have a card to play. That means them. Why do you think they're *alive*?"

"Carlos," the woman said as Prax came to the corner of the bay. "We can have this conversation later. There's a hostile enemy force on the base right now, and if you're still here when they come through that hatch—"

"Yeah," Amos interrupted, "what happens then?"

The bay was just like the others. Strickland—it was unmistakably Strickland—stood beside a gray metal transport crate that went from the floor to just above his hip. In the specimen cages, a half dozen children lay motionless, sleeping or drugged. Strickland also had a small gun in his hand, pointed at the woman from the video. She was in a harshly cut uniform, the sort of thing that security forces adopted to make their staff look hard and intimidating. It worked for her.

"We came in the other hatch," Prax said, pointing back over his shoulder.

"Da?"

One syllable, spoken softly. It rang out from the transport cart louder than all the weeks of explosions and gauss rounds and screams of the wounded and dying. Prax couldn't breathe; he couldn't move. He wanted to tell them all to put the guns away, to be careful. There was a child. His child.

Strickland's pistol barked, and some sort of high-explosive round destroyed the woman's neck and face in a spray of blood and cartilage. She tried to scream once, but with significant portions of her larynx already compromised, what she managed was more of a powerful, wet exhalation. Amos lifted the shotgun, but Strickland—Merrian, whatever his name was—put his pistol on the top of the crate and seemed almost to sag with relief. The woman drifted to the floor, blood and flesh fanning out and falling gently to the ground like a blanket of red lace.

"Thank God you came," the doctor said. "Oh, thank God you came. I was stalling her as long as I could. Dr. Meng, I can't imagine how hard this has been for you. I am so, *so* sorry."

Prax stepped forward. The woman took another jerking breath, her nervous system firing at random now. Strickland smiled at him, the same reassuring smile he recognized from any number of doctor's visits over the previous years. Prax found the transport's control pad and knelt to open it. The side panel clicked as the magnetic locks gave up their grip. The panel rolled up, disappearing into the cart's frame.

For a terrible, breathless moment, it was the wrong girl. She had the black, lustrous hair, the egg-brown skin. She could have been Mei's older sister. And then the child moved. It wasn't much more than shifting her head, but it was all that his brain needed to see his baby in this older girl's body. All the months on Ganymede, all the weeks to Tycho and back, she'd been growing up without him.

"She's so big," he said. "She's grown so much."

Mei frowned, tiny ridges popping into being just above her brow. It made her look like Nicola. And then her eyes opened. They were blank and empty. Prax yanked at the release on his helmet and lifted it off. The station air smelled vaguely of sulfur and copper.

Mei's gaze fastened on him and she smiled.

"Da," she said again, and put out one hand. When he reached for her, she took his finger in her fist and pulled herself into his arms. He held her to his chest; the warmth and mass of her small body—no longer tiny, only small—was overwhelming. The void between the stars was smaller than Mei was at that moment.

"She's sedated," Strickland said. "But her health is perfect. Her immune system has been performing at peak."

"My baby," Prax said. "My perfect girl."

Mei's eyes were closed, but she smiled and made a small, animal grunt of satisfaction.

"I can't tell you how sorry I am for all this," Strickland said. "If I had any way of reaching you, of telling you what was happening, I swear to you I would have. This has been beyond a nightmare."

"So you're saying they kept you prisoner here?" Amos asked.

"Almost all the technical staff was here against their will," Strickland said. "When we signed on, we were promised resources and freedom of a kind most of us had only dreamed about. When I started, I thought I could make a real difference. I was terribly, terribly wrong, and I will never be able to apologize enough."

Prax's blood was singing. A warmth spread from the center of his body, radiating out to his hands and feet. It was like being dosed with the most perfect euphoric in the history of pharmacy. Her hair smelled like the cheap lab shampoo he'd used to wash dogs in the laboratories of his youth. He stood too quickly, and her mass and momentum pulled him a few centimeters off the floor. His knees and feet were slick, and it took him a moment to realize he'd been kneeling in blood.

"What happened to these kids? Are there others somewhere else?" Amos asked.

"These are the only ones I was able to save. They've all been sedated for evacuation," Strickland said. "But right now, we need to leave. Get off the station. I have to get to the authorities."

"And why do you need to do that?" Amos asked.

"I have to tell them what's been going on here," Strickland said. "I have to tell everyone about the crimes that were committed here."

"Yeah, okay," Amos said. "Hey, Prax? You think you could get that?" He pointed his shotgun at something on a nearby crate.

Prax turned to look at Amos. It was almost a struggle to remember where he was and what they were doing.

"Oh," he said. "Sure."

Holding Mei against him with one arm, he took Strickland's gun and trained it on the man.

"No," Strickland said. "You don't... you don't understand. I'm the victim here. I had to do all this. They forced me. She forced me."

"You know," Amos said, "maybe I'm coming across as what a guy like you might call working class. Doesn't mean I'm stupid. You're one of Protogen's pet sociopaths, and I ain't buying any damn thing you're trying to sell."

Strickland's face turned to cold rage like a mask had fallen away.

"Protogen's dead," he said. "There is no Protogen."

"Yeah," Amos said. "I got the brand name wrong. That's the problem here."

Mei murmured something, her hand reaching up behind Prax's ear to grip his hair. Strickland stepped back, his hands in fists.

"I saved her," he said. "That girl's alive because of me. She was slated for the second-generation units, and I pulled her off the project. I pulled all of them. If it wasn't for me, every child here would be worse than dead right now. Worse than dead."

"It was the broadcast, wasn't it?" Prax said. "You saw that we might find out, so you wanted to make sure that you had the girl from the screen. The one everyone was looking for."

"You'd rather I hadn't?" Strickland said. "It was still me that saved her."

"Actually, I think that makes it Captain Holden," Prax said. "But I take your point."

Strickland's pistol had a simple thumb switch on the back. He pressed it to turn the safety on.

"My home is gone," Prax said, speaking slowly. "My job is gone. Most of the people I've ever known are either dead or scattered through the system. A major government is saying I abuse women and children. I've had more than eighty explicit death threats from absolute strangers in the last month. And you know what? I don't care."

Strickland licked his lips, his eyes shifting from Prax to Amos and back again.

"I don't need to kill you," Prax said. "I have my daughter back. Revenge isn't important to me."

Strickland took a deep breath and let it out slowly. Prax could see the man's body relax, and something on the dividing line of relief and pleasure appeared at the corners of his mouth. Mei twitched once when Amos' auto-shotgun fired, but she lay back down against Prax's shoulder without crying or looking around. Strickland's body drifted slowly to the ground, the arms falling to the sides. The space where the head had been gouted bright arterial blood against the walls, each pulse smaller than the one before.

Amos shrugged.

"Or that," Prax said.

"So you got any ideas how we—"

The hatch behind them opened and a man ran in.

"What happened? I heard—"

Amos raised the auto-shotgun. The new man backpedaled, a thin whine of fear escaping from him as he retreated. Amos cleared his throat.

"Any idea how we get these kids out of here?"

Putting Mei back in the transport cart was one of the hardest things Prax had ever done. He wanted to carry her against him, to press his face against hers. It was a primate reaction, the deepest centers of his brain longing for the reassurance of physical contact. But his suit wouldn't protect her from the radiation or near vacuum of Io's sulfuric atmosphere, and the transport would. He nestled her gently against two other children while Amos put the other four in a second cart. The smallest of them was still in newborn diapers. Prax wondered if she had come from Ganymede too. The carts glided against the station flooring, only rattling when they crossed the built-in tracks.

"You remember how to get back to the surface?" Amos asked.

"I think so," Prax said.

"Uh, Doc? You really want to put your helmet back on."

"Oh! Right. Thank you."

At the T intersection, half a dozen men in security uniforms had built a barricade, preparing to defend the lab against attack. Because Amos tossed in his grenades from the rear, the cover was less effective than the locals had anticipated, but it still took a few minutes to clear the bodies and the remains of the barricade to let the carts roll through.

There was a time, Prax knew, that the violence would have bothered him. Not the blood or bodies. He'd spent more than enough time doing dissections and even autonomous-limb vivisection to be able to wall off what he was seeing from any particular sense of visceral horror. But that it was something done in anger, that the men and women he'd just seen blown apart hadn't donated their bodies or tissues, would have affected him once. The universe had taken that from him, and he couldn't say now exactly when it had happened. Part of him was numb, and maybe it always would be. There was a feeling of loss in that, but it was intellectual. The only emotions he felt were a glowing, transforming relief that Mei was here and alive and a vicious animal protectiveness that meant he would never let her leave his sight, possibly until she left for university.

On the surface, the transports were rougher, the wheels less suited to the uneven surface of the land. Prax followed Amos' example, turning the boxes around to pull them rather than push. Looking at the vectors, it made sense, but it wouldn't have occurred to him if he hadn't seen Amos doing it.

Bobbie was walking slowly toward the *Rocinante*. Her suit was charred and stained and moving poorly. A clear fluid was leaking down the back.

"Don't get close to me," she said. "I've got protomolecule goo all over this thing."

"That's bad," Amos said. "You got a way to clean that off?"

"Not really," she replied. "How'd the extraction go?"

"Got enough kids to start a singing group, but a little shy of a baseball team," Amos said.

"Mei's here," Prax said. "She's all right."

"I'm glad to hear that," Bobbie said, and even though she was clearly exhausted, she sounded like she meant it.

At the airlock, Amos and Prax got in and nestled the transports against the back wall while Bobbie stood on the rough ground outside. Prax checked the transport indicators. There was enough onboard air to last another forty minutes.

"All right," Amos said. "We're ready."

"Going for emergency blow," Bobbie said, and her armored suit came apart around her. It was a strange sight, the hard curves and layers of combat plate peeling themselves back, blooming out like a flower and then falling apart, and the woman, eyes closed and mouth open, being revealed. When she put her hand out for Amos to pull her in, the gesture reminded Prax of Mei seeing him again.

"Now, Doc," Amos said.

"Cycling," Prax said. He closed the outer door and started fresh air coming into the lock. Ten seconds later, Bobbie's chest started to pump like a bellows. Thirty seconds, and they were at seven-eighths of an atmosphere.

"Where do we stand, guys?" Naomi asked as Prax opened the

transport. The children were all asleep. Mei was sucking on her first two fingers, the way she had when she was a baby. He couldn't get past how much older she looked.

"We're solid," Amos said. "I say we get the fuck out of here and glass the place."

"A-fucking-men," Avasarala's voice said in the background.

"Copy that," Naomi said. "We're prepping for launch. Let me know when you've got all our new passengers safely in."

Prax pulled off his helmet and sat beside Bobbie. In the black sheath of her base garments, she looked like someone just coming back from the gym. She could have been anybody.

"Glad you got your kid back," she said.

"Thank you. I'm sorry you lost the suit," he said.

She shrugged.

"At this point, it was mostly a metaphor anyway," she said, and the inner airlock opened.

"Cycle's done, Naomi," Amos said. "We're home."

Chapter Fifty-Two: Avasarala

It was over, except that it wasn't. It never was.

"We're all friends now," Souther said. Talking to him without lag was a luxury she was going to miss. "But if we all limp back to our corners, we're more likely to stay that way. I'm thinking it's going to be a question of years before either of our fleets are back up to what we were. There was a lot of damage."

"The children?"

"Processing them. My medical officer's in communication with a list of doctors who deal with pediatric immune problems. It's just about finding their parents and getting them all home now."

"Good," she said. "That's what I like to hear. And the other thing?"

Souther nodded. He looked younger in low gravity. They both did. Skin didn't sag when there was nothing to tug it down, and she could see what he'd looked like as a boy.

"We've got transponder locks on a hundred and seventy-one packages. They're all moving sunward pretty fast, but they're not accelerating or evading. Pretty much we're standing back and letting them get close enough to Mars that disposal is trivial."

"You sure that's a good idea?"

"By 'close,' I mean still weeks away at current speed. Space is big."

There was a pause that meant something other than distance.

"I wish you'd ride back on one of ours," Souther said.

"And be stuck out here for another few weeks with the paperwork? Not going to happen. And besides, heading back with James Holden and Sergeant Roberta Draper and Mei Meng? It has all the right symbolism. Press will eat it up. Earth, Mars, the Outer Planets, and whatever the hell Holden is now."

"Celebrity," Souther said. "A nation of its own."

"He's not that bad once you get past the self-righteousness. And anyway, this is the ship I'm on, and there's nothing it's waiting to repair before it starts its burn. And I've already hired him. No one's giving me any shit about discretionary spending right now."

"All right," Souther said. "Then I'll see you back down the well."

"See you there," she said, and cut the connection.

She pulled herself up and launched gently across the ops deck. It would have been easy to push down the crew ladder shaft, flying the way she'd dreamed of as a child. It tempted. In practice, she figured she'd either push too hard and slam into something or else too gently and have air resistance stop her with nothing solid close enough to reach. She used the handholds and pulled herself slowly down toward the galley. Pressure doors opened at her approach and closed behind her with soft hydraulic hisses and metallic bangs. When she reached the crew deck, she heard the voices before she could make out the words, and the words before she saw the people.

"...have to shut it down," Prax was saying. "I mean, it's false pretenses now. You don't think I could be sued, do you?"

"You can always be sued," Holden said. "Chances are they wouldn't win."

"But I don't want to be sued in the first place. We have to shut it down."

"I put a notice on the site so it gives a status update and asks for confirmation before any more money gets moved."

She pulled herself into the galley. Prax and Holden were floating near the coffee machine. Prax wore a stunned expression, whereas Holden looked slightly smug. They both had bulbs of coffee, but Prax seemed to have forgotten his. The botanist's eyes were wide and his mouth hung open, even in the microgravity.

"Who's getting sued?" Avasarala asked.

"Now that we have Mei," Holden said, "Prax wants people to stop giving him money."

"It's too much," the botanist said, looking at her as if he expected her to do something about it. "I mean..."

"Surplus funds?" Avasarala asked.

"He can't *quite* retire on what he's got," Holden said. "Not in luxury, anyway."

"But it's yours," Prax said, turning to Holden with something like hope. "You set up the account."

"I took the *Rocinante*'s fees already. Trust me, you paid us generously," Holden said, hand out in a gesture of refusal. "What's still in there's all yours. Well, yours and Mei's."

Avasarala scowled. That changed her personal calculus a little. She'd thought this would be the right time to lock Prax into a contract, but Jim Holden had once again ridden in at the last moment and screwed everything up.

"Congratulations," Avasarala said. "Has either of you seen Bobbie? I need to talk to her."

"Last I saw, she was heading for the machine shop."

"Thanks," Avasarala said, and kept pulling herself along. If Praxidike Meng was independently wealthy, that made him less likely to take on the job of rebuilding Ganymede for purely financial reasons. She could probably work the civic pride angle. He and his daughter were the face of the tragedy there, and having him running the show would mean more to people than all the facts and figures of how screwed they'd all be without the food supplies back online. He might be the kind of man who'd be swayed by that. She needed to think about it.

Once again, she was moving slowly and carefully enough that she heard the voices before she reached the machine shop. Bobbie and Amos, both of them laughing. She couldn't believe that she was walking in on an intimate moment, but it had that tickle-fight sound to it. Then Mei shrieked with delight, and Avasarala understood.

The machine shop was the last place in the ship, with the possible exception of engineering, that Avasarala would have thought about playing with a little girl, but there she was, arms and legs flailing through the air. Her shoulder-length black hair flowed around her in a whirl, following the gentle end-over-end spin of her body. Her face was bright with pleasure. Bobbie and Amos stood at opposite ends of the shop. As Avasarala watched, Bobbie caught the little girl out of the air and launched her back toward Amos. Soon, Avasarala thought, the girl would start losing her milk teeth. She wondered how much of all this Mei would remember when she was an adult.

"Are you people crazy?" Avasarala said as Amos caught the girl. "This isn't a playground."

"Hey there," Amos said, "we weren't planning on staying long. The captain and the doc needed a minute, so I figured I'd haul the kiddo down here. Give her the tour."

"When they send you to play catch with a child, they don't mean that she's the f— that she's the ball," Avasarala said, moving across to him. "Give that child to me. None of you people has any idea how to take care of a little girl. It's amazing you all lived to adulthood."

"Ain't wrong about that," Amos said amiably, holding out the kid.

"Come to your nana," Avasarala said.

"What's a nana?" Mei asked.

"I'm a nana," Avasarala said, gathering the child to her. Her body wanted to put the girl against her hip, to feel the weight bearing down on her. In microgravity holding a child felt odd. Good, but odd. Mei smelled of wax and vanilla. "How much longer before we can get some thrust? I feel like a f— like a balloon floating around in here."

"Soon as Alex and Naomi finish maintenance on the drive computers, we're out of here," Amos said.

"Where's my daddy?" Mei asked.

"Good," Avasarala said. "We've got a schedule to keep, and I'm not paying you people for floating lessons. Your daddy's talking to the captain, Mei-Mei."

"Where?" the girl demanded. "Where is he? I want my da!"

"I'll get you back to him, kiddo," Amos said, holding out a massive hand. He shifted his attention to Avasarala. "She's good for about five minutes, then it's 'Where's Daddy?'"

"Good," Avasarala said. "They deserve each other."

"Yeah," the big mechanic said. He pulled the child close to his center of gravity and launched up toward the galley. No handhold for him. Avasarala watched him go, then turned to Bobbie.

Bobbie floated, her hair sprayed softly out around her. Her face and body were more relaxed than Avasarala remembered ever having seen them. It should have made her seem at peace, but all she could think was that the girl looked drowned.

"Hey," Bobbie said. "Did you hear back from your tech guys on Earth?"

"I did," Avasarala said. "There was another energy spike. Bigger than the last ones. Prax was right. They are networked, and worse than that, they don't suffer lag. Venus reacted before the information about the battle could have reached it."

"Okay," Bobbie said. "That's bad, right?"

"It's weird as tits on a bishop, but who knows if it means anything? They're talking about spin-entanglement webs, whatever the hell those are. The best theory we've got is that it's like a little adrenaline rush for the protomolecule. Some part of it is involved with violence, and the rest goes on alert until it's clear the danger's passed."

"Well, then it's scared of something. Nice to know it might have a vulnerability somewhere."

They were silent for a moment. Somewhere far off in the ship, something clanged and Mei shrieked. Bobbie tensed, but Avasarala didn't. It was interesting to see people who hadn't been around a child react to Mei. They couldn't tell the difference between pleasure and alarm. Avasarala found that on this ship, she and Prax were the only experts in children's screaming.

"I was looking for you," Avasarala said.

"I'm here," Bobbie said, shrugging.

"Is that a problem?"

"I don't follow. Is what a problem?"

"That you're here?"

She looked away, her expression closing down. It was what Avasarala had expected.

"You were going down there to die, only the universe fucked you over again. You won. You're alive. None of the problems go away."

"Some of them do," Bobbie said. "Just not all. And at least we won your game."

Avasarala's cough of a laugh was enough to set her spinning slightly. She reached out to the wall and steadied her drift.

"That's the game I play. You never win. You just don't lose yet. Errinwright? He lost. Soren. Nguyen. I took them out of the game and I stayed in, but now? Errinwright's going to retire with extreme prejudice, and I'm going to be given his job."

"Do you want it?"

"It doesn't matter if I want it. I'll be offered it because if the bobble-head doesn't offer it, people will think he's slighting me. And I'll take it because if I don't, people will think I'm not hungry enough to be afraid of any longer. I'll be answering directly to the secretary-general. I'll have more power, more responsibility. More friends and more enemies. It's the price of playing."

"Seems like there should be an alternative."

"There is. I could retire."

"Why don't you?"

"Oh, I will," Avasarala said. "The day my son comes home. What about you? Are you looking to quit?"

"You mean am I still planning to get myself killed?"

"Yes, that."

There was a pause. That was good. It meant Bobbie was actually thinking about her answer.

"No," she said. "I don't think so. Going down in a fight's one thing. I can be proud of that. But just getting out to get out. I can't do that."

"You're in an interesting position," Avasarala said. "You think about what to do with it."

"And what position is that? Ronin?"

"A traitor to your government and a patriotic hero. A martyr who didn't die. A Martian whose best and only friend is about to run the government of Earth."

"You're not my only friend," Bobbie said.

"Bullshit. Alex and Amos don't count. They only want to get into your pants."

"And you don't?"

Avasarala laughed again. Bobbie was at least smiling. It was more than she'd done since she'd come back. Her sigh was deep and melancholy.

"I still feel haunted," she said. "I thought it would go away. I thought if I faced it, it would all go away."

"It doesn't go away. Ever. But you get better at it."

"At what?"

"At being haunted," Avasarala said. "Think about what you want to do. Think about who you want to become. And then see me, and I will make it happen for you if I can."

"Why?" Bobbie asked. "Seriously, why? I'm a soldier. I did the mission. And yes, it was harder and stranger than anything I've ever done, but I *got* it done. I did it because it needed doing. You don't owe me anything."

Avasarala hoisted an eyebrow.

"Political favors are how I express affection," she said.

"Okay, people," Alex's voice said across the ship's PA. "We're back up and commencing burn in thirty seconds unless someone says otherwise. Everybody get ready to weigh something."

"I appreciate the offer," Bobbie said. "But it may be a while before I know if I want to take it."

"What will you do, then? Next, I mean."

"I'm going home," she said. "I want to see my family. My dad. I think I'll stay there for a while. Figure out who I am. How to start over. Like that."

"The door's open, Bobbie. Whenever you want it, the door is open."

The flight back to Luna was a pain in the ass. Avasarala spent seven hours a day in her crash couch, sending messages back and forth against different levels of lag. On Earth, Sadavir Errinwright was quietly celebrated, his career with the UN honored with a small and private ceremony, and then he went off to spend more time with his family or farm chickens or whatever he was going to do with the remaining decades until death. Whatever it was, it wouldn't involve wielding political power.

The investigation into the Io base was ongoing, and heads were quietly rolling on Earth. But not on Mars. Whoever in the Martian government had been bidding against Errinwright, they were going to get away with it. By losing the most powerful biological weapon in human history, they'd saved their own careers. Politics was full of little ironies like that.

Avasarala put together her own new office in absentia. By the time she stepped into it, it would already have been running for a month. It felt like driving a car while sitting in the backseat. She hated it.

In addition, Mei Meng had decided she was funny, and spent part of each day monopolizing her attention. She didn't have time to play with a little girl, except that of course she did. So she did. And she had to exercise so that they wouldn't have to put her in a nursing home when she got back to a full g. The steroid cocktail gave her hot flashes and made it hard to sleep. Both her granddaughters had birthdays she could attend only on a screen. One had twenty minutes' lag; one had four.

When they passed the cloud of protomolecule monsters speeding in toward the sun, she had nightmares for two nights running, but they gradually stopped. Every one of them was being tracked by two governments, and Errinwright's little packets of death were all quiescent and speeding quietly and happily toward their own destruction.

She couldn't wait to be home.

When they docked on Luna, it was like a starving woman with a slice of apple touched to her lips, but not allowed to bite. The soft blue and white of the daylight planet, the black and gold of night. It was a beautiful world. Unmatched in the solar system. Her garden was down there. Her office. Her own bed.

But Arjun was not.

He was waiting for her on the landing pad in his best suit with a spray of fresh lilacs in his hand. The low gravity made him look younger too, if a little bloodshot about the eyes. She could feel the curiosity of Holden and his crew as she walked toward him. Who was this man that he could stand to be married to someone as abrasive and hard as Chrisjen Avasarala? Was this her master or her victim? How would that even work?

"Welcome home," Arjun said softly as she leaned into his arms.

He smelled like himself. She put her head against his shoulder, and she didn't need Earth so badly any longer.

This was home enough.

Chapter Fifty-Three: Holden

"Hi, Mom. We're on Luna!"

The light delay from Luna was less than six seconds for a round trip, but it was enough to add an awkward pause before each response. Mother Elise stared out at him from his hotel room's video screen for five long heartbeats; then her face lit up. "Jimmy! Are you coming down?"

She meant down the well. Coming home. Holden felt an ache to do exactly that. It had been years since he'd been to the farm in Montana that his parents owned. But this time he had Naomi with him, and Belters didn't go to Earth. "No, Mom, not this time. But I want all of you to come meet me up here. The shuttle ride is my treat. And UN Undersecretary Avasarala is hosting, so the accommodations are pretty posh."

When there was comm lag, it was difficult not to ramble on. The other person never sent the subtle physical cues that signaled it was their turn to talk. Holden forced himself to stop babbling and wait for a reply. Elise stared at the screen, waiting out the lag. Holden could see how much she'd aged in the years since his last trip home. Her dark brown, almost black, hair was streaked with gray, and the laugh lines around her eyes and mouth had deepened. After five seconds, she waved a hand at the screen in a dismissive gesture. "Oh, Tom will never ride a shuttle to Luna. You know that. He hates microgravity. Just come down and see us here. We'll throw a party. You can bring your friends here."

Holden smiled at her. "Mom, I need you guys to come up here because I have someone I want you to meet. Remember the woman? Naomi Nagata, the one I told you about? I told you I've been seeing her. I think it might be more than that. In fact, I'm kind of sure about it now. And now we'll be on Luna while a whole lot of political bullshit gets straightened out. I really want you guys to come up. See me, meet Naomi."

It was almost too subtle to catch, the way his mother flinched five seconds later. She covered it with a big smile. "More than that? What does that mean? Like, getting married? I always thought you'd want kids of your own someday..." She trailed off, maintaining an uncomfortably stiff smile.

"Mom," Holden said. "Earthers and Belters can have kids just fine. We're not a different species."

"Sure," she said a few seconds later, nodding too quickly. "But if you have children out there—" She stopped, her smile fading a bit.

"Then they'll be Belters," Holden said. "Yeah, you guys are just going to have to be okay with that."

After five seconds, she nodded. Again, too quickly. "Then I guess we better come up and meet this woman you're willing to leave Earth behind for. She must be very special."

"Yeah," Holden said. "She is."

Elise shifted uncomfortably for a second; then her smile came back, far less forced. "I'll get Tom on that shuttle if I have to drag him by the hair."

"I love you, Mom," Holden said. His parents had spent their whole lives on Earth. The only outer planets types they knew were the caricature villains that showed up on bad entertainment feeds. He didn't hold their ingrained prejudices against them, because he knew that meeting Naomi would be the cure for it. A few days spent in her company and they wouldn't be able to help falling in love with her. "Oh, one last thing. That data I sent you a while back? Hang on to that for me. Keep it quiet, but keep it. Depending on how things fall out over the next couple of months, I may need it."

"My parents are racists," Holden said to Naomi later that night. She lay curled against his side, her face against his ear. One long brown leg thrown across his hips.

"Okay," she whispered.

The hotel suite Avasarala had provided for them was luxurious to the point of opulence. The mattress was so soft that in the lunar gravity it was like floating on a cloud. The air recycling system pumped in subtle scents handcrafted by the hotel's in-house per-fumer. That night's selection was called Windblown Grass. It didn't exactly smell like grass to Holden, but it was nice. Just a hint of earthiness to it. Holden had a suspicion that all perfumes were named randomly, anyway. He also suspected that the hotel ran the oxygen just a little higher than normal. He felt a little *too* good.

"They're worried our babies will be Belters," he said.

"No babies," Naomi whispered. Before Holden could ask what she meant, she was snoring in his ear.

The next day, he woke before Naomi, dressed in the best suit he owned, and headed out into the station. There was one last thing he had to do before he could call this whole bloody affair truly over.

He had to see Jules Mao.

Avasarala had told him that Mao was one of several dozen high-ranking politicians, generals, and corporate leaders rounded up in the mass of arrests following Io. He was the only one Avasarala was going to see personally. And, since they'd caught him on his L5 station frantically trying to get on a fast ship to the outer planets, she'd just had him brought to her on Luna.

That day was the day of their meeting. He'd asked Avasarala if he could be there, expecting a no. Instead, she laughed a good, long time and said, "Holden, there is literally nothing I can think of that will be more humiliating to that man than having you watch me dismantle him. Fuck yes, you can come."

So Holden hurried out of the hotel and onto the streets of Lovell City. A quick pedicab ride got him to the tube station, and a twenty-minute tube ride took him to the New Hague United Nations complex. A perky young page was waiting for him when he arrived, and he was escorted efficiently through the complex's twisty maze of corridors to a door marked CONFERENCE ROOM 34.

"You can wait inside, sir," the perky page chirped at him.

"No, you know?" Holden said, clapping the boy on the shoulder. "I think I'll wait out here."

The page dipped his head slightly and bustled off down the corridor, already looking at his hand terminal for whatever his next task was. Holden leaned against the corridor wall and waited. In the low gravity, standing was hardly any more effort than sitting, and he really wanted to see Mao perp-walked down the hallway to his meeting.

His terminal buzzed, and he got a short text message from Avasarala. It said ON OUR WAY.

Less than five minutes later, Jules-Pierre Mao climbed off an elevator into the corridor, flanked by two of the largest military police officers Holden had ever seen. Mao had his hands cuffed in front of him. Even wearing a prisoner's jumpsuit, hands in restraints, and with armed guards escorting him, he managed to look arrogant and in control. As they approached, Holden stood up straight and stepped in their way. One of the MPs yanked on Mao's arm to stop him and gave Holden a subtle nod. It seemed to say, *I'm down for whatever with this guy.* Holden had a sense that if he yanked a pistol out of his pants and shot Mao right there in the corridor, the two MPs would discover they had both been struck with blindness at the same moment and failed to see anything.

But he didn't want to shoot Mao. He wanted what he always seemed to want in these situations. He wanted to know *why.*

"Was it worth it?"

Even though they were the same height, Mao managed to frown down at him. "You are?"

"Awww, come on," Holden said with a grin. "You know me. I'm James Holden. I helped bring down your pals at Protogen, and now I'm about to finish that job with you. I'm also the one that found your daughter after the protomolecule had killed her. So I'll ask again: Was it worth it?"

Mao didn't answer.

"A dead daughter, a company in ruins, millions of people slaughtered, a solar system that will probably never have peaceful stability again. *Was it worth it?*"

"Why are you here?" Mao finally asked. He looked smaller when he said it. He wouldn't make eye contact.

"I was there, in the room, when Dresden got his and I'm the man who killed your pet admiral. I just feel like there's this wonderful symmetry in being there when you get yours."

"Antony Dresden," Mao said, "was shot in the head three times execution style. Is that what passes for justice with you?"

Holden laughed. "Oh, I doubt Chrisjen Avasarala is going to shoot you in the face. Do you think what's coming will be better?"

Mao didn't reply, and Holden looked at the MP and gestured toward the conference room door. They almost looked disappointed as they pushed Mao into the room and attached his restraints to a chair.

"We'll be waiting out here, sir, if you need us," the larger of the two MPs said. They took up flanking positions next to the door.

Holden went into the conference room and took a chair, but he didn't say anything else to Mao. A few moments later, Avasarala shuffled into the room, talking on her hand terminal.

"I don't give a fuck whose birthday it is, you make this happen before my meeting is over or I'll have your nuts as paperweights." She paused as the person on the other end said something. She grinned at Mao and said, "Well, go fast, because I have a feeling my meeting will be short. Good talking to you."

She sank into a chair directly across the table from Mao. She didn't look at Holden or acknowledge him at all. He suspected that the record would never reflect his presence in the room. Avasarala put her terminal on the tabletop and leaned back in her chair. She didn't speak for several tense seconds. When she did, it was to Holden. She still didn't look at him.

"You've gotten paid for hauling me back here?"

"Payment's cleared," Holden said.

"That's good. I wanted to ask you about a longer-term contract. It would be civilian, of course, but—"

Mao cleared his throat. Avasarala smiled at him.

"I know you're there. I'll be right with you."

"I've already got a contract," Holden said. "We're escorting the first reconstruction flotilla to Ganymede. And after that, I'm thinking we'll probably be able to get another escort gig from there. Still a lot of people relocating who'd rather not get stopped by pirates along the way."

"You're sure?"

Mao's face was white with humiliation. Holden let himself enjoy it.

"I've just gotten done working for a government," Holden said. "I didn't wear it well."

"Oh please. You worked for the OPA. That's not a government, it's a rugby scrum with a currency. Yes, Jules, what is it? You need to go to the potty?"

"This is beneath you," Mao said. "I didn't come here to be insulted."

Avasarala's smile was incandescent.

"You're sure about that? Let me ask, do you remember what I said the first time we met?"

"You asked me to tell you about any involvement I might have had with the protomolecule project run by Protogen."

"No," Avasarala replied. "I mean, yes, I did ask that. But that's not the part that you should be caring about right now. You lied to me. Your involvement with weaponizing the Protogen project is fully exposed, and that question is like asking what color Tuesday was. It's meaningless."

"Let's get down to brass tacks," Mao said. "I can—"

"No," Avasarala interrupted. "The part you should be caring about is what I said just before you left. Do you remember that?"

He looked blankly up at her.

"I didn't think so. I told you that if I found out later you'd hidden something from me, I wouldn't take it well."

"Your exact words," Mao said with a mocking grin, "were 'I am not someone you want to fuck with.'"

"So you do remember," she said, not a hint of humor in her tone. "Good. This is where you get to find out what that means."

"I have additional information that could be of benefit—"

"Shut the fuck up," Avasarala said, real anger creeping into her voice for the first time. "Next time I hear your voice, I have those two big MPs in the hallway hold you down and beat you with a fucking chair. Do you understand me?"

Mao didn't reply, which showed that he did.

"You don't have any idea what you've cost me," she said. "I'm being promoted. The economic planning council? I run it now. The public health service? I never had to worry about it because that was Errinwright's pain in the ass. It's mine now. The committee on financial regulation? Mine. You've fucked up my calendar for the next two decades.

"This is not a negotiation," Avasarala continued. "This is me gloating. I'm going to drop you into a hole so deep even your wife will forget you ever existed. I'm going to use Errinwright's old position to dismantle everything you ever built, piece by piece, and scatter it to the winds. I'll make sure you get to watch it happening. The one thing your hole will have is twenty-four-hour news. And since you and I will never meet again, I want to make sure my name is on your mind every time I destroy something else you left behind. I am going to *erase* you."

Mao stared back defiantly, but Holden could see it was just a shell. Avasarala had known exactly where to hit him. Because men like him lived for their legacy. They saw themselves as the architects of the future. What Avasarala was promising was worse than death.

Mao shot a quick look at Holden, and it seemed to say, *I'll take those three shots to the head now, please.*

Holden smiled at him.

Chapter Fifty-Four: Prax

Mei sat on Prax's lap, but her attention was focused with a laser intensity to her left. She put her hand up to her mouth and gently, deliberately deposited a wad of half-chewed spaghetti into her palm, then held it out toward Amos.

"It's yucky," she said.

The big man chuckled.

"Well, if it wasn't before, it sure is now, pumpkin," he said, unfolding his napkin. "Why don't you put that right here?"

"I'm sorry," Prax said. "She's just—"

"She's just a kid, Doc," Amos said. "This is what she's supposed to do."

They didn't call the dinner a dinner. It was a reception sponsored by the United Nations at the New Hague facilities on Luna. Prax couldn't tell if the wall was a window or an ultrahigh-definition screen. On it, Earth glowed blue and white on the horizon. The tables were spread around the room in a semi-organic array that Avasarala had explained was the current fashion. *Makes it look like some asshole just put them up anywhere.*

The room was almost equally people he knew and people he didn't, and watching them segregate was fascinating in its way. To his right, several small tables were filled with short, stocky men and women in professional suits and military uniforms orbiting around Avasarala and her amused-looking husband, Arjun. They gossiped about funding-system analysis and media-relations control. Every outer planets hand they shook was an inclusion that their subjects of conversation denied. To his left, the scientific group was dressed in the best clothes they had, dress jackets that had fit ten years before, and suits representing at least half a dozen different design seasons. Earthers and Martians and Belters all mixed in that group, but the talk was just as exclusionary: nutrient grades, adjustable permeability membrane technologies, phenotypic force expressions. Those were both his people from the past and his future. The shattered and reassembled society of Ganymede. If it hadn't been for the middle table with Bobbie and the crew of the *Rocinante*, he would have been there, talking about cascade arrays and non-visible-feeding chloroplasts.

But in the center, isolated and alone, Holden and his crew were as happy and at peace as if they'd been in their own galley, burning through the vacuum. And Mei, who had taken a fancy to Amos, still wouldn't be physically parted from Prax without starting to yell and cry. Prax understood exactly how the girl felt, and didn't see it as a problem.

"So living on Ganymede, you know a lot about low-gravity childbearing, right?" Holden said. "It's not really that much riskier for Belters, is it?"

Prax swallowed a mouthful of salad and shook his head.

"Oh, no. It's tremendously difficult. Especially if it's just a shipboard situation without extensive medical controls. If you look at naturally occurring pregnancies, there's a developmental or morphological abnormality five times out of six."

"Five..." Holden said.

"Most of them are germ line issues, though," Prax said. "Nearly all of the children born on Ganymede were implanted after a full genetic analysis. If there's a lethal equivalent, they just drop the zygote and start over. Non–germ line abnormalities are only twice as common as on Earth, though, so that's not so bad."

"Ah," Holden said, looking crestfallen.

"Why do you ask?"

"No reason," Naomi said. "He's just making conversation."

"Daddy, I want tofu," Mei said, grabbing his earlobe and yanking it. "Where's tofu?"

"Let's see if we can't find you some tofu," Prax said, pushing his chair back from the table. "Come on."

As he walked across the room, scanning the crowd for a dark, formal suit belonging to a waiter as opposed to a dark, formal suit belonging to a diplomat, a young woman came up to him with a drink in one hand and a flush on her cheeks.

"You're Praxidike Meng," she said. "You probably don't remember me."

"Um. No," he said.

"I'm Carol Kiesowski," she said, touching her collarbone as if to clarify what she meant by *I.* "We wrote to each other a couple of times right after you put out the video about Mei."

"Oh, right," Prax said, trying desperately to remember anything about the woman or the comments she might have left.

"I just want to say I think both of you are just so, so brave," the woman said, nodding. It occurred to Prax that she might be drunk.

"Son of a fucking *whore*," Avasarala said, loud enough to cut through the background buzz of conversations.

The crowd turned to her. She was looking at her hand terminal.

"What's a whore, Daddy?"

"It's a kind of frost, honey," Prax said. "What's going on?"

"Holden's old boss beat us to the punch," Avasarala said. "I guess we know what happened to all those fucking missiles he stole."

Arjun touched his wife's shoulder and pointed at Prax. She actually looked abashed.

"Sorry for the language," she said. "I forgot about her."

Holden appeared at Prax's shoulder.

"My boss?"

"Fred Johnson just put on a display," Avasarala said. "Nguyen's monsters? We've been waiting for them to come closer to Mars before we took them down. Transponders are all chirping away, and we've got them all tracked tighter than a fly's...Well, they crossed into the Belt, and he nuked them. All of them."

"That's good, though," Prax said. "I mean, isn't that good?"

"Not if he's doing it," Avasarala said. "He's flexing muscles. Showing that the Belt's got an offensive arsenal now."

A man in uniform to Avasarala's left started talking at the same time as a woman just behind her, and in a moment, the need to declaim had spread through the whole group. Prax pulled away. The drunk woman was pointing at a man and talking rapidly, Prax and Mei forgotten. He found a waiter at the edge of the room, extracted a promise of tofu, and went back to his seat. Amos and Mei immediately started playing at who could blow their nose the hardest, and Prax turned to Bobbie.

"Are you going to go back to Mars, then?" he asked. It seemed like a polite, innocuous question until Bobbie pressed her lips tight and nodded.

"I am," she said. "Turns out my brother's getting married. I'm going to try to get there in time to screw up his bachelor party. What about you? Taking the old lady's position?"

"Well, I think so," Prax said, a little surprised that Bobbie had heard about Avasarala's offer. It hadn't been made public yet. "I mean, all of the basic advantages of Ganymede are still there. The magnetosphere, the ice. If even some of the mirror arrays can be salvaged, it would still be better than starting again from nothing. I mean, the thing you have to understand about Ganymede..."

Once he started on the subject, it was hard for him to stop. In many ways, Ganymede had been the center of civilization in the outer planets. All the cutting-edge plant work had been there. All the life sciences issues. But it was more than that. There was something exciting about the prospect of rebuilding that was, in its fashion, even more interesting than the initial growth. To do something the first time was an exploration. To do it again was to take all the things they had learned, and refine, improve, perfect. It left Prax a little bit giddy. Bobbie listened with a melancholy smile on her face.

And it wasn't only Ganymede. All of human civilization had been built out of the ruins of what had come before. Life itself was a grand chemical improvisation that began with the simplest replicators and grew and collapsed and grew again. Catastrophe was just one part of what always happened. It was a prelude to what came next.

"You make it sound romantic," Bobbie said, and the way she said it was almost an accusation.

"I don't mean to—" Prax began, and something cold and wet wriggled its way into his ear. He pulled back with a yelp, turning to face Mei's bright eyes and brilliant smile. Her index finger dripped with saliva, and beyond her Amos was laughing himself crimson, one hand grasping at his belly and the other slapping the table hard enough to make the plates rattle.

"What was *that*?"

"Hi, Daddy. I love you."

"Here," Alex said, passing Prax a clean napkin. "You're gonna want that."

The startling thing was the silence. He didn't know how long it had been going on, but the awareness of it washed over him like a wave. The political half of the room was still and quiet. Through the forest of their bodies, he saw Avasarala bending forward, her elbows on her knees, her hand terminal inches in front of her face. When she stood up, they parted before her. She was such a small woman, but she commanded the room just by walking out of it.

"That's not good," Holden said, rising to his feet. Without another word, Prax and Naomi, Amos and Alex and Bobbie all followed after her. The politicians and the scientists came too, all of them mixing at last.

The meeting room was across a wide hall and set up in the model of an ancient Greek amphitheater. The podium at the front stood before a massive high-definition screen. Avasarala marched down to a seat, talking fast and low into her hand terminal. The others trailed in after her. The sense of dread was physical. The screen went black and someone dimmed the lights.

In the darkness of the screen, Venus stood in near silhouette against the sun. It was an image Prax had seen hundreds of times before. The feed could have come from any of a dozen monitoring stations. The time stamp on the lower left said they were looking back in time forty-seven minutes. A ship name, the *Celestine*, floated beneath the numbers.

Every time the protomolecule soldiers had been involved in violence, Venus had reacted. The OPA had just destroyed a hundred of its half-human soldiers. Prax felt himself caught between excitement and dread.

The image scattered and re-formed, some kind of interference confusing the sensors. Avasarala said something sharp that could have been *show me*. A few seconds later, the image stopped and reframed. A detail screen showing a gray-green ship. A heads-up display marked it the *Merman*. The image scattered again, and when it re-formed, the *Merman* had moved half an inch to the left and was spinning end over end, tumbling. Avasarala spoke again. A few seconds' lag, and the screen went back to its original image. Now that Prax knew to look, he could see the tiny dot of the *Merman* moving near the penumbra. There were other tiny specks like it.

The dark side of Venus pulsed like a sudden, planetary flash of lightning under the obscuring clouds. And then it glowed.

Vast filaments thousands of kilometers long like spokes on a wheel lit white and vanished. The clouds of Venus shifted, disturbed from below. Prax had the powerful memory of seeing a wake on the surface of a water tank when a fish passed close underneath. Vast and glowing, it rose through the cloud cover. Spoke-like strands of iridescence arced with vast lightning storms, coming together like the arms of an octopus but connected to a rigid central node. Once it had climbed out of Venus' thick cloud cover, it launched itself away from the sun, toward the viewing ship, but passing it. The other ships in its path were scattered and hurled away. A long plume of displaced Venusian atmosphere caught the sun and glowed like snowflakes and slivers of ice. Prax tried to make sense of the scale. As large as Ceres Station. As large as Ganymede. Larger. It folded its arms—its tentacles—together, accelerating without any visible drive plume. It swam in the void. His heart was racing, but his body was still as stone.

Mei patted his cheek with her open palm and pointed to the screen.

"What's that?" she asked.

Epilogue: Holden

Holden started the replay again. The wall screen in the *Roci-nante*'s galley was too small to really catch all the details of the high-resolution imagery the *Celestine* had taken. But Holden couldn't stop watching it no matter what room he was in. An ignored cup of coffee cooled on the table in front of him next to the sandwich he hadn't eaten.

Venus flashed with light in an intricate pattern. The heavy cloud cover swirled as though caught in a planetwide storm. And then it rose from the surface, pulling a thick contrail of Venus' atmosphere in its wake.

"Come to bed," Naomi said, then leaned forward in her chair and took his hand. "Get some sleep."

"It's so big. And the way it swatted all those ships out of the way. Effortless, like a whale swimming through a school of guppies."

"Can you do anything about it?"

"This is the end, Naomi," Holden said, pulling his eyes away from the screen to look at her. "What if this is the end? This isn't some alien virus anymore. This thing is what the protomolecule came here to make. This is what it was going to hijack all life on the Earth to make. It could be *anything*."

"Can you do anything about it?" she repeated. Her words were harsh, but her voice was kind and she squeezed his fingers affectionately.

Holden turned back to the screen, restarting the image. A dozen ships blew away from Venus as though a massive wind had caught them and sent them spinning like leaves. The surface of the atmosphere began to roil and twist.

"Okay," Naomi said, standing up. "I'm going to bed. Don't wake me when you come in. I'm exhausted."

Holden nodded to her without looking away from the video feed. The massive shape folded itself into a streamlined dart, like a piece of wet cloth plucked up from the center, then flew away. The Venus it left behind looked diminished, somehow. As though something vital had been stolen from it to construct the alien artifact.

And here it was. After all the fighting, with human civilization left in chaos just from its presence, the protomolecule had finished the job it came billions of years before to do. Would humanity survive it? Would the protomolecule even notice them, now that it had finished its grand work?

It wasn't the ending of one thing that left Holden terrified. It was the prospect of something beginning that was utterly outside the human experience. Whatever happened next, no one could be prepared for it.

It scared the hell out of him.

Behind him, a man cleared his throat.

Holden turned reluctantly away from the image on the screen. The man stood next to the galley refrigerator as if he'd always been there, rumpled gray suit and dented porkpie hat. A bright blue firefly flew off his cheek, then hung in the air beside him. He waved it away like it was a gnat. His expression was one of discomfort and apology.

"Hey," Detective Miller said. "We gotta talk."

Acknowledgments

The process of making a book is never as solitary as it seems. This book and this series wouldn't exist without the hard work of Shawna McCarthy and Danny Baror and the support and dedication of DongWon Song, Anne Clarke, Alex Lencicki, the inimitable Jack Womack, and the brilliant crew at Orbit. Also gratitude goes to Carrie, Kat, and Jayné for feedback and support, and also to the whole Sakeriver gang. Much of the cool in the book belongs to them. The errors and infelicities and egregious fudging was all us.

extras

orbit

meet the author

JAMES S. A. COREY is the pen name of fantasy author Daniel Abraham and Ty Franck. They both live in Albuquerque, New Mexico. Find out more about this series at www.the-expanse.com.

introducing

If you enjoyed
CALIBAN'S WAR,
look out for

ABADDON'S GATE

Book Three of The Expanse

by James S. A. Corey

PROLOGUE: MANÉO

Manéo Jung-Espinoza—Néo to his friends back on Ceres Station—huddled in the cockpit of the little ship he'd christened the *Y Que*. After almost three months, there was maybe fifty hours left before he made history. The food had run out two days before. The only water that was left to drink was half a liter of recycled piss that had already gone through him more times than he could count. Everything he could turn off, he'd turned off. The reactor was shut down. He still had passive monitors, but no active sensor arrays. The only light in the cockpit came from the backsplash of the display terminals. The blanket he'd wrapped himself in, corners tucked into his restraints so it wouldn't float away, wasn't even powered. His broadcast and tight-beam transmitters were both shut off, and he'd slagged the transponder even before he'd painted the name on her hull. He hadn't flown this far just to have some kind of accidental blip alert the flotillas that he was coming.

Fifty hours—less than that—and the only thing he had to do was not be seen. And not run into anything, but that part was in *los manos de Dios*.

His cousin Evita had been the one who'd introduced him to the underground society of slingshots. That had been three years earlier, just before his fifteenth birthday. He'd been hanging at his family hole, his mother gone to work at the water treatment plant, his father at a meeting with the grid maintenance group he oversaw. Néo had stayed home, cutting school for the fourth time in a month. When the system announced someone waiting at the door, he'd figured it was school security busting him for being truant. Instead, Evita was there.

She was two years older and his mother's sister's kid. A real Belter. They had the same long, thin bodies, but she was *from* there. He'd had a thing for Evita since the first time he saw her. He'd had dreams about what she'd look like with her clothes off. What it would feel like to kiss her. Now here she was, and the place to himself. His heart was going three times standard before he opened the door.

"Esá, unokabátya," she said, smiling and shrugging with one hand.

"Hoy," he'd said, trying to act cool and calm. He'd grown up in the massive city in space that was Ceres Station, just the way she had, but his father had the low, squat frame that marked him as an Earther. He had as much right to the cosmopolitan slang of the Belt as she had, but it sounded natural on her. When he said it, it was like he was putting on someone else's jacket.

"Some cayos meeting down portside. Silvestari Campos back," she said, her hip cocked, her mouth soft as a pillow, and her lips shining. "Doch mit?"

"Que no?" he'd said. "Got nothing better."

He'd figured out afterward that she'd brought him because Mila Sana, a horse-faced Martian girl a little younger than him, had a thing, and they all thought it was funny to watch the ugly inner girl padding around after the half-breed, but by then he didn't care. He'd met Silvestari Campos and he'd heard of slingshotting.

Went like this: Some coyo put together a boat. Maybe it was salvage. Maybe it was fabbed. Probably at least some of it was stolen. Didn't need to be much more than a torch drive, a crash couch, and enough air and water to get the job done. Then it was all about plotting the trajectory. Without an Epstein, a torch drive burned pellets too fast to get anyone anywhere. At least without help. The trick was to plot it so that the burn—and the best only ever used one burn—would put the ship through a gravity assist, suck up the velocity of a planet, and head out as deep as the push would take them. Then figure out how to get back without getting dead. Whole thing got tracked by a double-encrypted black net as hard to break as anything that the Loca Greiga or Golden Bough had on offer. Maybe they ran it. It was illegal as hell, and somebody was taking the bets. Dangerous, which was the point. And then when you got back, everyone knew who you were. You could lounge around in the warehouse party and drink whatever you wanted and talk however you wanted and drape your hand on Evita Jung's right tit and she wouldn't even move it off.

And just like that, Néo, who hadn't ever cared about anything very much, developed an ambition.

"The thing people have to remember is that the Ring isn't magical," the Martian woman said. Néo had spent a lot of time in the past months watching the newsfeeds about the Ring, and so far, he liked her the best. Pretty face. Nice accent. She wasn't as thick as an Earther, but she didn't belong to the Belt either. Like him. "We don't entirely understand it yet, and we may not for decades. But the last two years have given us some of the most interesting and exciting breakthroughs in materials technology since the wheel. Within the next ten or fifteen years, we're going to start seeing the applications of what we've learned from watching the protomolecule, and it will—"

"Fruit. Of. A poisoned. Tree," the old, leathery-looking coyo beside her said. "We cannot allow ourselves to forget that this was built from mass murder. The criminals and monsters at Protogen and Mao-Kwik released this weapon on a population of innocents.

That slaughter began all of this, and profiting from it makes us all complicit."

The feed cut to the moderator, who smiled and shook his head at the leathery one.

"Rabbi Kimble," the moderator said, "we've had contact with an undisputed alien artifact that took over Eros Station, spent a little over a year preparing itself in the vicious pressure cooker of Venus, then launched a massive complex of structures just outside the orbit of Uranus and built a thousand-kilometer-wide ring. You can't be suggesting that we are morally required to ignore those facts."

"Himmler's hypothermia experiments at Dachau—" the leathery coyo began, wagging his finger in the air, but now it was the pretty Martian's turn to interrupt.

"Can we move past the 1940s, please?" she said, smiling in a way that said, *I'm being friendly but shut the fuck up.* "We're not talking about space Nazis here. This is the single most important event in human history. Protogen's role in it was terrible, and they've been punished for it. But now we have to—"

"Not *space* Nazis!" the old coyo yelled. "The Nazis aren't from *space*. They are right here among us. They are the beasts of our worst nature. By profiting from these discoveries, we *legitimize* the path by which we came to them."

The pretty one rolled her eyes and looked at the moderator like she wanted help. The moderator shrugged at her, which only made the old one angrier.

"The Ring is a temptation to sin," the old coyo shouted. There were little flecks of white at the corners of his mouth, which the video editor had chosen to leave visible.

"We don't know what it is," the pretty one said. "Given that it was intended to do its work on primordial Earth with single-celled organisms and wound up on Venus with an infinitely more complex substrate, it probably doesn't work at all, but I can say that temptation and sin have nothing to do with it."

"They are victims. Your 'complex substrate'? It is the corrupted bodies of the innocent!"

Néo turned down the feed volume and just watched them gesture at each other for a while.

It had taken him months to plan out the trajectory of the *Y Que*, finding the time when Jupiter, Europa, and Saturn were all in the right positions. The window was so narrow it had been like throwing a dart from a half klick away and pinning a fruit fly's wing with it. Europa had been the trick. A close pass on the Jovian moon, then down so close to the gas giant that there was almost drag. Then out again for the long trip past Saturn, sucking more juice out of its orbital velocity, and then farther out into the black, not accelerating again, but going faster than anyone would imagine a little converted rock hopper could manage. Through millions of klicks of vacuum to hit a bull's-eye smaller than a mosquito's asshole.

Néo imagined the expressions of all the science and military ships parked around the Ring when a little ship, no transponder and flying ballistic, appeared out of nowhere and shot straight through the Ring at 150 thousand kilometers per hour. After that, he'd have to move fast. He didn't have enough fuel left to kill all his velocity, but he'd slow down enough that they could get a rescue ship to him.

He'd do some time in slam, that was sure. Maybe two years, if the magistrates were being pissy. It was worth it, though. Just the messages from the black net, where all his friends were tracking him with the constant and rising chorus of *Holy Shit It's Going to Work*, made it worth it. He was going down in history. In a hundred years, people were still going to be talking about the biggest-balled slingshot ever. He'd lost months building the *Y Que*, more than that in transit, then jail time after. It was worth it. He was going to live forever.

Twenty hours.

The biggest danger was the flotilla surrounding the Ring. Earth and Mars had kicked each other's navies into creaky old men months earlier, but what was left was mostly around the Ring. Or else down in the inner planets, but Néo didn't care about them. There were maybe twenty or thirty big military ships watching each other while every science vessel in the system peeked and listened and floated gently a couple thousand klicks from the Ring. All the Navy muscle there to make sure no one touched. No one even got close. Scared, all of them. Even with all that metal and ceramic crammed into the same tiny corner of space, even with the relatively tiny thousand klicks across that was the inner face of the Ring, the chances that he'd run into anything were tiny. There was a lot more nothing than something. And if he did hit one of the flotilla ships, he wasn't going to be around to worry about it, so he just gave it up to *Dios y la Virgen María* and started setting up the high-speed camera. When it finally happened, it would be so fast he wouldn't even know whether he'd made the mark until he analyzed the data. And he was making sure there was going to be a record. He turned his transmitters back on.

"Hoy," he said into the camera, "Néo here. Néo solo. Captain and crew of souverän Belt-racer *Y Que*. Mielista me. Got six hours until biggest slipper since God made man. Esta being for me Mama, the sweet Sophia Brun, and Jesus our lord and savior. Watch close. Blink it and miss, que sa?"

He watched the file. He looked like crap. He probably had time; he could shave the ratty little beard off and at least tie back his hair. He wished now he'd kept up with his daily exercises so he wouldn't look so chicken-shouldered. Too late now. Still, he could mess with the camera angle. He was ballistic. Wasn't like there was any thrust gravity to worry about.

He tried again from two other angles until his vanity was satisfied, then switched to the external cameras. His introduction was a little over ten seconds long. He'd start the broadcast twenty seconds out, then switch to the exterior cameras. More than a thousand frames per second, and it still might miss the Ring between images. He had to hope for the best. Wasn't like he could get another camera now, even if a better one existed.

He drank the rest of his water and wished that he'd packed just a little more food. A tube of protein slush would have gone down really well. It'd be done soon. He'd be in some Earther or Martian brig where there would be a decent toilet and water to drink and prisoners' rations. He was almost looking forward to it.

His sleeping comm array woke up and squawked about a tight-beam. He opened the connection. The encryption meant it was from the black net and sent long enough before that it would reach him here. Someone besides him was showing off.

Evita was still beautiful, but more like a woman now than she'd been when he'd started getting money and salvage to build the *Y Que*. Another five years, she'd be plain. He'd still have a thing for her, though.

"Esá, unokabátya," she said. "Eyes of the world. Toda auge. Mine too."

She smiled, and just for a second, he thought maybe she'd lift her shirt. For good luck. The tightbeam dropped.

Two hours.

"I repeat, this is Martian frigate *Lucien* to the unidentified ship approaching the Ring. Respond immediately or we will open fire."

Three minutes. They'd seen him too soon. The Ring was still three minutes away, and they weren't supposed to see him until he had less than one.

Néo cleared his throat.

"No need, que sa? No need. This is the *Y Que*, racer out sa Ceres Station."

"Your transponder isn't on, *Y Que*."

"Busted, yeah? Need some help with that."

"Your radio's working just fine, but I'm not hearing a distress beacon."

"Not distressed," he said, pulling the syllables out for every extra second. He could keep them talking. "Ballistic is all. Can fire up the reactor, but it's going to take a couple minutes. Maybe you can come give a hand, eh?"

"You are in restricted space, *Y Que*," the Martian said, and Néo felt the grin growing on his face.

"No harm," Néo said. "No harm. Surrender. Just got to get slowed down a little. Firing it up in a few seconds. Hold your piss."

"You have ten seconds to change trajectory away from the Ring or we will open fire."

The fear felt like victory. He was doing it. He was on target for the Ring and it was freaking them out. One minute. He started warming up the reactor. At this point, he wasn't even lying anymore. The full suite of sensors started their boot sequence.

"Don't fire," he said as he made a private jacking-off motion. "Please, sir, please don't shoot me. I'm slowing down as fast as I can."

"You have five seconds, *Y Que*."

He had thirty seconds. The friend-or-foe screens popped up as soon as the full ship system was on. The *Lucien* was going to pass close by. Maybe seven hundred klicks. No wonder they'd seen him. At that distance, the *Y Que* would light up the threat boards like it was Christmas. Just bad luck, that.

"You can shoot if you want, but I'm stopping as fast as I can," he said.

The status alarm sounded. Two new dots appeared on the display. *Hijo de puta* had actually launched torpedoes.

Fifteen seconds. He was going to make it. He started the broadcast and the exterior camera. The Ring was out there somewhere, its thousand-kilometer span still too small and dark to make out with the naked eye. There was only the vast spill of stars.

"Hold fire!" he shouted at the Martian frigate. "Hold fire!"

Three seconds. The torpedoes were gaining fast.

One second.

As one, the stars all blinked out.

Néo tapped the monitor. Nothing. Friend-or-foe didn't show anything. No frigate. No torpedoes. Nothing.

"Now that," he said to no one and nothing, "is weird."

On the monitor, something glimmered blue, and he pulled himself closer, as if being a few inches closer to the screen would make it all make sense.

The sensors that triggered the high-g alert took five-hundredths of a second to trip. The alert, hardwired, took another three-hundredths of a second to react, pushing power to the red LED and the emergency Klaxon. The little console telltale that pegged out with a ninety-nine-g deceleration warning took a glacial half second to excite its light-emitting diodes. But by that time Néo was already a red smear inside the cockpit. The ship's deceleration throwing him forward through the screen and into the far bulkhead in less time than it took a synapse to fire.

In the unbroken darkness, the exterior high-speed camera kept up its broadcast, sending out a thousand frames per second of nothing.

And then, of something else.

It took two hours with a torch and prying tools from the machine shop to cut through the hatch.

With the hydraulics compromised, she had to crank it open by hand. A gust of warm wet air blew out, carrying a hospital scent without the antiseptic. A coppery, nauseating smell. The torture chamber, then. Her friends would be inside, beaten or cut to pieces. Julie hefted her wrench and prepared to bust open at least one head before they killed her. She floated down.

The engineering deck was huge, vaulted like a cathedral. The fusion reactor dominated the central space. Something was wrong with it. Where she expected to see readouts, shielding, and monitors, a layer of something like mud seemed to flow over the reactor core. Slowly, Julie floated toward it, one hand still on the ladder. The strange smell became overpowering.

The mud caked around the reactor had structure to it like nothing she'd seen before. Tubes ran through it like veins or airways. Parts of it pulsed. Not mud, then.

Flesh.

An outcropping of the thing shifted toward her. Compared to the whole, it seemed no larger than a toe, a little finger. It was Captain Darren's head.

"Help me," it said.

LEVIATHAN WAKES

BOOK ONE OF THE EXPANSE

JAMES S. A. COREY

![orbit]

orbit

www.orbitbooks.net

Orbit
Hachette Book Group
1290 Avenue of the Americas, New York, NY 10104
HachetteBookGroup.com

First Edition: June 2011

Orbit is an imprint of Hachette Book Group, Inc. The Orbit name and logo are trademarks of Little, Brown Book Group Limited.

Library of Congress Cataloging-in-Publication Data
Corey, James S. A.
  Leviathan wakes / James S. A. Corey.—1st ed.
    p. cm.
  ISBN 978-0-316-12908-4
  1. Interplanetary voyages—Fiction.   2. Space warfare—Fiction.   I. Title.
  PS3601.B677L48 2011
  813'.6—dc22

                                                                    2010046442

20 19 18 17

Printed in the United States of America

*For Jayné and Kat, who encourage me
to daydream about spaceships*

Prologue: Julie

The *Scopuli* had been taken eight days ago, and Julie Mao was finally ready to be shot.

It had taken all eight days trapped in a storage locker for her to get to that point. For the first two she'd remained motionless, sure that the armored men who'd put her there had been serious. For the first hours, the ship she'd been taken aboard wasn't under thrust, so she floated in the locker, using gentle touches to keep herself from bumping into the walls or the atmosphere suit she shared the space with. When the ship began to move, thrust giving her weight, she'd stood silently until her legs cramped, then sat down slowly into a fetal position. She'd peed in her jumpsuit, not caring about the warm itchy wetness, or the smell, worrying only that she might slip and fall in the wet spot it left on the floor. She couldn't make noise. They'd shoot her.

On the third day, thirst had forced her into action. The noise of the ship was all around her. The faint subsonic rumble of the reactor and drive. The constant hiss and thud of hydraulics and steel bolts as the pressure doors between decks opened and closed. The clump of heavy boots walking on metal decking. She waited until all the noise she could hear sounded distant, then pulled the environment suit off its hooks and onto the locker floor. Listening for any approaching sound, she slowly disassembled the suit and took out the water supply. It was old and stale; the suit obviously hadn't been used or serviced in ages. But she hadn't had a sip in days, and the warm loamy water in the suit's reservoir bag was the best thing she had ever tasted. She had to work hard not to gulp it down and make herself vomit.

When the urge to urinate returned, she pulled the catheter bag out of the suit and relieved herself into it. She sat on the floor, now cushioned by the padded suit and almost comfortable, and wondered who her captors were—Coalition Navy, pirates, something worse. Sometimes she slept.

On day four, isolation, hunger, boredom, and the diminishing number of places to store her piss finally pushed her to make contact with them. She'd heard muffled cries of pain. Somewhere nearby, her shipmates were being beaten or tortured. If she got the attention of the kidnappers, maybe they would just take her to the others. That was okay. Beatings, she could handle. It seemed like a small price to pay if it meant seeing people again.

The locker sat beside the inner airlock door. During flight, that usually wasn't a high-traffic area, though she didn't know anything about the layout of this particular ship. She thought about what to say, how to present herself. When she finally heard someone moving toward her, she just tried to yell that she wanted out. The dry rasp that came out of her throat surprised her. She swallowed, working her tongue to try to create some saliva, and tried again. Another faint rattle in the throat.

The people were right outside her locker door. A voice was

talking quietly. Julie had pulled back a fist to bang on the door when she heard what it was saying.

No. Please no. Please don't.

Dave. Her ship's mechanic. Dave, who collected clips from old cartoons and knew a million jokes, begging in a small broken voice.

No, please no, please don't, he said.

Hydraulics and locking bolts clicked as the inner airlock door opened. A meaty thud as something was thrown inside. Another click as the airlock closed. A hiss of evacuating air.

When the airlock cycle had finished, the people outside her door walked away. She didn't bang to get their attention.

They'd scrubbed the ship. Detainment by the inner planet navies was a bad scenario, but they'd all trained on how to deal with it. Sensitive OPA data was scrubbed and overwritten with innocuous-looking logs with false time stamps. Anything too sensitive to trust to a computer, the captain destroyed. When the attackers came aboard, they could play innocent.

It hadn't mattered.

There weren't the questions about cargo or permits. The invaders had come in like they owned the place, and Captain Darren had rolled over like a dog. Everyone else—Mike, Dave, Wan Li— they'd all just thrown up their hands and gone along quietly. The pirates or slavers or whatever they were had dragged them off the little transport ship that had been her home, and down a docking tube without even minimal environment suits. The tube's thin layer of Mylar was the only thing between them and hard nothing: hope it didn't rip; goodbye lungs if it did.

Julie had gone along too, but then the bastards had tried to lay their hands on her, strip her clothes off.

Five years of low-gravity jiu jitsu training and them in a confined space with no gravity. She'd done a lot of damage. She'd almost started to think she might win when from nowhere a gauntleted fist smashed into her face. Things got fuzzy after that. Then the locker, and *Shoot her if she makes a noise.* Four days of not making noise while they beat her friends down below and then threw one of them out an airlock.

After six days, everything went quiet.

Shifting between bouts of consciousness and fragmented dreams, she was only vaguely aware as the sounds of walking, talking, and pressure doors and the subsonic rumble of the reactor and the drive faded away a little at a time. When the drive stopped, so did gravity, and Julie woke from a dream of racing her old pinnace to find herself floating while her muscles screamed in protest and then slowly relaxed.

She pulled herself to the door and pressed her ear to the cold metal. Panic shot through her until she caught the quiet sound of the air recyclers. The ship still had power and air, but the drive wasn't on and no one was opening a door or walking or talking. Maybe it was a crew meeting. Or a party on another deck. Or everyone was in engineering, fixing a serious problem.

She spent a day listening and waiting.

By day seven, her last sip of water was gone. No one on the ship had moved within range of her hearing for twenty-four hours. She sucked on a plastic tab she'd ripped off the environment suit until she worked up some saliva; then she started yelling. She yelled herself hoarse.

No one came.

By day eight, she was ready to be shot. She'd been out of water for two days, and her waste bag had been full for four. She put her shoulders against the back wall of the locker and planted her hands against the side walls. Then she kicked out with both legs as hard as she could. The cramps that followed the first kick almost made her pass out. She screamed instead.

Stupid girl, she told herself. She was dehydrated. Eight days without activity was more than enough to start atrophy. At least she should have stretched out.

She massaged her stiff muscles until the knots were gone, then stretched, focusing her mind like she was back in dojo. When she was in control of her body, she kicked again. And again. And again, until light started to show through the edges of the locker. And again, until the door was so bent that the three hinges and the locking bolt were the only points of contact between it and the frame.

And one last time, so that it bent far enough that the bolt was no longer seated in the hasp and the door swung free.

Julie shot from the locker, hands half raised and ready to look either threatening or terrified, depending on which seemed more useful.

There was no one on the whole deck: the airlock, the suit storage room where she'd spent the last eight days, a half dozen other storage rooms. All empty. She plucked a magnetized pipe wrench of suitable size for skull cracking out of an EVA kit, then went down the crew ladder to the deck below.

And then the one below that, and then the one below that. Personnel cabins in crisp, almost military order. Commissary, where there were signs of a struggle. Medical bay, empty. Torpedo bay. No one. The comm station was unmanned, powered down, and locked. The few sensor logs that still streamed showed no sign of the *Scopuli*. A new dread knotted her gut. Deck after deck and room after room empty of life. Something had happened. A radiation leak. Poison in the air. Something that had forced an evacuation. She wondered if she'd be able to fly the ship by herself.

But if they'd evacuated, she'd have heard them going out the airlock, wouldn't she?

She reached the final deck hatch, the one that led into engineering, and stopped when the hatch didn't open automatically. A red light on the lock panel showed that the room had been sealed from the inside. She thought again about radiation and major failures. But if either of those was the case, why lock the door from the inside? And she had passed wall panel after wall panel. None of them had been flashing warnings of any kind. No, not radiation, something else.

There was more disruption here. Blood. Tools and containers in disarray. Whatever had happened, it had happened here. No, it had started here. And it had ended behind that locked door.

It took two hours with a torch and prying tools from the machine shop to cut through the hatch to engineering. With the hydraulics compromised, she had to crank it open by hand. A gust of warm wet air blew out, carrying a hospital scent without the antiseptic. A coppery, nauseating smell. The torture chamber, then. Her friends would be inside, beaten or cut to pieces. Julie hefted her wrench and prepared to bust open at least one head before they killed her. She floated down.

The engineering deck was huge, vaulted like a cathedral. The fusion reactor dominated the central space. Something was wrong with it. Where she expected to see readouts, shielding, and monitors, a layer of something like mud seemed to flow over the reactor core. Slowly, Julie floated toward it, one hand still on the ladder. The strange smell became overpowering.

The mud caked around the reactor had structure to it like nothing she'd seen before. Tubes ran through it like veins or airways. Parts of it pulsed. Not mud, then.

Flesh.

An outcropping of the thing shifted toward her. Compared to the whole, it seemed no larger than a toe, a little finger. It was Captain Darren's head.

"Help me," it said.

Chapter One: Holden

A hundred and fifty years before, when the parochial disagreements between Earth and Mars had been on the verge of war, the Belt had been a far horizon of tremendous mineral wealth beyond viable economic reach, and the outer planets had been beyond even the most unrealistic corporate dream. Then Solomon Epstein had built his little modified fusion drive, popped it on the back of his three-man yacht, and turned it on. With a good scope, you could still see his ship going at a marginal percentage of the speed of light, heading out into the big empty. The best, longest funeral in the history of mankind. Fortunately, he'd left the plans on his home computer. The Epstein Drive hadn't given humanity the stars, but it had delivered the planets.

Three-quarters of a kilometer long, a quarter of a kilometer wide—roughly shaped like a fire hydrant—and mostly empty space inside, the *Canterbury* was a retooled colony transport.

Once, it had been packed with people, supplies, schematics, machines, environment bubbles, and hope. Just under twenty million people lived on the moons of Saturn now. The *Canterbury* had hauled nearly a million of their ancestors there. Forty-five million on the moons of Jupiter. One moon of Uranus sported five thousand, the farthest outpost of human civilization, at least until the Mormons finished their generation ship and headed for the stars and freedom from procreation restrictions.

And then there was the Belt.

If you asked OPA recruiters when they were drunk and feeling expansive, they might say there were a hundred million in the Belt. Ask an inner planet census taker, it was nearer to fifty million. Any way you looked, the population was huge and needed a lot of water.

So now the *Canterbury* and her dozens of sister ships in the Pur'n'Kleen Water Company made the loop from Saturn's generous rings to the Belt and back hauling glaciers, and would until the ships aged into salvage wrecks.

Jim Holden saw some poetry in that.

"Holden?"

He turned back to the hangar deck. Chief Engineer Naomi Nagata towered over him. She stood almost two full meters tall, her mop of curly hair tied back into a black tail, her expression halfway between amusement and annoyance. She had the Belter habit of shrugging with her hands instead of her shoulders.

"Holden, are you listening, or just staring out the window?"

"There was a problem," Holden said. "And because you're really, really good, you can fix it even though you don't have enough money or supplies."

Naomi laughed.

"So you weren't listening," she said.

"Not really, no."

"Well, you got the basics right anyhow. *Knight*'s landing gear isn't going to be good in atmosphere until I can get the seals replaced. That going to be a problem?"

"I'll ask the old man," Holden said. "But when's the last time we used the shuttle in atmosphere?"

"Never, but regs say we need at least one atmo-capable shuttle."

"Hey, Boss!" Amos Burton, Naomi's earthborn assistant, yelled from across the bay. He waved one meaty arm in their general direction. He meant Naomi. Amos might be on Captain McDowell's ship; Holden might be executive officer; but in Amos Burton's world, only Naomi was boss.

"What's the matter?" Naomi shouted back.

"Bad cable. Can you hold this little fucker in place while I get the spare?"

Naomi looked at Holden, *Are we done here?* in her eyes. He snapped a sarcastic salute and she snorted, shaking her head as she walked away, her frame long and thin in her greasy coveralls.

Seven years in Earth's navy, five years working in space with civilians, and he'd never gotten used to the long, thin, improbable bones of Belters. A childhood spent in gravity shaped the way he saw things forever.

At the central lift, Holden held his finger briefly over the button for the navigation deck, tempted by the prospect of Ade Tukunbo—her smile, her voice, the patchouli-and-vanilla scent she used in her hair—but pressed the button for the infirmary instead. Duty before pleasure.

Shed Garvey, the medical tech, was hunched over his lab table, debriding the stump of Cameron Paj's left arm, when Holden walked in. A month earlier, Paj had gotten his elbow pinned by a thirty-ton block of ice moving at five millimeters a second. It wasn't an uncommon injury among people with the dangerous job of cutting and moving zero-g icebergs, and Paj was taking the whole thing with the fatalism of a professional. Holden leaned over Shed's shoulder to watch as the tech plucked one of the medical maggots out of dead tissue.

"What's the word?" Holden asked.

"It's looking pretty good, sir," Paj said. "I've still got a few nerves. Shed's been tellin' me about how the prosthetic is gonna hook up to it."

"Assuming we can keep the necrosis under control," the medic said, "and make sure Paj doesn't heal up too much before we get to Ceres. I checked the policy, and Paj here's been signed on long enough to get one with force feedback, pressure and temperature sensors, fine-motor software. The whole package. It'll be almost as good as the real thing. The inner planets have a new biogel that regrows the limb, but that isn't covered in our medical plan."

"Fuck the Inners, and fuck their magic Jell-O. I'd rather have a good Belter-built fake than anything those bastards grow in a lab. Just wearing their fancy arm probably turns you into an asshole," Paj said. Then he added, "Oh, uh, no offense, XO."

"None taken. Just glad we're going to get you fixed up," Holden said.

"Tell him the other bit," Paj said with a wicked grin. Shed blushed.

"I've, ah, heard from other guys who've gotten them," Shed said, not meeting Holden's eyes. "Apparently there's a period while you're still building identification with the prosthetic when whacking off feels just like getting a hand job."

Holden let the comment hang in the air for a second while Shed's ears turned crimson.

"Good to know," Holden said. "And the necrosis?"

"There's some infection," Shed said. "The maggots are keeping it under control, and the inflammation's actually a good thing in this context, so we're not fighting too hard unless it starts to spread."

"Is he going to be ready for the next run?" Holden asked.

For the first time, Paj frowned.

"Shit yes, I'll be ready. I'm always ready. This is what I *do,* sir."

"Probably," Shed said. "Depending on how the bond takes. If not this one, the one after."

"Fuck that," Paj said. "I can buck ice one-handed better than half the skags you've got on this bitch."

"Again," Holden said, suppressing a grin, "good to know. Carry on."

Paj snorted. Shed plucked another maggot free. Holden went back to the lift, and this time he didn't hesitate.

The navigation station of the *Canterbury* didn't dress to impress. The great wall-sized displays Holden had imagined when he'd first volunteered for the navy did exist on capital ships but, even there, more as an artifact of design than need. Ade sat at a pair of screens only slightly larger than a hand terminal, graphs of the efficiency and output of the *Canterbury*'s reactor and engine updating in the corners, raw logs spooling on the right as the systems reported in. She wore thick headphones that covered her ears, the faint thump of the bass line barely escaping. If the *Canterbury* sensed an anomaly, it would alert her. If a system errored, it would alert her. If Captain McDowell left the command and control deck, it would alert her so she could turn the music off and look busy when he arrived. Her petty hedonism was only one of a thousand things that made Ade attractive to Holden. He walked up behind her, pulled the headphones gently away from her ears, and said, "Hey."

Ade smiled, tapped her screen, and dropped the headphones to rest around her long slim neck like technical jewelry.

"Executive Officer James Holden," she said with an exaggerated formality made even more acute by her thick Nigerian accent. "And what can I do for you?"

"You know, it's funny you should ask that," he said. "I was just thinking how pleasant it would be to have someone come back to my cabin when third shift takes over. Have a little romantic dinner of the same crap they're serving in the galley. Listen to some music."

"Drink a little wine," she said. "Break a little protocol. Pretty to think about, but I'm not up for sex tonight."

"I wasn't talking about sex. A little food. Conversation."

"I was talking about sex," she said.

Holden knelt beside her chair. In the one-third g of their current thrust, it was perfectly comfortable. Ade's smile softened. The log spool chimed; she glanced at it, tapped a release, and turned back to him.

"Ade, I like you. I mean, I really enjoy your company," he said. "I don't understand why we can't spend some time together with our clothes on."

"Holden. Sweetie. Stop it, okay?"

"Stop what?"

"Stop trying to turn me into your girlfriend. You're a nice guy. You've got a cute butt, and you're fun in the sack. Doesn't mean we're engaged."

Holden rocked back on his heels, feeling himself frown.

"Ade. For this to work for me, it needs to be more than that."

"But it isn't," she said, taking his hand. "It's okay that it isn't. You're the XO here, and I'm a short-timer. Another run, maybe two, and I'm gone."

"I'm not chained to this ship either."

Her laughter was equal parts warmth and disbelief.

"How long have you been on the *Cant*?"

"Five years."

"You're not going anyplace," she said. "You're comfortable here."

"Comfortable?" he said. "The *Cant*'s a century-old ice hauler. You can find a shittier flying job, but you have to try really hard. Everyone here is either wildly under-qualified or seriously screwed things up at their last gig."

"And you're comfortable here." Her eyes were less kind now. She bit her lip, looked down at the screen, looked up.

"I didn't deserve that," he said.

"You didn't," she agreed. "Look, I told you I wasn't in the mood tonight. I'm feeling cranky. I need a good night's sleep. I'll be nicer tomorrow."

"Promise?"

"I'll even make you dinner. Apology accepted?"

He slipped forward, pressed his lips to hers. She kissed back, politely at first and then with more warmth. Her fingers cupped his neck for a moment, then pulled him away.

"You're entirely too good at that. You should go now," she said. "On duty and all."

"Okay," he said, and didn't turn to go.

"Jim," she said, and the shipwide comm system clicked on.

"Holden to the bridge," Captain McDowell said, his voice compressed and echoing. Holden replied with something obscene. Ade laughed. He swooped in, kissed her cheek, and headed back for the central lift, quietly hoping that Captain McDowell suffered boils and public humiliation for his lousy timing.

The bridge was hardly larger than Holden's quarters and smaller by half than the galley. Except for the slightly oversized captain's display, required by Captain McDowell's failing eyesight and general distrust of corrective surgery, it could have been an accounting firm's back room. The air smelled of cleaning astringent and someone's overly strong yerba maté tea. McDowell shifted in his seat as Holden approached. Then the captain leaned back, pointing over his shoulder at the communications station.

"Becca!" McDowell snapped. "Tell him."

Rebecca Byers, the comm officer on duty, could have been bred from a shark and a hatchet. Black eyes, sharp features, lips so thin they might as well not have existed. The story on board was that she'd taken the job to escape prosecution for killing an ex-husband. Holden liked her.

"Emergency signal," she said. "Picked it up two hours ago. The transponder verification just bounced back from *Callisto*. It's real."

"Ah," Holden said. And then: "Shit. Are we the closest?"

"Only ship in a few million klicks."

"Well. That figures," Holden said.

Becca turned her gaze to the captain. McDowell cracked his knuckles and stared at his display. The light from the screen gave him an odd greenish cast.

"It's next to a charted non-Belt asteroid," McDowell said.

"Really?" Holden said in disbelief. "Did they run into it? There's nothing else out here for millions of kilometers."

"Maybe they pulled over because someone had to go potty. All we have is that some knucklehead is out there, blasting an emergency signal, and we're the closest. Assuming..."

The law of the solar system was unequivocal. In an environment as hostile to life as space, the aid and goodwill of your fellow humans wasn't optional. The emergency signal, just by existing, obligated the nearest ship to stop and render aid—which didn't mean the law was universally followed.

The *Canterbury* was fully loaded. Well over a million tons of ice had been gently accelerated for the past month. Just like the little glacier that had crushed Paj's arm, it was going to be hard to slow down. The temptation to have an unexplained comm failure, erase the logs, and let the great god Darwin have his way was always there.

But if McDowell had really intended that, he wouldn't have called Holden up. Or made the suggestion where the crew could hear him. Holden understood the dance. The captain was going to be the one who would have blown it off except for Holden. The grunts would respect the captain for not wanting to cut into the ship's profit. They'd respect Holden for insisting that they follow the rule. No matter what happened, the captain and Holden would both be hated for what they were required by law and mere human decency to do.

"We have to stop," Holden said. Then, gamely: "There may be salvage."

McDowell tapped his screen. Ade's voice came from the console, as low and warm as if she'd been in the room.

"Captain?"

"I need numbers on stopping this crate," he said.

"Sir?"

"How hard is it going to be to put us alongside CA-2216862?"

"We're stopping at an asteroid?"

"I'll tell you when you've followed my order, Navigator Tukunbo."

"Yes, sir," she said. Holden heard a series of clicks. "If we flip the ship right now and burn like hell for most of two days, I can get us within fifty thousand kilometers, sir."

"Can you define 'burn like hell'?" McDowell said.

"We'll need everyone in crash couches."

"Of course we will," McDowell sighed, and scratched his scruffy beard. "And shifting ice is only going to do a couple million bucks' worth of banging up the hull, if we're lucky. I'm getting old for this, Holden. I really am."

"Yes, sir. You are. And I've always liked your chair," Holden said. McDowell scowled and made an obscene gesture. Rebecca snorted in laughter. McDowell turned to her.

"Send a message to the beacon that we're on our way. And let Ceres know we're going to be late. Holden, where does the *Knight* stand?"

"No flying in atmosphere until we get some parts, but she'll do fine for fifty thousand klicks in vacuum."

"You're sure of that?"

"Naomi said it. That makes it true."

McDowell rose, unfolding to almost two and a quarter meters and thinner than a teenager back on Earth. Between his age and never having lived in a gravity well, the coming burn was likely to be hell on the old man. Holden felt a pang of sympathy that he would never embarrass McDowell by expressing.

"Here's the thing, Jim," McDowell said, his voice quiet enough that only Holden could hear him. "We're required to stop and make an attempt, but we don't have to go out of our way, if you see what I mean."

"We'll already have stopped," Holden said, and McDowell patted at the air with his wide, spidery hands. One of the many Belter gestures that had evolved to be visible when wearing an environment suit.

"I can't avoid that," he said. "But if you see anything out there that seems off, don't play hero again. Just pack up the toys and come home."

"And leave it for the next ship that comes through?"

"And keep yourself safe," McDowell said. "Order. Understood?"

"Understood," Holden said.

As the shipwide comm system clicked to life and McDowell began explaining the situation to the crew, Holden imagined he could hear a chorus of groans coming up through the decks. He went over to Rebecca.

"Okay," he said, "what have we got on the broken ship?"

"Light freighter. Martian registry. Shows Eros as home port. Calls itself *Scopuli*..."

Chapter Two: Miller

Detective Miller sat back on the foam-core chair, smiling gentle encouragement while he scrambled to make sense of the girl's story.

"And then it was all pow! Room full up with bladeboys howling and humping shank," the girl said, waving a hand. "Look like a dance number, 'cept that Bomie's got this look he didn't know nothing never and ever amen. You know, que?"

Havelock, standing by the door, blinked twice. The squat man's face twitched with impatience. It was why Havelock was never going to make senior detective. And why he sucked at poker.

Miller was very good at poker.

"I totally," Miller said. His voice had taken on the twang of an inner level resident. He waved his hand in the same lazy arc the girl used. "Bomie, he didn't see. Forgotten arm."

"Forgotten fucking arm, yeah," the girl said as if Miller had spoken a line of gospel. Miller nodded, and the girl nodded back like they were two birds doing a mating dance.

The rent hole was three cream-and-black-fleck-painted rooms—bathroom, kitchen, living room. The struts of a pull-down sleeping loft in the living room had been broken and repaired so many times they didn't retract anymore. This near the center of Ceres' spin, that wasn't from gravity so much as mass in motion. The air smelled beery with old protein yeast and mushrooms. Local food, so whoever had bounced the girl hard enough to break her bed hadn't paid enough for dinner. Or maybe they did, and the girl had chosen to spend it on heroin or malta or MCK.

Her business, either way.

"Follow que?" Miller asked.

"Bomie vacuate like losing air," the girl said with a chuckle. "Bang-head hops, kennis tu?"

"Ken," Miller said.

"Now, all new bladeboys. Overhead. I'm out."

"And Bomie?"

The girl's eyes made a slow track up Miller, shoes to knees to porkpie hat. Miller chuckled. He gave the chair a light push, sloping up to his feet in the low gravity.

"He shows, and I asked, que si?" Miller said.

"Como no?" the girl said. *Why not?*

The tunnel outside was white where it wasn't grimy. Ten meters wide, and gently sloping up in both directions. The white LED lights didn't pretend to mimic sunlight. About half a kilometer down, someone had rammed into the wall so hard the native rock showed through, and it still hadn't been repaired. Maybe it wouldn't be. This was the deep dig, way up near the center of spin. Tourists never came here.

Havelock led the way to their cart, bouncing too high with every step. He didn't come up to the low gravity levels very often, and it made him awkward. Miller had lived on Ceres his whole life, and truth to tell, the Coriolis effect up this high could make him a little unsteady sometimes too.

"So," Havelock said as he punched in their destination code, "did you have fun?"

"Don't know what you mean," Miller said.

The electrical motors hummed to life, and the cart lurched forward into the tunnel, squishy foam tires faintly squeaking.

"Having your outworld conversation in front of the Earth guy?" Havelock said. "I couldn't follow even half of that."

"That wasn't Belters keeping the Earth guy out," Miller said. "That was poor folks keeping the educated guy out. And it was kind of fun, now you mention it."

Havelock laughed. He could take being teased and keep on moving. It was what made him good at team sports: soccer, basketball, politics.

Miller wasn't much good at those.

Ceres, the port city of the Belt and the outer planets, boasted two hundred fifty kilometers in diameter, tens of thousands of kilometers of tunnels in layer on layer on layer. Spinning it up to 0.3 g had taken the best minds at Tycho Manufacturing half a generation, and they were still pretty smug about it. Now Ceres had more than six million permanent residents, and as many as a thousand ships docking in any given day meant upping the population to as high as seven million.

Platinum, iron, and titanium from the Belt. Water from Saturn, vegetables and beef from the big mirror-fed greenhouses on Ganymede and Europa, organics from Earth and Mars. Power cells from Io, Helium-3 from the refineries on Rhea and Iapetus. A river of wealth and power unrivaled in human history came through Ceres. Where there was commerce on that level, there was also crime. Where there was crime, there were security forces to keep it in check. Men like Miller and Havelock, whose business it was to track the electric carts up the wide ramps, feel the false gravity of spin fall away beneath them, and ask low-rent glitz whores about what happened the night Bomie Chatterjee stopped collecting protection money for the Golden Bough Society.

The primary station house for Star Helix Security, police force and military garrison for the Ceres Station, was on the third level from the asteroid's skin, two kilometers square and dug into the rock so high Miller could walk from his desk up five levels without ever leaving the offices. Havelock turned in the cart while Miller went to his cubicle, downloaded the recording of their interview with the girl, and reran it. He was halfway through when his partner lumbered up behind him.

"Learn anything?" Havelock asked.

"Not much," Miller said. "Bomie got jumped by a bunch of unaffiliated local thugs. Sometimes a low-level guy like Bomie will hire people to pretend to attack him so he can heroically fight them off. Ups his reputation. That's what she meant when she called it a dance number. The guys that went after him were that caliber, only instead of turning into a ninja badass, Bomie ran away and hasn't come back."

"And now?"

"And now nothing," Miller said. "That's what I don't get. Someone took out a Golden Bough purse boy, and there's no payback. I mean, okay, Bomie's a bottom-feeder, but…"

"But once they start eating the little guys, there's less money coming up to the big guys," Havelock said. "So why hasn't the Golden Bough meted out some gangster justice?"

"I don't like this," Miller said.

Havelock laughed. "Belters," he said. "One thing goes weird and you think the whole ecosystem's crashing. If the Golden Bough's too weak to keep its claims, that's a good thing. They're the bad guys, remember?"

"Yeah, well," Miller said. "Say what you will about organized crime, at least it's organized."

Havelock sat on the small plastic chair beside Miller's desk and craned to watch the playback.

"Okay," Havelock said. "What the hell is the 'forgotten arm'?"

"Boxing term," Miller said. "It's the hit you didn't see coming."

The computer chimed and Captain Shaddid's voice came from the speakers.

"Miller? Are you there?"

"Mmm," Havelock said. "Bad omen."

"What?" the captain asked, her voice sharp. She had never quite overcome her prejudice against Havelock's inner planet origins. Miller held up a hand to silence his partner.

"Here, Captain. What can I do for you?"

"Meet me in my office, please."

"On my way," he said.

Miller stood, and Havelock slid into his chair. They didn't speak. Both of them knew that Captain Shaddid would have called them in together if she'd wanted Havelock to be there. Another reason the man would never make senior detective. Miller left him alone with the playback, trying to parse the fine points of class and station, origin and race. Lifetime's work, that.

Captain Shaddid's office was decorated in a soft, feminine style. Real cloth tapestries hung from the walls, and the scent of coffee and cinnamon came from an insert in her air filter that cost about a tenth of what the real foodstuffs would have. She wore her uniform casually, her hair down around her shoulders in violation of corporate regulations. If Miller had ever been called upon to describe her, the phrase *deceptive coloration* would have figured in. She nodded to a chair, and he sat.

"What have you found?" she asked, but her gaze was on the wall behind him. This wasn't a pop quiz; she was just making conversation.

"Golden Bough's looking the same as Sohiro's crew and the Loca Greiga. Still on station, but...distracted, I guess I'd call it. They're letting little things slide. Fewer thugs on the ground, less enforcement. I've got half a dozen mid-level guys who've gone dark."

He'd caught her attention.

"Killed?" she asked. "An OPA advance?"

An advance by the Outer Planets Alliance was the constant bogeyman of Ceres security. Living in the tradition of Al Capone and Hamas, the IRA and the Red Martials, the OPA was beloved by the people it helped and feared by the ones who got in its way.

Part social movement, part wannabe nation, and part terrorist network, it totally lacked an institutional conscience. Captain Shaddid might not like Havelock because he was from down a gravity well, but she'd work with him. The OPA would have put him in an airlock. People like Miller would only rate getting a bullet in the skull, and a nice plastic one at that. Nothing that might get shrapnel in the ductwork.

"I don't think so," he said. "It doesn't smell like a war. It's... Honestly, sir, I don't know what the hell it is. The numbers are great. Protection's down, unlicensed gambling's down. Cooper and Hariri shut down the underage whorehouse up on six, and as far as anyone can tell, it hasn't started up again. There's a little more action by independents, but that aside, it's all looking great. It just smells funny."

She nodded, but her gaze was back on the wall. He'd lost her interest as quickly as he'd gotten it.

"Well, put it aside," she said. "I have something. New contract. Just you. Not Havelock."

Miller crossed his arms.

"New contract," he said slowly. "Meaning?"

"Meaning Star Helix Security has accepted a contract for services separate from the Ceres security assignment, and in my role as site manager for the corporation, I'm assigning you to it."

"I'm fired?" he said.

Captain Shaddid looked pained.

"It's additional duty," she said. "You'll still have the Ceres assignments you have now. It's just that, in addition...Look, Miller, I think this is as shitty as you do. I'm not pulling you off station. I'm not taking you off the main contract. This is a favor someone down on Earth is doing for a shareholder."

"We're doing favors for shareholders now?" Miller asked.

"You are, yes," Captain Shaddid said. The softness was gone; the conciliatory tone was gone. Her eyes were dark as wet stone.

"Right, then," Miller said. "I guess I am."

Captain Shaddid held up her hand terminal. Miller fumbled at his side, pulled out his own, and accepted the narrow-beam transfer. Whatever this was, Shaddid was keeping it off the common network. A new file tree, labeled JMAO, appeared on his readout.

"It's a little-lost-daughter case," Captain Shaddid said. "Ariadne and Jules-Pierre Mao."

The names rang a bell. Miller pressed his fingertips onto the screen of his hand terminal.

"Mao-Kwikowski Mercantile?" he asked.

"The one."

Miller whistled low.

Maokwik might not have been one of the top ten corporations in the Belt, but it was certainly in the upper fifty. Originally, it had been a legal firm involved in the epic failure of the Venusian cloud cities. They'd used the money from that decades-long lawsuit to diversify and expand, mostly into interplanetary transport. Now the corporate station was independent, floating between the Belt and the inner planets with the regal majesty of an ocean liner on ancient seas. The simple fact that Miller knew that much about them meant they had enough money to buy and sell men like him on open exchange.

He'd just been bought.

"They're Luna-based," Captain Shaddid said. "All the rights and privileges of Earth citizenship. But they do a lot of shipping business out here."

"And they misplaced a daughter?"

"Black sheep," the captain said. "Went off to college, got involved with a group called the Far Horizons Foundation. Student activists."

"OPA front," Miller said.

"Associated," Shaddid corrected him. Miller let it pass, but a flicker of curiosity troubled him. He wondered which side Captain Shaddid would be on if the OPA attacked. "The family put it down to a phase. They've got two older children with controlling interest, so if Julie wanted to bounce around vacuum calling herself a freedom fighter, there was no real harm."

"But now they want her found," Miller said.

"They do."

"What changed?"

"They didn't see fit to share that information."

"Right."

"Last records show she was employed on Tycho Station but maintained an apartment here. I've found her partition on the network and locked it down. The password is in your files."

"Okay," Miller said. "What's my contract?"

"Find Julie Mao, detain her, and ship her home."

"A kidnap job, then," he said.

"Yes."

Miller stared down at his hand terminal, flicking the files open without particularly looking at them. A strange knot had tied itself in his guts. He'd been working Ceres security for thirty years, and he hadn't started with many illusions in place. The joke was that Ceres didn't have laws — it had police. His hands weren't any cleaner than Captain Shaddid's. Sometimes people fell out airlocks. Sometimes evidence vanished from the lockers. It wasn't so much that it was right or wrong as that it was justified. You spent your life in a stone bubble with your food, your water, your *air* shipped in from places so distant you could barely find them with a telescope, and a certain moral flexibility was necessary. But he'd never had to take a kidnap job before.

"Problem, Detective?" Captain Shaddid asked.

"No, sir," he said. "I'll take care of it."

"Don't spend too much time on it," she said.

"Yes, sir. Anything else?"

Captain Shaddid's hard eyes softened, like she was putting on a mask. She smiled.

"Everything going well with your partner?"

"Havelock's all right," Miller said. "Having him around makes people like me better by contrast. That's nice."

Her smile's only change was to become half a degree more genuine. Nothing like a little shared racism to build ties with the boss. Miller nodded respectfully and headed out.

His hole was on the eighth level, off a residential tunnel a hundred meters wide with fifty meters of carefully cultivated green park running down the center. The main corridor's vaulted ceiling was lit by recessed lights and painted a blue that Havelock assured him matched the Earth's summer sky. Living on the surface of a planet, mass sucking at every bone and muscle, and nothing but gravity to keep your air close, seemed like a fast path to crazy. The blue was nice, though.

Some people followed Captain Shaddid's lead by perfuming their air. Not always with coffee and cinnamon scents, of course. Havelock's hole smelled of baking bread. Others opted for floral scents or semipheromones. Candace, Miller's ex-wife, had preferred something called EarthLily, which had always made him think of the waste recycling levels. These days, he left it at the vaguely astringent smell of the station itself. Recycled air that had passed through a million lungs. Water from the tap so clean it could be used for lab work, but it had been piss and shit and tears and blood and would be again. The circle of life on Ceres was so small you could see the curve. He liked it that way.

He poured a glass of moss whiskey, a native Ceres liquor made from engineered yeast, then took off his shoes and settled onto the foam bed. He could still see Candace's disapproving scowl and hear her sigh. He shrugged apology to her memory and turned back to work.

Juliette Andromeda Mao. He read through her work history, her academic records. Talented pinnace pilot. There was a picture of her at eighteen in a tailored vac suit with the helmet off: pretty girl with a thin, lunar citizen's frame and long black hair. She was grinning like the universe had given her a kiss. The linked text said she'd won first place in something called the Parrish/Dorn

500K. He searched briefly. Some kind of race only really rich people could afford to fly in. Her pinnace—the *Razorback*—had beaten the previous record and held it for two years.

Miller sipped his whiskey and wondered what had happened to the girl with enough wealth and power to own a private ship that would bring her here. It was a long way from competing in expensive space races to being hog-tied and sent home in a pod. Or maybe it wasn't.

"Poor little rich girl," Miller said to the screen. "Sucks to be you, I guess."

He closed the files and drank quietly and seriously, staring at the blank ceiling above him. The chair where Candace used to sit and ask him about his day stood empty, but he could see her there anyway. Now that she wasn't here to make him talk, it was easier to respect the impulse. She'd been lonely. He could see that now. In his imagination, she rolled her eyes.

An hour later, his blood warm with drink, he heated up a bowl of real rice and fake beans—yeast and fungus could mimic anything if you had enough whiskey first—opened the door of his hole, and ate dinner looking out at the traffic gently curving by. The second shift streamed into the tube stations and then out of them. The kids who lived two holes down—a girl of eight and her brother of four—met their father with hugs, squeals, mutual accusations, and tears. The blue ceiling glowed in its reflected light, unchanging, static, reassuring. A sparrow fluttered down the tunnel, hovering in a way that Havelock assured him they couldn't on Earth. Miller threw it a fake bean.

He tried to think about the Mao girl, but in truth he didn't much care. Something was happening to the organized crime families of Ceres, and it made him jumpy as hell.

This thing with Julie Mao? It was a sideshow.

Chapter Three: Holden

After nearly two full days in high gravity, Holden's knees and back and neck ached. And his head. Hell, his feet. He walked in the crew hatch of the *Knight* just as Naomi was climbing up the ladder from its cargo bay. She smiled and gave him a thumbs-up.

"The salvage mech is locked down," she said. "Reactor is warming up. We're ready to fly."

"Good."

"We got a pilot yet?" she asked.

"Alex Kamal is on the ready rotation today, so he's our man. I kind of wish Valka had been up. He's not the pilot Alex is, but he's quieter, and my head hurts."

"I like Alex. He's ebullient," Naomi said.

"I don't know what *ebullient* means, but if it means Alex, it makes me tired."

Holden started up the ladder to ops and the cockpit. In the

shiny black surface of a deactivated wall panel, Naomi's reflection smirked at his back. He couldn't understand how Belters, thin as pencils, bounced back from high g so quickly. Decades of practice and selective breeding, he assumed.

In ops, Holden strapped into the command console, the crash couch material silently conforming to his body. At the half g Ade put them on for the final approach, the foam felt good. He let a small groan slip out. The switches, plastic and metal made to withstand hard g and hundreds of years, clicked sharply. The *Knight* responded with an array of glowing diagnostic indicators and a near-subliminal hum.

A few minutes later, Holden glanced over to see Alex Kamal's thinning black hair appear, followed by his round cheerful face, a deep brown that years of shipboard life couldn't pale. Martian-raised, Alex had a frame that was thicker than a Belter's. He was slender compared to Holden, and even so, his flight suit stretched tight against his spreading waistline. Alex had flown in the Martian navy, but he'd clearly given up on the military-style fitness routine.

"Howdy, XO," he drawled. The old west affectation common to everyone from the Mariner Valley annoyed Holden. There hadn't been a cowboy on Earth in a hundred years, and Mars didn't have a blade of grass that wasn't under a dome, or a horse that wasn't in a zoo. Mariner Valley had been settled by East Indians, Chinese, and a small contingent of Texans. Apparently, the drawl was viral. They all had it now. "How's the old warhorse today?"

"Smooth so far. We need a flight plan. Ade will be bringing us to relative stop in"—he checked the time readout—"forty, so work fast. I want to get out, get it done, and get the *Cant* back on course to Ceres before she starts rusting."

"Roger that," Alex said, climbing up to the *Knight*'s cockpit.

Holden's headset clicked; then Naomi's voice said, "Amos and Shed are aboard. We're all ready down here."

"Thanks. Just waiting on flight numbers from Alex and we'll be ready to go."

The crew was the minimum necessary: Holden as command,

Alex to get them there and back, Shed in case there were survivors to treat, Naomi and Amos for salvage if there weren't.

It wasn't long before Alex called down, "Okay, Boss. It'll be about a four-hour trip flyin' teakettle. Total mass use at about thirty percent, but we've got a full tank. Total mission time: eleven hours."

"Copy that. Thanks, Alex," Holden said.

Flying teakettle was naval slang for flying on the maneuvering thrusters that used superheated steam for reaction mass. The *Knight*'s fusion torch would be dangerous to use this close to the *Canterbury* and wasteful on such a short trip. Torches were pre-Epstein fusion drives and far less efficient.

"Calling for permission to leave the barn," Holden said, and clicked from internal comm to the link with the *Canterbury*'s bridge. "Holden here. *Knight* is ready to fly."

"Okay, Jim, go ahead," McDowell said. "Ade's bringing her to a stop now. You kids be careful out there. That shuttle is expensive and I've always sort of had a thing for Naomi."

"Roger that, Captain," Holden said. Back on the internal comm, he buzzed Alex. "Go ahead and take us out."

Holden leaned back in his chair and listened to the creaks of the *Canterbury*'s final maneuvers, the steel and ceramics as loud and ominous as the wood planks of a sailing ship. Or an Earther's joints after high g. For a moment, Holden felt sympathy for the ship.

They weren't really stopping, of course. Nothing in space ever actually stopped; it only came into a matching orbit with some other object. They were now following CA-2216862 on its merry millennium-long trip around the sun.

Ade sent them the green light, and Holden emptied out the hangar bay air and popped the doors. Alex took them out of the dock on white cones of superheated steam.

They went to find the *Scopuli*.

CA-2216862 was a rock a half kilometer across that had wandered away from the Belt and been yanked around by Jupiter's enormous gravity. It had eventually found its own slow orbit around the sun in the vast expanse between Jupiter and the Belt, territory empty even for space.

The sight of the *Scopuli* resting gently against the asteroid's side, held in place by the rock's tiny gravity, gave Holden a chill. Even if it was flying blind, every instrument dead, its odds of hitting such an object by chance were infinitesimally low. It was a half-kilometer-wide roadblock on a highway millions of kilometers in diameter. It hadn't arrived there by accident. He scratched the hairs standing up on the back of his neck.

"Alex, hold us at two klicks out," Holden said. "Naomi, what can you tell me about that ship?"

"Hull configuration matches the registry information. It's definitely the *Scopuli*. She's not radiating in the electromagnetic or infrared. Just that little distress beacon. Looks like the reactor's shut down. Must have been manual and not damage, because we aren't getting any radiation leakage either," Naomi said.

Holden looked at the pictures they were getting from the *Knight*'s scopes, as well as the image the *Knight* created by bouncing a laser off the *Scopuli*'s hull. "What about that thing that looks like a hole in the side?"

"Uh," Naomi said. "Ladar says it's a hole in the side."

Holden frowned. "Okay, let's stay here for a minute and recheck the neighborhood. Anything on the scope, Naomi?"

"Nope. And the big array on the *Cant* can spot a kid throwing rocks on Luna. Becca says there's nobody within twenty million klicks right now," Naomi said.

Holden tapped out a complicated rhythm on the arm of his chair and drifted up in the straps. He felt hot, and reached over to aim the closest air-circulation nozzle at his face. His scalp tingled with evaporating sweat.

If you see anything out there that seems off, don't play hero again. Just pack up the toys and come home. Those were his orders. He looked at the image of the *Scopuli*, the hole in its side.

"Okay," he said. "Alex, take us in to a quarter klick, and hold station there. We'll ride to the surface on the mech. Oh, and keep the torch warmed up and ready. If something nasty is hiding in that ship, I want to be able to run away as fast as I can and melt anything behind us into slag while I do it. Roger?"

"Got it, Boss. *Knight*'s in run-like-a-bunny mode till you say otherwise," Alex replied.

Holden looked over the command console one more time, searching for the flashing red warning light that would give him permission to go back to the *Cant*. Everything remained a soft green. He popped open his buckles and shoved himself out of the chair. A push on the wall with one foot sent him over to the ladder, and he descended headfirst with gentle touches on the rungs.

In the crew area, Naomi, Amos, and Shed were still strapped into their crash couches. Holden caught the ladder and swung around so that his crew didn't look upside down. They started undoing their restraints.

"Okay, here's the situation. The *Scopuli* got holed, and someone left it floating next to this rock. No one is on the scopes, so maybe that means it happened a while ago and they left. Naomi, you'll be driving the salvage mech, and the three of us will tether on and catch a ride down to the wreck. Shed, you stay with the mech unless we find an injured person, which seems unlikely. Amos and I will go into the ship through that hole and poke around. If we find anything even remotely booby trap–like, we will come back to the mech, Naomi will fly us back to the *Knight,* and we will run away. Any questions?"

Amos raised one beefy hand. "Maybe we oughta be armed, XO. Case there's piratey types still lurking aboard."

Holden laughed. "Well, if there are, then their ride left without them. But if it makes you feel more comfortable, go ahead and bring a gun."

If the big, burly Earther mechanic was carrying a gun, it would make *him* feel better too, but better not to say it. Let them think the guy in charge felt confident.

Holden used his officer's key to open the weapon locker, and

Amos took a high-caliber automatic that fired self-propelled rounds, recoilless and designed for use in zero g. Old-fashioned slug throwers were more reliable, but in null gravity they were also maneuvering thrusters. A traditional handgun would impart enough thrust to achieve escape velocity from a rock the size of CA-2216862.

The crew drifted down to the cargo bay, where the egg-shaped, spider-legged open cage of Naomi's mech waited. Each of the four legs had a manipulator claw at the end and a variety of cutting and welding tools built into it. The back pair could grip on to a ship's hull or other structure for leverage, and the front two could be used to make repairs or chop salvage into portable pieces.

"Hats on," Holden said, and the crew helped each other put on and secure their helmets. Everyone checked their own suit and then someone else's. When the cargo doors opened, it would be too late to make sure they were buttoned up right.

While Naomi climbed into her mech, Amos, Holden, and Shed secured their suit tethers to the cockpit's metal cage. Naomi checked the mech and then hit the switch to cycle the cargo bay's atmosphere and open the doors. Sound inside Holden's suit faded to just the hiss of air and the faint static of the radio. The air had a slight medicine smell.

Naomi went first, taking the mech down toward the asteroid's surface on small jets of compressed nitrogen, the crew trailing her on three-meter-long tethers. As they flew, Holden looked back up at the *Knight:* a blocky gray wedge with a drive cone stuck on the wider end. Like everything else humans built for space travel, it was designed to be efficient, not pretty. That always made Holden a little sad. There should be room for aesthetics, even out here.

The *Knight* seemed to drift away from him, getting smaller and smaller, while he didn't move. The illusion vanished when he turned around to look at the asteroid and felt they were hurtling toward it. He opened a channel to Naomi, but she was humming to herself as she flew, which meant she, at least, wasn't worried. He didn't say anything, but he left the channel open to listen to her hum.

Up close, the *Scopuli* didn't look all that bad. Other than the gaping hole in its flank, it didn't have any damage. It clearly hadn't hit the asteroid; it had just been left close enough that the microgravity had slowly reeled it in. As they approached, he snapped pictures with his suit helmet and transmitted them to the *Canterbury*.

Naomi brought them to a stop, hovering three meters above the hole in the *Scopuli*'s side. Amos whistled across the general suit channel.

"That wasn't a torpedo did this, XO. This was a breaching charge. See how the metal's bent in all around the edges? That's shaped charges stuck right on her hull," Amos said.

In addition to being a fine mechanic, Amos was the one who used explosive surgery to crack open the icebergs floating around Saturn and turn them into more manageable chunks. Another reason to have him on the *Knight*.

"So," Holden said, "our friends here on the *Scopuli* stop, let someone climb onto their hull and plant a breaching charge, and then crack them open and let all the air out. Does that make sense to anyone?"

"Nope," Naomi said. "It doesn't. Still want to go inside?"

If you see anything out there that seems off, don't play hero again. Just pack up the toys and come home.

But what could he have expected? Of course the *Scopuli* wasn't up and running. Of course something had gone wrong. *Off* would have been not seeing anything strange.

"Amos," Holden said, "keep that gun out, just in case. Naomi, can you make us a bigger hole? And be careful. If anything looks wrong, back us off."

Naomi brought the mech in closer, nitrogen blasts no more than a white breath on a cold night. The mech's welding torch blazed to life, red hot, then white, then blue. In silence, the mech's arms unfurled—an insectile movement—and Naomi started cutting. Holden and Amos dropped to the ship's surface, clamping on with magnetic boots. He could feel the vibration in his feet when Naomi pulled a length of hull free. A moment later the torch turned off, and Naomi blasted the fresh edges of the hole with the mech's fire-suppression gear to cool them. Holden gave Amos the thumbs-up and dropped himself very slowly into the *Scopuli.*

The breaching charge had been placed almost exactly amidships, blasting a hole into the galley. When Holden landed and his boots grabbed on to the galley wall, he could feel flash-frozen bits of food crunch under them. There were no bodies in sight.

"Come on in, Amos. No crew visible yet," Holden called over the suit comm.

He moved off to the side and a moment later Amos dropped in, gun clutched in his right hand and a powerful light in his left. The white beam played across the walls of the destroyed galley.

"Which way first, XO?" Amos asked.

Holden tapped on his thigh with one hand and thought. "Engineering. I want to know why the reactor's off-line."

They took the crew ladder, climbing along it toward the aft of the ship. All the pressure doors between decks were open, which was a bad sign. They should all be closed by default, and certainly if the atmosphere-loss alarm had sounded. If they were open, that meant there were no decks with atmosphere left in the ship. Which meant no survivors. Not a surprise, but it still felt like a defeat. They passed through the small ship quickly, pausing in the machine shop. Expensive engine parts and tools were still in place.

"Guess it wasn't robbery," Amos said.

Holden didn't say, *Then what was it?* but the question hung between them anyway.

The engine room was neat as a pin, cold, and dead. Holden waited while Amos looked it over, spending at least ten minutes just floating around the reactor.

"Someone went through the shutdown procedures," Amos said. "The reactor wasn't killed by the blast, it was turned off afterward. No damage that I can see. Don't make sense. If everyone is dead from the attack, who shut it down? And if it's pirates, why not take the ship? She'll still fly."

"And before they turned off the power, they went through and opened every interior pressure door on the ship. Emptied out the air. I guess they wanted to make sure no one was hiding," Holden said. "Okay, let's head back up to ops and see if we can crack the computer core. Maybe it can tell us what happened."

They floated back toward the bow along the crew ladder, and up to the ops deck. It too was undamaged and empty. The lack of bodies was starting to bother Holden more than the presence of them would have. He floated over to the main computer console and hit a few keys to see if it might still be running on backup power. It wasn't.

"Amos, start cutting the core out. We'll take it with us. I'm going to check comms, see if I can find that beacon."

Amos moved to the computer and started taking out tools and sticking them to the bulkhead next to it. He began a profanity-laced mumble as he worked. It wasn't nearly as charming as Naomi's humming, so Holden turned off his link to Amos while he moved to the communications console. It was as dead as the rest of the ship. He found the ship's beacon.

No one had activated it. Something else had called them. Holden moved back, frowning.

He looked through the space, searching for something out of place. There, on the deck beneath the comm operator's console. A small black box not connected to anything else.

His heart took a long pause between beats. He called out to Amos, "Does that look like a bomb to you?"

Amos ignored him. Holden turned his radio link back on.

"Amos, does that look like a bomb to you?" He pointed at the box on the deck.

Amos left his work on the computer and floated over to look, then, in a move that made Holden's throat close, grabbed the box off the deck and held it up.

"Nope. It's a transmitter. See?" He held it up in front of Holden's helmet. "It's just got a battery taped to it. What's it doing there?"

"It's the beacon we followed. Jesus. The ship's beacon never even turned on. Someone made a fake one out of that transmitter and hooked it up to a battery," Holden said quietly, still fighting his panic.

"Why would they do that, XO? That don't make no kinda sense."

"It would if there's something about this transmitter that's different from standard," Holden said.

"Like?"

"Like if it had a second signal triggered to go when someone found it," Holden said, then switched to the general suit channel. "Okay, boys and girls, we've found something weird, and we're out of here. Everyone back to the *Knight,* and be very careful when you—"

His radio crackled to life on the outside channel, McDowell's voice filling his helmet. "Jim? We may have a problem out here."

Chapter Four: Miller

Miller was halfway through his evening meal when the system in his hole chirped. He glanced at the sending code. The Blue Frog. It was a port bar catering to the constant extra million non-citizens of Ceres that advertised itself as a near-exact replica of a famous Earth bar in Mumbai, only with licensed prostitutes and legal drugs. Miller took another forkful of fungal beans and vat-grown rice and debated whether to accept connection.

Should have seen this one coming, he thought.

"What?" he asked.

A screen popped open. Hasini, the assistant manager, was a dark-skinned man with eyes the color of ice. The near smirk on his face was the result of nerve damage. Miller had done him a favor when Hasini had had the poor judgment to take pity on an unlicensed prostitute. Since then, security detective and portside barman had traded favors. The unofficial, gray economics of civilization.

"Your partner's here again," Hasini said over the pulse and wail of bhangra music. "I think he's having a bad night. Should I keep serving him?"

"Yeah," Miller said. "Keep him happy for...Give me twenty minutes."

"He doesn't want to be kept happy. He very much wants a reason to get unhappy."

"Make it hard to find. I'll be there."

Hasini nodded, smirking his damaged smirk, and dropped the connection. Miller looked at his half-eaten meal, sighed, and shoved the remains into the recycling bin. He pulled on a clean shirt, then hesitated. The Blue Frog was always warmer than he liked, and he hated wearing a jacket. Instead, he put a compact plastic pistol in his ankle holster. Not as fast a draw, but if it got that far, he was screwed anyway.

Ceres at night was indistinguishable from Ceres in the daytime. There had been a move, back when the station first opened, to dim and brighten the lights through the traditional human twenty-four-hour cycle, mimicking the spin of Earth. The affectation had lasted four months before the council killed it.

On duty, Miller would have taken an electric cart down the wide tunnels and down to the port levels. He was tempted even though he was off duty, but a deep-seated superstition stopped him. If he took the cart, he was going as a cop, and the tubes ran just fine. Miller walked to the nearest station, checked the status, and sat on the low stone bench. A man about Miller's age and a girl no more than three came in a minute later and sat across from him. The girl's talk was as fast and meaningless as a leaking seal, and her father responded with grunts and nods at more or less appropriate moments.

Miller and the new man nodded to each other. The girl tugged at her father's sleeve, demanding his attention. Miller looked at her—dark eyes, pale hair, smooth skin. She was already too tall to be mistaken for an Earth child, her limbs longer and thinner. Her skin had the pink flush of Belter babies, which came with the pharmaceutical cocktail that assured that their muscles and bones would grow strong. Miller saw the father notice his attention. Miller smiled and nodded toward the kid.

"How old?" he asked.

"Two and a half," the father said.

"Good age."

The father shrugged, but he smiled.

"Kids?" he asked.

"No," Miller said. "But I've got a divorce about that old."

They chuckled together as if it was funny. In his imagination, Candace crossed her arms and looked away. The soft oil-and-ozone-scented breeze announced the tube's arrival. Miller let father and child go first, then chose a different compartment.

The tube cars were round, built to fit into the evacuated passages. There were no windows. The only view would have been stone humming by three centimeters from the car. Instead, broad screens advertised entertainment feeds or commented on inner planet political scandals or offered the chance to gamble away a week's pay at casinos so wonderful that your life would seem richer for the experience. Miller let the bright, empty colors dance and ignored their content. Mentally, he was holding up his problem, turning it one way and then the other, not even looking for an answer.

It was a simple mental exercise. Look at the facts without judgment: Havelock was an Earther. Havelock was in a portside bar again and looking for a fight. Havelock was his partner. Statement after statement, fact after fact, facet after facet. He didn't try to put them in order or make some kind of narrative out of them; that would all come later. Now it was enough to wash the day's cases out of his head and get ready for the immediate situation. By the time the tube reached his station, he felt centered. Like he was walking on his whole foot, was how he'd described it, back when he had anyone to describe it to.

The Blue Frog was crowded, the barn-heat of bodies adding to the fake-Mumbai temperature and artificial air pollution. Lights glittered and flashed in seizure-inducing display. Tables curved and undulated, the backlight making them seem darker than merely black. Music moved through the air with a physical presence, each beat a little concussion. Hasini, standing in a clot of steroid-enhanced bouncers and underdressed serving girls, caught Miller's eyes and nodded toward the back. Miller didn't acknowledge anything; he just turned and made his way through the crowd.

Port bars were always volatile. Miller was careful not to bump into anyone if he could help it. When he had to choose, he'd run into Belters before inner planet types, women before men. His face was a constant mild apology.

Havelock was sitting alone, with one thick hand wrapping a fluted glass. When Miller sat down beside him, Havelock turned toward him, ready to take offense, nostrils flared and eyes wide. Then the surprise registered. Then something like sullen shame.

"Miller," he said. In the tunnels outside, he would have been shouting. Here, it was barely enough to carry as far as Miller's chair. "What're you doing here?"

"Nothing much to do at the hole," Miller said. "Thought I'd come pick a fight."

"Good night for it," Havelock said.

It was true. Even in the bars that catered to inner planet types, the mix was rarely better than one Earther or Martian in ten. Squinting out at the crowd, Miller saw that the short, stocky men and women were nearer a third.

"Ship come in?" he asked.

"Yeah."

"EMCN?" he asked. The Earth-Mars Coalition Navy often passed through Ceres on its way to Saturn, Jupiter, and the stations of the Belt, but Miller hadn't been paying enough attention to the relative position of the planets to know where the orbits all stood. Havelock shook his head.

"Corporate security rotating out of Eros," he said. "Protogen, I think." A serving girl appeared at Miller's side, tattoos gliding over her skin, her teeth glowing in the black light. Miller took the drink she offered him, though he hadn't ordered. Soda water.

"You know," Miller said, leaning close enough to Havelock that even his normal conversational voice would reach the man, "it doesn't matter how many of their asses you kick. Shaddid's still not going to like you."

Havelock snapped to stare at Miller, the anger in his eyes barely covering the shame and hurt.

"It's true," Miller said.

Havelock rose lurching to his feet and headed for the door. He was trying to stomp, but in the Ceres spin gravity and his inebriated state, he misjudged. It looked like he was hopping. Miller, glass in hand, slid through the crowd in Havelock's wake, calming with a smile and a shrug the affronted faces that his partner left behind him.

The common tunnels down near the port had a layer of grime and grease to them that air scrubbers and astringent cleaners could never quite master. Havelock walked out, shoulders hunched, mouth tight, rage radiating from him like heat. But the doors of the Blue Frog closed behind them, the seal cutting off the music like someone hitting mute. The worst of the danger had passed.

"I'm not drunk," Havelock said, his voice too loud.

"Didn't say you were."

"And you," Havelock said, turning and stabbing an accusing finger at Miller's chest. "You are not my nanny."

"Also true."

They walked together for maybe a quarter of a kilometer. The bright LED signs beckoned. Brothels and shooting galleries, coffee bars and poetry clubs, casinos and show fights. The air smelled like piss and old food. Havelock began to slow, his shoulders coming down from around his ears.

"I worked homicide in Terrytown," Havelock said. "I did three years vice at L-5. Do you have any idea what that was like? They were shipping kids out of there, and I'm one of three guys that stopped it. I'm a good cop."

"Yes, you are."

"I'm damn good."

"You are."

They walked past a noodle bar. A coffin hotel. A public terminal, its displays running a free newsfeed: COMMUNICATION PROBLEMS PLAGUE PHOEBE SCIENCE STATION. NEW ANDREAS K GAME NETS 6 BILLION DOLLARS IN 4 HOURS. NO DEAL IN MARS, BELT TITANIUM CONTRACT. The screens glowed in Havelock's eyes, but he was staring past them.

"I'm a damn good cop," he said again. Then, a moment later: "So what the hell?"

"It's not about you," Miller said. "People look at you, they don't see Dmitri Havelock, good cop. They see Earth."

"That's crap. I was eight years in the orbitals and on Mars before I ever shipped out here. I worked on Earth maybe six months total."

"Earth. Mars. They're not that different," Miller said.

"Try telling that to a Martian," Havelock said with a bitter laugh. "They'll kick your ass for you."

"I didn't mean...Look, I'm sure there are all kinds of differences. Earth hates Mars for having a better fleet. Mars hates Earth for having a bigger one. Maybe soccer's better in full g; maybe it's worse. I don't know. I'm just saying anyone this far out from the sun? They don't care. From this distance, you can cover Earth and Mars with one thumb. And..."

"And I don't belong," Havelock said.

The door of the noodle bar behind them opened and four Belters in gray-green uniforms came out. One of them wore the split circle of the OPA on his sleeve. Miller tensed, but the Belters didn't come toward them, and Havelock didn't notice them. Near miss.

"I knew," Havelock said. "When I took the Star Helix contract, I knew I'd have to work to fit in. I thought it'd be the same as anywhere, you know? You go, you get your chops busted for a while.

Then, when they see you can take it, they treat you like one of the team. It's not like that here."

"It's not," Miller said.

Havelock shook his head, spat, and stared at the fluted glass in his hand.

"I think we just stole some glasses from the Blue Frog," Havelock said.

"We're also in a public corridor with unsealed alcohol," Miller said. "Well, you are, anyway. Mine's soda water."

Havelock chuckled, but there was despair in the sound. When Havelock spoke again, his voice was only rueful.

"You think I'm coming down here, picking fights with people from the inner planets so that Shaddid and Ramachandra and all the rest of them will think better of me."

"It occurred to me."

"You're wrong," Havelock said.

"Okay," Miller said. He knew he wasn't.

Havelock raised his fluted glass. "Take these back?" he asked.

"How about Distinguished Hyacinth?" Miller countered. "I'll buy."

The Distinguished Hyacinth Lounge was up three levels, far enough that foot traffic from the port levels was minimal. And it was a cop bar. Mostly Star Helix Security, but some of the minor corporate forces—Protogen, Pinkwater, Al Abbiq—hung out there too. Miller was more than half certain that his partner's latest breakdown had been averted, but if he was wrong, better to keep it in the family.

The décor was pure Belt—old-style ships' folding tables and chairs set into the wall and ceiling as if the gravity might shut off at any moment. Snake plant and devil's ivy—staples of first-generation air recycling—decorated the wall and freestanding columns. The music was soft enough to talk over, loud enough to keep private conversations private. The first owner, Javier Liu, was a structural engineer from Tycho who'd come out during the big spin and liked Ceres enough to stay. His grandchildren ran it now. Javier the Third was standing behind the bar, talking with half of the vice and exploitation team. Miller led the way to a back table, nodding to the men and women he knew as he passed. While he'd been careful and diplomatic at the Blue Frog, he chose a bluff masculinity here. It was just as much a pose.

"So," Havelock said as Javier's daughter Kate — a fourth generation for the same bar — left the table, Blue Frog glasses on her tray, "what is this supersecret private investigation Shaddid put you on? Or is the lowly Earther not supposed to know?"

"Is that what got to you?" Miller asked. "It's nothing. Some shareholders misplaced their daughter and want me to track her down, ship her home. It's a bullshit case."

"Sounds more like their backyard," Havelock said, nodding toward the V and E crowd.

"Kid's not a minor," Miller said. "It's a kidnap job."

"And you're good with that?"

Miller sat back. The ivy above them waved. Havelock waited, and Miller had the uncomfortable sense that a table had just been turned.

"It's my job," Miller said.

"Yeah, but we're talking about an adult here, right? It's not like she couldn't go back home if she wanted to be there. But instead her parents get security to take her home whether she wants to go or not. That's not law enforcement anymore. It's not even station security. It's just dysfunctional families playing power games."

Miller remembered the thin girl beside her racing pinnace. Her broad smile.

"I told you it was a bullshit case," Miller said.

Kate Liu returned to the table with a local beer and a glass of whiskey on her tray. Miller was glad for the distraction. The beer was his. Light and rich and just the faintest bit bitter. An ecology based on yeasts and fermentation meant subtle brews.

Havelock was nursing his whiskey. Miller took it as a sign that he was giving up on his bender. Nothing like being around the boys from the office to take the charm out of losing control.

"Hey, Miller! Havelock!" a familiar voice said. Yevgeny Cobb from homicide. Miller waved him over, and the conversation turned to homicide's bragging about the resolution of a particularly ugly case. Three months' work figuring out where the toxins came from ending with the corpse's wife awarded the full insurance settlement and a gray-market whore deported back to Eros.

By the end of the night, Havelock was laughing and trading jokes along with the rest of them. If there was occasionally a narrowed glance or a subtle dig, he took it in stride.

Miller was on his way up to the bar for another round when his terminal chimed. And then, slowly throughout the bar, fifty other chimes sounded. Miller felt his belly knot as he and every other security agent in the place pulled out their terminals.

Captain Shaddid was on the broadcast screen. Her eyes were bleary and filled with banked rage; she was the very picture of a woman of power wakened early from sleep.

"Ladies and gentlemen," she said. "Whatever you're doing, drop it and go to your stations for emergency orders. We have a situation.

"Ten minutes ago, an unencrypted, signed message came in from the rough direction of Saturn. We haven't confirmed it as true, but the signature matches the keys on record. I've put a hold on it, but we can assume some asshole's going to put it on the network, and the shit should hit the fan about five minutes after that. If you're in earshot of a civilian, turn off now. For the rest of you, here's what we're up against."

Shaddid moved to one side, tapping her system interface. The screen went black. A moment later a man's face and shoulders appeared. He was in an orange vacuum suit with the helmet off. An Earther, maybe in his early thirties. Pale skin, blue eyes, dark short-cropped hair. Even before the man opened his mouth, Miller saw the signs of shock and rage in his eyes and the way he held his head forward.

"My name," the man said, "is James Holden."

Chapter Five: Holden

Ten minutes at two g, and Holden's head was already starting to ache. But McDowell had called them home at all haste. The *Canterbury* was warming up its massive drive. Holden didn't want to miss his ride.

"Jim? We may have a problem out here."
"Talk to me."
"Becca found something, and it is sufficiently weird to make my balls creep up. We're getting the hell out of here."

"Alex, how long?" Holden asked for the third time in ten minutes.
"We're over an hour out. Want to go on the juice?" Alex said.
Going on the juice was pilot-speak for a high-g burn that would

knock an unmedicated human unconscious. *The juice* was the cocktail of drugs the pilot's chair would inject into him to keep him conscious, alert, and hopefully stroke-free when his body weighed five hundred kilos. Holden had used the juice on multiple occasions in the navy, and coming down afterward was unpleasant.

"Not unless we have to," he said.

"What kind of weird?"

"Becca, link him up. Jim, I want you seeing what we're seeing."

Holden tongued a painkiller tab from his suit's helmet and reran Becca's sensor feed for the fifth time. The spot in space lay about two hundred thousand kilometers from the *Canterbury*. As the *Cant* had scanned it, the readout showed a fluctuation, the gray-black false color gradually developing a warm border. It was a small temperature climb, less than two degrees. Holden was amazed Becca had even spotted it. He reminded himself to give her a glowing review the next time she was up for promotion.

"Where did that come from?" Holden asked.

"No idea. It's just a spot faintly warmer than the background," Becca said. *"I'd say it was a cloud of gas, because we get no radar return from it, but there aren't supposed to be any gas clouds out here. I mean, where would it come from?"*

"Jim, any chance the Scopuli *killed the ship that killed it? Could it be a vapor cloud from a destroyed ship?"* McDowell asked.

"I don't think so, sir. The Scopuli *is totally unarmed. The hole in her side came from breaching charges, not torpedo fire, so I don't think they even fought back. It might be where the* Scopuli *vented, but…"*

"Or maybe not. Come back to the barn, Jim. Do it now."

"Naomi, what slowly gets hotter that gives no radar or ladar return when you scan it? Wild-ass guess here," Holden said.

"Hmmmm…" Naomi said, giving herself time to think. "Anything that was absorbing the energy from the sensor package wouldn't give a return. But it might get hotter when it shed the absorbed energy."

The infrared monitor on the sensor console next to Holden's chair flared like the sun. Alex swore loudly over the general comm.

"Are you seein' that?" he said.

Holden ignored him and opened a channel to McDowell.

"Captain, we just got a massive IR spike," Holden said.

For long seconds, there was no reply. When McDowell came on the channel, his voice was tight. Holden had never heard the old man sound afraid before.

"Jim, a ship just appeared in that warm spot. It's radiating heat like a bastard," McDowell said. "Where the hell did that thing come from?"

Holden started to answer but then heard Becca's voice coming faintly through the captain's headset. "No idea, sir. But it's smaller than its heat signature. Radar shows frigate-sized," she said.

"With what?" McDowell said. "Invisibility? Magical wormhole teleportation?"

"Sir," Holden said, "Naomi was speculating that the heat we picked up might have come from energy-absorbing materials. Stealth materials. Which means that ship was hiding on purpose. Which means its intentions are not good."

As if in answer, six new objects appeared on his radar, glowing yellow icons appearing and immediately shifting to orange as the system marked their acceleration. On the *Canterbury*, Becca yelled out, "Fast movers! We have six new high-speed contacts on a collision course!"

"Jesus H. Christ on a pogo stick, did that ship just fire a spread of torpedoes at us?" McDowell said. "They're trying to slap us down?"

"Yes, sir," Becca said.

"Time to contact."

"Just under eight minutes, sir," she replied.

McDowell cursed under his breath.

"We've got pirates, Jim."

"What do you need from us?" Holden said, trying to sound calm and professional.

"I need you to get off the radio and let my crew work. You're an hour out at best. The torpedoes are eight minutes. McDowell out," the captain said, his comm clicking off and leaving Holden listening to the faint hiss of static.

The general comm exploded with voices, Alex demanding to go on the juice and race the torpedoes to the *Cant,* Naomi chattering about missile-jamming strategies, Amos cursing at the stealth ship and questioning the parenting of its crew. Shed was the only quiet one.

"Everyone, shut up!" Holden yelled into his headset. The ship fell into shocked silence. "Alex, plot the fastest course to the *Cant* that won't kill us. Let me know when you have it. Naomi, set up a three-way channel with Becca, you, and me. We'll help however we can. Amos, keep cussing but turn your mic off."

He waited. The clock ticked toward impact.

"Link is up," Naomi said. Holden could hear two distinct sets of background noise over the comm channel.

"Becca, this is Jim. I've got Naomi on this channel too. Tell us what we can do to help. Naomi was talking about jamming techniques?"

"I'm doing everything I know to do," Becca said, her voice astonishingly calm. "They're painting us with a targeting laser. I'm broadcasting garbage to scramble it, but they've got really, really good shit. If we were any closer, that targeting laser would be burning a hole in our hull."

"What about physical chaff?" Naomi asked. "Can you drop snow?"

While Naomi and Becca talked, Jim opened a private channel to Ade. "Hey, this is Jim. I have Alex working on a fast-burn solution so we can get there before..."

"Before the missiles turn us into a flying brick? Good idea. Taken by pirates isn't something you want to miss," Ade said. He could hear the fear behind the mocking tone.

"Ade, please, I want to say something—"

"Jim, what do you think?" Naomi said on the other channel.

Holden cursed. To cover, he said, "Uh, about which thing?"

"Using the *Knight* to try and draw those missiles," Naomi said.

"Can we do that?" he asked.

"Maybe. Were you listening at all?"

"Ah…something happened here, drew my attention for a minute. Tell me again," Holden said.

"We try to match the frequency of the light scatter coming off the *Cant* and broadcast it with our comm array. Maybe the torpedoes will think we're the target instead," Naomi said like she was speaking to a child.

"And then they come blow us up?"

"I'm thinking we run away while pulling the torpedoes toward us. Then, when we get them far enough past the *Cant,* we kill the comm array and try to hide behind the asteroid," Naomi said.

"Won't work," Holden said with a sigh. "They follow the targeting laser's scatter for general guidance, but they also take telescope shots of the target on acquisition. They'll take one look at us and know we aren't their target."

"Isn't it worth a shot?"

"Even if we manage it, torpedoes designed to disable the *Cant* would make us into a greasy stretch of vacuum."

"All right," Naomi said. "What else have we got?"

"Nothing. Very smart boys in the naval labs have already thought of everything we are going to think of in the next eight minutes," Holden said. Saying it out loud meant admitting it to himself.

"Then what are we doing here, Jim?" Naomi asked.

"Seven minutes," Becca said, her voice still eerily calm.

"Let's get there. Maybe we can get some people off the ship

after it's hit. Help with damage control," Holden said. "Alex, got that plot figured out?"

"Roger that, XO. Bleeding-g burn-and-flip laid in. Angled approach course so our torch won't burn a hole in the *Cant.* Time to rock and roll?" Alex replied.

"Yeah. Naomi, get your people strapped in for high g," Holden said, then opened up a channel to Captain McDowell. "Captain, we're coming in hot. Try to survive, and we'll have the *Knight* on station for pickup or to help with damage control."

"Roger," McDowell said, and killed the line.

Holden opened up his channel to Ade again. "Ade, we're going to burn hard, so I won't be talking, but leave this channel open for me, okay? Tell me what's happening. Hell, hum. Humming is nice. I just really need to hear you're all right."

"Okay, Jim," Ade said. She didn't hum but she left the channel open. He could hear her breathing.

Alex began the countdown over the general comm. Holden checked the straps on his crash couch and palmed the button that started the juice. A dozen needles stuck into his back through membranes in his suit. His heart shuddered and chemical bands of iron gripped his brain. His spine went dead cold, and his face flushed like a radiation burn. He pounded a fist into the arm of the crash couch. He hated this part, but the next one was worse. On the general comm, Alex whooped as the drugs hit his system. Belowdecks, the others were getting the drugs that kept them from dying but kept them sedated through the worst of it.

Alex said, "One," and Holden weighed five hundred kilos. The nerves at the back of his eye sockets screamed at the massive load of his eyeballs. His testicles crushed themselves against his thighs. He concentrated on not swallowing his tongue. Around him, the ship creaked and groaned. There was a disconcerting bang from belowdecks, but nothing on his panel went red. The *Knight*'s torch drive could deliver a lot of thrust, but at the cost of a prodigious fuel-burn rate. But if they could save the *Cant,* it wouldn't matter.

Over the blood pounding in his ears, Holden could hear Ade's gentle breathing and the click of her keyboard. He wished he could just go to sleep to that sound, but the juice was singing and burning in his blood. He was more awake than he'd ever been.

"Yes, sir," Ade said over the comm.

It took Holden a second to realize she was talking to McDowell. He turned up the volume to hear what the captain was saying.

"—the mains online, full power."

"We're fully loaded, sir. If we try to burn that hard, we'll tear the drive right off the mounts," Ade replied. McDowell must have asked her to fire up the Epstein.

"Mr. Tukunbo," McDowell said, "we have…four minutes. If you break it, I won't bill you."

"Yes, sir. Bringing mains online. Setting for maximum burn," Ade said, and in the background Holden could hear the high-g warning Klaxon. There was a louder clicking as Ade strapped herself in.

"Mains online in three…two…one…execute," Ade said.

The *Canterbury* groaned so loud Holden had to turn the comm volume down. It moaned and shrieked like a banshee for several seconds, and then there was a shattering crash. He pulled up the exterior visual, fighting against the g-induced blackout at the edge of his vision. The *Canterbury* was in one piece.

"Ade, what the hell was that?" McDowell said, his speech slurred.

"The drive tearing a strut. Mains are off-line, sir," Ade replied, not saying *Exactly like I said would happen.*

"What did that buy us?" McDowell asked.

"Not much. The torpedoes are now at over forty klicks a second and accelerating. We're down to maneuvering thrusters," Ade said.

"Shit," McDowell said.

"They're going to hit us, sir," Ade said.

"Jim," McDowell said, his voice suddenly loud over the direct channel he'd opened. "We're going down, and there's no way around it. Click twice to acknowledge."

Jim clicked his radio twice.

"Okay, so, now we need to think about surviving after the hit. If they're looking to cripple us before boarding, they'll take out our drive and our comm array. Becca's been broadcasting an SOS ever since the torpedoes were fired, but I'd like you to keep yelling if we stop. If they know you're out there, they are less likely to toss everyone out an airlock. Witnesses, you know," McDowell said.

Jim clicked twice again.

"Turn around, Jim. Hide behind that asteroid. Call for help. Order."

Jim clicked twice, then signaled all-stop to Alex. In an instant, the giant sitting on his chest disappeared, replaced by weightlessness. The sudden transition would have made him throw up if his veins hadn't been coursing with antinausea drugs.

"What's up?" Alex said.

"New job," Holden said, teeth chattering from the juice. "We're calling for help and negotiating a release of prisoners once the bad guys have the *Cant*. Burn back to that asteroid, since it's the closest we can get to cover."

"Roger that, Boss," Alex said. He added in a lower voice, "I'd kill for a couple of tubes or a nice keel-mounted rail gun right now."

"I hear you."

"Wake up the kids downstairs?"

"Let them sleep."

"Roger that," Alex said, then clicked off.

Before the heavy g started up again, Holden turned on the *Knight*'s SOS. The channel to Ade was still open, and now that McDowell was off the line, he could hear her breathing again. He turned the volume all the way up and lay back in the straps, waiting to be crushed. Alex didn't disappoint him.

"One minute," Ade said, her voice loud enough to distort through his helmet's speakers. Holden didn't turn the volume down. Her voice was admirably calm as she called out the impact countdown.

"Thirty seconds."

Holden wanted desperately to talk, to say something comforting, to make ludicrous and untrue assertions of love. The giant standing on his chest just laughed with the deep rumble of their fusion torch.

"Ten seconds."

"Get ready to kill the reactor and play dead after the torpedoes hit. If we're not a threat, they won't hit us again," McDowell said.

"Five," Ade said.

"Four.

"Three.

"Two.

"One."

The *Canterbury* shuddered and the monitor went white. Ade took one sharp intake of breath, which cut off as the radio broke up. The static squeal almost ruptured Holden's eardrums. He chinned the volume down and clicked his radio at Alex.

The thrust suddenly dropped to a tolerable two g and all the ship's sensors flared into overload. A brilliant light poured through the small airlock porthole.

"Report, Alex, report! What happened?" Holden yelled.

"My God. They nuked her. They nuked the *Cant*," Alex said, his voice low and dazed.

"What's her status? Give me a report on the *Canterbury*! I have zero sensors down here. Everything's just gone white!"

There was a long pause; then Alex said, "I have zero sensors up here too, Boss. But I can give you a status on the *Cant*. I can see her."

"See her? From here?"

"Yeah. She's a cloud of vapor the size of Olympus Mons. She's gone, Boss. She's gone."

That can't be right, Holden's mind protested. That doesn't happen. Pirates don't nuke water haulers. No one wins. No one gets paid. And if you just want to murder fifty people, walking into a restaurant with a machine gun is a *lot* easier.

He wanted to shout it, scream at Alex that he was wrong. But he had to keep it together. *I'm the old man now.*

"All right. New mission, Alex. Now we're witnesses to murder. Get us back to that asteroid. I'll start compiling a broadcast. Wake everyone up. They need to know," Holden said. "I'm rebooting the sensor package."

He methodically shut down the sensors and their software, waited two minutes, then slowly brought them back online. His hands were shaking. He was nauseated. His body felt like he was operating his flesh from a distance, and he didn't know how much was the juice and how much was shock.

The sensors came back up. Like any other ship that flew the space lanes, the *Knight* was hardened against radiation. You couldn't get anywhere near Jupiter's massive radiation belt unless you were. But Holden doubted the ship's designers had half a dozen nuclear weapons going off nearby in mind when they'd created the specs. They'd gotten lucky. Vacuum might protect them from an electromagnetic pulse, but the blast radiation could still have fried every sensor the ship had.

Once the array came back up, he scanned the space where the *Canterbury* had been. There was nothing larger than a softball. He switched over to the ship that killed it, which was flying off sunward at a leisurely one g. Heat bloomed in Holden's chest.

He wasn't scared. Aneurysm-inducing rage made his temples pound and his fists squeeze until his tendons hurt. He flipped on the comms and aimed a tightbeam at the retreating ship.

"This message is to whoever ordered the destruction of the *Canterbury*, the civilian ice freighter that you just blew into gas. You don't get to just fly away, you murderous son of a bitch. I don't care what your reasons are, but you just killed fifty friends of mine. You need to know who they were. I am sending to you the name and photograph of everyone who just died in that ship. Take a good look at what you did. Think about that while I work on finding out who you are."

He closed the voice channel, pulled up the *Canterbury*'s

personnel files, and began transmitting the crew dossiers to the other ship.

"What are you doing?" asked Naomi from behind him, not from his helmet speakers.

She was standing there with her helmet off. Sweat plastered her thick black hair to her head and neck. Her face was unreadable. Holden took off his helmet.

"I'm showing them the *Canterbury* was a real place where real people lived. People with names and families," he said, the juice making his voice less steady than he would have liked. "If there's something resembling a human being giving the orders on that ship, I hope it haunts him right up to the day they put him in the recycler for murder."

"I don't think they appreciate it," Naomi said, pointing at the panel behind him.

The enemy ship was now painting them with its targeting laser. Holden held his breath. No torpedoes launched, and after a few seconds, the stealth ship turned off its laser and the engine flared as it scooted off at high g. He heard Naomi let out a shuddering breath.

"So the *Canterbury*'s gone?" Naomi asked.

Holden nodded.

"Fuck me sideways," said Amos.

Amos and Shed stood together at the crew ladder. Amos' face was mottled red and white, and his big hands clenched and unclenched. Shed collapsed to his knees, slamming against the deck in the heavy two-g thrust. He didn't cry. He just looked at Holden and said, "Cameron's never going to get that arm, I guess," then buried his head in his hands and shook.

"Slow down, Alex. No need to run now," Holden said into the comm. The ship slowly dropped to one g.

"What now, Captain?" Naomi said, looking at him hard. *You're in charge now. Act like it.*

"Blowing them out of the sky would be my first choice, but since we don't have the weapons... follow them. Keep our eyes on them until we know where they're going. Expose them to everyone," Holden replied.

"Fuckin' A," said Amos loudly.

"Amos," Naomi said over her shoulder, "take Shed below and get him into a couch. If you need to, give him something to put him to sleep."

"You got it, Boss." Amos put a thick arm around Shed's waist and took him below.

When he was gone, Naomi turned back to Holden.

"No, sir. We are *not* chasing that ship. We are going to call for help, and then go wherever the help tells us to go."

"I—" Holden started.

"Yes, you're in charge. That makes me XO, and it's the XO's job to tell the captain when he's being an idiot. You're being an idiot, sir. You already tried to goad them into killing us with that broadcast. Now you want to chase them? And what will you do if they let you catch them? Broadcast another emotional plea?" Naomi said, moving closer to him. "You are going to get the remaining four members of your crew to safety. And that's all. When we're safe, you can go on your crusade. Sir."

Holden unbuckled the straps on his couch and stood up. The juice was starting to burn out, leaving his body spent and sickened. Naomi lifted her chin and didn't back up.

"Glad you're with me, Naomi," he said. "Go see to the crew. McDowell gave me one last order."

Naomi looked him over critically; he could see her distrust. He didn't defend himself; he just waited until she was done. She nodded at him once and climbed down the ladder to the deck below.

Once she was gone, he worked methodically, putting together a broadcast package that included all the sensor data from the *Canterbury* and the *Knight*. Alex climbed down from the cockpit and sat down heavily in the next chair.

"You know, Captain, I've been thinkin'," he said. His voice had the same post-juice shakes as Holden's own.

Holden bit back his irritation at the interruption and said, "What about?"

"That stealth ship."

Holden turned away from his work.

"Tell me."

"So, I don't know any pirates that have shit like that."

"Go on."

"In fact, the only time I've seen tech like that was back when I was in the navy," Alex said. "We were working on ships with energy-absorbing skins and internal heat sinks. More of a strategic weapon than a tactical one. You can't hide an active drive, but if you can get into position and shut the drive down, store all your waste heat internally, you can hide yourself pretty good. Add in the energy-absorbing skin, and radar, ladar, and passive sensors don't pick you up. Plus, pretty tough to get nuclear torpedoes outside of the military."

"You're saying the Martian navy did this?"

Alex took a long shuddering breath.

"If *we* had it, you know the Earthers were workin' on it too," he said.

They looked at each other across the narrow space, the implications heavier than a ten-g burn. Holden pulled the transmitter and battery they'd recovered from the *Scopuli* out of the thigh pocket of his suit. He started pulling it apart, looking for a stamp or an insignia. Alex watched, quiet for once. The transmitter was generic; it could have come from the radio room of any ship in the solar system. The battery was a nondescript gray block. Alex reached out and Holden handed it to him. Alex pried off the gray plastic cover and flipped the metal battery around in his hands. Without saying a word, he held the bottom up to Holden's face. Stamped in the black metal on the bottom of the battery was a serial number that began with the letters *MCRN*.

Martian Congressional Republic Navy.

The radio was set to broadcast on full power. The data package was ready to transmit. Holden stood in front of the camera, leaning a little forward.

"My name is James Holden," he said, "and my ship, the *Canterbury*, was just destroyed by a warship with stealth technology and what appear to be parts stamped with Martian navy serial numbers. Data stream to follow."

Chapter Six: Miller

The cart sped through the tunnel, siren masking the whine of motors. Behind them, they left curious civilians and the scent of overheated bearings. Miller leaned forward in his seat, willing the cart to go faster. They were three levels and maybe four kilometers from the station house.

"Okay," Havelock said. "I'm sorry, but I'm missing something here."

"What?" Miller said. He meant *What are you yammering about?* Havelock took it as *What are you missing?*

"A water hauler millions of klicks from here got vaporized. Why are we going to full alert? Our cisterns will last months without even going on rationing. There are a lot of other haulers out there. Why is this a crisis?"

Miller turned and looked at his partner straight on. The small, stocky build. The thick bones from a childhood in full g. Just like the asshole in the transmission. They didn't understand. If Havelock had been in this James Holden's place, he might have done the same stupid, irresponsible, idiotic bullshit. For the space of a breath, they weren't security anymore. They weren't partners. They were a Belter and an Earther. Miller looked away before Havelock could see the change in his eyes.

"That prick Holden? The one in the broadcast?" Miller said. "He just declared war on Mars for us."

The cart swerved and bobbed, its internal computer adjusting for some virtual hiccup in the traffic flow half a kilometer ahead. Havelock shifted, grabbing for the support strut. They hit a ramp up to the next level, civilians on foot making a path for them.

"You grew up where the water's maybe dirty, but it falls out of the sky for you," Miller said. "The air's filthy, but it's not going away if your door seals fail. It's not like that out here."

"But we're not on the hauler. We don't need the ice. We aren't under threat," Havelock said.

Miller sighed, rubbing his eyes with thumb and knuckle until ghosts of false color bloomed.

"When I was homicide," Miller said, "there was this guy. Property management specialist working a contract out of Luna. Someone burned half his skin off and dropped him out an airlock. Turned out he was responsible for maintenance on sixty holes up on level thirty. Lousy neighborhood. He'd been cutting corners. Hadn't replaced the air filters in three months. There was mold growing in three of the units. And you know what we found after that?"

"What?" Havelock asked.

"Not a goddamn thing, because we stopped looking. Some people need to die, and he was one. And the next guy that took the job cleaned the ducting and swapped the filters on schedule. That's what it's like in the Belt. Anyone who came out here and didn't put environmental systems above everything else died young. All us still out here are the ones that cared."

"Selective effect?" Havelock said. "You're seriously arguing in favor of selective effect? I never thought I'd hear that shit coming out of you."

"What's that?"

"Racist propaganda bullshit," Havelock said. "It's the one that says the difference in environment has changed the Belters so much that instead of just being a bunch of skinny obsessive-compulsives, they aren't really human anymore."

"I'm not saying that," Miller said, suspecting that it was exactly what he was saying. "It's just that Belters don't take the long view when you screw with basic resources. That water was future air, propellant mass, and potables for us. We have no sense of humor about that shit."

The cart hit a ramp of metalwork grate. The lower level fell away below them. Havelock was silent.

"This Holden guy didn't say it was Mars. Just that they found a Martian battery. You think people are going to…declare war?" Havelock said. "Just on the basis of this one guy's pictures of a battery?"

"The ones that wait to get the whole story aren't our problem."

At least not tonight, he thought. *Once the whole story gets out, we'll see where we stand.*

The station house was somewhere between one-half and three-quarters full. Security men stood in clumps, nodding to each other, eyes narrow and jaws tight. One of the vice cops laughed at something, his amusement loud, forced, smelling of fear. Miller saw the change in Havelock as they walked across the common area to their desks. Havelock had been able to put Miller's reaction down to one man's being oversensitive. A whole room, though. A whole station house. By the time they reached their chairs, Havelock's eyes were wide.

Captain Shaddid came in. The bleary look was gone. Her hair was pulled back, her uniform crisp and professional, her voice as calm as a surgeon in a battlefield hospital. She stepped up on the first desk she came to, improvising a pulpit.

"Ladies and gentlemen," she said. "You've seen the transmission. Any questions?"

"Who let that fucking Earther near a radio?" someone shouted. Miller saw Havelock laugh along with the crowd, but it didn't reach his eyes. Shaddid scowled and the crowd quieted.

"Here's the situation," she said. "No way we can control this information. It was broadcast everywhere. We have five sites on the internal network that have been mirroring it, and we have to assume it's public knowledge starting ten minutes ago. Our job now is to keep the rioting to a minimum and ensure station integrity around the port. Station houses fifty and two thirteen are helping on it too. The port authority has released all the ships with inner planet registry. That doesn't mean they're all gone. They still have to round up their crews. But it does mean they're going."

"The government offices?" Miller said, loud enough to carry.

"Not our problem, thank God," Shaddid said. "They have infrastructure in place. Blast doors are already down and sealed. They've broken off from the main environmental systems, so we aren't even breathing their air right now."

"Well, that's a relief," Yevgeny said from the cluster of homicide detectives.

"Now the bad news," Shaddid said. Miller heard the silence of a hundred and fifty cops holding their breath. "We've got eighty known OPA agents on the station. They're all employed and legal, and you know this is the kind of thing they've been waiting for. We have an order from the governor that we're not going to do any proactive detention. No one gets arrested until they do something."

Angry voices rose in chorus.

"Who does he think he is?" someone called from the back. Shaddid snapped at the comment like a shark.

"The governor is the one who contracted with us to keep this station in working order," Shaddid said. "We'll follow his directives."

In his peripheral vision, Miller saw Havelock nod. He wondered what the governor thought of the question of Belter independence. Maybe the OPA weren't the only ones who'd been waiting for something like this to happen. Shaddid went on, outlining the security response they were permitted. Miller listened with half an ear, so lost in speculating on the politics behind the situation he almost missed it when Shaddid called his name.

"Miller will take the second team to the port level and cover sectors thirteen through twenty-four. Kasagawa, team three, twenty-five through thirty-six, and so on. That's twenty men apiece, except for Miller."

"I can make it with nineteen," Miller said, then quietly to Havelock, "You're sitting this one out, partner. Having an Earther with a gun out there isn't going to make things better."

"Yeah," Havelock said. "Saw that coming."

"Okay," Shaddid said. "You all know the drill. Let's move."

Miller rounded up his riot squad. All the faces were familiar, all men and women he'd worked with over his years in security. He organized them in his mind with a nearly automatic efficiency. Brown and Gelbfish both had SWAT experience, so they would lead the wings if it came to crowd control. Aberforth had three write-ups for excessive violence since her kid had been busted for drug running on Ganymede, so she was second string. She could work out her anger-management issues another time. Around the station house, he heard the other squad commanders making similar decisions.

"Okay," Miller said. "Let's suit up."

They moved away in a group, heading for the equipment bay. Miller paused. Havelock remained leaning against his desk, arms folded, eyes locked on the middle distance. Miller was torn between sympathy for the man and impatience. It was hard being on the team but not on the team. On the other hand, what the hell had he expected, taking a contract in the Belt? Havelock looked up, meeting Miller's gaze. They nodded to each other. Miller was the first to turn away.

The equipment bay was part warehouse, part bank vault, designed by someone more concerned with conserving space than getting things out efficiently. The lights—recessed white LEDs—gave the gray walls a sterile cast. Bare stone echoed every voice and footfall. Banks of ammunition and firearms, evidence bags and test panels, spare servers and replacement uniforms lined the walls and filled most of the interior space. The riot gear was in a side room, in gray steel lockers with high-security electronic locks. The standard outfit consisted of high-impact plastic shields, electric batons, shin guards, bullet-resistant chest and thigh armor, and helmets with reinforced face guards—all of it designed to make a handful of station security into an intimidating, inhuman force.

Miller keyed in his access code. The seals released; the lockers opened.

"Well," Miller said conversationally. "Fuck me."

The lockers were empty, gray coffins with the corpses all gone. Across the room, he heard one of the other squads shouting in outrage. Miller systematically opened every riot control locker he could get to. All of them were the same. Shaddid appeared at his side, her face pale with rage.

"What's plan B?" Miller asked.

Shaddid spat on the floor, then closed her eyes. They shifted under her lids like she was dreaming. Two long breaths later, they opened.

"Check the SWAT lockers. There should be enough in there to outfit two people in each squad."

"Snipers?" Miller said.

"You have a better idea, Detective?" Shaddid said, leaning on the last word.

Miller raised his hands in surrender. Riot gear was meant to intimidate and control. SWAT gear was made to kill with the greatest efficiency possible. Seemed their mandate had just changed.

On any given day, a thousand ships might be docked on Ceres Station, and activity there rarely slowed and never stopped. Each sector could accommodate twenty ships, the traffic of humanity and cargo, transport vans, mesocranes, and industrial forklifts, and his squad was responsible for twenty sectors.

The air stank of refrigerant and oil. The gravity was slightly above 0.3 g, station spin alone lending the place a sense of oppression and danger. Miller didn't like the port. Having vacuum so close under his feet made him nervous. Passing the dockworkers and transport crews, he didn't know whether to scowl or smile. He was here to scare people into behaving and also to reassure them that everything was under control. After the first three sectors, he settled on the smile. It was the kind of lie he was better at.

They had just reached the junction of sectors nineteen and twenty when they heard screaming. Miller pulled his hand terminal out of his pocket, connected to the central surveillance network, and called up the security camera array. It took a few seconds to find it: a mob of fifty or sixty civilians stretching almost all the way across the tunnel, traffic blocked on both sides. There were weapons being waved over heads. Knives, clubs. At least two pistols. Fists pumped in the air. And at the center of the crowd, a huge shirtless man was beating someone to death.

"Showtime," Miller said, waving his squad forward at a run.

He was still a hundred meters from the turn that would take them to the clot of human violence when he saw the shirtless man knock his victim to the ground, then stomp on her neck. The head twisted sideways at an angle that didn't leave any question. Miller slowed his team to a brisk walk. Arresting the murderer while surrounded by a crowd of his friends would be tough enough without being winded.

There was blood in the water now. Miller could sense it. The mob was going to turn out. To the station, to the ships. If the people started joining the chaos...what path would it be likely to take? There was a brothel one level up from there and half a kilometer anti-spinward that catered to inner planet types. The tariff inspector for sector twenty-one was married to a girl from Luna and had bragged about it maybe once too often.

There were too many targets, Miller thought even as he motioned his snipers to spread out. He was trying to reason with a fire. Stop it here, and no one else got killed.

In his imagination, Candace crossed her arms and said, *What's plan B?*

The outer edge of the mob raised the alarm well before Miller reached it. The surge of bodies and threats shifted. Miller tipped back his hat. Men, women. Dark skin, pale, golden brown, and all with the long, thin build of Belters, all with the square-mouthed angry gape of chimpanzees at war.

"Let me take a couple of them down, sir," Gelbfish said from his terminal. "Put the fear of God into them."

"We'll get there," Miller said, smiling at the angry mob. "We'll get there."

The face he expected floated to the front. Shirtless. The big man, blood covering his hands and splattered on his cheek. The seed crystal of the riot.

"That one?" Gelbfish asked, and Miller knew that a tiny infrared dot was painting Shirtless' forehead even as he glowered at Miller and the uniforms behind him.

"No," Miller said. "That'll only set the rest of them off."

"So what do we do?" Brown said.

It was a hell of a question.

"Sir," Gelbfish said. "The big fucker's got an OPA tattoo on his left shoulder."

"Well," Miller said, "if you do have to shoot him, start there."

He stepped forward, tying his terminal into the local system, overriding the alert. When he spoke, his voice boomed from the overhead speakers.

"This is Detective Miller. Unless you all want to be locked up as accessories to murder, I suggest you disperse now." Muting the microphone in his terminal, he said to Shirtless, "Not you, big fella. Move a muscle and we shoot you."

Someone in the crowd threw a wrench, the silver metal arcing low through the air toward Miller's head. He almost stepped out of the way, but the handle caught him across the ear. His head filled with the deep sound of bells, and the wet of blood tracked down his neck.

"Hold fire," Miller shouted. "Hold your fire."

The crowd laughed, as if he'd been talking to them. Idiots. Shirtless, emboldened, strode forward. The steroids had distended his thighs so badly that he waddled. Miller turned the mic on his terminal back on. If the crowd was watching them face each other down, they weren't breaking things. It wasn't spreading. Not yet.

"So. Friend. You only kick helpless people to death, or can anybody join in?" Miller asked, his voice conversational but echoing out of the dock speakers like a pronouncement from God.

"The fuck you barking, Earth dog?" Shirtless said.

"Earth?" Miller said, chuckling. "I look like I grew up in a gravity well to you? I was born on this rock."

"Inners kibble you, bitch," Shirtless said. "You they dog."

"You think?"

"Fuckin' dui," Shirtless said. *Fucking true.* He flexed his pectorals. Miller suppressed the urge to laugh.

"So killing that poor bastard was for the good of the station?" Miller said. "The good of the Belt? Don't be a chump, kid. They're playing you. They want you to act like a bunch of stupid riotboys so they have a reason to shut this place down."

"*Schrauben sie sie weibchen,*" Shirtless said in Belter-inflected gutter German, leaning forward.

Okay, second time I've been called a bitch, Miller thought.

"Kneecap him," Miller said. Shirtless' legs blew out in twin sprays of crimson and he went down howling. Miller walked past his writhing body, stepping toward the mob.

"You're taking your orders from this *pendejo*?" he said. "Listen to me, we all know what's coming. We know dance starting, now, like pow, right? They fucked tu agua, and we all know the answer. Out an airlock, no?"

He could see it in their faces: the sudden fear of the snipers, then the confusion. He pressed on, not giving them time to think. He switched back to the lower-level lingo, the language of education, authority.

"You know what Mars wants? They want you, doing this. They want this piece of shit here to make sure that everyone looks at Belters and thinks we're a bunch of psychopaths who tear up their own station. They want to tell themselves we're just like them. Well, we aren't. We're Belters, and we take care of our own."

He picked a man at the edge of the mob. Not as pumped as Shirtless, but big. He had an OPA split circle on his arm.

"You," Miller said. "You want to fight for the Belt?"

"Dui," the man said.

"I bet you do. He did too," Miller said, jerking a thumb back at Shirtless. "But now he's a cripple, and he's going down for murder. So we've already lost one. You see? They're turning us against each other. Can't let them do that. Every one of you I have to arrest or cripple or kill, that's one less we have when the day comes. And it's coming. But it's not now. You understand?"

The OPA man scowled. The mob drew back from him, making space. Miller could feel it like a current against him. It was shifting.

"Day's coming, hombre," the OPA man said. "You know your side?"

The tone was a threat, but there was no power behind it. Miller took a slow breath. It was over.

"Always the side of the angels," he said. "Why don't you all go back to work? Show's over here, and we've all got plenty that needs doing."

Momentum broken, the mob fell apart. First one and two peeling off from the edges, and then the whole knot untying itself at once. Five minutes after Miller had arrived, the only signs that anything had happened were Shirtless mewling in a pool of his own blood, the wound on Miller's ear, and the body of the woman fifty good citizens had stood by and watched be beaten to death. She was short and wearing the flight suit of a Martian freight line.

Only one dead. Makes it a good night, Miller thought sourly.

He went to the fallen man. The OPA tattoo was smeared red. Miller knelt.

"Friend," he said. "You are under arrest for the murder of that lady over there, whoever the hell she is. You are not required to participate in questioning without the presence of an attorney or union representative, and if you so much as look at me wrong, I'll space you. Do we understand each other?"

From the look in the man's eyes, Miller knew they did.

Chapter Seven: Holden

Holden could drink coffee at half a g. Actually sit and hold a mug under his nose and let the aroma drift up. Sip it slowly and not burn his tongue. Drinking coffee was one of the activities that didn't make the transition to microgravity well, but at half a g, it was fine.

So he sat and tried very hard to think about coffee and gravity in the silence of the *Knight*'s tiny galley. Even the normally talkative Alex was quiet. Amos had set his big handgun on the table and was staring at it with frightening concentration. Shed was asleep. Naomi was sitting across the room, drinking tea and keeping one eye on the wall panel next to her. She'd routed ops to it.

As long as he kept his mind on his coffee, he didn't have to think about Ade giving one last gasp of fear and then turning into a glowing vapor.

Alex ruined it by speaking.

"At some point, we need to decide where we're goin'," he said.

Holden nodded, took a sip of his coffee, and closed his eyes. His muscles vibrated like plucked strings, and his peripheral vision was dappled with points of imaginary light. The first twinges of the post-juice crash were starting, and it was going to be a bad one. He wanted to enjoy these last few moments before the pain hit.

"He's right, Jim," Naomi said. "We can't just fly in a big circle at half a g forever."

Holden didn't open his eyes. The darkness behind his lids was bright and active and mildly nauseating.

"We aren't waiting forever," he said. "We're waiting fifty minutes for Saturn Station to call me back and tell me what to do with their ship. The *Knight* is still P and K property. We're still employees. You wanted me to call for help, I called for help. Now we are waiting to see what that looks like."

"Shouldn't we start flying toward Saturn Station, then, Boss?" Amos asked, directing his question at Naomi.

Alex snorted.

"Not on the *Knight*'s engine. Even if we had the fuel for that trip, which we don't, I don't want to sit in this can for the next three months," he said. "Naw, if we're goin' somewhere, it's gotta be the Belt or Jupiter. We're as close to exactly between 'em as you can get."

"I vote we continue on to Ceres," Naomi said. "P and K has offices there. We don't know anyone in the Jupiter complex."

Without opening his eyes, Holden shook his head.

"No, we wait for them to call us back."

Naomi made an exasperated sound. It was funny, he thought, how you could make someone's voice out from the smallest sounds. A cough or a sigh. Or the little gasp right before she died.

Holden sat up and opened his eyes. He placed his coffee mug on the table carefully, with hands that were starting to palsy.

"I don't want to fly sunward to Ceres, because that's the direction the torpedo ship went, and your point about chasing them is well taken, Naomi. I don't want to fly out to Jupiter, because we only have the fuel for one trip, and once we fly that direction for a while, we're locked in. We are sitting here and drinking coffee because I need to make a decision, and P and K gets a say in that decision. So we wait for them to answer, and then I decide."

Holden got up slowly, carefully, and began moving toward the crew ladder. "I'm going to crash for a few minutes, let the worst of the shakes wear off. If P and K calls, let me know."

Holden popped sedative tabs—thin, bitter pills with an aftertaste like bread mold—but he didn't sleep. Over and over, McDowell placed a hand on his arm and called him Jim. Becca laughed and cursed like a sailor. Cameron bragged about his prowess on the ice.

Ade gasped.

Holden had flown the Ceres-to-Saturn circuit on the *Canterbury* nine times. Two round-trips a year, for almost five years. Most of the crew had been there the entire time. Flying on the *Cant* might be the bottom of the barrel, but that meant there was nowhere else to go. People stayed, made the ship their home. After the near-constant duty transfers of the navy, he appreciated stability. Made it his home too. McDowell said something he couldn't quite make out. The *Cant* groaned like she was under a hard burn.

Ade smiled and winked at him.

The worst leg cramp in history hit every muscle in his body at once. Holden bit down hard on his rubber mouth guard, screaming. The pain brought an oblivion that was almost a relief. His mind shut off, drowned out by the needs of his body. Fortunately or not, the drugs started to kick in. His muscles unknotted. His nerves stopped screaming, and consciousness returned like a reluctant schoolboy. His jaw ached as he pulled out the guard. He'd worn toothmarks in the rubber.

In the dim blue cabin light, he thought about the kind of man who followed an order to kill a civilian ship.

He'd done some things in the navy that had kept him awake nights. He'd followed some orders he vehemently disagreed with. But to lock on to a civilian ship with fifty people aboard and press the button that launched six nuclear weapons? He would have refused. If his commanding officer had insisted, he'd have declared it an illegal order and demanded that the executive officer take control of the ship and arrest the captain. They'd have had to shoot him to get him away from the weapon post.

He'd known the sort of people who would have followed the order, though. He told himself that they were sociopaths and animals, no better than pirates who'd board your ship, strip your engine, and take your air. That they weren't human.

But even as he nursed his hatred, drug-hazed rage offering its nihilistic comforts, he couldn't believe they were idiots. The itch at the back of his head was still *Why? What does anyone gain from killing an ice hauler? Who gets paid? Someone always gets paid.*

I'm going to find you. I'm going to find you and end you. But before I do, I am going to make you explain.

The second wave of pharmaceuticals exploded in his bloodstream. He was hot and limp, his veins filled with syrup. Just before the tabs finally knocked him out, Ade smiled and winked.

And blew away like dust.

The comm beeped at him. Naomi's voice said, "Jim, the P and K response finally came in. Want me to send it down there?"

Holden struggled to make sense of the words. Blinked. Something was wrong with his bunk. With the ship. Slowly, he remembered.

"Jim?"

"No," he said. "I want to watch it up in ops with you. How long was I out?"

"Three hours," she said.

"Jesus. They took their sweet time getting back to us, didn't they?"

Holden rolled out of his couch and wiped off the crust that held his eyelashes together. He'd been weeping in his sleep. He told himself it was from the juice crash. The deep ache in his chest was only stressed cartilage.

What were you doing for three hours before you called us back? he wondered.

Naomi waited for him at the comm station, a man's face frozen mid-word on the screen in front of her. He seemed familiar.

"That isn't the operations manager."

"Nope. It's the P and K legal counsel on Saturn Station. The one who gave that speech after the crackdown on supply pilfering?" Naomi said. " 'Stealing from us is stealing from you.' That one."

"Lawyer," Holden said with a grimace. "This is going to be bad news, then."

Naomi restarted the message. The lawyer sprang into motion.

"James Holden, this is Wallace Fitz calling from Saturn Station. We've received your request for help, and your report of the incident. We've also received your broadcast accusing Mars of destroying the *Canterbury*. This was, to say the least, ill advised. The Martian representative on Saturn Station was in my office not five minutes after your broadcast was received, and the MCR is quite upset by what they view as unfounded accusations of piracy by their government.

"To further investigate this matter, and to aid in discovering the true wrongdoers, if any, the MCRN is dispatching one of their ships from the Jupiter system to pick you up. The MCRN *Donnager* is the name of this vessel. Your orders from P and K are as follows: You will fly at best possible speed to the Jupiter system. You will cooperate fully with instructions given you by the MCRN *Donnager*, or by any officer of the Martian Congressional Republic Navy. You will assist the MCRN in their investigation into the destruction of the *Canterbury*. You will *refrain* from any further broadcasting except to us or the *Donnager*.

"If you fail to follow these instructions from the company and from the government of Mars, your contract with P and K will be terminated, and you will be considered in illegal possession of a P and K shuttle craft. We will then prosecute you to the fullest extent of the law.

"Wallace Fitz out."

Holden frowned at the monitor, then shook his head.

"I never said Mars did it."

"You sort of did," Naomi replied.

"I didn't say anything that wasn't entirely factual and backed up by the data I transmitted, and I engaged in no speculation about those facts."

"So," Naomi said. "What do we do?"

"No fucking way," Amos said. "No *fucking* way."

The galley was a small space. The five of them filled it uncomfortably. The gray laminate walls showed whorls of bright scrapes where mold had grown once and been cleaned off with microwaves and steel wool. Shed sat with his back against the wall, Naomi across the table. Alex stood in the doorway. Amos had started pacing along the back — two fast paces, then a turn — before the lawyer had finished his first sentence.

"I'm not happy about it either. But that's the word from the home office," Holden said, pointing at the galley's display screen. "Didn't mean to get you guys in trouble."

"No problem, Holden. I still think you did the right thing," Shed replied, running one hand through his limp blond hair. "So what do you think the Martians will do with us?"

"I'm thinking pull our fucking toes off until Holden goes back on the radio and says it wasn't them," Amos said. "What in the holy hell is this? They attacked us, and now we're supposed to *cooperate*? They killed the captain!"

"Amos," Holden said.

"Sorry, Holden. Captain," Amos said. "But Jesus *wept*. We're getting fucked here and not the nice way. We're not gonna do this, are we?"

"I don't want to disappear into some Martian prison ship forever," Holden said. "The way I see it, we have two options. Either we go along with this, which is basically throwing ourselves on their mercy. Or we run, try to make it to the Belt and hide."

"I'm voting for the Belt," Naomi said, her arms crossed. Amos raised a hand, seconding the motion. Shed slowly raised his own.

Alex shook his head.

"I know the *Donnager*," he said. "She's not some rock hopper. She's the flagship for the MCRN's Jupiter fleet. Battleship. Quarter million tons of bad news. You ever serve on a ship that size?"

"No. I wasn't on anything bigger than a destroyer," Holden replied.

"I served on the *Bandon*, with the home fleet. We can't go anywhere that a ship like that can't find us. She's got four main engines, each one bigger than our whole ship. She's designed for long periods at high g with every sailor on board juiced to the gills. We can't run, sir, and even if we did, her sensor package could track a golf ball and hit it with a torpedo from half the solar system away."

"Oh, fuck that, sir," Amos said, standing up. "These Martian needle dicks blew up the *Cant*! I say run. At least make it hard for them."

Naomi put one hand on Amos' forearm, and the big mechanic paused, shook his head, and sat down. The galley was silent. Holden wondered if McDowell had ever had to make a call like this, and what the old man would have done.

"Jim, this is your decision," she said, but her eyes were hard. *No, what you are going to do is get the remaining four members of your crew to safety. And that's all.*

Holden nodded and tapped his fingers against his lips.

"P and K doesn't have our back on this one. We probably can't get away, but I don't want to disappear either," Holden said. And then: "I think we go, but we don't go quietly. Why don't we go disobey the spirit of an order?"

Naomi finished working on the comm panel, her hair now float-ing around her like a black cloud in the zero g.

"Okay, Jim, I'm dumping every watt into the comm array. They'll be getting this loud and clear all the way out to Titania," she said.

Holden reached up to run one hand through his sweat-plastered hair. In the null gravity, that just made it stick straight out in every direction. He zipped up his flight suit and pressed the record button.

"This is James Holden, formerly of the *Canterbury,* now on the shuttle *Knight.* We are cooperating with an investigation into who destroyed the *Canterbury* and, as part of that cooperation, are agreeing to be taken aboard your ship, the MCRN *Donnager.* We hope that this cooperation means that we will not be held prisoner or harmed. Any such action would only serve to reinforce the idea that the *Canterbury* was destroyed by a Martian vessel. James Holden out."

Holden leaned back. "Naomi, send that out broadband."

"That's a dirty trick, Boss," said Alex. "Pretty hard to disap-pear us now."

"I believe in the ideal of the transparent society, Mr. Kamal," said Holden. Alex grinned, pushed off, and floated down the gangway. Naomi tapped the comm panel, making a small, satis-fied sound in the back of her throat.

"Naomi," Holden said. She turned, her hair waving lazily, like they were both drowning. "If this goes badly, I need you...I need you to..."

"Throw you to the wolves," she said. "Blame everything on you and get the others back to Saturn Station safely."

"Yeah," Holden said. "Don't play the hero."

She let the words hang in the air until the last of the irony leeched out of them.

"Hadn't crossed my mind, sir," she said.

"*Knight,* this is Captain Theresa Yao of the MCRN *Donnager,*" said the severe-looking woman on the comm screen. "Message received. Please refrain from further general broadcasts. My navigator will be sending course information shortly. Follow that course exactly. Yao out."

Alex laughed.

"I think you pissed her off," he said. "Got the course info. They'll be picking us up in thirteen days. Give her time to really stew on it."

"Thirteen days before I'm clapped in irons and have needles shoved under my fingernails," Holden sighed, leaning back in his couch. "Well, best begin our flight toward imprisonment and torture. You may lock in the transmitted course, Mr. Kamal."

"Roger that, Cap— Huh," said Alex.

"A problem?"

"Well, the *Knight* just did her pre-burn sweep for collision objects," Alex said. "And we have six Belt objects on an intercept course."

"Belt objects?"

"Fast contacts with no transponder signal," Alex replied. "Ships, but flyin' dark. They'll catch us just about two days before the *Donnager* does."

Holden pulled up the display. Six small signatures, yellow-orange shifting toward red. Heavy burn.

"Well," Holden said to the screen. "And who the hell are *you?*"

Chapter Eight: Miller

Aggression against the Belt is what Earth and Mars survive on. Our weakness is their strength," the masked woman said from Miller's terminal screen. The split circle of the OPA draped behind her, like something painted on a sheet. "Don't be afraid of them. Their only power is your fear."

"Well, that and a hundred or so gunships," Havelock said.

"From what I hear," Miller said, "if you clap your hands and say you believe, they can't shoot you."

"Have to try that sometime."

"We must rise up!" the woman said, her voice growing shrill. "We have to take our destiny before it is taken from us! Remember the *Canterbury*!"

Miller shut the viewer down and leaned back in his chair. The station was at its change-of-shift surge, voices raised one over the other as the previous round of cops brought the incoming

ones up to speed. The smell of fresh coffee competed with cigarette smoke.

"There's maybe a dozen like her," Havelock said, nodding
toward the dead terminal screen. "She's my favorite, though.
There're times I swear she's actually foaming at the mouth."

"How many more files?" Miller asked, and his partner shrugged.

"Two, three hundred," Havelock said, and took a drag on his
cigarette. He'd started smoking again. "Every few hours, there's a
new one. They aren't coming from one place. Sometimes they're
broadcast on the radio. Sometimes the files show up on public
partitions. Orlan found some guys at a portside bar passing out
those little VR squids like they were pamphlets."

"She bust them?"

"No," Havelock said as if it was no big deal.

A week had passed since James Holden, self-appointed martyr,
had proudly announced that he and his crew were going to go talk
to someone from the Martian navy instead of just slinging shit and
implications. The footage of the *Canterbury*'s death was everywhere, debates raging over every frame. The log files that documented the incident were perfectly legitimate, or they were
obviously doctored. The torpedoes that had slaughtered the hauler
were nukes or standard pirate fare that breached the drive by mistake, or it was all artifice lifted from old stock footage to cover up
what had really killed the *Cant*.

The riots had lasted for three days on and off, like a fire hot
enough to reignite every time the air pumped back in. The administrative offices reopened under heavy security, but they reopened.
The ports fell behind, but they were catching up. The shirtless
bastard who Miller had ordered shot was in the Star Helix detainment infirmary, getting new knees, filling out protests against
Miller, and preparing for his murder trial.

Six hundred cubic meters of nitrogen had gone missing from a
warehouse in sector fifteen. An unlicensed whore had been beaten
up and locked in a storage unit; as soon as she was done giving
evidence about her attackers, she'd be arrested. They'd caught the

kids who'd been breaking the surveillance cameras on level sixteen. Superficially, everything was business as usual.

Only superficially.

When Miller had started working homicide, one of the things
that had struck him was the surreal calm of the victims' families.
People who had just lost wives, husbands, children, and lovers.
People whose lives had just been branded by violence. More often
than not, they were calmly offering drinks and answering questions, making the detectives feel welcome. A civilian coming in
unaware might have mistaken them for whole. It was only in the
careful way they held themselves and the extra quarter second it
took their eyes to focus that Miller could see how deep the damage was.

Ceres Station was holding itself carefully. Its eyes were taking a
quarter second longer to focus. Middle-class people—storekeepers,
maintenance workers, computer techs—were avoiding him on
the tube the way petty criminals did. Conversations died when
Miller came near. In the station, the sense of being under siege was
growing. A month earlier, Miller and Havelock, Cobb and Rich-
ter, and the rest had been the steadying hand of the law. Now they
were employees of an Earth-based security contractor.

The difference was subtle, but it was deep. It made him want to
stand taller, to show with his body that he was a Belter. That he
belonged there. It made him want to win people's good opinion
back. Let by a bunch of guys passing out virtual reality propaganda with a warning, maybe.

It wasn't a smart impulse.

"What've we got on the board?" Miller asked.

"Two burglaries that look like that same ring," Havelock said.
"That domestic dispute from last week still needs the report closed
up. There was a pretty good assault over by Nakanesh Import
Consortium, but Shaddid was talking to Dyson and Patel about
that, so it's probably spoken for already."

"So you want…"

Havelock looked up and out to cover the fact that he was looking away. It was something he'd been doing more often since things had gone to shit.

"We've really got to get the reports done," Havelock said. "Not just the domestic. There're four or five folders that are only still open because they need to be crossed and dotted."

"Yeah," Miller said.

Since the riots, he'd watched everyone in a bar get served before Havelock. He'd seen how the other cops from Shaddid down went out of their way to reassure Miller that *he* was one of the good guys, a tacit apology for saddling him with an Earther. And he'd seen Havelock see it too.

It made Miller want to protect the man, to let Havelock spend his days in the safety of paperwork and station house coffee. Help the man pretend that he wasn't hated for the gravity he'd grown up in.

That wasn't a smart impulse either.

"What about your bullshit case?" Havelock asked.

"What?"

Havelock held up a folder. The Julie Mao case. The kidnap job. The sideshow. Miller nodded and rubbed his eyes. Someone at the front of the station house yelped. Someone else laughed.

"Yeah, no," Miller said. "Haven't touched it."

Havelock grinned and held it out to him. Miller accepted the file, flipped it open. The eighteen-year-old grinned out at him with perfect teeth.

"I don't want to saddle you with all the desk driving," Miller said.

"Hey, you're not the one that kept me off that one. That was Shaddid's call. And anyway…it's just paperwork. Never killed anyone. You feel guilty about it, you can buy me a beer after work."

Miller tapped the case against the corner of his desk, the small impacts settling the contents against the folder's spine.

"Right," he said. "I'll go do some follow-up on the bullshit. I'll be back by lunch, write something up to keep the boss happy."

"I'll be here," Havelock said. Then, as Miller rose: "Hey. Look.

I didn't want to say anything until I was sure, but I also don't want you to hear it someplace else…"

"Put in for a transfer?" Miller said.

"Yeah. Talked to some of those Protogen contractors that passed through. They say their Ganymede office is looking for a new lead investigator. And I thought…" Havelock shrugged.

"It's a good move," Miller said.

"Just want to go someplace with a sky, even if you look at it through domes," Havelock said, and all the bluff masculinity of police work couldn't keep the wistfulness out of his voice.

"It's a good move," Miller said again.

Juliette Andromeda Mao's hole was in the ninth level of a fourteen-tiered tunnel near the port. The great inverted V was almost half a kilometer wide at the top, and no more than a standard tube width at the bottom, the retrofit of one of a dozen reaction mass chambers from the years before the asteroid had been given its false gravity. Now thousands of cheap holes burrowed into the walls, hundreds on each level, heading straight back like shotgun shacks. Kids played on the terraced streets, shrieking and laughing at nothing. Someone at the bottom was flying a kite in the constant gentle spin breeze, the bright Mylar diamond swerving and bucking in the microturbulence. Miller checked his terminal against the numbers painted on the wall. *5151-I.* Home sweet home to the poor little rich girl.

He keyed his override, and the dirty green door popped its seals and let him pass.

The hole canted up into the body of the station. Three small rooms: general living space at the front, then a bedroom hardly larger than the cot it contained, then a stall with shower, toilet, and half sink all within elbow distance. It was a standard design. He'd seen it a thousand times.

Miller stood for a minute, not looking at anything in particular, listening to the reassuring hiss of air cycling through ductwork. He reserved judgment, waiting as the back of his head built an impression of the place and, through it, of the girl who'd lived there.

Spartan was the wrong word. The place was simple, yes. The only decorations were a small framed watercolor of a slightly abstracted woman's face over the table in the front room and a cluster of playing-card-sized plaques over the cot in the bedroom. He leaned close to read the small script. A formal award granting Julie Mao — not Juliette — purple belt status by the Ceres Center for Jiu Jitsu. Another stepping her up to brown belt. They were two years apart. Tough school, then. He put his fingers on the empty space on the wall where one for black could go. There was none of the affectation — no stylized throwing stars or imitation swords. Just a small acknowledgment that Julie Mao had done what she had done. He gave her points for that.

The drawers had two changes of clothes, one of heavy canvas and denim and one of blue linen with a silk scarf. One for work, one for play. It was less than Miller owned, and he was hardly a clotheshorse.

With her socks and underwear was a wide armband with the split circle of the OPA. Not a surprise, for a girl who'd turned her back on wealth and privilege to live in a dump like this. The refrigerator had two takeaway boxes filled with spoiled food and a bottle of local beer.

Miller hesitated, then took the beer. He sat at the table and pulled up the hole's built-in terminal. True to Shaddid's word, Julie's partition opened to Miller's password.

The custom background was a racing pinnace. The interface was customized in small, legible iconography. Communication, entertainment, work, personal. *Elegant.* That was the word. Not Spartan, but elegant.

He paged quickly through her professional files, letting his mind take in an overview, just as he had with the whole living space. There would be time for rigor, and a first impression was usually more useful than an encyclopedia. She had training videos on several different light transport craft. Some political archives, but nothing that raised a flag. A scanned volume of poetry by some of the first settlers in the Belt.

He shifted to her personal correspondence. It was all kept as neat and controlled as a Belter's. All incoming messages were filtered to subfolders. Work, Personal, Broadcast, Shopping. He popped open Broadcast. Two or three hundred political news-feeds, discussion group digests, bulletins and announcements. A few had been viewed here and there, but nothing with any sort of religious observation. Julie was the kind of woman who would sacrifice for a cause, but not the kind who'd take joy in reading the propaganda. Miller filed that away.

Shopping was a long tracking of simple merchant messages. Some receipts, some announcements, some requests for goods and services. A cancellation for a Belt-based singles circle caught his eye. Miller re-sorted for related correspondence. Julie had signed up for the "low g, low pressure" dating service in February of the previous year and canceled in June without having used it.

The Personal folder was more diverse. At a rough guess there were sixty or seventy subfolders broken down by name. Some were people—Sascha Lloyd-Navarro, Ehren Michaels. Others were private notations—Sparring Circle, OPA.

Bullshit Guilt Trips.

"Well, this could be interesting," he said to the empty hole.

Fifty messages dating back five years, all marked as originating at the Mao-Kwikowski Mercantile stations in the Belt and on Luna. Unlike the political tracts, all but one had been opened.

Miller took a pull from the beer and considered the most recent two messages. The most recent, still unread, was from JPM. Jules-Pierre Mao, at a guess. The one immediately before it showed three drafted replies, none of them sent. It was from Ariadne. The mother.

There was always an element of voyeurism in being a detective. It was legal for him to be here, poking through the private life of a woman he'd never met. It was part of his legitimate investigation to know that she was lonely, that the only toiletries in her bathroom were her own. That she was proud. No one would have any complaints to make, or at least any that carried repercussions for his job, if he read every private message on her partition. Drinking her beer was the most ethically suspect thing he'd done since he'd come in.

And still he hesitated for a few seconds before opening the second-to-last message.

The screen shifted. On better equipment, it would have been indistinguishable from ink on paper, but Julie's cheap system shuddered at the thinnest lines and leaked a soft glow at the left edge. The handwriting was delicate and legible, either done with a calligraphic software good enough to vary letter shape and line width, or else handwritten.

> *Sweetheart:*
>
> *I hope everything's going well for you. I wish you would write to me on your own sometimes. I feel like I have to put in a request in triplicate just to hear how my own daughter is doing. I know this adventure of yours is all about freedom and self-reliance, but surely there's still room in there to be considerate.*
>
> *I wanted to get in touch with you especially because your father is going through one of his consolidation phases again, and we're thinking of selling the Razorback. I know it was important to you once, but I suppose we've all given up on your racing again. It's just racking up storage fees now, and there's no call to be sentimental.*

It was signed with the flowing initials *AM*.

Miller considered the words. Somehow he'd expected the parental extortions of the very rich to be more subtle. *If you don't do as we say, we'll get rid of your toys. If you don't write. If you don't come home. If you don't love us.*

Miller opened the first incomplete draft.

Mother, if that's what you call yourself:
    Thank you so much for dropping yet another turd onto my day. I can't believe how selfish and petty and crude you are. I can't believe you sleep at night or that you ever thought I could

Miller skimmed the rest. The tone seemed consistent. The second draft reply was dated two days later. He skipped to it.

Mom:
    I'm sorry we've been so estranged these last few years. I know it's been hard for you and for Daddy. I hope you can see that the decisions I've made were never meant to hurt either of you.
    About the Razorback, I wish you'd reconsider. She's my first boat, and I

It stopped there. Miller leaned back.

"Steady on, kid," he said to the imaginary Julie, then opened the last draft.

Ariadne:
    Do what you have to.

Julie

Miller laughed and raised his bottle to the screen in toast. They'd known how to hit her where it hurt, and Julie had taken the blow. If he ever caught her and shipped her back, it was going to be a bad day for both of them. All of them.

He finished the beer, dropped the bottle into the recycling chute, and opened the last message. He more than half dreaded learning the final fate of the *Razorback*, but it was his job to know as much as he could.

Julie:

This is not a joke. This is not one of your mother's drama fits. I have solid information that the Belt is about to be a very unsafe place. Whatever differences we have we can work out later.

FOR YOUR OWN SAFETY COME HOME NOW.

Miller frowned. The air recycler hummed. Outside, the local kids whistled high and loud. He tapped the screen, closing the last Bullshit Guilt Trip message, then opened it again.

It had been sent from Luna, two weeks before James Holden and the *Canterbury* raised the specter of war between Mars and the Belt.

This sideshow was getting interesting.

Chapter Nine: Holden

The ships are still not responding," Naomi said, punching a key sequence on the comm panel.

"I didn't think they would. But I want to show the *Donnager* that we're worried about being followed. It's all covering our asses at this point," Holden said.

Naomi's spine popped as she stretched. Holden pulled a protein bar out of the box in his lap and threw it at her.

"Eat."

She peeled the wrapping off while Amos clambered up the ladder and threw himself into the couch next to her. His coverall was so filthy it shined. Just as with the others, three days on the cramped shuttle hadn't helped his personal hygiene. Holden reached up and scratched his own greasy hair with distaste. The *Knight* was too small for showers, and the zero-g sinks were too small to stick your head in. Amos had solved the hair-washing problem by shaving all of his off. Now he just had a ring of stubble around his bald spot. Somehow, Naomi's hair stayed shiny and mostly oil free. Holden wondered how she did that.

"Toss me some chow, XO," Amos said.

"Captain," Naomi corrected.

Holden threw a protein bar at him too. Amos snatched it from the air, then considered the long, thin package with distaste.

"Goddamn, Boss, I'd give my left nut for food that didn't look like a dildo," Amos said, then tapped his food against Naomi's in mock toast.

"Tell me about our water," Holden said.

"Well, I've been crawling around between hulls all day. I've tightened everything that can be tightened, and slapped epoxy on anything that can't, so we aren't dripping anywhere."

"It'll still be right down to the wire, Jim," Naomi said. "The *Knight*'s recycling systems are crap. She was never intended to process five people's worth of waste back into potables for two weeks."

"Down to the wire, I can handle. We'll just learn to live with each other's stink. I was worried about 'nowhere near enough.'"

"Speaking of which, I'm gonna head to my rack and spray on some more deodorant," Amos said. "After all day crawling in the ship's guts, my stink's even keeping me awake tonight."

Amos swallowed the last of his food and smacked his lips with mock relish, then climbed out of his couch and headed down the crew ladder. Holden took a bite of his own bar. It tasted like greased cardboard.

"What's Shed up to?" he asked. "He's been pretty quiet."

Naomi, frowning, put her half-eaten bar down on the comm panel.

"I wanted to talk to you about that. He's not doing well, Jim. Out of all of us, he's having the hardest time with...what's happened. You and Alex were both navy men. They train you to deal with losing shipmates. Amos has been flying so long this is actually the *third* ship that's gone down under him, if you can believe that."

"And you are made entirely of cast iron and titanium," Holden said, only pretending to joke.

"Not entirely. Eighty, ninety percent. Tops," Naomi said with a half smile. "Seriously, though. I think you should talk to him."

"And say what? I'm no psychiatrist. The navy version of this speech involves duty and honorable sacrifice and avenging fallen comrades. Doesn't work as well when your friends have been murdered for no apparent reason and there's essentially no chance you can do anything about it."

"I didn't say you had to fix him. I said you needed to talk to him."

Holden got up from his couch with a salute.

"Yes, sir," he said. At the ladder he paused. "Again, thank you, Naomi. I'd really—"

"I know. Go be the captain," she said, turning back to her panel and calling up the ship ops screen. "I'll keep waving at the neighbors."

Holden found Shed in the *Knight*'s tiny sick bay. Really more a sick closet. Other than a reinforced cot, the cabinets of supplies, and a half dozen pieces of wall-mounted equipment, there was just enough room for one stool stuck to the floor on magnetic feet. Shed was sitting on it.

"Hey, buddy, mind if I come in?" Holden asked. *Did I actually say "Hey, buddy"?*

Shed shrugged and pulled up an inventory screen on the wall panel, opening various drawers and staring at the contents. Pretending he'd been in the middle of something.

"Look, Shed. This thing with the *Canterbury* has really hit everyone hard, and you've—" Holden said. Shed turned, holding up a white squeeze tube.

"Three percent acetic acid solution. Didn't realize we had this out here. The *Cant*'s run out, and I've got three people with GW who could really use it. Why'd they put it on the *Knight*, I wonder," Shed said.

"GW?" was all Holden could think to reply.

"Genital warts. Acetic acid solution is the treatment for any visible warts. Burns 'em off. Hurts like hell, but it does the job. No reason to keep it on the shuttle. Medical inventory is always so messed up."

Holden opened his mouth to speak, found nothing to say, and closed it again.

"We've got acetic acid cream," Shed said, his voice increasingly shrill, "but no elemcet for pain. Which do you think you'd need more on a rescue shuttle? If we'd found anyone on that wreck with a bad case of GW, we'd have been set. A broken bone? You're out of luck. Just suck it up."

"Look, Shed," Holden said, trying to break in.

"Oh, and look at this. No coagulant booster. What the hell? Hey, no chance anyone on a rescue mission could, you know, start *bleeding*. Catch a case of red bumps on your crank, sure, but bleeding? No way! I mean, we've got four cases of syphilis on the *Cant* right now. One of the oldest diseases in the book, and we still can't get rid of it. I tell those guys, 'The hookers on Saturn Station are banging every ice bucker on the circuit, so put the glove on,' but do they listen? No. So here we are with syphilis and not enough ciprofloxacin."

Holden felt his jaw slide forward. He gripped the side of the hatch and leaned into the room.

"Everyone on the *Cant* is dead," Holden said, making each word clear and strong and brutal. "Everyone is dead. No one needs the antibiotics. No one needs wart cream."

Shed stopped talking, and all the air went out of him like he'd been gut punched. He closed the drawers in the supply cabinet and turned off the inventory screen with small precise movements.

"I know," he said in a quiet voice. "I'm not stupid. I just need some time."

"We all do. But we're stuck in this tiny can together. I'll be honest, I came down here because Naomi is worried about you, but now that I'm here, you're freaking me the hell out. That's okay, because I'm the captain now and it's my job. But I can't have you freaking Alex or Amos out. We're ten days from being grabbed by a Martian battleship, and that's scary enough without the doctor falling apart."

"I'm not a doctor, I'm just a tech," Shed said, his voice very small.

"You're *our* doctor, okay? To the four of us here with you on this ship, you're our doctor. If Alex starts having post-traumatic stress episodes and needs meds to keep it together, he'll come to you. If you're down here jabbering about warts, he'll turn around and go back up to the cockpit and just do a really bad job of flying. You want to cry? Do it with all of us. We'll sit together in the galley and get drunk and cry like babies, but we'll do it together where it's safe. No more hiding down here."

Shed nodded.

"Can we do that?" he said.

"Do what?" Holden asked.

"Get drunk and cry like babies?"

"Hell yes. That is officially on the schedule for tonight. Report to the galley at twenty hundred hours, Mr. Garvey. Bring a cup."

Shed started to reply when the general comm clicked on and Naomi said, "Jim, come back up to ops."

Holden gripped Shed's shoulder for a moment, then left.

In ops, Naomi had the comm screen up again and was speaking to Alex in low tones. The pilot was shaking his head and frowning. A map glowed on her screen.

"What's up?" Holden asked.

"We're getting a tightbeam, Jim. It locked on and started transmitting just a couple minutes ago," Naomi replied.

"From the *Donnager*?" The Martian battleship was the only thing he could think of that might be inside laser communications range.

"No. From the Belt," Naomi said. "And not from Ceres, or Eros, or Pallas either. None of the big stations."

She pointed at a small dot on her display.

"It's coming from here."

"That's empty space," Holden said.

"Nope. Alex checked. It's the site of a big construction project Tycho is working on. Not a lot of detail on it, but radar returns are pretty strong."

"Something out there has a comm array that'll put a dot the size of your anus on us from over three AU away," Alex said.

"Okay, wow, that's impressive. What is our anus-sized dot saying?" Holden asked.

"You'll never believe this," Naomi said, and turned on the playback.

A dark-skinned man with the heavy facial bones of an Earther appeared on the screen. His hair was graying, and his neck was ropy with old muscle. He smiled and said, "Hello, James Holden. My name is Fred Johnson."

Holden hit the pause button.

"This guy looks familiar. Search the ship's database for that name," he said.

Naomi didn't move; she just stared at him with a puzzled look on her face.

"What?" he said.

"That's *Frederick Johnson*," she said.

"Okay."

"Colonel Frederick Lucius Johnson."

The pause might have been a second; it might have been an hour.

"Jesus," was all Holden could think to say.

The man on the screen had once been among the most decorated officers in the UN military, and ended up one of its most embarrassing failures. To Belters, he was the Earther Sheriff of Nottingham who'd turned into Robin Hood. To Earth, he was the hero who'd fallen from grace.

Fred Johnson started his rise to fame with a series of high-profile captures of Belt pirates during one of the periods of tension between Earth and Mars that seemed to ramp up every few decades and then fade away again. Whenever the system's two superpowers rattled their sabers at each other, crime in the Belt rose. Colonel Johnson—Captain Johnson at the time—and his small wing of three missile frigates destroyed a dozen pirate ships and two major bases in a two-year span. By the time the Coalition had stopped bickering, piracy was actually *down* in the Belt, and Fred Johnson was the name on everyone's lips. He was promoted and given command over the Coalition marine division tasked with policing the Belt, where he continued to serve with distinction.

Until Anderson Station.

A tiny shipping depot almost on the opposite side of the Belt from the major port Ceres, most people, including most Belters, would not have been able to find Anderson Station on a map. Its only importance was as a minor distribution station for water and air in one of the sparsest stretches of the Belt. Fewer than a million Belters got their air from Anderson.

Gustav Marconi, a career Coalition bureaucrat on the station, decided to implement a 3-percent handling surcharge on shipments passing through the station in hopes of raising the bottom line. Less than 5 percent of the Belters buying their air from Anderson were living bottle to mouth, so just under fifty thousand Belters might have to spend one day of each month not breathing. Only a small percentage of those fifty thousand lacked the leeway in their recycling systems to cover this minor shortfall. Of those, only a small portion felt that armed revolt was the correct course.

Which was why of the million affected, only 170 armed Belters came to the station, took over, and threw Marconi out an airlock. They demanded a government guarantee that no further handling surcharges would be added to the price of air and water coming through the station.

The Coalition sent Colonel Johnson.

During the Massacre of Anderson Station, the Belters kept the station cameras rolling, broadcasting to the solar system the entire time. Everyone watched as Coalition marines fought a long, grue-some corridor-to-corridor battle against men with nothing to lose and no reason to surrender. The Coalition won—it was a fore-gone conclusion—but it took three days of broadcast slaughter. The iconic image of the video was not one of the fighting, but the last image the station cameras caught before they were cut off: Colonel Johnson in station ops, surrounded by the corpses of the Belters who'd made their last stand there, surveying the carnage with a flat stare and hands limp at his sides.

The UN tried to keep Colonel Johnson's resignation quiet, but he was too much a public figure. The video of the battle domi-nated the nets for weeks, only displaced when the former Colonel Johnson made a public statement apologizing for the massacre and announcing that the relationship between the Belt and the inner planets was untenable and heading toward ever greater tragedy.

Then he vanished. He was almost forgotten, a footnote in the history of human carnage, until the Pallas colony revolt four years later. This time refinery metalworkers kicked the Coalition gov-ernor off station. Instead of a tiny way station with 170 rebels, it was a major Belt rock with more than 150,000 people on it. When the Coalition ordered in the marines, everyone expected a blood-bath.

Colonel Johnson came out of nowhere and talked the metal-workers down; he talked the Coalition commanders into holding back the marines until the station could be handed over peace-fully. He spent more than a year negotiating with the Coalition governor to improve working conditions in the refineries. And suddenly, the Butcher of Anderson Station was a Belt hero and an icon.

An icon who was beaming private messages to the *Knight*.

Holden hit the play button, and *that* Fred Johnson said, "Mr. Holden, I think you're being played. Let me say straight out that I am speaking to you as an official representative of the Outer Planets Alliance. I don't know what you've heard, but we aren't all a bunch of cowboys itching for a chance to shoot our way to freedom. I've spent the last ten years working to make life for the Belters better without *anyone* getting shot. I believe in this idea so deeply that I gave up my Earth citizenship when I came out here.

"I tell you that so you'll know how invested I am. I may be the one person in the solar system who wants war the least, and my voice is loud in OPA councils.

"You may have heard some of the broadcasts beating on the war drums and calling for revenge against Mars for what happened to your ship. I've talked to every OPA cell leader I know, and no one's claiming responsibility.

"Someone is working very hard to start a war. If it's Mars, then when you get on that ship, you'll never say another word in public that isn't fed to you by Martian handlers. I don't want to think it *is* Mars. I can't see how they would get anything out of a war. So my hope is that even after the *Donnager* picks you up, you can still be a player in what follows.

"I am sending you a keyword. Next time you broadcast publicly, use the word *ubiquitous* within the first sentence of the broadcast to signal that you're not being coerced. Don't use it, and I'll assume you are. Either way, I want you to know you have allies in the Belt.

"I don't know who or what you were before, but your voice matters now. If you want to use that voice to make things better, I will do anything I can to help you do it. If you get free, contact me at the address that follows. I think maybe you and I have a lot to talk about.

"Johnson out."

The crew sat in the galley drinking a bottle of ersatz tequila Amos had scrounged from somewhere. Shed was politely sipping from a small cup of it and trying to hide his grimace each time. Alex and Amos drank like sailors: a finger full in the bottom of the cup, tossed back all at once. Alex had a habit of saying "Hooboy!" after each shot. Amos just used a different profanity each time.

He was up to his eleventh shot and so far had not repeated himself.

Holden stared at Naomi. She swirled the tequila in her cup and stared back. He found himself wondering what sort of genetic mashup had produced her features. Definitely some African and South American in there. Her last name hinted at Japanese ancestry, which was only barely visible, as a slight epicanthic fold. She'd never be conventionally pretty, but from the right angle she was actually fairly striking.

Shit, I'm drunker than I thought.

To cover, he said, "So…"

"So Colonel Johnson is calling you now. Quite the important man you've become, sir," Naomi replied.

Amos put down his cup with exaggerated care.

"Been meaning to ask about that, sir. Any chance we might take up his offer of help and just head back to the Belt?" he said. "Don't know about you, but with the Martian battleship in front, and the half dozen mystery ships behind, it's starting to feel pretty fuckin' crowded out here."

Alex snorted. "Are you kidding? If we flipped now, we'd be just about stopped by the time the *Donnager* caught up to us. She's burnin' the furniture to catch us before the Belter ships do. If we start headin' their direction, the *Donnie* might take that as a sign we've switched teams, frag the whole lot of us."

"I agree with Mr. Kamal," Holden said. "We've picked our course and we're going to see it through. I won't be losing Fred's contact information anytime soon. Speaking of which, have you deleted his message yet, Naomi?"

"Yes, sir. Scrubbed it from the ship's memory with steel wool. The Martians will never know he talked to us."

Holden nodded and unzipped his jumpsuit a little further. The galley was starting to feel very hot with five drunk people in it. Naomi raised an eyebrow at his days-old T-shirt. Embarrassed, he zipped back up.

"Those ships don't make any sense to me, Boss," Alex said. "A half dozen ships flyin' kamikaze missions with nukes strapped to their hulls *might* make a dent in a battlewagon like the *Donnie,* but not much else would. She opens up with her point defense network and rail guns, she can create a no-fly zone a thousand klicks across. They could be killin' those six ships with torpedoes already, 'cept I think they're as confused about who they are as we are."

"They'll know they can't catch us before the *Donnager* picks us up," Holden said. "And they can't take her in a fight. So I don't know what they're up to."

Amos poured the last of the tequila into everyone's cups and held his up in a toast.

"I guess we'll fucking find out."

Chapter Ten: Miller

Captain Shaddid tapped the tip of her middle finger against her thumb when she started getting annoyed. It was a small sound, soft as a cat's paws, but ever since Miller first noticed her habit, it had seemed louder. Quiet as it was, it could fill her office.

"Miller," she said, smiling as if she meant it. "We're all on edge these days. These have been hard, hard times."

"Yes, sir," Miller said, lowering his head like a fullback determined to muscle his way through all defenders, "but I think this is important enough to deserve closer—"

"It's a favor for a shareholder," Shaddid said. "Her father got jumpy. There's no reason to think he meant Mars blasting the *Canterbury*. Tariffs are going up again. There was a mine blowout on one of the Red Moon operations. Eros is having trouble with their yeast farm. We don't go through a day without something happening in the Belt that would make a daddy scared for his precious little flower."

"Yes, sir, but the timing—"

Her fingers upped tempo. Miller bit his lips. The cause was lost.

"Don't go chasing conspiracies," Shaddid said. "We've got a full board of crimes we know are real. Politics, war, system-wide cabals of inner planet bad guys searching for ways to screw us over? Not our mandate. Just get me a report that says you're looking, I'll send it back up the line, and we can get back to our jobs."

"Yes, sir."

"Anything else?"

"No, sir."

Shaddid nodded and turned back to her terminal. Miller plucked his hat from the corner of her desk and headed out. One of the station house air filters had gone bad over the weekend, and the replacement gave the rooms a reassuring smell of new plastic and ozone. Miller sat at his desk, fingers laced behind his head, and stared at the light fixture above him. The knot that had tied itself in his gut hadn't loosened up. That was too bad.

"Not so good, then?" Havelock asked.

"Could have gone better."

"She pull the job?"

Miller shook his head. "No, it's still mine. She just wants me to do it half-assed."

"Could be worse. At least you get to find out what happened. And if you maybe spend a little time after hours digging into it just for practice, you know?"

"Yeah," Miller said. "Practice."

Their desks were unnaturally clean, his and Havelock's both. The barrier of paperwork Havelock had created between himself and the station had eroded away, and Miller could tell from his partner's eyes and the way his hands moved that the cop in Havelock wanted to get back into the tunnels. He couldn't tell if it was to prove himself before his transfer went through, or just to break a few heads. Maybe those were two ways of saying the same thing.

Just don't get yourself killed before you get out of here, Miller thought. Aloud, he said, "What have we got?"

"Hardware shop. Sector eight, third level in," Havelock said. "Extortion complaint."

Miller sat for a moment, considering his own reluctance as if it belonged to someone else. It was like Shaddid had given a dog just one bite of fresh meat, then pointed it back toward kibble. The temptation to blow off the hardware shop bloomed, and for a moment he almost gave in. Then he sighed, swung his feet down to the decking, and stood.

"All right, then," he said. "Let's go make the station safe for commerce."

"Words to live by," Havelock said, checking his gun. He'd been doing that a lot more recently.

The shop was an entertainment franchise. Clean white fixtures offering up custom rigs for interactive environments: battle simulations, exploration games, sex. A woman's voice ululated on the sound system, somewhere between an Islamic call to prayer and orgasm with a drumbeat. Half the titles were in Hindi with Chinese and Spanish translations. The other half were English with Hindi as the second language. The clerk was hardly more than a boy. Sixteen, seventeen years old with a weedy black beard he wore like a badge.

"Can I help you?" the boy said, eyeing Havelock with disdain just short of contempt. Havelock pulled his ID, making sure the kid got a good long look at his gun when he did it.

"We'd like to talk to"—Miller glanced at the complaint form on his terminal screen—"Asher Kamamatsu. He here?"

The manager was a fat man, for a Belter. Taller than Havelock, the man carried fat around his belly and thick muscles through the shoulders, arms, and neck. If Miller squinted, he could see the seventeen-year-old boy he had been under the layers of time and disappointment, and it looked a lot like the clerk out front. The office was almost too small for the three of them and stacked with boxes of pornographic software.

"You catch them?" the manager said.

"No," Miller said. "Still trying to figure out who they are."

"Dammit, I already told you. There's pictures of them off the store camera. I gave you his fucking name."

Miller looked at his terminal. The suspect was named Mateo Judd, a dockworker with an unspectacular criminal record.

"You think it's just him, then," Miller said. "All right. We'll just go pick him up, throw him in the can. No reason for us to find out who he's working for. Probably no one who'll take it wrong, anyway. My experience with these protection rackets, the purse boys get replaced whenever one goes down. But since you're sure this guy's the *whole* problem…"

The manager's sour expression told Miller he'd made his point. Havelock, leaning against a stack of boxes marked сиротливые девушки, smiled.

"Why don't you tell me what he wanted," Miller said.

"I already told the last cop," the manager said.

"Tell me."

"He was selling us a private insurance plan. Hundred a month, same as the last guy."

"Last guy?" Havelock said. "So this happened before?"

"Sure," the manager said. "Everyone has to pay some, you know. Price of doing business."

Miller closed his terminal, frowning. "Philosophical. But if it's the price of doing business, what're we here for?"

"Because I thought you…you people had this shit under control. Ever since we stopped paying the Loca, I've been able to turn a decent profit. Now it's all starting up again."

"Hold on," Miller said. "You're telling me the Loca Greiga stopped charging protection?"

"Sure. Not just here. Half of the guys I know in the Bough just stopped showing up. We figured the cops had actually done something for once. Now we've got these new bastards, and it's the same damn thing all over again."

A crawling feeling made its way up Miller's neck. He looked up at Havelock, who shook his head. He hadn't heard of it either. The Golden Bough Society, Sohiro's crew, the Loca Greiga. All the organized crime on Ceres suffering the same ecological collapse, and now someone new moving into the evacuated niche. Might be opportunism. Might be something else. He almost didn't want to ask the next questions. Havelock was going to think he was paranoid.

"How long has it been since the old guys called on you for protection?" Miller asked.

"I don't know. Long time."

"Before or after Mars killed that water hauler?"

The manager folded his thick arms; his eyes narrowed.

"Before," he said. "Maybe a month or two. S'that got to do with anything?"

"Just trying to get the time scale right," Miller said. "The new guy. Mateo. He tell you who was backing his new insurance plan?"

"That's your job, figuring it. Right?"

The manager's expression had closed down so hard Miller imagined he could hear the click. Yes, Asher Kamamatsu knew who was shaking him down. He had balls enough to squeak about it but not to point the finger.

Interesting.

"Well, thanks for that," Miller said, standing up. "We'll let you know what we find."

"Glad you're on the case," the manager said, matching sarcasm for sarcasm.

In the exterior tunnel, Miller stopped. The neighborhood was at the friction point between sleazy and respectable. White marks showed where graffiti had been painted over. Men on bicycles swerved and weaved, foam wheels humming on the polished stone. Miller walked slowly, his eyes on the ceiling high above them until he found the security camera. He pulled up his terminal, navigated to the logs that matched the camera code, and cross-referenced the time code from the store's still frames. For a moment, he thumbed the controls, speeding people back and forth. And there was Mateo, coming out of the shop. A smug grin deformed the man's face. Miller froze the image and enhanced it. Havelock, watching over his shoulder, whistled low.

The split circle of the OPA was perfectly clear on the thug's armband—the same kind of armband he'd found in Julie Mao's hole.

What kind of company have you been keeping, kid? Miller thought. *You're better than this. You have to know you're better than this.*

"Hey, partner," he said aloud. "Think you can write up the report on that interview? I've got something I'd like to do. Might not be too smart to have you there. No offense."

Havelock's eyebrows crawled toward his hairline.

"You're going to question the OPA?"

"Shake some trees, is all," Miller said.

Miller would have thought that just being a security contractor in a known OPA-convivial bar would be enough to get him noticed. In the event, half the faces he recognized in the dim light of John Rock Gentlemen's Club were normal citizens. More than one of those were Star Helix, just like him, when they were on duty. The music was pure Belter, soft chimes accompanied by zither and guitar with lyrics in half a dozen languages. He was on his fourth beer, two hours past the end of his shift, and on the edge of giving up his plan as a losing scheme when a tall, thin man sat down at the bar next to him. Acne-pocked cheeks gave a sense of damage to a face that otherwise seemed on the verge of laughter. It wasn't the first OPA armband he'd seen that night, but it was worn with an air of defiance and authority. Miller nodded.

"I heard you've been asking about the OPA," the man said. "Interested in joining up?"

Miller smiled and lifted his glass, an intentionally noncommittal gesture.

"You who I'd talk to if I did?" he asked, his tone light.

"Might be able to help."

"Maybe you could tell me about a couple other things, then," he said, taking out his terminal and putting it on the fake bamboo bar with an audible click. Mateo Judd's picture glowed on the screen. The OPA man frowned, turning the screen to see it better.

"I'm a realist," Miller said. "When Chucky Snails was running protection, I wasn't above talking to his men. When the Hand took over and then the Golden Bough Society after them. My job isn't to stop people from bending the rules, it's to keep Ceres stable. You understand what I'm saying?"

"I can't say I do," the pock-marked man said. His accent made him sound more educated than Miller had expected. "Who is this man?"

"His name's Mateo Judd. He's been starting a protection business in sector eight. Says it's backed by the OPA."

"People say things, Detective. It is Detective, isn't it? But you were discussing realism."

"If the OPA's making a move on the Ceres black economy, it's going to be better all around if we can talk to each other. Communicate."

The man chuckled and pushed the terminal back. The bartender paced by, a question in his eyes that wasn't asking if they needed anything. It wasn't meant for Miller.

"I had heard that there was a certain level of corruption in Star Helix," the man said. "I admit I'm impressed by your straightforward manner. I'll clarify. The OPA isn't a criminal organization."

"Really? My mistake. I figured from the way it killed a lot of people..."

"You're baiting me. We defend ourselves against people who are perpetrating economic terrorism against the Belt. Earthers. Martians. We are in the business of protecting Belters," the man said. "Even you, Detective."

"Economic terrorism?" Miller said. "That seems a little overheated."

"You think so? The inner planets look on us as their labor force. They tax us. They direct what we do. They enforce their laws and ignore ours in the name of stability. In the last year, they've doubled the tariffs to Titania. Five thousand people on an ice ball orbiting Neptune, months from anywhere. The sun's just a bright star to them. Do you think they're in a position to get redress? They've blocked any Belter freighters from taking Europa contracts. They charge us twice as much to dock at Ganymede. The science station on Phoebe? We aren't even allowed to *orbit* it. There isn't a Belter in the place. Whatever they do there, we won't find out until they sell the technology back to us, ten years from now."

Miller sipped his beer and nodded toward his terminal.

"So this one isn't yours?"

"No. He isn't."

Miller nodded and put the terminal back in his pocket. Oddly, he believed the man. He didn't hold himself like a thug. The bravado wasn't there. The sense of trying to impress the world. No, this man was certain and amused and, underneath it all, profoundly tired. Miller had known soldiers like that, but not criminals.

"One other thing," Miller said. "I'm looking for someone."

"Another investigation?"

"Not exactly, no. Juliette Andromeda Mao. Goes by Julie."

"Should I know the name?"

"She's OPA," Miller said with a shrug.

"Do you know everyone in Star Helix?" the man said, and when Miller didn't answer, he added, "We are considerably larger than your corporation."

"Fair point," Miller said. "But if you could keep an ear out, I'd appreciate it."

"I don't know that you're in a position to expect favors."

"No harm asking."

The pock-faced man chuckled, put a hand on Miller's shoulder.

"Don't come back here, Detective," he said, and walked away into the crowd.

Miller took another drink of his beer, frowning. An uncomfortable feeling of having made the wrong step fidgeted in the back of his mind. He'd been sure that the OPA was making a move on Ceres, capitalizing on the death of the water hauler and the Belt's uptick in fear and hatred of the inner planets. But how did that fit with Julie Mao's father and his suspiciously well-timed anxiety? Or the disappearance of Ceres Station's supply of usual suspects in the first place? Thinking about it was like watching a video that was just out of focus. The sense of it was almost there, but only almost.

"Too many dots," Miller said. "Not enough lines."

"Excuse me?" the bartender said.

"Nothing," Miller said, pushing the half-empty bottle across the bar. "Thanks."

In his hole, Miller turned on some music. The lyrical chants that Candace had liked, back when they were young and, if not hopeful, at least more joyful in their fatalism. He set the lights to half power, hoping that if he relaxed, if for just a few minutes he let go of the gnawing sense that he had missed some critical detail, the missing piece might arrive on its own.

He'd half expected Candace to appear in his mind, sighing and looking crossly at him the way she had in life. Instead, he found himself talking with Julie Mao. In the half sleep of alcohol and exhaustion, he imagined her sitting at Havelock's desk. She was the wrong age, younger than the real woman would be. She was the age of the smiling kid in her picture. The girl who had raced in the *Razorback* and won. He had the sense of asking her questions, and her answers had the power of revelation. Everything made sense. Not only the change in the Golden Bough Society and her own abduction case, but Havelock's transfer, the dead ice hauler, Miller's own life and work. He dreamed of Julie Mao laughing, and he woke up late, with a headache.

Havelock was waiting at his desk. His broad, short Earther face seemed strangely alien, but Miller tried to shake it off.

"You look like crap," Havelock said. "Busy night?"

"Just getting old and drinking cheap beer," Miller said.

One of the vice squad shouted something angry about her files being locked again, and a computer tech scuttled across the station house like a nervous cockroach. Havelock leaned closer, his expression grave.

"Seriously, Miller," Havelock said. "We're still partners, and... honest to God, I think you may be the only friend I've got on this rock. You can trust me. If there's anything you want to tell me, I'm good."

"That's great," Miller said. "But I don't know what you're talking about. Last night was a bust."

"No OPA?"

"Sure, OPA. Anymore, you swing a dead cat in this station, you'll hit three OPA guys. Just no good information."

Havelock leaned back, lips pressed thin and bloodless. Miller's shrug asked a question, and the Earther nodded toward the board. A new homicide topped the list. At three in the morning, while Miller had been having inchoate dream conversations, someone had opened Mateo Judd's hole and fired a shotgun cartridge full of ballistic gel into his left eye.

"Well," Miller said, "called that one wrong."

"Which one?" Havelock said.

"OPA's not moving in on the criminals," Miller said. "They're moving in on the cops."

Chapter Eleven: Holden

The *Donnager* was ugly.

Holden had seen pictures and videos of the old oceangoing navies of Earth, and even in the age of steel, there had always been something beautiful about them. Long and sleek, they had the appearance of something leaning into the wind, a creature barely held on the leash. The *Donnager* had none of that. Like all long-flight spacecraft, it was built in the "office tower" configuration: each deck one floor of the building, ladders or elevators running down the axis. Constant thrust took the place of gravity.

But the *Donnager* actually *looked* like an office building on its side. Square and blocky, with small bulbous projections in seemingly random places. At nearly five hundred meters long, it was the size of a 130-story building. Alex had said it was 250,000 tons dry weight, and it looked heavier. Holden reflected, not for the first time, on how so much of the human sense of aesthetics had been formed in a time when sleek objects cut through the air. The *Donnager* would never move through anything thicker than interstellar gas, so curves and angles were a waste of space. The result was ugly.

It was also intimidating. As Holden watched from his seat next to Alex in the cockpit of the *Knight*, the massive battleship matched course with them, looming close and then seeming to stop above them. A docking bay opened, breaking up the *Donnager*'s flat black belly with a square of dim red light. The *Knight* beeped insistently, reminding him of the targeting lasers painting their hull. Holden looked for the point defense cannons aimed at him. He couldn't find them.

When Alex spoke, Holden jumped.

"Roger that, *Donnager*," the pilot said. "We've got steering lock. I'm killing thrust."

The last shreds of weight vanished. Both ships were still moving at hundreds of kilometers a minute, but their matched courses felt like stillness.

"Got docking permission, Cap. Take her in?"

"It seems late to make a run for it, Mr. Kamal," Holden said. He imagined Alex making a mistake that the *Donnager* interpreted as threatening, and the point defense cannons throwing a couple hundred thousand Teflon-coated chunks of steel through them.

"Go slowly, Alex," he said.

"They say one of those can kill a planet," Naomi said over the comm. She was at the ops station a deck below.

"Anyone can kill a planet from orbit," Holden replied. "You don't even need bombs. Just push anvils out the airlock. That thing out there could kill... Shit. Anything."

Tiny touches shifted them as the maneuvering rockets fired. Holden knew that Alex was guiding them in, but he couldn't shake the feeling that the *Donnager* was swallowing them.

Docking took nearly an hour. Once the *Knight* was inside the bay, a massive manipulator arm grabbed *her* and put it down in an empty section of the deck. Clamps grabbed the ship, the *Knight*'s hull reverberating with a metallic bang that reminded Holden of a brig cell's maglocks.

The Martians ran a docking tube from one wall and mated up to the *Knight*'s airlock. Holden gathered the crew at the inner door.

"No guns, no knives, no anything that might look like a weapon," he said. "They'll probably be okay with hand terminals, but keep them turned off just in case. If they ask for it, hand it over without complaint. Our survival here may rest on them thinking we're very compliant."

"Yeah," Amos said. "Fuckers killed McDowell, but *we* have to act nice…"

Alex started to respond, but Holden cut him off.

"Alex, you did twenty flying with the MCRN. Anything else we should know?"

"Same stuff you said, Boss," Alex replied. "Yes sir, no sir, and snap to when given an order. The enlisted guys will be okay, but the officers get the sense of humor trained out of 'em."

Holden looked at his tiny crew, hoping he hadn't killed them all by bringing them here. He cycled open the lock, and they drifted down the short docking tube in the zero g. When they reached the airlock at the end—flat gray composites and immaculately clean—everyone pushed down to the floor. Their magnetic boots grabbed on. The airlock closed and hissed at them for several seconds before opening into a larger room with about a dozen people standing in it. Holden recognized Captain Theresa Yao. There were several others in naval officers' dress, who were part of her staff; one man in an enlisted uniform with a look of thinly veiled impatience; and six marines in heavy combat armor, carrying assault rifles. The rifles were pointed at him, so Holden put up his hands.

"We're not armed," he said, smiling and trying to look harmless.

The rifles didn't waver, but Captain Yao stepped forward.

"Welcome aboard the *Donnager*," she said. "Chief, check them."

The enlisted man clumped toward them and quickly and professionally patted them all down. He gave the thumbs-up to one of the marines. The rifles went down, and Holden worked hard not to sigh with relief.

"What now, Captain?" Holden asked, keeping his voice light.

Yao looked Holden over critically for several seconds before answering. Her hair was pulled tightly back, the few strands of gray making straight lines. In person, he could see the softening of age at her jaw and the corners of her eyes. Her stony expression had the same quiet arrogance that all the naval captains he'd known shared. He wondered what she saw, looking at him. He resisted the urge to straighten his greasy hair.

"Chief Gunderson will take you down to your rooms and get you settled in," she replied. "Someone will be along shortly to debrief you."

Chief Gunderson started to lead them from the room when Yao spoke again, her voice suddenly hard.

"Mr. Holden, if you know anything about the six ships that are following you, speak now," she said. "We gave them a two-hour deadline to change course about an hour ago. So far they haven't. In one hour I'm going to order a torpedo launch. If they're friends of yours, you could save them a great deal of pain."

Holden shook his head emphatically.

"All I know is they came out of the Belt when you started out to meet us, Captain," Holden said. "They haven't talked to us. Our best guess is they're concerned citizens of the Belt coming to watch what happens."

Yao nodded. If she found the thought of witnesses disconcerting, it didn't show.

"Take them below, Chief," she said, then turned away.

Chief Gunderson gave a soft whistle and pointed at one of the two doors. Holden's crew followed him out, the marines bringing up the rear. As they moved through the *Donnager*, Holden took his first really up-close look at a Martian capital ship. He'd never served on a battleship in the UN Navy, and he'd stepped foot on them maybe three times in seven years, always in dock, and usually for a party. Every inch of the *Donnager* was just a little sharper than any UN vessel he'd served on. *Mars really does build them better than we do.*

"Goddamn, XO, they sure do keep their shit squeaky clean," Amos said behind him.

"Ain't much to do on a long flight for most of the crew, Amos," Alex said. "So when you aren't doin' somethin' else, you clean."

"See, that's why I work haulers," Amos said. "Clean decks or get drunk and screw, and I've got a preference."

As they walked through a maze of corridors, the ship started a slight vibration, and gravity slowly reappeared. They were under thrust. Holden used his heels to touch his boots' slide controls, turning the magnets off.

They saw almost no one, and the few they did see moved fast and said little, barely sparing them a glance. With six ships closing on them, everyone would be at their duty stations. When Captain Yao had said she'd fire her torpedoes in an hour, there hadn't been a hint of threat in her voice. It was just a flat statement of fact. For most of the young sailors on this ship, it would probably be the first time they'd ever been in a live combat situation—if it came to that. Holden didn't believe it would.

He wondered what to make of the fact that Yao was prepared to take out a handful of Belt ships just because they were running quiet and close. It didn't suggest that they'd hesitate to kill a water hauler, like the *Cant*, if they thought there was reason to.

Gunderson brought them to a stop in front of a hatch with *OQ117* printed on it. He slid a card through the lock and gestured everyone inside.

"Better than I'd expected," Shed said, sounding impressed.

The compartment was large by ship standards. It had six high-g couches and a small table with four chairs stuck to the deck with magnetic feet. An open door in one bulkhead showed a smaller compartment with a toilet and sink. Gunderson and the marine lieutenant followed the crew inside.

"This is your rack for the time being," the chief said. "There's a comm panel on the wall. Two of Lieutenant Kelly's people will be stationed outside. Buzz them and they'll send for anything you need."

"How about some chow?" Amos said.

"We'll have some sent up. You are to remain here until called for," Gunderson said. "Lieutenant Kelly, you have anything to add, sir?"

The marine lieutenant looked them over.

"The men outside are there for your protection, but they will react unpleasantly if you make any trouble," he said. "You read me?"

"Loud and clear, Lieutenant," Holden said. "Don't worry. My people will be the easiest houseguests you've ever had."

Kelly nodded at Holden with what seemed like genuine gratitude. He was a professional doing an unpleasant job. Holden sympathized. Also, he'd known enough marines to know how unpleasant it could get if they felt challenged.

Gunderson said, "Can you take Mr. Holden here to his appointment on your way out, El Tee? I'd like to get these folks squared away."

Kelly nodded and took Holden's elbow.

"Come with me, sir," he said.

"Where am I going, Lieutenant?"

"Lieutenant Lopez asked to see you as soon as you landed. I'm taking you to him."

Shed looked nervously from the marine to Holden and back. Naomi nodded. They'd all see each other again, Holden told himself. He even thought it was likely to be true.

Kelly led Holden at a brisk pace through the ship. His rifle was no longer at the ready but hanging from his shoulder loosely. Either he'd decided Holden wasn't going to cause trouble, or that he could take him down easily if he did.

"Can I ask who Lieutenant Lopez is?"

"He's the guy who asked to see you," Kelly said.

Kelly stopped at a plain gray door, rapped once, then took Holden inside a small compartment with a table and two uncomfortable-looking chairs. A dark-haired man was setting up a recorder. He waved one hand vaguely in the direction of a chair. Holden sat. The chair was even less comfortable than it looked.

"You can go, Mr. Kelly," the man Holden assumed was Lopez said. Kelly left and closed the door.

When Lopez had finished, he sat down across the table from Holden and reached out one hand. Holden shook it.

"I'm Lieutenant Lopez. Kelly probably told you that. I work for naval intelligence, which he almost certainly didn't tell you. My job isn't secret, but they train jarheads to be tight-lipped."

Lopez reached into his pocket, took out a small packet of white lozenges, and popped one into his mouth. He didn't offer one to Holden. Lopez's pupils contracted to tiny points as he sucked the lozenge. Focus drugs. He'd be watching every tic of Holden's face during questioning. Tough to lie to.

"First Lieutenant James R. Holden, of Montana," he said. It wasn't a question.

"Yes, sir," Holden said anyway.

"Seven years in the UNN, last posting on the destroyer *Zhang Fei*."

"That's me."

"Your file says you were busted out for assaulting a superior officer," Lopez said. "That's pretty cliché, Holden. You punched the old man? Seriously?"

"No. I missed. Broke my hand on a bulkhead."

"How'd that happen?"

"He was quicker than I expected," Holden replied.

"Why'd you try?"

"I was projecting my self-loathing onto him. It's just a stroke of luck that I actually wound up hurting the right person," Holden said.

"Sounds like you've thought about it some since then," Lopez said, his pinprick pupils never moving from Holden's face. "Therapy?"

"Lots of time to think on the *Canterbury*," Holden replied.

Lopez ignored the obvious opening and said, "What did you come up with, during all that thinking?"

"The Coalition has been stepping on the necks of the people out here for over a hundred years now. I didn't like being the boot."

"An OPA sympathizer, then?" Lopez said, his expression not changing at all.

"No. I didn't switch sides. I stopped playing. I didn't renounce my citizenship. I like Montana. I'm out here because I like flying, and only a Belter rust trap like the *Canterbury* will hire me."

Lopez smiled for the first time. "You're an exceedingly honest man, Mr. Holden."

"Yes."

"Why did you claim that a Martian military vessel destroyed your ship?"

"I didn't. I explained all that in the broadcast. It had technology only available to inner planet fleets, and I found a piece of MCRN hardware in the device that tricked us into stopping."

"We'll want to see that."

"You're welcome to it."

"Your file says you were the only child of a family co-op," Lopez said, acting as though they'd never stopped talking about Holden's past.

"Yes, five fathers, three mothers."

"So many parents for only one child," Lopez said, slowly unwrapping another lozenge. The Martians had lots of space for traditional families.

"The tax break for eight adults only having one child allowed them to own twenty-two acres of decent farmland. There are over thirty billion people on Earth. Twenty-two acres is a national park," Holden said. "Also, the DNA mix is legit. They aren't parents in name only."

"How did they decide who carried you?"

"Mother Elise had the widest hips."

Lopez popped the second lozenge into his mouth and sucked on it a few moments. Before he could speak again, the deck shook. The video recorder jiggled on its arm.

"Torpedo launches?" Holden said. "Guess those Belt ships didn't change course."

"Any thoughts about that, Mr. Holden?"

"Just that you seem pretty willing to kill Belt ships."

"You've put us in a position where we can't afford to seem weak. After your accusations, there are a lot of people who don't think much of us."

Holden shrugged. If the man was watching for guilt or remorse from Holden, he was out of luck. The Belt ships had known what they were going toward. They hadn't turned away. But still, something bothered him.

"They might hate your living guts," Holden said. "But it's hard to find enough suicidal people to crew six ships. Maybe they think they can outrun torpedoes."

Lopez didn't move, his whole body preternaturally still with the focus drugs pouring through him.

"We—" Lopez began, and the general quarters Klaxon sounded. It was deafening in the small metal compartment.

"Holy shit, did they shoot *back*?" Holden asked.

Lopez shook himself, like a man waking up from a daydream. He got up and hit the comm button by the door. A marine came through seconds later.

"Take Mr. Holden back to his quarters," Lopez said, then left the room at a run.

The marine gestured at the corridor with the barrel of his rifle. His expression was hard.

It's all fun and games till someone shoots back, Holden thought.

Naomi patted the empty couch next to her and smiled.

"Did they put slivers under your fingernails?" she asked.

"No, actually, he was surprisingly human for a naval intelligence wonk," Holden replied. "Of course, he was just getting warmed up. Have you guys heard anything about the other ships?"

Alex said, "Nope. But that alarm means they're takin' them seriously all of a sudden."

"It's insane," Shed said quietly. "Flying around in these metal bubbles, and then trying to poke holes in each other. You ever seen what long-term decompression and cold exposure does? Breaks all the capillaries in your eyes and skin. Tissue damage to the lungs can cause massive pneumonia followed by emphysema-like scarring. I mean, if you don't just die."

"Well, that's awful fucking cheerful, Doc. Thanks for that," Amos said.

The ship suddenly vibrated in a syncopated but ultra-high-speed rhythm. Alex looked at Holden, his eyes wide.

"That's the point defense network openin' up. That means incoming torpedoes," he said. "Better strap in tight, kids. The ship might start doin' some violent maneuvering."

Everyone but Holden was already belted into the couches. He fastened his restraints too.

"This sucks. All the real action is happenin' thousands of klicks from here, and we got no instruments to look at," Alex said. "We won't know if somethin' slipped through the flack screen till it rips the hull open."

"Boy, everybody is just a fucking pile of fun right now," Amos said loudly.

Shed's eyes were wide, his face too pale. Holden shook his head.

"Not going to happen," he said. "This thing is unkillable. Who-ever those ships are, they can put on a good show, but that's it."

"All respect, Captain," Naomi said. "But whoever those ships are, they should be dead already, and they aren't."

The distant noises of faraway combat kept up. The occasional rumble of a torpedo firing. The near-constant vibration of the high-speed point defense guns. Holden didn't realize he'd fallen asleep until he was jerked awake by an earsplitting roar. Amos and Alex were yelling. Shed was screaming.

"What happened?" Holden yelled over the noise.

"We're hit, Cap!" Alex said. "That was a torpedo hit!"

The gravity suddenly dropped away. The *Donnager* had stopped its engines. Or they'd been destroyed.

Amos was still yelling, "Shit shit shit," over everything. But at least Shed had stopped screaming. He was staring wide eyed out of his couch, his face white. Holden unbuckled his straps and pushed off toward the comm panel.

"Jim!" Naomi called out. "What are you doing?"

"We need to find out what's going on," Holden said over his shoulder.

When he reached the bulkhead by the hatch, he punched the comm panel call button. There was no reply. He hit it again, then started pounding on the hatch. No one came.

"Where are our damn marines?" he said.

The lights dimmed, came back up. Then again, and again, in a slow cadence.

"Gauss turrets firing. Shit. It's CQB," Alex said in awe.

In the history of the Coalition, no capital ship had ever gotten into a close-quarters battle. But here they were, firing the ship's big cannons, which meant that the range was sufficiently short that a nonguided weapon was viable. Hundreds or even dozens of kilometers, not thousands. Somehow the Belt ships had survived *Donnager*'s torpedo barrage.

"Anyone else think this is desperate fucking queer?" Amos asked, a touch of panic in his voice.

The *Donnager* began to ring like a gong struck over and over again by a massive hammer. Return fire.

The gauss round that killed Shed didn't even make a noise. Like a magic trick, two perfectly round holes appeared on either side of the room in a line that intersected Shed's couch. One moment, the medic was there; the next, his head was gone from the Adam's apple up. Arterial blood pumped out in a red cloud, pulled into two thin lines, and whirled to the holes in the walls of the room as the air rushed out.

Chapter Twelve: Miller

For thirty years, Miller had worked security. Violence and death were familiar companions to him. Men, women. Animals. Kids. Once he'd held a woman's hand while she bled to death. He'd killed two people, could still see them die if he closed his eyes and thought about it. If anyone had asked him, he'd have said there wasn't much left that would shake him.

But he'd never watched a war start before.

The Distinguished Hyacinth Lounge was in the shift-change rush. Men and women in security uniforms—mostly from Star Helix, but a few smaller companies too—were either drinking their after-work liquor and winding down or making trips to the breakfast buffet for coffee, textured fungi in sugar sauce, sausage with meat maybe one part in a thousand. Miller chewed the sausage and watched the display monitor on the wall. A Star Helix external relations head looked sincerely out, his demeanor radiating calm and certainty as he explained how everything was going to hell.

"Preliminary scans suggest that the explosion was the result of a failed attempt to connect a nuclear device to the docking station. Officials from the Martian government have referred to the incident only as an 'alleged terrorist action' and refused comment pending further investigation."

"Another one," Havelock said from behind him. "You know, eventually, one of those assholes is going to get it right."

Miller turned in his seat, then nodded to the chair beside him. Havelock sat.

"That'll be an interesting day," Miller said. "I was about to call you."

"Yeah, sorry," his partner said. "I was up kind of late."

"Any word on the transfer?"

"No," Havelock said. "Figure my paperwork's hung on a desk someplace in Olympus. What about you? Any word on your special-project girl?"

"Not yet," Miller said. "Look, the reason I wanted to meet up before we went in...I need to take a couple days, try to run down some leads on Julie. With all this other shit going on, Shaddid doesn't want me doing much more than phoning this one in."

"But you're ignoring that," Havelock said. It wasn't a question.

"I've got a feeling about this one."

"So how can I help?"

"I need you to cover for me."

"How am I going to do that?" Havelock asked. "It's not like I can tell them you're sick. They've got access to your medical records same as everyone else's."

"Tell 'em I've been getting drunk a lot," Miller said. "That Candace came by. She's my ex-wife."

Havelock chewed his sausage, brow furrowed. The Earther shook his head slowly—not a refusal, but the prelude to a question. Miller waited.

"You're telling me you'd rather have the boss think you're

missing work because you're on a dysfunctional, heartbroken bender than that you're doing the work she assigned you? I don't get it."

Miller licked his lips and leaned forward, elbows on the smooth off-white table. Someone had scratched a design into the plastic. A split circle. And this was a cop bar.

"I don't know what I'm looking at," Miller said. "There's a bunch of things that belong together somehow, and I'm not sure yet what it is. Until I know more, I need to stay low. A guy has a fling with his ex, hits the bottle for a few days? That's not going to light up anyone's panels."

Havelock shook his head again, this time in mild disbelief. If he'd been a Belter, he'd have made the gesture with his hands, so you could see it when he had an environment suit on. Another of the hundred small ways someone who hadn't grown up on the Belt betrayed himself. The wall monitor cut to the image of a blond woman in a severe uniform. The external relations head was talking about the Martian navy's tactical response and whether the OPA was behind the increased vandalism. That was what he called fumbling an overloaded fusion reactor while setting up a ship-killing booby trap: vandalism.

"That shit just doesn't follow," Havelock said, and for a moment Miller didn't know if he meant the Belter guerrilla actions, the Martian response, or the favor he'd asked. "Seriously. Where's Earth? All this shit's going on, and we don't hear a damn thing from them."

"Why would we?" Miller asked. "It's Mars and the Belt going at it."

"When was the last time Earth let anything major happen without them in the middle of it?" Havelock said, then sighed. "Okay. You're too drunk to come in. Your love life's a mess. I'm trying to cover for you."

"Just for a couple days."

"Make sure you get back before someone decides it's the perfect chance for a random shooting to take out the Earther cop."

"I'll do that," Miller said, rising from the table. "You watch your back."

"Don't need to tell me twice," Havelock said.

The Ceres Center for Jiu Jitsu was down near the port, where the spin gravity was strongest. The hole was a converted storage space from before the big spin. A cylinder flattened where flooring had been set in about a third of the way from the bottom. Racks bearing various lengths of staffs, bamboo swords, and dull plastic practice knives hung from the vaulted ceiling. The polished stone echoed with the grunting of men working a line of resistance machines and the soft thud of a woman at the back punishing a heavy bag. Three students stood on the central mat, speaking in low voices.

Pictures filled the front wall on either side of the door. Soldiers in uniform. Security agents for half a dozen Belter corporations. Not many inner planet types, but a few. Plaques commemorating placements in competitions. A page of small type outlining the history of the studio.

One of the students shouted and collapsed, carrying one of the others to the mat with her. The one still standing applauded and helped them back up. Miller searched through the wall of pictures, hoping to find Julie.

"Can I help you?"

The man was half a head shorter than Miller and easily twice as broad. It should have made him look like an Earther, but everything else about him said Belt. He wore pale sweats that made his skin seem even darker. His smile was curious and as serene as a well-fed predator. Miller nodded.

"Detective Miller," he said. "I'm with station security. There's one of your students I wanted to get some background on."

"This is an official investigation?" the man asked.

"Yeah," Miller said. "I'm afraid it is."

"Then you'll have a warrant."

Miller smiled. The man smiled back.

"We don't give out any information on our students without a warrant," he said. "Studio policy."

"I respect that," Miller said. "No, I really do. It's just that… parts of this particular investigation are maybe a little more official than others. The girl's not in trouble. She didn't do anything. But she has family on Luna who want her found."

"A kidnap job," the man said, folding his arms. The serene face had gone cool without any apparent movement.

"Only the official part," Miller said. "I can get a warrant, and we can do the whole thing through channels. But then I have to tell my boss. The more she knows, the less room I have to move."

The man didn't react. His stillness was unnerving. Miller struggled not to fidget. The woman working the heavy bag at the far end of the studio went through a flurry of strikes, shouting out with each one.

"Who?" the man asked.

"Julie Mao," Miller said. He could have said he was looking for the Buddha's mother for all the reaction he got. "I think she's in trouble."

"Why do you care if she is?"

"I don't know the answer to that one," Miller said. "I just do. If you don't want to help me, then you don't."

"And you'll go get your warrant. Do this through channels."

Miller took off his hat, rubbed a long, thin hand across his head, and put the hat back in place.

"Probably not," he said.

"Let me see your ID," the man said. Miller pulled up his terminal and let the man confirm who he was. The man handed it back and pointed to a small door behind the heavy bags. Miller did as he was told.

The office was cramped. A small laminate desk with a soft sphere behind it in lieu of a chair. Two stools that looked like they'd come out of a bar. A filing cabinet with a small fabricator that stank of ozone and oil that was probably where the plaques and certificates were made.

"Why does the family want her?" the man asked, lowering himself onto the sphere. It acted like a chair but required constant balance. A place to rest without actually resting.

"They think she's in harm's way. At least, that's what they're saying, and I don't have reason to disbelieve them yet."

"What kind of harm?"

"Don't know," Miller said. "I know she was on station. I know she shipped out for Tycho, and after that, I've got nothing."

"Her family want her back on their station?"

The man knew who her family was. Miller filed the information away without missing a beat.

"I don't think so," Miller said. "The last message she got from them routed through Luna."

"Down the well." The way he said it made it sound like a disease.

"I'm looking for anyone who knows who she was shipping with. If she's on a run, where she was going and when she was planning to get there. If she's in range of a tightbeam."

"I don't know any of that," the man said.

"You know anyone I should ask?"

There was a pause.

"Maybe. I'll find what I can for you."

"Anything else you can tell me about her?"

"She started at the studio five years ago. She was...angry when she first came. Undisciplined."

"She got better," Miller said. "Brown belt, right?"

The man's eyebrows rose.

"I'm a cop," Miller said. "I find things out."

"She improved," her teacher said. "She'd been attacked. Just after she came to the Belt. She was seeing that it didn't happen twice."

"Attacked," Miller said, parsing the man's tone of voice. "Raped?"

"I didn't ask. She trained hard, even when she was off station.

You can tell when people let it slide. They come back weaker. She never did."

"Tough girl," Miller said. "Good for her. Did she have friends? People she sparred with?"

"A few. No lovers that I know of, since that's the next question."

"That's strange. Girl like that."

"Like what, Detective?"

"Pretty girl," Miller said. "Competent. Smart. Dedicated. Who wouldn't want to be with someone like that?"

"Perhaps she hadn't met the right person."

Something in the way he said it hinted at amusement. Miller shrugged, uncomfortable in his skin.

"What kind of work did she do?" he asked.

"Light freighter. I don't know of any particular cargo. I had the impression that she shipped wherever there was a need."

"Not a regular route, then?"

"That was my impression."

"Whose ships did she work? One particular freighter, or whatever came to hand? A particular company?"

"I'll find what I can for you," the man said.

"Courier for the OPA?"

"I'll find out," the man said, "what I can."

The news that afternoon was all about Phoebe. The science station there—the one that Belters weren't allowed even to dock at—had been hit. The official report stated that half the inhabitants of the base were dead, the other half missing. No one had claimed responsibility yet, but the common wisdom was that some Belter group—maybe the OPA, maybe someone else—had finally managed an act of "vandalism" with a body count. Miller sat in his hole, watching the broadcast feed and drinking.

It was all going to hell. The pirate casts from the OPA calling for war. The burgeoning guerrilla actions. All of it. The time was coming that Mars wasn't going to ignore them anymore. And when Mars took action, it wouldn't matter if Earth followed suit. It would be the first real war in the Belt. The catastrophe was coming, and neither side seemed to understand how vulnerable they were. And there was nothing — not one single goddamned thing — that he could do to stop it. He couldn't even slow it down.

Julie Mao grinned at him from the still frame, her pinnace behind her. Attacked, the man had said. There was nothing about it in her record. Might have been a mugging. Might have been something worse. Miller had known a lot of victims, and he put them into three categories. First there were the ones who pretended nothing had happened, or that whatever it was didn't really matter. That was well over half the people he talked to. Then there were the professionals, people who took their victimization as permission to act out any way they saw fit. That ate most of the rest.

Maybe 5 percent, maybe less, were the ones who sucked it up, learned the lesson, and moved on. The Julies. The good ones.

His door chimed three hours after his official shift was over. Miller stood up, less steady on his feet than he'd expected. He counted the bottles on the table. There were more than he'd thought. He hesitated for a moment, torn between answering the door and throwing the bottles into the recycler. The door chimed again. He went to open it. If it was someone from the station, they expected him to be drunk, anyway. No reason to disappoint.

The face was familiar. Acne-pocked, controlled. The OPA armband from the bar. The one who'd had Mateo Judd killed.

The cop.

"Evening," Miller said.

"Detective Miller," the pocked man said. "I think we've gotten off on the wrong foot. I was hoping we could try again."

"Right."

"May I come in?"

"I try not to take strange men home," Miller said. "I don't even know your name."

"Anderson Dawes," the pocked man said. "I'm the Ceres liaison for the Outer Planets Alliance. I think we can help each other. May I come in?"

Miller stood back, and the pocked man—Dawes—stepped inside. Dawes took in the hole for the space of two slow breaths, then sat as if the bottles and the stink of old beer were nothing to comment on. Silently cursing himself and willing a sobriety he didn't feel, Miller sat across from him.

"I need a favor from you," Dawes said. "I'm willing to pay for it. Not money, of course. Information."

"What do you want?" Miller asked.

"Stop looking for Juliette Mao."

"No sale."

"I'm trying to keep the peace, Detective," Dawes said. "You should hear me out."

Miller leaned forward, elbows on the table. Mr. Serene Jiu Jitsu Instructor was working for the OPA? The timing of Dawes' visit seemed to be saying so. Miller filed that possibility away but said nothing.

"Mao worked for us," Dawes said. "But you'd guessed that."

"More or less. You know where she is?"

"We don't. We are looking for her. And we need to be the ones to find her. Not you."

Miller shook his head. There was a response, the right thing to say. It was rattling in the back of his head, and if he just didn't feel quite so fuzzy…

"You're one of *them*, Detective. You may have lived your whole life out here, but your salary is paid by an inner planet corporation. No, wait. I don't blame you. I understand how it is. They were hiring and you needed the work. But…we're walking on a bubble right now. The *Canterbury*. The fringe elements in the Belt calling for war."

"Phoebe Station."

"Yes, they'll blame us for that too. Add a Luna corporation's prodigal daughter…"

"You think something's happened to her."

"She was on the *Scopuli*," Dawes said, and when Miller didn't immediately respond, he added, "The freighter that Mars used as bait when they killed the *Canterbury*."

Miller thought about that for a long moment, then whistled low.

"We don't know what happened," Dawes said. "Until we do, I can't have you stirring up the water. It's muddy enough now."

"And what information are you offering?" Miller asked. "That's the trade, right?"

"I'll tell you what we find. After we find her," Dawes said. Miller chuckled, and the OPA man went on. "It's a generous offer, considering who you are. Employee of Earth. Partner of an Earther. Some people would think that was enough to make you the enemy too."

"But not you," Miller said.

"I think we've got the same basic goals, you and I. Stability. Safety. Strange times make for strange alliances."

"Two questions."

Dawes spread his arms, welcoming them.

"Who took the riot gear?" Miller asked.

"Riot gear?"

"Before the *Canterbury* died, someone took our riot gear. Maybe they wanted to arm soldiers for crowd control. Maybe they didn't want our crowds controlled. Who took it? Why?"

"It wasn't us," Dawes said.

"That's not an answer. Try this one. What happened to the Golden Bough Society?"

Dawes looked blank.

"Loca Greiga?" Miller asked. "Sohiro?"

Dawes opened his mouth, closed it. Miller dropped his beer bottle into the recycler.

"Nothing personal, friend," he said, "but your investigative techniques aren't impressing me. What makes you think you can find her?"

"It's not a fair test," Dawes said. "Give me a few days, I'll get answers for you."

"Talk to me then. I'll try not to start an all-out war while you do, but I'm not letting go of Julie. You can go now."

Dawes rose. He looked sour.

"You're making a mistake," he said.

"Won't be my first."

After the man left, Miller sat at his table. He'd been stupid. Worse, he'd been self-indulgent. Drinking himself into a stupor instead of doing the work. Instead of finding Julie. But he knew more now. The *Scopuli*. The *Canterbury*. More lines between the dots.

He cleaned away his bottles, took a shower, and pulled up his terminal, searching what there was about Julie's ship. After an hour, a new thought occurred to him, a small fear that grew the more he looked at it. Near midnight, he put a call through to Havelock's hole.

His partner took two full minutes to answer. When he did, his image was wild-haired and bleary-eyed.

"Miller?"

"Havelock. You have any vacation time saved up?"

"A little."

"Sick leave?"

"Sure," Havelock said.

"Take it," Miller said. "Take it now. Get off station. Someplace safe if you can find it. Someplace they're not going to start killing Earthers for shits and giggles if things go pear-shaped."

"I don't understand. What are you talking about?"

"I had a little visit with an OPA agent tonight. He was trying to talk me into dropping my kidnap job. I think...I think he's nervous. I think he's scared."

Havelock was silent for a moment while the words filtered into his sleep-drunk mind.

"Jesus," he said. "What scares the OPA?"

Chapter Thirteen: Holden

Holden froze, watching the blood pump from Shed's neck, then whip away like smoke into an exhaust fan. The sounds of combat began to fade as the air was sucked out of the room. His ears throbbed and then hurt like someone had put ice picks in them. As he fought with his couch restraints, he glanced over at Alex. The pilot was yelling something, but it didn't carry through the thin air. Naomi and Amos had gotten out of their couches already, kicked off, and were flying across the room to the two holes. Amos had a plastic dinner tray in one hand. Naomi, a white three-ring binder. Holden stared at them for the half second it took to understand what they were doing. The world narrowed, his peripheral vision all stars and darkness.

By the time he'd gotten free, Amos and Naomi had already covered the holes with their makeshift patches. The room was filled with a high-pitched whistle as the air tried to force its way out through the imperfect seals. Holden's sight began to return as the air pressure started to rise. He was panting hard, gasping for breath. Someone slowly turned the room's volume knob back up and Naomi's yells for help became audible.

"Jim, open the emergency locker!" she screamed.

She was pointing at a small red-and-yellow panel on the bulkhead near his crash couch. Years of shipboard training made a path through the anoxia and depressurization, and he yanked the tab on the locker's seal and pulled the door open. Inside were a white first aid kit marked with the ancient red-cross symbol, half a dozen oxygen masks, and a sealed bag of hardened plastic disks attached to a glue gun. The emergency-seal kit. He snatched it.

"Just the gun," Naomi yelled at him. He wasn't sure if her voice sounded distant because of the thin air or because the pressure drop had blown his eardrums.

Holden yanked the gun free from the bag of patches and threw it at her. She ran a bead of instant sealing glue around the edge of her three-ring binder. She tossed the gun to Amos, who caught it with an effortless backhand motion and put a seal around his dinner tray. The whistling stopped, replaced by the hiss of the atmosphere system as it labored to bring the pressure back up to normal. Fifteen seconds.

Everyone looked at Shed. Without the vacuum, his blood was pouring out into a floating red sphere just above his neck, like a hideous cartoon replacement for his head.

"Jesus Christ, Boss," Amos said, looking away from Shed to Naomi. He snapped his teeth closed with an audible click and shook his head. "What..."

"Gauss round," Alex said. "Those ships have rail guns."

"*Belt* ships with *rail* guns?" Amos said. "Did they get a fucking navy and no one told me?"

"Jim, the hallway outside and the cabin on the other side are both in vacuum," Naomi said. "The ship's compromised."

Holden started to respond, then caught a good look at the binder Naomi had glued over the breach. The white cover was stamped with black letters that read MCRN EMERGENCY PROCEDURES. He had to suppress a laugh that would almost certainly go manic on him.

"Jim," Naomi said, her voice worried.

"I'm okay, Naomi," Holden replied, then took a deep breath. "How long do those patches hold?"

Naomi shrugged with her hands, then started pulling her hair behind her head and tying it up with a red elastic band.

"Longer than the air will last. If everything around us is in vacuum, that means the cabin's running on emergency bottles. No recycling. I don't know how much each room has, but it won't be more than a couple hours."

"Kinda makes you wish we'd worn our fucking suits, don't it?" Amos asked.

"Wouldn't have mattered," Alex said. "We'd come over here in our enviro suits, they'd just have taken 'em away."

"Could have tried," Amos said.

"Well, if you'd like to go back in time and do it over, be my guest, partner."

Naomi sharply said, "Hey," but then nothing more.

No one was talking about Shed. They were working hard not to look at the body. Holden cleared his throat to get everyone's attention, then floated to Shed's couch, drawing their eyes with him. He paused a moment, letting everyone get a good look at the decapitated body, then pulled a blanket from the storage drawer beneath the couch and strapped it down over Shed's body with the couch's restraints.

"Shed's been killed. We're in deep peril. Arguing won't extend our lives one second," Holden said, looking at each member of his crew in turn. "What will?"

No one spoke. Holden turned to Naomi first.

"Naomi, what will keep us alive longer that we can do right now?" he asked.

"I'll see if I can find the emergency air. The room's built for six, and there're only . . . there are four of us. I might be able to turn the flow down and stretch it longer."

"Good. Thank you. Alex?"

"If there's anyone other than us, they'll be lookin' for survivors. I'll start poundin' on the bulkhead. They won't hear it in the vacuum, but if there're cabins with air, the sound'll travel down the metal."

"Good plan. I refuse to believe we're the only ones left on this ship," Holden said, then turned to Amos. "Amos?"

"Lemme check on that comm panel. Might be able to get the bridge or damage control or...shit, *something*," Amos replied.

"Thanks. I'd love to let someone know we're still here," Holden said.

People moved off to work while Holden floated in the air next to Shed. Naomi began yanking access panels off the bulkheads. Alex, hands pressed against a couch for leverage, lay on the deck and began to kick the bulkhead with his boots. The room vibrated slightly with each booming kick. Amos pulled a multi-tool out of his pocket and began taking the comm panel apart.

When Holden was sure everyone was busy, he put one hand on Shed's shoulder, just below the blanket's spreading red stain.

"I'm sorry," he whispered to the body. His eyes burned and he pressed them into the back of his thumbs.

The comm unit was hanging out of the bulkhead on wires when it buzzed once, loudly. Amos yelped and pushed off hard enough to fly across the room. Holden caught him, wrenching his shoulder by trying to arrest the momentum of 120 kilos of Earther mechanic. The comm buzzed again. Holden let Amos go and floated to it. A yellow LED glowed next to the unit's white button. Holden pressed the button. The comm crackled to life with Lieutenant Kelly's voice.

"Move away from the hatch, we're coming in," he said.

"Grab something!" Holden yelled to the crew, then grabbed a couch restraint and wrapped it around his hand and forearm.

When the hatch opened, Holden expected all the air to rush out. Instead, there was a loud crack and the pressure dropped slightly for a second. Outside in the corridor, thick sheets of plastic had been sealed to the walls, creating an ad hoc airlock. The walls of the new chamber bowed out dangerously with the air pressure, but they held. Inside the newly created lock, Lieutenant Kelly and three of his marines wore heavy vacuum-rated armor and carried enough weaponry to fight several minor wars.

The marines moved quickly into the room, weapons ready, and then sealed the hatch behind them. One of them tossed a large bag at Holden.

"Five vac suits. Get them on," Kelly said. His eyes moved to the bloody blanket covering Shed, then to the two improvised patches. "Casualty?"

"Our medic, Shed Garvey," Holden replied.

"Yeah. What the fuck?" Amos said loudly. "Who's out there shooting the shit out of your fancy boat?"

Naomi and Alex said nothing but started pulling the suits from the bag and handing them out.

"I don't know," Kelly said. "But we're leaving right now. I've been ordered to get you off this ship in an escape craft. We've got less than ten minutes to make it to the hangar bay, take possession of a ship, and get out of this combat area. Dress fast."

Holden put on his suit, the implications of their evacuation racing through his mind.

"Lieutenant, is the ship coming apart?" he asked.

"Not yet. But we're being boarded."

"Then why are we leaving?"

"We're losing."

Kelly didn't tap his foot while waiting for them to seal into their suits; Holden guessed this was only because the marines had their magnetic boots turned on. As soon as everyone had given the thumbs-up, Kelly did a quick radio check on each suit, then headed back into the corridor. With eight people in it, four of them in powered armor, the mini-airlock was tight. Kelly pulled a heavy knife from a sheath on his chest and slashed the plastic barrier open in one quick movement. The hatch behind them slammed shut, and the air in the corridor vanished in a soundless ripple of plastic flaps. Kelly charged into the corridor with the crew scrambling to keep up.

"We are moving with all speed to the keel elevator banks," Kelly said through the radio link. "They're locked down because of the boarding alarm, but I can get the doors open on one and we'll float down the shaft to the hangar bay. Everything is on the double. If you see boarders, do not stop. Keep moving at all times. We'll handle the hostiles. Roger that?"

"Roger, Lieutenant," Holden gasped out. "Why board you?"

"The command information center," Alex said. "It's the holy grail. Codes, deployments, computer cores, the works. Takin' a flagship's CIC is a strategist's wet dream."

"Cut the chatter," Kelly said. Holden ignored him.

"That means they'll blow the core rather than let that happen, right?"

"Yep," Alex replied. "Standard ops for boarders. Marines hold the bridge, CIC, and engineering. If any of the three is breached, the other two flip the switch. The ship turns into a star for a few seconds."

"Standard ops," Kelly growled. "Those are my friends."

"Sorry, El Tee," Alex replied. "I served on the *Bandon*. Don't mean to make light."

They turned a corner and the elevator bank came into view. All eight elevators were closed and sealed. The heavy pressure doors had slammed shut when the ship was holed.

"Gomez, run the bypass," Kelly said. "Mole, Dookie, watch those corridors."

Two of the marines spread out, watching the hallways through their gun sights. The third moved to one of the elevator doors and started doing something complicated to the controls. Holden motioned his crew to the wall, out of the firing lines. The deck vibrated slightly from time to time beneath his feet. The enemy ships wouldn't still be firing, not with their boarders inside. It must be small-arms fire and light explosives. But as they stood there in the perfect quiet of vacuum, everything that was happening took on a distant and surreal feeling. Holden recognized that his mind wasn't working the way it should be. Trauma reaction. The destruction of the *Canterbury*, the deaths of Ade and McDowell. And now someone had killed Shed in his bunk. It was too much; he couldn't process it. He felt the scene around him grow more and more distant.

Holden looked behind him at Naomi, Alex, and Amos. His crew. They stared back, faces ashen and ghostly in the green light of their suit displays. Gomez pumped his fist in triumph as the outer pressure door slid open, revealing the elevator doors. Kelly gestured to his men.

The one called Mole turned around and started to walk to the elevator when his face disintegrated in a spray of pebble-shaped bits of armored glass and blood. His armored torso and the corridor bulkhead beside him bloomed in a hundred small detonations and puffs of smoke. His body jerked and swayed, attached to the floor by magnetic boots.

Holden's sense of unreality washed away in adrenaline. The fire spraying across the wall and Mole's body was high-explosive rounds from a rapid-fire weapon. The comm channel filled with yelling from the marines and Holden's own crew. To Holden's left, Gomez yanked the elevator doors open using the augmented strength of his powered armor, exposing the empty shaft behind them.

"Inside!" Kelly shouted. "Everybody inside!"

Holden held back, pushing Naomi in, and then Alex. The last marine—the one Kelly had called Dookie—fired his rifle on full auto at some target around the corner from Holden. When the weapon ran dry, the marine dropped to one knee and ejected the clip in the same motion. Almost faster than Holden could follow, he pulled a new magazine from his harness and slapped it into his weapon. He was firing again less than two seconds after he'd run out.

Naomi yelled at Holden to get into the elevator shaft, and then a viselike hand grabbed his shoulder, yanked him off his magnetic grip on the floor, and hurled him through the open elevator doors.

"Get killed when I'm not babysitting," Lieutenant Kelly barked.

They shoved off the walls of the elevator shaft and flew down the long tunnel toward the aft of the ship. Holden kept looking back at the open door, receding into the distance behind them.

"Dookie isn't following us," he said.

"He's covering our exit," Kelly replied.

"So we better get away," Gomez added. "Make it mean something."

Kelly, at the head of the group, grabbed at a rung on the wall of the shaft and came to a jerking stop. Everyone else followed suit.

"Here's our exit. Gomez, go check it out," Kelly said. "Holden, here's the plan. We'll be taking one of the corvettes from the hangar bay."

That made sense to Holden. The corvette class was a light frigate. A fleet escort vessel, it was the smallest naval ship equipped with an Epstein drive. It would be fast enough to travel anywhere in the system and outrun most threats. Its secondary role was as a torpedo bomber, so it would also have teeth. Holden nodded inside his helmet at Kelly, then gestured for him to continue. Kelly waited until Gomez had finished opening the elevator doors and gone into the hangar bay.

"Okay, I've got the key card and activation code to get us inside and the ship fired up. I'll be heading straight for it, so all of you stick right on my ass. Make sure your boot mags are off. We're going to push off the wall and fly to it, so aim straight or you miss your ride. Everyone with me?"

Affirmative replies all around.

"Outstanding. Gomez, what's it look like out there?"

"Trouble, El Tee. Half a dozen boarders looking over the ships in the hangar. Powered armor, zero-g maneuvering packs, and heavy weapons. Loaded for bear," Gomez whispered back. People always whispered when they were hiding. Wrapped in a space suit and surrounded by vacuum, Gomez could have been lighting fireworks inside his armor and no one would have heard it, but he whispered.

"We run for the ship and shoot our way through," Kelly said. "Gomez, I'm bringing the civvies in ten seconds. You're covering fire. Shoot and displace. Try and make them think you're a small platoon."

"You callin' me small, sir?" Gomez said. "Six dead assholes coming up."

Holden, Amos, Alex, and Naomi followed Kelly out of the elevator shaft and into the hangar bay and stopped behind a stack of military-green crates. Holden peeked over them, spotting the boarders immediately. They were in two groups of three near the *Knight,* one group walking on top of it and the other on the deck below it. Their armor was flat black. Holden hadn't seen the design before.

Kelly pointed at them and looked at Holden. Holden nodded back. Kelly pointed across the hangar at a squat black frigate about twenty-five meters away, halfway between them and the *Knight.* He held up his left hand and began counting down from five on his fingers. At two, the room strobed like a disco: Gomez opening fire from a position ten meters from their own. The first barrage hit two of the boarders on top of the *Knight* and hurled them spinning off. A heartbeat later, a second burst was fired five meters from where Holden had seen the first. He would have sworn it was two different men.

Kelly folded up the last finger on his hand, planted his feet on the wall, and pushed off toward their corvette. Holden waited for Alex, Amos, and Naomi, then shoved off last. By the time he was in motion, Gomez was firing from a new location. One of the boarders on the deck pointed a large weapon toward the muzzle flash from Gomez's gun. Gomez and the crate he'd been taking cover behind disappeared in fire and shrapnel.

They were halfway to the ship and Holden was starting to think they might make it when a line of smoke crossed the room and intersected with Kelly, and the lieutenant disappeared in a flash of light.

Chapter Fourteen: Miller

The *Xinglong* died stupid. Afterward, everyone knew she was one of thousands of small-time rock-hopping prospector ships. The Belt was lousy with them: five- or six-family operations that had scraped together enough for a down payment and set up operations. When it happened, they'd been three payments behind, and their bank—Consolidated Holdings and Investments—had put a lien on the ship. Which, common wisdom had it, was why they had disabled her transponder. Just honest folks with a rust bucket to call their own trying to keep flying.

If you were going to make a poster of the Belter's dream, it would have been the *Xinglong*.

The *Scipio Africanus*, a patrol destroyer, was due to head back down toward Mars at the end of its two-year tour of the Belt. They both headed for a captured cometary body a few hundred thousand kilometers from Chiron to top off their water.

When the prospecting ship first came in range, the *Scipio* saw a fast-moving ship running dark and headed more or less in their direction. The official Martian press releases all said that the *Scipio* had tried repeatedly to hail her. The OPA pirate casts all said it was crap and that no listening station in the Belt had heard anything like that. Everyone agreed that the *Scipio* had opened its point defense cannons and turned the prospecting ship into glowing slag.

The reaction had been as predictable as elementary physics. The Martians were diverting another couple dozen ships to help "maintain order." The OPA's shriller talking heads called for open war, and fewer and fewer of the independent sites and casts were disagreeing with them. The great, implacable clockwork of war ticked one step closer to open fighting.

And someone on Ceres had put a Martian-born citizen named Enrique Dos Santos through eight or nine hours of torture and nailed the remains to a wall near sector eleven's water reclamation works. They identified him by the terminal that had been left on the floor along with the man's wedding ring and a thin faux-leather wallet with his credit access data and thirty thousand Europa-script new yen. The dead Martian had been affixed to the wall with a single-charge prospector's spike. Five hours afterward, the air recyclers were still laboring to get the acid smell out. The forensics team had taken their samples. They were about ready to cut the poor bastard down.

It always surprised Miller how peaceful dead people looked. However godawful the circumstances, the slack calm that came at the end looked like sleep. It made him wonder if when his turn came, he'd actually feel that last relaxation.

"Surveillance cameras?" he said.

"Been out for three days," his new partner said. "Kids busted 'em."

Octavia Muss was originally from crimes against persons, back before Star Helix split violence up into smaller specialties. From there, she'd been on the rape squad. Then a couple of months of crimes against children. If the woman still had a soul, it had been pressed thin enough to see through. Her eyes never registered anything more than mild surprise.

"We know which kids?"

"Some punks from upstairs," she said. "Booked, fined, released into the wild."

"We should round 'em back up," Miller said. "It'd be interesting to know whether someone paid them to take out these particular cameras."

"I'd bet against it."

"Then whoever did this had to know that these cameras were busted."

"Someone in maintenance?"

"Or a cop."

Muss smacked her lips and shrugged. She'd come from three generations in the Belt. She had family on ships like the one the *Scipio* had killed. The skin and bone and gristle hanging in front of them were no surprise to her. You dropped a hammer under thrust, and it fell to the deck. Your government slaughtered six families of ethnic Chinese prospectors, someone pinned you to the living rock of Ceres with a three-foot titanium alloy spike. Same same.

"There's going to be consequences," Miller said, meaning *This isn't a corpse, it's a billboard. It's a call to war.*

"There ain't," Muss said. *The war is here anyway, banner or no.*

"Yeah," Miller said. "You're right. There ain't."

"You want to do next of kin? I'll go take a look at outlying video. They didn't burn his fingers off here in the corridor, so they had to haul him in from somewhere."

"Yeah," Miller said. "I've got a sympathy form letter I can fire off. Wife?"

"Don't know," she said. "Haven't looked."

Back at the station house, Miller sat alone at his desk. Muss already had her own desk, two cubicles over and customized the way she liked it. Havelock's desk was empty and cleaned twice over, as if the custodial services had wanted the smell of Earth off their good Belter chair. Miller pulled up the dead man's file, found the next of kin. Jun-Yee Dos Santos, working on Ganymede. Married six years. No kids. Well, there was something to be glad of, at least. If you were going to die, at least you shouldn't leave a mark.

He navigated to the form letter, dropped in the new widow's name and contact address. *Dear Mrs. Dos Santos, I am very sorry to have to tell you* blah blah blah. *Your* [he spun through the menu] *husband was a valued and respected member of the Ceres community, and I assure you that everything possible will be done to see that her* [Miller toggled that] *his killer or killers will be brought to answer for this. Yours...*

It was inhuman. It was impersonal and cold and as empty as vacuum. The hunk of flesh on that corridor wall had been a real man with passions and fears, just like anyone else. Miller wanted to wonder what it said about him that he could ignore that fact so easily, but the truth was he knew. He sent the message and tried not to dwell on the pain it was about to cause.

The board was thick. The incident count was twice what it should have been. *This is what it looks like,* he thought. No riots. No hole-by-hole military action or marines in the corridors. Just a lot of unsolved homicides.

Then he corrected himself: *This is what it looks like so far.*

It didn't make his next task any easier.

Shaddid was in her office.

"What can I do for you?" she asked.

"I need to make some requisitions for interrogation transcripts," he said. "But it's a little irregular. I was thinking it might be better if it came through you."

Shaddid sat back in her chair.

"I'll look at it," she said. "What are we trying to get?"

Miller nodded, as if by signaling *yes* himself, he could get her to say the same.

"Jim Holden. The Earther from the *Canterbury.* Mars should

be picking his people up around now, and I need to petition for the debriefing transcripts."

"You have a case that goes back to the *Canterbury*?"

"Yeah," he said. "Seems like I do."

"Tell me," she said. "Tell me now."

"It's the side job. Julie Mao. I've been looking into it…"

"I saw your report."

"So you know she's associated with the OPA. From what I've found, it looks like she was on a freighter that was doing courier runs for them."

"You have proof of that?"

"I have an OPA guy that said as much."

"On the record?"

"No," Miller said. "It was informal."

"And it tied into the Martian navy killing the *Canterbury* how?"

"She was on the *Scopuli*," Miller said. "It was used as bait to stop the *Canterbury*. The thing is, you look at the broadcasts Holden makes, he talks about finding it with a Mars Navy beacon and no crew."

"And you think there's something in there that'll help you?"

"Won't know until I see it," Miller said. "But if Julie wasn't on that freighter, then someone had to take her off."

Shaddid's smile didn't reach her eyes.

"And you would like to ask the Martian navy to please hand over whatever they got from Holden."

"If he saw something on that boat, something that'll give us an idea what happened to Julie and the other—"

"You aren't thinking this through," Shaddid said. "The Mars Navy killed the *Canterbury*. They did it to provoke a reaction from the Belt so they'd have an excuse to roll in and take us over. The only reason they're 'debriefing' the survivors is so that no one could get to the poor bastards first. Holden and his crew are either dead or getting their minds cored out by Martian interrogation specialists right now."

"We can't be sure…"

"And even if I could get a full record of what they said as each toenail got ripped off, it would do you exactly no good, Miller. The Martian navy isn't going to ask about the *Scopuli*. They know good and well what happened to the crew. They planted the *Scopuli*."

"Is that Star Helix's official stand?" Miller asked. The words were barely out of his mouth before he saw they'd been a mistake. Shaddid's face closed down like a light going out. Now that he'd said it, he saw the implied threat he'd just made.

"I'm just pointing out the source reliability issue," Shaddid said. "You don't go to the suspect and ask where they think you should look next. And the Juliette Mao retrieval isn't your first priority."

"I'm not saying it is," Miller said, chagrined to hear the defensiveness in his voice.

"We have a board out there that's full and getting fuller. Our first priorities are safety and continuity of services. If what you're doing isn't directly related to that, there are better things for you to be doing."

"This war—"

"Isn't our job," Shaddid said. "Our job is Ceres. Get me a final report on Juliette Mao. I'll send it through channels. We've done what we could."

"I don't think—"

"I do," Shaddid said. "We've done what we could. Now stop being a pussy, get your ass out there, and catch bad guys. Detective."

"Yes, Captain," Miller said.

Muss was sitting at Miller's desk when he got back to it, a cup in her hand that was either strong tea or weak coffee. She nodded toward his desktop monitor. On it, three Belters—two men and one woman—were coming out of a warehouse door, an orange plastic shipping container carried between them. Miller raised his eyebrows.

"Employed by an independent gas-hauling company. Nitrogen, oxygen. Basic atmospherics. Nothing exotic. Looks like they had the poor bastard in one of the company warehouses. I've sent forensics over to see if we can get any blood splatters for confirmation."

"Good work," Miller said.

Muss shrugged. *Adequate work,* she seemed to say.

"Where are the perps?" Miller asked.

"Shipped out yesterday," she said. "Flight plan logs them as headed for Io."

"Io?"

"Earth-Mars Coalition central," Muss said. "Want to put any money on whether they actually show up there?"

"Sure," Miller said. "I'll lay you fifty that they don't."

Muss actually laughed.

"I've put them on the alert system," she said. "Anyplace they land, the locals will have a heads-up and a tracking number for the Dos Santos thing."

"So case closed," Miller said.

"Chalk another one up for the good guys," Muss agreed.

The rest of the day was hectic. Three assaults, two of them overtly political and one domestic. Muss and Miller cleared all three from the board before the end of shift. There would be more by tomorrow.

After he clocked out, Miller stopped at a food cart near one of the tube stations for a bowl of vat rice and textured protein that approximated teriyaki chicken. All around him on the tube, normal citizens of Ceres read their newsfeeds and listened to music. A young couple half a car up from him leaned close to each other, murmuring and giggling. They might have been sixteen. Seventeen. He saw the boy's wrist snake up under the girl's shirt. She didn't protest. An old woman directly across from Miller slept, her head lolling against the wall of the car, her snores almost delicate.

These people were what it was all about, Miller told himself. Normal people living small lives in a bubble of rock surrounded by hard vacuum. If they let the station turn into a riot zone, let order fail, all these lives would get turned into kibble like a kitten in a meat grinder. Making sure it didn't happen was for people like him, Muss, even Shaddid.

So, a small voice said in the back of his mind, *why isn't it your job to stop Mars from dropping a nuke and cracking Ceres like an egg? What's the bigger threat to that guy standing over there, a few unlicensed whores or a Belt at war with Mars?*

What was the harm that could come from knowing what happened to the *Scopuli*?

But of course he knew the answer to that. He couldn't judge how dangerous the truth was until he knew it—which was itself a fine reason to keep going.

The OPA man, Anderson Dawes, was sitting on a cloth folding chair outside Miller's hole, reading a book. It was a real book— onionskin pages bound in what might have been actual leather. Miller had seen pictures of them before; the idea of that much weight for a single megabyte of data struck him as decadent.

"Detective."

"Mr. Dawes."

"I was hoping we could talk."

Miller was glad, as they went inside together, that he'd cleaned up a little. All the beer bottles had gone to the recycler. The tables and cabinets were dusted. The cushions on the chairs had all been mended or replaced. As Dawes took his seat, Miller realized he'd done the housework in anticipation of this meeting. He hadn't realized it until now.

Dawes put his book on the table, dug in his jacket pocket, and slid a thin black filmdrive across the table. Miller picked it up.

"What am I going to see on this?" he asked.

"Nothing you can't confirm in the records," Dawes answered.

"Anything fabricated?"

"Yes," Dawes said. His grin did nothing to improve his appearance. "But not by us. You asked about the police riot gear. It was signed for by a Sergeant Pauline Trikoloski for transfer to special services unit twenty-three."

"Special services twenty-three?"

"Yes," Dawes said. "It doesn't exist. Nor does Trikoloski. The equipment was all boxed up, signed for, and delivered to a dock. The freighter in the berth at the time was registered to the Corporação do Gato Preto."

"Black Cat?"

"You know them?"

"Import-export, same as everyone else," Miller said with a shrug. "We investigated them as a possible front for the Loca Greiga. Never tied them down, though."

"You were right."

"You prove it?"

"Not my job," Dawes said. "But this might interest you. Automated docking logs for the ship when she left here and when she arrived on Ganymede. She's three tons lighter, not even counting reaction mass consumption. And the transit time is longer than the orbital mechanics projections."

"Someone met her," Miller said. "Transferred the gear to another ship."

"There's your answer," Dawes said. "Both of them. The riot gear was taken off the station by local organized crime. There aren't records to support it, but I think it's safe to assume that they also shipped out the personnel to use that gear."

"Where to?"

Dawes lifted his hands. Miller nodded. They were off station. Case closed. Another one for the good guys.

Damn.

"I've kept my part of our bargain," Dawes said. "You asked for information. I've gotten it. Now, are you going to keep your end?"

"Drop the Mao investigation," Miller said. It wasn't a question, and Dawes didn't act is if it were. Miller leaned back in his chair.

Juliette Andromeda Mao. Inner system heiress turned OPA courier. Pinnace racer. Brown belt, aiming for black.

"Sure, what the hell," he said. "It's not like I would have shipped her back home if I'd found her."

"No?"

Miller shifted his hands in a gesture that meant *Of course not.*

"She's a good kid," Miller said. "How would you feel if you were all grown up and Mommy could still pull you back home by your ear? It was a bullshit job from the start."

Dawes smiled again. This time it actually did help a little.

"I'm glad to hear you say that, Detective. And I won't forget the rest of our agreement. When we find her, I *will* tell you. You've got my word on it."

"I appreciate that," Miller said.

There was a moment of silence. Miller couldn't decide if it was companionable or awkward. Maybe there was room for both. Dawes rose, put out his hand. Miller shook it. Dawes left. Two cops working for different sides. Maybe they had something in common.

Didn't mean Miller was uncomfortable lying to the man.

He opened his terminal's encryption program, routed it to his communication suite, and started talking into the camera.

"We haven't met, sir, but I hope you'll find a few minutes to help me out. I'm Detective Miller with Star Helix Security. I'm on the Ceres security contract, and I've been tasked with finding your daughter. I've got a couple questions."

Chapter Fifteen: Holden

Holden grabbed for Naomi. He struggled to orient himself as the two of them spun across the bay with nothing to push off of and nothing to arrest their flight. They were in the middle of the room with no cover.

The blast had hurled Kelly five meters through the air and into the side of a packing crate, where he was floating now, one magnetic boot connected to the side of the container, the other struggling to connect with the deck. Amos had been blown down, and lay flat on the floor, his lower leg stuck out at an impossible angle. Alex crouched at his side.

Holden craned his neck, looking toward the attackers. There was the boarder with the grenade launcher who had blasted Kelly, lining up on them for the killing shot. *We're dead,* Holden thought. Naomi made an obscene gesture.

The man with the grenade launcher shuddered and dissolved in a spray of blood and small detonations.

"Get to the ship!" Gomez screamed from the radio. His voice was grating and high, half shrieking pain and half battle ecstasy.

Holden pulled the tether line off Naomi's suit.

"What are you...?" she began.

"Trust me," he said, then put his feet into her stomach and shoved off, hard. He hit the deck while she spun toward the ceiling. He kicked on his boot mags and then yanked the tether to pull her down to him.

The room strobed with sustained machine gun fire. Holden said, "Stay low," and ran as quickly as his magnetic boots would allow toward Alex and Amos. The mechanic moved his limbs feebly, so he was still alive. Holden realized he still had the end of Naomi's tether in his hand, so he clipped it on to a loop on his suit. No more getting separated.

Holden lifted Amos off the deck, then checked the inertia. The mechanic grunted and muttered something obscene. Holden attached Amos' tether to his suit too. He'd carry the whole crew if that was what it took. Without saying a word, Alex clipped his tether to Holden and gave him a weary thumbs-up.

"That was...I mean, *fuck*," Alex said.

"Yeah," Holden said.

"Jim," Naomi said. "Look!"

Holden followed her gaze. Kelly was staggering toward them. His armor was visibly crushed on the left side of his torso, and hydraulic fluid leaked from his suit into a trail of droplets floating behind him, but he was moving—toward the frigate.

"Okay," Holden said. "Let's go."

The five of them moved as a group to the ship, the air around them filled with pieces of packing crates blown apart by the ongoing battle. A wasp stung Holden's arm, and his suit's head-up display informed him that it had sealed a minor breach. He felt something warm trickle down his bicep.

Gomez shouted like a madman over the radio as he dashed

around the outer edge of the bay, firing wildly. The return fire was constant. Holden saw the marine hit again and again, small explosions and ablative clouds coming off his suit until Holden could hardly believe that there could be anything inside it still living. But Gomez kept the enemy's attention, and Holden and the crew were able to limp up to the half cover of the corvette's airlock.

Kelly pulled a small metal card from a pocket on his armor. A swipe of the card opened the outer door, and Holden pulled Amos' floating body inside. Naomi, Alex, and the wounded marine came in after, staring at each other in shocked disbelief as the airlock cycled and the inner doors opened.

"I can't believe we…" Alex said; then his voice trailed off.

"Talk about it later," Kelly barked. "Alex Kamal, you served on MCRN ships. Can you fly this thing?"

"Sure, El Tee," Alex replied, then visibly straightened. "Why me?"

"Our other pilot's outside getting killed. Take this," Kelly said, handing him the metal card. "The rest of you, get strapped in. We've lost a lot of time."

Up close, the damage to Kelly's armor was even more apparent. He had to have severe injuries to his chest. And not all the liquid coming out of the suit was hydraulic fluid. There was definitely blood as well.

"Let me help you," Holden said, reaching for him.

"Don't touch me," Kelly said, with an anger that took Holden by surprise. "You get strapped in, and you shut the fuck up. Now."

Holden didn't argue. He unhooked the tethers from his suit and helped Naomi maneuver Amos to the crash couches and strap him in. Kelly stayed on the deck above, but his voice came over the ship's comm.

"Mr. Kamal, are we ready to fly?" he said.

"Roger that, El Tee. The reactor was already hot when we got here."

"The *Tachi* was the ready standby. That's why we're taking her. Now go. As soon as we clear the hangar, full throttle."

"Roger," Alex said.

Gravity returned in tiny bursts at random directions as Alex lifted the ship off the deck and spun it toward the hangar door. Holden finished putting on his straps and checked to see that Naomi and Amos were squared away. The mechanic was moaning and holding on to the edge of the couch with a death grip.

"You still with us, Amos?" Holden said.

"Fan-fucking-tastic, Cap."

"Oh shit, I can see Gomez," Alex said over the comm. "He's down. Aw, you goddammed bastards! They're shootin' him while he's down! Son of a bitch!"

The ship stopped moving, and Alex said in a quiet voice, "Suck on this, asshole."

The ship vibrated for half a second, then paused before continuing toward the lock.

"Point defense cannons?" Holden asked.

"Summary roadside justice," Alex grunted back.

Holden was imagining what several hundred rounds of Teflon-coated tungsten steel going five thousand meters per second would do to human bodies when Alex threw down the throttle and a roomful of elephants swan dived onto his chest.

Holden woke in zero g. His eye sockets and testicles ached, so they'd been at high thrust for a while. The wall terminal next to him said it had been almost half an hour. Naomi was moving in her couch, but Amos was unconscious, and blood was coming out of a hole in his suit at an alarming rate.

"Naomi, check Amos," Holden croaked, his throat aching with the effort. "Alex, report."

"The *Donnie* went up behind us, Cap. Guess the marines didn't hold. She's gone," Alex said in a subdued voice.

"The six attacking ships?"

"I haven't seen any sign of them since the explosion. I'd guess they're toast."

Holden nodded to himself. Summary roadside justice, indeed. Boarding a ship was one of the riskiest maneuvers in naval combat. It was basically a race between the boarders rushing to the engine room and the collective will of those who had their fingers on the self-destruct button. After even one look at Captain Yao, Holden could have told them who'd lose *that* race.

Still. Someone had thought it was worth the risk.

Holden pulled his straps off and floated over to Amos. Naomi had opened an emergency kit and was cutting the mechanic's suit off with a pair of heavy scissors. The hole had been punched out by a jagged end of Amos' broken tibia when the suit had pushed against it at twelve g.

When she'd finished cutting the suit away, Naomi blanched at the mass of blood and gore that Amos' lower leg had turned into.

"What do we do?" Holden asked.

Naomi just stared at him, then barked out a harsh laugh.

"I have no idea," she said.

"But you—" Holden started. She talked right over him.

"If he were made of metal, I'd just hammer him straight and then weld everything into place," she said.

"I—"

"But he *isn't* made out of ship parts," she continued, her voice rising into a yell, "so why are you asking *me* what to do?"

Holden held up his hands in a placating gesture.

"Okay, got it. Let's just stop the bleeding for now, all right?"

"If Alex gets killed, are you going to ask me to fly the ship too?"

Holden started to answer and then stopped. She was right. Whenever he didn't know what to do, he handed off to Naomi. He'd been doing it for years. She was smart, capable, usually unflappable. She'd become a crutch, and she'd been through all the same trauma he had. If he didn't start paying attention, he'd break her, and he needed not to do that.

"You're right. I'll take care of Amos," he said. "You go up and check on Kelly. I'll be there in a few minutes."

Naomi stared at him until her breathing slowed, then said, "Okay," and headed to the crew ladder.

Holden sprayed Amos' leg with coagulant booster and wrapped it in gauze from the first aid kit. Then he called up the ship's database on the wall terminal and did a search on compound fractures. He was reading it with growing dismay when Naomi called.

"Kelly's dead," she said, her voice flat.

Holden's stomach dropped, and he gave himself three breaths to get the panic out of his voice.

"Okay. I'll need your help setting this bone. Come on back down. Alex? Give me half a g of thrust while we work on Amos."

"Any particular direction, Cap?" Alex asked.

"I don't care, just give me half a g and stay off the radio till I say so."

Naomi dropped back down the ladder well as the gravity started to come up.

"It looks like every rib on the left side of Kelly's body was broken," she said. "Thrust g probably punctured all his organs."

"He had to know that was going to happen," Holden said.

"Yeah."

It was easy to make fun of the marines when they weren't listening. In Holden's navy days, making fun of jarheads was as natural as cussing. But four marines had died getting him off the *Donnager,* and three of them had made a conscious decision to do so. Holden promised himself that he'd never make fun of them again.

"We need to pull the bone straight before we set it. Hold him still, and I'll pull on his foot. Let me know when the bone has retracted and lined up again."

Naomi started to protest.

"I know you're not a doctor. Just best guess," Holden said.

It was one of the most horrible things Holden had ever done. Amos woke up screaming during the procedure. He had to pull the leg out twice, because the first time the bones didn't line up, and when he let go, the jagged end of the tibia popped back out the hole in a spray of blood. Fortunately, Amos passed out after that and they were able to make the second attempt without the screaming. It seemed to work. Holden sprayed the wound down with antiseptics and coagulants. He stapled the hole closed and slapped a growth-stimulating bandage over it, then finished up with a quick-form air-cast and an antibiotic patch on the mechanic's thigh.

Afterward he collapsed onto the deck and gave in to the shakes. Naomi climbed into her couch and sobbed. It was the first time Holden had ever seen her cry.

Holden, Alex, and Naomi floated in a loose triangle around the crash couch where Lieutenant Kelly's body lay. Below, Amos was in a heavily sedated sleep. The *Tachi* drifted through space toward no particular destination. For the first time in a long time, no one followed.

Holden knew the other two were waiting for him. Waiting to hear how he was going to save them. They looked at him expectantly. He tried to appear calm and thoughtful. Inside, he panicked. He had no idea where to go. No idea what to do. Ever since they'd found the *Scopuli,* everywhere that should have been safe had turned into a death trap. The *Canterbury,* the *Donnager.* Holden was terrified of going *anywhere,* for fear that it would be blown up moments later.

Do something, a mentor of a decade earlier said to his young officers. *It doesn't have to be right, it just has to be something.*

"Someone is going to investigate what happened to the *Donnager,*" Holden said. "Martian ships are speeding to that spot as we speak. They'll already know the *Tachi* got away, because our transponder is blabbing our survival to the solar system at large."

"No it ain't," Alex said.

"Explain that, Mr. Kamal."

"This is a torpedo bomber. You think they want a nice transponder signal to lock on to when they're makin' runs on an enemy capital ship? Naw, there's a handy switch up in the cockpit that says 'transponder off.' I flipped it before we flew out. We're just another moving object out of a million like us."

Holden was silent for two long breaths.

"Alex, that may be the single greatest thing anyone has ever done, in the history of the universe," he said.

"But we can't land, Jim," Naomi said. "One, no port is going to let a ship with no transponder signal anywhere near them, and two, as soon as they make us out visually, the fact that we're a Martian warship will be hard to hide."

"Yep, that's the downside," Alex agreed.

"Fred Johnson," Holden said, "gave us the network address to get in touch with him. I'm thinking that the OPA might be the one group that would let us land our stolen Martian warship somewhere."

"It ain't stolen," Alex said. "It's legitimate salvage now."

"Yeah, you make that argument to the MCRN if they catch us, but let's try and make sure they don't."

"So, we just wait here till Colonel Johnson gets back to us?" Alex asked.

"No, I wait. You two prep Lieutenant Kelly for burial. Alex, you were MCRN. You know the traditions. Do it with full honors and record it in the log. He died to get us off that ship, and we're going to accord him every respect. As soon as we land anywhere, we'll bounce the full record to MCRN command so they can do it officially."

Alex nodded. "We'll do it right, sir."

Fred Johnson replied to his message so fast that Holden wondered if he'd been sitting at his terminal waiting for it. Johnson's message consisted only of coordinates and the word *tightbeam*. Holden aimed the laser array at the specified location—it was the same one Fred had beamed his first message from—then turned on his mic and said, "Fred?"

The coordinates given were more than eleven light-minutes

away. Holden prepared to wait twenty-two minutes for his answer. Just to have something to do, he fed the location up to the cockpit and told Alex to fly in that direction at one g as soon as they'd finished with Lieutenant Kelly.

Twenty minutes later the thrust came up and Naomi climbed the ladder. She'd stripped off her vacuum suit and was wearing a red Martian jumpsuit that was half a foot too short for her and three times too big around. Her hair and face looked clean.

"This ship has a head with a shower. Can we keep it?" she said.

"How'd it go?"

"We took care of him. There's a decent-sized cargo bay down by engineering. We put him there until we can find some way to send him home. I turned off the environment in there, so he'll stay preserved."

She held out her hand and dropped a small black cube into his lap.

"That was in a pocket under his armor," she said.

Holden held up the object. It looked like some sort of data-storage device.

"Can you find out what's on it?" he asked.

"Sure. Give me some time."

"And Amos?"

"Blood pressure's steady," Naomi said. "That's got to be a good thing."

The comm console beeped at them, and Holden started the playback.

"Jim, news of the *Donnager* has just started hitting the net. I admit I am extremely surprised to be hearing from you," said Fred's voice. "What can I do for you?"

Holden paused a moment while he mentally prepared his response. Fred's suspicion was palpable, but he'd sent Holden a keyword to use for exactly that reason.

"Fred. While our enemies have become *ubiquitous,* our list of friends has grown kind of short. In fact, you're pretty much it. I am in a stolen—"

Alex cleared his throat.

"A *salvaged* MCRN gunboat," Holden went on. "I need a way to hide that fact. I need somewhere to go where they won't just shoot me down for showing up. Help me do that."

It was half an hour before the reply came.

"I've attached a datafile on a subchannel," Fred said. "It's got your new transponder code and directions on how to install it. The code will check out in all the registries. It's legitimate. It's also got coordinates that will get you to a safe harbor. I'll meet you there. We have a lot to talk about."

"New transponder code?" Naomi said. "How does the OPA get new transponder codes?"

"Hack the Earth-Mars Coalition's security protocols or get a mole in the registry office," Holden said. "Either way, I think we're playing in the big league now."

Chapter Sixteen: Miller

Miller watched the feed from Mars along with the rest of the station. The podium was draped in black, which was a bad sign. The single star and thirty stripes of the Martian Congressional Republic hung in the background not once, but eight times. That was worse.

"This cannot happen without careful planning," the Martian president said. "The information they sought to steal would have compromised Martian fleet security in a profound and fundamental way. They failed, but at the price of two thousand and eighty-six Martian lives. This aggression is something the Belt has been preparing for years at the least."

The Belt, Miller noticed. Not the OPA—the Belt.

"In the week since first news of that attack, we have seen thirty incursions into the security radius of Martian ships and bases, including Pallas Station. If those refineries were to be lost, the economy of Mars could suffer irreversible damage. In the face of an armed, organized guerrilla force, we have no choice but to enforce a military cordon on the stations, bases, and ships of the Belt. Congress has delivered new orders to all naval elements not presently involved in active Coalition duty, and it is our hope that our brothers and sisters of Earth will approve joint Coalition maneuvers with the greatest possible speed.

"The new mandate of the Martian navy is to secure the safety of all honest citizens, to dismantle the infrastructures of evil presently hiding in the Belt, and bring to justice those responsible for these attacks. I am pleased to say that our initial actions have resulted in the destruction of eighteen illegal warships and—"

Miller turned off the feed. That was it, then. The secret war was out of the closet. Papa Mao had been right to want Julie out, but it was too late. His darling daughter was going to have to take her chances, just like everyone else.

At the very least, it was going to mean curfews and personnel tracking all through Ceres Station. Officially, the station was neutral. The OPA didn't own it or anything else. And Star Helix was an Earth corporation, not under contractual or treaty obligation to Mars. At best, Mars and the OPA would keep their fight outside the station. At worst, there would more riots on Ceres. More death.

No, that wasn't true. At worst, Mars or the OPA would make a statement by throwing a rock or a handful of nuclear warheads at the station. Or by blowing a fusion drive on a docked ship. If things got out of hand, it would mean six or seven million dead people and the end of everything Miller had ever known.

Odd that it should feel almost like relief.

For weeks, Miller had known. Everyone had known. But it hadn't actually happened, so every conversation, every joke, every chance interaction and semi-anonymous nod and polite moment of light banter on the tube had seemed like an evasion. He couldn't fix the cancer of war, couldn't even slow down the spread, but at least he could admit it was happening. He stretched, ate his last bite of fungal curds, drank the dregs of something not entirely unlike coffee, and headed out to keep peace in wartime.

Muss greeted him with a vague nod when he got to the station house. The board was filled with cases—crimes to be investigated, documented, and dismissed. Twice as many entries as the day before.

"Bad night," Miller said.

"Could be worse," Muss said.

"Yeah?"

"Star Helix could be a Mars corporation. As long as Earth stays neutral, we don't have to actually be the Gestapo."

"And how long you figure that'll last?"

"What time is it?" she asked. "Tell you what, though. When it does come down, I need to make a stop up toward the core. There was this one guy back when I was rape squad we could never quite nail."

"Why wait?" Miller asked. "We could go up, put a bullet in him, be back by lunch."

"Yeah, but you know how it is," she said. "Trying to stay professional. Anyway, if we did that, we'd have to investigate it, and there's no room on the board."

Miller sat at his desk. It was just shoptalk. The kind of over-the-top deadpan you did when your day was filled with underage whores and tainted drugs. And still, there was a tension in the station. It was in the way people laughed, the way they held themselves. There were more holsters visible than usual, as if by showing their weapons they might be made safe.

"You think it's the OPA?" Muss asked. Her voice was lower now.

"That killed the *Donnager,* you mean? Who else could? Plus which, they're taking credit for it."

"Some of them are. From what I heard, there's more than one OPA these days. The old-school guys don't know a goddamn thing about any of this. All shitting their pants and trying to track down the pirate casts that are claiming credit."

"So they can do what?" Miller asked. "You can shut down every loudmouth caster in the Belt, it won't change a thing."

"If there's a schism in the OPA, though…" Muss looked at the board.

If there was a schism within the OPA, the board as they saw it now was nothing. Miller had lived through two major gang wars. First when the Loca Greiga displaced and destroyed the Aryan Flyers, and then when the Golden Bough split. The OPA was bigger, and meaner, and more professional than any of them. That would be civil war in the Belt.

"Might not happen," Miller said.

Shaddid stepped out of her office, her gaze sweeping the station house. Conversations dimmed. Shaddid caught Miller's eye. She made a sharp gesture. *Get in the office.*

"Busted," Muss said.

In the office, Anderson Dawes sat at ease on one of the chairs. Miller felt his body twitch as that information fell into place. Mars and the Belt in open, armed conflict. The OPA's face on Ceres sitting with the captain of the security force.

So that's how it is, he thought.

"You're working the Mao job," Shaddid said as she took her seat. Miller hadn't been offered the option of sitting, so he clasped his hands behind him.

"You assigned it to me," he said.

"And I told you it wasn't a priority," she said.

"I disagreed," Miller said.

Dawes smiled. It was a surprisingly warm expression, especially compared to Shaddid's.

"Detective Miller," Dawes said. "You don't understand what's happening here. We are sitting on a pressure vessel, and you keep swinging a pickax at it. You need to stop that."

"You're off the Mao case," Shaddid said. "Do you understand that? I am officially removing you from that investigation as of right now. Any further investigation you do, I will have you disciplined for working outside your caseload and misappropriating

Star Helix resources. You will return any material on the case to me. You will wipe any data you have in your personal partition. And you'll do it before the end of shift."

Miller's brain spun, but he kept his face impassive. She was taking Julie away. He wasn't going to let her. That was a given. But it wasn't the first issue.

"I have some inquiries in process..." he began.

"No, you don't," Shaddid said. "Your little letter to the parents was a breach of policy. Any contact with the shareholders should have come through me."

"You're telling me it didn't go out," Miller said. Meaning *You've been monitoring me.*

"It did not," Shaddid said. *Yes, I have. What are you going to do about it?*

And there wasn't anything he could do.

"And the transcripts of the James Holden interrogation?" Miller said. "Did those get out before..."

Before the *Donnager* was destroyed, taking with it the only living witnesses to the *Scopuli* and plunging the system into war? Miller knew the question sounded like a whine. Shaddid's jaw tensed. He wouldn't have been surprised to hear teeth cracking. Dawes broke the silence.

"I think we can make this a little easier," he said. "Detective, if I'm hearing you right, you think we're burying the issue. We aren't. But it's not in anyone's interests that Star Helix be the one to find the answers you're looking for. Think about it. You may be a Belter, but you're working for an Earth corporation. Right now, Earth is the only major power without an oar in the water. The only one who can possibly negotiate with all sides."

"And so why wouldn't they want to know the truth?" Miller said.

"That isn't the problem," Dawes said. "The problem is that Star Helix and Earth can't appear to be involved one way or the other. Their hands need to stay clean. And this issue leads outside your contract. Juliette Mao isn't on Ceres, and maybe there was a time you could have jumped a ship to wherever you found her and done the abduction. Extradition. Extraction. Whatever you want to call it. But that time has passed. Star Helix is Ceres, part of Ganymede, and a few dozen warehouse asteroids. If you leave that, you're going into enemy territory."

"But the OPA isn't," Miller said.

"We have the resources to do this right," Dawes said with a nod. "Mao is one of ours. The *Scopuli* was one of ours."

"And the *Scopuli* was the bait that killed the *Canterbury*," Miller said. "And the *Canterbury* was the bait that killed the *Donnager.* So why exactly would anyone be better off having you be the only ones looking into something you might have done?"

"You think we nuked the *Canterbury*," Dawes said. "The OPA, with its state-of-the-art Martian warships?"

"It got the *Donnager* out where it could be attacked. As long as it was with the fleet, it couldn't have been boarded."

Dawes looked sour.

"Conspiracy theories, Mr. Miller," he said. "If we had cloaked Martian warships, we wouldn't be losing."

"You had enough to kill the *Donnager* with just six ships."

"No. We didn't. Our version of blowing up the *Donnager* is a whole bunch of tramp prospectors loaded with nukes going on a suicide mission. We have many, many resources. What happened to the *Donnager* wasn't part of them."

The silence was broken only by the hum of the air recycler. Miller crossed his arms.

"But...I don't understand," he said. "If the OPA didn't start this, who did?"

"That is what Juliette Mao and the crew of the *Scopuli* can tell us," Shaddid said. "Those are the stakes, Miller. Who and why and please Christ some idea of how to stop it."

"And you don't want to find them?" Miller said.

"I don't want *you* to," Dawes said. "Not when someone else can do it better."

Miller shook his head. It was going too far, and he knew it. On the other hand, sometimes going too far could tell you something too.

"I'm not sold," he said.

"You don't have to be *sold*," Shaddid said. "This isn't a negotiation. We aren't bringing you in to ask you for a goddamn favor. I am your boss. I am telling you. Do you know those words? Telling. You."

"We have Holden," Dawes said.

"What?" Miller said at the same time Shaddid said, "You're not supposed to talk about that."

Dawes raised an arm toward Shaddid in the Belt's physical idiom of telling someone to be quiet. To Miller's surprise, she did as the OPA man said.

"We have Holden. He and his crew didn't die, and they are or are about to be in OPA custody. Do you understand what I'm saying, Detective? Do you see my point? I can do this investigation because I have the resources to do it. *You* can't even find out what happened to your own riot gear."

It was a slap. Miller looked at his shoes. He'd broken his word to Dawes about dropping the case, and the man hadn't brought it up until now. He had to give the OPA operative points for that. Added to that, if Dawes really did have James Holden, there was no chance of Miller's getting access to the interrogation.

When Shaddid spoke, her voice was surprisingly gentle.

"There were three murders yesterday. Eight warehouses got broken into, probably by the same bunch of people. We've got six people in hospital wards around the station with their nerves falling apart from a bad batch of bathtub pseudoheroin. The whole station's jumpy," she said. "There's a lot of good you can do out there, Miller. Go catch some bad guys."

"Sure, Captain," Miller said. "You bet."

Muss leaned against his desk, waiting for him. Her arms were crossed, her eyes as bored looking at him as they had been looking at the corpse of Dos Santos pinned to the corridor wall.

"New asshole?" she asked.

"Yeah."

"It'll grow closed. Give it time. I got us one of the murders. Mid-level accountant for Naobi-Shears got his head blown off outside a bar. It looked fun."

Miller pulled up his hand terminal and took in the basics. His heart wasn't in it.

"Hey, Muss," he said. "I got a question."

"Fire away."

"You've got a case you don't want solved. What do you do?"

His new partner frowned, tilted her head, and shrugged.

"I hand it to a fish," she said. "There was a guy back in crimes against children. If we knew the perp was one of our informants, we'd always give it to him. None of our guys ever got in trouble."

"Yeah," Miller said.

"For that matter, I need someone to take the shitty partner, I do the same thing," Muss went on. "You know. Someone no one else wants to work with? Got bad breath or a shitty personality or what-ever, but he needs a partner. So I pick the guy who maybe he used to be good, but then he got a divorce. Started hitting the bottle. Guy still thinks he's a hotshot. Acts like it. Only his numbers aren't bet-ter than anyone else's. Give him the shit cases. The shit partner."

Miller closed his eyes. His stomach felt uneasy.

"What did you do?" he asked.

"To get assigned to you?" Muss said. "One of the seniors made the moves on me and I shot him down."

"So you got stuck."

"Pretty much. Come on, Miller. You aren't stupid," Muss said. "You had to know."

He'd had to know that he was the station house joke. The guy who used to be good. The one who'd lost it.

No, actually he hadn't known that. He opened his eyes. Muss didn't look happy or sad, pleased at his pain or particularly dis-tressed by it. It was just work to her. The dead, the wounded, the injured. She didn't care. Not caring was how she got through the day.

"Maybe you shouldn't have turned him down," Miller said.

"Ah, you're not that bad," Muss said. "And he had back hair. I hate back hair."

"Glad to hear it," Miller said. "Let's go make some justice."

"You're drunk," the asshole said.

" 'M a cop," Miller said, stabbing the air with his finger. "Don't fuck with me."

"I know you're a cop. You've been coming to my bar for three years. It's me. Hasini. And you're drunk, my friend. Seriously, dangerously drunk."

Miller looked around him. He was indeed at the Blue Frog. He didn't remember having come here, and yet here he was. And the asshole was Hasini after all.

"I…" Miller began, then lost his train of thought.

"Come on," Hasini said, looping an arm around him. "It's not that far. I'll get you home."

"What time is it?" Miller asked.

"Late."

The word had a depth to it. *Late.* It was late. All the chances to make things right had somehow passed him. The system was at war, and no one was even sure why. Miller himself was turning fifty years old the next June. It was late. Late to start again. Late to realize how many years he'd spent running down the wrong road. Hasini steered him toward an electric cart the bar kept for occasions like this one. The smell of hot grease came out of the kitchen.

"Hold on," Miller said.

"You going to puke?" Hasini asked.

Miller considered for a moment. No, it was too late to puke. He stumbled forward. Hasini laid him back in the cart and engaged the motors, and with a whine they steered out into the corridor. The lights high above them were dimmed. The cart vibrated as they passed intersection after intersection. Or maybe it didn't. Maybe that was just his body.

"I thought I was good," he said. "You know, all this time, I thought I was at least good."

"You do fine," Hasini said. "You've just got a shitty job."

"That I was good at."

"You do fine," Hasini repeated, as if saying it would make it true.

Miller lay on the bed of the cart. The formed plastic arch of the wheel well dug into his side. It ached, but moving was too much effort. Thinking was too much effort. He'd made it through his day, Muss at his side. He'd turned in the data and materials on Julie. He had nothing worth going back to his hole for, and no place else to be.

The lights shifted into and out of his field of view. He wondered if that was what it would be like to look at stars. He'd never looked up at a sky. The thought inspired a certain vertigo. A sense of terror of the infinite that was almost pleasant.

"There anyone who can take care of you?" Hasini said when they reached Miller's hole.

"I'll be fine. I just...I had a bad day."

"Julie," Hasini said, nodding.

"How do you know about Julie?" Miller asked.

"You've been talking about her all night," Hasini said. "She's a girl you fell for, right?"

Frowning, Miller kept a hand on the cart. Julie. He'd been talking about Julie. That was what this was about. Not his job. Not his reputation. They'd taken away Julie. The special case. The one that mattered.

"You're in love with her," Hasini said.

"Yeah, sort of," Miller said, something like revelation forcing its way through the alcohol. "I think I am."

"Too bad for you," Hasini said.

Chapter Seventeen: Holden

The *Tachi*'s galley had a full kitchen and a table with room for twelve. It also had a full-size coffeepot that could brew forty cups of coffee in less than five minutes whether the ship was in zero g or under a five-g burn. Holden said a silent prayer of thanks for bloated military budgets and pressed the brew button. He had to restrain himself from stroking the stainless steel cover while it made gentle percolating noises.

The aroma of coffee began to fill the air, competing with the baking-bread smell of whatever Alex had put in the oven. Amos was thumping around the table in his new cast, laying out plastic plates and actual honest-to-god metal silverware. In a bowl Naomi was mixing something that had the garlic scent of good hummus. Watching the crew work at these domestic tasks, Holden had a sense of peace and safety deep enough to leave him light-headed.

They'd been on the run for weeks now, pursued the entire time by one mysterious ship or another. For the first time since the *Canterbury* was destroyed, no one knew where they were. No one was demanding anything of them. As far as the solar system was concerned, they were a few casualties out of thousands on the *Donnager*. A brief vision of Shed's head disappearing like a grisly magic trick reminded him that at least one of his crew *was* a casualty. And still, it felt so good to once again be master of his own destiny that even regret couldn't entirely rob him of it.

A timer rang, and Alex pulled out a tray covered with thin, flat bread. He began cutting it into slices, onto which Naomi slathered a paste that did in fact look like hummus. Amos put them on the plates around the table. Holden drew fresh coffee into mugs that had the ship's name on the side. He passed them around. There was an awkward moment when everyone stared at the neatly set table without moving, as if afraid to destroy the perfection of the scene.

Amos solved this by saying, "I'm hungry as a fucking bear," and then sitting down with a thump. "Somebody pass me that pepper, wouldja?"

For several minutes, no one spoke; they only ate. Holden took a small bite of the flat bread and hummus, the strong flavors making him dizzy after weeks of tasteless protein bars. Then he was stuffing it into his mouth so fast it made his salivary glands flare with exquisite agony. He looked around the table, embarrassed, but everyone else was eating just as fast, so he gave up on propriety and concentrated on food. When he'd finished off the last scraps from his plate, he leaned back with a sigh, hoping to make the contentment last as long as possible. Alex sipped coffee with his eyes closed. Amos ate the last bits of the hummus right out of the serving bowl with his spoon. Naomi gave Holden a sleepy look through half-lidded eyes that was suddenly sexy as hell. Holden quashed that thought and raised his mug.

"To Kelly's marines. Heroes to the last, may they rest in peace," he said.

"To the marines," everyone at the table echoed, then clinked mugs and drank.

Alex raised his mug and said, "To Shed."

"Yeah, to Shed, and to the assholes who killed him roasting in hell," Amos said in a quiet voice. "Right beside the fucker who killed the *Cant*."

The mood at the table got somber. Holden felt the peaceful moment slipping away as quietly as it had come.

"So," he said. "Tell me about our new ship. Alex?"

"She's a beaut, Cap. I ran her at twelve g for most of half an hour when we left the *Donnie*, and she purred like a kitten the whole time. The pilot's chair is comfy too."

Holden nodded.

"Amos? Get a chance to look at her engine room yet?" he asked.

"Yep. Clean as a whistle. This is going to be a boring gig for a grease monkey like me," the mechanic replied.

"Boring would be nice," Holden said. "Naomi? What do you think?"

She smiled. "I love it. It's got the nicest showers I've ever seen on a ship this size. Plus, there's a truly amazing medical bay with a computerized expert system that knows how to fix broken marines. We should have found it rather than fix Amos on our own."

Amos thumped his cast with one knuckle.

"You guys did a good job, Boss."

Holden looked around at his clean crew and ran a hand through his own hair, not pulling it away covered in grease for the first time in weeks.

"Yeah, a shower and not having to fix broken legs sounds good. Anything else?"

Naomi tilted her head back, her eyes moving as though she was running through a mental checklist.

"We've got a full tank of water, the injectors have enough fuel pellets to run the reactor for about thirty years, and the galley is fully stocked. You'll have to tie me up if you plan to give her back to the navy. I love her."

"She is a cunning little boat," Holden said with a smile. "Have a chance to look at the weapons?"

"Two tubes and twenty long-range torpedoes with high-yield plasma warheads," Naomi said. "Or at least that's what the manifest says. They load those from the outside, so I can't physically verify without climbing around on the hull."

"The weapons panel is sayin' the same thing, Cap," Alex said. "And full loads in all the point defense cannons. You know, except..."

Except the burst you fired into the men who killed Gomez.

"Oh, and, Captain, when we put Kelly in the cargo hold, I found a big crate with the letters MAP on the side. According to the manifest, it stands for 'Mobile Assault Package.' Apparently navy-speak for a big box of guns," Naomi said.

"Yeah," Alex said. "It's full kit for eight marines."

"Okay," Holden said. "So with the fleet-quality Epstein, we've got legs. And if you guys are right about the weapons load out, we've also got teeth. The next question is what do we do with it? I'm inclined to take Colonel Johnson's offer of refuge. Any thoughts?"

"I'm all for that, Captain," Amos said. "I always did think the Belters were getting the short end of the stick. I'll go be a revolutionary for a while, I guess."

"Earthman's burden, Amos?" Naomi asked with a grin.

"What the fuck does that even mean?"

"Nothing, just teasing," she said. "I know you like our side because you just want to steal our women."

Amos grinned back, suddenly in on the joke.

"Well, you ladies do have the legs that go *all* the way up," he said.

"Okay, enough," Holden said, raising his hand. "So, two votes for Fred. Anyone else?"

Naomi raised her hand.

"I vote for Fred," she said.

"Alex? What do you think?" Holden asked.

The Martian pilot leaned back in his chair and scratched his head.

"I got nowhere in particular to be, so I'll stick with you guys, I guess," he said. "But I hope this don't turn into another round of bein' told what to do."

"It won't," Holden replied. "I have a ship with guns on it now, and the next time someone orders me to do something, I'm using them."

After dinner, Holden took a long, slow tour of his new ship. He opened every door, looked in every closet, turned on every panel, and read every readout. He stood in engineering next to the fusion reactor and closed his eyes, getting used to the almost subliminal vibration she made. If something ever went wrong with it, he wanted to feel it in his bones before any warning ever sounded. He stopped and touched all the tools in the well-stocked machine shop, and he climbed up to the personnel deck and wandered through the crew cabins until he found one he liked, and messed up the bed to show it was taken. He found a bunch of jumpsuits in what looked like his size, then moved them to the closet in his new room. He took a second shower and let the hot water massage knots in his back that were three weeks old. As he wandered back to his cabin, he trailed his fingers along the wall, feeling the soft give of the fire-retardant foam and anti-spalling webbing over the top of the armored steel bulkheads. When he arrived at his cabin, Alex and Amos were both getting settled into theirs.

"Which cabin did Naomi take?" he asked.

Amos shrugged. "She's still up in ops, fiddling with something."

Holden decided to put off sleep for a while and rode the keel ladder-lift—*we have a lift!*—up to the operations deck. Naomi was sitting on the floor, an open bulkhead panel in front of her and what looked like a hundred small parts and wires laid out around her in precise patterns. She was staring at something inside the open compartment.

"Hey, Naomi, you should really get some sleep. What are you working on?"

She gestured vaguely at the compartment.

"Transponder," she said.

Holden moved over and sat down on the floor next to her.

"Tell me how to help."

She handed him her hand terminal; Fred's instructions for changing the transponder signal were open on the screen.

"It's ready to go. I've got the console hooked up to the transponder's data port just like he says. I've got the computer program set up to run the override he describes. The new transponder code and ship registry data are ready to be entered. I put in the new name. Did Fred pick it?"

"No, that was me."

"Oh. All right, then. But…" Her voice trailed off, and she waved at the transponder again.

"What's the problem?" Holden asked.

"Jim, they make these things *not* to be fiddled with. The civilian version of this device fuses itself into a solid lump of silicon if it thinks it's being tampered with. Who knows what the military version of the fail-safe is? Drop the magnetic bottle in the reactor? Turn us into a supernova?"

Naomi turned to look at him.

"I've got it all set up and ready to go, but now I don't think we should throw the switch," she said. "We don't know the consequences of failure."

Holden got up off the floor and moved over to the computer console. A program Naomi had named Trans01 was waiting to be run. He hesitated for one second, then pressed the button to execute. The ship failed to vaporize.

"I guess Fred wants us alive, then," he said.

Naomi slumped down with a noisy, extended exhale.

"See, this is why I can't ever be in command," she said.

"Don't like making tough calls with incomplete information?"

"More I'm not suicidally irresponsible," she replied, and began slowly reassembling the transponder housing.

Holden punched the comm system on the wall. "Well, crew, welcome aboard the gas freighter *Rocinante.*"

"What does that name even mean?" Naomi said after he let go of the comm button.

"It means we need to go find some windmills," Holden said over his shoulder as he headed to the lift.

Tycho Manufacturing and Engineering Concern was one of the first major corporations to move into the Belt. In the early days of expansion, Tycho engineers and a fleet of ships had captured a small comet and parked it in stable orbit as a water resupply point decades before ships like the *Canterbury* began bringing ice in from the nearly limitless fields in Saturn's rings. It had been the most complex, difficult feat of mass-scale engineering humanity had ever accomplished until the next thing they did.

As an encore, Tycho had built the massive reaction drives into the rock of Ceres and Eros and spent more than a decade teaching the asteroids to spin. They had been slated to create a network of high-atmosphere floating cities above Venus before the development rights fell into a labyrinth of lawsuits now entering its eighth decade. There was some discussion of space elevators for Mars and Earth, but nothing solid had come of it yet. If you had an impossible engineering job that needed to be done in the Belt, and you could afford it, you hired Tycho.

Tycho Station, the Belt headquarters of the company, was a massive ring station built around a sphere half a kilometer across, with more than sixty-five million cubic meters of manufacturing and storage space inside. The two counter-rotating habitation rings that circled the sphere had enough space for fifteen thousand workers and their families. The top of the manufacturing sphere was festooned with half a dozen massive construction waldoes that looked like they could rip a heavy freighter in half. The bottom of the sphere had a bulbous projection fifty meters across, which housed a capital-ship-class fusion reactor and drive system, making Tycho Station the largest mobile construction platform in the solar system. Each compartment within the massive rings was built on a swivel system that allowed the chambers to reorient to thrust gravity when the rings stopped spinning and the station flew to its next work location.

Holden knew all this, and his first sight of the station still took his breath away. It wasn't just the size of it. It was the idea that four generations of the smartest people in the solar system had been living and working here as they helped drag humanity into the outer planets almost through sheer force of will.

Amos said, "It looks like a big bug."

Holden started to protest, but it did resemble some kind of giant spider: fat bulbous body and all its legs sprouting from the top of its head.

Alex said, "Forget the station, look at *that* monster."

The vessel it was constructing dwarfed the station. Ladar returns told Holden the ship was just over two kilometers long and half a kilometer wide. Round and stubby, it looked like a cigarette butt made of steel. Framework girders exposed internal compartments and machinery at various stages of construction, but the engines looked complete, and the hull had been assembled over the bow. The name *Nauvoo* was painted in massive white letters across it.

"So the Mormons are going to ride that thing all the way to Tau Ceti, huh?" Amos asked, following it up with a long whistle. "Ballsy bastards. No guarantee there's even a planet worth a damn on the other end of that hundred-year trip."

"They seem pretty sure," Holden replied. "And you don't make the money to build a ship like that by being stupid. I, for one, wish them nothing but luck."

"They'll get the stars," Naomi said. "How can you not envy them that?"

"Their great-grandkids'll get maybe *a* star if they don't all starve to death orbiting a rock they can't use," Amos said. "Let's not get grandiose here."

He pointed at the impressively large comm array jutting from the *Nauvoo's* flank.

"Want to bet that's what threw our anus-sized tightbeam message?" Amos said.

Alex nodded. "If you want to send private messages home from a couple light-years away, you need serious beam coherence. They probably had the volume turned down to avoid cuttin' a hole in us."

Holden got up from the copilot's couch and pushed past Amos. "Alex, see if they'll let us land."

Landing was surprisingly easy. The station control directed them to a docking port on the side of the sphere and stayed on the line, guiding them in, until Alex had married the docking tube to the airlock door. The tower control never pointed out that they had a lot of armaments for a transport and no tanks for carrying compressed gas. She got them docked, then wished them a pleasant day.

Holden put on his atmosphere suit and made a quick trip to the cargo bay, then met the others just inside the *Rocinante's* inner airlock door with a large duffel.

"Put your suits on, that's now standard ops for this crew anytime we go someplace new. And take one of these," he said, pulling handguns and cartridge magazines from the bag. "Hide it in a pocket or your bag if you like, but I will be wearing mine openly."

Naomi frowned at him.

"Seems a bit…confrontational, doesn't it?"

"I'm tired of being kicked around," Holden said. "The *Roci's* a good start toward independence, and I'm taking a little piece of her with me. Call it a good luck charm."

"Fuckin' A," said Amos, and strapped one of the guns to his thigh.

Alex stuffed his into the pocket of his flight suit. Naomi wrinkled her nose and waved off the last gun. Holden put it back into his duffel, led the crew into the *Rocinante*'s airlock, and cycled it. An older, dark-skinned man with a heavy build waited for them on the other side. As they came in, he smiled.

"Welcome to Tycho Station," said the Butcher of Anderson Station. "Call me Fred."

Chapter Eighteen: Miller

The death of the *Donnager* hit Ceres like a hammer striking a gong. Newsfeeds clogged themselves with high-power telescopic footage of the battle, most if not all of it faked. The Belt chatter swam with speculation about a secret OPA fleet. The six ships that had taken down the Martian flagship were hailed as heroes and martyrs. Slogans like *We did it once and we can do it again* and *Drop some rocks* cropped up even in apparently innocuous settings.

The *Canterbury* had stripped away the complacency of the Belt, but the *Donnager* had done something worse. It had taken away the fear. The Belters had gotten a sudden, decisive, and unexpected win. Anything seemed possible, and the hope seduced them.

It would have scared Miller more if he'd been sober.

Miller's alarm had been going off for the past ten minutes. The grating buzz took on subtones and overtones when he listened to it long enough. A constant rising tone, fluttering percussion throbbing under it, even soft music hiding underneath the blare. Illusions. Aural hallucinations. The voice of the whirlwind.

The previous night's bottle of fungal faux bourbon sat on the bedside table where a carafe of water usually waited. It still had a couple fingers at the bottom. Miller considered the soft brown of the liquid, thought about how it would feel on his tongue.

The beautiful thing about losing your illusions, he thought, was that you got to stop pretending. All the years he'd told himself that he was respected, that he was good at his job, that all his sacrifices had been made for a reason fell away and left him with the clear, unmuddied knowledge that he was a functional alcoholic who had pared away everything good in his own life to make room for anesthetic. Shaddid thought he was a joke. Muss thought he was the price she paid not to sleep with someone she didn't like. The only one who might have any respect for him at all was Havelock, an Earther. It was peaceful, in its way. He could stop making the effort to keep up appearances. If he stayed in bed listening to the alarm drone, he was just living up to expectations. No shame in that.

And still there was work to be done. He reached over and turned off the alarm. Just before it cut off, he heard a voice in it, soft but insistent. A woman's voice. He didn't know what she'd been saying. But since she was just in his head, she'd get another chance later.

He levered himself out of bed, sucked down some painkillers and rehydration goo, stalked to the shower, and burned a day and a half's ration of hot water just standing there, watching his legs get pink. He dressed in his last set of clean clothes. Breakfast was a bar of pressed yeast and grape sweetener. He dropped the bourbon from the bedside table into the recycler without finishing it, just to prove to himself that he still could.

Muss was waiting at the desk. She looked up when he sat.

"Still waiting for the labs on the rape up on eighteen," she said. "They promised them by lunch."

"We'll see," Miller said.

"I've got a possible witness. Girl who was with the vic earlier in the evening. Her deposition said she left before anything happened, but the security cameras aren't backing her up."

"Want me in the questioning?" Miller asked.

"Not yet. But if I need some theater, I'll pull you in."

"Fair enough."

Miller didn't watch her walk away. After a long moment staring at nothing, he pulled up his disk partition, reviewed what still needed doing, and started cleaning the place up.

As he worked, his mind replayed for the millionth time the slow, humiliating interview with Shaddid and Dawes. *We have Holden,* Dawes said. *You can't even find out what happened to your own riot gear.* Miller poked at the words like a tongue at the gap of a missing tooth. It rang true. Again.

Still, it might have been bullshit. It might have been a story concocted just to make him feel small. There wasn't any proof, after all, that Holden and his crew had survived. What proof could there be? The *Donnager* was gone, and all its logs along with it. There would have to have been a ship that made it out. Either a rescue vessel or one of the Martian escort ships. There was no way a ship could have gotten out and not been the singular darling of every newsfeed and pirate cast since. You couldn't keep something like that quiet.

Or sure you could. It just wouldn't be easy. He squinted at the empty air of the station house. Now. How *would* you cover up a surviving ship?

Miller pulled up a cheap navigation plotter he'd bought five years before — transit times had figured in a smuggling case — and plotted the date and position of the *Donnager*'s demise. Anything running under non-Epstein thrust would still have been out there, and Martian warships would have either picked it up or blasted it into background radiation by now. So if Dawes wasn't just handing him bullshit, that meant an Epstein drive. He ran a couple quick calculations. With a good drive, someone could have made Ceres in just less than a month. Call it three weeks to be safe.

He looked at the data for almost ten minutes, but the next step didn't come to him, so he stepped away, got some coffee, and pulled up the interview he and Muss had done with a Belter ground-crew grunt. The man's face was long and cadaverous and subtly cruel. The recorder hadn't had a good fix on him, so the picture kept bouncing around. Muss asked the man what he'd seen, and Miller leaned forward to read the transcribed answers, checking for incorrectly recognized words. Thirty seconds later, the grunt said *clip whore* and the transcript read *clipper.* Miller corrected it, but the back of his mind kept churning.

Probably eight or nine hundred ships came into Ceres in a given day. Call it a thousand to be safe. Give it a couple days on either side of the three-week mark, that was only four thousand entries. Pain in the ass, sure, but not impossible. Ganymede would be the other real bitch. With its agriculture, there would be hundreds of transports a day there. Still, it wouldn't double the workload. Eros. Tycho. Pallas. How many ships docked on Pallas every day?

He'd missed almost two minutes of the recording. He started again, forcing himself to pay attention this time, and half an hour later, he gave up.

The ten busiest ports with two days to either side of an estimated arrival of an Epstein-drive ship that originated when and where the *Donnager* died totaled twenty-eight thousand docking records, more or less. But he could cut that down to seventeen thousand if he excluded stations and ports explicitly run by Martian military and research stations with all or nearly all inner planet inhabitants. So how long would it take him to check all the porting records by hand, pretending for a minute that he was stupid enough to do it? Call it 118 days — if he didn't eat or sleep. Just working ten-hour days, doing nothing else, he could almost get through it in less than a year. A little less.

Except no. Because there were ways to narrow it. He was only looking for Epstein drive ships. Most of the traffic at any of the ports would be local. Torch drive ships flown by prospectors and short-hop couriers. The economics of spaceflight made relatively few and relatively large ships the right answer for long flights. So take it down by, conservatively, three-quarters, and he was back in the close-to-four-thousand range again. Still hundreds of hours of work, but if he could think of some other filter that would just feed him the likely suspects...For instance, if the ship couldn't have filed a flight plan before the *Donnager* got killed.

The request interface for the port logs was ancient, uncomfortable, and subtly different from Eros to Ganymede to Pallas and on and on. Miller tacked the information requests on to seven different cases, including a month-old cold case on which he was only a consultant. Port logs were public and open, so he didn't particularly need his detective status to hide his actions. With any luck Shaddid's monitoring of him wouldn't extend to low-level, public-record poking around. And even if it did, he might get the replies before she caught on.

Never knew if you had any luck left unless you pushed it. Besides, there wasn't a lot to lose.

When the connection from the lab opened on his terminal, he almost jumped. The technician was a gray-haired woman with an unnaturally young face.

"Miller? Muss with you?"

"Nope," Miller said. "She's got an interrogation."

He was pretty sure that was what she'd said. The tech shrugged.

"Well, her system's not answering. I wanted to tell you we got a match off the rape you sent us. It wasn't the boyfriend. Her boss did it."

Miller nodded. "You put in for the warrant?" he asked.

"Yep," she said. "It's already in the file."

Miller pulled it up: STAR HELIX ON BEHALF OF CERES STATION AUTHORIZES AND MANDATES THE DETENTION OF IMMANUEL CORVUS DOWD PENDING ADJUDICATION OF SECURITY INCIDENT CCS-4949231. The judge's digital signature was listed in green. He felt a slow smile on his lips.

"Thanks," he said.

On the way out of the station, one of the vice squads asked him where he was headed. He said lunch.

The Arranha Accountancy Group had their offices in the nice part of the governmental quarter in sector seven. It wasn't Miller's usual stomping grounds, but the warrant was good on the whole station. Miller went to the secretary at the front desk—a good-looking Belter with a starburst pattern embroidered on his vest—and explained that he needed to speak with Immanuel Corvus Dowd. The secretary's deep-brown skin took on an ashy tone. Miller stood back, not blocking the exit, but keeping close.

Twenty minutes later, an older man in a good suit came through the front door, stopped in front of Miller, and looked him up and down.

"Detective Miller?" the man said.

"You'd be Dowd's lawyer," Miller said cheerfully.

"I am, and I would like to—"

"Really," Miller said. "We should do this now."

The office was clean and spare with light blue walls that lit themselves from within. Dowd sat at the table. He was young enough that he still looked arrogant, but old enough to be scared. Miller nodded to him.

"You're Immanuel Corvus Dowd?" he said.

"Before you continue, Detective," the lawyer said, "my client is involved with very high-level negotiations. His client base includes some of the most important people in the war effort. Before you make any accusations, you should be aware that I can and will have everything you've done reviewed, and if there is one mistake, you will be held responsible."

"Mr. Dowd," Miller said. "What I am about to do to you is literally the only bright spot in my day. If you could see your way clear to resisting arrest, I'd really appreciate it."

"Harry?" Dowd said, looking to his lawyer. His voice cracked a little.

The lawyer shook his head.

Back at the police cart, Miller took a long moment. Dowd,

handcuffed in the back, where everyone walking by could see him, was silent. Miller pulled up his hand terminal, noted the time of arrest, the objections of the lawyer, and a few other minor comments. A young woman in professional dress of cream-colored linen hesitated at the door of the accountancy. Miller didn't recognize her; she was no one involved with the rape case, or at least not the one he was working. Her face had the expressionless calm of a fighter. He turned, craning his neck to look at Dowd, humiliated and not looking back. The woman shifted her gaze to Miller. She nodded once. *Thank you.*

He nodded back. *Just doing my job.*

She went through the door.

Two hours later, Miller finished the last of the paperwork and sent Dowd off to the cells.

Three and a half hours later, the first of his docking log requests came in.

Five hours later, the government of Ceres collapsed.

Despite being full, the station house was silent. Detectives and junior investigators, patrolmen and desk workers, the high and the low, they all gathered before Shaddid. She stood at her podium, her hair pulled back tight. She wore her Star Helix uniform, but the insignia had been removed. Her voice was shaky.

"You've all heard this by now, but starting now, it's official. The United Nations, responding to requests from Mars, is withdrawing from its oversight and...protection of Ceres Station. This is a peaceful transition. This is not a coup. I'm going to say that again. This isn't a coup. Earth is pulling out of here, we aren't pushing."

"That's bullshit, sir," someone shouted. Shaddid raised her hand.

"There's a lot of loose talk," Shaddid said. "I don't want to hear any of it from you. The governor's going to make the formal announcement at the start of the next shift, and we'll get more details then. Until we hear otherwise, the Star Helix contract is still in place. A provisional government is being formed with members drawn from local business and union representation. We are still the law on Ceres, and I expect you to behave appropriately. You will all be here for your shifts. You will be here on time. You will act professionally and within the scope of standard practice."

Miller looked over at Muss. His partner's hair was still unkempt from the pillow. It was pushing midnight for them both.

"Any questions?" Shaddid said in a voice that implied there ought not be.

Who's going to pay Star Helix? Miller thought. *What laws are we enforcing? What does Earth know that makes walking away from the biggest port in the Belt the smart move?*

Who's going to negotiate your peace treaty now?

Muss, seeing Miller's gaze, smiled.

"Guess we're hosed," Miller said.

"Had to happen," Muss agreed. "I better go. Got a stop to make."

"Up at the core?"

Muss didn't answer, because she didn't have to. Ceres didn't have laws. It had police. Miller headed back to his hole. The station hummed, the stone beneath him vibrating from the countless docking clamps and reactor cores, tubes and recyclers and pneumatics. The stone was alive, and he'd forgotten the small signs that proved it. Six million people lived here, breathed this air. Fewer than in a middle-sized city on Earth. He wondered if they were expendable.

Had it really gone so far that the inner planets would be willing to lose a major station? It seemed like it had if Earth was abandoning Ceres. The OPA would step in, whether it wanted to or not. The power vacuum was too great. Then Mars would call it an OPA coup. Then…Then what? Board it and put it under martial law? That was the good answer. Nuke it into dust? He couldn't quite bring himself to believe that either. There was just too much money involved. Docking fees alone would fuel a small national economy. And Shaddid and Dawes—much as he hated it—were right. Ceres under Earth contract had been the best hope for a negotiated peace.

Was there someone on Earth who didn't *want* that peace? Someone or something powerful enough to move the glacial bureaucracy of the United Nations to take action?

"What am I looking at, Julie?" he said to the empty air. "What did you see out there that's worth Mars and the Belt killing each other?"

The station hummed to itself, a quiet, constant sound too soft for him to hear the voices within it.

Muss didn't come to work in the morning, but there was a message on his system telling him she'd be in late. "Cleanup" was her only explanation.

To look at it, nothing about the station house had changed. The same people coming to the same place to do the same thing. No, that wasn't true. The energy was high. People were smiling, laughing, clowning around. It was a manic high, panic pressed through a cheesecloth mask of normalcy. It wasn't going to last.

They were all that separated Ceres from anarchy. They were the law, and the difference between the survival of six million people and some mad bastard forcing open all the airlocks or poisoning the recyclers rested on maybe thirty thousand people. People like him. Maybe he should have rallied, risen to the occasion like the rest of them. The truth was the thought made him tired.

Shaddid marched by and tapped him on the shoulder. He sighed, rose from his chair, and followed her. Dawes was in her office again, looking shaken and sleep deprived. Miller nodded to him. Shaddid crossed her arms, her eyes softer and less accusing than he'd become used to.

"This is going to be tough," she said. "We're facing something harder than anything we've had to do before. I need a team I can trust with my life. Extraordinary circumstances. You understand that?"

"Yeah," he said. "I got it. I'll stop drinking, get myself together."

"Miller. You're not a bad person at heart. There was a time you were a pretty good cop. But I don't trust you, and we don't have time to start over," Shaddid said, her voice as near to gentle as he had ever heard it. "You're fired."

Chapter Nineteen: Holden

Fred stood alone, hand outstretched, a warm and open smile on his broad face. There were no guards with assault rifles behind him. Holden shook Fred's hand and then started laughing. Fred smiled and looked confused but let Holden keep a grip on his hand, waiting for Holden to explain what was so funny.

"I'm sorry, but you have no idea how pleasant this is," Holden said. "This is *literally* the first time in over a month that I've gotten off a ship without it blowing up behind me."

Fred laughed with him now, an honest laugh that seemed to originate somewhere in his belly.

After a moment the man said, "You're quite safe here. We are the most protected station in the outer planets."

"Because you're OPA?" Holden asked.

Fred shook his head.

"No. We make campaign contributions to Earth and Mars

politicians in amounts that would make a Hilton blush," he said. "If anyone blows us up, half the UN assembly and all of the Martian Congress will be howling for blood. It's the problem with politics. Your enemies are often your allies. And vice versa."

Fred gestured to a doorway behind him and motioned for everyone to follow. The ride was short, but halfway through, gravity reappeared, shifting in a disorienting swoop. Holden stumbled. Fred looked chagrined.

"I'm sorry. I should have warned you about that. The central hub's null g. Moving into the ring's rotational gravity can be awkward the first time."

"I'm fine," Holden said. Naomi's brief smile might only have been his imagination.

A moment later the elevator door opened onto a wide carpeted corridor with walls of pale green. It had the reassuring smell of air scrubbers and fresh carpet glue. Holden wouldn't have been surprised to find they were piping "new space station" scent into the air. The doors that led off the corridor were made of faux wood distinguishable from the real thing only because nobody had that much money. Of all his crew, Holden was almost certainly the only one who had grown up in a house with real wooden furniture and fixtures. Amos had grown up in Baltimore. They hadn't seen a tree there in more than a century.

Holden pulled off his helmet and turned around to tell his crew to do the same, but theirs were already off. Amos looked up and down the corridor and whistled.

"Nice digs, Fred," he said.

"Follow me, I'll get you settled in," Fred replied, leading them down the corridor. As he walked, he spoke. "Tycho Station has undergone a number of refurbishments over the last hundred years, as you might guess, but the basics haven't changed much. It was a brilliant design to begin with; Malthus Tycho was an engineering genius. His grandson, Bredon, runs the company now. He isn't on station at the moment. Down the well at Luna negotiating the next big deal."

Holden said, "Seems like you have a lot on your plate already, with that monster parked outside. And, you know, a war going on."

A group of people in jumpsuits of various colors walked past, talking animatedly. The corridor was so wide that no one had to give way. Fred gestured at them as they went by.

"First shift's just ending, so this is rush hour," he said. "It's actually time to start drumming up new work. The *Nauvoo* is almost done. They'll be loading colonists on her in six months. Always have to have the next project lined up. The Tycho spends eleven million UN dollars every day she's in operation, whether we make money that day or not. It's a big nut to cover. And the war...well, we're hoping that's temporary."

"And now you're taking in refugees. That won't help," Holden said.

Fred just laughed and said, "Four more people won't put us in the poorhouse anytime soon."

Holden stopped, forcing the others to pull up short behind him. It was several steps before Fred noticed, then turned around with a confused look.

"You're dodging," Holden said. "Other than a couple billion dollars' worth of stolen Martian warship, we haven't got anything of value. Everyone thinks we're dead. Any access of our accounts ruins that, and I just don't live in a universe where Daddy Warbucks swoops in and makes everything okay out of the goodness of his heart. So either tell us why you're taking the risk of putting us up, or we go get back on our ship and try our hand at piracy."

"Scourge of the Martian merchant fleet, they'll call us," Amos growled from somewhere behind him. He sounded pleased.

Fred held up his hands. There was a hardness in his eyes, but also an amused respect.

"Nothing underhanded, you have my word," he said. "You're armed, and station security will allow you to carry guns whenever you like. That alone should reassure you that I'm not planning foul play. But let me get you settled in before we do much more talking, okay?"

Holden didn't move. Another group of returning workers was going by in the corridor, and they watched the scene curiously as they passed. Someone from the knot of people called out, "Everything okay, Fred?"

Fred nodded and waved them by impatiently. "Let's get out of the corridor at least."

"We aren't unpacking until we get some answers," Holden replied.

"Fine. We're almost there," Fred said, and then led them off again at a somewhat faster pace. He stopped at a small inset in the corridor wall with two doors in it. Opening one with the swipe of a card, he led the four of them into a large residential suite with a roomy living space and lots of seating.

"Bathroom is that door back there on the left. The bedroom is the one on the right. There's even a small kitchen space over here," Fred said, pointing to each thing as he spoke.

Holden sat down in a large brown faux-leather recliner and leaned it back. A remote control was in a pocket of the armrest. He assumed it controlled the impressively large screen that took up most of one wall. Naomi and Amos sat on a couch that matched his chair, and Alex draped himself over a loveseat in a nice contrasting cream color.

"Comfortable?" Fred asked, pulling a chair away from the six-seat dining area and sitting down across from Holden.

"It's all right," Holden said defensively. "My ship has a really nice coffeemaker."

"I suppose bribes won't work. You are all comfortable, though? We have two suites set aside for you, both this basic layout, though the other suite has two rooms. I wasn't sure of the, ah, sleeping arrangements..." Fred trailed off uncomfortably.

"Don't worry, Boss, you can bunk with me," Amos said with a wink at Naomi.

Naomi just smiled faintly.

"Okay, Fred, we're off the street," she said. "Now answer the captain's questions."

Fred nodded, then stood up and cleared his throat. He seemed to review something. When he spoke, the conversational facade was gone. His voice carried a grim authority.

"War between the Belt and Mars is suicide. Even if every rock hopper in the Belt were armed, we still couldn't compete with the Martian navy. We might kill a few with tricks and suicide runs. Mars might feel forced to nuke one of our stations to prove a point. But we can strap chemical rockets onto a couple hundred rocks the size of bunk beds and rain Armageddon down on Martian dome cities."

Fred paused, as if looking for words, then sat back down on his chair.

"All of the war drums ignore that. It's the elephant in the room. Anyone who doesn't live on a spaceship is structurally vulnerable. Tycho, Eros, Pallas, Ceres. Stations can't evade incoming missiles. And with all of the enemy's citizens living at the bottom of huge gravity wells, we don't even have to aim particularly well. Einstein was right. We will be fighting the next war with rocks. But the Belt has rocks that will turn the surface of Mars into a molten sea.

"Right now everyone is still playing nice, and only shooting at ships. Very gentlemanly. But sooner or later, one side or the other will be pressed to do something desperate."

Holden leaned forward, the slick surface of his environment suit making an embarrassing squeak on the leather textured chair. No one laughed.

"I agree. What does that have to do with us?" he asked.

"Too much blood has already been shed," Fred said.

Shed.

Holden winced at the bleak, unintentional pun but said nothing.

"The *Canterbury,*" Fred continued. "The *Donnager.* People aren't just going to forget about those ships, and those thousands of innocent people."

"Seems like you just crossed off the only two options, Chief," Alex said. "No war, no peace."

"There's a third alternative. Civilized society has another way of dealing with things like this," Fred said. "A criminal trial."

Amos' snort shook the air. Holden had to fight not to smile himself.

"Are you fucking serious?" Amos asked. "And how do you put a goddamn Martian stealth ship on trial? Do we go question all the stealth ships about their whereabouts, double-check their alibis?"

Fred held up a hand.

"Stop thinking of the *Canterbury's* destruction as an act of war," he said. "It was a crime. Right now, people are overreacting, but once the situation sinks in, heads will cool. People on both sides will see where this road goes and look for another way out. There is a window where the saner elements can investigate events, negotiate jurisdiction, and assign blame to some party or parties that both sides can agree to. A trial. It's the only outcome that doesn't involve millions of deaths and the collapse of human infrastucture."

Holden shrugged, a gesture barely visible in his heavy environment suit.

"So it goes to a trial. You still aren't answering my question."

Fred pointed at Holden, then at each of the crew in turn.

"You're the ace in the hole. You four people are the only eyewitnesses to the destruction of *both* ships. When the trial comes, I need you and your depositions. I have influence already through our political contacts, but you can buy me a seat at the table. It will be a whole new set of treaties between the Belt and the inner planets. We can do in months what I'd dreamed of doing in decades."

"And you want to use our value as witnesses to force your way into the process so you can make those treaties look the way you want them to," Holden said.

"Yes. And I'm willing to give you protection, shelter, and run of my station for as long as it takes to get there."

Holden took a long, deep breath, got up, and started unzipping his suit.

"Yeah, okay. That's just self-serving enough I believe it," he said. "Let's get settled in."

Naomi was singing karaoke. Just thinking about it made Holden's head spin. Naomi. Karaoke. Even considering everything that had happened to them over the past month, Naomi up onstage with a mic in one hand and some sort of fuchsia martini in the other, screaming out an angry Belt-punk anthem by the Moldy Filters, was the strangest thing he'd ever seen. She finished to scattered applause and a few catcalls, then staggered off the stage and collapsed across from him in the booth.

She held up her drink, sloshing a good half of it onto the table, then threw the other half back all at once.

"Whadja think?" Naomi asked, waving at the bartender for another.

"It was terrible," Holden replied.

"No, really."

"It was truly one of the most awful renditions of one of the most awful songs I've ever heard."

Naomi shook her head, blowing an exasperated raspberry at him. Her dark hair fell across her face and, when the bartender brought her a second brightly colored martini, foiled all her attempts at drinking. She finally grabbed her hair and held it above her head in a clump while she drank.

"You don't get it," she said. "It's *supposed* to be awful. That's the point."

"Then it was the best version of that song I've ever heard," Holden said.

"Damn straight." Naomi looked around the bar. "Where're Amos and Alex?"

"Amos found what I'm pretty sure was the most expensive hooker I've ever seen. Alex is in the back playing darts. He made some claims about the superiority of Martian darts players. I assume they're going to kill him and throw him out an airlock."

A second singer was onstage, crooning out some sort of Vietnamese power ballad. Naomi watched the singer for a while, sipping her drink, then said, "Maybe we should go save him."

"Which one?"

"Alex. Why would Amos need saving?"

"Because I'm pretty sure he told the expensive hooker he was on Fred's expense account."

"Let's mount a rescue mission; we can save them both," Naomi said, then drank the rest of her cocktail. "I need more rescue fuel, though."

She started waving at the bartender again, but Holden reached out and grabbed her hand and held it on the table.

"Maybe we should take a breather instead," he said.

A flush of anger as intense as it was brief lit her face. She pulled back her hand.

"You take a breather. I've just had two ships and a bunch of friends shot out from underneath me, and spent three weeks of dead time flying to get here. So, no. I'm getting another drink, and then doing another set. The crowd loves me," Naomi said.

"What about our rescue mission?"

"Lost cause. Amos will be murdered by space hookers, but at least he'll die the way he lived."

Naomi pushed her way up from the table, grabbed her martini off the bar, and headed toward the karaoke stage. Holden watched her go, then finished off the scotch he'd been nursing for the past two hours and got up.

For a moment there, he'd had a vision of the two of them staggering back to the room together, then falling into bed. He'd have hated himself in the morning for taking advantage, but he'd still have done it. Naomi was looking at him from the stage, and he realized he'd been staring. He gave a little wave, then headed out the door with only ghosts—Ade, Captain McDowell, Gomez and Kelly and Shed—to keep him company.

The suite was comfortable and huge and depressing. He'd lain on the bed less than five minutes before he was up and out the door again. He walked the corridor for half an hour, finding the big intersections that led to other parts of the ring. He found an electronics store and a teahouse and what on closer inspection turned out to be a very expensive brothel. He declined the video menu of services the desk clerk offered and wandered out again, wondering if Amos was somewhere inside.

He was halfway down a corridor he hadn't seen before when a small knot of teenage girls passed him. Their faces looked no older than fourteen, but they were already as tall as he was. They got quiet as he walked by, then burst out laughing when he was behind them, and hurried away. Tycho was a city, and he suddenly felt very much like a foreigner, unsure of where to go or what to do.

It was no surprise to him when he looked up from his wanderings and discovered he'd come to the elevator to the docking area. He punched the button and climbed inside, remembering to turn on his boot mags just in time to avoid being flung off his feet when the gravity twisted sideways and vanished.

Even though he'd only had possession of the ship for three weeks, climbing back onto the *Rocinante* felt like going home. Using gentle touches on the keel ladder, he made his way up to the cockpit. He pulled himself into the copilot's couch, strapped in, and closed his eyes.

The ship was silent. With the reactor off-line, and no one aboard, nothing was moving at all. The flexible docking tube that connected the *Roci* to the station transmitted very little vibration to the ship. Holden could close his eyes and drift in the straps and disconnect from everything around him.

It would have been peaceful except that every time he'd closed his eyes for the past month, the fading ghost lights behind his eyelids had been Ade winking and blowing away like dust. The voice at the back of his head was McDowell's as he tried to save his ship right up to the very last second. He wondered if he'd have them for the rest of his life, coming out to haunt him every time he found a moment of quiet.

He remembered the old-timers from his navy days. Grizzled lifers who could soundly sleep while two meters away their shipmates played a raucous game of poker or watched the vids with the volume all the way up. Back then he'd assumed it was just learned behavior, the body adapting so it could get enough rest in an environment that never really had downtime. Now he wondered if those vets found the constant noise preferable. A way to keep their lost shipmates away. They probably went home after their twenty and never slept again. He opened his eyes and watched a small green telltale blink on the pilot's console.

It was the only light in the room, and it illuminated nothing. But its slow fade in and out was somehow comforting. A quiet heartbeat for the ship.

He told himself that Fred was right; a trial was the right thing to hope for. But he wanted that stealth ship in Alex's gun sights. He wanted that unknown crew to live through the terrifying moment when all the countermeasures have failed, the torpedoes are seconds from impact, and absolutely nothing can stop them.

He wanted them to have that same last gasp of fear he'd heard through Ade's mic.

For a time, he displaced the ghosts in his head with violent vengeance fantasies. When they stopped working, he floated down to the personnel deck, strapped into his cot, and tried to sleep. The *Rocinante* sang him a lullaby of air recyclers and silence.

Chapter Twenty: Miller

Miller sat at an open café, the tunnel wide above him. Grass grew tall and pale in the public commons, and the ceiling glowed full-spectrum white. Ceres Station had come unmoored. Orbital mechanics and inertia kept it physically where it had always been, but the stories about it had changed. The point defenses were the same. The tensile strength of the port blast doors was the same. The ephemeral shield of political status was all they'd lost, and it was everything.

Miller leaned forward and sipped his coffee.

There were children playing on the commons. He thought of them as children, though he remembered thinking of himself as an adult at that age. Fifteen, sixteen years old. They wore OPA armbands. The boys spoke in loud, angry voices about tyranny and freedom. The girls watched the boys strut. The ancient, animal story, the same whether it was on a spinning rock surrounded by hard vacuum or the stamp-sized chimpanzee preserves on Earth. Even in the Belt, youth brought invulnerability, immortality, the unshakable conviction that for you, things would be different. The laws of physics would cut you a break, the missiles would never hit, the air would never hiss out into nothing. Maybe for other people—the patched-together fighting ships of the OPA, the water haulers, the Martian gunships, the *Scopuli,* the *Canterbury,* the *Donnager,* the hundred other ships that had died in small actions since the system had turned itself into a battlefield—but not you. And when youth was lucky enough to survive its optimism, all Miller had left was a little fear, a little envy, and the overwhelming sense of life's fragility. But he had three month's worth of company script in his account and a lot of free time, and the coffee wasn't bad.

"You need anything, sir?" the waiter asked. He didn't look any older than the kids on the grass. Miller shook his head.

Five days had passed since Star Helix pulled its contract. The governor of Ceres was gone, smuggled out on a transport before the news had gone wide. The Outer Planets Alliance had announced the inclusion of Ceres among official OPA-held real estate, and no one had said otherwise. Miller had spent the first day of his unemployment drunk, but his bender had an oddly pro forma feel. He'd descended into the bottle because it was familiar, because it was what you did when you'd lost the career that defined you.

The second day, he'd gotten through the hangover. The third, he'd gotten bored. All through the station, security forces were making the kind of display he'd expected, preemptive peacekeeping. The few political rallies and protests ended fast and hard, and the citizens of Ceres didn't much care. Their eyes were on their monitors, on the war. A few locals with busted heads getting thrown into prison without charges were beneath notice. And Miller was personally responsible for none of it.

The fourth day, he'd checked his terminal and discovered that 80 percent of his docking log requests had come through before

Shaddid had shut his access down. Over a thousand entries, any one of which could be the only remaining lead to Julie Mao. So far, no Martian nukes were on their way to crack Ceres. No demands of surrender. No boarding forces. It could all change in a moment, but until it did, Miller was drinking coffee and auditing ship records, about one every fifteen minutes. Miller figured that if Holden was the last ship in the log, he'd find him in about six weeks.

The *Adrianopole,* a third-gen prospector, had docked at Pallas within the arrival window. Miller checked the open registration, frustrated again at how little information was there compared to the security databases. Owned by Strego Anthony Abramowitz. Eight citations for substandard maintenance, banned from Eros and Ceres as a danger to the port. An idiot and an accident waiting to happen, but the flight plan seemed legitimate, and the history of the ship was deep enough not to smell new-minted. Miller deleted the entry.

The *Badass Motherfucker,* a freight hauler doing a triangle between Luna, Ganymede, and the Belt. Owned by MYOFB Corporation out of Luna. A query to the public bases at Ganymede showed it had left the port there at the listed time and just hadn't bothered to file a flight plan. Miller tapped the screen with a fingernail. Not exactly how he'd fly under the radar. Anyone with authority would roust that ship just for the joy of doing it. He deleted the entry.

His terminal chimed. An incoming message. Miller flipped over to it. One of the girls on the commons shrieked and the others laughed. A sparrow flew past, its wings humming in the constant recycler-driven breeze.

Havelock looked better than when he'd been on Ceres. Happier. The dark circles were gone from his eyes, and the shape of his face had subtly softened, as if the need to prove himself in the Belt had changed his bones and now he was falling back into his natural form.

"Miller!" the recording said. "I heard about Earth cutting Ceres just before I got your message. Bad luck. I'm sorry to hear Shaddid fired you. Between the two of us, she's a pompous idiot. The rumor I've heard is Earth is doing everything it can to stay out of the war, including giving up any station that it's expecting to be a point of contention. You know how it is. You've got a pit bull on one side of you and a rottweiler on the other, first thing you do is drop your steak."

Miller chuckled.

"I've signed on with Protogen security, big-company private army bullshit. But the pay is worth putting up with their delusions of grandeur. The contract's supposed to be on Ganymede, but with the crap going on right now, who knows how it'll really play out? Turns out Protogen's got a training base in the Belt. I'd never heard about it, but it's supposed to be quite the gymnasium. I know they're hiring on, and I'd be happy to put in a word for you. Just let me know, and I'll get you together with the induction recruiter, get you off that damned rock."

Havelock smiled.

"Take care of yourself, partner," the Earther said. "Keep in touch."

Protogen. Pinkwater. Al Abbiq. Small corporate security forces that the big transorbital companies used as private armies and mercenary forces to rent out as needed. AnnanSec had the Pallas security contract, and had for years, but it was Mars-based. The OPA was probably hiring, but probably not him.

It had been years since he'd tried to find work. He'd assumed that particular struggle was behind him, that he was going to die working the Ceres Station security contract. Now that events had thrown him out, everything had an odd floating feeling. Like the gap between getting hit and feeling the pain. He needed to find another job. He needed to do more than send a couple messages out to his old partners. There were employment firms. There were bars on Ceres that would hire an ex-cop for a bouncer. There were gray markets that would take anyone capable of giving them a veneer of legality.

The last thing that made sense was to sit around, ogling girls in the park and chasing down leads on a case that he hadn't been meant to follow up on in the first place.

The *Dagon* had come into Ceres just a little ahead of the arrival window. Owned by the Glapion Collective, who were, he was pretty sure, an OPA front. That made it a good fit. Except the flight plan had been put in just a few hours after the *Donnager* blew, and the exit record from Io looked solid. Miller shifted it into a file he was keeping for ships that earned a second look.

The *Rocinante,* owned by Silencieux Courant Holdings out of Luna, was a gas hauler that had landed at Tycho just hours before the end of the arrival window. Silencieux Courant was a medium-sized corporate entity with no obvious ties to the OPA, and the flight plan from Pallas was plausible. Miller put his fingertip over the delete key, then paused. He sat back.

Why was a gas hauler going between Pallas and Tycho? Both stations were gas *consumers.* Flying from consumer to consumer without hitting a supply in the middle was a good way to not cover your docking fees. He put in a request for the flight plan that had taken the *Rocinante* to Pallas from wherever it had been before, then sat back to wait. If the records were cached in the Ceres servers, the request shouldn't take more than a minute or two. The notification bar estimated an hour and a half, so that meant the request was getting forwarded to the docking systems at Pallas. It hadn't been in the local backup.

Miller stroked his chin; five days of stubble had almost reached the beginning of a beard. He felt a smile starting. He did a definition search on *Rocinante.* Literally meaning "no longer a workhorse," its first entry was as the name of Don Quixote's horse.

"That you, Holden?" Miller said to the screen. "You out tilting at windmills?"

"Sir?" the waiter said, but Miller waved him away.

There were hundreds of entries still to be looked at and dozens at least in his second-look folder. Miller ignored them, staring at the entry from Tycho as if by sheer force of will he could make more information appear on the screen. Then, slowly, he pulled up the message from Havelock, hit the respond key, and looked into the tiny black pinprick of the terminal's camera.

"Hey, partner," he said. "Thanks for the offer. I may take you up on it, but I've got some kinks I need to work out before I jump. You know how it is. If you can do me a favor, though...I need to keep track of a ship, and I've only got the public databases to work from, plus which Ceres may be at war with Mars by now. Who knows, you know? Anyway, if you can put a level one watch on any flight plans for her, drop me a note if anything comes up...I'd buy you a drink sometime."

He paused. There had to be something more to say.

"Take care of yourself, partner."

He reviewed the message. On-screen, he looked tired, the smile a little fake, the voice a little higher than it sounded in his head. But it said what it needed to say. He sent it.

This was what he'd been reduced to. Access gone, service gun confiscated—though he still had a couple of drops in his hole— money running out. He had to play the angles, call in favors for things that should have been routine, outthink the system for any scrap. He'd been a cop, and they'd turned him into a mouse. *Still,* he thought, sitting back in the chair. *Pretty good work for a mouse.*

The sound of detonation came from spinward, then voices raised in anger. The kids on the commons stopped their games of touch-me touch-you and stared. Miller stood up. There was smoke, but he couldn't see flames. The breeze picked up as the station air cleaners raised the flow to suck away particulates so the sensors didn't think there was a risk of fanning a fire. Three gunshots rang out in fast succession, and the voices came together in a rough chant. Miller couldn't make words out of it, but the rhythm told him all he needed to know. Not a disaster, not a fire, not a breach. Just a riot.

The kids were walking toward the commotion. Miller caught one by the elbow. She couldn't have been more than sixteen, her eyes near black, her face a perfect heart shape.

"Don't go over there," he said. "Get your friends together and walk the other way."

The girl looked at him, his hand on her arm, the distant commotion.

"You can't help," he said.

She pulled her arm free.

"Gotta try, yeah?" she said. "Podría intentar, you know." *You could too.*

"Just did," Miller said as he put his terminal in its case and walked away. Behind him, the sounds of the riot grew. But he figured the police could take care of it.

Over the next fourteen hours, the system net reported five riots on the station, some minor structural damage. Someone he'd never heard of announced a tri-phase curfew; people out of their holes more than two hours before or after their work shifts would be subject to arrest. Whoever was running the show now thought they could lock down six million people and create stability and peace. He wondered what Shaddid thought about that.

Outside Ceres, things were getting worse. The deep astronomy labs on Triton had been occupied by a band of prospectors sympathetic to the OPA. They'd turned the array in-system and had been broadcasting the location of every Martian ship in the system along with high-definition images of the surface of Mars, down to the topless sunbathers in the dome parks. The story was that a volley of nukes was on its way to the station, and the array would be bright dust within a week. Earth's imitation of a snail was picking up the pace as Earth- and Luna-based companies pulled back down the gravity well. Not all of them, not even half, but enough to send the Terran message: *Count us out.* Mars appealed for solidarity; the Belt appealed for justice or, more often, told the birthplace of humanity to go fuck itself.

It wasn't out of control yet, but it was ramping up. Another few incidents and it wouldn't matter how it had started. It wouldn't matter what the stakes were. Mars knew the Belt couldn't win, and the Belt knew it had nothing to lose. It was a recipe for death on a scale humanity had never seen.

And, like Ceres, there wasn't much Miller could do about that either. But he could find James Holden, find out what had happened to the *Scopuli*, follow the leads back to Julie Mao. He was a detective. It was what he did.

As he packed up his hole, throwing out the collected detritus that grew over decades like a crust, he talked to her. He tried to explain why he'd given up everything to find her. After his discovery of the *Rocinante*, he could hardly avoid the word *quixotic*.

His imaginary Julie laughed or was touched. She thought he was a sad, pathetic little man, since just tracking her down was the nearest to a purpose in life he could find. She dressed him down as being a tool of her parents. She wept and put her arms around him. She sat with him in some almost unimaginable observation lounge and watched the stars.

He fit everything he had into a shoulder bag. Two changes of clothes, his papers, his hand terminal. A picture of Candace from back in better days. All the hard copy of Julie's case he'd made before Shaddid wiped his partition, including three pictures of Julie. He thought that everything he'd lived through should have added up to more, and then changed his mind. It was probably about right.

He spent one last day ignoring the curfew, making his rounds of the station, saying goodbye to the few people he felt he might miss or might miss him. To his surprise, Muss, who he found at a tense and uncomfortable police bar, actually teared up and hugged him until his ribs ached from it.

He booked passage on a transport to Tycho. His bunk ran him a quarter of his remaining funds. It occurred to him, not for the first time, that he had to find Julie pretty damn quick or find a job to support him through the investigation. But it hadn't happened yet, and the universe wasn't stable enough anymore to make long-range planning more than a sour joke.

As if to prove the point, his terminal chimed as he was in the line to board the transport.

"Hey, partner," Havelock said. "That favor you needed? I got a bite. Your package just put in a flight plan for Eros. I'm sending the public-access data attached. I'd get you the good stuff, but these Protogen guys are tight. I mentioned you to the recruiter and she seemed interested. So let me know, right? Talk to you soon."

Eros.

Great.

Miller nodded at the woman behind him, stepped out of line, and walked to the kiosk. By the time a screen was open, they were calling final boarding for the Tycho transport. Miller turned in his ticket, got a nominal refund, and spent a third of what he still had in his account for a ticket to Eros. Still, it could have been worse. He could have been on the way before he got word. He had to start thinking about it as good luck, not bad.

The passage confirmation came through with a chime like a gently struck triangle.

"I hope I'm right about this," he said to Julie. "If Holden's not there, I'm gonna feel pretty stupid."

In his mind, she smiled ruefully.

Life is risk, she said.

Chapter Twenty-One: Holden

Ships were small. Space was always at a premium, and even on a monster like the *Donnager,* the corridors and compartments were cramped and uncomfortable. On the *Rocinante,* the only rooms where Holden could spread out his arms without touching two walls were the galley and the cargo bay. No one who flew for a living was claustrophobic, but even the most hardened Belt prospector could recognize the rising tension of being ship-bound. It was the ancient stress response of the trapped animal, the subconscious knowledge that there was literally nowhere to go that you couldn't see from where you were already standing. Getting off the ship at port was a sudden and sometimes giddying release of tension.

It often took the form of a drinking game.

Like all professional sailors, Holden had sometimes ended long flights by drinking himself into a stupor. More than once he'd wandered into a brothel and left only when they threw him out with an emptied account, a sore groin, and a prostate as dry as the Sahara desert. So when Amos staggered into his room after three days on station, Holden knew exactly what the big mechanic felt like.

Holden and Alex were sharing the couch and watching a news-feed. Two talking heads were discussing the Belter actions with words like *criminal, terrorist,* and *sabotage.* The Martians were "peacekeepers." It was a Martian news channel. Amos snorted and collapsed on the couch. Holden muted the screen.

"Having a good shore leave, sailor?" Holden asked with a grin.

"I'll never drink again," Amos groaned.

"Naomi's comin' over with some chow she got at that sushi place," Alex said. "Nice raw fish wrapped in fake seaweed."

Amos groaned again.

"That's not nice, Alex," Holden said. "Let the man's liver die in peace."

The door to the suite slid open again, and Naomi came in carrying a tall stack of white boxes.

"Food's here," she said.

Alex opened all the boxes and started handing around small disposable plates.

"Every time it's your turn to get food, you get salmon rolls. It shows a lack of imagination," Holden said as he began putting food on his plate.

"I like salmon," Naomi replied.

The room got quiet as people ate; the only sounds were the clack of plastic chopsticks and the wet squish of things being dipped in wasabi and soy. When the food was gone, Holden wiped his eyes, made runny by the heat in his sinuses, and leaned his chair all the way back. Amos used one of his chopsticks to scratch under the cast on his leg.

"You guys did a pretty good job setting this," he said. "It's the thing on my body that hurts the least right now."

Naomi grabbed the remote off Holden's armrest and turned

the volume back on. She began spooling through the different feeds. Alex closed his eyes and slid down on the loveseat, lacing his fingers across his belly and sighing contentedly. Holden felt a sudden and irrational annoyance at his crew for being so comfortable.

"Everyone had enough of sucking on Fred's teat yet?" he said. "I know I have."

"What the fuck are you talking about?" Amos said, shaking his head. "I'm just getting started."

"I mean," Holden said, "how long are we going to hang around on Tycho, drinking and whoring and eating sushi on Fred's expense account?"

"As long as I can?" Alex said.

"You have a better plan, then," Naomi said.

"I don't have a plan, but I want to get back in the game. We were full of righteous anger and dreams of vengeance when we got here, and a couple of blowjobs and hangovers later, it's like nothing ever happened."

"Uh, vengeance kinda requires someone to avenge upon, Cap," Alex said. "Case you ain't noticed, we're lackin' in that department."

"That ship is still out there, somewhere. The people who ordered it to shoot are, too," Holden said.

"So," Alex replied slowly, "we take off and start flyin' in a spiral until we run into it?"

Naomi laughed and threw a soy packet at him.

"I don't know what we do," Holden said, "but sitting here while the people who killed our ship keep doing whatever it is *they're* doing is making me nuts."

"We've been here three days," Naomi said. "We deserve some comfortable beds and decent food and a chance to blow off steam. Don't try to make us feel bad for taking it."

"Besides, Fred said we'll get those bastards at the trial," Amos said.

"If there's a trial," Holden replied. "*If.* It won't happen for months, or maybe even years. And even then, Fred's looking at those treaties. Amnesty might be another bargaining chip, right?"

"You were quick enough to agree to his terms, Jim," Naomi said. "Changed your mind?"

"If Fred wants depositions in exchange for letting us patch up and rest, the price was cheap. That doesn't mean I think a trial will fix everything, or that I want to be sidelined until it happens."

He gestured at the faux-leather couch and huge wall screen around them.

"Besides, this can be a prison. It's a nice one, but as long as Fred controls the purse strings, he owns us. Make no mistake."

Naomi's brow crinkled; her eyes grew serious.

"What's the option, sir?" she asked. "Leave?"

Holden folded his arms, his mind turning over everything he'd said as if he was hearing it for the first time. Saying things out loud actually made them clearer.

"I'm thinking we look for work," he said. "We've got a good ship. More importantly, we have a sneaky ship. It's fast. We can run without a transponder if we need to. Lots of people will need things moved from place to place with a war on. Gives us something to do while we wait for Fred's trial, and a way to put money in our pockets so we can get off the dole. And, as we fly from place to place, we can keep our ears and eyes open. Never know what we'll find. And seriously, how long can you three stand to be station rats?"

There was a moment's silence.

"I could station rat for another . . . week?" Amos said.

"It ain't a bad idea, Cap," Alex said with a nod.

"It's your decision, Captain," Naomi said. "I'll stick with you, and I like the idea of getting my own money again. But I hope you're not in a hurry. I could really use a few more days off."

Holden clapped his hands and jumped to his feet.

"Nope," he said. "Having a plan makes all the difference. Downtime's easier to enjoy when I know it'll end."

Alex and Amos got up together and headed for the door. Alex

had won a few dollars playing darts, and now he and Amos were in the process of turning it into even more money at the card tables.

"Don't wait up, Boss," Amos said to Naomi. "I'm feeling lucky today."

They left, and Holden went to the small kitchen nook to make coffee. Naomi followed him in.

"One other thing," she said.

Holden tore open the sealed coffee packet, the strong odor filling the room.

"Shoot," he said.

"Fred is taking care of all the arrangements for Kelly's body. He'll hold it here in state until we go public with our survival. Then he'll ship it back to Mars."

Holden filled the coffeemaker with water from the tap and started the machine. It made soft gurgling sounds.

"Good. Lieutenant Kelly deserves all the respect and dignity we can give him."

"It got me thinking about that data cube he had. I haven't been able to hack it. It's some kind of military über-encryption that makes my head hurt. So..."

"Just say it," Holden said with a frown.

"I want to give it to Fred. I know it's a risk. We have no idea what's on it, and for all his charm and hospitality, Fred's still OPA. But he was also high-ranking UN military. And he's got a serious brain trust here on the station. He might be able to open it up."

Holden thought for a moment, then nodded.

"Okay, let me sit with that. I want to know what Yao was trying to get off the ship, but—"

"Yeah."

They shared a companionable silence as the coffee brewed. When it was finished, Holden poured two mugs and handed one to Naomi.

"Captain," she said, then paused. "Jim. I've been a pain-in-the-ass XO so far. I've been stressed out and scared shitless about eighty percent of the time."

"You do an amazing job of hiding that fact," Holden replied.

Naomi nodded the compliment away.

"Anyway, I've been pushy about some things that I probably shouldn't have been."

"Not a big deal."

"Okay, let me finish," she said. "I want you to know I think you've done a great job of keeping us alive. You keep us focused on the problems we can solve instead of feeling sorry for ourselves. You keep everyone in orbit around you. Not everyone can do that, I couldn't do it, and we've needed that stability."

Holden felt a glow of pride. He hadn't expected it, and he didn't trust it, but it felt good all the same.

"Thank you," Holden said.

"I can't speak for Amos and Alex, but I plan to stick it out. You're not just the captain because McDowell is dead. You're *our* captain, as far as I'm concerned. Just so you know."

She looked down, blushing as if she'd just confessed something. Maybe she had.

"I'll try not to blow it," he said.

"I'd appreciate that, sir."

Fred Johnson's office was like its occupant: big, intimidating, and overflowing with things that needed to be done. The room was easily two and a half square meters, making it larger than any single compartment on the *Rocinante*. His desk was made of actual wood, looked at least a hundred years old, and smelled of lemon oil. Holden sat in a chair that was just a little lower than Fred's, and looked at the mounds of file folders and papers covering every flat surface.

Fred had sent for him and then spent the first ten minutes after he'd arrived speaking on the phone. Whatever he was talking about, it sounded technical. Holden assumed it was related to the giant generation ship outside. It didn't bother him to be ignored for a few minutes, since the wall behind Fred was entirely covered by a bleedingly high-definition screen pretending to be a window. It was showing a spectacular view of the *Nauvoo* moving past as the station spun. Fred spoiled the scene by putting the phone down.

"Sorry about that," he said. "The atmosphere processing system has been a nightmare from day one. When you're going a hundred plus years on only the air you can bring with you, the loss tolerances are…stricter than usual. Sometimes it's difficult to impress the importance of fine details on the contractors."

"I was enjoying the view," Holden said, gesturing at the screen.

"I'm starting to wonder if we'll be able to get it done on schedule."

"Why?"

Fred sighed and leaned his chair back with a squeak.

"It's the war between Mars and the Belt."

"Material shortages, then?"

"Not just that. Pirate casts claiming to speak for the OPA are working into a frenzy. Belt prospectors with homemade torpedo launchers are firing on Martian warships. They get wiped out in response, but every now and then one of those torpedoes hits and kills a few Martians."

"Which means Mars starts shooting first."

Fred nodded and then got up and started pacing the room.

"And then even honest citizens on legitimate business start getting worried about going out of the house," he said. "We've had over a dozen late shipments so far this month, and I'm worried it will stop being delays and start being cancellations."

"You know, I've been thinking about the same thing," Holden said.

Fred acted as though he hadn't heard.

"I've been on that bridge," Fred said. "Unidentified ship coming on you, and a decision to make? No one wants to press the button. I've watched a ship get bigger and bigger on the scope while my finger was on the trigger. I remember begging them to stop."

Holden said nothing. He'd seen it too. There was nothing to say. Fred let silence hang in the air for a moment, then shook his head and straightened up.

"I need to ask you a favor," Fred said.

"You can always ask, Fred. You've paid for that much," Holden replied.

"I need to borrow your ship."

"The *Roci*?" Holden said. "Why?"

"I need to have something picked up and delivered here, and I need a ship that can stay quiet and run past Martian picket ships if it needs to."

"The *Rocinante* is definitely the right ship, then, but that didn't answer my question. Why?"

Fred turned his back to Holden and looked at the view screen. The nose of the *Nauvoo* was just vanishing from sight. The view turned to the flat, star-speckled black of forever.

"I need to pick someone up on Eros," he said. "Someone important. I've got people who can do it, but the only ships we've got are light freighters and a couple of small shuttles. Nothing that can make the trip quickly enough or have a hope of running away if trouble starts."

"Does this person have a name? I mean, you keep saying you don't want to fight, but the other unique thing about my ship is that it's the only one here with guns. I'm sure the OPA has a whole list of things they'd like blown up."

"You don't trust me."

"Nope."

Fred turned back around and gripped the back of his chair. His knuckles were white. Holden wondered if he'd gone too far.

"Look," Holden said, "you talk a good game about peace and trials and all that. You disavow the pirate casts. You have a nice station filled with nice people. I have every reason to believe you are what you say you are. But we've been here three days, and the first time you tell me about your plans, you ask to borrow my ship for a secret mission. Sorry. If I'm part of this, I get full access; no secrets. Even if I knew for a fact, which I don't, that you had nothing but good intentions, I still wouldn't go along with the cloak-and-dagger bullshit."

Fred stared at him for a few seconds, then came around his chair and sat down. Holden found he was tapping his fingers on his thigh nervously and forced himself to stop. Fred's eyes flicked down at Holden's hand and then back up. He continued to stare.

Holden cleared his throat.

"Look, you're the big dog here. Even if I didn't know who you used to be, you'd scare the shit out of me, so don't feel the need to prove it. But no matter how scared I am, I'm not backing down on this."

Fred's hoped-for laughter didn't come. Holden tried to swallow without gulping.

"I bet every captain you ever flew under thought you were a gigantic pain in the ass," Fred said finally.

"I believe my record reflects that," Holden said, trying to hide his relief.

"I need to fly to Eros and find a man named Lionel Polanski, and then bring him back to Tycho."

"That's only a week out if we push," Holden said, doing the math in his head.

"The fact that Lionel doesn't actually exist complicates the mission."

"Yeah, okay. Now I'm confused," Holden agreed.

"You wanted in?" Fred said, the words taking on a quiet ferocity. "Now you're in. Lionel Polanski exists only on paper, and owns things that Mr. Tycho doesn't want to own. Including a courier ship called the *Scopuli*."

Holden leaned forward in his chair, his face intense.

"You now have my undivided attention," he said.

"The nonexistent owner of the *Scopuli* checked into a flophouse on one of the shit levels of Eros. We only just got the message. We have to work on the assumption that whoever got the room knows our operations intimately, needs help, and can't ask for it openly."

"We can leave in an hour," Holden said breathlessly.

Fred held up his hands in a gesture that was surprisingly Belter for an Earth man.

"When," Fred asked, "did this turn into *you* leaving?"

"I won't loan my ship, but I'll definitely rent it out. My crew and I were talking about getting jobs, actually. Hire us. Deduct whatever's fair for services you've already rendered."

"No," Fred said. "I need *you.*"

"You don't," Holden replied. "You need our depositions. And we're not going to sit here waiting a year or two for sanity to reign. We'll all do video depositions, sign whatever affidavits you want us to as to their authenticity, but we're leaving to find work one way or the other. You might as well make use of it."

"No," Fred said. "You're too valuable to take risks with your lives."

"What if I throw in the data cube the captain of the *Donnager* was trying to liberate?"

The silence was back, but it had a different feel to it.

"Look," Holden said, pressing on. "You need a ship like the *Roci.* I've got one. You need a crew for her. I've got that too. And you're as hungry to know what's on that cube as I am."

"I don't like the risk."

"Your other option is to throw us in the brig and commandeer the ship. There's some risks in that too."

Fred laughed. Holden felt himself relax.

"You'll still have the same problem that brought you here," Fred said. "Your ship looks like a gunship, no matter what its transponder is saying."

Holden jumped up and grabbed a piece of paper from Fred's desk. He started writing on it with a pen snatched from a decorative pen set.

"I've been thinking about that. You've got full manufacturing facilities here. And we're supposed to be a light gas freighter. So," he said as he sketched a rough outline of the ship, "we weld on a bunch of empty compressed-gas storage tanks in two bands around the hull. Use them to hide the tubes. Repaint the whole thing. Weld on a few projections to break up the hull profile and hide us from ship-recognition software. It'll look like shit and screw up the aerodynamics, but we won't be near atmo anytime soon. It'll look exactly like what it is: something a bunch of Belters slapped together in a hurry."

He handed the paper to Fred. Fred began laughing in earnest, either at the terrible drawing or at the absurdity of the whole thing.

"You could give a pirate a hell of a surprise," he said. "If I do this, you and your crew will record my depositions and hire on as an independent contractor for errands like the Eros run and appear on my behalf when the peace negotiations start."

"Yes."

"I want the right to outbid anyone else who tries to hire you. No contracts without my counteroffer."

Holden held out his hand, and Fred shook it.

"Nice doing business with you, Fred."

As Holden left the office, Fred was already on the comm with his machine-shop people. Holden pulled out his portable terminal and called up Naomi.

"Yeah," she said.

"Pack up the kids, we're going to Eros."

Chapter Twenty-Two: Miller

The people-mover to Eros was small, cheap, and overcrowded. The air recyclers had the plastic-and-resin smell of long-life industrial models that Miller associated with warehouses and fuel depots. The lights were cheap LEDs tinted a false pink that was supposed to flatter the complexion but instead made everyone look like undercooked beef. There were no cabins, only row after row of formed laminate seating and two long walls with five-stacks of bunks that the passengers could hot-swap. Miller had never been on a cheapjack transport before, but he knew how they worked. If there was a fight, the ship's crew would pump riot gas into the cabin, knock everyone out, and put anyone who'd been in the scuffle under restraint. It was a draconian system, but it did tend to keep passengers polite. The bar was always open and the drinks were cheap. Not long ago Miller would have found that enticing.

Instead, he sat on one of the long seats, his hand terminal open.

Julie's case file—what he had reconstructed of it—glowed before him. The picture of her, proud and smiling, in front of the *Razorback*, the dates and records, her jiu jitsu training. It seemed like very little, considering how large the woman had grown in his life.

A small newsfeed crawled down the terminal's left side. The war between Mars and the Belt escalated, incident after incident, but the secession of Ceres Station was the top news. Earth was taken to task by Martian commentators for failing to stand united with its fellow inner planet, or at least for not handing over the Ceres security contract to Mars. The scattershot reaction of the Belt ran the gamut from pleasure at seeing Earth's influence fall back down the gravity well, to strident near-panic at the loss of Ceres' neutrality, to conspiracy theories that Earth was fomenting the war for its own ends.

Miller reserved judgment.

"I always think of pews."

Miller looked over. The man sitting next to him was about Miller's age; the fringe of gray hair, the soft belly. The man's smile told Miller the guy was a missionary, out in the vacuum saving souls. Or maybe it was the name tag and Bible.

"The seats, I mean," the missionary said. "They always make me think of going to church, the way they're all lined up, row after row. Only instead of a pulpit, we have bunk beds."

"Our Lady of Sleeping Through It," Miller said, knowing he was getting drawn into conversation but unable to stop himself. The missionary laughed.

"Something like that," he said. "Do you attend church?"

"Haven't in years," Miller said. "I was a Methodist when I was anything. What flavor are you selling?"

The missionary lifted his hands in a gesture of harmlessness that went back to the African plains of the Pleistocene. *I have no weapon; I seek no fight.*

"I'm just going back to Eros from a conference on Luna," he said. "My proselytizing days are long behind me."

"I didn't think those ever ended," Miller said.

"They don't. Not officially. But after a few decades, you come to a place where you realize that there's really no difference between trying and not trying. I still travel. I still talk to people. Sometimes we talk about Jesus Christ. Sometimes we talk about cooking. If someone is ready to accept Christ, it doesn't take much effort on my part to help them. If they aren't, no amount of hectoring them does any good. So why try?"

"Do people talk about the war?" Miller asked.

"Often," the missionary said.

"Anyone make sense of it?"

"No. I don't believe war ever does. It's a madness that's in our nature. Sometimes it recurs; sometimes it subsides."

"Sounds like a disease."

"The herpes simplex of the species?" the missionary said with a laugh. "I suppose there are worse ways to think of it. I'm afraid that as long as we're human, it will be with us."

Miller looked over at the wide, moon-round face.

"As long as we're human?" he said.

"Some of us believe that we shall all eventually become angels," the missionary said.

"Not the Methodists."

"Even them, eventually," the man said, "but they probably won't go first. And what brings you to Our Lady of Sleeping Through It?"

Miller sighed, sitting back against the unyielding chair. Two rows down, a young woman shouted at two boys to stop jumping on the seats and was ignored. A man behind them coughed. Miller took a long breath and let it out slowly.

"I was a cop on Ceres," he said.

"Ah. The change of contract."

"That," Miller said.

"Taking up work on Eros, then?"

"More looking up an old friend," Miller said. Then, to his own surprise, he went on. "I was born on Ceres. Lived there my whole life. This is the...fifth? Yeah, fifth time I've been off station."

"Do you plan to go back?"

"No," Miller said. He sounded more certain than he'd known. "No, I think that part of my life is pretty much over."

"That must be painful," the missionary said.

Miller paused, letting the comment settle. The man was right; it should have been painful. Everything he'd ever had was gone. His job, his community. He wasn't even a cop anymore, his checked-in-luggage handgun notwithstanding. He would never eat at the little East Indian cart at the edge of sector nine again. The receptionist at the station would never nod her greeting to him as he headed in for his desk again. No more nights at the bar with the other cops, no more off-color stories about busts gone weird, no more kids flying kites in the high tunnels. He probed himself like a doctor searching for inflammation. Did it hurt here? Did he feel the loss there?

He didn't. There was only a sense of relief so profound it approached giddiness.

"I'm sorry," the missionary said, confused. "Did I say something funny?"

Eros supported a population of one and a half million, a little more than Ceres had in visitors at any given time. Roughly the shape of a potato, it had been much more difficult to spin up, and its surface velocity was considerably higher than Ceres' for the same internal g. The old shipyards protruded from the asteroid, great spiderwebs of steel and carbon mesh studded with warning lights and sensor arrays to wave off any ships that might come in too tight. The internal caverns of Eros had been the birthplace of the Belt. From raw ore to smelting furnace to annealing platform and then into the spines of water haulers and gas harvesters and prospecting ships. Eros had been a port of call in the first generation of humanity's expansion. From there, the sun itself was only a bright star among billions.

The economics of the Belt had moved on. Ceres Station had

spun up with newer docks, more industrial backing, more people. The commerce of shipping moved to Ceres, while Eros remained a center of ship manufacture and repair. The results were as predictable as physics. On Ceres, a longer time in dock meant lost money, and the berth fee structure reflected that. On Eros, a ship might wait for weeks or months without impeding the flow of traffic. If a crew wanted a place to relax, to stretch, to get away from one another for a while, Eros was the port of call. And with the lower docking fees, Eros Station found other ways to soak money from its visitors: Casinos. Brothels. Shooting galleries. Vice in all its commercial forms found a home in Eros, its local economy blooming like a fungus fed by the desires of Belters.

A happy accident of orbital mechanics put Miller there half a day ahead of the *Rocinante*. He walked through the cheap casinos, the opioid bars and sex clubs, the show fight areas where men or women pretended to beat one another senseless for the pleasure of the crowds. Miller imagined Julie walking with him, her sly smile matching his own as he read the great animated displays. RANDOLPH MAK, HOLDER OF THE BELT FREEFIGHT CHAMPIONSHIP FOR SIX YEARS, AGAINST MARTIAN KIVRIN CARMICHAEL IN A FIGHT TO THE DEATH!

Surely not fixed, Julie said drily in his mind.

Wonder which one's going to win, he thought, and imagined her laughing.

He'd stopped at a noodle cart, two new yens' worth of egg noodles in black sauce steaming in their cone, when a hand clapped on his shoulder.

"Detective Miller," a familiar voice said. "I think you're outside your jurisdiction."

"Why, Inspector Sematimba," Miller said. "As I live and breathe. You give a girl the shakes, sneaking up like that."

Sematimba laughed. He was a tall man, even among Belters, with the darkest skin Miller had ever seen. Years before, Sematimba and Miller had coordinated on a particularly ugly case. A smuggler with a cargo of designer euphorics had broken with his supplier. Three people on Ceres had been caught in the crossfire, and the smuggler had shipped out for Eros. The traditional competitiveness and insularity of the stations' respective security forces had almost let the perp slip away. Only Miller and Sematimba had been willing to coordinate outside the corporate channels.

"What brings you," Sematimba said, leaning against a thin steel railing and gesturing at the tunnel, "to the navel of the Belt, the glory and power that is Eros?"

"Following up on a lead," Miller said.

"There's nothing good here," Sematimba said. "Ever since Protogen pulled out, things have been going from bad to worse."

Miller sucked up a noodle.

"Who's the new contract?" he asked.

"CPM," Sematimba said.

"Never heard of them."

"*Carne Por la Machina*," Sematimba said, and pulled a face: exaggerated bluff masculinity. He thumped his breast and growled, then let the imitation go and shook his head. "New corporation out of Luna. Mostly Belters on the ground. Make themselves out to be all hard core, but they're mostly amateurs. All bluster, no balls. Protogen was inner planets, and that was a problem, but they were serious as hell. They broke heads, but they kept the peace. These new assholes? Most corrupt bunch of thugs I've ever worked for. I don't think the board of governors is going to renew when the contract's up. I didn't say that, but it's true."

"I've got an old partner signed up with Protogen," Miller said.

"They're not bad," Sematimba said. "Almost wish I'd picked them in the divorce, you know?"

"Why didn't you?" Miller asked.

"You know how it is. I'm from here."

"Yeah," Miller said.

"So. You didn't know who was running the playhouse? You aren't here looking for work."

"Nope," Miller said. "I'm on sabbatical. Doing some travel for myself these days."

"You've got money for that?"

"Not really. But I don't mind going on the cheap. For a while, you know. You heard anything about a Juliette Mao? Goes by Julie?"

Sematimba shook his head.

"Mao-Kwikowski Mercantile," Miller said. "Came up the well and went native. OPA. It was an abduction case."

"Was?"

Miller leaned back. His imagined Julie raised her eyebrows.

"It's changed a little since I got it," Miller said. "May be connected to something. Kind of big."

"How big are we talking about?" Sematimba said. All trace of jocularity had vanished from his expression. He was all cop now. Anyone but Miller would have found the man's empty, almost angry face intimidating.

"The war," Miller said. Sematimba folded his arms.

"Bad joke," he said.

"Not joking."

"I consider us friends, old man," Sematimba said. "But I don't want any trouble around here. Things are unsettled as it stands."

"I'll try to stay low-profile."

Sematimba nodded. Down the tunnel, an alarm blared. Only security, not the earsplitting ditone of an environmental alert. Sematimba looked down the tunnel as if squinting would let him see through the press of people, bicycles, and food carts.

"I'd better go look," he said with an air of resignation. "Probably some of my fellow officers of the peace breaking windows for the fun of it."

"Great to be part of a team like that," Miller said.

"How would you know?" Sematimba said with a smile. "If you need something…"

"Likewise," Miller said, and watched the cop wade into the sea of chaos and humanity. He was a large man, but something about the passing crowd's universal deafness to the alarm's blare made him seem smaller. *A stone in the ocean,* the phrase went. One star among millions.

Miller checked the time, then pulled up the public docking records. The *Rocinante* showed as on schedule. The docking berth was listed. Miller sucked down the last of his noodles, tossed the foam cone with the thin smear of black sauce into a public recycler, found the nearest men's room, and when he was done there, trotted toward the casino level.

The architecture of Eros had changed since its birth. Where once it had been like Ceres—webworked tunnels leading along the path of widest connection—Eros had learned from the flow of money: All paths led to the casino level. If you wanted to go anywhere, you passed through the wide whale belly of lights and displays. Poker, blackjack, roulette, tall fish tanks filled with prize trout to be caught and gutted, mechanical slots, electronic slots, cricket races, craps, rigged tests of skill. Flashing lights, dancing neon clowns, and video screen advertisements blasted the eyes. Loud artificial laughter and merry whistles and bells assured you that you were having the time of your life. All while the smell of thousands of people packed into too small a space competed with the scent of heavily spiced vat-grown meat being hawked from carts rolling down the corridor. Greed and casino design had turned Eros into an architectural cattle run.

Which was exactly what Miller needed.

The tube station that arrived from the port had six wide doors, which emptied to the casino floor. Miller accepted a drink from a tired-looking woman in a G-string and bared breasts and found a screen to stand at that afforded him a view of all six doors. The crew of the *Rocinante* had no choice but to come through one of those. He checked his hand terminal. The docking logs showed the ship had arrived ten minutes earlier. Miller pretended to sip his drink and settled in to wait.

Chapter Twenty-Three: Holden

The casino level of Eros was an all-out assault on the senses. Holden hated it.

"I love this place," Amos said, grinning.

Holden pushed his way through a knot of drunk middle-aged gamblers, who were laughing and yelling, to a small open space near a row of pay-by-the-minute wall terminals.

"Amos," he said, "we'll be going to a less touristy level, so watch our backs. The flophouse we're looking for is in a rough neighborhood."

Amos nodded. "Gotcha, Cap."

While Naomi, Alex, and Amos blocked him from view, Holden reached behind his back to adjust the pistol that pulled uncomfortably on his waistband. The cops on Eros were pretty uptight about people walking around with guns, but there was no way he was going to "Lionel Polanski" unarmed. Amos and Alex were both carrying too, though Amos kept his in the right pocket of his jacket and his hand never left it. Only Naomi flatly refused to carry a gun.

Holden led the group toward the nearest escalators, with Amos, casting the occasional glance behind, in the rear. The casinos of Eros stretched for three seemingly endless levels, and even though they moved as quickly as possible, it took half an hour to get away from the noise and crowds. The first level above was a residential neighborhood and disorientingly quiet and neat after the casino's chaos and noise. Holden sat down on the edge of a planter with a nice array of ferns in it and caught his breath.

"I'm with you, Captain. Five minutes in that place gives me a headache," Naomi said, and sat down next to him.

"You kidding me?" Amos said. "I wish we had more time. Alex and I took almost a grand off those fish at the Tycho card tables. We'd probably walk out of here fucking millionaires."

"You know it," Alex said, and punched the big mechanic on the shoulder.

"Well, if this Polanski thing turns out to be nothing, you have my permission to go make us a million dollars at the card tables. I'll wait for you on the ship," Holden said.

The tube system ended at the first casino level and didn't start again until the level they were on. You could choose not to spend your money at the tables, but they made sure you were punished for doing so. Once the crew had climbed into a car and started the ride to Lionel's hotel, Amos sat down next to Holden.

"Somebody's following us, Cap," he said conversationally. "Wasn't sure till he climbed on a couple cars down. Behind us all through the casinos too."

Holden sighed and put his face in his hands.

"Okay, what's he look like?" he said.

"Belter. Fifties, or maybe forties with a lot of mileage. White shirt and dark pants. Goofy hat."

"Cop?"

"Oh yeah. But no holster I can see," Amos said.

"All right. Keep an eye on him, but no need to get too worried. Nothing we're doing here is illegal," Holden said.

"You mean, other than arriving in our stolen Martian warship, sir?" Naomi asked.

"You mean our *perfectly legitimate* gas freighter that all the paperwork and registry data says is *perfectly legitimate*?" Holden replied with a thin smile. "Yeah, well, if they'd seen through that, they would have stopped us at the dock, not followed us around."

An advertising screen on the wall displayed a stunning view of multicolored clouds rippling with flashes of lightning, and encouraged Holden to take a trip to the amazing dome resorts on Titan. He'd never been to Titan. Suddenly he wanted to go there very much. A few weeks of sleeping late, eating in fine restaurants, and lying on a hammock, watching Titan's colorful atmosphere storm above him sounded like heaven. Hell, as long as he was fantasizing, he threw in Naomi walking over to his hammock with a couple of fruity-looking drinks in her hands.

She ruined it by talking.

"This is our stop," she said.

"Amos, watch our friend, see if he gets off the train with us," Holden said as he got up and headed to the door.

After they got off and walked a dozen steps down the corridor, Amos whispered, "Yep," at his back. *Shit.* Well, definitely a tail, but there wasn't really any reason not to go ahead and check up on Lionel. Fred hadn't asked them to do anything *with* whoever was pretending to be the *Scopuli*'s owner. They couldn't very well be arrested for knocking on a door. Holden whistled a loud and jaunty tune as he walked, to let his crew and whoever was following them know he wasn't worried about a thing.

He stopped when he saw the flophouse.

It was dark and dingy and exactly the sort of place where people got mugged or worse. Broken lights created dark corners, and there wasn't a tourist in sight. He turned to give Alex and Amos meaningful looks, and Amos shifted his hand in his pocket. Alex reached under his coat.

The lobby was mostly empty space, with a pair of couches at one end next to a table covered with magazines. A sleepy-looking older woman sat reading one. Elevators were recessed into the wall at the far end, next to a door marked STAIRS. In the middle was the check-in desk, where, in lieu of a human clerk, a touch screen terminal let guests pay for their rooms.

Holden stopped next to the desk and turned around to look at the woman sitting on the couch. Graying hair, but good features and an athletic build. In a flophouse like this, that probably meant a prostitute reaching the end of her shelf life. She pointedly ignored his stare.

"Is our tail still with us?" Holden asked in a quiet voice.

"Stopped outside somewhere. Probably just watching the door now," Amos replied.

Holden nodded and hit the inquiry button on the check-in screen. A simple menu would let him send a message to Lionel Polanski's room, but Holden exited the system. They knew Lionel was still checked in, and Fred had given them the room number. If it was someone playing games, no reason to give him a heads-up before Holden knocked on the door.

"Okay, he's still here, so let's—" Holden said, and then stopped when he saw the woman from the couch standing right behind Alex. He hadn't heard or seen her approach.

"You need to come with me," she said in a hard voice. "Walk to the stairwell slowly, stay at least three meters ahead of me the entire time. Do it now."

"Are you a cop?" Holden asked, not moving.

"I'm the person with the gun," she said, a small weapon appearing like magic in her right hand. She pointed it at Alex's head. "So do what I say."

Her weapon was small and plastic and had some kind of battery pack. Amos pulled his heavy slug thrower out and aimed it at her face.

"Mine's bigger," he said.

"Amos, don't—" was all Naomi had time to say before the

stairwell door burst open and half a dozen men and women armed with compact automatic weapons came into the room, yelling at them to drop their guns.

Holden started to put his hands up when one of them opened fire, the weapon coughing out rounds so fast it sounded like someone ripping construction paper; it was impossible to hear the separate shots. Amos threw himself to the floor. A line of bullet holes stitched across the chest of the woman with the taser, and she fell backward with a soft, final sound.

Holden grabbed Naomi by one hand and dragged her behind the check-in desk. Someone in the other group was yelling, "Cease fire! Cease fire!" but Amos was already shooting back from his position, prone on the floor. A yelp of pain and a curse told Holden he'd probably hit someone. Amos rolled sideways to the desk, just in time to avoid a hail of slugs that tore up the floor and wall and made the desk shudder.

Holden reached for his gun, but the front sight caught in his waistband. He yanked it out, tearing his underwear, then crawled on his knees to the edge of the desk and looked out. Alex was lying on the floor on the other side of one of the couches, gun drawn and face white. As Holden looked, a burst of gunfire hit the couch, blowing stuffing into the air and making a line of holes in the back of the couch not more than twenty centimeters above Alex's head. The pilot reached his pistol around the corner of the couch and blindly fired off half a dozen shots, yelling at the same time.

"Fucking assholes!" Amos yelled, then rolled out and fired a couple more shots and rolled back before the return fire started.

"Where are they?" Holden yelled at him.

"Two are down, the rest in the stairwell!" Amos yelled back over the sound of return fire.

Out of nowhere a burst of rounds bounced off the floor past Holden's knee. "Shit, someone's flanking us!" Amos cried out, then moved farther behind the desk and away from the shots.

Holden crawled to the other side of the desk and peeked out.

Someone was moving low and fast toward the hotel entrance. Holden leaned out and took a couple shots at him, but three guns opened up from the stairwell doorway and forced him back behind the desk.

"Alex, someone's moving to the entrance!" Holden screamed at the top of his lungs, hoping the pilot might be able to get off a shot before they were all chopped to pieces by crossfire.

A pistol barked three times by the entrance. Holden risked a look. Their tail with the goofy hat crouched by the door, a gun in his hand, the machine gun–toting flanker lying still at his feet. Instead of looking at them, the tail was pointing his gun toward the stairwell.

"No one shoot the guy with the hat!" Holden yelled, then moved back to the edge of the desk.

Amos put his back to the desk and popped the magazine from his gun. As he fumbled around in his pocket for another, he said, "Guy is probably a cop."

"Extra especially do *not* shoot any cops," Holden said, then fired a few shots at the stairwell door.

Naomi, who'd spent the entire gunfight so far on the floor with her arms over her head, said, "They might all be cops."

Holden squeezed off a few more shots and shook his head.

"Cops don't carry small, easily concealable machine guns and ambush people from stairwells. We call those death squads," he said, though most of his words were drowned out by a barrage of gunfire from the stairwell. Afterward came a few seconds of silence.

Holden leaned back out in time to see the door swing shut.

"I think they're bugging out," he said, keeping his gun trained on the door anyway. "Must have another exit somewhere. Amos, keep your eye on that door. If it opens, start shooting." He patted Naomi on the shoulder. "Stay down."

Holden rose from behind the now ruined check-in kiosk. The desk facade had splintered and the underlying stone showed through. Holden held his gun barrel-up, his hands open. The man in the hat stood, considering the corpse at his feet, then looked up as Holden came near.

"Thanks. My name is Jim Holden. You are?"

The man didn't speak for a second. When he did, his voice was calm. Almost weary. "Cops will be here soon. I need to make a call or we're all going to jail."

"Aren't you the cops?" Holden asked.

The other man laughed; it was a bitter, short sound, but with some real humor behind it. Apparently Holden had said something funny.

"Nope. Name's Miller."

Chapter Twenty-Four: Miller

Miller looked at the dead man—the man he'd just killed—and tried to feel something. There was the trailing adrenaline rush still ramping up his heartbeat. There was a sense of surprise that came from walking into an unexpected firefight. Past that, though, his mind had already fallen into the long habit of analysis. One plant in the main room so Holden and his crew wouldn't see anything too threatening. A bunch of trigger-happy yahoos in the stairwell to back her up. *That* had gone well.

It was a slapdash effort. The ambush had been set by people who either didn't know what they were doing or didn't have the time or resources to do it right. If it hadn't been improvised, Holden and his three buddies would have been taken or killed. And him along with them.

The four survivors of the *Canterbury* stood in the remains of the firefight like rookies at their first bust. Miller felt his mind shift back half a step as he watched everything without watching anything in particular. Holden was smaller than he'd expected from the video feeds. It shouldn't have been surprising; he was an Earther. The man had the kind of face that was bad at hiding things.

"Thanks. My name is Jim Holden. You are?"

Miller thought of six different answers and turned them all aside. One of the others—a big man, solid, with a bare scalp—was pacing out the room, his eyes unfocused the same way Miller's were. Of Holden's four, that was the only guy who'd seen serious gunplay before.

"Cops will be here soon," Miller said. "I need to make a call or we're all going to jail."

The other man—thinner, taller, East Indian by the look of him—had been hiding behind a couch. He was sitting on his haunches now, his eyes wide and panicky. Holden had some of the same look, but he was doing a better job of keeping control. The burdens, Miller thought, of leadership.

"Aren't you the cops?"

Miller laughed.

"Nope," he said. "Name's Miller."

"Okay," the woman said. "Those people just tried to kill us. Why did they do that?"

Holden took a half step toward her voice even before he turned to look at her. Her face was flushed, full lips pressed thin and pale. Her features showed a far-flung racial mix that was unusual even in the melting pot of the Belt. Her hands weren't shaking. The big one had the most experience, but Miller put the woman down as having the best instincts.

"Yeah," Miller said. "I noticed."

He pulled out his hand terminal and opened a link to Sematimba. The cop accepted a few seconds later.

"Semi," Miller said. "I'm really sorry about this, but you know how I was going to stay low-profile?"

"Yes?" the local cop said, drawing the word out to three syllables.

"Didn't work out. I was heading to a meeting with a friend..."

"A meeting with a friend," Sematimba echoed. Miller could imagine the man's crossed arms even though they didn't show in the frame.

"And I happened to see a bunch of tourists in the wrong place at the wrong time. It got out of hand."

"Where are you?" Sematimba asked. Miller gave him the station level and address. There was a long pause while Sematimba consulted with some internal communication software that would have been part of Miller's tool set once. The man's sigh was percussive. "I don't see anything. Were there shots fired?"

Miller looked at the chaos and ruin around them. About a thousand different alerts should have gone out with the first weapon fired. Security should have been swarming toward them.

"A few," he said.

"Strange," Sematimba said. "Stay put. I'll be there."

"Will do," Miller said, and dropped the connection.

"Okay," Holden said. "Who was that?"

"The real cops," Miller said. "They'll be here soon. It'll be fine."

I think it'll be fine. It occurred to him that he was treating the situation like he was still on the inside, a part of the machine. That wasn't true anymore, and pretending it was might have consequences.

"He was following us," the woman said to Holden. And then, to Miller, she said, "You were following us."

"I was," Miller said. He didn't think he sounded rueful, but the big guy shook his head.

"It was the hat," the big one said. "Stood out some."

Miller swept off his porkpie and considered it. Of course the big one had been the one to make him. The other three were competent amateurs, and Miller knew that Holden had done some time in the UN Navy. But Miller gave it better than even money that the big one's background check would be interesting reading.

"Why were you following us?" Holden asked. "I mean, I appreciate the part where you shot the people who were shooting at us, but I'd still like to know that first part."

"I wanted to talk to you," Miller said. "I'm looking for someone."

There was a pause. Holden smiled.

"Anyone in particular?" he asked.

"A crew member of the *Scopuli*," Miller said.

"The *Scopuli*?" Holden said. He started to glance at the woman and stopped himself. There was something there. The *Scopuli* meant something to him beyond what Miller had seen on the news.

"There was nobody on her when we got there," the woman said.

"Holy shit," the shaky one behind the couch said. It was the first thing he'd said since the firefight ended, and he repeated it five or six more times in quick succession.

"What about you?" Miller asked. "*Donnager* blew you to Tycho, and now here. What's that about?"

"How did you know that?" Holden said.

"It's my job," Miller said. "Well, it used to be."

The answer didn't appear to satisfy the Earther. The big guy had fallen in behind Holden, his face a friendly cipher: No trouble, unless there was trouble, and then maybe a whole lot of trouble. Miller nodded, half to the big guy, half to himself.

"I had a contact in the OPA who told me you didn't die on the *Donnager*," Miller said.

"They just *told* you that?" the woman asked, banked outrage in her voice.

"He was making a point at the time," Miller said. "Anyway, he said it, and I took it from there. And in about ten minutes, I'm going to make sure Eros security doesn't throw all of you in a hole, and me with you. So if there's anything at all you want to tell me—like what you're doing here, for instance—this would be the right time."

The silence was broken only by the sound of recyclers laboring to clear the smoke and particulate dust of gunfire. The shaky one stood. Something about the way he held himself looked military. Ex-something, Miller assumed, but not a ground pounder. Navy, maybe; Martian at a guess. He had the vocal twang some of them affected.

"Ah, fuck it, Cap'n," the big one said. "He shot the flank guy for us. He may be an asshole, but he's okay by me."

"Thank you, Amos," Holden said. Miller filed that. The big one was Amos. Holden put his hands behind his back, returning his gun to his waistband.

"We're here to look for someone too," he said. "Probably someone from the *Scopuli.* We were just double-checking the room when everyone decided to start shooting at us."

"Here?" Miller said. Something like emotion trickled into his veins. Not hope, but dread. "Someone off the *Scopuli* is in this flop right now?"

"We think so," Holden said.

Miller looked out the flophouse lobby's front doors. A small, curious crowd had started to gather in the tunnel. Crossed arms, nervous glances. He knew how they felt. Sematimba and his police were on the way. The gunmen who'd attacked Holden and his crew weren't mounting another attack, but that didn't mean they were gone. There might be another wave. They could have fallen back to a better position to wait for Holden to advance.

But what if Julie was here right now? How could he come this far and stop in the lobby? To his surprise, he still had his gun drawn. That was unprofessional. He should have holstered it. The only other one still drawn was the Martian's. Miller shook his head. Sloppy. He needed to stop that.

Still, he had more than half a magazine left in the pistol.

"What room?" he asked.

The flophouse corridors were thin and cramped. The walls had the impervious gloss of warehouse paint, and the carpet was carbon-silicate weave that would wear out more slowly than bare stone. Miller and Holden went first, then the woman and the Martian—Naomi and Alex, their names were—then Amos, trailing and looking back over his shoulder. Miller wondered if anyone but he and Amos understood how they were keeping the others safe. Holden seemed to know and be irritated by it; he kept edging ahead.

The doors of the rooms were identical fiberglass laminates, thin enough to be churned out by the thousands. Miller had kicked in a hundred like them in his career. A few here and there were decorated by longtime residents—with a painting of improbably red flowers, a whiteboard with a string where a pen had once been attached, a cheap reproduction of an obscene cartoon acting out its punch line in a dimly glowing infinite loop.

Tactically, it was a nightmare. If the ambushing forces stepped out of doors in front of and behind them, all five could be slaughtered in seconds. But no slugs flew, and the only door that opened disgorged an emaciated, long-bearded man with imperfect eyes and a slack mouth. Miller nodded at the man as they passed, and he nodded back, possibly more surprised by someone's acknowledging his presence than by the drawn pistols. Holden stopped.

"This is it," he murmured. "This is the room."

Miller nodded. The others came up in a clump, Amos casually hanging back, his eyes on the corridor retreating behind them. Miller considered the door. It would be easy to kick in. One strong blow just above the latch mechanism. Then he could go in low and to the left, Amos high and to the right. He wished Havelock were there. Tactics were simpler for people who'd trained together. He motioned Amos to come up close.

Holden knocked on the door.

"What are you...?" Miller whispered fiercely, but Holden ignored him.

"Hello?" Holden called. "Anyone there?"

Miller tensed. Nothing happened. No voice, no gunfire. Nothing. Holden seemed perfectly at ease with the risk he'd just taken.

From the expression on Naomi's face, Miller took it this wasn't the first time he'd done things this way.

"You want that open?" Amos said.

"Kinda do," Miller said at the same moment Holden said, "Yeah, kick it down."

Amos looked from one to the other, not moving until Holden nodded at him. Then Amos shifted past them, kicked the door open in one blow, and staggered back, cussing.

"You okay?" Miller asked.

The big man nodded once through a pale grimace.

"Yeah, busted my leg a while back. Cast just came off. Keep forgetting about that," he said.

Miller turned back to the room. Inside, it was as black as a cave. No lights came on, not even the dim glow of monitors and sensory devices. Miller stepped in, pistol drawn. Holden was close behind him. The floor made the crunching sound of gravel under their feet, and there was an odd astringent smell that Miller associated with broken screens. Behind it was another smell, much less pleasant. He chose not to think about that one.

"Hello?" Miller said. "Anyone here?"

"Turn on the lights," Naomi said from behind them. Miller heard Holden patting the wall panel, but no light came up.

"They're not working," Holden said.

The dim spill from the corridor gave almost nothing. Miller kept his gun steady in his right hand, ready to empty it toward muzzle flash if anyone opened fire from the darkness. With his left, he took out his hand terminal, thumbed on the backlight, and opened a blank white writing tablet. The room came into monochrome. Beside him, Holden did the same.

A thin bed pressed against one wall, a narrow tray beside it. The bedding was knotted like the remnant of a bad night's sleep. A closet stood open, empty. The hulking form of an empty vacuum suit lay on the floor like a mannequin with a misplaced head. An old entertainment console hung on the wall across from the cot, its screen shattered by half a dozen blows. The wall was dimpled where blows intended to break the LED sconces had missed. Another hand terminal added its glow, and another. Hints of color started to come into the room—the cheap gold of the walls, the green of the blankets and sheet. Under the cot, something glimmered. An older-model hand terminal. Miller crouched as the others stepped in.

"Shit," Amos said.

"Okay," Holden said. "Nobody touches anything. Period. Nothing." It was the most sensible thing Miller had heard the man say.

"Someone put up a bitch of a fight," Amos muttered.

"No," Miller said. It had been vandalism, maybe. It hadn't been a struggle. He pulled a thin-film evidence bag out of his pocket and turned it inside out over his hand like a glove before picking up the terminal, flipping the plastic over it, and setting off the sealing charge.

"Is that…blood?" Naomi asked, pointing to the cheap foam mattress. Wet streaks pooled on the sheet and pillow, not more than a fingers' width, but dark. Too dark even for blood.

"No," Miller said, shoving the terminal into his pocket.

The fluid marked a thin path toward the bathroom. Miller raised a hand, pushing the others back as he crept toward the half-open door. Inside the bathroom, the nasty background smell was much stronger. Something deep, organic, and intimate. Manure in a hothouse, or the aftermath of sex, or a slaughterhouse. All of them. The toilet was brushed steel, the same model they used in prisons. The sink matched. The LED above it and the one in the ceiling had both been destroyed. In the light of his terminal, like the glow of a single candle, black tendrils reached from the shower stall toward the ruined lights, bent and branching like skeletal leaves.

In the shower stall, Juliette Andromeda Mao lay dead.

Her eyes were closed, and that was a mercy. She'd cut her hair differently since she'd taken the pictures Miller had seen, and it changed the shape of her face, but she was unmistakable. She was nude, and barely human. Coils of complex growth spilled from her mouth, ears, and vulva. Her ribs and spine had grown spurs like knives that stretched pale skin, ready to cut themselves free of her. Tubes stretched from her back and throat, crawling up the walls behind her. A deep brown slush had leaked from her, filling the shower pan almost three centimeters high. He sat silently, willing the thing before him not to be true, trying to force himself awake.

What did they do to you? he thought. *Oh, kid. What did they do?*

"Ohmygod," Naomi said behind him.

"Don't touch anything," he said. "Get out of the room. Into the hall. Do it now."

The light in the next room faded as the hand terminals retreated. The twisting shadows momentarily gave her body the illusion of movement. Miller waited, but no breath lifted the bent rib cage. No flicker touched her eyelids. There was nothing. He rose, carefully checking his cuffs and shoes, and walked out to the corridor.

They'd all seen it. He could tell from the expressions, they'd all seen. And they didn't know any better than he did what it was. Gently, he pulled the splintered door closed and waited for Sematimba. It wasn't long.

Five men in police riot armor with shotguns made their way down the hall. Miller walked forward to meet them, his posture better than a badge. He could see them relax. Sematimba came up behind them.

"Miller?" he said. "The hell is this? I thought you said you were staying put."

"I didn't leave," he said. "Those are the civilians back there. The dead guys downstairs jumped them in the lobby."

"Why?" Sematimba demanded.

"Who knows?" Miller said. "Roll them for spare change. That's not the problem."

Sematimba's eyebrows rose. "I've got four corpses down there, and they're not the problem."

Miller nodded down the corridor.

"Fifth one's up here," he said. "It's the girl I was looking for."

Sematimba's expression softened. "I'm sorry," he said.

"Nah," Miller said. He couldn't accept sympathy. He couldn't accept comfort. A gentle touch would shatter him, so he stayed hard instead. "But you're going to want the coroner on this one."

"It's bad, then?"

"You've got no idea," Miller said. "Listen, Semi. I'm in over my head here. Seriously. Those boys down there with the guns? If they weren't hooked in with your security force, there would have been alarms as soon as the first shot was fired. You know this was a setup. They were waiting for these four. And the squat fella with the dark hair? That's James Holden. He's not even supposed to be alive."

"Holden that started the war?" Sematimba said.

"That's the one," Miller said. "This is deep. Drowning deep. And you know what they say about going in after a drowning man, right?"

Sematimba looked down the corridor. He nodded.

"Let me help you," Sematimba said, but Miller shook his head.

"I'm too far gone. Forget me. What happened was you got a call. You found the place. You don't know me, you don't know them, you've got no clue what happened. Or you come along and drown with me. Your pick."

"You don't leave the station without telling me?"

"Okay," Miller said.

"I can live with that," Sematimba said. Then, a moment later: "That's really Holden?"

"Call the coroner," Miller said. "Trust me."

Chapter Twenty-Five: Holden

Miller gestured at Holden and headed for the elevator without waiting to see if he was following. The presumption irritated him, but he went anyway.

"So," Holden said, "we were just in a gunfight where we killed at least three people, and now we're just leaving? No getting questioned or giving a statement? How exactly does that happen?" Holden asked.

"Professional courtesy," Miller said, and Holden couldn't tell if he was joking.

The elevator door opened with a muffled ding, and Holden and the others followed Miller inside. Naomi was closest to the panel, so she reached out to press the lobby button, but her hand was shaking so badly that she had to stop and clench it into a fist. After a deep breath, she reached out a now steady finger and pressed the button.

"This is bullshit. Being an ex-cop doesn't give you a license to get in gunfights," Holden said to Miller's back.

Miller didn't move, but he seemed to shrink a little bit. His sigh was heavy and unforced. His skin seemed grayer than before.

"Sematimba knows the score. Half the job is knowing when to look the other way. Besides, I promised we wouldn't leave the station without letting him know."

"Fuck that," Amos said. "You don't make promises for us, pal."

The elevator came to a stop and opened onto the bloody scene of the gunfight. A dozen cops were in the room. Miller nodded at them and they nodded back. He led the crew out of the lobby to the corridor, then turned around.

"We can work that out later," Miller said. "Right now, let's get someplace we can talk."

Holden agreed with a shrug. "Okay, but you're paying."

Miller headed off down the corridor toward the tube station.

As they followed, Naomi put a hand on Holden's arm and slowed him down a bit so that Miller could get ahead. When he was far enough away, she said, "He knew her."

"Who knew who?"

"He," Naomi said, nodding at Miller, "knew her." She jerked her head back toward the crime scene behind them.

"How do you know?" Holden said.

"He wasn't expecting to find her there, but he knew who she was. Seeing her like that was a shock."

"Huh, I didn't get that at all. He's seemed like Mr. Cool all through this."

"No, they were friends or something. He's having trouble dealing with it, so maybe don't push him too hard," she said. "We might need him."

The hotel room Miller got was only slightly better than the one they'd found the body in. Alex immediately headed for the bathroom and locked the door. The sound of water running in the sink wasn't quite loud enough to cover the pilot's retching.

Holden plopped down on the small bed's dingy comforter, forcing Miller to take the room's one uncomfortable-looking chair. Naomi sat next to Holden on the bed, but Amos stayed on his feet, prowling around the room like a nervous animal.

"So, talk," Holden said to Miller.

"Let's wait for the rest of the gang to finish up," Miller replied with a nod toward the bathroom.

Alex came out a few moments later, his face still white, but now freshly washed.

"Are you all right, Alex?" Naomi asked in a soft voice.

"Five by five, XO," Alex said, then sat down on the floor and put his head in his hands.

Holden stared at Miller and waited. The older man sat and played with his hat for a minute, then tossed it onto the cheap plastic desk that cantilevered out from the wall.

"You knew Julie was in that room. How?" Miller said.

"We didn't even know her name was Julie," Holden replied. "We just knew that it was someone from the *Scopuli*."

"You should tell me how you knew that," Miller said, a frightening intensity in his eyes.

Holden paused a moment. Miller had killed someone who had been trying to kill them, and that certainly helped make the case that he was a friend, but Holden wasn't about to sell out Fred and his group on a hunch. He hesitated, then went halfway.

"The fictional owner of the *Scopuli* had checked into that flophouse," he said. "It made sense that it was a member of the crew raising a flag."

Miller nodded. "Who told you?" he said.

"I'm not comfortable telling you that. We believed the information was accurate," Holden replied. "The *Scopuli* was the bait that someone used to kill the *Canterbury*. We thought someone from the *Scopuli* might know why everyone keeps trying to kill us."

Miller said, "Shit," and then leaned back in his chair and stared at the ceiling.

"You've been looking for Julie. You'd hoped we were looking for her too. That we knew something," Naomi said, not making it a question.

"Yeah," Miller said.

It was Holden's turn to ask why.

"Parents sent a contract to Ceres looking for her to be sent home. It was my case," Miller said.

"So you work for Ceres security?"

"Not anymore."

"So what are you doing here?" Holden asked.

"Her family was connected to something," Miller replied. "I just naturally hate a mystery."

"And how did you know it was bigger than just a missing girl?"

Talking to Miller felt like digging through granite with a rubber chisel. Miller grinned humorlessly.

"They fired me for looking too hard."

Holden consciously decided not to be annoyed by Miller's non-answer. "So let's talk about the death squad in the hotel."

"Yeah, seriously, what the fuck?" Amos said, finally pausing in his pacing. Alex took his head out of his hands and looked up with interest for the first time. Even Naomi leaned forward on the edge of the bed.

"No idea," Miller replied. "But someone knew you were coming."

"Yeah, thanks for the brilliant police work," Amos said with a snort. "No way we woulda figured that out on our own."

Holden ignored him. "But they didn't know why, or they would have already gone up to Julie's room and gotten whatever they wanted."

"Does that mean Fred's been compromised?" Naomi said.

"Fred?" Miller asked.

"Or maybe someone figured out the Polanski thing too, but didn't have a room number," Holden said.

"But why come out guns blazing like that?" Amos said. "Doesn't make any sense to shoot us."

"*That* was a mistake," Miller said. "I saw it happen. Amos here drew his gun. Somebody overreacted. They were yelling cease-fire right up until you folks started shooting back."

Holden began ticking off points on his fingers.

"So someone finds out we're headed to Eros, and that it is related to the *Scopuli.* They even know the hotel, but not the room."

"They don't know it's Lionel Polanski either," Naomi said. "They could have looked it up at the desk, just like we did."

"Right. So they wait for us to show, and have a squad of gunmen ready to take us in. But that goes to shit and it turns into a gunfight in the lobby. They absolutely *don't* see you coming, Detective, so they aren't omniscient."

"Right," Miller said. "The whole thing screams last minute. Grab you guys and find out what you're looking for. If they'd had more time, they could have just searched the hotel. Might have taken two or three days, but it could have been done. They didn't, so that means grabbing you was easier."

Holden nodded. "Yes," he said. "But that means that they already had teams here. Those didn't seem like locals to me."

Miller paused, looking disconcerted.

"Now you say it, me either," he agreed.

"So whoever it is, they already have teams of gunmen on Eros, and they can redeploy them to come at a moment's notice to pick us up," Holden said.

"And enough pull with security that they could have a firefight and nobody came," Miller said. "Police didn't know anything was happening until I called them."

Holden cocked his head to one side, then said, "Shit, we really need to get out of here."

"Wait a minute," Alex said loudly. "Just wait a goddamn minute here. How come no one is talkin' about the *mutant horror show* in that room? Was I the only one that saw that?"

"Yeah, Jesus, what was that all about?" Amos said quietly.

Miller reached into his coat pocket and took out the evidence bag with Julie's hand terminal in it.

"Any of you guys a techie?" he asked. "Maybe we could find out."

"I could probably hack it," Naomi said. "But there's no way I'm touching that thing until we know what did that to her and that it isn't catching. I'm not pushing my luck by handling anything she's touched."

"You don't have to touch it. Keep the bag sealed. Just use it right through the plastic. The touch screen should still work."

Naomi paused for a second, then reached out and took the bag.

"Okay, give me a minute," she said, then set to work on it.

Miller leaned back in his chair again, letting out another heavy sigh.

"So," Holden said. "Did you know Julie before this? Naomi seems to think finding her dead like that really knocked you for a loop."

Miller shook his head slowly. "You get a case like that, you look into whoever it is. You know, personal stuff. Read their e-mail. Talk to the people they know. You get a picture."

Miller stopped talking and rubbed his eyes with his thumbs. Holden didn't push him, but he started talking again anyway.

"Julie was a good kid," Miller said as if he were confessing something. "She flew a mean racing ship. I just...I wanted to get her back alive."

"It's got a password," Naomi said, holding up the terminal. "I could hack the hardware, but I'd have to open the case."

Miller reached out and said, "Let me give it a try."

Naomi handed the terminal to him, and he tapped a few characters on the screen and handed it back.

"*Razorback*," Naomi said. "What's that?"

"It's a sled," Miller replied.

"Is he talking to us?" Amos said, pointing his chin at Miller. " 'Cause there's no one else here, but I swear half the time I don't know what the fuck he's on about."

"Sorry," Miller said. "I've been working more or less solo. Makes for bad habits."

Naomi shrugged and went back to work with Holden and Miller now looking over her shoulders.

"She's got a lot of stuff on here," Naomi said. "Where to start?"

Miller pointed at a text file simply labeled NOTES sitting on the terminal's desktop.

"Start there," he said. "She's a fanatic about putting things in the right folders. If she left that on the desktop, it means she wasn't sure where it went."

Naomi tapped on the document to open it up. It expanded into a loosely organized collection of text that read like someone's diary.

First off, get your shit together. Panic doesn't help. It never helps. Deep breaths, figure this out, make the right moves. Fear is the mind-killer. Ha. Geek.

Shuttle Pros:
No reactor, just batteries. V. low radiation.
Supplies for eight
Lots of reaction mass

Shuttle Cons:
No Epstein, no torch
Comm not just disabled, but physically removed *(feeling a little paranoid about leaks, guys?)*

Closest transit is Eros. Is that where we were going? Maybe go someplace else? On just teakettle, this is gonna be a **slow** *boat. Another transit adds seven more weeks. Eros, then.*

I've got the Phoebe bug, no way around it. Not sure how, but that brown shit was everywhere. It's anaerobic, must have touched some. Doesn't matter how, just work the problem.

I just slept for THREE WEEKS. Didn't even get up to pee. What does that?

I'm so fucked.

Things you need to remember:

* BA834024112
* Radiation kills. No reactor on this shuttle, but keep the lights off. Keep the e-suit on. Video asshat said this thing eats radiation. Don't feed it.
* Send up a flag. Get some help. You work for the smartest people in the system. They'll figure something out.
* Stay away from people. Don't spread the bug. Not coughing up the brown goo yet. No idea when that starts.
* Keep away from bad guys — as if you know who they are. Fine. So keep away from everyone. Incognito is my name. Hmm. Polanski?

Damn. I can feel it. I'm hot all the time, and I'm starving. Don't eat. Don't feed it. Feed a cold, starve a flu? Other way around? Eros is a day out, and then help is on the way. Keep fighting.

Safe on Eros. Sent up the flag. Hope the home office is watching. Head hurts. Something's happening on my back. Lump over my kidneys. Darren turned into goo. Am I going to be a suit full of jelly?

Sick now. Things coming out of my back and leaking that brown stuff everywhere. Have to take the suit off. If you read this, don't let anyone touch the brown stuff. Burn me. I'm burning up.

Naomi put the terminal down, but no one spoke for a moment. Finally, Holden said, "Phoebe bug. Anyone have an idea?"

"There was a science station on Phoebe," Miller said. "Inner planets place, no Belters allowed. It got hit. Lots of dead people, but..."

"She talks about being on a shuttle," Naomi said. "The *Scopuli* didn't have a shuttle."

"There had to be another ship," Alex said. "Maybe she got the shuttle off it."

"Right," Holden said. "They got on another ship, they got infected with this Phoebe bug, and the rest of the crew...I don't know. Dies?"

"She gets out, not realizing she's infected till she's on the shuttle," Naomi continued. "She comes here, she sends up the flag to Fred, and she dies in that hotel room of the infection."

"Not, however, turned to goo," Holden said. "Just really badly...I don't know. Those tubes and bone spurs. What kind of disease does that?"

The question hung in the air. Again no one spoke. Holden knew they were all thinking the same thing. They hadn't touched anything in the flophouse room. Did that mean they were safe from it? Or did they have the Phoebe bug, whatever the hell it was? But she'd said anaerobic. Holden was pretty sure that meant you couldn't get it by breathing it in the air. *Pretty* sure...

"Where do we go from here, Jim?" Naomi asked.

"How about Venus?" Holden said, his voice higher and tighter than he'd expected. "Nothing interesting happening on Venus."

"Seriously," Naomi said.

"Okay. Seriously, I think Miller there lets his cop friend know the story, and then we get the hell off of this rock. It's got to be a bioweapon, right? Someone steals it off a Martian science lab, seeds this shit in a dome, a month later every human being in the city is dead."

Amos interrupted with a grunt.

"There's some holes in that, Cap'n," Amos said. "Like what the fuck does that have to do with taking down the *Cant* and the *Donnager*?"

Holden looked Naomi in the eye and said, "We have a place to look now, don't we?"

"Yeah, we do," she said. "BA834024112. That's a rock designation."

"What do you think is out there?" Alex asked.

"If I was a betting man, I'd say it's whatever ship she stole that shuttle from," Holden replied.

"Makes sense," Naomi said. "Every rock in the Belt is mapped. You want to hide something, put it in a stable orbit next to one and you can always find it later."

Miller turned toward Holden, his face even more drawn.

"If you're going there, I want in," he said.

"Why?" Holden asked. "No offense, but you found your girl. Your job's over, right?"

Miller looked at him, his lips a thin line.

"Different case," Miller said. "Now it's about who killed her."

Chapter Twenty-Six: Miller

Your police friend put a lockdown order on my ship," Holden said. He sounded outraged.

Around them, the hotel restaurant was busy. Last shift's prostitutes mixed with the next shift's tourists and businessmen at the cheap pink-lit buffet. The pilot and the big guy—Alex and Amos—were vying for the last bagel. Naomi sat at Holden's side, her arms crossed, a cup of bad coffee cooling before her.

"We did kill some people," Miller said gently.

"I thought you got us out of that with your secret police handshake," Holden said. "So why's my ship in lockdown?"

"You remember when Sematimba said we shouldn't leave the station without telling him?" Miller said.

"I remember you making some kind of deal," Holden said. "I don't remember agreeing to it."

"Look, he's going to keep us here until he's sure he won't get fired for letting us go. Once he knows his ass is covered, the lock goes down. So let's talk about the part where I rent a berth on your ship."

Jim Holden and his XO exchanged a glance, one of those tiny human burst communications that said more than words could have. Miller didn't know either of them well enough to decode all of it, but he guessed they were skeptical.

They had reason to be. Miller had checked his credit balance before he'd called them. He had enough left for another night in the hotel or a good dinner, but not both. He was spending it on a cheap breakfast that Holden and his crew didn't need and probably wouldn't enjoy, buying goodwill.

"I need to make very, very sure I understand what you're saying," Holden said as the big one—Amos—returned and sat at his other side holding the bagel. "Are you saying that unless I let you on my ship, your friend is going to keep us here? Because that's blackmail."

"Extortion," Amos said.

"What?" Holden said.

"It's not blackmail," Naomi said. "That would be if he threatened to expose information we didn't want known. If it's just a threat, that's extortion."

"And it's not what I'm talking about," Miller said. "Freedom of the station while the investigation rolls? That's no trouble. Leaving jurisdiction's another thing. I can't hold you here any more than I can cut you loose. I'm just looking for a ride when you go."

"Why?" Holden said.

"Because you're going to Julie's asteroid," Miller said.

"I'm willing to bet there's no port there," Holden said. "Did you plan on going anyplace after that?"

"I'm kind of low on solid plans. Haven't had one yet that actually happened."

"I hear that," Amos said. "We've been fucked eighteen different ways since we got into this."

Holden folded his hands on the table, one finger tapping a

complicated rhythm on the wood-textured concrete top. It wasn't a good sign.

"You seem like a...well, like an angry, bitter old man, actually. But I've been working water haulers for the past five years. That just means you'd fit in."

"But," Miller said, and let the word hang there.

"But I've been shot at a lot recently, and the machine guns yesterday were the least lethal thing I've had to deal with," Holden said. "I'm not letting anyone on my ship that I wouldn't trust with my life, and I don't actually know you."

"I can get the money," Miller said, his belly sinking. "If it's money, I can cover it."

"It's not about negotiating a price," Holden said.

"Get the money?" Naomi said, her eyes narrowing. " 'Get the money,' as in you don't have it now?"

"I'm a little short," Miller said. "It's temporary."

"You have an income?" Naomi said.

"More like a strategy," Miller said. "There's some independent rackets down on the docks. There always are at any port. Side games. Fights. Things like that. Most of them, the fix is in. It's how you bribe cops without actually bribing cops."

"That's your plan?" Holden said, incredulity in his voice. "Go collect some police bribes?"

Across the restaurant, a prostitute in a red nightgown yawned prodigiously; the john across the table from her frowned.

"No," Miller said reluctantly. "I play the side bets. A cop goes in, I make a side bet that he's going to win. I know who the cops are mostly. The house, they know because they're bribing them. The side bets are with fish looking to feel edgy because they're playing unlicensed."

Even as he said it, Miller knew how weak it sounded. Alex, the pilot, came and sat beside Miller. His coffee smelled bright and acidic.

"What's the deal?" Alex asked.

"There isn't one," Holden said. "There wasn't one before and there still isn't."

"It works better than you'd think," Miller said gamely, and four hand terminals chimed at once. Holden and Naomi exchanged another, less complicit glance and pulled up their terminals. Amos and Alex already had theirs up. Miller caught the red-and-green border that meant either a priority message or an early Christmas card. There was a moment's silence as they all read something; then Amos whistled low.

"Stage three?" Naomi said.

"Can't say as I like the sound of that," Alex said.

"You mind if I ask?" Miller said.

Holden slid his terminal across the table. The message was plaintext, encoded from Tycho.

CAUGHT MOLE IN TYCHO COMM STATION.
YOUR PRESENCE AND DESTINATION LEAKED TO
UNKNOWN PERSONS ON EROS. BE CAREFUL.

"Little late on that," Miller said.

"Keep reading," Holden said.

MOLE'S ENCRYPTION CODE ALLOWED INTERCEPT
OF SUBSIGNAL BROADCAST FROM EROS FIVE
HOURS AGO.
    INTERCEPTED MESSAGE FOLLOWS:
HOLDEN ESCAPED BUT PAYLOAD SAMPLE
RECOVERED. REPEAT: SAMPLE RECOVERED.
PROCEEDING TO STAGE THREE.

"Any idea what that means?" Holden asked.

"I don't," Miller said, pushing the terminal back. "Except…if the payload sample is Julie's body."

"Which I think we can assume it is," Holden said.

Miller tapped his fingertips on the tabletop, unconsciously copying Holden's rhythm, his mind working through the combinations.

"This thing," Miller said. "The bioweapon or whatever. They were shipping it here. So now it's here. Okay. There's no reason to take out Eros. It's not particularly important to the war when you hold it up to Ceres or Ganymede or the shipyard at Callisto. And if you wanted it dead, there're easier ways. Blow a big fusion bomb on the surface, and crack it like an egg."

"It's not a military base, but it is a shipping hub," Naomi said. "And, unlike Ceres, it's not under OPA control."

"They're shipping her out, then," Holden said. "They're taking their sample out to infect whatever their original target was, and once they're off the station, there's no way we're going to stop it."

Miller shook his head. Something about the chain of logic felt wrong. He was missing something. His imaginary Julie appeared across the room, but her eyes were dark, black filaments pouring down her cheeks like tears.

What am I looking at here, Julie? he thought. *I'm seeing something here, but I don't know what it is.*

The vibration was a slight, small thing, less than a transport tube's braking stutter. A few plates rattled; the coffee in Naomi's cup danced in a series of concentric circles. Everyone in the hotel went silent with the sudden shared dread of thousands of people made aware of their fragility in the same moment.

"Oh-kay," Amos said. "The fuck was that?" and the emergency Klaxons started blaring.

"Or possibly stage three is something else," Miller said over the noise.

The public-address system was muddy by its nature. The same voice spoke from consoles and speakers that might have been as close as a meter from each other or as far out as earshot would take them. It made every word reverberate, a false echo. Because of that, the voice of the emergency broadcast system enunciated very carefully, each word bitten off separately.

"Attention, please. Eros Station is in emergency lockdown. Proceed immediately to the casino level for radiological safety confinement. Cooperate with all emergency personnel. Attention, please. Eros station is in emergency lockdown…"

And on in a loop that would continue, if no one coded in the override, until every man, woman, child, animal, and insect on the station had been reduced to dust and humidity. It was the nightmare scenario, and Miller did what a lifetime on pressurized rocks had trained him to do. He was up from the table, in the corridor, and heading down toward the wider passages, already clogged with bodies. Holden and his crew were on his heels.

"That was an explosion," Alex said. "Ship drive at the least. Maybe a nuke."

"They are going to kill the station," Holden said. There was a kind of awe in his voice. "I never thought I'd miss the part where they just blew up the ships I was on. But now it's stations."

"They didn't crack it," Miller said.

"You're sure of that?" Naomi asked.

"I can hear you talking," Miller said. "That tells me there's air."

"There are airlocks," Holden said. "If the station got holed and the locks closed down…"

A woman pushed hard against Miller's shoulder, forcing her way forward. If they weren't damn careful, there was going to be a stampede. This was too much fear and not enough space. It hadn't happened yet, but the impatient movement of the crowd, vibrating like molecules in water just shy of boiling, made Miller very uncomfortable.

"This isn't a ship," Miller said. "It's a station. This is rock we're on. Anything big enough to get to the parts of the station with atmosphere would crack the place like an egg. A great big pressurized egg."

The crowd was stopped, the tunnel full. They were going to

need crowd control, and they were going to need it fast. For the first time since he'd left Ceres, Miller wished he had a badge. Someone pushed into Amos' side, then backed away through the press when the big guy growled.

"Besides," Miller said, "it's a rad hazard. You don't need air loss to kill everyone in the station. Just burn a few quadrillion spare neutrons through the place at C, and there won't be any trouble with the oxygen supply."

"Cheerful fucker," Amos said.

"They build stations inside of rocks for a reason," Naomi said. "Not so easy to force radiation through this many meters of rock."

"I spent a month in a rad shelter once," Alex said as they pushed through the thickening crowd. "Ship I was on had magnetic containment drop. Automatic cutoffs failed, and the reactor kept runnin' for almost a second. Melted the engine room. Killed five of the crew on the next deck up before they knew we had a problem, and it took them three days to carve the bodies free of the melted decking for burial. The rest of us wound up eighteen to a shelter for thirty-six days while a tug flew to get us."

"Sounds great," Holden said.

"End of it, six of 'em got married, and the rest of us never spoke to each other again," Alex said.

Ahead of them, someone shouted. It wasn't in alarm or even anger, really. Frustration. Fear. Exactly the things Miller didn't want to hear.

"That may not be our big problem," Miller said, but before he could explain, a new voice cut in, drowning out the emergency-response loop.

"Okay, everybody! We're Eros security, *que no*? We got an emergency, so you do what we tell you and nobody gets hurt."

About time, Miller thought.

"So here's the rule," the new voice said. "Next asshole who pushes anyone, I'm going to shoot them. Move in an orderly fashion. First priority: orderly. Second priority is *move*! Go, go, go!"

At first nothing happened. The knot of human bodies was tied too tightly for even the most heavy-handed crowd control to free quickly, but a minute later, Miller saw some heads far ahead of him in the tunnel start to shift, then move away. The air in the tunnel was thickening and the hot plastic smell of overloaded recyclers reached him just as the clot came free. Miller's breath started coming easier.

"Do they have hard shelters?" a woman behind them asked her companion, and then was swept away by the currents. Naomi plucked Miller's sleeve.

"Do they?" she asked.

"They should, yes," Miller said. "Enough for maybe a quarter million, and essential personnel and medical crews would get first crack at them."

"And everyone else?" Amos said.

"If they survive the event," Holden said, "station personnel will save as many people as they can."

"Ah," Amos said. Then: "Well, fuck that. We're going for the *Roci*, right?"

"Oh, hell yes," Holden said.

Ahead of them, the fast-shuffling crowd in their tunnel was merging with another flow of people from a lower level. Five thick-necked men in riot gear were waving people on. Two of them were pointing guns at the crowd. Miller was more than half tempted to go up and slap the little idiots. Pointing guns at people was a lousy way to avoid panic. One of the security men was also far too wide for his gear, the Velcro fasteners at his belly reaching out for each other like lovers at the moment of separation.

Miller looked down at the floor and slowed his steps, the back of his mind suddenly and powerfully busy. One of the cops swung his gun out over the crowd. Another one—the fat guy—laughed and said something in Korean.

What had Sematimba said about the new security force? All bluster, no balls. A new corporation out of Luna. Belters on the ground. Corrupt.

The name. They'd had a name. CPM. *Carne Por la Machina.*
Meat for the machine. One of the gun-wielding cops lowered his
weapon, swept off his helmet, and scratched violently behind one
ear. He had wild black hair, a tattooed neck, and a scar that went
from one eyelid down almost to the joint of his jaw.

Miller knew him. A year and a half ago, he'd arrested him for
assault and racketeering. And the equipment—armor, batons,
riot guns—also looked hauntingly familiar. Dawes had been
wrong. Miller had been able to find his own missing equipment
after all.

Whatever this was, it had been going on a long time before the
Canterbury had picked up a distress call from the *Scopuli*. A long
time before Julie had vanished. And putting a bunch of Ceres
Station thugs in charge of Eros crowd control using stolen Ceres
Station equipment had been part of the plan. The third phase.

Ah, he thought. *Well. That can't be good.*

Miller slid to the side, letting as many bodies as he plausibly
could fill the space between him and the gunmen dressed as
police.

"Get down to the casino level," one of the gunmen shouted over
the crowd. "We'll get you into the radiation shelters from there,
but you've got to get to the casino level!"

Holden and his crew hadn't noticed anything odd. They were
talking among themselves, strategizing about how to get to their
ship and what to do once they got there, speculating about who
might have attacked the station and where Julie Mao's twisted,
infected corpse might be headed. Miller fought the impulse to
interrupt them. He needed to stay calm, to think things through.
They couldn't attract attention. He needed the right moment.

The corridor turned and widened. The press of bodies light-
ened a little bit. Miller waited for a dead zone in the crowd control, a space where none of the fake security men could see them.
He took Holden by the elbow.

"Don't go," he said.

Chapter Twenty-Seven: Holden

What do you mean, don't go?" Holden asked, yanking his elbow out of Miller's grasp. "Somebody just nuked the station. This has escalated beyond our capacity to respond. If we can't get to the *Roci,* we're doing whatever they tell us to until we can."

Miller took a step back and put up his hands; he was clearly doing his best to look nonthreatening, which just pissed Holden off even more. Behind him, the riot cops were motioning the people milling in the corridors toward the casinos. The air echoed with the electronically amplified voices of the police directing the crowds and the buzz of anxious citizens. Over it all, the public-address system told everyone to remain calm and cooperate with emergency personnel.

"See that bruiser over there in the police riot gear?" Miller said. "His name is Gabby Smalls. He supervises a chunk of the Golden Bough protection racket on Ceres. He also runs a little dust on the side, and I suspect he's tossed more than a few people out airlocks."

Holden looked at the guy. Wide shoulders, thick gut. Now that Miller pointed him out, there was something about him that didn't seem right for a cop.

"I don't get it," Holden said.

"A couple months ago, when you started a bunch of riots by saying Mars blew up your water hauler, we found out—"

"I never said—"

"—*found out* that most of the police riot gear on Ceres was missing. A few months before that, a bunch of our underworld muscle went missing. I just found out where both of them are."

Miller pointed at the riot-gear-equipped Gabby Smalls.

"I wouldn't go wherever he's sending people," he said. "I really wouldn't."

A thin stream of people bumped past.

"Then where?" Naomi asked.

"Yeah, I mean, if the choice is radiation or mobsters, I gotta go with the mobsters," Alex said, nodding emphatically at Naomi.

Miller pulled out his hand terminal and held it up so everyone could see the screen.

"I've got no radiation warnings," he said. "Whatever happened outside isn't a danger on this level. Not right now. So let's just calm down and make the smart move."

Holden turned his back on Miller and motioned to Naomi. He pulled her aside and said in a quiet voice, "I still think we go back to the ship and get out of here. Take our chances getting past these mobsters."

"If there's no radiation danger, then I agree," she said with a nod.

"I disagree," Miller said, not even pretending he hadn't been eavesdropping. "To do that we have to walk through three levels of casino filled with riot gear and thugs. They're going to tell us to get in one of those casinos for our own protection. When we don't, they'll beat us unconscious and throw us in anyway. For our own protection."

Another crowd of people poured out of a branch corridor, heading for the reassuring presence of the police and the bright casino lights. Holden found it difficult not to be swept along with the crowd. A man with two enormous suitcases bumped into Naomi, almost knocking her down. Holden grabbed her hand.

"What's the alternative?" he asked Miller.

Miller glanced up and down the corridor, seeming to measure the flow of people. He nodded at a yellow-and-black-striped hatch down a small maintenance corridor.

"That one," he said. "It's marked HIGH VOLTAGE, so the guys sweeping for stragglers won't bother with it. It's not the kind of place citizens hide."

"Can you get that door open quickly?" Holden said, looking at Amos.

"Can I break it?"

"If you need to."

"Then sure," Amos said, and began pushing his way through the crowd toward the maintenance hatch. At the door, he pulled out his multi-tool and popped off the cheap plastic housing for the card reader. After he twisted a couple of wires together, the hatch slid open with a hydraulic hiss.

"Ta-da," Amos said. "The reader won't work anymore, so anyone who wants in comes in."

"Let's worry about that if it happens," Miller replied, then led them into the dimly lit passageway beyond.

The service corridor was filled with electrical cable held together with plastic ties. It stretched through the dim red light for thirty or forty feet before falling into gloom. The light came from LEDs mounted on the metal bracing that sprouted from the wall every five feet or so to hold the cable up. Naomi had to duck to enter, her frame about four centimeters too tall for the ceiling. She put her back to the wall and slid down onto her haunches.

"You'd think they'd make the maintenance corridors tall enough for Belters to work in," she said irritably.

Holden touched the wall almost reverently, tracing a corridor identification number carved right into the stone.

"The Belters who built this place weren't tall," he said. "These are some of the main power lines. This tunnel goes back to the first Belt colony. The people who carved it grew up in gravity."

Miller, who also had to duck his head, sat on the floor with a grunt and popping knees.

"History lesson later," he said. "Let's figure a way off this rock."

Amos, studying the bundles of cable intently, said over his shoulder, "If you see a frayed spot, don't touch it. This thick fucker right here is a couple million volts. That'd melt your shit down real good."

Alex sat down next to Naomi, grimacing when his butt hit the cold stone floor.

"You know," he said, "if they decide to seal up the station, they might pump all the air outta these maintenance corridors."

"I get it," Holden said loudly. "It's a shitty and uncomfortable hiding spot. You have my permission to now shut up about that."

He squatted down across the corridor from Miller and said, "Okay, Detective. Now what?"

"Now," Miller said, "we wait for the sweep to pass us by, and get behind it, try to get to the docks. The folks in the shelters are easy to avoid. Shelters are up deep. Trick's going to be getting through the casino levels."

"Can't we just use these maintenance passages to move around?" Alex asked.

Amos shook his head. "Not without a map, we won't. You get lost in here, you're in trouble," he said.

Ignoring them, Holden said, "Okay, so we wait for everyone to move to the radiation shelters and then we leave."

Miller nodded at him, and then the two men sat staring at each other for a moment. The air between them seemed to thicken, the silence taking on a meaning of its own. Miller shrugged like his jacket itched.

"Why do you think a bunch of Ceres mobsters are moving everyone to radiation shelters when there's no actual radiation danger?" Holden finally said. "And why are the Eros cops letting them?"

"Good questions," Miller said.

"If they were using these yahoos, it helps explain why their attempted kidnapping at the hotel went so poorly. They don't seem like pros."

"Nope," Miller said. "That's not their usual area of expertise."

"Would you two be quiet?" Naomi said.

For almost a minute they were.

"It'd be really stupid," Holden said, "to go take a look at what's going on, wouldn't it?"

"Yes. Whatever's going on at those shelters, you know that's where all the guards and patrols will be," Miller said.

"Yeah," Holden said.

"Captain," Naomi said, a warning in her voice.

"Still," Holden said, talking to Miller, "you hate a mystery."

"I do at that," Miller replied with a nod and a faint smile. "And you, my friend, are a damn busybody."

"It's been said."

"Goddamn it," Naomi said quietly.

"What is it, Boss?" Amos asked.

"These two just broke our getaway plan," Naomi replied. Then she said to Holden, "You guys are going to be very bad for each other and, by extension, us."

"No," Holden replied. "You aren't coming along. You stay here with Amos and Alex. Give us"—he looked at his terminal—"three hours to go look and come back. If we aren't here—"

"We leave you to the gangsters and the three of us get jobs on Tycho and live happily ever after," Naomi said.

"Yeah," Holden said with a grin. "Don't be a hero."

"Wouldn't even consider it, sir."

Holden crouched in the shadows outside the maintenance hatch and watched as Ceres mobsters dressed in police riot gear led the citizens of Eros away in small groups. The PA system continued to declare the possibility of radiological danger and exhorted the citizens and guests of Eros to cooperate fully with emergency personnel. Holden had selected a group to follow and was getting ready to move when Miller placed a hand on his shoulder.

"Wait," Miller said. "I want to make a call."

He quickly dialed up a number on his hand terminal, and after a few moments, a flat gray *Network Not Available* message appeared.

"Phone is down?" Holden asked.

"That's the first thing I'd do, too," Miller replied.

"I see," Holden said even though he really didn't.

"Well, I guess it's just you and me," Miller said, then took the magazine out of his gun and began reloading it with cartridges he pulled out of his coat pocket.

Even though he'd had enough of gunfights to last him the rest of his life, Holden took out his gun and checked the magazine as well. He'd replaced it after the shoot-out in the hotel, and it was full. He racked it and put it back in the waistband of his pants. Miller, he noticed, kept his out, holding it close to his thigh, where his coat mostly covered it.

It wasn't difficult following the groups up through the station toward the inner sections where the radiation shelters were. As long as they kept moving in the same direction as the crowds, no one gave them a second look. Holden made a mental note of the many corridor intersections where men in riot gear stood guard. It would be much tougher coming back down.

When the group they were following eventually stopped outside a large metal door marked with the ancient radiation symbol, Holden and Miller slipped off to the side and hid behind a large planter filled with ferns and a couple of stunted trees. Holden watched the fake riot cops order everyone into the shelter and then seal the door behind them with the swipe of a card. All but one of them left, the remaining one standing guard outside the door.

Miller whispered, "Let's ask him to let us in."

"Follow my lead," Holden replied, then stood up and began walking toward the guard.

"Hey, shithead, you supposed to be in a shelter or in the casino, so get the fuck back to your group," the guard said, his hand on the butt of his gun.

Holden held up his hands placatingly, smiled, and kept walking. "Hey, I lost my group. Got mixed up somehow. I'm not from here, you know," he said.

The guard pointed down the corridor with the stun baton in his left hand.

"Go that way till you hit the ramps down," he said.

Miller seemed to appear out of nowhere in the dimly lit corridor, his gun already out and pointed at the guard's head. He thumbed off the safety with an audible click.

"How about we just join the group already inside?" he said. "Open it up."

The guard looked at Miller out of the corners of his eyes, not turning his head at all. His hands went up, and he dropped the baton.

"You don't want to do that, man," the fake cop said.

"I kind of think he does," Holden said. "You should do what he says. He's not a very nice person."

Miller pushed the barrel of his gun against the guard's head and said, "You know what we used to call a 'no-brainer' back at the station house? It's when a shot to the head actually blows the entire brain out of someone's skull. It usually happens when a gun is pressed to the victim's head right about here. The gas's got nowhere to go. Pops the brain right out through the exit wound."

"They said not to open these up once they'd been sealed, man," the guard said, speaking so fast he ran all the words together. "They were pretty serious about that."

"This is the last time I ask," Miller said. "Next time I just use the card I took off your body."

Holden turned the guard around to face the door and pulled the handgun out of the man's belt holster. He hoped all Miller's threats were just threats. He suspected they weren't.

"Just open the door, and we'll let you go, I promise," Holden said to the guard.

The guard nodded and moved up to the door, then slid his card through it and punched in a number on the keypad. The heavy blast door slid open. Beyond it, the room was even darker than the corridor outside. A few emergency LEDs glowed a sullen red. In the faint illumination, Holden could see dozens...*hundreds* of bodies scattered across the floor, unmoving.

"Are they dead?" Holden asked.

"I don't know nothing about—" the guard said, but Miller cut him off.

"You go in first," Miller said, and pushed the guard forward.

"Hold on," Holden said. "I don't think it's a good idea to just charge in here."

Three things happened at once. The guard took four steps forward and then collapsed on the floor. Miller sneezed once, loudly, and then started to sway drunkenly. And both Holden's and Miller's hand terminals began an angry electric buzzing.

Miller staggered back and said, "The door..."

Holden hit the button and the door slid shut again.

"Gas," Miller said, then coughed. "There's gas in there."

While the ex-cop leaned against the corridor wall and coughed, Holden took out his terminal to shut off the buzzing. But the alarm flashing on its screen wasn't an air-contamination alert. It was the venerable three wedge shapes pointing inward. Radiation. As he watched, the symbol, which should have been white, shifted through an angry orange color to dark red.

Miller was looking at his too, his expression unreadable.

"We've been dosed," Holden said.

"I've never actually seen the detector activate," Miller said, his voice rough and faint after his coughing fit. "What does it mean when the thing is red?"

"It means we'll be bleeding from our rectums in about six hours," Holden said. "We have to get to the ship. It'll have the meds we need."

"What," Miller said, "the *fuck*...is going on?"

Holden grabbed Miller by the arm and led him back down the

corridor toward the ramps. Holden's skin felt warm and itchy. He didn't know if it was radiation burn or psychosomatic. With the amount of radiation he'd just taken, it was a good thing he had sperm tucked away in Montana and on Europa.

Thinking that made his balls itch.

"They nuke the station," Holden said. "Hell, maybe they just *pretend* to nuke it. Then they drag everyone down here and toss them into radiation shelters that are only radioactive on the inside. Gas them to keep them quiet."

"There are easier ways to kill people," Miller said, his breathing coming in ragged gasps as they ran down the corridor.

"So it has to be more than that," Holden said. "The bug, right? The one that killed that girl. It...fed on radiation."

"Incubators," Miller said, nodding in agreement.

They arrived at one of the ramps to the lower levels, but a group of citizens led by two fake riot cops were coming up. Holden grabbed Miller and pulled him to one side, where they could hide in the shadow of a closed noodle shop.

"So they infected them, right?" Holden said in a whisper, waiting for the group to pass. "Maybe fake radiation meds with the bug in it. Maybe that brown goo just spread around on the floor. Then whatever was in the girl, Julie—"

He stopped when Miller walked away from him straight at the group that had just come up the ramp.

"Officer," said Miller to one of the fake cops.

They both stopped, and one of them said, "You supposed to be—"

Miller shot him in the throat, right below his helmet's faceplate. Then he swiveled smoothly and shot the other guard in the inside of the thigh, just below the groin. When the man fell backward, yelling in pain, Miller walked up and shot him again, this time in the neck.

A couple of the citizens started screaming. Miller pointed his gun at them and they got quiet.

"Go down a level or two and find someplace to hide," he said.

"Do not cooperate with these men, even though they're dressed like police. They do not have your best interests at heart. Go."

The citizens hesitated, then ran. Miller took a few cartridges out of his pocket and began replacing the three he'd fired. Holden started to speak, but Miller cut him off.

"Take the throat shot if you can. Most people, the faceplate and chest armor don't quite cover that gap. If the neck is covered, then shoot the inside of the thigh. Very thin armor there. Mobility issue. Takes most people down in one shot."

Holden nodded, as though that all made sense.

"Okay," Holden said. "Say, let's get back to the ship before we bleed to death, right? No more shooting people if we can help it." His voice sounded calmer than he felt.

Miller slapped the magazine back into his gun and chambered a round.

"I'm guessing there's a lot more people need to be shot before this is over," he said. "But sure. First things first."

Chapter Twenty-Eight: Miller

The first time Miller killed anyone was in his third year working security. He'd been twenty-two, just married, talking about having kids. As the new guy on the contract, he'd gotten the shit jobs: patrolling levels so high the Coriolis made him seasick, taking domestic disturbance calls in holes no wider than a storage bin, standing guard on the drunk tank to keep predators from raping the unconscious. The normal hazing. He'd known to expect it. He'd thought he could take it.

The call had been from an illegal restaurant almost at the mass center. At less than a tenth of a g, gravity had been little more than a suggestion, and his inner ear had been confused and angered by the change in spin. If he thought about it, he could still remember the sound of raised voices, too fast and slurred for words. The smell of bathtub cheese. The thin haze of smoke from the cheap electric griddle.

It had happened fast. The perp had come out of the hole with a gun in one hand, dragging a woman by the hair with the other. Miller's partner, a ten-year veteran named Carson, had shouted out the warning. The perp had turned, swinging the gun out at arm's length like a stuntman in a video.

All through training, the instructors had said that you couldn't know what you'd do until the moment came. Killing another human being was hard. Some people couldn't. The perp's gun came around; the gunman dropped the woman and shouted. It turned out that, for Miller at least, it wasn't all that hard.

Afterward, he'd been through mandatory counseling. He'd cried. He'd suffered the nightmares and the shakes and all the things that cops suffered quietly and didn't talk about. But even then, it seemed to be happening at a distance, like he'd gotten too drunk and was watching himself throw up. It was just a physical reaction. It would pass.

The important thing was he knew the answer to the question. Yes, if he needed to, he could take a life.

It wasn't until now, walking through the corridors of Eros, that he'd taken joy in it. Even taking down the poor bastard in that first firefight had felt like the sad necessity of work. Pleasure in killing hadn't come until after Julie, and it wasn't really pleasure as much as a brief cessation of pain.

He held the gun low. Holden started down the ramp, and Miller followed, letting the Earther take point. Holden walked faster than he did and with the uncommented athleticism of someone who lived in a wide variety of gravities. Miller had the feeling he'd made Holden nervous, and he regretted that a little. He hadn't intended to, and he really needed to get aboard Holden's ship if he was going to find Julie's secrets.

Or, for that matter, not die of radiation sickness in the next few hours. That seemed a finer point than it probably was.

"Okay," Holden said at the bottom of the ramp. "We need to get back down, and there are a lot of guards between us and Naomi that are going to be really confused by two guys walking the wrong direction."

"That's a problem," Miller agreed.

"Any thoughts?"

Miller frowned and considered the flooring. The Eros floors were different than Ceres'. Laminate with flecks of gold.

"Tubes aren't going to be running," he said. "If they are, it'll be in lockdown mode, where it only stops at the holding pen down in the casino. So that's out."

"Maintenance corridor again?"

"If we can find one that goes between levels," Miller said. "Might be a little tricky, but it seems like a better bet than shooting our way past a couple dozen assholes in armor. How long have we got before your friend takes off?"

Holden looked at his hand terminal. The radiation alarm was still deep red. Miller wondered how long those took to reset.

"A little more than two hours," Holden said. "Shouldn't be a problem."

"Let's see what we can find," Miller said.

The corridors nearest the radiation shelters—the death traps, the incubators—had been emptied. Wide passages built to accommodate the ancient construction equipment that had carved Eros into a human habitation were eerie with only Holden's and Miller's footsteps and the hum of the air recyclers. Miller hadn't noticed when the emergency announcements had stopped, but the absence of them now seemed ominous.

If it had been Ceres, he would have known where to go, where everything led, how to move gracefully from one stage to another. On Eros, all he had was an educated guess. That wasn't so bad.

But he could tell it was taking too long, and worse than that—they weren't talking about it; neither one spoke—they were walking more slowly than normal. It wasn't up to the threshold of consciousness, but Miller knew that both of their bodies were starting to feel the radiation damage. It wasn't going to get better.

"Okay," Holden said. "Somewhere around here there has to be a maintenance shaft."

"Could also try the tube station," Miller said. "The cars run in vacuum, but there might be some service tunnels running parallel."

"Don't you think they'd have shut those down as part of the big roundup?"

"Probably," Miller said.

"Hey! You two! What the fuck you think you're doing up here?"

Miller looked back over his shoulder. Two men in riot gear were waving at them menacingly. Holden said something sharp under his breath. Miller narrowed his eyes.

The thing was these men were amateurs. The beginning of an idea moved in the back of Miller's mind as he watched the two approach. Killing them and taking their gear wouldn't work. There was nothing like scorch marks and blood to make it clear something had happened. But...

"Miller," Holden said, a warning in his voice.

"Yeah," Miller said. "I know."

"I said what the fuck are you two doing here?" one of the security men said. "The station's on lockdown. Everyone goes down to the casino level or up to the radiation shelters."

"We were just looking for a way to...ah...get down to the casino level," Holden said, smiling and being nonthreatening. "We're not from around here, and—"

The closer of the two guards jabbed the butt of his rifle neatly into Holden's leg. The Earther staggered, and Miller shot the guard just below the faceplate, then turned to the one still standing, mouth agape.

"You're Mikey Ko, right?" Miller said.

The man's face went even paler, but he nodded. Holden groaned and stood.

"Detective Miller," Miller said. "Busted you on Ceres about four years ago. You got a little happy in a bar. Tappan's, I think? Hit a girl with a pool cue?"

"Oh, hey," the man said with a frightened smile. "Yeah, I remember you. How you been doing?"

"Good and bad," Miller said. "You know how it is. Give the Earther your gun."

Ko looked from Miller to Holden and back, licking his lips and judging his chances. Miller shook his head.

"Seriously," Miller said. "Give him the gun."

"Sure, yeah. No problem."

This was the kind of man who'd killed Julie, Miller thought. Stupid. Shortsighted. A man born with a sense for raw opportunity where his soul should have been. Miller's mental Julie shook her head in disgust and sorrow, and Miller found himself wondering if she meant the thug now handing his rifle to Holden or himself. Maybe both.

"What's the deal here, Mikey?" Miller asked.

"What do you mean?" the guard said, playing stupid, like they were in an interrogation cell. Stalling for time. Walking through the old script of cop and criminal as if it still made sense. As if everything hadn't changed. Miller was surprised by a tightness in his throat. He didn't know what it was there for.

"The job," he said. "What's the job?"

"I don't know—"

"Hey," Miller said gently. "I just killed your buddy."

"And that's his third today," Holden said. "I saw him."

Miller could see it in the man's eyes: the cunning, the shift, the move from one strategy to another. It was old and familiar and as predictable as water moving down.

"Hey," Ko said, "it's just a job. They told us about a year ago how we were making a big move, right? But no one knows what it is. So a few months back, they start moving guys over. Training us up like we were cops, you know?"

"Who was training you?" Miller said.

"The last guys. The ones who were working the contract before us," Ko said.

"Protogen?"

"Something like that, yeah," he said. "Then they took off, and we took over. Just muscle, you know. Some smuggling."

"Smuggling what?"

"All kinds of shit," Ko said. He was starting to feel safe, and it showed in the way he held himself and the way he spoke. "Surveillance equipment, communication arrays, serious-as-fuck servers with their own little gel software wonks already built in. Scientific equipment too. Stuff for checking the water and the air and shit. And these ancient remote-access robots like you'd use in a vacuum dig. All sorts of shit."

"Where was it going to?" Holden asked.

"Here," Ko said, gesturing to the air, the stone, the station. "It's all here. They were like months installing it all. And then for weeks, nothing."

"What do you mean, nothing?" Miller asked.

"Nothing nothing. All this buildup and then we sat around with our thumbs up our butts."

Something had gone wrong. The Phoebe bug hadn't made its rendezvous, but then Julie had come, Miller thought, and the game had turned back on. He saw her again as if he were in her apartment. The long, spreading tendrils of whatever the hell it was, the bone spurs pressing out against her skin, the black froth of filament pouring from her eyes.

"The pay's good, though," Ko said philosophically. "And it was kind of nice taking some time off."

Miller nodded in agreement, leaned close, tucking the barrel of his gun through the interleaving of armor at Ko's belly, and shot him.

"What the fuck!" Holden said as Miller put his gun into his jacket pocket.

"What did you think was going to happen?" Miller said, squatting down beside the gut-shot man. "It's not like he was going to let us go."

"Yeah, okay," Holden said. "But..."

"Help me get him up," Miller said, hooking an arm behind Ko's shoulder. Ko shrieked when Miller lifted him.

"What?"

"Get his other side," Miller said. "Man needs medical attention, right?"

"Um. Yes," Holden said.

"So get his other side."

It wasn't as far back to the radiation shelters as Miller had expected, which had its good points and its bad ones. On the upside, Ko was still alive and screaming. The chances were better that he'd be lucid, which wasn't what Miller had intended. But as they came near the first group of guards, Ko's babbling seemed scattered enough to work.

"Hey!" Miller shouted. "Some help over here!"

At the head of the ramp, four of the guards looked at one another and then started moving toward them, curiosity winning out over basic operating procedures. Holden was breathing hard. Miller was too. Ko wasn't that heavy. It was a bad sign.

"What the hell is this?" one of the guards said.

"There's a bunch of people holed up back there," Miller said. "Resistance. I thought you people swept this level."

"That wasn't our job," the guy said. "We're just making sure the groups from the casino get to the shelters."

"Well, someone screwed up," Miller snapped. "You have transport?"

The guards looked at each other again.

"We can call for one," a guy at the back said.

"Never mind," Miller said. "You boys go find the shooters."

"Wait a minute," the first guy said. "Exactly who the hell are you?"

"The installers from Protogen," Holden said. "We're replacing the sensors that failed. This guy was supposed to help us."

"I didn't hear about that," the leader said.

Miller dug a finger under Ko's armor and squeezed. Ko shrieked and tried to writhe away from him.

"Talk to your boss about it on your own time," Miller said. "Come on. Let's get this asshole to a medic."

"Hold on!" the first guard said, and Miller sighed. Four of them. If he dropped Ko and jumped for cover...but there wasn't much cover. And who the hell knew what Holden would do?

"Where are the shooters?" the guard asked. Miller kept himself from smiling.

"There's a hole about a quarter klick anti-spinward," Miller said. "The other one's body's still there. You can't miss it."

Miller turned down the ramp. Behind him, the guards were talking among themselves, debating what to do, who to call, who to send.

"You're completely insane," Holden said over Ko's semiconscious weeping.

Maybe he was right.

When, Miller wondered, *does someone stop being human?* There had to be a moment, some decision that you made, and before it, you were one person, and after it, someone else. Walking down through the levels of Eros, Ko's bleeding body slung between him and Holden, Miller reflected. He was probably dying of radiation damage. He was lying his way past half a dozen men who were only letting him by because they were used to people being scared of them and he wasn't. He had killed three people in the last two hours. Four if he counted Ko. Probably safer to say four, then.

The analytical part of his mind, the small, still voice he had cultivated for years, watched him move and replayed all his decisions. Everything he'd done had made perfect sense at the time. Shooting Ko. Shooting the other three. Leaving the safety of the crew's hideout to investigate the evacuation. Emotionally, it had all been obvious at the time. It was only when he considered it from outside that it seemed dangerous. If he'd seen it in someone else—Muss, Havelock, Sematimba—he wouldn't have taken more than a minute to realize they'd gone off the rails. Since it was him, he had taken longer to notice. But Holden was right. Somewhere along the line, he'd lost himself.

He wanted to think it had been finding Julie, seeing what had happened to her body, knowing he hadn't been able to save her, but that was only because it seemed like the sentimental moment. The truth was his decisions before then—leaving Ceres to go on a wild hunt for Julie, drinking himself out of a career, remaining a cop for even a day after that first kill all those years earlier—none of them seemed to make sense, viewed objectively. He'd lost a marriage to a woman he'd loved once. He'd lived hip deep in the worst humanity had to offer. He'd learned firsthand that he was capable of killing another human being. And nowhere along the line could he say that there, at that moment, he had been a sane, whole man, and that afterward, he hadn't.

Maybe it was a cumulative process, like smoking cigarettes. One didn't do much. Five didn't do much more. Every emotion he'd shut down, every human contact he'd spurned, every love and friendship and moment of compassion from which he'd turned had taken him a degree away from himself. Until now, he'd been able to kill men with impunity. To face his impending death with a denial that let him make plans and take action.

In his mind, Julie Mao tilted her head, listening to his thoughts. In his mind, she held him, her body against his in a way that was more comforting than erotic. Consoling. Forgiving.

This was why he had searched for her. Julie had become the part of him that was capable of human feeling. The symbol of what he could have been if he hadn't been this. There was no reason to think his imagined Julie had anything in common with the real woman. Meeting her would have been a disappointment for them both.

He had to believe that, the same way he'd had to believe everything that had cut him off from love before.

Holden stopped, the body—corpse now—of Ko tugging Miller back to himself.

"What?" Miller said.

Holden nodded at the access panel in front of them. Miller looked at it, uncomprehending, and then recognized it. They'd made it. They were back at the hideout.

"Are you all right?" Holden said.

"Yeah," Miller said. "Just woolgathering. Sorry."

He dropped Ko, and the thug slid to the floor with a sad thud. Miller's arm had fallen asleep. He shook it, but the tingling didn't go away. A wave of vertigo and nausea passed through him. *Symptoms,* he thought.

"How'd we do for time?" Miller asked.

"We're a little past deadline. Five minutes. It'll be fine," Holden said, and slid the door open.

The space beyond, where Naomi and Alex and Amos had been, was empty.

"Fuck me," Holden said.

Chapter Twenty-Nine: Holden

Fuck me," Holden said. And a moment later: "They left us."

No. *She* had left *him*. Naomi had said she would, but confronted with the reality of it, Holden realized that he hadn't really believed her. But here it was—the proof. The empty space where she used to be. His heart hammered and his throat tightened, breath coming in gasps. The sick feeling in his gut was either despair or his colon sloughing off its lining. He was going to die sitting outside a cheap hotel on Eros because Naomi had done exactly what she'd said she would. What he himself had ordered her to do. His resentment refused to listen to reason.

"We're dead," he said, and sat down on the edge of a fern-filled planter.

"How long do we have?" Miller asked, looking up and down the corridor while he fidgeted with his gun.

"No idea," Holden replied, gesturing vaguely at his terminal's flashing red radiation symbol. "Hours before we really start to feel it, I think, but I don't know. God, I wish Shed was still here."

"Shed?"

"Friend of mine," Holden said, not feeling up to elaborating. "Good med tech."

"Call her," Miller said.

Holden looked at his terminal and tapped the screen a few times.

"Network's still down," he said.

"All right," Miller said. "Let's go to your ship. See if it's still in dock."

"They'll be gone. Naomi's keeping the crew alive. She warned me, but I—"

"So let's go anyway," Miller said. He was shifting from one foot to the other and looking down the corridor as he spoke.

"Miller," Holden said, then stopped. Miller was clearly on edge, and he'd shot four people. Holden was increasingly frightened of the former cop. As if reading his mind, Miller stepped close, the two-meter man towering over him where he sat. Miller smiled ruefully, his eyes unnervingly gentle. Holden would almost have preferred they be threatening.

"Way I see it, there's three ways this can go," Miller said. "One, we find your ship still in dock, get the meds we need, and maybe we live. Two, we try to get to the ship, and along the way we run into a bunch of mafia thugs. Die gloriously in a hail of bullets. Three, we sit here and leak out of our eyes and assholes."

Holden said nothing; he just stared up at the cop and frowned.

"I'm liking the first two better than the last one," Miller said. His voice made it sound like an apology. "How about you come with?"

Holden laughed before he could catch himself, but Miller didn't look like he was taking offense.

"Sure," Holden said. "I just needed to feel sorry for myself for a minute. Let's go get killed by the mafia."

He said it with much more bravado than he felt. The truth was he didn't want to die. Even during his time in the navy, the idea of dying in the line of duty had always seemed distant and unreal. *His* ship would never be destroyed, and if it was, *he* would make it to the escape shuttle. The universe without him in it didn't make any sense at all. He'd taken risks; he'd seen other people die. Even people he loved. Now, for the first time, his own death was a real thing.

He looked at the cop. He'd known the man less than a day, didn't trust him, and wasn't sure he much liked him. And this was who he'd die with. Holden shuddered and stood up, pulling his gun out of his waistband. Under the panic and fear, there was a deep feeling of calm. He hoped it would last.

"After you," Holden said. "If we make it, remind me to call my mothers."

The casinos were a powder keg waiting for a match. If the evacuation sweeps had been even moderately successful, there were probably a million or more people crammed into three levels of the station. Hard-looking men in riot gear moved through the crowds, telling everyone to stay put until they were taken to the radiation shelters, keeping the crowd frightened. Every now and then, a small group of citizens would be led away. Knowing where they were going made Holden's stomach burn. He wanted to yell out that the cops were fake, that they were killing people. But a riot with this many people in such a confined space would be a meat grinder. Maybe that was inevitable but he wasn't going to be the one to start it.

Someone else did.

Holden could hear raised voices, the angry rumble of the mob, followed by the electronically amplified voice of someone in a riot helmet yelling for people to get back. And then a gunshot, a brief pause, then a fusillade. People screamed. The entire crowd around Holden and Miller surged in two opposing directions, some of the people rushing toward the sound of the conflict, but many more of them running away from it. Holden spun in the current of bodies; Miller reached out and grabbed the back of his shirt, gripping it in his fist and yelling for Holden to stay close.

About a dozen meters down the corridor, in a coffee shop seating area separated by a waist-high black iron fence, one of the mafia thugs had been cut off from his group by a dozen citizens. Gun drawn, he was backing up and yelling at them to move aside. They kept advancing, their faces wild with the drunken frenzy of mob violence.

The mafia thug fired once, and one small body staggered forward, then fell to the ground at the thug's feet. Holden couldn't tell if it was a boy or a girl, but they couldn't be more than thirteen or fourteen years old. The thug moved forward, looking down at the small thin figure at his feet, and pointed his gun at them again.

It was too much.

Holden found himself running down the corridor toward the thug, gun drawn and screaming for people to get out of the way. When he was about seven meters away, the crowd split apart enough for him to begin firing. Half his shots went wild, hitting the coffee shop counter and walls, one round blowing a stack of ceramic plates into the air. But a few of them hit the thug, staggering him back.

Holden vaulted the waist-high metal fence and came to a sliding halt about three meters from the fake cop and his victim. Holden's gun fired one last time and then the slide locked in the open position to let him know it was empty.

The thug didn't fall down. He straightened up, looked down at his torso, and then looked up and pointed his gun at Holden's face. Holden had time to count the three bullets that were smashed against the heavy chest armor of the thug's riot gear. *Die gloriously in a hail of bullets,* he thought.

The thug said, "Stupid mother fu—" and his head snapped back in a spray of red. He slumped to the floor.

"Gap at the neck, remember?" Miller said from behind him. "Chest armor's too thick for a pistol."

Suddenly dizzy, Holden bent over at the waist, gasping for air. He tasted lemon at the back of his throat and swallowed twice to stop himself from throwing up. He was afraid it would be full of blood and stomach lining. He didn't need to see that.

"Thanks," he gasped out, turning his head toward Miller.

Miller just nodded vaguely in his direction, then walked over to the guard and nudged him with one foot. Holden stood up and looked around the corridor, waiting for the inevitable wave of vengeful mafia enforcers to come crashing down on them. He didn't see any. He and Miller were standing in a quiet island of calm in the midst of Armageddon. All around them, tendrils of violence were whipping into high gear. People were running in every direction; the mafia goons were yelling in booming amplified voices and punctuating the threats with periodic gunfire. But there were only hundreds of them, and there were many thousands of angry and panicked civilians. Miller gestured at the chaos.

"This is what happens," he said. "Give a bunch of yahoos the equipment, and they think they know what they're doing."

Holden crouched beside the fallen child. It was a boy, maybe thirteen, with Asian features and dark hair. His chest had a gaping wound in it, blood trickling out instead of gushing. He didn't have a pulse that Holden could find. Holden picked him up anyway, looking around for someplace to take him.

"He's dead," Miller said as he replaced the cartridge he'd fired.

"Go to hell. We don't know. If we can get him to the ship, maybe..."

Miller shook his head, a sad but distant expression on his face as he looked at the child in Holden's arms.

"He took high-caliber round to the center of mass," Miller said. "He's gone."

"Fuck me," Holden said.

"You keep saying that."

A bright neon sign flashed above the corridor that led out of the casino levels and onto the ramps down to the docks. THANK YOU FOR PLAYING, it read. And YOU'RE ALWAYS A WINNER ON EROS. Below it, two ranks of men in heavy combat armor blocked the way. They might have given up on crowd control in the casinos, but they weren't letting anyone go.

Holden and Miller crouched behind an overturned coffee cart a hundred meters from the soldiers. As they watched, a dozen or so people made a dash toward the guards and were summarily mowed down by machine gun fire, then fell to the deck beside those who had tried before.

"I count thirty-four of them," Miller said. "How many can you handle?"

Holden spun to look at him in surprise, but Miller's face told him the former cop was joking.

"Kidding aside, how *do* we get past that?" Holden said.

"Thirty men with machine guns and a clear line of sight. No cover to speak of for the last twenty meters or so," Miller said. "We don't get past that."

Chapter Thirty: Miller

They sat on the floor with their backs to a bank of pachinko machines no one was playing, watching the ebb and flow of the violence around them like it was a soccer game. Miller's hat was perched on his bent knee. He felt the vibration against his back when one of the displays cycled through its dupe-call. The lights glittered and glowed. Holden, beside him, was breathing hard, like he'd run a race. Out beyond them, like something from Hieronymus Bosch, the casino levels of Eros prepared for death.

The riot's momentum had spent itself for now. Men and women gathered together in small groups. Guards strode through, threatening and scattering any bunch that got too large or unruly. Something was burning fast enough that the air scrubbers couldn't get out the smell of melting plastic. The bhangra Muzak mixed with weeping and screaming and wails of despair. Some idiot was shouting at one of the so-called cops: he was a lawyer; he was getting all of this on video; whoever was responsible was going to be in big trouble. Miller watched a bunch of people start to gather around the confrontation. The guy in the riot gear listened, nodded, and shot the lawyer once in the kneecap. The crowd dispersed except for one woman, the lawyer's wife or girlfriend, bent down over him screaming. And in the privacy of Miller's skull, everything slowly fell apart.

He was aware of having two different minds. One was the Miller he was used to, familiar with. The one who was thinking about what was going to happen when he got out, what the next step would be in connecting the dots between Phoebe Station, Ceres, Eros, and Juliette Mao, how to work the case. That version of him was scanning the crowd the way he might have watched the line at a crime scene, waiting for some detail, some change to catch his attention. Send him in the right direction to solve the mystery. It was the shortsighted, idiotic part of him that couldn't conceive of his own personal extinction, and it thought surely, *surely* there was going to be an after.

The other Miller was different. Quieter. Sad, maybe, but at peace. He'd read a poem many years before called "The Death-Self," and he hadn't understood the term until now. A knot at the middle of his psyche was untying. All the energy he'd put into holding things together—Ceres, his marriage, his career, himself—was coming free. He'd shot and killed more men in the past day than in his whole career as a cop. He'd started—only started—to realize that he'd actually fallen in love with the object of his search after he knew for certain that he'd lost her. He'd seen unequivocally that the chaos he'd dedicated his life to holding at bay was stronger and wider and more powerful than he would ever be. No compromise he could make would be enough. His death-self was unfolding in him, and the dark blooming took no effort. It was a relief, a relaxation, a long, slow exhale after decades of holding it in.

He was in ruins, but it was okay, because he was dying.

"Hey," Holden said. His voice was stronger than Miller had expected it might be.

"Yeah?"

"Did you ever watch *Misko and Marisko* when you were a kid?"

Miller frowned. "The kids' show?" he asked.

"The one with the five dinosaurs and the evil guy in the big pink hat," Holden said, then starting humming a bright, boppy tune. Miller closed his eyes and then started singing along. The music had had words once. Now it was only a series of rises and falls, runs up and down a major scale, with every dissonance resolved in the note that followed.

"Guess I must have," Miller said when they reached the end.

"I loved that show. I must have been eight or nine last time I saw it," Holden said. "Funny how that stuff stays with you."

"Yeah," Miller said. He coughed, turned his head, and spat out something red. "How are you holding together?"

"I think I'm okay," Holden said. Then, a moment later, he added, "As long as I don't stand up."

"Nauseated?"

"Yeah, some."

"Me too."

"What is this?" Holden asked. "I mean, what the hell is this all about? Why are they *doing* this?"

It was a fair question. Slaughtering Eros—slaughtering any station in the Belt—was a pretty easy job. Anyone with first-year orbital mechanics skills could find a way to sling a rock big enough and fast enough to crack the station open. With the effort Protogen had put in, they could have killed the air supply or drugged it or whatever the hell they wanted to do. This wasn't a murder. This wasn't even a genocide.

And then there was all the observation equipment. Cameras, communications arrays, air and water sensors. There were only two reasons for that kind of shit. Either the mad bastards at Protogen got off on watching people die, or...

"They don't know," Miller said.

"What?"

He turned to look at Holden. The first Miller, the detective, the optimist, the one who needed to know, was driving now. His death-self didn't fight, because of course it didn't. It didn't fight anything. Miller raised his hand, like he was giving a lecture to a rookie.

"They don't know what it's about, or... you know, at least they don't know what's going to happen. This isn't even built like a torture chamber. It's all being watched, right? Water and air sensors. It's a petri dish. They don't know what that shit that killed Julie does, and this is how they're finding out."

Holden frowned.

"Don't they have laboratories? Places where you could maybe put that crap on some animals or something? Because as experimental design goes, this seems a little messed up."

"Maybe they need a really big sample size," Miller said. "Or maybe it's not about the people. Maybe it's about what happens to the station."

"There's a cheery thought," Holden said.

The Julie Mao in Miller's mind brushed a lock of hair out of her eyes. She was frowning, looking thoughtful, interested, concerned. It all had to make sense. It was like one of those basic orbital mechanics problems where every hitch and veer seemed random until all the variables slipped into place. What had been inexplicable became inevitable. Julie smiled at him. Julie as she had been. As he imagined she had been. The Miller who hadn't resigned himself to death smiled back. And then she was gone, his mind shifting to the noise from the pachinko machines and the low, demonic wailing of the crowds.

Another group—twenty men hunkered low, like linebackers—made a rush toward the mercenaries guarding the opening to the port. The gunmen mowed them down.

"If we had enough people," Holden said after the sound of machine guns fell away, "we could make it. They couldn't kill all of us."

"That's what the patrol goons are for," Miller said. "Make sure no one can organize a big enough push. Keep stirring the pot."

"But if it was a mob, I mean a really big mob, it could..."

"Maybe," Miller agreed. Something in his chest clicked in a way it hadn't a minute before. He took a slow, deep breath, and the click happened again. He could feel it deep in his left lung.

"At least Naomi got away," Holden said.

"That is good."

"She's amazing. She'd never put Amos and Alex in danger if she could help it. I mean, she's serious. Professional. Strong, you know? I mean, she's really, really..."

"Pretty, too," Miller said. "Great hair. Love the eyes."

"No, that wasn't what I meant," Holden said.

"You don't think she's a good-looking woman?"

"She's my XO," Holden said. "She's...you know..."

"Off-limits."

Holden sighed.

"She got away, didn't she?" Holden asked.

"Almost for sure."

They were silent. One of the linebackers coughed, stood up, and limped back into the casino, trailing blood from a hole in his ribs. The bhangra gave way to an afropop medley with a low, sultry voice singing in languages Miller didn't know.

"She'd wait for us," Holden said. "Don't you think she'd wait for us?"

"Almost for sure," Miller's death-self said, not particularly caring if it was a lie. He thought about it for a long moment, then turned to face Holden again. "Hey. Just so you know it? I'm not exactly at my best right now."

"Okay."

"All right."

The glowing orange lockdown lights on the tube station across the level clicked to green. Miller sat forward, interested. His back felt sticky, but it was probably just sweat. Other people had noticed the change too. Like a current in a water tank, the attention of the nearby crowds shifted from the mercenaries blocking the way to the port to the brushed-steel doors of the tube station.

The doors opened, and the first zombies appeared. Men and women, their eyes glassy and their muscles slack, stumbled out through the open doors. Miller had seen a documentary feed about hemorrhagic fevers as part of his training on Ceres Station. Their movements were the same: listless, driven, autonomic. Like rabid dogs whose minds had already been given over to their disease.

"Hey," Miller said, his hand on Holden's shoulder. "Hey, it's happening."

An older man in a pair of emergency services scrubs approached the shambling newcomers. His hands were out before him, as if he could corral them by simple force of will. The first zombie in the pack turned empty eyes toward him and vomited up a spray of very familiar brown goo.

"Look," Holden said.

"I saw."

"No, *look*!"

All down the casino level, tube station lights were going off lockdown. Doors were opening. The people were pulsing toward the open tubes and the implicit, empty promise of escape, and away from the dead men and women walking out from them.

"Vomit zombies," Miller said.

"From the rad shelters," Holden said. "The thing, the organism. It goes faster in radiation, right? That's why what's-her-name was so freaky about the lights and the vac suit."

"Her name's Julie. And yeah. Those incubators were for this. Right here," Miller said, and sighed. He thought about standing up. "Well. We may not die of radiation poisoning after all."

"Why not just pump that shit into the air?" Holden asked.

"Anaerobic, remember?" Miller said. "Too much oxygen kills 'em."

The vomit-covered emergency medicine guy was still trying to treat the shambling zombies like they were patients. Like they were still humans. There were smears of the brown goo on people's clothes, on the walls. The tube doors opened again, and Miller saw half a dozen people dodge into a tube car coated in brown. The mob churned, unsure what to do, the group mind stretched past its breaking point.

A riot cop jumped forward and started spraying down the zombies with gunfire. The entrance and exit wounds spilled out fine loops of black filament, and the zombies went down. Miller chuckled even before he knew what was funny. Holden looked at him.

"They didn't know," Miller said. "The bully boys in riot gear? They aren't gonna get pulled out. Meat for the machine, just like the rest of us."

Holden made a small approving sound. Miller nodded, but something was niggling at the back of his mind. The thugs from Ceres in their stolen armor were being sacrificed. That didn't mean everyone was. He leaned forward.

The archway leading to the port was still manned. Mercenary fighters in formation, guns at the ready. If anything, they looked more disciplined now than they had before. Miller watched as the guy in the back with extra insignia on his armor barked into a mic.

Miller had thought hope was dead. He'd thought all his chances had been played, and then, like a bitch, it all hauled itself up out of the grave.

"Get up," Miller said.

"What?"

"Get up. They're going to pull back."

"Who?"

Miller nodded at the mercenaries.

"They knew," he said. "Look at them. They aren't freaking out. They aren't confused. They were waiting for this."

"And you think that means they'll fall back?"

"They aren't going to be hanging out. Stand up."

Almost as if he'd been giving the order to himself, Miller groaned and creaked to his feet. His knees and spine ached badly. The click in his lung was getting worse. His belly made a soft, complicated noise that would have been concerning under different circumstances. As soon as he started moving, he could feel how far the damage had gone, his skin not yet in pain but in the soft presentiment of it, like the gap between a serious burn and the blisters that followed. If he lived, it was going to hurt.

If he lived, *everything* was going to hurt.

His death-self tugged at him. The sense of release, of relief, of *rest* felt like something precious being lost. Even while the chattering, busy, machinelike mind kept grinding, grinding, grinding forward, the soft, bruised center of Miller's soul urged him to pause, sit back down, let the problems go away.

"What are we looking for?" Holden said. He'd stood up. A blood vessel in the man's left eye had given way, the white of the sclera turning a bright, meaty red.

What are we looking for? the death-self echoed.

"They're going to fall back," Miller said, answering the first question. "We follow. Just outside the range so whoever's going last doesn't feel like he has to shoot us."

"Isn't everyone going to do the same thing? I mean, once they're gone, isn't everyone in this place going to head in for the port?"

"I expect so," Miller said. "So let's try to slip in ahead of the rush. Look. There."

It wasn't much. Just a change in the mercenaries' stance, a shift in their collective center of gravity. Miller coughed. It hurt more than it should have.

What are we looking for? his death-self asked again, its voice more insistent. *An answer? Justice? Another chance for the universe to kick us in the balls? What is through that archway that there isn't a faster, cleaner, less painful version of in the barrel of our gun?*

The mercenary captain took a casual step back and strode down the exterior corridor and out of sight. Where he had been, Julie Mao sat, watching him go. She looked at Miller. She waved him on.

"Not yet," he said.

"When?" Holden said, his voice surprising Miller. Julie in his head flickered out, and he was back in the real world.

"It's coming," Miller said.

He should warn the guy. It was only fair. You got into a bad place, and at the very least, you owed your partner the courtesy of letting him know. Miller cleared his throat. That hurt too.

It's possible I may start hallucinating or become suicidal. You might have to shoot me.

Holden glanced over at him. The pachinko machines lit them blue and green and shrieked in artificial delight.

"What?" Holden said.

"Nothing. Getting my balance," Miller said.

Behind them, a woman shouted. Miller glanced back to see her pushing a vomit zombie away, a slick of brown goo already covering the live woman. At the archway, the mercenaries quietly stepped back and started down the corridor.

"Come on," Miller said.

He and Holden walked toward the archway, Miller pulling his hat on. Loud voices, screams, the low, liquid sound of people being violently ill. The air scrubbers were failing, the air taking on a deep, pungent odor like beef broth and acid. Miller felt like there was a stone in his shoe, but he was almost certain if he looked, there would be only a point of redness where his skin was starting to break down.

No one shot at them. No one told them to stop.

At the archway, Miller led Holden against the wall, then ducked his head around the corner. A quarter second was all it took to know the long, wide corridor was empty. The mercs were done here and leaving Eros to its fate. The window was open. The way was clear.

Last chance, he thought, and he meant both the last chance to live and the last one to die.

"Miller?"

"Yeah," he said. "It looks good. Come on. Before everyone gets the idea."

Chapter Thirty-One: Holden

Something was moving in Holden's gut. He ignored it and kept his eyes on Miller's back. The lanky detective barreled down the corridor toward the port, stopping occasionally at junctions to peek around the corner and look for trouble. Miller had become a machine. All Holden could do was try to keep up.

Always the same distance ahead were the mercenaries who'd been guarding the exit from the casino. When they moved, Miller moved. When they slowed down, he slowed. They were clearing a path to the port, but if they thought that any of the citizens were getting too close, they'd probably open fire. They were definitely shooting anyone they ran into along the way. They'd already shot two people who'd run at them. Both had been vomiting brown goo. *Where the hell did those vomit zombies come from so fast?*

"Where the hell did those vomit zombies come from so fast?" he said to Miller's back.

The detective shrugged with his left hand, his right still clutching his pistol.

"I don't think enough of that crap came out of Julie to infect the whole station," he replied without slowing down. "I'm guessing they were the first batch. The ones they incubated to get enough goo to infect the shelters with."

That made sense. And when the controlled portion of the experiment went to shit, you just turned them loose on the populace. By the time people figured out what was going on, half of them were infected already. Then it was just a matter of time.

They paused briefly at a corridor intersection, watching as the leader of the merc group stopped a hundred meters ahead and talked on his radio for a minute. Holden was gasping and trying to catch his breath when the group started up again, and Miller moved to follow. He reached out and grabbed the detective's belt and let Miller drag him along. Where did the skinny Belter keep this reserve of energy?

The detective stopped. His expression was blank.

"They're arguing," Miller said.

"Huh?"

"The leader of that group and some of the men. Arguing about something," Miller replied.

"So?" Holden asked, then coughed something wet into his hand. He wiped it off on the back of his pants, not looking to see if it was blood. *Please don't let it be blood.*

Miller shrugged with his hand again.

"I don't think everyone's on the same team here," he said.

The merc group turned down another corridor, and Miller followed, yanking Holden along behind him. These were the outer levels, filled with warehouse space and ship repair and resupply depots. They didn't see a lot of foot traffic at the best of times. Now the corridor echoed like a mausoleum with their footsteps. Up ahead, the merc group turned again, and before Miller and Holden could reach the junction, a lone figure wandered into view.

He didn't appear to be armed, so Miller moved toward him

cautiously, impatiently reaching behind himself and pulling Holden's hand off his belt. Once he was free, Miller held up his left hand in an unmistakably cop-like gesture.

"This is a dangerous place to be wandering around, sir," he said.

The man was now less than fifteen meters ahead of them and began moving toward them at a lurch. He was dressed for a party in a cheap tuxedo with a frilly shirt and sparkly red bow tie. He was wearing one shiny black shoe, the other foot covered with only a red sock. Brown vomit trickled from the corners of his mouth and stained the front of his white shirt.

"Shit," Miller said, and brought up his gun.

Holden grabbed his arm and yanked it back down.

"He's innocent in this," Holden said, the sight of the injured and infected man making his eyes burn. "He's innocent."

"He's still coming," Miller said.

"So walk faster," Holden said. "And if you shoot anyone else and I haven't given you permission to, you don't get a ride on my ship. Got me?"

"Trust me," Miller said. "Dying is the best thing that could happen to that guy today. You're not doing him any favors."

"You don't get to decide that," Holden replied, his tone edging into real anger.

Miller started to reply, but Holden held up one hand and cut him off.

"You want on the *Roci*? I'm the boss, then. No questions, no bullshit."

Miller's smirk turned into a smile. "Yes, sir," he said. "Our mercs are getting ahead of us." He pointed down the corridor.

Miller nodded and moved off again at his steady, machinelike pace. Holden didn't turn around, but he could hear the man Miller had almost shot crying in the corridor behind him for a long time. To cover up the sound, which probably existed only in his head once they'd made a couple more turns in the corridor, he began humming the theme to *Misko and Marisko* again.

Mother Elise, who'd been the one to stay home with him when he was very young, had always brought him something to eat while he watched, and then sat by him with her hand on his head, playing with his hair. She'd laughed at the dinosaur antics even harder than he had. One Halloween she'd made him a big pink hat to wear so that he could be the evil Count Mungo. Why had that guy been trying to capture the dinosaurs, anyway? It had never really been clear. Maybe he just liked dinosaurs. One time he'd used a shrink ray and—

Holden slammed into Miller's back. The detective had stopped suddenly and now moved quickly to one side of the corridor, crouching low to keep himself in the shadows. Holden followed suit. About thirty meters ahead, the mercenary group had gotten much bigger and had split into two factions.

"Yep," Miller said. "Whole lot of people having really bad days today."

Holden nodded and wiped something wet off his face. It was blood. He didn't think he'd hit Miller's back hard enough to bloody his nose, and he had a suspicion it wasn't going to stop on its own. Mucous membranes getting fragile. Wasn't that part of radiation burning? He tore strips off his shirt and stuffed them up his nostrils while he watched the scene at the end of the corridor.

There were two clear groups, and they did seem to be engaged in some sort of heated argument. Normally, that would have been fine. Holden didn't care about the social lives of mercenaries. But these mercenaries numbered by this time close to a hundred, were heavily armed, and blocked the corridor that led to his ship. That made their argument worth watching.

"Not everyone from Protogen left, I think," Miller said quietly, pointing at one of the two groups. "Those guys on the right don't look like the home team."

Holden looked at the group and nodded. They were definitely the more professional-looking soldiers. Their armor fit well. The other group looked like it was largely made up of guys dressed in police riot gear, with only a few men in combat armor.

"Want to guess what the argument is about?" Miller asked.

"Hey, can we have a ride too?" Holden said mockingly with a Ceres accent. *"Uh, no, we need you guys to stay here and, uh, keep an eye on things, which we promise will be* totally *safe and* absolutely not *involve you turning into vomit zombies."*

He actually got a chuckle from Miller and then the corridor erupted in a barrage of gunfire. Both sides of the discussion were firing automatic weapons at each other from point-blank range. The noise was deafening. Men screamed and flew apart, spraying the corridor and each other with blood and body parts. Holden dropped flat to the floor but continued watching the firefight.

After the initial barrage, the survivors from both groups began falling back in opposite directions, still firing as they moved. The floor at the corridor junction was littered with bodies. Holden estimated that twenty or more men had died in that first second of the fight. The sounds of gunfire grew more distant as the two groups fired at each other down the corridor.

In the middle of the junction, one of the bodies on the floor suddenly stirred and raised its head. Even before the wounded man could get to his feet, a bullet hole appeared in the middle of his face shield and he dropped back to the floor with limp finality.

"Where's your ship?" Miller asked.

"The lift is at the end of this corridor," Holden replied.

Miller spat what looked like bloody phlegm on the floor.

"And the corridor that crosses it is now a war zone, with armed camps sniping at each other from both sides," he said. "I guess we could try just running through it."

"Is there another option?" Holden asked.

Miller looked at his terminal.

"We're fifty-three minutes past the deadline Naomi set," he said. "How much more time do you want to waste?"

"Look, I was never particularly good at math," Holden said. "But I'd guess there are as many as forty guys in either direction down that other corridor. A corridor which is a good three, maybe three and a half meters wide. Which means that we give eighty guys three meters worth of shots at us. Even dumb luck means we get hit a lot and then die. Let's think of a plan B."

As if to underline his argument, another fusillade broke out in the cross corridor, gouging chunks out of the rubbery wall insulation and chewing up the bodies lying on the floor.

"They're still withdrawing," Miller said. "Those shots came from farther away. I guess we can just wait them out. I mean, if we can."

The rags Holden had stuffed up his nose hadn't stopped the bleeding; they had just dammed it up. He could feel a steady trickle down the back of his throat that made his stomach heave with nausea. Miller was right. They were getting down to the last of their ability to wait anyone out at this point.

"Goddamn, I wish we could call and see if Naomi is even there," Holden said, looking at the flashing *Network Not Available* on his terminal.

"Shhh," Miller whispered, putting one finger on his lips. He pointed back down the corridor in the direction they'd come, and now Holden could hear heavy footsteps approaching.

"Late guests to the party," Miller said, and Holden nodded. The two men swiveled around, pointing their guns down the corridor and waiting.

A group of four men in police riot armor rounded the corner. They didn't have their guns out, and two of them had their helmets off. Apparently they hadn't heard about the new hostilities. Holden waited for Miller to fire and, when he didn't, turned to look at him. Miller was staring back.

"I didn't dress real warm," Miller said, almost apologetically. It took Holden half a second to understand what he meant.

Holden gave him permission by shooting first. He targeted one of the mafia thugs without a helmet and shot him in the face, then continued firing at the group until his gun's slide locked open when the magazine was empty. Miller had begun firing a split second after Holden's first shot and also fired until his gun was empty. When it was over, all four thugs were lying facedown in the corridor. Holden let out a long breath that turned into a sigh, and sat down on the floor.

Miller walked to the fallen men and nudged each one in turn with his foot as he replaced the magazine in his gun. Holden didn't bother reloading his. He was done with gunfights. He put the empty pistol in his pocket and got up to join the cop. He bent down and began unbuckling the least damaged armor he could find. Miller raised an eyebrow but didn't move to help.

"We're making a run for it," Holden said, swallowing back the vomit-and-blood taste in his throat as he pulled the chest and back armor free of the first man. "But maybe if we wear this stuff, it will help."

"Might," Miller said with a nod, then knelt down to help strip a second man.

Holden put on the dead man's armor, working hard to believe that the pink trail down the back was absolutely not part of the man's brain. Undoing the straps was exhausting. His fingers felt numb and awkward. He picked up the thigh armor, then put it down again. He'd rather run fast. Miller had finished buckling his on too and picked up one of the undamaged helmets. Holden found one with just a dent in it and slipped it onto his head. It felt greasy inside, and he was glad he had no sense of smell. He suspected that its previous occupant hadn't bathed often.

Miller fiddled with the side of his helmet until the radio came on. The cop's voice was echoed a split second later over the helmet's tinny speakers as he said, "Hey, we're coming out into the corridor! Don't shoot! We're coming to join up!"

Thumbing off the mic, he turned to Holden and said, "Well, maybe one side won't be shooting at us now."

They moved back down the corridor and stopped ten meters from the intersection. Holden counted down from three and then took off at the best run he could manage. It was dishearteningly slow; his legs felt like they were filled with lead. Like he was running in a pool of water. Like he was in a nightmare. He could hear

Miller just behind him, his shoes slapping on the concrete floor, his breath coming in ragged gasps.

Then he heard only the sound of gunfire. He couldn't tell if Miller's plan had worked. Couldn't tell which direction the gunfire was coming from. It was constant and deafening and started the instant he entered the cross corridor. When he was three meters from the other side, he lowered his head and jumped forward. In Eros' light gravity, he seemed to fly, and he was nearly to the other side when a burst of bullets caught him in the armor over his ribs and slammed him into the corridor wall with a spine-jarring crack. He dragged himself the rest of the way as bullets continued to hit all around his legs, one of them passing through the meaty part of his calf.

Miller tripped over him, flying a few feet farther down the hall and then collapsing in a heap. Holden crawled to his side.

"Still alive?"

Miller nodded. "Got shot. Arm's broke. Keep moving," he gasped out.

Holden climbed to his feet, his left leg feeling like it was on fire as the muscle in his calf clenched around his gaping wound. He pulled Miller up and then leaned on him as they limped toward the elevator. Miller's left arm was dangling boneless at his side, and blood was pouring off his hand.

Holden punched the button to call the lift, and he and Miller leaned on each other while they waited. He hummed the *Misko and Marisko* theme to himself, and after a few seconds, Miller started too.

Holden punched the button for the *Rocinante*'s berth and waited for the elevator to stop at a blank gray airlock door with no ship beyond it. That would be when he finally had permission to lie down on the floor and die. He looked forward to that moment when his exertions could end with a relief that would have surprised him if he'd still been capable of surprise. Miller let go of him and slid down the lift wall, leaving a blood trail on the shiny metal and ending in a pile on the floor. The man's eyes were closed.

He could almost have been sleeping. Holden watched the detective's chest rise and fall in ragged, painful breaths that grew smoother and more shallow.

Holden envied him, but he had to see that closed airlock door before he could lie down. He began to feel faintly angry with the elevator for taking so long.

It stopped, lift doors sliding open with a cheerful ding.

Amos stood in the airlock on the other side, an assault rifle in each hand and two belts of magazines for the rifles slung on his shoulders. He looked Holden up and down once, then glanced over to Miller and back again.

"Jesus, Captain, you look like shit."

Chapter Thirty-Two: Miller

Miller's mind reassembled slowly and with several false starts. In his dreams, he was fitting a puzzle together as the pieces kept changing shape, and each time, just as he was on the verge of slipping the whole mechanism together, the dream began again. The first thing he became aware of was the ache at the small of his back, then the heaviness of his arms and legs, then the nausea. The nearer he came to consciousness, the more he tried to postpone it. Imaginary fingers tried to complete the puzzle, and before he could make it all fit, his eyes opened.

He couldn't move his head. Something was in his neck: a thick bundle of black tubes reaching out of him and up past the limits of his vision. He tried to lift his arms, to push the invading, vampiric thing away, but he couldn't.

It got me, he thought with a thrill of fear. *I'm infected.*

The woman appeared from his left. He was surprised she wasn't

Julie. Deep brown skin, dark eyes with just a hint of an epicanthic fold. She smiled at him. Black hair draped down the side of her face.

Down. There was a *down.* There was gravity. They were under thrust. That seemed very important, but he didn't know why.

"Hey, Detective," Naomi said. "Welcome back."

Where am I? he tried to say. His throat felt solid. Crowded like too many people in a tube station.

"Don't try to get up or talk or anything," she said. "You've been under for about thirty-six hours. Good news is we have a sick bay with a military-grade expert system and supplies for fifteen Martian soldiers. I think we burned half of what we've got on you and the captain."

The captain. Holden. That was right. They'd been in a fight. There had been a corridor and people shooting. And someone had been sick. He remembered a woman, covered in brown vomit, with vacant eyes, but he didn't know whether it was part of a nightmare.

Naomi was still talking. Something about full plasma flushes and cell damage. He tried to lift a hand, to reach out to her, but a strap restrained him. The ache in his back was his kidneys, and he wondered what exactly was getting filtered out of his blood. Miller closed his eyes, asleep before he could decide whether to rest.

No dreams troubled him this time. He roused again when something deep in his throat shifted, pulled at his larynx, and retreated. Without opening his eyes, he rolled to his side, coughed, puked, and rolled back.

When he woke, he was breathing on his own. His throat felt sore and abused, but his hands weren't tied down. Drainage tubes ran out of his belly and side, and there was a catheter the size of a pencil coming out his penis. Nothing particularly hurt, so he had to assume he was on pretty nearly all the narcotics there were. His clothes were gone, his modesty preserved only by a thin paper gown and a cast that held his left arm stony and immovable. Someone had put his hat on the next bed over.

The sick bay, now that he could see it, looked like a ward on a high-production entertainment feed. It wasn't a hospital; it was the matte-black-and-silver idea of what a hospital was supposed to be. The monitors hung suspended in the air on complex armatures, reporting his blood pressure, nucleic acid concentrations, oxygenation, fluid balance. There were two separate countdowns running, one to the next round of autophagics, the other for pain medication. And across the aisle, at another station, Holden's statistics looked more or less the same.

Holden looked like a ghost. His skin was pale and his sclera were red with a hundred little hemorrhages. His face was puffy from steroids.

"Hey," Miller said.

Holden lifted a hand, waving gently.

"We made it," Miller said. His voice sounded like it had been dragged down an alley by its ankles.

"Yeah," Holden said.

"That was ugly."

"Yeah."

Miller nodded. That had taken all the energy he had. He lay back down and fell, if not asleep, at least unconscious. Just before his mind flickered back into forgetfulness, he smiled. He'd made it. He was on Holden's ship. And they were going to find whatever Julie had left behind for them.

Voices woke him.

"Maybe you shouldn't, then."

It was the woman. Naomi. Part of Miller cursed her for disturbing him, but there was a buzz in her voice—not fear or anger, but close enough to be interesting. He didn't move, didn't even swim all the way back to awareness. But he listened.

"I need to," Holden said. He sounded phlegmy, like someone who needed to cough. "What happened on Eros…it's put a lot of things in perspective. I've been holding something back."

"Captain—"

"No, hear me out. When I was in there thinking that all I was going to have left was half an hour of rigged pachinko games and then death…when that happened, I knew what my regrets were. You know? I felt all the things that I wished I'd done and never had the courage for. Now that I know, I can't just ignore it. I can't pretend it isn't there."

"Captain," Naomi said again, and the buzz in her voice was stronger.

Don't say it, you poor bastard, Miller thought.

"I'm in love with you, Naomi," Holden said.

The pause lasted no longer than a heartbeat.

"No, sir," she said. "You aren't."

"I am. I know what you're thinking. I've been through this big traumatic experience and I'm doing the whole thing where I want to affirm life and make connections, and maybe some of that's part of it. But you have to believe that I know what I feel. And when I was down there, I knew that the thing that I wanted the most was to get back to you."

"Captain. How long have we served together?"

"What? I don't know exactly…"

"Ballpark estimate."

"Eight and a half runs makes it almost five years," Holden said. Miller could hear the confusion in his voice.

"All right. And in that time, how many of the crew did you share bunks with?"

"Does it matter?"

"Only a little."

"A few."

"More than a dozen?"

"No," he said, but he didn't sound sure.

"Let's call it ten," Naomi said.

"Okay. But this is different. I'm not talking about having a little shipboard romance to pass the time. Ever since—"

Miller imagined the woman holding up her hand or taking Holden's or maybe just glaring at him. Something to stop the flow of words.

"And do you know when I fell for you, sir?"

Sorrow. That was what the strain in her voice was. Sorrow. Disappointment. Regret.

"When...when you..."

"I can tell you the day," Naomi said. "You were about seven weeks into that first run. I was still smarting that some Earther had come in from out of the ecliptic and taken my XO job. I didn't like you much right at the start. You were too charming, too pretty, and too damn comfortable in my chair. But there was a poker game in the engine room. You and me and those two Luna boys out of engineering and Kamala Trask. You remember Trask?"

"She was the comm tech. The one who was..."

"Built like a refrigerator? Face like a bulldog puppy?"

"I remember her."

"She had the biggest crush on you. Used to cry herself to sleep at night all through that run. She wasn't in that game because she cared about poker. She just wanted to breathe some of your air, and everyone knew it. Even you. And all that night, I watched you and her, and you never once led her along. You never gave her any reason to think she had a chance with you. And you still treated her with respect. That was the first time I thought you might be a decent XO, and it was the first time I wished that I could be the girl in your bunk at shift's end."

"Because of Trask?"

"That and you've got a great ass, sir. My point is we flew together for four years and more. And I would have come along with you any day of that if you'd asked me."

"I didn't know," Holden said. He sounded a little strangled.

"You didn't ask. You always had your sights set someplace else. And, honestly, I think Belter women just put you off. Until the *Cant*...Until it was just the five of us. I've seen you looking at me. I know exactly what those looks mean, because I spent four years on the other side of them. But I only got your attention when I was the only female on board, and that's not good enough for me."

"I don't know—"

"No, sir, you don't. That's my point. I've watched you seduce a lot of women, and I know how you do it. You get fixed on her, you get excited by her. Then you convince yourself that the two of you have some kind of special connection, and by the time you believe it, she usually thinks it's true too. And then you sleep together for a while, and the connection gets a little faded. One or the other of you says something like *professional* or *appropriate boundaries* or starts worrying what the crew will think, and the whole thing slides away. Afterwards they still like you. All of them. You do it all so well they don't even feel like they get to hate you for it."

"That's not true."

"It is. And until you figure out that you don't have to love everyone you bed down with, I'm never going to know whether you love me or just want to bed down. And I won't sleep with you until *you* know which it is. The smart money isn't on love."

"I was just—"

"If you want to sleep with me," Naomi said, "be honest. Respect me enough for that. Okay?"

Miller coughed. He hadn't meant to, hadn't even been aware he was going to. His belly went tight, his throat clamped down, and he coughed wet and deep. Once he started, it was hard to stop. He sat up, eyes watering from the effort. Holden was lying back on his bed. Naomi sat on the next bed over, smiling like there had been nothing to overhear. Holden's monitors showed an elevated heart rate and blood pressure. Miller could only hope the poor bastard hadn't gotten an erection with the catheter still in.

"Hey, Detective," Naomi said. "How're you feeling?"

Miller nodded.

"I've felt worse," he said. Then, a moment later: "No. I haven't. But I'm all right. How bad was it?"

"You're both dead," Naomi said. "Seriously, we had to override the triage filters on both of you more than once. The expert system kept clicking you over into hospice care and shooting you full of morphine."

She said it lightly, but he believed her. He tried to sit up. His body still felt terribly heavy, but he didn't know if it was from weakness or the ship thrust. Holden was quiet, jaw clamped tight. Miller pretended not to notice.

"Long-term estimates?"

"You're both going to need to be checked for new cancers every month for the rest of your lives. The captain has a new implant where his thyroid used to be, since his real one was pretty much cooked down. We had to take out about a foot and a half of your small bowel that wouldn't stop bleeding. You're both going to bruise easy for a while, and if you wanted kids, I hope you have some sperm in a bank someplace, because all your little soldiers have two heads now."

Miller chuckled. His monitors blinked into alarm mode and then back out.

"You sound like you trained as a med tech," he said.

"Nope. Engineer. But I've been reading the printouts every day, so I've got the lingo down. I wish Shed was still here," she said, and sounded sad for the first time.

That was the second time someone had mentioned Shed. There was a story there, but Miller let it drop.

"Hair going to fall out?" he asked.

"Maybe," Naomi said. "The system shot you full of the drugs that are supposed to stop that, but if the follicles die, they die."

"Well. Good thing I've still got my hat. What about Eros?"

Naomi's false light tone failed her.

"It's dead," Holden said from his bed, turning to look at Miller. "I think we were the last ship out. The station isn't answering calls, and all the automatic systems have it in a quarantine lockdown."

"Rescue ships?" Miller asked, and coughed again. His throat was still sore.

"Not going to happen," Naomi said. "There were a million and a half people on station. No one has the resources to put into that kind of rescue op."

"After all," Holden said, "there's a war on."

The ship system dimmed the lights for night. Miller lay on his bed. The expert system had shifted his treatment regimen into a new phase, and for the past three hours, he'd alternated between spiking fevers and teeth-chattering chills. His teeth and the nail beds of his fingers and toes ached. Sleep wasn't an option, so he lay in the gloom and tried to pull himself together.

He wondered what his old partners would have made of his behavior on Eros. Havelock. Muss. He tried to imagine them in his place. He'd killed people, and he'd done it cold. Eros had been a kill box, and when the people in charge of the law wanted you dead, the law didn't apply anymore. And some of the dead ass-holes had been the ones who'd killed Julie.

So. Revenge killing. Was he really down to revenge killing? That was a sad thought. He tried to imagine Julie sitting beside him the way Naomi had with Holden. It was like she'd been waiting for the invitation. Julie Mao, who he'd never really known. She raised a hand in greeting.

And what about us? he asked her as he looked into her dark, unreal eyes. *Do I love you, or do I just want to love you so bad I can't tell the difference?*

"Hey, Miller," Holden said, and Julie vanished. "You awake?"

"Yeah. Can't sleep."

"Me either."

They were silent for a moment. The expert system hummed. Miller's left arm itched under its cast as the tissue went through another round of forced regrowth.

"You doing okay?" Miller asked.

"Why wouldn't I be?" Holden said sharply.

"You killed that guy," Miller said. "Back on the station. You shot him. I mean, I know you shot at guys before that. Back at the hotel. But right at the end there, you actually hit somebody in the face."

"Yeah. I did."

"You good with that?"

"Sure," Holden said, too quickly.

The air recyclers hummed, and the blood pressure cuff on Miller's good arm squeezed him like a hand. Holden didn't speak, but when Miller squinted, he could see the elevated blood pressure and the uptick in brain activity.

"They always made us take time off," Miller said.

"What?"

"When we shot someone. Whether they died or not, they always made us take a leave of absence. Turn in our weapon. Go talk to the headshrinker."

"Bureaucrats," Holden said.

"They had a point," Miller said. "Shooting someone does something to you. Killing someone…that's even worse. Doesn't matter that they had it coming or you didn't have a choice. Or maybe a little difference. But it doesn't take it away."

"Seems like you got over it, though."

"Maybe," Miller said. "Look. All that I said back there about how you kill someone? About how leaving them alive wasn't doing them any favors? I'm sorry that happened."

"You think you were wrong?"

"I wasn't. But I'm still sorry it happened."

"Okay."

"Jesus. Look, I'm saying it's good that it bothers you. It's good that you can't stop seeing it or hearing it. That part where it haunts you some? That's the way it's supposed to be."

Holden was quiet for a moment. When he spoke again, his voice was gray as stone.

"I've killed people before, you know. But they were blips in a radar track. I—"

"It's not the same, is it?" Miller said.

"No, it isn't," Holden replied. "Does this go away?"

Sometimes, Miller thought.

"No," he said. "Not if you've still got a soul."

"Okay. Thanks."

"One other thing?"

"Yeah?"

"I know it's none of my business, but I really wouldn't let her put you off. So you don't understand sex and love and women. Just means you were born with a cock. And this girl? Naomi? She seems like she's worth putting a little effort into it. You know?"

"Yeah," Holden said. Then: "Can we never talk about that again?"

"Sure."

The ship creaked and gravity shifted a degree to Miller's right. Course correction. Nothing interesting. Miller closed his eyes and tried to will himself to sleep. His mind was full of dead men and Julie and love and sex. There was something Holden had said about the war that was important, but he couldn't make the pieces fit. They kept changing. Miller sighed, shifted his weight so that he blocked one of his drainage tubes and had to shift back to stop the alarm.

When the blood pressure cuff fired off again, it was Julie holding him, pulling herself so close her lips brushed his ear. His eyes opened, his mind seeing both the imaginary girl and the monitors that she would have blocked if she'd really been there.

I love you too, she said, *and I* will *take care of you.*

He smiled at seeing the numbers change as his heart raced.

Chapter Thirty-Three: Holden

For five more days, Holden and Miller lay on their backs in sick
bay while the solar system burned down around them. The
reports of Eros' death ran from massive ecological collapse
brought about by war-related supply shortages, to covert Martian
attack, to secret Belt bioweapon laboratory accident. Analysis
from the inner planets had it that the OPA and terrorists like them
had finally shown how dangerous they could be to innocent civilian populations. The Belt blamed Mars, or the maintenance crews
of Eros, or the OPA for not stopping it.

And then a group of Martian frigates blockaded Pallas, a revolt
on Ganymede ended in sixteen dead, and the new government of
Ceres announced that all ships with Martian registry docked
on station were being commandeered. The threats and accusations, all set to the constant human background noise of war
drums, moved on. Eros had been a tragedy and a crime, but it was

finished, and there were new dangers popping up in every corner of human space.

Holden turned off his newsfeed, fidgeted in his bunk, and tried to wake Miller up by staring at him. It didn't work. The massive radiation exposure had failed to give him superpowers. Miller began to snore.

Holden sat up, testing the gravity. Less than a quarter g. Alex wasn't in a hurry, then. Naomi was giving him and Miller time to heal before they arrived at Julie's magical mystery asteroid.

Shit.

Naomi.

The last few times she'd come into sick bay had been awkward. She never brought the subject of his failed romantic gesture back up, but he could feel a barrier between them now that filled him with regret. And every time she left the room, Miller would look away from him and sigh, which just made it worse.

But he couldn't avoid her forever, no matter how much he felt like an idiot. He swung his feet off the edge of the bed and pressed down on the floor. His legs felt weak but not rubbery. The soles of his feet hurt, but quite a bit less than nearly everything else on his body. He stood up, one hand still on the bed, and tested his balance. He wobbled but remained upright. Two steps reassured him that walking was possible in the light gravity. The IV tugged at his arm. He was down to just one bag of something a faint blue. He had no idea what it was, but after Naomi's description of how close to death he'd come, he figured it must be important. He pulled it off the wall hook and held it in his left hand. The room smelled like antiseptic and diarrhea. He was happy to be leaving.

"Where you going?" Miller asked, his voice groggy.

"Out." Holden had the sudden, visceral memory of being fifteen.

"Okay," Miller said, then rolled onto his side.

The sick bay hatch was four meters from the central ladder, and Holden covered the ground with a slow, careful shuffle, his paper booties making a whispery scuffing sound on the fabric-covered metal floor. The ladder itself defeated him. Even though ops was only one deck up, the three-meter climb might as well have been a thousand. He pressed the button to call the lift, and a few seconds later, the floor hatch slid open and the lift climbed through with an electric whine. Holden tried to hop on but managed only a sort of slow-motion fall that ended with his clutching the ladder and kneeling on the lift platform. He stopped the lift, pulled himself upright, and started it again, then rode it up to the next deck in what he hoped was a less beaten and more captain-like pose.

"Jesus, Captain, you *still* look like shit," Amos said as the lift came to a stop. The mechanic was sprawled across two chairs at the sensor stations and munching on what looked like a strip of leather.

"You keep saying that."

"Keeps bein' true."

"Amos, don't you have work to do?" Naomi said. She was sitting at one of the computer stations, watching something flash by on the screen. She didn't look up when Holden came onto the deck. That was a bad sign.

"Nope. Most boring ship I ever worked, Boss. She don't break, she don't leak, she don't even have an annoying rattle to tighten down," Amos replied as he sucked down the last of his snack and smacked his lips.

"There's always mopping," Naomi said, then tapped out something on the screen in front of her. Amos looked from her to Holden and back again.

"Oh, that reminds me. I better get down to the engine room and look at that...thing I've been meaning to look at," Amos said, and jumped to his feet. " 'Scuse me, Cap."

He squeezed past Holden, hopped on the lift, and rode it sternward. The deck hatch closed behind him.

"Hey," Holden said to Naomi once Amos was gone.

"Hey," she said without turning around. That wasn't good either. When she'd sent Amos away, he'd hoped she wanted to talk. It didn't look like it. Holden sighed and shuffled over to the chair next to her. He collapsed into it, his legs tingling like he'd run a kilometer instead of just walking twenty-odd steps. Naomi had left her hair down, and it hid her face from him. Holden wanted to brush it back but was afraid she'd snap his elbow with Belter kung fu if he tried.

"Look, Naomi," he started, but she ignored him and hit a button on her panel. He stopped when Fred's face appeared on the display in front of her.

"Is that Fred?" he said, because he couldn't think of anything even more idiotic to say.

"You should see this. Got it from Tycho a couple hours ago on the tightbeam after I sent them an update on our status."

Naomi tapped the play button and Fred's face sprang to life.

"Naomi, sounds like you guys have had a tough time of it. The air's full of chatter on the station shutdown, and the supposed nuclear explosion. No one knows what to make of it. Keep us informed. In the meantime, we managed to hack open that data cube you left here. I don't think it'll help much, though. Looks like a bunch of sensor data from the *Donnager*, mostly EM stuff. We've tried looking for hidden messages, but my smartest people can't find anything. I'm passing the data along to you. Let me know if you find anything. Tycho out."

The screen went blank.

"What does the data look like?" Holden asked.

"It's just what the man said," Naomi said. "EM sensor data from the *Donnager* during the pursuit by the six ships, and the battle itself. I've dug through raw stuff, looking for anything hidden inside, but for the life of me, I can't find a thing. I've even had the *Roci* digging through the data for the last couple hours, looking for patterns. She has really good software for that sort of thing. But so far, nothing."

She tapped on the screen again and the raw data began spooling past faster than Holden could follow. In a small window inside the larger screen, the *Rocinante*'s pattern-recognition software worked to find meaning. Holden watched it for a minute, but his eyes quickly unfocused.

"Lieutenant Kelly died for this data," he said. "He left the ship while his mates were still fighting. Marines don't do that unless it matters."

Naomi shrugged and pointed at the screen with resignation.

"That's what was on his cube," she said. "Maybe there's something steganographic, but I don't have another dataset to compare it to."

Holden began tapping on his thigh, his pain and romantic failures momentarily forgotten.

"So let's say that this data is all that it is. There's nothing hidden. What would this information mean to the Martian navy?"

Naomi leaned back in her chair and closed her eyes in thought, one finger twisting and untwisting a curl of hair by her temple.

"It's mostly EM data, so lots of engine-signature stuff. Drive radiation is the best way to keep track of other ships. So that tells you where which ships were during the fight. Tactical data?"

"Maybe," Holden said. "Would that be important enough to send Kelly out with?"

Naomi took a deep breath and let it out slowly.

"I don't think so," she said.

"Me either."

Something tapped at the edge of his conscious mind, asking to be let in.

"What was that thing with Amos all about?" he said.

"Amos?"

"Him showing up at the airlock with two guns when we arrived," he said.

"There was some trouble on our trip back to the ship."

"Trouble for who?" Holden asked. Naomi actually smiled at that.

"Some bad men didn't want us to hack the lockdown on the *Roci*. Amos talked it over with them. You didn't think it was because we were *waiting* for you, did you, sir?"

Was there a smile in her voice? A hint of coyness? Flirtation? He stopped himself from grinning.

"What did the *Roci* say about the data when you ran it?" Holden asked.

"Here," Naomi replied, and hit something on her panel. The screen began displaying long lists of data in text. "Lots of EM and light spectrum stuff, some leakage from damaged—"

Holden yelped. Naomi looked up at him.

"I'm such an idiot," Holden said.

"Granted. Elaborate?"

Holden touched the screen and began scrolling up and down through the data. He tapped one long list of numbers and letters and leaned back with a grin.

"There, that's it," he said.

"That's what?"

"Hull structure isn't the only recognition metric. It's the most accurate, but it's also got the shortest range and"—he gestured around him at the *Rocinante*—"is the easiest to fool. The next best method is drive signature. Can't mask your radiation and heat patterns. And they're easy to spot even from really far away."

Holden turned on the screen next to his chair and pulled up the ship's friend/foe database, then linked it to the data on Naomi's screen.

"That's what this message is, Naomi. It's telling Mars who killed the *Donnager* by showing them what the drive signature was."

"Then why not just say, 'So-and-so killed us,' in a nice easy-to-read text file?" Naomi asked, a skeptical frown on her face.

Holden leaned forward and paused, opened his mouth, then closed it and sat back again with a sigh.

"I don't know."

A hatch banged open with a hydraulic whine; then Naomi looked past Holden to the ladder and said, "Miller's coming up."

Holden turned to watch the detective finish the slow climb up from the sick bay deck. He looked like a plucked chicken, pink-gray skin stippled with gooseflesh. His paper gown went poorly with the hat.

"Uh, there's a lift," Holden said.

"Wish I'd known that," Miller replied, then dragged himself up onto the ops deck with a gasp. "We there yet?"

"Trying to figure out a mystery," Holden said.

"I hate mysteries," Miller said, then hauled himself to his feet and made his way to a chair.

"Then solve this one for us. You find out who murdered someone. You can't arrest them yourself, so you send the information to your partner. But instead of just sending the perp's name, you send your partner all the clues. Why?"

Miller coughed and scratched his chin. His eyes were fixed on something, like he was reading a screen Holden couldn't see.

"Because I don't trust myself. I want my partner to arrive at the same conclusion I did, without my biasing him. I give him the dots, see what it looks like when he connects 'em."

"Especially if guessing wrong has consequences," Naomi said.

"You don't like to screw up a murder charge," Miller said with a nod. "Looks unprofessional."

Holden's panel beeped at him.

"Shit, I know why they were careful," he said after reading his screen. "The *Roci* thinks those were standard light-cruiser engines built by the Bush Shipyards."

"They were Earth ships?" Naomi said. "But they weren't flying any colors, and...Son of a *bitch*!"

It was the first time Holden had ever heard her yell, and he understood. If UNN black ops ships had killed the *Donnager*, then that meant Earth was behind the whole thing. Maybe even killing the *Canterbury* in the first place. It would mean that Martian warships were killing Belters for no reason. Belters like Naomi.

Holden leaned forward and called up the comm display, then tapped out a general broadcast. Miller caught his breath.

"That button you just pressed doesn't do what I think it does, does it?" he said.

"I finished Kelly's mission for him," Holden said.

"I have no idea who the fuck Kelly is," Miller said, "but please tell me that his mission wasn't broadcasting that data to the solar system at large."

"People need to know what's going on," Holden said.

"Yes, they do, but maybe we should actually know what the hell is going on before we tell them," Miller replied, all the weariness gone from his voice. "How gullible *are* you?"

"Hey," Holden said, but Miller got louder.

"You found a Martian battery, right? So you told everyone in the solar system about it and started the single largest war in human history. Only turns out the Martians maybe weren't the ones that left it there. Then, a bunch of mystery ships kill the *Donnager*, which Mars blames on the Belt, only, dammit, the Belt didn't even know it was *capable* of killing a Martian battle cruiser."

Holden opened his mouth, but Miller grabbed a bulb of coffee Amos had left behind on the console and threw it at his head.

"Let me finish! And now you find some data that implicates Earth. First thing you do is blab it to the universe, so that Mars *and* the Belt drag Earth into this thing, making the largest war of all time even bigger. Are you seeing a pattern here?"

"Yes," Naomi said.

"So what do you think's going to happen?" Miller said. "This is how these people work! They made the *Canterbury* look like Mars. It wasn't. They made the *Donnager* look like the Belt. It wasn't. Now it looks like the whole damn thing's Earth? Follow the pattern. It probably isn't! You never, *never* put that kind of accusation out there until you know the score. You look. You listen. You're quiet, fercrissakes, and when you know, *then* you can make your case."

The detective sat back, clearly exhausted. He was sweating. The deck was silent.

"You done?" Holden said.

Miller nodded, breathing heavily. "Think I might have strained something."

"I haven't accused anyone of doing anything," Holden said.

"I'm not building a case. I just put the data out there. Now it's not a secret. They're doing something on Eros. They don't want it interrupted. With Mars and the Belt shooting at each other, everyone with the resources to help is busy elsewhere."

"And you just dragged Earth into it," Miller said.

"Maybe," Holden said. "But the killers *did* use ships that were built, at least in part, at Earth's orbital shipyards. Maybe someone will look into that. And *that's* the point. If everyone knows everything, nothing stays secret."

"Yeah, well," Miller said. Holden ignored him

"Eventually, someone'll figure out the big picture. This kind of thing requires secrecy to function, so exposing all the secrets hurts them in the end. It's the only way this really, permanently stops."

Miller sighed, nodded to himself, took off his hat, and scratched his scalp.

"I was just going to put 'em out an airlock," Miller said.

BA834024112 wasn't much of an asteroid. Barely thirty meters across, it had long ago been surveyed and found completely devoid of useful or valuable minerals. It existed in the registry only to warn ships not to run into it. Julie had left it tethered to wealth measured in the billions when she flew her small shuttle to Eros.

Up close, the ship that had killed the *Scopuli* and stolen its crew looked like a shark. It was long and lean and utterly black, almost impossible to see against the backdrop of space with the naked eye. Its radar-deflecting curves gave it an aerodynamic look almost always lacking in space-going vessels. It made Holden's skin crawl, but it was beautiful.

"Motherfucker," Amos said under his breath as the crew clustered in the cockpit of the *Rocinante* to look at it.

"The *Roci* doesn't even see it, Cap," Alex said. "I'm pourin' ladar into it, and all we see is a slightly warmer spot on the asteroid."

"Like Becca saw just before the *Cant* died," Naomi said.

"Her shuttle's been launched, so I'm guessin' this is the right stealth ship someone left tied to a rock," Alex added. "Case there's more than one."

Holden tapped his fingers on the back of Alex's chair for a moment as he floated over the pilot's head.

"It's probably full of vomit zombies," Holden finally said.

"Want to go see?" said Miller.

"Oh yeah," Holden said.

Chapter Thirty-Four: Miller

The environment suit was better than Miller was used to. He'd only done a couple walks outside during his years on Ceres, and the Star Helix equipment had been old back then: thick corrugated joints, separable air-supply unit, gloves that left his hands thirty degrees colder than the rest of his body. The *Rocinante*'s suits were military and recent, no bulkier than standard riot gear, with integrated life support that could probably keep fingers warm after a hand got shot off. Miller floated, one hand on a strap in the airlock, and flexed his fingers, watching the sharkskin pattern of the knuckle joints.

It didn't feel like enough.

"All right, Alex," Holden said. "We're in place. Have the *Roci* knock for us."

A deep, rumbling vibration shook them. Naomi put a hand against the airlock's curved wall to steady herself. Amos shifted forward to take point, a reactionless automatic rifle in his hands. When he bent his neck, Miller could hear the vertebrae cracking through his radio. It was the only way he could have heard it; they were already in vacuum.

"Okay, Captain," Alex said. "I've got a seal. The standard security override isn't working, so give me a second...to..."

"Problem?" Holden said.

"Got it. I've got it. We have a connection," Alex said. Then, a moment later: "Ah. It doesn't look like there's much to breathe over there."

"Anything?" Holden asked.

"Nope. Hard vacuum," Alex said. "Both her lock doors are open."

"All right, folks," Holden said, "keep an eye on your air supply. Let's go."

Miller took a long breath. The external airlock went from soft red to soft green. Holden slid it open, and Amos launched forward, the captain just behind him. Miller gestured to Naomi with a nod. *Ladies first.*

The connecting gantry was reinforced, ready to deflect enemy lasers or slow down slugs. Amos landed on the other ship as the hatch to the *Rocinante* closed behind them. Miller had a moment's vertigo, the ship before them suddenly clicking from *ahead* to *down* in his perception, as if they were falling into something.

"You all right?" Naomi asked.

Miller nodded, and Amos passed into the other ship's hatch. One by one, they went in.

The ship was dead. The lights coming off their environment suits played over the soft, almost streamlined curves of the bulkheads, the cushioned walls, the gray suit lockers. One locker was bent out of shape, like someone or something had forced its way out from within. Amos pushed off slow. Under normal circumstances, hard vacuum would have been assurance enough that nothing was about to jump out at them. Right now, Miller figured it was only even money.

"Whole place is shut down," Holden said.

"Might be backups in the engine room," Amos said.

"So the ass end of the ship from here," Holden said.

"Pretty much."

"Let's be careful," Holden said.

"I'm heading up to ops," Naomi said. "If there's anything running off battery, I can—"

"No, you aren't," Holden said. "We aren't splitting up the group until we know what we're looking at. Stay together."

Amos moved down, sinking into the darkness. Holden pushed off after him. Miller followed. He couldn't tell from Naomi's body language whether she was annoyed or relieved.

The galley was empty, but signs of struggle showed here and there. A chair with a bent leg. A long, jagged scratch down the wall where something sharp had flaked the paint. Two bullet holes set high along one bulkhead where a shot had gone wide. Miller put a hand out, grabbed one of the tables, and swung slowly.

"Miller?" Holden said. "Are you coming?"

"Look at this," Miller said.

The dark spill was the color of amber, flaky and shining like glass in his flashlight beam. Holden hovered closer.

"Zombie vomit?" Holden said.

"Think so."

"Well. I guess we're on the right ship. For some value of right."

The crew quarters hung silent and empty. They went through each of them, but there were no personal markings—no terminals, no pictures, no clues to the names of the men and women who had lived and breathed and presumably died on the ship. Even the captain's cabin was indicated only by a slightly larger bunk and the face of a locked safe.

There was a massive central compartment as high and wide as the hull of the *Rocinante*, the darkness dominated by twelve huge cylinders encrusted with narrow catwalks and scaffolds. Miller saw Naomi's expression harden.

"What are they?" Miller asked.

"Torpedo tubes," she said.

"*Torpedo* tubes?" he said. "Jesus *Christ*, how many are they packing? A million?"

"Twelve," she said. "Just twelve."

"Capital-ship busters," Amos said. "Built to pretty much kill whatever you're aiming at with the first shot."

"Something like the *Donnager*?" Miller asked.

Holden looked back at him, the glow of his heads-up display lighting his features.

"Or the *Canterbury*," he said.

The four of them passed between the wide black tubes in silence.

In the machine and fabrication shops, the signs of violence were more pronounced. There was blood on the floor and walls, along with wide swaths of the glassy gold resin that had once been vomit. A uniform lay in a ball. The cloth had been wadded and soaked in something before the cold of space had frozen it. Habits formed from years of walking through crime scenes put a dozen small things in place: the pattern of scratches on the floor and lift doors, the spatter of blood and vomit, the footprints. They all told the story.

"They're in engineering," Miller said.

"Who?" Holden said.

"The crew. Whoever was on the ship. All except that one," he said, gesturing at half a footprint that led toward the lift. "You see how her footprints are over the top of everything else. And there, where she stepped in that blood, it was already dry. Flaked instead of smearing."

"How you know it was a girl?" Holden asked.

"Because it was Julie," Miller said.

"Well, whoever's in there, they've been sucking vacuum for a long time," Amos said. "Want to go see?"

No one said yes, but they all floated forward. The hatch stood open. If the darkness beyond it seemed more solid, more ominous, more *personal* than the rest of the dead ship had, it was only Miller's imagination playing tricks. He hesitated, trying to summon up the image of Julie, but she wouldn't come.

Floating into the engineering deck was like swimming into a cave. Miller saw the other flashlights playing over walls and panels, looking for live controls, or else controls that could come alive. He aimed his own beam into the body of the room, the dark swallowing it.

"We got batteries, Cap'n," Amos said. "And...looks like the reactor got shut down. Intentional."

"Think you can get it back up?"

"Want to run some diagnostics," Amos said. "There could be a reason they shut it off, and I don't want to find out the hard way."

"Good point."

"But I can at least get us...some...come *on,* you bastard."

All around the deck, blue-white lights flared up. The sudden brilliance blinded Miller for a half second. His vision returned with a sense of growing confusion. Naomi gasped, and Holden yelped. Something in the back of Miller's own mind started to shriek, and he forced it into silence. It was just a crime scene. They were only bodies.

Except they weren't.

The reactor stood before him, quiescent and dead. All around it, a layer of human flesh. He could pick out arms, hands with fingers splayed so wide they hurt to look at. The long snake of a spine curved, ribs fanning out like the legs of some perverse insect. He tried to make what he was seeing make sense. He'd seen men eviscerated before. He knew that the long, ropy swirl to the left of the thing were intestines. He could see where the small bowel widened to become a colon. The familiar shape of a skull looked out at him.

But then, among the familiar anatomy of death and dismemberment, there were other things: nautilus spirals, wide swaths of soft black filament, a pale expanse of something that might have been skin cut by a dozen gill-like vents, a half-formed limb that looked equally like an insect and a fetus without being either one.

The frozen, dead flesh surrounded the reactor like the skin of an orange. The crew of the stealth ship. Maybe of the *Scopuli* as well.

All but Julie.

"Yeah," Amos said. "This could take a little longer than I was thinking, Cap."

"It's okay," Holden said. His voice on the radio sounded shaky. "You don't have to."

"It's no trouble. As long as none of *that* freaky shit broke the containment, reactor should boot up just fine."

"You don't mind being around…it?" Holden said.

"Honest, Cap'n, I'm not thinking about it. Give me twenty minutes, I'll tell you if we got power or if we have to patch a line over from the *Roci*."

"Okay," Holden said. And then again, his voice more solid: "Okay, but don't touch any of that."

"Wasn't going to," Amos said.

They floated back out through the hatch, Holden and Naomi and Miller coming last.

"Is that…" Naomi said, then coughed and started again. "Is that what's happening on Eros?"

"Probably," Miller said.

"Amos," Holden said. "Do you have enough battery power to light up the computers?"

There was a pause. Miller took a deep breath, the plastic-and-ozone scent of the suit's air system filling his nose.

"I think so," Amos said dubiously. "But if we can get the reactor up first…"

"Bring up the computers."

"You're the captain, Cap'n," Amos said. "Have it to you in five."

In silence, they floated up—back—to the airlock, and past it to the operations deck. Miller hung back, watching the way Holden's trajectory kept him near Naomi and then away from her.

Protective and head-shy both, Miller thought. Bad combination.

Julie was waiting in the airlock. Not at first, of course. Miller slid back into the space, his mind churning through everything he'd seen, just like it was a case. A normal case. His gaze drifted toward the broken locker. There was no suit in it. For a moment, he was back on Eros, in the apartment where Julie had died. There had been an environment suit there. And then Julie was there with him, pushing her way out of the locker.

What were you doing there? he thought.

"No brig," he said.

"What?" Holden said.

"I just noticed," Miller said. "Ship's got no brig. They aren't built to carry prisoners."

Holden made a low agreeing grunt.

"Makes you wonder what they were planning to do with the crew of the *Scopuli*," Naomi said. The tone of her voice meant she didn't wonder at all.

"I don't think they were," Miller said slowly. "This whole thing...they were improvising."

"Improvising?" Naomi said.

"Ship was carrying an infectious something or other without enough containment to contain it. Taking on prisoners without a brig to hold 'em in. They were making this up as they went along."

"Or they had to hurry," Holden said. "Something happened that made them hurry. But what they did on Eros must have taken months to arrange. Maybe years. So maybe something happened at the last minute?"

"Be interesting to know what," Miller said.

Compared to the rest of the ship, the ops deck looked peaceful. Normal. The computers had finished their diagnostics, screens glowing placidly. Naomi went to one, holding the back of the chair with one hand so the gentle touch of her fingers against the screen wouldn't push her backward.

"I'll do what I can here," she said. "You can check the bridge."

There was a pause that carried weight.

"I'll be fine," Naomi said.

"All right. I know you'll...I...C'mon, Miller."

Miller let the captain float ahead into the bridge. The screens there were spooling through diagnostics so standard Miller recognized them. It was a wider space than he'd imagined, with five stations with crash couches customized for other people's bodies. Holden strapped in at one. Miller took a slow turn around the deck. Nothing seemed out of place here—no blood, no broken chairs or torn padding. When it happened, the fight had been down near the reactor. He wasn't sure yet what that meant. He sat at what, under a standard layout, would have been the security station, and opened a private channel to Holden.

"Anything you're looking for in particular?"

"Briefings. Overviews," Holden said shortly. "Whatever's useful. You?"

"See if I can get into the internal monitors."

"Hoping to find...?"

"What Julie found," Miller said.

The security assumed that anyone sitting at the console had access to the low-level feeds. It still took half an hour to parse the command structure and query interface. Once Miller had that down, it wasn't hard. The time stamp on the log listed the feed as the day the *Scopuli* had gone missing. The security camera in the airlock bay showed the crew—Belters, most of them—being escorted in. Their captors were in armor, with faceplates lowered. Miller wondered if they'd meant to keep their identities secret. That would almost have suggested they were planning to keep the crew alive. Or maybe they were just wary of some last-minute resistance. The crew of the *Scopuli* weren't wearing environment suits or armor. A couple of them weren't even wearing uniforms.

But Julie was.

It was strange, watching her move. With a sense of dislocation, Miller realized that he'd never actually seen her in motion. All the pictures he'd had in his file back on Ceres had been stills. Now here she was, floating with her chosen compatriots, her hair back out of her eyes, her jaw clamped. She looked very small surrounded by her crew and the men in armor. The little rich girl who'd turned her back on wealth and status to be with the down-trodden Belt. The girl who'd told her mother to sell the *Razor-back*—the ship she'd loved—rather than give in to emotional blackmail. In motion, she looked a little different from the imaginary version he'd built of her—the way she pulled her shoulders back, the habit of reaching her toes toward the floor even in null g—but the basic image was the same. He felt like he was filling in blanks with the new details rather than reimagining the woman.

The guards said something—the security feed's audio was playing to vacuum—and the *Scopuli* crew looked aghast. Then, hesitantly, the captain started taking his uniform off. They were stripping the prisoners. Miller shook his head.

"Bad plan."

"What?" Holden said.

"Nothing. Sorry."

Julie wasn't moving. One of the guards moved toward her, his legs braced on the wall. Julie, who'd lived through being raped, maybe, or something as bad. Who'd studied jiu jitsu to feel safe afterward. Maybe they thought she was just being modest. Maybe they were afraid she was hiding a weapon under her clothes. Either way, they tried to force the point. One of the guards pushed her, and she latched on to his arm like her life depended on it. Miller winced when he saw the man's elbow bend the wrong way, but he also smiled.

That's my girl, he thought. *Give 'em hell.*

And she did. For almost forty seconds, the airlock bay was a battleground. Even some of the cowed *Scopuli* crew tried to join in. But then Julie didn't see a thick-shouldered man launch from behind her. Miller felt it when the gauntleted hand hammered Julie's temple. She wasn't out, but she was groggy. The men with guns stripped her with a cold efficiency, and when there were no weapons or comm devices, they handed her a jumpsuit and shoved her in a locker. The others, they led down into the ship. Miller matched time stamps and switched feeds.

The prisoners were taken to the galley, then bound to the tables.

One of the guards spent a minute or so talking, but with his face-plate down, the only clues Miller had to the content of the sermon were the reactions of the crew—wide-eyed disbelief, confusion, outrage, and fear. The guard could have been saying anything.

Miller started skipping. A few hours, then a few more. The ship was under thrust, the prisoners actually sitting at the tables instead of floating near them. He flipped to other parts of the ship. Julie's locker was still closed. If he hadn't known better, he'd have assumed she was dead.

He skipped ahead.

One hundred and thirty-two hours later, the crew of the *Scopuli* grew a pair. Miller saw it in their bodies even before the violence started. He'd seen holding cells rise up before, and the prisoners had the same sullen-but-excited look. The feed showed the stretch of wall where he'd seen the bullet holes. They weren't there yet. They would be. A man came into the picture with a tray of food rations.

Here it comes, Miller thought.

The fight was short and brutal. The prisoners didn't stand a chance. Miller watched as they hauled one of them—a sandy-haired man—to the airlock and spaced him. The others were put in heavy restraints. Some wept. Some screamed. Miller skipped ahead.

It had to be in there someplace. The moment when it—whatever it was—got loose. But either it had happened in some unmonitored crew quarters or it had been there from the beginning. Almost exactly one hundred and sixty hours after Julie had gone into the locker, a man in a white jumper, eyes glassy and stance unsure, lurched out of the crew quarters and vomited on one of the guards.

"Fuck!" Amos shouted.

Miller was out of his chair before he knew what had happened. Holden was up too.

"Amos?" Holden said. "Talk to me."

"Hold on," Amos said. "Yeah, it's okay, Cap'n. It's just these fuckers stripped off a bunch of the reactor shielding. We've got her up, but I sucked down a few more rads than I'd have picked."

"Get back to the *Roci*," Holden said. Miller steadied himself against a wall, pushing back down toward the control stations.

"No offense, sir, but it ain't like I'm about to start pissing blood or anything fun like that," Amos said. "I got surprised more than anything. I start feeling itchy, I'll head back over, but I can get some atmosphere for us by working out of the machine shop if you give me a few more minutes."

Miller watched Holden's face as the man struggled. He could make it an order; he could leave it be.

"Okay, Amos. But you start getting light-headed or anything—I mean *anything*—and you get over to the sick bay."

"Aye, aye," Amos said.

"Alex, keep an eye on Amos' biomed feed from over there. Give us a heads-up if you see a problem," Holden said on the general channel.

"Roger," came Alex's lazy drawl.

"You finding anything?" Holden asked Miller on their private channel.

"Nothing unexpected," Miller said. "You?"

"Yeah, actually. Take a look."

Miller pushed himself to the screen Holden had been working. Holden pulled himself back into the station and started pulling up feeds.

"I was thinking that someone had to go last," Holden said. "I mean, there had to be someone who was the least sick when whatever it was got loose. So I went through the directory to see what activity was going on before the system went dead."

"And?"

"There's a whole bunch of activity that looks like it happened a couple days before the system shutdown, and then nothing for two solid days. And then a little spike. A lot of accessed files and system diagnostics. Then someone hacked the override codes to blow atmosphere."

"It was Julie, then."

"That's what I was thinking," Holden said. "But one of the feeds she accessed was…Shit, where is it? It was right…Oh. Here. Watch this."

The screen blinked, controls dropping to standby, and a high-res emblem, green and gold, came up. The corporate logo of Protogen, with a slogan Miller hadn't seen before. *First. Fastest. Furthest.*

"What's the time stamp on the file?" Miller asked.

"The original was created about two years ago," Holden said. "This copy was burned eight months ago."

The emblem faded, and a pleasant-faced man sitting at a desk took its place. He had dark hair, with just a scattering of gray at the temples, and lips that seemed used to smiling. He nodded at the camera. The smile didn't reach his eyes, which were as empty as a shark's.

Sociopath, Miller thought.

The man's lips began moving soundlessly. Holden said, "Shit," and hit a switch to have the audio transmitted to their suits. He rewound the video feed and started it over.

"Mr. Dresden," the man said. "I would like to thank you and the members of the board for taking the time to review this information. Your support, both financial and otherwise, has been absolutely essential to the incredible discoveries we've seen on this project. While my team has been point man, as it were, Protogen's tireless commitment to the advancement of science has made our work possible.

"Gentlemen, I will be frank. The Phoebe protomolecule has exceeded all our expectations. I believe it represents a genuinely game-changing technological breakthrough. I know that these kinds of corporate presentations are prone to hyperbole. Please understand that I have thought about this carefully and chosen my words: Protogen can become the most important and powerful entity in the history of the human race. But it will require initiative, ambition, and bold action."

"He's talking about killing people," Miller said.

"You've seen this already?" Holden said.

Miller shook his head. The feed changed. The man faded out, and an animation took his place. A graphic representation of the solar system. Orbits marked in wide swaths of color showed the plane of the ecliptic. The virtual camera swirled out from the inner planets, where Mr. Dresden and board members presumably were, and out toward the gas giants.

"For those of you on the board unfamiliar with the project, eight years ago, the first manned landing was made on Phoebe," the sociopath said.

The animation zoomed in toward Saturn, rings and planet flying past in a triumph of graphic design over accuracy.

"A small ice moon, the assumption was that Phoebe would eventually be mined for water, much like the rings themselves. The Martian government commissioned a scientific survey more out of a sense of bureaucratic completeness than from expectation of economic gain. Core samples were taken, and when silicate anomalies raised flags, Protogen was approached as cosponsor of a long-term research facility."

The moon itself—Phoebe—filled the frame, turning slowly to show all sides like a prostitute at a cheap brothel. It was a crater-marked lump, indistinguishable from a thousand other asteroids and planetesimals Miller had seen.

"Given Phoebe's extra-ecliptical orbit," the sociopath went on, "one theory has been that it was a body that originated in the Kuiper belt and had been captured by Saturn when it happened to pass through the solar system. The existence of complex silicon structures within the interior ice, along with suggestions of impact-resistant structures within the architecture of the body itself, have forced us to reevaluate this.

"Using analyses proprietary to Protogen and not yet shared with the Martian team, we have determined beyond any credible doubt that what you are seeing now is not a naturally formed planetesimal, but a weapon. Specifically, a weapon designed to carry its payload through the depths of interplanetary space and deliver it safely onto Earth two and one third billion years ago, when life itself was in its earliest stages. And the payload, gentlemen, is this."

The display clicked to a graphic that Miller couldn't quite parse. It looked like the medical text of a virus, but with wide, looping structures that were at once beautiful and improbable.

"The protomolecule first caught our interest for its ability to maintain its primary structure in a wide variety of conditions through secondary and tertiary changes. It also showed an affinity for carbon and silicon structures. Its activity suggested it was not in itself a living thing, but a set of free-floating instructions designed to adapt to and guide other replicating systems. Animal experiments suggest that its effects are not exclusive to simple replicators, but are, in fact, scalable."

"Animal tests," Miller said. "What, they dumped it on a cat?"

"The initial implication of this," the sociopath went on, "is that a larger biosphere exists, of which our solar system is only a part, and that the protomolecule is an artifact of that environment. That alone, I think you must agree, would revolutionize human understanding of the universe. Let me assure you, it's small beer. If accidents of orbital mechanics had not captured Phoebe, life as we know it would not presently exist. But something else would. The earliest cellular life on Earth would have been hijacked. Reprogrammed along lines contained within the structure of the protomolecule."

The sociopath reappeared. For the first time, smile lines appeared around his eyes, like a parody of themselves. Miller felt a visceral hatred growing in his gut and knew himself well enough to recognize it for what it was. Fear.

"Protogen is in a position to take sole possession of not only the first technology of genuinely extraterrestrial origin, but also a prefabricated mechanism for the manipulation of living systems and the first clues as to the nature of the larger—I will call it *galactic*—biosphere. Directed by human hands, the applications of this are limitless. I believe that the opportunity now facing not only us but life itself is as profound and transformative as anything that has ever happened. And, further, the control of this technology will represent the base of all political and economic power from now on.

"I urge you to consider the technical details I have outlined in the attached. Moving quickly to understand the programming, mechanism, and intent of the protomolecule, as well as its direct application to human beings, will mark the difference between a Protogen-led future and being left behind. I urge immediate and decisive action to take exclusive control of the protomolecule and move forward with large-scale testing.

"Thank you for your time and attention."

The sociopath smiled again, and the corporate logo reappeared. *First. Fastest. Furthest.* Miller's heart was racing.

"Okay. All right," he said. And then: "Fuck *me*."

"Protogen, protomolecule," Holden said. "They had no idea what it does, but they slapped their label on it like they'd made it. They found an alien weapon, and all they could think to do was *brand* it."

"There's reason to think these boys are pretty impressed with themselves," Miller replied with a nod.

"Now, I'm not a scientist or anything," Holden said, "but it seems to me like taking an *alien supervirus* and dropping it into a space station would be a bad idea."

"It's been two years," Miller said. "They've been doing tests. They've been...I don't know what the hell they've been doing. But Eros is what they decided on. And everyone knows what happened on Eros. The other side did it. No research and recovery ships because they're all fighting each other or guarding something. The war? It's a distraction."

"And Protogen is doing...what?"

"Seeing what their toy does when you take it out for a spin is my guess," Miller said.

They were silent for a long moment. Holden spoke first.

"So you take a company that seems to be lacking an institutional conscience, that has enough government research contracts to almost be a privately run branch of the military. How far will they go for the holy grail?"

"First, fastest, furthest," Miller replied.

"Yeah."

"Guys," Naomi said, "you should come down here. I think I've got something."

Chapter Thirty-Five: Holden

I've found the comm logs," Naomi said as Holden and Miller drifted into the room behind her.

Holden put a hand on her shoulder, pulled it back, and hated that he'd pulled back. A week earlier she'd have been fine with a simple gesture of affection like that, and he wouldn't have been afraid of her reaction. He regretted the new distance between them only slightly less than he would have regretted not saying anything at all. He wanted to tell her that.

Instead, he said, "Find anything good?"

She tapped the screen and pulled up the log.

"They were hard-core about comm discipline," she said, pointing at the long list of dates and times. "Nothing ever went out on radio, everything was tightbeam. And everything was double-speak, lots of obvious code phrases."

Miller's mouth moved inside his helmet. Holden tapped on his face shield. Miller rolled his eyes in disgust and then chinned the comm link to the general channel.

"Sorry. Don't spend a lot of time in suits," he said. "What've we got that's good?"

"Not much. But the last communication was in plain English," she said, then tapped the last line on the list.

THOTH STATION

CREW DEGENERATING. PROJECTING 100% CASUALTIES. MATERIALS SECURED. STABILIZING COURSE AND SPEED. VECTOR DATA TO FOLLOW. EXTREME CONTAMINATION HAZARD FOR ENTRY TEAMS.

CPT. HIGGINS

Holden read it several times, imagining Captain Higgins watching the infection spread through his crew, helpless to stop it. His people vomiting all over in a vacuum-sealed metal box, even one molecule of the substance on your skin a virtual death sentence. Black filament-covered tendrils erupting from their eyes and mouths. And then that...soup that covered the reactor. He let himself shudder, grateful that Miller wouldn't see it through the atmosphere suit.

"So this Higgins fella realizes his crew is turning into vomit zombies and sends a last message to his bosses, right?" Miller said, breaking into Holden's reverie. "What's this stuff about vector data?"

"He knew they'd all be dead, so he was letting his people know how to catch the ship," Holden replied.

"But they didn't, because it's here, because Julie took control and flew it somewhere else," Miller said. "Which means they're looking for it, right?"

Holden ignored that and put his hand back on Naomi's shoulder with what he hoped was companionable casualness.

"We have tightbeam messages and the vector info," he said. "Are they all going to the same place?"

"Sort of," she said, nodding with her right hand. "Not the same place, but all to what appear to be points in the Belt. But based on the changes in direction and the times they were sent, to one point in the Belt that is moving around, and not in a stable orbit either."

"A ship, then?"

Naomi gave another nod.

"Probably," she said. "I've been playing with the locations, and I can't find anything in the registry that looks likely. No stations or inhabited rocks. A ship would make sense. But—"

Holden waited for Naomi to finish, but Miller leaned forward impatiently.

"But what?" he said.

"But how did they know where it would be?" she replied. "I have no incoming comms in the log. If a ship was moving around randomly in the Belt, how'd they know where to send these messages?"

Holden squeezed her shoulder, lightly enough that she probably didn't even feel it in the heavy environment suit, then pushed off and allowed himself to drift toward the ceiling.

"So it's not random," he said. "They had some sort of map of where this thing would be at the time they sent the laser comms. Could be one of their stealth ships."

Naomi turned around in her chair to look up at him.

"Could be a station," she said.

"It's the lab," Miller broke in. "They're running an experiment on Eros, they need the white coats nearby."

"Naomi," Holden said. " 'Materials secured.' There's a safe in the captain's quarters that's still locked down. Think you can get it open?"

Naomi gave a one-handed shrug.

"I don't know," she said. "Maybe. Amos could probably blast it open with some of the explosives we found in that big box of weapons."

Holden laughed.

"Well," he said. "Since it's probably full of little vials of nasty alien viruses, I'm going to nix the blasting option."

Naomi shut down the comm log and pulled up a general ship's systems menu.

"I can look around and see if the computer has access to the safe," she said. "Try to open it that way. It might take some time."

"Do what you can," Holden said. "We'll get out of your hair."

Holden pushed himself off the ceiling and over to the ops compartment hatch, then pulled himself through, into the corridor beyond. A few moments later, Miller followed. The detective planted his feet on the deck with magnetic boots, then stared at Holden, waiting.

Holden floated down to the deck next to him.

"What do you think?" Holden asked. "Protogen being the whole thing? Or is this another one where it looks like them, so it isn't?"

Miller was silent for the space of two long breaths.

"This one smells like the real thing," Miller said. He sounded almost grudging.

Amos pulled himself up the crew ladder from below, dragging a large metal case behind him.

"Hey, Cap'n," he said. "I found a whole case of fuel pellets for the reactor in the machine shop. We'll probably want to take these with us."

"Good work," Holden said, holding up one hand to let Miller know to wait. "Go ahead and take those across. Also, I need you to work up a plan for scuttling this ship."

"Wait, what?" Amos said. "This thing is worth a *jillion* bucks, Captain. Stealth missile ship? The OPA would sell their grandmothers for this thing. And six of those tubes still have fish in them. Capital-ship busters. You could slag a small moon with those. Forget their grannies, the OPA would pimp their daughters for that gear. Why the fuck would we blow it up?"

Holden stared at him in disbelief.

"Did you forget what's in the engine room?" he asked.

"Hell, Cap," Amos snorted. "That shit is all frozen. Couple hours with a torch and I can chop it up and chuck it out the airlock. Good to go."

The mental image of Amos hacking the melted bodies of the ship's former crew apart with a plasma torch and then cheerfully hurling the chunks out an airlock tipped Holden over the edge into full-fledged nausea. The big mechanic's ability just to ignore anything that he didn't want to notice probably came in handy while he was crawling around in tight and greasy engine compartments. His ability to shrug off the horrible mutilation of several dozen people threatened to change Holden's disgust into anger.

"Forgetting the mess," he said, "and the very real possibility of infection by what *made* that mess, there is also the fact that someone is desperately searching for this very expensive and very stealthy ship, and so far *Alex can't find the ship that's looking.*"

He stopped talking and nodded at Amos while the mechanic mulled that over. He could see Amos' broad face working as he put it together in his head. *Found a stealth ship. Other people looking for stealth ship. We can't see the other people looking for it.*

Shit.

Amos' face went pale.

"Right," he said. "I'll set the reactor up to slag her." He looked down at the time on his suit's forearm display. "Shit, we've been here too long. Better get the lead out."

"Better had," Miller agreed.

Naomi was good. *Very* good. Holden had discovered this when he'd signed on with the *Canterbury,* and over the course of years, he'd added it to his list of facts, along with *space is cold* and *the direction of gravity is down.* When something stopped working on the water hauler, he'd tell Naomi to fix it, and then never think of it again. Sometimes she'd claim not to be able to fix something, but it was always a negotiating tactic. A short conversation would lead to a request for spare parts or an additional crewman hired on at the next port, and that would be that. There was no problem that involved electronics or spaceship parts she couldn't solve.

"I can't open the safe," she said.

She floated next to the safe in the captain's quarters, one foot resting lightly on his bunk to stabilize herself as she gestured. Holden stood on the floor with his boot mags on. Miller was in the hatchway to the corridor.

"What would you need?" Holden asked.

"If you won't let me blast it or cut it, I can't open it."

Holden shook his head, but Naomi either didn't see it or ignored him.

"The safe is designed to open when a very specific pattern of magnetic fields is played across that metal plate on the front," she said. "Someone has a key designed to do that, but that key isn't on this ship."

"It's at that station," Miller said. "He wouldn't send it there if they couldn't open it."

Holden stared at the wall safe for a moment, his fingers tapping on the bulkhead beside it.

"What're the chances cutting it sets off a booby trap?" he said.

"Fucking excellent, Cap," Amos said. He was listening in from the torpedo bay as he hacked the small fusion reactor that powered one of the six remaining torpedoes to go critical. Working on the ship's main reactor was too dangerous with the shielding stripped off.

"Naomi, I really want that safe and the research notes and samples it contains," Holden said.

"You don't know that's what's in there," Miller said, then laughed. "No, of course that's what's in there. But it won't help us if we get blown up or, worse, if some piece of goo-coated shrapnel makes a hole in our nice suits."

"I'm taking it," Holden replied, then pulled a piece of chalk from his suit's pocket and drew a line around the safe on the bulkhead. "Naomi, cut a small hole in the bulkhead and see if there's anything that would stop us from just cutting the whole damned thing out and taking it with us."

"We'd have to take out half the wall."

"Okay."

Naomi frowned, then shrugged, then smiled and nodded with one hand.

"All right, then," she said. "Thinking of taking it to Fred's people?"

Miller laughed again, a dry humorless rasp that made Holden uneasy. The detective had been watching the video of Julie Mao's fight with her captors over and over again while they'd waited on Naomi and Amos to finish their work. It gave Holden the disquieting feeling that Miller was storing the footage in his head. Fuel for something he planned to do later.

"Mars would give you your lives back in exchange for this," Miller said. "I hear Mars is nice if you're rich."

"Fuck rich," Amos said with a grunt as he worked on something below. "They'd build statues of us."

"We have an agreement with Fred to let him outbid any other contracts we take," Holden said. "Of course, this isn't really a contract per se..."

Naomi smiled and winked at Holden.

"So what is it, sir?" she said, her voice faintly mocking. "OPA heroes? Martian billionaires? Start your own biotech firm? What are we doing here?"

Holden pushed away from the safe and kicked out toward the airlock and the cutting torch that waited there with their other tools.

"I don't know yet," he said. "But it sure feels nice to have choices again."

Amos pushed the button again. No new stars flared in the dark. The radiation and infrared sensors remained quiet.

"There's supposed to be an explosion, right?" Holden asked.

"Fuck, yes," Amos said, then pushed the button on the black box in his hand a third time. "This isn't an exact science or anything. Those missile drives are as simple as it gets. Just a reactor with one wall missing. Can't exactly predict…"

"It isn't rocket science," Holden said with a laugh.

"What?" Amos asked, ready to be angry if he was being mocked.

"You know, 'it isn't rocket science,'" Holden said. "Like 'it isn't hard.' You're a rocket scientist, Amos. For real. You work on fusion reactors and starship drives for a living. Couple hundred years ago, people would have been lining up to give you their children for what you know."

"What the fu—" Amos started, but stopped when a new sun flared outside the cockpit window, then faded quickly. "See? Fucking told you it would work."

"Never doubted it," Holden said, then slapped Amos on one meaty shoulder and headed aft down the crew ladder.

"What the fuck was that about?" Amos asked no one in particular as Holden drifted away.

He headed through the ops deck. Naomi's chair was empty. He'd ordered her to get some sleep. Strapped down to loops inset in the deck was the stealth ship's safe. It looked bigger cut out of the wall. Black and imposingly solid. The kind of container in which one kept the end of the solar system.

Holden floated over to it and quietly said, "Open sesame."

The safe ignored him, but the deck hatch opened and Miller pulled himself up into the compartment. His environment suit had been traded in for a stale-smelling blue jumpsuit and his ever-present hat. There was something about the look on his face that made Holden uncomfortable. Even more so than the detective usually made him.

"Hey," Holden said.

Miller just nodded and pulled himself over to one of the workstations, then buckled in to one of the chairs.

"We decided on a destination yet?" he asked.

"No. I'm having Alex run the numbers on a couple of possibilities, but I haven't made up my mind."

"Been watching the news at all?" the detective asked.

Holden shook his head, then moved over to a chair on the other side of the compartment. Something in Miller's face was chilling his blood.

"No," he said. "What happened?"

"You don't hedge, Holden. I admire that about you, I guess."

"Just tell me," Holden said.

"No, I mean it. A lot of people claim to believe in things. 'Family is most important,' but they'll screw a fifty-dollar hooker on payday. 'Country first,' but they cheat on their taxes. Not you, though. You say everyone should know everything, and by God, you put your money where your mouth is."

Miller waited for him to say something, but Holden didn't know what. This speech had the feel of something the detective had prepared ahead of time. Might as well let him finish it.

"So Mars finds out that maybe Earth's been building ships on the side, ones with no flag on them. Some of them might have killed a Martian flagship. I bet Mars calls up to check. I mean, it's the Earth-Mars Coalition Navy, one big happy hegemony. Been policing the solar system together for almost a hundred years. Commanding officers are practically sleeping together. So it must be a mistake, right?"

"Okay," Holden said, waiting.

"So Mars calls," Miller said. "I mean, I don't know for sure, but I bet that's how it starts. A call from some bigwig on Mars to some bigwig on Earth."

"Seems reasonable," Holden said.

"What d'you think Earth says back?"

"I don't know."

Miller reached over and flipped on one of the screens, then pulled up a file with his name on it, date stamped from less than an hour before. A recording of video from a Martian news source, showing the night sky through a Martian dome. Streaks and flashes fill the sky. The ticker across the bottom of the feed says that Earth ships in orbit around Mars suddenly and without warning fired on their Martian counterparts. The streaks in the sky are missiles. The flashes are ships dying.

And then a massive white flare turns the Martian night into day for a few seconds, and the crawl says that the Deimos deep radar station has been destroyed.

Holden sat and watched the video display the end of the solar system in vivid color and with expert commentary. He kept waiting for the streaks of light to begin descending on the planet itself, for the domes to fly apart in nuclear fire, but it seemed someone had kept some measure of restraint, and the battle remained in the sky.

It couldn't stay that way forever.

"You're telling me that I did this," Holden said. "That if I hadn't broadcast that data, those ships would still be alive. Those people."

"That, yeah. And that if the bad guys wanted to keep people from watching Eros, it just worked."

Chapter Thirty-Six: Miller

The war stories flowed in. Miller watched the feeds five at a time, subscreens crowding the face of his terminal. Mars was shocked, amazed, reeling. The war between Mars and the Belt—the biggest, most dangerous conflict in the history of mankind—was suddenly a sideshow. The reactions of the talking heads of Earth security forces ran the gamut from calm, rational discussion of preemptive defense to foaming-at-the-mouth denunciations of Mars as a pack of baby-raping animals. The attack on Deimos had turned the moon into a slowly spreading ring of gravel in the moon's old orbit, a smudge on the Martian sky, and with that, the game had changed again.

Miller watched for ten hours as the attack became the blockade. The Martian navy, spread throughout the system, was turning home under heavy burn. The OPA feeds were calling it a victory, and maybe someone thought that was true. The pictures came through from the ships, from the sensor arrays. Dead warships, their sides ripped open by high-energy explosions, spinning out into their irregular orbital graves. Medical bays like the *Roci*'s filled with boys and girls half his age bleeding, burning, dying. Each cycle, new footage came in, new details of death and carnage. And each time some new clip appeared, he sat forward, hand on his mouth, waiting for the word to come. The one event that would signal the end of it all.

But it hadn't come yet, and every hour that didn't bring it gave another sliver of hope that maybe, *maybe* it wasn't going to happen.

"Hey," Amos said. "You slept at all?"

Miller looked up, his neck stiff. Red creases of his pillow still on his cheek and forehead, the mechanic stood in the open doorway of Miller's cabin.

"What?" Miller said. Then: "Yeah, no. I've been…watching."

"Anyone drop a rock?"

"Not yet. It's all still orbital or higher."

"What kind of half-assed apocalypse are they running down there?" Amos said.

"Give 'em a break. It's their first."

The mechanic shook his broad head, but Miller could see the relief under the feigned disgust. As long as the domes were still standing on Mars, as long as the critical biosphere of Earth wasn't in direct threat, humanity wasn't dead. Miller had to wonder what they were hoping for out in the Belt, whether they'd managed to talk themselves into believing that the rough ecological pockets of the asteroids would sustain life indefinitely.

"You want a beer?" Amos asked.

"You're having beer for breakfast?"

"Figure it's dinner for you," Amos said.

The man was right. Miller needed sleep. He hadn't managed more than a catnap since they'd scuttled the stealth ship, and that had been plagued by strange dreams. He yawned at the thought of yawning, but the tension in his gut said he was more likely to spend the day watching newsfeeds than resting.

"It's probably breakfast again," Miller said.

"Want some beer for breakfast?" Amos asked.

"Sure."

Walking through the *Rocinante* felt surreal. The quiet hum of the air recyclers, the softness of the air. The journey out to Julie's ship was a haze of pain medication and sickness. The time on Eros before that was a nightmare that wouldn't fade. To walk through the spare, functional corridors, thrust gravity holding him gently to the floor, with very little chance of anyone trying to kill him felt suspicious. When he imagined Julie walking with him, it wasn't so bad.

As he ate, his terminal chimed, the automatic reminder for another blood flush. He stood, adjusted his hat, and headed off to let the needles and pressure injectors do their worst. The captain was already there and hooked into a station when Miller arrived.

Holden looked like he'd slept, but not well. There weren't the bruise-dark marks under his eyes that Miller had, but his shoulders were tense, his brow on the edge of furrowed. Miller wondered whether he'd been a little too hard on the guy. *I told you so* could be an important message, but the burden of innocent death, of the chaos of a failing civilization might also be too much for one man to carry.

Or maybe he was still mooning over Naomi.

Holden raised the hand that wasn't encased in medical equipment.

"Morning," Miller said.

"Hey."

"Decided where we're going yet?"

"Not yet."

"Getting harder and harder to get to Mars," Miller said, easing himself into the familiar embrace of the medical station. "If that's what you're aiming for, you'd better do it soon."

"While there's still a Mars, you mean?"

"For instance," Miller agreed.

The needles snaked out on gently articulated armatures. Miller looked at the ceiling, trying not to tense up as the lines forced their way into his veins. There was a moment's stinging, then a low, dull ache, and then numbness. The display above him announced the state of his body to doctors who were watching young soldiers die miles above Olympus Mons.

"Do you think they'd stop?" Holden asked. "I mean, Earth has got to be doing this because Protogen owns some generals or senators or something, right? It's all because they want to be the only ones who have this thing. If Mars has it too, Protogen doesn't have a reason to fight."

Miller blinked. Before he could pick his answer—*They'd try to annihilate Mars completely,* or *It's gone too far for that,* or *Exactly how naive are you, Captain?*—Holden went on.

"Screw it. We've got the datafiles. I'm going to broadcast them."

Miller's reply was as easy as reflex.

"No, you aren't."

Holden propped himself up, storm clouds in his expression.

"I appreciate that you might have a reasonable difference of opinion," he said, "but this is still my ship. You're a passenger."

"True," Miller said. "But you have a hard time shooting people, and you are going to have to shoot me before you send that thing out."

"I'm *what*?"

The new blood flowed into Miller's system like a tickle of ice water crawling toward his heart. The medical monitors shifted to a new pattern, counting up the anomalous cells as they hit its filters.

"You are going to have to shoot me," Miller said, slowly this time. "Twice now you've had the choice of whether or not to break the solar system, and both times you've screwed it up. I don't want to see you strike out."

"I think you may have an exaggerated idea of how much influence the second-in-command of a long-distance water hauler actually has. Yes, there's a war. And yes, I was there when it started up. But the Belt has hated the inner planets since a long time before the *Cant* was attacked."

"You've got the inner planets divided up too," Miller said.

Holden tilted his head.

"Earth has always hated Mars," Holden said like he was reporting that water was wet. "When I was in the navy, we ran projections for this. Battle plans if Earth and Mars ever really got into it. Earth loses. Unless they hit first, hit hard, and don't let up, Earth just plain loses."

Maybe it was distance. Maybe it was a failure of imagination. Miller had never seen the inner planets as divided.

"Seriously?" he asked.

"They're the colony, but they have all the best toys and everyone knows it," Holden said. "Everything that's happening out there right now has been building up for a hundred years. If it hadn't been there to start with, this couldn't have happened."

"That's your defense? 'Not my powder keg; I just brought the match'?"

"I'm not making a defense," Holden said. His blood pressure and heart rate were spiking.

"We've been through this," Miller said. "So let me just ask, why is it you think this time will be different?"

The needles in Miller's arm seemed to heat up almost to the point of being painful. He wondered if that was normal, if every blood flush he had was going to feel the same way.

"This time *is* different," Holden said. "All the crap that's going on out there is what happens when you have imperfect information. Mars and the Belt wouldn't have been going after each other in the first place if they'd known what we know now. Earth and Mars wouldn't be shooting each other if everyone knew the fight was being engineered. The problem isn't that people know too much, it's that they don't know enough."

Something hissed and Miller felt a wave of chemical relaxation swim through him. He resented it, but there was no calling the drugs back.

"You can't just throw information at people," Miller said. "You have to know what it *means*. What it's going to *do*. There was a case back on Ceres. Little girl got killed. For the first eighteen hours, we were all sure Daddy did it. He was a felon. A drunk. He was the last one who saw her breathing. All the classic signs. Hour nineteen, we get a tip. Turned out Daddy owed a lot of money to one of the local syndicates. All of a sudden, things are more complicated. We have more suspects. Do you think if I'd been broadcasting everything I knew, Daddy would still have been alive when the tip came? Or would someone have put it all together and done the obvious thing?"

Miller's medical station chimed. Another new cancer. He ignored it. Holden's cycle was just finishing, the redness of his cheeks speaking as much to the fresh, healthy blood in his body as to his emotional state.

"That's the same ethos they have," Holden said.

"Who?"

"Protogen. You may be on different sides, but you're playing the same game. If everyone said what they knew, none of this would have happened. If the first lab tech on Phoebe who saw something weird had gotten on his system and said, 'Hey, everyone! Look, this is weird,' none of this would have happened."

"Yeah," Miller said, "because telling everyone there's an alien virus that wants to kill them all is a great way to maintain calm and order."

"Miller," Holden said. "I don't mean to panic you, but there's an alien virus. And it wants to kill everyone."

Miller shook his head and smiled like Holden had said something funny. "So look, maybe I can't point a gun at you and make you do the right thing. But lemme ask you something. Okay?"

"Fine," Holden said. Miller leaned back. The drugs were making his eyelids heavy.

"What happens?" Miller said.

There was a long pause. Another chime from the medical system. Another rush of cold through Miller's abused veins.

"What happens?" Holden repeated. It occurred to Miller he could have been more specific. He forced his eyes open again.

"You broadcast everything we've got. What happens?"

"The war stops. People go after Protogen."

"There's some holes in that, but let it go. What happens after that?"

Holden was quiet for a few heartbeats.

"People start going after the Phoebe bug," he said.

"They start experimenting. They start fighting for it. If that little bastard's as valuable as Protogen thinks, you can't stop the war. All you can do now is change it."

Holden frowned, angry lines at the corners of his mouth and eyes. Miller watched a little piece of the man's idealism die and was sorry that it gave him joy.

"So what happens if we get to Mars?" Miller went on, his voice low. "We trade out the protomolecule for more money than any of us have ever seen. Or maybe they just shoot you. Mars just wins against Earth. And the Belt. Or you go to the OPA, who are the best hope the Belt has of independence, and they're a bunch of crazy zealots, half of 'em thinking we can actually sustain out there without Earth. And trust me, they'll probably shoot you too. Or you just tell everyone everything and pretend that however it comes down, you kept your hands clean."

"There's a right thing to do," Holden said.

"You don't have a right thing, friend," Miller said. "You've got a whole plateful of maybe a little less wrong."

Holden's blood flush finished. The captain pulled the needles out of his arm and let the thin metallic tentacles retract. As he rolled down his sleeve, the frown softened.

"People have a right to know what's going on," Holden said. "Your argument boils down to you not thinking people are smart enough to figure out the right way to use it."

"Has anyone used anything you've broadcast as something besides an excuse to shoot someone they already didn't like? Giving them a new reason won't stop them killing each other," Miller said. "You started these wars, Captain. Doesn't mean you can stop them. But you have to try."

"And how am I supposed to do that?" Holden said. The distress in his voice could have been anger. It could have been prayer.

Something in Miller's belly shifted, some inflamed organ calming enough to slip back into place. He hadn't been aware he'd felt wrong until he suddenly felt right again.

"You ask yourself *what happens*," Miller said. "Ask yourself what Naomi'd do."

Holden barked out a laugh. "Is that how you make your decisions?"

Miller let his eyes close. Juliette Mao was there, sitting on the couch at her old apartment on Ceres. Fighting the crew of the stealth ship to a standstill. Burst open by the alien virus on the floor of her shower stall.

"Something like it," Miller said.

The report from Ceres, a break from the usual competing press releases, came that night. The governing council of the OPA announced that a ring of Martian spies had been rooted out. The video feed showed the bodies floating out an industrial airlock in what looked like the old docks in sector six. At a distance, the victims seemed almost peaceful. The feed cut to the head of security. Captain Shaddid looked older. Harder.

"We regret the necessity of this action," she said to everyone everywhere. "But in the cause of freedom, there can be no compromise."

That's what it's come to, Miller thought, rubbing a hand across his chin. *Pogroms after all. Cut off just a hundred more heads, just a thousand more heads, just ten thousand more heads, and then we'll be free.*

A soft alert sounded, and a moment later, gravity shifted a few degrees to Miller's left. Course change. Holden had made a decision.

He found the captain sitting alone and staring at a monitor in ops. The glow lit his face from below, casting shadows up into his eyes. The captain looked older too.

"You make the broadcast?" Miller asked.

"Nope. We're just one ship. We tell everyone what this thing is and that we've got it, we'll be dead before Protogen."

"Probably true," Miller said, sitting at an empty station with a grunt. The gimbaled seat shifted silently. "We're going someplace."

"I don't trust them with it," Holden said. "I don't trust any of them with that safe."

"Probably smart."

"I'm going to Tycho Station. There's someone there I...trust."

"Trust?"

"Don't actively distrust."

"Naomi think it's the right thing?"

"I don't know. I didn't ask her. But I think so."

"Close enough," Miller said.

Holden looked up from the monitor for the first time.

"You know the right thing?" Holden said.

"Yeah."

"What is it?"

"Throw that safe into a long collision course with the sun and find a way to make sure no one ever, ever goes to Eros or Phoebe again," Miller said. "Pretend none of this ever happened."

"So why aren't we doing that?"

Miller nodded slowly. "How do you throw away the holy grail?"

Chapter Thirty-Seven: Holden

Alex had the *Rocinante* running at three-quarters of a g for two hours while the crew prepared and ate dinner. He would run it back up to three when the break was over, but in the meantime, Holden enjoyed standing on his own two legs at something not too far off from Earth gravity. It was a little heavy for Naomi and Miller, but neither of them complained. They both understood the need for haste.

Once the gravity had dropped from the crush of high acceleration, the whole crew quietly gathered in the galley and started making dinner. Naomi blended together fake eggs and fake cheese. Amos cooked tomato paste and the last of their fresh mushrooms into a red sauce that actually smelled like the real thing. Alex, who had the duty watch, had forwarded ship ops down to a panel in the galley and sat at a table next to it, spreading the fake cheese paste and red sauce onto flat noodles in hopes that the end result would approximate lasagna. Holden had oven duty and had spent the lasagna prep time baking frozen lumps of dough into bread. The smell in the galley was not entirely unlike actual food.

Miller had followed the crew into the galley but seemed uncomfortable asking for something to do. Instead, he set the table and then sat down at it and watched. He wasn't exactly avoiding Holden's eyes, but he wasn't going out of his way to catch his attention. By unspoken mutual agreement, no one had any of the news channels on. Holden was sure everyone would rush back to check the current state of the war as soon as dinner was over, but for now they all worked in companionable silence.

When the prep was done, Holden switched off bread duty and on to moving lasagna-filled cookware into and out of the oven. Naomi sat down next to Alex and began a quiet conversation with him about something she'd seen on the ops screen. Holden split his time between watching her and watching the lasagna. She laughed at something Alex said and unconsciously twisted one finger into her hair. Holden felt his belly tighten a notch.

Out of the corner of his eye, he thought he saw Miller staring at him. When he looked, the detective had turned away, a hint of a smile on his face. Naomi laughed again. She had one hand on Alex's arm, and the pilot was blushing and talking as fast as his silly Martian drawl would let him. They looked like friends. That both made Holden happy and filled him with jealousy. He wondered if Naomi would ever be his friend again.

She caught him looking and gave him a conspiratorial wink that probably would have made a lot of sense if he'd been able to hear what Alex was saying. He smiled and winked back, grateful just to be included in the moment. A sizzling sound from inside the oven called his attention back. The lasagna was beginning to bubble and run over the sides of the dishes.

He pulled on his oven mitts and opened the door.

"Soup's on," he said, pulling the first of the dishes and putting it on the table.

"That's mighty ugly-looking soup," Amos said.

"Uh, yeah," Holden said. "It's just something Mother Tamara used to say when she'd finished cooking. Not sure where it comes from."

"One of your *three* mothers did the cooking? How traditional," Naomi said with a smirk.

"Well, she split it pretty evenly with Caesar, one of my fathers."

Naomi smiled at him, a genuine smile now.

"It sounds really nice," she said. "Big family like that."

"Yeah, it really was," he replied, a vision in his head of nuclear fire tearing apart the Montana farmhouse he'd grown up in, his family blowing into ash. If it happened, he was sure Miller would be there to let him know it was his fault. He wasn't sure he'd be able to argue anymore.

As they ate, Holden felt a slow release of tension in the room. Amos belched loudly, then reacted to the chorus of protests by doing it again even more loudly. Alex retold the joke that had made Naomi laugh. Even Miller got into the mood and told a long and increasingly improbable story about hunting down a black market cheese operation that ended in a gunfight with nine naked Australians in an illegal brothel. By the finish of the story, Naomi was laughing so hard she'd drooled on her shirt, and Amos kept repeating "No fucking way!" like a mantra.

The story was amusing enough, and the detective's dry delivery suited it well, but Holden only half listened. He watched his crew, saw the tension falling from their faces and shoulders. He and Amos were both from Earth, though if he had to guess, he'd say Amos had forgotten about his home world the first time he'd shipped out. Alex was from Mars and clearly still loved it. One bad mistake on either side and both planets might be radioactive rubble by the end of dinner. But right now they were just friends having a meal together. It was right. It was what Holden had to keep fighting for.

"I actually remember that cheese shortage," Naomi said once Miller had stopped talking. "Belt-wide. That was your fault?"

"Yeah, well, if they'd only been sneaking cheese past the government auditors, we wouldn't have had a problem," Miller said. "But they had this habit of shooting the other cheese smugglers. Makes the cops notice. Bad business."

"Over fucking *cheese*?" Amos said, tossing his fork onto his plate with a clack. "Are you serious? I mean, drugs or gambling or something. But cheese?"

"Gambling's legal, most places," Miller said. "And a chemistry class dropout can cook up just about any drug you like in his bathroom. No way to control supply."

"Real cheese comes from Earth, or Mars," Naomi added. "And after they tack on shipping costs and the Coalition's fifty percent in taxes, it costs more than fuel pellets."

"We wound up with one hundred and thirty kilos of Vermont Cheddar in the evidence lockup," Miller said. "Street value that would have probably bought someone their own ship. It had disappeared by the end of the day. We wrote it up as lost to spoilage. No one said a word, as long as everyone went home with a brick."

The detective leaned back in his chair with a distant look on his face.

"My God, that was good cheese," he said with a smile.

"Yeah, well, this fake stuff does taste like shit," Amos said, then added in a hurry, "No offense, Boss, you did a real good job whipping it up. But that's still weird to me, fighting over cheese."

"It's why they killed Eros," Naomi said.

Miller nodded but said nothing.

"How do you figure that?" Amos said.

"How long have you been flying?" Naomi asked.

"I dunno," Amos replied, his lips compressing as he did the mental math. "Twenty-five years, maybe?"

"Fly with a lot of Belters, right?"

"Yeah," Amos said. "Can't get better shipmates than Belters. 'Cept me, of course."

"You've flown with us for twenty-five years, you like us, you've learned the patois. I bet you can order a beer and a hooker on any station in the Belt. Heck, if you were a little taller and a lot skinnier, you could pass for one of us by now."

Amos smiled, taking it as a compliment.

"But you still don't get us," Naomi said. "Not really. No one who grew up with free air ever will. And that's why they can kill a million and a half of us to figure out what their bug really does."

"Hey now," Alex interjected. "You serious 'bout that? You think the inners and outers see themselves as that different?"

"Of course they do," Miller said. "We're too tall, too skinny, our heads look too big, and our joints too knobby."

Holden noticed Naomi glancing across the table at him, a speculative look on her face. *I like your head,* Holden thought at her, but the radiation hadn't given him telepathy either, because her expression didn't change.

"We've practically got our own language now," Miller said. "Ever see an Earther try to get directions in the deep dig?"

" 'Tu run spin, pow, Schlauch tu way acima and ido,' " Naomi said with a heavy Belter accent.

"Go spinward to the tube station, which will take you back to the docks," Amos said. "The fuck's so hard about that?"

"I had a partner wouldn't have known that after two years on Ceres," Miller said. "And Havelock wasn't stupid. He just wasn't...*from* there."

Holden listened to them talk and pushed cold pasta around on his plate with a chunk of bread.

"Okay, we get it," he said. "You're weird. But to kill a million and a half people over some skeletal differences and slang..."

"People have been getting tossed into ovens for less than that ever since they invented ovens," Miller said. "If it makes you feel better, most of us think you're squat and microcephalic."

Alex shook his head.

"Don't make a lick of sense to me, turnin' that bug loose, even if you hated every single human on Eros personally. Who knows what that thing'll do?"

Naomi walked to the galley sink and washed her hands, the running water drawing everyone's attention.

"I've been thinking about that," she said, then turned around, wiping her hands on a towel. "The point of it, I mean."

Miller started to speak, but Holden hushed him with a quick gesture and waited for Naomi to continue.

"So," she said. "I've been thinking of it as a computing problem. If the virus or nanomachine or protomolecule or whatever was designed, it has a purpose, right?"

"Definitely," Holden said.

"And it seems like it's trying to do something—something complex. It doesn't make sense to go to all that trouble just to kill people. Those changes it makes look intentional, just…not complete, to me."

"I can see that," Holden said. Alex and Amos nodded along with him but stayed quiet.

"So maybe the issue is that the protomolecule isn't smart enough yet. You can compress a lot of data down pretty small, but unless it's a quantum computer, processing takes space. The easiest way to get that processing in tiny machines is through distribution. Maybe the protomolecule isn't finishing its job because it just isn't smart enough to. Yet."

"Not enough of them," Alex said.

"Right," Naomi said, dropping the towel into a bin under the sink. "So you give them a lot of biomass to work with, and see what it is they are ultimately made to do."

"According to that guy in the video, they were made to hijack life on Earth and wipe us out," Miller said.

"And that," Holden said, "is why Eros is perfect. Lots of biomass in a vacuum-sealed test tube. And if it gets out of hand, there's already a war going on. A lot of ships and missiles can be used for nuking Eros into glass if the threat seems real. Nothing to make us forget our differences like a new player butting in."

"Wow," Amos said. "That is really, really fucked up."

"Okay. But even though that's probably what's happened," Holden said, "I still can't believe that there are enough evil people all in one place to do it. This isn't a one-man operation. This is the work of dozens, maybe hundreds, of very smart people. Does Protogen just go around recruiting every potential Stalin and Jack the Ripper it runs across?"

"I'll make sure to ask Mr. Dresden," Miller said, an unreadable expression on his face, "when we finally meet."

Tycho's habitat rings spun serenely around the bloated zero-g factory globe in the center. The massive construction waldoes that sprouted from the top were maneuvering an enormous piece of hull plating onto the side of the *Nauvoo.* Looking at the station on the ops screens while Alex finished up docking procedures, Holden felt something like relief. So far, Tycho was the one place no one had tried to shoot them, or blow them up, or vomit goo on them, and that practically made it home.

Holden looked at the research safe clamped securely to the deck and hoped that he hadn't just killed everyone on the station by bringing it there.

As if on cue, Miller pulled himself through the deck hatch and drifted over to the safe. He gave Holden a meaningful look.

"Don't say it. I'm already thinking it," Holden said.

Miller shrugged and drifted over to the ops station.

"Big," he said, nodding at the *Nauvoo,* on Holden's screen.

"Generation ship," Holden said. "Something like that will give us the stars."

"Or a lonely death on a long trip to nowhere," Miller replied.

"You know," Holden said, "some species' version of the great galactic adventure is shooting virus-filled bullets at their neighbors. I think ours is pretty damn noble in comparison."

Miller seemed to consider that, nodded, and watched Tycho Station swell on the monitor as Alex brought them closer. The detective kept one hand on the console, making the micro adjustments necessary to remain still even as the pilot's maneuvers threw unexpected bursts of gravity at them from every direction. Holden was strapped into his chair. Even concentrating, he couldn't handle zero g and intermittent thrust half that well. His brain just couldn't be trained out of the twenty-odd years he'd spent with gravity as a constant.

Naomi was right. It would be so easy to see Belters as alien. Hell, if you gave them time to develop some really efficient implantable oxygen storage and recycling and kept trimming the environment suits down to the minimum necessary for heat, you might wind up with Belters who spent more time outside their ships and stations than in.

Maybe that was why they were taxed to subsistence level. The bird was out of the cage, but you couldn't let it stretch its wings too far or it might forget it belonged to you.

"You trust this Fred?" Miller asked.

"Sort of," Holden said. "He treated us well last time, when everyone else wanted us dead or locked up."

Miller grunted, as if that proved nothing.

"He's OPA, right?"

"Yeah," Holden said. "But I think maybe the real OPA. Not the cowboys who want to shoot it out with the inners. And not those nuts on the radio calling for war. Fred's a politician."

"What about the ones keeping Ceres in line?"

"I don't know," Holden said. "I don't know about them. But Fred's the best shot we have. Least wrong."

"Fair enough," Miller said. "We won't find a political solution to Protogen, you know."

"Yeah," Holden said, then began unbuckling his harness as the *Roci* slid into its berth with a series of metallic bangs. "But Fred isn't *just* a politician."

Fred sat behind his large wooden desk, reading the notes Holden had written about Eros, the search for Julie, and the discovery of the stealth ship. Miller sat across from him, watching Fred like an entomologist might watch a new species of bug, guessing if it was likely to sting. Holden was a little farther away on Fred's right, trying not to keep looking at the clock on his hand terminal. On the huge screen behind the desk, the *Nauvoo* drifted by like the metal bones of some dead and decaying leviathan. Holden could see the tiny spots of brilliant blue light where workers used welding torches on the hull and frame. To occupy himself, he started counting them.

He'd reached forty-three when a small shuttle appeared in his field of view, a load of steel beams clutched in a pair of heavy manipulator arms, and flew toward the half-built generation ship. The shuttle shrank to a point no larger than the tip of a pen before it stopped. The *Nauvoo* suddenly shifted in Holden's mind from a large ship relatively nearby, to a gigantic ship farther away. It gave him a short rush of vertigo.

His hand terminal beeped at almost the same instant that Miller's did. He didn't even look at it; he just tapped the face to shut it up. He knew this routine by now. He pulled out a small bottle, took out two blue pills, and swallowed them dry. He could hear Miller pouring pills out of his bottle as well. The ship's expert medical system dispensed them for him every week with a warning that failing to take them on schedule would lead to horrific death. He took them. He would for the rest of his life. Missing a few would just mean that wasn't very long.

Fred finished reading and threw his hand terminal down on the desk, then rubbed his eyes with the heels of his hands for several seconds. To Holden, he looked older than the last time they'd seen each other.

"I have to tell you, Jim, I have no idea what to make of this," he finally said.

Miller looked at Holden and mouthed, *Jim,* at him with a question on his face. Holden ignored him.

"Did you read Naomi's addition at the end?" Holden asked.

"The bit with the networked nanobugs for increased processing power?"

"Yeah, that bit," Holden said. "It makes sense, Fred."

Fred laughed without humor, then stabbed one finger at his terminal.

"That," he said. "That only makes sense to a psychopath. No one sane could do that. No matter what they thought they might get out of it."

Miller cleared his throat.

"You have something to add, Mr. Muller?" Fred asked.

"Miller," the detective replied. "Yes. First—and all respect here—don't kid yourself. Genocide's old-school. Second, the facts aren't in question. Protogen infected Eros Station with a lethal alien disease, and they're recording the results. Why doesn't matter. We need to stop them."

"And," Holden said, "we think we can track down where their observation station is."

Fred leaned back in his chair, the fake leather and metal frame creaking under his weight even in the one-third g.

"Stop them how?" he asked. Fred knew. He just wanted to hear them say it out loud. Miller played along.

"I'd say we fly to their station and shoot them."

"Who is 'we'?" Fred asked.

"There are a lot of OPA hotheads looking to shoot it out with Earth and Mars," Holden said. "We give them some real bad guys to shoot at instead."

Fred nodded in a way that didn't mean he agreed to anything.

"And your sample? The captain's safe?" Fred said.

"That's mine," Holden said. "No negotiation on that."

Fred laughed again, though there was some humor in it this time. Miller blinked in surprise and then stifled a grin.

"Why would I agree to that?" Fred asked.

Holden lifted his chin and smiled.

"What if I told you that I've hidden the safe on a planetesimal booby-trapped with enough plutonium to break anyone who touches it into their component atoms even if they could find it?" he said.

Fred stared at him for a moment, then said, "But you didn't."

"Well, no," Holden said. "But I could tell you I did."

"You are too honest," Fred said.

"And you can't trust anyone with something this big. You already know what I'm going to do with it. That's why, until we can agree on something better, you're leaving it with me."

Fred nodded.

"Yes," he said, "I guess I am."

Chapter Thirty-Eight: Miller

The observation deck looked out over the *Nauvoo* as the behemoth slowly came together. Miller sat on the edge of a soft couch, his fingers laced over his knee, his gaze on the immense vista of the construction. After his time on Holden's ship and, before that, in Eros, with its old-style closed architecture, a view so wide seemed artificial. The deck itself was wider than the *Rocinante* and decorated with soft ferns and sculpted ivies. The air recyclers were eerily quiet, and even though the spin gravity was nearly the same as Ceres', the Coriolis felt subtly wrong.

He'd lived in the Belt his whole life, and he'd never been anywhere that was designed so carefully for the tasteful display of wealth and power. It was pleasant as long as he didn't think about it too much.

He wasn't the only one drawn to the open spaces of Tycho. A few dozen station workers sat in groups or walked through together. An hour before, Amos and Alex had gone by, deep in their own conversation, so he wasn't entirely surprised when, standing up and walking back toward the docks, he saw Naomi sitting by herself with a bowl of food cooling on a tray at her side. Her gaze was fixed on her hand terminal.

"Hey," he said.

Naomi looked up, recognized him, and smiled distractedly.

"Hey," she said.

Miller nodded toward the hand terminal and shrugged a question.

"Comm data from that ship," she said. It was always *that ship*, Miller noticed. The same way people would call a particularly godawful crime scene *that place*. "It's all tightbeam, so I thought it wouldn't be so hard to triangulate. But..."

"Not so much?"

Naomi lifted her eyebrows and sighed.

"I've been plotting orbits," she said. "But nothing's fitting. There could be relay drones, though. Moving targets the ship system was calibrated for that would send the message on to the actual station. Or another drone, and then the station, or who knows?"

"Any data coming off Eros?"

"I assume so," Naomi said, "but I don't know that it would be any easier to make sense of than this."

"Can't your OPA friends do something?" Miller asked. "They've got more processing power than one of these handhelds. Probably have a better activity map of the Belt too."

"Probably," she said.

He couldn't tell if she didn't trust this Fred that Holden had given them over to, or just needed to feel like the investigation was still hers. He considered telling her to back off it for a while, to let the others carry it, but he didn't see he had the moral authority to make that one stick.

"What?" Naomi said, an uncertain smile on her lips.

Miller blinked.

"You were laughing a little," Naomi said. "I don't think I've ever seen you laugh before. I mean, not when something was funny."

"I was just thinking about something a partner of mine told me about letting cases go when you got pulled from them."

"What did he say?"

"That it's like taking half a shit," Miller said.

"Had a way with words, that one."

"He was all right for an Earther," Miller said, and something tickled at the back of his mind. Then, a moment later: "Ah, Jesus. I may have something."

Havelock met him in an encrypted drop site that lived on a server cluster on Ganymede. The latency kept them from anything like real-time conversation. It was more like dropping notes, but it did the trick. The waiting made Miller anxious. He sat with his terminal set to refresh every three seconds.

"Would you like anything else?" the woman asked. "Another bourbon?"

"That'd be great," Miller said, and checked to see if Havelock had replied yet. He hadn't.

Like the observation deck, the bar looked out on the *Nauvoo,* though from a slightly different angle. The great ship looked foreshortened, and arcs of energy lit it where a layer of ceramic was annealing. A bunch of religious zealots were going to load themselves into that massive ship, that small self-sustaining world, and launch themselves into the darkness between the stars. Generations would live and die in it, and if they were mind-bendingly lucky enough to find a planet worth living on the end of the journey, the people who came out of it would never have known Earth or Mars or the Belt. They'd be aliens already. And if whatever had made the protomolecule was out there to greet them, then what?

Would they all die like Julie had?

There was life out there. They had proof of it now. And the proof came in the shape of a weapon, so what did that tell him?

380 JAMES S. A. COREY

Except that maybe the Mormons deserved a little warning about what they were signing their great-grandkids up for.

He laughed to himself when he realized that was exactly what Holden would say.

The bourbon arrived at the same moment his hand terminal chimed. The video file had a layered encryption that took almost a minute to unpack. That alone was a good sign.

The file opened, and Havelock grinned out from the screen. He was in better shape than he'd been on Ceres, and it showed in the shape of his jaw. His skin was darker, but Miller didn't know if it was purely cosmetic or if his old partner had been basking in false sunlight for the joy of it. It didn't matter. It made the Earther look rich and fit.

"Hey, buddy," Havelock said. "Good to hear from you. After what happened with Shaddid and the OPA, I was afraid we were going to be on different sides now. I'm glad you got out of there before the shit hit the fan.

"Yeah, I'm still with Protogen, and I've got to tell you, these guys are kind of scary. I mean, I've worked contract security before, and I'm pretty clear when someone's hard-core. These guys aren't cops. They're troops. You know what I mean?

"Officially, I don't know dick about a Belt station, but you know how it is. I'm from Earth. There are a lot of these guys who gave me shit about Ceres. Working with the vacuum-heads. That kind of thing. But the way things are here, it's better to be on the good side of the bad guys. It's just that kind of job."

There was an apology in his expression. Miller understood. Working in some corporations was like going to prison. You adopted the views of the people around you. A Belter might get hired on, but he'd never belong. Like Ceres, just pointed the other way. If Havelock had made friends with a set of inner planet mercs who spent their off nights curb-stomping Belters outside bars, then he had.

But making friends didn't mean he was one of them.

"So. Off the record, yeah, there's a black ops station in the Belt.

I hadn't heard it called Thoth, but it could be. Some sort of very scary deep research and development lab. Heavy science crew, but not a huge place. I think *discreet* would be the word. Lots of automated defenses, but not a big ground crew.

"I don't need to tell you that leaking the coordinates would get my ass killed out here. So wipe the file when you're done, and let's not talk again for a long, long time."

The datafile was small. Three lines of plaintext orbital notation. Miller put it into his hand terminal and killed the file off the Ganymede server. The bourbon still sat beside his hand, and he drank it off neat. The warmth in his chest might have been the alcohol or it might have been victory.

He turned on the hand terminal's camera.

"Thanks. I owe you one. Here's part of the payment. What happened on Eros? Protogen was part of it, and it's big. If you get the chance to drop your contract with them, do it. And if they try to rotate you out to that black ops station, don't go."

Miller frowned. The sad truth was that Havelock was probably the last real partner he'd had. The only one who'd looked on him as an equal. As the kind of detective Miller had imagined himself to be.

"Take care of yourself, partner," he said, then ended the file, encrypted it, shipped it out. He had the bone-deep feeling he wasn't ever going to talk to Havelock again.

He put through a connection request to Holden. The screen filled with the captain's open, charming, vaguely naive face.

"Miller," Holden said. "Everything okay?"

"Yeah. Great. But I need to talk to your Fred guy. Can you arrange that?"

Holden frowned and nodded at the same time.

"Sure. What's going on?"

"I know where Thoth Station is," Miller said.

"You know what?"

Miller nodded.

"Where the hell did you get that?"

Miller grinned. "If I gave you that information and it got out, a good man would get killed," he said. "You see how that works?"

It struck Miller as he, Holden, and Naomi waited for Fred that he knew an awful lot of inner planet types fighting against the inner planets. Or at least not for them. Fred, supposedly a high-ranking OPA member. Havelock. Three-quarters of the crew of the *Rocinante*. Juliette Mao.

It wasn't what he would have expected. But maybe that was shortsighted. He was seeing the thing the way Shaddid and Protogen did. There were two sides fighting—that was true enough—but they weren't the inner planets versus the Belters. They were the people who thought it was a good idea to kill people who looked or acted differently against the people who didn't.

Or maybe that was a crap analysis too. Because given the chance to put the scientist from the Protogen pitch, the board of directors, and whoever this Dresden piece of shit was into an airlock, Miller knew he'd agonize about it for maybe half a second after he blew them all into vacuum. Didn't put him on the side of angels.

"Mr. Miller. What can I do for you?"

Fred. The Earther OPA. He wore a blue button-down shirt and a nice pair of slacks. He could have been an architect or a mid-level administrator for any number of good, respectable corporations. Miller tried to imagine him coordinating a battle.

"You can convince me that you've really got what it takes to kill the Protogen station," Miller said. "Then I'll tell you where it is."

Fred's eyebrows rose a millimeter.

"Come into my office," Fred said.

Miller went. Holden and Naomi followed. When the doors closed behind them, Fred was the first to speak.

"I'm not sure exactly what you want from me. I'm not in the habit of making my battle plans public knowledge."

"We're talking about storming a station," Miller said. "Something with damn good defenses and maybe more ships like the one that killed the *Canterbury*. No disrespect intended, but that's a pretty tall order for a bunch of amateurs like the OPA."

"Ah, Miller?" Holden said. Miller held up a hand, cutting him off.

"I can give you the directions to Thoth Station," Miller said. "But if I do that and it turns out you haven't got the punch to see this through, then a lot of people die and nothing gets resolved. I'm not up for that."

Fred cocked his head, like a dog hearing an unfamiliar sound. Naomi and Holden shared a glance that Miller couldn't parse.

"This is a war," Miller said, warming to the subject. "I've worked with the OPA before, and frankly you folks are a lot better at little guerrilla bullshit than at coordinating anything real. Half of the people who claim to speak for you are crackpots who happened to have a radio nearby. I see you've got a lot of money. I see you've got a nice office. What I don't see—what I need to see—is that you've got what it takes to bring these bastards down. Taking out a station isn't a game. I don't care how many simulations you've run. This is real now. If I'm going to help you, I need to know you can handle it."

There was a long silence.

"Miller?" Naomi said. "You know who Fred is, right?"

"The Tycho mouthpiece for the OPA," Miller said. "That doesn't draw a whole lot of water with me."

"He's Fred *Johnson*," Holden said.

Fred's eyebrows rose another millimeter. Miller frowned and crossed his arms.

"Colonel Frederick Lucius Johnson," Naomi said, clarifying.

Miller blinked. "The Butcher of Anderson Station?" he said.

"The same," Fred said. "I have been talking with the central council of the OPA. I have a cargo ship with more than enough troops to secure the station. Air support is a state-of-the-art Martian torpedo bomber."

"The *Roci*?" Miller said.

"The *Rocinante*," Fred agreed. "And while you may not believe it, I actually know what I'm doing."

Miller looked at his feet, then up toward Holden.

"*That* Fred Johnson?" he said.

"I thought you knew," Holden said.

"Well. Don't I feel like the flaming idiot," Miller said.

"It'll pass," Fred said. "Was there anything else you wanted to demand?"

"No," Miller said. And then: "Yes. I want to be part of the ground assault. When we take that station crew, I want to be there."

"Are you sure?" Fred said. "'Taking out a station isn't a game.' What makes you think *you* have what it takes?"

Miller shrugged.

"One thing it takes is the coordinates," Miller said. "I have got those."

Fred laughed. "Mr. Miller. If you'd like to go down to this station and have whatever's waiting for us down there try to kill you along with the rest of us, I won't stand in your way."

"Thanks," Miller said. He pulled up his hand terminal and sent the plaintext coordinates to Fred. "There you go. My source is solid, but he's not working from firsthand data. We should confirm before we commit."

"I'm not an amateur," Colonel Fred Johnson said, looking at the file. Miller nodded, adjusted his hat, and walked out. Naomi and Holden flanked him. When they reached the wide, clean public hallway, Miller looked to his right, catching Holden's eyes.

"Really, I thought you knew," Holden said.

Eight days later, the message came. The cargo ship *Guy Molinari* had arrived, full up with OPA soldiers. Havelock's coordinates had been verified. Something was sure as hell out there, and it appeared to be collecting the tightbeamed data from Eros. If Miller wanted to be part of this, the time had come to move out.

He sat in his quarters in the *Rocinante* for what was likely the last time. He realized with a little twinge, equal parts surprise and sorrow, that he was going to miss the place. Holden, for all his faults and Miller's complaints, was a decent guy. In over his head and only half aware of the fact, but Miller could think of more than one person who fit that bill. He was going to miss Alex's odd, affected drawl and Amos' casual obscenity. He was going to wonder if and how Naomi ever worked things out with her captain.

Leaving was a reminder of things he'd already known: that he didn't know what would come next, that he didn't have much money, and that while he was sure he could get back from Thoth Station, where and how he went from there was going to be improvisation. Maybe there would be another ship he could sign on with. Maybe he'd have to take a contract and save up some money to cover his new medical expenses.

He checked the magazine in his gun. Packed his spare clothes into the small, battered pack he'd taken on the transport from Ceres. Everything he owned still fit in it.

He turned off the lights and made his way down the short corridor toward the ladder-lift. Holden was in the galley, twitching nervously. The dread of the coming battle was already showing in the corners of the man's eyes.

"Well," Miller said. "Here we go, eh?"

"Yep," Holden said.

"It's been a hell of a ride," Miller said. "Can't say it's all been pleasant, but…"

"Yeah."

"Tell the others I said goodbye," Miller said.

"Will do," Holden said. Then, as Miller moved past him toward the lift: "So assuming we all actually live through this, where should we meet up?"

Miller turned.

"I don't understand," he said.

"Yeah, I know. Look, I trust Fred or I wouldn't have come here. I think he's honorable, and he'll do the right thing by us. That doesn't mean I trust the whole OPA. After we get this thing done,

I want the whole crew together. Just in case we need to get out in a hurry."

Something painful happened under Miller's sternum. Not a sharp pain, just a sudden ache. His throat felt thick. He coughed to clear it.

"As soon as we get the place secure, I'll get in touch," Miller said.

"Okay, but don't take too long. If Thoth Station has a whorehouse left standing, I'm going to need help prying Amos out of it."

Miller opened his mouth, closed it, and tried again.

"Aye, aye, Captain," he said, forcing a lightness into his voice.

"Be careful," Holden said.

Miller left, pausing in the passageway between ship and station until he was sure he'd stopped weeping, and then making his way to the cargo ship and the assault.

Chapter Thirty-Nine: Holden

The *Rocinante* hurtled through space like a dead thing, tumbling in all three axes. With the reactor shut down and all the cabin air vented, it radiated neither heat nor electromagnetic noise. If it weren't for its speeding toward Thoth Station significantly faster than a rifle shot, the ship would be indistinguishable from the rocks in the Belt. Nearly half a million kilometers behind it, the *Guy Molinari* screamed the *Roci*'s innocence to anyone who would listen, and fired its engines in a long slow deceleration.

With the radio off, Holden couldn't hear what they were saying, but he'd helped write the warning, so it echoed in his head anyway. *Warning! Accidental detonation on the cargo ship* Guy Molinari *has broken large cargo container free. Warning to all ships in its path: Container is traveling at high speed and without independent control. Warning!*

There had been some discussion about not broadcasting at all.

Because Thoth was a black station, they'd be using only passive sensors. Scanning every direction with radar or ladar would light them up like a Christmas tree. It was possible that with its reactor off, the *Rocinante* could sneak up on the station without being noticed. But Fred had decided that if they were somehow spotted, it would be suspicious enough to probably warrant an immediate counterattack. So instead of playing it quiet, they'd decided to play it loud and count on confusion to help them.

With luck the Thoth Station security systems would scan them and see that they were in fact a big chunk of metal flying on an unchanging vector and lacking apparent life support, and ignore them just long enough to let them get close. From far away, the stations' defense systems might be too much for the *Roci*. But up close, the maneuverable little ship could dart around the station and cut it to pieces. All their cover story needed to do was buy them time while the station's security team tried to figure out what was going on.

Fred, and by extension everyone in the assault, was betting that the station wouldn't fire until they were absolutely certain they were under attack. Protogen had gone to a lot of trouble to hide their research lab in the Belt. As soon as they launched their first missile, their anonymity was lost forever. With the war going on, monitors would pick up the fusion torch trails and wonder what was up. Firing a weapon would be Thoth Station's last resort.

In theory.

Sitting alone inside the tiny bubble of air contained in his helmet, Holden knew that if they were wrong, he'd never even realize it. The *Roci* was flying blind. All radio contact was down. Alex had a mechanical timepiece with a glow-in-the-dark face, and a to-the-second schedule memorized. They couldn't beat Thoth at high-tech, so they were flying as low-tech as you could get. If they'd missed their guess and the station fired on them, the *Roci* would be vaporized without warning. Holden had once dated a Buddhist who said that death was merely a different state of being, and people only feared the unknown that lay behind that transition. Death without warning was preferable, as it removed all fear.

He felt he now had the counterargument.

To keep his mind busy, he ran through the plan again. When they were practically close enough to spit on Thoth Station, Alex would fire up the reactor and do a braking maneuver at nearly ten g's. The *Guy Molinari* would begin spraying radio static and laser clutter at the station to confuse its targeting package for the few moments the *Roci* would need to come around on an attack vector. The *Roci* would engage the station's defenses, disabling anything that could hurt the *Molinari,* while the cargo ship moved in to breach the station's hull and drop off her assault troops.

There were any number of things wrong with this plan.

If the station decided to fire early, just in case, the *Roci* could die before the fight even started. If the station's targeting system could cut the *Molinari*'s static and laser clutter, they might begin firing while the *Roci* was still getting into position. And even if all that worked perfectly, there was still the assault team, cutting their way into the station and fighting corridor to corridor to the nerve center to take control. Even the inner planets' best marines were terrified of breaching actions, and for good reason. Moving through unfamiliar metal hallways without cover while the enemy ambushed you at every intersection was a good way to get a lot of people killed. In training simulations back in the Earth navy, Holden had never seen the marines do better than 60 percent casualties. And these weren't inner planet marines with years of training and state-of-the-art equipment. They were OPA cowboys with whatever gear they could scrape together at the last minute.

But even that wasn't what really worried Holden.

What really worried him was the large, slightly-warmer-than-space area just a few dozen meters above Thoth Station. The *Molinari* had spotted it and warned them before cutting them loose. Having seen the stealth ships before, no one on the *Roci* doubted that this was another one.

Fighting the station would be bad enough, even up close, where most of the station's advantages were lost. But Holden didn't look forward to dodging torpedo fire from a missile frigate at the same time. Alex had assured him that if they could get in close enough to the station, they could keep the frigate from firing at them for fear of damaging Thoth, and that the *Roci*'s greater maneuverability would make it more than a match for the larger and more heavily armed ship. The stealth frigates were a strategic weapon, he'd said, not a tactical one. Holden hadn't said, *Then why do they have one here?*

Holden moved to glance down at his wrist, then snorted with frustration in the pitch black of the ops deck. His suit was powered down, chronometers and lights both. The only system on in his suit was air circulation, and that was strictly mechanical. If something got fouled up with it, no little warning lights would come on; he'd just choke and die.

He glanced around the dark room and said, "Come on, how much longer?"

As if in answer, lights began flickering on through the cabin. There was a burst of static in his helmet; then Alex's drawling voice said, "Internal comms online."

Holden began flipping switches to bring the rest of the systems back up.

"Reactor," he said.

"Two minutes," Amos replied from the engine room.

"Main computer."

"Thirty seconds to reboot," Naomi said, and waved at him from across the ops deck. The lights had come up enough for them to see each other.

"Weps?"

Alex laughed with something like genuine glee over the comm.

"Weapons are coming online," he said. "As soon as Naomi gives me back the targeting comp, we'll be cocked, locked, and ready to rock."

Hearing everyone check in after the long and silent darkness of their approach reassured him. Being able to look across the room and see Naomi working at her tasks eased a dread he hadn't even realized he'd been feeling.

"Targeting should be up now," Naomi said.

"Roger that," Alex replied. "Scopes are up. Radar, up. Ladar, up— Shit, Naomi, you seeing this?"

"I see it," Naomi said. "Captain, getting engine signatures from the stealth ship. They're powering up too."

"We expected that," Holden said. "Everyone stay on task."

"One minute," Amos said.

Holden turned on his console and pulled up his tactical display. In the scope, Thoth Station turned in a lazy circle while the slightly warm spot above it got hot enough to resolve a rough hull outline.

"Alex, that doesn't look like the last frigate," Holden said. "Does the *Roci* recognize it yet?"

"Not yet, Cap, but she's workin' on it."

"Thirty seconds," Amos said.

"Getting ladar searches from the station," Naomi said. "Broadcasting chatter."

Holden watched on his screen as Naomi tried to match the wavelength the station was using to target them, and began spraying the station with their own laser comm array to confuse the returns.

"Fifteen seconds," Amos said.

"Okay, buckle up, kids," Alex said. "Here comes the juice."

Even before Alex had finished saying it, Holden felt a dozen pinpricks as his chair pumped him full of drugs to keep him alive during the coming deceleration. His skin went tight and hot, and his balls crawled up into his belly. Alex seemed to be speaking in slow motion.

"Five...four...three...two..."

He never said *one*. Instead, a thousand kilos sat on Holden's chest and rumbled like a laughing giant as the *Roci*'s engine slammed on the brakes at ten g's. Holden thought he could actually feel his lungs scraping the inside of his rib cage as his chest did its best to collapse. But the chair pulled him into a soft gel-filled embrace, and the drugs kept his heart beating and his brain processing. He didn't black out. If the high-g maneuvering killed him, he'd be wide awake and lucid for the entire thing.

His helmet filled with the sound of gurgling and labored breathing, only some of which was his own. Amos managed part of a curse before his jaw was clamped shut. Holden couldn't hear the *Roci* shuddering with the strain of her course change, but he could feel it through the seat. She was tough. Tougher than any of them. They'd be long dead before the ship pulled enough g's to hurt itself.

When relief came, it came so suddenly that Holden almost vomited. The drugs in his system stopped that too. He took a deep breath and the cartilage of his sternum clicked painfully back into place.

"Check in," he muttered. His jaw hurt.

"Comm array targeted," Alex replied immediately. Thoth Station's comm and targeting array was the first item on their target priority list.

"All green," Amos said from below.

"Sir," Naomi said, a warning in her voice.

"Shit, I see it," Alex said.

Holden told his console to mirror Naomi's so he could see what she was looking at. On her screen, the *Roci* had figured out why it couldn't identify the stealth ship.

There were two ships, not one large and ungainly missile frigate that they could dance around and cut to pieces at close range. No, that would have been too easy. These were two much smaller ships parked close together to trick enemy sensors. And now they were both firing their engines and splitting up.

Okay, Holden thought. *New plan.*

"Alex, get their attention," he said. "Can't let them go after the *Molinari*."

"Roger," Alex replied. "One away."

Holden felt the *Roci* shudder as Alex fired a torpedo at one of the two ships. The smaller ships were rapidly changing speed and vector, and the torpedo had been fired hastily and from a bad angle. It wouldn't score a hit, but the *Roci* would be on everyone's scope as a threat now. So that was good.

Both of the smaller ships darted away in opposite directions at full burn, spraying chaff and laser chatter behind them as they went. The torpedo wobbled in its trajectory and then limped away in a random direction.

"Naomi, Alex, any idea what we're facing here?" Holden asked.

"*Roci* still doesn't recognize them, sir," Naomi said.

"New hull design," Alex said over her. "But they're flyin' like fast interceptors. Guessin' a torpedo or two on the belly, and a keel-mounted rail gun."

Faster and more maneuverable than the *Roci,* but they'd be able to fire in only one direction.

"Alex, come around to—" Holden's order was cut short when the *Rocinante* shuddered and jumped sideways, hurling him into the side of his restraints with rib-bruising force.

"We're hit!" Amos and Alex yelled at the same time.

"Station shot us with some sort of heavy gauss cannon," Naomi said.

"Damage," Holden said.

"Went clean through us, Cap," Amos said. "Galley and the machine shop. Got yellows on the board, but nothing that'll kill us."

Nothing that'll kill us sounded good, but Holden felt a pang for his coffeemaker.

"Alex," Holden said. "Forget the little ships, kill that comm array."

"Roger," Alex replied, and the *Roci* lurched sideways as Alex changed course to begin his torpedo run on the station.

"Naomi, as soon as the first one of those fighters comes around on his attack run, give him the comm laser in the face, full strength, and start dropping chaff."

"Yes, sir," she replied. Maybe the laser would be enough to screw up his targeting system for a few seconds.

"Station's openin' up with the PDCs," Alex said. "This'll get a mite bumpy."

Holden switched from mirroring Naomi's screen to watching Alex's. His panel filled with thousands of rapidly moving balls of light and Thoth Station rotating in the background. The *Roci*'s threat computer was outlining the incoming point defense cannon fire with bright light on Alex's HUD. It was moving impossibly fast, but at least with the system doing a bright overlay on each round, the pilot could see where the fire was coming from and which direction it was traveling. Alex reacted to this threat information with consummate skill, maneuvering away from the PDCs' direction of fire in quick, almost random movements that forced the automated targeting of the point defense cannons to adjust constantly.

To Holden, it looked like a game. Incredibly fast blobs of light flew up from the space station in chains, like long and thin pearl necklaces. The ship moved restlessly, finding the gaps between the threads and dodging away to a new gap before the strands could react and touch her. But Holden knew that each blob of light represented a chunk of Teflon-coated tungsten steel with a depleted uranium heart, going thousands of meters per second. If Alex lost the game, they'd know it when the *Rocinante* was cut to pieces.

Holden almost jumped out of his skin when Amos spoke. "Shit, Cap, got a leak somewhere. Three port maneuvering thrusters are losing water pressure. Going to patch it."

"Copy, Amos. Go fast," Holden said.

"You hang on down there, Amos," Naomi said.

Amos just snorted.

On his console, Holden watched as Thoth Station grew larger on the scope. Somewhere behind them, the two fighters were probably coming about. The thought made the back of Holden's head itch, but he tried to keep focus. The *Roci* didn't have enough torpedoes for Alex to fire shot after shot at the station from far off and hope one made it through the point defense fire. Alex had to bring them in so close that the cannons couldn't shoot the torpedo down.

A blue highlight appeared on the HUD surrounding a portion of the station's central hub. The highlighted portion expanded into a smaller subscreen. Holden could make out the dishes and antennas that made up the comm and targeting array.

"One away," Alex said, and the *Roci* vibrated as her second torpedo was fired.

Holden shook violently in his restraints and then slapped back into his chair as Alex took the *Roci* through a series of sudden maneuvers and then slammed down the throttle to evade the last of the PDC fire. Holden watched his screen as the red dot of their missile streaked toward the station and struck the comm array. A flash blanked out his screen for a second and then faded. Almost immediately the PDC fire stopped.

"Good sh—" Holden was cut off by Naomi yelling, "Bogey one has fired! Two fast movers!"

Holden flipped back to her screen and saw the threat system tracking both fighters and two smaller and much faster objects moving toward the *Roci* on an intercept course.

"Alex!" Holden said.

"Got it, Chief. Going defensive."

Holden slammed back into his chair again as Alex poured on the speed. The steady rumble of the engine seemed to stutter, and Holden realized he was feeling the constant fire of their own PDCs as they tried to shoot down the pursuing missiles.

"Well, fuck," Amos said almost conversationally.

"Where are you?" Holden asked, then flipped his screen to Amos' suit camera. The mechanic was in a dimly illuminated crawl space filled with conduit and piping. That meant he was between the inner and outer hulls. In front of him, a section of damaged pipe looked like snapped bones. A cutting torch floated nearby. The ship bounced violently, banging the mechanic around in the tight space. Alex whooped over the comm.

"Missiles did not impact!" he said.

"Tell Alex to stop jerking her around," Amos said. "Makes it hard to hang on to my tools."

"Amos, get back to your crash couch!" Naomi said.

"Sorry, Boss," Amos replied with a grunt as he yanked one end of the broken pipe free. "If I don't fix this and we lose pressure, Alex won't be able to turn to starboard anymore. Bet that'll fuck us up good."

"Keep working, Amos," Holden said over Naomi's protests. "But hang on. This is going to get worse."

Amos said, "Roger that."

Holden switched back to Alex's HUD display.

"Holden," Naomi said. There was fear in her voice. "Amos is going to get—"

"He's doing his job. Do yours. Alex, we have to take these two out before the *Molinari* gets here. Get me an intercept on one of them and let's kick its ass."

"Roger that, Cap," Alex said. "Going after bogey two. Could use some help with bogey one."

"Bogey one is Naomi's priority," Holden said. "Do what you can to keep it off of our backside while we kill his friend."

"Roger," Naomi said in a tight voice.

Holden switched back to Amos' helmet camera, but the mechanic seemed to be doing fine. He was cutting the damaged pipe free with his torch, and a length of replacement pipe floated nearby.

"Strap that pipe down, Amos," Holden said.

"All respect, Captain," Amos said, "but safety standards can kiss my ass. I'm getting this done fast and getting outta here."

Holden hesitated. If Alex had to make a course correction, the floating pipe could turn into a projectile massive enough to kill Amos or break the *Roci*. *It's Amos,* he told himself. *He knows what he's doing.*

Holden flipped to Naomi's screen as she poured everything the comm system had at the small interceptor, trying to blind it with light and radio static. Then he went back to his tactical display.

The *Roci* and bogey two flew toward each other at suicidal speeds. As soon as they passed the point where incoming torpedo fire couldn't be avoided, bogey two launched both his missiles. Alex flagged the two fast movers for the PDCs and kept up his intercept course but didn't launch missiles.

"Alex, why aren't we shooting?" Holden said.

"Gonna shoot his torpedoes down, then get in close and let the PDCs chew him up," the pilot replied.

"Why?"

"We've only got so many torpedoes and no resupply. No call to waste 'em on these munchkins."

The incoming torpedoes arced forward on Holden's display, and he felt the *Roci*'s PDCs firing to shoot them down.

"Alex," he said. "We didn't pay for this ship. Feel free to use it up. If I get killed so you can save ammo, I am going to put a reprimand in your permanent file."

"Well, you put it that way…" Alex said. Then: "One away."

The red dot of their torpedo streaked off toward bogey two. The incoming missiles got closer and closer, and then one disappeared from the display.

Alex said, "Shit," in a flat voice, and then the *Rocinante* slammed sideways hard enough that Holden broke his nose on the inside of his helmet. Yellow emergency lights began rotating on all the bulkheads, though with the ship evacuated of air, Holden mercifully couldn't hear the Klaxons that were trying to sound throughout it. His tactical display flickered, went out, and then came back after a second. When it came back up, all three torpedoes, as well as bogey two, were gone. Bogey one continued to bear down on them from astern.

"Damage!" Holden yelled, hoping the comm was still up.

"Major damage to the outer hull," Naomi replied. "Four maneuvering thrusters gone. One PDC nonresponsive. We've also lost O2 storage, and the crew airlock looks like it's slag."

"Why are we alive?" Holden asked while he flipped through the damage report and then over to Amos' suit camera.

"The fish didn't hit us," Alex said. "The PDC got it, but it was close. Warhead detonated and sprayed us down pretty good."

It didn't look like Amos was moving. Holden yelled, "Amos! Report!"

"Yeah, yeah, still here, Captain. Just hanging on in case we get knocked around like that again. I think I busted a rib on one of the hull braces, but I'm strapped down. Good fucking thing I didn't waste time with that pipe, though."

Holden didn't take time to answer. He flipped back to his tactical display and watched the rapidly approaching bogey one. It had already fired its torpedoes, but at close range it could still cut them apart with its cannon.

"Alex, can you get us turned around and get a firing solution on that fighter?" he said.

"Working on it. Don't have much maneuverability," Alex replied, and the *Roci* began rotating with a series of lurches.

Holden switched to a telescope and zoomed in on the approaching fighter. Up close, the muzzle of its cannon looked as big around as a corridor on Ceres, and it appeared to be aimed directly at him.

"Alex," he said.

"Working on it, Chief, but the *Roci*'s hurtin'."

The enemy ship's cannon flared open, preparing to fire.

"Alex, kill it. Kill it *kill it kill it.*"

"One away," the pilot said, and the *Rocinante* shuddered.

Holden's console threw him out of the scope view and back to the tactical view automatically. The *Roci*'s torpedo flew toward the fighter at almost the same instant that the fighter opened up with its cannon. The display showed the incoming rounds as small red dots moving too fast to follow.

"Incom—" he shouted, and the *Rocinante* came apart around him.

Holden came to.

The inside of the ship was filled with flying debris and bits of superheated metal shavings that looked like slow-motion showers of sparks. With no air, they bounced off walls and then floated, slowly cooling, like lazy fireflies. He had a vague memory of one corner of a wall-mounted monitor detaching and bouncing off three bulkheads in the world's most elaborate billiards shot, then hitting him right below the sternum. He looked down, and the little chunk of monitor was floating a few centimeters in front of him, but there was no hole in his suit. His guts hurt.

The ops console chair next to Naomi had a hole in it; green gel slowly leaked into small balls that floated away in the zero g. Holden looked at the hole in the chair, and the matching hole in the bulkhead across the room, and realized that the round must have passed within centimeters of Naomi's leg. A shudder swept through him, leaving him nauseated in its wake.

"What the fuck was that?" Amos asked quietly. "And how about we don't do it anymore?"

"Alex?" Holden said.

"Still here, Cap," the pilot replied, his voice eerily calm.

"My panel's dead," Holden said. "Did we kill that son of a bitch?"

"Yeah, Cap, he's dead. About half a dozen of his rounds actually hit the *Roci*. Looks like they went through us from bow to stern. That anti-spalling webbing on the bulkheads really keeps the shrapnel down, doesn't it?"

Alex's voice had started shaking. He meant *We should all be dead.*

"Open a channel to Fred, Naomi," Holden said.

She didn't move.

"Naomi?"

"Right. Fred," she said, then tapped on her screen.

Holden's helmet was filled with static for a second, then with Fred's voice.

"*Guy Molinari* here. Glad you guys are still alive."

"Roger that. Begin your run. Let us know when we can limp over to one of the station's docks."

"Roger," Fred replied. "We'll find you a nice place to land. Fred out."

Holden pulled the quick release on his chair's restraints and floated toward the ceiling, his body limp.

Okay, Miller. Your turn.

Chapter Forty: Miller

O i, Pampaw," the kid in the crash couch to Miller's right said. "Popped seal, you and bang, hey?"

The kid's combat armor was gray-green, articulated pressure seals at the joints and stripes across the front plates where a knife or flechette round had scraped the finish. Behind the face mask, the kid could have been fifteen. His hand gestures spoke of a childhood spent in vacuum suits, and his speech was pure Belt creole.

"Yeah," Miller said, raising his arm. "Saw some action recently. I'll be fine."

"Fine's fine as fine," the kid said. "But you hold to the foca, and neto can pass the air out to you, hey?"

No one on Mars or Earth would have the first clue what you're saying, Miller thought. *Shit, half the people on Ceres would be embarrassed by an accent that thick. No wonder they don't mind killing you.*

"Sounds good to me," Miller said. "You go first, and I'll try to keep anyone from shooting you in the back."

The kid grinned. Miller had seen thousands like him. Boys in the throes of adolescence, working through the normal teenage drive to take risks and impress girls, but at the same time they lived in the Belt, where one bad call meant dead. He'd seen thousands. He'd arrested hundreds. He'd watched a few dozen picked up in hazmat bags.

He leaned forward to look down the long rows of close-packed gimbaled crash couches that lined the gut of the *Guy Molinari*. Miller's rough estimate put the count at between ninety and a hundred of them. So by dinner, chances were good he'd have seen a couple dozen more die.

"What's your name, kid?"

"Diogo."

"Miller," he said, and gave the kid his hand to shake. The high-quality Martian battle armor Miller had taken from the *Rocinante* let his fingers flex a lot more than the kid's.

The truth was Miller was in no shape for the assault. He was still getting occasional waves of inexplicable nausea, and his arm ached whenever the medication level in his blood started thinning out. But he knew his way around a gun, and he probably knew more about corridor-to-corridor fighting than nine-tenths of the OPA rock jumpers and ore hogs like Diogo who were about to go in. It would have to be good enough.

The ship's address system clicked once.

"This is Fred. We've had word from air support, and we're green for breach in ten minutes. Final checks start now, people."

Miller sat back in his couch. The clicking and chattering of a hundred suits of armor, a hundred sidearms, a hundred assault weapons filled the air. He'd been over his own enough times now; he didn't feel the urge to do it again.

In a few minutes, the burn would come. The cocktail of high-g drugs was kept on the ragged edge, since they'd be going straight from the couches into a firefight. No point having your assault force more doped than necessary.

Julie sat on the wall beside him, her hair swirling around her like she was underwater. He imagined the dappled light flashing across her face. Portrait of the young pinnace racer as a mermaid. She smiled at the idea, and Miller smiled back. She would have been here, he knew. Along with Diogo and Fred and all the other OPA militia, patriots of the vacuum, she'd have been in a crash couch, wearing borrowed armor, heading into the station to get herself killed for the greater good. Miller knew he wouldn't have. Not before her. So in a sense, he'd taken her place. He'd become her.

They made it, Julie said, or maybe only thought. If the ground attack was going forward, it meant the *Rocinante* had survived — at least long enough to knock out the defenses. Miller nodded, acknowledging her and letting himself feel a moment's pleasure at the idea, and then thrust gravity pushed him into his couch so hard that his consciousness flickered, and the hold around him dimmed. He felt it when the braking burn came, all the crash couches spinning to face the new up. Needles dug into Miller's flesh. Something deep and loud happened, the *Guy Molinari* ringing like a gigantic bell. The breaching charge. The world pulled hard to the left, the couch swinging for the last time as the assault ship matched the station's spin.

Someone was shouting at him. "Go go go!" Miller lifted his assault rifle, tapped the sidearm strapped to his thigh, and joined the press of bodies making for the exit. He missed his hat.

The service corridor they'd cut into was narrow and dim. The schematics the Tycho engineers had worked up suggested they wouldn't see any real resistance until they got into the manned parts of the station. That had been a bad guess. Miller staggered in with the other OPA soldiers in time to see an automatic defense laser cut the first rank in half.

"Team three! Gas it!" Fred snapped in all their ears, and half a dozen blooms of thick white anti-laser smoke burst into the close air. The next time a defense laser fired, the walls flashed with mad iridescence, and the smoke of burning plastic filled the air, but no one died. Miller pressed forward and up a red metal ramp. A welding charge flared, and a service door swung open.

The corridors of Thoth Station were wide and roomy, with long swaths of ivy grown in carefully tended spirals, niches every few feet with tastefully lit bonsai. Soft light the pure white of sunlight made the place feel like a spa or a rich man's private residence. The floors were carpet.

The HUD in his armor flickered, marking the path the assault was meant to take. Miller's heart stepped up to a fast, constant flutter, but his mind seemed to grow perfectly still. At the first intersection, a riot barrier was manned by a dozen men in Protogen security uniforms. The OPA troops hung back, using the curve of the ceiling as cover. What suppressing fire there was came in kneecap low.

The grenades were perfectly round, not even a hole where the pin had been pulled. They didn't roll as well on the soft industrial carpet as they would have on stone or tiling, so one of the three went off before it reached the barrier. The concussion was like being hit in the ears with a hammer; the narrow, sealed corridors channeled the blast back at them almost as much as at the enemy. But the riot barrier shattered, and the Protogen security men fell back.

As they all rushed forward, Miller heard his new, temporary compatriots whooping with the first taste of victory. The sound was muffled, as if they were a long way away. Maybe his earpieces hadn't dampened the blast as much as they were supposed to. Making the rest of the assault with blown eardrums wouldn't be easy.

But then Fred came on, and his voice was clear enough.

"Do not advance! Hold back!"

It was almost enough. The OPA ground force hesitated, Fred's orders pulling at them like a leash. These weren't troops. They weren't even cops. They were a Belter irregular militia; discipline and respect for authority weren't natural to them. They slowed. They got careful. So rounding the corner, they didn't walk into the trap.

The next corridor was long and straight, leading—the HUD suggested—to a service ramp up toward the control center. It looked empty, but a third of the way to the curve horizon, the carpeting started to fly apart in ragged tufts. One of the boys beside Miller grunted and went down.

"They are using low-shrapnel rounds and bouncing them off the curve," Fred said into all their ears at once. "Bank-shot rico-chet. Stay low, and do exactly as I say."

The calm in the Earther's voice had more effect than his shout-ing had. Miller thought he might have been imagining it, but there also seemed to be a deeper tone. A certainty. The Butcher of Anderson Station doing what he did best, leading his troops against the tactics and strategies he'd helped create back when he'd been the enemy.

Slowly, the OPA forces moved forward, up one level, and then the next, then the next. The air grew hazy with smoke and ablated paneling. The wide corridors opened into broad plazas and squares, as airy as prison yards, with the Protogen forces in the guard towers. The side corridors were locked down, local security trying to channel them into situations where they could be caught in crossfire.

It didn't work. The OPA forced open the doors, taking cover in display-rich rooms, something between lecture halls and manu-facturing complexes. Twice, unarmored civilians, still at their work despite the ongoing assault, attacked them when they entered. The OPA boys mowed them down. Part of Miller's mind—the part that was still a cop and not a soldier—twitched at that. They were civilians. Killing them was, at the very least, bad form. But then Julie whispered in the back of his mind, *No one here is innocent,* and he had to agree.

The operations center was a third of the way up the station's slight gravity well, defended better than anything they had seen so far. Miller and five others, directed by the all-knowing voice of Fred, took cover in a narrow service corridor, keeping a steady suppressing fire up the main corridor toward ops, and making sure no Protogen counterattack would go unanswered. Miller checked his assault weapon and was surprised to see how much ammunition was left.

"Oi, Pampaw," the kid next to him said, and Miller smiled, recognizing Diogo's voice behind the face mask. "Day's the day, passa?"

"I've seen worse," Miller agreed, then paused. He tried to scratch his injured elbow, but the armor plates kept anything satisfying from happening.

"Beccas tu?" Diogo asked.

"No, I'm fine. It's just...this place. I don't get it. It looks like a spa, and it's built like a prison."

The boy's hands shifted in query. Miller shook his fist in response, thinking through the ideas as he spoke.

"It's all long sight lines and locked-down side passages," Miller said. "If I was going to build a place like this, I'd—"

The air sang, and Diogo went down, his head snapping back as he fell. Miller yelped and wheeled. Behind them in the side corridor, two figures in Protogen security uniform dove for cover. Something hissed through the air by Miller's left ear. Something else bounced off the breastplate of his fancy Martian armor like a hammer blow. He didn't think about raising his assault weapon; it was just there, coughing out return fire like an extension of his will. The other three OPA soldiers turned to help.

"Get back," Miller barked. "Keep your fucking eyes on the main corridor! I'm *on* this."

Stupid, Miller told himself, *stupid to let them get behind us. Stupid to stop and talk in the middle of a firefight.* He should have known better, and now, because he'd lost focus, the boy was...

Laughing?

Diogo sat up, lifted his own assault weapon, and peppered the side corridor with rounds. He got unsteadily to his feet, then whooped like a child who'd just gotten off a thrill ride. A wide streak of white goo stretched from his collarbone up across the right side of his face mask. Behind it, Diogo was grinning. Miller shook his head.

"What the hell are they using crowd suppression rounds for?" he said to himself as much as the boy. "They think this is a riot?"

"Forward teams," Fred said in Miller's ear, "get ready. We're moving in five. Four. Three. Two. Go!"

We don't know what we're getting into here, Miller thought as he joined the sprint down the corridor, pressing toward the assault's final target. A wide ramp led up to a set of blast doors done in wood-grain veneer. Something detonated behind them, but Miller kept his head low and didn't look back. The press of bodies jostling in their ragtag armor grew thicker, and Miller stumbled on something soft. A body in Protogen uniform.

"Give us some room!" a woman at the front shouted. Miller pushed toward her, cutting through the crowd of OPA soldiers with his shoulder and elbow. The woman shouted again as he reached her.

"What's the problem?" Miller shouted.

"I can't cut through this bitch with all these dick-lickers pushing me," she said, lifting a cutting torch already glowing white at the edge. Miller nodded and slid his assault rifle into the sling on his back. He grabbed two of the nearest shoulders, shook the men until they noticed him, and then locked his elbows with theirs.

"Just need to give the techs some room," Miller said, and together they waded into their own men, pushing them back. *How many battles, all through history, fell apart at moments like this?* he wondered. *The victory all but delivered until allied forces started tripping over each other.* The welder popped to life behind him, the heat pressing at his back like a hand even in armor.

At the edge of the crowd, automatic weapons gurgled and choked.

"How's it going back there?" Miller shouted over his shoulder.

The woman didn't answer. Hours seemed to pass, though it couldn't have been more than five minutes. The haze of hot metal and aerosolized plastic filled the air.

The welding torch turned off with a pop. Over his shoulder, Miller saw the bulkhead sag and shift. The tech placed a card-thin jack into the gap between plates, activated it, and stood back. The station around them groaned as a new set of pressures and strains reshaped the metal. The bulkhead opened.

"Come on," Miller shouted, then tucked his head and moved through the new passageway, up a carpeted ramp, and into the ops center. A dozen men and women looked up from their stations, eyes wide with fear.

"You're under arrest!" Miller shouted as the OPA soldiers boiled in around him. "Well, no you're not, but…shit. Put your hands up and back away from the controls!"

One of the men—tall as a Belter, but built solid as a man in full gravity—sighed. He wore a good suit, linen and raw silk, without the lines and folds that spoke of computer tailoring.

"Do what they say," the linen suit said. He sounded peeved, but not frightened.

Miller's eyes narrowed.

"Mr. Dresden?"

The suit raised a carefully shaped eyebrow, paused, and nodded.

"Been looking for you," Miller said.

Fred walked into the ops center like he belonged there. With a tighter set of the shoulders and a degree's shift of the spine, the master engineer of Tycho Station was gone, and the general was in his place. He looked over the ops center, sucking in every detail with a flicker of his eyes, then nodded at one of the senior OPA techs.

"All locked down, sir," the tech said. "The station's yours."

Miller had almost never been present to witness another man's moment of absolution. It was such a rare thing, and so utterly private that it approached the spiritual. Decades ago, this man—younger, fitter, not as much gray in his hair—had taken a space station, wading up to his knees in the gore and death of Belters, and Miller saw the barely perceptible relaxation in his jaw, the opening of his chest that meant that burden had lifted. Maybe it wasn't gone, but it was near enough. It was more than most people managed in a lifetime.

He wondered what it would feel like if he ever got the chance.

"Miller?" Fred said. "I hear you've got someone we'd like to talk to."

Dresden unfolded from his chair, ignoring the sidearms and assault weapons as if such things didn't apply to him.

"Colonel Johnson," Dresden said. "I should have expected that a man of your caliber would be behind all this. My name is Dresden."

He handed Fred a matte black business card. Fred took it as if by reflex but didn't look at it.

"You're the one responsible for this?"

Dresden gave him a chilly smile and looked around before he answered.

"I'd say you're responsible for at least part of it," Dresden said. "You've just killed quite a few people who were simply doing their jobs. But maybe we can dispense with the moral finger-pointing and get down to what actually matters?"

Fred's smile reached all the way to his eyes.

"And what exactly would that be?"

"Negotiating terms," Dresden replied. "You are a man of experience. You understand that your victory here puts you in an untenable position. Protogen is one of the most powerful corporations on Earth. The OPA has attacked it, and the longer you try to hold it, the worse the reprisals will be."

"Is that so?"

"Of course it is," Dresden said, waving Fred's tone away with a dismissing hand. Miller shook his head. The man genuinely didn't understand what was going on. "You've taken your hostages. Well, here we are. We can wait until Earth sends a few dozen battleships and negotiate while you look down the barrels, or we can end this now."

"You're asking me…how much money I want to take my people and just leave," Fred said.

"If money's what you want," Dresden said with a shrug. "Weapons. Ordinance. Medical supplies. Whatever it is you need to prosecute your little war and get this over with quickly."

"I know what you did on Eros," Fred said quietly.

Dresden chuckled. The sound made Miller's flesh crawl.

"Mr. Johnson," Dresden said. "*Nobody* knows what we did on Eros. And every minute I have to spend playing games with you is one I can't use more productively elsewhere. I will swear this: You are in the best bargaining position right now that you will ever have. There is no incentive for you to draw this out."

"And you're offering?"

Dresden spread his hands. "Anything you like and amnesty besides. As long as it gets you out of here and lets us return to our work. We both win."

Fred laughed. It was mirthless.

"Let me get this straight," he said. "You'll give me all the kingdoms of the Earth if I just bow down and do one act of worship for you?"

Dresden cocked his head. "I don't know the reference."

Chapter Forty-One: Holden

The *Rocinante* docked with Thoth Station on the last gasps from her maneuvering thrusters. Holden felt the station's docking clamps grab the hull with a thud, and then gravity returned at a low one-third g. The close detonation of a plasma warhead had torn off the outer door of the crew airlock and flooded the chamber with superheated gas, effectively welding it shut. That meant they'd be using the cargo airlock at the stern of the ship and spacewalking over to the station.

That was fine; they were still in their suits. The *Roci* had more holes now than the air cycling system could keep up with, and their shipboard O2 supply had been vented into space by the same explosion that killed the airlock.

Alex dropped from the cockpit, face hidden by his helmet, his belly unmistakable even in his atmosphere suit. Naomi finished locking her station and powering down the ship, then joined Alex, and the three of them climbed down the crew ladder to the ship's aft. Amos was waiting there, buckling an EVA pack onto his suit and charging it with compressed nitrogen from a storage tank. The mechanic had assured Holden that the EVA maneuvering pack had enough thrust to overcome the station's spin and get them back up to an airlock.

No one spoke. Holden had expected banter. He'd expected to want to banter. But the damaged *Roci* seemed to call for silence. Maybe awe.

Holden leaned against the cargo bay bulkhead and closed his eyes. The only sounds he could hear were the steady hiss of his air supply and the faint static of the comm. He could smell nothing through his broken and blood-clogged nose, and his mouth was filled with a coppery taste. But even so, he couldn't keep a smile off his face.

They'd won. They'd flown right up to Protogen, taken everything the evil bastards could throw at them, and bloodied *their* noses. Even now OPA soldiers were storming their station, shooting the people who'd helped kill Eros.

Holden decided that he was okay with not feeling any remorse for them. The moral complexity of the situation had grown past his ability to process it, so he just relaxed in the warm glow of victory instead.

The comm chirped and Amos said, "Ready to move."

Holden nodded, remembered he was still in his atmosphere suit, and said, "Okay. Hook on, everyone."

He, Alex, and Naomi pulled tethers from their suits and clamped them to Amos' broad waist. Amos cycled the cargo airlock and flew out the door on puffs of gas. They were immediately hurled away from the ship by station spin, but Amos quickly got them under control and flew back up toward Thoth's emergency airlock.

As Amos flew them past the *Roci*, Holden studied the outside of the ship and tried to catalog repair requirements. There were a dozen holes in both her bow and aft that corresponded to holes all along the inside of the ship. The gauss cannon rounds the interceptor had fired probably hadn't even slowed appreciably on their path through the *Roci*. The crew was just lucky none of them had found the reactor and punched a hole in it.

There was also a huge dent in the false superstructure that made the ship look like a compressed gas freighter. Holden knew it would match an equally ugly wound in the armored outer hull. The damage hadn't extended to the inner hull, or the ship would have cracked in two.

With the damage to the airlock, and the total loss of their oxygen storage tanks and recycling systems, there would be millions of dollars in damage and weeks in dry dock, assuming they could make it to a dry dock somewhere.

Maybe the *Molinari* could give them a tow.

Amos flashed the EVA pack's yellow warning lights three times, and the station's emergency airlock door cycled open. He flew them inside, where four Belters in combat armor waited.

As soon as the airlock finished cycling, Holden pulled his helmet off and touched his nose. It felt twice its normal size and throbbed with every heartbeat.

Naomi reached out and held his face still, her thumbs on either side of his nose, her touch surprisingly gentle. She turned his head from side to side, examining the injury, then let go.

"It'll be crooked without some cosmetic surgery," she said. "But you were too pretty before anyway. It'll give your face character."

Holden felt a slow grin coming on, but before he could reply, one of the OPA troops started talking.

"Watched the fight, hermano. You guys really kicked some ass."

"Thanks," said Alex. "How's it goin' in here?"

The soldier with the most stars on his OPA insignia said, "Less resistance than expected, but the Protogen security's been fighting for every foot of real estate. Even some of the eggheads have been coming at us. We've had to shoot a few."

He pointed at the inner airlock door.

"Fred's heading up to ops. Wants you people up there, pronto."

"Lead the way," Holden replied, his nose turning it into *lee da way*.

"How's that leg, Cap?" Amos asked as they walked along the station corridor. Holden realized he'd forgotten about the limp his gunshot to the calf had left him.

"Doesn't hurt, but the muscle doesn't flex as much," he replied. "Yours?"

Amos grinned and glanced down at the leg that still limped from the fracture he'd suffered on the *Donnager* months earlier.

"No biggie," he said. "The ones that don't kill you don't count."

Holden started to reply, then stopped when the group rounded a corner into a slaughterhouse. They were clearly coming up behind the assault team, because now the corridor floor was littered with bodies, the walls with bullet holes and scorch marks. To his relief, Holden saw a lot more bodies in Protogen security armor than in OPA gear. But there were enough dead Belters on the floor to make his stomach twist. When he passed a dead man in a lab coat, he had to stop himself from spitting on the floor. The security guys had maybe made a bad decision in going to work for the wrong team, but the scientists on this station had killed a million and a half people just to see what would happen. They couldn't be dead enough for Holden's comfort.

Something tugged at him, and he paused. Lying next to the dead scientist was what looked like a kitchen knife.

"Huh," Holden said. "He didn't come at you guys with that, did he?"

"Yeah, crazy, no?" said one of their escorts. "I heard of bringing a knife to a gunfight, but..."

"Ops is up ahead," said the ranking trooper. "General's waiting."

Holden entered the station's ops center and saw Fred, Miller, a bunch of OPA troops, and one stranger in an expensive-looking suit. A line of technicians and operations staff in Protogen uniform had their wrists cuffed and were being led away. The room was covered deck to ceiling in screens and monitors, most of which were spooling text data too fast to read.

"Let me get this straight," Fred was saying. "You'll give me all the kingdoms of the Earth if I just bow down and do one act of worship for you?"

"I don't know the reference," the stranger said.

Whatever else they were about to say stopped when Miller noticed Holden and tapped Fred on the shoulder. Holden could swear that the detective gave him a warm smile, though on his dour face it was hard to tell.

"Jim," Fred said, then gestured for him to come closer. He was reading a matte black business card. "Meet Antony Dresden, executive VP of bio research for Protogen, and the architect of the Eros project."

The asshole in the suit actually reached out like he was going to shake hands. Holden ignored him.

"Fred," he said. "Casualties?"

"Shockingly low."

"Half their security had non-lethals," Miller said. "Riot control. Sticky rounds. Like that."

Holden nodded and then shook his head and frowned.

"I saw a lot of Protogen security bodies out there in the corridor. Why have so many guys and then give them weapons that can't repel boarders?"

"Good question," Miller agreed.

Dresden chuckled.

"This is what I mean, Mr. Johnson," Dresden said. He turned to Holden. "Jim? Well then, Jim. The fact that you don't understand this station's security needs tells me that you have no idea what you've become involved with. And I think you know that as well as I do. As I was saying to Fred here —"

"Antony, you need to shut the fuck up," Holden said, surprised by the sudden flush of anger. Dresden looked disappointed.

The bastard had no right to be comfortable. Condescending. Holden wanted the man terrified, begging for his life, not sneering behind his cultured accent.

"Amos, if he talks to me again without being told to, break his jaw."

"My pleasure, Captain," Amos said, and took half a step forward.

Dresden smirked at the ham-fisted threat but kept his mouth shut.

"What do we know?" Holden asked, aiming the question at Fred.

"We know the Eros data is coming here, and we know this piece of shit is in charge. We'll know more once we've taken the place apart."

Holden turned to look at Dresden again, taking in the blue blood European good looks, the gym-sculpted physique, the expensive haircut. Even now, surrounded by men with guns, Dresden managed to look like he was in charge. Holden could imagine him glancing down at his watch and wondering how much more of his expensive time this boarding party was going to take.

Holden said, "I need to ask him something."

Fred nodded. "You earned it."

"Why?" Holden asked. "I want to know why."

Dresden's smile was almost pitying, and he stuck his hands into his pockets as casually as a man talking sports at a dockside bar.

" 'Why' is a very big question," Dresden said. "Because God wanted it that way? Or perhaps you want to narrow it for me."

"Why Eros?"

"Well, Jim—"

"You can call me Captain Holden. I'm the guy that found your lost ship, so I've seen the video from Phoebe. I know what the protomolecule is."

"Really!" Dresden said, his smile becoming half a degree more genuine. "I have you to thank for turning the viral agent over to us on Eros. Losing the *Anubis* was going to put our timeline back months. Finding the infected body already there on the station was a godsend."

I knew it. I fucking knew it, Holden thought. Out loud, he said, "Why?"

"You know what the agent is," Dresden said, at a loss for the first time since Holden had come into the room. "I don't know what more I can tell you. This is the most important thing to ever happen to the human race. It's simultaneously proof that we are not alone in the universe, and our ticket out of the limitations that bind us to our little bubbles of rock and air."

"You aren't answering me," Holden said, hating the way his broken nose made his voice slightly comical when he wanted to be threatening. "I want to know *why* you killed a million and a half people."

Fred cleared his throat, but he didn't interrupt. Dresden looked from Holden to the colonel and back again.

"I *am* answering, Captain. A million and a half people is small potatoes. What we're working with here is bigger than that," Dresden said, then moved over to a chair and sat down, pulling up his pants leg as he crossed his knees, so as not to stretch the fabric. "Are you familiar with Genghis Khan?"

"What?" Holden and Fred said at almost the same instant. Miller only stared at Dresden with a blank expression, tapping the barrel of his pistol against his own armored thigh.

"Genghis Khan. There are some historians who claim that Genghis Khan killed or displaced one quarter of the total human population of Earth during his conquest," Dresden said. "He did that in pursuit of an empire that would begin falling apart as soon as he died. In today's scale, that would mean killing nearly ten billion people in order to affect a generation. A generation and a half. Eros isn't even a rounding error by comparison."

"You really don't care," Fred said, his voice quiet.

"And unlike Khan, we aren't doing it to build a brief empire. I know what you think. That we're trying to aggrandize ourselves. Grab power."

"You don't want to?" Holden said.

"Of course we do." Dresden's voice was cutting. "But you're thinking too small. Building humanity's greatest empire is like building the world's largest anthill. Insignificant. There is a civilization out there that built the protomolecule and hurled it at us over two billion years ago. They were *already* gods at that point. What have they become since then? With another two billion years to advance?"

With a growing dread, Holden listened to Dresden speak. This speech had the air of something spoken before. Perhaps many times. And it had worked. It had convinced powerful people. It was why Protogen had stealth ships from the Earth shipyards and seemingly limitless behind-the-scenes support.

"We have a terrifying amount of catching up to do, gentlemen," Dresden was saying. "But fortunately we have the tool of our enemy to use in doing it."

"Catching up?" a soldier to Holden's left said. Dresden nodded at the man and smiled.

"The protomolecule can alter the host organism at the molecular level; it can create genetic change on the fly. Not just DNA, but any stable replicator. But it is only a machine. It doesn't think. It follows instructions. If we learn how to alter that programming, then *we* become the architects of that change."

Holden interrupted. "If it was supposed to wipe out life on Earth and replace it with whatever the protomolecule's creators wanted, why turn it loose?"

"Excellent question," Dresden said, holding up one finger like a college professor about to deliver a lecture. "The protomolecule doesn't come with a user's manual. In fact, we've never before been able to actually watch it carry out its program. The molecule requires significant mass before it develops enough processing power to fulfill its directives. Whatever they are."

Dresden pointed at the screens covered with data around them.

"We are going to watch it at work. See what it intends to do.

How it goes about doing it. And, hopefully, learn how to change that program in the process."

"You could do that with a vat of bacteria," Holden said.

"I'm not interested in remaking bacteria," Dresden said.

"You're fucking insane," Amos said, and took another step toward Dresden. Holden put a hand on the big mechanic's shoulder.

"So," Holden said. "You figure out how the bug works, and then what?"

"Then *everything*. Belters who can work outside a ship without wearing a suit. Humans capable of sleeping for hundreds of years at a time flying colony ships to the stars. No longer being bound to the millions of years of evolution inside one atmosphere of pressure at one g, slaves to oxygen and water. We decide what we want to be, and we reprogram ourselves to be that. That's what the protomolecule gives us."

Dresden had stood back up as he'd delivered this speech, his face shining with the zeal of a prophet.

"What we are doing is the best and only hope of humanity's survival. When we go out there, we will be facing *gods*."

"And if we don't go out?" Fred asked. He sounded thoughtful.

"They've already fired a doomsday weapon at us once," Dresden said.

The room was silent for a moment. Holden felt his certainty slip. He hated everything about Dresden's argument, but he couldn't quite see his way past it. He knew in his bones that something about it was dead wrong, but he couldn't find the words.

Naomi's voice startled him.

"Did it convince them?" she asked.

"Excuse me?" Dresden said.

"The scientists. The technicians. Everyone you needed to make it happen. They actually had to do this. They had to watch the video of people dying all over Eros. They had to design those radioactive murder chambers. So unless you managed to round up every serial killer in the solar system and send them through a postgraduate program, how did you do this?"

"We modified our science team to remove ethical restraints."

Half a dozen clues clicked into place in Holden's head.

"Sociopaths," he said. "You turned them into sociopaths."

"High-functioning sociopaths," Dresden said with a nod. He seemed pleased to explain it. "And extremely curious ones. As long as we kept them supplied with interesting problems to solve and unlimited resources, they remained quite content."

"And a big security team armed with riot control rounds for when they aren't," Fred said.

"Yes, there are occasional issues," Dresden said. He looked around, the slightest frown creasing his forehead. "I know. You think it's monstrous, but I am saving the human *race.* I am giving humanity the *stars.* You disapprove? Fine. Let me ask you this. Can you save Eros? Right now."

"No," Fred said, "but we can—"

"Waste the data," Dresden said. "You can make certain that every man, woman, and child who died on Eros died for nothing."

The room was silent. Fred was frowning, his arms crossed. Holden understood the struggle going on in the man's mind. Everything Dresden said was repulsive and eerie and rang too much of the truth.

"Or," Dresden said, "we can negotiate a price, you can go on your way, and I can—"

"Okay. That's enough," Miller said, speaking for the first time since Dresden had begun his pitch. Holden glanced over at the detective. His flat expression had gone stony. He wasn't tapping the barrel of his pistol against his leg.

Oh, shit.

Chapter Forty-Two: Miller

Dresden didn't see it coming. Even as Miller raised the pistol, the man's eyes didn't register a threat. All he saw was Miller with an object in his hand that happened to be a gun. A dog would have known to be scared, but not Dresden.

"Miller!" Holden shouted from a great distance. "Don't!"

Pulling the trigger was simple. A soft click, the bounce of metal against his glove-cushioned palm, and then again two more times. Dresden's head snapped back, blooming red. Blood spattered a wide screen, obscuring the data stream. Miller stepped close, fired two more rounds into Dresden's chest, considered for a moment, then holstered the pistol.

The room was silent. The OPA soldiers were all looking at each other or at Miller, surprised, even after the press of the assault, by the sudden violence. Naomi and Amos were looking at Holden, and the captain was staring at the corpse. Holden's injured face was set as a mask; fury, outrage, maybe even despair. Miller understood that. Doing the obvious thing still wasn't natural for Holden. There had been a time when it hadn't come so easily for Miller either.

Only Fred didn't flinch or look nervous. The colonel didn't smile or frown, and he didn't look away.

"What the fuck was that?" Holden said through his blood-plugged nose. "You shot him in cold blood!"

"Yeah," Miller said.

Holden shook his head. "What about a trial? What about justice? You just decide, and that's the way it goes?"

"I'm a cop," Miller said, surprised by the apology in his voice.

"Are you even human anymore?"

"All right, gentlemen!" Fred said, his voice booming out in the quiet. "Show's over. Let's get back to work. I want the decryption team in here. We've got prisoners to evacuate and a station to strip down."

Holden looked from Fred to Miller to the still-dying Dresden. His jaw was set with rage.

"Hey, Miller," Holden said.

"Yeah?" Miller said softly. He knew what was coming.

"Find your own ride home," the captain of the *Rocinante* said, then spun and stalked out of the room, his crew following. Miller watched them walk away. Regret tapped gently at his heart, but there was nothing to be done about it. The broken bulkhead seemed to swallow them. Miller turned to Fred.

"Hitch a lift?"

"You're wearing our colors," Fred said. "We'll get you as far as Tycho."

"I appreciate that," Miller said. Then, a moment later: "You know it had to be done."

Fred didn't reply. There wasn't anything to say.

Thoth Station was injured, but not dead. Not yet. Word of the sociopathic crew spread fast, and the OPA forces took the warning to heart. The occupation and control phase of the attack lasted forty hours instead of the twenty that it would have taken with normal prisoners. With humans. Miller did what he could with prisoner control.

The OPA kids were well intentioned, but most of them had never worked with captive populations before. They didn't know how to cuff someone at the wrist and elbow so that the perp couldn't get his hands out in front to strangle them. They didn't know how to restrain someone with a length of cord around the neck so that the prisoner couldn't choke himself to death, by accident or intentionally. Half of them didn't even know how to pat someone down. Miller knew all of it like a game he'd played since childhood. In five hours, he found twenty hidden blades on the science crew alone. He hardly had to think about it.

A second wave of transport ships arrived: personnel haulers that looked ready to spill their air out into the vacuum if you spat on them, salvage trawlers already dismantling the shielding and superstructure of the station, supply ships boxing and packing the precious equipment and looting the pharmacies and food banks. By the time news of the assault reached Earth, the station would be stripped to a skeleton and its people hidden away in unlicensed prison cells throughout the Belt.

Protogen would know sooner, of course. They had outposts much closer than the inner planets. There was a calculus of response time and possible gain. The mathematics of piracy and war. Miller knew it, but he didn't let it worry him. Those were decisions for Fred and his attachés to make. Miller had taken more than enough initiative for one day.

Posthuman.

It was a word that came up in the media every five or six years, and it meant different things every time. Neural regrowth hormone? Posthuman. Sex robots with inbuilt pseudo intelligence? Posthuman. Self-optimizing network routing? Posthuman. It was a word from advertising copy, breathless and empty, and all he'd ever thought it really meant was that the people using it had a limited imagination about what exactly humans were capable of.

Now, as he escorted a dozen captives in Protogen uniforms to a docked transport heading God-knew-where, the word was taking on new meaning.

Are you even human anymore?

All *posthuman* meant, literally speaking, was what you were when you weren't human anymore. Protomolecule aside, Protogen aside, Dresden and his Mengele-as-Genghis-Khan self-righteous fantasies aside, Miller thought that maybe he'd been ahead of the curve all along. Maybe he'd been posthuman for years.

The min-max point came forty hours later, and it was time to go. The OPA had skeletonized the station, and it was time to get out before anyone came along with vengeance in mind. Miller sat in a crash couch, his blood dancing with spent amphetamines and his mind slipping into and out of exhaustion psychosis. The thrust gravity was like a pillow over his face. He was vaguely aware that he was weeping. It didn't mean anything.

In Miller's haze, Dresden was talking again, pouring out promises and lies, half-truths and visions. Miller could see the words themselves like a dark smoke, coalescing into the spilling black filament of the protomolecule. The threads of it were reaching toward Holden, Amos, Naomi. He tried to find his gun, to stop it, to do the obvious thing. His despairing shout woke him, and he remembered he'd already won.

Julie sat beside him, her hand cool against his forehead. Her smile was gentle, understanding. Forgiving.

Sleep, she said, and his mind fell into the deep black.

"Oi, Pampaw," Diogo said. "Acima and out, sabez?"

It was Miller's tenth morning back on Tycho, his seventh hot-bunking in Diogo's closet-sized apartment. He could tell from the buzz in the boy's voice it would have to be one of the last. Fish and company start to smell after three days. He rolled off the thin bed, ran fingers through his hair, and nodded. Diogo stripped down and crawled into the bed without speaking. He stank of liquor and cheap tub-grown marijuana.

Miller's terminal told him that the second shift had ended two hours before, the third shift halfway into its morning. He gathered his things in his suitcase, turned off the lights on Diogo's already snoring form, and trundled out to the public showers to spend a few of his remaining credits trying to look less homeless.

The pleasant surprise of his return to Tycho Station was the boost of money in his account. The OPA, meaning Fred Johnson, had paid him for his time on Thoth. He hadn't asked for it, and there was part of him that wanted to turn the payment down. If there had been an alternative, he might have. Since there wasn't, he tried to stretch the funds out as far as they would go and appreciate the irony. He and Captain Shaddid were on the same payroll after all.

For the first few days after his return to Tycho, Miller had expected to see the attack on Thoth in the newsfeeds. EARTH CORPORATION LOSES RESEARCH STATION TO CRAZED BELTERS, or some such. He should have been finding a job or a place to sleep that wasn't charity. He meant to. But the hours seemed to dissolve as he sat in the bar or the lounges, watching the screens for just a few more minutes.

The Martian navy had suffered a series of harassing attacks by Belters. A half ton of super-accelerated gravel had forced two of their battleships to change course. A slowdown in water harvesting on Saturn's rings was either an illegal work stoppage, and therefore treasonous, or the natural response to increased security needs. Two Earth-owned mining operations had been attacked by either Mars or the OPA. Four hundred people were dead. Earth's blockade of Mars was entering its third month. A coalition of scientists and terraforming specialists were screaming that the cascading processes were in danger, and that while the war would be over in a year or two, the loss of supplies would set the terraforming effort back generations. Everyone blamed everyone else for Eros. Thoth Station didn't exist.

It would, though.

With most of the Martian navy still in the outer planets, Earth's siege was a brittle thing. Time was getting short. Either the Martians would go home and try facing down the somewhat older, somewhat slower, but more numerous ships of Earth, or they'd go straight for the planet itself. Earth was still the source of a thousand things that couldn't be grown elsewhere, but if someone got happy or cocksure or desperate, it wouldn't take much to start dropping rocks down the gravity wells.

All of it as a distraction.

There was an old joke. Miller didn't remember where he'd heard it. Girl's at her own father's funeral, meets this really cute guy. They talk, hit it off, but he leaves before she can get his number. Girl doesn't know how to track the guy down.

So a week later, she kills her mom.

Big laugh.

It was the logic of Protogen, of Dresden, of Thoth. *Here is the problem,* they said to themselves, *and there is the solution.* That it was drowned in innocent blood was as trivial as the font the reports were printed in. They had disconnected themselves from humanity. Shut off the cell clusters in their brains that made life besides their own sacred. Or valuable. Or worth saving. All it had cost them was every human connection.

Funny how familiar that sounded.

The guy who walked into the bar and nodded to Miller was one of Diogo's friends. Twenty years old or maybe a little south of that. A veteran of Thoth Station, just like Miller. He didn't remember the kid's name, but he'd seen him around often enough to know that the way he held himself was different than usual. Tightwound. Miller tapped the mute on his terminal's newsfeed and made his way over.

"Hey," he said, and the kid looked up sharply. The face was tense, but a softer, intentional ease tried to mask it. It was just

Diogo's old grandpa. The one, everyone on Thoth knew, who'd killed the biggest dick in the universe. It won Miller some points, so the kid smiled and nodded to the stool beside him.

"All pretty fucked up, isn't it?" Miller said.

"You don't know the half," the kid said. He had a clipped accent. Belter by his height, but educated. Technician, probably. The kid tabbed in a drink order, and the bar offered up a glass of clear fluid so volatile Miller could watch it evaporate. The kid drank it down with a gulp.

"Doesn't work," Miller said.

The kid looked over. Miller shrugged.

"They say drinking helps, but it doesn't," Miller said.

"No?"

"Nope. Sex sometimes, if you've got a girl who'll talk to you after. Or target practice. Working out, sometimes. Liquor doesn't make you feel better. Just makes you not so worried about feeling bad."

The kid laughed and shook his head. He was on the edge of talking, so Miller sat back and let the quiet do his work for him. He figured the kid had killed someone, probably on Thoth, and it was sneaking up on him. But instead of telling the story, the kid took Miller's terminal, keyed in a few local codes, and handed it back. A huge menu of feeds appeared—video, audio, air pressure and content, radiological. It took Miller half a second to understand what he was seeing. They'd cracked the encryption on the Eros feeds.

He was looking at the protomolecule in action. He was seeing Juliette Andromeda Mao's corpse writ large. For a moment, his imagined Julie flickered beside him.

"If you ever wonder if you did the right thing shooting that guy," the kid said, "look at that."

Miller opened a feed. A long corridor, wide enough for twenty people to walk abreast. The flooring was wet and undulating like the surface of a canal. Something small rolled awkwardly through the mush. When Miller zoomed in, it was a human torso—rib cage, spine, trailing lengths of what used to be intestines and were now the long black threads of the protomolecule—pushing itself along on the stump of an arm. There was no head. The feed output bar showed there was sound, and Miller undid the mute. The high, mindless piping reminded him of mentally ill children singing to themselves.

"It's all like that," the kid said. "Whole station's crawling with . . . shit like that."

"What's it doing?"

"Building something," the kid said, and shuddered. "I thought you should see it."

"Yeah?" Miller said, his gaze nailed to the screen. "What did I ever do to you?"

The kid laughed.

"Everyone thinks you're a hero for killing that guy," the kid said. "Everyone thinks we should push every last prisoner we took off that station out an airlock."

Probably should, Miller thought, *if we can't make them human again.* He switched the feed. The casino level where he and Holden had been, or else a section very like it. A webwork of something like bones linked ceiling and roof. Black sluglike things a yard long slithered up and between them. The sound was a hushing, like the recordings he'd heard of surf against a beach. He switched again. The port, with bulkheads closed and encrusted with huge nautilus spirals that seemed to shift while he watched them.

"Everyone thinks you're a fucking hero," the kid said, and this time, it bit a little. Miller shook his head.

"Nah," he said. "Just a guy who used to be a cop."

Why should going into a firefight, charging into an enemy station filled with people and automatic systems built to kill you, seem less frightening than talking to people who you shipped with for weeks?

And still.

It was third shift, and the bar at the observation platform was set to imitate night. The air was scented with something smoky that wasn't smoke. A piano and bass dueled lazily with each other while a man's voice lamented in Arabic. Dim lights glowed at the bases of the tables, casting soft shadows up across faces and bodies, emphasizing the customers' legs and bellies and breasts. The shipyards beyond the windows were busy as always. If he went close, he could pick out the *Rocinante,* still recovering from its wounds. Not dead, and being made stronger.

Amos and Naomi were at a table in a corner. No sign of Alex. No sign of Holden. That made it easier. Not easy, but closer. He made his way toward them. Naomi saw him first, and Miller read the discomfort in her expression, covered over as quickly as it appeared. Amos turned to see what she'd been reacting to, and the corners of his mouth and eyes didn't shift into a frown or a smile. Miller scratched his arm even though it didn't itch.

"Hey," he said. "Buy you folks a round?"

The silence lasted a beat longer than it should have, and then Naomi forced a smile.

"Sure. Just one. We've got…that thing. For the captain."

"Oh yeah," Amos said, lying even more awkwardly than Naomi had, making his awareness of the fact part of the message. "The thing. That's important."

Miller sat, lifted a hand for the waiter to see, and, when the man nodded, leaned forward with his elbows on the table. It was the seated version of a fighter's crouch, bent forward with his arms protecting the soft places in his neck and belly. It was the way a man stood when he expected injury.

The waiter came, and then beers all around. Miller paid for them with the OPA's money and took a sip.

"How's the ship?" he asked at last.

"Coming together," Naomi said. "They really banged the hell out of her."

"She'll still fly," Amos said. "She's one tough bitch."

"That's good. When—" Miller said, then tripped on his words and had to start again. "When are you folks shipping out?"

"Whenever the captain says," Amos said with a shrug. "We're airtight now, so could go tomorrow, if he's got someplace he wants to be."

"And if Fred lets us," Naomi said, and then grimaced like she wished she'd kept silent.

"That an issue?" Miller asked. "Is the OPA leaning on Holden?"

"It's just something I was thinking about," Naomi said. "It's nothing. Look, thanks for the drink, Miller. But I really think we'd better be going."

Miller took a long breath and let it out slow.

"Yeah," he said. "Okay."

"You head out," Amos said to Naomi. "I'll catch up."

Naomi shot a confused look at the big man, but Amos only gave back a smile. It could have meant anything.

"Okay," Naomi said. "But don't be long, okay? The thing."

"For the captain," Amos said. "No worries."

Naomi rose and walked away. Her effort not to look back over her shoulder was visible. Miller looked at Amos. The lights gave the mechanic a slightly demonic appearance.

"Naomi's a good person," Amos said. "I like her, you know? Like my kid sister, only smart and I'd do her if she let me. You know?"

"Yeah," Miller said. "I like her too."

"She's not like us," Amos said, and the warmth and humor were gone.

"That's why I like her," Miller said. It was the right thing to say. Amos nodded.

"So here's the thing. As far as the captain goes, you're dipped in shit right now."

The scrim of bubbles where his beer touched the glass glowed white in the dim light. Miller gave the glass a quarter turn, watching them closely.

"Because I killed someone who needed it?" Miller asked. The bitterness in his voice wasn't surprising, but it was deeper than he'd intended. Amos didn't hear it or else didn't care.

"Because you've got a habit of that," Amos said. "Cap'n's not like that. Killing people without talking it over first makes him jumpy. You did a lot of it on Eros, but...you know."

"Yeah," Miller said.

"Thoth Station wasn't Eros. Next place we go won't be Eros either. Holden doesn't want you around."

"And the rest of you?" Miller asked.

"We don't want you around either," Amos said. His voice wasn't hard or gentle. He was talking about the gauge of a machine part. He was talking about anything. The words hit Miller in the belly, just where he'd expected it. He couldn't have blocked them.

"Here's the thing," Amos went on. "You and me, we're a lot the same. Been around. I know what I am, and my moral compass? I'll tell you, it's fucked. A few things fell different when I was a kid. I could have been those ass-bandits on Thoth. I know that. Captain couldn't have been. It's not in him. He's as close to righteous as anyone out here gets. And when he says you're out, that's just the way it is, because the way I figure it, he's probably right. Sure as hell has a better chance than I do."

"Okay," Miller said.

"Yeah," Amos said. He finished his beer. Then he finished Naomi's. And then he walked away, leaving Miller to himself and his empty gut. Outside, the *Nauvoo* fanned a glittering array of sensors, testing something or else just preening. Miller waited.

Beside him, Julie Mao leaned on the table, just where Amos had been.

So, she said. *Looks like it's just you and me now.*

"Looks like," he said.

Chapter Forty-Three: Holden

A Tycho worker in blue coveralls and a welding mask sealed up the hole in one of the galley bulkheads. Holden watched with his hand shielding his eyes from the harsh blue glare of the torch. When the plate steel was secured in place, the welder flipped her mask up to check the bead. She had blue eyes and a small mouth in a heart-shaped pixie face and a mop of red hair pulled into a bun. Her name was Sam, and she was the team leader on the *Rocinante* repair project. Amos had been chasing her for two weeks now with no success. Holden was glad, because the pixie had turned out to be one of the best mechanics he'd ever met, and he'd hate for her to focus on anything other than his ship.

"It's perfect," he said to her as she ran one gloved hand over the cooling metal.

"It's okay," she said with a shrug. "We'll grind this down smooth enough, paint it nice, then you'll never even know your ship had a boo-boo." She had a surprisingly deep voice that contrasted with her looks and her habit of using mockingly childlike phrases. Holden guessed that her appearance combined with her chosen profession had led to a lot of people underestimating her in the past. He didn't want to make that mistake.

"You've done amazing work, Sam," he said. He guessed Sam was short for something, but he'd never asked and she'd never volunteered. "I keep telling Fred how happy we are to have you in charge of this job."

"Maybe I'll get a gold star in my next report card," she said while she put her torch away and stood up. Holden tried to think of something to say to that and failed.

"Sorry," she said, turning to face him. "I appreciate your praise to the boss. And to be honest, it's been a lot of fun working on your little girl. She's quite a ship. The beating she took would have blown anything we own into scrap."

"It was a close thing, even for us," Holden replied.

Sam nodded, then began putting the rest of her gear away. As she worked, Naomi climbed down the crew ladder from the upper decks, her gray coveralls hung with electrician's tools.

"How are things up there?" Holden asked.

"Ninety percent," Naomi said as she crossed the galley to the refrigerator and took out a bottle of juice. "Give or take." She took out a second bottle and tossed it to Sam, who caught it one-handed.

"Naomi," Sam said, raising the bottle in mock toast before downing half of it in one swallow.

"Sammy," Naomi said in return with a grin.

The two of them had hit it off right away, and now Naomi was spending a lot of her off time with Sam and her Tycho crowd. Holden hated to admit it, but he missed being the only social circle Naomi had. When he did admit it to himself, like now, it made him feel like a creep.

"Golgo comp in rec, tonight?" Sam said after she'd gulped down the last of her drink.

"Think those C7 chumps are tired of getting their asses handed to them?" Naomi said in return. To Holden, it sounded like they were speaking in code.

"We can throw the first one," Sam said. "Get 'em hooked tight before we drop the hammer and wipe their roll."

"Sounds good to me," Naomi said, then tossed her empty bottle into the recycling bin and started back up the ladder. "See you at eight, then." She tossed a little wave at Holden. "Later, Captain."

Holden said, "How much longer, do you think?" to Sam's back as she finished with her tools.

Sam shrugged. "Couple days, maybe, to get her to perfect. She could probably fly now, if you're not worried about nonessentials and cosmetics."

"Thanks, again," Holden said, holding out his hand to Sam as she turned around. She shook it once, her palm heavily calloused and her grip firm. "And I hope you mop the floor with those chumps from C7."

She gave him a predatory grin.

"It's not even in doubt."

Through Fred Johnson, the OPA had provided the crew with living quarters on the station during the renovation of the *Roci,* and over the past few weeks, Holden's cabin had almost come to feel like home. Tycho had money, and they seemed to spend a lot of it on their employees. Holden had three rooms to himself, including a bath and a kitchen nook off the public space. On most stations, you'd have to be the governor to have that kind of luxury. Holden had the impression it was fairly standard for management on Tycho.

He tossed his grimy jumpsuit into the laundry bin and started a pot of coffee before jumping into his private shower. A shower every night after work: another almost unthinkable luxury. It would be easy to get distracted. To start thinking of this period of ship repair and quiet home life as normalcy, not interlude. Holden couldn't let that happen.

Earth's assault on Mars filled the newsfeeds. The domes of Mars still stood, but two showers of meteors had pocked the wide slopes of Olympus Mons. Earth claimed that it was debris from Deimos, Mars that it was an intentional threat and provocation. Martian ships from the gas giants were burning hard for the inner planets. Every day, every hour brought the moment closer when Earth would have to commit to annihilating Mars or backing away. The OPA's rhetoric seemed built to ensure that whoever won would kill them next. Holden had just helped Fred with what Earth would see as the largest act of piracy in the history of the Belt.

And a million and a half people were dying right now on Eros. Holden thought of the video feed he'd seen of what was happening to the people on the station, and shuddered even in the heat of the shower.

Oh, and aliens. Aliens that had tried to take over the Earth two billion years ago, and failed because Saturn got in the way. *Can't forget the aliens.* His brain still hadn't figured out a way to process that, so it kept trying to pretend it didn't exist.

Holden grabbed a towel and turned on the wall screen in his living room while he dried off. The air was filled with the competing scents of coffee, humidity from the shower, and the faintly grassy and floral scent Tycho pumped into all the residences. Holden tried the news, but it was speculation about the war without any new information. He changed to a competition show with incomprehensible rules and psychotically giddy contestants. He flipped through a few feeds that he could tell were comedies, because the actors paused and nodded where they expected the laughs to be.

When his jaw started aching, he realized he was gritting his teeth. He turned off the screen and threw the remote onto his bed in the next room. He wrapped the towel around his waist, then poured a mug of coffee and collapsed onto the couch just in time for his door to chime.

"What?" he yelled at the top of his lungs. No one replied. Good insulation on Tycho. He went to the door, arranging his towel for maximum modesty along the way, and yanked it open.

It was Miller. He was dressed in a rumpled gray suit he'd probably brought from Ceres, and was fumbling around with that stupid hat.

"Holden, hey—" he started, but Holden cut him off.

"What the hell do you want?" Holden said. "And are you *really* standing outside my door with your hat in your hands?"

Miller smiled, then put the hat back on his head. "You know, I always wondered what that meant."

"Now you know," Holden replied.

"You got a minute?" Miller said.

Holden waited a moment, staring up at the lanky detective. He quickly gave up. He probably outweighed Miller by twenty kilos, but it was impossible to be intimidating when the person you were staring down was a foot taller than you.

"Okay, come in," he said, then headed for his bedroom. "Let me get dressed. There's coffee."

Holden didn't wait for a reply; he just closed the bedroom door and sat on the bed. He and Miller hadn't exchanged more than a dozen words since returning to Tycho. He knew they couldn't leave it at that, as much as he might like to. He owed Miller at least the conversation where he told him to get lost.

He put on a pair of warm cotton pants and a pullover, ran one hand through his damp hair, and went back out to the living room. Miller was sitting on his couch holding a steaming mug.

"Good coffee," the detective said.

"So, let's hear it," Holden replied, sitting in a chair across from him.

Miller took a sip of his coffee and said, "Well—"

"I mean, this is the conversation where you tell me how you were right to shoot an unarmed man in the face, and how I'm just too naive to see it. Right?"

"Actually—"

"I fucking told you," Holden said, surprised to feel the heat rise in his cheeks. "No more of that judge, jury, and executioner shit or you could find your own ride, and you did it anyway."

"Yes."

The simple affirmative took Holden off guard.

"Why?"

Miller took another sip of his coffee, then set the mug down. He reached up and took off his hat, tossed it onto the couch next to him, then leaned back.

"He was going to get away with it."

"Excuse me?" Holden replied. "Did you miss the part where he confessed to everything?"

"That wasn't a confession. That was a boast. He was untouchable, and he knew it. Too much money. Too much power."

"That's bullshit. No one gets to kill a million and a half people and get away with it."

"People get away with things all the time. Guilty as hell, but something gets in the way. Evidence. Politics. I had a partner for a while, name of Muss. When Earth pulled out of Ceres—"

"Stop," Holden said. "I don't care. I don't want to hear any more of your stories about how being a cop makes you wiser and deeper and able to face the truth about humanity. As far as I can tell, all it did was break you. Okay?"

"Yeah, okay."

"Dresden and his Protogen buddies thought they could choose who lives and who dies. That sound familiar? And don't tell me it's different this time, because everyone says that, every time. And it's not."

"Wasn't revenge," Miller said, a little too hotly.

"Oh really? This wasn't about the girl in the hotel? Julie Mao?"

"Catching him was. Killing him..."

Miller sighed and nodded to himself, then got up and opened the door. He stopped in the doorway and turned around, real pain on his face.

"He was talking us into it," Miller said. "All that about getting the stars and protecting ourselves from whatever shot that thing at Earth? I was starting to think maybe he should get away with it. Maybe things were just too big for right and wrong. I'm not saying he convinced me. But he made me think maybe, you know? Just maybe."

"And for that, you shot him."

"I did."

Holden sighed, then leaned against the wall next to the open door, his arms crossed.

"Amos calls you righteous," Miller said. "You know that?"

"Amos thinks he's a bad guy because he's done some things he's ashamed of," Holden said. "He doesn't always trust himself, but the fact that he cares tells me he *isn't* a bad guy."

"Yeah—" Miller started, but Holden cut him off.

"He looks at his soul, sees the stains, and wants to be clean," he said. "But you? You just shrug."

"Dresden was—"

"This isn't about Dresden. It's about you," Holden said. "I can't trust you around the people I care about."

Holden stared at Miller, waiting for him to reply, but the cop just nodded sadly, then put his hat on and walked away down the gently curving corridor. He didn't turn around.

Holden went back inside and tried to relax, but he felt jumpy and nervous. He would never have gotten off Eros without Miller's help. There was no question about it: Tossing him out on his ear felt wrong. Incomplete.

The truth was Miller made his scalp crawl every time they were in the same room. The cop was like an unpredictable dog that might lick your hand or take a bite out of your leg.

Holden thought about calling Fred and warning him. He called Naomi instead.

"Hey," she answered on the second chime. Holden could hear a bar's frantic, alcohol-fueled merriment in the background.

"Naomi," he said, then paused, trying to think of some excuse to have called. When he couldn't think of one, he said, "Miller was just here."

"Yeah, he cornered Amos and me a while back. What did he want?"

"I don't know," Holden said with a sigh. "Say goodbye, maybe."

"What are you doing?" Naomi asked. "Want to meet up?"

"Yes. Yes I do."

Holden didn't recognize the bar at first, but after ordering a scotch from a professionally friendly waiter, he realized it was the same place he'd watched Naomi sing karaoke to a Belter punk song what seemed like centuries before. She wandered in and plopped down across from him in the booth just as his drink showed up. The waiter gave her a questioning smile.

"Gah, no," she said quickly, waving her hands at him. "I've had plenty tonight. Just some water, thanks."

As the waiter bustled away, Holden said, "How did your, uh… What exactly is Golgo, anyway? And how did it go?"

"Game they play here," Naomi said, then took a glass of water from their returning waiter and drank half of it in one gulp. "Like a cross between darts and soccer. Never seen it before, but I seem to be good at it. We won."

"Great," Holden said. "Thanks for coming. I know it's late, but this Miller thing freaked me out a bit."

"He wants you to absolve him, I think."

"Because I'm 'righteous,'" Holden said with a sarcastic laugh.

"You are," Naomi said with no irony. "I mean, it's a loaded term, but you're as close to it as anyone I've ever known."

"I've fucked everything up," Holden blurted out before he could stop himself. "Everyone who's tried to help us, or that we've tried to help, has died spectacularly. This whole fucking war. And Captain McDowell and Becca and Ade. And Shed—" He had to stop and swallow a sudden lump in his throat.

Naomi just nodded, then reached across the table and took his hand in hers.

"I need a win, Naomi," he continued. "I need to do something that makes a difference. Fate or Karma or God or whatever dropped me in the middle of this thing, and I need to know I'm making a difference."

Naomi smiled at him and squeezed his hand.

"You're cute when you're being noble," she said. "But you need to stare off into the distance more."

"You're making fun of me."

"Yeah," she said. "I am. Want to come home with me?"

"I—" Holden started, then stopped and stared at her, looking for the joke. Naomi was still smiling at him, nothing in her eyes but warmth and a touch of mischief. While he watched, one curly lock of hair fell over her eye, and she pushed it up without looking away from him. "Wait, what? I thought you'd—"

"I said don't tell me you love me to get me into bed," she said. "But I also said I'd have gone to your cabin anytime you asked over the last four years. I didn't think I was being subtle, and I'm sort of tired of waiting."

Holden leaned back in the booth and tried to remember to breathe. Naomi's grin changed to pure mischief now, and one eyebrow went up.

"You okay, sailor?" she asked.

"I thought you were avoiding me," he said once he was capable of speech. "Is this your way of giving me a win?"

"Don't be insulting," she said, though there was no hint of anger in her voice. "But I've waited weeks for you to get your nerve up, and the ship's almost done. That means you'll probably volunteer us for something really stupid and this time our luck will run out."

"Well—" he said.

"If that happens without us at least giving this a try *once*, I will be very unhappy about it."

"Naomi, I—"

"It's simple, Jim," she said, reaching out for his hand and pulling him back toward her. She leaned across the table between them until their faces were almost touching. "It's a yes or no question."

"*Yes.*"

Chapter Forty-Four: Miller

Miller sat by himself, staring out the wide observation windows without seeing the view. The fungal-culture whiskey on the low black table beside him remained at the same level in the glass as when he'd bought it. It wasn't really a drink. It was permission to sit. There had always been a handful of drifters, even on Ceres. Men and women whose luck had run out. No place to go, no one to ask favors of. No connection to the vast net of humanity. He'd always felt a kind of sympathy for them, his spiritual kindred.

Now he was part of that disconnected tribe in earnest.

Something bright happened on the skin of the great generation ship—a welding array firing off some intricate network of subtle connection, maybe. Past the *Nauvoo*, nestled in the constant hive-like activity of Tycho Station, was a half-degree arc of the *Rocinante*, like a home he'd once had. He knew the story of Moses seeing a promised land he would never enter. Miller wondered how the old prophet would have felt if he'd been ushered in for a moment—a day, a week, a year—and then dropped back out in the desert. Kinder never to leave the wastelands. Safer.

Beside him, Juliette Mao watched him from the corner of his mind carved out for her.

I was supposed to save you, he thought. *I was supposed to find you. Find the truth.*

And didn't you?

He smiled at her, and she smiled back, as world-weary and tired as he was. Because of course he had. He'd found her, he'd found who killed her, and Holden was right. He'd taken revenge. All that he'd promised himself, he'd done. Only it hadn't saved him.

"Can I get you anything?"

For half a second, Miller thought Julie had said it. The serving girl had opened her mouth to ask him again before he shook his head. She couldn't. And even if she had been able to, he couldn't afford it.

You knew it couldn't last, Julie said. *Holden. His crew. You knew you didn't really belong there. You belong with me.*

A sudden shot of adrenaline revved his tired heart. He looked around for her, but Julie was gone. His own privately generated fight-or-flight reaction didn't have room for daydream hallucinations. And still. *You belong with me.*

He wondered how many people he'd known who had taken that path. Cops had a tradition of eating their guns that went back to long before humanity had lifted itself up the gravity well. Here he was, without a home, without a friend, with more blood on his hands from the past month than from his whole career before it. The in-house shrink on Ceres called it suicidal ideation in his yearly presentation to the security teams. Something to watch out for, like genital lice or high cholesterol. Not a big deal if you were careful.

So he'd be careful. For a while. See where it went.

He stood, hesitated for three heartbeats, then scooped up his bourbon and drank it in a gulp. Liquid courage, they called it, and it seemed to do the trick. He pulled up his terminal, put in a connect request, and tried to compose himself. He wasn't there yet. And if he was going to live, he needed a job.

"Sabez nichts, Pampaw," Diogo said. The kid was wearing a mesh-work shirt and pants cut in a fashion as youthful as it was ugly, and in his previous life, Miller would probably have written him off as too young to know anything useful. Now Miller waited. If anything could wring a prospect out of Diogo, it would be the promise of Miller getting a hole of his own. The silence dragged. Miller forced himself not to speak for fear of begging.

"Well…" Diogo said warily. "Well. There's one hombre might could. Just arm and eye."

"Security guard work's fine with me," Miller said. "Anything that pays the bills."

"Il conversa á do. Hear what's said."

"I appreciate anything you can do," Miller replied, then gestured at the bed. "You mind if I…?"

"Mi cama es su cama," Diogo said. Miller lay down.

Diogo stepped into the small shower, and the sound of water against flesh drowned out the air cycler. Even on board ship, Miller hadn't lived in physical circumstances this intimate with anyone since his marriage. Still, he wouldn't have gone as far as to call Diogo a friend.

Opportunity was thinner on Tycho than he'd hoped, and he didn't have much by way of references. The few people who knew him weren't likely to speak on his behalf. But surely there'd be something. All he needed was a way to remake himself, to start over and be someone different from who he'd been.

Assuming, of course, that Earth or Mars—whichever one came out on top of the war—didn't then wipe the OPA and all the stations loyal to it out of the sky. And that the protomolecule didn't escape Eros and slaughter a planet. Or a station. Or him. He had a moment's chill, recalling that there was still a sample of the thing on board the *Roci*. If something happened with it, Holden and Naomi, Alex and Amos might all join Julie long before Miller did.

He told himself that wasn't his problem anymore. Still, he hoped they'd be all right. He wanted them to be well, even if he wasn't.

"Oi, Pampaw," Diogo said as the door to the public hall slid open. "You hear that Eros started talking?"

Miller lifted himself to one elbow.

"Sí," Diogo said. "Whatever that shit is, it started broadcasting. There's even words and shit. I've got a feed. You want a listen?"

No, Miller thought. *No, I have seen those corridors. What's happened to those people almost happened to me. I don't want anything to do with that abomination.*

"Sure," he said.

Diogo scooped up his own hand terminal and keyed in something. Miller's terminal chimed that it had received the new feed route.

"Chicá perdída in ops been mixing a bunch of it to bhangra," Diogo said, making a shifting dance move with his hips. "Hardcore, eh?"

Diogo and the other OPA irregulars had breached a high-value research station, faced down one of the most powerful and evil corporations in a history of power and evil. And now they were making music from the screams of the dying. Of the dead. They were dancing to it in the low-rent clubs. *What it must be like*, Miller thought, *to be young and soulless*.

But no. That wasn't fair. Diogo was a good kid. He was just naive. The universe would take care of that, given a little time.

"Hard-core," Miller said. Diogo grinned.

The feed sat in queue, waiting. Miller turned out the lights, letting the little bed bear him up against the press of spin. He didn't want to hear. He didn't want to know. He had to.

At first, the sound was nothing—electric squeals and a wildly fluting static. Then, maybe somewhere deep in the back of it, music. A chorus of violas churning away together in a long, distant crescendo. And then, as clear as if someone were speaking into a microphone, a voice.

"Rabbits and hamsters. Ecologically unstabilizing and round and blue as moonbeams. August."

It almost certainly wasn't a real person. The computer systems on Eros could generate any number of perfectly convincing dialects and voices. Men's, women's, children's. And how many millions of hours of data could there be on the computers and storage dumps all through the station?

Another electronic flutter, like finches looped back against themselves. A new voice—feminine and soft this time—with a throbbing pulse behind it.

"Patient complains of rapid heartbeat and night sweats. Symptom onset reported as three months previous, but with a history..."

The voice faded, and the throbbing rose. Like an old man with Swiss cheese holes in his brain, the complex system that had been Eros was dying, changing, losing its mind. And because Protogen had wired it all for sound, Miller could listen to the station fail.

"I didn't tell him, I didn't tell him, I didn't tell him. The sunrise. I've never seen the sunrise."

Miller closed his eyes and slid down toward sleep, serenaded by Eros. As consciousness faded, he imagined a body in the bed beside him, warm and alive and breathing slowly in time with the rise and fall of the static.

The manager was a thin man, weedy, with hair combed high above his brow like a wave that never crashed. The office hunched close around them, humming at odd moments when the infrastructure—water, air, energy—of Tycho impinged on it. A business built between ducts, improvisational and cheap. The lowest of the low.

"I'm sorry," the manager said. Miller felt his gut tighten and sink. Of all the humiliations the universe had in store for him, this one he hadn't foreseen. It made him angry.

"You think I can't handle it?" he asked, keeping his voice soft.

"It's not that," the weedy man said. "It's...Look, between us, we're looking for a thumb, you know? Someone's idiot kid brother could guard this warehouse. You've got all this experience. What do we need with riot control protocols? Or investigative procedure? I mean, come on. This gig doesn't even come with a gun."

"I don't care," Miller said. "I need something."

The weedy man sighed and gave the exaggerated shrug of a Belter.

"You need something else," he said.

Miller tried not to laugh, afraid it would sound like despair. He stared at the cheap plastic wall behind the manager until the guy started to get uncomfortable. It was a trap. He was too experienced to start over. He knew too much, so there was no going back and doing fresh beginnings.

"All right," he said at last, and the manager across the desk from him let out a breath, then had the good grace to look embarrassed.

"Can I just ask," the weedy man said. "Why did you leave your old job?"

"Ceres changed hands," Miller said, putting on his hat. "I wasn't on the new team. That was all."

"Ceres?"

The manager looked confused, which in turn confused Miller. He glanced down at his own hand terminal. There was his work history, just the way he'd presented it. The manager couldn't have missed it.

"That's where I was," Miller said.

"For the police thing. But I meant the last job. I mean, I've been around, I understand not putting OPA work on your resume, but you have to figure we all know that you were part of the thing... you know, with the station. And all."

"You think I was working for the OPA," Miller said.

The weedy man blinked.

"You were," he said.

Which, after all, was true.

Nothing had changed in Fred Johnson's office, and everything had. The furnishings, the smell of the air, the sense of its existing somewhere between a boardroom and a command and control center. The generation ship outside the window might have been half a percent closer to completion, but that wasn't it. The stakes of the game had shifted, and what had been a war was something else now. Something bigger. It shone in Fred's eyes and tightened his shoulders.

"We could use a man with your skills," Fred agreed. "It's always the small-scale things that trip you up. How to frisk someone. That kind of thing. Tycho security can handle themselves, but once we're off our station and shooting our way into someone else's, not as much."

"Is that something you're looking to do more of?" Miller said, trying to make it a casual joke. Fred didn't answer. For a moment, Julie stood at the general's side. Miller saw the pair of them reflected in the screens, the man pensive, the ghost amused. Maybe Miller had gotten it wrong from the start, and the divide between the Belt and the inner planets was something besides politics and resource management. He knew as well as anyone that the Belt offered a harder, more dangerous life than Mars or Earth provided. And yet it called these people—the best people—out of humanity's gravity wells to cast themselves into the darkness.

The impulse to explore, to stretch, to leave home. To go as far as possible out into the universe. And now that Protogen and Eros offered the chance to become gods, to re-create humanity into beings that could go beyond merely human hopes and dreams, it occurred to Miller how hard it would be for men like Fred to turn that temptation away.

"You killed Dresden," Fred said. "That's a problem."

"It needed to happen."

"I'm not sure it did," Fred replied, but his voice was careful. Testing. Miller smiled, a little sadly.

"That's why it needed to happen," he said.

The small, coughing laugh told Miller that Fred understood him. When the general turned back to consider him again, his gaze was steady.

"When it comes to the negotiating table, someone's going to have to answer for it. You killed a defenseless man."

"I did," Miller said.

"When the time comes, I will hand-feed you to the wolves as the first chip I offer. I won't protect you."

"Wouldn't ask you to protect me," Miller said.

"Even if it meant being a Belter ex-cop in an Earth-side prison?"

It was a euphemism, and they both knew it. *You belong with me,* Julie said. And so what did it matter, really, how he got there?

"I've got no regrets," he said, and half a breath later was shocked to discover it was almost true. "If there's a judge out there who wants to ask me about something, I'll answer. I'm looking for a job here, not protection."

Fred sat in his chair, eyes narrow and thoughtful. Miller leaned forward in his seat.

"You've got me in a hard position," Fred said. "You're saying all the right things. But I have a hard time trusting that you'd follow through. Keeping you on the books would be risky. It could undermine my position in the peace negotiations."

"It's a risk," Miller said. "But I've been on Eros and Thoth Station. I flew on the *Rocinante* with Holden and his crew. When it comes to analysis of the protomolecule and how we got into this mess, there isn't anyone in a better position to give you information. You can argue I knew too much. That I was too valuable to let go."

"Or too dangerous."

"Sure. Or that."

They were silent for a moment. On the *Nauvoo,* a bank of lights glittered in a gold-and-green test pattern and then went dark.

"Security consultant," Fred said. "Independent. I won't give you a rank."

I'm too dirty for the OPA, Miller thought with a glow of amusement.

"If it comes with my own bunk, I'll take it," he said. It was only until the war was over. After that, he was meat for the machine. That was fine. Fred leaned back. His chair hissed softly into its new configuration.

"All right," Fred said. "Here's your first job. Give me your analysis. What's my biggest problem?"

"Containment," Miller said.

"You think I can't keep the information about Thoth Station and the protomolecule quiet?"

"Of course you can't," Miller said. "For one thing, too many people already know. For another thing, one of them's Holden, and if he hasn't already broadcast the whole thing on every empty frequency, he will soon. And besides that, you can't make a peace deal without explaining what the hell's going on. Sooner or later, it has to come out."

"And what do you advise?"

For a moment, Miller was back in the darkness, listening to the gibbers of the dying station. The voices of the dead calling to him from across the vacuum.

"Defend Eros," he said. "All sides are going to want samples of the protomolecule. Locking down access is going to be the only way you get yourself a seat at that table."

Fred chuckled.

"Nice thought," he said. "But how do you propose we defend something the size of Eros Station if Earth and Mars bring their navies to bear?"

It was a good point. Miller felt a tug of sorrow. Even though Julie Mao—his Julie—was dead and gone, it felt like disloyalty to say it.

"Then you have to get rid of it," he said.

"And how would I do that?" Fred said. "Even if we studded the thing with nukes, how would we be sure that no little scrap of the thing would make its way to a colony or down a well? Blowing that thing up would be like blowing dandelion fluff into the breeze."

Miller had never seen a dandelion, but he saw the problem. Even the smallest portion of the goo filling Eros might be enough to start the whole evil experiment over again. And the goo thrived on radiation; simply cooking the station might hurry the thing along its occult path rather than end it. To be sure that the protomolecule on Eros never spread, they'd need to break everything on the station down to its constituent atoms...

"Oh," Miller said.

"Oh?"

"Yeah. You're not going to like this."

"Try me."

"Okay. You asked. You drive Eros into the sun."

"Into the sun," Fred said. "Do you have any idea how much mass we're talking about here?"

Miller nodded to the wide, clear expanse of window, to the construction yards beyond it. To the *Nauvoo.*

"Big engines on that thing," Miller said. "Get some fast ships out to the station, make sure no one can get in before you get there. Run the *Nauvoo* into Eros Station. Knock it sunward."

Fred's gaze turned inward as he planned, calculated.

"Got to make sure no one gets into it until it hits corona. That'll be hard, but Earth and Mars are both just as interested in keeping the other guy from having it as in getting it themselves."

I'm sorry I couldn't do better, Julie, he thought. *But it'll be a hell of a funeral.*

Fred's breath grew slow and deep, his gaze flickering as if he were reading something in the air that only he could see. Miller didn't interrupt, even when the silence got heavy. It was almost a minute later that Fred let out a short, percussive breath.

"The Mormons are going to be pissed," he said.

Chapter Forty-Five: Holden

Naomi talked in her sleep. It was one of a dozen things Holden hadn't known about her before tonight. Even though they'd slept in crash couches a few feet apart on many occasions, he'd never heard it. Now, with her face against his bare chest, he could feel her lips move and the soft, punctuated exhalations of her words. He couldn't hear what she was saying.

She also had a scar on her back, just above her left buttock. It was three inches long and had the uneven edges and rippling that came from a tear rather than a slice. Naomi would never get herself knifed in a bar fight, so it had to have come on the job. Maybe she had been climbing through tight spaces in the engine room when the ship maneuvered unexpectedly. A competent plastic surgeon could have made it invisible in one visit. That she hadn't bothered and clearly didn't care was another thing he had learned about her tonight.

She stopped murmuring and smacked her lips a few times, then said, "Thirsty."

Holden slid out from under her and headed for the kitchen, knowing that this was the obsequiousness that always accompanied a new lover. For the next couple of weeks, he wouldn't be able to stop himself from fulfilling every whim Naomi might have. It was a behavior some men carried at the genetic level, their DNA wanting to make sure that first time wasn't just a fluke.

Her room was laid out differently than his, and the unfamiliarity made him clumsy in the dark. He fumbled around for a few minutes in her small kitchen nook, looking for a glass. By the time he found it, filled it, and headed back into the bedroom, Naomi was sitting up in bed. The sheet lay pooled on her lap. The sight of her half nude in the dimly lit room gave him an embarrassingly sudden erection.

Naomi panned her gaze up his body, pausing at his midsection, then at the water glass, and said, "Is that for me?"

Holden didn't know which thing she was asking about, so he just said, "Yes."

"You asleep?"

Naomi's face was on his belly, her breathing slow and deep, but to his surprise she said, "No."

"Can we talk?"

Naomi rolled off him and pulled herself up until her face lay next to his on the pillow. Her hair fell across her eyes, and Holden reached out and brushed it away in a move that felt so intimate and proprietary that he had to swallow a lump in his throat.

"Are you about to get serious on me?" she asked, her eyes half lidded.

"Yeah, I am," he said, and kissed her forehead.

"My last lover was over a year ago," she said. "I'm a serial monogamist, so as far as I'm concerned, this is an exclusive-rights deal until one of us decides it isn't. As long as I get advance warning that you've decided to end the deal, there won't be any hard feelings. I'm open to the idea of it being more than just sex, but in my experience that will happen on its own if it's going to. I have eggs in storage on Europa and Luna, if that matters to you."

She rolled up onto her elbow, her face hovering over his.

"Did I cover all the bases?" she asked.

"No," he said. "But I agree to the conditions."

She flopped onto her back, letting out a long contented sigh. "Good."

Holden wanted to hold her, but he felt too hot and sticky with sweat, so he just reached down and held her hand instead. He wanted to tell her that this meant something, that it was already more than sex for him, but all the words he tried out in his head came off sounding phony or maudlin.

"Thank you," he said instead, but she was already snoring quietly.

They had sex again in the morning. After a long night with too little sleep, it wound up being far more effort than release for Holden, but there was a pleasure in that too, as if less than mind-blowing sex somehow meant something different and funnier and gentler than what they'd already done together. Afterward, Holden went to the kitchen and made coffee, then brought it back to bed on a tray. They drank it without talking, some of the shyness they'd avoided the night before coming now in the artificial morning of the room's LEDs.

Naomi put her empty coffee cup down and touched the badly healed lump in his recently broken nose.

"Is it hideous?" Holden asked.

"No," she said. "You were too perfect before. It makes you seem more substantial."

Holden laughed. "That sounds like a word you use to describe a fat man or a history professor."

Naomi smiled and touched his chest lightly with her fingertips. It wasn't an attempt to arouse, just the exploration that came when satiation had removed sex from the equation. Holden tried to remember the last time the cold sanity following sex had been this comfortable, but maybe that had been never. He was making plans to spend the remainder of the day in Naomi's bed, running through a mental list of restaurants on the station that delivered, when his terminal began buzzing on the nightstand.

"God dammit," he said.

"You don't have to answer," Naomi replied, and moved her explorations to his belly.

"You've been paying attention the last couple months, right?" Holden said. "Unless it's a wrong number, then it's probably some end-of-the-solar-system-type shit and we have five minutes to evacuate the station."

Naomi kissed his ribs, which simultaneously tickled him and caused him to question his assumptions about his own refractory period.

"That's not funny," she said.

Holden sighed and picked up the terminal off the table. Fred's name flashed as it buzzed again.

"It's Fred," he said.

Naomi stopped kissing him and sat up.

"Yeah, then it's probably not good news."

Holden tapped on the screen to accept the call and said, "Fred."

"Jim. Come see me as soon as you get a chance. It's important."

"Okay," Holden replied. "Be there in half an hour."

He ended the call and tossed his hand terminal across the room onto the pile of clothes he'd left at the foot of the bed.

"Going to shower, then go see what Fred wants," he said, pulling off the sheet and getting up.

"Should I come, too?" Naomi asked.

"Are you kidding? I'm never letting you out of my sight again."

"Don't get creepy on me," Naomi replied, but she was smiling when she said it.

The first unpleasant surprise was Miller sitting in Fred's office when they arrived. Holden nodded at the man once, then said to Fred, "We're here. What's up?"

Fred gestured for them to sit, and when they had, he said, "We've been discussing what to do about Eros."

Holden shrugged. "Okay. What about it?"

"Miller thinks that someone will try to land there and recover some samples of the protomolecule."

"I have no trouble believing that someone will be that stupid," Holden said with a nod.

Fred stood up and tapped something on his desk. The screens that normally showed a view of the *Nauvoo* construction outside suddenly switched to a 2-D map of the solar system, tiny lights of different colors marking fleet positions. An angry swarm of green dots surrounded Mars. Holden assumed that meant the greens were Earth ships. There were a lot of red and yellow dots in the Belt and outer planets. Red was probably Mars, then.

"Nice map," Holden said. "Accurate?"

"Reasonably," Fred said. With a few quick taps on his desk, he zoomed in on one portion of the Belt. A potato-shaped lump labeled EROS filled the middle of the screen. Two tiny green dots inched toward it from several meters away.

"That is the Earth science vessel *Charles Lyell* moving toward Eros at full burn. She's accompanied by what we think is a Phantom-class escort ship."

"The *Roci*'s Earth navy cousin," Holden said.

"Well, the Phantom class is an older model, and largely relegated to rear-echelon assignments, but still more than a match for anything the OPA can quickly field," Fred replied.

"Exactly the sort of ship that would be escorting science ships around, though," Holden said. "How'd they get out there so quick? And why just the two of them?"

Fred backed the map up until it was a distant view of the entire solar system again.

"Dumb luck. The *Lyell* was returning to Earth from doing

non-Belt asteroid mapping when it diverted course toward Eros. It was close; no one else was. Earth must have seen a chance to grab a sample while everyone else was figuring out what to do."

Holden looked over at Naomi, but her face was unreadable. Miller was staring at him like an entomologist trying to figure out exactly where the pin went.

"So they know, then?" Holden said. "About Protogen and Eros?"

"We assume so," Fred said.

"You want us to chase them away? I mean, I think we can, but that will only work until Earth can reroute a few more ships to back them up. We won't be able to buy much time."

Fred smiled.

"We won't need much," he said. "We have a plan."

Holden nodded, waiting to hear it, but Fred sat down and leaned back in his chair. Miller stood up and changed the view on the screen to a close-up of the surface of Eros.

Now we get to find out why Fred is keeping this jackal around, Holden thought, but said nothing.

Miller pointed at the picture of Eros.

"Eros is an old station. Lots of redundancy. Lot of holes in her skin, mostly small maintenance airlocks," the former detective said. "The big docks are in five main clusters around the station. We're looking at sending six supply freighters to Eros, along with the *Rocinante.* The *Roci* keeps the science vessel from landing, and the freighters secure themselves to the station, one at each docking cluster."

"You're sending people in?" Holden said.

"Not in," Miller replied. "Just on. Surface work. Anyway, the sixth freighter evacuates the crews once the others are docked. Each abandoned freighter will have a couple dozen high-yield fusion warheads wired to the ship's proximity detectors. Anything tries to land at the docks, and there's a few-hundred-megaton fusion explosion. It should be enough to take out the approaching ship, but even if it doesn't, the docks will be too slagged to land at."

Naomi cleared her throat. "Uh, the UN and Mars both have bomb squads. They'll figure out how to get past your booby traps."

"Given enough time," Fred agreed.

Miller continued as though he hadn't been interrupted.

"The bombs are just a second line of deterrence. *Rocinante* first, bombs second. We're trying to buy Fred's people enough time to prep the *Nauvoo.*"

"The *Nauvoo?*" Holden said, and half a breath later, Naomi whistled low. Miller nodded to her almost as if he were accepting applause.

"The *Nauvoo*'s launching in a long parabolic course, building up speed. It'll hit Eros at a velocity and angle calculated to knock Eros toward the sun. Set off the bombs too. Between the impact energy and the fusion warheads, we figure the surface of Eros'll be hot and radioactive enough to cook anything that tries to land until it's too damn late," Miller finished, then sat back down. He looked up as if he was waiting for reactions.

"This was your idea?" Holden asked Miller.

"*Nauvoo* part was. But we didn't know about the *Lyell* when we first talked about it. The booby trap thing's kind of improvised. I think it'll work, though. Buy us enough time."

"I agree," Holden said. "We need to keep Eros out of anyone's hands, and I can't think of a better way to do it. We're in. We'll shoo the science ship away while you do your work."

Fred leaned forward in his chair with a creak and said, "I knew you'd be on board. Miller was more skeptical."

"Throwing a million people into the sun seemed like something you might balk at," the detective said with a humorless grin.

"There's nothing human left on that station. What's your part in all of this? You armchair quarterbacking now?"

It came out nastier than he'd intended, but Miller didn't appear offended.

"I'll be coordinating security."

"Security? Why will they need security?"

Miller smiled. All his smiles looked like he was hearing a good joke at a funeral.

"In case something crawls out of an airlock, tries to thumb a ride," he said.

Holden frowned. "I don't like to think those things can get around in vacuum. I don't like that idea at all."

"Once we bring the surface temp of Eros up to a nice balmy ten thousand degrees, I'm thinking it won't matter much," Miller replied. "Until then, best be safe."

Holden found himself wishing he shared the detective's confidence.

"What are the odds the impact and detonations just break Eros into a million pieces and scatter them all over the solar system?" Naomi asked.

"Fred's got some of his best engineers calculating everything to the last decimal to make sure that doesn't happen," Miller replied. "Tycho helped build Eros in the first place. They've got the blueprints."

"So," said Fred. "Let's deal with the last bit of business."

Holden waited.

"You still have the protomolecule," Fred said.

Holden nodded again. "And?"

"And," replied Fred. "And the last time we sent you out, your ship was almost wrecked. Once Eros has been nuked, it will be the only confirmed sample around, outside of what might still be on Phoebe. I can't find any reason to let you keep it. I want it to remain here on Tycho when you go."

Holden stood up, shaking his head.

"I like you, Fred, but I'm not handing that stuff over to anyone who might see it as a bargaining chip."

"I don't think you have a lot of—" Fred started, but Holden held up a finger and cut him off. While Fred stared at him in surprise, he grabbed his terminal and opened the crew channel.

"Alex, Amos, either of you on the ship?"

"I'm here," Amos said a second later. "Finishing up some—"

"Lock it down," Holden said over him. "Right now. Seal it up. If I don't call you in an hour, or if anyone other than me tries to board, leave the dock and fly away from Tycho at best possible speed. Direction is your choice. Shoot your way free if you have to. Read me?"

"Loud and clear, Cap," Amos said. If Holden had asked him to get a cup of coffee, Amos would have sounded exactly the same.

Fred was still staring at him incredulously.

"Don't force this issue, Fred," Holden said.

"If you think you can threaten me, you're mistaken," Fred said, his voice flat and frightening.

Miller laughed.

"Something funny?" Fred said.

"That wasn't a threat," Miller replied.

"No? What would you call it?"

"An accurate report of the world," Miller said. He stretched slowly as he talked. "If it was Alex on board, he might think the captain was trying to intimidate someone, maybe back down at the last minute. Amos, though? Amos will absolutely shoot his way free, even if it means he goes down with the ship."

Fred scowled, and Miller shook his head.

"It's not a bluff," Miller said. "Don't call it."

Fred's eyes narrowed, and Holden wondered if he'd finally gone too far with the man. He certainly wouldn't be the first person Fred Johnson had ordered shot. And he had Miller standing right next to him. The unbalanced detective would probably shoot him at the first hint someone thought it was a good idea. It shook Holden's confidence in Fred that Miller was even here.

Which made it a little more surprising when Miller saved him.

"Look," the detective said. "Fact is, Holden is the best person to carry that shit around until you decide what to do with it."

"Talk me into it," Fred said, his voice still tight with anger.

"Once Eros goes up, he and the *Roci* are going to have their asses hanging in the breeze. Someone might be angry enough to nuke him just on general principles."

"And how does that make the sample safer with him?" Fred asked, but Holden had understood Miller's point.

"They might be less inclined to blow me up if I let them know that I've got the sample and all the Protogen notes," he said.

"Won't make the sample safer," Miller said. "But it makes the mission more likely to work. And that's the point, right? Also, he's an idealist," Miller continued. "Offer Holden his weight in gold and he'll just be offended you tried to bribe him."

Naomi laughed. Miller glanced at her, a small shared smile at the corner of his mouth, then turned back to Fred.

"Are you saying he can be trusted and I can't?" Fred said.

"I was thinking more about the crew," Miller said. "Holden's got a small bunch, and they do what he says. They think he's righteous, so they are too."

"My people follow me," Fred said.

Miller's grin was weary and unassailable.

"There's a lot of people in the OPA," he said.

"The stakes are too high," Fred said.

"You're kind of in the wrong career for safe," Miller said. "I'm not saying it's a great plan. Just you won't get a better one."

Fred's slitted eyes glittered with equal parts frustration and rage. His jaw worked silently for a moment before he spoke.

"Captain Holden? I'm disappointed with your lack of trust after all I've done for you and yours."

"If the human race still exists a month from now, I'll apologize," Holden said.

"Get your crew out to Eros before I change my mind."

Holden rose, nodded to Fred, and left. Naomi walked at his side.

"Wow, that was close," she said under her breath.

Once they'd left the office, Holden said, "I think Fred was half a second from ordering Miller to shoot me."

"Miller's on our side. Haven't you figured that out yet?"

Chapter Forty-Six: Miller

Miller had known when he'd taken Holden's side against his new boss that there were going to be consequences. His position with Fred and the OPA was tenuous to start with, and pointing out that Holden and his crew were not only more dedicated but also more trustworthy than Fred's people wasn't the thing you did when you were kissing up. That it was the truth only made it worse.

He'd expected some kind of payback. He would have been naive not to.

"Rise up, O men of God, in one united throng," the resisters sang. *"Bring in the days of bro-ther-hood, and end the night of wrong…"*

Miller took off his hat and ran fingers through his thinning hair. It wasn't going to be a good day.

The interior of the *Nauvoo* showed more patchwork and process than its hull suggested. Two kilometers long, its designers had built it as more than a huge ship. The great levels stacked one atop the other; alloy girders worked organically with what would have been pastoral meadows. The structure echoed the greatest cathedrals of Earth and Mars, rising up through empty air and giving both thrust-gravity stability and glory to God. It was still metal bones and woven agricultural substrate, but Miller could see where it was all heading.

A generation ship was a statement of overarching ambition and utter faith. The Mormons had known that. They'd embraced it. They'd constructed a ship that was prayer and piety and celebration all at the same time. The *Nauvoo* would be the greatest temple mankind had ever built. It would shepherd its crew through the uncrossable gulfs of interstellar space, humanity's best hope of reaching the stars.

Or it would have been, if not for him.

"You want us to gas them, Pampaw?" Diogo asked.

Miller considered the resisters. At a guess, there might have been two hundred of them strung in linked chains across the access paths and engineering ducts. Transport lifts and industrial waldoes stood idle, their displays dark, their batteries shorted.

"Yeah, probably should," Miller sighed.

The security team—his security team—numbered fewer than three dozen. Men and women more unified by the OPA-issued armbands than by their training, experience, loyalties, or politics. If the Mormons had chosen violence, it would have been a bloodbath. If they'd put on environment suits, the protest would have lasted hours. Days, possibly. Instead, Diogo gave the signal, and three minutes later, four small comets arced out into the null-g space, wavering on their tails of NNLP-alpha and tetrahydrocannabinol.

It was the kindest, gentlest riot control device in the arsenal. Any of the protesters with compromised lungs could still be in trouble, but within half an hour, all of them would be relaxed into near stupor and high as a kite. NNLPa and THC wasn't a combination Miller had ever used on Ceres. If they'd tried to stock it, it would have been stolen for office parties. He tried to take some comfort in the thought. As if it would make up for the lifetimes of dreams and labor he was taking away.

Beside him, Diogo laughed.

It took them three hours to make the primary sweep of the ship, and another five to hunt down all the stowaways huddled in ducts and secure rooms, waiting to make their presence known at the last minute and sabotage the mission. As those were hauled weeping off the ship, Miller wondered whether he'd just saved their lives. If all he'd done with his life was keep Fred Johnson from deciding whether to let a handful of innocent people die with the *Nauvoo*, or risk keeping Eros around for the inner planets, that wasn't so bad.

As soon as Miller gave the word, the OPA tech team moved into action, reengaging the waldoes and transports, fixing the hundred small acts of sabotage that would have kept the *Nauvoo*'s engines from firing, clearing out equipment they wanted to save. Miller watched industrial lifts big enough to house a family of five shift crate after crate, moving out things that had only recently been moved in. The docks were as busy as Ceres at mid-shift. Miller half expected to see his old cohorts wandering among the stevedores and lift tubes, keeping what passed for the peace.

In the quiet moments, he set his hand terminal to the Eros feed. Back when he'd been a kid, there had been a performance artist making the rounds—Jila Sorormaya, her name was. As he recalled, she'd intentionally corrupted data-storage devices and then put the data stream through her music kit. She'd gotten into trouble when some of the proprietary code of the storage device software got incorporated into her music and posted. Miller hadn't been a sophisticate. He'd figured another nutcase artist had to get a real job, and the universe could only be a better place.

Listening to the Eros feed—Radio Free Eros, he called it—he thought maybe he'd been a little rough on old Jila. The squeaks and cross-chatter, the flow of empty noise punctuated by voices, were eerie and compelling. Just like the broken data stream, it was the music of corruption.

…asciugare il pus e che possano sentirsi meglio…

…ja minä nousivat kuolleista ja halventaa kohtalo pakottaa minut ja siskoni…

…do what you have to…

He'd listened to the feed for hours, picking out voices. Once, the whole thing had fluttered, cutting in and out like a piece of equipment on the edge of failure. Only after it had resumed did Miller wonder if the stutters of quiet had been Morse code. He leaned against the bulkhead, the overwhelming mass of the *Nauvoo* towering above him. The ship only half born and already marked for sacrifice. Julie sat beside him, looking up. Her hair floated around her face; her eyes never stopped smiling. Whatever trick of the imagination had kept his own internal Juliette Andromeda Mao from coming back to him as her corpse, he thanked it.

It would have been something, wouldn't it? she said. *Flying through vacuum without a suit. Sleeping for a hundred years and waking up in the light of a different sun.*

"I didn't shoot that fucker fast enough," Miller said aloud.

He could have given us the stars.

A new voice broke in. A human voice shaking with rage.

"Antichrist!"

Miller blinked, returning to reality, and thumbed off the Eros feed. A prisoner transport wound its lazy way through the dock, a dozen Mormon technicians bound to its restraint poles. One was a young man with a pocked face and hatred in his eyes. He was staring at Miller.

"You're the Antichrist, you vile excuse for a human! God knows you! He'll *remember* you!"

Miller tipped his hat as the prisoners ambled by.

"Stars are better off without us," he said, but too softly for anyone but Julie to hear.

A dozen tugs flew before the *Nauvoo,* the web of nanotubule tethers invisible at this distance. All Miller saw was the great behemoth, as much a part of Tycho Station as the bulkheads and air, shift in its bed, shrug, and begin to move. The tugs' drive flares lit the interior space of the station, flickering in their perfectly choreographed duties like Christmas lights, and a nearly subliminal shudder passed through the deep steel bones of Tycho. In eight hours, the *Nauvoo* would be far enough out that the great engines could be brought online without endangering the station with their exhaust plume. It might be more than two weeks after that before it reached Eros.

Miller would beat it there by eighty hours.

"Oi, Pampaw," Diogo said. "Done-done?"

"Yeah," Miller said with a sigh. "I'm ready. Let's get everyone together."

The boy grinned. In the hours since the commandeering of the *Nauvoo,* Diogo had added bright red plastic decorations to three of his front teeth. It was apparently deeply meaningful in the youth culture of Tycho Station, and signified prowess, possibly sexual. Miller felt a moment's relief that he wasn't hot-bunking at the boy's place anymore.

Now that he was running security ops for the OPA, the irregular nature of the group was clearer to him than ever. There had been a time when he'd thought the OPA might be something that could take on Earth or Mars when it came to a real war. Certainly, they had more money and resources than he'd thought. They had Fred Johnson. They had Ceres now, for as long as they could hold it. They'd taken on Thoth Station and won.

And yet the same kids he'd gone on the assault with had been working crowd control at the *Nauvoo,* and more than half of them would be on the demolitions ship when it left for Eros. It was the thing that Havelock would never understand. For that matter, it was the thing Holden would never understand. Maybe no one who had lived with the certainty and support of a natural atmosphere would ever completely accept the power and fragility of a society based in doing what needed doing, in becoming fast and flexible, the way the OPA had. In becoming articulated.

If Fred couldn't build himself a peace treaty, the OPA would never win against the discipline and unity of an inner planet navy. But they would also never lose. War without end.

Well, what was history if not that?

And how would having the stars change anything?

As he walked to his apartment, he opened a channel request on his hand terminal. Fred Johnson appeared, looking tired but alert.

"Miller," he said.

"We're getting ready to ship out if the ordinance is ready."

"It's loading now," Fred replied. "Enough fissionable material to keep the surface of Eros unapproachable for years. Be careful with it. If one of your boys goes down for a smoke in the wrong place, we aren't going to be able to replace the mines. Not in time."

Not *you'll all be dead*. The weapons were precious, not the people.

"Yeah, I'll watch it," Miller said.

"The *Rocinante*'s already on its way."

That wasn't something Miller needed to know, so there was some other reason Fred had mentioned it. His carefully neutral tone made it something like an accusation. The only controlled sample of protomolecule had left Fred's sphere of influence.

"We'll get out there to meet her in plenty of time to keep anybody off of Eros," Miller said. "Shouldn't be a problem."

On the tiny screen, it was hard to tell how genuine Fred's smile was.

"I hope your friends are really up for this," he said.

Miller felt something odd. A little hollowness just below his breastbone.

"They aren't my friends," he said, keeping his tone of voice light.

"No?"

"I don't exactly have friends. It's more I've got a lot of people I used to work with," he said.

"You put a lot of faith in Holden," Fred said, making it almost a question. A challenge, at least. Miller smiled, knowing that Fred would be just as unsure if his was genuine.

"Not faith. Judgment," he said.

Fred coughed out a laugh.

"And that's why you don't have friends, friend."

"Part of it," Miller said.

There was nothing more to say. Miller dropped the connection. He was almost at his hole, anyway.

It was nothing much. An anonymous cube on the station with even less personality to it than his place back on Ceres. He sat on his bunk, checked his terminal for the status of the demolitions ship. He knew that he should just go up to the docks. Diogo and the others were assembling, and while it wasn't likely that the drug haze of the pre-mission parties would allow them all to arrive on time, it was at least possible. He didn't even have that excuse.

Julie sat in the space behind his eyes. Her legs were folded under her. She was beautiful. She'd been like Fred and Holden and Havelock. Someone born in a gravity well who came to the Belt by choice. She'd died for her choice. She'd come looking for help and killed Eros by doing it. If she'd stayed there, on that ghost ship...

She tilted her head, her hair swinging against the spin gravity. There was a question in her eyes. She was right, of course. It would have slowed things down, maybe. It wouldn't have stopped them. Protogen and Dresden would have found her eventually. Would have found it. Or gone back and dug up a fresh sample. Nothing would have stopped them.

And he knew—knew the way he knew he was himself—that Julie wasn't like the others. That she'd understood the Belt and Belters, and the need to push on. If not for the stars, at least close to them. The luxury available to her was something Miller had never experienced, and never would. But she'd turned away. She'd come out here, and stayed even when they were going to sell her racing pinnace. Her childhood. Her pride.

That was why he loved her.

When Miller reached the dock, it was clear something had happened. It was in the way the dockworkers held themselves and the looks half amusement and half pleasure, on their faces. Miller signed in and crawled through the awkward Ojino-Gouch-style airlock, seventy years out of date and hardly larger than a torpedo tube, into the cramped crew area of the *Talbot Leeds*. The ship looked like it had been welded together from two smaller ships, without particular concern for design. The acceleration couches were stacked three deep. The air smelled of old sweat and hot metal. Someone had been smoking marijuana recently enough that the filters hadn't cleared it out yet. Diogo was there along with a half dozen others. They all wore different uniforms, but they also all had the OPA armband.

"Oi, Pampaw! Kept top bunk á dir."

"Thanks," Miller said. "I appreciate that."

Thirteen days. He was going to spend thirteen days sharing this tiny space with the demolitions crew. Thirteen days pressed into these couches, with megatons of fission mines in the ship's hold. And yet the others were all smiling. Miller hauled himself up to the acceleration couch Diogo had saved for him, and pointed to the others with his chin.

"Someone have a birthday?"

Diogo gave an elaborate shrug.

"Why's everyone in such a good fucking mood?" Miller said, more sharply than he'd intended. Diogo took no offense. He smiled his great red-and-white teeth.

"Audi-nichts?"

"No, I haven't heard, or I wouldn't be asking," Miller said.

"Mars did the right thing," Diogo said. "Got the feed off Eros, put two and two, and—"

The boy slammed a fist into his open palm. Miller tried to parse what he was saying. They'd attacked Eros? They'd taken on Protogen?

Ah. Protogen. Protogen and Mars. Miller nodded. "The Phoebe science station," he said. "Mars quarantined it."

"Fuck that, Pampaw. *Autoclaved* it, them. Moon is gone. Dropped enough nukes on it to split it subatomic."

They better have, Miller thought. It wasn't a big moon. If Mars had really destroyed it and there was any protomolecule left on a hunk of ejecta…

"Tu sabez?" Diogo said. "They're on our side now. They get it. Mars-OPA alliance."

"You don't really think that," Miller said.

"Nah," Diogo said, just as pleased with himself in admitting that the hope was fragile at best and probably false. "But don't hurt to dream, que no?"

"You don't think?" Miller said, and lay back.

The acceleration gel was too stiff to conform to his body at the dock's one-third g, but it wasn't uncomfortable. He checked the news on his hand terminal, and indeed someone in the Martian navy had made a judgment call. It was a lot of ordinance to use, especially in the middle of a shooting war, but they'd expended it. Saturn had one fewer moon, one more tiny, unformed, filamentous ring—if there was even enough matter left from the detonations to form that. It looked to Miller's unpracticed eye as if the explosions had been designed to drop debris into the protective and crushing gravity of the gas giant.

It was foolish to think it meant the Martian government wouldn't want samples of the protomolecule. It was naive to pretend that any organization of that size and complexity was univocal about anything, much less something as dangerous and transforming as this.

But still.

Perhaps it was enough just knowing that someone on the other side of the political and military divide had seen the same evidence they had seen and drawn the same conclusions. Maybe it left room for hope. He switched his hand terminal back to the Eros feed. A strong throbbing sound danced below a cascade of noise. Voices rose and fell and rose again. Data streams spewed into one another, and the pattern-recognition servers burned every spare cycle making something from the resultant mess. Julie took his hand, the dream so convincing he could almost pretend he felt it.

You belong with me, she said.

As soon as it's over, he thought. It was true he kept pushing back the end point of the case. First find Julie, then avenge her, and now destroy the project that had claimed her life. But after that was accomplished, he could let go.

He just had this one last thing he needed to do.

Twenty minutes later, the Klaxon sounded. Thirty minutes later, the engines kicked on, pressing him into the acceleration gel at a joint-crushing high-g burn for thirteen days, with one-g breaks for biological function every four hours. And when they were done, the half-trained jack-of-all-trades crew would be handling nuclear mines capable of annihilating them if they screwed it up.

But at least Julie would be there. Not really, but still.

It didn't hurt to dream.

Chapter Forty-Seven: Holden

Even the wet cellulose taste of reconstituted artificial scrambled eggs was not enough to ruin Holden's warm, self-satisfied glow. He shoveled the faux eggs into his mouth, trying not to grin. Sitting at his left around the galley table, Amos ate with lip-smacking enthusiasm. To Holden's right, Alex pushed the limp eggs around on his plate with a piece of equally fake toast. Across the table, Naomi sipped a cup of tea and looked at him from under her hair. He stifled the urge to wink at her.

They'd talked about how to break the news to the crew but hadn't come to any consensus. Holden hated to hide anything. Keeping it secret made it seem dirty or shameful. His parents had raised him to believe that sex was something you did in private not because it was embarrassing, but because it was intimate. With five fathers and three mothers, the sleeping arrangements were always complex at his house, but the discussions about who was bedding with whom were never hidden from him. It left him with a strong aversion to hiding his own activities.

Naomi, on the other hand, thought they shouldn't do anything to upset the fragile equilibrium they'd found, and Holden trusted her instincts. She had an insight into group dynamics that he often lacked. So, for now, he was following her lead.

Besides, it would have felt like boasting, and that would have been rude.

Keeping his voice neutral and professional, he said, "Naomi, can you pass the pepper?"

Amos' head snapped up, and he dropped his fork on the table with a loud clatter.

"Holy shit, you guys are doing it!"

"Um," Holden said. "What?"

"Something's been screwy ever since we got back on the *Roci*, but I couldn't figure. But that's *it*! You guys are finally playing hide the weasel."

Holden blinked twice at the big mechanic, unsure of what to say. He glanced at Naomi for support, but her head was down, and her hair completely covered her face. Her shoulders were shaking in silent laughter.

"Jesus, Cap," Amos said, a grin on his wide face. "It fucking took you long enough. If she'd been throwing herself at me like that, I'd have been neck deep in that shit."

"Uh," Alex said, looking shocked enough that it was clear he hadn't shared Amos' insights. "Wow."

Naomi stopped laughing and wiped tears away from the corners of her eyes.

"Busted," she said.

"Look. Guys, it's important that you know this doesn't affect our—" Holden said, but Amos cut him off with a snort.

"Hey, Alex," Amos said.

"Yo," Alex replied.

"XO boning the captain going to make you a really shitty pilot?"

"Don't believe it will," Alex said with a grin, exaggerating his drawl.

"And, oddly enough, I don't feel the need to be a lousy mechanic."

Holden tried again. "I think it's important that—"

"Cap'n?" Amos continued, ignoring him. "Consider that no one gives a fuck, it won't stop us from doing our jobs, and just enjoy it, since we'll probably all be dead in a few days anyway."

Naomi started laughing again.

"Fine," she said. "I mean, everyone knows I'm only doing it to get a promotion. Oh, wait, right. Already the second-in-command. Hey, can I be captain now?"

"No," Holden said, laughing. "It's a shit job. I'd never ask you to do it."

Naomi grinned and shrugged. *See? I'm not always right.* Holden glanced at Alex, who was looking at him with genuine affection, clearly happy about the idea of him and Naomi together. Everything seemed right.

Eros spun like a potato-shaped top, its thick skin of rock hiding the horrors inside. Alex brought them in close to do a thorough scan of the station. The asteroid swelled on Holden's screen until it looked close enough to touch. At the other ops station, Naomi swept the surface with ladar, looking for anything that might pose a danger to the Tycho freighter crews, still a few days behind. On Holden's tactical display, the UNN science ship continued to flare in a braking maneuver toward Eros, its escort right beside it.

"Still not talking, huh?" Holden asked.

Naomi shook her head, then tapped on her screen and sent the comm's monitoring information to his workstation.

"Nope," she said. "But they see us. They've been bouncing radar off of us for a couple hours now."

Holden tapped his fingers on the arm of his chair and thought about the choices. It was possible that the hull modifications Tycho had made to the *Roci* were fooling the Earth corvette's recognition software. They might just ignore the *Roci,* thinking she was a Belter gas runner that happened to be hanging around. But the *Roci* was running without a transponder, which made her illegal no matter what hull configuration she was showing. That the corvette wasn't trying to warn off a ship that was running dark made him nervous. The Belt and the inner planets were in a shooting war. A Belter ship with no identification was hanging around Eros while two Earth ships flew toward it. No way any captain with half a brain would just ignore them.

The corvette's silence meant something else.

"Naomi, I have a feeling that corvette is going to try and blow us up," Holden said with a sigh.

"It's what I'd do," she replied.

Holden tapped one last complicated rhythm on his chair, then put his headset on.

"All right, I guess I make the first overture, then," he said.

Not wishing to make their conversation public, Holden targeted the Earther corvette with the *Rocinante*'s laser array and signaled a generic linkup request. After a few seconds, the *link established* light went green, and his earplugs began to hiss with faint background static. Holden waited, but the UN ship offered no greeting. They wanted him to speak first.

He flicked off his mic, switching to the shipwide comm.

"Alex, get us moving. One g for now. If I can't bluff this guy, it'll be a shooting match. Be ready to open her up."

"Roger," drawled Alex. "Goin' on the juice, just in case."

Holden glanced over at Naomi's station, but she'd already switched to her tactical screen and had the *Roci* plotting firing solutions and jamming tactics on the two approaching ships. Naomi had been in only one battle, but she was reacting now like a seasoned veteran. He smiled at her back, then turned around before she had time to realize he was staring.

"Amos?" he said.

"Locked down and shipshape down here, Cap. The *Roci*'s pawing at the turf. Let's go kick some ass."

Let's hope we don't have to, Holden thought.

He turned his mic back on.

"This is Captain James Holden of the *Rocinante,* calling the captain of the approaching United Nations Navy corvette, call sign unknown. Please respond."

There was a static-filled pause, followed by *"Rocinante.* Leave our flight path immediately. If you do not begin moving away from Eros at best possible speed, you will be fired upon."

The voice was young. An aging corvette with the tedious task of following an asteroid-mapping ship around wouldn't be a much sought after command. The captain was probably a lieutenant without patrons or prospects. He'd be inexperienced, but he might see a confrontation as an opportunity to prove himself to his superiors. And that made the next few moments treacherous to navigate.

"Sorry," said Holden. "Still don't know your call sign, or your name. But I can't do what you want. In fact, I can't let anyone land on Eros. I'm going to need you to stop approaching the station."

"Rocinante, I don't think you—"

Holden took control of the *Roci*'s targeting system and began painting the approaching corvette with its targeting laser.

"Let me explain what's happening here," he said. "Right now, you're looking at your sensors, and you're seeing what looks like a thrown-together gas freighter that's giving your ship-recognition software fits. And all of a sudden, meaning *right now,* it's painting you with a state-of-the-art target-acquisition system."

"We don't—"

"Don't lie. I know that's what's happening. So here's the deal. Despite how it looks, my ship is newer, faster, tougher, and better armed than yours. The only way for me to really prove that is to open fire, and I'm hoping not to do that."

"Are you threatening me, *Rocinante?*" the young voice on Holden's headset said, its tone hitting just the right notes of arrogance and disbelief.

"You? No," said Holden. "I'm threatening the big, fat, slow-moving, and unarmed ship you're supposed to be protecting. You keep flying toward Eros, and I will unload everything I've got at it. I guarantee we will blow that flying science lab out of the sky. Now, it's possible you might get us while we do it, but by then your mission is screwed anyway, right?"

The line went silent again, only the hiss of background radiation letting him know his headset hadn't died.

When his answer came, it came on the shipwide comms.

Alex said, "They're stoppin', Captain. They just started hard brakin'. Tracking says they'll be relative stopped about two million klicks out. Want me to keep flyin' toward 'em?"

"No, bring us back to our stationary position over Eros," Holden replied.

"Roger that."

"Naomi," Holden said, spinning his chair around to face her. "Are they doing anything else?"

"Not that I can see through the clutter of their exhaust. But they could be tightbeaming messages the other direction and we'd never know," she said.

Holden flipped the shipwide comm off. He scratched his head for a minute, then unbuckled his restraints.

"Well, we stopped them for now. I'm going to hit the head and then grab a drink. Want anything?"

"He's not wrong, you know," Naomi said later that night.

Holden was floating in zero g on the ops deck, his station a few feet away. He'd turned down the deck lights, and the cabin was as dim as a moonlit night. Alex and Amos were sleeping two decks below. They might as well have been a million light-years away. Naomi was floating near her own station, two meters away, her hair unbound and drifting around her like a black cloud. The panel behind her lit her face in profile: the long forehead, flat nose, large lips. He could tell that her eyes were closed. He felt like they were the only two people in the universe.

"Who's not wrong?" he said, just to be saying something.

"Miller," she replied as though it were obvious.

"I have no idea what you're talking about."

Naomi laughed, then swatted with one hand to rotate her body and face him in the air. Her eyes were open now, though with the panel lights behind her, they were visible only as black pools in her face.

"I've been thinking about Miller," she said. "I treated him badly on Tycho. Ignored him because you were angry. I owed him better than that."

"Why?"

"He saved your life on Eros."

Holden snorted, but she kept going anyway.

"When you were in the navy," she finally said, "what were you supposed to do when someone went crazy on the ship? Started doing things that endangered everyone?"

Thinking they were talking about Miller, Holden said, "You restrain him and remove him as a danger to the ship and crew. But Fred didn't—"

Naomi cut him off.

"What if it's wartime?" she said. "The middle of a battle?"

"If he can't be easily restrained, the chief of the watch has an obligation to protect the ship and crew by whatever means necessary."

"Even shooting him?"

"If that's the only way to do it," Holden replied. "Sure. But it would only be in the most pressing circumstances."

Naomi nodded with her hand, sending her body slowly twisting the other way. She stopped her motion with one unconscious gesture. Holden was pretty good in zero g, but he'd never be that good.

"The Belt is a network," Naomi said. "It's like one big distributed ship. We have nodes that make air, or water, or power, or structural materials. Those nodes may be separated by millions of kilometers of space, but that doesn't make them any less interconnected."

"I see where this is going," Holden said with a sigh. "Dresden was a madman on the ship, Miller shot him to protect the rest of us. He gave me that speech back on Tycho. Didn't buy it then either."

"Why?"

"Because," Holden said. "Dresden wasn't an immediate threat. He was just an evil little man in an expensive suit. He didn't have a gun in his hand, or his finger on a bomb trigger. And I will never trust a man who believes he has the right to unilaterally execute people."

Holden put his foot against the bulkhead and tapped off just hard enough to float a few feet closer to Naomi, close enough to see her eyes, read her reaction to him.

"If that science ship starts flying toward Eros again, I will throw every torpedo we have at it, and tell myself I was protecting the rest of the solar system from what's on Eros. But I won't just start shooting at it now, on the idea that it *might* decide to head to Eros again, because that's murder. What Miller did was murder."

Naomi smiled at him, then grabbed his flight suit and pulled him close enough for a kiss.

"You might be the best person I know. But you're totally uncompromising on what you think is right, and that's what you hate about Miller."

"I do?"

"Yes," she said. "He's totally uncompromising too, but he has different ideas on how things work. You hate that. To Miller, Dresden was an active threat to the ship. Every second he stayed alive endangered everyone else around him. To Miller, it was self-defense."

"But he's wrong. The man was helpless."

"The man talked the UN Navy into giving his company state-of-the-art ships," she said. "He talked his company into murdering a million and a half people. Everything Miller said about why the protomolecule is better off with us was just as true about Dresden. How long is he in an OPA lockup before he finds the jailer who can be bought?"

"He was a prisoner," Holden said, feeling the argument slipping away from him.

"He was a monster with power, access, and allies who would have paid any price to keep his science project going," Naomi said. "And I'm telling you as a Belter, Miller wasn't wrong."

Holden didn't answer; he just continued to float next to Naomi, keeping himself in her orbit. Was he angrier about the killing of Dresden or about Miller's making a decision that disagreed with him?

And Miller had known. When Holden had told him to find his own ride back to Tycho, he'd seen it in the detective's sad basset hound face. Miller had known it was coming, and had made no attempt to fight or argue. That meant that Miller had made his choice fully cognizant of the cost and ready to pay it. That meant something. Holden wasn't sure exactly what, but something.

A red telltale began flashing on the wall, and Naomi's panel woke up and began throwing data onto the screen. She pulled herself down to it using the back of her chair, then tapped out several quick commands.

"Shit," she said.

"What is it?"

"The corvette or science ship must have called for help," Naomi said, pointing at her screen. "We've got ships on their way from all over the system."

"How many are coming?" Holden asked, trying to get a better look at her screen.

Naomi made a small sound in the back of her throat, halfway between a chuckle and a cough.

"At a guess? All of them."

Chapter Forty-Eight: Miller

Y ou are, and you aren't," the Eros feed said through a semi-random drumming of static. "You are, and you aren't. You are, and you aren't."

The little ship shuddered and bumped. From a crash couch, one of the OPA techs called out a string of obscenities remarkable more for inventiveness than actual rancor. Miller closed his eyes, trying to keep the micro-g adjustments of their nonstandard docking from nauseating him. After days of joint-aching acceleration and an equally bruising braking routine, the small shifts and movements felt arbitrary and strange.

"You are, are, are, are, *are, are, are*..."

He'd spent some time listening to the newsfeeds. Three days after they'd left Tycho, the news of Protogen's involvement with Eros broke. Amazingly, Holden hadn't been the one to do it. Since then, the corporation had gone from total denial, to blaming a rogue subcontractor, to claiming immunity under an Earth defense secrets statute. It didn't sound good for them. Earth's blockade of Mars was still in place, but attention had shifted to the power struggle within Earth, and the Martian navy had slowed its burn, giving the Earth forces a little more breathing room before any permanent decisions had to be made. It looked like they'd postponed Armageddon for a few weeks, anyway. Miller found he could take a certain joy in that. It also left him tired.

More often, he listened to the voice of Eros. Sometimes he watched the video feeds too, but usually, he just listened. Over the hours and days, he began to hear, if not patterns, at least common structures. Some of the voices spooling out of the dying station were consistent—broadcasters and entertainers who were over-represented in the audio files archives, he guessed. There seemed to be some specific tendencies in, for want of a better term, the music of it too. Hours of random, fluting static and snatched bits of phrases would give way, and Eros would latch on to some word or phrase, fixating on it with greater and greater intensity until it broke apart and the randomness poured back in.

"...are, are, are, ARE, ARE, ARE..."

Aren't, Miller thought, and the ship suddenly shoved itself up, leaving Miller's stomach about half a foot from where it had been. A series of loud clanks followed, and then the brief wail of a Klaxon.

"Dieu! Dieu!" someone shouted. "Bombs son vamen roja! Going to fry it! Fry us toda!"

There was the usual polite chuckle that the same joke had occasioned over the course of the trip, and the boy who'd made it—a pimply Belter no more than fifteen years old—grinned with pleasure at his own wit. If he didn't stop that shit, someone was going to beat him with a crowbar before they got back to Tycho. But Miller figured that someone wasn't him.

A massive jolt forward pushed him hard into the couch, and then gravity was back, the familiar 0.3 g. Maybe a little more. Except that with the airlocks pointing toward ship's down, the pilot had to grapple the spinning skin of Eros' belly first. The spin gravity made what had been the ceiling the new floor; the lowest rank of couches was now the top; and while they rigged the fusion bombs to the docks, they were all going to have to climb up onto a cold, dark rock that was trying to fling them off into the vacuum.

Such were the joys of sabotage.

Miller suited up. After the military-grade suits of the *Rocinante,* the OPA's motley assortment of equipment felt like third-hand clothes. His suit smelled of someone else's body, and the Mylar faceplate had a deformation where it had cracked and been repaired. He didn't like thinking about what had happened to the poor bastard who'd been wearing it. The magnetic boots had a thick layer of corroded plastic and old mud between the plates and a triggering mechanism so old that Miller could feel it click on and off even before he moved his foot. He had the image of the suit locking on to Eros and never letting go.

The thought made him smile. *You belong with me,* his own private Julie had said. It was true, and now that he was here, he felt perfectly certain that he wasn't going to leave. He'd been a cop for too long, and the idea of trying to reconnect to humanity again filled him with the presentiment of exhaustion. He was here to do the last part of his job. And then he was done.

"Oi! Pampaw!"

"I'm coming," Miller said. "Hold your damn horses. It's not like the station's going anyplace."

"A rainbow is a circle you can't see. Can't see. Can't see," Eros said in a child's singsong voice. Miller turned down the volume of his feed.

The rocky surface of the station had no particular purchase for the suits and control waldoes. Two other ships had made polar landings where there was no spin gravity to fight against, but the Coriolis would leave everyone with a subliminal nausea. Miller's team had to keep to the exposed metal plates of the dock, clinging like flies looking down into the starlit abyss.

Engineering the placement of the fusion bombs wasn't trivial work. If the bombs didn't pump enough energy into the station, the surface might cool enough to give someone another chance to put a science team on it before the penumbra of the sun swallowed it and whatever parts of the *Nauvoo* were still clinging to it. Even with the best minds of Tycho, there was still the chance that the detonations wouldn't sync up. If the pressure waves traveling through the rock amplified in ways they hadn't anticipated, the station could crack open like an egg, spreading the protomolecule through the wide, empty track of the solar system like scattering a handful of dust. But the difference between success and disaster might be literally a question of meters.

Miller crawled up the airlock and out to the station surface. The first wave of technicians were setting up resonance seismographs, the glow of the work lights and readouts the brightest thing in the universe. Miller set his boots on a wide swath of a ceramic steel alloy and let the spin stretch the kinks out of his back. After days in the acceleration couch, the freedom felt euphoric. One of the techs raised her hands, the physical Belter idiom that called for attention. Miller upped the suit volume.

"…insectes rampant sur ma peau…"

With a stab of impatience, he switched from the Eros feed to the team channel.

"Got to move," a woman's voice said. "Too much splashback here. We have to get to the other side of the docks."

"These go on for almost two kilometers," Miller said.

"Is," she agreed. "We can unmoor and move the ship under power or we can tow it. We've got enough lead line."

"Which one's fastest? We don't have a lot of spare time here."

"Towing."

"Tow it, then," Miller said.

Slowly, the ship rose, twenty small, crawling transport drones clinging to leads like they were hauling a great metallic zeppelin. The ship was going to stay with him, here on the station, strapped to the rock like a sacrifice to the gods. Miller walked with the crew as they crossed the wide, closed bay doors. The only sounds were the tapping of his soles as the electromagnets jolted onto the surface and then a tick when they let go again. The only smells were of his own body and the fresh plastic of the air recycler. The metal under his feet shone like someone had cleaned it. Any dust or pebbles had been hurled away long ago.

They worked fast to place the ship, arm the bombs, and fit the security codes, everyone tacitly aware of the great missile that had been the *Nauvoo* speeding toward them.

If another ship came down and tried to disarm the trap, the ship would send synchronizing signals to all the other OPA bomb ships studding the moon's surface. Three seconds later, the surface of Eros would be scrubbed clean. The spare air and supplies were loaded off the ship, bundled together and ready for reclamation. No reason to waste the resources.

Nothing horrific crawled out of an airlock and tried to attack the crew, which made Miller's presence during the mission entirely superfluous. Or maybe not. Maybe it was just a ride.

When everything was done that could be, Miller sent the all clear, relayed through the now-dead ship's system. The return transport appeared slowly, a dot of light that grew gradually brighter and then spread, the null-g boarding web strung out like scaffolding. At the new ship's word, Miller's team turned off their boots and fired simple maneuvering thrusters either from their suits or, if the suits were too old, from shared ablative evacuation shells. Miller watched them drop away.

"Call va and roll, Pampaw," Diogo said from someplace. Miller wasn't sure which of them he was at this distance. "This tube don't sit."

"I'm not coming," Miller said.

"Sa que?"

"I decided. I'm staying here."

There was a moment of silence. Miller had been waiting for this. He had the security codes. If he needed to crawl back into the shell of their old ship and lock the door behind him, he could. But he didn't want to. He'd prepared his arguments: He would only be going back to Tycho as a political pawn for Fred Johnson's negotiations; he was tired and old in a way that years didn't describe; he'd already died on Eros once, and he wanted to be here to finish it. He'd earned that much. Diogo and the others owed it to him.

He waited for the boy to react, to try to talk him out of it.

"All correct, then," Diogo said. "Buona morte."

"Buona morte," Miller said, and shut off his radio. The universe was silent. The stars below him shifted slowly but perceptibly as the station he hung from spun. One of those lights was the *Rocinante*. Two others were the ships Holden had been sent out to stall. Miller couldn't pick them out. Julie floated beside him, her dark hair floating in the vacuum, the stars shining through her. She looked peaceful.

If you had it to do again, she said. *If you could do it all over from the beginning?*

"I wouldn't," he said.

He watched the OPA transport ship start up its engines, glowing gold and white, and pull away until it was a star again. A small one. And then lost. Miller turned and considered the dark, empty moonscape and the permanent night.

He just needed to be with her for another few hours, and they would both be safe. They would *all* be safe. It was enough. Miller found himself smiling and weeping, the tears tracking up from his eyes and into his hair.

It's going to be fine, Julie said.

"I know," Miller said.

He stood silently for almost an hour, then turned and made his slow, precarious way back to the sacrificed ship, down the airlock, and into the dim belly. There was enough residual atmosphere that he didn't need to sleep in his suit. He stripped naked, chose an acceleration couch, and curled up on the hard blue gel. Not twenty meters away, five fusion devices powerful enough to outshine the sun waited for a signal. Above him, everything that had once been human in Eros Station changed and re-formed, pouring from one shape to another like Hieronymus Bosch made real. And still almost a day away, the *Nauvoo*, the hammer of God, hurtled toward him.

Miller set his suit to play some old pop tunes he'd enjoyed when he was young and let himself be sung to sleep. When he dreamed, he dreamed he'd found a tunnel at the back of his old hole on Ceres that meant he would at last, at *last,* be free.

His last breakfast was a hard kibble bar and a handful of chocolate scrounged from a forgotten survival pack. He ate it with tepid recycled water that tasted of iron and rot. The signals from Eros were almost drowned by the oscillating frequencies blasting out from the station above him, but Miller made out enough to know where things stood.

Holden had won, much as Miller had expected him to. The OPA was responding to a thousand angry accusations from Earth and Mars and, in the true and permanent style, factions within the OPA itself. It was too late. The *Nauvoo* was due in hours now. The end was coming.

Miller put on his suit for the last time, turned out the lights, and crawled back up the airlock. For a long moment, the exterior release didn't respond, the safety lights glowing red, and he had a stab of fear that he would spend his last moments there, trapped in a tube like a torpedo ready to fire. But he cycled the lock's power, and it opened.

The Eros feed was wordless now, with only a soft murmuring like water over stone. Miller walked out across the wide mouth of the docking bays. The sky above him turned, and the *Nauvoo* rose from the horizon like the sun. His splayed hand held at full arm's length wasn't big enough to cover the glow of its engines. He hung by his boots, watching the ship approach. The phantom Julie watched with him.

If he'd done the math right, the *Nauvoo*'s impact site would be at the center of Eros' major axis. Miller would be able to see it when it happened, and the giddy excitement in his chest reminded him of being young. It would be a show. Oh, it would be something to see. He considered recording it. His suit would be able to make a simple visual file and stream the data out in real time. But no. This was his moment. His and Julie's. The rest of humanity could guess what it had been like if they cared.

The massive glow of the *Nauvoo* filled a quarter of the sky now, and the full circle of it was free of the horizon. The Eros feed's soft murmur shifted to something more clearly synthetic: a rising, spiraling sound that reminded him for no particular reason of the green sweeping radar screens of ancient films. There were voices at the back of it, but he couldn't make out the words or even the language.

The great torch of the *Nauvoo* was a full half of the sky, the stars around it blotted out by the light of full burn. Miller's suit chirped a radiation warning and he shut it off.

A manned *Nauvoo* would never have sustained a burn like that; even in the best couch, the thrust gravity would have pulped bones. He tried to guess how fast the ship would be going when it hit.

Fast enough. That was all that mattered. Fast enough.

There, in the center of the fiery bloom, Miller saw a dark spot, no more than the dot of a pencil's tip. The ship itself. He took a deep breath. When he closed his eyes, the light pressed red through his lids. When he opened them again, the *Nauvoo* had length. Shape. It was a needle, an arrow, a missile. A fist rising from the depths. For the first time in memory, Miller felt awe.

Eros shouted.

"DON'T YOU *FUCKING* TOUCH ME!"

Slowly, the bloom of engine fire changed from a circle to an oval to a great feathery plume, the *Nauvoo* itself showing silver in rough profile. Miller gaped.

The *Nauvoo* had missed. It had turned. It was right now, right *now*, speeding past Eros and not into it. But he hadn't seen any kind of maneuvering rockets fire. And how would you turn something that big, moving that quickly, so abruptly that it would veer off between one breath and the next without also tearing the ship apart? The acceleration g alone...

Miller looked at the stars as if there was some answer written in them. And to his surprise, there was. The sweep of the Milky Way, the infinite scattering of stars were still there. But the angles had changed. The rotation of Eros had shifted. Its relation to the plane of the ecliptic.

For the *Nauvoo* to change course at the last minute without falling apart would have been impossible. And so it hadn't happened. Eros was roughly six hundred cubic kilometers. Before Protogen, it had housed the second-largest active port in the Belt.

And without so much as overcoming the grip of Miller's magnetic boots, Eros Station had dodged.

Chapter Forty-Nine: Holden

Holy shit," said Amos in a flat voice.

"Jim," Naomi said to Holden's back, but he waved her off and opened a channel to Alex in the cockpit.

"Alex, did we just see what my sensors say we saw?"

"Yeah, Cap," the pilot replied. "Radar and scopes are both sayin' Eros jumped two hundred klicks spinward in a little less than a minute."

"Holy shit," Amos repeated in exactly the same emotionless tone. The metallic bang of deck hatches opening and closing echoed through the ship, signaling Amos' approach up the crew ladder.

Holden shook off the flush of irritation he felt at Amos' leaving his post. He'd deal with that later. He needed to be sure that the *Rocinante* and her crew hadn't just experienced a group hallucination.

"Naomi, give me comms," he said.

Naomi turned around in her chair to face him, her face ashen.

"How can you be so calm?" she asked.

"Panic won't help. We need to know what's going on before we can plan intelligently. Please transfer the comms to me."

"Holy shit," Amos said as he climbed into the ops deck. The deck hatch shut with a punctuating bang.

"I don't remember ordering you to leave your post, sailor," Holden said.

"Plan intelligently," Naomi said like they were words in a foreign language that she almost understood. "Plan intelligently."

Amos threw himself at a chair hard enough that the cushioning gel grabbed him and kept him from bouncing off.

"Eros is really fucking big," Amos said.

"Plan intelligently," Naomi repeated, speaking to herself now.

"I mean, *really* fucking big," Amos said. "Do you know how much energy it took to spin that rock up? I mean, it took *years* to do that shit."

Holden put his headset on to drown Amos and Naomi out, and called up Alex again.

"Alex, is Eros still changing velocity?"

"No, Cap. Just sitting there like a rock."

"Okay," Holden said. "Amos and Naomi are vapor locked. How are you doing?"

"Not taking my hands off the stick while that bastard is anywhere in my space, that's for damn sure."

Thank God for military training, Holden thought.

"Good, keep us at a constant distance of five thousand klicks until I say otherwise. Let me know if it moves again, even an inch."

"Roger that, Cap," said Alex.

Holden took off his headset and turned to face the rest of the crew. Amos was looking at the ceiling, ticking points off with his fingers, his eyes unfocused.

"—don't really remember the mass of Eros off the top of my head..." he was saying to no one in particular.

"About seven thousand trillion kilos," Naomi replied. "Give or take. And the heat signature's up about two degrees."

"*Jesus*," the mechanic said. "I can't do that math in my head. That much mass coming up two degrees like that?"

"A lot," Holden said. "So let's move on—"

"About ten exajoules," Naomi said. "That's just off the top of my head, but I'm not off by an order of magnitude or anything."

Amos whistled.

"Ten exajoules is like, what, a two-gigaton fusion bomb?"

"It's about a hundred kilos converted directly to energy," Naomi said. Her voice began to steady. "Which, of course, we couldn't do. But at least whatever they did wasn't magic."

Holden's mind grabbed on to her words with an almost physical sensation. Naomi was, in fact, about the smartest person he knew. She had just spoken directly to the half-articulated fear he'd been harboring since Eros had jumped sideways: that this was magic, that the protomolecule didn't have to obey the laws of physics. Because if that was true, humans didn't stand a chance.

"Explain," he said.

"Well," she replied, tapping on her keypad. "Heating Eros up didn't move it. So I assume that means it was waste heat from whatever it was they actually did."

"And that means?"

"That entropy still exists. That they can't convert mass to energy with perfect efficiency. That their machines or processes or whatever they use to move seven thousand trillion kilos of rock wastes some energy. About a two-gigaton bomb's worth of it."

"Ah."

"You couldn't move Eros two hundred kilometers with a two-gigaton bomb," Amos said with a snort.

"No, you couldn't," Naomi replied. "This is just the leftovers. Heat by-product. Their efficiency is still off the charts, but it isn't perfect. Which means the laws of physics still hold. Which means it isn't magic."

"Might as well be," Amos said.

Naomi looked at Holden.

"So, we—" he started when Alex interrupted over the shipwide comm.

"Cap, Eros is movin' again."

"Follow it, get me a course and speed as soon as you can," Holden said, turning back to his console. "Amos, get back down to engineering. If you leave it again without a direct order, I'll have the XO beat you to death with a pipe wrench."

The only reply was the hiss of the deck hatch opening and the bang as it closed behind the descending mechanic.

"Alex," Holden said, staring at the data stream the *Rocinante* was feeding him about Eros. "Tell me something."

"Sunward is all we know for sure," Alex replied, his voice still calm and professional. When Holden had been in the military, he'd been officer track right from the start. He'd never been to military pilot school, but he knew that years of training had compartmentalized Alex's brain into two halves: piloting problems and, secondarily, everything else. Matching Eros and getting a course for it was the former. Extra-solar space aliens trying to destroy humanity wasn't a piloting issue and could be safely ignored until he left the cockpit. He might have a nervous breakdown afterward, but until then, Alex would keep doing his job.

"Drop back to fifty thousand klicks and maintain a constant distance," Holden told him.

"Huh," said Alex. "Maintainin' a constant distance might be tough, Cap. Eros just disappeared off the radar."

Holden felt his throat go tight.

"Say again?"

"Eros just disappeared off the radar," Alex was saying, but Holden was already punching up the sensor suite to check for himself. His telescopes showed the rock still moving on its new course toward the sun. Thermal imaging showed it as slightly warmer than space. The weird feed of voices and madness that had been leaking out of the station was still detectable, if faint. But radar said there was nothing there.

Magic, a small voice at the back of his mind said again.

No, not magic. Humans had stealth ships too. It was just a matter of absorbing the radar's energy rather than reflecting it. But suddenly, keeping the asteroid in visual range became all the more important. Eros had shown that it could move fast and maneuver wildly, and it was now invisible to radar. It was entirely possible that a mountain-sized rock could disappear completely.

Gravity began to pile up as the *Roci* chased Eros toward the sun.

"Naomi?"

She looked up at him. The fear was still in her eyes, but she was holding it together. For now.

"Jim?"

"The comm? Could you...?"

The chagrin on her face was the most reassuring thing he'd seen in hours. She shifted control to his station, and he opened a connection request.

"UNN corvette, this is the *Rocinante,* please respond."

"Go ahead, *Rocinante,*" the other ship said after half a minute of static.

"Calling to confirm our sensor data," Holden said, then transmitted the data regarding Eros' movement. "You guys seeing the same thing?"

Another delay, this one longer.

"Roger that, *Rocinante.*"

"I know we were just about to shoot each other and all, but I think we're a little past that now," Holden said. "Anyway, we're chasing the rock. If we lose sight of it, we might never find it again. Want to come with? Might be nice to have some backup if it decides to shoot at us or something."

Another delay, this one almost two minutes long; then a different voice came on the line. Older, female, and totally lacking the arrogance and anger of the young male voice he'd been dealing with so far.

"*Rocinante,* this is Captain McBride of the UNN Escort Vessel

Ravi." *Ah,* thought Holden. *I've been talking to the first officer all along. The captain finally took the horn. That might be a good sign.* "I've sent word to fleet command, but it's a twenty-three minute lag right now, and that rock's putting on speed. You have a plan?"

"Not really, *Ravi.* Just follow and gather intel until we find an opportunity to do something that makes a difference. But if you came along, maybe none of your people will shoot at us accidentally while we figure it out."

There was a long pause. Holden knew that the captain of the *Ravi* was weighing the chance that he was telling the truth against the threat he'd made against their science vessel. What if he was in on whatever was happening? He'd be wondering the same thing in their position.

"Look," he said. "I've told you my name. James Holden. I served as a lieutenant in the UNN. My records should be on file. It'll show a dishonorable discharge, but they'll also show that my family lives in Montana. I don't want that rock to hit Earth any more than you do."

The silence on the other end continued for another few minutes.

"Captain," she said, "I believe my superiors would want me to keep an eye on you. We'll be coming along for the ride while the brains figure this out."

Holden let out a long, noisy exhale.

"Thanks for that, McBride. Keep trying to get your people on the line. I'm going to make a few calls myself. Two corvettes are not going to fix this problem."

"Roger that," the *Ravi* replied, then killed the connection.

"I've opened a connection with Tycho," Naomi said.

Holden leaned back in his chair, the mounting gravity of their acceleration pressing against him. A watery lump was gathering low in his gut, the loose knot telling him that he had no idea what he was doing, that all the best plans had failed, and that the end was near. The brief hope he'd felt was already starting to slip away.

How can you be so calm?

I think I'm watching the end of the human race, Holden

thought. *I'm calling Fred so that it isn't my fault when no one has an idea how to stop it. Of course I'm not calm.*

I'm just spreading the guilt.

"How fast?" Fred Johnson asked incredulously.

"Four g's now and climbing," Holden replied, his voice thick as his throat compressed. "Oh, and it's invisible to radar now."

"*Four g. Do you know how heavy Eros is?*"

"There's, uh, been some discussion," Holden said, only the acceleration keeping his impatience from showing in his voice. "The question is, now what? The *Nauvoo* missed. Our plans are shot to shit."

There was another perceptible increase in pressure as Alex sped the ship up to keep up with Eros. A little while longer and speech wouldn't be possible.

"It's definitely headed for Earth?" Fred asked.

"Alex and Naomi are ninety percent or so. Hard to be totally accurate when we can only use visual data. But I trust them. I'd go to where there are thirty billion new hosts too."

Thirty billion new hosts. Eight of whom were his parents. He imagined Father Tom as a bundle of tubes oozing brown goo. Mother Elise as a rib cage dragging itself across the floor with one skeletal arm. And with that much biomass, what could it do then? Move Earth? Turn out the sun?

"Have to warn them," Holden said, trying not to strangle on his own tongue as he spoke.

"You don't think they know?"

"They see a threat. They may not see the end of all native life in the solar system," Holden said. "You wanted a reason to sit at the table? How about this one: Come together or die."

Fred was quiet for a moment. Background radiation spoke to Holden in mystic whispers full of dire portents while he waited. *Newcomer,* it said. *Hang around for fourteen billion years or so. See what I've seen. Then all this nonsense won't seem so important.*

"I'll see what I can do," Fred said, interrupting the universe's lecture on transience. "In the meantime, what are you going to do?"

Get outrun by a rock and then watch the cradle of humanity die.

"I'm open to suggestions," Holden said.

"Maybe you could detonate some of the surface nukes the demo team put down. Deflect Eros' course. Buy us time."

"They're on proximity fuses. Can't set them off," Holden said, the last word turning into a yelp as his chair stabbed him in a dozen different places and injected him full of fire. Alex had hit them with the juice, which meant Eros was still speeding up, and he was worried they'd all black out. How fast was it going to go? Even on the juice they couldn't sustain prolonged acceleration past seven or eight g without serious risk. If Eros kept this rate of increase up, it would outrun them.

"You can remote detonate," Fred said. "Miller will have the codes. Have the demo team calculate which ones to set off for maximum effect."

"Roger that," Holden said. "I'll give Miller a call."

"I'll work on the inners," Fred said, using the Belter slang without a hint of self-consciousness. "See what I can do."

Holden broke the connection, then linked up to Miller's ship.

"Yo," said whoever was manning the radio there.

"This is Holden, on the *Rocinante*. Give me Miller."

"Uh…" said the voice. "Okay."

There was a click, then static, then Miller saying hello with a faint echo. Still wearing his helmet, then.

"Miller, this is Holden. We need to talk about what just happened."

"Eros moved."

Miller sounded strange, his voice distant, as though he was only barely paying attention to the conversation. Holden felt a flush of irritation but tamped it back down. He needed Miller right now, whether he wanted to or not.

"Look," he said. "I've talked to Fred and he wants us to coordinate with your demo guys. You've got remote codes. If we set off all of them on one side, we can deflect its course. Get your techs on the line, and we'll work it out."

"Huh, yeah, that sounds like a good idea. I'll send the codes along," said Miller, his voice no longer distant, but holding back a laugh. Like a man about to tell the punch line of a really good joke. "But I can't really help you with the techs."

"Shit, Miller, you pissed those people off, too?"

Miller did laugh now, a free, soft sound that someone who wasn't piling on g could afford. If there was a punch line, Holden had missed it.

"Yeah," Miller said. "Probably. But that's not why I can't get them for you. I'm not on the ship with them."

"What?"

"I'm still on Eros."

Chapter Fifty: Miller

What do you mean you're on Eros?" Holden said.

"Pretty much that," Miller said, covering his growing sense of shame with a casual tone of voice. "Hanging upside down outside the tertiary docks, where we moored one of the ships. Feel like a freaking bat."

"But—"

"Funny thing, too. I didn't feel it when the thing moved. You'd think accelerating like that, it would have thrown me off or squashed me flat, one or the other. But there was nothing."

"Okay, hold on. We're coming to get you."

"Holden," Miller said. "Just stop it, all right?"

The silence didn't last more than a dozen seconds, but it carried a wealth of meaning. *It's not safe to bring the* Rocinante *to Eros,* and *I came here to die,* and *Don't make this harder than it is.*

"Yeah, I just…" Holden said. And then: "Okay. Let me…let

me coordinate with the technicians. I'll...Jesus. I'll let you know what they say."

"One thing, though," Miller said. "You're talking about deflecting this sonofabitch? Just keep in mind it's not a rock anymore. It's a ship."

"Right," Holden said. And a moment later: "Okay."

The connection dropped with a tick. Miller checked his oxygen supply. Three hours in-suit, but he could head back to his little ship and refill it well before that. So Eros was moving, was it? He still didn't feel it, but watching the curved surface of the asteroid, he could see micro-asteroids, all coming from the same direction, bouncing off. If the station kept accelerating, they'd start coming more often, more powerfully. He'd need to stay in the ship.

He turned his hand terminal back to the Eros feed. The station beneath him was chirping and muttering, long slow vowel sounds radiating out from it like recorded whale song. After the angry words and static, the voice of Eros sounded peaceful. He wondered what kind of music Diogo's friends would be making out of this. Slow dancing didn't seem like their style. An annoying itch settled in the small of his back, and he shifted in his suit, trying to rub it away. Almost without his noticing it, he grinned. And then laughed. A wave of euphoria passed into him.

There was alien life in the universe, and he was riding on it like a tick on a dog. Eros Station had moved of its own free will and by mechanisms he couldn't begin to imagine. He didn't know how many years it had been since he'd been overwhelmed by awe. He'd forgotten the feeling. He raised his arms to his sides, reaching out as if he could embrace the endless dark vacuum below him.

Then, with a sigh, he turned back toward the ship.

Back in the protective shell, he took off the vac suit and hooked the air supply to the recyclers to charge up. With only one person to care for, even low-level life support would have it ready to go within the hour. The ship batteries were still almost fully charged. His hand terminal chimed twice, reminding him that it was once again time for the anti-cancer meds. The ones he'd earned the last time he'd been on Eros. The ones he'd be on for the rest of his life. Good joke.

The fusion bombs were in the ship's cargo hold: gray square boxes about half again as long as they were tall, like bricks in a mortar of pink adhesive foam. It took Miller twenty minutes of searching through storage lockers to find a can of solvent that still had charge in it. The thin spray from it smelled like ozone and oil, and the stiff pink foam melted under it. Miller squatted beside the bombs and ate a ration bar that tasted convincingly like apples. Julie sat beside him, her head resting weightlessly on his shoulder.

There had been a few times that Miller had flirted with faith. Most had been when he was young and trying out everything. Then when he was older, wiser, more worn, and in the crushing pain of the divorce. He understood the longing for a greater being, a huge and compassionate intelligence that could see everything from a perspective that dissolved the pettiness and evil and made everything all right. He still felt that longing. He just couldn't convince himself it was true.

And still, maybe there was something like a plan. Maybe the universe had put him in the right place at the right time to do the thing that no one else would do. Maybe all the pain and suffering he'd been through, all the disappointments and soul-crushing years wallowing through the worst that humanity had to offer up, had been meant to bring him here, to this moment, when he was ready to die if it bought humanity a little time.

It would be pretty to think so, Julie said in his mind.

"It would," he agreed with a sigh. At the sound of his voice, the vision of her vanished, just another daydream.

The bombs were heavier than he'd remembered. Under a full g, he wouldn't have been able to move them. At only one-third, it was a struggle, but possible. An agonizing centimeter at a time, he dragged one of them onto a handcart and hauled it to the airlock. Eros, above him, sang to itself.

He had to rest before he tackled the hard work. The airlock was thin enough that only the bomb or he could fit through at a time.

He climbed on top of it to get out the outer airlock door, then had to lift the bomb out with straps he rigged from cargo netting. And once out, it had to be tethered to the ship with magnetic clamps to keep Eros' spin from slinging it out into the void. After he'd pulled it out and strapped it to the cart, he stopped to rest for half an hour.

There were more impacts now, a rough sign that Eros was indeed accelerating. Each one a rifle shot, capable of bouncing clean through him or the ship behind him if bad luck sent it in the right direction. But the odds were low of one of the occasional rocks lining up a killing shot with his tiny antlike figure crawling across the surface. Once Eros cleared the Belt, they'd stop, anyway. Was Eros leaving the Belt? He realized he had no idea where Eros was going. He'd assumed it was Earth. Holden would know by now, probably.

His shoulders ached a little from his efforts, but not badly. He worried that he'd overloaded the cart. Its wheels were stronger than his mag boots, but they could still be overcome. The asteroid above him lurched once, a new and unsettling motion that didn't repeat. His hand terminal cut off the Eros feed, alerting him that he had an incoming connection. He looked at it, shrugged, and let the call come through.

"Naomi," he said before she could speak. "How've you been doing?"

"Hey," she said.

The silence between them stretched.

"You talked to Holden, then?"

"I did," she said. "He's still talking about ways to get you off that thing."

"He's a good guy," Miller said. "Talk him out of it for me, okay?"

The silence hung long enough that Miller started to get uncomfortable.

"What are you doing there?" she asked. As if there were an answer for that. As if all his life could be summarized in answer to one simple question. He danced around what she meant and replied only to what she'd said.

"Well, I've got a nuclear bomb strapped to a cargo wagon. I'm hauling it over to the access hatch and taking it into the station."

"Miller—"

"The thing is, we were treating this like a rock. Now everyone knows that's a little simplistic, but it's going to take people time to adjust. Navies are still going to be thinking of this thing like a billiard ball when it's really a rat."

He was talking too fast. The words spilling out of him in a rush. If he didn't give her room, she wouldn't talk. He wouldn't have to hear what she had to say. He wouldn't have to keep her from talking him down.

"It's going to have structure. Engines or control centers. Something. If I truck this thing inside, get it close to whatever coordinates the thing, I can break it. Turn it back into a billiard ball. Even if it's just for a little while, that gives the rest of you a chance."

"I figured," she said. "It makes sense. It's the right thing to do."

Miller chuckled. A particularly solid impact tocked against the ship beneath him, the vibration of it jarring his bones. Gas started venting out of the new hole. The station was moving faster.

"Yeah," he said. "Well."

"I was talking to Amos," she said. "You need a dead man's switch. So that if something happens, the bomb still goes off. If you have the access codes...?"

"I do."

"Good. I've got a routine you can put on your hand terminal. You'll need to keep your finger on the select button. If you go away for five seconds, it sends the go signal. If you want, I can upload it to you."

"So I have to wander around the station with my finger mashed on a button?"

Naomi's tone made it an apology. "They might take you out

with a head shot. Or wrestle you down. The longer the gap, the more chance for the protomolecule to disable the bomb before it goes off. If you need more, I can reprogram it."

Miller looked at the bomb resting on its cart just outside the ship's airlock. Its readouts all glowed green and gold. His sigh briefly fogged the inside of his helmet.

"Yeah, no. Five is good. Upload the routine. Am I going to need to tweak it, or is there a simple place I can put the arm-and-fire string?"

"There's a setup section," Naomi said. "It prompts you."

The hand terminal chirped, announcing the new file. Miller accepted it, ran it. It was easy as keying in a door code. Somehow he felt that arming fusion bombs to detonate around him should have been more difficult.

"Got it," he said. "We're good to go. I mean, I still have to move this bastard, but other than that. How fast am I accelerating on this thing, anyway?"

"Eventually it will be faster than the *Roci* can go. Four g and ramping up with no sign of easing off the throttle."

"Can't feel it at all," he said.

"I'm sorry about before," Naomi said.

"It was a bad situation. We did what we had to do. Same as always."

"Same as always," she echoed.

They didn't speak for a few seconds.

"Thanks for the trigger," Miller said. "Tell Amos I appreciate it."

He cut the connection before she could answer. Long goodbyes weren't anyone's strong suit. The bomb rested in the handcart, magnetic clamps in place and a wide woven-steel belt around the whole mess. He moved slowly across the metallic surface of the port docks. If the cart lost its grip on Eros, he wouldn't be strong enough to hold it back. Of course, if one of the increasingly frequent strikes hit him, it would be a lot like getting shot, so waiting around wasn't a good solve either. He put both dangers out of his mind and did the work. For ten nervous minutes, his suit smelled of overheating plastic. All the diagnostics showed within the error bars, and by the time the recyclers cleared it, his air supply still looked good. Another little mystery he wasn't going to solve.

The abyss above him shone with unflickering stars. One of the dots of light was Earth. He didn't know which one.

The service hatch had been tucked in a natural outcropping of stone, the raw-ferrous cart track like a ribbon of silver in the darkness. Grunting, Miller hauled the cart and the bomb and his own exhausted body up around the curve, and spin gravity once again pressed down on his feet instead of stretching his knees and spine. Light-headed, he keyed in the codes until the hatch opened.

Eros lay before him, darker than the empty sky.

He ran the hand terminal connection through the suit, calling Holden for what he expected was the last time.

"Miller," Holden said almost immediately.

"I'm heading in now," he said.

"Wait. Look, there's a way we might be able to get an automated cart. If the *Roci*—"

"Yeah, but you know how it is. I'm already here. And we don't know how fast this sonofabitch can go. We've got a problem we need to fix. This is how we do it."

Holden's hope had been weak, anyway. Pro forma. A gesture and, Miller thought, maybe even heartfelt. Trying to save everyone, right to the last.

"I understand," Holden finally said.

"Okay. So once I've broken whatever the hell I find in there...?"

"We're working on ways to annihilate the station."

"Good. I'd hate to go through the trouble for nothing."

"Is there...Is there anything you want me to do? After?"

"Nah," Miller said, and then Julie was at his side, her hair floating around her like they were underwater. She glowed in more starlight than was actually there. "Wait. Yes. A couple things. Julie's parents. They run Mao-Kwikowski Mercantile. They knew the war was going to start before it did. They've got to have links to Protogen. Make sure they don't get away with it. And if you see them, tell them I'm sorry I didn't find her in time."

"Right," Holden said.

Miller squatted in the darkness. Was there anything else? Shouldn't there be more? A message to Havelock, maybe? Or Muss. Or Diogo and his OPA friends? But then there would have to be something to say.

"Okay," Miller said. "That's it, then. It was good working with you."

"I'm sorry it came down this way," Holden said. It wasn't an apology for what he'd done or said, for what he'd chosen and refused.

"Yeah," Miller said. "But what can you do, right?"

It was as close to goodbye as either of them could get. Miller shut the connection, brought up the script Naomi had sent him, and enabled it. While he was at it, he turned the Eros feed back on.

A soft hushing sound, like fingernails scratching down an endless sheet of paper. He turned on the cart's lights, the dark entrance of Eros brightening to industrial gray, shadows scattering to the corners. His imagined Julie stood in the glare like it was a spotlight, the glow illuminating her and all the structures behind her at the same time, the remnant of a long dream, almost over.

He took off the brakes, pushed, and went inside Eros for the last time.

Chapter Fifty-One: Holden

Holden knew that humans could tolerate extremely high g-forces over short durations. With proper safety systems, professional daredevils had sustained impacts in excess of twenty-five g's and survived. The human body deformed naturally, absorbed energy in soft tissues, and diffused impacts across larger areas.

He also knew that the problem with extended exposure to high g was that the constant pressure on the circulatory system would begin exposing weaknesses. Have a weak spot in an artery that could turn into an aneurysm in forty years? A few hours at seven g might just pop it open now. Capillaries in the eyes started to leak. The eye itself deformed, sometimes causing permanent damage. And then there were the hollow spaces, like the lungs and digestive tract. You piled on enough gravity, and they collapsed.

And while combat ships might maneuver at very high g for

short durations, every moment spent under thrust multiplied the danger.

Eros didn't need to shoot anything at them. It could just keep speeding up until their bodies exploded under the pressure. His console was showing five g, but even as he watched, it shifted to six. They couldn't keep this up. Eros was going to get away. There was nothing he could do about it.

But he still didn't order Alex to stop accelerating.

As if Naomi were reading his mind, WE CAN'T KEEP THIS UP popped up on his console, her user ID in front of the text.

FRED'S WORKING ON IT. THEY MIGHT NEED US TO BE WITHIN RANGE OF EROS WHEN THEY COME UP WITH A PLAN, he replied. Even moving his fingers the millimeters necessary to use the controls built into his chair for exactly this reason was painfully difficult.

WITHIN RANGE FOR WHAT? Naomi typed.

Holden didn't answer. He had no idea. His blood was burning with drugs to keep him awake and alert even while his body was being crushed. The drugs had the contradictory effect of making his brain run at double speed while not allowing him to actually think. But Fred would come up with something. Lots of smart people were thinking about it.

And Miller.

Miller was lugging a fusion bomb through Eros right now. When your enemy had the tech advantage, you came at him as low-tech as you could get. Maybe one sad detective pulling a nuclear weapon on a wagon would slip through their defenses. Naomi had said they weren't magic. Maybe Miller could make it and give them the opening they needed.

Either way, Holden had to be there, even if it was just to see.

FRED, Naomi typed to him.

Holden opened the connection. Fred looked to him like a man suppressing a grin.

"Holden," he said. "How are you guys holding up?"

SIX G'S. SPIT IT OUT.

"Right. So it turns out that the UN cops have been ripping Protogen's network apart, looking for clues as to what the hell's been going on. Guess who showed up as public enemy number one for the Protogen bigwigs? Yours truly. Suddenly all is forgiven, and Earth welcomes me back into her warm embrace. The enemy of my enemy thinks I am a righteous bastard."

GOODY. MY SPLEEN IS COLLAPSING. HURRY UP.

"The idea of Eros crashing into Earth is bad enough. Extinction-level event, even if it's just a rock. But the UN people have been watching the Eros feeds, and it's scaring the shit out of them."

AND.

"Earth is preparing to launch her entire ground-based nuclear arsenal. *Thousands* of nukes. They're going to vaporize that rock. The navy will intercept what's left after the initial attack and sterilize that entire area of space with constant nuclear bombardment. I know it's a risk, but it's what we have."

Holden resisted the urge to shake his head. He didn't want to wind up with one cheek stuck to the chair permanently.

EROS DODGED THE *NAUVOO*. IT'S GOING SIX G'S RIGHT NOW, AND ACCORDING TO NAOMI, MILLER FEELS NO ACCELERATION. WHATEVER IT'S DOING, IT DOESN'T HAVE THE SAME INERTIAL LIMITATIONS WE HAVE. WHAT'S TO STOP IT FROM JUST DODGING AGAIN? AT THESE SPEEDS, THE MISSILES WILL NEVER BE ABLE TO TURN AROUND AND CATCH IT. AND WHAT THE HELL ARE YOU TARGETING ON? EROS DOESN'T REFLECT RADAR ANYMORE.

"That's where you come in. We need you to try bouncing a laser off of it. We can use the *Rocinante*'s targeting system to guide the missiles in."

I HATE TO BREAK IT TO YOU, BUT WE'LL BE OUT OF THIS GAME LONG BEFORE THOSE MISSILES SHOW. WE CAN'T KEEP UP. WE CAN'T GUIDE THE MISSILES IN FOR YOU. AND ONCE WE LOSE VISUAL, NO ONE WILL BE ABLE TO TRACK WHERE EROS IS.

"You might have to put it on autopilot," Fred said.

Meaning *You might all have to die in the seats you're in right now.*

I'VE ALWAYS WANTED TO DIE A MARTYR AND ALL, BUT WHAT MAKES YOU THINK THE ROCI CAN BEAT THIS THING ON ITS OWN? I'M NOT KILLING MY CREW BECAUSE YOU CAN'T COME UP WITH A GOOD PLAN.

Fred leaned toward the screen, his eyes narrowing. For the first time, Fred's mask slipped and Holden saw the fear and helplessness behind it.

"Look, I know what I'm asking, but you know the stakes. This is what we have. I didn't call you to hear how it won't work. Either help or give up. Right now devil's advocate is just another name for asshole."

I'm crushing myself to death, probably doing permanent damage, just because I wouldn't *give up, you bastard. So sorry I didn't sign my crew up to die the minute you said to do it.*

Having to type everything out had the advantage of restraining emotional outbursts. Instead of ripping into Fred for questioning his commitment, Holden just typed LET ME THINK ABOUT IT and cut the connection.

The optical tracking system watching Eros flashed a warning to him that the asteroid was increasing speed again. The giant sitting on his chest added a few pounds as Alex pushed the *Rocinante* to keep up. A flashing red indicator informed Holden that because of the duration they'd spent at the current acceleration, he could expect as much as 12 percent of the crew to stroke out. It would go up. Enough time, and it would reach 100 percent. He tried to remember the *Roci*'s maximum theoretical acceleration. Alex had already flown it at twelve g briefly when they'd left the *Donnager*. The actual limit was one of those trivial numbers, a way to brag about something your ship would never really do. Fifteen g, was it? Twenty?

Miller hadn't felt any acceleration at all. How fast could you go if you didn't even *feel* it?

Almost without realizing he was going to do it, Holden activated the master engine cutoff switch. Within seconds he was in free fall, wracked with coughs as his organs tried to find their original resting places inside his body. When Holden had recovered enough to take one really deep breath, his first in hours, Alex came on the comm.

"Cap, did you kill the engines?" the pilot said.

"Yeah, that was me. We're done. Eros is getting away no matter what we do. We were just prolonging the inevitable, and risking some crew deaths in the process."

Naomi turned her chair and gave him a sad little smile. She was sporting a black eye from the acceleration.

"We did our best," she said.

Holden shoved out of his chair hard enough that he bruised his forearms on the ceiling, then shoved off hard again and pinned his back to a bulkhead by grabbing on to a fire extinguisher mount. Naomi was watching him from across the deck, her mouth a comical O of surprise. He knew he probably looked ridiculous, like a petulant child throwing a tantrum, but he couldn't stop himself. He broke free of his grip on the fire extinguisher and floated into the middle of the deck. He hadn't known he'd been pounding on the bulkhead with his other fist. Now that he did, his hand hurt.

"God dammit," he said. "Just God dammit."

"We—" Naomi started, but he cut her off.

"We did our best? What the hell does that matter?" Holden felt a red haze in his mind, and not all of it was from the drugs. "I did my best to help the *Canterbury*, too. I tried to do the right thing when I let us be taken by the *Donnager*. Did my good intentions mean jack shit?"

Naomi's expression went flat. Now her eyelids dropped, and she stared at him from narrow slits. Her lips pressed together until they were almost white. *They wanted me to kill you*, Holden thought. *They wanted me to kill my crew just in case Eros can't break fifteen g, and I couldn't do it.* The guilt and rage and sorrow played against each other, turning into something thin and unfamiliar. He couldn't put a name to the feeling.

"You're the last person I'd expect to hear self-pity from," she said, her voice tight. "Where's the captain who's always asking, 'What can we do right now to make things better?'"

Holden gestured around himself helplessly. "Show me which button to push to stop everyone on Earth from being killed, I'll push it."

Just as long as it doesn't kill you.

Naomi unbuckled her harness and floated toward the crew ladder.

"I'm going below to check on Amos," she said, then opened the deck hatch. She paused. "I'm your operations officer, Holden. Monitoring communication lines is part of the job. I know what Fred wanted."

Holden blinked, and Naomi pulled herself out of sight. The hatch slammed behind her with a bang that couldn't have been any harder than normal but felt like it was anyway.

Holden called up to the cockpit and told Alex to take a break and get some coffee. The pilot stopped on his way through the deck, looking like he wanted to talk, but Holden just waved him on. Alex shrugged and left.

The watery feeling in his gut had taken root and bloomed into a full-fledged, limb-shaking panic. Some vicious, vindictive, self-flagellating part of his mind insisted on running nonstop movies of Eros hurtling toward Earth. It would come screaming down out of the sky like every religion's vision of apocalypse made real, fire and earthquakes and pestilential rain sweeping the land. But each time Eros hit the Earth in his mind, it was the explosion of the *Canterbury* he saw. A shockingly sudden white light, and then nothing but the sound of ice pebbles rattling across his hull like gentle hail.

Mars would survive, for a while. Pockets of the Belt would hold out even longer, probably. They had a culture of making do, surviving on scraps, living on the bleeding edge of their resources. But in the end, without Earth, everything would eventually die. Humans had been out of the gravity well a long time. Long enough to have developed the technology to cut that umbilical cord, but they'd just never bothered to do it. Stagnant. Humanity, for all its desire to fling itself into every livable pocket it could reach, had become stagnant. Satisfied to fly around in ships built half a century before, using technology that hadn't changed in longer than that.

Earth had been so focused on her own problems that she'd ignored her far-flung children, except when asking for her share of their labors. Mars had bent her entire population to the task of remaking the planet, changing its red face to green. Trying to make a new Earth to end their reliance on the old. And the Belt had become the slums of the solar system. Everyone too busy trying to survive to spend any time creating something new.

We found the protomolecule at exactly the right time for it to do the most damage to us, Holden thought.

It had looked like a shortcut. A way to avoid having to do any of the work, to just jump straight to godhood. And it had been so long since anything was a real threat to humanity outside of itself that no one was even smart enough to be scared. Dresden had said it himself: The things that had made the protomolecule, loaded it into Phoebe, and shot it at the Earth were already godlike back when humanity's ancestors thought photosynthesis and the flagellum were cutting-edge. But he'd taken their ancient engine of destruction and turned the key anyway, because when you got right down to it, humans were still just curious monkeys. They still had to poke everything they found with a stick to see what it did.

The red haze in Holden's vision had taken on a strange strobing pattern. It took him a moment to realize that a red telltale on his panel was flashing, letting him know that the *Ravi* was calling. He kicked off a nearby crash couch, floated back to his station, and opened the link.

"*Rocinante* here, *Ravi,* go ahead."

"Holden, why are we stopped?" McBride asked.

"Because we weren't going to keep up anyway, and the danger of crew casualties was getting too high," he replied. It sounded weak even to him. Cowardly. McBride didn't seem to notice.

"Roger. I'm going to get new orders. Will let you know if anything changes."

Holden killed the connection and stared blankly at the console. The visual tracking system was doing its very best to keep Eros in sight. The *Roci* was a good ship. State of the art. And since Alex had tagged the asteroid as a threat, the computer would do everything in its power to keep track of it. But Eros was a fast-moving, low-albedo object that didn't reflect radar. It could move unpredictably and at high speed. It was just a matter of time before they lost track of it, especially if it wanted to be lost track of.

Next to the tracking information on his console, a small data window opened to inform him that the *Ravi* had turned on its transponder. It was standard practice even for military ships to keep them on when there was no apparent threat or need for stealth. The radio man on the little UNN corvette must have flipped it back on out of habit.

And now the *Roci* registered it as a known vessel and threw it onto the threat display with a gently pulsing green dot and a name tag. Holden looked at it blankly for a long moment. He felt his eyes go wide.

"*Shit,*" Holden said, then opened the shipwide comm. "Naomi, I need you in ops."

"I think I'd rather stay down here for a bit," she replied.

Holden hit the battle station's alert button on his console. The deck lights shifted to red and a Klaxon sounded three times.

"XO Nagata to ops," he said. Let her chew him out later. He'd have it coming. But right now he didn't have any time to waste.

Naomi was on the ops deck in less than a minute. Holden had already buckled back into his crash couch and was pulling up the comm logs. Naomi pushed over to her chair and belted in as well. She gave him an inquiring look—*Are we going to die after all?*— but said nothing. If he said so, she would. He felt a spike of equal parts admiration for and impatience with her. He found what he was looking for in the logs before speaking.

"Okay," he said. "We've had radio contact with Miller after Eros dropped off of radar. Is that right?"

"Yes, that's right," she said. "But his suit isn't powerful enough to transmit through the shell of Eros out to much distance, so one of the moored ships is boosting the signal for him."

"Which means that whatever Eros is doing to kill the radar isn't killing all radio transmissions from outside."

"That seems right," Naomi said, a growing curiosity in her voice.

"And you still have the control codes for the five OPA freighters on the surface, right?"

"Yes, sir." And then a moment later: "Oh, *shit.*"

"Okay," Holden said, turning in his chair to face Naomi with a grin. "Why do the *Roci* and every other naval ship in the system have a switch to turn off their transponders?"

"So the enemy can't get a missile lock on the transponder signal and blow them up," she said, sharing his grin now.

Holden spun his chair back around and began opening a comm channel to Tycho Station.

"XO, would you be so kind as to use the control codes Miller gave you to turn those five OPA freighters back on and fire up their transponders? Unless our visitor on Eros can outrun radio waves, I think we've gotten around the acceleration problem."

"Aye, aye, Captain," Naomi replied. Even looking the other way, Holden could hear the smile in her voice, and it melted the last of the ice in his gut. They had a plan. They were going to make a difference.

"Call coming in from the *Ravi,*" Naomi said. "You want it before I turn the transponders on?"

"Hell yes."

The line clicked.

"Captain Holden. We've got our new orders. Seems we're going to be chasing that thing a little further."

McBride sounded almost like someone who hadn't just been sent to her death. Stoic.

"You might want to hold off on that for a couple minutes," Holden said. "We have an alternative."

As Naomi activated the transponders on the five OPA freighters

Miller had left moored to the surface of Eros, Holden laid out the plan to McBride and then, on a separate line, Fred. By the time Fred had gotten back to him with an enthusiastic approval of the plan from both him and the UN Naval command, the five freighters were pinging away, telling the solar system where they were. An hour after that, the largest swarm of interplanetary nuclear weapons in the history of humanity had been fired and were winging their way toward Eros.

We're going to win, Holden thought as he watched the missiles take flight like a swarm of angry red dots on his threat display. *We're going to beat this thing.* And what was more, his crew was going to see the end of it. No one else had to die.

Except...

"Miller's calling," Naomi said. "Probably noticed we turned his ships back on."

Holden had a wrenching feeling in his stomach. Miller would be there, on Eros, when those missiles arrived. Not everyone would get to celebrate the coming victory.

"Hey. Miller. How you doing?" he said, not quite able to keep the funereal tone out of his voice.

Miller's voice was choppy, and half drowned by static, but not so garbled that Holden couldn't hear the tone in it and know that he was about to take a piss all over their parade.

"Holden," Miller said. "We have a problem."

Chapter Fifty-Two: Miller

One. Two. Three.

Miller pushed down on the hand terminal, resetting the trigger again. The double doors in front of him had once been one of thousands of quietly automated mechanisms. They had run reliably in their subtle magnetic tracks, maybe for years. Now something black with the texture of tree bark grew like creepers around their sides, deforming the metal. Past them lay the port corridors, the warehouses, the casino. Everything that had been Eros Station and was now the vanguard of an invading alien intelligence. But to reach it, Miller had to pry open a stuck door. In less than five seconds. While wearing an environment suit.

He put the hand terminal down again and reached quickly for the thin crack where the two doors met. One. Two. The door shifted a centimeter, flakes of black matter sifting down. Three.

Four.

He grabbed the hand terminal again, resetting the trigger.

This shit just wasn't going to work.

Miller sat on the ground beside the cart. The Eros feed whispered and muttered, apparently unaware of the tiny invader scratching at the station's skin. Miller took a long, deep breath. Door didn't move. He had to get past it.

Naomi wasn't going to like this.

With his one free hand, Miller loosened the woven metal strap around the bomb until it could rock back and forth a little. Carefully, slowly, he lifted the corner of it. Then, watching the status readouts, he wedged the hand terminal under it, the metal corner digging hard into the touch screen over the enter button. The trigger stayed green. If the station shook or shifted, he'd still have five seconds to get to it.

Good enough.

Braced with both hands, Miller tugged at the doors. More of the black crust fell away as he levered the doors open far enough to see through. The corridor beyond was nearly round; the dark growth had filled in the corners until the passage looked like a huge desiccated blood vessel. The only lights were his suit's headlights and a million tiny luminescent dots that swirled in the air like blue fireflies. When the Eros feed pulsed, growing momentarily louder, the fireflies dimmed and then returned. The environment suit reported breathable air with higher than expected concentrations of argon, ozone, and benzene.

One of the luminescent dots floated past him, swirling on currents he couldn't feel. Miller ignored it, pushing at the doors, widening the gap centimeter by centimeter. He could put in an arm to feel the crust. It seemed solid enough to support the cart. That was a godsend. If it had been thigh-high alien mud, he would have had to find some other way to carry the bomb. It was going to be bad enough hauling the cart up to the rounded surface.

No rest for the wicked, Julie Mao said in his mind. *No peace for the good.*

He went back to work.

By the time he'd shoved the doors wide enough to get through, he was sweating. His arms and back ached. The dark crust had started growing down the corridor, tendrils shooting out toward the airlock, keeping to the edges, where walls met floor or ceiling. The blue glow had colonized the air. Eros was heading out the corridor as quickly as he was heading in. Faster, maybe.

Miller hauled the cart up with both hands, watching the hand terminal closely. The bomb rocked, but not so much it lost its grip on the trigger. Once he was safely in the corridor, he took the terminal back.

One. Two.

The heavy bomb casing had carved a little divot in the touch pad, but it still worked. Miller took the cart handle and leaned forward, the uneven, organic surface beneath him translated into the rough tug and flutter of the cart's vibration.

He'd died here once. He'd been poisoned. Shot. These halls, or ones much like them, had been his battleground. His and Holden's. They were unrecognizable now.

He passed through a wide, nearly empty space. The crust had thinned here, the metal walls of the warehouse showing through in places. One LED still glowed in the ceiling, the cool white light spilling onto the darkness.

The path led him to the casino level, the architecture of commerce still bringing visitors to the same spot. The alien bark was nearly gone, but the space had been transformed. Pachinko machines stood in their rows, half melted or exploded or, like a few, still glittering and asking for the financial information that would unlock the gaudy lights and festive, celebratory sound effects. The card tables were still visible under mushroom caps of clear glutinous gel. Lining the walls and cathedral-high ceilings, black ribs rippled with hairlike threads that glowed at the tips without offering any illumination.

Something screamed, the sound muffled by Miller's suit. The broadcast feed of the station sounded louder and richer now that he was under its skin. He had the sudden, transporting memory of being a child and watching a video feed of a boy who'd been swallowed by a monstrous whale.

Something gray and the size of Miller's two fists together flew by almost too fast to see. It hadn't been a bird. Something scuttled behind an overturned vending machine. He realized what was missing. There had been a million and a half people on Eros, and a large percentage of them had been here, on the casino level, when their own personal apocalypse came. But there were no bodies. Or, no. That wasn't true. The black crust, the millions of dark rills above him with their soft, oceanic glow. Those were the corpses of Eros, re-created. Human flesh, remade. A suit alarm told him he was starting to hyperventilate. Darkness started to creep in at the edge of his vision.

Miller sank to his knees.

Don't pass out, you son of a bitch, he told himself. *Don't pass out, or if you do, at least land so your weight's on the damned trigger.*

Julie put her hand on his. He could almost feel it, and it steadied him. She was right. They were only bodies. Just dead people. Victims. Just another slab of recycled meat, same as every unlicensed whore he'd seen stabbed to death in the cheap hotels on Ceres. Same as all the suicides who'd thrown themselves out of airlocks. Okay, the protomolecule had mutilated the flesh in weird ways. Didn't change what it was. Didn't change what he was.

"When you're a cop," he told Julie, repeating something he'd told every rookie he'd been partnered with in his career, "you don't have the luxury of feeling things. You have to do the job."

So do the job, she said gently.

He nodded. He stood. *Do the job.*

As if in response, the sound in his suit changed, the Eros feed fluting up through a hundred different frequencies before exploding in a harsh flood of what he thought was Hindi. Human voices. *Till human voices wake us,* he thought, without quite being able to recall where the phrase came from.

Somewhere in the station, there was going to be…something.

A control mechanism or a power supply or whatever the proto-molecule was using instead of an engine. He didn't know what it would look like or how it would be defended. He didn't have any idea how it worked, apart from the assumption that if he blew it up, it wouldn't keep going very well.

So we go back, he told Julie. *We go back to what we do know.*

The thing that was growing inside Eros, using the stone skin of the asteroid as its own unarticulated exoskeleton, hadn't cut off the ports. It hadn't moved the interior walls or re-created the chambers and passages of the casino level. So the station's layout should be pretty near what it had always been. Okay.

Whatever it used to drive the station through space, it was using a shitload of energy. Okay.

So find the hot spot. With his free hand, he checked the environment suit. Ambient temperature was twenty-seven degrees: hot but far from unbearable. He walked briskly back toward the port corridor. The temperature dropped by less than a hundredth of a degree, but it did drop. All right, then. He could go to each of the corridors, find which one was hottest, and follow it. When he found a place in the station that was, say, three or four degrees hotter than the rest, that would be the place. He'd roll the cart up beside it, let up his thumb, and count to five.

No problem.

When he got back to the cart, something golden with the soft look of heather was growing around the wheels. Miller scraped it off as best he could, but one of the wheels had still developed a squeak. Nothing to be done about that.

With one hand hauling the cart and the other mashing down on his hand terminal's dead-man's-switch, Miller headed up, deeper into the station.

"She's mine," mindless Eros said. It had been stuck on the phrase for the better part of an hour. "She's *mine*. She's...*mine*."

"Fine," Miller muttered. "You can have her."

His shoulder ached. The squeak in the cart's wheel had grown worse, the whine of it cutting through the souls-of-the-damned madness of the Eros feed. His thumb was starting to tingle from the constant, relentless pressure of not annihilating himself quite yet. With each level he rose, the spin gravity grew lighter and the Coriolis a little more noticeable. It wasn't quite the same as on Ceres, but it was close and felt like coming home. He found himself looking forward to when the job was done. He imagined himself back in his hole, a six-pack of beer, some music on the speakers that had an actual composer instead of the wild, empty-minded glossolalia of the dead station. Maybe some light jazz.

Who ever thought the idea of light jazz would be appealing?

"Catch me if you can, cocksuckers," Eros said. "I am gone and gone and gone. Gone and gone and gone."

The inner levels of the station were both more familiar and stranger. Away from the mass grave of the casino level, more of Eros' old life showed through. Tube stops still glowed, announcing line errors and counseling patience. Air recyclers hummed. The floors were relatively clean and clear. The sense of near normalcy made the changes stand out eerily. Dark fronds coated the walls with swirling nautilus patterns. Flakes of the stuff drifted down from above, whirling in the spin gravity like soot. Eros still had spin gravity but didn't have gravity from the massive acceleration it was under. Miller chose not to try to figure that out.

A flock of softball-sized spiderlike things crawled through the corridor, leaving a slick sheen of glowing slime behind them. It wasn't until he paused to knock one off the cart that he recognized them as severed hands, the trailing wrist bones charred black and remade. Part of his mind was screaming, but it was a distant one and easy to ignore.

He had to respect the protomolecule. For something that had been expecting prokaryotic anaerobes, it was doing a bang-up job of making do. He paused to check his suit's sensor array. The temperature had risen half a degree since he'd left the casino and a tenth of a degree since he'd entered this particular main hall. The background radiation was also climbing, his poor abused flesh sucking in more rads. The concentration of benzene was going down, and his suit was picking up more exotic aromatic molecules—tetracene, anthracene, naphthalene—with behavior sufficiently strange to confuse the sensors. So it was the right direction. He leaned forward, the cart resisting his pull like a bored kid. As he recalled, the structural layout was roughly like Ceres', and he knew Ceres like he knew his name. One more level up—maybe two—there would be a confluence of services from the lower, high-g levels and the supply and energy systems that did better at lower gravity. It seemed as likely a place to grow a command and control center as any. As good a location for a brain.

"Gone and gone and gone," Eros said. "And gone."

It was funny, he thought, how the ruins of the past shaped everything that came after. It seemed to work on all levels; one of the truths of the universe. Back in the ancient days, when humanity still lived entirely down a well, the paths laid down by Roman legions had become asphalt and later ferroconcrete without ever changing a curve or a turn. On Ceres, Eros, Tycho, the bore of the standard corridor had been determined by mining tools built to accommodate the trucks and lifts of Earth, which had in turn been designed to go down tracks wide enough for a mule cart's axle.

And now the alien—the thing from out in the vast dark—was growing along the corridors, ducts, tube routes, and water pipes laid out by a handful of ambitious primates. He wondered what it would have been like if the protomolecule hadn't been captured by Saturn, had actually found its way into the soup of primordial Earth. No fusion reactors, no navigation drives, no complex flesh to appropriate. What would it have done differently if it hadn't had to build around some other evolution's design choices?

Miller, Julie said. *Keep moving.*

He blinked. He was standing in the empty passageway at the base of an access ramp. He didn't know how long he'd been lost in his own mind.

Years, maybe.

He blew out a long breath and started up the ramp. The corridors above him were reading as considerably hotter than ambient. Almost three degrees. He was getting close. There was no light, though. He took his tingling, half-numbed thumb off the select button, turned on the hand terminal's little utility LED, and got back to the dead man's switch just before the count of four.

"Gone and gone and…and…and and and *and*."

The Eros feed squealed, a chorus of voices chattering in Russian and Hindi clamoring over the old singular voice and being drowned out in turn by a deep creaking howl. Whale song, maybe. Miller's suit mentioned politely that he had half an hour of oxygen left. He shut the alarm down.

The transfer station was overgrown. Pale fronds swarmed along the corridors and twisted into ropes. Recognizable insects—flies, cockroaches, water spiders—crawled along the thick white cables in purposeful waves. Tendrils of something that looked like articulated bile swept back and forth, leaving a film of scurrying larvae. They were as much victim of the protomolecule as the human population. Poor bastards.

"You can't take the razor back," Eros said, and its voice sounded almost triumphant. "You can't take the razor back. She is gone and gone and gone."

The temperature was climbing faster now. It took him a few minutes to decide that spinward might be slightly warmer. He hauled the cart. He could feel the squeaking, a tiny, rattling tremor in the bones of his hand. Between the mass of the bomb and the failing wheel bearings, his shoulders were starting to really ache. Good thing he wasn't going to have to haul this damn thing back down.

Julie was waiting for him in the darkness; the thin beam from his hand terminal cut through her. Her hair floated, spin gravity having, after all, no effect on phantoms of the mind. Her expression was grave.

How does it know? she asked.

Miller paused. Every now and then, all through his career, some daydreamed witness would say something, use some phrase, laugh at the wrong thing, and he'd know that the back of his mind had a new angle on the case.

This was that moment.

"You can't take the razor back," Eros crowed.

The comet that took the protomolecule into the solar system in the first place was a dead drop, not a ship, Julie said, her dark lips never moving. *It was just ballistic. Any ice bullet with the protomolecule in deep freeze. It was aimed at Earth, but it missed and got grabbed by Saturn instead. The payload didn't steer it. Didn't drive it. Didn't navigate.*

"It didn't need to," Miller said.

It's navigating now. It's going to Earth. How does it know to go to Earth? Where did that information come from? It's talking. Where did that grammar come from?

Who is the voice of Eros?

Miller closed his eyes. His suit mentioned that he only had twenty minutes of air.

"You can't take the *Razorback*! She is gone and gone and gone!"

"Oh fuck," Miller said. "Oh *Jesus.*"

He let go of the cart, turning back toward the ramp and the light and the wide station corridors. Everything was shaking, the station itself trembling like someone on the edge of hypothermia. Only of course it wasn't. The only one shaking was him. It was all in the voice of Eros. It had been there all the time. He should have known.

Maybe he had.

The protomolecule didn't know English or Hindi or Russian or any of the languages it had been spouting. All of that had been in the minds and softwares of Eros' dead, coded in the neurons and grammar programs that the protomolecule had eaten. Eaten, but not destroyed. It had kept the information and languages and complex cognitive structures, building itself on them like asphalt over the roads the legions built.

The dead of Eros weren't dead. Juliette Andromeda Mao was alive.

He was grinning so hard his cheeks ached. With one gloved hand, he tried the connection. The signal was too weak. He couldn't get through. He told his uplink on the surface ship to crank up the power, got a connection.

Holden's voice came over the link.

"Hey. Miller. How you doing?"

The words were soft, apologetic. A hospice worker being gentle to the dying. An incandescent spark of annoyance lit his mind, but he kept his voice steady.

"Holden," he said. "We have a problem."

Chapter Fifty-Three: Holden

Actually, we've sort of figured out how to solve the problem," Holden replied.

"I don't think so. I'm linking you to my suit's med data," Miller said.

A few seconds later, four columns of numbers popped up in a small window on Holden's console. It all looked fairly normal, though there were subtleties that only a med-tech, like Shed, would be able to interpret correctly.

"Okay," Holden said. "That's great. You're getting a little irradiated, but other than that—"

Miller cut him off.

"Am I suffering from hypoxia?" he said.

The data from his suit showed 87 mmHg, comfortably above baseline.

"No," Holden said.

"Anything that would make a guy hallucinate or get demented? Alcohol, opiates. Something like that?"

"Not that I can see," Holden said, growing impatient. "What's this about? Are you seeing things?"

"Just the usual," Miller replied. "I wanted to get that shit out the way, because I know what you're going to say next."

He stopped talking, and the radio hissed and popped in Holden's ear. When Miller spoke again after several seconds of silence, his voice had taken on a different tone. It wasn't quite pleading, but close enough to make Holden shift uncomfortably in his seat.

"She's alive."

There was only one *she* in Miller's universe. Julie Mao. "Uh, okay. Not sure how to respond to that."

"You'll have to take my word that I'm not having a nervous breakdown or psychotic episode or anything like that. But Julie's in here. She's driving Eros."

Holden looked at the suit's medical data again, but it kept reporting normal readings, all the numbers except for radiation comfortably in the green. His blood chemistry didn't even look like he was particularly stressed for a guy carrying a fusion bomb to his own funeral.

"Miller, Julie's dead. We both saw the body. We saw what the protomolecule…did to it."

"We saw her body, sure. We just assumed she was dead because of the damage—"

"She didn't have a *heartbeat*," Holden said. "No brain activity, no metabolism. That's pretty much the definition of *dead*."

"How do we know what dead looks like to the protomolecule?"

"We—" Holden started, then stopped. "We don't, I guess. But no heartbeat, that's a pretty good start."

Miller laughed.

"We've both seen the feeds, Holden. Those rib cages equipped with one arm that drag themselves around, think they have a heartbeat? This shit hasn't been playing by our rules since day one, you expect it to start now?"

Holden smiled to himself. Miller was right.

"Okay, so what makes you think Julie isn't just a rib cage and a mass of tentacles?"

"She might be, but it's not her body I'm talking about," Miller said. "*She's* in here. Her mind. It's like she's flying her old racing pinnace. The *Razorback*. She's been babbling about it on the radio for hours now, and I just didn't put it together. But now that I have, it's pretty goddamn clear."

"Why is she headed toward Earth?"

"I don't know," Miller said. He sounded excited, interested. More alive than Holden had ever heard him. "Maybe the proto-molecule wants to get there and it's messing with her. Julie wasn't the first person to get infected, but she's the first one that survived long enough to get somewhere. Maybe she's the seed crystal and everything that the protomolecule's doing is built on her. I don't know that, but I can find out. I just need to find her. Talk to her."

"You need to get that bomb to wherever the controls are and set it off."

"I can't do that," Miller said. Because of course he couldn't.

It doesn't matter, Holden thought. *In a little less than thirty hours, you're both radioactive dust.*

"All right. Can you find your girl in less than"—Holden had the *Roci* do a revised time of impact for the incoming missiles— "twenty-seven hours?"

"Why? What happens in twenty-seven hours?"

"Earth fired her entire interplanetary nuclear arsenal at Eros a few hours ago. We just turned the transponders on in the five freighters you parked on the surface. The missiles are targeting them. The *Roci* is guessing twenty-seven hours to impact based on the current acceleration curve. The Martian and UN navies are on their way to sterilize the area after detonation. Make sure nothing survives or slips the net."

"Jesus."

"Yeah," Holden said with a sigh. "I'm sorry I didn't tell you sooner. I've had a lot going on, and it sort of slipped my mind."

There was another long silence on the line.

"You can stop them," Miller said. "Shut down the transponders."

Holden spun his chair around to face Naomi. Her face had the same *what did he just say?* look that he knew was on his own. She pulled the suit's medical data over to her console, then called up the *Roci*'s medical expert system and began running a full medical diagnostic. The implication was clear. She thought something was wrong with Miller that wasn't immediately apparent from the data they were getting. If the protomolecule had infected him, used him as a last-ditch misdirection...

"Not a chance, Miller. This is our last shot. If we blow this one, Eros can orbit the Earth, spraying brown goo all over it. No way we take that risk."

"Look," Miller said, his tone alternating between the earlier pleading and a growing frustration. "*Julie is in here.* If I can find her, a way to talk to her, I can stop this without the nukes."

"What, ask the protomolecule to pretty please not infect the Earth, when that was what it was designed to do? Appeal to its better nature?"

Miller paused for a moment before speaking again.

"Look, Holden, I think I know what's going on here. This thing was intended to infect single-celled organisms. The most basic forms of life, right?"

Holden shrugged, then remembered there was no video feed and said, "Okay."

"That didn't work, but it's a smart bastard. Adaptive. It got into a human host, a complex multicelled organism. Aerobic. Huge brain. Nothing like what it was built for. It's been improvising ever since. That mess on the stealth ship? That was its first try. We saw what it was doing with Julie in that Eros bathroom. It was learning how to work with us."

"Where are you going with this?" Holden said. There was no time pressure yet, with the missiles still more than a day away, but he couldn't quite keep the impatience out of his voice.

"All I'm saying is Eros now isn't what the protomolecule's

designers planned on. It's their original plan laid over the top of billions of years of our evolution. And when you improvise, you use what you've got. You use what works. Julie's the template. Her brain, her emotions are all over this thing. She sees this run to Earth as a race, and she's crowing about winning. Laughing at you because you can't keep up."

"Wait," Holden said.

"She's not attacking Earth, she's going home. For all we know, she's not heading for Earth at all. Luna, maybe. She grew up there. The protomolecule piggybacked on her structure, her brain. And so she infected it as much as it infected her. If I can make her understand what's really going on, then maybe I can negotiate with her."

"How do you know that?"

"Call it a hunch," Miller said. "I'm good with hunches."

Holden whistled, the entire situation doing a flip-flop in his head. The new perspective was dizzying.

"But the protomolecule still wants to obey its program," Holden said. "And we have no idea what that is."

"I can damn sure tell you it isn't wiping humans out. The things that shot Phoebe at us two billion years ago didn't know what the hell humans were. Whatever it wants to do needed biomass, and it's got that now."

Holden couldn't stop himself from snorting at that.

"So, what? They don't mean us any harm? Seriously? You think if we explain that we'd rather not have it land on Earth, then it will just agree and go somewhere else?"

"Not it," Miller said. "Her."

Naomi looked up at Holden, shaking her head. She wasn't seeing anything organic wrong with Miller either.

"I've been working this case for, shit, almost a year," Miller said. "I've climbed into her life, read her mail, met her friends. I know her. She's about as independent as a person can be, and she loves us."

"Us?" Holden asked.

"People. She loves humans. She gave up being the little rich girl and joined the OPA. She backed the Belt because it was the right thing to do. No way she kills us if she knows that's what's happening. I just need to find a way to explain. I can do this. Give me a chance."

Holden ran a hand through his hair, grimacing at the accumulating grease. A day or two at high g was not conducive to regular showering.

"Can't do it," Holden said. "Stakes are too high. We're going ahead with the plan. I'm sorry."

"She'll beat you," Miller said.

"What?"

"Okay, maybe she won't. You've got a shitload of firepower. But the protomolecule's figured out how to get around inertia. And Julie? She's a fighter, Holden. If you take her on, my money's on her."

Holden had seen the video of Julie fighting off her attackers on board the stealth ship. She'd been methodical and ruthless in her own defense. She'd fought without giving quarter. He'd seen the wildness in her eyes when she felt trapped and threatened. Only her attackers' combat armor had kept her from doing a lot more damage before they took her down.

Holden felt the hair on the back of his neck stand up at the idea of Eros actually fighting. So far it had been content to run from their clumsy attacks. What happened when it went to *war*?

"You could find her," Holden said, "and use the bomb."

"If I can't get through to her," Miller said, "that's my deal. I'll find her. I'll talk to her. If I can't get through, I'll take her out, and you can turn Eros into a cinder. I'm fine with that. But you have to give me time to try it my way first."

Holden looked at Naomi looking back at him. Her face was pale. He wanted to see the answer in her expression, to know what he should do based on what she thought. He didn't. It was his call.

"Do you need more than twenty-seven hours?" Holden finally asked.

He heard Miller exhale loudly. There was gratitude in his voice that was, in its own way, worse than the pleading had been.

"I don't know. There are a couple thousand kilometers of tunnels down here, and none of the transit systems work. I have to walk everywhere pulling this damn wagon. Not to mention the fact that I don't really know what I'm even looking for. But give me a little time, I'll figure it."

"And you know that if this doesn't work, you'll have to kill her. Yourself and Julie?"

"I know."

Holden had the *Roci* calculate how long it would take Eros to reach the Earth at the current rate of acceleration. The missiles from Earth were covering the distance a lot faster than Eros was. The IPBMs were just overpowered Epstein drives with nuclear bombs riding up front. Their acceleration limits were the functional limits of the Epstein drive itself. If the missiles didn't arrive, it would still take nearly a week for Eros to get to Earth, even if it kept a constant rate of acceleration.

There was some flexibility in there.

"Hold on, let me work something out here," Holden said to Miller, then muted the connection. "Naomi, the missiles are flying in a straight line toward Eros, and the *Roci* thinks they'll intercept it in about twenty-seven hours, give or take. How much time do we buy if we turn that straight line into a curve? How much of a curve can we do and still give the missiles a chance to catch Eros before it gets too close?"

Naomi tipped her head to one side, looking at him suspiciously through narrowed eyes.

"What are you about to do?" she said.

"Maybe give Miller a chance to head off the first interspecies war."

"You trust *Miller*?" she said with surprising vehemence. "You think he's insane. You threw him off the ship because you thought he was a psychopath and a killer, and now you're going to let him speak for humanity to an alien God-thing that wants to rip us to shreds?"

Holden had to suppress a smile. Telling an angry woman how

attractive her anger made her would make it stop being cute very quickly. And besides that, he needed it to make sense to her. That was how he'd know if he was right.

"You told me once that Miller was right, even when I thought he was wrong."

"I didn't make it a blanket statement," Naomi said, spacing her words out like she was speaking to an idiot child. "I said he was right to shoot Dresden. That doesn't mean Miller's *stable.* He's in the process of committing suicide, Jim. He's fixated on this dead girl. I can't even begin to imagine what might be going through his head right now."

"Agreed. But he's there, on the scene, and he's got a keen eye for observation and just plain figuring shit out. This guy tracked us to Eros based on the ship name we picked. That's pretty damned impressive. He'd never even met me, and he knew me well enough from researching me to know I'd like naming my ship after Don Quixote's horse."

Naomi laughed. "Really? Is that where that comes from?"

"So when he says that he knows Julie, I believe him."

Naomi started to say something, then paused.

"You think she'll beat the nukes?" Naomi said, more softly.

"He thinks she can. And he thinks he can talk her into not killing us all. I have to give him that chance. I owe it to him."

"Even if it means killing Earth?"

"No," Holden said. "Not that much."

Naomi paused again. Her anger faded.

"So delay the impact, not abort," Naomi said.

"Buy him some time. How much can we get?"

Naomi frowned, looking at the readouts. He could almost see the options clicking through her mind. She smiled, her fierceness gone now, replaced by the mischievous look she got when she knew she was being really clever.

"As much as you want."

"You want to do what?" Fred asked.

"Pull the nukes off course for a while to buy Miller some time, but not so much that we can't still use them to destroy Eros if we need to," Holden said.

"It's simple," Naomi added. "I'm sending you detailed instructions."

"Give me the overview," Fred said.

"Earth has targeted their missiles on the five freighter transponders on Eros," Naomi said, pulling her plan up as an overlay on the comm video. "You have ships and stations all over the Belt. You use the transponder reconfiguring program you gave us way back when, and you keep shifting those transponder codes to ships or stations along these vectors to pull the missiles into a long arc that eventually wraps back around to Eros."

Fred shook his head.

"Won't work. The minute UNN Command sees we're doing it, they'll just tell the missiles to stop following those particular codes, and they'll try to figure out some other way to target Eros," he said. "And they'll also be really pissed at us."

"Yeah, they're going to be pissed all right," Holden said. "But they're not going to get their missiles back. Just before you start leading the missiles off course, we're going to launch a massive hacking attempt from multiple locations on the missiles."

"So they'll assume an enemy is trying to trick them, and shut down mid-flight reprogramming," Fred said.

"Yep," Holden replied. "We'll tell them we're going to trick them so they stop listening, and once they're not listening, we'll trick them."

Fred shook his head again, this time giving Holden the vaguely frightened look of a man who wanted to back slowly out of the room.

"There is no way in hell I am going along with this," he said. "Miller isn't going to work some magical deal with the aliens. We're going to wind up nuking Eros no matter what. Why delay the inevitable?"

"Because," Holden said. "I'm starting to think it might be less dangerous this way. If we use the missiles without taking out Eros' command center...brain...whatever, we don't know if it'll work, but I'm pretty sure our chances go down. Miller's the only one who can do that. And these are his terms."

Fred said something obscene.

"If Miller doesn't manage to talk to it, he'll take it out. I do trust him for that," Holden said. "Come on, Fred, you know these missile designs as well as I do. Better. They put enough fuel pellets in those drives to fly around the solar system twice. We aren't losing anything by giving Miller a little more time."

Fred shook his head a third time. Holden saw his face go hard. He wasn't going to buy it. Before he could say no, Holden said, "Remember that box with the protomolecule samples, and all the lab notes? Want to know what my price is for it?"

"You," Fred said slowly, drawing it out, "are out of your God damn mind."

"Want to buy it or what?" Holden replied. "You want the magic ticket to a seat at the table? You know my price now. Give Miller his chance, and the sample's yours."

"I'd be curious to know how you talked them into it," Miller said. "I was thinking I was probably screwed."

"Doesn't matter," Holden said. "We bought you your time. Go find the girl and save humanity. We'll be waiting to hear back." *And ready to nuke you into dust if we don't* remained unsaid. There was no need.

"I've been thinking about where to go, if I can talk to her," Miller said. He had the already lost hopefulness of a man with a lottery ticket. "I mean, she's got to park this thing somewhere."

If we live. If I can save her. If the miracle is true.

Holden shrugged, even though no one could see it.

"Give her Venus," he said. "It's an awful place."

Chapter Fifty-Four: Miller

I don't and I don't," the voice of Eros muttered. Juliette Mao, talking in her sleep. "I don't and I don't and I don't..."

"Come on," Miller said. "Come *on,* you sonofabitch. *Be* here."

The medical bays were lush and overgrown, black spirals with filaments of bronze and steel climbing the walls, encrusting the examination tables, feeding on the supplies of narcotics, steroids, and antibiotics spilling out of the broken supply cabinets. Miller dug through the clutter with one hand, his suit alarm chiming. His air had the sour taste that came from being through the recyclers too many times. His thumb, still mashed on the dead man's switch, tingled when it wasn't shooting with pain.

He brushed the almost fungal growth off a storage box that wasn't broken yet, found the latch. Four medical gas cylinders: two red, one green, one blue. He looked at the seal. The protomolecule hadn't gotten them yet. Red for anesthetic. Blue nitrogen.

He picked up the green. The sterile shield on the delivery nipple was in place. He took a deep sighing breath of dying air. Another few hours. He put down his hand terminal (*one...two...*), popped the seal (*three...*), fed the nipple into his suit's intake (*four...*), and put a finger on the hand terminal. He stood, feeling the cool of the oxygen tank in his hand while his suit revised his life span. Ten minutes, an hour, four hours. The medical cylinder's pressure hit equality with the suit's, and he popped it off. Four more hours. He'd won himself four more hours.

It was the third time he'd managed an emergency resupply since he'd talked to Holden. The first had been at a fire-suppression station, the second at a backup recycling unit. If he went back down to the port, there would probably be some uncompromised oxygen in some of the supply closets and docked ships. If he went all the way back to the surface, the OPA ships would have plenty.

But there wasn't time for that. He wasn't looking for air; he was looking for Juliette. He let himself stretch. The kinks in his neck and back were threatening to turn into cramps. The CO_2 levels in the suit were still on the high side of acceptable, even with the new oxygen coming into the mix. The suit needed maintenance and a new filter. It'd have to wait. Behind him, the bomb in its cart kept its own counsel.

He had to find her. Somewhere in the maze of corridors and rooms, the dead city, Juliette Mao was driving them back to Earth. He'd tracked four hot spots. Three had been decent candidates for his original plan of vast nuclear immolation: hubs of wire and black alien filament tangling into huge organic-looking nodes. The fourth had been a cheap lab reactor churning on its way to meltdown. It had taken him fifteen minutes to get the emergency shutdown going, and he probably shouldn't have wasted the time. But wherever he went, no Julie. Even the Julie of his imagination was gone, as if the ghost had no place now that he knew the real woman was still alive. He missed having her around, even if she'd only been a vision.

A wave went through the medical bays, all the alien growth rising and falling like iron filings with a magnet passed beneath them. Miller's heart sped up, adrenaline leaking into his blood, but it didn't happen again.

He had to find her. He had to find her soon. He could feel exhaustion grinding at him, little teeth chewing at the back of his mind. He already wasn't thinking as clearly as he should. Back on Ceres, he'd have gone back to his hole, slept for a day, and come back to the problem whole. Not an option here.

Full circle. He'd come full circle. Once, in a different life, he'd taken on the task of finding her; then, when he'd failed, there'd been taking vengeance. And now he had the chance to find her again, to save her. And if he couldn't, he was still pulling a cheap, squeaky-wheeled wagon behind him that would do for revenge.

Miller shook his head. He was having too many moments like this, getting lost in his own thoughts. He took a fresh grip on the cart full of fusion bomb, leaned forward, and headed out. The station around him creaked the way he imagined an old sailing ship might have, timbers bent by waves of salt water and the great tidal tug-of-war between earth and moon. Here, it was stone, and Miller couldn't guess what forces were acting on it. Hopefully nothing that would interfere with the signal between his hand terminal and his cargo. He didn't want to be reduced to his component atoms unintentionally.

It was getting more and more clear that he couldn't cover the whole station. He'd known that from the start. If Julie had gotten herself someplace obscure—hidden in some niche or hole like a dying cat—he wouldn't find her. He'd become a gambler, betting against all hope on drawing the inside straight. The voice of Eros shifted, different voices now, singing something in Hindi. A child's round, Eros harmonizing with itself in a growing richness of voices. Now that he knew to listen for it, he heard Julie's voice threading its way among the others. Maybe it had always been there. His frustration verged on physical pain. She was so close, but he couldn't quite reach her.

He pulled himself back into the main corridor complex. The

hospital bays had been a good place to look for her too. Plausible. Fruitless. He'd looked at the two mercantile bio-labs. Nothing. He'd tried the morgue, the police holding tanks. He'd even gone through the evidence room, bin after plastic bin of contraband drugs and confiscated weapons scattered on the floor like oak leaves in one of the grand parks. It had all meant something once. Each one had been part of a small human drama, waiting to be brought out into the light, part of a trial or at least a hearing. Some small practice for judgment day, postponed now forever. All points were moot.

Something silver flew above him, faster than a bird, and then another, and then a flock, streaming by overhead. Light glittered off the living metal, bright as fish scales. Miller watched the alien molecule improvising in the space above him.

You can't stop here, Holden said. *You have to stop running and get on the right road.*

Miller looked over his shoulder. The captain stood, real and not, where his inner Julie would have been.

Well, that's interesting, Miller thought.

"I know," he said. "It's just…I don't know where she went. And…well, look around. Big place, you know?"

You can stop her or I will, his imaginary Holden said.

"If I just knew where she went," Miller said.

She didn't, Holden said. *She never* went.

Miller turned to look at him. The swarm of silver roiled overhead, chittering like insects or a badly tuned drive. The captain looked tired. Miller's imagination had put a surprising swath of blood at the corner of the man's mouth. And then it wasn't Holden anymore; it was Havelock. The other Earther. His old partner. And then it was Muss, her eyes as dead as his own.

Julie didn't go anyplace. Miller had seen her in the hotel room, back when he still hadn't believed that anything but a bad smell could rise from the grave. Back before. She'd been taken away in a body bag. And then taken somewhere else. The Protogen scientists had recovered her, harvested the protomolecule, and spread

Julie's remade flesh through the station like bees pollinating a field of wildflowers. They'd given her the station, but before they'd done it, they'd put her someplace they thought they would be safe.

Safe room. Until they were ready to distribute the thing, they'd want to contain it. To pretend it could be contained. It wasn't likely they'd have gone to the trouble of cleaning up after they'd gotten what they needed. It wasn't as if anyone else was going to be around to use the space, so chances were good she was still there. That narrowed things.

There would be isolation wards in the hospital, but Protogen wouldn't have been likely to use facilities where non-Protogen doctors and nurses might wonder what was happening. Unnecessary risk.

All right.

They could have set up in one of the manufacturing plants down by the port. There were plenty of places there that required all-waldo work. But again, it would have been at the risk of being discovered or questioned before the trap was ready to spring.

It's a drug house, Muss said in his mind. *You want privacy, you want control. Extracting the bug from the dead girl and extracting the good shit from the poppy seeds might have different chemistry, but it's still crime.*

"Good point," Miller said. "And near the casino level…No, that's not right. The casino was the second stage. The first was the radiation scare. They put a bunch of people in the radiation shelters and cooked them to get the protomolecule good and happy, then *they* infected the casino level."

So where would you put a drug kitchen that was close to the rad shelters? Muss asked.

The roiling silver stream overhead veered left and then right, pouring through the air. Tiny curls of metal began to rain down, drawing thin trails of smoke behind them as they did.

"If I had the access? The backup environment controls. It's an emergency facility. No foot traffic unless someone's running inventory. It's got all the equipment for isolation built in already. Wouldn't be hard."

And since Protogen ran Eros security even before they put the disposable thugs in place, they'd be able to arrange it, Muss said, and she smiled joylessly. *See? I knew you could think that through.*

For less than a second, Muss was gone and Julie Mao—his Julie—was in her place. She was smiling and beautiful. Radiant. Her hair floated around her as if she were swimming in zero g. And then she was gone. His suit alarm warned him about an increasingly corrosive environment.

"Hang tight," he said to the burning air. "I'll be right there."

It was just less than thirty-three hours from the moment he'd realized that Juliette Andromeda Mao wasn't dead to the one when he cycled down the emergency seals and pulled his cart into Eros' backup environmental control facility. The clean, simple lines and error-reducing design of the place still showed under the outgrowth of the protomolecule. Barely. Knots of dark filament and nautilus spirals softened the corners of wall and floor and ceiling. Loops hung from the ceiling like Spanish moss. The familiar LED lights still shone under the soft growth, but more illumination came from the swarm of faint blue dots glowing in the air. His first step onto the floor sank him into a thick carpet up the ankle; the bomb cart would have to stay outside. His suit reported a wild mix of exotic gases and aromatic molecules, but all he smelled was himself.

All the interior rooms had been remade. Transformed. He walked through the wastewater treatment control areas like a scuba diver in a grotto. The blue lights swirled around him as he passed, a few dozen adhering to his suit and glittering there. He almost didn't brush them off the helmet's faceplate, thinking they would smear like dead fireflies, but they only swirled back up into the air. The air recycling monitors still danced and glowed, the thousand alarms and incident reports silhouetting the latticework of protomolecule that covered the screens. Water was flowing somewhere close by.

She was in a hazmat analysis node, lying on a bed of the dark thread that spilled out from her spine until it was indistinguishable from a massive fairy-tale cushion of her own flowing hair. Tiny points of blue light glittered on her face, her arms, her breasts. The bone spurs that had been pressing out of her skin had grown into sweeping, almost architectural connections with the lushness around her. Her legs were gone, lost in the tangle of dark alien webs; she reminded Miller of a mermaid who had traded her fins for a space station. Her eyes were closed, but he could see them shifting and dancing under the lids. And she was breathing.

Miller stood beside her. She didn't have quite the same face as his imagined Julie. The real woman was wider through the jaw, and her nose wasn't as straight as he remembered it. He didn't notice that he was weeping until he tried to wipe the tears away, batting his helmet with a gloved hand. He had to make do with blinking hard until his sight cleared.

All this time. All this way. And here was what he'd come for.

"Julie," he said, putting his free hand on her shoulder. "Hey. Julie. Wake up. I need you to wake up now."

He had his suit's medical supplies. If he needed to, he could dose her with adrenaline or amphetamines. Instead, he rocked her gently, like he had Candace on a sleepy Sunday morning, back when she'd still been his wife, back in some distant, near-forgotten lifetime. Julie frowned, opened her mouth, closed it.

"Julie. You need to wake up now."

She moaned and lifted an ineffectual arm to push him away.

"Come back to me," he said. "You need to come back now."

Her eyes opened. They weren't human anymore—the sclera etched with swirls of red and black, the iris the same luminous blue as the fireflies. Not human, but still Julie. Her lips moved soundlessly. And then:

"Where am I?"

"Eros Station," Miller said. "The place isn't what it used to be. Not even *where* it used to be, but…"

He pressed the bed of filament with his hand, judging it, and then rested his hip at her side like he was sitting on her bed. His body felt achingly tired and also lighter than it should. Not like low gravity. The unreal buoyancy had nothing to do with the weary flesh.

Julie tried to talk again, struggled, stopped, tried again.

"Who are you?"

"Yeah, we haven't officially met, have we? My name's Miller. I used to be a detective for Star Helix Security back on Ceres. Your parents contracted with us, only it was really more a friends-in-high-places thing. I was supposed to track you down, grab you, ship you back down the well."

"Kidnap job?" she said. Her voice was stronger. Her gaze seemed more focused.

"Pretty standard," Miller said, then sighed. "I kind of cocked it up, though."

Her eyes fluttered closed, but she kept talking.

"Something happened to me."

"Yeah. It did."

"I'm scared."

"No, no, no. Don't be scared. It's all right. In an ass-backward kind of way, but it's all right. Look, right now the whole station is heading back for Earth. Really fast."

"I dreamed I was racing. I was going home."

"Yeah, we need to stop that."

Her eyes opened again. She looked lost, anguished, alone. A tear streaked down from the corner of her eye, glowing blue.

"Give me your hand," Miller said. "No, really, I need you to hold something for me."

She lifted her hand slowly, seaweed in a soft current. He took his hand terminal, settled it in her palm, pressed her thumb to the dead man's switch.

"Just hold that there. Don't let it up."

"What is it?" she asked.

"Long story, just don't let up."

His suit alarms shrieked at him when he undid his helmet seals. He turned them off. The air was strange: acetate and cumin and a deep, powerful musk that made him think of hibernating animals. Julie watched him as he stripped off his gloves. Right then, the protomolecule was latching on to him, burrowing into his skin and eyes, getting ready to do to him what it had done to everyone on Eros. He didn't care. He took the hand terminal back and then laced his fingers through hers.

"You're driving this bus, Julie," he said. "Do you know that? I mean, can you tell?"

Her fingers were cool in his, but not cold.

"I can feel...something," she said. "I'm hungry? Not hungry, but...I want something. I want to go back to Earth."

"We can't do that. I need you to change course," Miller replied. What had Holden said? *Give her Venus.* "Head for Venus instead."

"That's not what it wants," she said.

"It's what we've got on offer," Miller said. Then, a moment later: "We can't go home. We need to go to Venus."

She was quiet for a long moment.

"You're a fighter, Julie. You've never let anyone call your shots for you. Don't start now. If we go to Earth—"

"It'll eat them too. The same way it ate me."

"Yeah."

She looked up at him.

"Yeah," he said again. "Like that."

"What happens on Venus?"

"We die maybe. I don't know. But we don't take a lot of people with us, and we make sure no one gets a hold of this crap," he said, gesturing at the grotto around them. "And if we don't die, then... well, that'll be interesting."

"I don't think I can."

"You can. The thing that's doing all this? You're smarter than it is. You're in control. Take us to Venus."

546 **JAMES S. A. COREY**

The fireflies swirled around them, the blue light pulsing slightly: bright and dim, bright and dim. Miller saw it in her face when she made the decision. All around them, the lights went bright, the grotto flooding in soft blue, and then dimmed back to where they had been before. Miller felt something catch at the back of his neck like the first warning of a sore throat. He wondered if he'd have time to deactivate the bomb. And then he looked at Julie. Juliette Andromeda Mao. OPA pilot. Heir to the Mao-Kwikowski corporate throne. The seed crystal of a future beyond anything he'd ever dreamed. He'd have plenty of time.

"I'm afraid," she said.

"Don't be," he said.

"I don't know what's going to happen," she said.

"No one ever does. And, look, you don't have to do this alone," he said.

"I can feel something in the back of my mind. It wants something I don't understand. It's so *big*."

Reflexively, he kissed the back of her hand. There was an ache starting deep in his belly. A sense of illness. A moment's nausea. The first pangs of his transformation into Eros.

"Don't worry," he said. "We're gonna be fine."

Chapter Fifty-Five: Holden

Holden dreamed.

He'd been a lucid dreamer most of his life, so when he found himself sitting in his parents' kitchen in the old house in Montana, talking to Naomi, he knew. He couldn't quite understand what she was saying, but she kept pushing her hair out of her eyes as she munched cookies and drank tea. And while he found that he wasn't ever able to pick a cookie up and take a bite out of it, he could smell them, and the memory of Mother Elise's chocolate chip oatmeal cookies was a very good one.

It was a good dream.

The kitchen strobed red once, and something changed. Holden felt the wrongness of it, felt the dream slipping from warm memory into nightmare. He tried to say something to Naomi but couldn't form the words. The room strobed red again, but she didn't seem to notice. He got up and went to the kitchen window and looked out. When the room strobed a third time, he saw what was causing it. Meteors were falling out of the sky, leaving behind them fiery trails the color of blood. He somehow knew they were chunks of Eros as it crashed through the atmosphere. Miller had failed. The nuclear attack had failed.

Julie had come home.

He turned around to tell Naomi to run, but black tendrils had burst through the floor and wrapped her up, pierced her body in multiple places. They poured from her mouth and eyes.

Holden tried to run to her, to help her, but he couldn't move, and when he looked down, he saw that the tendrils had come up and grabbed him too. One wrapped around his waist and held him. Another pressed into his mouth.

He woke with a yell in a dark room that was strobing with red light. Something was holding him around the waist. In a panic he began clawing at it, threatening to tear a fingernail loose on his left hand, before his rational mind reminded him where he was. On the ops deck, in his chair, belted down in zero g.

He popped his finger into his mouth, trying to soothe the abused fingertip he'd damaged on one of the chair buckles, and took a few deep breaths through his nose. The deck was empty. Naomi was asleep down in her cabin. Alex and Amos were off duty and presumably sleeping too. They'd spent almost two days without rest during the high-g chase of Eros. Holden had ordered everyone to get some shut-eye and had volunteered to take first watch.

And then had promptly fallen asleep. Not good.

The room flashed red again. Holden shook his head to clear the last of the sleep away, and refocused his attention on his console. A red warning light pulsed, and he tapped the screen to open up the menu. It was his threat panel. Someone was hitting them with a targeting laser.

He opened up the threat display and turned on the active sensors. The only ship within millions of kilometers was the *Ravi*, and it was the ship that was targeting them. According to the automatic logs, it had just started a few seconds earlier.

He reached out to activate the comm and call the *Ravi* as his incoming-message light flickered on. He opened the connection, and a second later, McBride's voice said, "*Rocinante*, cease maneuvering, open your outer airlock door, and prepare to be boarded."

Holden frowned at his console. Was that a weird joke?

"McBride, this is Holden. Uh, what?"

Her reply was in a clipped tone that was not encouraging.

"Holden, open your outer airlock and prepare for boarding. If I see a single defensive system wake up, I will fire on your ship. Is that understood?"

"No," he said, not quite able to keep the annoyance out of his voice. "It's not understood. And I'm not going to let you board me. What the hell is going on?"

"I've been ordered by UNN Command to take control of your vessel. You're charged with interfering with UNN military operations, unlawfully commandeering UNN military assets, and a list of other crimes I'm not going to bother reading right now. If you do not surrender immediately, we will be forced to fire on you."

"Oh," said Holden. The UNN had discovered that their missiles were changing course, had attempted to reprogram them, and had discovered that the missiles weren't listening.

They were upset.

"McBride," Holden said after a moment. "Boarding us won't do any good. We can't give you those missiles back. And it's unnecessary, anyway. They're just taking a little detour."

McBride's laugh sounded more like the sharp bark of an angry dog just before it bit.

"Detour?" she said. "You handed three thousand five hundred and seventy-three high-yield thermonuclear interplanetary ballistic missiles over to a traitor and accused war criminal!"

It took Holden a minute.

"You mean *Fred*? I think traitor is a bit harsh—"

McBride cut in.

"Deactivate the false transponders leading our missiles away from Eros, and reactivate the transponders on the surface, or we will fire on your ship. You have ten minutes to comply."

The connection dropped with a click. Holden looked at the console with something between disbelief and outrage, then shrugged and hit the battle stations alarm. Deck lights came on all over the ship in an angry red. The warning Klaxon sounded three times. In less than two minutes, Alex rushed up the ladder to the cockpit, and half a minute behind him, Naomi threw herself into her ops station.

Alex spoke first.

"The *Ravi* is four hundred kilometers away," he said. "Ladar says her tube is open, and she's got us locked."

Clearly enunciating his words, Holden said, "Do not—I repeat, do not—open our tubes or attempt to get a target lock on the *Ravi* at this time. Just keep a close eye on her, and prepare to go defensive if she looks like she's firing. Let's not do anything to provoke her."

"Shall I begin jamming?" Naomi said from behind him.

"No, that would look aggressive. But prep a countermeasures package and have your finger on the ready button," Holden said. "Amos, you in engineering?"

"Roger that, Cap. Ready to go down here."

"Bring the reactor up to one hundred percent and pull control of the point defense cannons to your console down there. If they shoot at us at this range, Alex won't have time to fly and shoot back. You see a red dot on the threat console, you open up with the PDCs immediately. Copy?"

"Roger that," Amos said.

Holden blew a long breath through his teeth, then opened the channel to the *Ravi* again.

"McBride, this is Holden. We are not surrendering, we are not going to let you board us, and we aren't going to comply with your demands. Where do we go from here?"

"Holden," McBride said. "Your reactor is coming up. Are you getting ready to fight with us?"

"No, just getting ready to try and survive. Why, are we fighting?"

Another short harsh laugh.

"Holden," McBride said. "Why do I get the feeling you aren't taking this seriously?"

"Oh, I absolutely am," Holden replied. "I don't want you to kill me, and believe it or not, I have no desire to kill you. The nukes are on a little detour, but this isn't something we need to go down in flames over. I can't give you what you want, and I'm not interested in spending the next thirty years in a military prison. You gain nothing by shooting us, and I will fight back if it comes to that."

McBride cut the channel.

"Captain," Alex said. "The *Ravi* is startin' to maneuver. She's spraying clutter. I think she's gettin' ready to make an attack run."

Shit. Holden had been so sure he could talk her out of it.

"Okay, go defensive. Naomi, start your countermeasures. Amos? Got your finger on that button?"

"Ready," Amos replied.

"Don't hit it until you see a missile launch. Don't want to force their hand."

Sudden crushing g's hit Holden, stuffing him into his chair. Alex had started maneuvering.

"At this distance, maybe I can out-turn her. Keep her from bein' able to take a shot," the pilot said.

"Do it, and open the tubes."

"Roger," Alex said, his professional pilot's calm not quite able to keep the excitement about a possible battle out of his voice.

"I've broken the targeting lock," Naomi said. "Their laser array is not nearly as good as the *Roci*'s. I'm just drowning it in clutter."

"Hooray for bloated Martian defense budgets," Holden replied.

The ship jerked suddenly through a series of wild maneuvers.

"Damn," Alex said, his voice strained by the g-force of the sharp turns. "The *Ravi* just opened up on us with her PDCs."

Holden checked his threat display and saw the long glowing pearl strands of incoming rounds displayed there. The shots were falling well behind them. The *Roci* reported the distance between the ships as 370 kilometers—pretty long range for computer targeting systems to hit a wildly maneuvering ship with a ballistic shot from another wildly maneuvering ship.

"Return fire?" Amos yelled into the comm.

"No!" Holden yelled back. "If she wanted us dead, she'd be throwing torpedoes. Don't give her a reason to want us dead."

"Cap, we're out-turnin' her," Alex said. "The *Roci*'s just too fast. We'll have a firing solution in less than a minute."

"Roger," Holden said.

"Do I take the shot?" Alex asked, his silly Martian cowboy accent fading as his tension rose.

"No."

"Their targeting laser just shut off," Naomi said.

"Which means they've given up trying to cut our jamming," Holden replied, "and have just switched their missiles over to radar tracking."

"Not as accurate," Naomi said hopefully.

"A corvette like that carries at least a dozen fish. They only need to hit us with one to make us dead. And at this range…"

A gentle sound came from his threat console, letting him know that the *Roci* had calculated a firing solution to the *Ravi*.

"I've got tone!" Alex yelled. "Fire?"

"No!" Holden said. He knew that inside the *Ravi*, they were getting the loud warning buzz of an enemy lock. *Stop*, Holden willed them. *Please don't make me kill you.*

"Uh," Alex said in a low voice. "Huh."

Behind Holden, at almost the same moment, Naomi said, "Jim?"

Before he could ask, Alex came back on the general comm.

"Hey, Captain, Eros just came back."

"What?" Holden said, a brief image of the asteroid sneaking up like a cartoon villain on the two circling warships popping into his head.

"Yeah," Alex said. "Eros. It just popped back up on radar.

Whatever it was doing to block our sensors, it just stopped doing it."

"What's it doing?" Holden said. "Get me a course."

Naomi pulled the tracking information to her console and began working on it, but Alex was done a few seconds sooner.

"Yeah," he said. "Good guess. It's changing course. Still heading sunward, but deflecting away from the Earth vector it was on."

"If it keeps this course and speed," Naomi chimed in, "I'd say it was heading toward Venus."

"Wow," said Holden. "That was a joke."

"Good joke," Naomi said.

"Well, someone tell McBride she doesn't need to shoot us now."

"Hey," Alex said, his voice thoughtful. "If we made those nukes stop listening, that means we can't shut 'em down, right? Wonder where Fred's going to drop those."

"Hell if I know," Amos said. "Just disarmed Earth, though. That's gotta be fucking embarrassing."

"Unintended consequences," Naomi sighed. "Always with the unintended consequences."

Eros crashing into Venus was the most widely broadcast and recorded event in history. By the time the asteroid reached the sun's second planet, several hundred ships had taken up orbits there. Military vessels tried to keep the civilian ships away, but it was no use. They were just outnumbered. The video of Eros' descent was captured by military gun cameras, civilian ship telescopes, and the observatories on two planets and five moons.

Holden wished he could have been there to see it up close, but Eros had picked up speed after it had turned, almost as though the asteroid were impatient for the journey to end now that the destination was in sight. He and the crew sat in the galley of the *Rocinante* and watched it on the broadcast newsfeeds. Amos had dug up yet another bottle of faux tequila from somewhere and was liberally splashing it into coffee cups. Alex had them flying toward Tycho at a gentle one-third g. No need to hurry now.

It was all over but the fireworks.

Holden reached out, took Naomi's hand, and held it tightly as the asteroid entered Venus orbit and then seemed to stop. He felt like he could feel the entire human race holding their breath. No one knew what Eros—no, what *Julie*—would do now. No one had spoken to Miller after the last time Holden had, and he wasn't answering his hand terminal. No one knew for sure what had happened on the asteroid.

When the end came, it was beautiful.

In orbit around Venus, Eros came apart like a puzzle box. The giant asteroid split into a dozen chunks, stringing out around the equator of the planet in a long necklace. Then those dozen pieces split into a dozen more, and then a dozen after that, a glittering fractal seed cloud spreading out across the entire surface of the planet, disappearing into the thick cloud layer that usually hid Venus from view.

"Wow," Amos said, his voice almost reverent.

"That was gorgeous," Naomi said. "Vaguely unsettling, but gorgeous."

"They won't stay there forever," Holden said.

Alex tossed off the last of the tequila in his glass, then refilled it from the bottle.

"What d'ya mean, Cap?" he asked.

"Well, I'm just guessing. But I doubt the things that built the protomolecule just wanted to store it here. This was part of a bigger plan. We saved the Earth, Mars, the Belt. Question is, what happens now?"

Naomi and Alex exchanged glances. Amos pursed his lips. On-screen, Venus glittered as arcs of lightning danced all across the planet.

"Cap," Amos said. "You are seriously harshing my buzz."

Epilogue: Fred

Frederick Lucius Johnson. Former colonel in Earth's armed forces, Butcher of Anderson Station. Thoth Station now too. Unelected prime minister of the OPA. He had faced his own mortality a dozen times, lost friends to violence and politics and betrayal. He'd lived through four assassination attempts, only two of which were on any record. He'd killed a pistol-wielding attacker using only a table knife. He'd given the orders that had ended hundreds of lives, and stood by his decisions.

And yet public speaking still made him nervous as hell. It didn't make sense, but there it was.

Ladies and gentlemen, we stand at a crossroads—

"General Sebastian will be at the reception," his personal secretary said. "Remember not to ask after her husband."

"Why? I didn't kill him, did I?"

"No, sir. He's having a very public affair, and the general's a bit touchy about it."

"So she might *want* me to kill him."

"You can make the offer, sir."

The "greenroom" was actually done in red and ochre, with a black leather couch, a mirrored wall, and a table laid out with hydroponic strawberries and carefully mineralized drinking water. The head of Ceres security, a dour-faced woman named Shaddid, had escorted him from the dock to the conference facilities three hours earlier. Since then, he'd been pacing—three steps in one direction, turn, three steps back—like the captain of an ancient ship of the line on his quarterdeck.

Elsewhere in the station, the representatives of the formerly warring factions were in rooms of their own, with secretaries of their own. Most of them hated Fred, which wasn't particularly a problem. Most of them feared him too. Not because of his standing in the OPA, of course. Because of the protomolecule.

The political rift between Earth and Mars was probably irreparable; the Earth forces loyal to Protogen had engineered a betrayal too deep for apologies, and too many lives had been lost on both sides for the coming peace to look anything like it had been before. The naive among the OPA thought this was a good thing: an opportunity to play one planet against the other. Fred knew better. Unless all three forces—Earth, Mars, and the Belt—could reach a real peace, they would inevitably fall back into a real war.

Now if only Earth or Mars thought of the Belt as something more than an annoyance to be squashed after their true enemy was humiliated...But in truth, anti-Mars sentiment on Earth was higher now than it had been during the shooting war, and Martian elections were only four months away. A significant shift in the Martian polity could ease the tensions or make things immeasurably worse. Both sides had to see the big picture.

Fred stopped before a mirror, adjusted his tunic for the hundredth time, and grimaced.

"When did I turn into a damned marriage counselor?" he said.

"We aren't still talking about General Sebastian, are we, sir?"

"No. Forget I said anything. What else do I need to know?"

"There's a possibility that Blue Mars will try to disrupt your presentation. Hecklers and signs, not guns. Captain Shaddid has several Blues in custody, but some may have slipped past her."

"All right."

"You have interviews scheduled with two political narrowcasts and a news source based on Europa. The Europa interviewer is likely to ask about Anderson Station."

"All right. Anything new from Venus?"

"Something's happening down there," his secretary said.

"It's not dead, then."

"Apparently not, sir."

"Great," he said bitterly.

Ladies and gentlemen, we stand at a crossroads. On one hand there is the very real threat of mutual annihilation, and on the other—

And on the other, there's the bogeyman of Venus, getting ready to crawl up out of its well and slaughter you all in your sleep. I have the live sample, which is your best, if not only, hope of divining what its intentions and capabilities are, and which I have hidden so that you can't just march over and take it from me. It's the only reason any of you are listening to me in the first place. So how about a little respect here?

His secretary's terminal chirped, and she consulted it briefly.

"It's Captain Holden, sir."

"Do I have to?"

"It would be best if he felt he was part of the effort, sir. He has a track record of amateur press releases."

"Fine. Bring him in."

The weeks that had passed since Eros Station had come apart in the thick skies of Venus had been good to Holden, but prolonged high-g dives like the one the *Rocinante* had sustained chasing Eros had long-lasting effects. The burst blood vessels in the man's sclera had healed; the pressure bruising was gone from around his eyes and the back of his neck. Only a little hesitation in the way he walked spoke of the deep joint pain, cartilage still on its way back to its natural form. Acceleration swagger, they'd called it, back when Fred had been a different man.

"Hey," Holden said. "You're looking pretty. Did you see the latest feed from Venus? Two-kilometer-high crystal towers. What do you think that is?"

"Your fault?" Fred suggested, keeping the tone friendly. "You could have told Miller to drive it into the sun."

"Yes, because two-kilometer-high crystal towers coming out of the sun wouldn't be creepy at all," Holden said. "Are those strawberries?"

"Have some," Fred said. He hadn't been able to eat anything since that morning.

"So," Holden said around a mouthful of fruit, "are they really going to sue me over this?"

"Unilaterally giving away all mineral and development rights to an entire planet on an open radio channel?"

"Yeah," Holden said.

"I would guess the people who actually owned those rights are probably going to sue you," Fred said. "If they ever figure out who they are."

"Could you give me a hand with that?" Holden asked.

"I'll be a character witness," Fred said. "I don't actually make the law."

"Then what exactly *are* you all doing here? Couldn't there be some kind of amnesty? We retrieved the protomolecule, tracked down Julie Mao on Eros, broke Protogen, and saved Earth."

"*You* saved Earth?"

"We helped," Holden said, but his voice had a more somber tone. Miller's death still bothered the captain. Fred knew how that felt. "It was a joint effort."

Fred's personal secretary cleared her throat and glanced toward the door. They'd need to go soon.

"I'll do what I can," Fred said. "I've got a lot of other things on the plate, but I'll do what I can."

"And Mars can't have the *Roci* back," Holden said. "Right of salvage says that's my ship now."

"They aren't going to see it that way, but I will do what I can."

"You keep saying that."

"It keeps being all I can do."

"And you'll tell them about him, right?" Holden said. "Miller. He deserves the credit."

"The Belter who went back into Eros of his own free will in order to save Earth? You're damn right I'm going to tell them about him."

"Not 'the Belter.' Him. Josephus Aloisus Miller."

Holden had stopped eating the free strawberries. Fred crossed his arms.

"You've been reading up," Fred said.

"Yeah. Well. I didn't know him all that well."

"Neither did anybody else," Fred said, and then softened a little. "I know it's hard, but we don't need a real man with a complex life. We need a symbol of the Belt. An icon."

"Sir," the secretary said. "We really do need to go now."

"That's what got us here," Holden said. "Icons. Symbols. People without names. All of those Protogen scientists were thinking about biomass and populations. Not Mary who worked in supply and raised flowers in her spare time. None of them killed *her*."

"You think they wouldn't have?"

"I think if they were going to, they owed it to her to know her name. All their names. And you owe it to Miller not to make him into something he wasn't."

Fred laughed. He couldn't help it.

"Captain," he said, "if you're saying that I should amend my address to the peace conference so that it wasn't a noble Belter sacrificing himself to save the Earth—if you're suggesting that I say something like 'We happened to have a suicidal ex-cop on-site' instead—you understand this process less than I thought you did. Miller's sacrifice is a tool, and I'm going to use it."

"Even if it makes him faceless," Holden said. "Even if it makes him something he never was?"

"Especially if it makes him something he never was," Fred said. "Do you remember what he was like?"

Holden frowned and then something flickered in his eyes. Amusement. Memory.

"He was kind of a pain in the ass, wasn't he?" Holden said.

"That man could take a visitation from God with thirty under-dressed angels announcing that sex was okay after all and make it seem vaguely depressing."

"He was a good man," Holden said.

"He wasn't," Fred said. "But he did his job. And now I've got to go do mine."

"Give 'em hell," Holden said. "And amnesty. Keep talking up the amnesty."

Fred walked down the curving hallway, his secretary close behind him. The conference halls had been designed for smaller things. Petty ones. Hydroponics scientists getting away from their husbands and wives and children to get drunk and talk about rais-ing bean sprouts. Miners coming together to lecture each other about waste minimization and tailings disposal. High school band competitions. And instead, these work carpets and brushed-stone walls were going to have to bear the fulcrum of history. It was Holden's fault that the shabby, small surroundings reminded him of the dead detective. They hadn't before.

The delegations were seated across the aisle from each other. The generals and political appointees and general secretaries of Earth and Mars, the two great powers together at his invitation to Ceres, to the Belt. Territory made neutral because neither side took it seriously enough to be concerned about their demands.

All of history had brought them here, to this moment, and now, in the next few minutes, Fred's job was to change that trajectory.

The fear was gone. Smiling, he stepped up to the speaker's dais, the podium.

The pulpit.

There was a scattering of polite applause. A few smiles, and a few frowns. Fred grinned. He wasn't a man anymore. He was a symbol, an icon. A narrative about himself and about the forces at play in the solar system.

And for a moment, he was tempted. In that hesitation between drawing breath and speaking, part of him wondered what would happen if he shed the patterns of history and spoke about himself as a man, about the Joe Miller who he'd known briefly, about the responsibility they all shared to tear down the images they held of one another and find the genuine, flawed, conflicted people they actually were.

It would have been a noble way to fail.

"Ladies and gentlemen," he said. "We stand at a crossroads. On one hand, there is the very real threat of mutual annihilation. On the other..."

He paused for effect.

"On the other, the stars."

Acknowledgments

Like most children, this book took a village. I would like to express my deep gratitude to my agents, Shawna and Danny, and to my editors DongWon and Darren. Also instrumental in the early formation of the book were Melinda, Emily, Terry, Ian, George, Steve, Walter, and Victor, of the New Mexico Critical Mass writers group, and also Carrie, who read an early draft. An additional thanks goes to Ian, who helped with some of the math, and who is responsible for none of the mistakes I made understanding it. I also owe an enormous debt to Tom, Sake Mike, Non-Sake Mike, Porter, Scott, Raja, Jeff, Mark, Dan, and Joe. Thanks, guys, for doing the beta testing. And finally, a special thanks to the *Futurama* writers and Bender Bending Rodriguez for babysitting the kid while I wrote.

extras

orbit

meet the author

JAMES S. A. COREY is the pen name of fantasy author Daniel Abraham and Ty Franck, George R. R. Martin's assistant. They both live in Albuquerque, New Mexico. Find out more about this series at www.the-expanse.com.

interview

Leviathan Wakes *is the first book in a series called The* **Expanse.** *What kind of story are you telling in this series?*

There's a lot of science fiction that talks about the near future. There's a lot about great galaxy-spanning empires of the distant future. But there's not much that talks about the part in between. The Expanse is playing on that bridge. Whatever drives us off Earth to the rest of the solar system or from there to the stars, the problems we have are the ones we bring with us. What I want to do is write good old-fashioned space opera centered around human stories, but with an increasingly large backdrop.

It seems like **Leviathan Wakes** *is a science fiction book, but it borrows from a lot of other genres as well, including horror and noir. Did you intend to blend those genres? What kind of book do you feel this is?*

It's definitely science fiction of the old-school space opera variety. That's the story I wanted to tell. But half of the story was a detective story, and as soon as Detective Miller hit the page, he told me in a loud voice that he was a classic noir character. It was in his voice and the way he talked about things, you know? As for the horror feel, that's just the way I roll. I've never written anything in my life that didn't at least blur the line into horror. If I wrote greeting cards, they'd probably have a squick factor.

Leviathan Wakes *has two protagonists with very different worldviews, which are often in conflict. Can you describe those views and why you chose that particular conflict?*

You know how they say science fiction is about the future you're writing about, but it's also about the time you're writing in? Holden and Miller have got two different views on the ethical use of information. That's very much a current argument. Holden's my holy fool. He's an idealist, a man who faces things with this very optimistic view of humanity. He believes that if you give people all of the information, they'll do the right thing with it, because people are naturally good. Miller is a cynic and a nihilist. He looks at the dissemination of information as a game you play. He doesn't have faith in anyone else's moral judgment. Control of information is how you get people to do what you want, and he doesn't trust anyone else to make that call. I picked those two characters because they're both right, and they're both wrong. By having them in the same story, I can have them talk to each other. And that central disagreement is sort of underneath everything else that happens.

Leviathan Wakes *has a gritty and realistic feel. How much research did you do on the technology side of things, and how important was it to you that they be realistic and accurate?*

Okay, so what you're really asking me there is if this is hard science fiction. The answer is an emphatic no. I have nothing but respect for well-written hard science fiction, and I wanted everything in the book to be plausible enough that it doesn't get in the way. But the rigorous how-to with the math shown? It's not that story. This is working man's science fiction. It's like in *Alien,* we meet the crew of the *Nostromo* doing their jobs in this very blue-collar environment. They're truckers, right? Why is there a room in the *Nostromo* where water leaks down off of chains suspended from the ceiling? Because it looks cool and makes the world feel a little messy. It gives you the feel of the world. Ridley Scott doesn't explain why that room exists, and when most people watch the film, it never even occurs to them to ask. What kind of drive does the *Nostromo* use? I bet no one walked out of the film asking that question. I wanted to tell a story about humans living and working in a well-populated solar system. I wanted to convey a feeling of what that would be like, and then tell a story about the people who live there.

So how does the Epstein drive work?
Very well. Efficiently.

In your acknowledgments you thank the New Mexico Critical Mass writers group. What effect did having that workshop environment have on your work?
Well, Critical Mass is a lot more than a workshop or critical group. It's more like a writer's mafia. Just about anything you might need, someone in the group can get it for you. Walter Jon Williams, who wrote the brilliant Dread Empire's Fall space opera series, was there to give important tips about writing in that genre. S. M. Stirling and Victor Milan write some of the best action in the business, and there was a lot of action for them to critique. Ian Tregillis is an actual astrophysicist and made himself available for technical questions. Melinda Snodgrass is pretty much the Yoda of letting you know when you've wandered too far away from your plot. And the entire group, including Emily Mah, Terry England, and George R. R. Martin, was there to read and critique the early drafts of the book, and a lot of changes were made based on their advice.

You've worked with George R. R. Martin a lot in the past. What kind of advice did he have for this project?
Yes, I've done a number of projects with him in one incarnation or another. In this case, he was mostly just encouraging. He likes old-fashioned space opera, and he followed my progress on the book with great interest. He was also the first to read the final version. He was very complimentary. He said at one point that it

was the best book about vomit zombies he'd ever read. That was nice.

Where do you see the Expanse series going from here?

Well, I'm contracted with Orbit for at least two more books. They are titled *Caliban's War* and *Dandelion Sky*. I hope to keep exploring the idea of human expansion into the solar system and beyond, and balancing the very real threats that the galaxy poses for the fledgling human diaspora against the threats that those same humans will bring with them. For up-to-date information on what I'm up to and where the project is headed, people can visit www.the-expanse.com and get the latest.

introducing

If you enjoyed
LEVIATHAN WAKES,
look out for

CALIBAN'S WAR

Book Two of The Expanse

by James S. A. Corey

"Snoopy's out again," Private Hillman said. "I think his CO must be pissed at him."

Gunnery Sergeant Roberta Draper of the Martian Marine Corps upped the magnification on her armor's head-up display and looked in the direction Hillman was pointing. Twenty-five hundred meters away, a squad of four United Nations marines were tromping around their outpost, backlit by the giant greenhouse dome they were guarding. A greenhouse dome identical in nearly all respects to the dome that was behind her.

One of the four UN marines had black smudges on the sides of his helmet that looked like beagle ears.

"Yep, that's Snoopy," Bobbie said. "Been on every patrol detail so far today. Wonder what he did."

Guard duty around the greenhouses on Ganymede meant doing what you could to keep your mind occupied. Including speculating on the lives of the marines on the other side.

The other side. Eighteen months before, there hadn't been sides. The inner planets had all been one big, happy, slightly dysfunctional family. Then the Eros incident, and now the two superpowers were dividing up the solar system between them, and the one moon neither side was willing to give up was Ganymede, breadbasket of the Jovian system.

As the only moon with any magnetosphere, it was the only place where dome-grown crops stood a chance in Jupiter's harsh radiation belt, and even there, the domes and habitats had to be shielded to protect civilians from the eight rems a day burning off Jupiter and onto the moon's surface.

Bobbie's armor had been designed to let a soldier walk through a nuclear bomb crater an hour after the blast. It also worked well at keeping Jupiter from frying Martian marines.

Behind the Earth soldiers on patrol, their dome glowed in a shaft of weak sunlight captured by enormous orbital mirrors. Even with the mirrors, most terrestrial plants would have died, starved of sunlight. Only the heavily modified versions the Ganymede scientists cranked out could hope to survive in the trickle of light the mirrors fed them.

"Be sunset soon," Bobbie said, still watching the Earth marines outside their little guard hut, knowing they were watching her too. In addition to Snoopy, she spotted the one they called Stumpy because he or she couldn't be much more than a meter and a half tall. She wondered what their nickname for her was. Maybe Big Red. Her armor still had the Martian surface camouflage on it. She hadn't been on Ganymede long enough to get it resurfaced with mottled gray and white.

One by one, over the course of five minutes, the orbital mirrors winked out as Ganymede passed behind Jupiter for a few hours. The glow from the greenhouse behind her changed to actinic blue as the artificial lights came on. While the overall light level didn't go down much, the shadows shifted in strange and subtle ways. Above, the sun — not even a disk from here as much as the brightest star — flashed as it passed behind Jupiter's limb, and for a moment the planet's faint ring system was visible.

"They're going back in," Corporal Travis said. "Snoop's bringing up the rear. Poor guy. Can we bail too?"

Bobbie looked around at the featureless dirty ice of Ganymede. Even in her high-tech armor she could feel the moon's chill.

"Nope."

Her squad grumbled but fell in line as she led them on a slow low-gravity shuffle around the dome. In addition to Hillman and Travis, she had a green private named Gourab on this patrol. And even though he'd been in the marines all of about a minute and a half, he grumbled just as loud as the other two in his Mariner Valley drawl.

She couldn't blame them. It was make-work. Something for the Martian soldiers on Ganymede to do to keep them busy. If Earth decided it needed Ganymede all to itself, four grunts walking around the greenhouse dome wouldn't stop them. With dozens of Earth and Mars warships in a tense standoff in orbit, if hostilities broke out, the ground pounders would probably find out only when the surface bombardment began.

To her left, the dome rose to almost half a kilometer: triangular glass panels separated by gleaming copper-colored struts that turned the entire structure into a massive Faraday cage. Bobbie had never been inside one of the greenhouse domes. She'd been sent out from Mars as part of a huge surge in troops to the outer planets and had been walking patrols on the surface almost since day one. Ganymede to her was a spaceport, a small marine base, and the even smaller guard outpost she currently called home.

As they shuffled around the dome, Bobbie watched the unremarkable landscape. Ganymede didn't change much without a catastrophic event. The surface was mostly silicate rock and water ice a few degrees warmer than space. The atmosphere was oxygen so thin it could pass as an industrial vacuum. Ganymede didn't weather. It changed when rocks fell on it from space, or when warm water from the liquid core forced itself onto the surface and created short-lived lakes. Neither thing happened all that often. At home on Mars, wind and dust changed the landscape hourly. Here, she was walking through the footsteps of the day before and the day before and the day before. And if she never came back, those footprints would outlive her. Privately, she thought it was sort of creepy.

A rhythmic squeaking started to cut through the normally smooth hiss and thump sounds her powered armor made. She usually kept the suit's HUD minimized. It got so crowded with information that a marine knew everything except what was actually in front of her. Now she pulled it up, using blinks and eye movements to page over to the suit's diagnostic screen. A yellow telltale warned her that the suit's left knee actuator was low on hydraulic fluid. Must be a leak somewhere, but a slow one, because the suit couldn't find it.

"Hey, guys, hold up a minute," Bobbie said. "Hilly, you have any extra hydraulic fluid in your pack?"

"Yep," said Hillman, already pulling it out.

"Give my left knee a squirt, would you?"

While Hillman crouched in front of her, working on her suit, Gourab and Travis began an argument that seemed to be about sports. Bobbie tuned it out.

"This suit is ancient," Hillman said. "You really oughta upgrade. This sort of thing is just going to happen more and more often, you know."

"Yeah, I should," Bobbie said. But the truth was that was easier said than done. Bobbie was not the right shape to fit into one of the standard suits, and the marines made her jump through a series of flaming hoops every time she requisitioned a new custom one. At two meters tall, she was only a bit above average height for a Martian male, but thanks in part to her Polynesian ancestry, she weighed in at more than 140 kilos at one g. It wasn't fat, but her muscles seemed to get bigger every time she even walked through a weight room, and as a marine, she trained all the time.

The suit she had now was the first one in twelve years of active duty that actually seemed to fit well. And even though it was beginning to show its age, it was just easier to try to keep it running than beg and plead for a new one.

Hillman was just starting to put his tools away when Bobbie's radio crackled to life.

"Outpost four to stickman. Come in, stickman."

"Roger four," Bobbie replied. "This is stickman one. Go ahead."

"Stickman one, where are you guys? You're half an hour late and some shit is going down over here."

"Sorry four, some equipment trouble here," Bobbie said, wondering what sort of shit might be going down, but not enough to ask about it over an open frequency.

"Return to the outpost immediately. We have shots fired at the UN outpost. We're going into lockdown."

It took Bobbie a moment to parse that. She could see her men staring at her, their faces a mix of puzzlement and fear.

"Uh, the Earth guys are shooting at you?" she finally asked.

"Not yet, but they're shooting. Get your asses back here."

Hillman jumped to his feet. Bobbie flexed her knee once and got greens on her diagnostic. She gave Hilly a nod of thanks, then said, "Double-time it back to the outpost. Go."

Bobbie and her squad were still half a kilometer from the outpost when the general alert went out. Her suit's HUD came up on its own, switching to combat mode. The sensor package went to work looking for hostiles and linked up to one of the satellites for a top-down view. She felt the click as the gun built into the suit's right arm switched to free-fire mode.

A thousand alarms would be sounding if an orbital bombardment had begun, but she couldn't help looking up at the sky anyway. No flashes or missile trails. Nothing but Jupiter's bulk.

Bobbie took off for the outpost at a dead run. Her squad followed without a word. A person trained in the use of a strength-augmenting suit running in low gravity could cover a lot of ground quickly. The outpost came into view around the curve of the dome in just a few seconds, and a few seconds after that, the cause of the alarm.

UN marines were charging at the Martian outpost. The year-long cold war was going hot. Somewhere deep behind the cool mental habits of training and discipline, she was surprised. She hadn't really thought this day would come.

The rest of her platoon were out of the outpost and arranged in a firing line facing the UN position. Someone had driven *Yojimbo* out onto the line, and the four-meter-tall combat mech towered over the other marines, looking like a headless giant in power armor, his massive cannon moving slowly as it tracked the incoming Earth troops. The UN soldiers were covering the 2,500 meters between the two outposts at full speed.

Why isn't anyone talking? she wondered. The silence coming from her platoon was eerie.

And then, just as her squad got to the firing line, her suit squealed a jamming warning at her. The top-down vanished as she lost contact with the satellite. Her team's life signs and equipment status reports went dead as her link to their suits was cut off. The faint static of the open comm channel disappeared, leaving an even more unsettling silence.

She used hand motions to place her team at the right flank, then moved up the line to find Lieutenant Givens, her CO. She spotted his suit right at the center of the line, almost directly under *Yojimbo*. She ran up and placed her helmet against his.

"What the fuck is going on, El Tee?" she shouted.

He gave her an irritated look and yelled, "Your guess is as good as mine. We can't tell them to back off because of the jamming, and visual warnings are being ignored. Before the radio cut out, I got authorization to fire if they come within half a klick of our position."

Bobbie had a couple hundred more questions, but the UN troops would cross the five-hundred-meter mark in just a few more seconds, so she ran back to anchor the right flank with her squad. Along the way, she had her suit count the incoming forces and mark them all as hostiles. The suit reported seven targets. Less than a third of the UN troops at their outpost.

This makes no sense.

She had her suit draw a line on the HUD at the five-hundred-meter mark. She didn't tell her boys that was the free-fire zone. She didn't need to. They'd open fire when she did without needing to know why.

The UN soldiers had crossed the one-kilometer mark, still without firing a shot. They were coming in a scattered formation, with six out front in a ragged line, and a seventh bringing up the rear about seventy meters behind. Her suit HUD selected the figure on the far left of the enemy line as her target, picking the one closest to her by default. Something itched at the back of her brain and she overrode the suit and selected the target at the rear and told it to magnify.

The small figure suddenly enlarged in her targeting reticule. She felt a chill move down her back and magnified again.

The figure chasing the six UN marines wasn't wearing a suit. Nor was it, properly speaking, human. Its skin was covered in chitinous plates, like large black scales. Its head was a massive horror, easily twice as large as it should be and covered in strange protruding growths.

But most disturbing of all were its hands. Far too large for its body, and too long for their width, they were a childhood-nightmare version of hands. The hands of the troll under the bed or the witch sneaking in through the window. They flexed and grasped at nothing with a constant manic energy.

The Earth forces weren't attacking. They were retreating.

"Shoot the thing chasing them," Bobbie yelled to no one.

Before the UN soldiers could cross the half kilometer that would cause the Martians to open fire, the thing caught them.

"Oh, holy shit," Bobbie whispered. "Holy *shit.*"

It grabbed one UN marine in its huge hands and tore the man in half like paper. Titanium and ceramic armor tore as easily as the flesh inside, spilling broken bits of technology and wet human viscera indiscriminately onto the ice. The remaining five soldiers ran even harder, but the monster chasing them barely slowed as it killed.

"Shoot it shoot it shoot it," Bobbie screamed and opened fire. Bobbie's training and the technology of her combat suit combined to make her an extremely efficient killing machine. As soon as her finger pulled the trigger on her suit's gun, a stream of two-millimeter armor-piercing rounds streaked out at the creature at a thousand meters per second. In just under one second, she fired nearly fifty rounds at it. It was a relatively slow-moving human-sized target, running in a straight line. Her targeting computer could do ballistic corrections that would let her hit a softball-sized object moving at supersonic speeds. Every bullet she fired at the monster hit.

It didn't matter.

The rounds went through it, probably not slowing appreciably before they exited. Each exit wound sprouted a spray of black filaments that fell onto the snow instead of blood. It was like shooting water. The wounds closed almost faster than they were created; the only sign the thing had even been hit was the trail of black fibers in its wake.

And then it caught a second UN marine. Instead of tearing him to pieces like it had the last one, it spun and hurled the fully armored Earther—probably massing more than five hundred kilos total—toward Bobbie. Her HUD tracked the UN soldier on his upward arc and helpfully informed her that the monster had thrown him not *toward* her, but *at* her. In a very flat trajectory. Which meant fast.

She dove to the side as quickly as her suit would let her. The hapless UN marine swiped Hillman, who'd been standing next to her, and then both of them were gone, bouncing down the ice at lethal speeds.

By the time she turned back to the monster, it had killed two more UN soldiers.

The entire Martian line opened fire on it, including *Yojimbo*'s big cannon. The two remaining Earth soldiers diverged and ran at angles away from the thing, trying to give their Martian counter-parts an open firing lane. The creature was hit hundreds, thousands of times. It stitched itself back together while remaining at a full run, never more than slowing when one of *Yojimbo*'s cannon shots detonated nearby.

Bobbie, back on her feet, joined in the barrage but it didn't make any difference. The creature slammed into the Martian line, killing two marines faster than the eye could follow. *Yojimbo* slid to one side, far more nimble than a machine of its size should be. Bobbie though Sa'id must be driving it. He swore he could make the big mech dance the tango when he wanted to. It didn't matter. Even before Sa'id could bring the mech's cannon around for a point-blank shot, the creature ran right up its side, gripped the pilot hatch, and tore the door off its hinges. Sa'id was snatched from his cockpit harness and hurled sixty meters straight up.

The other marines had begun to fall back, firing as they went. Without radio, there was no way to coordinate the retreat. Bobbie found herself running toward the dome with the rest. The small and distant part of her mind that wasn't panicking knew that the dome's glass and metal would offer no protection against something that could tear an armored man in half and rip a nine-ton mech to pieces. That part of her mind recognized the futility in attempting to override her terror.

By the time she found the external door to the dome, there was only one other marine left with her. Gourab. Up close, she could see his face through the armored glass of his helmet. He was screaming something at her she couldn't hear. She started to lean forward to touch helmets with him when he shoved her backward onto the ice. He was hammering on the door controls with one metal fist, trying to smash his way in in his mindless panic, when the creature caught him and peeled the helmet off his suit. Gourab stood for one moment, face in vacuum, eyes blinking and mouth open in a soundless scream; then the creature tore off his head as easily as it had his helmet.

It turned and looked at Bobbie, still flat on her back.

Up close, she could see that it had bright blue eyes. A glowing, electric blue. They were beautiful. She raised her gun and held down the trigger for half a second before she realized she'd run out of ammo long before. The creature looked at her gun with what she would have sworn was curiosity, then looked into her eyes and cocked its head to one side.

This is it, she thought. *This is how I go out, and I'm not going to know what did it, or why.* Dying she could handle. Dying without any answers seemed terribly cruel.

The creature took one step toward her, then stopped and shuddered. A new pair of limbs burst out of its midsection and writhed in the air like tentacles. Its head, already grotesque, seemed to swell up. The blue eyes flashed as bright as the lights in the domes.

And then it exploded in a ball of fire that hurled her away across the ice and slammed her into a low ridge hard enough for the impact-absorbing gel in her suit to go rigid, freezing her in place.

She lay on her back, fading toward unconsciousness. The night sky above her began to flash with light. The ships in orbit, shooting.

Cease fire, she thought, pressing the thought out into the blackness. *They were retreating. Cease fire.* Her radio was still out. She couldn't tell anyone that the UN marines hadn't been attacking.

Or that something else had.